# The Growing

## Susanne M. Beck
### and
## Okasha Skat'si

P.D. Publishing, Inc.
Clayton, North Carolina

Copyright © 2006 by Susanne M. Beck and Okasha Skat'si

All rights reserved. No part of this publication may be reproduced, transmitted in any form or by any means, electronic or mechanical, including photocopy, recording, or any information storage and retrieval system, without permission in writing from the publisher. The characters herein are fictional and any resemblance to a real person, living or dead, is purely coincidental.

ISBN-13: 978-0-9754366-9-1
ISBN-10: 0-9754366-9-4

9 8 7 6 5 4 3 2 1

Cover photo by Penelope Warren
Cover design by Stephanie Solomon-Lopez
Edited by Day Petersen/Linda Daniel

Published by:

P.D. Publishing, Inc.
P.O. Box 70
Clayton, NC 27528

http://www.pdpublishing.com

Acknowledgements:

Dedicated to my Godmother, Ilene, who loves me enough to read my work and feel pride in my accomplishments; to my Mom and Dad, whom I love very much; to my brother, his wife, and family who I wish I could see more of, to Elizabeth, who has always been there to listen and to hug, and lastly, to Sheri. No matter what, babe, I'll always love you. Sue.

Many thanks are due to Sue, who invited me to participate in this project, and to Barb and Linda, who had faith in the book and were willing to take the risk of publishing it in one volume as the epic monster it is. Special gratitude goes to Toni, for encouragement and support; and to Moses Thunderpurr, Robin Pouncemaster and Pele Pear, lions and lioness in small. Okasha.

In memory of the best damn dog a woman could ever have: Kricket Beck. I miss you, old girl. Twenty years wasn't nearly long enough.

~ Sue

The air-raid sirens wail discordantly, unendingly, as Dakota Rivers bulls her old, much beloved truck down the snowy highways and byways leading out from Rapid City. The noise rises above the howling wind, the shriek of metal on metal as cars and trucks plow into one another at high speed, even the panicked screams of men and women running for their lives. *Music to end the world by*, she thinks, squinting through the heavy lines of snow blowing directly at her.

The sound of the sirens drills into her ears with such wicked persistence that she feels she must surely go mad. A quick look at the devastation around her, and she wonders if she's already there. She brakes as she sees a man dressed in a heavy parka and boots running up the middle of the highway, dodging overturned trucks and mangled cars, waving his hands and screaming for help. Behind him, two men, less well dressed but infinitely more sure-footed, march grimly after him. As she watches, one raises a rifle. The sound of the shot is buried beneath the wailing of the sirens, but its effect is readily seen as the man, his arms still high over his head, does an almost graceful swan dive onto the snowpacked road, dead before he hits the ground.

"Fuck," Koda mutters as the men, and their weapons, turn her way. Her hands tighten on the steering wheel and she guns the engine, which causes her tires to spin uselessly. "Come on, baby," she whispers. "Come on, you can do it." She eases off the gas, then gooses the pedal a little, grimly staring through the snow at her calm assassins. Her headlights catch a wink of metal around one's neck, and she bares her teeth as the wheels continue to spin and spin, the heavy chains doing little to help. "C'mon, *cantesukye,* just a little more...a little more..."

The right side of her windshield suddenly exhibits a starburst pattern, and she gives up all pretense at gentleness. "Go, you bitch! GO!" The heavy engine growls as the chains finally catch, and she sluices ahead like a horse just out of the gate. Her shooter and his companion don't move an inch as she heads right for them. She doesn't have to hear the sounds of the slugs hitting the body of her truck to know that they are, in fact, adding to the vehicle's already rustic charm. Yelling out a battle cry, she doesn't even slow as she plows into both men, bearing them under her truck and shredding them with the tire chains.

The sirens continue to wail as she slips between two cars, their hoods accordioned by a head-on collision. She swallows sickly as she rides over the dead body of one of the drivers and continues, faster than she dares. Her sense of urgency, the overwhelming need to see to her family right now is the only thing that keeps her on the road. If she must die, and all the signs are pointing in that direction, she will do it among people she loves.

She pulls up on the narrow divider to get around an overturned semi, and, like an answer to a prayer, sees that the way beyond is clear. The traffic, what little of it is still moving, is going in the other direction — toward the city and its flaming wreckage. She wants to yell at these people, to demand that they turn around and run, to tell them that they will be infinitely safer in the wild lands than they will be in the carnage she has just left, but she knows that even if she tried, her words would fall on deaf ears.

Panic is a strange taskmaster, and logic falls prostrate in the face of it.

"*Ina, Até,*" she whispers, her words plumes of smoke that linger in the air, fogging her windshield. "Please wait for me. I'm coming home."

**Scrambling around her** townhouse, Kirsten shoves clothing and the bare necessities of travel into her duffel bag: soap, toothbrush, toothpaste, a bottle of aspirin. Her computer and other equipment are already packed in her SUV, and she needs no more now than will keep her warm and well until she can reach her goal.

She listens to the screaming of sirens that sound as if the city is under attack around her. Not surprising; it is, and defenses are doubtful at best. She has to get out. Fast. As she grabs a heavy coat off the rack by the door, she chastises herself for not having anything ready sooner. She has had a bad feeling for months, and now she knows she has been right all along. Not that that is any comfort.

Carefully she opens the door, peering out to be sure the parking lot is empty. Satisfied that it's safe, she steps outside and pulls her door shut behind her. She crosses the parking lot at a dead run, Asi keeping pace beside her as she dodges in and out among the cars sitting in their orderly ranks. Two rows to go. One. She pulls up before her truck, fumbling with the keys already in her hand. Almost out. Almost. As she slips the key into the lock, the rattle of automatic fire echoes between the buildings of her apartment complex. The shooting is somewhere out in the street, too near for safety.

*Shit.* The adrenaline courses through her body as she manages to key the truck unlocked and get inside, clambering into the seat with the duffel bag flung heedlessly down behind her. Asi, whining, settles beside it, his gaze quizzical. "It's okay, boy," she pants. "It's okay. Just keep your head down and stay quiet."

Kirsten takes her own advice, her hand on the big dog's scruff, as two police cars whip by with lights and sirens blaring. Drawing a deep breath, Kirsten starts the truck and pulls out of her parking space. This will be the last time she will see her home, or at least what she has called home for the last three years. Her real home, her family— But she cannot think of them now, only of the urgency of her escape.

This will be forever burned into her mind as the day her world ended.

She drives slowly down the street, trying to look as normal as possible. The last thing she wants to do is call attention to herself. Getting well away from the city is the only hope she has. And she knows it. Kirsten turns left onto a side street lined mostly by small businesses. She needs to keep out of residential areas, out of the range of their sensors. She hears still more sirens and something that sounds like muffled gunfire. Her foot presses down slightly on the accelerator. Discretion is the better part of valor; even her soldier father says so.

There is a growl from the back seat, and Asi, contrary to all good order and discipline, raises his head. "Easy, Asimov. It's okay, boy. We're getting the hell out of Dodge."

The dog climbs over the back of the seat and takes his regular place in the front across from his favorite human. Kirsten reaches over and give him a scratch on the head. "We're gonna be okay, boy. I promise."

Despite the sounds of fighting the streets are deserted. And somewhere in the back of her mind, little voices whisper that that can't be good. *Hard to please, aren't you, King?* The thought sneaks its way into her consciousness. Streets full of gunmen are not good. Streets full of dead gunmen are worse. As she makes another turn, speeding up to get past a large apartment complex, Asimov raises his head and begins growling in earnest. She watches him as he faces the window and barks furiously.

Suddenly the truck impacts against something and Kirsten's head jerks up as a man rolls onto the hood. He is still alive, panicked and obviously running for his life. "Help me!" he screams as he pounds on the windshield with his hand. "For God's sake, please help me!"

Kirsten slams the brake and he slides drunkenly to hang half on, half off the hood. Asimov's barking grows more intense and she knows what she has to do. Looking the man directly in the eye, she says, "I'm sorry."

Throwing the truck into reverse, she backs up quickly. The force of the acceleration throws the man from the hood to the ground. Hitting the gas, she speeds past him. In the rearview mirror she can see three of them moving in on him, one of them pointing a rifle at the man's head. The blast seems to follow her as she speeds up and heads for the freeway that will take her away from the madness.

**Dakota's truck, a** decades old campaigner who has been with her since she learned to drive, growls low and moves with confident speed over the packed and blowing snow covering the roads. The sound of the chains rattling as they cut through the icepack can be heard even over the fiercely blowing wind.

In this part of South Dakota, where distances between neighbors are often-times measured in miles instead of yards or feet, she knows that at the very least, under optimal conditions, it will take her a half hour to reach her parents' house. With the blizzard, the more likely estimate is forty five minutes, minimum.

She glares at the racked mic of her dashboard CB, listening as static, very much like what was on the television, hisses at her. It is the only response to the constant calls she's been putting out. Her parents have a big base unit in their home, and her youngest brother, Washington, an absolute radio fiend, is never more than three steps away from it.

"You bastards better not have hurt my family, or I'll rip you apart with my bare hands."

It's pretty impotent as threats go, but a part of her feels better for having said it. Without bothering to signal, she makes the looping left turn that leads her to her parents' road, hoping against hope that time is still on her side.

**Two hours later,** Kirsten finally slows down and takes a moment to breathe. Her route has taken her off the freeway and onto two lane state highways, less frequently used and completely desolate in some places. Pulling onto a wide spot on the road, she puts the truck in park and takes a deep breath, letting it out slowly. Asimov sits up, his tongue lolling and his ears perked. "Bet you need a break, doncha?" She nods, answering for him, and ruffles the winter fur around his neck. "Okay, but make it quick."

Getting out of the truck and walking around the front, she can see spots of blood on the grillwork. Sick to her stomach, she reaches over and grasps the handle of the passenger door and lets the dog out.  While Asimov paces the road shoulder, sniffing at the edge of the asphalt and at the fence posts that run parallel to it, Kirsten leans against the truck and takes a deep breath.  Looking up into the night sky, the normal twinkling of the stars gives her a sense of security that she knows is false.  "God," she sighs, looking down at Asimov, now done with business and waiting patiently in front of her.  "Well pal, it's just us, and it's going to be that way for a while, I think.  We have to stay low and try to figure out how to stop this insanity."

Suddenly all of the adrenaline coursing through her during her frantic escape from the city is gone, and exhaustion sets in.  "Tonight, we sleep in the truck.  Tomorrow, we head to the facility and try to get some answers."

Opening the door, she motions for the dog to jump in.  Once he is inside, she gets back in and pulls the truck into a thicket of trees just off the road.  As she shuts off the lights and the engine, her head slumps forward to rest on the steering wheel.  "I'm tired, Asimov.  You get to keep watch tonight."

She crawls into the back of the truck, shoving and pulling her supplies around until she finds her sleeping bag and pillow.  Asimov remains in the front seat and watches as his human settles down to try to sleep.  Before she feels completely safe, Kirsten removes her gun from the duffle bag and snicks off the safety.  She knows it probably won't stop them, but if her aim is good, it might at least slow them down.

"Sleep," she mutters.  "I need sleep.  It'll all be better in the morning."

**Dakota leaves the** motor running and the lights blazing as she jumps down from her truck and starts toward the front door.

The lights being on likely saves her life, as she is able to see the rifle barrel poke out of one of the front windows seconds before it goes off, bullet piercing the air where she'd been not a split second before.

"Who's there?" comes the quavering sound of a young man's voice, caught in a quandary of puberty and terror.

"Damn it, Phoenix, is that you, goober?"

"Koda?"

"Yeah, it's me.  Now do you wanna put that gun away before you blow my head off?"

"Sorry."

Dakota takes no more than two steps toward the porch when the door flies open and her mother, a short, stocky woman, rushes out into the snow, her arms flung open.  "Dakota!  My daughter, you're home!  I was so worried."

The younger woman takes her mother into her arms and returns the crushing hug, chilled fingers tenderly stroking the thick, silver threaded black hair that is tied back in a fat braid.  "I'm home, *Ina*.  It's okay, I'm home."  After a moment, she pulls away, large hands descending on her mother's broad shoulders.  "Let's get inside.  It's freezing out here."

"But your truck..."

"Leave it that way for now.  We need to talk."

Stepping inside the huge ranch house, she is immediately comforted by the sounds and scents of home, a place she has done no more than visit in the past five years.  Her brothers and sisters, seven in this bunch, surround her in a tight press, hugging and touching and talking, all at once. Dakota finally wriggles her hands free and holds them up in a gesture of calm.

"One at a time. One at a time."

They look at her with shining, hopeful faces. Though only the third born, she has always been their rock, and their love for her is boundless. In turn, she is fiercely, utterly, devoted to them, like a mother bear protecting her newborn cubs.

Looking around the room, she notices that two family members are conspicuously absent. "Where's *Até*? And Tacoma?"

"They're both down at the MacGregor's ranch. Kimberly called, screaming for help. I couldn't understand her, and she hung up before I was able to know what was wrong. Your father and brother went out there."

Dakota stiffens. "How long ago?"

Her mother looks at the clock. "No more than ten or fifteen minutes. With the storm, they probably just got there." Reaching out, she clamps her daughter's arm in a very strong grip. "Dakota, what's going on?"

It's a demand, not a question. Koda answers, "I wish I could tell you, *Ina*, but I just don't know. Something's happening, something big, I think, but I need more information to go on."

"I won't accept that, Dakota," her mother replies, deep black eyes flashing with a light she knows only too well.

Dakota smiles, just slightly, and lays a gentle hand over her mother's. "You'll have to, Mother, if for just a little while longer. I need to get to Father and Tacoma."

"Are they in danger?"

Dakota considers lying, but in the end, just can't bring herself to do it. "I don't know," she says softly.

Her mother releases her arm immediately, drawing back just a step. "I'll let it go then. For now. Do what you need to, and bring them both back safely."

"I'll do my best."

Smiling, her mother pulls her head down for a kiss, then releases her. "I know you will."

Turning to leave, Dakota is surprised when a small missile — in the shape of her youngest brother — launches itself into her arms. "I wanna go with you, Koda! Can I, please?"

She hugs the ten-year-old close against her, taking in his young boy scent. "You can't, Wash. Not this time."

"But I wanna! Please?" He draws the last word out and looks at her with big, pleading dark eyes. "Please?"

"Washington."

The young boy stiffens in his sister's arms at the sound of his mother's voice.

"Wash, I need you here to man the CB. You're the only one who knows how to work the da — ah — darn thing, right?"

Washington reluctantly nods.

"And if I need help with Father and Tacoma, who do you think I'm gonna call?"

"Me?"

"Of course you. You're the only one I can count on with this, and you know it."

The boy smiles, his narrow chest puffing out with pride. "I won't let you down, Koda."

Grinning, Dakota releases her brother and swats him on the behind, which earns a yelp and a scowl. "See you guys later."

With a wave and a grin, Dakota is gone.

**The morning sun** is too bright and very warm when it shines directly into Kirsten's eyes. Yawning, she rolls over to feel a kink in her neck. "Well, it's not my water bed, that's for sure." Lifting her head, she looks to her furry companion. "You okay, buddy?"

Asimov yawns too, and rests his head on the back of the seat.

"Okay, let's dig out the map and see where we need to go."

Rifling through a computer case, she removes the map and unfolds it. "Okay, we're here. And we need to be..." she follows a route with her finger, "...here. Looks like about sixteen hundred miles." She sighs. "Well, that sucks. It's going to take days to get there, and we need to be careful. Maybe it won't be as bad as we head out west."

Even as she speaks the words, she knows she's lying to herself. They are everywhere, and no one is safe. She has come to the conclusion that her parents are dead. They had three of the monsters in their house and could never understand Kirsten's demand that they get rid of them. She couldn't make them understand what she knew. There was no way to make anybody believe it.

She remembers her mother tending her rose garden and her father trimming the hedges and what she considered an almost idealistic way to grow up. She had been an only child, and her parents had encouraged her and given her the support she needed to follow her dreams. She realizes that eventually she will have to go to Georgia to find out if they're alive, but the incessant ringing of her parents' phone has given her all the answers she really needs.

Folding the map, she tosses it into the front and crawls into the driver's seat. She looks over to Asimov. "You don't want to drive, do you?"

The dog squirms in his seat and lays his head down to get some sleep.

"I didn't think so."

Starting the truck, she pulls back out onto the road and turns left toward her destination.

**She knows the** roads between the two ranches well, and before too much time has passed, Dakota has parked her truck behind a high bank of snow, lights off, engine shut down to silence. She can see her father's large, burly body propped against another snowbank overlooking the valley where the ranch house sits sprawled like a dog sunning itself.

She hoots low, twice, using a call learned from the man propped against the snowbank. A hand is raised, slightly, and she moves forward, taking care to keep her head below the level of the bank. Within seconds, she's laid out carefully beside her father, whose sheer size dwarfs her own not inconsiderable height, being a couple inches over six feet without her boots on.

Her oldest brother, Tacoma, lies on her other side. He shares his father's height but not his girth, instead sporting a swimmer's build that is all the rage in the few scattered nightclubs around town. Women literally fall over themselves trying to get his attention. Unfortunately for them, he's as gay as old dad's hatband. Still, he doesn't mind the attention. It's a source of great teasing in the Rivers' household.

"Hey," Dakota whispers to them both. They reply with silent nods. Both are armed. Her father carries a Winchester Black Shadow rifle, and her brother, a Black Shadow pump action shotgun.

Feeling the cold bite into her even through several layers of clothing, she eases her head up just slightly to peer over the top of the bank. What she sees causes her jaw to tighten, muscles bunching and jumping.

Ian MacGregor, a big, bluff, and kindly Scotsman, lies dead, half on, half off of his large wrap porch, his wide eyes staring blankly into whatever eternity exists for him. His two adult sons, both strapping like their father, lie one to either side of Ian, a gruesome trinity.

Dakota has known them all since she was in the cradle, and the sight of their lifeless bodies twists something deep inside her guts. Her face, likewise, twists, into a grimace she's not aware of displaying. The door to the house is splintered to kindling, and if she listens hard enough, she can hear the faint sounds of screaming above the howling of the wind. "How many?" she asks her father.

"I don't know," he replies, shifting his heavy bulk on the packed snow and ice. "Was like this when we came."

A shadow passes over the threshold, and a moment later, a tall, broad shouldered male strides out into the cold, holding two screaming young girls by their long, dark hair. They're trying their best to break free, but it's as if the man doesn't even notice he's holding them; the kicks, gouges and punches have absolutely no effect whatsoever. He turns and faces the house, as if waiting for something within.

Dakota lets out a breath that sounds like a growl and reaches out a hand. Her father hands over his gun willingly. Then she turns to her brother. "Can you still shoot the balls off a gnat at a hundred yards?"

"Yeah," Tacoma replies with no pride in his voice.

"Trade me, then." Grasping the shotgun, she trades for the rifle.

Though he knows his father keeps his guns immaculate, he checks the rifle over carefully, a habit he hasn't lost since his Army days, seemingly a lifetime ago. Satisfied, he nods to her, eyebrows raised to his hairline.

"All right. When I say 'go,' I want you to wing him. Shoulder, arm, it doesn't matter. Just don't hit those girls."

"But..."

"Listen to me, Tac, 'cause we don't have much time. Just get his attention. Make him turn, maybe loosen his grip a little, all right?"

"If you say so, sis."

"I do."

Tacoma looks over at his father, who nods. He nods back. "Okay. I'm ready."

Taking off her gloves, Dakota flexes her fingers, then eases them around the pump action of the shotgun. "All right. Ready? Go!"

Tacoma rises up in a perfect marksman's stance and eases the trigger back. The sound of the rifle firing is almost insignificant, but the bullet hits its mark, and the man spins. The two girls stumble off their feet, still tethered to this man by their hair. Both scream in agony.

Dakota jumps to her feet, shotgun socketed and ready. "Let them go, you bastard!" The last word hangs in the air, only to be obliterated a split second later by the huge roar of the shotgun's blasting. Most of the man's face disappears, and he topples back into the snow. "Katie! Kelly! RUN!"

They try, but they're still in the ungiving grip of the man's hands. Screaming in terror, they finally find the strength to pull away, leaving sizable hunks of brown hair behind.

"RUN!" Dakota starts forward, shotgun aimed and ready. Sinking into thigh-deep snow with every step, her gait is slow and plodding. Everything seems preternaturally bright as she moves forward, keeping a wary eye on the fallen stranger.

A moment later, a second man darts outside. He's armed with an Uzi, which he immediately fires, spraying bullets all over the compound. Dakota drops into the snow an instant too late. She can feel the hot bloom of pain welling up from her side. She doesn't know how badly she's hurt, but her body freezes, stunned for a brief moment, and she loses her grip on the gun. "Shit!"

"Dakota!"

She can hear the screams of her father and brother, but the sound of Tacoma's frantic rifle fire is drowned out by the noise of the Uzi firing again and again.

"Stay down!"

She thinks she's screaming, but the sound is only a gasp. She struggles to move, but the snow has her cocooned, and her body still isn't ready to work the way it should. Long fingers, reddened and chapped from the icy snow and bitter wind, scramble desperately for the gun she's lost.

"DAKOTA!"

Rounds of fire streak over her head. *It sounds like a war zone, and in a way*, she muses, *that's exactly what it is*. She knows her father and brother are pinned down by the Uzi fire. To move forward would be suicide, but she also knows that either one would willingly risk his life for hers. And she would do the same, without hesitation.

*Dear God, let them be safe. Please let them be safe. If I have to die, fine. Just...don't take them too, okay?*

*Finally!* Luck puts her hand in the path of her shotgun, and with a spastic, clamping grip, she drags it through the snow to cradle against her chest. She can't really feel it; her hands are blocks of wood, but her finger finds the trigger by pure instinct, and she waits, eyes open to whatever fate awaits her.

She can hear footsteps, and knows they're coming from the wrong direction. Her already tense body tenses even further, causing fresh blood to gush from her wound, staining the snow a garish red.

*Snow cone, anyone?*

Gallows humor makes its appearance right on time, as always. A face and the muzzle of an Uzi make a simultaneous appearance within Dakota's reduced field of vision. The face is completely blank; no emotions can be read in those shining, soulless eyes.

She sees him hesitate, and it's all the opening her body needs. Levering her shotgun's muzzle up, she pulls the trigger. "Eat shit, you bastard!"

The force of the blast blows him off his feet, and she forces her body to roll up to a seated, and finally standing, position. She sways for a moment, then walks steadily toward the prone figure lying in the deep snow. She can sense her family closing quickly, but this is something she has to do for herself. White teeth flash in a wolf's smile and she points the gun downward. "Die, you miserable, stinking piece of shit."

A pull of the trigger, and the face is totally obliterated. A pump of the action, and she places the muzzle against the shoulder joint. Another blast and the arm disintegrates from the shoulder. A third blast takes the second arm. Finally satisfied, she relaxes slightly, still staring down at the mangled figure in the snow.

A warm hand clasps her shoulder, and she turns her head to look up into the concerned face of her father. "I'll be all right. Are you guys okay?"

"That was some shooting, sis," Tacoma remarks, grinning. Then he notices the blood on her shirt and his smile disappears. "Shit, Koda, you got busted."

"I'll live," she replies dryly, though now that the fight is over, her pain begins to make itself felt. "We need to go up to the house and see if anyone else is still alive."

Reaching down, her father picks up the Uzi, then straightens. "Your brother and I will take care of that. You just get back to your truck and wait for us there."

Though many years from her childhood, Dakota knows an order when she hears one, and nods. "Yes, sir."

A rare hint of a smile crosses her father's handsome face. "You did well, Daughter. I'm proud."

*Funny, even after all these years, how good that still makes me feel.* Even so, as she watches her father and brother enter the house, she resists going back to the warmth of her truck. Clamping a hard hand on her wound to help staunch the sluggish bleeding, she stares down at her handiwork. The figure is twitching. The legs are moving in slow motion, like a dog dreaming of chasing butterflies. That fierce grin comes again, but she doesn't raise her gun. *Not yet. Not yet.*

"I might not be able to kill you, you bastard, but I can make damn sure you don't ever hurt anyone again."

# CHAPTER TWO

It's been two days since the shooting, and Dakota's wound, not much more than a graze, is healing, though still painful. When the crowded rooms and the close press of humanity gets to be too much, she escapes to the glassed-in porch, closing the door behind her and reveling in the silence of a South Dakota winter evening. It's snowing again. The flakes, heavy and wet, hiss through the air in a soothing monotone.

The storm door squeals in protest as it is opened again, and the floorboards groan out accompaniment as Dakota's father joins her on the porch. She hears a slight rustle, then the flick of a match being struck against the wooden casement, and soon the air is filled with the sweet smell of pipe tobacco. Its scent takes Dakota back to the days of her childhood, when her whole world was the man standing beside her and her only goal in life was to see the light of pride in his eyes. Eyes that are, like hers, a brilliant, pale blue, a queer genetic anomaly going back as long as anyone can remember. For long moments, the porch is silent save for quiet breaths and the hissing of the snow.

The remnants of the MacGregor family — Kimberly, her two grown daughters and two granddaughters — have taken up residence in a small house just to the west of the main home. Dakota's mother is helping them through their grief as best she can, trying to break through the silent, staring shock that melds them to their beds and chairs, living statues crafted by the hand of a madman.

The rest of the family spends its days huddled around the CB radio, gleaning and hoarding each bit of information the way a prospector panned for gold dust. Wild speculation paints the airwaves in crazy, neon colors: space aliens have landed in Washington DC; Peter Westerhaus has sold out to certain Middle Eastern interests, handing them the United States on a silver platter; and the most popular, God is using Satan's tools to cleanse the Earth in preparation for the return of His Son.

Each rumor is treated as Gospel truth, examined like a diamond for clarity and flaws, and kept or discarded based on its possible merit.

"Your spirit wanders."

Shaken from her reverie, Dakota lets out a small sigh, tips her head slightly, and leans a shoulder against the sturdy frame of the porch. She eyes her father directly, taking in his gentle, somber countenance.

"Where will you go?"

"Home. At least, at first. I need to..."

Her voice trails off, but her father nods his understanding. "And then?"

"South, I think. To Rapid City."

"To the base?"

"Yes."

"Very dangerous."

"I know."

"Your mother will forbid it."

Dakota nods, dropping her gaze to the worn boards. "I know that, too." Her voice is no more than a whisper, its timbre blending with the falling snow.

A soft rustle of cloth eases the silence, and when Dakota raises her eyes, her father is holding an object out to her. Her eyes widen as the significance of the object becomes abundantly clear. "Your medicine pouch..."

"Take it."

"But—"

"*Le icu wo, chunkshi.*"

Reaching out, she allows her fingers to curl around the small, worn pouch. In turn, her father's warm fingers curl around hers. Their eyes meet. He gives her a rare and precious smile.

"If I were younger and did not have a family to protect, I would do as you do now, Dakota." His face sobers and he releases her hand. "Go now. Say goodbye to your brothers and sisters. I will talk to your mother."

Rising to his feet, he is gone before she can open her mouth to thank him.

**Twenty minutes later**, Dakota stands by her truck, gazing one last time upon her family, whose faces are pressed against the large windows, fogging them and making the watching figures dreamy and indistinct.

Her mother's face is the only one she can see clearly, and her expression is a swirling thundercloud of anger, love, and fear. Her heavy arms are crossed against her ample bosom, and as Dakota meets her eyes, she scowls and turns away.

Clenching her jaw in frustration, Dakota also turns and opens the door to her truck. Before she can step in, her mother comes at her from behind, wrapping her arms around Dakota's slim waist and pulling her back.

"*Yé shni ye, chunkshi. Yé shni ye.*"

Dakota turns in her mother's arms, bringing up chilled hands to cup soft, careworn cheeks. "I have to go, Mother. I need to do this."

"And I need you here, Dakota. Here, with your family, where you belong."

"*Ina...*"

"Wife."

Dakota's mother turns to look at her husband, then back at her daughter. "Please. I'm asking you. Stay."

"*Ina,* I...can't."

The older woman's face hardens. "Then you are no daughter of mine." She takes in a breath. "Is that what you want?"

Dakota shakes her head. "No, that's not what I want at all."

Her mother smiles, triumphant.

Dakota continues. "But, if that's how you feel it must be, then there's nothing I can do to stop you, Mother. This is something I have to do." Releasing her mother, she steps away. "I love you, Mother. Always."

A long, tense moment passes between them.

"I need to go." Dakota's voice is soft, regretful.

Before she can turn away, her arms are once again filled with the solid, firm body of her mother. They embrace tightly, almost desperately, before finally parting. Turning quickly, Dakota jumps into her truck, starts it, and drives off, savagely ignoring the tears sparkling in her eyes.

**"Shit," Kirsten grumps** as her truck, a valiant old campaigner, wheezes its last and coasts to a stop along the curb in a tiny town in western Pennsylvania. She is completely out of gas. Slamming the steering wheel with one gloved hand, she opens the door and steps out into the cold air, a great deal further from her destination than she'd planned.

The turnpike and vast east-west highways she'd planned to use are almost completely impassable. The news of the uprising has taken the country by sudden storm, people jumping into their cars with just the clothes on their backs, desperate to flee a hopeless situation. Some have been murdered where they sat, behind the wheel. Still others have been killed in multi-vehicle pile-ups or smashed under the wreckage of hurtling semis.

Kirsten has passed several hastily erected, and now abandoned, military checkpoints at which ordinary, innocent citizens have been heartlessly mown down by the supposed protectors of their freedom and constitutional rights to life, liberty, and the pursuit of happiness. Sickened, she has abandoned the highways for secondary roads. Even there, signs of death loom everywhere, and she has spent hours and hours of precious time skirting roads blocked by smashed cars and shattered bodies. When she reaches the outskirts of western Pennsylvania, her truck finally sputters and stops.

She finds herself in a ghost town in the likes of which old Spaghetti Westerns were made. There is no sign of life anywhere she looks, and the air is devoid of sound save for a howling wind and the rusted protest of a sign hanging from long chains hooked to the eaves of a roof. Thompson's Realty, the sign says. A Great Place to call Home.

"Not anymore," Kirsten says, then laughs a little at the poor joke. As if in response, Asimov whines, and she widens the door, beckoning him out. They both hear the hiss of a startled cat, and before she can even open her mouth, Asimov is off like a shot, chasing the fleeing feline down the empty street.

"You'd better get your ass back here or I'll leave without you!" Kirsten shouts, then listens as her words echo off the storefronts that border both sides of the street. She waits long enough to realize that her threat has gone unheeded. "Great. Now even my dog doesn't believe me."

She turns as she picks up another sound, one she can't quite decipher. Her heart gathers speed and, reaching into the open cab of her truck, she grabs her pistol and hauls it out, aiming in the direction of the sound. "Who's there?"

The question echoes, and when it finally dies off, the sound, still indecipherable, is still there. Curiosity sets her feet in motion, and she heads for a staid, brick-faced church sitting on the corner. Rounding the corner, she stops dead, as the source of the noise becomes readily apparent.

A huge cross dominates the church's lawn, and upon that cross, two bodies hang, one from each arm. Their faces are purple, their tongues and eyes, protruding. Each head is cocked identically, almost comically, lolling from the stalk of a broken neck. Both wear cardboard placards around their necks, each bearing the same crudely written phrase: REPENT! FOR THE HOUR OF GOD IS AT HAND!

"Jesus."

Turning away from the gruesome sight, her gaze is captured by the front of the church. The doors, red as barn paint, have been broken inward and lie shattered and crazy-canted in the vestibule. Unable to stop herself, she climbs the steps and enters the church itself, then almost reverses her course as the overwhelming stench of death and decay permeates her nostrils and twists her guts into a heaving uproar.

"Dear God. Oh, Jesus."

The church must have, at one time, been filled to capacity. Now all that remains are the men, the very old, and the very young. She doesn't have to look to know that each body bears at least one bullet hole, adult and child alike. They lie in the pews and in the aisles, their limbs canted at angles impossible to living flesh. These people didn't die easily. As she looks up toward the altar, she freezes, jaw dropping silently open like a trap door at the end of well-oiled hinges.

The Lector, clad in a dark, somber suit, lies draped over the altar, half of his head missing. His stiffened fingers curl inward as if trying to form fists. A huge, gold-leafed Bible, its thin pages dotted with blood, lies open before him. He almost appears to be reading it with the one eye he has left.

But even that isn't the worst atrocity in this room. That honor belongs to the life-sized cross hanging above the altar. Instead of the requisite figure of the crucified Jesus staring up into the heavens through sorrowing eyes, the Priest, clad in heavy purple, white and gold vestments, hangs, long nails driven through his wrists and feet. A crude facsimile of the Crown of Thorns — in actuality some barbed wire from the local hardware store — is pressed upon his bald head, and runnels of dried blood paint his face like ruby tears.

A sign loops around his neck, bearing only one word. HERETIC

"Oooookay, then. That's quite enough of this. I think I'd best be going now."

With deliberate steps, Kirsten turns and walks out of the church as quickly as her feet will carry her. Only when she has turned the corner and is out of sight of the two hanging corpses does she stop, one hand pressed to her chest. Her heart thumps crazily against it as if trying to exit through muscle and bone.

Finally, her breathing and heart rate calm, and she chances a look around. The town is as empty, and as silent, as it was when she first entered. This helps to calm her further.

"All right then, let's get down to business."

**It is well** past midnight, and the only light that glows in the fair-sized ranch house comes from the large, roaring fire in the fieldstone fireplace. The electricity and phones are out, but for South Dakota in winter, that's almost a given. An unlit oil lantern sits on a low table that borders a long, low-slung couch.

Koda sits on the couch, one long leg tucked beneath her, the other thrown casually over the stout wooden arm. With steady hands, she works through a fat stack of glossy photos. Some she lingers over, a smile creasing her face. Others she flips quickly past, pain darkening the blue of her eyes. On the mantle, a brass clock in the shape of a galloping horse ticks, keeping a time that she senses will no longer be needed in this world.

The last in the stack of pictures comes up, and, smiling, she lifts it closer to her face, placing the others down on the rough-hewn coffee table. The photo is of a slim, beautiful Lakota woman, her coal-black almond eyes sparkling with love and laughter. Clad in a white, beaded gown, she grins with mischievous intent as her hands, filled with a large piece of cake dripping with frosting, begin to move forward as if to shove said cake into the face of the picture taker.

"Got me good, didn't ya," Dakota whispers, trailing a gentle thumb over the woman's grinning features. "I miss you."

Holding the picture to her chest, she unfolds herself and lies full length on the couch, staring into the crackling flames until sleep finally overtakes her.

**The sound of** trashcans rattling in an alleyway almost causes Kirsten's heart to leap out through her mouth, and she spins, pointing her gun in the direction of the noise. A slat-thin, mangy dog runs out of the alley, grinning at her, and she comes a hairsbreadth away from blowing it to Kingdom Come. The dog stops and growls, its hackles rising in spiky tufts over bony shoulders, its teeth white and glimmering.

"Nice doggy. Niiiice doggy."

The dog growls again, dropping low on its haunches and slinking forward.

Kirsten follows its progress with the muzzle of her gun. "Oh, c'mon, pooch, you really don't want to be doing this." She waggles her gun. "Trust me, there are easier ways to get some dinner, dog. I bet I don't even taste that good." She pauses. "Well, figuratively speaking, anyway."

Continuing its advance, the dog gathers its legs underneath itself, muscles tensing, preparing to leap.

"Aw hell," Kirsten sighs, her finger tightening on the trigger.

Before either party can move, a blur of black and silver bisects the invisible line between them, and the dog yelps as it is driven away, rolling several times before it lands on its side, chest aspirating weakly like a bellows running out of air.

"Asimov! It's about time you showed up!"

Asimov looks over his shoulder, tongue lolling.

"Don't play innocent with me, you flea-bitten throw rug. Now, if you're done playing with your little friend there, we need to get moving. It won't stay light forever, ya know."

Lifting a gigantic paw, Asimov graciously allows his prey to escape, yelping and whining, back into the darkness of the alley from which it came, scrawny tail tucked between its legs.

Sticking the gun into the waistband of her jeans, Kirsten rubs her hands together. "All right, then. First things first. We need to get us some wheels. A van, I think. With a full gas tank. And keys in the ignition."

Asimov gives her a look.

"All right, all right. So I'm a little picky. Is that a crime?"

Rolling her eyes, Kirsten moves down the road, away from the church and its gruesome inhabitants. Rounding another corner, her eyes light up as she spies a used car lot. Its red, white and blue pennants flicker and flap in the freshening breeze, displaying their wares in a manic frenzy to no one.

She walks slowly along the sidewalk, looking over the selection — what there is of one. The cars are, for the most part, dusty, dented, and gently rusting as they rest on slowly softening, tread-worn tires. The hand-lettered signs, once bright and eye-catching, are now faded and cracked under the harsh mercies of the glaring sun and bitter wind.

Asimov looks up at his mistress and whines.

"I know, boy. We'll find something. Don't worry."

Turning in at the gate, she makes her way into the lot, stepping over several fallen bodies with a resolve not to look.

*Deadwood,* she thinks to herself. *Just deadwood, piles of it, like the stuff that lies outside our cabin on the Cape, waiting for winter.*

Near the back of the lot, there is a service bay, and just outside that service bay is a large, white cargo van which looks to be perfect for her needs. It has a few dents, and the driver's side rocker panel has seen a better decade, but the tires look new, and as long as the battery is well juiced, she thinks she can run with it.

As she steps around to the passenger's side, she stops cold. The body of a young man, barely out of his teens, lies half in and half out of the van. He was obviously once a detailer, since there is a cloth in one hand and a sponge in the other. If not for the now-familiar unnatural cock of his head, she would think that he was just resting; taking a break from what she believes has to be one of the world's most monotonous jobs. His face is young and handsome in a Midwestern, corn-fed way, and the wind whips his curly blond hair into a halo around his head. He should be on a football field somewhere tackling behemoths and scoring cheerleaders.

Her eyes begin to well, and she wipes at them savagely, unable to spare the time she'd need to mourn.

*Not now. Just keep going. You need to keep it together, K, or you're gonna end up just like him.*

Taking in a deep breath, she reaches forward and, as gently as she possibly can, eases the young man from his place inside the van. As soon as he is flat on the ground, she stands up and wipes her hands on the fabric of her jeans, then takes the large step up into the van.

The boy has done his job well. The van is immaculately clean inside and smells fresh, despite housing a corpse for God knows how many days. There are two bench seats — one in front, one behind. The rest of the huge van is completely empty. She looks over at the control panel. Though old, the transmission is automatic, and, best of all, the keys are dangling from the ignition. This brings a smile to her face and she turns to look down at the whining dog waiting just outside. "Asimov, I think we're in business."

**The morning dawns** bitterly cold and thankfully clear. Dakota has been up for several hours. Her sturdy knapsack is packed to the brim with clothing and non-perishable foodstuffs. The fire is out, and the hearth has been swept clean of ashes. Dakota's breath emerges in frosty plumes as she walks through the rooms of her home, saying a quiet goodbye to things she knows she'll never see again. Crossing through the living room, she stops at a door just to the left of the stairs leading up to the loft and twists the knob, entering into another large and chilled room.

A flip of the switch, and brilliant fluorescent lights flicker and hum to life, powered by the backup generator located at the rear of the house. The lights reveal a sterile space in white and chrome. Two examination tables sit side by side, their surfaces sparkling and immaculate. Two walls sport inlaid counters which hold a wide variety of surgical instruments covered in sterile wrap. A huge autoclave sits in a corner, silent, cold and dark. Along the third wall are several rows of large wire kennels, stacked three high, and four incubators and one warmer bed rest along the fourth. All are empty.

As a Doctor of Veterinary Medicine and Licensed Wildlife Rehabilitation Specialist, Dakota has spent the majority of her adult life in this room, patiently coaxing warmth, food, and life back into injured or abandoned animals native to her home state. When she listens closely enough, she fancies she can hear the meeps, howls, growls, purrs, and screeching cries of each and every animal she has treated here. She has mourned each death and celebrated each second chance at life that her skills, and luck, have been able to grant. Her sharp eyes scan the room, imprinting each piece of equipment, each warm success, each sad defeat, indelibly to memory. And then, with a soft sigh, she turns to leave, plunging the room into blackness once again.

**Her truck packed** and warming, Dakota makes one last trip, plowing through thigh-deep snow to the back of her sprawling house. Her horses have been fed and watered and set free to wander or to stay as they will. Her house has been raided of all useful items, and only this one thing is left to do before she can begin her trek into the unknown.

The piled stone marker is covered with snow, a fanciful little hillock protruding from an otherwise flat landscape. Bending down, she carefully brushes the snow away until the rocks are uncovered to her gaze.

The front of the cairn is inlaid with a small, stone marker, carved in loving detail. The marker holds three simple words. *Tali. Mitháwichu ki.*

Tali. My wife.

Ungloving her left hand, she brushes the very tips of her fingers against the words, eyes dim with remembering. A long moment passes in this utter silence, until the sun spreads its rays over the barn and highlights the cairn in lines of dazzling gold.

With a slow blink to clear the tears welling in her eyes, Dakota reaches up and twists the simple gold band from her finger. She stares at it, watching as it sparkles in the newborn sunlight, then she tucks it reverently into a seam in the rocks, drawing her fingers over its warmth one last time before withdrawing.

"I'll never forget you."

**She moves through** a world gone all to white. White earth, white sky, bare, snow-covered trees. Ice swirls in netted patterns like her grandmother's best crocheted tablecloth where the steady thump of the windshield wipers does not reach. Her breath makes a white cloud about her in the unheated cabin of her truck.

White is the color of the north. White is the color of death.

Before her the white road lies unmarked. Ten miles from home, and no traffic has passed here since the snowfall stopped just at dawn. The only sign of life is a line of small four-toed prints running along a barbed wire fence line. A fox, moving fast.

Koda's gloved fingers curl stiffly about the rim of the steering wheel. Her feet, numb despite three pairs of wool and silk socks and the fleece linings of her boots, somehow manage to find the accelerator and the brake as needed. Snow and ice limit her speed, even with the chains. Which, she thinks, is just as well. She cannot afford an accident.

She can't afford to turn on the heater, either. It is not that she fears sensors or spy satellites; her truck's V-8 will show up half the size of Mount Rushmore in the infrared regardless. She has more than enough gas in her double tanks to make the forty miles to Rapid City and back, taking farm-to-market roads like this one to avoid the Interstate, enough to scout the extent of the devastation in this corner of South Dakota. The trouble is that she has no idea if she will be able to buy or scavenge so much as another drop between now and her return.

"Take nothing for granted," her father said as she hugged him good-bye. "Trust nothing and no one. Come back safe."

The wound in her side aches with the cold. She holds the pain away from her, just as she does the memories of the massacre the night before. There will be a time again for rage, a time for mourning; she cannot afford them now.

Twelve miles further and a sign appears on her right, to the north of the road. Standing Buffalo Ranch, home to Paul and Virginia Hurley and their five kids. The welded pipe gate leans open, the cattle guard clotted with snow. There are no tire marks on the narrow road that leads up to the ranch house and barns, out of sight over a low ridge. Koda can just see the spokes of a generator windmill, its three blades and their hub hung with ice. No tire marks, possibly no electricity. No one out doing anything about it.

She swerves the truck in to the turnoff, the chains racketing on the metal grille as she crosses the cattle guard. Beside her on the seat, blunt and angular in its functional ugliness, is the Uzi she took from one of the things that killed the MacGregors. If what she has begun to fear is true, she will not need it. Still, it gives her comfort. Blasting another of the things to atoms would give her more.

How many dead? How many taken? She has no answers to those questions.

*Why? Dear God and all the saints, spirits of my ancestors, why?*

She has no answer to that question, either.

Koda does not realize that she has some spark of hope left until she sees the ranch house door swinging open and the snow in the entryway. The point of light, infinitely small as it is, winks out. Gone. Darkness. The white expanse between house and barn is unmarked. Two vehicles are drawn up in the carport. One is Paul Hurley's Dodge Ram crew cab; the other is an SUV she does not recognize. She pulls up behind them, cross-wise, and waits. There is no movement behind the gauzy front curtains, none behind the smaller window near the driveway where a bottle of Dawn dish soap and a long-handled sponge perch on the sill beneath a gingham ruffle. When she thinks she has waited long enough, she waits as long again. Still nothing.

Slowly Koda takes her hands from the steering wheel. She lifts the Uzi from its resting place beside her and slings the strap across her body, maneuvering it past the wide brim of her hat. Briefly she checks the magazine. Very carefully, she eases her door open and slithers down and forward to crouch behind the bulk of the still-running engine. There is a moment when she is, blessedly, almost warm with its heat. Then the wind, not strong but straight off six feet of packed snow and ice, reasserts itself, and her feet remind her that she is standing calf-deep in more of the same.

Koda whips from behind the truck and runs for the front porch as low and as fast as the snow will let her. She draws up short with her back against the wall, her weapon raised. For the first time she hears a sound from within the house, a small dog barking incessantly, somewhere toward the back and up. She eases through the doorframe and into the front hall. Nothing. Beyond is the living room, where a feathery dusting of snow lies across the dark green carpet and under the ornament-hung Douglas fir, covering the gaily wrapped presents with swirls of frost. A small aquarium holds angelfish, brilliant and ethereal, suspended like jewels in ice. The dining room, separated from the parlor by an open arch, seems in order, Virginia's proud collection of majolica serving dishes still stately in their place of honor along the sideboard. Only the CD tower is out of place, lying across the door to the den with its flat plastic cases spilled out beside it.

She braces herself for what she knows she will find when she enters the room. Paul Hurley is there, still on the couch in front of the television, empty eyes staring at the ceiling with his head bent back against the cushions at a ninety-degree angle. A Budweiser can tilts floorward in his half-open hand. David, youngest of the five children, lies at his feet, an obscene red blossom of blood and torn flesh in the middle of his back. Shotgun. Eddie, older by five years, sprawls in the lounger, neck broken like his father's, a bag of potato chips still in his lap.

Cold inside now, no longer feeling the frigid air, Koda takes the can from Paul's hand and gently attempts to move his fingers. Their rigidity tells her what she already knows must be true. When she turns David over, as much not to have to see the terrible hole in his body as to see his face and know for certain that he is David, he slips from her stiff hands and thumps solidly against the television cabinet. Frozen. Frozen cold and dead.

It is a line from a poem from some forgotten moment of her childhood, lifetimes, eons distant from this time and this place. It goes 'round in her head, over and over. Frozen. Frozen cold and dead. Her own horror is beyond her understanding. She has seen harder deaths, has dissected human bodies as part of her training. Still the line of the poem goes 'round, as if to keep her mind from worse things.

Frozen. Frozen cold and dead.

The dog's yapping is louder here in the den. Koda steps carefully around the coffee table and climbs the stairs, setting her feet soundlessly on the treads. The barking grows clearer with each step, higher and more frantic. At the landing, she has a clear view of the master bedroom through the open door. The blue-and-russet log cabin quilt lies undisturbed, forming an angular pattern with the brass bars of the Hurleys' antique bed. In another room, curlers and makeup litter the dresser. Double closets stand open, with girls' jeans and sweaters strewn over the floor amid broken glass from a framed poster of Britney Spears that tilts crazily against the wall. Despite the clear signs of a struggle, there are no bodies in the room.

The yapping comes from behind a third bedroom door, this one closed. As Koda turns the knob and pushes it open, a small furry body flings itself against her knees, alternately panting and barking. She swings the Uzi behind her back, out of the dog's reach, and hunkers down to soothe the frantic creature, gently rubbing its ears. "There, fella," she croons. "There, baby, it's all right. I've got you. There, there."

As it calms, reassured by her experienced touch and the low monotone of her voice, she ascertains that it is a neutered male Yorkshire terrier, dehydrated and not recently fed. A bedraggled blue bow clinging to a tuft of fur above his eyes matches the polish on his manicured nails. Not a country dog. The tag on his rhinestone-studded collar identifies him as Louie and his mistress as Adele Hurley of Pierre, with address and telephone number. *Which*, she notes with an unexpected sense of relief, *explains the Suburban.*

When she finally enters the room, Louie now quiet at her heels except for a low whine, she finds Adele toppled forward on the rug, the legs of her walker jutting absurdly past her hips. Blood has soaked her short grey hair, stiffened by the freezing cold into scarlet spikes. An elderly man lies half on and half off the bed, his battered skull partly concealed by a fold of the comforter. Clumsy with the bulk of her gloves, Koda removes his billfold from his hip pocket and thumbs through the plasticine card pockets until she finds his driver's license. He is — *he was*, she corrects herself — Theodore Hurley, also of Pierre.

Koda knows that Paul's father is long dead, having attended his funeral three years before. Theodore must have been an uncle.

A search of the rest of the house yields no sign of Virginia or her three adolescent daughters. In the kitchen, Koda discovers that the hot tap is dripping; there is still water. *Thank you God for propane.* She sets about feeding and watering Louie and examining the contents of Virginia's pantry. As she counts the cans of beans and the Mason jars filled with bright gold and purple preserves, spiced peaches, and pickled beets, a shudder creeps over her that has nothing to do with the cold. She feels like a ghoul, pawing through the remnants of a woman's life.

Remnants that will help feed her own family and the refugees gathered in their home. Virginia would not want her good food to go to waste. *There will*, she tells herself, *be no more trips to the Safeway anytime soon.*

Koda finds the matches and lights a burner to make herself a cup of the Hurleys' instant Maxwell House, then lights the oven, leaving it open so the room will warm. She closes the swinging door behind her as she returns upstairs to search the linen cabinet. Five blankets she carries down and sets out on a chair in the den; one, the thickest quilt she can find, she makes into a bed for Louie beside the stove. She is almost comfortable as she sips the dark brew — *almost coffee*, she thinks wryly — warming her fingers that seem to be gone all to cold bone against the thick earthenware of the cup. She finds herself almost smiling as Louie turns twice widdershins and thumps down onto the mounded bedspread with a wheezy sigh, full-bellied, and secure for the first time in days. Within seconds, he begins to snore.

Promising herself another cup before she leaves, Koda pulls her gloves back on and slogs through the snow to the barn. The doors are closed but not locked. When her eyes accustom themselves to the dim light, she finds a pair of Holstein cows and a heifer huddled together amid the hay, their breath making cloudy weather about them. An Appaloosa turns his head toward her expectantly as she approaches his stall; his quarterhorse stablemate, more impatient, whinnies loudly and stamps. Speaking softly, she rubs each of their noses in turn.

Half an hour later, the cows and horses are fed and watered, the stalls mucked out. In the process of finding and dragging out a sack of feed, Koda has also discovered a dozen red hens and a rooster along a shelf in an empty stall. Now replete, they are back on their perch, clucking softly, settling down once more. Like Louie, they are as comfortable and safe as she can make them.

Only one thing left to do.

Koda takes the snow shovel from its place against the barn wall and makes her way to the north side of the house, where the sun, when it comes out, will be slow to melt the drifts, where more fall will pile high. She digs a shallow trench, long and narrow, under the eaves. The ground beneath is frozen.

One by one, she brings the dead from the house and lays them in all the grave she can make for them. She expects the children to be the hardest. But while her heart clenches as she wraps their bodies, cold as any stone, and bears them out to their burials, it is the death of the old folk that comes nearest to breaking it. They should have died in their beds, at home, their children and grandchildren about them. Wise, content in their passing.

*Até*, she promises her father as the silent tears spill from her eyes, *Ina, my mother: I will not let you die like this.*

Gently Koda drops the snow over the bodies, gently smoothes the surface so that there will be no sign of disturbance with the next fall. She turns to go.

It is too stark; there should be some ceremony, some leave-taking. The Hurleys are Irish Catholic, every man jack and woman of them for four generations all the way back to Ellis Island and a thousand years before that. She cannot find their priest in Rapid City and send him back; it is far too dangerous, even if he is somehow still alive. She will have to do, heathen that she is.

She searches her memory for the words, and they come to her, the Church's prayer for those about to step onto the Blue Road of the spirit. She signs a cross above the snow and murmurs, "Go forth, Christian souls, out of this world: in the name of the Father, who has created you; in the name of the Son, who has redeemed you; in the name of the Holy Spirit, who sanctifies you. Into Paradise may the angels lead you; at your coming may the martyrs receive you, and lead you into the Holy City, Jerusalem. Amen."

Koda stands a moment more by the grave, head bowed in respect. Then she turns once again to the care of the living.

Back in the house, the second and not nearly so satisfying cup of not-quite-coffee in her hand, Koda wrestles briefly with herself whether to leave the oven on for Louie. In the end she opts for safety and her mother's training, turns it off, ruffles the sleeping dog's ears a last time, and returns to her truck. As she swings back out of the driveway, she thumbs her CB on. "Wash. Washington, come in."

"Hey, Koda! You comin' home already? You got a flat? You need me to come help you?"

"Hey yourself, bro. We've been there, done that. Mom and Dad need you at home."

"Yeah, sure." A whole world of adolescent male discouragement is loaded into the two words.

*Eddie. David.* Koda's hand clenches on the mic. *I won't let that happen to you either, little brother. Not while I live.* But she says steadily, "Is Dad around? Tacoma?"

"I'll get 'em. Hang on."

It is Tacoma who takes the call. "Dad's out in the barn. What's up?"

Guardedly, Koda describes what she has found at the Hurley ranch. "It's the same pattern. Paul and the boys are dead. So are an elderly couple I think were his aunt and uncle. The girls and Virginia are missing. Soon as you can, you and Dad need to come get the food out of the pantry and take the livestock, including a small shaggy dog named Louie."

"Louie?" There is laughter in Tacoma's voice.

"Yeah, Louie. Mom'll like him. There are trailers here; you just need to bring the trucks."

"Gotcha."

"And listen. Nobody's been here since they were killed. If you see more tracks than mine, one set coming and another set going—"

"Gotcha again," he interrupts. "We'll be careful. You do the same."

"Yeah. Later."

"Later," he echoes, and breaks the connection.

**Kirsten pulls along** the drop-off curb in front of the Shop 'n Go Market. Jumping out of the van, she walks to the back and opens the large cargo doors, displaying an interior which now has a number of five- and ten-gallon gas cans, filled to the brim with fuel. Gas had taken her a while to get; without electricity to power the pumps, she had to resort to siphoning, which left her nauseated and with the foul taste of gasoline in her mouth.

Asimov whines at her from the rear bench seat, and she looks at him. "You stay here and guard the truck, boy. No chasing cats, or dogs, or rats, or whatever else strikes your fancy. You just stay here, all right? I'll be back in a little while."

The large dog whines again but settles down, propping his big head on the top of the seat and looking at her through soulful brown eyes.

"Not this time, boy. I'm sorry, but I need to move quick and not be chasing you around the store. We'll be on the road soon, I promise."

With a long suffering sigh that would have done a Jewish mother proud, Asimov seems to accept his mistress's terms and drops his head off the seat, stretching his body along the back in preparation for a nap.

Nodding in satisfaction, Kirsten steps away from the van and walks toward the wide glass doors of the supermarket. Engaged in her thoughts, she doesn't stop until she feels a thick sheet of glass pressed tight against her body. Stunned, she takes a step back and stares at the door for a moment, perplexed. Then she utters a shaky laugh and mentally slaps her head. Without electricity, the automatic doors have become as useful as a flag to a hen. Stepping forward, more cautiously this time as though the doors might suddenly grow fangs and attempt to bite, she wraps a hand around the small handle and pulls. It takes most of her strength, but she manages to bully the door open wide enough to slip through. And immediately steps back outside again as the high, sweet stench of decaying food and rotting human assaults her senses for the second time that afternoon. It's a good thing that her stomach is filled with nothing but hunger, or she would be adding to the stench. Wiping heavily watering eyes with both hands, she takes a few deep breaths of cold, outside air and contemplates her options.

There aren't many. The next store down is a SavMor Pharmacy, but unless she plans to spend the rest of her time on the road subsisting on cheese crackers washed down by swigs of cherry-flavored laxative, the grocery store is the only game in town. Reaching into her back pocket, she pulls out a grey bandana, flaps it out, and ties it securely around her nose and mouth. It won't do much, she's quite sure, but it's better than nothing. She hopes.

Figuratively girding her loins, Kirsten steps back to the door and again bullies it open by sheer strength. Her stomach immediately twists and growls out its outrage as the stench assaults her senses anew, but she silently commands it to shut up and takes a step forward into the store. Her gaze is immediately drawn upwards by a large, bright sign that catches the rays of the slowly dying sun: Wednesdays are Senior Days at Shop 'n Go! Golden age discounts for our golden age members!

Without looking down, she mentally calculates the days, and a grimace spreads over her face as she realizes that today is Friday. Finally allowing her gaze to lower, she finds herself in the middle of an abattoir. Elderly men and women had heeded the sign and died in droves. They are scattered through the aisles like fallen trees, still dressed in their Sunday best. A smattering of younger people, mostly adolescent boys and a couple of grown men, lie sprawled out by the cash registers and the manager's booth. The enemy caught them unaware, and they'd never had time to defend themselves, not that they could have had any success against their inhuman murderers.

The lights flicker and hum, dimming and brightening in a pulsing rhythm courtesy of the backup generator that is obviously breathing its last.

The aisles are so tightly packed with corpses that she'll never get a cart down any of them. Resigning herself, she grabs two hand baskets and carefully makes her way over and around the dead, searching for what she'll need to survive the long trip she has ahead of her.

An hour, and five trips later, she's finally done. Canned goods, dog food, the few fresh vegetables and fruits she could find, water by the gallon, and several butane stoves she found in the clearance aisle share space with the gas cans in the van's large cargo hold. A quick trip to the neighboring pharmacy, not nearly as crowded with rotting corpses, yields first aid items, personal care items, and enough narcotics to land her in jail, were there anyone around to arrest her.

She thinks for a moment, then steps into the cargo hold, grabbing her backpack and pulling out a fresh set of clothes. The ones she's wearing reek of death and decay, and once she's stripped them off — wishing mightily for a bath — she tosses them onto the pavement of the lot never to be used again.

Jumping out of the van, she closes the cargo doors, locks them against accidental opening, and returns to the driver's seat. Asimov wakes up from his nap and jumps into the front seat beside her. Smiling and ruffling his ears, she tosses him a chew-hoof she picked up in the market, starts the ignition, and drives quickly away from the small town, leaving it deserted once again.

**She returns to** a world of undisturbed whiteness. There has been no further snowfall, but neither has any melted. The flat white stretches away in all directions, broken only by fence posts jutting through the drifts at intervals. Icicles hang from barbed wire strung between like Christmas tinsel. The blank sky offers no light, casts no shadows. It is a world of the dead, for the dead.

For the first time, Koda is grateful for the miserable cold. Without it, without the growl of the powerful engine under her truck's hood, her senses would have nothing to cling to. She has lived on the northern plains all her life, has lived with the winters that come sliding down over open country from the blue pack ice of the Arctic Circle. She has driven snowy roads in the depths of January, when, like now, her truck has been the only moving thing besides the howling wind. This is different.

She is a woman on whom solitude rests easily. This is not solitude. This is isolation from the very idea of life.

Koda strikes the rim of the steering wheel with the flat of her hand, hard. *Damn. Damn again.* She hates being helpless before a disaster she does not understand, cannot quite piece together. *All right, Rivers. Break it down and sort it out. Treat it as an epidemic. Find patient zero, chart the spread.*

She knows her data set is incomplete, but the basic pattern has held true for the MacGregors, for the Hurleys and for all the survivors who have managed to make it to a CB.

*Item. The uprising seems to be spread at least across North America.* She does not know what has happened in Europe or Africa, Asia or South America. It is fairly obvious that less technologically oriented cultures are likely to have more survivors. At least temporarily.

*Item. In all cases the men and boys have been slaughtered, together with the older women. Girls and younger women have disappeared.*

*Item. Two thousand years ago, the pattern would have been familiar. Kill the men, rape the women, sell the virgin girls as slaves.*

*Which makes no sense. Try again.*

*Foreign attack?*

South Dakota has been riddled for decades with nuclear weapons and the missiles to deliver them. So has North Dakota. The prospect of mutual assured destruction has kept them in their silos. Could the Defense Department codes have fallen into enemy hands? And if so, which enemy? And if so, why now?

Abruptly she brakes the truck. There, cut deep in the snow ahead of her, are the tracks of another vehicle. She studies the marks carefully. Wide body. Wide, heavy tires, heavily chained. The asphalt shows through in places where the links have bitten through the ice. A truck of some kind, possibly heavily loaded.

She gets out of the pickup, Uzi slung again over her shoulder. Slowly, she walks up the road between the ruts but sees nothing that can tell her more. No conveniently dropped candy wrappers, no cigarette butts, no beer cans, nothing to tell her whether the occupants of the other truck are human or not. When she has gone a couple hundred yards she gives it up and turns back.

*Now what?*

She scans the flat landscape in all directions. White drifts, bare trees, the dark lines of fences. In the field to her left, there are humps in the snow that may be hay bales or frozen cattle. Most of her route into Rapid City will be through open country like this. She is a little more than five miles north of Elm Creek. There is a bridge.

The snow lies too deep for her to cut across country. The next intersection with another road is on the other side of that bridge. She can turn around, or she can go on.

No choice. Back behind the wheel of the pickup, Koda pulls the fleece-lined leather glove off her right hand. Underneath it is another of knitted wool, below that a silk mitt. She turns the key in the ignition, then drives with her left hand. The right rests on the freezing metal grip of the Uzi in her lap.

A mile along she sees the first living thing that has crossed her path since she set out from the Hurleys. Far out in a rolling meadow to her left, just this side of a line of trees, there is a spill of black across the snow. It moves, separates, shifts again. Ravens. Her gaze follows the line of the rise. There, high above, another bird soars with its wings held in a shallow V. Its form is black against the sky; in the poor light all she can see is a silhouette. Raptor. Not an owl. Not a falcon by the shape of the wings. Hawk or eagle, then.

The sight warms her slightly from within. She is not quite sure why, except that she is pleased to see other living things in this barren landscape, going about their lives, unaffected by the disaster that has overtaken their two-legged relations. As she watches, the bird banks and turns south, toward the creek, and disappears from sight.

A half mile from the bridge, she is still following the tracks of the unknown vehicle. The road curves here, a long, slow, shallow arc that passes through a stand of lodgepole pine and will put her onto a straight stretch no more than a couple hundred yards from the creek. If there is danger, it will be here.

It is waiting for her at the bridge.

A cold stillness spreads around her heart as Koda takes in the blockade. Two troop-carrier trucks are drawn up across the road, blocking the bridge. Four figures in military green winter fatigues stand in front of them, three of them with M-16s held ready, the fourth with a mobile launcher on its shoulder and a bandolier of grenades strung across its chest. Even beneath the bulky clothing, she can make out the bulge of pistols at their belts. In her rear view mirror, she sees two more muffled and heavily armed figures step out of the trees and take up position behind her.

There is no hope of driving around them and through the creek. It is too deep at this point, the bank's too steep. Koda brakes the pickup halfway between the woods and the barricade. She waits.

One of the figures has a bullhorn. The voice that comes through has no human tone, only the flat, tinny quality of the amplifier. "You in the truck. Get out slowly with your hands on top of your head!"

There are three possibilities. These soldiers may be droids. They may be marauders set loose by the spreading chaos. Or they may be what they seem. Deliberately, keeping her right hand in full view through the windshield, Koda slides out, placing both hands firmly on the crown of her Stetson and keeping the door between herself and the soldiers.

"Stand clear of the vehicle!"

Koda hesitates for a heartbeat. Once she is in the open, the Uzi will be in full view. She calculates the odds that she can reach it and take a few of these bastards, if bastards they are, with her before they shoot her down.

Another of the figures steps forward, arm raised. There is a grenade in its hand. "Stand clear NOW!"

The voice is female, deep and furry in the way of the Louisiana bayous. Almost certainly it belongs to a human. Between the soldier's cap and the high collar that conceals most of her face, Koda can just make out the glint of dark eyes. Warily, stepping sideways, she comes out from behind the door.

She shouts, "You guys wanna introduce yourselves?" just as one exclaims, "Shit! He has a gun!"

The figure with the grenade takes a step forward. "Keep your hands away from your weapon!"

"They are away! Who the fuck are you?"

"We're the free people of the United States! Take your left hand off your head and unbutton your coat and shirt! Let us see your throat!"

"After you!"

"Do it! Or I'll frag your truck and incinerate you along with it!"

Non-negotiable. No more time to decide.

The woman brings her hands forward to pull the pin. Before she can reach it, a hawk plunges toward her out of the sky, screaming. It hurtles downward to within inches of her face, pulling up nanoseconds short of collision, talons outstretched to strike. Then it shoots upward again at an almost vertical angle. The woman yells, recoils, wavers, and topples backward into the snow, the grenade disappearing somewhere in the drift.

Laughter catches in Koda's throat as one of the other soldiers raises a gun to shoot at the bird. "No!" she shouts, pulling furiously at the collar of her coat with her right hand, raising her left in a fist. She whistles loud, piercingly. "Wiyo! Wiyo Cetan!"

She whistles three times. At the third, the hawk hovers briefly at her zenith, then stoops again, making straight for Koda. Koda whistles a fourth time, at a lower pitch, and the hawk's body swings forward. Great wings backing air, it comes to light gently, almost delicately, on her upraised fist. Then, mantling and hissing at the dumbstruck soldiers, it sidesteps its way up her arm to her shoulder. One of its wings strikes Koda's hat, knocking it off her head, and her hair comes tumbling down. The hawk settles, glaring.

The leader has regained her feet. A wide grin splits her dark face as she opens her own collar, showing unmarked human flesh. "Colonel Margaret Allen, United States Air Force. Pleased to meet you."

"Dakota Rivers, Lakota Nation."

The colonel offers her hand to shake, and Koda takes it. "You a vet?"

"Yeah."

"I saw your license plate." Koda follows her gaze back to her truck, where the registration numbers are split by a caduceus overlaying a V. "Figured you were human, but we're not taking any chances."

"You from the base?"

The colonel grimaces. "What's left of it." Then, "What are you doing out on the road? You have people in the city?"

Koda shakes her head. "Scouting."

"With a hawk? That's a red-tail, isn't it?"

"Not it. She."

Another of the soldiers has gotten himself sufficiently together to approach. Koda stares at him. He is the first living man she has seen in three days who is not her kin. Her right hand drops to her waist, near the Uzi. He follows her gaze, then opens the throat of his coat. "I'm real, too. August Schimmel. That's a hell of a pet you've got there."

Wiyo mantles again and Koda smiles. It is not a particularly reassuring smile. "Not a pet. A friend."

Colonel Allen bends down and retrieves Koda's hat, hands it to her. "Come on over to one of the carriers, where it's warm. We need to talk."

Koda nods. As she follows the other woman toward the dark olive-green trucks, Wiyo leaves her shoulder with a hiss and rises to settle in a bare sycamore by the bridge. The small flicker of hope that had gone out when she found the Hurleys massacred rekindles itself in a far recess of Koda's mind. There are other people alive, and fighting. She is not alone.

# CHAPTER THREE

Kirsten pulls her jacket more closely about her, balancing the scrapbook between her knees and the rim of the steering wheel. The night is freezing cold, her breath frosting even within the confines of the van, but she cannot afford to waste fuel to run the heater. The cold glare of a halogen flashlight shows her the clippings she has gathered over the years, ever since the news had broken of Westerhaus's stunning advance in robotics. She turns the pages slowly, searching for a pattern, some hint of the inevitability of the present disaster. It is all there, laid out in black and white in yellowing newsprint.

*Advisors Axe Androids, Heckle Hoaxer*

New York (New York Post)  The Chairman of the newly developed President's Committee on Robotics, Howard Mexenbaum, issued a press release today stating that Peter Westerhaus's revolutionary invention is no more revolutionary "...than a child's Halloween costume." Mr. Mexenbaum is quoted as saying, "It's obvious to anyone with two eyes in their head that this android business is a hoax of the highest order. George Lucas showed more ingenuity in stuffing that little man into his R2D2 costume than Westerhaus has yet shown the American people."

When asked, in a private interview, whether Mr. Mexenbaum had actually seen the android in question, he stated that he had not, but that he had heard reports and that those reports were "virtually unanimous" in their disparagement of Westerhaus's "invention."

The press release went on to say that the Committee was drafting a letter to the President asking that the FBI and possibly the CIA open up preliminary investigations on this "...modern day P.T. Barnum."

::flip::

*President is "Utterly Convinced"*

Washington DC (AP)  In a Press Conference in the Rose Garden today, President Hillary Clinton stated that she is "utterly convinced" that Peter Westerhaus's android inventions are, in fact, "the genuine article".

In a private meeting with the President earlier today, Westerhaus unveiled two prototypes of his androids, affectionately named C4PO and R2D3 in a sarcastic reply to Howard Mexenbaum's earlier accusations of huckstering. The President reportedly stood in awe as the androids walked up to her, shook her hand, greeted her by name, and returned to the side of their inventor. One of the androids apparently asked Ms. President if she would like him to fix the squeaky hinge in the door leading to the Oval Office. It is unknown how she replied.

When asked if she would be the first in line to purchase one of the androids when they became commercially available, the President smiled and said, "No, that's why I have Bill."

::flip::

*Westerhaus Announces Household Robot*

New York (AP) Westerhaus Inc. today announced the unveiling of its new home robot, the revolutionary Maid Marian. "We are pleased to offer American householders the greatest time- and labor-saving device since the introduction of the automatic washing machine," company spokesperson Melinda Deliganis said. "The Maid Marian is a highly programmable model that can take over such tedious jobs as cleaning, cooking, and even a limited degree of routine errand-running, such as picking up parcels. She can walk at a maximum speed of 4 miles per hour, and her feet will never get tired!"

Deliganis characterized Microsoft's crash program to develop a competing product as "irrelevant". "We have the patents and the proprietary technology. While it is true that the first Maid Marians will be priced in the high-ticket range, we expect demand to be great enough to support a mass-market version within eighteen months."

::flip::

*Bishop Says There Are No Religious Implications*

Washington (MSNBC)  In an interview with MSNBC's Chris Matthews yesterday, the Right Reverend William S. MacDermott, Presiding Bishop of the Episcopal Church in the United States, stated flatly that the introduction of android robots "...does not pose any theological questions. Does your car pose a theological question?" the Bishop asked rhetorically. "Does your alarm clock?  A robot is a machine, property that can be bought and sold. Nuts and bolts and printed circuits, nothing more."

Asked to respond to Televangelist Pat Robertson's claim that the robots are "the work of the devil", the Bishop referred Matthews to his previous response.  "I'll be surprised if the Rev. Robertson doesn't have one mowing his lawn by the Fourth of July," he quipped.

::flip::

*Royals to Replace Staff with Bots?*

London (Reuters)  A spokesperson for Queen Camilla today declined to confirm or deny that Palace maids and other maintenance personnel will be replaced with androids.  "Her Majesty welcomes technological change, and as you know, has sponsored several scholarships for promising computer-technical students.  This has nothing to do with the current nation-wide shortage of domestic employees."

In a related story (A 14)  the Palace responded, "No comment" to Tonight Show host Jay Leno's  remark that His Majesty King Charles is an early, unmarketable Westerhaus test model.

::flip::

*Phelps Campaign Interrupts Commendation Ceremony*

Minneapolis (CNN)  Jedadiah Phelps, the grandson of Fred Phelps, the late Minister of the Westboro Baptist Church, gathered his faithful flock in protest of a commendation ceremony held in Minneapolis today.  Holding handmade signs and shouting "God Hates Droids!" the group of twenty managed to disrupt the proceedings at least twice before police clad in riot gear ushered them from the premises.

The ceremony, presided over by Mayor Tim "The Rule Man" Taylor, was to commemorate and commend the heroic actions of Android 77-EDY-823 (Eddie) during the recent bout of arson-related fires in the city.  Fire-droid Eddie, it will be remembered, managed a rescue total of twenty three humans, five dogs, seventeen cats, two birds and one chinchilla during the three-day siege.

The mayor...

*::flip::*

*Defense Secretary Announces Android Soldiers*

Washington (AP)  Secretary of Defense Humberto X. Palacios today announced that initial tests of android infantry soldiers have been "a stunning success. These new models, co-developed by Westerhaus and Boeing Defense Industries, have exceeded all expectations in target recognition, accuracy, versatility in weapons usage and deployment capability. The day is coming when no young American soldier will ever again have to face enemy fire head-on." Palacios indicated that if these new models perform well in further tests which more closely simulate actual battlefield conditions, initial deployment could take place as soon as next year.

When asked if these new military androids could pose a danger to the American people, Palacios replied, "These androids will be deployed under very strict, very controlled military situations and will never come into contact with American civilians."

Dr. Kirsten King, the Government's top expert in robotics and a noted skeptic of the current "android rage", was unavailable for comment.

*::flip::*
*Android Troops to be Deployed in Gulf*
Camp David (Reuters) *The Guardian* has learned today that President Clinton will order the first deployment of android infantry to the Gulf theater next week. "I inherited this war, as you know," Ms. Clinton said. "Now I mean to put a stop to it."

*::flip::*
*Loser Demands Gold Medalist Step Down*
Copenhagen (Reuters) Ekaterina Petrovna Schevaryedna, Silver Medalist in the 2012 Winter Olympics, has filed a complaint alleging that Britney Chung, the U. S. skater who glided to a stunning upset over the top-rated Russian in the Women's Figure Skating last night, should be disqualified. Schevaryedna alleges that her competitor is "not a human at all. She is a robot!"

Olympic officials here issued a brief statement this morning, saying only that Chung has consented to undergo X-ray examination and to submit blood samples. Off the record, one Commissioner quipped, "At least this is easier to deal with than crooked judges."

*::flip::*
*Android Involved in Assault on Driver*
Kalamazoo (MSNBC) Today an android allegedly assaulted the driver of a vehicle which struck it as it was crossing the street in this Midwestern city. Neither the name of the driver nor the model of the android was made public. Details remain spotty.

*::flip::*
"Why'd you do it, Peter?" Kirsten asks, voice soft as her eyes trace a grainy, newspaper photo of the diminutive Westerhaus dwarfed by the size of the yacht he stood aboard, platinum blondes dripping off of him like voluptuous beads of sweat. "You had it all, and more. Why this? Why now?"

Sighing, she closes the scrapbook and places it atop the dozen others she managed to secret away when she began the run for her life. She sighs again, clicking off the flashlight in her hand and slumping back against the seat. The night sky is brilliantly clear, the stars a smattering of jewels thrown across a velvet tapestry by a careless hand. She stares through the windshield into that sky, lost in her thoughts.

The paper is right, of course. About most things in her life, and the androids especially, Kirsten King is a skeptic of the highest order. The religious zealots and jealous corporations had praised her to the highest heaven during her first public stands against Westerhaus's creations. Others had looked at her as if she'd grown a second head. Her peers, mostly, laughed behind their hands and dubbed her with the affectionate title "Chicken Little". Not because of any perceived cowardice on her part, but because of what they felt to be her sudden propensity toward running around shouting "The sky is falling! The sky is falling!"

"It fell, all right."

Her voice is unnaturally loud in the absolute silence of the night, and her breath fogs the windshield, rendering her view hazy and indistinct.

Smothering a yawn with her cupped palm, Kirsten stretches out her cramped shoulders and back, rolling her neck from side to side and hearing its crackle with a soft grunt of satisfaction. Behind her, Asimov moans in his doggy dreams and shifts slightly into a more comfortable position.

"Okay, mutt," she says, turning to look over her shoulder at her slumbering canine companion, "time for you to give up your—"

The sound of shattering glass cuts through the rest of her sentence like a knife. Before she can react, Kirsten feels a hand slip into her hair and pull tightly, slamming her head hard against the window's support. Her vision lights up with interior stars that swirl in a dizzying pattern before her. A breath that sounds very much like a scream is forced from her lungs, and her survival instinct kicks in with a vengeance. Her scalp shrieks as she jerks her head away and rolls sideways across the bench seat.

She jerks back as a second arm blasts through the passenger's side window, splattering her face and clothing with icy shards of safety glass. This time, it's a definite scream that shoots forth, and Kirsten crab-crawls backward, hands and feet slipping and sliding along the vinyl seat-cover.

Snarling, Asimov jumps over the seat and clamps his huge, dripping teeth into the arm that pokes into the passenger's side of the truck, searching for the door handle.

Pulling her legs out from beneath her dog's heavy weight, Kirsten reaches for the keys still in the ignition, but before she can grab the switch, her hair is again grabbed and she is hauled bodily across the rest of the seat, slamming against the door hard enough to drive the breath from her lungs and the thoughts from her mind.

The world greys out for a moment, then rushes back with startling clarity. *I'm going to die.*

The thought is strangely free of accompanying emotion, and part of her wonders if she's not dead already, simply existing as some amorphous ghost-thing, doomed forever to haunt a truck.

"I don't believe in ghosts." Setting her jaw, she jerks forward again, only to be dragged back when a strong forearm clamps itself against her throat, cutting off her breathing in a savage motion.

Her right arm shoots out, trying desperately to reach the keys, but all she can do is flop her fingers uselessly against the steering wheel. Black roses begin to bloom in her vision, and with all of her strength she tries again. Nothing.

Her hand rebounds off the steering wheel to land at her side. Her fingers trace along the chilled metal of some object that her oxygen starved brain refuses to identify. Working on blind instinct alone, she grabs the object, hand curling around it naturally. Hefting it, she brings her arm up and across her body and pulls the trigger of the gun in her hand, again and again and again until it only responds with empty, impotent clicks.

In deep shock, and temporarily deafened by her own gun, Kirsten doesn't realize that the arm around her neck has loosened until her head begins pounding with the rush of life-giving oxygen returning her red blood cells to their normal function.

Her lungs respond automatically, in heaving gasps of fresh, cold air, and even before her second intake of breath, she's straightened out, dropped the gun, and is reaching for the keys in the ignition. This time, her fingers score a direct hit, and the van starts up with a howling growl.

"Asimov, release!" she shouts as she swings her leg down and jams her foot on the accelerator. Human and canine are driven against the backs of their seats as the van goes from stop to go in what seems to be a nanosecond. The stench of burning rubber accompanies the screech of new Michelins. The van rockets away from the curb, shimmies a bit on a small patch of black ice, then straightens admirably and roars down the street as if being pursued by Lucifer himself.

Her attacker is still hanging on, though now it's to the doorframe. Shards of safety glass cut cruelly into its unfeeling palms, but it holds on, uncaring. Kirsten knows better than to try and pry the fingers away from the frame. She lacks the strength and leverage it would require, and it would further draw her attention away from the road she is blistering down at sixty and still gaining.

A grin devoid of any charm or humor curls her lips as she sees a delivery truck parked against the curb to her left. A quick twist of the wheel, and the van heads in that direction.

"Die, you fucker!"

Another jerk of the wheel and the side of the van crashes against the delivery truck and bounces off. It shudders, then sideswipes the truck again, paint and metal screeching their last. The screeching stops as the two vehicles finally separate. The truck remains stationary, rocking on its springs. The van continues forward, sounding a little worse for wear.

Kirsten chances a look to her left and crows in delight when the only sign of her inhuman attacker is the two hands it's left behind, still gripping the window frame hard enough to dent the metal beneath the vinyl and foam padding.

At her side, Asimov yelps, and Kirsten quickly returns her attention to the road just in time to see a moving van parked crossways along the pavement, blocking it completely.

"Oh shiiiiiiiiiiiiiiiii..."

Yanking the wheel hard, she almost overturns the van in an attempt to turn at a nearly right angle while still doing somewhere close to fifty miles an hour.

"...iiiiiiiiiiiiiiii..."

Going up on two wheels for a terror-filled moment, the van finally drops home on all four and continues on at an angle, the truck in its sights and growing larger by the second.

"...iiiiiiiiiii..."

All four wheels leave the road as the van jumps the curb, missing the rear corner of the moving truck by less than the width of a hair.

"...iiiiiiiiiiiiit!"

The front wheels land first. Kirsten's head jerks forward, pounding against the steering wheel and slicing a large gash just above her hairline. Asimov yelps again as he is thrown against the glove compartment, rebounds into the seat and collapses, panting and whining in pain.

The rear wheels hit then, and Kirsten's head tips back. A rich fan of bright blood splashes across the windshield and the ceiling. A second fan joins the first as the van drops down off the curb and shoots down a narrow side street, careening out of control.

The side street widens out, then curves gently, becoming a freeway onramp. Kirsten holds the curve, blinking the streaming blood from eyes as big and round and white as saucers. She lets out a breath of relief as the van rockets onto the empty freeway, then sucks that breath back in as the tires hit another patch of black ice and slide across the lanes as if they've suddenly grown skate blades.

The sideways glide, almost balletic really, comes to an abrupt end as the van sideswipes a steel divider, further abusing the already crumpled driver's side from bumper to bumper. More metal and paint are sacrificed to the gods of destruction, and the van gradually slows, half on and half off the smoothly paved freeway. It finally rolls to a complete stop, and Kirsten sits staring through the window as her mind tries to wrap itself around the events just preceding.

Her hand moves up to wipe her brow. It comes away bloody as she hisses at the sting. "You all right, boy?" she asks Asimov. His ears perk, followed by his body as he comes to a sitting position and leans over to lick at her face. It tickles, and she giggles a little before pushing him away. The laugh sounds a little breathless, a little tremulous, and she knows that her system is just waiting out the shock she's just given it. And if that happens...

Reaching into her pocket, she pulls out another handkerchief, dabs gingerly at the blood on her brow, then ties the kerchief around her head just below the level of the cut. The mediocre first aid will have to do for now. She can't spare time for anything else.

The battered van starts forward again, though grudgingly, and soon she's driving west as if trying to outrun the dawn shading the eastern sky.

**Setting her hat** back on her head, Koda follows Allen to the back of the nearer troop truck. She swings herself easily up onto the bumper, then ducks through the narrow door. Inside, the carrier has been transformed into a mobile field office. A table has been bolted to the floor between the two long side benches; over their heads — not more than a couple millimeters over Koda's — a battery-powered fluorescent tube runs almost the length of the compartment.

A topo map of the area is taped by its corners to the table, which also holds a compact laptop no thicker than a weekly newsmagazine. Best of all, a camp stove backed by a wide reflector radiates heat through the entire space. The colonel unbuttons her heavy parka and drops it onto a folding chair. Koda follows suit, adding hat and gloves to the pile.

The colonel raises a mug with a squadron logo on the side: a bobcat standing on its hind feet and twirling a six-gun in either paw, a crooked, very human grin spread across its whiskered face under a Stetson. Behind it is the shape of a steeply climbing fighter jet, with "Bobcats SR" in looping script across its tail. "Coffee?"

Koda settles on one of the benches, stretching her booted feet out to the stove. "Real?"

"Real." Allen rummages in a thermal chest under the table and comes up with another cup and a vacuum jug. "Sugar? Creamer?"

"Black, thanks."

She hands Koda the hot, fragrant drink and settles across from her. She is tall and spare, though not so tall as Koda, with elegant long hands. There is a scattering of grey in her hair, worn natural and close to her scalp. Her only ornament is a single gold ear cuff, also in the form of a bobcat. She smiles faintly, but her eyes remain sharp and more than a little wary. "So," she says, "truth or dare time. You want me to go first?"

Koda raises her mug in salute. "Be my guest, Colonel."

"Maggie."

"Koda, then."

Maggie nods, then settles herself, leaning back against the wall of the truck. "Okay."

"We were in the air when we got word of the uprising. We'd only been up about half an hour or so — myself, half a dozen instructors with their student pilots. Flying echelon, doing some formation training on the way up to Minot. We were doing the tour, landings and takeoffs at half a dozen bases with mid-air refueling. Standard exercise."

*So they have planes.* Not quite quickly enough, Koda lowers her eyes as she takes a sip from the cup.

"Right," Maggie confirms with a negligent wave of her hand. "When we heard, we turned around and put down on a long, straight stretch of farm road a couple miles from here. We found a ranch house that had already been hit. The folks there apparently kept a couple domestic droids, maybe a field hand or two. The men were all dead and the women all gone."

She pauses, and Koda recognizes that it is her turn. "That's the pattern we've seen. The night it happened, we destroyed a pair of droids that had gone to raid our neighbors' ranch. We weren't in time to help the men, but we got the women and girls away from them. Same at another place a few miles up the road, except that the things were long gone."

"We?"

"My family and I. My dad has a large spread up near the Cheyenne. I have my own place next to it."

"Can your people hold it?"

"So far."

"Good. We need to find other resisters, too. Right now, we're holding about fifteen square miles, closing off the roads and bridges and running a tight perimeter with relay patrols."

"How many troops?"

Maggie ticks them off. "We have the fighter crews; that's fourteen of us. Then we have another thirty, weekend infantry we picked up when we went to raid the National Guard armory at Box Elder for vehicles and small arms. Plus survivors and refugees that managed to get away from Ellsworth itself. Sixty-five of us altogether."

"So what's going on? It's not just a mutiny. Hell," Koda thumps her cup down on the table, sloshing the still-scalding liquid halfway up the side of the mug. "It's a goddam third-rate science-fiction story: kill the men and carry off Earth's Fairest Daughters. It's worse than goddam Fay Wray with the goddam gorilla up on the goddam Empire State Building!"

"You're right about that," Maggie says softly. "Most of the men on the base were killed."

"Young, prime males, sure." Koda shrugs. "Steers go to market; cows and heifers make more steers, with the bull or with the turkey baster. It does, however," she says very carefully, "seem unlikely that the droids are raising beef. Or long pig."

"Well, they haven't eaten anybody yet. I've always hated the damn things. Hated the idea of them, the risk they just might not be controllable in a crisis. Hated making them humanoid." A wry grin splits Maggie's dark face. "But I don't think they've gotten human enough to turn to cannibalism. No, it's something else. Want to help us find out what?"

"What do you have in mind?"

"Some recon tomorrow, on to the base, and maybe into Rapid City."

It was what she had intended to do in any case; she had not expected to have allies. Koda nods. "Count me in."

Half an hour later, as part of the small convoy that has picked up the colonel and the bridge guards and left others in their place, Koda is back on the road toward the ranch house that serves as headquarters for the guerilla force. The driver ahead of her, one Corporal Lizzie Montoya, is a maniac, her tires spraying snow in arcing fountains as she bumps and crunches along through the ice at reckless speed. Koda drives with one foot half on the brake in case Montoya skids off the road or into the lead vehicle. Miraculously, the corporal does not kill herself or anyone else.

A mile and a half from the bridge, they come to clear pavement, and the sudden change jolts through Koda's back and shoulders. Ahead of them on the road, coming nearer, seven huge silver shapes loom against the sky like prehistoric beasts. Wings canted back, bristling with missiles that jut out from underneath their bellies like spines, they might be pterodactyls set down to roost. Movement catches her eye and Koda glances up.

A hawk glides smoothly across the white sky. Something eases inside Koda, a tension she scarcely has known was there. *It is a good sign*, she thinks. *Lelah wakan.*

When she takes the turn that leads toward a slim column of smoke to the west, the hawk follows.

**An old, old** song pounds through Kirsten's head. She navigates the Interstate with the attention of a barrel rider, avoiding wrecked trucks, spilled cargo, here and there a corpse. As the frozen asphalt stretches out between her van and the city, obstacles become fewer. She still passes the occasional abandoned vehicle, doors broken and hanging open like the valves of a plundered clamshell. She has no way of knowing whether the occupants have escaped or been taken. She cannot slow down to find out, cannot concern herself with the wounded or the possibly salvageable; her own survival is paramount. She tells herself over and over again that this is not the Highway to Hell. Through Hell, maybe, but not to Hell. It is the highway to Minot, North Dakota, and it is already more than all the hell she ever thought she would see.

*Keep it simple. Keep it literal.*

Somewhere around noon she crosses the thin spike of West Virgina that juts up between Pennsylvania and Ohio. Her forehead and scalp, which have ached dully since her collision with the steering wheel, have begun to itch with the dried blood from her wound. Little rusty flakes sift down every now and then into her eyes, momentarily blurring her vision. Her bladder, in fact her entire abdomen, has felt for the last half hour as though a whole firing squad of porcupines has used her for target practice. For twice that time, in fifteen-minute increments, she has been promising herself to hold on. Finally, Asimov settles the matter for her, whining piteously and batting at the door handle with one huge paw.

"Okay, boy. I get you. Hang on just a few minutes more." She reaches over to ruffle his ears and receives an exceptionally slobbery lick in return. "God," she mutters, "how I do love gratitude."

Just over the Ohio line, the Interstate dips to pass under a railroad bridge. Kirsten pulls over and ducks into an embrasure between the concrete struts. Asimov finds himself a satisfactory pillar near the further side of the overpass and irrigates it copiously. The puddle steams in the frigid air.

Asimov quarters the patch of highway, nose down and tail stiff, snuffling ecstatically at a sprayed stain on the cement and lifting his leg to obliterate it with one last, joyful squirt. Kirsten allows him to run off some of the stiffness of the hours in the van, stretching her own cramped legs and shoulders at the same time. When the cold begins to seep through her insulated boots, she whistles her dog back to the van. "Asimov, come! Let's go!"

He wheels to obey, then freezes, ears straight up. He gives two sharp barks, whines, and repeats the alarm. Without even thinking, Kirsten grabs the gun off the van's seat. "What is it, boy? Where?"

Asimov barks yet again, and this time she hears what he hears. Faint at first but coming steadily nearer, the steady whup-whup of a helicopter's rotor sweeps toward them down the highway.

"Asimov!"

Her voice is sharp, and he comes to her. Holding his collar with her left hand, her right gripping the automatic, Kirsten crouches down behind the bulk of the van. In her thoughts, she makes herself small. Transparent. Not there.

The noise grows louder and louder until it seems to Kirsten that the chopper must be hovering directly above them, maybe even landing on the tracks over her head. By the sound it is a large craft, a Black Hawk, maybe, or an Apache gunship. Definitely not a two-seater bubble. It is low enough that the rotor wash kicks up snow, making little funnel clouds and eddies in the drifts piled against the sides of the culvert. The racket is deafening.

There are two possibilities. The helicopter may be operated by human soldiers or law enforcement officers. If it is, they might be able to get her to Minot in half a day. Or the crew may not be human. In that case, she will destroy as many as she can.

Finding out is not worth the risk.

The pitch of the rotor changes, intensifies unbearably for half a minute. Then the sound begins to recede, fading finally somewhere to the west and north of the overpass. Whatever has drawn the pilot's attention, it is not one more derelict vehicle on the highway. It is only when her heart dislodges itself from her throat and begins to slow that she realizes it has been beating like a trip hammer to the rhythm of the blades. Her mouth feels cotton-dry. From somewhere deep in her mind, a childhood memory rises: Ms. Tannenbaum's Sunday School class, little Passover lambs molded of papier maché and covered with fringed and curled white tissue paper.

*Take some of the blood and put it on the sides and tops of the door-frames...eat with your cloak tucked into your belt, your sandals on your feet and your staff in your hand. Eat it in haste; it is the Lord's Passover. On that same night I will pass through Egypt and strike down every firstborn... The blood will be a sign for you on the houses where you are; and when I see the blood, I will pass over you.*

Somehow the words have remained with her, overlaid by the smell of polymer glue and newsprint on a hot spring morning in Southern California, where her father had been stationed at Twenty-Nine Palms.

Shakily, Kirsten gets to her feet and sets down the gun. "Stay, Asimov."

As he waits patiently, she tops off the gas tank from the jerry cans she has stashed in the back of the van. Then she wets her bandana with as little water as possible and scrubs the dried blood from her forehead. There is a faint tinge of red when she brings it away; she is still bleeding slightly. She ties a fresh strip around her forehead, then eats a granola bar while she studies the map. When she is certain the helicopter will not return, she whistles Asimov onto the front seat and sets out again on the open road.

**The ranch is** good sized, though smaller than her family's. Which isn't all that surprising, given Clan Rivers has managed to hold on to their piece of land since Time Immemorial, or so it seems. The main house here is a long, rectangular structure with several outbuildings trailing behind like goslings to their mother.

Dakota steps out of her truck into snow that is nearly knee deep and watches as the others exit their vehicles and head for the promising warmth of the house. She follows along slightly behind, taking careful inventory of those with whom she's thrown in her lot, for better or for worse.

For the tough Air Force colonel, she feels a rather immediate kinship, which gives her pause. Outside of her family, she trusts very few. While more than intelligent enough to realize that circumstances sometimes make for strange bedfellows, she believes that in this case, perhaps, circumstances have very little to do with things.

The others — those she's met, anyway — seem capable, and very loyal to their commanding officer.

Her musings are interrupted by Montoya, who, with a rakish grin and a flourishing bow, ushers her inside the house. The interior is overly warm, given the bitterness of the outside air, and she pauses for a moment as the flush of blood hits her tanned skin, painting her in a rosy hue. Montoya notices the flush and, mistaking the reason for it, tips the striking vet a wink, which is abruptly abandoned as cool blue eyes laser into hers.

"I'll...um...you know...just go over...there..."

The young corporal is gone with a speed that surprises even her commander. Allen tries hard to keep a smile from her lips as she rapidly deduces the reason for the young woman's alacrity. It's a failed effort as those same blue eyes move to meet her own, twinkling with wry amusement. Allen covers her mouth and laughs, shoulders shaking with mirth.

"Dakota?"

Koda swings around to see a handsome, well-built man standing just inside the doorway, his dark eyes wide with surprise. "Manny?"

The young man's face breaks into a beaming grin and he crosses the room in three long strides, arms wide. The two embrace tightly for long seconds while the others, bemused, look on. Finally, Manny pulls away and looks up. "Damn, woman, when are you gonna stop growing?"

"You're just shrinking, sprout," Dakota replies, reaching up and scrubbing her hand over the bristles of his buzz-cut.

Ducking his head, the younger man smiles ruefully and rubs his own hand over his scalp, remembering when his hair was as long, glossy, and lush as Dakota's. Then he stiffens and the smile drops from his face. "Koda, your family?"

"They're fine, Manny. As are yours. Mother told me they'd been talking on the CB."

Manny lets out a breath of relief. "Thank God. I tried to contact them, but the phones are out." He looks up at her, face wreathed in sorrow. "I'm sorry about Tali, Koda. She was a good person." He clears his throat. "I tried to make it for the funeral, but we were on maneuvers."

Dakota smiles. "It's okay, *hankashi*. She knew you loved her, and that's what counts, right?"

Sighing, Manny nods, then turns at the sound of his commander clearing her throat. A faint blush colors his skin. "Sorry, Colonel. This is Dakota, my *shic'eshi*."

"Cousin, right?"

The younger man grins. "That's right. See, you're learning!"

Allen chuckles.

"We practically grew up together. I haven't seen her or her family in, what is it now, four years?"

"About that," Dakota agrees.

"Good. I'm glad I could help get the two of you back together then." Allen waves at her junior. "Why don't you show your cousin where she'll be bunking for the night. We're leaving for the base first thing in the morning."

Before Manny can respond, the front door bursts open to admit a florid-faced young man wearing lieutenant's stripes. "Corporal, that little girl we found, I can't stop the bleeding."

Allen nods, already throwing her coat back on. "All right, let's see what we can do."

Dakota steps between the two. Allen looks at her, eyebrow raised.

"Maybe I can help."

Maggie continues to stare.

"You have any medics?"

Allen shakes her head. "Just pilots. We've got basic first aid training, but not much more than that."

"Then I'm the best you've got for now." Dakota holds up the triage kit she always carries with her. "I know my way around the human body pretty well."

Allen smiles, relieved. "I'll take that offer. C'mon."

**They walk along** a shoveled and salted pathway bracketed by several heavily armed soldiers who take up positions along the walk, ever vigilant for intruders. Bypassing the first small cottage, they come to the second just to its right, and Koda follows the colonel inside.

The house is stuffed to the veritable rafters with hollow-eyed refugees, all women and girl-children. It is very warm inside and it reeks of despair and too many bodies packed too tightly together. The rescued women shuffle out of their way like zombies, making a path to a door along the narrow hallway. Opening the door, Allen gestures Koda to precede her.

The stench of putrescence is overpowering, but Koda, having smelled far worse in her life, keeps her face carefully neutral as she walks over to the small cot upon which lies a young girl, no more than four. Her dark, almond eyes are huge and glassy with a fever that paints clown spots of color high on her already ruddy cheeks. Her long, black hair is matted with sweat and dirt, and she stirs restlessly, further tangling the sheet that does not cover her tiny body.

"She was found—" Maggie starts, but quiets at Dakota's upheld hand.

"Hi, sweetheart," Koda murmurs, looking down into eyes so large that they seem to swallow the youngster's face whole. "Not feelin' so good, huh?"

The girl shifts her gaze, not looking so much to Dakota as through her. Deep, dark, almost insanely calm pools of helplessness and hopelessness sear into the vet, touching off a sparkstone of rage deep inside. She fights it down with everything she has, keeping her gaze gentle and as warm as she can make it.

The girl is Cheyenne. This she can tell by the shape of her face and the color of her skin. "My name is Koda," she murmurs in the girl's own language. "And I'm going to help make you feel better, okay?"

The girl blinks slowly, a tiny spark of surprise shining in the depths of her glassy, huge eyes.

Dakota responds with a small smile. "Can you tell me your name, little one?"

"He'kase," the girl whispers, voice cracked and dry.

Allen murmurs in surprise. It's the first time the girl has spoken since they found her two days ago. Dakota shoots the colonel a look, then gazes back down at her tiny patient.

"I'm happy to meet you, He'kase," she says softly.

The young girl's eyes widen as Dakota bends slightly forward, causing her medicine pouch to slip past the buttons of her shirt. A small, pudgy arm reaches up to brush trembling fingers reverently against the deerhide pouch, causing it to swing slightly.

Dakota smiles. "Can you do me a favor, He'kase?"

The little girl nods somberly.

Reaching up, Koda slips the pouch over her head and presses it into the girl's hand. "Can you keep this safe for me? I don't want it to get in the way when I look at your leg, okay?"

He'kase nods again, eyes shining with a light that goes beyond the fever eating at her bones. She holds the pouch tight against her chest, covering it with both hands.

"Thank you." Stepping down to the foot of the cot, Dakota gently lifts the sheet away from He'kase's legs. The high, powerful smell of raging infection wafts out from beneath the sheet, causing Maggie to cough softly and turn away for a long moment. She turns back to see Dakota eyeing her, and tries out a weak smile. "I'm okay."

Dakota looks at her for a moment longer before finally returning her attention to her patient. He'kase's left thigh is swollen, taut and shiny. Dakota tenderly unwraps the blood encrusted bandage and pulls it away, exposing the wound. The young girl moans in pain but keeps remarkably still, her trust in Dakota plainly evident.

There is a grotesque starburst of black, purple, red, and green surrounding what can only be a bullet hole, black and charred against her tender flesh. The wound seeps blood and a thick green pus that eats into the flesh beyond.

Dakota feels the rage flash through her again, a raging sea of red, but she tamps it down with savage intent, her fingers gentle against He'kase's skin. She can feel a weak, thready pulse both behind the knee and in the foot; she thinks that there's a fair chance to save the leg if the wound can be properly drained and cleansed.

After another moment, she replaces the sheet and smiles at the somber child. Reaching down, she hefts her kit, unbuckles the straps, and looks inside for what she needs. A vial of clear liquid sits close by a number of syringes. She removes both vial and syringe and sets them on the table next to the cot.

"Sweetheart, I'm going to give you some medicine. It will help take the pain away, and it might make you sleepy, but that's okay."

He'kase's eyes move from the syringe to Dakota and back again. She swallows once, then nods her quiet acceptance. She doesn't even flinch when the needle pierces her skin and the stinging fluid burns its way into her muscle.

Disposing of the syringe, Dakota walks again to the head of the cot and, smiling slightly, she tenderly brushes the thick, sweaty bangs from He'kase's forehead. After a moment, the girl's eyes close and she falls into a deep, troubled sleep, the medicine pouch cradled safely between her hands.

Maggie quietly approaches, laying a hand on Dakota's shoulder. She can feel the anger coursing through the tall vet, an anger she knows all too well.

Straightening to her full height, Dakota looks down at the Air Force colonel, her face a stony mask.

"We found her inside a ranch house about five miles south of here," Allen begins. "Her family, what was left of it, were butchered, like cattle." She takes in a deep breath, then lets it out slowly, trying to cool her own rage. "We found her halfway underneath what we assumed to be her father. He was obviously trying to protect her, and I can only guess that those bastards thought they'd done their job. By the time we got there," she sighs again, "she was already like this. We did the best we could, but..." Her hands lift, as if in supplication to an uncaring god.

"I'll need some help."

"I can—"

"No, you've got a camp to run. If you could get Manny; he used to help me in the clinic when he was younger. I don't think he's forgotten what to do."

Maggie nods. "I'll get him for you right away."

"Thanks."

"No," Allen replies. "Thank you."

**The road is** clear for the rest of the morning. Toward midday, the sky begins to clear, showing streaks of bright blue through the flat grey of the clouds. The glint of the sun off ice is almost a shock, and Kirsten fumbles one-handed in her pack for her dark glasses. Asimov has stretched out across the bench seat with his hind feet in her lap and is snoring and twitching by turns as he chases rabbits or Frisbees or the neighbors' female golden retriever in his doggy dreams.

The breaking clouds mean increasing cold come nightfall. She will have to find some better shelter than the van for the night or expend precious fuel to run the heater. She does not particularly care for the idea of sipping Shamrock through a straw again if she can help it. "Damn," Kirsten mutters to the oblivious Asimov. "I never thought I'd miss Motel 6."

Or maybe she need not miss it. An empty, deserted motel just might offer possibilities. Better yet, an abandoned house. She is passing through Ohio farm country, small towns slipping past along the Interstate like beads on a string. Many of these homes, built in the previous century, will have working fireplaces, complete with a couple of cords of wood piled outside.

Many of them will be tenanted by the dead, murdered and left where they fell. Kirsten's hands flex against the steering wheel, tighten. She can deal with death. She has dealt with it. At least here, after several days and nights of snow and ice with the utilities out, the dead will be decently frozen. Grotesque, perhaps, an offense to the eyes, but not to the nose and stomach.

For the first time, she spares a thought for her future self. *What will I be when the world is set to rights, assuming it can be?*

But that one's easy. Dead, probably.

Dead long before.

At Zaneville, Kirsten turns off the freeway onto state roads. They will be snowed over and more dangerous, will slow her down even more than the sheen of ice on the Interstate. But they will lead her around Columbus and its suburbs in a wide arc to the south. Even more importantly, they will lead her around Wright Patterson AFB, where droids are likely to be concentrated. Pulling off into the shelter of a derelict Whataburger beside the exit ramp, Kirsten maps out the route she will take, west and south. There are, she notes, a number of state parks associated with early Native American ruins scattered throughout the Hopewell valley. They might be an even better prospect for overnight than deserted farmhouses. Most have cabins, and most of those cabins would have fireplaces or wood stoves. Because they would have been sparsely populated at best at this season, they would have drawn minimal attention from raiders. Certainly there would be no reason for the droids to stake them out or occupy them. The danger, if any, would come from other refugees like herself.

Highway 22 winds through vacant farmland, the fields blanketed with knee-high drifts of snow. The trees stand bare to the winds, skeletal shapes against the western sky as the sun stands down toward evening. Here and there a dark shape perches in the branches, head hunched down into its shoulders; sometimes there are two huddled together. Owls or ravens — she cannot be sure at the distance. Except for the growl of the truck's engine and Asimov's occasional whine as a foraging hare makes its way laboriously through the snow, the landscape is utterly silent.

It lulls her as she should not let it, and so she is shocked and momentarily disoriented when she sees the roadblock ahead. The vehicles drawn up on the sides of the pavement are pickups and SUVs, none of them with flashers or official markings. Among them she can make out burly shapes muffled in two or three layers each of Polartec and down. Some wear balaclavas or ski masks; others have pulled their caps down so far they almost meet the scarves and turned-up collars around their necks. As she slows, Kirsten can see the clouds of mist that rise about them with their breath. One man's greying eyebrows and beard are stiff with crusted frost. He holds a shotgun braced with its butt against his hip.

Even the most lifelike of the droids do not breathe warm air that clouds with the cold. Humans, then.

There are only two possibilities. These are free people defending their land, or they are the scum that disaster always brings to the surface. If she stops, she may find help. Or she may be robbed, killed, raped, and handed over to the droids. The choices are the same as they were under the railroad bridge.

Without hesitation, Kirsten shoves her foot down hard on the accelerator, and the van, still gaining speed when it crashes through the sawhorse barriers at 80 miles an hour, scatters the startled guards in all directions. From behind her she hears the boom of the shotgun, and a sharp crack that can only be a rifle, but she is already beyond their range. Asimov, rudely awakened by the sudden speed, has regained his balance and is sitting backwards in the front seat, paws draped over the headrest, barking maniacally in her ear. Then the yaps give way to a deep-chested baying that sends atavistic tingles up her spine. "Wonderful, just wonderful," she mutters. "The Hound of the Baskervilles, alive and well and — what the fuck?"

A moving shape has appeared in her rear-view mirror, hurtling along behind her through the rutted snow. It is close enough that she can see a gun barrel protruding from the passenger window. "Down, Asimov!" she snaps. "Lie down, now!"

Aggrieved but obedient, he settles once again along the bench seat, his head below the level of the windows.

"Stay!" she orders, and pushes the accelerator clear down to the floor.

The van lurches, half-skidding down the road, spraying snow from its tires in sheeting arcs as high as the roof. A bullet whangs by, hitting the edge of the mirror frame and kicking shards of metal loose to ping against the plexiglass windshield. Spiderweb cracks appear suddenly before her eyes, breaking the flat white expanse before her into a kaleidoscope pattern in monotone. The van buckets and lurches beneath her, so that all her concentration goes into wrestling the steering wheel to keep them from running off the road.

The van sits high off the road. Unless her pursuers are inexplicably stupid or too drunk to think at all, they will eventually start shooting low, for her tires. She cannot afford that. Nor can she risk a hit to the gas cans in the back, which will send her, Asimov, and quite possibly the remaining human population of the United States, up in a cloud of greasy smoke. "Asimov!" she orders. "Play dead!"

Asimov, already denied the canine pleasures of the hunt, glances over his shoulder at her, offended and disbelieving.

"Play dead, dammit!"

With a sigh of almost human frustration, Asimov sags loose-limbed onto the seat as Kirsten brakes abruptly and sends the van into a wild skid that whips it, tailpipe first, across the opposite lane, hauling so hard on the wheel that her shoulders ache. The truck comes to a stop facing her pursuers, whose pickup swerves wide to avoid her and ends half in and half out of a roadside ditch concealed by the mounded snow. Kirsten pulls the bandage off her head, bringing fresh blood, and slumps across the steering wheel. Her finger presses lightly on the trigger of the gun in her lap.

She hears both doors of the pickup open and close, to the accompaniment of obscenities. Then feet, scrunching through ice and crusted snow. The latch on her own door clicks, and she can smell burnt cordite. Then a voice.

"Oh, hell, Brad, it's just a girl and her dog. She's bleeding." There is another click as Brad opens the passenger door.

Kirsten shoots the first man, angling the barrel of her gun high, to take him in the chest. As she squeezes the trigger, she yells, "Take him, Asimov! Hold!" and feels the dog's weight launch itself out of the van. A roar fills her ears as a shotgun discharges less than a yard away, followed by an angry, human yell. "Off! Get off me, goddam you!"

Kirsten raises her head, getting a firmer grip on her gun, and slides out of the van. The man she has shot is sprawled on his back, arms flung wide, blood pouring from his mouth into his beard and grey plaid muffler. As she watches, his eyes fix, staring somewhere past her shoulder.

"Steve! Steve? What the fuck's going on here? Answer—"

The voice is suddenly cut off, and Kirsten hears a flurry of movement, ending in a low growl from Asimov. "Hold, boy!" she calls to him. "Hold!"

"Goddam you, you bitch, what've you done to my bro—"

This time Asimov's growl is deeper as it cuts off the voice. "Good boy, Asimov! Hold!"

Steve has fallen partly onto his rifle. Wishing that she did not have to know his name, Kirsten has to shift him to extract it. A last, wheezing sigh escapes his lungs as she turns him; it startles her so that she almost drops the weapon. The man on the other side of the truck, Brad, is yelling again. She wishes that she did not know his name, either.

Very deliberately, avoiding thinking about their humanity, Kirsten walks around the front of the truck. Asimov's outsize paws are planted on Brad's chest, his jaws clamped onto the man's throat. He has not drawn blood, only snarls and clamps down a little tighter each time his prey cries out. The man's eyes follow Kirsten's movements. She sees his death in his eyes.

Slowly, very deliberately, not thinking, Kirsten shoulders the rifle and shoots Brad in the head. Blood blossoms on the snow, unfolding in crimson and scarlet like the petals of a rose. Flower of evil.

Just as deliberately, Kirsten picks up Brad's 12-guage and lays it on the floor of the van. In the foundered pickup, she finds shells for both the shotgun and the rifle. Two sleeping bags lie rolled up on the back bench; Kirsten takes them. Finally she reaches under the dash and tears out the ignition wires, cutting them off short with a pair of snippers she finds on the console between the seats. It is quicker than shooting out the tires, and it makes less noise.

Her hands are sweating inside her gloves. On her way back to the van she begins to shake. At first it is only a fine shiver, like a chill over her skin. Then reaction takes possession of her, adrenaline rattling her bones and buckling her knees beneath her. She makes her way around Brad's corpse and hauls herself back up onto the seat. Asimov follows and huddles up against her, nudging her shoulder with his nose. He whimpers softly as she gasps, half-choking, for breath.

Part of it, she knows in a rational corner of her mind, is pure physiology. That part will pass if she does not feed it. The other part, which may never pass at all, is that she has just killed two men who were almost certainly innocent of harm. Because she could not take the chance.

She tells herself she needs to get moving again. The sound of the shots will have carried. When Brad and Steve do not return to their companions promptly, the other men at the barricade will come looking for them. And then they will come looking for her.

She needs to throw them off her trail, and she needs to find shelter. And she needs to do both by nightfall. She has perhaps two hours.

When her hands are steady enough, she starts the van again, turns carefully so that she does not run over the two dead men, and sets out again toward the south.

**Several hours later,** Dakota leaves her patient's room, wiping her hands on a towel supplied by her cousin. He'kase is resting comfortably in the care of one of the rescued women who has had some nurse's aide training. Her wound is clean and dry, and antibiotics are pumping their way through her tiny system. In place of the medicine pouch, which is in its customary place around Koda's neck, the youngster holds an eagle feather, the sacred icon that Manny has held onto since he was shorn of his flowing locks upon first entering the Air Force.

"Damn, Koda. I forgot how good you were at this stuff."

"You're not so bad yourself."

The cousins share a rueful laugh as they walk through the late November evening, nodding to the soldiers as they pass. Inside the main house, Manny takes his leave, scurrying off to the shower.

Maggie looks up from her place at the kitchen table and beckons Dakota over with a smile. A mug of steaming black coffee is already there, awaiting her. Dakota accepts gratefully, sitting down with a groan and stretching out her long legs as she lifts the mug to her lips, inhaling the fragrance with a sigh of approval.

"Things went okay?" Maggie guesses from the look on Koda's face.

"As well as can be expected," Dakota replies, taking a bracing sip of coffee, letting it warm her from the inside out. "Manny hasn't lost his touch. He's got the makings of a damn decent medic."

"Better that than a pilot," Maggie jokes.

"Hey!" Manny yells, filling the doorway with his towel-girded bulk. "I heard that!"

Both women laugh, knowing that the young man before them is as good as anyone gets when it comes to flying. Absolutely fearless, he can make a jet walk and talk and turn on a dime. He's one of the best of the best, and everyone knows it.

"All right, flyboy, get your ass to bed. We're on the road at 0430."

Snapping off a crisp salute while still managing to retain the hold on both towel and dignity, Manny grins, winks, and turns back down the hall. The soft click of his door ends the conversation.

Silence falls between them, a soft ethereal mist. Peering at Dakota over the rim of her coffee cup, Allen takes in the sharp, clean lines of her face and the energy that seems to hum around her even now, while sitting quietly, apparently lost in thought. It's a sweet siren's song, one that Maggie is in no way adverse to hearing.

"See anything interesting?"

Dakota's warm contralto rolls over her, and Maggie is suddenly glad that her mocha skin hides her flush well. Though not, perhaps, quite as well as she might have liked, given the sparkle of amusement in the crystal eyes turned her way. "I might," she allows, responding to the tease with a small one of her own. A smile curves her lips, and her gaze is bold and direct, though not overly aggressive. Maggie Allen knows what she wants and isn't shy about reaching for it. As career Air Force, she's seen her share of too many wars and too many deaths, and when opportunities for warmth and life present themselves on gilt-edged platters, she rarely hesitates.

The silence between them is almost palpable, filling the shadowed and cobwebby corners of the open great room with a turbulent, humming energy. Their gazes break at the same time. Maggie looks over at a painting hanging above the mantle. Dakota looks down at her hands. The ring finger of her left hand looks strangely naked; the small band of paler flesh highlighted like an after-image of a life long past.

*Seven years*, Dakota thinks, her thumb rubbing over the pale, soft skin. A time for beginnings. A time for endings. A generation. An itch. Seven virtues and seven vices. Paradise and damnation. Confusion? Maybe. Guilt? A little of that, too. She sighs.

"I have a room to myself in the back of the house," Allen says, very softly. "One of the perks of being CO." She smiles a little. "I'd like to share it with you tonight." Dakota looks up then, her gaze piercing and direct. The sharply etched planes of her face soften just slightly, and Allen is stunned once again by the woman's striking beauty.

"I'd like that."

**When Dakota next** awakens, it's still dark, and she knows without looking that dawn is a long way off. She stretches slightly, then settles, arms comfortably curled around the warm body in her arms. For a moment, she thinks she's dreaming, but the hair that brushes against her chest is shorter and coarser than what she's used to, and the body draped across her is more muscular and compact. It awakens her to the reality of her situation, but the reality is not all that unpleasant.

Maggie hums sleepily and, lifting her head just slightly, presses a kiss to the warm, bare breast upon which she is resting her head. "Mmm. Good morning."

Her voice is deep and sleep burred and the sound of it reaches into Koda's belly and twists it pleasantly. "It is that."

"What time is it?"

In an automatic reflex, Dakota looks over at the nightstand, but of course, the clock is blank without the electricity needed to run it.

"Damn," Maggie says, chuckling. "Forgot about that." Reaching across Koda's body, she picks up the watch she's left on the nightstand and peers into it through sleep blurred eyes. "0320. Good thing I don't need much sleep, hmm?"

"You could always grab a little more."

Maggie laughs, a throaty chuckle. "With you here? Naked? Darling, sleep is the last thing I plan on grabbing."

A strong hand slides up a muscled thigh, and Maggie slides with it, reaching Dakota's tempting lips and entangling her own in a deep, luscious kiss. "Dear God, woman," she pants when she finally pulls away, "I never thought I'd say this to another human being, but you've got flying beat by a long mile."

Dakota's deep chuckle follows her down to sensual oblivion.

# CHAPTER FOUR

Kirsten huddles before the dying fire, watching the play of scarlet and orange amid the black remains of the embers. She is wrapped in her own sleeping bag, shielded from the concrete floor by a pair of thin mattresses pulled off one of the bunk beds. Asimov is stretched out on another with his head in her lap. She rubs his ears absently.

The small cabin is warm. She has before her the prospect of the first comfortable night since the insurrection began. She has a hot meal inside her, even if it was only canned stew set in the ashes, and has cleaned up as best she can with water warmed the same way and a bar of looted soap. She needs to sleep.

Over and over in her mind, Kirsten replays her encounter with the men at the barricade. Over and over she imagines it differently: introducing herself as a refugee fleeing toward her family in Indiana, perhaps. Shaking hands, accepting their hospitality and a temporary alliance. She is almost certain she could have trusted them far enough to set her safely on her way.

And over and over, she imagines what would have happened if she had been wrong. And what would have happened after that, will probably still happen if she doesn't get through to the droid facility at Minot.

Outside the snow is falling again, hissing softly as it drifts past the windows. It is the one bit of luck she has had today — the new fall obscuring the ruts made by her tires on the deserted roads. The dead men's companions had not followed her, or if they had, they had set out too late to catch up before the light failed and the clouds closed in again. Rural areas are as dangerous to her as the urban centers. In the cities, the droids will still be hunting down humans. In the farm counties, the humans who remain will be defending their homes and families against the droids.

But it's not that simple. All wars have collaborators. If there are not yet humans who have been spared as decoys, there will be. If there are none who cooperate for their own safety and that of their families, there will be. And she can never, never, take a chance that another person is not a collaborator. Too much rides on her own survival for her to be trusting or merciful.

Kirsten banks the fire and pulls her makeshift bed closer to the hearth. Because there is nothing else to do, she stretches out full length on the mattress, Asimov rousing just long enough to move up beside her. She does not expect to sleep, but can at least allow her aching muscles as much ease as warmth and rest allow.

She moves through a twilight world. All about her the snow lies heavy: on the ground, in the forks of the branches that spread bare above her head. The sky is white, too, the light diffused and dim. Asimov paces at her side, his huge paws spread to carry him across the surface, lynx-fashion. Her own feet do not sink into the snow. When she looks down, she sees only a faint, shadowless impression in the crust where she has stepped.

Above her, in the sky over a clearing, a hawk hangs at the hover. It gives one long and ringing cry, then banks and flies off toward what she knows to be the west, though there is no sun to give direction.

Then she sees it, a shape drifting through the trees, keeping pace with her. Kirsten's heart seems to stop, then slams against her breastbone, but strangely it is not fear that sets her blood to racing. Somewhere deep in her mind is the knowledge that this is something she has searched for, has waited for, longer than she can remember. She tries to call out to whatever it is, but her throat closes around the words.

The ground begins to rise abruptly, and she realizes that she is climbing one of the ancient earthworks that dot the Hopewell Valley. The forest thins as she scales the top, and there laid out before her, stretching away infinitely far into horizonless space, is a long, sinuous mound in the shape of a serpent, coiling and uncoiling, doubling back on itself in rhythmic curves only to spiral outward again. There are tracks here, the prints of a large animal moving swiftly. Kirsten sets out to follow, placing her own feet in the pad marks that somehow remain undisturbed behind her. Asimov lopes along beside her, a strange eagerness in the play of rippling muscle under his black and silver coat.

Then she sees it. Straight ahead, directly in her path where nothing but air had been a nanosecond before, is a wolf. Its black fur is covered in rimefrost, and it regards her with eyes of a startling sky-blue.

Its gaze lasts only a moment. Without warning, the ground gives way beneath Kirsten's feet, and she is falling, falling through space as the stars streak past, plunging into atmosphere finally as clouds billow around her, plummeting toward a black rock island in a mighty river where she will shatter into atoms. For a moment she thinks that she may survive with no more than a few bones broken, or that she can perhaps deflect her trajectory for a landing in that impossibly blue water.

*Don't be a damned idiot*, she tells herself. *You know you're going to die.*

The rock rises up to meet her, and she strikes with an impact that jerks her bolt upright in her sleeping bag, to find the hearth still warm and Asimov whuffling softly in his own dreams.

Kirsten's hands are trembling, and she feels a cold runnel of sweat as it slips between her shoulderblades. "Goddam," she breathes. "Goddam." Her heart lays down a rapid, thready beat, counterpoint to the rhythm of her shocked lungs.

*What the hell was that?*

*Who the hell was that?*

But she has no answers. She has seen wolves before, camping in Yellowstone with her parents when she was a teenager; she has no doubt at all that a wolf is what she has dreamed. She tries to call up the Psych 101 lectures that bored her straight into an afternoon nap more often than not, but other than a vague recollection that almost everything, according to Dr. Werbow, signified either sex or death, she cannot connect the blue-eyed wolf with any standard interpretation.

Eventually she steadies and lies down again, yawning. She has no idea where the dream came from, though she is fairly certain that it was not something she ate. *Dinty Moore's psychedelic stew, oh yeah.*

She slips off to sleep again with unexpected ease, and does not wake until the morning.

**The big truck** shakes, rattles, and rolls as it bounds over the ice-rutted roads, last in a fair sized convoy of impressive military vehicles. Manny sits beside his cousin, a military handset in his lap and a machine pistol at his side. He eyes Dakota at odd intervals, trying to discover without asking exactly what is different about his cousin this morning. She seems...relaxed somehow, as if she'd spent the night... His eyes widen, but then he gives himself a mental shake. *Nah. Couldn't be. Could it?*

"See something interesting?"

The low voice startles him, and he blinks, then blushes at being caught out. Scrubbing a hand over his face, he shakes his head in the negative. "Just woolgathering." He smiles weakly. "Really."

"Mmhm."

They both fall silent, listening to the military radio as it crackles out its continuing stream of routine messages from members of the caravan. Suddenly, the taillights in front of them flash once, twice, then stay on as the troop carrier comes to a quick stop. Koda works her own brakes. The truck wants to skid, but in the end, it behaves and rolls to a stop, front bumper inches away from the rear of the carrier.

The radio crackles to life.

"Chief? You might wanna come look at this."

"Everybody down!"

The sound of gunfire shatters the morning. Dropping the radio, Manny grabs his gun and levers himself outside the passenger door. Only to duck back inside again in order to keep his head from being blown off of his neck. He stares, wide-eyed, past Dakota and out into the brightness of the morning, his jaw dropped. "Great Father, protect us," he whispers.

Koda turns her head and sees a scene out of an Orwellean nightmare.

A long line of military droids block the roadway and the areas beyond. These are not the generically handsome, lantern-jawed, poster children for America's Idealized Infantryman that have filled newspapers and news broadcasts over the past several years. Instead, they resemble nothing so much as a mechanized creature straight out of a 1980s blockbuster science fiction, action/adventure movie. Shining a blinding, mirrorlike silver, the only humanoid resemblance is in the head and torso region. The "legs" end below the knees, replaced by the thick treads usually seen propelling heavy tanks over uncertain ground. The "arms" end in lethal weaponry currently pointed at the convoy.

Dakota turns to her cousin. "You ever seen them before?"

"No. I heard they existed, but no. Never. Jesus."

He runs a hand over his short, buzzed hair in a gesture of nervousness familiar to Dakota.

The radio crackles to life. Maggie Allen's voice is terse. "Check off, people!"

"Rivers here, Colonel," Manny replies, keying the handset.

"Manny? We're gonna lay down a line of grenade cover. You get the civvie out of here. Go back the way you came, and don't stop until you're sure you're out of danger."

Dakota grabs the radio away from her cousin and holds it up to her mouth. "Sorry, Colonel, but the 'civvie' is the one driving this beast, and the only direction I'm going is forward."

"Dakota!"

"Can't hear you, Colonel. You're breaking up."

"Rivers!"

Releasing the talk button, Dakota tosses the handset down on the floorboards at Manny's feet, pinning her cousin in place with a look. "Don't even think about it," she warns.

"Who, me? Not a chance, cuz. I've still got bruises from the last time you pounded me, thanks."

The two listen momentarily to Allen's increasingly irate squawking. "She's gonna bust me down to Airman for this, you know."

Pulling down the mirrored lenses of her sunglasses, Dakota gives him a look that makes him laugh. "All right, I get your point, Koda. So...what do we do now?"

As if hearing the question, the radio crackles back to life. "Listen up, everybody. This means you too, 'Airman' Rivers."

Dakota winces. Manny gulps.

"Here's the deal. These bastards aren't like anything we've faced before, and we're gonna need to be creative in figuring out a way to get past them without getting ourselves fragged to Canada in little pieces. Rule number one, people — no shooting at them. They're bulletproof, and anything you fire at them will ricochet God knows where. We can't risk it, so put your guns away for another fight, understand?"

Affirmatives buzz across the radio.

"Our friends from the Guard were kind enough to bring along a few little toys we're going to try out instead, so everybody just sit tight for a bit, and I'll get back to you."

Since Koda and Manny can see very little from behind the massive troop carrier they are following, they do exactly as Allen suggests and cool their heels while keeping a wary eye on the metallic monstrosities lined up across the roadway and beyond.

A loud, whooshing roar is followed immediately by an explosion so powerful that Dakota and Manny are tossed about like rag dolls as the truck bounces and rolls on its springs. The shaking no sooner stops than gunfire erupts from all around them. The distinctive sounds of bullets hitting the metal of the truck cause the cousins to duck down. The driver's side window shatters, raining glass over them both. The roar of gunfire is punctuated here and there by the horrific screams of men and women in agony.

Unable to lie passively by and do nothing, Dakota reaches over and unlocks the passenger's side door, then begins to crawl over the top of Manny, who grabs her by the waistband of her jeans.

"What the hell are you doing, cuz? They're killing us out there!"

"Exactly," Dakota replies, prying Manny's hand from her waist and continuing to crawl until she is out of the truck. Coming up on to her haunches, she surveys the damage. Men and women are scattered like tenpins, many of them bleeding their lives into the snow and pleading with an uncaring sky to save them. As she watches, a soldier becomes a corpse, jittering like a puppet on the hard-packed snow under the constant, unremitting onslaught of artillery.

Drawing in a deep breath, she lowers her head and charges out into the fray. Bullets slice the air around her, but she keeps her head down and keeps running, sinking past her knees in the snow. Reaching the first two injured soldiers, she lowers her arms and grabs them by their jackets, dragging them until they are behind the cover of a military vehicle.

Another whooshing roar sounds from very close by, and the resulting explosion knocks her to the ground. A shadow falls over her, and when she looks up, Manny is there, two more injured soldiers in his grasp. His face is grim, but his eyes are shining.

"Couldn't let you have all the fun," he grumbles, voice almost lost within the continuing gun battle.

Getting back to her feet, Koda pounds on the panel of the vehicle before her, then pounds harder when there's no response. "Watch them!" she commands over her shoulder as she makes her way up to the cab of the vehicle. Two men lie in the cab, dead beyond any possibility of resurrection, destroyed beyond any possibility of recognition.

"Uh...Koda?"

Dakota whirls around. "What?"

"They're bleeding pretty bad over here. What should I do?"

Koda thinks for a moment. "Pack snow in their wounds. It should slow the bleeding until we can get them under some kind of cover. I need to get my kit."

"I'll do it."

"No. Stay with the injured. I'll be right back."

Knowing better than to argue with his cousin, Manny kneels in the snow and begins scooping handsful of it onto the bleeding chests and bellies and limbs of his comrades, warning himself all the while not to look at their faces. As long as he doesn't see their faces, he can pretend that they are simply strangers on a battlefield, strangers he will do his best to save.

Dakota makes her way back to the truck and retrieves her kit without much difficulty, but then becomes pinned down by furious gunfire. A man stumbles by, half of his face blown off, a smoking stump where his arm used to be. As she watches, he tumbles into the snow, and dies, open-eyed.

"Koda!"

Ripping her gaze away from the dead soldier, Dakota looks over to Manny, who is frantically compressing the chest of one of the women he's dragged out of the line of fire. He is looking at Koda through eyes as wide as saucers.

"Hang on! I'll be right there!"

She's about to move when her attention is distracted. Looking on, she tracks a shoulder-launched missile as it flies across the gap that separates human from android and explodes into the noticeably thinned android ranks. A huge fireball erupts, and Koda ducks down, covering her head with both arms as bits and pieces of androids rain down on her in a blazing storm. She slams back against the truck just in time to avoid being turned into a stain by a basketball sized lump of molten metal which lands in the snow not more than a foot away. It hisses violently, sending up clouds of vapor as it melts a hole in the snow several feet deep.

"Dakota!"

Peering through the swirling, dissipating vapor, Koda watches as Manny takes a desperate step toward her position, only to be blown back by a bullet that pierces his arm and drops him to the ground.

"Manny! *Hankashi!* Shit."

Grabbing her pack, she rushes across the space separating herself from her fallen cousin. Manny is already picking himself up as Koda reaches him. Aiding him to his feet, she looks into his eyes, her own flashing all kinds of warnings. "Damn it, Manny, this is no time to be playing John Wayne. How many times do I have to tell you — you're no cowboy."

"Yeah, yeah, whatever. Like you'd just sit by and watch me almost get blown to bits, right?"

Scowling, Koda grabs his arm and turns it over. "You're lucky. It's just a graze."

"Yeah, I know. Stings like fire, though." He looks to his right. His face crumples. "Oh, holy damn," he whispers, looking at the carnage lying around him. "Jesus, Koda, I'm sorry."

"It's all right. It wasn't your fault. You couldn't have protected them from the shrapnel." She looks over at the pieces of dead bodies lying in the snow and closes her eyes tightly for a moment. When she opens them again, they are clear and resolute. "Let's go find some people we can help."

**The sound of** men and women screaming and moaning in pain within the close confines of the troop carrier seems to encompass the whole world, and it's all Manny can do not to jab an icepick through his eardrums just to stop the gut-churning noise. Koda has set up a field hospital of sorts within the vehicle, and the most grievously injured patients lie on makeshift cots, bleeding their lives away while the harried vet tries frantically to save them.

The battle outside is slowly winding down. Shoulder-fired rockets have done the trick, and the mission has been reduced to a simple mop-up, if anything about this terrifying monstrosity can be considered as mundane as "simple".

Unless the androids have buddies out there.

Somewhere.

Manny pushes down a chill that humps up his flesh as he rushes from injured woman to injured man, doing what he can to offer comfort while his cousin goes about the business of patching and stitching. He's been through war, but it was never anything like this. A pilot sits above it all like an armored god, dropping his cargo and speeding away, never seeing the damage and pain and misery he causes.

Manny's reverie is broken by the man before him, lying on a cot and holding the glistening loops of his guts in his hands. His voice, a deep basso, spirals up and up into a castrato's soprano as he holds a scream that pierces the veil of eternity. His eyes, though, are dead already, staring through the young pilot as if staring into an infinity worthy of Poe's worst nightmares.

The woman lying next to him covers her ears and adds a scream of her own. "Oh God, shut him up, please! Please shut him up! Shut him up!"

"Koda!"

Dakota looks up from her place by the side of a young woman whose puckered and twisted face is a horror film's mask. The young woman is seizing, her body sunfishing and bucking mindlessly, her tongue black and protruding from the charred remains of her mouth. "Give him some morphine!" the vet shouts over the din.

"I can't! There isn't any more!"

"Shit." She turns to an airman pressed into service as a nurse.

"Watch her. I'll be right back."

The soldier nods.

The man is still screaming as Koda approaches and looks down into what is left of his belly. His guts roil and twist like snakes in a cave, moving and tumbling over one another as his agonized body writhes on the cot.

"Can you do anything for him?" Manny asks, willing himself not to be sick.

Grabbing her medical kit, Dakota rummages through it, and comes out with a single glass morphine cartridge. It's empty, and she throws it down on the ground, where it shatters. Her eyes tell Manny everything he needs to know. She startles a bit as a surprisingly strong hand, covered in blood and gore, grasps the front of her shirt and twists, pulling her forward slightly. She looks down into the pain-wracked face of the mortally injured soldier. His eyes are very bright, very clear, and almost supernaturally aware.

"Please." His strained voice is no more than a breath on the wind.

Dakota looks at the hand gripping her, then into the man's open wound, a part of her in awe that he's managed to last this long, then back to his too bright, too aware eyes. "I can't save you," she says, gently as possible. "Your wound's too severe."

The man gives a solemn nod, no more than the barest twitch of the muscles in his neck. "Please," he breathes again.

Another airman, shot in the groin but currently stable, looks up. "You're a vet, aren't you?"

Koda nods.

"I don't mean to sound ungrateful or anything, but would you let a dying dog suffer the way he is right now?"

Koda stiffens, then relaxes, knowing the man is right. "No. I wouldn't."

"Then pardon me if I don't see the difference here." The young man gives her a pointed look. "He's begging you, man! Help him!"

"That's enough, Roberts," Manny snaps, chest puffing, shoulders straightening, fists clenching.

Dakota's sure she would smell the testosterone in the air if it wasn't for the blood and death already polluting it.

"Keep it zipped."

The airman scowls, but holds his peace, slamming his head back down on the rolled uniform jacket he's using in lieu of a pillow and glaring at the both of them.

Sure that the danger, what there was of it, has passed for the moment, Manny looks over to his cousin. Their gazes meet and meld in brief, silent communication. Manny nods, once, then looks away.

Hitching a deep sigh, Koda reaches back into her bag and pulls out a pre-filled syringe. The mortally wounded soldier has his eyes glued to her every move. "You know what this will do," Dakota says, giving the young man every chance to back out.

He nods, more surely this time.

"And this is what you want."

"Please."

*Third time pays for all*, Dakota thinks as she reaches for the IV tubing, her eyes never leaving the soldier's.

A second later, it's done. The man's grip convulsively tightens on her shirt, then falls away as his eyes, once bright and shining, become flat and dull, the eyes of a discarded doll on a trash heap as large as the world. Dakota closes those eyes gently, then rests her hand briefly on an already cooling forehead, whispering a prayer so ancient it seems inborn rather than taught.

Manny grips her shoulder and squeezes once in comfort. After a moment, Dakota shrugs off the grip and walks across the cramped space to her next patient, never looking back.

**The air is** cold with wind and melting snow, but not too cold to carry the mingled scents of burned wood and living pine needles. Tumbled into random hummocks of brick and charred beams, the remains of the park office lie before her. Those cabins she can see in the dim light are in no better condition, and when the wind shifts slightly, clocking about to the east, she can smell dead flesh among the ashes and the firs. Asimov whimpers softly at her side, and Kirsten stretches out a hand to pat him almost absently.

She has driven now for two days and a night without rest. She needs a place to lie up and sleep, or she will become a danger to herself on the road. *Ain't life a bitch. And then you die.* She sighs. It's the truck or nothing. Kirsten tugs at Asimov's collar. "Come on, boy. Gotta get some sleep. Both of us."

She turns back toward the vehicle, glancing up at the clearing sky. It is near dawn, but in the west the stars blaze down with undiminished brilliance. All the hackneyed metaphors — ice, glass, diamonds — march by for inspection, and none is adequate. The stars blaze down, cold and detached as the eyes of angels, so that for the first time Kirsten believes with her heart as well as her scientist's brain that they truly are lifetimes distant. From somewhere among the trees comes an unidentified grunt. *Deer? Bear? Skunk?*

The exalted speculations of a moment before come crashing down, and she petrifies there on the edge of day, trying not to make a sound, not to breathe, most of all not to smell attractive to bear or polecat. In the east the stars begin to pale, not so much a dimming of their light as the gradual leaching of the darkness. A white shadow ghosts along the treetops with the rising wind, its wings making no sound as it hunts the last of the night.

Kirsten's breath catches in her throat, and her belly tightens. Abruptly tensed, the long muscles in leg and back relax just as abruptly. She does not fling herself flat, praying not to be noticed. The rational part of her brain, that bit of it not befogged by need for sleep, observes sarcastically that owls do not eat humans and reminds her that pterodactyls are long since stone. Yet death has passed over. Hunting someone else, this time. Next time, maybe her.

Last time, it was her. And the time before and the time before that. She knows she will be prey again.

*God, I need to sleep. Afraid of an owl. Next thing you know I'll be hallucinating.*

Above her head, the first rays of the sun strike the tips of pine needles to blazing gold. From somewhere behind her, Kirsten hears the beat of great wings lifting. She turns, and a hawk sweeps past her, all bright bronze and copper, climbing into the dawn. A blood stopping *kreeee-eeeer*! rings out over the forest. The hawk cries again, twice, and spirals up toward the strengthening sun and her day's work.

As Kirsten moves back toward her truck, a stray breeze carries a half-charred piece of blue paper between her feet. She jerks away from it, startled, then catches her breath and picks it up. *Christ, spooked at a goddam tourist flyer. Gotta get some sleep. Now.* Idly, she glances at the brochure in the growing light. It is a map of the park, showing lake, fishing dock, cabins (now demolished), and a network of deep limestone caves underlying the bluff along the river. Phrases register disjointedly in her mind. Walkways. Stairs. Constant 60° Fahrenheit.

Salvation.

"C'mon, Asimov." She whistles the dog to her, climbs into the truck and heads toward the first prospect of real comfort she has known in days.

An hour later, she has established a camp several hundred feet below the surface of the bluff and half a mile in. Two trips from the van have set her up with a Coleman stove, now heating yet another can of stew because she is ravenously hungry as well as weary, a pile of sleeping bags apiece for Asimov and herself, and an electric lantern. For the first time since leaving Washington, she is able to take off her jacket and double layer of sweaters and sit lightly in her shirtsleeves. Her shoulders feel as though half the world has rolled off them to go bouncing down the pale rock flows of the cave. From above her comes a low thrumming sound, almost below the threshold of her hearing, that she knows is the voice of the river, singing.

Singing, singing...singing her to sleep like a mother, rocking her in her rock cradle, loose, light, stoned in her house of stone, the deep waters singing of warmth and refuge and release from pain, singing, singing...

She has just enough presence of mind to turn off the stove before she sinks back onto her bed and into the darkness where there is only the voice of the river, singing the song of the earth, rocking her home, singing and singing now and forever...

It seems to Kirsten that she has not slept at all. Yet she rises up lightly, easily, borne almost on a breath of air. The small stove no longer burns but still radiates warmth, a visible glow in the darkness around her. That seems strange to her, though not so strange as to be disturbing. Nor is she alarmed that Asimov, too, seems to shed his own light where he lies snoring, lost in dreams.

Kirsten glances down at her hands, and they, too, seem to glow palely. Just under the skin, she sees the outlines of a double spiral and a lightning bolt forming, rising to the surface in red and black and ochre paint. When she raises her hands to her face, she can feel the same sigils taking shape beneath her cheekbones, patterns traceable under her fingers. Her palms are painted with sun and crescent moon. Strangely unalarmed, she turns to see her body still lying where she has left it, sprawled with no particular grace across the blankets.

So. She does not seem to be dead. At least, this is not how she has ever seen the experience described. With no more than a thought, she finds herself kneeling by her body, which is still breathing, the chest rising in deep, slow inhalations. Rising on another thought, she drifts across the rock floor to Asimov, who whimpers softly at the faint ruffling of his fur made by her passing.

*Not dead then. But if not dead, what?*

She can feel a force, gentle but insistent, pulling her further into the depths of the cave. With a last insubstantial brush at Asimov's ears, she allows it to draw her as it will. She has no idea how long her journey takes her, or what distance. Where she is there is no time, no space beyond that which surrounds her. Her bare feet skim the limestone floor of the cave without feeling its chill.

Like the walls, like the pillars of calcite that seem to extend upward without end, milk-white as the columns of some great temple, the stone itself is suffused with a soft light. Rising up to the roof, she drifts among colonies of bats in their thousands, tens of thousands perhaps, all lost in their winter's sleep. Some part of her scientist self remains even now, and she notes that they are *Myotis socialis*, hanging single file in long, precisely aligned rows, so neatly arrayed that she can see the nose of every bat in each rank. A bat army. Bat Marines. She raises a hand to her forehead in salute and drifts on. She passes lace curtains formed of glittering mica, crosses a pool setting each foot precisely into the surface tension of the water. *Always wanted to do that. Move over, Jesus!*

The voice of the river becomes louder as she descends into parts of the cave where there is no further human sign. No walkways here, no blank lamps hanging from iron stanchions to mar the beauty of the great vault above her. Effortlessly she glides down the spill of petrified water-falls, past small pools where eyeless fish swim. With a breath, she ascends sheer walls rising ten meters or more to make her way along a path that skirts the high wall, no more than inches wide. The dust here has not been disturbed for centuries, yet she can make out the marks left by human feet along the ledge. Here the pull is exponentially stronger, and she knows in some part of her soul that the holy one whose footprints she walks in without disturbing a grain of sand came, one day long ago, from the very place where she is going.

She comes upon it suddenly, where the path ends abruptly at a fissure in the sheer wall. Like a breath of smoke she passes through it, to find herself within a geological miracle. The dome is perhaps twelve feet across, and lined from floor to apex with clear crystals. Some are slender as pen-cils, others as large as her forearm. Energy pulses from them to the rhythm of the water that seems to flow no more than a meter or so above, some-times slipping lightly over its stone bed, sometimes roaring. In the center of the chamber is a stone slab perhaps a meter high. Around its sides are painted spirals, blazing suns, the forms of bear and wolf, eagle and puma. Carved into its surface are the shapes of hands, one to either side, and a hollow for the back of a human head.

Kirsten understands that it is a place of vision. She understands, too, that it is perhaps mortally perilous.

But danger is irrelevant. She approaches the slab and stretches her incorporeal body out upon it, head in the depression at one end, hands in the carved prints. She is not surprised to find them exactly to her measure.

As she lies there, the voice of the river changes, grows deeper, begins to form words. It is not any language she knows, but she understands its meaning nonetheless. It is the earth herself speaking to her — of violation, of anger, of terrible grief at the murder of her children. Images shift before her eyes so fast that she can barely keep track of them.

The terrible wound of a strip mine gouged out of the sacred Black Hills.

Forests falling to the rasp of saws and lumbering mechanical behemoths.

A yellow butterfly, last of its kind, dying in the summer sun on a strip of asphalt.

Dead buffalo lying skinned by the thousands.

Dead men and dead women, skins bronze and coppery red, lying dead and mutilated across fields of snow and grassy meadows.

A coyote with its rotting foot caught in a trap like a shark's jaw.

And last, the world she has just left, humans slaughtered by the tens and hundreds of thousands, corpses left frozen in the snow or rotting in the heat of a tropical beach, scavenged by gulls.

And suddenly she finds herself once again on the surface of the world, in the forest now lit by a full moon. The cold does not touch her nakedness, nor the wind burn her skin. Before her stands a woman clothed in fringed buckskin worked with porcupine quills in the shape of a hummingbird across her breast, bands of turquoise and white shell circling her neck and wrists. Her long black hair drifts on the air, framing a face that is old and wrinkled and wise beyond knowing in one instant, young and radiantly beautiful the next.

Kirsten folds down on her bare knees before her, wailing soundlessly. *What must I do, Mother? It is too much, too much!*

*Of course it is too much, my daughter,* the woman answers. *Too much and too long. Yet you will not be alone.*

*I have Asi.*

*Him, too.* The woman smiles. *But not only him. See, and remember when the time is right.*

The woman vanishes, and in her place stands the wolf of her dream. Its dark fur gleams white with frost, white as the snow in which it stands, and its eyes are blue flecked with gold like lapis. Above it circles a red-tailed hawk. Its hunting cry rises into the night and is answered from a half-dozen other circling shapes above. Moonlight glints off their wings like silver.

For time unmeasured, Kirsten kneels in the snow looking into the wolf's blue eyes. It regards her with a cool and level interest, nothing of hostility in it, nor of warmth either. Then it turns and trots into the thicket, followed by the cry of the hawk and the strange birds swarming above them.

And without warning, Kirsten finds herself slamming back into her body with a force that should kill her outright but somehow does not. Her sleeping form jerks once where it lies. Asimov rouses slightly with a grunt and a sound that is not quite a bark. Then he turns and lays his great head on his paws, dreaming peacefully. After that, there is only the dark and the slow, steady beat of her own heart.

**She sleeps.**

And as she sleeps, she dreams.

She is standing in a pure white vista, cold and sharp as the edge of an obsidian knife. Gone are the houses, the trees and the mountains. Gone are the animals of land and sky. The white is everything, and everywhere. Nothing and nowhere. It is the alpha, and the omega.

The bitter wind is a constant shriek, like the souls of the damned in a Hell that really has frozen over.

The tone of the shriek changes, melding, as it will in dreams, into a cry she knows well. Looking up into the vast white sky, she watches, smiling as a dot on the horizon grows larger and larger still until it is directly overhead, gliding on the currents of the icy air.

Their eyes meet, two wild souls bound by mutual trust and respect, and with no effort at all, Koda is swept up and welcomed into the body of Cetan Tate, an old and cherished friend.

The wind is not so biting now, buffered as it is by down and feathers. Her vision is sharpened, crisp, like a winter morning after a long spell of snow. As she flies, the mountains thrust up out of the ground, granite giants rising from their winter dens. Trees spring up and gather into communes of forestland, their tips swaying and nodding in the constant wind, speaking to each other in a language as old as time.

Recognizing the landmarks, she knows they are headed north. Land passes beneath them with incredible, heart stopping speed. Mountains rise up and fall away, at times close enough to touch, at others, seeming only a dim memory of a murky past. Forests blend, separate, change, making fanciful patterns in the virgin snow, like clouds marching slowly by on a fine summer day.

After a seeming joyful eternity, Cetan Tate circles once, a wide, looping arc, and gives a piercing cry. When Koda looks down, she recognizes the place beneath immediately. With a silent thank you to her cherished friend, she closes her eyes and feels a sense of quiet displacement. The feeling is not one of pain, as such, but rather a sorrowful emptiness.

*'Til we meet again, old friend.*

With another cry, the hawk is gone, winging toward the east and a rising sun.

Koda is falling. When she lands, she knows without looking that she has assumed the form of her dream spirit *Shungmanitu tanka.* The wolf.

She pads through the snow, a silent shadow, taking in the beauty and stillness around her, allowing it to calm a soul far too weary for far too long. This dreaming place gives her comfort, and she soaks it up greedily, storing it deep within against the horror that has become her waking reality. A rock altar comes gradually into view, and she sits on her haunches, waiting for the One she knows has drawn her here.

She feels it then; a warm, comforting sensation that reminds her of childhood and being wrapped by her mother in a woven woolen blanket, warm and safe and very much loved.

The Wise One appears before the stone slab and places a gnarled hand on Koda's broad head, giving her a fond scratch behind the ears. Koda lowers her eyes in respect. The old woman laughs and tips Koda's jaw up, and their eyes meet, shining.

*Ina Maka.*

*Welcome, my child.*

As she sees the slow tears wending their way down a much-seamed face, Koda pushes her strong body against the Crone, offering her strength and support as best she can.

*Mother, why do you weep?*

*An abomination has come into my home. My children lie dead in their cradles. If I do not weep, I will destroy the world with my wrath.*

*What must I do, Mother? How can I help?*

Ina Maka smiles fondly through her tears. *You are precious to me, blessed daughter. So fierce, and so giving. You are my joy.* Her countenance sobers. *There is one who must be shown the way. She has great knowledge, and with it, great power.*

*Where is she, Mother? Who is she?*

*She is running, child. Hunted like prey, by kin and non alike. She seeks answers to the North. You will need to find and protect her. She is the key.*

*The key to what?*

*Salvation.*

There is a pause as Koda drinks this in. She shakes her great, shaggy head, then meets the Mother's eyes straight on. *How will I know her?*

*I have summoned her here. Watch, and see.*

With an almost human nod, Koda turns and trots into the woods, silent as a shadow. Once sufficiently hidden, she turns and watches. She notes first the face and form of the young woman, surely too young and too frail to bear the heavy weight thrust upon her. Hearing gentle laughter in her mind, she chides herself for too-quick assumptions.

The sigils on the woman's face and hands glow with the touch of the Mother. Koda is intrigued. And when the young woman falls to her knees with a cry of anguish so heart rending that the very forest seems to pause in tribute, Koda is drawn forward as if an unseen tie binds her to the woman whose grief seems to fill the world to the sky and beyond.

Their eyes meet and lock and hold. Neither notices when Ina Maka fades from view. The woman's gaze holds a look that Koda knows well, having seen it in the mirror every morning since the androids seized power.

Hollow. Frightened. Suddenly old beyond telling, as if she stares into eternity. There is a naked vulnerability there, which Koda can't help but respond to. And yet, if she looks deep enough, she can see a core of steel, a tensile strength not noticed on first glance. Will it be enough? Will it allow her to continue her journey alone until Koda can join her? *I will find you.*

Have those eyes, green as the new leaves of spring, brightened just a bit? Has she heard the vow? As she breaks eye contact and trots back into the forest, Dakota can only hope she has.

*I will find you.*

*I will protect you.*

*You are not alone.*

# CHAPTER FIVE

Koda comes to full wakefulness quickly and silently. Her dream remains with her even as her body and mind awaken to reality. She smiles as she feels the compact body in her arms, melded against and atop her like a second skin. Reaching up, she strokes the thick, soft black hair, chuckling inwardly as the woman in her arms purrs very much like a cat while trying to burrow further into her embrace, still fast asleep.

After another moment, Dakota slips out from beneath the Air Force colonel and makes her way, still unclothed, to the small, polarized window. The night beyond is crisp, clear, and unremittingly cold. As she peers off to the north, now knowing her destination, she thinks back on the past two days.

As the remains of the military caravan wound nearer the base like an injured snake, it was held up by a long line of soldiers armed to the teeth. Koda could hear, via the open mic, the orders of those soldiers, demanding that everyone step out of their vehicles to verify that they were human.

Up to her elbows in a downed airman's chest cavity, Dakota, of course, refused. When the gun's muzzle came into view, it was only Manny's fast reflexes, which had been courted by colleges across the country and a few major league teams as well, that saved her from being splattered like an ink blot all over the truck's interior.

Four heads poked immediately through the truck's doors, military faces cut from the same cookie cutter mold, down to the deep cleft in their chins. Fortunately for everyone, they immediately relaxed when they realized that Allen was, in fact, telling the truth. Three of the men hopped aboard and began helping the beleaguered vet, while the fourth ran back to his mates and ordered the gates opened so the caravan could proceed with all due haste.

Dakota saw very little of the compound itself, though she could smell the thick, acrid smoke that hung in the air like a pall. The base had, thankfully, a fairly modern hospital and several surviving doctors and medics to tend to the men in her care.

The electricity was running, thanks to a small hydroelectric plant on the grounds, and Koda spent the next thirty-six hours helping the harried staff tend to the wounds of the injured soldiers.

When she was finally approached by a very insistent Allen, she didn't fight the firm hand encircling her wrist or the tug that forced her legs to move away from the patients she was watching over.

She stopped and stared, though, when her first sight of the compound settled over her. It looked like it had been deluged by bombs. Many of the buildings were nothing but still-smoking rubble, and almost all of the uniformed men and women who scuttled about like ants bore some mark of its passing, whether a bandaged appendage or a shell-shocked expression and deep, hollow eyes.

Mounds of fresh snow covered the bodies of those who would never rise again. Twenty across and at least that many deep, the bodies were watched over by a full military color-guard, honored in the only way they knew.

"C'mon," Maggie had said, gently tugging Dakota's arm. "Let's get you somewhere warm where you can get some food in your belly before you pass out."

"I'm fine." Koda's voice was a distracted mumble as she eyed the hillocks of snow covering the bodies of the fallen.

"You're as pale as the snow out here, Koda, and your pulse is racing to beat the band. I'll make it an order if I have to." Allen resolutely withstood the colorless eyes that came to rest on hers. "Yeah, I know, you're a civvie, but I can be mighty persuasive when I want to be." That earned her a smile that, while small, cheered her considerably.

The mess was pretty much what Dakota expected a military mess to be, and she ate her food without really tasting it, just glad to have something warm and substantial in her belly after more than a day of existing on black coffee. The housing was, however, somewhat of a surprise, and when Maggie led her into the small, private cottage, she looked around approvingly, giving the arrangements her first real smile of the day.

A shower had been the first thing on her agenda, and it took almost an hour of scrubbing to get all of the encrusted blood and body fluids removed from her skin and hair. Clad in a fresh T-shirt and soft sweatpants, she tumbled into the king-sized bed and was asleep before her head hit the pillow.

Maggie had returned late that evening, and when Koda awoke, they fell into an embrace and a loving that was more needing than tender. Primal and passionate, it was the connection of two bodies trying to reaffirm life after having seen so much death.

They had fallen asleep soon after, completely drained of the last of their energy.

**There is a** body in the road. Young, female, bleeding. Unfortunately, despite the presence of half a dozen expectant ravens, it is also still alive. Even with snow falling, Kirsten can see the faint, warding flutter of a hand when one of the birds ventures too close. *Damn. Goddam. I. So. Do. Not. Need. This.* Risky. Way too risky.

Yet even as she begins to steer in an arc that will carry her past on the other side, Kirsten's foot settles on the brake. Asimov, on the seat beside her, stands to attention, ears pricked forward, tail stiff at half-mast. He whines, low in his throat, and gives a short, sharp bark of alarm.

"Yeah, boy," she mutters. "I see her."

For several minutes, Kirsten does just that, examining the scene before her. The woman — no, a girl, slender and still almost flat-chested under the bulk of her jacket, with generic Midwestern features and light brown hair spilling out from beneath the brim of a knitted cap — lies some ten feet from the verge of the road, in the westbound lane of the Interstate. A wavering line of footprints, now rapidly filling with the new snow, dots the empty field to the north of the road.

Halfway across there are slip marks and a hollow where someone has fallen, presumably the annoyance in front of her. Even at a distance, she can make out a pink tinge to patches of the snow. Closer too, crimson spatters the fresh cover, with a long streak where the girl has skidded and fallen again.

There are half a dozen ways it could be a trap. The girl could be microchipped or wearing a transponder. She might have a weapon under her jacket. There could be droids waiting behind the line of trees that runs along a ridge to the other side of the road. Almost as bad, there might be human predators who have left their latest victim as bait for the next.

As the possibilities sort through her mind, one of the ravens stalks up to the girl on the road, waddling a little on the still soft surface. Cocking its head, it seems to study her face for a moment, then grasps a strand of her long hair in its bill and tugs. And tugs again, backing up in the snow. The girl thrashes and cries out weakly, "No! Oh, no! Jesus, help me!"

Kirsten has never placed much credence in the idea of a fate worse than death, but being eaten alive qualifies. In spades. She pauses only to check the magazine of her pistol, slides out of the seat and slogs toward the young woman who has suddenly become her unwelcome charge. Less inhibited, Asimov streaks past her and bounds over the girl's body in a flying arc, landing splay-legged in the middle of the ravens and snapping at the air. The birds, not much impressed, step away from the dog with a haughty stare and a ruffle of wing feathers.

The girl, though, cries out in terror, "A wolf! Oh my God, noooooo!"

"No, he isn't. He just think he's one," Kirsten snaps. She whistles sharply. "Come, Asi!"

The girl turns to look at Kirsten, floundering in the snow. Closer to, Kirsten can see that the right leg of her jeans is ripped and soaked with red, fresh blood pooling and melting the snow where she lies. Her eyes are all pupil, so wide with pain and terror that Kirsten cannot tell what color they are. Scratches streak her face, though they seem superficial, perhaps the result of fleeing through the underbrush of the woods along the ridge. Her left arm lies at a strange angle, either broken or dislocated.

*Oh, wonderful*, Kirsten thinks. *Multiple choice: a) put her out of her misery; b) take her with me; or c) leave her for the ravens.*

Leaving her for the birds is not an option. If it were, Kirsten would already be five miles further down the road, five supremely important miles closer to the end of her own journey. Euthanasia by 9mm round? She cannot quite bring herself to do it, at least not without knowing for certain that the life seeping out onto the road at her feet is unsalvageable. *All right, then. That leaves b.*

"**Go back to** sleep. It's still the middle of the night."

The soft, deep voice startles Maggie from her rapt, if a bit sleepy, moonlit contemplation of surely the most perfect body that God, in His infinite wisdom, has ever created. Feeling warmth steal over her face, she's glad of the darkness. "How did you—"

"Know you were awake? I have my ways."

"Mm," Maggie all but purrs. "I'll testify to that."

When the expected chuckle doesn't follow, the colonel scoots up in the bed until her back is resting against the headboard and the blanket is comfortably wrapped around her chest. There she returns to her inspection, though this time with a more professional eye. She notices the new lines of tension stretched across the broad shoulders and along the column of Koda's elegant spine. "Is something wrong?" she hazards, knowing it's a crap shoot whether or not she'll get an answer.

After a long moment of silence, Dakota releases a small sigh, slightly fogging the polarized window. "What are your plans?"

The question pulls the colonel up short. There are several shades of meaning behind the all too forthright words. "You mean...with my troops?"

Koda nods, still looking out the window. "Yes."

It's Maggie's turn to sigh. "Much as I don't like it, I think I'm going to have to split them into smaller squads."

"Why?"

"Well, while you were busy patching and sewing, I was talking to the acting base commander, Major General Hart. There's been a small but steady line of survivors coming in since the 'incident,' as he calls it. Mostly men and children. Some older women. One or two younger women, but that's all." Maggie pauses for a moment, ordering her thoughts. "Word is that the droids are taking the young women, all of child-bearing age, like we guessed, and housing them in the local jails. Nobody knows why, or what they're doing to them in there. But it can't be pretty, whatever it is."

"So you're going after them. Try to break them out."

Maggie nods. "That's the plan, yes." She looks down at her hands. "Most of the jails down in this part of the state are, as you know, pretty damn small. And it's a damn sure bet that the droids are armed to their beady glass eyeballs with whatever weapons they can get their hands on. Which means that if we send out huge squads, they'll likely shoot the prisoners before we can even break through the front door. With fewer people, we just might be able to do it."

"Sounds like fun."

Maggie's mouth drops open in shock. Koda turns from the window, giving a little smirk that tells the colonel that she's not entirely joking. Maggie can't help but grin back, that part of her that's been a soldier since she was a little girl suddenly warming to the challenge. "Well, I'm not exactly used to being this up close and personal with the enemy, but...yeah, it could be fun at that." With a sexy little smile, she draws the blanket down so that just the tops of her full breasts show. "Care to join me?"

Another question with a variety of meanings. Koda, regretfully, declines all of the offers. "I need to go north."

Maggie hides her disappointment. "Worried about your family?"

Shaking her head, Dakota smiles a little. "My family can take care of themselves."

"Then why north?"

Dakota looks at her so long and so penetratingly that she's afraid she's crossed an invisible line. She finds herself holding her breath as she waits for an answer, all the while praising God that this intent, intense woman is on her side.

"I had a dream."

Koda's voice is only a whisper, but in the otherwise tomb-silent room, Maggie has no trouble hearing. The phrase is so incongruous that she finds herself flipping back to the age of seven, sitting in the front row of Mrs. Dobbin's Country Day class and watching the monitor as an ancient, grainy image of a dark-skinned man mouths those same words from the steps of the Lincoln Memorial. *Looks like your dream finally came true, Reverend King*, Maggie thinks. *Thank God you're not around to see the result.*

Pushing the maudlin thought away, she realizes that Koda is still pinning her with those too-brilliant gemcut eyes. The aura of tension has returned, strumming around the vet's body like an electrical charge. "And in this dream, you're headed north?"

Koda nods, the tension still swirling around her body. Maggie swears she can feel the fine hairs on her arms prick up. "It must be very important to you, then." Like the breaking of a vacuum seal, the tension immediately dissipates from the room. Maggie knows she has responded correctly.

Dakota nods. "It is."

"How far will you go?"

"Very far."

Maggie stiffens as the answer seeps into her brain, as if by osmosis. "Not Minot."

Koda nods again.

"Dakota, that's—"

"Crazy?" The vet gives a half smile, but her eyes are twin glaciers.

"You know damn well it is," Maggie replies, letting her anger show. Taking in a deliberate breath, she reins in her legendary temper. "Koda," she begins again, softly, "this is in no way meant to diminish your dream, but you don't need to go up there. I'm already planning to take a couple of my fighters and blast that damn factory into a mega-mall parking lot. And you know I've got the payload to do it."

"And the humans inside that factory?"

"You actually think they've left any alive in there?" Maggie is incredulous. "What would be the point? That whole factory is completely automated. The droids do everything!"

"I can't take that chance, Colonel," Koda replies, turning back to the window. "Every human life is precious. Especially now."

"And what about yours?" Maggie demands, hands fisted in the blanket. The colonel's answer is a sad smile reflected in the window's glass.

**With a sigh,** Kirsten thumbs on her gun's safety catch and tucks the weapon into her belt. *No good deed ever goes unpunished*, she reminds herself wryly, and this one will probably have an exorbitant cost. Saving this girl's life, if she can, will make her that much later getting to the manufacturing facility at Minot. And that will almost certainly be paid for in other lives, elsewhere. She has already killed innocent people to get as far as she has. She is not willing to do it again except under circumstances more extreme than this.

She kneels in the snow beside the wounded girl, whose huge black eyes have never left her own. Forcing her voice to the gentleness that always marked her mother's, Kirsten takes the girl's hand, lifting it from where it still scrabbles at the snow, fighting for purchase. "It's all right. I'm not going to hurt you. What's your name?"

The girl's only answer is a whimper, deep in her throat. When Kirsten reaches for the zip of her jacket, she shrinks away, trying to make herself small. "All right. My name's — my name's Annie. I'm going to look at your leg, if you'll let me. I'll try really hard not to hurt you." *Damn. It's like talking to a half-feral dog.*

*You would do this for a dog. Pretend she is one if that's what it takes. Patience.* "Easy," she whispers. "Easy, now."

Without waiting for a response, Kirsten folds the torn denim back from the girl's thigh. There is a puncture wound, probably from a large caliber bullet.  The good news, insofar as there is any, is that the blood slowly seeping from its depths is dark, almost black, venous blood.  Which means it's just possible that her new responsibility is not going to bleed to death on her.  *If the femoral artery had been hit, she would be dead by now.  And we would not be having this charming conversation.*  Unfortunately, she cannot see the exit wound and has no idea how much of the flesh has been torn away in the passage of the projectile.  There is no way at all she can deal with the arm until she gets the jacket off, and she cannot do that with her patient lying in the snow.

"Listen to me," Kirsten says gently.  "I can't tend to you like this.  I'm going to bring the van over here and lift you into it.  I've got some medicines and other supplies that will help you.  Do you understand?"

Silence.  The eyes fixed on her remain huge and black.  Kirsten begins to wonder if there's a concussion along with the other injuries, or if the girl is deaf.  *But she can speak; that is certain.  Damn.*  "Okay, you don't have to talk to me if you don't want to.  Can you raise your hand if you understand me?"  Nothing.  Then, very slowly, two fingers rise up out of the snow.

Kirsten lets out a long breath.  "Good.  I'll only be gone a minute.  This is Asimov."  She points to the dog, where he sits on the girl's other side, tongue lolling and a happy idiot expression on his face as he watches the ravens.  "He'll keep the birds away from you.  He is not a wolf."  *No matter what he might think.*

It takes Kirsten more time than she would like to maneuver the truck to within a couple feet of her patient.  Once alongside, she slides open the side door and clears out a spot on the floor.  Her task is easier than it would have been a few days ago, and she frowns.  Her supplies are getting low.  She has enough gas in the jerry cans to get her across the rest of Minnesota and half of North Dakota, with maybe a tank and a half to spare.  She cannot take this waif with her; neither can she expend much of her precious fuel looking for a safe haven.

In this sparsely populated country, there would have been fewer droids than in the cities.  Somewhere she had read — National Geographic, Scientific American? — that there were still bands of Mennonites here on the northern plains who had refused to come out of the nineteenth century even so far as to use electricity, much less modern farm machinery.  In the last hundred miles, Kirsten has seen the occasional tracks of a wheeled vehicle, and even more occasionally a thin column of smoke from a chimney.  *Almost any group of survivors ought to be glad of another pair of hands, even if they come accompanied by a young and healthy appetite.*

*They ought to be willing to take a good, well-trained dog, too.*

The idea comes unbidden.  It is something she has been trying very hard not to think about, though she has known from the beginning that she cannot take Asimov where she is going.  Simply abandoning him is unthinkable, just as leaving him behind had been.  Far in the back of her mind is the even harder choice she had known she might face.  With a bit of luck, now, it will not come to that.

The thought is almost enough to make her feel kindly toward the Nameless One as she spreads out a sleeping bag, then tops it with a blanket-covered tarp as a makeshift treatment table.  Kirsten also lays out a box of bandages, an ampoule of penicillin — still a staple drug after three-quarters of a century, a five cc syringe, and a precious vial of morphine.  *Per-*

*haps*, she thinks, *I can leave the drugs, too, with anyone willing to give Asimov a home. Even an aspirin should be worth its weight in diamonds, now.*

Worth more. Worth lives to those fortunate enough to have it.

The world has changed irrevocably, and she knows it. Even if she succeeds in stopping the droids, even if there are enough surviving chemists, physicists, microbiologists, AI wonks like herself to rebuild the technology, the life she has known is gone. The social order likely to emerge from the ruins will be radically different, with few men and almost no elders. Nations are destroyed. What will rise in their stead, she fears even to imagine. *City-states? Tribes? The Empire of Miami?*

She gives her head a shake to force herself to focus on the present. *Whatever comes, I probably will not live to see it.*

**"For the last** time, Manny, no."

Manny Rivers' face, already ruddy, goes a deeper shade of red, becoming nearly plum as his hands fist at his sides and his chest expands enough to put a serious strain on the zipper of his jumpsuit. The other members of the small group fidget nervously. Manny is usually the most placid of men, but when his anger sparks, the results aren't always pretty.

Taking a quick look at the crowd they are drawing, Dakota signals to her cousin and the two walk downwind to a relatively empty section of the bombed-out base.

"I'm not the little boy you can boss around anymore, *shic'eshi.*"

"I know you aren't, Manny, and I apologize if I'm making you feel that way."

Manny relaxes a little, but the tension is still plain in the lines on his youthful face. "At least tell me why."

"Because I need you here."

"For what? That's the part you're not explaining, Koda."

Mustering what's left of her patience, Koda pulls a military map out of the generous pocket of her coat. Laying it across some overturned cans, she trails a long finger north along a micro-thin line.

"That's pretty out of the way," Manny observes, cocking his head to get a better look.

"Less chance of being detected," Koda replies. Her finger stops close to the border. "This is the only jail we'll pass. It's small, no more than twenty cells, max."

"You've gotta take me, Koda! I'm the best fighter you've got. The rest of these guys couldn't shoot fish in a barrel."

"Niiice. And you picked them out for me all by yourself, hmm?"

He scowls. "You know what I mean."

"Once we break those women out, we're gonna need some temporary place to put them. It's pretty barren up this way, but I think I know of a good spot or two."

Manny gives a grudging smile, remembering when he was young, praying for a visit from his older cousin, who would sweep him away in her truck, taking him places where their ancestors had once made a home. They were his favorite times as a boy, and he remembers them fondly still.

Koda looks at him as he remembers, a faint hint of a smile on her face. When he comes back to the present, she nods. "I'll need to communicate their position to the base somehow so they can be picked up."

Manny shrugs his shoulders. "So? You've got the world's most powerful satellite phone in your hand there. Where's the problem?"

"And let every droid east and west of the Mississippi know their position? Think, Manny."

"So what are you gonna do? Make like injuns in a John Wayne movie and blow smoke signals from the top of the Black Hills?"

Koda rolls her eyes. "Listen to me, Manny, because I'm only gonna say this once, okay?"

Manny gives a reluctant nod.

"There's a way I can use this phone and keep the droids from knowing where the women are."

"How?"

"*Uniyapi Lakota.*"

Understanding draws over his face like the wakening dawn. His brow is a squiggle of conflicting emotion — part wanting to lift in an admiring grin, part wanting to lower in a defeated scowl.

"I spoke to the base commander this morning. As far as he knows, the droids have never been programmed with the Lakota language. It'll give us an advantage that we sorely need right now, and before you say anything, I checked. We're the only Lakota here." She looks at her cousin for a long moment. When she speaks again, her voice is soft. "Now do you see why I need you here?"

The scowl wins. "I see it. I don't like it, but I see it."

"Good."

"I'm giving you ten days," he warns, pointing a finger at her. "Ten days, and then I'm getting in my Tomcat and coming after your ass, hear me?"

Folding her map and storing it in her pocket, she nods. He takes a step closer and flings his arms around her, no longer the soldier, the crack pilot, the man, but rather the boy she remembers so long ago clinging desperately to her in a silent plea for her not to leave. Her own arms gentle themselves around his trim, hard body. She breathes in the warm, familiar scent of him as a guard against the demons of the unknown she will soon face.

All too soon, the moment ends, and they both step back, neither acknowledging, except in their hearts, the sheen of tears in the other's eyes.

**Carefully Kirsten lets** herself down into the snow next to the Nameless One. "Listen to me," she says softly. "I'm going to lift you up and back and into the truck. I need you to help me if you can. Do you understand?"

This time there is a nod. Progress.

Kirsten straddles the girl's body, getting a firm grip under her arms. "Okay, on the count of three."

Another nod.

At "three!" Kirsten straightens and heaves, stepping forward in the same motion to sit the girl in the open door of the van. It is easier than she expected, with the Nameless One able to take some of her own weight on her good leg and support herself with her uninjured arm.

After that it is Emergency First Aid 101. Kirsten cuts away the right half of the girl's jeans and applies pressure compresses until the wound stops bleeding. The exit hole is larger than the entry, but not measurably worse; not a military round, then, or a dum-dum. She pours it full of anti-septic and winds bandages around the leg. The arm is more difficult. An enormous purple bruise and swelling above the elbow indicate a fracture. Kirsten does not have the skill to set the bone, so she splints it with triple thicknesses of cardboard cut from a carton of dog food and straps it to the girl's side to immobilize it. She replaces the stained blanket under her patient with a fresh one. Finally she pumps five hundred units of penicillin into her. The repairs have taken the better part of two hours. The light is fading as Kirsten reaches for the percodan.

The girl has borne the pain in silence, all the while watching her with those great dark eyes. Kirsten uncaps another syringe with her teeth and inserts it into the ampoule of painkiller. "I'll give you something that will make you sleep, now. I can't promise you'll feel better when you wake up, but at least you'll have a fighting chance. We need to find someone I can leave you with, though." Gently she slides the needle home. "I can't take you where I'm going."

"Where's that?"

The girl's voice is hardly more than a breath, but it startles Kirsten so that she straightens suddenly. "Well," she says, after a moment, "so you are going to talk to me."

"Sorry. I was scared."

"Of course you were." Kirsten gives the girl's unbroken arm an awkward pat. "Can you tell me what happened to you? And what do I call you?"

"Lizzie. Lizzie Granger. My folks call me Elizabeth, but..." Lizzie chokes suddenly, turning her face away. "Oh God, they're all dead. My mom, my dad, my baby brother. The Beast's locusts killed them."

"Beast? Locusts?"

"The Beast. You know, the Beast, 666."

"You mean the one from the Bible? The Anti-Christ?"

"No, no. The one that comes before the Anti-Christ. You're not a Christian, are you?"

"I was raised Methodist. Does that count?"

"Christian. Gotta be a real Christian." The girl's voice is slurring with the effect of the morphine. "Not like me. Not good enough. The locusts came, the ones with faces like men but with lions' teeth. Breastplates of iron. Stings. Killed them all."

*This is*, Kirsten decides, *the most bizarre conversation I have had in decades.* Not even the Jehovah's Witnesses who came to the door when her dad was stationed in Corpus Christi, the ones who thought the United Nations was the Devil's own bureaucracy and the flag was an idol, were quite this weird. *Droids running out of control and the girl is worried about grasshoppers. Grasshoppers with human faces and metal bodies and...oh bloody hell, of course.* "Droids," she says. "You mean droids?"

"Droids," Lizzie murmurs. Her voice is fading. "Ran. Scared. Got left. Behind. Left..."

Lizzie's eyes slide closed, and her breathing deepens. It is still faster than it should be, and shallower, but she is in no immediate danger. That will come later. For all of them.

Kirsten drapes a blanket over the girl's unconscious form and climbs back into the front seat. She whistles Asimov up beside her, puts the truck in gear and heads again into the west, into the settling darkness.

**She finds herself** again in a world of white. Monotonous, perhaps, but expected.

The effect is magnified by the all-white machine humming between her legs. The soldiers call them "stink bugs", and it's more or less an apt term, given the military snowmobiles' reliance on methane as a fuel for propulsion, together with the wasp-like drone that marks their passing.

Adding to the monotony is the group's mode of dress. Camo-white is the uniform of the day, and Koda flashes back to a movie she'd seen as a child. Willie...somebody, she remembers. Something about a chocolate factory and a young boy, dressed almost exactly as she is now, who gets reduced to his component atoms and flies across the room to materialize inside a television, a shadow of his former self. "And here I am, off to rescue the natives of Oompa Loompa Land."

Her wry thoughts are whipped away by the wind. As she rides on, she smiles, remembering Maggie's goodbye to her. A quick, if heartfelt hug, a quiet "Be safe" and it was over. It was as if the woman had read her mind and had given her exactly what she needed.

A shadow crosses over her and, looking up, her smile broadens. Wiyo rides the winds above her, sleek elegance personified.

ANGEL or demon! thou, — whether of light
    The minister, or darkness — still dost sway
This age of ours; thine eagle's soaring flight
    Bears us, all breathless, after it away.
    The eye that from thy presence fain would stray
Shuns thee in vain; thy mighty shadow thrown
    Rests on all pictures of the living day.

The past stares at her through a curtain not quite opaque. She can smell chalk dust, hear the quiet hum of the clock as it limps its way toward the final bell, and feel the filtered, somnolent sun resting on her shoulder. She can even see Mr. Hancock's pinched face and the bald pate that shines in the harsh fluorescent lighting of the tiny classroom. He wants her to slip up. She can feel it, just as she can feel the ancient prejudice that runs through his veins like tainted, bilious blood. It is not a new feeling for her, living as she does in a country that proclaims freedom for all but those it has conquered.

She won't slip, though. She never slips. The hunger of her intellect far outstrips his paltry teaching skills, and he knows it. The anger sharpens the grey of his eyes to flinty chips, and his permanently sour expression becomes more so. Had she been raised any differently, she might feel a spark of bitter pride in his anger. Instead, she feels only sadness.

A piercing cry from high above draws closed the curtain to the past, and Dakota once again looks up, eyes narrowing as Wiyo banks left, flutters, then swings around and low in warning.

"Ho' up," she murmurs into the mic at her throat.

Though she wears no stripes on her arm nor brass on her collar, the soldiers obey as if she does. They split formation — half the group pulling to a smooth stop against the left side of the road, the other half doing the same on the right. As a unit, they unsling their weapons while still astride their snowmobiles, ready and waiting for anything.

Koda lifts an arm and Wiyo settles on it, folding her wings comfortably as her eyes stare directly forward at a danger only she can see.

"Damn good watchdog you got there, ma'am," the young lieutenant on her left comments, voice quiet with awe.

Wiyo, surprisingly, takes no exception to the comment, and Koda smiles a secret grin as the hawk settles more comfortably against her.

A moment later, they all can hear the loud, blatting roar of a truck running out the last of its life as it heads toward them. As the vehicle barrels drunkenly into view, Wiyo lifts easily away, strong wings bearing her once again into the cutting air.

Weapons are immediately raised to high port, zeroing in on the oncoming truck with deadly purpose. Koda raises her arm again. "Steady. Let's find out who it is, first."

Not a droid, surely. Dakota can easily see the blood painted across the inside remains of a shattered windshield. And the man, or woman, inside leans like a potato sack against the steering wheel, head bobbing violently with each rut the truck's bounding wheels hit.

"He's gonna hit us," the young lieutenant — *Andrews*, Koda remembers — softly warns, his hands tightening their grip on his weapon.

"Steady..."

"Ma'am?"

"Steady..."

Then the man, for it is a man, sees them and his eyes widen. He yanks the steering wheel sharply to the right, but it's too late. The front tire catches a patch of black ice, and, sliding, the front bumper plows into the snowbank on the left side of the road. The truck flips, end over end. The shattered windshield gives way and the man is ejected out into the winter air, a wingless bird with his own peculiar, dying elegance.

The truck ends its own flight smashed against a tree. There isn't enough gasoline left for an explosion. Instead it shudders, and dies.

Dakota moves first, bounding over the snowbank and racing to the downed man as fast as she can plow through the two feet of snow under her boots. He lies in a bloody heap in the snow, limbs bent in ways human appendages aren't meant to bend. There are two ragged holes in his heavy parka, each tinged with soot and coated in dark, viscous blood. His eyes, surprisingly, are open. One is crazy-canted, filled with blood and staring off to the side. The other, however, is very much aware and filled with terror. Discerning the reason for the terror, Koda immediately reaches up and loosens her collar, displaying her bare neck to the man. At her side yet again, Andrews does the same.

The man relaxes slightly. The fear leaches from his eyes, but horror remains. One hand, at the end of a terribly mangled arm, reaches up and grabs the leg of Koda's pants, spasming into a shaking fist. "D-Daughter," he rasps, coughing on the blood pooling around his lips. "My daughter. Help — help my daughter."

"Where is your daughter?" Andrews asks.

"P-Prison. They — they took her aw-away from me...sh-sh-shot me — tw-twice, couldn't hold...on...help her...please."

"We will. We will," Andrews hastens to reassure. "We'll help her, buddy. But we gotta help you too. You're..." The young lieutenant's voice trails off as the light and awareness in the man's good eye slowly fades to a blank, glassy stare. "Damn. Goddamn." He looks up as a hand descends on his shoulder, squeezes briefly, and lets go. "This blows, ma'am."

"You're right. It does." Koda looks down at the corpse lying at her feet. "Let's cover him with snow. We'll relay his position back to the base once we've gotten the women out, alright?"

After a moment, Andrews nods, his shoulders slumped in defeat and resignation. "He deserves better. Hell, we all do. But I guess you're right. It's the best we can do for now."

# CHAPTER SIX

It is a repeating nightmare. Stretched across the road a hundred meters ahead is a line of pickups strung nose to bumper, a steel wall she can neither drive through nor veer around. To the left of the barricade is a six-foot deep concrete-lined drainage ditch. Something metallic and vaguely human-shaped at its bottom glints in the late sunlight, light that also runs along the barrels of the half dozen long guns swinging up to aim at Kirsten and her vehicle. As she begins to brake, she runs through a quick assessment of her options. The list is very brief. Zero to zero, in fact.

The drainage ditch on one side, possibly with a demolished droid in it — a potentially good sign. A wide gate of welded pipe on the other, topped by a wrought iron sign announcing Shiloh Farm. A bad sign, given that it is closed.

She could throw the truck into reverse at 80 miles per hour and turn around again a half mile up the road. The scopes on several of the rifles make it unlikely that she would get that far without a blown-out tire or punctured gas tank. If these are real people, she might be able to talk her way through. Or buy her way out with the supplies and drugs she will not need much longer. On the other hand, they may well kill her and take them anyway. And that would be a shame.

Kirsten rolls to a stop half a dozen meters from the blockade. Carefully she slides her pistol into her lap. A glance behind the seat tells her that her patient is again sleeping soundly under the effects of the morphine given her when Kirsten changed the dressing on the gunshot wound. Asimov raises his head just high enough to peer over the dashboard, then settles again beside her.

Which is either reassuring or terrifying, depending upon what happens next.

Three of the guards step away from the barricade, stopping halfway to the van. One shouts, "Unlock your doors! Then put your hands on the steering wheel where we can see them!"

Kirsten pauses only to slip the 9mm into her waistband, where it will remain hidden, however briefly, under the bulk of her down vest. Then she presses the button to pop the locks and places her hands in plain view, clasped on the rim of the wheel.

As they approach again, one of the men pauses to spit out a long stream of caramel-colored liquid, and Kirsten allows herself an infinitesimal measure of relaxation. Droids don't chew tobacco. Brigands would have shot her already. Unlike the other two, the third member of the group carries no weapon. Shorter than his companions and slightly built, he sports thin white hair combed optimistically over a scalp flushed bright pink with the cold and a week's genuine human stubble above a Roman collar. Kirsten glances at the perfectly calm Asimov, now sitting straight up in the seat. "Stay, boy," she mutters. Probably unnecessary; he looks as if he has taken root. "Some guard dog you are."

The priest opens the driver's door of the van and looks up at her with the clearest grey eyes Kirsten has ever seen. They are like glass, almost, or spring water running over flint pebbles, worn smooth with the stream's passing. "Good afternoon," he says pleasantly. His voice is unexpectedly deep and resonant. "I'm Dan Griffin."

There is a moment's pause, and Kirsten realizes she is expected to return the courtesy. The alias comes to her tongue without hesitation. "Annie Hutchinson. Pleased to meet you."

Her voice is a bit dryer than she intends, and Griffin's eyes glint in amusement. "I do hope so. Do you have any weapons with you, Annie?" When she does not answer immediately, he adds, "You can tell me about them, or we can search your van. Let's do this the easy way, shall we?"

She nods. "In the back. There's an injured girl, too."

"Keep your hands on the wheel, please," he says, and steps back to slide open the side door. There is the sound of his sharply indrawn breath behind her, and a rustle of cloth as he lays back the blanket tucked about the unconscious Lizzie. "What happened?"

"I don't know exactly. She's been shot in the leg. The arm's broken."

"Yes, I see. How long has she been unconscious like this?"

She can tell the truth or be caught in the lie. "Since I gave her a shot of painkiller. It's the only thing I could do for the fracture."

"You're a medic?"

"My grandmother had diabetes. She couldn't take the pills." Kirsten knows that she has answered only half his real question — where did she get the drug? — but he lets it pass.

"All right." With that, he appears again at the driver's door. "Now then, Annie, if you and your dog will step down for a bit and let my friends check out what you're carrying, we can take the young lady here up to the farm and see to her injuries."

**"What's the count?"**

"Twenty nine," Andrews murmurs, pulling the nightscope from his face. "Can't find one damn metalhead, though. Fuckers don't put out any heat."

In the nearly pitch darkness, the jail rises up before them like an ancient monolith, cold and uncaring, blind and deaf to the suffering within. The structure is tall but narrow, a finger thrust upward, pointing toward an uncaring Heaven. Lights blaze from within, indicating an independent power source of some type.

"How many do you think there are?" asks a slight, red-headed woman who would look more at home sitting behind a desk in junior high than clad in an Army uniform and toting a rather large automatic weapon.

"Damned if I know. Could be one, could be a hundred."

"Doubtful." Dakota gives each of her squad members a look before continuing. "These droids are nothing if not efficient. Two or three of them could easily handle the twenty nine women in there."

"Two?" the young woman responds, hefting her weapon. "What the hell are we waiting for, then? Let's go!"

"Not so fast," Koda warns, lifting a hand. "They obviously want these women alive for a reason, so they're likely looking after them with special interest."

"More droids?"

"More droids. Say six to do the grunt work, and two or three to take care of whatever administrative details droids take care of. And because I'm fond of even numbers, round it up to ten to be on the safe side."

The woman's face falls. "Ten. Damn, that's a lotta metalheads in such a small space."

"Be a lot fewer when we're done with 'em," Andrews growls.

Koda feels the group respond as the energy level cranks up another notch. The men and women around her are almost vibrating with anticipation. The plan, conceived by Maggie back at the base, is firm and set in everyone's minds. They have their jobs, they know what to do. Koda gives them all a final, slow look before nodding.

"Stay behind us, ma'am," Andrews warns as the squad breaks up into two groups and heads, silent as the night, toward the heavy door at the front of the prison.

Drilling holes through his back with her eyes, Dakota says nothing as she follows along behind the group, staying in the shadows as the plastique is carefully placed and then detonated. With a muted whuff, the door falls inward and, weapons drawn, the soldiers enter the prison two by two.

Two silent human chains flow along the interior walls, like water pouring into a basin.

"Down!" Andrews yells a split-second before gunfire erupts over their heads. As one, they duck down, grabbing cover where they can find it. Overturned tables, shattered wooden boxes, and other less identifiable objects litter the floor.

"Remember," Koda cautions as they ready their weapons in preparation for returning fire, "aim at their arms and hands. They can't fire what they can't hold."

The others nod, deferring to her greater experience in fighting the droids.

"And if you can't get a good shot there, aim for their optical sensors. Should throw their own aim off."

Using hand signals, Andrews draws the others into position, and with a quiet command into his mic, the squad rises and begins the assault. Gunfire explodes in bursts of deadly hail as the soldiers begin an inexorable march forward.

Two go down. Then a third. But the group marches onward, fingers depressed on the triggers of their high-powered weapons, never giving an inch of the ground they've gained.

The first wave of droids, four in all, goes down relatively quickly as the group advances upon, and captures, the first set of steel risers that will lead them up to the cells where the women are kept.

Koda makes it to the third step before something slams into her chest and blows her off her feet. She is driven back and down, landing on the cement floor with force enough to rob what little breath she has left from her lungs. Her gun flies from her hand, clattering along the rough concrete until it hits a wall and discharges, filling her world with its roar.

As she lies stunned, she watches with something close to clinical interest — *shock*, she supposes — as Andrews swoops down upon her like some sort of gangly, prehistoric bird, shouting things that she can't quite get her mind to unravel.

*So, this is what dying feels like. Not too bad, actually.*

Andrews' homely, freckled face looms over her like the pitted moon. His lips continue move in incomprehensible patterns, spitting out syllables she can't seem to care enough to understand. Suddenly, her vision is obscured as his body closes down over her. The force of his collapse fires the nerves in her diaphragm, releasing it from its paralysis. She can feel herself taking in great, heaving gasps of air, and the agony of expanding bruised and cracked ribs lets her know that she's not quite dead yet. A moment later, her vision clears and it's his concerned face she sees once again.

"Are you all right?"

Finally, some words that make sense. Taking quick mental stock of her body, she nods.

A smile wreathes his face as he gently helps her to a sitting position. She looks down at her chest. A rather large hole has been ripped through the white flak jacket just below her heart, and she stares down at it with a sense of awed wonder.

"Amazing what they're doing with ceramics these days, huh?" Andrews asks cheerfully.

"Damn" is all Koda can think to reply.

Climbing slowly back to her feet, she allows Andrews to steady her as her legs become reaccustomed to the fact that they're not going to be feeding the buzzards anytime soon.

"M-Maybe you should wait outside, ma'am," a concerned Andrews murmurs.

Koda shoots him a look that vaporizes the spit in his mouth. "*Chesli.*"

"Um — do I wanna know what that means, ma'am?"

The look comes again.

"Didn't think so."

Prudently, the young man turns away for a moment, then back. "They — they've cleared the second and third tiers. Hobbs and Jackson have gone to the control room to try and get the doors opened."

A loud buzz echoes through the building, indicating the venture's success. Koda starts forward at a run, taking the steps two at a time. Andrews shakes his head and follows.

The scene on the second tier is controlled chaos. Several droids have been temporarily disabled, shoved into a cell, and the door manually locked behind them. Shell-shocked women, shabbily dressed, bruised, some of them bloodied, mill about like frightened cattle bound for slaughter. More stream down from the tiers above. Sporadic gunfire erupts, causing the women to scream and the soldiers to look around wildly in the hopes of spotting the remaining droids before they themselves are spotted.

"Hanson, Siebert, Reeves, start getting these women secure. Johnson and Larke, go on ahead, act as lookouts. Shoot anything that moves." Dakota's orders are crisp and clear. The selected soldiers nod, faces set and grave.

Andrews and Koda spot the shadowed movement from the next tier up at the same time and, pushing soldiers and civilians down and away, begin firing. Two droids advance through the gunfire, mechanical fingers constantly depressed on their Uzis. Bullets whiz by like hungry, deadly gnats, ricocheting off the steel of the cell doors.

"Move!" Koda yells to the soldiers guarding the women. "Now!!"

The shout breaks their paralysis, and they begin herding the women down the stairs, weapons at the ready.

One droid falls to Koda's blast to his optical sensors, but the second, continues its advance. Its Uzi is firing sporadically now. They can almost feel the heat from the nearly spent weapon from where they stand.

"Die, you motherfucker!" Running up several stairs, Andrews pulls the pin on a grenade and shoves it down the tight metallic singlet the droid is wearing.

Dakota catches the soldier as he leaps backward, and both are driven to their knees by the resulting explosion.

"That was the last one, Lieutenant!" a feminine voice calls through the smoke and falling debris.

Andrews and Koda come to their feet to the sound of boots hitting the steel steps. Bodies materialize through the smoke as the rest of the prisoners gather on the landing. Koda's eyes narrow. "Who are they?"

Martinez looks at the three dirt-covered men who stand in the group with the rest and shrugs. "Found 'em with the others. They're human."

A stone mask drops over Koda's face as she notices the women shying away from the men in question. "I wouldn't be too sure about that," she mutters, half under her breath. Ignoring Andrews' questioning look, she searches the small crowd. A pair of dark, calm eyes meet her own, and she gestures the woman forward.

Older than the rest by almost a decade, the woman displays an almost regal bearing as she steps up to the vet. "Thank you," she says in a voice heavy with sincerity.

"You're welcome," Dakota replies in kind before looking over her shoulder at the men. "What's their story?"

"They were here when we were captured." The woman's voice is now a flat monotone, devoid of any emotion. "Prisoners, I'd guess."

"And?" Koda asks, eyebrow raised.

"Our rapists."

Hissing through his teeth, Andrews raises his weapon and gestures for the others to move away.

"Hold it," Koda warns, one hand raised. She looks back to the woman. "All of you?"

"Yes."

"Were they coerced?"

"No. They were quite willing."

"The bitch lies!" one of the men shouts, struggling against the sudden grips of iron around his biceps. He might as well be tied between a boulder and a mountain for all the good his efforts net him. "She's lying! Fucking bitch!" He falls silent when the muzzle of a gun is pressed to his temple.

Koda looks over at him, then lets her gaze trail down the line until she spies a young girl of no more than thirteen. "Her too?"

The woman nods.

"All right, that's it," Andrews growls, aiming his weapon. "Motherfucker dies now."

"Hold it," Koda warns again.

"But—"

"Please."

Slowly, uncertainly, Andrews lowers his weapon, his eyes full of questions.

"Put them in those cells back there," Koda orders. "One to a cell."

As the soldiers move to do her bidding, Andrews turns to her, face ruddy with rage. "Why? Why are you letting these scumbags live?"

"Live?" Koda shrugs. "Oh, I suppose they'll live. For a while, anyway. 'Til they starve to death from lack of food and water." Her smile is ice. "There won't be anyone around to take care of them. Or let them out."

Her voice carries easily to the men, and they begin their fruitless struggles anew, screaming and pleading for mercy. The pleas are cut short as the heavy steel doors slam shut for the final time. Then Koda turns back to Andrews. "I think a quick death is too easy for them." She eyes the woman standing before her. "Don't you?"

After a moment, a predatory smile curves the lips of the woman. She nods as the other women surge forward, calling out their own thanks.

"All right then. Let's get the hell outta here."

**Kirsten moves out** just after dawn. The world is faded to mono-chrome in the thin light, sky washed blue-white. Her medicines have been offloaded, as have the empty jerry cans. Their places have been taken by a thermal chest filled with what she has come to think of, reverently, as Real Food, more water, more gasoline. A couple of Pelican cases, no longer hidden under the mounds of other supplies, hold items that should help her get into Minot. The lingering fear that she has forgotten something will not leave her.

The highway is snow-covered over a layer of ice. The going is slow, and a sense of urgency nags at Kirsten. The world beyond her newly-patched window is white as far as she can see, wide flat expanses of fallow field, the occasional hump of a hill or low shed covered by the ten-days' fall. Drifts lie deep along fence lines, completely burying some of the posts, leaving half a foot of others to jut up out of the snow in long, straight lines.

Dan Griffen had recognized her the evening before. Drawing her aside as the members of the commune searched her truck, he had asked pointedly, "You're headed to Minot, aren't you? To the droid facility."

Her mouth dry as cotton, she could only nod and accept his offer of sanctuary for her passenger and supplies for herself. She and Asimov had spent the night in the comfort of a bed — an actual bed with a mattress — and she had fully intended to ask the priest for haven for the dog along with the waif. She had not been able to do it. And now—

She refuses to think about what now. She strikes the steering wheel with her hand, so hard she knows there will be a bruise. "Damn! Goddam! Stupid..."

A bark, high-pitched and unmistakably joyful, answers her. She sighs and reaches out to lay a hand on the dog's broad head. There will be someone else along the way, someone who can give him a good home. There will have to be. Kirsten blinks hard, forcing back tears. Asimov leans against her, whining, and quite without volition, her arm goes around him, holding tight.

**Koda's glance takes** in the semi-circle of survivors there in the jail's guardroom. It is an oddly tidy place: no McDonald's wrappers, no Pepsi or Coke cans, no papers piled in multi-colored triplicate on the watch officer's desk. If not for the ghosts of bloodstains that linger on floor and walls, it would be almost as clean as an examining room. But that had been part of the droids' appeal: no more mess than a pet rock. She takes a quick tally of the women huddled in one corner — twenty-six.

But no, that's wrong. There are twenty-five women and one little girl.

A red haze passes over Koda's mind. There is a legend in the family from generations past, of a white lawman who violated her grandmother's younger sister. The sister's husband and his brother had waylaid the deputy one night on a lonely road and left him deep in an abandoned mine shaft with his testicles nailed to a beam. They had also left him a knife, and a choice.

But she has more practical matters before her. She raps out, "Siebert. Hobbs."

"Ma'am."

"Find a store with women's clothing. Bring back something warm for these ladies. White, if you can find it."

"Ma'am."

"There's a sports shop two blocks north," says the older woman who has spoken for the group. "There was, at any rate." Then, "Who are you?"

"Sorry. These are the free forces of the United States, Colonel Margaret Allen commanding. I'm Dakota Rivers."

"Oh, thank God," the woman breathes on a long sigh. "We didn't know, you see, if there were any survivors at all, much less..." A wave of her hand encompasses the soldiers in the room.

"What's going to happen to us now?" The speaker is a younger woman, no more than twenty, whose long, pale hair lies perfectly combed across her shoulders.

It is not vanity, Koda realizes, but some small attempt at a semblance of dignity where dignity is impossible. "We need to get you to someplace safe. You know the area better than we do — where can we leave you when we move out again?"

"There's the Scout camp." It is the thirteen-year-old. "No one will be there now. I used to go there every summer, and so did my—" She pauses, swallowing hard, but her eyes are dry. "My two brothers. Brian was an Eagle Scout; he was a counselor."

Koda silently curses to hell and worse the unknown persons responsible for the disaster. A child ought not to be forced into the emotional wasteland beyond tears; that is the province of adults. She takes a step toward the girl, meaning to hug her, but reads the minuscule flinch in the child's shoulders, the rejection in her eyes. A touch will break her.

Again the blood-crimson mist filters through Koda's mind. She wants to kill someone, badly. Her vision narrows, shrinks to a point. *This,* she thinks, *must be what Wiyo feels when she holds at hover before she stoops on her prey. Or the wolf, when she sees the elk flounder in the snow.* It is a yearning for hot blood slipping over the tongue that cannot be satisfied by the shattering of cold metal.

She shakes her head to clear it, and her vision returns to normal. "That sounds good. How do the rest of you feel about that?"

There are nods along the line, slow and wary. One woman objects. "No! I have to try to find my family."

"Honey." It is the older woman again. "Honey, if your family is someplace safe, you won't be able to find them. If they aren't safe — better you don't."

"She's right, you know, ma'am," Andrews puts in softly. "If your family is alive, the best thing you can do for them is make sure you survive."

"All right," says Koda, fishing under her camos for a list she has prepared and a pen. She addresses the youngster. "Do you—" Then, more gently, "Can I call you something besides 'you'?"

"Donna."

"Donna. Do you know how to get to the camp?"

Donna nods.

"Great. Can you show Lieutenant Andrews on the map, please?"

As they spread the unwieldy sheet out on one of the desks, Koda scribbles *mifepristone* and *oxytocin* at the top of the priority one drugs. "Johnson and Martinez. Find a pharmacy and bring back everything they have on this list. If they have herbal meds, get these, too." Blue and black cohosh, motherwort, long used by her people to ease delivery or to end an unwanted pregnancy. If this jail is the pattern, every milligram is precious.

Johnson scans the list quickly, then meets Koda's eyes. She salutes. "Right away, ma'am."

"Hanson, Larke, food and trucks, per plan. Check the jail garage. See if the sheriff's vans will do and if you can get anything useful out of their gas pump. Reeves, collect all the guns and ammo you can find here, then help Hanson and Larke."

"Yes, ma'am."

The soldiers scatter to her orders, and Koda marvels at their cohesion. They are a mixture of Air Force, Marines, regular Army, working as smoothly as if they had all been together since basic training. And all of them under the unlikely command of a veterinarian. "Hump it," she adds. "We move out in an hour and a half."

In the end, they set out fifteen minutes early, a box truck packed with supplies and the rescued women riding double and triple behind the soldiers on their snowmobiles. A couple more of the machines have been liberated from the sports outfitters and are now piloted by some of the former captives themselves. A half dozen of the troops have no passengers, ranging loose before and beside the small procession, weapons ready. Koda watches them swing out onto the road, then glides into position at the front. A small warm spot has taken hold somewhere under her rib cage. It is one thing to stop the enemy; it is another to take back what they have stolen. Counting coup. Koda glances upward, where a hawk keeps pace with them, her rust colored tail spread against the hard blue of the winter sky. *Lelah wakan.* It is a good sign indeed.

**Three nights later** Kirsten camps in a stand of woods beside the Lac aux Mortes. Tomorrow she will go on to Minot.

She is still far enough away from the base to risk a proper campfire. The pines give shelter from aerial surveillance; infrared sensors will pick up body heat and the residual warmth of the van's engine in any case. Bowl in hand, Kirsten scrapes the bottom of the Dinty Moore can hopefully, then sets it in front of Asimov. "Here you go, boy. There's barely a molecule left."

At Kirsten's feet, Asimov raises his head and whines, his tongue making the circuit of his jaws.

She reaches down absently to ruffle his fur. He whines again, a deeper sound, and she sets aside the map that lies across her knees. The map is for tomorrow. This night, she is acutely aware that every time she touches Asi, every word she speaks to him, brings her closer to the moment when she will have to leave him and enter the base.

The chance that she will survive, that she will ever see him again, is too small to measure. Alone, there is at least some small likelihood that he can feed and protect himself. His odds are better than hers. That does not make the thought of abandoning him any less bitter. *God damn you, Westerhaus. Damn you to deepest Hell. And God damn me for not being able to give him up.*

Rising, she calls the dog and escapes into the trees. They are not so thick overhead that they hide the sky, and a full moon shines down, its reflection a luminous mist upon the snow. The Shepherd lopes loose-limbed alongside her, his black and silver mingling with the shadows and the snow.

Another ten yards and she picks it up faintly, just on the margins of her hearing, soft footfalls under the trees. On the edge of a small clearing, Asi freezes, coming to a sudden stop with ears forward. Almost imperceptibly, shadow moving upon shadow, the tip of his tail twitches from side to side. Kirsten's hand goes to her gun.

She stands without breathing for a long moment, as the sounds become less faint, moving nearer. Not human, not droid. Wrong season for bear. Asimov whines again, almost eagerly. Just across the glade she thinks she sees a form moving, pale against the paler reflection of moon off snow. Asi gives a sharp yip, a greeting. There is no answer.

Kirsten takes a step backward, her eyes never leaving the space between the trees where she has sensed movement. "Come on, boy. Time to go back."

As she steps back again, a wolf paces into the clearing, its coat leached white under the moon. Asimov looks back at Kirsten. Then, as if suddenly slipped off the leash, he crosses the space with a bound and disappears into the pines. For half a second the wolf remains, staring at Kirsten with eyes that gleam red in the pale light. Then it, too, is gone.

*I should go after him*, she thinks. But she does not move, and after a time she turns to make her way back to camp.

Better that he be free.

As she is free, too. And alone.

**The moon swings** low above the pine trees, framed in the old-fashioned divided window pane. Its brightness hangs in a mist above the snow, a shifting of light and shadow like old ghosts wandering. From somewhere in the woods there comes a deep-throated baying, a sound that seems to begin somewhere down in the vitals of the earth itself, passing up through the crevices of the mountains to find its way at last into a mortal throat. It is answered by a second voice, and a third. Others join in until the sound begins to invade Koda's bones, sliding along her muscles in a chant older than her people, older than her species. She feels her tendons flex; her spine reconfigures. Smells bring her the history of the past day: sweat, blood, the scent of human mating. Over it all lingers the acrid stench of gunpowder, which is death to her and her kind. Her legs gather under her to flee, and bring her abruptly to her feet and awake before the dying embers in the fireplace, M-16 at the ready.

*Dream. Just a dream.*

Not quite a dream. The wolf pack, miles away across the hills, still sings as it courses through the snow. Close to, she can still smell the black-powder smoke that clings to her clothing. Yet the night is peaceful. The freed captives of Mandan jail sleep quietly in the cabin's sturdy double bunks, some snoring softly, others whimpering now and again in their sleep. Koda bends to poke at the embers glowing in the grate of the massive fireplace and sets another couple of pieces of split oak above them. Built by WPA workers in the 1930s, Camp Sitting Bull — formerly, judging by the not-quite-obliterated sign over the cabin door, Camp Custer — is low-tech and therefore comfortable this winter's night.

Koda makes her way, soft-footed, between the tiers of bunks. All is well. Still quietly, she slips outside. The moon is full, bright enough to cast shadows, and she finds her way easily to a stone bench set under the tall pines. From it, she can see smoke curling from the chimneys of three more cabins, one housing more of the freed women, the other two temporary barracks for her troops.

*My troops.* She turns that phrase over in her mind, examining it from all angles. She comes from a long line of warriors. Her grandfather's grandfather followed Tschunka Witco, the one the whites called Crazy Horse, on the Powder River and at the Greasy Grass by the Little Big Horn. A hundred years and more removed, her mother is a cousin of Red Cloud. Battle is in her blood, and she has known it for as long as she can remember knowing anything. More than once as a girl, she cried for the vision that would call her to fight for her nation and her land, to return the sacred Black Hills to a free Lakota people. It has never come, but she has been true — as a healer, as a woman — to those visions that have.

Her troops. A Lakota chieftain did not command troops. Warriors followed him because he was successful, not because rank or organization compelled them. Despite the cultural dissonance, despite her strictly legal status as a civilian, she knows that she has somehow become a commander and that these men and women following her north into danger are her troops. Andrews may be the nominal leader of the mission, but he defers to her, as do all the others. Some of their respect may reflect the obvious awe in which they hold her top-gun, kick-ass, take-no-prisoners cousin Manny; some may have rubbed off onto her from the colonel, who seems to be indistinguishable from God in the eyes of her squadron. But that does not explain the easy companionship or the instant equality she has found with Maggie herself. It does not explain the familiarity.

Perhaps it is a memory of another time, when she was not Dakota Rivers. Perhaps it is the memory of Ina Maka, Mother Earth herself, seeping into her mind and her bones from this land that has so long been a battleground, so drenched in the blood of the Lakota and other Nations. If she listens with the ears of her spirit, she can almost hear the war cries, the clash of metal, almost smell the sweat and blood. As she looks up at the sky, she can almost see the stars shift about the pole through the frozen light years. Almost.

As she watches, a silver pinprick of light makes its way across the sky beneath the stars. A meteor, flaring as it plunges to earth. Perhaps a satellite, part of another world now, pacing its orbit, or like the meteor, burning in the air.

"My mother used to say a falling star meant a death."

Koda turns to look up at the speaker. It is Sonia Mandelbaum, the older woman from the jail, now bundled against the cold in Polartec and boots. "Are you having trouble sleeping?" she asks. "I could get you something for that."

The woman shakes her head. "No," she says, "thank you. I'd rather face my ghosts than try to drug them out of existence."

Koda slides to one side of the bench in invitation, and the woman settles herself, her breath forming a cloud about her. Even in the pale light, Koda can see that her eyes are swollen, the faint glint of frozen crystals on her eyelashes.

Sonia is silent for a long moment, her gaze following the path of the meteorite. Then, "Do you understand this?"

"You mean the uprising?"

Sonia nods. "That. And what's happened to us."

"The uprising — no. All we do know is that it seems to have been world-wide and coordinated. The other — how much do you feel able to tell me?"

"There's not much." After a time, she goes on, "We had a bakery, my husband and I, with half a dozen employees and a couple droids to clean and do deliveries and run errands. Maid Marians, both of them brand new. Nick always liked to have state-of-the-art equipment."

"Nick is your husband?"

"Was my husband." The emphasis is very slight. Sonia pauses, then goes on. "I was finishing a wedding cake. Nick had some French bread just out of the oven and was bagging it. I heard some shouting in the street, and went to the front of the store to look out the window. We've had trouble with skinhead demonstrations in Mandan before, some of those 'Christian Nation' people from Idaho. Once we had swastikas painted all over the display window. But it wasn't the brownshirts this time."

"The droids." It was not a question.

"The droids. One of ours grabbed Nick from behind and broke his neck." She makes a snapping motion with her hands. "Just like that. Then they killed Bill and Lalo, who did most of the breads." Again the snapping motion. "Just like that."

"But not the women."

"No, not the women. They herded us into the delivery truck and took us to the jail."

She flinches as boots crunch through the crusted snow behind them. Koda turns, half rising with her hands on the grips of her gun as Reese passes on his guard round. He is clearly surprised to find them outside in the cold, but much too disciplined to remark on their presence. He salutes. "Ma'am."

"Carry on." Koda nods, resisting the urge to return the salute, and settles again on the bench. As footsteps recede down the path toward the next cabin, she says, "They took only the women of childbearing age?"

"Yes. They asked us about when we'd had our last periods when we got to the jail, before they locked us up." She turns haunted eyes to Koda. "I said last month; it's been almost a year."

Very gently, Koda asks, "How did you know that was the right answer?"

"There was one girl who told them she'd had a hysterectomy; I think she was a teacher at the middle school. They took her outside, and we heard her scream. We never saw her again."

"I see."

"So I lied. The rapes began the next day."

Koda's mind flashes back to her first conversation with Maggie. Slaughter the steers, keep the cows and heifers to make more steers, send the old cows to auction when they can no longer produce calves. But that doesn't make sense. Droids do not eat. If not food, then what? Slaves?

That possibility seems no more likely than the first. True, slaves bred to servitude from the womb, who had never known any other life, might be more docile than those taken as adults or even as children, but slaves require a slavemaster. Droids need slaves as little as they need food.

Someone controlling the droids, then? Koda says, "Sonia, did you ever see or hear the droids receive transmissions from anyone?"

"No. After that first day, they never spoke to us. They never spoke to each other either."

It is three in the morning, and Koda's head is beginning to ache. She needs coffee, she needs sleep; she will get neither. Tomorrow she and her troops must settle the women in the camp, and the day after they must move out again, toward Minot. "Black helicopters," she says suddenly.

"Pardon?" Sonia looks up at her, puzzled.

"Sorry. Twenty years ago, there were a lot of people, especially out in this part of the country, who thought the government was part of some vast international banking conspiracy. It was going to take over and create a corporate state with its capital at Zurich. They thought they were being spied on from black helicopters."

"Do you think that's what it is?"

Koda stands and stretches; her legs and shoulders feel like lead. Another pinprick of light scuds across the sky as they turn back toward the cabins, and a shiver passes up her spine that has nothing to do with the temperature. "No," she says. "I think that whatever it is, is worse than that. Much, much worse."

**The whole world** seems to hold its breath as the first grey streaks of dawn paint themselves over the roof of the earth. Seated crosslegged on a tallish boulder about a mile from the base, Kirsten faces east and watches as the earth prepares to give birth to another day. Watching sunrises is, she believes, a pastime best left to dreamers and fools, and she considers herself neither. But the odd sense of peace that descends over her makes the break in her fastidious habits worth the effort.

She's alone now. More alone than she's ever been, and that thought brings with it a surprising twinge of sadness. Surprising because she's quite sure that somewhere on some dusty library shelf, there's a dictionary that sports her picture next to the word "loner". Born into a family of loners, she's always figured she came by it honestly. Add to that the fact that it's hard to make friends when kids your age are sitting in kindergarten exploring the pleasures of eating paste while you're in a fifth grade classroom calculating the square root of pi, and you have the recipe for a person whose mind is her own best company.

When she had come down with an anomalous case of measles at the age of twelve the complete loss of her hearing hardly fazed her. If keeping the noises of the outside world at bay allowed her to delve more deeply into the rigid structure of her private thoughts and aspirations, well, that was pretty much fine by her.

She laughs now as she remembers that day, so many years ago now, when she woke up in the recovery room of Brooke Army Medical Center, able to hear again for the first time in two years. How joyful her parents had been, and how their faces had crumpled as she cried for the loss of her deafness.

"I'm sorry, Mom and Dad," she says softly into the wakening world. "I know you only wanted what was best for me, and you did a damn good job giving it to me, too. Thank you for that. I appreciate it, and you, more than you'll ever know."

As if in answer, the rim of the sun peeks over the horizon, and, surprised, she wipes a dampness from her cheeks.

She laughs again, this time in self-derision. "All right, Kirsten, enough of this foolishness. You've got a job to do, and it's about damn time you started doing it."

Like a rude guest who's bound and determined to pull up a chair and stay a while, the strange but welcome sense of peace travels with her to the back of the van. Opening the doors, she crawls inside the cool dimness, sharp eyes scanning the interior until they light upon the items she needs.

A powerful battery operated lantern illuminates the dim interior, and she settles once again into her cross-legged position, grabbing a set of carefully packed items and placing them within easy reach around her.

First she pulls out her laptop, the steroidal super-computer some of her staff jokingly named "Arnold". The joke had to be explained to her before she got it. Movie watching had never been on her top ten list of things to do.

The computer obediently boots up, courtesy of a special, long lasting battery and a solar panel tucked into one corner of the cover. Nimble fingers fly over the keyboard, opening a succession of windows. Seconds later, she sits back with a self-satisfied smirk, green eyes seeming to glow as the light from the screen flickers across her face. Multiple incomprehensible lines of text are highlighted, but only one blinking and bolded word changes the smirk to a full-blown smile: active. She wants to laugh, but holds it in as her quick mind replays the steps necessary to set her plan into motion.

Androids aren't The Borg. Though each is connected to a massive data hub deep underground in the Silicone Valley, they are no more connected to each other than two refrigerators in two different houses are connected. It was the one concession she was able to receive as the newly-minted Secretary of Technology, Cabinet-level wonk. And it is a concession that will make her life, what remains of it, a good deal easier.

Though the droids are in no way colony creatures, they do have ways of recognizing one another and of sending streams of information along pre-set pathways that human beings don't possess. With that problem in mind, Kirsten drags over a second item, a box about half the size of her laptop. Carefully opening the lid, she withdraws a second box, this one much smaller than the other. The tiny, plastic-encased hinges give a soft squeal when she pries open the lid of this box to reveal two large brown contact lenses resting in saline solution. Kirsten smiles when they are revealed, touching on the memory of her brief foray into the world of virtual reality.

Her college classmates, all much older than her, seemed addicted to the fantasy of being able to instantly transport themselves into a world of their choosing just for the thinking. Pre-adolescent curiosity drew her into the web, and before she quite knew what was happening, a sizable amount of her scholarship money went toward the purchase of the items she now holds in her hands.

Placing the contacts aside for the moment, she lifts and opens a third, very small, box. Inside this box rests a small, flesh colored button no larger than half the size of the nail on her smallest finger. An earpiece that no audiologist has ever seen, it was used in VR to impart a sense of movement and sound to the wearer, shattering the bounds of computer-generated reality.

For Kirsten, however, the effect had been somewhat different. When combined with the workings of her cochlear implants, she discovered that what she was hearing was the actual wireless data being streamed into the microchip implanted into the ear piece. With a little tweaking, she was able to effect a sort of data translator, and from there on, she recouped her scholarship losses by developing VR games for her classmates at a substantially reduced cost. She'd quickly become the darling of the Student Union at the ripe old age of fourteen.

Laughing softly, she pulls out the earpiece and slips it into her ear canal. Once it is seated comfortably, she hits a key on her computer. After a moment of disorientation, the signal comes through clearly and she nods, satisfied.

Pressing the key again, she cuts off the noise, then grabs a hand mirror and positions it just so. The contact lenses go in smoothly, though her eyes, at first, rebel at the unexpected intrusion. Blinking one last time, she clears her vision and glances into the mirror. A stranger stares back at her. A stranger with the brown, dead dolls' eyes that mark an android. She shudders at the image, then settles.

*Need to get over those whim-whams, little K.*

She can almost hear her dad's voice, as if he were standing right over her shoulder urging her to jump from the highest board at the community pool. The memory of that gruff, husky voice has helped her through more than a few of life's little roadblocks. Maybe the magic will hold for one, final try. *Please. Let it hold. Just let me do this one last thing.*

Nodding to herself, she takes one final object from the nest of boxes before her, lifting it to shine in the light, twisting it between her fingers. What should have been a final, tragic insult instead will become, she hopes, her ultimate triumph.

*"Here you go, doll,"* he had said, painted blondes dripping off his arms like water. *His insolent smirk made his homely face all the uglier, but the diamond-studded whores didn't seem to care. "The working microchip is inside. Give it a good, long look-see, and if you can figure it out, call me. We'll do lunch."* Laughing heartily, he tossed her a shining, metallic silver strip and walks away, people trailing him like apostles to the One True God.

*Though almost loathe to touch the thing, she nevertheless grabbed it from the air and stuffed it into the bodice of her sequined evening gown.*

"You're a real prick, Westerhaus," she murmurs, coming back to the present. "And I just hope I'll live long enough to tell you that. And to thank you for this. Right before I shove it up your pockmarked little candy ass."

She slips the silver collar around her neck and fastens it securely. It's snug, but not too tight, as if it's been crafted just for her. Knowing that little asshole, it probably was.

With a final pat to the collar, she looks back down into the mirror. Her lips form a stunned O as she sees the final results of her handiwork.

"Damn."

Her soft exhalation briefly fogs the mirror, breaking the spell she's cast over herself. A small breath of relief, and she looks over at the still blinking monitor.

Active.

With a few quick changes, she has transformed herself from Kirsten King, Ph.D. in Robotics, to BD-1499081-Z-2A6-13, biodroid currently in service to Chalmatech Pharmaceuticals, the largest drug company in the world.

Biodroids had been the first androids developed by Westerhaus, touted as a superior alternative to animal research. Designed to mimic the human body in every way, including a beating "heart", breathing "lungs", measurable "blood pressure" and a body "chemistry" that could mimic any disease known to man, and efficiently and accurately predict the effects of medicines used to fight said diseases, the biodroid had been a smashing success.

And it is Kirsten's ticket onto the base. Her only chance to try and undo the damage Westerhaus has created. Her tightly clenched fist pounds on her leg, and she nods once, sharply. "All right. Let's do it."

# CHAPTER SEVEN

"*Shic'eshi*," Koda greets Manny.

"*Hankashi*," he answers in Lakota.

"Listen, this has got to be quick. *Winan iyoheyapi ekta Mandan — hochoken Tatanka Watanka.*"

"*Toná?*"

"*Wikcemna yamni.*"

"*Iyeyathi,*" he promises.

"*Pilámayaye.*"

"*Wakan Tanka nici un.*"

Koda gives the communications handset back to Johnson, who returns to her own sleep, taking the unit with her. The women they have left at Camp Sitting Bull will be safe. Koda and Manny's brief communication in Lakota would avoid detection by the droids.

She paces for a time, restless. The moon is in her blood again this night, and Koda slips quietly across the perimeter of the camp and onto the shore of the frozen lake beyond. She passes Martinez on his sentry rounds, accepting his salute quietly with a murmured acknowledgement and a nod. The feeling of disquieting familiarity with the mantle of command slips along her veins beside the other summons. It is something she now knows she will have to deal with, though when or how is not certain.

Her grandfather would have known how to confront this new aspect of herself. But then again, he would not have needed or wanted to be forewarned. "Well, Tshunkila," he would have said, "it will come when all such things come — when you have no time for it and when you are not prepared. Any fool can deal with a challenge that comes in broad daylight across an open field. Only a real warrior or a true *winan wakan* will survive an ambush."

"Fox" had been Tunkashila's name for her then. "Fox Ears", her mother had sometimes amended when she found Koda had overheard some dully adult thing that wasn't "fit" for a child. Mostly about sex, of course, but how many times could you see the stallion stand with the mares and your baby brother out of his diapers, and not figure it out? Then there was the other thing she'd figured out, with no assistance from the horses, and her mother had simply kissed her and said, "Yes, I thought so." Once, teasing, Tali had sworn she had married Koda just to have a decent mother-in-law.

A yard or so from the edge of the ice, a sandstone outcropping thrusts up through the snow. Koda brushes the powdery new fall off the top of the boulder, clambers up and settles crosslegged, facing north. Between the tops of the pines and the moon, now just off the full, the Northern Lights flare across the sky in ripples of green and blue and gold and lilac. Her grandfather had called them the outrunners of *waziya ahtah*, the blizzard, but she had pointed to them one night and said, "*Wápata, tunkashila.*" "Flags?" he had asked, laughing, and she had insisted, "Banners, of many warriors on great horses, wearing gold." He had looked at her then, long and hard, and she had seen decision form in his eyes. He had said, "You are the one I will teach." He taught her what she is about to do now.

Laying her hands on her knees and closing her eyes, she begins to breathe slowly, deeply. Gradually she becomes aware of the breath as it passes in and out of her lungs, follows the thrum and hiss of her own blood as it beats in throat and ankle. She begins to chant softly to the rhythm of her body's drum, first in its own tempo, then slowing and feeling her heart slow with it. *Hey-ah. Hey-ah. Heeyy-aaahh.* It is the blood song, one of the first of her grandfather's teachings. It can be used to stop bleeding, in human or birthing mare or wire-entangled deer. Or it can be used as she uses it now, to quiet the noise of physical life and let the spirit slip free.

When the chant has slowed almost to stillness, she feels herself rise upward, out of her body, past the trees and the floating banners. Above her the stars flare close and huge, cold as the   northern ice below them. Across the snow fields she hears again the wolf pack racing under the waning moon, calling to each other in the chase, calling to her, Tshunkmanitou Wakan Winan of the Lakota people, to run with them.

She follows the baying as she slides along the air, miles slipping away under her with a thought. When she finds them, they are a string of dark shadows, moving over the snow in great leaping bounds from north to south across a rise. As she descends, she feels the beginning of the change come over her. Her spine reconfigures itself, hips and shoulders twisting beneath its line. Eyes and ears become almost unbearably keen. She hears each padded footfall as it breaks the crust of the snow, sees each hair in the feathery ruff of each wolf as they streak toward her, never breaking stride.

As the big male in the lead passes by her, she swings into the line after him. She feels her spine coil and release with each plunge into the snow, feels the power as muscles of hip and thigh lift her free of it again and into the air. Yellow eyes gleam like fireflies around her; the breath of a dozen mouths streams behind her in a plume. It is only gradually that she becomes aware that there is something strange in this running. There is no crashing of underbrush as escaping prey flees before them; her nose catches no scent of elk or deer or antelope.

She senses amusement from the pack leader at her discovery, and something that, had it been a human word, would have been, "Wait."

A mile further along, she picks up the scent — wolf-like but not, with faint but still perceptible overtones of human. Dog. Male. A ripple of tension runs through the lower-ranking members of the pack behind her, but she senses nothing of threat or fear in the lead male. Instead there is purpose, and the feeling of a task almost completed.

When they come upon him at last he is stretched out along a fallen log in a larch pine clearing, front paws straight out in front of him, the brush of his tail draped elegantly to one side, facing forward with ears erect. Almost as if he has been waiting for them. And almost — almost he is familiar to her. A big dog, almost as large as the alpha wolf, with silver fur on face and flank, legs and belly, marked with a black saddle and a four-pointed black star between his eyes.

The pack comes to a halt, and the stranger descends to meet them. He sniffs noses with the leader, and they stalk around each other stiff-legged for a moment, tails straight up, hackles rising. Then the dog steps back, lowering his head to make submission. The ritual repeats itself down the line. Then the pack wheels and sets off south again, running under the moon toward the frozen lake and the small band of humans encamped there.

When Koda's spirit comes again into her body, her muscles are sore, and she is painfully hungry. Sound asleep on the rock beside her is a large silver and black German Shepherd. Levering herself up, she grabs him by the scruff of the neck and gives him a shake. "C'mon, boy," she says. "Let's go find something to eat."

**Walking up to** the retinal sensor, Kirsten experiences a feeling of terror unknown in her life before this time. If she fails this one simple test, she will be killed outright. No second chances, no recriminations. Dead. As a doornail, as her father has been known to say on occasion. Her analytic mind could never quite make sense of that particular idiom before, but now it seems painfully clear. Taking a deep breath, Kirsten steps in front of the sensor and prays her contacts will do their job.

The wait seems interminable; she has time to see various scenes of her life flash through her mind in all their Technicolor glory. She hears a soft hum and has only time enough to think, *I'm a dead woman*, before the gate slides open noiselessly and she steps through, unencumbered and still very much alive.

She fights to keep her face and body completely without expression as her eyes trail over what she first takes to be scattered hillocks in the snow. It is only on further, seemingly casual inspection that she notices those hillocks are actually snow-covered bodies, left to die, and freeze, where they have fallen.

*Don't start, K. Don't stare. You're an emotionless android. Remember that, or you'll be joining your frozen friends here.*

Thus fortified, she begins the trek across the wide expanse of grounds toward the large, low-slung and windowless building directly ahead. It looks more like a bomb shelter than a business, but given that the facility is, for the most part, a fully self contained unit, and further given that the androids that operate there wouldn't appreciate an outside view, Kirsten supposes it all makes sense.

A second retinal scanner awaits her at the main entrance to the building, but she isn't nearly as petrified to step before it. A half-second later, a small beep tells her she's been processed and her identity accepted. The door hisses open, and she slips through easily.

The normalcy of the scene boggles her. For one heart-stopping moment, it seems as if the events of the recent past have been swept clean away, like the cobwebs of a nightmare upon full awakening. She could be walking into her own lab, nodding pleasant good mornings to her employees as they bustle by, intent on one task or another. If she looks hard enough, wishes hard enough, she can almost see Peterson, her gangly, nerdish assistant, start toward her in his peculiar, shuffling gait, steaming cup of strong black coffee in one freckled hand.

It is a dangerous mind trap when there is no hope, and Kirsten only manages to scramble out when she notices the shining silver bands around the necks of what she now recognizes to be androids.

A hard bite to the inside of her cheek jerks her back to the reality of her situation. With only a slight hitch in her step, she continues forward with all the poise and confidence she can manage. The first of the wireless messages tickles her implants with its stream of incoming data, and within seconds, the building's entire layout is completely known to her, as if she'd been drawn a map. She finds herself surprised by the low hum of verbal communication among the droids, never having figured that, in the absence of humans, the droids would still resort to speaking to one another aloud. There isn't much conversation, to be sure, more like the low hive drone one would hear in the waiting room of a dentist's office, but it is there nonetheless. Its very presence is something she'll have to carefully consider. Help or hindrance, she doesn't know.

Passing into a long, downward slanting hallway, she peers off to the left, where a bank of polarized windows gives her a view into one of what she knows is many "clean rooms" where the droids and their component parts are assembled.

She pauses a moment to wonder at the perfect, robotic efficiency of the androids as they assemble their fellows. There's not a wasted movement, not a second's hesitation as they go about their work with a single-minded focus which nothing can disrupt. She can't help but feel a bit of professional envy as she looks on. The scientist in her admires the extreme proficiency, even as the human in her screams out its rage.

With a quick jerk of her head, she draws her eyes away from the scene and continues her walk through the hall. Several more doors — each guarded by the ever-present retinal sensor — bar her way, but she passes each test and is admitted further and further into the true nerve center of the facility. She passes few androids this deep, and those she does pass don't give her so much a look as she walks by. She's been accepted, it's as simple as that, and she suppresses a smirk only by the strongest exercise of will, knowing their efficiency in such matters may, if she is supremely lucky, ultimately be their undoing.

Finally, she reaches her destination. The door slides open and she steps in. At last, an island of humanity in a sea of androids. The small room smells of stale smoke, stale coffee, stale sweat, and stale food, and she can't ever remember savoring a scent more than she does at this very moment in time.

Her gaze is caught by a framed picture on the desk, facing outward. A family of four smiles for the camera, their expressions innocent and care-free, their family bond evident beyond their similar looks. The two girls, obviously twins, bear identical gap-toothed grins. *Where are they now?* Kirsten wonders, drawn to the photo in a way she can't understand. *Dead, most likely.* Killed, indirectly, by the very person who likely shot the picture. Their father, the man who sat in this very room controlling this mini empire that churns out death by the hundreds and thousands and hundreds of thousands. She wonders if he ever understood the irony she sees now, staring into the sweet, innocent eyes of these two girls who will never grow up to have girls of their own.

She shakes her head to dispel the thought, knowing if she freezes now, she's dead, with the rest of humanity likely following in short order.

Walking over to the scarred desk, she lays her laptop on it, then slowly circles the room, examining it from every angle by the light of the harsh overhead fluorescents. Bank upon bank of softly humming CPUs, stacked from the cool tiled floor nearly to the ceiling, take up three of the four walls. The front wall is a massive bank of monitors, each tuned to a different part of the facility. Each screen shows the androids hard at work, never wavering from the task of creating others of their kind. Never wavering, never pausing, never stopping; they are relentless in the pursuit of their preprogrammed goal.

She returns to the desk, pulls out the chair, and seats herself in its faux-leather comfort. While the desk has seen better decades, the computer is spanking new and top of the line. It is also fully booted and running, though a password prompt blinks at her ominously. She knows she can easily crack the password, but it will likely leave a trace if she forces it.

Contemplative, her gaze settles upon the photograph once again. In a plastic frame, the back of the picture is easily visible. Childish letters are scrawled across the back. Squinting slightly, Kirsten tries to decipher the scribbling.

Happy Father's Day, Daddy! Love, Adam, Ashely and Amber.

Kirsten smiles. Returning to the keyboard, she types in a string of letters and hits the "enter" button.

"Bingo." A welcome screen appears and, smirking, Kirsten prepares to get down to work.

Her heart jumps into her throat when the door buzzes softly and opens, admitting a male droid. Her implants hum as a long data stream flows into them. The stream abruptly stops, and the droid eyes her, clearly expecting a response. She sends a silent thank-you heavenward for her contacts, which, she hopes, hide the deer-in-the-headlights look she's sure she's wearing.

"I am a biodroid, IC6-47A, and am not programmed to respond in the way you are expecting." If it were possible for an android to show surprise, Kirsten is sure it would be showing some now.

After a second's hesitation, it speaks. "I received no communication that this room was to be occupied. Explain your presence here, BD-1499081."

Kirsten doesn't hesitate. "I have not been programmed with the information requisite to aiding in assembly of the units. I came to offer my services as a data technician. When I noticed that this office was unoccupied, I set to work. If there is another task that you wish me to perform, I shall comply with your orders to the best of my capabilities."

There is another moment's hesitation as the android runs the possible responses through its microchip mind. Kirsten fancies that she can almost hear the circuits humming.

"Negative. Continue with your duties here. You will be notified if other tasks require your presence."

Kirsten returns her attention to the computer screen without acknowledgement, and it is only after she hears the door slip closed that she allows herself to sag against the desk. The taste of fear coats her mouth, high and bright, like copper, or what she imagines copper might taste like. Her heart pounds, and she can feel the tickle of sweat as it beads across her temples and her upper lip. "Jesus," she breathes, wiping it away. "That'll teach you to get cocky, King. Now just get to work."

Her fingers fly over the keys, opening and closing screens in the blink of an eye. The database is massive, larger even than she thought it would be. The security is immense, and she knows it will take hours, even days, just to break through that alone. Doing it live will assure her of nothing but a quick death.

With a deep sigh, she draws her laptop closer and sets it up for a wireless transfer. Downloading the massive database onto her laptop takes time she cannot afford, but she can think of no other options. The codes she needs are buried deep, she knows, and only patience will yield the harvest she's after.

**Ten hours later,** the download is almost completed and Kirsten sags back in her chair, resisting the urge to rub her burning eyes. Eyestrain has given her a headache strong enough to fell a moose, and her stomach howls out its emptiness while her kidneys throb and ache like rotting teeth. Grimacing, she damns herself for forgetting the most important thing of all. Androids, no matter how human they seem, have no need for the intake of food or liquids, nor the elimination of their by-products. Not even biodroids, which are the most "human" of all.

Suppressing a groan, she uses the edge of the desk to help push her to feet gone numb with extended inactivity. The world around her greys out momentarily as her head swims and her muscles tremble. Tending toward hypoglycemia since childood, she realizes that ten hours at a computer with nothing to eat or drink has put her in a bad spot.

*Stupid*, her mind supplies helpfully. *Stupid, stupid, stupid.*

She grasps the desk more tightly as her head spins, and for a long moment, it's a tossup as to whether or not she's going to faint. With true desperation, she manages to release her grip long enough to claw open the top drawer of the desk, pawing through assorted pencils, pens and paperclips until her fingers touch what can only be a cellophane wrapper. As she grabs for purchase, the wrapper slips further back into the desk, and she scrapes the skin of her forearm scrabbling in after it. Finally managing to snag the object between two trembling fingers, Kirsten pulls out her prize — a red and white striped mint.

"Thank you, God," she whispers, twisting off the wrapper and shoving the hard candy into her mouth. The glucose in the candy hits her system almost immediately, calming the tremors, easing her headache slightly, and lending her a much needed strength. This high won't last long, and she knows it; but for now, as it's all she has, it will have to do.

She presses several buttons on her still downloading laptop. Two small chips eject into her hands. After a moment's thought, she reaches down the neck of her shirt and deposits the backup chips into the cups of her bra, shifting slightly to settle them comfortably beneath her breasts. Then, taking steady, deliberate steps across the office, she stands before the door sensor and continues through the portal as it opens.

It's as if nothing has changed during her ten hours of isolation, and indeed, nothing has. The same droids stand before the same stations doing the same work in the same manner. While she feels as if shattered glass has replaced her bones and joints, the androids all look newly-minted.

Seeing this and, perhaps, fully realizing its implications for the first time, a depression far blacker than any she's experienced before descends over her like a blanket. For the smallest of instants, she struggles with the mighty temptation to just let it fall, to wallow in the solace it seems to offer her.

*How can I hope to defeat this? Alone. I'm alone with all this surround-*

*ing me. Dear God!*

A remnant of a recent dream slides before her eyes and she gazes, from a distance, at the old woman — *Goddess? Earth? Who?* — she has promised to help. Another memory of childhood hours spent in catechism melds with the vision. *Mother, please take this cup from my lips.*

The non-answer is all the answer she needs. She must drink the brew, no matter the bitterness. For one crystal second, she feels a sense of profound empathy with the plight of a man she's not sure ever existed. *This Savior stuff really sucks.*

Cheered by her mind's wicked turn — sacrilege has always done that for her — she tosses off the threatening depression and continues onward, a new strength to her step and her emotions.

**"You sure you** know where this thing is?"

"Sure, I'm sure," Reese answers, consulting his global positioning readout for the hundredth time. "Start poking..." he takes a last look at the sky, turning to take in the whole circle of the horizon, "...right about...over...there." He points to a patch of snow in no way distinguishable from the flat expanse of white that stretches out all about them, unbroken except for the low, dark silhouette of buildings to the north. Minot Air Force Base, probably the most secure military facility in the Western hemisphere, is about to be burglarized by a couple of ragtag platoons strung together from at least three different branches of the armed services, a veterinarian and a dog.

Not for the first time, Koda feels as though she has dropped down the rabbit hole on Alice's heels. Her universe has become an unstable place where not even an Oxbridge jackrabbit in a Saville Row suit would surprise her. She watches as her soldiers — there it is again, her soldiers — set to work prodding at the drifts, using tent poles, shovels, their own feet. Koda herself scans the distant buildings through high-powered binoculars, searching for signs of movement, sweeping the sky for the inevitable gunship that should by rights be strafing them to ribbons at this instant.

Nothing.

Nothing on the long, rippled avenues of unbroken white that her map tells her are Bomber Boulevard and the miles long runways. Nothing among the hundred and fifty Minuteman III ICBM silos arrayed along their looping tracks, folded and refolded like the guts of some huge animal. Her men are the only moving things against the dead white of the landscape, the only color, the only sound. High above, a solitary hawk etches a spiral against the hard blue sky, riding the thermal created by the base's presence. Now and again the sun catches the rust-red of her tail feathers as she banks in her turnings, and a high-pitched *kreeee-eeeerr* spills through the air. The morning holds a strange stillness, as if time has wound down to a crawl.

Absently, Koda reaches down to pat the big dog who has become the troop's mascot overnight. MRE — so christened because he is the only being they have ever met who seems to enjoy the pre-packaged rations — thumps his tail, sweeping out a one-winged snow angel behind him. He, too, is remarkably quiet, all the rambunctiousness run off him the night before. And he, too, seems to be waiting.

A sudden scrape of metal against concrete brings a shout from

Andrews. "Got, it, ma'am!"

MRE at her heels, Koda moves away from the parked snowmobiles to watch as the troops brush the snow from a cement platform perhaps a meter high and ten across, looking for the much smaller personnel hatch that should be somewhere near the perimeter. As expected, the entrance is sealed; a winking green telltale light signals its connection to the rest of the base security system. There is almost certainly a manual lock, too.

"Ma'am?" It is Andrews again.

Without warning, in a single word, the ambush her grandfather had warned her about is upon her. Koda can turn responsibility back to the lieutenant and walk away from the instinct for command that she now knows to be grappled to her bones. She can deny the power that lures her with the easy excuse of familiarity, leave the job to professionals.

Or she can give the order that will commit the lives of these men and women to mortal hazard. Once the hatchway is breached, an alarm will flash across monitor screens in the base's control rooms, tripping klaxons, giving them away as surely as if they had marched up to the front gate and politely asked for admittance. Once into the silo, they will be trapped, easy prey for defenders — human or android.

"Reese," she says, "you're absolutely sure this is the way your father showed you into the command shelter? Absolutely?"

"Yes'm." He nods toward the electronic device in his hand. "My dad was a flight commander, and he told us to get in through here if missiles ever came over the Pole. We wouldn't be allowed in, normally."

"All right. Hanson."

"Ma'am?"

"Set the charge."

"Ma'am!"

Hanson opens a small case he has carried with him ever since Rapid City, extracting a packet with vari-colored protruding wires. It looks not unlike a spider, and Hanson sets about attaching it to the outside locking mechanism. "One Black Widow Special, coming up!"

The effect is remarkably modest. The plastic explosive emits a muffled thump, a bit of smoke. But when Koda rises from her crouch, a foot wide hole gapes in the entry cover, clearly exposing the lever beneath. Hanson reaches into the opening and turns the bar. Reaching for her flashlight, Koda plays the beam down the steeply descending spiral staircase. "Stay," she says to MRE, and steps carefully into the darkness of the rabbit hole.

**Were it not** for the light of the moon on the mostly virgin snow, the darkness would be complete. No overhead lights, no flickering headlights, not even a flashlight carried loosely by a careless night watchman to bisect the encompassing black.

With a deep, silent breath, Kirsten steps forward, tripping the infrared beam and causing the outer door to slide open. The cold hits her immediately, and she fights her weakened body's urge to step back into the warmth of building. Her bladder pangs, its summons unimpeachable, and her course is decided. Hatless, gloveless, and without more than a simple woolen sweater to protect her from the Arctic night, she knows that her physical needs must be attended to with the speed of lightning, or she'll join the snow-covered corpses already liberally scattered about the grounds.

One step leads to another, and another. Completely numb, her strides take her along the building's faux-brick walls as her mind plays over the locations of the security cameras and the blind spots between each. The snow beneath is white and virgin. None have come this way, and this gives her hope as she sticks to the shadows created by the slight overhang of the roof.

She's not alone. She can feel them out there, somewhere. She can't see them, can't hear them, but she knows they're there, just as she knows that if they choose to, they can see and hear her as if she were standing in the brightest sunshine no more than a foot away.

Her nape hairs stand at stiff attention. Adrenaline floods her body in a fight or flight instinct as old as time. Still, her bladder urges her onward and it is only with the strongest of wills that she prevents her numb, wooden legs from shambling into a quick and deadly sprint.

Finally, she comes to a spot that her senses tell her will be adequate for her needs. Leaning against the wall for support, her deadened fingers fumble with the button and zipper on her jeans as her bladder gives out its final warning. Hands curled into claws yank her jeans down at the last possible instant, and she can't help the soft groan that issues from her lips as she finally finds the relief she's sought.

Her eyes dart furtively, knowing that if she's caught in this position, her life is forfeit.

**Koda leads her** troops down the spiral stairs of the silo, booted feet clanging on metal risers behind her. It is cold, brutally cold, surrounded as they are by struts and platforms of reinforced steel that rise up toward them out of the pit like the bones of some Mesozoic beast. Their breath creates a mist about them, shot through with the beams of their torches. Before them, behind them, beside them at every turn looms the hundred-and-fifty-foot bulk of the Minuteman IV missile, set as softly into its cradle of springs and blast absorbers as an egg into isinglass. Under the shell of its nosec-one lie multiple warheads, each bearing death cloaked in a blaze of light. A shudder passes through her that has nothing to do with the frigid air. Like all the people of the high plains, Koda has known life long of the dragons sleeping beneath her earth, has known that one day fire may rain down from the sky and parch to ashes the land and all that lives on it.

And now the end of days is upon them in truth, and it is nothing fore-known except in the lightly dismissed rantings of a handful of Luddites and the gut-deep discomfort of folk like her own family. Ambush, just as her grandfather had said.

Three turnings of the stair bring them to a steel door. A keypad is built into its handle; a small glass circle at head height is obviously a retinal scan. Koda steps to one side. "Hanson."

Hanson rigs the small shaped device in matter of seconds. "Okay, folks," he says, "Black Widow II. Duck and cover."

The charge is smaller than the one used to break open the hatch above, but here the report of the explosion clangs off the steel plates of floor and ceiling, loose-mounted to survive shock, reverberates off the steel pylons that rock the sleeping monster in its springs, sets their coils to humming.  The clatter echoes and reechoes around the length of the missile itself, like thunder walking over the men and women huddled in the dark, hands clamped futilely against their ears.  It is, Koda thinks, like being trapped inside John Bonham's drum kit about halfway through "Dazed and Confused" with all the tower amps turned up to max.

When the puff of smoke clears, Koda motions Martinez and Larke forward with their crowbars.  More clanging as they work the forked ends of the pries between the door and the jamb, and at last it creaks open.  Six feet ahead of them is another entry just like it.  In normal use — if nuclear war could ever be considered "normal" — neither door would open unless the other were closed.  The arrangement reminds Koda of the sterile airlocks found in medical labs, sometimes in surgical theaters.  She turns to the tapping of a hand against her shoulder to see Hanson mouthing "Ma'am?" at her.

"Go on, do the other one."

Again the silent goldfish "Ma'am?" and Koda realizes that he is shouting at her.  He obviously cannot hear her, either.

She points toward the other blast door and he nods, motioning her and the couple of other soldiers who have followed them out of the airlock.  He gives the timer an extra sixty seconds, and he and Andrews push the first door almost shut behind them before the charge detonates.  This time it is not nearly so painful.  *Either we're all stone deaf, or closing the door did the job.*  But the ringing in her ears is already less, and she can hear her own voice, high and tinny, yelling, "Come on!" to the men and women behind her.

The second blast door opens onto a long corridor that is nothing but a bridge suspended inside a twelve-foot wide pipe.  Koda's flashlight plays over arm-thick cables hanging from their staples in loops like boa constrictors.  The floor of the passage sways beneath their feet, and from somewhere back in the line, Johnson yells, "Break step!"

The tunnel seems to go on forever into the darkness, and its swaying beneath her feet calls up childhood panics: her first time on the high diving board with only one way down through an infinity of empty air; daring Tacoma to walk the two-by-four laid over the twenty-foot drop from the hayloft to the barn floor; making her way along an eight-inch wide deer trail after an injured fawn, with sheer rockface to her left and an even sheerer sixty-foot plunge into a frozen creek on the right.  She stifles the impulse to run and get it over with.  Showing fear is not an option.  Not now; maybe never again.

After what seems like an eon in Purgatory, the tunnel ends at another door.  This one, by miracle or negligence, is not locked, and they emerge into the missile crew's living quarters.  They plunge down another three flights of metal stairs, past the ghostly remains of lives spent here beneath the earth in the imminent expectation of holocaust: beds still neatly made, a table with a game of checkers still half-played.  On the bottom floor is a common area with a wide-screen television and disc player, a pool table, a stove and refrigerator, and a wall papered with photographs of families — wives and husbands, parents and children.  Koda takes it all in at a glance as they sweep through, heading for yet another stretch of tunnel that will lead them into the command center and ultimately, if Reeves is right, into daylight inside the shelter compound that now serves as the droid factory.

The bridge here sways, too, but it is only a fraction of the length of the distance from the silo to the crew quarters. In the darkness of their approach, Koda can see green and amber telltales winking on control panels and the soft glow of monitor screens. This area must have its own generator, but there is no time to search for a light switch. Guided by the beams from the flashes, they make for the staircase leading upward into the darkness. Koda has her foot on the first step when the field telephone buzzes.

Johnson has the pack. She answers, listens for perhaps five seconds, then says, "Ma'am, it's the colonel."

Koda takes the handset. "Rivers. What is it?"

Allen's voice comes through blurred by distance and thirty feet of earth and concrete. "Abort mission immediately. Return to base."

"We're almost into the compound yard, Colonel."

"I don't care where you are, Rivers. Get yourself and your people out. Now."

"I can't do that, Colonel," she says quietly. "There's something or someone here I have to find. We've been over this."

"Goddammit!" Maggie pauses, and when she speaks again, her voice is even. "There are half a dozen F-18s on their way to bomb Minot right now. I couldn't talk the base commander out of it. The planes were in the air before I knew; they've been up for fifteen minutes. Get out. Get out now."

"Understood. Over and out." Koda clicks off and hands the set back to Johnson. She turns to the soldiers behind her, their faces in semi-shadow or starkly lit by their torches. "The colonel informs me that the general at Ellsworth has called an immediate strike on this facility. I intend to go on. The rest of you get topside and prepare to leave the area. If I don't come back within twenty minutes, or you see or hear the planes coming, get out." There is no movement behind her. "Turn around," she yells. "Go!"

"I volunteer to accompany you, ma'am." It is Andrews, but his offer is drowned almost immediately in the shouting. "Yeah!" "Right on!" "Me too!"

*Oh Christ. There is no time for this.* She cannot stop to argue with them. "All right, count off by ones and twos." They obey her reluctantly, knowing what she intends. "Now, ones come with me, twos prepare vehicles for departure. Make sure you strap MRE in good and tight. Eighteen minutes. Now, let's go!"

This time they do as ordered, and the thunder of feet in the tunnel carries to her even as she storms up the staircase to the roof of the command center and its hatch. She silently thanks all the gods when the lever turns beneath her hand and she pushes it open onto moonlit snow. Her vision, already dark-adapted, sharpens. She is in an open yard between buildings, punctuated here and there by shadowed hummocks that she realizes must be the frozen corpses of the installation's human workers. Above, its feathers bleached by the cold light, an owl drifts by on soundless wings.

"Stay here while I scout," she says, and steps out into the empty space.

**After a seeming** eternity, her bladder is finally emptied and she yanks her jeans back up over flesh as warm and as feeling as the inside of a metal freezer door. Taking several careful and agonizing steps, she stoops on frozen knees, scoops up a handful of snow, and shoves it into her mouth, sucking and chewing as fast as she is able. A brilliant spike of pain knifes into her brain, almost toppling her to the ground, but she continues feeding the snow into her mouth, her body desperate for the moisture it offers. Then she freezes as her implants detect a sound almost directly in front of her.

**Just as she** shuts the door behind her, Dakota senses something and looks to her left. There, crouched against the building, is a figure. It is short and female-shaped, with pale hair that falls over a high forehead. Moonlight glints off the dark optics and titanium throat-band of an android. "Bastard!" Koda spits, and raises her gun to fire, setting the sight just between those wide, limpid eyes.

## CHAPTER EIGHT

Perhaps it is the way those dark eyes widen at the sight of her — an action quite undroid-like. Or perhaps it is a sense of familiarity that steals over Koda's senses and makes her hesitate. Whatever the reason, the hesitation costs her dearly as something heavy and blunt connects with the junction of her neck and shoulder, paralyzing her arm and dropping her into the snow as if pole axed. She fights to keep her eyes open, needing to meet her death head on.

The droid, male this time, looks down at her, its eyes expressionless. With a smooth economy of motion, it lifts the Uzi it's holding and points it directly between the intruder's eyes.

"Hold!"

The voice is female, that much she can tell, but whether issued through living or manufactured vocal cords is another question entirely, one that she's amazed she even has time to contemplate. The gun's muzzle never wavers, but the finger doesn't tighten on the trigger, either, and Koda lets out a small breath, not daring to drag her eyes away from her imminent demise.

Kirsten strides purposefully across the short span separating her from the action. Simple deduction tells her that the fallen figure is human. It is the only reason the android would have attacked, after all. Reaching them both, she stops and looks down just as the moon sails from behind a lowering cloud. Pale blue eyes look back at her, and she freezes for a moment as a queer sense of *déjà vu* settles over her.

*Those eyes...*

Forcing herself to look away, she meets the dispassionate gaze of the android and says the first thing that comes to mind. "Human female."

Taking another look, the android nods in a very human gesture of acknowledgement. "It will be of use to us."

As the droid bends at the waist, preparing to lift the woman, Kirsten again stops it. "I will take this one to the facility. There may be others. She entered from that direction."

"Acknowledged."

After the android is swallowed by the blackness, Kirsten lowers herself into a painful crouch, staring down at the woman in the snow. "Are you crazy?" she hisses. "This place is crawling with androids! What were you thinking?" Glittering, too-familiar eyes center themselves on her neck, and Kirsten feels an unaccountable blush warm her frozen cheeks. "I'm human," she whispers, her hand drifting up to brush against the droid collar at her throat.

"Seems I'm not the only crazy one, then."

The voice is low and melodious, and it hums pleasantly in Kirsten's ears. Her sensitive hearing picks up another sound, and she reaches out, clamping down onto an arm. "Hurry, they're coming back. We need to get you inside. I'll figure out what to do with you after we're there."

"No time," Koda replies, shaking off the arm and rolling to her feet. "We need to get out of here. Now."

Dark eyes widen in amazement. "You are crazy. Do you have any idea that you're in the middle of one of the largest android factories in the world?"

"It's also gonna be one of the flattest android factories in the world in about eight minutes. We need to move."

Kirsten freezes, dread skittering down her spine. "What? What are you saying?"

Dakota sighs, impatient. "Look, there's a squadron of F-18s headed up here from Ellsworth to turn this place into a smoking crater."

"Military! You're with the Army?"

"No, I'm—"

"Great! Do you have any idea what you've just done? Jesus Christ!"

"Listen, I don't make the orders here. I just—"

Once again her words are cut off by an irate Kirsten. "Of all the stupid... Jesus! I've got to get back inside before it's too late!"

She makes ready to run back into the building, only to be halted in her tracks by a very strong hand clamped around her bicep. "You don't understand. It's already too late."

Kirsten whirls around, eyes blazing behind her contacts. "You're the one who doesn't understand! Your damn planes are going to ruin everything!"

"They're not my... Dammit!" Dakota runs after the woman who has so adroitly slipped her grip. Her long legs easily eat up the distance between them, and she lowers a hard hand onto the fleeing woman's shoulder. "Wait a minute! Please!"

They both stop as both heads cock in identical listening postures.

"They're early," Dakota whispers, her eyes searching the as yet empty sky.

"No!" Kirsten shouts, once again shaking off Koda's strong grip. "I need to—"

"You need to go!" Koda replies, grabbing her again. "Now!" Spinning, she all but tosses the woman back the way they've come, then sprints after her, gun at the ready. "Don't stop! Keep moving!" Her voice is raised in a shout to be heard over the ever increasing roar of the planes.

Kirsten stumbles and only avoids making a snow angel by the strong grip on the back of her sweater which tears the fabric and almost lifts her off of her feet. "Keep running! Go! Go! Go!"

The door looms in front of her, growing larger with every step she takes. She nearly screams as something that can only be a bullet whines past her ear close enough to make her hair flutter. Then she finds herself face first in the snow as bullets erupt from everywhere at once.

Hearing the firestorm, Andrews flings open the door and rushes out, followed by his compatriots. Bracketing Dakota on either side, they empty their weapons into the darkness as the roar of the planes becomes almost overwhelming.

"We need to leave now, ma'am!" Andrews shouts over the din.

Koda nods to signal her understanding, and, with a final burst of gunfire, turns and heads for the door, the others in tow.

Kirsten turns herself over in the snow just in time to see the barrel of a gun shoved in her face by a very angry looking woman.

"No!" Koda shouts, knocking Johnson's weapon away just in time. The bullet pierces the ground not more than a foot to the left of Kirsten's arm. "She's human!"

Johnson looks stunned, then pales as she realizes what she almost did. Koda shoves her in the direction of the door, then grabs Kirsten and hauls her to her feet. "Move! Now!"

They can hear the planes directly overhead as they dart into the darkness of the underground tunnel.

The first of the bombs hits as the group thunders down the stairs and into the crew quarters. The entire underground structure shakes, and men and women are thrown into walls and over tables as they struggle to move away from the conflagration overhead. Kirsten's knees buckle, but the arm around her waist keeps her from falling. It is all she can do just to concentrate on putting one foot in front of the other. Soaked, freezing, numb and dizzy, survival is the only thing that matters. The anger will return later, and when it does, Kirsten will give these people a little King-sized conflagration of her own.

Through the swaying bridge and into the crew's quarters they run, resisting the instinctive urge to duck and cover as gigantic explosion after gigantic explosion shudders the underground complex like an earthquake.

Kirsten trips going up the first set of stairs. Her numb legs simply do not have the feeling or the strength left to do the job. Instead of falling, however, she is borne up with the tide of bodies running for their lives.

Shooting out of the crew quarters, the group runs into the tunnel and its swaying, never-ending bridge. Then falls the most titanic explosion yet, seemingly directly overhead. Trapped on the bridge, the group collapses to their knees, grabbing the struts for dear life as it sways alarmingly. A series of massive explosions follows like the finale of a fireworks display. With each concussion, the bridge swings more violently until it tips almost sideways. Her half-frozen hands useless, Kirsten wraps both arms around the center strut, placing her face against the icy metal and holding with all her will.

Ramirez, a young airman, shouts as he topples over the guardrail. Dakota and Andrews both manage to snag him before he plummets to what likely would be his death.

"Stop kicking!" His fear sweat provides a greasy grip, and Koda feels her hand slipping. The bridge rocks again, and Andrews loses his grip on the young man, who screams loud and long. "Goddamnit, Ramirez! Stop kicking!" With a grunt, Koda readjusts her grip and manages to keep hold of the panicking airman. "Andrews! Get back up here and give me some help!"

Stumbling to his feet, Andrews manages to shoot an arm out just as another bomb falls and rocks the bridge. "Fuck! I'm losing him! I'm losing him!"

"On three, pull! One, two, three, now!"

With the last of their strength, Koda and Andrews yank Ramirez up and over the guardrails. The airman grunts as he lands on his back, driving the breath from his lungs. Bending over, Andrews grabs the man by the front of his jumpsuit and hauls him to his feet. "Now move! Move!"

Kirsten feels hands on her arms, and she looks up into concerned blue eyes. Her implants are ringing so loudly that she can't hear what the tall woman is trying to say to her. Even lip-reading is out of the question as the bridge continues to rock back and forth at an alarming rate. She feels her death grip on the strut loosened, and a second later, she's pulled back to her feet and herded through the tunnel like a steer to market.

Finally outside the interminable tunnel, she sees, for the first time, the objects sharing this underground bunker with her. Long and sleek, they are Earth's total destruction in fragile metal shells.

Her eyes go wide with shock, and the anger, so much a part of her anymore, comes roaring back. She turns to the woman behind her, lips spread in a snarl. Though she can't even hear the sound of her own voice, she's sure it's loud enough to be heard on the moon. "A nuclear missile silo? You brought us into a nuclear missile silo with half the world's bombs dropping on our heads?"

"Keep moving!" Koda orders, punctuating her shout with a shove to Kirsten's back, which starts her legs moving again.

Another set of steps rises up seemingly to the heavens and, once again, Kirsten allows herself to surge along with the tide of humanity. Anything to escape the deathtrap she finds herself in. Even being in a factory full of androids hadn't scared her this badly.

Up ahead, like a beacon of hope, an open door lets in the meager light of a newly dawned day. Kirsten feels the strength surging into limbs deadened by the cold, and she pushes for the door and freedom.

Suddenly, the light is cut off as the door slams shut, plunging them into darkness once again. A hail goes down the line. "What's happening?" "What's going on?" "Hey! Who turned out the lights?"

"Firefight," Johnson replies, leaning against the now closed door and breathing heavily. "There must be a hundred of 'em out there!"

Dakota pushes her way to the front of the group, Andrews following on her heels like a well trained puppy. A quick nod is exchanged before Koda grabs the handle and yanks back hard. The sound of gunfire is almost inconsequential compared to what they've just been through — small, like the pop-pop-pop of a Daisy air rifle shooting at tin cans in a summer field.

Johnson wasn't far off in her assessment. Dakota eyeballs at least one hundred armed androids firing at her handful of soldiers hunkered down behind a small cement abutment. There is a football-field sized span of distance between the bunker door and the beleaguered squad.

Andrews looks up at her, a question in his eyes. The weight of an unasked for command sits heavy on her shoulders once again — an unwelcome guest with no apparent plans for departure. Her quick mind sorts through and discards several possible scenarios. Suddenly, she smiles, and Andrews' eyes bug nearly out of his head.

"Ma'am?"

"Listen."

He does. A slow smile spreads across his face as he hears a telltale whut-whut-whut-whut-whut-whut.

The smile morphs into an outright grin as a squadron of Black Hawk attack helicopters come over the rise like a swarm of black, terminally pissed-off wasps. Fire spits from their gunports, and droids scatter like autumn leaves in the snow. Line after line of androids fall, blown to bits by the awesome firepower of the flying destroyers.

The small group trapped behind the abutment cheers as the Black Hawks destroy the last of the androids and set down in a clear patch of snow. Their rotors still turn at a brisk clip as the pilots jump down and stride over to the group. One in particular is very familiar, and as he spots

Koda, he gives a big, boyish grin and changes his course to head in her direction.

"Move out, everyone!" Dakota orders, then steps aside as grateful men and women push past her and into the fresh, open air of a new day.

"Didn't think I'd let you have all the fun, did ya, cuz?" Manny grins, wrapping Koda in a tight embrace.

"You're a sight for sore eyes, Manny, I'll give you that." Pulling away, she notices her charge leaning heavily against the door. Wet and shivering, Kirsten looks the very picture of misery, and Koda immediately removes her jacket and walks back to her. "Here." Easing the young woman away from the door, she slips the large coat around her shoulders and pulls it close around the neck. From the corner of her eye, she notices Manny's stunned look and turns to face him directly. "She's one of us."

"Da-yum. Good costume!"

Kirsten gives a short nod, too miserable to do anything else at the moment.

From several feet away, a commotion springs up, and before Koda can turn, a black and silver blur bolts past her and drives Kirsten back down into the snow.

"Shit!" Manny yells, reaching for his gun.

"Wait." Dakota narrows her eyes, then relaxes as she recognizes the dog's posture. The big dog is all squiggles as he greets his mistress with mighty kisses and soft whimpers. Grabbing the Shepherd by his heavy ruff, Koda pulls him back and looks down into the young woman's slobber covered face. A slight smirk curls her lip. "Friend of yours?"

"Asimov! M-my dog! Where did you find him?"

"Long story," Koda replies, reaching down and helping the woman to her feet. "C'mon, let's get you back to the base and into something warm and dry, all right?"

"Ellsworth?"

Dakota nods.

Kirsten's smile is anything but pleasant. "Lead the way."

**After doing an** amazing rendition of a mule refusing to follow the carrot, Kirsten manages to convince Manny to set the helicopter down just a short distance away from her dilapidated van. The area is swarming with droids drawn to the copter, but the closest is still a good distance away. Koda hops out after Kirsten and pins her cousin with a look. "Get ready to get this beast off the ground in a split second, got me? Even if you have to leave us behind."

"Can't promise that, cuz. You just be careful. I'll be waiting."

Shaking her head, Dakota trots off after her charge, gun at the ready.

Already at the van, Kirsten yanks the doors open and dives inside, blindly searching for what she needs. She pulls out her spare laptop first, followed by her eyeglass case, which she slips into one of the myriad of roomy pockets of her borrowed jacket. Her burning, stinging eyes remind her that her contacts are still in place, and with a quick blink, she removes them and tosses them back into their saline bed. The earbud follows. Before she can reach for the sack containing what's left of her clothes, she hears a low voice through the ringing still in her ears.

"It's time to move. Come on."

Though the voice is perfectly calm, conversational almost, Kirsten can easily detect the subtle undercurrent of urgency, like the hint of oak in a fine white wine. She responds without thinking, backing out of the truck until she is once again standing in knee-deep snow.

"Move. Now. Don't stop until you're in the helicopter."

She can hear them now, all around, making no attempt at stealth. Her pulse quickens, and her legs move into a trot, and then an all-out sprint before she's even aware she's running.

Manny is leaning out the side of the helicopter, his SA58 Mini FAL laying down bursts of covering fire. Stopping for a split-second, he reaches out and pulls Kirsten inside before returning to his task, covering his sprinting cousin.

Leaping, Koda dives head first into the chopper, tosses down her spent Uzi, and grabs Manny's weapon, firing into the thick brush that surrounds the van as Manny jumps into the pilot's seat and wrestles the Black Hawk skyward. The androids break out of cover by the dozens, all firing their weapons at the swiftly rising chopper. It is only Manny's excellent skill that keeps them alive and in one piece as he dips and dodges in an aerial ballet worthy of Baryshnikov.

Once they're fully airborne and away from the androids' deadly menace, only then does Koda allow a small, silent sigh of relief escape from between her lips.

The rest of the trip is made in complete silence.

**Kirsten jumps from** the helicopter before it has even fully touched down, her laptop swinging by her side with each step she takes. Asimov, hackles raised by his mistress's obvious anger, follows along directly at her heel.

Manny makes as if to take off after the strange, but admittedly attractive, woman, but is stopped by a hand on his shoulder. Looking up at his cousin in question, he notices a familiar little twinkle in her eyes — the same twinkle she'd sport when they were kids, daring him to go on an adventure he knew he'd get his hide tanned for. He'd never been able to resist it then, and becoming an adult hasn't changed that any. Relaxing, he follows her lead as they make their way through the knots of soldiers and civilians toward a large, empty hangar.

Kirsten bulls her way through the same throng, her eyes fixed steadily on one person alone. Sebastian Hart, obviously the commander of this base, stands in the middle of a crowd, towering above them all. His uniform is immaculately pressed, the brass polished to a blinding shine. His smile is part politician, part kindly grandfather, and all fake.

She's met him before, at one or another of the myriad of insufferable cabinet meetings she'd been forced to attend as the rookie Secretary in the Cabinet. To her, he is just another military blowhard, willing to do anything with anyone just to get the funding he desires. She trusts him and his cohorts about as far as she could throw a tank.

As she continues to push through a crowd filled with happy pilots celebrating their successful mission, a small part of her recognizes that what she is about to do will likely significantly dampen ebullient spirits. Happiness is an emotion hard to come by lately, and part of her is loath to put an end to it. Her father's voice, as it often does now, soothes into her mind, reminding her that winning small battles is nothing if the war itself is lost. And it is that which spurs her on until she is standing in front of the general, eyes flashing.

"General Hart?"

The general looks down at the small, bedraggled woman standing before him. "Yes?"

The smack of palm against cheek is loud in the suddenly silent square. Blinking owlishly, Hart lifts a hand to his lips. It comes away tinged with blood. Asimov growls low in his throat, a warning to the soldiers who are staring at Kirsten as if at a viper poised to strike. "Do you have any idea what you've just done?"

Silence answers her.

"You don't recognize me, do you?"

After a moment, horrified comprehension dawns, and the general pales as his eyes widen still further. "M-Madame Secretary!"

A murmur goes through the crowd.

Kirsten smiles. It's not a very pleasant expression.

"But how...where...when...?"

"I'm curious, General. Did you check to see if there were any human beings left alive in Minot before you decided to blow the base to kingdom come?"

Hart's face reddens. "Impossible," he declares flatly. "Minot was an android factory. They would have left no one alive."

"Mm. That sure, were you? Were you even aware that there were at least a dozen of your own soldiers on that base when you sent those planes up?"

"They were ordered to turn back!"

"And if they refused to obey your orders because, unlike you, they weren't positive that everyone was dead?"

"Impossible."

"Oh, very possible, General. I was on that base when you sent your planes in, General Hart. And I would have been blown to bits if your soldiers hadn't risked their own lives rescuing me."

The redness drains from the man's face like water through sand. His normally ruddy cheeks turn a color best suited to curdling milk and his Adam's apple bobs as he takes a hard swallow. "I — didn't..."

Kirsten smiles again. "But that's not even the worst part," she continues in a conversational tone. "Do you want to guess what the worst part is, General?"

Hart slowly shakes his head.

"The worst part is that in your zeal to destroy a couple of thousand androids, you also destroyed what might have been our only hope to deactivate the several million still left." She pauses a moment, watching as he lifts a slightly shaking hand to his brow. "The deactivation codes were in the computers on that base, General Hart. Computers which are now in billions of tiny little pieces so small that not all the general's horses nor the general's men will ever have the hope of putting them back together again."

"I — I didn't — think..."

"No, you didn't, did you? You might want to start trying that in the future." And with that, Kirsten turns and walks away, leaving the stunned crowd behind.

Manny looks up at his cousin, an almost awed smile on his face. "Wow."

Koda chuckles in agreement.

"I thought I recognized her. Kirsten King, isn't it? The robotics guru?" At Koda's nod, he continues. "Sure looks different without those damned contacts in, that's for sure." Then he grins. "The colonel's gonna prang when she finds out the good doctor's here. They think the same way about those metalheads." He scratches his head. "Too bad she's not here."

"Where is she?" Koda asks, surprised.

"Got called out to escort some civvies in. A couple of them were hurt, from what we heard. She should be back this evening some time."

Both look on as Kirsten exits the hangar, the crowd easily parting before her as if she bears the staff of Moses. Koda eyes her cousin. "Looks like I'm pulling some escort duty of my own. Catch you later, huh?"

"I'm headed for the mess. Stop by later if you've got time."

"Will do."

**"Dr. King!"**

Kirsten stops and whirls, fully prepared to confront this latest interruption of her royal blue funk. She hesitates as she realizes the intruder is the woman who has saved her several times already this day. If for no other reason than that, she swallows her temper and even manages to try a smile out for size. It fits rather poorly.

"Yes," Kirsten pauses, looking at the insignia on the uniform covering the woman's rather well-maintained form, "...Lieutenant?"

Koda gives an easy grin. "Just Dakota, or Koda if you prefer. I'm a vet."

"Ex-lieutenant, then," Kirsten replies, smirking.

Koda rolls her eyes. "A vet as in veterinarian. I'm not military, ex or otherwise."

Kirsten's eyebrows climb into her hairline. "You're a civilian? Then how...why...?"

Koda sobers. "Let's just say it was something I had to do." She looks the smaller woman over carefully, a frown creasing her striking features. "I think maybe a trip to the hospital would be in order. We've got a good one on base here, and you've been out in sub-optimal conditions without adequate clothing for far too long."

This smile is more genuine, though sorrowfully brief. "You have a gift for understatement."

"So I've been told," Koda replies in kind.

"Well, I thank you for your generous offer, but I'll pass right now. My chest is clear and I'm regaining feeling in my limbs, so I think I'm all right for now."

"Well, then, how about if I get you to a place where you can dry off and warm up?"

Kirsten eyes the tall vet carefully, her ingrained distrust once again springing to the fore. *For Christ's sweet sake, K,* a small corner of her mind clamors, *this woman just saved your life, almost at the cost of her own. I really think you can trust her, don't you?*

It's a bit of a struggle, but she finally gives in to that insistent inner voice and manages a nod at her benefactor. "That's an offer I'll be happy to accept."

"Good," Koda replies, smiling. "If you'll follow me?"

**Kirsten steps into** the small but cozy house with a sigh of profound relief. Warmth from the heater immediately seeps into limbs just now waking from their frozen sleep. The tingling starts immediately, and she knows that knifing pain is soon to follow, but she keeps her reactions pushed down deep inside, as is her custom when in the presence of others.

Dakota disappears for a moment, returning with a neat stack of dry clothing in her hands. "Bathroom's right behind that door there." She gestures as she transfers the small bundle to Kirsten's arms. "Fresh towels are in the closet, and the shower should even have some hot water left, if you're so inclined."

Dakota turns away before Kirsten can say a word and disappears back into what Kirsten can see from her current vantage point is the bedroom. The door closes softly, leaving Kirsten alone in the short hallway, clothes in her hands and a perplexed look on her face. After a moment, she shrugs and heads into the bathroom.

After so long doing without, the shower is simply much too large a temptation to resist. Turning on the "hot" tap to full blast, she sheds her sodden garments as a warm fog rolls out from the shower to fill the small, tiled room. Adding a little cold to the mix, she turns on the shower itself and steps inside.

The first touch of water on her skin is an almost religious experience — pleasure wrapped around pain wrapped around a feeling of relief so muscle-jarring that her head spins. Bracing herself against the cool tiled wall, she waits for the feeling to pass before grabbing the bar of soap and lathering up. Days of dirt and sweat swirl down the drain, and she wonders for a moment if her anger, and her fear, and every other negative emotion she's currently clinging to as tightly as a miser to his cash, will be so easily washed away.

It is only when the water starts to go tepid that she drags her weary — blessedly clean — body from the shower. The towel is soft and gentle on her skin, and the clothes she slips into, though a bit large, bring with them a comfort of their own simply by being dry. After a quick drag of a comb through her hair, she leaves the warm, moist haven of the bathroom for the house beyond.

Koda smiles up at her from her place on the tatty couch. Dressed in a pair of well-worn jeans and a simple white T-shirt, she displays a body that, to Kirsten's scientific eye, is as close to perfection as she's ever seen. She pauses a moment, wondering at her body's response to the picture presented, then shoves the thought down with the rest of them, to be explored at a later time. For the first time in a very long time, she feels that there may actually be a later.

Noticing the odd look directed her way, she summons up a smile in response and continues into the living room, where her meager stockpile of belongings has been carefully set on the coffee table.

"Feeling better?"

"Much, thank you."

"Good." Dakota once again looks over the young scientist, taking in the bloom of roses on her cheeks and eyes which, if not exactly sparkling with good humor, have at least lost their haunted dullness. Still, exhaustion has drawn dark, sooty smudges beneath each eye, and Koda spends a moment wondering when it was that the doctor had last slept. "You're probably tired. You're welcome to the bed, if you'd like."

"No...thank you, but I need to figure out if I was able to salvage anything from Minot's computers." She pulls the two chips from a pocket in the soft sweatpants she's been given to wear. "I took these with me when I went outside." She picks up her backup laptop, replaces the chips, and looks to Koda. "Hopefully they've got something on them I can use."

"There's an office right next to the bathroom, there. It doesn't have much in it, but you're welcome to whatever's there."

"Thank you."

"Not a problem." Dakota rises to her full height, stretching slightly to work out the kinks in a back much abused this day. "I'm headed for the mess. If you're hungry, I could bring some back for you. It's military food, but it's edible."

Kirsten nods, wondering at the simple, unaffected kindness of this stranger. In her world, offers are made with the expectation of gain. Nothing is for free, and each act of faux-kindness is greed dressed in sheep's clothing. "Thank you. I...thank you."

A casual grin leaves Kirsten feeling dazzled. A moment later, Dakota is gone.

Left alone, Kirsten blinks twice to clear her head and with a deep sigh turns and enters the small office. Setting her laptop on the desk, she sinks into a chair that is a little rickety, but serviceable. She rubs her head as her ears continue to ring from the bombs dropped earlier. It is an unfortunate side-effect of her implants, and one she wishes she knew how to correct. For now, she does the only thing she knows will help. Reaching up with both hands, she touches the almost imperceptible bulges above the processors behind her ears, and the world falls away into wondrous silence.

She then boots up her laptop, inserts the chips, and is soon lost in the world of streaming data.

**"Yo, cuz, I** know you're hungry, but man...eating for two?"

Koda shoots Manny a look over her shoulder and continues to scoop unidentifiable, but presumably edible substances onto two plates. "I'm getting our guest settled."

"Ah, the good doctor. Has she warmed up any?"

"Physically."

Manny laughs softly. "Yeah, she's a tough nut, that one. And she really hates the press. I remember watching CNN once. Damn, she almost fed a reporter his microphone. Enema style."

"I'll be sure to remember that the next time I decide to apply for press credentials," is Koda's dry response.

"I'm warnin' ya, cuz. She may be small, but she's got brass ones."

"I'll...keep that in mind."

Manny claps his cousin on the back, grinning. "If you're not doing anything later, drop by rec. We're getting up a dart game, and I feel the need to pull you in for a ringer. Later, all right?"

"Later."

**When Dakota re-enters** the house, Asi greets her with a soft bark and a furiously wagging tail. Placing the dinner trays on the kitchen table, Koda gives the dog a fond scratch behind the ears before straightening and calling out to Kirsten.

"Guess she fell asleep after all, huh boy?"

Approaching the closed office door, she gives another soft call, accompanied by a knock. Neither is answered. Turning the knob, she opens the door and enters the room to see Kirsten, quite unexpectedly, wide awake and enraptured by whatever it is that is on her computer screen.

"Dr. King? I have your dinner."

Still no answer.

Dakota watches for a moment, then crosses the room and lays a gentle hand on the scientist's shoulder. Only to pull back and catch a swinging hand a split second away from clouting her across the face. "Whoa. I'm a friend, remember?"

Stone deaf, Kirsten stares up into impossibly blue eyes, trying to ignore the radiant warmth emanating from the large hand encircling her wrist. Dakota's lips are moving, but Kirsten can't quite find the wherewithal to decipher what she's saying.

It is only after the hand releases its grip on her that she is able to gather herself enough to realize what she's almost done, and why. Flushing, she touches the spots behind her ears, and sounds once again flood into her consciousness.

"You startled me." She winces internally, part of her wishing that those words didn't sound quite as accusatory as they do.

"I apologize for that," Koda replies smoothly. "I didn't realize you had implants."

"Well, it's not exactly something I needed others to know."

Accepting the rather terse answer, Dakota nods, then gestures to the door. "Your dinner's in the kitchen."

"If you don't mind, I'll take it in here. I'm in the middle of some things that I don't want to leave."

"No problem. I'll get it for you and leave you in peace."

"Thank you."

**Several hours later,** Kirsten's body wins the battle it's having with her mind and, with some resentment, she finally shuts down her laptop. Her work thus far has been far less successful than she'd hoped.

*Damn General Hart and his damn bombs. Ten minutes more, an hour at the most, and I would have had those goddamned codes in my hands. Now? I'll be lucky if I find a goddamned recipe for carrot cake in this goddamned mess.*

Heaving a deep sigh, she pushes herself away from the desk and looks through the slats in the blinds covering the office's only window. Darkness and snow have fallen once again. "Great. Just what the world needs, more snow."

Stretching, she turns from the window and heads for the door, fully intending to take up Dakota's earlier offer, if that offer is still on the table. Asi greets her as she steps outside, rubbing his face and body along her own as his tail beats a steady tattoo against the wall.

Kirsten looks over at the bedroom door, surprised to find it closed. "Must be later than I thought." Listening, she hears quiet murmurs coming from the room in question, then once again damns the acute sensitivity of her implants as those murmurs resolve themselves into something quite a bit more intimate. The blush starts from the inside, warming her belly before spreading its way up her neck and face until her ears are burning with heat.

"C'mon, Asi," she grunts, walking over to grab her borrowed coat, "a bit of cold air seems about right right now. Let's go for a walk."

Asimov follows happily.

**A burst of** warm air greets Kirsten as she pushes open the front door of the colonel's house. The luxury of it almost unsettles her, familiar as she has become with the cold and the nearly offhand acceptance of her own death. She is not quite yet resigned to life, still less to comfort. Like the restoration of her hearing years ago, this seems more an intrusion than a healing — something she has never asked for, a prosthesis that does not fit, rubbing insidiously against her accustomed rawness. She feels as death row inmates must when, at the fifty-ninth minute of the eleventh hour, the phone call from the governor arrives, granting them a temporary reprieve.

Asi has no such qualms. He shoulders past her, still shedding snow onto the entryway rug, and makes a dash for the warm tiles of the hearth. At least that is where he comes to a sprawling stop. Perhaps it is only coincidence that the Lakota she-giant with the improbable blue eyes — *full-blood, my ass!* — sits on the couch with her outsized boots propped on the hassock, strategically placed to deliver a down and dirty belly rub. As if he is reading her mind, Asi rolls over onto his back with a whine and cocks his head up at the woman, tongue lolling. Rivers laughs, lowers one foot, and commences scratching. Asi's tail thumps.

Sitting beside her is another woman, dressed in flight fatigues and boots, her long, elegant legs crossed before her as she laughs, a low and throaty sound. It seems to Kirsten that the distance between the two women is both entirely decorous and non-existent, as if they have slipped into some Riemannian fold of space-time. Kirsten's sense of exclusion is acute, an ache she has known and largely ignored since childhood.

*Outside looking in. Again.*

Deliberately, Kirsten stamps her feet to dislodge the last clinging snow from her boots, rattling the clasps of her jacket as she hangs it on the old-fashioned hall tree. Nice and noisy. Sister King's Traveling Resentment and Incoherent Outrage Band, tuning up the drum kit for the concert of the century.

*Damn them for snatching me out of the droid factory just as I was within seconds of having the codes I needed to shut the goddam things down.*

BANG!

*Damn them for bombing the droid factory in the first place and sending its codes and programs into a cyber-oblivion of melted fiber optics and fused circuit boards.*

THUMP!

*Damn them because my dog — my dog, goddammit — can't wait to roll over for that overgrown hyperthyroid bitch in heat.*

CRASH!

*And damn them for the easy intimacy that is so fucking in-your-face obvious that even I can see it.*

CLANG!

The woman rises as Kirsten hesitates in the foyer. "Dr. King? Won't you join us by the fire?"

Kirsten can see the brass eagles on her lapels; a full colonel, then. Part of her wants to stamp into the middle of the cozy little scene and haul Asi off to the cramped office where she has been working, space that is at least temporarily hers. Another part simply wants to slink by silently and hope not to be noticed. Neither course is now possible.

"Colonel?" she says, and moves toward the old-fashioned green leather chair that sits at right angles to the couch.

"Maggie Allen," the other woman answers, extending her hand.

Kirsten accepts the handshake with as much grace as she can muster. "Kirsten King. Pleased to meet you, Colonel Allen." Then, with an effort, she adds, "Dr. Rivers."

"Evening," says the veterinarian with a wry smile, continuing to scratch Asimov's stomach.

From a tray on the weathered oak chest that serves as a coffee table, Allen pours a cup of steaming liquid and hands it to Kirsten. It is a tea, something herbal, with overtones of apple and citrus. The warmth of the cup against her hands is pure pleasure. "Thanks," she says, because manners dictate that she say something. At her feet, Asimov rolls halfway toward her, whining.

*Damn dog wants a goddam harem,* she thinks even as she bends to ruffle his ears.

Allen is still standing. Grudgingly, Kirsten takes in her height, the elegant modeling of her head emphasized by her short, natural hair, her long hands unspoiled by rings. The firelight glints off the single ornament she wears, an earcuff in the shape of a bobcat. There is a sense of stillness in her, of sufficiency with not so much as an atom's excess. Unbidden, something of the warmth that drove her out of the house rises again in Kirsten. She feels the blood spread across her cheeks and hopes that the other woman will attribute it to the steaming liquid she holds to her lips. From beneath her lashes she darts a quick glance at Rivers, who seems to be wholly absorbed in her attentions to Asimov.

*Oh great. First a spot of voyeurism, and now the colonel's a turn-on.* Kirsten drinks and sets down her cup. "Thanks," she says again. "That's good."

Allen's lips curve up slightly at the corners and for a moment she looks distinctly feline. A bobcat perhaps, or a slender serval cat, and just as enigmatic. She says, "Dr. King, I want to thank you for what you did."

Kirsten gives a dismissive wave of her hand, but the colonel continues. "No, it needs to be said. Of course we're all grateful for your courage in infiltrating the droid factory. That will be repeated again and again, and I suggest you get used to it. What I'm personally thankful for is your slugging the general in the chops. If you hadn't, I would have. And I'd be facing a court martial."

Rivers, who has been giving her entire attention to Asimov, gives a soft snort. Kirsten feels her eyes slide toward the Lakota woman again, taking in the high cheekbones and deep blue eyes, the jeans-clad legs that go on forever. To her chagrin, she also knows that Allen has seen before she can regain control of her face. "I appreciate that, Colonel," she says evenly.

"I'd have had his hide regardless, if any of my people had been harmed," Allen says, the faintest of emphasis on "any". "The general didn't just bomb the droid codes into oblivion, he nearly killed a couple dozen of my troops, not to mention the chopper squadron Manny Rivers led into Minot to haul their asses out." The colonel takes a sip of her own drink and sits down. "Not to mention your own."

"With respect, Colonel Allen, I'd have been perfectly all right if none of your people had interfered. And I'd have the codes necessary to disable the droids. That's the real cost of your general's stupidity, in lives we can't even begin to count."

Abruptly Rivers gets to her feet. "I'm going to bed. Good night, Dr. King." She pauses only to give Asi's belly a final tickle, then crosses the hallway to the bedroom, shutting the door behind her.

"I didn't mean—" Kirsten begins.

"To offend? But of course you did, Dr. King."

The colonel's expression does not change, but Kirsten has the distinct sense that the other woman is suppressing laughter.

"Still, don't be concerned that you've chased Dr. Rivers out of the room. She's faced" — and the smile does break through — "considerably worse than yourself. Good night." Halfway across the room, Allen pauses and turns. "When you're ready to sleep, blankets are in the hall closet. I'm afraid you'll have to make do with the couch tonight. We'll try to find better accomodations for you tomorrow."

Kirsten watches as the colonel disappears into the bedroom. The sound of soft voices comes to her, blurred, though the door. She raises a hand to turn off her implants, but lowers it after a moment's hesitation. She cannot follow the words; it is not as if she is eavesdropping. After a time, the strip of light beneath the door goes dark, and the voices fall silent.

Quietly, Kirsten makes up the couch with a pair of blankets she finds in the cabinet and turns out the lights. Asi manages to wedge himself onto the cushions beside her, his great head lowered onto his paws. Kirsten stares past him into the dying embers on the hearth, watching as their red glow fades and finally turns to ash. She has the uncomfortable feeling that something vital is hovering just beyond her understanding. She cannot come at it through reason, try as she will. Over and over she turns the question in her mind, looking for even the slightest intellectual purchase. But the answer lies elsewhere, and she does not know how to approach it.

When only ashes remain on the hearth, she sleeps.

## CHAPTER NINE

Dawn slowly filters through the slats of the blinds as Kirsten sits huddled on the lumpy couch, a cup of slowly chilling coffee in her hands and a threadbare military blanket draped over her shoulders. That the coffee is real, and therefore quite welcome, is of little comfort to her this morning — a morning on which she can count upon the fingers of one hand how many hours of sleep she has gotten, and still have enough fingers left to bowl a strike in any smoky ten-pin alley in town.

Sensitive as always to her moods, Asi whines and lifts his massive head from her lap. His head cocks, his eyes giving a look so human and so caring that, for a moment, her chest tightens and her eyes sting. But only for a moment.

Smiling at him to show she is fine, she once again lapses into thoughts that have chased each other round and round like a dog its tail for the better part of eight hours. Thoughts that on the face of things make no sense. Just random snatches of words and images glued together without any order or logic that her scientist's mind can comprehend, rather like a ransom note made from letters and pictures cut out of ladies' magazines.

"God, I could use a cigarette right about now." Though shed of the addiction for five years now, sometimes the urges come at her like a mugger waiting in a blind alley, and right now the mugger is twelve feet tall. And fanged.

She sits quietly, waiting for the urge to pass, then wonders why she even bothers fighting it. It's not as if cigarettes cost anything anymore, and after spending the better part of the last one hundred hours literally staring death in the face, the dangers of smoking have lost, so to speak, their power to scare.

She snorts softly. "Sure. I'll just go into the commissary or whatever they're calling it these days, grab a few cartons and smoke myself sick." Raising her coffee cup, she toasts the morning. "Happy days, huh?"

With a small whine and a louder groan, Asi heaves himself up off the floor and trots, tail wagging wildly, over to the door of the bedroom. A moment later, the door opens and Koda and Maggie, dressed identically in pristine white jumpsuits, step into the living room, their shoulders brushing casually together.

For reasons she can't fathom, the sight tugs at Kirsten in a most unpleasant way, and she finds she can breathe more easily only when the colonel has absented herself from the tableau, moving on into the kitchen, while the Lakota woman stays behind to scratch a positively ecstatic Azimov behind the ears.

Kirsten takes in the scene as her dog emits sounds like the late-late-late-show on a rent-by-the-hour motel's coin operated television set, and she can't help but watch wonderingly as graceful, long fingers magically hit every single perfect spot on her normally standoffish canine companion.

As if sensing the rapt attention, Koda looks up from her pleasurable task, and their eyes meet and lock. Kirsten feels the fiery heat of the blush that crawls upward across her skin; embarrassed at being caught staring, embarrassed at the noises her dog is making, embarrassed, most of all, by her attitude of the night before. It suddenly seems okay, somehow, despite the embarrassment and, if she goes deep enough within to admit it, her remorse. Things seem...possible. As if the chasm between them could be healed as simply as an "I'm sorry" or a "good morning".

Part of her knows this is true, knows it would take no more than that, and her mouth opens, more ready to say those simple words than she's ever been ready for anything in her life.

Maggie returns, two cups of steaming coffee in her hands, and the moment is broken like a child's brightly colored party balloon that drifts too close to the fireplace.

Kirsten turns resentful eyes to the intruder and is met with a friendly smile and a salute from a coffee mug.

"Thanks for brewing this."

"No problem," Kirsten manages before levering herself up off the couch and giving them the most civil nod she can. "If you don't mind, now that you're both up, I'll shower and get ready for my day."

"Not at all," Maggie replies, completely unfazed by Kirsten's grumpiness. "We won't be here when you get out. We're taking down a prison up north." Her smile turns conspiratorial. "If we're lucky, we'll bring back a working droid for you."

"That's a very dangerous thing to do."

Maggie actually laughs at this, though what she could possibly find funny in the situation is something Kirsten can't begin to fathom. "Of course it is. That's why I'm a soldier." With a wink and another coffee cup salute, the young Air Force colonel turns away, leaving Kirsten flat-footed and speechless in the middle of the living room.

Asimov simply whines, tosses himself on the floor, and covers his snout with his massive paws.

**The compound huddles** low against the snow, its walls seeming to rise out of the drifts piled against them in a seamless extension of the frozen earth. The central building appears to be both Administration and cell block, its colorless concrete block façade broken only by ranks of steel louvers over the high, narrow windows. None of them is open to the fading light. Even those closest to the heavy metal door, which must have been offices or reception rooms for the Corrections Corporation of the Northwest personnel, are shuttered tightly. Coil upon coil of concertina wire tops the eight-foot walls which surround exercise yard and parking lots. Here and there the low sun strikes off its razor edges; the barbs take the light in bursts of flame. The frigid air lies over the jail and its snowy matrix like glass, trapping the evening for all time in its clarity: the rising dark in the east, bands of gold and crimson fading in the west; the land and the double handful of humans crouched to the south in a stream bed long since gone to ice.

"How many?" Allen's voice is no more than a raspy whisper. The heat of their bodies will give them away well before they become audible to sensors at the jail, but habit dies hard.

"Metalheads?" Andrews consults his readouts again. "Colonel, I'm getting only a dozen for sure. There are a couple blips that might be double — say fifteen, max."

Koda frowns. "That's not many for a jail this size. There were more than that at Mandan — twice that. Will that thing pick them up if they're deactivated or on standby?"

"It should, ma'am." Andrews points to the LED display, which is broken down into a series of arcane number strings. "It reads off their metal mass, specifically the titanium. It doesn't pick up their transmissions."

Allen gives a wry grin. "Yeah. The first models kept picking up filing cabinets and calling them military droids. Goddam near got a couple Marine units fried the first time we used them in Baghdad. The troops steered clear of the 'droids' and ran smack into the mujahadeen instead."

"Okay," says Koda. With a frozen sycamore twig, she rapidly sketches out the plan of the jail, courtesy of an overflight by one of the gunships that await their signal a couple miles off. "Show us where they are."

Glancing back and forth between his readout and the diagram, Andrews positions their enemies. Ten in the building, apparently stationed at doors and along corridors; two in what may be the kitchen. The others seem to be a moving patrol, working the perimeter in mathematically precise rounds at equally precise intervals. "With a bit of luck," he says, "these will be less sophisticated models than we encountered at Minot, with fewer built-in logic branches and more stereotyped responses. No bio-droids, no 'creative' types with psuedo-HumIntel capacities."

Allen nods. "Johnson."

"Ma'am!"

"You're smallest; there's a chance you'll read as a large dog or a deer on their heat sensors. When I give the word, and the patrols are here and here," Allen jabs the diagram with her white-gloved finger, "you scramble out there and set the charge on the east gate. Then get back around to the south side. Give yourself thirty seconds. Andrews."

"Colonel?"

"Give me your droid reader. Rivers, you take him and half a dozen others and get through that gate when it blows. Make lots of noise; you're partly a diversion. While they're busy with you, I'll take the rest in through the front. Meet in the middle. Everybody got it?"

Koda nods, and with Andrews and the rest of her troops behind her, begins to move upstream — what would be upstream if the water were not frozen blue to the bottom — under the shelter of the bank. Crawling on hands and knees where the overhang is high enough, humping seal-fashion on knees and elbows where it is not, she breaks trail through the snow for them. White snow, white Arctic camo from head to foot, white breath hovering in clouds about them. White faces, even her own, smeared with grease paint where the ski mask does not cover the skin around the eyes.

White is the color of the North, and in the North there is death. A shiver passes over her that has nothing to do with the temperature. As she looks up, the shadow of an owl passes overhead, great wings spread on the silent air. Without thought, Koda brings a hand to her medicine pouch where it hangs about her neck. *Lelah sica.* The white owl, *Hinhan ska*, is an unpropitious sign. *Ina Maka*, she breathes silently, *Mother of us all. Do not let me lead my people into death.*

Behind her she hears a muffled curse as someone catches his foot in a root of one of the centuries-old sycamores that line the stream. Someone else sets too much weight on a branch invisible beneath the snow, and she turns to see Larke pitch forward abruptly as it snaps, only to be caught by his belt by the man behind him. No harm done. Koda slows as the creek leads them in a wide curve around to the east of the compound, the light growing dimmer here where night already spreads across the horizon. Peering above the stream bank, she can just see the outline of the wide metal gates that control vehicular traffic in and out of the prison. For several meters in front of it, shallower snow lies in a wide, straight band that must mark the driveway.

As she points to it, Andrews nods and gives a thumbs up. "Gotcha."

"Straight in when—" Koda breaks off as the com unit at her waist vibrates and buzzes softly. She thumbs it on. "Rivers."

"Allen. It's time." The unit clicks off abruptly.

"...the time comes," Koda continues. "Johnson! Now!"

The woman flings herself up over the stream bank in a gymnast's clean vault and is on her feet and streaking for the gate before Koda finishes the order. She covers the hundred yards in seconds, plants the charge and sprints for the corner. Thirty interminable seconds later, the plastique goes off with a whump and the clang of metal against metal as the lock blows away from the heavy steel panels.

"Let's go!"

Koda swings up out of the gully and is running full out even as the echoes of the explosion reverberate against the high walls of the compound. Andrews is beside her, the rest in a tight knot behind. They crash into the gate and keep going. The panels swing back to reveal an empty yard perhaps fifty meters square, the snow stained with grey sludge along the mathematically straight path the sentry droid has followed as it makes its circuit of the wall. A number of trucks are pulled up beneath a carport to one side of the central building, all white except for the CCNW logo of Justice's scales enclosed within a wreath of laurel leaves. The building itself is white and featureless, its blankness relieved only by the steel blind windows, its single story sprawling off from its original axis in half a dozen ill-proportioned wings.

The loading bay is at the end of the carport, close but difficult because of its double-door airlock construction. Koda opts for the kitchen entrance instead, cutting across the open space from gate to carport, then hugging the cell-block wall as she leads her unit through the deepening shadows around one wing and across a second yard to another.

"What the fuck?" Andrews mutters. "Where the hell are they?"

"There," says Koda as they turn the corner of the second wing.

Six droids stand in a perfectly straight line across the service entrance to the prison. All are armed with Uzis and M-16s.

Bracing her rifle at waist level, Koda stitches a row of holes as neatly as her mother's sewing machine across the middle of one of the droids. It drops its weapon, and Koda raises her own to her shoulder to fire straight into its optics, large and luminous in the half-light. Her squad beside her looses a storm of gunfire. She hears a scream from somewhere to the right but cannot take her attention off her targets to see who is hit. "Grenades!" she yells, plucking one from her belt, pitching forward and rolling in the snow, coming back up with a perfect overhand lob into the middle of the four droids still standing. It explodes like lightning struck too near, but the smell is of gunpowder and hot metal, not the clean ozone of the walking thunder. Two more grenades arc down upon the droids, then two more again, and the step before the kitchen door stands clear except for shrapnel and shards of Lexan, fragments of printed circuits and twisted copper wire scattered over the snow.

"Larke's hit, ma'am."

Andrews, his own sleeve streaked crimson, kneels beside the corporal where he lies in the in the open yard, a wide scarlet stain seeping through the snow beneath him. The layers of his battle dress are soaked with it. Larke is conscious, but his lips are ashen with pain as much as cold. His wry smile, isolated by the bone-white of his ski mask, seems to Koda the macabre grinning of a skull. "Just a flesh wound, ma'am."

Her hand goes to the medicine pouch about her neck, but she says crisply, "Reese, Martinez, get him up the steps and into the building. As they move to comply, assisted rather too eagerly by the lieutenant, she adds, "Andrews?"

"It's only a graze, ma'am. Just took off a bit of skin." He pulls down the frayed edge of the tear in his jacket to expose a long, narrow scrape. "Really."

"You'll live," Koda concedes, stepping over the jagged fragments of metal and plastic that are all that remain of their enemies.

The entrance leads into a large institutional kitchen. Pots and pans hover just above their heads, suspended from the ceiling by stainless steel hooks. Choppers and graters occupy the countertops, together with piles of bowls and spoons. On the stove a huge tub of rice boils energetically, foam overflowing its sides to sizzle on the burner. Its smell recalls her grandmother's washdays, the stiffly starched blouses and shirts into which she and her brothers had been buttoned every school day of every year until their high school graduations. *"Because you must always look better and do better."* Prison uniforms, she and Tacoma had called them.

Reese and Martinez set Larke down on a large central worktable, with his pack under the calf of his injured leg and a stack of clean dishtowels to hand. Quickly but gently, Koda cuts the fabric away from the wound, which lies about a hand's breadth down from the groin. She folds a pair of towels into a compress and slips it under the exit wound. From the open door she can hear the muffled rattle of gunfire and men shouting. "Andrews," she says, "take everyone but Martinez and start moving up the central hall. I'll be right behind you."

To Larke she says, "You know what 'flesh wound' really means? Severed tendons, ripped muscle, shredded veins. Still, you got off fairly light." She slaps another compress into place on the entry wound and bears down hard on the torn flesh.

Larke gasps, turning even paler. "Oh Lord, ma'am. You wouldn't take advantage of a guy when he's down, would you?"

The attempt at a joke is the best sign from the wounded man yet. "Nope," says Koda, maintaining pressure with one hand and swinging her rifle back down to the ready with the other. "Martinez is going to do that." As Martinez's hand replaces hers, she says, "Press down as hard as you can. Change towels when they get soaked. We'll be back for you."

"Got it, ma'am."

Koda sprints down the branching hallway, following the increasingly sharp reports of automatic weapons. As she runs, she can hear prisoners shouting encouragement to their jailers' unseen enemies, the sparse metal furniture of the prison banging against walls and doors. Somewhere up ahead the shouting becomes a chant, reverberating rhythmically in the narrow passageways, taking strength from the beat of steel on steel within the cells.

"Kill the droids! Kill the droids! Kill the droids!"

As she turns a sharp corner, Koda almost slams into Andrews, skews off to the right and slides in beside him and the rest of the unit where they hunker behind an improvised barricade of overturned desks. The space before them is an open intersection where three hallways meet. Two droids, their heads blown to fragments, lie frozen in a bizarre mechanical rigor mortis, joints still bent at elbow and knee. Another form sprawls between them, an enormous charred red hole where its right ribs should be and no arm or shoulder at all. The blood beneath it has already begun to congeal with the cold.

"Johnson?"

"Yeah. She went down just as we got here. The droids are over there," Andrews points toward a corridor to the right. "...and they've got a fifty-caliber. The colonel and the rest are around the corner to our left. They've got a couple injured, but she doesn't want to call in the gunships yet. We'd lose too many civilians if we did."

"Damn. We need to get behind them."

"There's another entrance over on the other side; we might be able to get through there."

Koda shakes her head. "That would take too long. There's a quicker way."

"Yeah?"

Koda points upward, toward the acoustic ceiling tiles. "You're not claustrophobic, are you?"

Andrews' bright blue eyes take on a sparkle in the midst of his featureless ski mask. "No, ma'am! Lead the way."

Koda drags a chair over to a spot beneath a light fixture, climbs up onto it and begins tossing down the large tiles. Wiring runs thickly tangled under the first two; the darkness behind the third glints with the lights' reflection off the aluminum sheathing of the HVAC ducts. The fourth gives access to the crawl space. "Paydirt," she observes, turns on her flashlight and pulls herself up and into ceiling and its snarl of pipes and wires.

The going is incredibly slow. The prison is carefully built, and the wire ends she can see are all properly capped. One exception, though, will fry them and the mission with them. Koda squirms forward on her elbows, avoiding the brightly colored strands as much as she can, lifting her weight gingerly over pipes they cannot afford to break. Behind her she half senses, half hears, her soldiers, some of them slithering along with the ease of rattlesnakes, others with about as much finesse as a bear raiding a dumpster.

"Shhhhh, dammit."

Reese, two behind her, tries to quiet the others. With the droids' sensors, though, they cannot be quiet enough. Andrews knows it, too. "We need more cover, ma'am."

"Right," she says. By dead reckoning, they should be over a cell facing the corridor they have just left, some distance behind their abandoned redoubt. "There should be somebody..." she pulls off her mask and pries a tile loose "...right about...here."

In the dim light of the cell, two startled women stare up at her. One holds the room's only stool, battered half to splinters where she has been pounding it against the door. The other has a metal bowl in each hand, their unpalatable contents spilled dirty white along the floor. Cymbals.

"We need more noise, please," Koda says simply. "Cover us."

The younger woman of the two, perhaps eighteen, loses her frozen expression and bares more teeth than Koda has seen outside an alligator's mouth. "You got it!"

Koda nods her thanks, and as they push themselves again along the narrow crawlway, the redoubled clamor becomes a vibration in the walls of the prison itself, a low, deep drumming of voices and metal shifting into a simpler, more primal rhythm. Cold creeps along Koda's spine as the chant pounds through her blood, an echo of war drums pounding down the centuries.

"Kill! Kill! Kill! Kill!"

She hears her men behind her take it up in breathy whispers, keeping with the women's voices as the mantra spreads, intersecting at first with the earlier chant and running counterpoint to it, then overwhelming the more complicated rhythm with its purer line.

"Kill! Kill! Kill! Kill!"

They have traveled perhaps fifteen meters in little more than half an hour. It feels like an eternity, though. Koda does not panic in elevators, but nor does she have any love of spaces that fit her like underwear. Motioning Andrews and the others to wait, she creeps forward alone for another few meters, pausing every couple of feet to listen with an ear pressed hard against the ceiling struts. Once she lifts a tile a centimeter or so and sees only a darkened cell with a dim form doubled up almost into fetal position; once she freezes like a rabbit who sees an eagle soar above its meadow, straining to pick up the oddly musical electronic tones or voder-generated voices by which the droids communicate with each other. In the end it is the shockingly loud burst of fire from the large-calibre machine gun almost directly beneath her that charts her location for her, and she waves her troops forward.

They drop from the ceiling directly behind the droids, howling. The sound that rips from Koda's throat is none that she has ever made before in her flesh, a full-throated baying that speaks of the spoor tracked to its source, of blood and death. Andrews, plummeting down beside her, screams like a panther as he raises his M-16 and presses the trigger down onto full automatic, spraying destruction across the brilliant metal surfaces of the droids, the dull green walls, the light fixtures that shatter and fall in minute glass shards like snow. "The gun!" Koda bellows as she braces her own rifle against her hip, raining armor-piercing rounds upon the nightmare things before her. "Get the machine gun, dammit!"

But one of the droids, quicker than the rest, is already turning the heavy weapon to face them. Spinning on her heel, Koda turns her fire on the M-50 and its operator. Andrews takes down the droid sliding into position to reinforce the gunner, the fall of its metal body indistinguishable from the cacophony of battle. Reese, though, darts from behind and charges the machine gun head-on, falling over the barrel and toppling it just as its fire rips through him, spattering blood and gouts of flesh over the walls, the ceiling, his comrades behind him. Andrew screams again and empties his magazine into the droid gunner. Hardly audible through the gunfire and the incessant chanting of the prisoners, Koda hears the clatter of booted feet stampeding across the concrete floor. Allen's troops, the Colonel herself in the lead and snarling like the bobcat emblazoned on her sleeve, come swarming over the barricade, pinning the droids between the two forces.

It is over, then, in a matter of seconds. As Koda raises her weapon to destroy the last of them, Allen yells, "No, take it!" and swings the butt of her M-16 to send its Uzi skidding down the passageway, out of reach.

Andrews makes a flying tackle that topples the droid, followed by Koda. It bucks under them, its mechanical limbs flailing to throw them off with a strength that is literally inhuman. To Koda it is like nothing so much as her one attempt to ride her grandfather's bull on a summer day when she was ten. Now as then, she can feel her spine rattle with the frantic twisting beneath her, now as then she can only hold on and try to keep astride. Then two more soldiers are sitting across its legs, keeping them still by their sheer weight, and yet another pair pins its arms.

"Good work, guys," Allen commends them, panting. She has both hands clamped down on the thing's wrist, a knee jammed into its elbow. "Somebody get a hand in my pack and take out the shackles. We're going to take Dr. King a little present."

Koda, just behind her, fumbles with the zipper and then draws out a length of bright titanium chain attached to a metal belt and four manacles, two each for hands and ankles.

The droid fights frantically to break free, striking Ramirez in the jaw with its foot, almost throwing Andrews and Koda from its back. Limb by limb, though, they struggle to immobilize it, sliding the belt under its waist to fasten in back, bending back the arms to chain each hand to its opposite foot. Just as the last shackle snaps shut, the droid gives up the struggle and lies still.

It is not disabled, certainly not destroyed. Its logic chains have simply returned a null set upon evaluating the possible success of further resistance.

Koda pushes herself up from the steel caracass, suddenly weary beyond telling, and makes her way toward Reese, still slumped across the disabled machine gun. She knows there is no hope of life, yet she kneels and turns him over onto his back gently, not to hurt him further. His blood smears the white of her winter camo, already stained from tending Larke's wounds. Marked, too, by Reese's torn flesh. She feels a void open inside her, black and deep as space beyond the stars. Her fingers clench in the folds of Reese's clothing, almost as if somehow she could hold him back from this last journey. But his eyes are fixed and vacant. The blood trickling from his mouth has already begun to congeal.

Maggie kneels softly beside her, setting a hand on her shoulder. "It's tough, leading men to their deaths. Especially the first one."

Almost as if in a dream, Koda turns toward the other woman. The warrior of only minutes past is gone. Allen's eyes are huge and sad in the brown face of a grieving Madonna, the face almost of Ina Maka herself. As if from a distance, Koda hears her own voice. "Does it get any easier? Ever?"

"No." Maggie shakes her head slightly. "It never does." A moment of silence stretches out, then Allen squeezes her shoulder gently and asks,

"Larke? Martinez?"

"Larke's hurt. Martinez is taking care of him in the kitchen."

"Good," she says. "Very good. Let's start clearing this place out."

The chanting of the prisoners has fallen silent. Laying Reese down gently, Koda gets to her feet beside Maggie. "I'll go check on Larke."

The Colonel nods. "Make it quick. I'm going to need you when we get these cells open." Then, more loudly, "Anybody got any idea where they keep the freaking keys?"

Koda sprints down the corridor toward the kitchen. She finds Larke as pale as his camouflage but conscious and not in shock. On the floor at Martinez's feet is a small mountain of bloody and discarded dishtowels. Koda is pleased, though, to see that the compress that he has bound tightly into place is not soaked through. When she lifts it up to check the wound, she can see that the blood that still oozes slowly from the wound is dark, with no evidence of arterial spurting. Larke's pulse is shallow and faster than she would like, but steady nonetheless. "So how am I doin', Doc?" he asks with a faint attempt at a smile. "Gonna live?"

Koda tightens the cotton strips that hold the compress in place. "Going to live; going to walk. And you're going to get to keep everything you were born with, which is more than I can say for a lot of my male patients."

Martinez starts to snicker, but apparently thinks better of it. "Hey, buddy." Larke lifts his head slightly to stare at his fellow trooper with mock indignation. "You just remember it could be you lying here next time." He makes a snipping motion with two fingers of his right hand.

Koda flashes a grin at the PFC. "He been giving you a hard time, Martinez?"

"Ma'am, he's a rotten patient. If he hadn't made himself dizzy just trying to sit up, he'd have taken off after you and Andrews."

"Oh, yeah? Ma'am, Leo was gonna help me get up. He wanted to go himself. Told him to go on, but he wouldn't."

"And good for you that he didn't." She turns to Martinez. "We're starting to mop up." Koda jabs a long finger at Larke, "He stays here," then at Martinez, "You stay with him and keep an eye on the bleeding. If anything changes, come get me. Otherwise just wait here 'til we call the choppers in. We'll take him out to the Medevac on a litter."

She turns to go, but Martinez touches her sleeve lightly. "Ma'am?"

Koda can see the question in his hazel eyes, pleading with her. She does not want to answer, but she says, "We lost two. Johnson and Reese. Otherwise, Larke here's the worst hurt."

"The droids?"

"All destroyed but one. We're taking it back to Dr. King to see if she can get any information out of it."

Martinez's fists clench once and unclench. "You know, ma'am, sometimes I wish they were human. It just doesn't seem fair that they can't feel anything."

"I know," she says quietly. Images of the last week tumble through her mind: the dead Hurley boys; the women from the Mandan jail; the quiet desperation she has sensed in Kirsten King. "We'll find out who's behind this. And they will pay."

"I wanna help collect, ma'am," Larke adds, just as quietly, and Martinez nods.

"Me, too."

"There will come a time, I promise you." Then, more sharply, "For now, stay put. It'll be maybe half an hour."

As Koda sprints once again for the central hub of the prison, a speaker over her head crackles a couple times, then sputters fully to life. "It's on? Yeah, that's got it. Good."

Then Allen's voice comes through, clear and strong. "Attention. Attention, please. This is Colonel Margaret Allen, United States Air Force. A combined services tactical force has destroyed the prison's android guard contingent and is now in command of this facility. Evacuation of prisoners will begin immediately on a corridor by corridor basis. If you have immediate medical needs, please inform the soldiers who will escort you from your cells to the dining area to await pickup."

The microphone clicks off, and there is perhaps a second's silence. Then the prison erupts in sound once again. This time, though, the roar is a cheer, starting deep and sliding up the scale until it pierces the air with the sharpness of a hawk's cry, the scream of a hunting eagle.

Koda finds the colonel in what appears to be the central guard station. The intercom equipment occupies one long counter, together with a couple computers and a bank of monitor screens that placidly record the undisturbed snow in most of the prison yards. It is still, strangely, only twilight. The entire operation has taken perhaps an hour. Allen looks up as Koda enters. "Larke?"

"Holding on," she reports. "Tried to get up, with Martinez aiding and abetting. He'll be fine, once we get him into a real hospital."

"Good. The locks here are electronic. We don't have the codes, but we do have the emergency switches. I want you to be there as each group comes out, in case we've got anything medically urgent on our hands." Allen pauses a moment, and her voice softens. "You did pretty damn good today, you know. You're a natural at this."

"I know," Koda answers in a voice so low that it is almost a whisper. "It's something that's just been — there — all my life. Like a memory, almost."

"We'll talk when we get back to base and can have a little quiet," Allen mumurs. "Meantime..." Her voice sharpens, and she is once again a line officer. "Andrews, take a couple more troops and accompany Dr. Rivers to A Wing. Give her a hand with anything medical if she needs it. I'm going to go ahead and call that other, overly creative Rivers of ours to have those birds here in another half hour."

Koda extracts her emergency kit from her pack and follows Andrews, Ramirez, and Hanson as they make their way down Corridor A. The women who come streaming out into the hallway here have little about them of the beaten and terrified prisoners of the Mandan jail. It may be only that they have known for an hour that their rescue is underway and have done what they can both to defy the enemy and to put heart into the soldiers facing the actual battle. One woman, her skin pink with excitement, grabs Andrews by the arms and kisses him soundly, then proceeds to reward Ramirez, Hanson, and Koda with equal enthusiasm. When a second makes for the startled lieutenant, he fends her off gently but firmly as he shepherds her toward the dining room with the rest. "Ma'am, please, time is limited. We appreciate your — ahm, we appreciate your appreciation — but we need to get you the hell out of this place. If you'll pardon my language. Uh, ma'am."

Koda is pleased to see that the women are, superficially, largely uninjured. Most have bruises, some yellow-green with age, others newly crimson. One prisoner has a long, shallow cut down her forearm, and Koda takes a moment to wrap it in Kurlex to await stitching when they reach base. "It's mah own fault, Doctah," she says, in a delicate voice that smacks of the Georgia peaches and cream that match her red-blonde hair and ivory skin. "Ah broke the leg off mah stool bangin' it against the doah. Ah wish it had been ovah one of those bastahdly thing's heahds."

Despite herself, a thread of amusement winds its way through Koda's anger. *Move over, Miz Scarlett.* Like her own people, the South has always bred its women tough. It is a breeding that will help this woman survive, as it has kept the *winan Lakota* alive through a century and a half of attempted extermination.

She leaves the latter-day Scarlett with the colonel and the rest of the troop in the cafeteria, where the soldiers have located clean cups and are passing out water and juice. Allen makes the rounds, speaking with each woman in turn, reassuring, comforting those with haunted eyes, answering what questions she can. One woman, pale and agitated, asks over and over again, "Where are the children? What have they done with the children?"

Koda pauses on her way out to evacuate D Wing as Allen answers, "Ma'am, I'm sorry. As far as we can tell, the droids have killed all the boys they found and kept only the girls past puberty. Were your children with you when you were taken?" The woman is close to hyperventilating, and Koda kneels down in front of her with the colonel, capturing her wrist to check her pulse.

"Yes! Christ, why is it so hard to make you understand!" She chokes for a moment, gasping for breath. "They took my kids with me! Why haven't you found them? Where are they, damn you?" Her voice rises to a shriek. "Where are they?"

One of the other prisoners comes to sit beside her, putting her arms around the now weeping woman. "It's true, Colonel. Deb's kids were with her when we were caught at the K-Mart. I haven't seen them since that first day, though."

"Deb?" Koda asks softly. "We'll look for your children. We won't leave, I promise, until we've found them or know for sure they're not here. Can you tell us how old they are? Boys? Girls?"

"Two boys," the second woman answers. "They were about four or five."

"Right." The colonel rises, motioning to two of her troops who are foraging behind the serving counter. "O'Donnell, Markovic!" she shouts. "Start searching the place for kids. Not the cells, we'll get all of those — try the garages and offices and tool sheds! Move it out! On the double!"

Koda returns to her task of evaluating the women as they exit the cells. On Wing D, they find a woman together with her young daughter, thirteen at most. The woman's clothes have obviously not seen the inside of a washing machine in days, perhaps more, but they are intact — no rips, no bloodstains, and her arms and face are equally unmarked. Unlike the others, they seem almost diffident, with none of the lava-hot undercurrent of anger Koda has sensed running thick and murderous below the bravado of the rest of the prisoners. Fear and bewilderment, yes, but no hatred. "I'm Millie Buxton," the woman introduces herself hesitantly. "My husband is here, too. Have you found him, yet?"

"They never touched you, did they?" a dark-haired woman sneers in passing, before Koda can answer. "Bitch! Droid lover!"

Andrews blocks the speaker as she moves to spit at the other woman and hustles her along the hallway. Koda says slowly, "No, we haven't. Was he an employee?"

"A prisoner. Erin and I were visiting when — when — it happened."

"And you haven't been harmed?"

"No. Not... I know what she meant, you see. I've heard when..." Millie glances back at her daughter, "...things happened to the other women. But they left us alone. I don't know why. I'm just glad because — because of Erin, you see."

Koda does not see, not quite, but an idea has begun to form. "We'll find your husband if he's here, Ms. Buxton." And to Andrews, more quietly, as the woman falls into step with the rest, "That last wing's been pretty near silent, all along."

Andrews nods. "Gotcha. We'll pick up a couple more guys before we go over there. That's where we dropped down, isn't it?"

"That's where I saw what I'm pretty sure was a man, one time when I lifted up a tile to see where we were. We'd better go cell by cell, there, not spring them all at once."

"Better see how the colonel wants to handle them. I'm all for leaving them to starve, but she may have other ideas."

In the end, there are four. Three are much like their counterparts from Mandan, foul-mouthed and full of bluster. The fourth, though, will not answer them when his cell is opened, remaining curled tightly on top of the blanket with his knees drawn up to his chest. Only the rise and fall of his ribs shows that he is still alive.

"All right," says Andrews after the prisoner has ignored him three times. "Let's haul him out."

"Wait a minute." Koda walks silently up to the bunk where the man remains unresponsive. "Mr. Buxton?"

Nothing.

"Mr Buxton?" she tries again. "Millie and Erin are worried about you. They're safe. Whatever deal you made, the droids kept it that far."

A sound that is not quite a sob, not quite a groan comes from the huddled form on the cot. "Just leave me, please. Or shoot me. Just don't tell them — please, I don't want them to know. Tell them I'm dead, please?"

Andrews reaches forward and hauls the man into a sitting position. Unkempt hair falls over a forehead pale with lack of sun and eyes that water with the dim light that enters through the half-open door. "Look here, Buxton. You just might get your wish. I don't know what the colonel's going to want to do with you — maybe shoot you on spot, maybe not. If I were you, I'd still want to see my wife and kid one last time. And I sure as hell know they want to see you."

"Mr. Buxton, Millie and Erin will find out exactly what you've done from the other women." Koda takes a deep breath and forces her voice to remain neutral. "Now, I don't know whether they'll forgive you; God knows the rest of these women won't, and shouldn't. But it should count for something that you bought your family's lives. Whatever happens, you can take that with you."

In the end, he comes with them, still half-unwillingly, his head down. Allen meets them just outside the entrance to the cafeteria and rakes the four men over with fury in her dark eyes. "Just like the other jail. Hold them in that office over there for now." She points to a small cubicle with a desk and computer and what seem to be endless piles of invoices. "Hanson, if one of these motherfuckers turns a hair wrong, shoot him."

Buxton raises his head and holds her withering gaze for a moment. "Ma'am, they tell me my wife and daughter are here. Whatever goes down, I'd like to know they're safe."

"Hostages for his performance," Koda says quietly.

"I see." There is what may be a minuscule softening in Allen's expression. "We're taking them back to base. They'll have a trial. Andrews, Rivers, come with me. Hanson, you sit on 'em, and sit on 'em tight. They go out on the last chopper where these women won't have to see their lousy faces."

"Ma'am."

Koda and Andrews follow the colonel back into the cafeteria. From overhead comes the steady whup-whup-whup of approaching helicopters, the noise intensifying until it becomes an unholy clatter as the great blades beat the air. From the doorway, Koda can see their noselights growing larger and larger, finally sweeping the snow before her as the pilots check for obstructions before easing in to a landing. There are at least a dozen; most are Black Hawk and Apache gunships; one is a carrier. The lead bird is another Black Hawk, a red cross painted prominently on its side. The rotor wash kicks up little eddies of snow, sending it spraying outward as the great, grasshopper-like hulks settle, wobbling, into the snow. Just as the high-pitched whine of the engines becomes an almost physical pain, it stops.

"Load up," yells Allen, and with that the former prisoners are running for the helicopters, clambering in with the help of their crews and the rescue unit. Two corpsmen from the Medevac fetch Larke from the kitchen, Martinez trotting alongside the litter. They load the remains of Johnson and Reese, too, decently wrapped in blankets for their last journey. The captive droid goes with the living prisoners, trussed and hauled along by the manacles that bind it hand and foot.

When all the rest are loaded, Allen hops aboard the Medvac chopper, Koda inches behind her. "Get us in the air, Rivers," she shouts as the engines once again begin to whine. "And give me the mic."

Manny complies, with a wave and a mouthed "*Hinkashi*" at Koda.

"*Schic'shi*," she answers, too weary to do more than lift a hand as she settles her back against the hull of the chopper. She can feel the vibration in every cell of her body as the rotors begin to turn, then pick up speed. *I should move*, she tells herself, but her muscles refuse to obey her. The Black Hawk rocks slightly on its wheels, then lifts off with its tail high and its nose low. It is the nature of this peculiar airborne beast that there is nowhere more comfortable than the spot where Koda half-slouches on the deck, unless it is one of the litters suspended on heavy straps from the opposite side of the craft, or the pilots's seats.

Just audible above the chopper's racket, she can hear Allen shouting into the mic.

"We're clear!  Send 'em in!"

Koda closes her eyes as the chopper begins its ascent, banking to the north and west.  When she opens them after a moment, she can see the half moon riding high, glinting off the snowscape as it falls away beneath them.  The winter stars spangle the night, Orion and his dog, the Bull, and the Ram.  As she watches, two of the stars seem to move toward them at tremendous speed, and it is only when she sees the green and red lights winking at their wingtips that she recognizes them for what they are.

Then she sees them dip and streak in low above the prison compound they have just left, their afterburners glowing like small suns in the enveloping dark.  As they pass, fire blooms behind them, reaching into the night sky in unfolding petals of flame.  She nods at Maggie in acknowledgment.  Her mind tells her that they have denied a tactical advantage to the enemy, but deep in her soul she knows that the fire is necessary to cleanse the evil from the place.  She leans back once more against the vibrating hull of the aircraft and lets the darkness take her.

# CHAPTER TEN

As she stands off to one side with the others, holding her hair back out of her eyes as the beating rotors of the approaching helicopters stir the air into a mini-hurricane, Kirsten tells herself that her reasons for being on the landing field are purely scientific. If her heartbeat is slightly faster than normal, it is because she will soon have a working android to examine. The sense of anticipation warming her from within is surely only a scientist's eagerness when given the experimental opportunity of a lifetime.

And if she finds herself looking for a particular glossy black head that towers above the sea of mostly red and gold, and if she imagines she can see, even from this distance, a pair of piercing eyes that rival the winter sky, well, those things are inconsequential. She is a scientist, and scientists are trained to notice things. Or so she makes herself believe.

The injured come off the helicopters first, young men and women bleeding their lives away on litters borne up by strong, resolute soldiers who double time toward the bright red cross of the ambulances. The dead follow, pristine white sheets covering their faces. Their entrance onto the base is more stately, as befits their heroic sacrifice.

Three men follow, heavily guarded and chained at the belly, ankles and wrists. Three sport an unkempt jailhouse pallor that is a perfect accompaniment to their frightened, darting eyes and heavily tattooed flesh. The fourth wears his shame like a shroud. Shoulders slumped, head bowed, he shuffles along staring only at the slush-covered ground beneath his feet, all but cringing at every new sound he hears. Kirsten feels a tiny shard of pity for him, though it's obvious what he's done and why he's chained and guarded so very heavily.

The victims disembark next, their faces displaying a wide range of emotions, from the hollow-eyed pallor of an Auschwitz camp survivor to a kind of quiet joy, to everything and nothing mixed in between. Those with enough awareness looked around curiously, taking in their new surroundings with a distinct lack of surprise, but with, perhaps, a burgeoning hope that their lot might, indeed, be improving.

A group of ten women, most of them former captives themselves, approach these newly freed survivors, offering soft words, soft expressions, soft touches as they lead the group toward the base hospital and the first step on the road to eventual — much hoped for — recovery.

Last to come off the choppers is a small group of heavily armed men and women, Dakota and the colonel included, who surround what Kirsten can easily recognize as a fully functioning android bound by titanium chains and cuffs. She finds herself biting back a smirk. They might as well have bound the thing with construction paper chains made by first graders for all even titanium will hold against the unsurpassed strength of even a single determined android. The very fact that it has allowed itself to be captured, and chained, and is making no effort to escape to fulfill its obviously prime directive to kill them all gives Kirsten a moment's pause, though she waves her concerns off for the moment, confident in her ability to have at least that one question answered by the droid itself. Eventually.

She meets the group halfway, nodding to Allen and Rivers and carefully examining the android as it approaches. Through the receiver in her ear, she can hear the almost desperate data streams it is sending out in an attempt to contact others of its kind. This alone is enough to tell her that it is "injured" in some way that is making it difficult, if not impossible, to fulfill its primary mission. Finding the source, and the cause, of the "injury" is, she knows, the first step toward learning how to disable them all. For the first time since the disaster of Minot, Kirsten allows a shard of hope to enter into the bleak landscape of her thoughts.

"General Hart was kind enough to give me an interrogation room in the brig. If you'll please follow me."

Allen gives a nod. Dakota and Manny continue to bracket the android, weapons at the ready, while the rest peel off, headed for some much deserved down time. The colonel stays with the smaller group, falling into step beside Kirsten as they head for the brig.

**"Don't bother with** those," Kirsten orders, casually waving away the chains Dakota and Manny are preparing to use to strap the android to the chair directly behind the desk she has commandeered. A smile curls her lips as she looks directly into its optical sensors. "If it wanted to kill us, we'd be dead already." A beat of silence. "Isn't that right, RJ-252711-RTLL-2199-RC?"

Again, that look of near shock that she'd seen at Minot. Clue or red herring? Without enough evidence to structure a credible hypothesis, she lets the information sit at the back of her thoughts as she continues her visual inspection of the android. Standing, she rounds the desk, seeing the others back off in the periphery of her vision. She feels a little like a star player in a "good cop/bad cop" melodrama of her hardly misspent youth as she stalks the helpless droid, her lips curved in a shark's feeding-time grin.

"I'm confusing you, aren't I," she remarks conversationally, touching it briefly on one shoulder as she circles. "I'm receiving all of your transmissions, but you're receiving none of mine. What does that make me?" Her smile is almost seductive as she stands before it, one finger rubbing across her full lower lip, as if in serious contemplation. "One of you?" Her smile broadens. "One of them?" One rather elegant hand flips a careless gesture toward Dakota, who stares back, eyebrow perfectly arched, arms folded across her chest. "You can't tell, can you. You don't know what the truth is, and that makes things...difficult...for you, doesn't it."

The android doesn't answer, though its fingers twitch on the arms of the chair, much like a nervous suspect who has been brought into the police station for questioning. It is sending out continuous pulses of data, an SOS beacon that Kirsten can read as clearly as if it were printed on a scrolling board in the middle of Times Square. She smiles and, temporarily turning down the heat, returns to her desk and sits down, spreading her hands against the rough wooden top.

"Tell me," she resumes after a long moment of silence, "why are you breeding humans? What do you hope to gain from this venture?"

The fingers twitch again. "This unit is not programmed to respond in that area."

"Ah. Just a drone, then. If you can't tell me why, can you tell me who? Who gave you these orders?"

"This unit is not..."

"...programmed to respond in that area. Yes, I understand that." She sits back in the chair, eyeing the droid. "I can't help you, RJ-252711, if you don't help me. You have data circuits that need repairing. I need answers. So..."

The data pulses are almost frantic now, and Kirsten hides a wince as a high pitched squeal of feedback enters her implants and loops through her brain. "I can help you, you know. You can feel it. You want to trust me, don't you?" Her voice is soft, seductive.

A louder blast of feedback slices through her, and her eyes close for a long moment, willing the pain away. There is something almost...compelling...in the messages traveling along her nerve bundles. She fights off a heaviness, a lethargy that seeps into the very marrow of her bones; a sweet siren's song to an end she's sure she'd be better off not knowing.

Dakota notices, and takes one step forward, only to be waved back by Kirsten who straightens and leans forward. "Answer my questions, RJ-252711. Answer my questions and I'll give you the help you need."

"I...am...not...programmed...to...to...to...to...to..."

"Answer me, RJ-252711."

"...cannot..."

"Answer me."

The android stiffens, all electronic joints locked as a whine emits from its vocal sensors. Subliminal at first, it grows in pitch until the humans present instinctively step back and raise desperate hands to their ears in a fruitless attempt to block out the sound.

Kirsten feels the code as it buzzes along her nerves like electric shock. She tries to raise her hands to snatch at her earpiece and dislodge the implants, but her muscles will not obey her. She cannot speak; only attend, helplessly, as the systems shutdown command speeds its way to her lungs, her heart, her brain. Koda has risen, leaning over the table to grasp her wrist, but she feels nothing, hears nothing as the other woman's lips form urgent words. Absently, she notes that the improbable blue eyes have gone wide with — fear? Surely not. And surely not for her. That amuses her for some reason, but she cannot laugh, only stare, her own gaze fixed on the wide black pupils that spread and spread like ripples in a midnight pond, and she is drawn into their blackness, falling infinitely down and down, drawn into the deep, into the dark and the silence, falling, falling down the rabbit hole to lose herself in the infinite lightlessness of space beyond the stars.

How long she falls she does not know nor care. The blackness slips past her as she spirals downward, accompanied by wind that whispers with the voices of her dead. *So precocious... That's my girl... I worry sometimes...* Then there are the other sounds: the staccato rattle of machine gun fire; electronic devices speaking to each other in strange tongues, *dit-ditDAHdit,* oddly musical as it speeds along the fiberoptics; the thrum of the blood in her veins as it slows, grows sluggish, stops. They ride along the rising wind that carries her spinning toward a point of light star light star bright, infinitesimally small, somehow above her now as she falls upward — and how did *that* happen, she wonders — with up so floating many bells down and voices are in the wind's singing, singing its own song now. Its blast strips the flesh from her, whistles through the cage of her bones. Yet it cannot drown out the deep baying of the hunter who runs lithe beside her now along moonlit snow and is gone again in a glimpse of driving muscles rippling under black fur that turns in upon itself, moebius-like, to become a small pointed face with eyes burning like molten gold out of a black mask. The narrow muzzle opens, and the creature speaks in a voice to silence thunder, one long-fingered hand raised to bar her passage.

*Go back. The time is not yet.*

But she hurtles past him as the pinprick of light suddenly bursts, brighter than a thousand suns. Pure thought now, with no crude matter to hold her back, she streaks toward its incandescent heart. Out of its center a woman leaps to meet her, brandishing a spear and an oval shield with a boss of bronze. Her naked body is painted with blue spirals and runes of power, and her hair streams behind her like flame. From somewhere behind her comes the slow rhythm of a drum. Her shout rises above its pounding.

*Go back. The time is not yet.*

The warrior fades, gives way to another woman, this one clothed in scarlet silk that flutters about her like tongues of fire. Her nut-brown face is serene with age, though the deep furrows at brow and mouth tell of wisdom bought at cost. The drumming grows louder now, but her gentle voice carries easily above it.

*Go back. The time is not yet.*

Still she moves forward, helpless to stop her steady advance into the sun.

And out of the heart of that sun a third woman comes striding, dressed in white buckskin with a hummingbird worked in shell beads and quills across her breast. Turquoise and white shell adorn her wrists and her slender neck, hang like stars amid the cloud of her hair. Her feet as she walks beat out the song of the drum, though her moccasins touch nothing more solid than air.

*You are astray, my daughter,* she says. *You must turn back.*

*Mother,* Kirsten wails soundlessly. *I have failed.*

*You have suffered a setback, certainly,* the woman acknowledges. *Will you let it defeat you, and all my children with it?*

*I am not strong enough. Not wise enough.*

*By yourself, you are not. But I have given you companions, for knowledge and for comfort.* The woman pauses, smiling. *And for something more, if you have the courage to lay hold of the gift. Will you refuse it? Look.*

An eddy forms in the brilliance, light swirling like the waters of a whirlpool. An opening appears, and Kirsten finds herself looking down from an infinite distance. A slight figure with pale hair lies sprawled on the floor, its face already waxy with the spirit's passing. A tall woman, dark, with a cloud of black hair wild about her face, kneels beside her, her fist rising and descending again and again to the rhythm of the drum. It comes to Kirsten that her own body is the drum, the fierce pounding a summons to return. There are words in that calling, but they skim past her awareness to be lost in the light and the voice of the drum.

There is, really, no choice.

*I will go back,* she says.

The woman's smile becomes radiant, like the sun, bright beyond comprehension, yet not painful to look upon. A long-fingered hand, smooth, so smooth it is the bottom of a rock-bottomed stream, lays itself upon Kirsten and a benediction flows into her soul. It is cool, cool like the spring, like the morning, like the dew that bleeds across her bare ankles as she runs through a clover-filled meadow, a bounding, black-furred beast at her side, matching her stride for stride, lope for lope.

The massive head turns, and she falls into eyes piercing and clear and blue, blue as the spring, like the morning, like the dew that slides across her naked flesh as she falls and falls and falls until her whole world is falling and nothing but.

Her landing is soft, but she awakens with a gasp and her hand clenched to a chest which is burning and throbbing to the rhythm of a newly beating heart. Disoriented, she calls out for an anchor. "Dakota!"

The hoarse call pulls Maggie Allen away from her conversation with a nearby medic. Approaching the bed, she lays a gentle hand on Kirsten's shoulder and smiles. "Welcome back to the land of the living, Doctor."

The sudden, absolute silence is something she can control, and Kirsten reaches behind her ear, only to have the motion stopped by Allen.

"Whoa, whoa, wait a minute there, Doc. You remember what happened, right?"

Easily reading the colonel's lips, a skill she's had for longer than she cares to remember, Kirsten nods. "I got caught in a self destruct feedback loop."

"Exactly. The metalhead is out of the picture, but the base's audiologist got fragged when the droids went over the wall in the first attack. We don't know if your implants are still working, and if they are, whether or not that feedback loop is still active. Turn them back on, and you could short circuit yourself all over again."

Kirsten knows enough military lingo to get a good sense of what Allen is trying to tell her, and nods again. "My computer?"

Reaching down by the side of the bed, Maggie grabs Kirsten's computer and hauls it onto the bed. "Maybe you better tell me what to do, huh? You've had a rough time of it." The look she receives causes Maggie to throw her hands up and step back. "You're the doc, Doc."

Opening the case, Kirsten boots the machine quickly, pleased to see that it wasn't harmed in what she is quickly coming to term "the event". Reaching into one zippered pouch, she pulls out a small wire that ends in an electrode and plugs it into a port in her laptop. The electrode she places behind her left ear, pressing softly until it adheres to her skin. One pale finger depresses the "enter" key, and she watches intently as data streams by in strings unintelligible to the normal mortal.

With a satisfied grunt, she ends the program and peels off the electrode before turning on her implants. Sound flows back into her world once again. She smiles briefly before slumping back against the wall, suddenly more weary than she can ever remember being. The ache is back in her chest, and it sets off a spasm of coughing that makes her feel as if a giant hand has reached down her throat and is even now tearing her lungs from their moorings. Breath is an elusive beast, and her gasps chase after it with all their might, capturing only small slices before it slips away again.

She feels herself pushed back into bed by firm hands as a soft oxygen mask is pressed down over her face. Words, unintelligible as an insect's hum, swirl around her head, but she wastes no energy deciphering their meaning. She knows she's being chided, in any event.

After another moment, the sweet, cool, dry oxygen flows into her lungs, and her hoarse gasping becomes winded pants, and then, as her constricted breathing passages open up, the quiet inspiration of normal breathing.

Standing above her, Maggie's shoulders slump in relief. "A little warning before you start playing Superwoman next time would be appreciated, Doctor King."

"Sorry," Kirsten replies, hoarse voice muffled behind the oxygen mask.

Maggie blinks, mildly shocked at the apology and the slight blush of embarrassment that dusts the younger woman's cheeks. "Yes. Well..." She clears her throat. "I'm going to leave you alone for a bit, then. Please, Doctor, have the good sense to stay in this bed for a while, okay? I've heard that bumping noses with the Grim Reaper takes something out of a person. Even a person as self-sufficient as you."

Pulling the mask off of her face, Kirsten nods. "I'll stay. I could use a nap, anyway."

"I'd imagine so." Maggie's tone is wry, to match the small smirk that curves one corner of her mouth. "I'll see you later, then." She is almost to the door of the small hospital room when Kirsten's voice reaches her again.

"Colonel?"

"Yes?"

"Dakota...Doctor Rivers...she was the one who saved me, wasn't she."

Maggie turns to face her. "It was pretty much a team effort, but yes, she's the one who figured out what was wrong first and started CPR on you. She also shut off your implants. How did you know?"

Her dreamlike trek into the afterworld is slowly fading from her memory, but certain things stand out with crystal clarity. She also knows, with the same clarity of thought, that the experience is something she is loath to share. "I just...had a feeling."

Maggie nods, knowing there's much more to the story, but accepting the statement at face value. Pulling teeth from a rabid wolf would be a cakewalk compared to getting information this woman. "I'll tell her you're awake and doing well when I see her."

"Thank you."

"Not a problem." With a final smile, she exits the room, closing the door softly behind her.

Left alone, Kirsten sinks back into the bed's soft comfort and stares blankly at the white cork ceiling. The words of the Mother — or whatever it is that the image represents — come back to her as if being whispered just now into her ear.

*And for something more, if you have the courage to lay hold of the gift. Will you refuse it?*

"What gift?" she asks the ceiling, frustrated. "How can I refuse something if I don't know what it is?"

But some voice, one that she recognizes comes from within the depths of her own soul, tells her that she already knows the answer to that question, and needs nothing but the courage to listen and understand.

Pondering that voice, she falls into a light, troubled sleep.

**Koda stretches luxuriously,** planting her feet against the front of the tub. Her shoulders, higher than she would like because the damned thing is not made for six-footers, press against its back. Lightly scented with lavender, steam rises up about her, soothing her sore body, easing the soreness that lingers in mind and spirit. For the first time since setting out into the snow and the alien place her world has become, Koda misses her own home. She misses the firm platform bed; she misses the fireplace, larger than most people's closets; most of all she misses her bath. The tub, almost deep enough to paddle in, long and wide enough to accommodate more than three quarters of her, had been the first renovation she had made to the hundred-year-old house, even before she and Tali had decided to marry.

Sharp and sweet as the lavender, the memory slips into her consciousness:

*Late at night, walking Tali into the bath with her hands over those laughing eyes, both of them naked and languorous from lovemaking, leading her down into the warm water where candles float and the scents of rose and lily of the valley mingle in the rising steam. Tali, laughing still as they pursue each other through the water like otters, rolling and tumbling, declaring that Koda must have been Cleopatra in a past life. "If I had been," Koda answers, "I wouldn't have bartered my kingdom away with men. I'd have ruled alone except for my favorite handmaiden."*

*"Me?" Tali asks.*

*"Who else?" And she draws Tali close, pinching out the candles one by one until a lone flame casts their shadow, also single, on the wall and lights their wet skin like molten gold.*

It had been a lifetime ago, in a different world. As surely as if there were an angel with a flaming sword at its gate, Koda knows she can never go back. It is not only that the world has changed. She has changed, become something new, a creature that can no longer live in the environment that gave birth to her. *It is time*, she tells herself wryly, *to recognize that I cannot go back into the trees. Time to come out of the water and grow legs.*

Figuratively, that is. This is her second soak, and she estimates that she has at least another fifteen minutes before the water begins to cool. She had taken ten minutes to shower off the dirt and blood, the acrid stench of black powder that clung to clothing and skin alike. Then she had soaked, her wet hair piled up on top of her head. When the first tub had cooled, she had run a second in defiance of all self-discipline and conservation of resources. She rubs now at the sore spot between her shoulders where she can feel the muscles still bunched. Maybe Maggie can get the knots out later. Maggie, of the long, clever hands and many skills.

*Maggie had known without being told to snatch up the phone and order in a medic and a portable defibrillator when Kirsten had arrested while probing the captured droid. Koda still is not entirely sure what had happened or how, but she remembers in every cell of brain and body her horror as the self-assured — all right, be honest, the more than slightly arrogant — scientist turned pale, her lips and eyelids going blue as she slumped over her terminal, her lungs emptying in a sigh as her chest stilled and her pulse grew silent.*

*Koda's nerves and muscles responded before her brain knew what was happening, clearing the airway, starting the regular compressions of the sternum that would keep the failed heart pumping.* One-two. One-two.

One-two. *At some point the count had become* Hey-ah, hey-ah, hey-ah, *and from somewhere she had heard the deep resonance of her grandfather's drum as it beat out the rhythm of the blood chant. Her hands and shoulders pressed down and released in perfect synch, precise as the steps of her brother Tacoma as he stamped out the figures of the grass dance, remaining steady even as she felt her own spirit gather and hurtle out of her body in pursuit of the dying woman's soul. She streaked down the spiraling dark after her, howling wordlessly, feeling the insubstantial spine of her spirit form coil and release like a spring as she gave chase. The way was barred, then, by another in animal form like herself, but still Kirsten plunged toward the pinprick of brightness that lighted the Blue Road. A woman of power, Koda could walk that path and return, but for someone untrained it led irrevocably into death. Half-panicking then, she felt herself somehow divided, leaping forward to block Kirsten's way, warning her back even as she kept pace alongside. Twice, she was so split, and twice she failed to catch the other woman's soul.*

*Then a blinding light burst on her just as someone grabbed her roughly by the shoulders and pushed her out of the way, making room for the defibrillator and the medics with it. Her eyes wide and sightless, Koda's body reeled backward and collapsed onto the tiles. As Koda hurtled down toward it from an infinite height, she heard Maggie's low* "Damn!" *distinct amid the shouts of the medics, then felt the almost physical impact as her spirit slammed back into her flesh with the shock of a meteor burying itself deep in the earth's rock strata.*

*Maggie was holding her when she came to, half in and half out of her lap. Her dark face was ashen with fear, but she spoke steadily enough.* "You okay?"

"Yeah. Rough landing, that's all."

"Hmph," *Maggie snorted.* "I've set down easier after one of Osama's boys tried to put a SAM up my tailpipe."

*Koda gathered her screaming muscles and sat up, only to lower her head into her hands with a groan. The drum was still with her, only this time it was pounding right behind her eyes.*

"Doctor Rivers?" *Maggie again, formal as always in the presence of subordinates.*

"'M okay," *she said softly, not to reinforce the thunder in her head.* "Shamanism 101. Never touch a body whose proprietor is temporarily absent. Bad things can happen."

"Thought for a moment we had two patients here." *That was the medic, wanting to check her vitals as a pair of orderlies carried the now steadily breathing Kirsten toward the infirmary. Koda let him take her blood pressure and her temperature simply because that would take less time than arguing with him. Then she headed straight for the bath and the now cooling water.*

Carefully, Koda grips the handle on the soap holder and pulls herself up, reaching for the pair of heated towels on the nearby rack. She feels infinitely better, the headache receding now to a dull pain no worse than ordinary tiredness. She needs food. She needs sleep.

She needs to know why Kirsten's near-death fills her with a terror beyond anything she has ever known. And she needs to know why that fear is so very familiar, a rooted ache in her heart.

*Mitakuye oyasin.* We are all related. It is the first teaching of her people. But there is more to it than that. Somehow this woman is part of the
hoop of her own life.

She does not yet know how, or why. But she will.

**Through lowered lashes** Koda gazes at the soft brown globes before
her. She runs her tongue over her lips, remembering their velvet smooth-
ness, the firm but yielding texture between her teeth. Her hand moves
toward them, hesitates, withdraws. *I shouldn't. I really shouldn't.* It would
be too much.

Maggie leans toward her, laughing softly. "Go ahead."

"No, I really shouldn't..."

Maggie laughs again, "You know you want it. Go ahead."

Koda meets the other woman's eyes, feeling color rising beneath her
own cheeks. "Are you sure?"

"Sure I'm sure." Maggie pushes the wicker basket with the one
remaining roll across the table. "I've never seen you so starved. Have at
it."

Koda knows she is blushing and not for the first time is glad of the
coppery skin that masks her embarrassment. But she takes the bread ,
breaks it in her fingers and begins to mop up the creamy sauce on her
plate. From his place under the table, Asi whines pitifully, pawing at her
knee. Koda pauses in her pursuit of the last streaks of gravy just long
enough to deposit her chop bone in his dish. "Sorry, fella. I didn't leave
you much."

"You certainly didn't." Maggie rises and begins to collect the frying
pan and other utensils, scraping them into the compacter beneath the small
sink. "I know I'm a decent cook, but I'm not that good. Battle agrees with
you."

There is silence for a moment, then Koda says, "It does, you know."
Her voice is very quiet, barely audible even to her own ears.

Maggie meets her eyes across the room. "I do know. Want to talk
about it once I get the dishwasher going and we can be comfortable?"

Koda hesitates, then nods. Her plate looks as if it has already been
washed. Without warning, her stomach growls again.

"Dessert?" Maggie offers. "I think I still have some frozen berries."

To hell with embarrassment. "Yes, please. I'm sorry — this isn't the
fighting. It's being out of the body. Exaggerated hunger is a textbook
response."

Maggie stows the last of the dishes and hits the button. The motor
whines, gears grating. The colonel swears and gives it a smart kick; with a
reassuring sound of water jets, it finally turns over. "Don't know what I'll do
when this damn thing gives out now." Returning her attention to Koda, she
raises an eyebrow. "Textbook. Like the low temperature and blood pressure that had the medic wanting to put you into the hospital, too?"

"Just like that."

"You know, I don't think I'd have believed it if I hadn't seen it. Hell, if
I'd seen it happen to anyone else, I don't think I'd have believed it."

"You should have seen my grandfather conduct a *yuwipi.* What I did
was nothing in comparison."

"*Yuwipi*?" Maggie pauses with the freezer door open, a bag of small wild blueberries in her hand.

"A spirit-calling ceremony."

"Well," says Maggie, "I'm willing to believe what I see with my own eyes. But if you're going to do something more flamboyant than take a little stroll in the spirit world or the astral plane or whatever, try to give me five minutes warning next time."

Koda laughs as she accepts a bowl of berries and they move toward the living room. "Count on it. Just as long as I have a bit of warning myself."

A quarter of an hour later, Koda sets her empty bowl on the low chest between sofa and fireplace. Asimov has reclaimed his place on the hearth tiles, lying on his back with his forepaws resting on his chest. His tongue lolls out of his mouth as if in his dreams he is licking some last succulent morsel from his whiskers. His soft snoring mingles with the snap and hiss of burning pine branches. *The sleep of the just*, Koda notes wryly to herself. She glances at Maggie whose face, underlit by the fire, is a study in bronze and shadow, the only points of brightness the reflected flame in her eyes and the glint off the golden bobcat cuff on one ear. *She might be some ancient battle goddess,* Koda thinks. *African or Egyptian.*

Sekhmet the lion-headed, Beloved of Ra her father, the One who holds back darkness, Lady of the scarlet-colored garment, Pre-eminent One in the boat of millions of years. As if from a great distance, almost beyond the range of hearing, there comes the soft sound of a small drum and a silvery tinkling of sistrums. Voices, too, though Koda cannot make out their words. Then the music is gone, and there is only Maggie and the sleeping dog and the light of the fire.

*And where, for all the gods' sake, did that come from?* Very deliberately, she leans forward and places both hands on the wrought metal hinges of the chest.

Maggie says nothing until Koda pushes herself back against the sofa cushions with a sigh. Then, "Cold iron?"

"Residual effect. Sometimes you stay a bit sensitive for a while."

"How long?" Maggie makes a circular gesture with one hand that encompasses a myriad of questions.

How long have you been seeing things?

How long have you been wigging out?

How long will it be before you go entirely round the bend?

But that is unfair. Maggie has been far more accepting than any other person of any race but Koda's own has ever been. She tries to imagine having this conversation with Kirsten King and cannot. *Cold iron, indeed.*

She says slowly, "I started — being aware — of things other people couldn't see or hear when I was six or seven. But my grandfather truly began to teach me when I was twelve, after I had done my *hanblecheyapi* — my first vision quest. What I saw then led me to be a healer, particularly a healer for the four-footed and winged peoples."

Maggie nods, setting down her coffee cup. "And you are extremely good at it. If it hadn't been for your license plate, I would never have suspected that you weren't an MD. Not after the fine work you did on some of my troops that day we ran into the droids."

"But, see, that's not the vision I wanted." Koda meets Maggie's dark eyes across the small space between them. "I wanted to be a warrior.

More than a warrior — Dakota Rivers, liberator of the Lakota Nation." She feels one side of her mouth quirk up wryly. "Don't say it. Grandiosity — pass the Thorazine."

"No, there's nothing wrong with that," Maggie says softly. "Do you know, when I was a little girl I had two heroes. One was Sojourner Truth. The other—" Maggie hesitates for a moment, then goes on. "The other was Joan of Arc. See, there was this old movie on the late, late video one night, called *The Messenger*. Everybody said it was a terrible film, and they're probably right. But what I saw in Joan was a woman absolutely possessed by her calling — a woman who needed to be a warrior because that's what her soul was. And her society wouldn't let her. She found her way, though, even if she died for it in the end."

"Because that's what her soul was." Koda repeats the words slowly. "That's exactly how it feels. Like some part of me is locked away, trying to get out."

"And now it is out. How do you feel about that?"

"Relieved." The word comes to her lips without thought. "Lighter. Like I've been wearing boots a size too small, and suddenly I can run barefoot."

"What about killing? You haven't blown away anything but droids so far, have you? What happens when it's another human being aiming an M-16 at you?"

Koda starts to give the easy answer, then checks herself. After a moment she says, "I don't know. I gave one of the men at the bridge that day an overdose, but he was suffering and beyond saving. That's different."

"That's different, yes. If you're lucky, the first time you have to kill a man or a woman it will go by so fast you won't have time to think about it. You have the fighting instinct, and I think that will carry you through. There's something to be said for losing yourself in the battle." She pauses. "*Rise up like fire, and sweep all before you.* That's in a poem somewhere. What's harder is to order your own troops into a situation they won't survive. But that you do know about."

Reeves. Johnson. More to come. "I know," she says softly. "I hate it."

"And that, my dear, is the price of leadership. Because you are not just a warrior, you are a born leader." Maggie smiles suddenly. "God, I wish I'd gotten my hands on you ten years ago. You'd be the goddamned youngest brigadier in the Air Force."

Koda smiles in return, tension she has refused to acknowledge draining out of her muscles. "If you'd gotten your hands on me ten years ago, it would have been fraternization and we'd both have been in trouble."

"Oh, yeah." Maggie's face splits in a grin. "But me, I like trouble." She rises and moves to extinguish the fire. "And so do you, my dear. So do you."

**As Kirsten wakes** up from the pleasant grip of a rapidly dissipating dream, she finds herself looking into the very eyes that dominated that dream. The transition is so seamless that she can't help but smile, a rare and radiant smile that transforms her entire face into something beyond simple beauty.

It's a smile that Dakota, caught totally unaware, can't help but respond to, and she wonders at that response, even as she wonders at the less than subtle response of her own body as it notices exactly what a smile does for the woman lying on the pristine white sheets of a narrow hospital bed.

After a long moment, both women realize, simultaneously, that they're grinning at one another like idiots, and each looks away, smiles slowly fading even as roses of embarrassment bloom on their cheeks.

Kirsten finds the weave of her blanket utterly fascinating and plucks at it as Koda rubs the back of her neck, not quite fidgeting, but close.

"I..."

"Are you..."

Koda chuckles a bit, and steps back. "You first." The gaze that meets hers is almost — not quite, but almost — shy, and Koda ponders if this morning of wonders portends an omen of some sort.

"I...just wanted to thank you. For saving my life. I, um..."

"It's all right," Koda replies, smiling. "I'm glad I was there to help." Pausing, she looks the young woman over with a clinical eye. "How are you feeling? Any residual effects?"

"I'm feeling...pretty well, actually."

"Good, good."

Silence, dense and uncomfortable, settles over them once again. "Well, I guess I'd better leave you to your rest. I'll talk to you later, all right?"

Kirsten smiles. "All right. And Doctor?"

"Dakota. Please. Just...Dakota."

Another almost shy smile, and Kirsten nods. "Dakota, then. Thank you, again, for saving my life. I know that sounds painfully inadequate, but..."

"No thanks necessary," Dakota replies, laying a quick touch on a blanket-covered foot. "I'm glad I was there." White teeth flash in a brief smile. "Rest up and get stronger, okay?"

"I will. Thanks."

"No problem."

As the door clicks softly closed, Kirsten leans her head back into the pillow and once again stares into the blank ceiling, her mind busily replaying her most out-of-character behavior. "Jesus," she whispers. "What in the hell is happening to me?"

# CHAPTER ELEVEN

*Captain Jack met a mermaid when he went asea*
*O my young ladies go and kiss him goodbye.*
*In the blink of an eye he forgot about me.*
*O tell him young laides, go and tell him for me*
*He can marry the mermaid that lives in the sea.*

*So my Jackie has left in the teeth of a gale.*
*For to marry some sea slug with crabs on her tail.*
*Now he wails on the rocks for he's found much too late*
*That the creatures of ocean and land cannot mate.*

As she pulls her new truck into Maggie's carport, Koda finds herself actually humming along with the jaunty tune. *And how long has it been*, she asks herself, *since I've done that?* The truck, and the truck's stash of Celtic and Celtic rock discs, are her unexpected inheritance from the base's veterinarian, currently missing in action and presumed taken or killed in the last attack on Ellsworth. Dr. LeFleur's practice has become hers, at least temporarily. Koda has spent the morning vaccinating and treating minor injuries and infections among the survivors' pets, as well as examining the MPs' canine contingent. It is the closest thing she has had to a normal day's work since the uprising began.

As the song ends with the self-satisfied assertion that "for he left all his gold and his best friend with me," Koda switches off the engine and collects the filled syringes she has brought from the clinic. She doesn't know when Asi was last vaccinated, or when the chance to give him his boosters may come again. *Might as well do it while I can.*

He greets her at the door with a bark and a furiously wagging tail, rising up on his hind legs to investigate the stranger smells that cling to her shirt, her boots, her jeans. He follows her into the kitchen, snuffling furiously at her heels and at her knees where she has braced the MPs' dogs against her for their shots. He barks again, sharply, and trots over to the table where Kirsten is seated with her laptop. She looks up from her screen and holds out a hand, which he licks with enthusiasm. The blonde woman smiles slightly, rubbing his ears. While it is not the transforming brilliance Koda remembers from the hospital room, even the small upturn of her lips warms Kirsten's face almost past recognition.

She feels the heat rise in her face. To cover her embarrassment she says, "It's good to see you feeling well enough to sit up. I though I'd go ahead and give Asi his boosters while I have the chance, but I seem to have offended him."

"How's that?" The smile, miraculously, has not faded.

"Infidelity." Koda indicates the dog and cat hairs that still cling to her jeans and the sleeves of her flannel shirt. "I've been with other critters all morning. Have you had lunch?"

Kirsten shrugs. "I forgot to."

"Let's see what we've got, then." Koda rummages in the fridge for the tub with last night's leftover soup and a wedge of cheese; the pantry yields a box of whole wheat crackers and some canned peaches. As she is setting the soup to heat, Maggie's sportscar pulls up behind the dark blue truck. With an odd sense of mingled disappointment and relief, Koda sets out a third bowl and adds another measure of coffee to the brewer. As she turns to tend to the soup, Koda catches a glimpse of Kirsten's face. One instant the smile is still there. In the next, Maggie crosses the space in front of the kitchen window and the smile freezes, shatters, falls from the woman's face. Koda imagines she can almost hear the chime of ice shards against the tiles of the floor.

Maggie strides through the door with a burst of the south breeze that has been blowing all morning, sweeping away the clouds. It is cold still but carries with it a hint that somewhere, far away, snow is melting into spring freshets while crooked shoots push up through the earth toward the sun and the year's turning. Maggie's jacket is half off before she closes the door behind her with a shove of her foot. She is back in her flight fatigues and boots, and a delighted grin spreads across her face when she sees Koda. "It's flying weather — no ceiling and visibility all the way to Denver! Want to come up on recon with me?"

"This minute?" Koda asks with an answering smile. "Or do we get to eat our soup?"

Maggie drapes her jacket over one of the chairs and makes for the sink to wash her hands. "After lunch is fine." She turns to Kirsten. "Dr. King, I'm glad you're feeling stronger. When the medics give the okay, I'll be happy to take you up too, if you'd like."

"Thank you, Colonel. I appreciate the offer." Kirsten turns back to the data streaming across her screen.

The temperature in the room seems to sink to near-polar levels. Maggie darts a puzzled glance at Koda, who shrugs almost imperceptibly. Lunch has become, in the military dialect Koda is rapidly picking up, a Situation.

As conversation fails entirely and the only sounds are the thump of the oblivious Asi's tail against the floor and the spoons clinking against the soup bowls, the next twenty minutes are among the most awkward Koda can remember. It feels rather like the preternaturally stretched out time spent in the hall outside Mother Superior's office in grade school, never quite certain what offense she had committed, never quite sure how to defend herself.

After lunch, she gives Asimov his shots while Kirsten holds him, crooning soothing sounds in his ear and rubbing his neck. As she follows Maggie out to her car to head for the flightline, Koda glances back through the window. Kirsten remains seated at her computer as before, one hand absently stroking the dog's head resting in her lap. The other hand props up her forehead as she stares at the screen, her glasses off and her gaze open and unfocused, all the anger gone. It is a curiously vulnerable look, and Koda senses an isolation behind it that is somehow different from her own aloneness — not so much a longing for what has gone, but a refusal to acknowledge the possibility of what might be.

She almost turns back. She knows she will not be welcome, though, not now. The other woman's defenses are all back up, the barriers impregnable. *Someday*, Koda promises herself as she settles into the passenger seat of the elegant little car. *One day.*

**The plane sits** on the apron waiting for them, its canopy up, its ladder down, underwings bristling with missiles. The winter sun gleams off its metal skin, running like liquid silver over the sleek length of the fuselage, striking off the extended wings and the double tail that rises above the afterburners like a pair of ancient banners. The squadron's gunfighter bobcat is emblazoned in gold and black on both panels, together with the base's call letters. Like the fighters parked on the snowbound road the day she first met Maggie and her band of resisters, this machine of titanium and steel and lexan seems somehow alive, a beast of prey lost in time. A frisson that is half fear, half excitement runs along her spine. The warplane is freedom and feral grace, and unrestrained power. It calls to her spirit in the wolf tongue that is as much hers as human speech.

Something of her feelings must show on her face, because Maggie touches her lightly on the shoulder and says, "Oh, yeah. It gets to everybody first time."

Koda turns to the pilot with a smile. "Even to you?"

"Especially to me. It's never stopped getting to me." Maggie's eyes go soft, the way they do in bed. "The first time I ever saw one of these beasts I wanted to run off into the woods with it and have its cubs."

"Cubs?"

"Or chicks." Maggie settles her helmet on her head and motions to the ground crew who have gathered in a sunny spot where the enormous bulk of a C-5 breaks the wind. "Whatever. It's a primal urge kind of thing."

The tech chief takes up his place at the foot of the ladder while the others slip their protective earmuffs into place and the traffic director positions herself to guide the plane onto the runway. Maggie takes a moment to double-check Koda's flight suit and helmet, adjusts the automatic pistol strapped under her arm. Apparently satisfied, the colonel gives her a small push. "Up you go."

The ladder only reaches halfway to the cockpit. From there, Koda finds the hand and foot holds built into the side of the plane, and with an upward push maneuvers herself into the rear seat, ducking a little so as not to hit her helmeted head against the edge of the canopy. She fits into the confined space as if it had been molded to her. As she settles, she takes note of the bank of lights and switches and dials that occupy the control panel. The plane can be flown from her station, but ordinarily the second seat is occupied by the radar intercept officer, and two LED screens and other readouts take up most of the space in front of her.

Maggie follows her up, and from her perch on the fixed portion of the wing supervises as Koda secures herself to the ejection seat and straps her oxygen mask into place. She points to a red-lighted button on the panel. "See that?"

Koda nods. The weight of the helmet carries her head forward; is not uncomfortable, exactly, but it is uncomfortably reminiscent of a morning after.

"Good. That's the ejection button. Don't go anywhere near it unless I tell you to or you know for sure I'm dead or unconscious. Your chute should open automatically in that case, but if it doesn't," she reaches for a cord attached to the seat and drapes it over Koda's shoulder, "here's your manual."

Koda grins up at her. "The things normal flight attendants don't tell you."

Maggie snorts, an entire dissertation on commercial aviation in a single sound. She points to a couple of toggles by the screens. "There's your camera switch; I'll tell you when to turn it on. That's the zoom — you've probably heard that these babies can pick up the dimples on a golf ball. This one can pick up a flea sitting in the dimple of a golf ball. Anything interesting you see on either of these screens — moving blip on the radar, moving anything on the video — you pass it up to me with this. Capiche?"

"Got it," Koda answers.

"Good." Maggie switches on her mic, gives her passenger a pat on the shoulder and, with grace born of long practice, swings along the fuselage and up into her own seat in front. After a moment or two, Koda's earphone crackles. "You all right back there?"

"Fine."

"Okay. Let's take her up."

As Maggie starts the engines, the Tomcat shudders and begins to vibrate, sending a tingle of excitement through Koda's nerves. She has flown before and loves it, but has never before felt this sense of intimacy with the craft. Following the hand signals of the traffic director, the plane begins its taxi onto the runway, turning stately onto the long stretch of pavement, making for the northern end. Maggie's voice comes through the speaker. "Watch your head. I'm putting the lid down."

As the canopy descends, the plane makes its second turn to face south, into the wind. Maggie kicks the engines in full, and the plane shudders a second time with the force that, once in the air, will send it racing ahead of its own sound. For long moments the plane remains stationary, its power held in check. Then Maggie throws the throttle open, and the jet is streaking down the runway at a speed that presses Koda into her seat and takes her breath away. Her heart pounds against her sternum and shouts to be let out, blood running in her ears with the roar of the Colorado in spring flood. Between one breath and the next, it seems, she feels the nose come up and the lift of air beneath the wings, and they are airborne, climbing steeply into the clear, impossible blue of the afternoon. The ascent goes on and on, leveling out finally when the land beneath is no more than intricate swirls of brown and green and white, with the course of the occasional river cut into it like the trunk of a vast tree, its tributary streams forking off into branches and twigs.

The craft banks into a turn, and sun glints off the wing and the canopy in bursts like small stars gone nova. When they level off again, the wings sweep back close to the body of the plane, like a falcon stooping. All around her now is the open sky, and with it a sense of perfect freedom. There is only herself and the blue air and the wings that carry her.

*This must be how it feels to be Wiyo.*

The tang of oxygen flowing into her mask startles her out of her reverie, followed closely by Maggie's voice.

"Engage the camera and radar now. We're going to make a sweep up the Cheyenne and then follow the Missouri into North Dakota."

Koda thumbs the toggles and stares at the images that rise to her screen. She can make out the rectangular shapes of roofs, outlined in shadow, as they pass over the small villages that dot this part of the state. Beside them stand tall hardwoods, winter-naked, or evergreens with fans of needles spread against the unvarying snow. When she engages the zoom, antennas and chimneys stand out of the snow that blankets the roofs. Once she sees a pair of deer, or elk, perhaps, breaking their way through the snow that covers the main street of a small town. Abandoned cars and farm machinery form mounds in the spaces between the houses, anonymous under the snow.

"See anything?"

"Negative," she responds. "Mostly snow, apparently abandoned homes, buried vehicles."

"Hang on, then."

With no more warning than that, Maggie flips the fighter over in a barrel roll. Koda gasps with surprise, then yells into her mic. "Do that again!"

Maggie rolls the plane twice more, then streaks out of the third flip upside down, with earth turned suddenly to sky and the blue depths of the sky below. Koda feels the adrenaline pouring into her blood, hitting her brain in a rush of pure physical pleasure. Then they are right side up again, and Maggie is laughing through the mic.

"Liked that, did you?"

"Gods, yes!" she yells. "That was wonderful!"

"Okay. Tell me if this gets uncomfortable."

The fighter begins to climb, straight up, corkscrewing. The ascent becomes a curve becomes a loop, and they are upside down again, sweeping into a descent that has left all sound behind except the low whisper of breath, and Maggie brings them out again into even flight for a space before the plane skims along its upward trajectory for the second time. The G-force holds Koda motionless, back pressed into her cushions, the whole force of their speed against her solar plexus. The sensation rides the thin line between pain and pleasure , pleasure and sensory overload. Then they are plunging down from the sky to skim no more than three or four meters above the snow along a thin flat stretch of road, only to climb again at an impossibly steep angle, reaching toward the edge of the envelope of air that is the first frontier between Earth and space. When Maggie levels off again, five miles up, Koda's breath comes in little gasps and her rational mind has gone AWOL. When a thought finally forces its way upward from the part of her brain that is still functioning, it is sex. *It feels like sex.* Her blood sings in her veins, her sated muscles hum. *I want to have its babies, too. Hatch its eggs. Whatever.*

The sensation fades gradually over the next half hour as they quarter the landscape beneath them. Maggie flies a straight line grid pattern over the ruins that were once population centers, but they can detect no gathering of humans or droids, no movement that is not solitary. Roads have become largely impassable and look as if they will remain so 'til spring thaw. Many will still be blocked then, by storm-felled trees or the tangled remains of accidents.

They have been flying for a little more than two hours when Koda picks up a line of something moving on the highway leading south from Bismarck. She zooms in on it, tweaking the fine focus. "Maggie, have a look."

She transfers the image to the pilot's readout, but she knows already what she sees. It is a column of troops, some droid, some apparently human, preceded by a coterie of snowplows and followed by a contingent of armor. There are personnel carriers, several tanks, a dozen flatbed trucks loaded with something long and rectangular. *Construction materials?* She tweaks the image again and the cargo comes into focus. *Mobile missile launchers.*

"This," Maggie says dryly, "is not good. I'm gonna take 'em out here and now. Hang onto your hat."

Maggie kicks in the afterburners, and the Tomcat comes streaking down out of the sky with the sun behind it. Half a mile above the column, she releases a long stick of precision-guided five-hundred pounders, laying them down with mathematical exactitude in the center of the long column, spaced precisely to destroy everything on the road. The explosions are muffled by distance and the roar of the jet's engines. On the video screen, Koda watches as the mobile launcher swivels on its truckbed to get them in its sights. A puff of smoke in the frigid air, and a long, lean shape rises toward them. Maggie has already seen it; even as Koda forwards the image to the pilot, she feels a faint thump as a Sparrow missile leaves its roost on the plane's flank and streaks to intercept the enemy fire. The kill is almost instantaneous, a burst of flame and vapor in the cold air. The plane swerves wildly as a second ground-to-air missile passes by without harm, a clean miss.

There is no third try. Maggie turns to make her second bombing run, and when she slows for the final pass to check and record results, nothing moves along the road at all. "And that," she says quietly, "is the end of that."

The flight back to Ellsworth is swift and straight. When the Tomcat once again comes to rest by its hanger, Koda finds, like a child at the carnival, that she does not want the afternoon to be over. As she climbs down the ladder, she runs her hand over the plane's sleek skin, all cool steel and titanium, belying the fire within.

"In love, are you?" Maggie smiles at her, unstrapping her helmet and tucking it under her arm.

"A little," Koda admits. She feels the silly grin spread across her face and can do nothing to stop it. "When can we do it again?"

At that, Maggie laughs outright. "You know, I really do wish I could have gotten my hands on you years ago. You'd have made one hell of a pilot. You got the tape?"

Koda hands the colonel the small cassette with the record of their engagement. It is the first indication they have that humans are collaborating with the droids. It is also the first evidence of large scale droid movements since the uprising. Serious matters both, and they are on their way to the general with their report without bothering to change their flight suits. But sheer joy runs in Koda's veins and will not be denied. "You'd have been a hell of a teacher. But don't you think one Rivers in your squadron is enough?"

It is a rare warm — if temperatures in the single digits can be considered warm — winter's morning, and Dakota drives along the snow packed roads with her window rolled halfway down and her gloved hand curled around the door's support, long fingers splayed against the roof. She's humming softly to herself, a song heard, and remembered from long ago. One of Tali's favorites, if she recalls correctly.

The truck rattles and buzzes and screeches, but she pays it no mind as her fingers tap out the rhythm of her humming on the salt-dusty roof. Nor does she pay special heed to the scent — old coffee, old sweat, and something high and sour and rank that she doesn't even want to identify — that emanates from the truck's interior. She's soaring high, caught up in the exhilarating memories of flying with Maggie the day before. The sense of unbounded, heady freedom is something she has only felt during her dream journeys, journeys always taken in a form other than human. The incandescent rush is with her still, and she wraps it around her like a blanket, feeling very much as she did when she first kissed Tali, behind the stables in the moonlight.

"Kiss? Hell," she snorts into the truck's warm cab. "It felt closer to what we did on our wedding night! Jesus." A pleasant shiver skitters down the length of her spine, and her limbs break out in temporary gooseflesh.

"Okay," she intones as her inattention to detail almost runs her off the road, "that's quite enough of that. Mind on the road, Rivers, and outta your pants, if you please."

Looking up into the pristine winter sky, she sees a large flock of birds pacing her truck. The flock is suddenly split almost directly down the middle, and wheels off to the left and to the right as another airborne object dives down through the vacated space like a star falling from the heavens.

Koda's face splits into a grin as the dive bomber levels out and casts its shadow along the unbroken snow just to the right of her truck. "Welcome back, old friend."

As if hearing her, Wiyo's call pierces the silence of the still morning as the red-tail glides on currents of air, shadowing Dakota's return to the place of her birth.

Still grinning, she turns left over the cattle-guard that marks the entrance to her parents' property and starts down the long, snow covered and ruler-straight road that will lead her to the family compound. She is being watched, she knows, by creatures human and non, but she senses no danger from the watching and so continues on, still humming.

Off in the distance, to her left, she sees a white mist rising. *It's either a vehicle moving in this direction, or...* "Ah," Koda says, laughing as the mist resolves itself into something easily recognizable. Her laughter is rich and full-bodied, breathing life into the woman she had once been and might yet be again.

The herd moves closer, with Wakinyan Lutah, her huge blood bay stallion, leading them. His black mane flutters like a war banner as he approaches the fence and rears, slashing forefeet pawing at the air, clots of snow flinging from his well-shod hooves.

Her laugh is that of a young girl: boundless, full of life and joy. Pulling over to the side of the road, she jumps out of the truck before it has come to a complete stop, striding across the road even as the heavy beating of air above her head almost knocks her hat off.

Wiyo lands on the top rung of the fence and proceeds to strut across it and back, like a miniature general before a platoon.

Wakinyan Lutah rears again, slashing hooves coming perilously close to the red-tail. Wiyo stares at him, completely unperturbed, and settles her wings more comfortably over her back before resuming her walk along the fence.

"C'mere, ya big baby," Koda says, rolling her eyes and holding her hand out over the fence.

Nervously eyeing the red-tail (Dakota believes she can see the proud gleam in Wiyo's eye even from where she's standing), the stallion sidesteps closer to the fence until he is able to nudge Koda's hand with his nose, whuffling a great, warm breath into her palm.

"Hey, boy," Koda says fondly, rubbing his nose and that spot between his ears that has him all but groaning in ecstasy. His coat is winter thick and gleams in the sunlight like freshly spilled blood. The comparison causes Dakota to wince and swallow hard as it dredges up memories best left buried until she has time to dissect them.

After a moment, Wakinyan backs up and tosses his head in an unmistakable invitation. When Dakota doesn't respond to his satisfaction, he whickers, tosses his great head again, and paws at the snow, digging deep ruts into the frozen ground beneath. Breath streams from his nose in foggy jets.

Unhappy with the sudden wind that ruffles her feathers, Wiyo hops onto Koda's forearm, then sidesteps up to her shoulder and expresses her displeasure with a loud hiss. These two are rivals of old, and Koda can't help but chuckle at their long familiar, and much beloved, antics.

After the stallion gives a final call, Koda shakes her head and sighs. "Oh, all right," she says, sounding more aggrieved than she really is. After taking one last look over her shoulder at the truck parked by the side of the road, she hitches in a breath and vaults over the fence, dislodging the red-tail, who hisses again and beats at the air with her huge wings, taking low flight.

"Ready, goober?"

Wakinyan nods his head, shaking out his mane.

"All right, then."

Another deep breath, and she vaults aboard the stallion's broad, muscular back, threading her fingers firmly in his mane. A light touch of her heels to his flank, and he wheels, and takes off flying across the snow packed ground, the herd following close behind.

Dakota whoops with pleasure. Her hair, exactly matching the color of her horse's mane, streams behind her in inky waves; her eyes flash, and her full, perfect lips split in a wide, take-no-prisoners grin. Her spirit soars as the land passes beneath her in a blur of white on white, and she feels a sense of connectedness that has been absent for a long, long time.

She is wild.

She is free.

She is home.

**With a grunt** of frustration, Kirsten wrenches the glasses from her face and tosses them on the battered desk upon which her computer rests. *Hours upon hours upon hours of searching, and nothing worth a fart in a windstorm to show for it.*

Leaning back in her chair, she rubs a numb hand over weary eyes, then looks down at Asi, who lifts his head and thumps his tail in a canine hello. The house is quiet, almost sterile in a way that only military housing can sometimes be. Outside the window, the afternoon is crisp, clear, and blessedly sunny. Looking upon the colorful parade of passersby, she once again feels that unwanted but familiar sense of dispossession and dislocation. *On the outside looking in. Again.*

*It doesn't have to be that way, Little K.* Her father's voice intrudes into her thoughts, frustrating her with its always maddening logic. *Nothing's keeping you locked inside. Nothing except you.*

"Shut up, Dad," she mutters, pinching the bridge of her nose where a headache threatens to erupt. "Just...shut up. Please."

She realizes that little internal thought masquerading as her father's voice might have a point, though. Perhaps some fresh air would do her good, a distraction that might help her subconscious continue to unravel the mystery of the code on its own with no further help from her.

"Worth a shot, anyway," she comments to the bare walls surrounding her. Rising to her feet, she steps from the room and into the short hallway. Quite without meaning to, she finds her glance drawn into the open portal of the master bedroom. There, draped across the comforter, lies the colonel's robe, and casually draped across that is the very shirt Kirsten had seen Dakota wear the day before.

The simple, careless, wholly domestic intimacy of the vision twists something deep inside, and although she's completely unaware of the sneer that twists her features, a mirror would tell her that it is, in fact, there.

*We're not going there. Not even partway.* She deliberately turns her attention away. *Air. That's what you need. Fresh air, and sunshine, and...damn!* Tears sting her eyes, liquid accusations that she rubs away with a savage forearm, denying all they might stand for.

"Let's go, Asi. Time for a walk."

Asi streaks by her like a bullet, dancing and panting at the doorway as his favorite word is spoken. His antics draw a reluctant chuckle from Kirsten, and, with the sense almost of taking a dare, she grabs one of Dakota's jackets from its post on the coat-rack. Lighter than the heavy, military issue parka she had been wearing, it also brings with it a sense of...comfort? The scent of the woman who had previously worn it permeates the cloth, and Kirsten wraps it around her in a moment of pure — and exceedingly rare — self indulgence.

Asimov's impatient whine demands her attention, and she quickly twists the doorknob. Asi bolts out before the door is more than partly open, barking and kicking up huge fans of snow in a burst of wholly canine energy.

Kirsten follows behind at a more leisurely pace, accepting and returning smiles and nods from the soldiers and civilians passing by. Without thought, she allows her feet to take her where they will. Asimov, his burst of hyperactivity quelled for the moment, returns to her and follows along, glued to her heel.

As she walks, her gaze darts here and there, capturing isolated images that fit, like puzzle pieces, into a greater tableau.

A group of soldiers, armed to the teeth, drilling in precision step.

A small group of children — far too few in number, now — preparing for a battle of their own, with snowballs and snow forts instead of bullets and battlements.

Uniformed young men, bearing the scars of an undeclared war, limping along shoveled paths.

Civilian-clad young women, bearing the scars of the same undeclared war, shuffling along those same paths, their expressions lost and frightened and alone.

Others, seemingly unaffected, pass quickly by, laughing and joking with friends newly met. Kirsten yearns to scream at them, to tell them to stop, to have respect for the hurt and the grieving and the dead. The dead, who are now no more than mounds of slowly melting snow, watched over by an honor guard and a tattered flag.

Holding back her anger by the barest of frayed threads, she continues her walk past row upon row of military housing. The faces that stare back at her through heavy glass tell tales of their own, and for the first time, she feels a sense of kinship with these people, these strangers, these survivors of a war none had asked for and all had suffered through.

In another first, she admits — even if only in the tiniest corner of her heart — that perhaps it has been her own pride that has fueled her anger and frustration. Perhaps it is her own savage joy at being proven right all along, and her need to stand upon those unbestowed laurels, and in so standing, further prove herself savior of this newly begotten world that has alienated her from the very people she is trying to save.

It's not that her pride, her need to point her finger into the face of humanity and shout "I told you so!" is a deliberate attempt to prolong suffering as a form of payback for the laughter that's followed her these last years. No, nothing so vile as that. But still...

Most of her turns its internal back on these newfound revelations in a sort of primitive self-defense mechanism. Self-blame is an emotion this world can ill-afford. But still...

Resolving to think on this later, she abruptly turns and begins the trek back to her temporary home, her agile mind already returning to the problem of the code, the code, that damnable code.

**Grunting softly, Koda** lowers her weary body onto the top support of the corral fence, hooking one leg behind the middle support and resting gloved hands against thighs tense and more than a bit sore. The warm spell has continued, making spring a promise instead of a fantasy dreamt only by poets. Stripped of her heavy jacket, she sits at ease in a down-filled vest, flannel shirt, and jeans. Well-sprung cowboy boots are clotted with mud and snow and muck, and will need to come off before she gets within shouting distance of the family home. She smiles, all but hearing her mother's warning tones.

To the west, the sun is preparing to set beyond winter-bare trees. The sky is a riot of color and the clouds are gilded with rose and purple and gold. It is a peaceful time that appeals to her need for solitude.

For the past three days she has been immersed in the concerns and troubles of her immediate family and neighbors. Her family's huge ranch has become a haven for the dispossessed. Orphans, widows, widowers, and the occasional full family unit now take up residence on the thirty thousand acre spread. The house and all its outbuildings are jammed with grieving people, each with a story to tell. Koda believes she's heard them all, most more than once. A new oral tradition is forming, a history kept in the mind and on the tongue, like the history of old. Her oldest sister, Virginia, has already set several of the stories to song as a way of remembering. It is the way of their people, a way of making sure that these stories are never forgotten.

For the past seventy two hours, her mother has stuck to her as if glued, finding reasons to touch her, to hug her, to simply look at her through deep, fathomless eyes.

"The prodigal daughter returneth home," Koda says softly, a wry laugh escaping into the slight breeze.

An answering cry sounds from overhead, and scant moments later, Wiyo lands on the fence next to her, settles her feathers, and looks up at her, head cocked inquisitively.

"Good hunting?" Koda asks, grinning at her friend.

Wiyo sidles closer until they are touching, then settles and begins to preen. Dakota feels tears sting her eyes at the simple and sacred beauty of the moment. It is something she will profoundly miss when she leaves again, quite probably for the last time.

Blinking those tears away, she looks back at the setting sun and all that surrounds her. This is her home, the place where her soul knows its only peace. And yet, to be who she must, to become who she will, she must leave behind both it and the peace it offers.

She senses the presence behind her a split second before a light touch descends on her shoulder.

"*Han, thiblo.*"

A deep laugh sounds behind her as Tacoma moves to the fence. "Those eyes in the back of your head have grown larger, I see. *Hau, tanski. Hau, Wiyo.*"

The redtail cocks a disinterested eye toward the large man before returning to her preening.

"Beautiful evening," Tacoma remarks, leaning forward to rest his forearms against the top rail.

"That it is," Koda agrees. With the sound of thunder, the herd comes over the ridge and runs by, Wakinyan leading them. The herd's size has nearly doubled in the weeks Koda has been away, and she looks on, impressed. "He covering them all?"

"Oh yeah. He's gonna be one happy boy come spring."

Koda shoots him a look before returning her attention to the setting sun. The two sit in companionable silence until the sun disappears behind the horizon and twilight descends, bringing with it a soft peace of its own.

Finally, Tacoma speaks. "I'm coming with you, you know."

Shifting on the fence rail, Koda looks down at her brother. "What?"

"When you leave. I figure that's gonna be either tomorrow or the day after. I recognize the signs."

"What signs?"

Tacoma grins, a touch smugly. "How long have I known you? You're as restless as a cougar in heat, *tanski*. You love this." A large hand splays, indicating the ranch. "But your soul is calling you elsewhere."

Koda dips her head, a touch embarrassed at being so easily read.

Tacoma chuckles softly, soothing her with a light touch to her broad back. "You always were a wandering spirit," he continues, tone reflective. "It surprised the hell out of me when you bought the ranch down the road and settled in."

"Tali," Koda answers, her own voice quiet as her brother's. "She was happy here. And I...a big part of me was too." A pause, then softer still, "Still is."

"But that other part, it's gotten bigger, hasn't it?"

Koda nods.

"You've changed, *tanski*." Tacoma holds up a hand. "No, no, not in a bad way. It's just..." He sighs, trying to put his thoughts into words. "*Ina* always said that you were born *wakan*."

Dakota turns wide eyes to him, and he laughs. "No, not to your face. You got into far too much mischief for her to ever let you know that out loud. But she's always been proud of you. *Até*, too. And you know the younger ones worship you. Hell, even I do."

Feeling a hot blush coming on, Koda turns away, glad for the evening breeze which has sprung up with the setting of the sun. It cools her skin, but does nothing for the rapid beat of her heart.

Caught up in his own thoughts, Tacoma doesn't notice — or has the sense, at least, to pretend he hasn't. "As I said, you were always self-possessed and mature, even when you were a wild child." He laughs, remembering. "Which was most of the time. But now...now you have...*wakan*. I can feel it coming off of you, even when you're sitting still, like now. It's just..." Head lowered, he sighs again. "I wish I had better words to explain."

"I've experienced many things in these past weeks," Koda replies, still looking to the horizon.

"I've heard the stories. Though I assume you edited them for *Ina* and *Até*. *Ina* especially."

Koda turns finally to look at him. "Wouldn't you?"

The two siblings share a quiet laugh, and then Dakota sobers. "There's a great battle coming, *thiblo*. I can feel it here." She pounds her thigh. "In my bones."

"Not here." Tacoma indicates the ranch again.

"No. This place is safe enough. For now, at least."

"Ellsworth, then?"

"I believe so. I don't know how I know, I just know that I do."

"Which is why I'm coming with you."

Koda rounds on him. "No, Tacoma. You can't. You need..."

"To stay here?" His voice is strong, steady, and brooks no contention. "You yourself just admitted that this place is safe."

"For now, I said."

"For now," he concedes. "But it's as well guarded as any Army camp, Dakota. You've seen it with your own eyes. We've got enough weapons and ammunition to last us for years, if need be, and everyone on this ranch, from the youngest on up, knows how to use them."

"But—"

"No buts. I am Tacoma Rivers, Staff Sergeant in the U.S. Army. I am a Lakota warrior. I can no more stand by than you can. If there is to be a battle, I mean to be there."

"*Ina* will never let that happen."

"*Ina* doesn't have a choice in the matter. I am *wichasha*. I run my own life, rule my own destiny."

"And cower like a *hokshila* when *Ina* shoots one look at you," Koda replies, smirking.

Tacoma can't help but laugh, knowing his sister's words for truth. Their mother runs the house with an iron fist, and no one dares deny her reign, not even her husband. "I need to do this, Dakota," he says finally. "No matter what, I need to do this."

Taking her brother's hand in hers, she gives it a firm squeeze and looks deep into his eyes. "I know."

Falling silent again, both turn to the sliver of the moon as it rises over the skeletons of trees as old as time.

**"No. You won't** go. I forbid it."

"*Ina.*"

"Mother."

"No. This discussion is finished. Now leave me, both of you. I have dinner to prepare."

Stepping away from the juggernaut who is their mother, Tacoma shoots a pleading look at Koda, who rolls her eyes and steps forward, careful not to touch. "*Ina*, please."

Themunga whirls, eyes fierce and filled with tears she won't allow to fall. "I told you to leave me be, Dakota."

"I can't do that, Mother. I won't do that."

"Who is *winan* here?" she demands, her brow like thunderheads amassing before a storm.

"We both are." Her eyes soften. "Please, *Ina*. We need to talk about this."

Sighing, Themunga looks at her daughter, then past her to where several not-quite familiar faces stare back with varying degrees of discomfiture. "Go on with you!" she demands, scowling and flapping her arm at them. "I'll let you know when the meal has been prepared."

The small group scatters like startled quail, leaving only mother, daughter, and son behind.

"Start talking." Arms folded across her chest, Themunga is a formidable sight.

Tacoma swallows hard, but Dakota refuses to be cowed. "I'll talk only when you are ready to listen to my words, *Ina*."

The thunderheads reappear, then scatter. Proud neck unbent, Themunga nevertheless lets her daughter know by her body language that she's ready to listen.

"The danger, it isn't over, *Ina*."

"All the more reason you are needed here, Dakota. To protect your *thihawe*. There is no greater need than that."

"Our family is protected, *Ina*. I have seen it. I have spoken with our neighbors, the men and women and children who have come to live here. They will protect this place, and everyone in it, with their lives."

Themunga's voice carries with it deep, biting sarcasm. "Oh, and you are demanding that they do what you will not?"

"I demand nothing from them, *Ina*. They do what they do of their own free will. As I do. As Tacoma does."

"And that is supposed to make me feel better?" her mother shouts, all but shaking the rafters. "That they will stay and fight, and you will run?"

"I'm not running, Mother. You know this."

"All I know is what I see. You are leaving us to defend ourselves while you go who knows where and take my oldest son with you."

Tacoma steps in, his voice even but firm. "I would go with or without

Dakota, Mother."

Themunga turns to her son, tears finally spilling over onto her rounded cheeks. "*Takuwe?*"

"Because I am needed."

"You are needed here!"

Tacoma shakes his head, saddened by his mother's tone, yet resolute. "I am needed there more."

Themunga turns away, her face almost ugly in its anger. "Let the *washichun* take care of himself."

"*Ina!*" Tacoma gasps.

She rounds on them both. "It's true!" she shouts again. "Where were they when our land was stripped from us? Where were they when our women were raped and our men were slaughtered like sheep? Where?"

"Not even born," Dakota replies, her voice flat, devoid of any emotion. Tacoma stares on, shocked at his mother's sudden bigotry.

"Oh?" Themunga retorts. "And I suppose it was ghosts who sent you home battered and bloody from school? It was ghosts who spat in your face when you walked into town? Who called you names that took the light out of your eyes and put a stone mask on your face instead? Was it, *chunksi?*"

"You know it wasn't, *Ina.*"

With a savage nod of her head, Themunga puts her hands on ample hips and stares at them both, obviously believing the matter decided to her satisfaction.

"Mother," Dakota begins softly, "you raised me to be the woman I am. A woman who will fight for what is right and just and good. There are thousands of innocent women and children trapped in prisons all over this country. Thousands more wander, lost and alone and in fear for their lives. If I turn my back on them because they are not Lakota, I am no better than the people who beat and spit on me because I am." Lowering her head just slightly, she levels her gaze into her mother's bottomless eyes. "Is that the woman you raised me to become?"

She sighs when there is no answer. "If so, then I'm sorry I failed you, *Ina.*" Turning to Tacoma, she says, "I'll be leaving at sunrise. With you or without you."

"I'll be ready," Tacoma replies.

After a last, long look at their mother, brother and sister turn away and leave the room.

When they are gone, Themunga's face crumples. Her body shakes with sobs finally released. A soft tread heralds the entrance of Wanbli Wakpa, who approaches his wife and wraps her tenderly in his massive arms. Stroking her hair, he comforts her as best he can, knowing it can never be enough.

# CHAPTER TWELVE

The light from the setting moon shines into the window as Koda wakens and slips out of the too-narrow, too-short bed. Placing her stockinged feet carefully on the floor, she uses the moon's light and her own uncanny hearing to determine the positions of her two youngest brothers, snoring softly on the floor directly ahead. Housing space being pinched as it is, Phoenix and Washington now share this room, and both spent the better part of the previous evening begging and cajoling their eldest sister to spend her last night at home with them. It took even longer for her to finally give up and agree to use the one bed they both shared, which had, as she'd predicted, made for a mostly sleepless night for her.

Straightening, she suppresses a groan as her stiffened and cramped muscles protest the abrupt change in position. She arches, hearing her spine crack along its length, then freezes as one of her brothers — Phoenix, she thinks — snuffles at the disturbance, turns, and falls back into a deep sleep.

*Think I'm gonna need a Maggie Allen special when I get back.*

The tiny smirk slides from her face as she realizes that this is the first time she has thought of Maggie in three days.

On the other hand, at odd times during those same days, she's found thoughts of the scientist, Kirsten King, sliding effortlessly into her mind. Random thoughts, really, nothing very specific. That they're there at all is somewhat of a surprise to her, however. Surely she has better things to think about than how that radiant smile had transformed the young woman into someone beyond beautiful, or how her eyes sparkled like clear-cut emeralds. Or even how her hair, so reminiscent of the summer sun, might feel to her fingers.

*Jesus, Dakota. You already have a woman who shares part of her life, and her bed, with you. Who respects you and cares for you. Why the interest in an arrogant, overbearing, close minded, close mouthed scientist who has about as much warmth as a North Dakota winter?*

*Because,* another voice, still her own, tells her, *she's not like that. Not deep inside, where it counts.*

Knowing that this internal conflict isn't something she's going to resolve any time soon, she pads silently to the window and takes a quick look outside. The fading night is clear as crystal, though she can tell by simply feeling the glass that the warm spell has continued to hold. Traveling should be good.

Turning away from the window, she looks down upon her sleeping brothers. Both sleep like the dead, and the picture clenches a fist in her heart. For the first time, she wonders if leaving is truly the right thing to do. The image of Phoenix, thirteen, and Washington, barely eleven, clutching rifles too big for them and falling silent beneath a hail of android ammunition causes her belly to roil and her palms to become slick with clammy sweat.

Suddenly, the room seems too cramped, and a primitive part of her considers panic. The door slips open and Tacoma comes partway through, a look of concern on his face. The siblings' eyes meet, and Koda immediately finds herself begin to calm. Releasing a slow breath, she holds up one finger. Tacoma nods and steps back out of the room, leaving the door the tiniest crack open.

Looking down once again, she tries to memorize the shape of their faces, knowing all the while that should she ever see them again, they will have become men instead of the boys who sleep so peacefully before her. *Will I even recognize you? Or will you have become strangers to me, merely another face passing by in my life?* She wipes a tear from her eye. *Please, never let that happen. Please.*

Squatting down, she kisses the tips of her fingers, then brushes them lightly against the downy cheeks of her brothers. "I love you," she whispers. "Never forget that. Never."

Rising, she pads silently to the door before turning and giving them both one last, lingering look. Then, eyes full, she opens the door and steps through, closing it quietly behind her.

Tacoma meets her in the hallway and slings a gentle arm around her shoulders. "You okay?" he whispers.

Nodding, she gives him a half-smile. "You should have been a shaman."

He laughs softly. "Remember what I told you, *tanski. Wakan Tanka* had a little mix-up with the two of us. He gave me the warrior vision and you the shaman vision, and we're stuck walking these paths."

"Not always," she replies, threading an arm around his waist as they start down the long, dark hall. "Not always."

They are met by a shadowed figure who steps out of his room and stands before them.

"Hey, Houston," Koda whispers, giving his thick chest a poke. At sixteen, he stands on the cusp of manhood, and is already showing the stamp of the handsome, rugged man he will shortly become.

"*Hau,* Koda. *Hau* Tacoma."

"You remember what I told you, right? If you get even the faintest whiff of trouble, you SOS Ellsworth and there'll be a squadron of Tomcats here so fast you won't be able to sneeze."

"Yeah, I remember. I'll keep an eye out, don't worry."

"All right, then."

"So...I guess this is it, huh? Do you..." He falters for a moment, then regains himself. "Will you come back?"

Reaching out, she places a hand on her younger brother's shoulder, squeezes it. "I will. When this is over, I will. I promise."

Nodding, he swallows hard, fighting tears they all know are a hairsbreadth from falling. "We'll all hold you to that, you know. Both of you."

"We'll be back, little bro," Tacoma remarks, slapping Houston's side. "Count on it."

With a final nod, he steps aside, then joins them as they continue their walk down the hallway.

They enter the brightly lit kitchen, then stop in surprise. Themunga stands with her back to them, stuffing the last of some frybread wrapped in waxed paper into a large cloth sack. Dusting her hands on the apron she wears, she turns to her children. Her eyes are circled by sooty smudges, betraying a lack of sleep, and her face is set like stone. But she shows them none of her previous anger as she lifts the sack from the counter and hands it to Dakota. "Food. For your journey. Eat it before it gets cold."

Dakota takes the sack, looking at her mother. *"Ina, I—"*

"No. No more words. They've all been said. Now go. Both of you."

Handing the sack to Tacoma, Dakota boldly steps forward and wraps her arms tight around Themunga's still, stiff form. "I love you, *Ina*," she whispers into one warm ear. "I will always love you."

After a moment, Themunga softens, returns the hug, then grabs Koda's face and covers it with small kisses. "I love you, *chunksi*. With all my heart." Releasing her daughter, she steps back. "Be safe. Come home."

"I will." It is as solemn a vow as she knows how to give. Without bothering to wipe the tears from her eyes, she turns, grabs the sack from Tacoma's limp hand, and leaves.

Five minutes later, Tacoma joins her in the truck, tears of his own rolling slowly down his cheeks. Their father stands outside of the driver's window, bending down to look inside. "Safe journeys to you both. Fight with honor, and come home to us."

"We will, *Até*," Tacoma replies.

With a nod, Wanbli Wakpa steps away. Koda starts the truck, and pulls out of the long drive, straining to see through tear-trebled vision. "Let's get outta here."

**Kirsten's fingers dance** lightly over the keyboard, calling up string after string of data, highlighting, selecting, discarding. She has spent sixteen hours a day at it since she signed herself out of the base hospital "against the advice of the attending physician" as the CYA-Against-Torts form so politely phrased it. *Sixteen hours a day of searching — no*, she amends, *excavating — this damned alphanumeric midden of junk code, and I have found not one damned thing to give me a clue to shutting down these damned, motherfucking droids.* The gentle Methodist minister of her childhood had taught, counter to orthodoxy, that the infinite love of God precluded the existence of Hell. Kirsten was one ahead of him there, believing for most of her life that the hellish existence of a large percentage of the globe's population precluded both the reality and the mercy of God in any measure. *Which was a shame*, she thinks, *because at this moment I would cheerfully spend eternity in the cosmic barbecue pit for the privilege of spitting and roasting the military idiot who ordered the strike on Minot.* With a small sound of disgust, Kirsten saves the mile-long strip of useless code, pops the disc and inserts another. Just in case there's something there that may prove useful later.

*Fat chance of that. Twice nothing is still bloody damn nothing.*

From his place under the table, Asi whines, lifting his head to peer at her as she bends over her work at the kitchen table. Absently she reaches down to scratch his ears, and, satisfied that she is well, he subsides again into his sleep.

Even with Asi within arm's reach, the house seems strangely empty. *And that*, Kirsten reflects, *is strange in itself.* She has always preferred her own company and that of her dog. Asimov now, Flandry before him, Altair earlier still.

Kirsten has been made at home in what was originally the second bedroom of the house, more recently Colonel Allen's music-cum-tv room-cum library. The colonel herself is presently out on one of the reconnaissance missions that have become more and more frequent in the last few days. Even though the base housing is comfortably away from the flight line, the takeoff noise of a supersonic fighter jet is hard to miss, and she has noted the increasing number of flights and landings, especially at night. The Lakota woman — *Dakota*, some deep part of her reminds, *she asked you to call her Dakota, remember?* — has also gone missing, haring off to see her family, according to the colonel. Dutifully, Kirsten tries to be glad that someone still has a family to go home to. Still the abrupt departure does feel oddly like a slight.

*And if that isn't the silliest thought you've had in six months*, she scolds herself. *You don't really miss either of them. It's just a matter of having gotten used to having another human or two about. Any human. Habit, that's all.* And if she keeps telling herself that enough times, maybe she'll actually start believing it.

"And won't that be a joy for all mankind?" She snorts softly. "God, Kirsten. You're pathetic. Did anyone ever tell you that? Just pathetic." With a shake of her head, she returns her attention to the scrolling alphanumerics on her screen. *Nothing. Nothing. More nothing.*

Abruptly she pushes her chair away from the table, crosses the room to the coffee maker and sets a fresh pot to brew. The tile floor is cool under her booted and double-socked feet, despite the central heating. As the coffee maker gurgles and hisses, she leans her back against the edge of the counter and scrubs at her eyes with both hands. Even with her glasses, the endless strings of numbers are starting to blur and run together on the screen as well as in her mind.

*There has to be some other way to do this besides just going through the columns of numbers and letters.* It is not just that visual searches could run on into the next Ice Age at the rate she's going, it's that she might actually find, and miss, what she's looking for in her state of fatigue. If this were *Star Trek* or *Time Enough for Love* or any other of her childhood favorites, she would simply ask the computer to find the shutdown code, and the computer would produce it. *Given that that's not going to happen here, let's try going at it from the other end. Weed out everything that's not a vital command.*

Cup in hand, she sets to work again, sorting out anything that does not fit the parameters of a basic command. It is not quite as simple as it sounds, and she spends the next hour selecting and downloading material that may be useful at some point but is little more than digital garbage now.

Two hours later, she is left with half a dozen files. Of those half dozen, three are passworded, and one is passworded and encrypted.

*Yes!* She waggles her aching fingers at the screen. *Think you're a match for the Orange County Hacker, do you? Prepare to meet your doom!*

*Orange County Hacker? Doom? Christ,* she thinks, *I am terminally punch drunk.*

The passwords are moderately difficult to break, but she has them within half an hour. The encryption key takes longer, but by the time the sun has slipped halfway down the afternoon sky, she has it, too. She hits the "Apply" button and holds her breath.

The commands scroll down the screen, endless columns of alphanumerics. Somewhere in them, if she is lucky — if the whole human race is lucky — is the code that will shut down the droids and allow the survivors to return the world to something close to normal. It will never be what it was; she knows that. The simple fact that women now outnumber men by perhaps a hundred to one or even more — maybe a thousand to one — will change the way the world goes about its business. Power will be defined differently, used differently. With her heart in her throat, Kirsten retrieves the saved code that shut down the prisoner droid and nearly killed her. She clicks on "Find similar" and waits, her forehead pressed against her clenched hands.

*Please God, any god, all gods, whatever. Let this work.*

When she looks up at the screen again, there is a match. Her hands shaking, she watches the symbols stream across the screen, matching her search criterion letter for letter, digit for digit. Then they begin to change: a related command, but different. *Yes. Yes!*

A small, cautious voice in the back of her mind warns her that this may not be what she is searching for, but she refuses to believe it. The information flows steadily, varying from the prototype command here, identical there. Abruptly it stops.

Kirsten runs the match again, and again the code plays out before reaching the end of the command. Incomplete. Kirsten runs it a third time. Still incomplete. A fourth time. Nothing is different. She has part of the code, no more. She lowers her forehead to her clenched hands again, and silent, bitter tears slip down her cheeks.

After a time, she raises her eyes and turns off the computer. If she does not have the complete code, she has at least a part of it and can perhaps build on that when her mind is rested. She is realist enough to know that she can accomplish nothing of worth in her present state of exhaustion. Rising, she takes her jacket from the row of hooks by the back door and whistles Asi to her side. He all but knocks her down, jostling her against the door frame, as he bounds out into the carport and down the snow-powdered street, turning to wait for her half a block away, tongue lolling, breath clouding in the frosty air.

Angry at her failure and at herself, refusing to think, Kirsten allows Asimov to choose their itinerary. He leads her through the half-derelict housing section, where vehicles that have not moved since the day of the uprising remain shrouded in snow and abandoned homes stand open to the elements. There has been no time to set them to rights or to reclaim what might be salvaged. No time, and no people. Those that are left have more immediate concerns.

At the end of a cul-de-sac, Asi veers away from the residential area into a strip of woodland growing on the banks of a long, narrow pond. The water, frozen now, gleams in the low sun with swirls of gold and crimson. *Fire*, Kirsten thinks. *Fire in the lake.*

Sudden overthrow. Revolution. As omens go, it is a bit belated. And no damned use in any case.

Asimov dances ahead of her, running a short distance, turning, barking, running again. Glad to be free of the confines of the house, clearly wanting to play. Too well trained to ignore him, Kirsten picks up a fallen limb a yard long and breaks it over her knee into shorter segments. "Asi!" she calls. "Fetch!"

She pitches the stick ahead of them some fifteen feet, and Asi bounds through the snow after it, for all the world as if it mattered to him. He returns, grinning around the piece of branch, and drops it at her feet, looking up at her expectantly. She picks it up again and feigns a throw. He wheels to run but stops in his tracks when she fails to release the stick, looking back at her reproachfully. Twice more she aborts her throw, then sends the improvised toy spinning ahead through the bare trees. Asi follows like a shot, sailing over the small rise, that may be only a drift or may be a massive tree root under the snow, and racing down the long line of naked sycamores that marks the edge of the water in warmer seasons. Kirsten slogs after him, clambering over the hump that does indeed feel like ancient, twisted wood beneath her feet. It is knobbed and knotted with age, and it takes all her attention to keep her balance as she climbs cautiously up and over to the other side, stumbling slightly when her foot catches on a protrusion near the ground. She flings out her arms to balance herself, fails, and sprawls in the snow. It is only when she is on her feet again and brushing herself off again that she realizes that Asi is nowhere to be seen.

"Asi! Asimov! Come!"

No answer.

"Asi! Come! Now!" Her voice rises and breaks with something near panic.

Still no Asimov, but from some yards ahead and to her left, she hears a high-pitched, plaintive whine. Following his prints, she trails him to the trunk of a huge tree whose bare branches extend almost halfway across the narrow inlet of the pond, where a feeder stream flows into it. He sits beneath the sycamore , staring upward, his tail brushing a half-circle in the loose powder that covers the frozen water. He whines again, this time almost pleadingly.

Twenty feet up, a raccoon sits in the fork of a branch. It is an older male, perhaps a third of Asimov's size and weight, his fur fluffed about him for warmth. He nibbles delicately at an acorn, holding it with both long-fingered paws as he turns it around and around before his narrow muzzle. He pauses as Kirsten arrives, regarding her with eyes like molten gold from behind his black mask.

Unbidden, images tumble through her mind. A naked woman painted in blue spirals and sunbursts, brandishing a spear and a shield of polished bronze. Another woman, her face printed with the years and with wisdom, enveloped in a billow of vermilion silk like flame. A raised hand of not quite human form, and a voice on the churning wind. *Turn back. The time is not yet.* Then they are gone, and she is standing under a tree with a disappointed dog and a raccoon who stares disdainfully down at them both, calmly eating his dinner.

Kirsten whistles, and this time Asimov obeys. They trudge back to the house through the gathering dark, as the eastern sky deepens to ultramarine and a flush of scarlet and purple still colors the west. The cold deepens as the sun slips finally beneath the horizon and the first stars appear. As Kirsten makes the final turn into Maggie's street, Asimov breaks from her side and goes pelting down the block, baying like the hound of the Baskervilles.

A long-bedded, heavy blue truck is pulled up in the driveway, a blue truck with the insignia of the veterinarian's V and caduceus just visible in the failing light. *Koda is back.*

Without conscious direction, Kirsten's feet carry her forward at a pace just short of a jog. Her heart picks up its rhythm to match, her mouth suddenly dry. She watches as Koda slides out of the driver's side of the pickup and is joined by a second figure, taller and broader shouldered, but with much the same erect carriage and proud tilt of the head. With a deliberate effort, Kirsten slows her pace and joins the two new arrivals just as Koda unlocks the kitchen door. Under the carport light, Kirsten can see the striking likeness of their features, and a small, unacknowledged fear shrinks in upon itself and dies.

"Hi," she says, as Koda turns to her with a smile. "Welcome back."

"Well, look who the dog dragged in," Koda teases gently, returning the smile as she reaches down to give Asi's ears a good scratch. Asimov all but turns into jelly, and for the first time, Kirsten finds herself not minding so much that her dog has obviously fallen head over heels in love with this woman.

To Asi's dismay, Koda all too soon retires her hand from scratching duty and lifts it to the doorknob instead. "Let's get in out of the cold, shall we?"

A blast of warmth and light hits them all as the door swings open and the group steps inside. Asi immediately claims his place in front of the fireplace and begins to attack the large soupbone Maggie had left for him earlier. With a sigh of satisfaction, Koda places her heavy pack on the kitchen table and gestures for her brother to do the same. Then she turns her smile back to the young scientist. "Doctor King, this is my brother, Tacoma. Tacoma, this is Doctor Kirsten King."

With a grin so identical to his sister's that they could be — and should be — twins, Tacoma holds out a massive hand that gently engulfs Kirsten's much smaller one. "A pleasure to meet you, ma'am."

Kirsten utters a sardonic chuckle. "I'd like to think I'm a little young for the 'ma'am' stage, Mr. Rivers, but it's a pleasure to meet you, as well."

"Tell you what. You call me Tacoma, and I'll drop the ma'am, all right, ma'am?"

Charmed, Kirsten's grin flashes just briefly as she releases Tacoma's hand. "It's a deal...Tacoma."

With a respectful incline of his head, Tacoma takes a short step back and looks around. "Nice digs."

"Colonel's quarters." Koda's succinct response tells it all. "And don't get too used to them. You'll be bunking with Manny."

"Figures," Tacoma replies, smirking. "The regs say that canon fodder like me isn't adapted to the rarified air of this place." The twinkle in his deep, black eyes lets Kirsten know the joke is old and well loved.

Rummaging through the litter on the table, Koda pulls the food sack her mother had given her. "Let me just split this stuff up."

Tacoma holds up a hand. "No, it's all right, *tanski*. I'm gonna have to get re-used to military chow sooner or later. For the sake of my belly, it's just as well that it be sooner. You keep it."

Unheeding, she pulls out two thick slices of frybread wrapped in waxed paper, a packet of meat filling, and hands both over to her brother. "Give one of them to Manny. I'm sure he'll appreciate it."

"Appreciate it?" Tacoma exclaims, grinning. "He'll just about have an..." His face turning an even deeper reddish hue, he nearly bites his tongue and gives Kirsten a positively hangdog look. "Um...sorry, ma'am."

Frozen to the spot, Kirsten shoots her gaze from Tacoma's mortified look to Dakota. The mirth swimming in those striking eyes almost causes her to lose it, and she bites down on the inside of her cheeks hard enough to draw blood just to keep herself from braying laughter like some demented donkey. The slight pain clears her head, and she manages what she hopes passes for a dignified nod. "It's quite all right, Tacoma. If that food tastes as good as it looks, I can understand the reaction."

Tacoma's sense of relief is almost palpable as he humbly receives his sister's food offering and stuffs it into his military pack.

Unable to help herself, Dakota laughs, grabs her brother's arm and, with the barest ghost of a wink to the onlooking Kirsten, drags Tacoma out of the house and into the dark of the South Dakota night.

**An hour or** so later, Koda slips quietly into the house. The interior is perfectly dark, save for the sliver of light that slices through the partially opened door to the room Kirsten is using as her office. Silent as a shadow, Koda tracks the light and peers into the office. Kirsten sits at the desk, her head propped up on one closed fist. Her glasses reflect the light from her computer, a light that washes over her face with the greenish pallor of a seasickness victim.

As if sensing Dakota's presence, Kirsten blinks, then slowly turns her head away from the scrolling lines of formula painting themselves across the display before her.

Her welcoming smile is wan and, drawn by that, Koda crosses the threshold and into the room, coming to stand beside the desk. "Hey."

"Hey. Did you get your brother settled in?"

Dakota smirks. "Oh yeah, he's settled in all right. When I left, he was busy regaling them with a bunch of 'flyboy' jokes he learned in the Army."

Kirsten winces.

"Nah. He served with a bunch of them in the wars. It's like old home week there right about now."

"He's a nice man."

"Tacoma? He's all right."

Dakota's smile is fond, and it warms something deep inside Kirsten upon seeing it. "Is he your only sibling?"

"If only," Dakota replies, laughing softly. "No, I'm one of ten. Tacoma's the oldest. I'm third in line. I also have an older sister, Virginia."

"Tacoma, Virginia, Dakota..."

"...Washington, Houston, Phoenix, Montana, Carolina, Dallas, and Orlando. My mother's a geography nut."

"You don't say."

Kirsten's tone is as dry as dust, but her eyes twinkle in a way that Dakota finds quite attractive. "Oh, I do. Very much so." There is a brief pause. "What about you? Any brothers or sisters?" A veil drops over Kirsten's eyes, leaching out the vibrant green and leaving a muddy brown behind, and Koda holds up a hand, even as she takes a step back, fully intending to end the conversation. "No, it's all right. I'll...see you tomorrow. Good night."

"I was an only child," Kirsten spits out rapidly, her words as staccato as machine gun fire. She looks on, feeling what can only be relief as Dakota stops her retreat and levels her an unreadable but not unfriendly look. "They wanted a big family, but my father had a run-in with an Iraqi landmine and, well..."

"Damn," Koda softly replies.

"Yeah. He was in the hospital for a while, but things were basically okay after that. I was pretty much spoiled rotten." She gives up a wry smile. "As if you didn't know that already."

Koda manages, by the skin of her teeth, to remain silent and stone-faced.

Kirsten flushes a little and turns away. The soft, low timbre of Dakota's voice draws her back.

"You're gonna be all right." The expression on Kirsten's face gives Koda a glimpse of the young woman's childhood more clearly than any photograph ever could. The naked, aching need for acceptance and reassurance pulls her in like a fish on a line. Her feet pad noiselessly across the floor, and the shoulder suddenly beneath her hand seems as fragile and complex as a bird's broken wing.

At the touch, Kirsten breathes in a soft hiss of air between clenched teeth. The gentle grip burns like a brand, soothes like a balm, engendering a paradox of calm and disquiet.

*But it's not disquiet you're feeling, is it?*

*Shut up.*

*It's time to buck it up and call a spade a spade, little K.*

*Shut. Up.*

*You can't live this new life you're trying to forge for yourself with your head buried in the sand, Kirsten. Examine your feelings. Face up to them. And then maybe you'll actually start living instead of just existing. Think about it.*

The voice fades into nothingness, and Kirsten only realizes her eyes have closed once she opens them. Koda is looking down at her, an odd mix of concern and compassion on her arresting features. Kirsten manages to conjure up a bit of a smile, which Koda returns, as if it is the most natural thing in the world.

*Examine your feelings. Face up to them.*

The voice is pushed away by the sound of her own. "Thank you."

Dakota's eyebrows lift. "For?"

Kirsten lifts one shoulder in a half-shrug. "Being here, I guess. I sometimes forget what it's like to have a normal conversation with another human being. Asi is my life, but...he doesn't do the talking thing real well."

Laughing, Koda releases Kirsten's shoulder and steps back, providing some needed distance between them. "Give him a little time. You might be surprised at what he has to say."

Kirsten shoots her an odd look. "If you say so."

"I say so," Koda returns, grinning. And again, the barest ghost of a wink. "See you tomorrow. Sleep well."

"I'll definitely try. You too."

"Thanks. Night."

Once the door is closed again, and Kirsten is alone, she pulls out the feeling of Dakota's simple touch, wrapping it around her like a warm winter coat. Her eyes slip closed again, and she crosses the boundary between wakefulness and sleep without ever being aware of the change.

**In her dream,** Koda wanders the Paha Sapa, the Black Hills sacred to her people from the time before time. Its cliffs rise up about her like shadow solidified in stone, their ramparts folded and refolded along the rockface, ledges jutting out at odd angles. Some of those folds mark caves that lead back into the heart of the Earth, some shelter springs no deeper than a sheen of sweat on a summer day, others, wells whose depths reach down beyond measure. It is the place where the Lakota came forth from the womb of Ina Maka herself, ascending into the light of the Sun for the first time as a human species and a nation. She goes here in a form older yet, one that pads without sound on four feet over the sharply ridged basalt that forms the canyon floor. To her left a bobcat moves like silk over the fissured volcanic rock, her wide paws scarcely touching the surface. The cat's ears and vibrissae stand stiffly forward, interrogating the night air for sign of prey or menace. On her right paces a cougar, gold-silver in the moonlight, the depths of his eyes spangled with reflected stars.

A fourth goes with them, a smaller being with nimble, clever hands and the black half-mask of a bandit. The cats she knows. Even in her dream, Koda is aware of the bobcat's human form lying warm beside her under the down comforter. The mountain lion, lean muscles rippling like river water under his fur, is the spirit of her warrior brother, Tacoma. As she puzzles over the fourth, scudding clouds blot out the moon and stars, and thunder rolls down, echoing from cliff to promontory and back like the pounding of the great drum of the Sun Dance. She and the other creatures who accompany her scramble for higher ground, leaping now from ledge to ledge, the unknown fourth keeping pace with the rest. Lightning splits the sky above, and thunder crashes about them again and again until the whole world shakes with it. It splits the shelf where the four have taken refuge, sending it plummeting away from the rockface and them with it, and they are falling, falling into the night, into the unformed world from which they came forth at Ina Maka's summoning, plunging headlong down and down...

"What the hell?"

Somehow the words penetrate the cacophony of thunder and falling rock. Koda is vaguely aware of Maggie as she rolls over and reaches across her for the switch of the bedside lamp.

"Sorry," she adds as the too-bright light stabs at Koda's eyes and she sits up, half-caught still in her dream.

"What—?"

"Somebody at the door." Maggie slips from beneath the comforter and into the robe she has left folded over the back of a chair. From the bedside table she takes her pilot's sidearm and slides a round into the chamber with a metallic chunk. "Be right back."

Koda reaches for her own shirt as Maggie closes the door softly behind her. Her mind snaps sharply back into the present as she pads barefoot after the other woman. Pounding on the door at 4:30 in the morning can mean nothing but trouble. A blast of chill air from the open door raises goosebumps on her bare legs as she steps into the entryway. Directly across the hall from her, Asimov stands at guard in the living room door, tail erect. Kirsten holds his ruff with one hand and her .45 in the other. Despite the shadows about her eyes, her gaze is as sharp and brittle as obsidian.

Koda flashes her a grin, an acknowledgement of one member of the hunting pack to another. Kirsten bares her teeth slightly in return just as Maggie draws the visitor on the doorstep into the foyer and shuts the door behind him. Bundled to the eyes and further masked by the cloud of his own breath, he snaps a salute at Maggie, then, looking past her shoulder, another at Koda and Kirsten. Maggie smiles as she turns to find her unexpected backup behind her. "Go on, Corporal," she says evenly. "Dr. Rivers and Dr. King have a stake in this, too."

"Yes'm," he says, averting his eyes carefully from Koda's bare legs and Kirsten's neat figure, which is covered but is not hidden by her form-fitting thermals. He appears to be addressing the hall tree with its array of hats and jackets. "The general's compliments, ma'am. There will be a meeting of all staff and senior officers at Wing Headquarters at oh-five-hundred. A number of small forces appear to be moving north from Peterson at Colorado Springs and from the Space Wing at Warren. Threat assessment and response to be discussed." The trooper salutes yet again. "Ma'am."

"Thank you, Corporal. My compliments to the general, and I'm on my way."

Maggie shuts the door behind the courier and turns to Koda and Kirsten with a smile. "Thanks for the backup." Her eyes become suddenly solemn. "This is the way it's going to be from now on, you know," she says softly. "Every unknown person will represent a possible danger. Everything unexplained will be potentially lethal until it is either explained or neutralized." The colonel's gaze shifts to Kirsten. "Women will hold most of the positions of authority in whatever society we have left. We will occupy most of the professions that survive. We will do most of the fighting until the droids are contained. After that happens, we'll still do most of the fighting — against other women, most likely, and the nation building. The rest of our lives will look a whole lot like tonight."

A tight smile pulls at Kirsten's mouth, but there is no irony in her voice. "Forward...into the past."

"Back to the beginning," Koda murmurs. And her dream is with her again, the landscape of first creation before humans grew away from Ina Maka and her other children, and power belonged to her and her daughters only. With the eyes of vision Koda watches as Kirsten fades, to be replaced by a woman in a brief leather skirt and halter and a towering mask with a bird's face and a mane of grass and feathers. When she tears her eyes away, Maggie is gone, too, her form melted into the shape of a woman with golden skin with knives glittering in either hand. Between one breath and the next the images vanish, and she is standing in the hallway with two other half-clothed women, cold and in need of coffee. "I'll make breakfast," she says, and follows Maggie back to the bedroom to dress.

Fifteen minutes later, Maggie pulls out of the drive with an insulated mug of coffee and a slice of Themunga's fry bread wrapped around a scrambled egg. Koda can hear water splashing in the bathroom a couple yards down the small cross-hall that connects the entrance to the back of the house as Kirsten showers, and a hint of Maggie's lavender-scented soap mingles with the aromas of dark-roasted Columbian coffee and melting butter. Koda sets out more of Themunga's frybread, together with the fresh milk and eggs her mother has sent with her. The eggs are brown, and while Koda's scientific mind knows very well that their shells merely reflect the color of the hens who laid them, she cannot quite shed her mother's utter conviction that they are somehow tastier and more nutritious than the white variety. A psychologist might put that down to her mother's feelings about race, she muses, but she knows too many white farmers and ranchers who are equally convinced. *Face it*, she tells herself as she sets to chopping sweet onion and tomato, *they are better, and there's no particular reason why.*

As Kirsten pulls on her boots and sweater, the rich aroma of sautééd onion and tomato wafts into her room and mingles in an odd harmony with the herbal soap whose fragrance lingers on her skin. It reminds her, a little, of weekend forays across the border into Tijuana and the exotic prizes waiting in the open air markets for a ten-year-old child with too little companionship and perhaps too much imagination. It reminds her, too, of Twenty-Nine Palms and Los Jacales, the tiny but imcomparable Mexican restaurant just outside the base where she and her parents had breakfast every Sunday. The memory is a small pang in her heart, almost physical, sharper than the ache left by the defibrillators and the bruises that linger on her chest. Carefully she removes a small woven straw box from the pants she wore the previous day and transfers it to her pocket. Guatemalan worry dolls, nearly twenty years old now, bought for her one bright summer day by her father. She still remembers the names she gave each of them, the stories she built about each bright, thread-wrapped figure.

They are one of her few remaining material links to the past. Oddly, they seem now as much a talisman of the future as a relic of her childhood. The indigenous peoples they represent, the traditional societies, have the best chance of survival now. As she opens her door and steps into the hall, it comes to her that somehow in the last few days the past has loosened its hold on her. Or she on it; she is not quite sure which it is. For the first time since her flight from Washington, the future has a habitation and a name. It is not just that the Earth has not, despite the horror, ground to a halt in its orbit. Somewhere in the depths of her mind is the recognition that, against all odds, she may somehow live to see the birth of a new and very different world. *And that may not be a bad thing. Not a bad thing at all.*

She has Asi, whose return she would call miraculous if she were inclined to believe in miracles. And she has — no, not friends exactly — colleagues and companions who share her purpose. "Morning," she says to one of them as she steps into the kitchen. The window over the sink frames a square of black sky, and she winces. "Middle of the night. Whatever."

Dakota turns her attention briefly from the stove to smile at her. "Morning. Breakfast's almost ready." She nods at the table, where a cup of coffee already steams on one of the two placemats. "Have a seat."

Kirsten shovels sugar into her cup, together with a generous dollop of cream. The adrenaline rush of an hour ago is gone, and she can feel reaction beginning to set in, her blood sugar starting to slide. The caffeine and glucose hit her system like a thunderbolt, finishing the job the hot water has begun. From underneath her lashes, she watches the other woman as she prepares their meal, moving around the room with the abrupt, angular grace of one of the great predators — a cheetah, perhaps, or a wolf. She wears the same plaid flannel shirt she had on earlier, but now it is tucked neatly into the waistband of the jeans that do little to conceal the taut elegance of her legs. Her hair, which had flowed over her shoulders like a river at midnight, is now caught back with a rubber band. It still sets off the sharp planes of her cheekbones and forehead, the generous lines of her mouth, the inexplicable blue eyes.

Kirsten feels heat rising in her cheeks that has nothing to do with the coffee or its effects. She feels suddenly disoriented, as if the room has suddenly turned itself upside down to leave her hanging weightless from the ceiling. To cover her confusion, she asks, "What do you think is going on?"

Dakota — Koda — gives the thickening eggs a stir and slaps two rounds of frybread down on the stove's surface to heat. "The droids have to take us out if they can. There's too much still functional. We've raided them successfully," with a swift movement of her bare fingers, she turns both pieces of bread, "and that makes us too big a threat for them to leave alone."

"So those small groups the corporal was talking about are likely to join up and attack the base again?"

"If we sit still for them." Koda dishes up the eggs onto the frybread, rolls them up and drops them onto warmed plates. "My guess is, we won't."

"At least the number of the military models is limited. That's some small comfort."

"Not enough to make up for bombing the factory, though." Koda sets down the plates and takes a seat. Her eyes meet Kirsten's across the table. "If not for that—"

"I'd have more than the partial code. It might all be over." Kirsten holds that intense blue gaze, unwilling to be less than honest. "Look, I come from a military family. You don't have to explain the brass's fuck-ups to me. It's par for the course."

Koda nods. "Tacoma has some stories that would curl your hair. Insufficient ammunition, garbled orders."

Kirsten reaches for a fork, then stops as Dakota picks up her roll taco-style and bites into it. Following suit, she reaches for a napkin as butter runs down her chin. "Good," she says. "You're a good cook."

"Not especially. I grew up helping my mother get meals for a large family. Lots of practice, is all."

From underneath the table, Asi whines, and Kirsten pinches a bit off the end of her roll. Koda does the same, dropping the bite into his bowl. It disappears in less than a nanosecond. Dakota grins. "Spoiled."

"Rotten," Kirsten agrees, breaking off a second morsel. It vanishes from her fingers in even less time. "You going to the clinic again today?"

"For the morning, anyway. You?"

"Work on the code 'til it drives me nuts. Take Asi for a walk 'til I can think straight again."

"Anything I can get you that would help? Discs, a printer?"

Kirsten shakes her head and pushes her chair away from the table. "I had a good supply in my truck." As she rises, an odd thought strikes her, and she asks, "Animals mean something in your traditions, don't they? Symbolically, that is."

The Lakota woman's withdrawal is both instant and almost imperceptible. *There was a time*, Kirsten thinks, *when I wouldn't have noticed that*. "I don't mean to be disrespectful. Asi found a raccoon yesterday, and I just thought it was odd. Don't they hibernate?"

"No, not exactly. They sleep a lot, living off their fat. They come out of their dens to feed periodically, though."

"So it doesn't necessarily mean the cold is going to let up some?" Shift the context. For some reason it is important to her not to offend this woman. "I've never seen so damned much snow in my life."

"No, I'm afraid not."

"Too bad." Kirsten shrugs and moves toward the door. Koda's voice stops her where she stands.

"It means disguise, Kirsten, and the need to let go of old identities. It means transformation."

And it is with her again, that long spiraling plunge toward death and the deep baying of the hunter who runs lithe beside her, a glimpse of driving muscles rippling under black fur that turns in upon itself, moebius-like, to become a small pointed face with eyes burning like molten gold out of a black mask. The narrow muzzle opens, and the creature speaks in a voice to silence thunder, one long-fingered hand raised to bar her passage. *Go back. The time is not yet.*

Kirsten's heart pounds in her chest like a trip hammer; sweat prickles along her skin. *The time is not yet.* "Thank you," she says, and flees. Again.

# CHAPTER THIRTEEN

The room is as grey as a November day. Grey walls, set off by a tasteful strip of white PVC running along the bottom in lieu of baseboard. Grey carpet, with tone-on-tone USAF logos imposed on diagonally offset laurel wreaths. Grey curtains, likewise. On the wall hang photographs of warplanes based at Ellsworth, the intensely turquoise skies behind and below the airborne Tomcats and SuperHornets virtually the only color in the room. On a table in one corner sits an unwatered Norfolk pine, its pot wrapped in peeling red-black foil and its wilting branches hung with miniature lights and iridescent glass globes, dull in the dim light that penetrates the heavily lined window coverings. The long conference table is grey steel; its vinyl-upholstered chairs match. Koda has, she thinks wryly, seen cheerier coffins.

Maggie says it for her. "Somebody get me a happy pill. This place would depress goddam Shirley Temple."

"Never mind goddam Shirley Temple. It depresses me." Tacoma gives a half-suppressed snort, not unlike a big cat's disdainful whuffle. "Droids get the psych-ops staff?"

Maggie shakes her head. "Hart got rid of the decorators, years ago. Too touchy-feely."

"It could be worse," Koda offers. "It could be pecan laminate and stuffed deers' heads."

Tacoma winces visibly as he shrugs out of his jacket and drapes it across the back of a chair about halfway down the table. He has resumed his Army uniform, the brass of his greens newly shined, his campaign ribbons proud in their many colors over his left pocket. Koda knows them as well as he does: the Afghan Meritorious Service Ribbon, bright green with its silver crescent; the Kingdom of Jordan Honor Legion; the Medal for Humane Action; Combat Action Ribbon; Bronze and Silver Stars, both with oak leaf. And there is the one she hates, purple with white edges. Wounded in action, gone missing in the frozen mountains of the Panjir for two weeks and more when no one, not his commander, not his family, knew whether he was alive or dead, and neither she nor her father, for all their special skills, had been able to find him in the spirit world. Her eyes meet Tacoma's as she seats herself across from his place, numbering his honors. Their father, veteran of VietNam, calls the tunic with the array of medals her brother's scalp shirt, boasting that it is even more lavish than his own.

"Hey," Tacoma says softly, reaching over the space between to touch her arm, calling her back to the present.

"Hey yourself. You didn't cut your hair."

"Not going to." He grins suddenly at Maggie, now seated beside him. "You able to live with that, Colonel?"

Maggie, in her own spruce blues and even more fruit salad, grins back at him. "We'll average it. You've got enough for Manny, yourself and me put together. Hart's not going to like it, though."

"Somebody mention my name?" Manny appears in the doorway, accompanied by two other men. One is in Marine uniform, the other in flannel shirt and jeans. Manny pulls out the chair next to Koda and glances around the room. "No coffee?"

"It's on its way," offers a newcomer, a blond youngster in fatigues whose sleeves carry airman's stripes. "What's up, Lieutenant?"

Manny shrugs and glances at Allen. "Colonel?"

"Something to do with recon, as I understand it."

The airman is followed by another man in civilian clothes, then by two women with wind-weathered faces. Koda sweeps the company with her eyes, not recognizing individuals but acknowledging the indelible signs of a life lived between earth and open sky. She says, "Everyone here is local, right?"

Nods answer her, responding to more than the single question. Local, and familiar with the countryside.

"Scouts," Koda says. "Ground reconnaissance."

"You've stolen my thunder, Dr. Rivers." Hart stands in the doorway, waving his officers back to their seats as they push their chairs back to stand and salute. "We do need people who know the area to become involved in recon. I'll be briefing all of you, then asking for volunteers." He moves to the head of the table, spine stiffly erect, allowing the carts bearing coffee and a projector-cum-laptop to follow him into the room. He motions toward the urn and stack of cups. "Please, help yourselves. We've even managed to requisition some doughnuts."

*Must be his own private stash of Krispy Kremes*, Koda observes wryly to herself as she fills her cup. She catches Tacoma's eye as he does the same and feels the thought pass easily between them. He winks at her, snagging a cinnamon cruller for himself and dropping another onto her plate. *Wants us bad.*

When the table has settled, Hart begins. "As you know, we have been fortunate at Ellsworth in that we have been able to repel the initial attacks of the mutinous androids, both military and civilian. We have, of course, suffered extensive casualties, but many of our officer corps have survived and we are still operational. At a reduced level, of course.

"We have also had the benefit of intelligence and reinforcements from the civilian population of the surrounding area." Hart pauses to smile at Koda and to single out the other ranchers with a nod. When he comes to Tacoma, the smile freezes for a moment, then becomes deliberately brighter.

Koda feels a light tap against her boot and looks up at Tacoma's suspiciously expressionless face. *Counting coup.*

"Lights, please." When the room is dark, the general switches on the projector and fiddles briefly with the focus. The images that gradually form against the wall are night-sight green, but fairly clear for all that:

Troop transport trucks, moving along narrow roads, no more than three or four in a convoy.

Columns of the inhuman soldier androids, churning along cleared highway surfaces on their caterpillar tracks, slowly but inexorably, never breaking rank, never tiring.

Armored vehicles, their guns at ready, crunching through the snow.

Small groups of men, platoon-size, no more than a dozen at a time, slipping along back roads and game trails, fully outfitted in helmet, backpack and weapons. Shepherded, invariably, by one or two of the military droids ahead, another pair behind.

Koda hears a small hiss of indrawn breath at the last sequence. Across the table from her, Maggie's face is drawn into a tight mask of anger and disgust. Closer to, Manny's fists clench against the table. The civilian woman two places down, her skin reddened from years of High Plains wind, her face hard as the bones of the land itself, looks nauseated in the flickering green light. Koda's own stomach turns over.

"Indeed," says General Hart as he switches off the projector, and the room lights come back up. "We have not only droids on the move, but we have human collaborators as well. This is something Colonel Allen and Dr. Rivers have encountered, but not quite in this capacity or in these numbers." He flicks another switch and a map of South Dakota, with Wyoming and Colorado to the south, appears on the wall. "These videos were taken by Colonel Allen and her squadron over the last several days. They show a disturbingly large number of small companies moving toward our position. They seem to come from Warren Space Wing in Wyoming and Peterson Air Force Base in Colorado. Presumably they will rendezvous at some point and position themselves for a second assault on the base. This is not a favorable development."

"General." Tacoma waits for recognition, and when Hart nods, continues. "We are assuming from these movements that there is no longer any resistance at Warren or Peterson?"

"Or in between?" Koda adds.

"Sergeant, Doctor, I have no reason to believe that is not correct." For a moment, Hart's normally ruddy face is as grey as the light filtering in through the windows. "We have no hope of reinforcement from either of those installations. Nor, I think, of further influx of civilians from the surrounding area. What we have now, is, barring the unexpected, what we will have to face the enemy."

"We're outnumbered," Manny observes.

"And except for air cover, probably outgunned," adds Maggie.

"Correct."

"But not," Tacoma answers, grinning, "outthought."

"Also correct, Sergeant." Hart's smile is a bit less stiff this time. "Every one of you in this room has immediate and intimate knowledge of the area surrounding Ellsworth. Some of you, like Mr. Marshak," he indicates the gentleman in the flannel shirt, "or Mmes. Tilbury-Laduque," a nod at the women ranchers, "have lived and worked in the region for decades. Some, like Marine Ensign Guell and Airman Mainz, are local residents who have experience camping or hunting in the vicinity. We need you all, assuming you are willing, to act as scouts — to move out into the countryside and track these units, discover as much about their movements, and, if possible, their plans, as you can."

"Why don't you just bomb the hell out of them?" asks one Ms. Tilbury-Laduque. Her thin face is stark with determination under her greying red hair; the question clearly does not come from cowardice. "It seems to me that human resources are what's scarcest here."

"If I may?" Maggie glances at Hart. At the general's nod, she proceeds. "We still have both adequate jet fuel and sufficient munitions to bomb these bastards back to atoms, ma'am. And we'll do that if we have to. But it's the best judgment of this base's senior officers that for the time being we would do best to conserve those resources for civilian defense.

There are a surprising number of survivor enclaves still out there in the countryside who are not equipped to repel, say, an attack by the military model androids. We need to hold the airborne defenses in reserve for them as long as we can."

There is a pause, then the rancher nods. "I see. Okay, I'm with you."

"Me, too," adds the other Ms. Tilbury-Laduque.

As the woman's work-roughened hand closes over her partner's fingers, Koda feels a tug of memory, brief and poignant. It is not so sharp as it would once have been, though, and she lowers her eyes to her own hands where a barely perceptible band of lighter skin remains on the third finger of her left hand.

It has become almost a phantom pain, like nerves still wired to the ghost of a missing limb. She has seen it in one or two of Tacoma's friends who did not come home from battle with all they had left home with, and who could or would not be fitted with cyberlimbs or old-fashioned prostheses. She has seen it, too, in her own surgical patients, cows whose hip muscles twitch, attempting to move a leg no longer there, a fox biting at a gangrenous tail she has been forced to amputate. She glances up at Maggie, intent now on the speaker across the table from her, her handsome features animated by an underlying lust for life so strong that Koda cannot begin to imagine her dampened by injury or illness. *And that*, she tells herself, *is a dangerous thing not to be able to imagine about a battle-companion, much less a battle-companion who is also a friend.*

"I'll do it," says Manny, glancing up at Maggie.

"So will I," adds the colonel. "I'd like to have some of the same troops that have been with me from the onset of the mutiny, General. They may not be strictly local, but they've had experience in skirmish encounters and in liberating civilians. We may run into caches of prisoners along the way, too."

"Anything you need, Colonel." Under his standard issue smile, Hart looks relieved. "This operation is in your hands. What about the rest of you? Are you with Colonel Allen, Sergeant Rivers?"

"Of course." Tacoma grins. "Anyone who can handle Flyboy here," he gestures toward his cousin, "has my utmost respect."

"Doctor?"

Koda nods her assent and watches as the rest repeat the gesture. There is a strange sense of slippage in her mind, as if time has somehow faulted and folded back upon itself. Scouts for the U. S. Army — "friendlies" cooperating in their own ultimate destruction as the Plains grew barren not only of the buffalo but of the human nations who lived with them and by them. She feels her hands clench like Manny's. *Never again. It will be different this time.* With the thought comes the recognition — the unshakable certainty that she has come to recognize as the mark of spiritual knowledge — that the world has changed irrevocably. Whatever she, and Manny with her, and Tacoma, help to bring to birth out of the wreckage of the old order will resemble nothing that has gone before.

Lakota *oyate*.

A Lakota nation, but not only a nation of Lakota. It is the time of the White Buffalo, the return seen, if seen unclearly, by the Paiute holy man Wovoka, the fulfillment of prophecy.

She blinks to clear the thought, and finds Manny looking at her oddly.

The general has resumed his briefing, something about forming small parties and communications problems.

"Koda?" Her cousin's voice is very soft. "You with us?"

"Yeah, I'm fine. Thanks." His face is a question. Tacoma, across the table, is watching her intently. "I'm fine," she repeats. "Later."

Without warning, the door opens. Kirsten stands framed in the opening, Asimov alert beside her. Her face is white with the rage that flares in her eyes, colder than the wailing heart of a blizzard. She says nothing. Sound dies in the room as all eyes at the table turn toward her.

After an awkward moment, Hart breaks the silence. "Dr. King, are you looking for someone? My secretary can direct you. Now, if you'll excuse us?"

Still Kirsten says nothing. Koda can feel the anger as it comes off her in waves, almost palpable in its strength. And with it there is a power she has not felt in the other woman before, something similar to the force she has sensed in Maggie. For a moment she is absurdly relieved that Kirsten is not holding a weapon. There is an authority in her that Koda has never seen before, not even in the moment when she stalked up to Hart and struck him across the face after the bombing of Minot.

*Ithanchan winan.* The thought comes unbidden. *This woman is a chief.*

Koda starts to push her chair back and rise to her feet, but Tacoma is there before her. Straight as a birch tree, he snaps to attention and salutes the woman in the doorway. Eyes on Kirsten, he stands motionless.

Manny follows by a heartbeat, then Allen. "Madame Secretary," the colonel says pointedly.

The Marine and the airman are on their feet next, together with the civilians. Koda's heart rises and lodges somewhere in her throat. Finally Hart does what he must. He moves away from the wall and salutes. "At your service, ma'am."

Kirsten holds them all with her eyes for a moment longer. Then she gives a brief wave of her hand. "At ease."

Hart pulls out his own chair at the head of the table for her, and Kirsten makes her way toward the front of the room. Asi paces with the dignity of a wolf beside her, for once ignoring his new friends. Koda's memory flashes on her first meeting with the big dog in the snowy clearing, his formal pose atop the log suddenly connecting with an image older by thousands of years, the jackal-god stretched out on a mastaba bench before the shrine of Pharaoh. Anubis the Watcher. Guardian of the King.

Quietly Kirsten takes her seat, Asimov still standing at her side. "Thank you, General Hart," she says. "Please begin the briefing."

Koda watches as Tacoma struggles manfully not to grin, gives up and coughs, turning his face away from the defeated general. The sparkle in his eyes is contagious, though, and it spreads up and down the table like February sun on new-melted springwater. The general is visibly relieved when he is able, finally, to order the lights off and run the video again. As it plays a second time, Koda memorizes the terrain: shapes of hills, angles of the moon, bare trees lining a rise against the sky, the course of a freshening stream, contours of barren fields where the dark earth begins to break through the blanket of snow.

When it is over, the colonel reviews the information that cannot be gotten onto film, and Kirsten listens without comment. When Maggie falls silent, she says, "General, is it your estimation that this base is the only regional defense installation still operable in this area?"

"Ma'am, it is." He gestures back toward the map. "If Ellsworth goes under, the droids will not only have access to all our remaining armaments, but will be able to overcome any resistance the surviving civilian population can offer. So far they have no air power, possibly because other installation commanders have disabled their planes; possibly because some, like Colonel Allen and her squadron, were in the air at the time of the mutiny; possibly because some aircraft were destroyed in the fighting. Possibly, too, because they have no human pilots and none of the military droids, that I'm aware of, are programmed to fly. We can't allow those assets to fall into their hands. Nor can we abandon our remaining civilian population."

"I agree." Kirsten glances down the table at volunteers that are suddenly hers, her gaze lingering on Koda for an infinitesimal fraction of a second before moving on. Again there is that small, phantom pain in her heart, coupled with a sense of finality. *It is not just the world that has changed,* she realizes. *It is* my *world, and the change is forever.*

"Colonel."

"Ma'am."

"Organize your scout parties. Put me on one of them."

All hell breaks loose. Koda finds herself wanting to shout with the rest, but clamps her teeth shut on words she knows will be useless.

"Dr. King—"

"Madame Secretary—"

"Ma'am, begging your pardon, but you can't go. You're too valuable to risk." Hart wins out above the clamor. "You're the only one who has any hope at all of shutting these godammed — I beg your pardon, ma'am — these droids down. I can't allow — that is, you can't put yourself in danger."

"It's not for you to allow or not, General." Koda speaks softly but firmly. "Dr. King fought her way — alone — from Washington all the way to Minot to get the shut-down code for the droids. She infiltrated the base there and successfully passed herself off as a droid." She hesitates for a moment, weighing her words, but there is no further virtue in diplomacy. "But for the destruction of Minot, her mission would have succeeded, and we would not presently be facing a second attack."

For the first time since entering the room, Kirsten smiles, a slight lift of the corners of her mouth. It strikes Koda between one breath and the next and almost stops her heart. She can count on one hand — maybe one finger — the times she has seen that expression on the other woman's face.

"Not quite alone." Gently Kirsten ruffles Asi's ears. "Can you understand droid-to-droid transmissions, General?" When he does not answer, she says, "I can. We can't afford for me not to go." There is an uncomfortable silence. "I am going," Kirsten repeats. "Do I make myself clear?"

"Oh, ma'am, you certainly do," Manny says on an outrush of breath that is not quite laughter. "No offense, but God missed the target when you weren't born a Lakota."

**A blast of** static comes through Dakota's earpiece.

"...Tshunka...20...come back?" She taps the earpiece, wincing as it lets off another, louder, blast of static. "Tacoma, is that you?"

"Han...your 20? GPS...fucked...can't...you."

Koda looks down at her own positioning unit, frowning as snow and wavery lines cross through the normally steady display. She cocks a look at Manny, who shakes his head.

"Maybe the metalheads are screwing with the signal?" he asks.

"Doubtful," Kirsten responds. "They might have advanced technologies, but even they need to rely on the GPS to fix a firm position. Most likely, the problem is with the satellites themselves. With no one around to monitor them, their orbits are starting to decay. Pretty soon these units will make attractive paperweights for all the good they'll be."

"Cheery thought," Manny mutters half under his breath.

Another blast of static makes its way into Dakota's ear. "...Tshunka...20..."

"Keep your pants on, *thiblo*. We're working on it."

Slipping the communications piece from her ear, Koda looks around, trying to manually triangulate their position by known landmarks. Darkness, and the fact that they've traveled several miles in that dark, most of them on foot — actually by snowshoe (and trying to teach Kirsten, a city girl at heart with an aversion to snow and anything associated with it, how to snowshoe is a story in and of itself), makes it a difficult task at best.

"Tell him that we're halfway between the big rock and the tree that looks like the Hunchback of Notre Dame, two steps off the nearest cow path."

Feeling her jaw drop, Koda slowly turns her head until Kirsten's stony, black streaked face is perfectly in her sight.

Manny, just as shocked, voices what Koda cannot. "Did...did you just crack a joke, ma'am?" Green eyes blaze from blackface, and Manny gulps. Hard. "Didn't think so, ma'am."

Koda clamps her jaw shut and settles for shaking her head. She scans the area ahead and, once she has their position firmly in her mind, slips the communications piece back in her ear. Through the static, she relays their position in Lakota to her brother.

Satisfied with her response, Tacoma cuts communication, and the world around Dakota falls back into blessed quiet. In the silence, she notices Kirsten staring blankly into the distance, her expression intent. Closing the distance between them, Dakota stops just outside the other woman's body space and waits patiently.

Sensing Dakota's presence, Kirsten blinks, draws back into herself, and gives the tall woman a questioning look.

"Hear anything?"

"Garbled," Kirsten replies, slipping the bud from her ear. "They're definitely headed this way, though." She looks around, then back at Koda. "If they've got humans with them, it would make sense to take a main road, even if it hasn't been plowed. Are there any of those near here?"

"About ten paces directly ahead. A main highway."

"That close, huh?"

Koda grins, a flash of pure white against the black greasepaint on her face. "We'll be long gone before they get within sniffing distance." As Kirsten nods her understanding and replaces her earbud, Koda sobers.

She opens her mouth as if to speak, then closes it, unable or unwilling to risk this new bit of warmth between them.

Kirsten notices. "What is it?"

Koda takes in a deep breath, considering her words. "I believe...in being prepared. I know this is just a recon mission, but something unexpected could happen, and if it does..."

Kirsten bristles. "I assure you, I'm perfectly capable of handling—"

"It's not that," Koda replies, holding her hand up. "It's..." Pausing, she fights for words again. "Look, if we need to shoot up some of those drones, and you're tapped into one of them at the time, I don't think Manny and I can keep you alive long enough for the others to get here and get us back to base."

A smile comes unbidden to Kirsten's lips. She feels a wash of tenderness so foreign to her that for a moment, she's taken aback by the strength of the simple, undeniably powerful emotion. "I'll be okay," she assures softly, reaching out one gloved hand to touch, only briefly, Koda's strong wrist. "The problem's been corrected. I won't be getting caught in any more self destruct feedback loops; I promise."

Koda looks deep into Kirsten's eyes, twin sparks of high color among the monochrome of lampblack and full moon. Her memories guide her spirit to the beat of the drums, to the pulse of the ether, the brightness of the Star-that-has-no-Name, and the ever-present pull of the seductive wind. "The time is not yet," she whispers.

Kirsten freezes, a living statue in a land humanity has forsworn. "What?"

The soft voice shakes Koda from her memories. "Nothing. It was..."

The words on the tip of Kirsten's tongue dry out as several streams of data pour into her implants. She cocks her head, still looking at Dakota. "They're headed this way. Ten armored military droids, twenty two regulars, almost fifty humans traveling on foot...or treads...or...whatever. They're picking up more as they move along. They're broadcasting everywhere. I can hear chatter from at least seven more groups nearby."

"This isn't good," Manny mutters, his eyes darting, trying to look everywhere at once.

"Strengths?" Koda asks, tightening her grip on her weapon.

"Don't know yet. They're definitely heading for the base, though."

"And the humans. Coerced or voluntary?"

"I don't know that yet, either," Kirsten bites off, shaking her head. "No particular mention of them in the routine communications I'm picking up."

Manny steps forward. "As much as I don't believe I'm saying this, Koda, I think we should treat them like unfriendlies no matter what their circumstances."

Kirsten gazes over at him, shocked. "Is that what they're teaching you in the military these days?"

"No, ma'am," Manny replies, spine so straight it crackles. "Exactly the opposite, in fact. But right now, I don't think we can afford to take any chances, ma'am."

Dismissing him with a look, Kirsten concentrates on the chatter coming over her implants. Koda flips on her com unit and quietly relays Kirsten's reports to Tacoma in Lakota. When she's done, she looks back to Kirsten. "Any more info?"

"Nothing specific. They're still headed this way. If the GPS was working, I could tell you exactly how far."

"It's all right." Grinning, she hefts a large, heavy sack and slings it over her back. "Manny, stay here and keep an eye out. I'll be back in a bit."

"Wait! Where are you—" Kirsten cuts off her question as she realizes she's speaking to thin air. She turns to Manny. "Where is she going?"

Manny smirks, then shrugs. "Dunno. I wouldn't worry about it, though. Dakota's real good at taking care of business. And herself."

Rubbing her chin thoughtfully, Kirsten stares down the most likely path of Koda's disappearance. "Yes," she comments softly, more to the air than the man standing just a few paces away. "Yes, I suppose she is." *The time is not yet.*

**Having been taught** to snowshoe as soon as she had learned to walk, Dakota moves effortlessly across the snowy plain, leaving no discernable tracks behind. Headed south, away from the droids and their human collaborators (or captives, if one possesses a glass half-full attitude), she parallels the road for a little over two miles, then back, and back again, until she comes to the perfect spot. She knows this particular stretch of road very well. Long, straight, and utterly monotonous, it's exactly what she needs.

Slinging the pack away from her body, she unzips the front and reaches inside, gloved fingers gingerly clamping onto a thick metal container. Pulling it out, she sets the pack on the snow, then unscrews the lid of the container and reaches inside. She removes a flat metallic disc the same size and shape as an old-time DVD. An anti-tank mine, it is smaller, lighter, more accurate, and much deadlier than the mines of just a decade ago. Placed correctly, it will allow the humans and non-military droids to step directly on it without tripping the trigger. Such would not be the case when the heavy treads of a military android descend.

Calmly and with precision, Koda places her stash of mines, ten in all, into the natural cracks and divots of the snow and ice that packs the road. Even in the deep of an icy night, nature flows over, around, and through her, accepting her as its own, even in her destructive task. A sharp wind cuts across the naked flesh of her face, but she pays it no mind, intent on her work and the ebb and flow of life around her.

An hour later, she steps back and, hands on hips, views her work by the light of the moon. A grunt of satisfaction, and she zips her pack, reseats the straps across her broad shoulders, and turns back the way she came.

**The soft hoot** of an owl brings Manny to instant attention. When the sound is repeated, he hoots back, which catches Kirsten's attention. Slipping the bud from her ear, she turns in Manny's direction and is almost launched into orbit when the empty space of a split-second ago is suddenly filled by Dakota's very living presence. "Holy Jesus," she breathes, holding a hand up to her chest. "You just scared the crap out of me."

"Sorry," Koda replies, contrite. She glances at Manny. "All quiet?"

"Clear blue."

"Good." She turns back to Kirsten. "Anything else on the targets?"

Recovering, Kirsten nods. "Still headed this way. I was able to do some triangulation. They're about five miles out now, give or take a few hundred feet. They've picked up two passengers. One regular droid, one human."

"Anything from the other groups?"

"I'm picking up two other definites, both smaller than the one we're tracking now. Maybe twenty or thirty in each party, mostly regular droids and a few humans here and there. Nothing more specific than that."

"How far out?"

"Ten, maybe fifteen miles. Both headed east southeast, toward Ellsworth. At the rate they're traveling, they'll probably join up about six miles east of here."

Koda nods, intuition satisfied. "I know the place." She spares them both a pointed glance. "Ready to haul out?"

Kirsten straightens. "Where are we going? And where did you go?"

"Left a few surprises for our friends," Koda replies, grinning.

"Surprises?"

"Land mines." Kirsten's exclamation is forestalled by an upraised hand. "Anti-tank mines. Any humans in the group will pass over them without a problem. These little gifts are for the military droids."

Kirsten looks unconvinced.

"We either get them now, away from innocent lives, or we'll have to deal with them later when there's no choice in the matter."

Looking down at her feet, Kirsten nods. The image of the two men she's killed flashes in front of her, and she finds herself clenching jaws and fists to keep it pushed down, far down out of sight and mind and thought.

Sensing Kirsten's inner turmoil, Koda takes a step closer. "You all right?" The gaze that meets hers is clear and direct, but she can see the struggle within and again it calls to her. "Is there something I can—"

"No," Kirsten interrupts, back in full control. "It's nothing." Her shoulders square and set. "I'm ready to move out when you are."

"Let's go, then."

**"Ouch! God...dammit!"**

From her point position, Koda hears Kirsten's pained cry and hurries back to investigate. "What is it? What's wrong?"

"Cramp," Kirsten bites out, snatching off a glove with her teeth and reaching down to work frozen fingers into an equally frozen knot of muscle in her calf. "Damn snowshoes. Should have left them to the rabbits, where they belong."

"Hang on, hang on." Tossing her weapon to Manny, Koda gets down on one knee and gently displaces Kirsten's stiff, digging fingers. "Take some deep slow breaths. In and out. In and out."

"I already know how to breathe," Kirsten snaps. "Been doing it since I was a baby."

"Just do it," Koda orders, working her fingers into the thick straps of knotted muscle.

Startled by Koda's uncharacteristic display of temper, Kirsten complies. Under the ministrations of Dakota's skilled hands, the cramp gradually loosens. Only to seize up again, hard enough to cause her leg to buckle. Saved from an ignominious topple onto her backside by Koda's strong arm, she tenses, then relaxes as she finds herself half carried, half dragged a few steps back to where a flat-topped rock juts out from its bed of snow. With a soft grunt of pain, she lowers herself onto the rock, not protesting as her boot is removed and her triply socked foot is grabbed and manipulated until her toes point almost toward her chest. This eases the tension on her calf somewhat, and when Dakota's fingers return to the knotted muscle, it begins to loosen in a way that Kirsten knows will be lasting.

As the cramp starts to relax, the rest of her does as well, as the stress and the hours without sleep begin to catch up with her. Her chin dips, and she gazes at the very top of Koda's uncovered head. The moonlight brings out the bluish highlights in the deep black hair, and Kirsten, to her private horror, watches as her hand lifts from its place on her lap and reaches out to brush gently against the shining mass. It is just the briefest of touches, but it lingers sweetly in some deep part of her that isn't hotly debating between crawling beneath the very rock she's sitting on and — the current frontrunner — running as fast and as far as she can and not stopping until she reaches, say, Outer Mongolia.

Manny notices and quickly looks away, suspecting that he's unintentionally intruding on a very private moment.

As quickly as it's come upon her, the panic fades away at the sight of arresting blue eyes and a sweetly crooked smile that now fills her field of vision. There is no judgment in Koda's striking features, only kindness, compassion, and caring.

"Better now?" Koda asks, her voice low and soft.

Kirsten clears her throat, suddenly aware of its dryness. "Yes." She swallows. "Much. Thank you."

"Anytime." A canteen is thrust into Kirsten's hands. "Here. Drink this. You're dehydrated."

"You mean it wasn't the snowshoes?"

"A little of both, maybe," Dakota concedes, slipping the heavy boot back over Kirsten's foot, fastening it securely, then rising to her full height. "Take a little more. Yeah, that's it. We've still got a few hours ahead of us, if you think you're up to it."

With a nod, Kirsten hands back the canteen and gets up on legs that are steady and blessedly pain free. "I'm up to it. Let's get going."

With an amused glance at her cousin, Koda starts out after the fully recovered and determined young woman striding ahead.

Manny just rolls his eyes and follows along.

**A chill wind,** heavy with the scent of snow, cuts sharply through the small grove of trees. The winter-bare limbs rattle like the bones of a hundred skeletons in a hundred closets. At the sound, Dakota looks up from her task of planting the last of the anti-tank mines. The sky is thick with turbulent clouds, angry in a way she knows all too well.

Manny follows her glance upward and winces. "Shit. Base said no weather tonight."

"Probably fucked up those satellites too," Koda grunts, turning back to her work.

"I'm guessing this is a bad thing," Kirsten remarks, walking over from her spot a few yards away.

"Depends on your definition of 'bad'," Dakota deadpans, not looking up from her precise placing of the mine beneath the snow.

The barest glint of a smirk sharpens Kirsten's eyes. "Would you like the Merriam-Webster-Turner version, or would you be content with the Oxford Condensed Unabridged?"

Manny's slow motion head turn is the stuff of old-time silent movie classics, and Kirsten enjoys every second of it. She's not exactly sure why she derives such pleasure from getting this brash young pilot's goat. Perhaps it's her way of telling him that she will be accepted on her own terms. Why she desires acceptance from a man who is, for all intents and purposes, a stranger is another question she doesn't have an answer for.

*Deer in the headlights*, she thinks, raising an eyebrow and daring him to respond. And he looks as if he's going to, right up until the time that his military training and the realization of exactly who she is both conspire to ambush him. His snappy comeback dies on his lips, and he turns away, pretending to study the roiling sky.

Perfectly aware of the little drama taking place mere feet away, Koda takes her time placing the last mine. Rising, she casually dusts her gloves on her thighs, then gives Kirsten a deliberately pointed look before clapping her cousin on the back. "All right, flyboy. Time to make tracks."

"Bless you," Manny half whispers before looking through the copse of trees directly ahead. "Uh oh."

Koda looks up just in time to see the heavy squall move toward them with the speed of an oncoming train. "Shit." She glances over her shoulder. "Kirsten, grab onto my pack. Don't let go no matter what, understand?"

"Whiteout!" Manny shouts just as the storm descends, enveloping them in a world of blinding, pure white.

# CHAPTER FOURTEEN

Kirsten becomes immediately disoriented as the howling wind whips the snow around her face and body, blinding her completely and stinging the exposed areas of her skin like a studded whip. "Dakota!"

"It's all right! You're safe!" Koda shouts to be heard above the shrieking wind. Reaching out blindly, she manages to capture Kirsten's arm and she pulls the other woman forward and tight against what little shelter her larger, longer body can offer. "Don't let go!"

"Not on your life!"

A massive bolt of lightning splits the sky, and the resulting crack of thunder shakes the earth around them with brutal force. Kirsten's implants howl in outrage, and she lifts her free hand to her forehead, trying fruitlessly to numb the spike of pain chiseling itself into her skull. The air stinks of burning rubber, and she can taste metal in the back of her mouth. *Thunder? In the middle of a snowstorm? What the hell?*

"Manny! Get us out of here!"

"Any suggestions? I'm blind here!"

"Shit!" She turns her head slightly to the side. "Kirsten, can you move?"

"Yes! I'm fine!"

"Come with me, then! Manny, stay close!"

"Like flies on horseshit, cuz!"

With determined steps, Dakota leads her small group forward, eyes straining to see through the lashing snow. It's absolutely useless; the only thing she can rely on is the instinct she's honed through her life on this land.

When lightning again splits the sky, she uses that same instinct to pull Kirsten to the side and shield her with her own body a split second before the scraping, brittle branches of a giant tree crash down, dealing her a glancing blow on the shoulder.

"Jesus!" Kirsten shouts. "What was that?"

"Tree! Keep moving!"

"Tree? We're in a whole forest of trees! What if we wind up running into them?"

"We'll all get bloody noses! Now move!"

Not moving isn't really an option as Kirsten feels herself pulled forward by the strength of Dakota's inexorable grip. Her mind rebels against the less than gentle handling, but her body knows a good deal when it senses one and moves her along complacently.

A chant to the Mother soft upon her lips, Dakota continues to use blind instinct to lead her party out of the dangerous woodland as lightning and thunder continue to do battle around them.

Then comes a flash of light and a loud coughing sound that is neither lightning nor thunder. "The mines," Koda remarks, still moving them through the thick grove of trees with uncanny precision and not a little stealth.

"Hoo yah!" Manny yells from his place glued to her right side. "Die, you motherfuckers!"

A second, third, and fourth explosion follow in quick succession. With a soft cry, Kirsten falls to her knees, arms wrapped around her head as the feedback of the dying droids — sounding amazingly like human screams — sears through her implants, robbing the strength from her body and the thoughts from her mind.

Koda stops immediately and squats down on her haunches, barely able to see the other woman's pain wracked face even from scant inches away. She grabs Kirsten's shoulders tight in her hands and barely keeps herself from shaking the young woman like a rag doll. "What is it? What's wrong?" Kirsten's mouth is frozen in a rictus of absolute agony, and Dakota divines the problem immediately. "Turn them off!" she all but screams. "Turn them off!"

If Kirsten can hear her, she gives no sign. A keening moan continues uninterrupted from the very back of her throat as her body rocks in an instinctive attempt at self-comfort as old as time.

Squinting through the hard-driving snow, Dakota unwraps Kirsten's arms from around her head and, praying silently that she's doing the right thing, feels for the tiny bumps behind each of the young scientist's ears. With deft, gentle pressure, she presses inward. Relief flows through her in a tangible wave as Kirsten's body begins to relax almost immediately, slumping weakly against her. Pulling off a glove with her teeth, Koda raises a warm palm to Kirsten's chin, tilting the other woman's gaze up to meet her own. Her mouth carefully forms one word. "Better?"

After a moment, Kirsten nods. "Much. Thank you."

Koda can't help the smile that spills out, and Kirsten responds with one of her own, all the more glorious for barely being seen, like the tantalizing flash of a deeply desired gift.

Another moment goes by, the sounds of exploding landmines slashing through the air around them. Releasing Kirsten's chin almost reluctantly, Dakota slips her glove back on and looks carefully at Kirsten, asking a question with her eyes. Kirsten nods and, with a deep breath, Koda rises, pulling the other woman up with her and holding her until Kirsten is more or less steady on her feet.

Kirsten moves up to turn her implants back on, only to be stopped by Koda, who catches her hand and curls it firmly around her bicep. Understanding the silent message, Kirsten gives another nod and begins walking forward in step with her companion. Effectively blind, and now completely deaf, she has no choice but to trust the tall Lakota woman who has, for the second time this day, saved, if not her life, at least her sanity.

Trust is the one emotion she has never truly felt able to give anyone. But with this woman, she relinquishes the fetters in her soul without a second's hesitation. There is something very freeing in this simple, if profound, act, and in this giving, she finds herself changed in a way she could never have predicted.

**When the explosions** start, Tacoma immediately clicks his com unit, then winces as static crackles directly into his ear. Undeterred, he clicks the unit again and again, willing to hear his sister's voice through the interference. "Tanski, come in. Dakota, if you hear me, come in." As more explosions rip through the night, Tacoma looks over at the colonel with wide eyes.

She holds out a hand. "Let me try."

Slipping the earpiece off, Tacoma hands the unit over to Allen. She situates the piece, then clicks to open transmission. "Allen to Rivers. Allen to Rivers. Do you read me. Over." Static answers her, and she tries again. "Allen to Rivers. Dakota, Manny, damn it, if you're receiving me, answer."

Nothing.

She shoots a quick look over her shoulder. "Mendoza, do you have a fix on their position?"

The young corporal looks at her with a hangdog expression. "No, ma'am. Nothing but interference across the board."

"Shit."

Allen's epithet is softly spoken, but Tacoma's sharp hearing picks it up, and he shares with her a brief look of concern and commiseration.

"Allen to Rivers. Dakota, can you read me?"

Another moment passes in silence.

Tacoma shoulders his weapon and straightens his jacket.

"What are you doing?" Allen asks, eyes narrowed.

"I'm gonna find them. Now."

"Wait." She doesn't back down from the tall man's fierce glare. Swallowing her colonel's pride, she deliberately softens both face and voice. "Please, wait. You don't even know where they are!"

"She's my *tanski*, my sister. I don't need a map. I just need this." A meaty fist thumps against his heart. "I'll find them."

Static crackles. And then, "...ta he...rea...u."

"Dakota! Dakota, can you read me? Come back." Allen knows her voice has a note of obvious desperation in it, but she can't seem to dredge up the will to care.

Tacoma freezes, turns, and looks back at the colonel, who nods and beckons him back while listening through the static to Koda's broken words.

"...read...Colonel...t..."

"Dakota, you're breaking up. Listen to me. We can hear explosions coming from your last noted position. Are you okay?"

"...fine...mines...we're..."

Allen's eyes widen. "Excuse me? I didn't copy. Did you say 'mines'?"

The static clears for one miraculous moment. "I said mines, Colonel. Anti-tank mines."

"But where? How?"

"From the supply sergeant at the base. Now if you'll excuse me—"

"Wait a minute!" Maggie yells as Tacoma hides a chuckle behind a faked cough. "You're saying you took anti-tank mines from the base? Do you know how dangerous that was? You could have been killed!"

Dakota's return transmission is succinct. "I do, we weren't, they worked, and with all respect, Colonel," Dakota deliberately emphasizes Maggie's title, "yell at me later. We're in the middle of a whiteout here and I need to get my team to safety. Rivers out."

Allen looks down at the dead com link in her hands, then up at Tacoma, whose dark eyes are shining with mirth. "Do you find this the least bit funny, Sergeant?" she snaps.

Tacoma sobers slightly. "Respectfully, Colonel, this is Dakota we're talking about. No one commands her." A slight smirk curves his lips. "Unless she wants them to, of course."

Allen simply glares.

**Dakota continues forward** as she clicks the com link closed. Manny, who has heard the entire conversation, turns his head in her direction, though the snow is still far too furious for him to clearly see her, only half a foot away. "Ooooh, she's not gonna like that, cuz."

"Let her fire me if she wants to," Koda mutters in return, trying fruitlessly to peer through the swirling snow. "I just want this damn squall to stop."

As if only awaiting those very words, the snow does just that. It doesn't just taper off. It stops completely, vanishing as if it had never been.

Manny comes to a halt and blinks. The abrupt end of the storm reveals their APC not more than ten feet away, blanketed in at least eight inches of newfallen snow. "Holy Mother," he breathes before turning to his cousin, eyes wide as saucers. "I can't believe you just did this. I knew you were half *Hupaki glake*. I fucking knew it!"

Koda rolls her eyes at him. "You've got the ears for one."

Blushing slightly, Manny instinctively reaches up for the aforementioned appendages. "Not fair."

"Take that up with Ina Maka. Right now, I just want to get home. You drive."

"You got it, cuz."

She looks to Kirsten, who is staring at her with an odd expression on her face. "What? What is it?"

Reaching up to turn her implants back on, she removes the ear bud from her ear and takes a step closer to Dakota. "You're bleeding."

Koda looks down, for the first time noticing the red stain covering much of her left chest. Her camo suit is raggedly torn and fresh blood oozes slowly from the hole. "Oh. It's just a scratch."

"How did it happen?"

"From the tree that fell. I think."

Their eyes meet. "The one that would have hit me if you hadn't shielded me with your body. Why did you do that?"

Koda shrugs. "Because I could."

It is a simple reply, and the truth of it shines through in her words, and eyes, leaving Kirsten to look at her in wonder.

Manny ends the moment with a quick toot of the horn. "Come on, guys! Time's a'wasting."

As Koda starts forward, more blood flows from the wound, soaking her camos. Kirsten stops her with a touch to the wrist.

"That's more than a scratch. Sit in the back with me. I'll tend it as we're driving back to the base."

"It'll be fine," Koda demurs. "It can wait."

"Please."

One simple word, so softly spoken, opens up a side of the young scientist that Dakota had long suspected was there, but had never really seen. Until now. She smiles, a cockeyed half-grin. "Okay."

**"Geez, Manny!"** Koda hisses as the APC hits yet another deep rut, bouncing its occupants, particularly the ones in the back seat, around like rag dolls. "We're not at the local tractor pull, you know."

"Sorry, cuz. The roads are a bitch out here. I'm doing my best."

"It's all right. Just...try to be a little smoother."

"You got it."

Kirsten pulls up the heavy first-aid kit from its place bolted to the floor-boards of the armored vehicle. Popping the clips, she opens the metal lid and peers inside. Her hands light upon a pair of bandage scissors, and she pulls them out, then looks up at Dakota. "If you can unzip your camos, I'm going to have to cut your thermals away from the wound."

Nodding, Koda unzips the suit to just above her navel.

Kirsten quickly averts her gaze as she gets an unexpected view of Dakota's small, firm breasts, clearly outlined against the thin, skin-tight fab-ric. She can feel her face go a flaming red and guesses Koda can likely feel the heat of it from her place against the opposite door. "I...um..."

"It's okay," Koda replies softly, smiling. "Like I said, this can wait."

"No." Kirsten clears her throat and tries again. "No. I can..." Forgo-ing any further attempts at talking, she grabs the proverbial bull by the horns, reaches for the neckline of Dakota's thermals, and gently cuts down to mid chest. Peeling the blood-sodden fabric away, she exposes the deep, sluggishly bleeding cut. She then tracks up to meet Koda's eyes. "It's um...it's..."

"On my breast. I know." She smiles again. "If you can wet down a bandage, I'll get some of this blood off, then tape a pressure dressing to it. It'll hold until we reach base."

"I'll do it," Kirsten replies firmly, trying desperately to rein in her pro-fessional demeanor, which seems to have fled with the rest of her common sense. *God, you'd think I was some giddy schoolgirl. Get your act together, Kirsten. You offered to help, so help. Think about her breasts later.*

And she would. Of that, she was sure.

Forcing her hands to remain steady, she uncaps a bottle of sterile water and wets a gauze dressing sponge. She begins to blot at the wound, though the task is made harder by the fact that she has nothing to gain pur-chase from. Manny driving them like he's riding a steer in a rodeo doesn't help matters any.

Finally, blessedly, most of the blood is cleaned away. Kirsten then unwraps a sterile 4X4, doubles it, then doubles it again and presses it tightly against the wound. The APV hits its biggest rut yet, and in pure instinct, Kirsten lifts her free hand and cups Koda's entire breast in order to maintain pressure on the wound.

"I guess this means we're married now."

The amusement in the low voice causes Kirsten to realize the position-ing of her hands, and she looks up at Koda with something very akin to hor-ror blazing from her features.

Dakota can't help the soft laugh that escapes. "Relax," she soothes. "You're doing a good job."

Kirsten's fiery blush deepens.

Koda rolls her eyes. "Breathe," she orders softly. "I can't have my nurse passing out on me like this. What would people think?"

The vehicle hits yet another rut, and Kirsten, already off balance, falls forward, diving nose first into Koda's warm cleavage. Dakota's arms come around her instinctively, protecting her from further jostling as the APV stut-ters and bucks its way down the unplowed road.

"Could this possibly get any worse?" comes the plaintive wail from between her breasts.

Koda laughs out loud. "Well, we could be walking."

**Wearing a freshly** pressed jumpsuit from the base hospital, Koda steps quietly into the darkened, cool house. Her head is lightly buzzing from the four or five shots of pure octane that her brother and cousin had all but poured down her throat in celebration. Of what, she still isn't quite sure, but their good spirits and warm companionship were a fine enough inducement to stay. Her wound is neatly stitched and dressed, and quite complacent beneath the numbing weight of the alcohol she's consumed.

The light from the fireplace leads her through the darkened kitchen and into the living room. Asi's tail thumps against the tattered rug, but he doesn't remove his head from its resting place atop Kirsten's thigh. The woman in question is sprawled along the couch, her head lolling against one ragged arm, a thick — and doubtless dry as dust — robotics tome resting, spine up, on her chest. Her glasses hang askew on her face, and she is snoring lightly, obviously deeply asleep.

Coming closer, Dakota squats on her haunches and lays a hand in Asimov's warm fur, stroking it as she gazes down at Kirsten, watching the firelight as it plays over her spun-gold hair. She follows one tendril that lies across one twitching eye, caught up in thick, dusky lashes. The face she looks upon is that of an innocent untouched by the ravages of war or time. It is a kind face, a compassionate face imbued with an innate goodness that the young scientist tries so hard to conceal. With infinite tenderness, Koda gently sweeps the tendril loose from its confinement, smiling as Kirsten's nose twitches briefly, before relaxing once again beneath the weight of her slumber.

A soft footfall sounds, and Koda looks up to see Maggie, her well-worn robe casually belted at the waist. Her face is solemn, brown eyes intent on Koda's face.

"She's getting inside, isn't she?"

Though the words carry with them a faint accusation, the tone itself is soft, perhaps even warm. Koda chooses to keep silent, well knowing that her face speaks a truth mere words can't convey.

"Thought so," Maggie responds in a whisper, walking over to the foot of the couch and staring down at the almost fragile looking woman taking up its length. "Sparks like that don't fly for nothing."

"Sparks?"

Maggie's smile, when it comes, is wry. "Yeah." As she swallows, a brief look of sadness crosses her features, and is gone.

"Maggie, I—"

Allen lifts a hand. "Don't say it, Koda. Don't say that you're sorry."

Rising gracefully to her feet, Dakota grasps the upraised hand and pulls it gently to her chest. "I wasn't going to." She pins Maggie with her eyes. "I'm not."

That brief, sad smile flashes but a moment as Maggie lifts her free hand and tenderly trails it against Dakota's warm cheek. "C'mon," she says softly. "Let's go to bed."

**The general's conference** room is still grey, but this time, at least, the coffee arrives promptly. As steam curls up from the mug before her, Koda is pleased to note that it is also hot. Kirsten's sudden status as possible Commander-in-Chief of whatever is left of the armed forces may not make Amtrak run on time — has not made the trains run at all, in fact — but it has had an immediate and positive effect on the base's coffeemakers.

Kirsten has taken her seat at the head of the table without question this time, Hart claiming the second-ranking chair at the foot. Otherwise the seating arrangement reflects the tension that has been building in the room for the past two hours. One side is wall-to-wall brass: Air Force light colonels, majors, a stray captain to fill out the line. Like Hart, they are all in formal uniform, all of them bristling with theatre ribbons and good conduct medals. Studying the decorations surreptitiously as she sips her coffee, Koda counts the presence of only one pair of pilot's wings and zero Purple Hearts. *Desk jockeys and rearguards.* Facing them across the table are the scouts who have just returned from the prospective battleground, Tacoma and Manny in unmarked and rankless fatigues, the rest in an assortment of jeans and work shirts. One of the majors — Grueneman, H., according to his name tag — darts his eyes repeatedly from Koda to Tacoma. She has no need of her shamanic talent to know what he is thinking: they look just like identical twins, but they can't be. There is, too, something of the offended grade school principal in the down-the-nose-on-a-long-slalom look that lingers on Tacoma's hair, caught back like her own with a beaded band at the nape. Definitely not regulation.

*Live with it, asshole. If you want Lakota allies, accept Lakota customs.* Koda sips at her coffee and winks slyly the next time Grueneman, H. allows his eyes to wander to her and her brother.

The major averts his gaze instantly, and Koda turns her attention back to Maggie Allen. The colonel stands at the front of the room, marking the positions of enemy units on a holographic topo map. Its contours are dotted with small red laser X's that show a clear pattern of convergence upon Ellsworth, troops grinding south from Minot, north from Warren and Offut. A scattering of green circles represents possible disposition of Ellsworth's own assets, mostly ground and mechanical forces with a couple squadrons of Black Hawks and Apaches to back them up from the air.

"That's an extremely conservative strategy, Colonel," Hart observes. "We do have an operational fighter squadron. Counting Lieutenant Rivers and yourself, we have a good dozen pilots."

Maggie turns from rearranging red and green marks on the screen to answer the base commander. "It is conservative, General. 'Conservative' as in preserving our assets. I would prefer to hold back our air power to use as a last resort."

"What aircraft do the droids have, Colonel?" Kirsten's question is quiet, but it draws the immediate attention of the entire assembly. "It's my understanding that they have no fighters and no air transport. And they would have no one to fly them if they did." Her attention shifts, then, and her green eyes flash, for an instant feral as a hunting cat's. "I can tell you for certain, General, that no military droids were ever programmed to operate aircraft or airborne weapons systems. I fought your own Air Force Chief of Staff over that in the House Armed Services Committee. I won."

"All the more reason to take advantage of...well, our advantage." Grueneman, H. has found his voice. "There is limited time remaining in which we can expect our satellite-guided systems to continue to function.

We might as well make use of them while we can."

"What about outlying civilian communities?" asks Lorena, the red-headed Ms. Tilbury-Laduque. "The jets are the only way help can reach them in time if they're attacked."

"Risk them — waste the ammo, waste the fuel — and they'll be entirely on their own," her partner adds.

"Ma'am, we're at war," says Hart. "Under these circumstances, the armed forces' first duty is to preserve itself and the government."

"No!" Kirsten is on her feet, hands flat on the surface of the table. Her mouth is straight and tight; the effort she is making to keep her voice even is almost palpable. "Don't you understand? There is no government at the moment. By itself, Ellsworth..." a wave of her hand encompasses the base, "...is not a viable unit. The population is skewed in half a dozen ways that mean it can't survive except as part of a wider social spectrum. Protecting those outlying communities has to be our first priority, not our last."

"I agree with Dr. King, General," Maggie says quietly. "Let's use our planes if we need them, but only if we can't get the job done otherwise. The droids do have SAMs; we don't want to risk a shoot-down unnecessarily."

"All right." Hart leans back in his chair, stretching his legs under the table. "Let's game it out without the air cover."

Maggie turns once again to the holoboard. "We have enemy units coming in here, here, here." She highlights the red X's with a pointer. "From what we've picked up from their communications and can guess by the routes they're taking, they'll converge in force here — in the foothills just north and east of the base."

"They'll have to cross the Elk Creek branch of the Cheyenne," Tacoma observes. "There's only one bridge."

Maggie flashes him a grin. "There's only one bridge. We split our forces. One party waits for them here, on the south bank. The land is rough, with plenty of cover, including some wooded areas. The other party..." She pauses, a good teacher waiting for her students to supply the answer.

"The other party," Koda answers slowly, "gets into position behind them before they arrive. We squeeze them between the two forces and the river. Dr. King can monitor the androids' communications. Manny and Tacoma and I can relay the information without worrying about interception."

"Classic pincer," observes Grueneman.

"Not quite," Manny counters. "When do we blow the bridge?"

"On my order, Lieutenant," says Hart. He gives Allen a nod and a complacent smile. "It's a good plan, Colonel, assuming we can get by without committing our air superiority."

An awkward silence falls in the room. Kirsten breaks it. "You mean to command the operation personally, General?"

"Why, yes."

"After your brilliant success at Minot?" she spits. "General, your leadership is what got us where we are now."

It seems to Koda that the temperature in the room drops a good ten degrees. The silence that follows is glacial. The muscles around Tacoma's mouth twitch almost imperceptibly; Lorena Tilbury-Laduque coughs sharply and covers the lower half of her face with a well-faded bandana. Without sound, Manny's lips form the words, "Holy Ina Maka, Mother of God."

The quiet stretches out interminably. Finally, Hart draws a long breath and says quietly. "Very well, Dr. King. Allow me to recommend Lieutenant Colonel Frank Maiewski."

Maiewski, Koda notes, is the lone uniformed pilot at the table.

He turns an unattractive shade of fuschia, bright pink scalp showing through thinning hair. "General, thank you, but I don't believe—"

"Colonel Allen has rank," Kirsten observes quietly.

"And experience," adds Manny. "We spent the first week after the uprising fighting these things out in the countryside."

The general's mouth curves upward in an expression that stiffens Koda's spine and sets off alarms all along her nerves. *That's how a snake would look if it could smile.* Beside her, Tacoma has picked up on it, too; he turns to stare straight at Hart.

His fingers, spread flat on the table, twitch as if trying to form themselves into fists, but Hart says only, "Colonel? Are you up to the job?"

Maggie's face has gone grey, but her voice is steady when she answers. "I will be happy to accept whatever assignment you or Dr. King gives me, sir."

"All right. You're in command of this operation. Just be sure of your targets this time." Hart pushes out his chair and rises. "Half hour break."

The colonel remains standing by the holo screen as the other officers and civilians file out. Koda is the last to go; just short of the door, though, Maggie calls her back. "Dakota."

Koda stops and shuts the door. Her voice is soft. "What's wrong?"

"Hart." Maggie lays down her pointer, making an oddly pleading gesture toward the general's now empty seat. "There's something you need to know."

*Be sure of your targets.* It had been a threat. *Missed targets.* With a sudden sense of conviction, Koda knows what Maggie is about to say. *Damn the bastard.* Aloud she says, "No. There's nothing I need to know."

"Yes, there is. Dr. King needs to know, too."

Koda speaks levelly, acknowledging what she knows is coming, denying nothing. "You hit the wrong target once."

"Oh, not just the wrong target." Maggie crosses the room and opens a pair of the grey-on-grey curtains. Thin grey light shines in, muted by cloud cover and dirty snow. "I hit the wrongest target there is."

"Civilians?"

"A village in the Panjir. Farmers and goatherders. Old women. Kids." Her voice hardens. "Half a dozen five-hundred pounders right on top of them. No goddamned excuse at all."

Koda says very carefully. "It's not the first time such a thing has happened, it won't be the last."

"No, it's not. But those other times I wasn't responsible. This time I was." Maggie turns to meet her eyes. "I should have left the service after that, but I didn't. I still loved it too much — the flying, the feeling of power."

*And you've demanded perfection of yourself ever since.* "Maggie?"

"Yes?"

"I've seen you in the field. I trust you, and so do the troops."

"Thanks." A small smile twitches at Maggie's mouth. "You have the

talent to be one of the best fighters I've ever met. If I've taught you anything, I can be proud of that."

Koda opens the door. "Not just that. Would you like me to tell Kirsten
you'd like to speak to her?"

"Please."

Koda nods, steps into the corridor and, very softly closes the door.

**Koda slips quietly** out of her sleeping bag, careful not to disturb Maggie or Kirsten, still stretched out on the floor of the troop carrier on either
side of her. Kirsten does not wake, but murmurs in her sleep, reaching out
toward the now-empty space where Koda had been a moment ago. She
misses Asi. With the thought, a twinge of — what? Not guilt, exactly, not
quite regret either — passes through Koda. The dog had howled and flung
himself against the gate of the clinic kennel when they had turned to leave
him not quite a day ago. Hidden behind her darkened lenses, Kirsten's
eyes had been red and swollen for the next twelve hours. "Allergies," she
had claimed, but even with a warming breeze from the south, it is still too
early for the spring miseries of blowing pollen.

In the light of the small ceramic heater, Koda begins to pull on her battle dress over her thermals. Because she and Kirsten will be stationed with
the com unit back in the woods that crown a rise behind the intended battle
line, her Arctic white camo is streaked in the grey-brown of bare branches,
the spider tracery of dead grass. She is not sure, exactly, of the time, but
even here in the enclosed warmth of the truck, she can smell the changes
that come with the wind that rises before dawn, bearing with it the hint of
far places where the snow has loosed its grip on the land. Places, even,
where ice never clamps down upon the earth at all, and winter means relief
from pounding heat.

*Heraklion.*

The thought comes to her with the vivid urgency of a child's wish. *If I
live through this — if any of us live; if there is anything human left at all —
someday I want to go back to Crete and lie on the beach at Heraklion.*

She can see it still, the white sand and the thousand-year-old Byzan-
tine domes whitewashed to perfect brightness under the white glare of the
sun; the white wings of gulls dipping and wheeling above the impossible
deep blue of the water that stretches on and on to the horizon.

For an instant it seems to her that time slips, and she is looking out
over the curling breakers at strong brown arms and legs flashing in the surf
as a dolphin arcs above the water's surface and the spray off its sleek form
catches the light like a shower of falling stars. The angle of the sun shifts,
and the swimmer is no longer Tali, but a fair-haired woman whose face she
cannot see. The ancient monastery that broods down from the sea-cliff has
acquired fluted columns and a marble altar that smokes with incense, the
sharp smell of myrrh sliding along the salt air. And the sun dips again, and
there is nothing but the white beach and the woman whose hair gleams like
cornsilk, calling to her from the water where the dolphins leap under the
endless sky.

Koda shakes her head to clear it, reaching for her sidearm and cinch-
ing down the straps that hold the shoulder holster in place against her side.
The images carry the feel of truth, but she cannot spare the attention now
to sort past from future, desire from fate.

Carefully she steps between the two women and lets herself out the insulated flap at the back of the truck. The plastic sheeting clacks softly behind her as she steps onto the rear bumper, then jumps lightly onto the snow beneath. The night is clear. The moon rides high above the bare limbs of beech and sycamore, its reflection on the snow casting ghost light about her feet. The wind creaks among the branches, unfurls the frost of her breath in streamers.

In an hour or a little more, she knows, the sun will rise, and the quiet woods and fields in this lonely corner of South Dakota will explode with the noise of battle. The thought does not frighten her; she has spent the last weeks with a gun scarcely out of her hand. She has condemned men to the slow death of thirst and starvation in the Mandan jail; has blown gods know how many androids into electronic oblivion; killed a man with her own hands. There will be nothing new to her in the violence to come. The difference tomorrow will be in her assigned role as communicator to the divided wings of the troops gathered here to close on the enemy force at the appointed time.

And there is Kirsten, whose safety will be her primary responsibility, on whose skills their survival beyond tomorrow may well depend.

Without sound, two shadows separate from the trees behind the line of trucks and move toward her. One, tall and bareheaded, is her brother; the other, shorter and stockier, is Manny. "*Hau, tanski,*" Tacoma greets her.

"*Han, thiblo. Shick'shi.*"

Tacoma draws a small leather bag out of his jacket. From it he takes a bundle of dried sweetgrass and sage tied with a red thread and half a dozen packets of folded buckskin. Carefully he lays them out on the truck's wide bumper. "I'm glad you're up." A grin lights his face. "Or did you already know we were coming?"

She smiles in return. "I should have."

"Other things on your mind?" Manny nods toward the truck.

"*Han.* It's not good for so much to depend on one person."

"No," her brother agrees quietly. "But she's our best bet to stop the droids. You're our best bet to keep her alive to do it. That is not in question."

"It ought to be."

"No. It shouldn't." Manny gestures back toward the stretch of highway where a squadron of Black Hawks and Apaches are parked. "You've got to know that my orders are to get you two out of here safely if it all goes to hell when the sun comes up."

"Damn it, Manny—"

"And I don't want any argument from you or Dr. Ice Maiden if it comes to that. There won't be time — oh, damn," he says very softly.

Silhouetted by the faint glow of the heater, Kirsten stands holding the open flap above them. There is no chance at all that she has not heard Manny's reference to her, and Koda can almost feel the heat of embarrassment radiating from him. But Kirsten speaks evenly, looking down at the small packets on the bumper. "I'm sorry, I've interrupted you. I'll go out the other way."

"No." It is Tacoma, his voice firm. "Please join us." He reaches up to hand her down, and after a moment's hesitation, she accepts. "You're a warrior, too."

Kirsten stands motionless for a moment, then says softly, "Thank you. I'm honored."

Tacoma hands Koda the sweetgrass bundle, and shielding a match with his big hands, carefully lights it. Smoke billows up from the herbs, and, closing her eyes, Koda waves it toward herself, over her head and shoulders, breathing in its fragrance. Calm settles over her, a stillness that begins just under her heart and ripples outward until mind and body alike are quiet. She passes the smudge stick to Tacoma, who repeats the ritual before handing it to Kirsten. Her face pale as the snow, Kirsten follows their example, bowing her head in reverence as the peace of the ritual takes possession of her. When Manny has completed the purification, Tacoma gingerly opens the small leather bundles. Five packets hold finely ground colors: white and black and red; red and yellow ochre. In the sixth is a knob of rendered buffalo fat.

Tacoma dips a finger in the tallow and mixes it with a sprinkling of the red ochre. Carefully he draws a blazing sun on his forehead and the pug marks of a large cat on either cheek. Manny follows suit, marking his face with black arrows tipped in red.

Kirsten, who has watched with a look of rapt attention, accepts a bit of the fat from the bundle as Manny offers it to her, together with some of the red and black pigment. There is unexpected certainty in her movements, and Koda stifles the impulse to offer help. Deliberately, precisely, the other woman traces a double spiral in red on the back of each of her hands, a black lightning bolt down her cheek.. When she has finished, she turns to offer the paints to Koda.

Tacoma's hand intercepts them. "Let me."

Koda opens her mouth to protest, but Tacoma says, very gently, "No, *tanski. Tshunkmanitou Wakan Winan.* Let me."

A tightening in her solar plexus sends alarm along her nerves, something near panic screaming down her blood. The calm of a few moments before is shattered, its fragments falling about her in brittle shards. All unexpectedly, she has arrived at a moment of crisis, something she knows she is not prepared for, something there is no way to prepare for. Her mouth goes dry as cotton, and her tongue feels thick and unwieldly as she forms the simple word she does not want to speak and knows she must speak. "*Ohan.*" No sound carries her consent, and she repeats, whispering, "*Ohan.*"

"*Washté,*" Tacoma answers quietly, and begins to mix white pigment in his hand.

Koda feels the pressure of his finger as he draws a jagged lightning bolt from her hairline to her chin. She swallows hard against the fear that rises in her, knowing somehow what is coming. When her brother begins to dot the paint onto her cheeks, she grabs his wrist. "Tacoma, no!"

He makes no effort to resist her, but says quietly, "It is right."

The night has begun to fade around them, and she can see her brother's eyes. They are a warrior's, deep brown and steady, but there is a spark of the shaman's gift in them as well.

He says again, "It is right."

She submits, then, allowing him to paint on her face the symbols that Tshunka Witco of the Oglala, Crazy Horse, saw when he cried for a vision. *Ina Maka,* she prays silently as a weight settles across her shoulders, a weight that now only death will lift from her. *Mother of us all, help me to carry this burden and not to fail.*

Above her in the fading darkness, she hears the high scream of a hawk. Just as the sun clears the horizon, a red-tail settles in the bare sycamore above her. Crazy Horse had worn a red-tailed hawk in his hair. Wiyo, though, looks down at her with a clear golden gaze that is somehow both loving and pitiless. It is validation of her office, and completion.

Tacoma follows her gaze as she looks up at the hawk. "*Hoka hey,*" he says. "It is a good day."

"It is a good day," Kirsten echoes. "A good day to fight."

# CHAPTER FIFTEEN

The early sun lies lightly on the valley, spreading a transparent wash of gold over the new snow that blankets the meadow to the southeast of the river. From the low bank to the woods, still bare with the lingering cold, it lies porcelain smooth for almost a quarter of a mile. Branches of beech and sycamore cast their shadows across it in a grey-blue web as delicate as a spider's. Here and there among the trees, a peeling of bark takes the light in a flash of silver, almost indistinguishable from the occasional glint off metal where the line of soldiers stands along the margin of the trees. Koda can make out the long barrels of the two howitzers drawn up behind them, only because she already knows where to look. Below the down-slope of the hill where she stands, mist rises off the Cheyenne to curl around the pylons and rails of the narrow bridge, coiling, loosing and coiling again as it spirals across the meadow, breaking like surf where it climbs against the steeply rising piedmont of the Paha Sapa to the northwest. Tacoma and most of their infantry lie concealed in the folds of those basalt ridges. The mist gives them further cover as it seeps by fissure and rock chimney into the badlands, though it cannot hide them from heat or infrared sensors. By the time the enemy picks them up, though, it should be too late.

"I feel as if I've slipped back in time."

Koda lowers her binoculars and turns to face Maggie. She gestures at her face, with its painted lightning bolt and hailstones, the devices worn almost a hundred and fifty years ago by Tshunka Witco, Crazy Horse of the Oglala. "You mean this?"

Maggie shakes her head slightly. "I mean this." The sweep of her hand takes in the valley and its troop emplacements, open and concealed. "The conventional doctrine of modern warfare is to pound the enemy down with bombs and missiles first. The ground forces only go in when you're ready to mop up or have to fight house to house. There hasn't been a true set battle like this in...oh, a century, not since the first of the World Wars."

"Forward into the past." The voice is soft, the tone lightly humorous.

Koda and Maggie both turn startled eyes on Kirsten where she sits in the back of the troop carrier. Her laptop is deployed on the folding table in the center, connected by a rat's nest of wire and cables to the bank of communications consoles stacked up along and below one of the benches. A small smile starts just at the edges of her mouth, widens as Koda and the colonel stare. Then she turns demurely back to her readouts, clicking rapidly through a series of equipment checks.

"All on line, Colonel," she says, serious again. "Please try your audio links now, Dakota."

Koda slips off the hood of her jacket and secures the headset in place. "Tacoma. Tacoma. *Ayupte.*"

"*Hau, tanksi. Manah'i blezela.*"

She nods to Maggie and Kirsten, both of whom look relieved. They had been concerned that the radio signal might be blocked by the same rock formations that conceal the troops. Runners are not going to work in this kind of fight, not with a river in between them. And line-of-sight signals would only draw the enemy's attention to the command post, where it is least wanted.

"*Wikcemna-topa*," she acknowledges. "Manny."

"*Manah'i hotanka na blezela.*"

Koda gives a thumbs-up as Manny breaks the link. He and his squadron of Black Hawks and Apaches wait five miles to the north of their position, set down on a straight stretch of farm road to await Maggie's signal.

"Jurgensen. Major Jurgensen. *Ayupte*," Koda calls.

Frank Jurgensen is a blond Wisonsin farm boy turned Marine major who has not a drop of Lakota blood. He has not a word of the language, either, except for the half-dozen signals Koda has drilled into him. His answer is awkward but clear: "*Ma-na-hee blay-zay-luh.*" Then, for a flourish, because he is a Marine, "*Wikeem-nah topa.*"

"*Wikcemna-topa*," she answers. Turning to Kirsten, she smiles briefly. "All good to go. No static, no language problems."

"Good," says Maggie. "At least we can get a courier to the guys on this side if we lose the major or he loses his vocabulary list." To Kirsten she says, "Are you picking up any droid chatter?"

Kirsten enters a code on the laptop and listens intently for a moment. "They're coming straight down the road. They should be getting into the first of the anti-tank mines—"

A sudden soft thump sounds to the northwest where the road winds through a stretch of lava flats. Koda turns on her heel, focusing on a thin column of smoke that rises into the clear air.

"—right about now," Kirsten finishes. She scowls, adjusting her headset. "They weren't expecting that. They've stopped. An armored personnel carrier hit the mine; the passengers are all dead — they were all human, apparently — and the shrapnel's taken out a couple droids."

"That one of yours?" Maggie asks Koda with a grin.

"Mine or Tacoma's. They—"

"They're going off road," Kirsten interrupts.

Maggie shoots Koda a questioning look and she answers, "They can't go overland in this terrain, Colonel. They'll have to get back on the highway. Not that it matters."

A second muffled explosion follows, and a third.

"Off-road mines?"

Koda nods, focusing the binoculars, searching for smoke. There is none this time. "Military droids?" she asks Kirsten.

Kirsten holds up her hand for quiet. After a moment she says, "They're going to stay on the road. They figure we can't have mined the whole stretch of highway. ... They're sorting their troops out. ... Humans in front ... regular droids off to the side. ... Their armor ... heavy-duty metalheads last and further out."

"They've sure as hell got their priorities sorted out," Maggie snorts. "You know, I keep forgetting they're machines. I keep hating the bastards."

"I keep hating Westerhaus." Kirsten bites the words off. "I keep hoping he's alive."

Koda opens her mouth to speak, then shuts it abruptly. She remembers the sharp crack of Kirsten's hand against General Hart's cheek upon her arrival at Ellsworth, the sense of contained rage coming off the woman's skin like heat. She turns her attention back toward the road. It is a matter of minutes before she hears another explosion, this one slightly louder, slightly nearer. A second follows, and a third, then nothing. She says, "They're through the first stretch of mines. They'll come on the next in about a mile."

"Gods, I hope the fog holds," Maggie mutters. "They're what, about an hour away?"

"At regular marching pace, yes. They can go faster if they get all the humans and regular droids up onto vehicles, but from what I'm picking up they don't have the wheels to do that." Kirsten pauses, listening. "They know there's a bridge here. They're sending out a couple of scouts in a truck."

"Damn," Maggie says quietly. "Can you fake their signals, Dr. King? Like all clear, come on?"

"I don't have the codes for that, Colonel."

"All right, we'll do it the old-fashioned way. Rivers, tell Dietrich to get half a dozen men down under the bridge. We're gonna play Billy Goat Gruff when the fuckers show up."

Koda raises the major again. "Wichasha sakpe kuta ceyakto. Numpa toka."

There is a pause, then the double click they have arranged as a signal for "say again". Koda repeats herself, more slowly. There is a long pause, and the sound of paper rustling. Just as she has resigned herself to English, the major says. "*Hau. Washte*," and the line goes dead.

A moment or two later, she can just see the squad, moving shapes of solid white darting through the fog toward the bridge. As they scramble down the bank to position themselves beneath the span, a Jeep painted in incongruous tropical camo, all deep green and blood-brown, comes to a sudden halt at the other end. Two forms, rifles at the ready, begin to work their way down its length, pausing to look over the railing at ten or twelve feet intervals.

Maggie, like Koda, has her binoculars up. "Can you tell what they are?"

"I'm not getting any signal off them, Colonel," says Kirsten. "If they're droids, they're not talking to each other."

In the distance, a mine goes off, and a thin curl of smoke rises. The column is closer now, and the sound echoes against the rocks. The two figures on the bridge pause, turning their heads in the direction of the blast. Then they resume their inspection, slowly working their way toward the end where ambush awaits them.

"Come on, come on," Maggie urges.

The scouts reach the southeast bank and step onto the road. One gestures back toward the river, pointing downward. Then both begin the descent, disappearing into the fog.

The sounds of the struggle come clearly over the water, little muffled by the fog. It is brief, and when it is over, five men in white camo emerge from beneath the bridge. One breaks away from the others, sprinting for the other side of the river. He picks up a com unit and speaks into it, then drives the Jeep off the road and down the sloping bank, to park it somewhere beneath the first pair of pylons. When he reappears he is running flat out, making for the single approach on the southeast side that has been left free of mines.

After that, there is little time to wait. A couple thousand yards from the bridge, the sun catches a glint of metal. Maggie sees it as the same time Koda does. "They're here."

Koda smiles slowly, her blood beginning to sing as it slips along her veins. "Hoka hey," she says. "It is a good day to fight."

"Here they come."

It is not a sound so much as it is a vibration, a wave propagating through earth and rock. There is a rhythm to it, of booted feet, human and not, tramping up the thin strip of highway, of metal treads crunching their way through snow and biting into the tarmac. From somewhere just out of sight around a basalt outcropping, the sun catches a glint of steel, then another and another as the enemy column winds its way through the maze of low rock walls and shallow gullies.

Koda swings her binoculars back up to try to catch first sight of the approaching force. They emerge between a pair of buttes, foot soldiers in uneven ranks, carrying an assortment of automatic rifles, grenade launchers, shoulder-fired LAAWS rockets. Some are in uniform, some not. "Conscripts?"

Beside her, Maggie scans the oncoming ranks, her mouth tightening. "Can't tell. We'll spare them if we can, as long as we can. But we don't take risks. The first one that fires a shot, we take 'em out."

Koda's com unit crackles to life. She listens briefly, then reports, "Tacoma says the column is about halfway past his position. They have a couple of mobile SAM missile launchers and some heavy guns, three howitzers. About fifteen percent of the enemy are the heavy military droids, pretty much what we figured. The rest are half-and-half humans and various domestic models — firedroids, Maid Marians, a few nannydroids. He says there's one in an old-fashioned parlor maid's uniform, toting an M-16." She listens again. "They've lost what appears to be about a third of their armored vehicles. They still have four tanks that Tacoma can see and a dozen APCs."

Maggie nods. "Could be better, but that cuts them down some. Good work with those mines, Rivers." She turns back to watching the enemy advance. "Tell that cousin of yours to start his engines and stand by. As soon as they get about half the heavy stuff out in the open, they're all his."

Koda relays the message swiftly. Like the colonel, she never takes her eyes from the oncoming troops.

"Dakota?" The voice is Kirsten's, a surprising hint of laughter in it.

"Yeah?"

"How the hell do you say 'parlor maid's uniform' in Lakota?"

Koda smiles in answer. "Simple. 'Silly-ass black and white dress with a frilly apron and ribbons.'"

Kirsten laughs briefly, then turns back to her com set. "Okay. An order is going up the line. They're going to go straight across the bridge. They bought the fake 'all clear'."

The human contingent is fully in the open now, strung out along the highway between the bridge and the point where the road emerges from the foothills. A band of general-use droids follows, a few out-liers of the military type ranging to the sides of the column. Koda spots the parlor maid, incongruous in its curly blonde doll's wig and beribboned cap. Another wears a firefighter's uniform, its blue shirt stained dark brown along its sleeves. Koda's blood sounds like a drum in her ears, and she struggles for control of her anger. *Fight cold, dammit.*

Finally the armor emerges onto the open highway, escorted by a hundred or so of the military droids. Koda locates one of the trucks carrying the SAMS, their launch tubes angled up at the ready. A pair of tanks follow, their cannons swiveled forward. They are close enough now that she can hear the characteristic whine of their engines. She glances to one side, but Maggie's attention is on the advancing enemy below them.

"Okay, come on," the colonel mutters softly. "Come on, you motherfuckers, come on...come on...come on...NOW!"

Koda keys her com and speaks sharply into the mic. "*Shic'eshi! Takpaye! Wana!*"

An ear-splitting whoop comes back through her earpiece. "*Unyanpi! Hoka hey!*" Then, still breathlessly but more quietly, "*Wikcemna-topa.*"

Koda echoes the sign-off, then turns to Kirsten and Maggie. "They're on their way."

It seems a lifetime, but is perhaps five minutes later that Kirsten raises a hand to her earpiece. "They're here."

Koda turns to see the sky above the hilltop swarming with monstrous locusts, the shriek of their turbo engines like the whine of plagues sweeping over the hapless grasslands, the pylons hanging like legs beneath their foreshortened wings bristling with chainguns and Hellfire missiles. They go over in a clamor of blades and the sweep of rotor wash, rattling the branches of the bare tree that spreads above the command post. Straining to see, Koda waves as the lead bird sweeps over the last of the low hills, giving them their first sight of the battleground.

From his side window, Manny picks out the three figures perched on the hillside, one of whom is waving at the mixed squadron of Black Hawks and Apaches as they descend on the enemy advancing toward the narrow bridge. He waves back, knowing she cannot see him, but feeling the tie of blood all the same. The green-lit screens on his console — one for radar, one for the laser-targeting mechanism — show the droids and the heavy armor strung out in formation. "Okay, Littleton," he says to the gunner seated in the nose of the craft below and in front of him. "Start picking your targets. Get the SAMs first."

"Gotcha, bro."

The target indicator appears above the shape of a launcher truck on the left hand LED screen as the aiming laser locks on; half a second later he feels a *whomp!* as the Hellfire leaves its perch beneath the port wing. It streaks away above the fog, its contrail curving slightly as its fins maneuver to set a straight course. Suddenly one of the SAMS is away, a blip on the radar screen. Manny leans on the joystick, putting the Apache over hard so that his shoulders ache where they press against his harness, and the missile speeds harmlessly by. On the ground, fire blossoms gold and red where the Hellfire strikes its target, secondary explosions adding to the roiling cloud of flame and smoke as it rises out of the mist and into the clear air. Briefly he notes the blazes set by other hits as he pulls back on the controls, taking them up and over and behind the enemy, and momentarily out of the range of their guns. "Report," he snaps into his mic. "Any casualties?"

One by one the squadron checks in. Only Andrews reports a hit. "Took a round to the fuselage, Apache One, but we're good to go."

"Okay, then. Let's go back for seconds."

They swoop down for a second pass over the column, which has almost reached the near end of the bridge. This time Littleton cuts loose with the chain guns, and Manny can see ordinary droids going down along the center of the line, but they seem to be doing very little damage to the military models on the perimeter. He dodges a couple of rockets, swerving wildly, tipping the bird almost over on its side. Not for the first time, he wishes he had his Tomcat under him, laying down a long stick of five-hundred-pounders the length of the road and ending the whole fucking mess right then and there. He understands why the brass have decided to hold back on the jets, and he agrees, at least in principle. He just wishes he had that kind of firepower now. Which does him no good whatsoever. *If wishes were buffalo...*

The backsweep takes out the second missile launcher and a tank, as well as several armored personnel carriers. And, he notes with satisfaction, any personnel they might have been carrying.

Littleton reads his mind. "'Spose we got some of the goddam metalheads with those APCs, Manny?"

"Let's hope—" He breaks off abruptly as Koda's voice crackles in his earpiece.

"*Washte,* Manny. *Ake.*"

"*Hau. Wikcemna-topa.*"

"What's that?" asks Littleton.

"She says do it again, bro. So," he clicks the com through to the other choppers, "we do it again."

Manny takes the squadron back over the command post hill to loop around for the third pass, waving again at the figures below him. There is no chance that they can spot him, but he can see them and know that they are secure, screened as they are by the lines of trees behind and in front of them. In the chill of battle, it makes a small warm spot of both affection and pride. Hell, he admits to himself, he's even developing a soft spot for the little blonde ice cube.

Mind you, not *that* way. As far as he's concerned, she has all the sex appeal of a circular saw. Run into her the wrong way and BZZZZZZZZZ.

He swings the Apache about and comes in low for the third pass, the squadron in loose formation behind him. Off to his right, a Black Hawk takes a direct hit, its fuel tank exploding in billows of smoke and flame still in midair, its fuselage wheeling drunkenly out of the sky to plunge into a company of droids, incinerating them instantly. Littleton lets fly their last two Hellfires, then turns the chaingun and the small-gauge rockets onto the line of foot soldiers. One with a LAAWS tube braced against its shoulder goes sprawling satisfyingly on the tarmac under the hail of thirty-millimeter rounds. As they sweep up the rise of the piedmont behind, Manny can see another file of armed men and women moving into position down a dry creek bed: Tacoma and the front line of his force, preparing to close the trap they have so carefully set.

Time for the last pass. "Give 'em the works this time through," he orders Littleton. "Whatever we've got left." Manny feels the thump as the rocket tubes discharge the last of the Hydras. "Okay, that's it. We're headed—"

The impact jars all his bones together, snapping his jaw shut and bloodying his tongue between his teeth. The Apache seems to hang suspended for a moment, hovering, and it almost feels normal. Then the bird begins to spin laterally, the tail and tail rotor no longer answering to the steering column. "Oh, shit," Manny says, very softly, just as Littleton yells out, loud enough to hear even over the sudden grating noise of the engines, "We're hit!"

"I know damn well that's not normal!" Kirsten exclaims, watching beside Koda as the Apache spins slowly, almost gracefully, on the axis of its mast. "Isn't Manny in one of the Apaches?"

Koda feels the blood drain from her face, sinking to her heart with the weight of lead. "He's in that Apache." She points to the bundle of red-tipped arrows newly painted on the side of the fuselage. "That's his sign."

Maggie steps closer to her, gripping Koda's other hand hard. "If anyone can get that bird down in one piece, Manny can."

Kirsten has moved up beside her, too, silently offering her presence. Koda can feel the fear in the other women, resonating with her own. Yet there is comfort there, too. "I know. He always did manage to walk away from — Goddam!"

Her voice dies in her throat as the chopper begins to cartwheel, heeling over half onto its side and spinning counterrhythm to its rotor as it falls out of the sky, plunging toward the broad meadow between the bridge and the woods beyond. Koda watches as it descends, not breathing, not daring to breathe.

*Got 'bout as much chance of survival as a goldfish in a shark tank,* Manny reflects wryly as he loses control of the Apache altogether and can only fold himself up per procedure and brace for the impact.

It comes with a crash like thunder walking in the mountains, reverberating in his ears and along his bones. Manny opens his eyes to find the nose of the Apache buried in the snow and himself hanging suspended by his straps just over his control panel. Out the front port he can see two of the rotor blades broken off where they have sliced into the earth. The buckle of his harness presses hard into his solar plexus, and he carefully eases himself off the end of his control stick, broken off just below the grip. If not for catching in the buckle, it would presently be jutting out his back ribs. The pressure and the thought both turn his stomach, and he pukes up his guts as he hangs there over the display panels, spattering them and the back of Littleton's helmet liberally with his breakfast. When the nausea passes, it occurs to him that he needs to get the hell out of here, and he reaches for his boot knife to cut himself out of this witch's cradle. His right arm does not move. *Shit.*

It doesn't hurt, particularly, but that doesn't mean anything. More encouraging is the fact that he cannot see any blood on the sleeve of his flight suit, or any splinters of bone protruding. *Okay. Let's try this...*

Twisting his left shoulder and lifting his right leg, he manages to grasp the knife's hilt and draw it. Carefully he saws himself loose, setting first one foot, then the other, down on the back of his gunner's seat, gingerly straddling the shattered steering column. Littleton has not moved.

One hand on the altimeter, the other on the fuel gauge to avoid the slick of half-digested egg and cereal, he touches the other man's shoulder. "Joe. Hey, Joe."

No answer.

*Shit.* Pulling his left glove off with his teeth, Manny feels for the pulse where the great veins thrum in the neck, working his fingers down under Littleton's collar. Nothing. *Shit, again. Sorry, bro.*

The door, of course, is stuck.

*Of course. Why get lucky now?* With the butt of his handgun Manny hammers repeatedly at the Lexan of the window until it gives and he can break the jagged pieces out of their steel frame. He slithers out through the too-small opening, pushing stubbornly with his feet and pulling with his good left arm. Somewhere around the halfway mark, the nerves in his dislocated right arm wake up, and he feels himself go light-headed with the pain. His mouth is dry as tinder. Shock.

He can't afford it. He gives one last shove with all the strength of his back and legs behind it, and suddenly he is free, tumbling out into the snow. Up onto his feet then, and running for the line of the woods and the friendly forces he knows are there, stumbling, his right arm dangling uselessly at his side as a rocket lands less than five meters behind him, picks him up and tosses him over a hump in the ground, and he is sliding, tobogganing down the slope on his back and butt, just like he used to do as a kid with Tacoma and Koda streaking along beside him.

He reaches the bottom with a thump and surely he is dreaming because a figure detaches itself from one of the century-old sycamores and comes running toward him, levering him up out of the snow and shoving him forward toward the woods, one foot after the other, head down, breath tearing at his throat and it suddenly comes to him that safety is ten feet in front of him and...

"He's going to make it! Koda, look!"

Dakota turns her head to follow Kirsten's pointing finger. A man has fought his way out of the downed copter, bit by bit wriggling and pushing through one of the windows. Koda puts up her binoculars, desperately attempting to focus on his face. She cannot, but she knows the anatomy of an Apache, and she can see clearly that the broken window is the one above as the copter sits crazily tilted on its nose in the snow. The pilot's seat.

*Thank you, Ina Maka*, she breathes silently. She watches, her heart still in her throat as her cousin makes his way drunkenly over the meadow to the woods beyond, then disappears from sight as another soldier emerges to help him to shelter. Aloud she says, "I knew he'd make it. Manny's just too damn contrary to die."

"Family trait?" Maggie asks with a cant of her eyebrow.

"Yeah, I guess it is." Koda cannot stop her mouth from pulling into a grin. "Just got good Lakota genes, that's all."

Koda lets out a long, relieved breath and turns her attention back to the battlefield. Even without binoculars, it is evident that the droid army is reforming its column, shifting and eddying around the burned out shells of tanks and APCs that stand in the roadway. A couple hundred meters from the bridge, one of the few remaining carriers has been pressed into service as a wrecker, nosing the shattered hulks off the tarmac to make way for what is left of the heavy weapons and armor. Fragments of bright titanium litter the shoulders of the road where chaingun and rocket have found their marks; elsewhere the snow is stained red, and the motionless figures torn and twisted into nightmare shapes by slug and shrapnel are of flesh, not metal. The half-melted frame of the downed Black Hawk rests on bare earth where ice and snow have melted away from it, a ring of motionless forms around it. From this distance it is impossible to tell whether they are droid or human. One of the howitzers crawls slowly back into line midway the column, behind the human troops and in front of the military droid contingent. Eerily, it seems to move on its own, its driver invisible behind the housing of the barrel.

Beside her, Maggie observes, "Damn good job, all things considered. That big gun is getting too close to do us damage, and things are a lot more equal than they were half an hour ago."

"We're losing our cover, Colonel," Kirsten observes. Except for the lowest elevations, in hollows of ridges and along the river's surface, the fog has begun to burn away. The meadow between the bridge and the woods gleams in the sudden sun, the snow refracting the light like prisms.

"It's okay. We've almost reached the point where it won't matter." Maggie glances over her shoulder at Kirsten, back at her com board, the fingers of one hand pressed behind her ear as if to strengthen the signals she is picking up. "Any change on the other side?"

"Negative, Colonel. They still don't know we're here; they think the choppers were a sortie flying out of the base. No indication they know Manny survived, either."

Maggie shakes her head, half in perplexity. "Much as I hate the things, there's something to be said for an enemy that doesn't think anything it's not told to think."

"What's really interesting," Koda adds, "is that none of the humans seem to have caught on, either."

"You think?"

"I think some of them think. They're just not telling."

"That does seem likely, doesn't it? We'll know for sure where they stand real soon now," Maggie says thoughtfully. After a long moment, she adds, "Go ahead and pass the word to spare them if we can, but anyone or anything that shoots at us is a fair target."

Koda repeats the order into her mic in Lakota, and is relieved to find that the new com officer with Jurgensen's company is her scapegrace cousin. "That was fast," she says, after he acknowledges the order and repeats it in English for Major Jurgensen.

He laughs. "Medics got my arm shot full of novocaine and strapped to my side. Mouth works fine, though. We got one happy CO over here, now he doesn't have to worry about his vocabulary list."

"We've got a happy CO over here who's relieved your worthless butt's in one piece."

"She ain't the only one. Take care, cuz. *Wikcemna-topa.*"

"*Wikcemna-topa,*" she signs off.

On the flat ground below, the enemy column has fallen in and is slowly beginning to move toward the bridge. Koda catches herself clenching her teeth and deliberately relaxes her muscles as they advance. *Come on, come on, come on,* she chants silently to herself. When the first of the troops sets foot on the span, she feels her spine unwind like an uncoiling spring.

"Okay, that's it. They're committed," Maggie says softly. "Wait 'til they get that howitzer within ten or fifteen meters of the bridge, then give

Tacoma the signal to blow it."

Koda watches as the enemy troops make the crossing, humans to the fore, keeping to the straight line of unmined highway when they reach the eastern bank. They are close enough now that Koda can hear the irregular tramp of their feet. Droids next, oddly matched as they are, metal feet ringing against the pavement, following the men and women in front.

The first of the remaining APCs grinds onto the bridge, followed by the two surviving tanks. The big gun lumbers along, now twenty meters away from the riverbank.

"Almost," Maggie murmurs. "Almost..."

"Nothing untoward on their com, Colonel," Kirsten reports. "Situation nominal."

After a long moment's pause, Maggie says, "Rivers, give the order."

Koda clicks through to Tacoma. "*Wana, thiblo. Ceyakto ihagyeye.*"

"*Washte,*" comes his response, clipped and brief. "*Wikcemna-topa.*"

A few seconds stretch out, become an impossibly long minute, expand into infinity. When it comes, the explosion roars like thunder in the earth, a rumbling under their feet that shakes the rocks of the hill where they stand, sets the branches of the bare tree above them to thrashing. Underneath the moving army, the pylons begin to buckle. A jagged crack splits the asphalt and its concrete bed; the report is as sharp as a rifle shot magnified a thousand times. The span sags in the middle, tipping crazily down toward the water, spilling human and machine alike into the swift current of the Cheyenne. A cloud of dust and smoke boils up from the mist, a dirty grey pall that covers bridge and river, rolling along the meadow to overtake the soldiers who have just crossed, enveloping them, sending them blind and directionless into the minefields that bracket the road and riverbanks.

Dulled by fog and distance, the muffled thump of explosions of the anti-personnel charges, interspersed with the screams of the enemy troops, comes to Koda where she stands on the hill. She watches as others plunge toward the water, humans and human limbs and bright machine parts thrown out by the force of the blast. The wind carries the acrid smell of dynamite and plastique, the iron odor of blood. "*Washte,*" she whispers to herself, and raises her eyes to the foothills of the Paha Sapa where another storm pours down the lava slopes.

Tacoma and his warriors, four hundred of them, swarm down the slope to cut off the enemy retreat and push them into their own rearguard and the river. He leaps from rock outcrop to ridge as easily as a mountain cat, half his troops following straight behind, the other half fanning out to block the churned and rutted road. His breath comes easily, his heart beating out the rhythm of the war chant and his blood singing in his veins. He struggles to keep the broad expanse of the field in his view, fighting the predator's instinct that narrows his vision to the enemy and the clear path to it. From his high ground, he can see that Jurgensen's smaller contingent on the other side of the stream has broken cover from the woods and is charging down on the humans and domestic androids now trapped between them and the minefield laid along the bank. On the near side, the military droids and their vehicles have begun to lose formation and mill about without direction in tight knots; their mechanical drone reaches him even here.

Beneath him the earth shudders, and with a high, whining buzz like all the hornets of the world singing in harmony, an 81-mm mortar shell sails overhead to land with a roar just short of the last few APCs in the armored column. Earth and spraying snow fountain up from the point of impact in the road, and Tacoma throws himself flat behind a low ridge of black rock, the rest of his contingent following suit as best they can. "You're too high, man!" he yells into his com. "Just a degree or two shorter!"

The next round arcs down over his position just as the line of mechanical demons sorts itself out. These are not just artificial humans with weapons, tin men with a coder chip for a heart. These are the Pentagon's best, or worst, only vaguely humanoid, self-propelled multiple weapons systems with real-time self-adapting programs and the resistance of tanks. Their heads are multiple sensor arrays, optics that span the visible spectrum and beyond into the infrared and ultraviolet, able to locate and map an enemy force by their body heat as well as their shape against the landscape. Their arms and hands are chaingun barrels, the ammunition feed housed in the long rectangle of the titanium thorax. Some are set on gearboxes with belt drives; others, in a parody of human shape, possess jointed lower extensions ending in smaller treads. They advance with the rhythmical slouching walk of antique zoot-suiters. With a slow grinding of metal limbs, they begin to bear down on the company crouching at the edge of the piedmont, clustered tubes at their arms' ends spraying death. Tacoma can hear the rounds whining over his head, the sharp crack when one strikes the stone behind him.

Another mortar shell rises to meet them, and this time the shell strikes the margin of their advance. Tacoma yells, "Got 'em! Mark your baseline!"

In his peripheral vision, he can see a second group, their treads tearing up gouts of snow and earth, moving off to meet the company now deployed across and to either side of the road. There is a certain terrible beauty to them as they begin to move inexorably toward the human lines, sun striking their titanium hides and splintering into sprays of light like shooting stars, even as the gunners hidden in a rock-cut gully figure their speed and the mortar rounds begin to hammer down on them. It is almost, he thinks, like a dance as the droids' internal computers calculate the rate of fire and the big guns' range, and they begin to dash forward at broken intervals to put themselves just behind or just in front of the steep arc cut by the artillery fire. Where it strikes them full on, it leaves a row of craters gouged into the earth, ringed in a fine fall of silver ash.

Tacoma watches them come on, inexorable and unthinking, counting off the seconds until they come within reach of smaller weapons. Gaps appear in their ranks, kill after kill, and still they come on. Softly Tacoma speaks into his com. "Almost, almost; all units hold your fire. Remember not to waste bullets on these tin cans."

*Come on, you motherfuckers, come on.* It is almost a prayer.

"*Thiblo!*" His com crackles to life. "*Wana! Khuteye!*"

"All right!" Tacoma bellows. "Give 'em hell!" Twisting his neck to look behind, he can just see the blunt ends of the launchers as they empty their load straight into the line of oncoming droids, the LAAWS rockets and grenades striking their targets straight on, blasting off the heads with their sensor arrays, tearing huge holes in the magazines where chest and abdomen should be.

Koda cannot see individual droids fall, but she does see the sudden flares as the explosives strike their targets, the wavering of the line as they re-form and begin to advance more slowly on the ridge where her brother's troops lie in wait. They do not waver. The rattle of gunfire and the deeper voice of the mortars comes to her sharply, refracted off the water's surface and the lift of rock to the northwest.

"Kirsten, are you getting anything?"

Seated in the back of the truck, Kirsten adjusts controls on two of her units, listening intently. "Negative. There's no pullback order yet."

Beside her, Maggie lowers her own field glasses and remarks, "You know, this plan depends on those damned things working the way they're supposed to. If their 'save your own metal ass' code doesn't kick in fairly soon, we're fucked."

Koda trains her own binoculars on the field below her. Remains of droids litter the field behind their line, their bright fragments taking the sunlight in among the mangled remains of APCs and troop transports. After what seems an eternity, the advance on her brother's position seems to slow as the droids' line shortens, begins to take longer and longer to straggle back into order after each wave of rocket fire. The mortars continue to hail destruction down on them. "They've got to run out of ammo fairly soon," says Koda.

Maggie's mouth crooks up in a wry smile. "Them or us?" Then she says, "The good news is on the other bank. Have a look."

Closer to, to the southeast of the river, Jurgensen's men are pressing the remainder of the enemy humans and household androids steadily back toward the water. Remains both metal and human lie scattered over the meadow, the latter identifiable by red stains spreading in the snow around them. Here and there, a human form kneels with its hands tied behind its back — surrendered prisoners left behind the advancing line to await either death at their allies' hands or judgement at their captors'. No one can be spared to escort them to the relative safety of the woods.

"There goes the Geneva Convention," Koda observes.

Maggie pauses, sweeping the field with her binoculars. "I expected more would give themselves up. I don't like it that we have this few. I don't like it at all."

"What the hell is in it for them? The bastards at the jail collaborated to save their lives, but these—"

"Threats. Promises." Maggie interrupts her. "Hatred. Any of those—" An exclamation from Kirsten interrupts.

"That's it! There's the code for retreat. They're going to pull back toward the river and try to lure our forces out."

Koda sees the faint hollowing of Maggie's chest, even under layers of thermal insulation, as the colonel breathes a relieved sigh. "Good. Thank Goddess the son-of-a-bitch who programmed those damned things never had an original tactic to his name."

Kirsten shakes her head. "Somebody did. They're not just going to pull back; they're going to try to cross the river."

"Shit," Maggie says quietly.

Following her gaze, Koda sees what the other woman dreads. Their own forces have pressed the enemy back up against the water and the minefields on the near bank. If the droids cross the remnants of the bridge, the best defense will be the guns hidden in the woods. They are not precision instruments. Their own troops may die indiscriminately. A movement above the treetops draws her eye. High up, no more than a shadow against the blue depths, a hawk rides a thermal, spiraling outward in widening circles. Her scream comes to them on the wind, high and piercing.

Tacoma turns his head to see one of his men go down, a spatter of blood and brain where his head had been. A ripple seems to go through the ranks of the droids, and they turn without warning, beginning to make their way back toward the bridge at speed. A flurry of mortar rounds lands short, sending up a cloud of dirt and snow, but knocking over no more than a half dozen of the enemy. Two of them lever themselves up, their joints stiff, and begin to grind their way back toward the river, following the rest.

"Goddam!" Tacoma springs to his own feet, yelling to the squads behind him. "They're headed back toward the bridge! They're going to try to cross!" Then into his com, "Recalibrate! They're retreating!"

"Got it," the gunner answers through a crackle of static. "I'm gonna put up a spotter. Give me some distance between you and them."

"You keep firing as long as you have ammo! Never mind where anyone is!"

"Sarge—"

"Goddammit, you keep shooting, you hear me? They don't have the ordnance to deal with those things on the other side! We gotta get 'em before they make the crossing! You got that, goddammit?"

"Got it," says the gunner meekly.

A half second later, a mortar round comes flying over Tacoma's head, landing in the rear rank of the now retreating droids. It leaves a quite satisfactory hole where a half dozen of them had been.

Tacoma's world shrinks to a small sphere of space where the only sound is a cacophony of explosions: mortars, grenades, shoulder-fired rockets going off all about him. His actions become mechanical, repeated by troops up and down the length of the line. There are fewer than there were before; as near as he can tell, he has lost a quarter of his troops. A straggle of men and women, some of them hobbling, others trailing bloody arms and legs, stumble forward from the position they have held across the road. Load, raise the launcher, fire. Load, raise the launcher, fire. Over and over again.

And always the retreating backs of the enemy, spattered with earth and snow as they go down one after the other onto the rutted ground. The advance of his troops, step by step, leaves fresh blood in the snow.

Some of it is his own. Something, he is not quite sure what, has struck him on the forehead. Without breaking stride, he raises his hand to swipe at the blood pouring into his eyes. And he keeps moving without thought.

Load.

Raise the launcher.

Fire.

Over and over again.

"What the hell's that?"

Koda swings the M-16 riding her shoulder down into position and raises her binoculars. A plume of dust from the rutted and drying road appears halfway down the hill where the command post stands, curving and backswitching as the path makes its crooked way up the slope. "It's a couple of Jeeps, I think."

Maggie turns her attention from the field of battle to scan the newcomers. "It's a couple of Jeeps full of idiot flyboys."

As the small convoy comes into closer focus, Koda can make out the unmistakable freckled face of Andrews at the wheel of the first vehicle. He has not bothered to change out of his flight suit or helmet and handles the bucking Jeep with much the same offhand élan as his Black Hawk. Some of the other pilots have changed into standard ground combat head buckets, but not bothered with the rest of their gear. The vehicles bristle with armaments: an M-60 apiece, grenade launchers, LAAWS.

"Just can't leave well enough alone," Maggie remarks tartly, but there is pride in her voice as much as exasperation.

"You lead by example, Colonel," Kirsten says quietly.

Koda turns swiftly to look at her, but there is no irony in the other woman's face. That pleases her, in a quiet way she cannot now take time to analyze.

Maggie, too, has taken it as the compliment intended. She grins. "Never did know when to quit."

One more steep climb and the Jeeps pull, brakes squealing, into the small flat space where the troop carrier cum com center sits. Andrews climbs out and salutes smartly, somehow managing to cover Maggie, Koda, and Kirsten all in the single gesture. "The Third Damn Fools, reporting for duty, ma'am."

Maggie looks them up and down with a drill sergeant's scowl. "You can't leave well enough alone, huh? Just gotta get in there and mix it up mano a mano."

"YES, MA'AM!"

"Goddam Hallelujah Chorus," she says. "Okay, here's the deal—"

"Colonel!" Kirsten's voice cuts through the banter. "The droids are almost to the bridge head. Sergeant Rivers just came through on clear. He's going to try to get in front of them but doesn't think he can hold all of them."

Instantly serious, Maggie snaps, "And—"

"He requests covering fire from the mortars back in the woods."

Maggie's face goes grey. Then, quietly she says, "Tell Jurgensen to shell what's left of the bridge. We'll try that first."

Kirsten turns back to her mic, speaking into it in English. The battle has reached the melee stage; strategic surprise is no longer possible.

Fear catches at Koda's throat. Shelling the bridge is a stalling tactic, a forlorn hope. Its complete destruction would require a howitzer, a bigger gun than they have, with a range too long for the relatively confined space of the valley below. Without speaking she turns her field glasses on the fight at the northwest end of the bridge. A company of the heavy military model droids grinds its way slowly toward the bridgehead, flanked on one side by a much smaller human force that ducks and runs and ducks again, firing off grenade launchers and shoulder rockets at every possibly opening. The troops on the southeast side are completely engaged with the remnants of the human and domestic droid forces; they cannot spare a squad.

She searches the forces on the far bank, looking for one man. Tacoma is down there. She knows it. She cannot make out his face or tell one shape from another under the camo and the layers of Polartec and thermal nylon, but there is one soldier out front and to the side that she knows with utter certainty is her brother. Her brother Tacoma, who has just called down a strike on his own position.

A red haze passes over her eyes. Her vision narrows to that one point where she knows he runs along the basalt table, sprawling where he can behind a low rise, heaving up the tube of his grenade launcher to fire when feasible. Impossibly keen, her ears bring her the clang of M-16 rounds on the metal skin of the droids on the near side; the scream of a soldier suddenly shot in the gut, doubling over in pain as his lifeblood runs out between his fingers. The hot metallic smell comes to her on the wind. Hardly aware of what she does, she passes her tongue over her teeth, tasting the richness of the odor.

With movements that seem ponderous, she slips loose of her rifle, lets the binoculars fall from her hand to go tumbling down the slope of the hill. Two long strides carry her to the back bumper of the last Jeep, another into the driver's seat. Human voices batter at her, shouting, a jumble of words that she neither heeds nor cares to.

KODANOSTOPWAITDAMMIT

MAAMYOUCANTDOTHAT

ATLEASTWAITFORMEYOUIDIOT

And she is bouncing down the hill in the Jeep, accelerator to the floor on a forty-degree downslope that probably ought to send her flying hood over tailpipe, but somehow she manages to keep the damn donkey of a machine on the road. There are other people in it with her, hanging on for their lives — a tall, lean, dark-faced woman yelling something into her ear, and a smaller one with hair that burns like white flame in the sunlight shrieking unintelligibly — and behind her she hears the roar and clatter of other engines as they speed down the hill straight toward the fighting, toward the near end of the bridge. As she pulls the vehicle onto the flat meadow at the foot of the rise, the first of the mortar shells streaks toward the far bridgehead, landing just short of the northwest bank and impacting the shattered concrete with a roar and a cloud of grey-white dust that clears to show a few large pieces of the bridge smashed to smaller pieces, but not much effect otherwise. A second shell screams over, and another, and another.

In the narrow focus of her vision, Koda can see a figure scrambling out onto the spars of half-collapsed asphalt and cement where broken slabs jut up against each other at unlikely angles like some strange rock formation on a sea-beaten coast. She shifts gears and sets the Jeep straight for the near end, steering her way somehow through grenade craters and over the splintered remains of droids. Her helmet flies off her head, and her hair unfurls behind her with her speed. A huge shout goes up around her, but she pays no attention, noting only out of the edges of her sight a convoy, no larger than the one she leads, streaking down on the battle out of nowhere, spilling out of the Black Hills, truck-mounted machine guns spraying bullets that bounce as harmlessly as pebbles off the titanium hides of the androids.

Just short of the near end of the bridge Koda stands on the brakes, bringing the Jeep to a shuddering halt that nearly throws her free. Snatching a belt of grenades and a launcher from the back of the vehicle, she speeds for the bridge, her eyes on that lone figure now firing on the advancing droids from the meager cover of a broken pylon. Behind her someone is shouting CEASEFIRECEASEFIREDAMMIT, and the broken

structure shakes beneath her as she leaps from concrete boulder to concrete boulder, grasping an upright length of rebar to steady herself as she
plants her feet and fires. She pushes off from her position, finds footing
again a meter ahead, fires again, catches a foot in a cage of steel supports
and shakes herself free to kneel and fire yet again on the advancing metal
demons. She is dimly aware of voices behind her, screaming out her name,
a warcry, curses. She cannot tell and does not care. She feels the recoil of
weapons loosed behind her, though, and knows that more of the droids are
going down than she can reasonably account for. *Thank you, Ina Maka.*
The thought winds through her mind, never touching the part of her brain
that drives her feet forward, powers her arms through the routine of load,
lift and fire, again and again as the droids clustered at the far end of the
bridge go down, crashing into those pressing forward behind them, some of
those behind falling forward to strike the ruins of the span and tumble down
into the metal-clotted water below.

There are fewer and fewer of them standing between her and the hills
beyond, and finally, there are none. She stares into a face inches from
hers, her fingers caught up in gentle hands as a voice says, again and
again, "*Tanksi? Tanski!* Koda, you in there? Answer me!"

Slowly the world takes shape around her. She is looking into the deep
brown of her brother's eyes, blurred where blood has run into them and carried streaks of his warpaint down his face in runnels crusted with dust and
minute grains of cement. There is a strange silence — no more shooting,
no more shouting. She can hear the rush of the current as the Cheyenne
finds its way in small rapids around the debris that juts out of the water.

Gingerly she glances around her. Andrews perches on a slab of concrete, teeth clenched, grimly cutting his left boot away from an ankle
already swollen half again its size. *I need to get up and tend to that*, she
thinks vaguely. Maggie, beside her, leans on the tube of a rocket launcher,
favoring her right foot. There is a streak of bright blood on the leg of her
pants above it, but her face is clear and bright. Kirsten, face as pale as her
hair, rubs at her shoulder where the end of a grenade launcher is printed
into the padded fabric of her jacket.

Koda's eyes return to her own hands, scraped raw and bloody in her
scramble across the ruins of the bridge. Gently she looses them from
Tacoma's grasp and looks around her, taking in the battlefield with its scattered dead and the deliberate movements of survivors walking among the
fallen, looking for wounded. She glances back at Maggie, then at her
brother again. "We won?"

"Yeah," he says, slipping his hands under her arms and levering them
both to their feet.

Even at her height, he is taller still as she gazes up at him. Slowly he
turns her to face the others. Somehow she cannot seem to find her bound-
aries; some part of her is still Koda Rivers, but she feels herself spread
thin, strung out, strands of her substance mingled with her brother's, Maggie's, Kirsten's, the thoughts of Andrews on his perch and the men still
scattered on the field beyond.

"That's the goddammedest thing I ever saw, ma'am, like something out
of a storybook," Andrews says, images tumbling through his mind of Lance-
lot stampeding across an English meadow toward a dragon, a Greek general in a mountain pass called the Hot Gates, a long haired man in a kilt,

wild with freedom, brandishing a sword almost as tall as himself.

Maggie shoots him a sharp glance, more than half-amused at the blatant hero-worship, but why the hell not? It's the bravest thing she's ever seen in her life, too. She tells herself that the pride she feels in this woman is totally irrational; she has not had the teaching of her, and yet the pride is there. Pride and regret both. She glances briefly upward, to the high reach of sky where the hawk still circles, and knows that an ending has been reached, an ending that, like the rising circles of the red-tail's spiral, is also a beginning. She lets her rocket launcher fall among the tumbled wreckage of the bridge and steps forward to put an arm around Koda's shoulders. "You were born for this," she says simply.

Koda's eyes are still wide, still not focused entirely on the reality in front of her. "You're the commander. You followed me."

Maggie feels her mouth stretch into a grin. "Well, you didn't exactly give us a choice. You were out front and running away without a word. We had to follow or be left behind."

The words echo in Kirsten's mind: *left behind, left behind, alone.* And suddenly she knows, directly, the same way she knows that her side hurts where she has pulled a muscle in the mad dash for the Jeep and then the insane stumble over the wreckage of the bridge, firing a weapon she's barely touched before, that she is not alone. From somewhere in the depth of her mind, an image forms: a dark-haired woman in a beaded dress, promising...promising, it seems, this woman who has just pulled them all out of themselves and drawn from them a courage and a passion they never knew was in them. Drawn them straight into the heart of the flame and through it, to come out tempered steel on the other side. "Hey," she says quietly, moving to support Koda on her other side.

Koda feels their arms around her, Tacoma still half-holding her up from behind, and they begin to make their slow progress back toward the southeast end of the bridge. *It was easier,* she thinks, *when I was not thinking at all.* A couple of times she stumbles and nearly falls to hands and knees on the jagged concrete. Somewhere someone is shouting. The sound starts small: one man, and then a woman joining him, and another, until it seems the whole small army is yelling, some of them waving their weapons in the air in a decidedly dangerous fashion. It seems odd that Maggie does not have something sharp to say about that. "What's the matter?" she asks. "What the hell's with all the noise?"

"You are," Kirsten says quietly. "Wave at them."

"Huh?" *This makes no sense. I am not drunk. I may, however, be losing my mind.* The thought is surprisingly clear.

"Wave," Maggie repeats from her other side. "They've fought like the devil themselves. They deserve the acknowledgement."

Koda raises her arm from Maggie's shoulders and waves at the troops. Their cheering — because that's what it is, she suddenly realizes — goes on and on and on. Finally her arm will no longer hold itself up, and her knees buckle with sudden weariness. "I'm sorry, I can't do anymore," she says. Maggie bears her up again, Kirsten still firm on the other side.

"Come on," she says in her best no-backtalk scientist voice. "Let's get you home."

# CHAPTER SIXTEEN

The room is as dark as guilty secrets. Only the faint light from the hallway enters, laying a wedge-shaped pattern across the carpet. It reaches the very edge of the bed and goes no further, as if afraid to disturb the vigil being kept above.

Kirsten sits on a chair that has seen better decades, staring down at Koda, who is so deeply unconscious that she appears, for all the world, dead. Only the slight rise and fall of her chest reassures her silent watcher. Heavily bandaged hands lie quiescent on the dark coverlet, as still as the body that bears them. Dakota looks small, almost fragile as she lies so still, a lost and broken child in her parents' bed. Kirsten swallows the lump in her throat, blinking to dispel the vision. She looks up, startled, at a soft sound from the doorway.

Maggie enters, bearing two steaming mugs. Smiling slightly, she walks to Kirsten's side and hands her one. "Thought you could use this."

Kirsten accepts the offered mug eagerly, wrapping her chilled hands around it and inhaling the comforting aroma with a sigh of pleasure. "Thank you. This is perfect." Taking a small sip, she lets the coffee roll over her tongue, savoring it for a timeless moment before swallowing. "Bless you, Colonel," she breathes. "This is just what the doctor ordered."

"Seeing as you're sitting in my bedroom," Maggie replies, smirking, "I think we could dispense with the formalities, don't you?"

Kirsten glances up, the expression of a guilty child plain upon her face. She begins to rise, but Maggie motions her back down. "No. It's all right. Stay." Her smirk softens into a true smile. "I have a strange sense of humor, sometimes."

Nodding, Kirsten returns the smile with a hesitant one of her own. The space between them is like a chasm; one which she suddenly wishes she could cross. If she only knew how.

Maggie lowers herself to perch casually on the lower corner of the large bed. Koda doesn't twitch. The colonel captures Kirsten in her steady regard. "You were pretty impressive out there," she murmurs. "Didn't know you could handle a grenade launcher." Her lips twitch with a smirk just dying to come out. "Learn that in Bionics 101?"

This time, Kirsten gets the joke and chuckles, saluting Maggie with her mug. Her grin fades. "Absolute terror," she admits, looking back down at the still figure on the bed. "It was like...I don't know...like I knew what she was going to do before she did it. And I knew that I wasn't going to be left behind." She swallows hard, vision trebling as some strange almost-memory steals through her consciousness like a thief in the night. "Not again."

Maggie raises an eyebrow in silent inquiry. Kirsten shakes off both the question and the strange feeling with a deliberate closing of her eyes. When she opens them again, she is more her old self — more or less. Her smile, when it comes, is natural, unbidden. "She was a sight to see, though, wasn't she?"

"That she was," Maggie replies. "I had myself half-convinced I was watching some old Audie Murphy flick." A frown creases her forehead. "The top kick in me is furious with her. It was completely foolhardy and dangerous in the extreme." The frown disappears as she shrugs. "But it worked, and we're alive to tell the tale. And I guess that's all that really matters in the end."

"So that means you won't take it out of her hide later?" Kirsten queries with a small smirk of her own.

Maggie snorts. "As if I could."

Looking back down at the occupant of the bed, Kirsten sobers. "There will be a later, though, right?" She looks up, startled once again, this time by the warm hand that clasps her wrist.

"There will be," Maggie affirms in a tone that brooks no contradiction. "Things like this...take a lot out of her. Almost everything, I think." She looks down at Koda, her smile warm and affectionate.

The adoration on her face causes Kirsten a brief stab of discomfort before she savagely pushes it away.

"She just needs some time to get those batteries of hers recharged, and she'll be good as new."

When Maggie releases her wrist, Kirsten lifts her arm to finish the last of her coffee. Then she makes as if to rise. "I'll...um..."

"No. Stay."

Kirsten looks at her, eyes slightly widened.

Maggie smiles. "Stay. I need to go tell everyone that she's doing well, and debrief the general as well. I don't expect to be back until morning, at least. And..." She takes a deep breath and lets it out slowly, opting for the truth, even though the words are like shards of glass in her mouth. "I think she knows you're here, and I think that's very important to her."

"But—"

"Please." Keeping her emotions under tight control, Maggie rises gracefully from her perch on the bed and quickly strides across the room. A soft voice halts her in her tracks.

"Maggie?"

She doesn't, can't, turn, but the stiffness of her shoulders shows Kirsten that she's listening.

"Thank you."

Unable to speak for fear her voice will betray her, Maggie settles for a nod and continues out of the room.

**Eyes closed, Koda** finds herself floating on a current of...something. Air, water, she can't tell which, nor does she especially care. It is neither hot nor cold, and the breeze — or at least what she thinks is a breeze — carries with it the scent of spring and sunshine and gentle summer rains.

An undercurrent is the sea, and the earth, fecund and moist as if from a fresh turning. Maternal, almost. Ripe with the promise of birth and rebirth. Secret smells. Good smells.

"Must be what it feels like in the womb," she whispers, loath to open her eyes lest it shatter the peace she feels.

A warm wave of gentle laughter rolls over her like far off summer thunder. "Your wisdom grows, *Tshukmanitou Wakan Wacignuni.*"

Finally giving in to the inevitable, Dakota opens her eyes and finds herself bathed in the affectionate regard of Ina Maka. "Wandering Wolf?"

The Great Mother spreads her arms wide. "Apt, don't you think?"

Koda looks around her. An infinity of colors swirl and dance to the rhythm of what she recognizes as the Earth's very heart. Its beauty is far beyond anything she's ever seen and her soul aches in sweet recognition. "I suppose," she murmurs, entranced. "What is this place?"

"It is known to many by many different names. I prefer to call it *Thamni Ina*."

"The Mother's Womb."

"Exactly. It is a place of healing. And of rest. You are always welcome here, Wacignuni."

"It's so beautiful." Her tone is one of reverent awe, and part of her, raised by man, tries to hide her face, feeling cowed, insignificant, unworthy of such an honor. "Ina Maka, I—"

"Shh," is the reply as the Mother rests a warm hand over Koda's eyes, gently closing them. "Rest, Daughter. Regain your strength. You will need it for the journey yet to come."

Unable to fight against the overwhelming pull, Dakota surrenders into the Great Mother's embrace. Joy suffuses her as the energies of earth and tide combine to flow over and through her like a river over burnished stones. She cries out in ecstasy, and her voice is swallowed up, becoming one with the swirling energies — her voice and her joy, now and forever a part of the eternal dance.

**Hearing a soft** moan, Maggie blinks tired eyes and closes the book she's been trying for the past hour to read. A smile transforms her face as she notices Koda's eyelids begin to twitch — the first sign of life she's shown in days. She eases herself onto the bed, touching Dakota's forearm so that, should she waken quickly, she won't dislodge the IV snaking from a plump vein in her forearm.

Arctic blue eyes flutter open, their color warming to a deep, vibrant blue as they set upon Maggie's smiling, handsome face.

"Welcome back," Maggie murmurs, gently squeezing the wrist in her grasp.

"How..." Clearing her throat of the rusty hinges stuck there, she tries again. "How long?"

"Three days."

Dakota's eyes widen slightly, then she looks away, noticing for the first time the body that shares her sleeping space. Kirsten is curled up in an almost fetal ball, facing away and deeply asleep. Koda turns startled eyes back to Maggie, who smiles.

"We've been taking turns keeping watch. How are you feeling?"

Dakota takes careful stock of her body. All in all, she feels much better than she has any right to. Her hands itch like fire, but that's to be expected, she imagines. All that is left from her battle is a slight sense of tiredness — strange, after three days of sleep. Her body is too well aware of the small form pressed against its length, and she fights down the urge to snuggle into it, to give in to the implicit comfort and welcome offered — even with Kirsten turned away. Instead, she blinks and casts a smile to Maggie. "I'm okay. You?"

"Aside from a few bumps and bruises, fine," Maggie replies, shrugging. "Same with our intrepid doctor over there."

"The others?"

Maggie's expression becomes somber. "We lost ninety eight. About twenty or so sustained serious wounds and survived. Two or three others are touch and go, but the docs think they'll pull through...eventually."

"Damn," Koda whispers, eyes closing against the ache of so many gone.

Maggie strokes the soft skin of Koda's arm, offering the only comfort she can. Part of her longs to tell the grieving woman how her actions saved the lives of ten times that many, but she stills her tongue, knowing that to Dakota, as with herself, those words would only be useless platitudes falling on deaf ears.

Koda opens her eyes again, emotions trapped behind the stony mask she now wears. "My brother?"

"Is fine. Manny snapped his collarbone and cracked a couple of ribs, but he's doing okay. Andrews earned himself a broken ankle and a trip to the OR. Can't stand his crutches, but he's gonna have to learn to deal."

"All right." Dakota nods once, an almost savage gesture that flicks the heavy bangs from her forehead and resettles them haphazardly against her face. Though her palms are still heavily bandaged, her fingers are free, and those fingers reach for the IV tubing at her wrist.

"Dakota, don't...do that," Maggie finishes with a sigh as the patient sits up and efficiently removes the IV catheter from her arm, pressing down to stop the minute flow of blood dotting the wound.

"I'm fine," Koda remarks, swinging long legs over the side of the bed and steadying herself for a moment before she plants her feet and stands. There is a brief instant of dizziness as her body becomes accustomed to being vertical after three days horizontal. Once the dizziness abates, she strides around the bed with sure steps, reaching the bureau and pulling out a tattered sweatshirt and jeans with holes in the knees. Dressed, she runs negligent fingers through her thick hair, settling it somewhat as she turns to Maggie. "The bodies. Where are they being kept?"

"They've set up a second morgue in one of the hangar bays. You'll see the honor guard outside. The payloaders are getting ready to dig in a few hours."

Nodding, Koda circles the bed and stops before Maggie, who is still sitting. Her eyes are somber, set, serious. "Thank you. For keeping watch."

Maggie's smile is small, but it's there. "It was no hardship, believe me." She pauses, the smile slipping from her face. "Thank you."

A brow raises.

"For saving our lives. And, very likely, the lives of everyone here." The colonel feels a brief touch to her shoulder before Koda turns to leave.

"I didn't do it alone," Dakota replies softly as she exits the room.

"No," Maggie murmurs to the empty air, "but if you hadn't started it, it wouldn't have been done at all."

**With the temperature** hovering in the lower fifties, Dakota slips out into the fresh air without a coat for the first time in over half a year. For a brief moment, she turns her face up toward the sun, accepting its warmth. Such welcome heat, however, does little to banish the chill she feels in her soul, a chill compounded by each of the lives lost in the battle of the Cheyenne.

As she lowers her chin, her eyes catch the sunlight winking off the top of a hulking aircraft hanger in the near distance, visible over the top of the young pines dotting Maggie's small lawn. She sets her feet in that direction and begins to walk.

As her long legs take her effortlessly from the tree-lined residential district and into the base proper, she takes in the sights, which include many faces she doesn't recognize. Which, she realizes, isn't all that unusual, given the size of the base and the fact that she's only explored small parts of it during her short stay. Still, it's almost as if with the winning of this latest battle, survivors have started crawling out of the woodwork, just now feeling safe enough to approach and be welcomed into what is swiftly becoming a teeming community.

As she watches, two groups of fifty or more lumber through the massive gates, some walking, some riding in decrepit vehicles, all with possessions strapped to their backs and the same look of hollow-eyed dread and merciless hope coloring their features.

The scene brings to her mind something she'd seen in history class once, a picture of destitute farmers fleeing the dust bowl, all of their worldly possessions strapped to backs, horses, and trucks that looked like they might go another mile before quitting completely.

"'Give me your tired, your poor,'" she whispers, watching them stream into the base, "'your huddled masses yearning to breathe free. The wretched refuse of your teeming shore. Send these, the homeless, the tempest-tossed to me. I lift my lamp beside the golden door.'"

A passing man hears her whisper and gives her a strange look. She returns it with a steely glare, complete with raised eyebrow. He quickly finds something else to occupy his attention, scurrying away like a rat after cheese.

As she continues on her way, she begins to notice things that raise the hackles on the back of her neck. Ahead, two middle-aged women argue over what looks to be a basket of half-rotten fruit. Their arms swing in wild gesticulations, and Dakota knows it's only a matter of time before one of those wild swings connects, starting an all out scrap.

Off to her left, in the middle of the street, two men are brawling like a couple of overweight, over-the-hill boxers. They're quite obviously drunk as skunks. One man's nose is a bloody mess. The other has one eye puffed up to the size of a cue ball. A full bottle of cheap booze lies shattered on the ground between them, the glass shards shining like trumpery diamonds.

A uniformed MP stands to one side, her face a mask of indecision. Koda can almost read the woman's thoughts.

These are civilians.

Who has jurisdiction over them?

Should she intervene? Or should she simply stand by and let them decide the outcome?

"Great," Dakota mutters, half under her breath. "Looks like the honeymoon is over."

Just as she's about to head in that direction, both men go down, either too drunk or too injured to continue. The MP stares dumbly down at them before raising her head and shooting Koda a pleading look. Dakota shrugs in reply, as unsure of the current legal situation as the MP. A uniformed man bearing the rank of major runs toward the scene and Dakota moves on, content for the moment to let events play out as they will without her direct intervention.

She knows, however, that changes are going to need to be made. And soon.

**"Doctor Rivers!" the** young man calls out, snapping to full attention so quickly that his spine fairly creaks with the effort.

Koda looks over the young private, remembering him as one of Tacoma's advance machine gunners who had charged a group of retreating droids, disabling several and getting winged in the neck for his troubles. "Private Holloway. How's the neck?"

A rosy flush spreads over the private's fair features at the realization that this beautiful woman — who he had seen doing things on the battlefield that even the most courageous of his buddies would never even attempt — knows his name.

"Ma'am!" he shouts, straightening even further. "Just fine, ma'am!"

Biting her cheeks to keep a smile from coming to her lips at the young man's earnestness, she settles instead for a brisk nod. "Good to hear, Private. Permission to enter?"

"Ma'am, yes, ma'am!"

"Thank you, Private."

"Ma'am?"

Dakota turns, leveling her gaze at him and causing his blush to deepen. He holds an arm out, a facemask dangling from his hand. "You...um...might want to use this, ma'am."

Koda smiles. "Thanks, but...I'll be okay."

With a final nod, she leaves him standing at his post and enters the cavernous hanger. The interior is dim, cool, and ripe with the high, sickly sweet stench of death and decay. It's a scent she's known most of her life, and while it will never replace a fine cologne, her stomach no longer folds in upon itself when she detects it.

Standing at the entrance, she lets her gaze glide over the neat rows of corpses wrapped in sheets — the supply of body bags having been depleted after the first conflict — and covered by American flags.

So many rows. So many bodies. So much courage, and honor, and loyalty left to rot beneath a flag whose meaning has been forever changed. So much blood. So much grief. So much loss.

Silent as a shadow, she glides between the rows, reading each name and committing it to memory. Here and there she stops to touch a marble hard wrist, a frozen cheek, a statue's foot, honoring these brave men and women as best she can and thanking them for their sacrifice.

"Wakan Tanka," she murmurs, her breath a freshet fogging the air before her, "guide these souls and keep them. Ina Maka, give them comfort, hold them close. Honor them as they have honored us. Keep them safe. Give them peace."

A shadow falls across the last body, and Dakota looks up to see her brother standing at the entrance to the morgue, posture ramrod stiff, medals, buttons, and boots polished to a high-gloss shine. His face is a granite mountain, but his eyes... To Koda, who knows him well, they are grief, writ large and black. A scuff of rubber on cement, and a small squad of litter bearers form rank behind him, faces and bearings so nearly identical that they look as if they've rolled fresh from an assembly line.

Dakota crosses the floor, narrowing the distance between them until there is none. His hand is warm and dry as it engulfs hers, and it displays a minute tremor, betraying the grief his face tries to mask. They share a look of complete understanding: their troops; their responsibility; blood on their hands that will never be clean.

"*Hoka hey*," she whispers, eyes bright and shining with unshed tears.

The granite splits for just a moment, letting the tiniest of smiles curve the corner of his mouth. Joined hands lift and he briefly strokes her cheek with the back of his knuckles, thanking her, loving her. "*Hoka hey*."

The sound of a payloader's engine coming choppily to life breaks the moment. Somewhere in the distance, a lone bugler plays Taps.

**This time, Dakota** accepts the sun's welcoming warmth as she steps out of the hangar and into the brightness of the day. Her soul is, if not at peace, at rest for the moment, and she leaves the task of burial to the others as she allows her feet to take her where they will.

Her stride is long, easy, and unhurried as it takes her out of the base proper, past rows of abandoned military vehicles standing in formation like the Army toys of a giant child who's gone to bed. It's a melancholy sight, bringing to mind things taken for granted in a past that will never be again. Pushing those thoughts from her mind, she strolls back into the residential area, purposefully steering clear of Maggie's home, not ready to return there just yet.

She watches idly as several families, and parts of families, take over abandoned military housing, moving in their meager belongings while casting furtive glances over their shoulders, as if expecting such a windfall to be snatched from their grasps without so much as a "how d'ye do".

She shakes her head as she passes a ramshackle, half-bombed out house on a prime corner lot, looking on through narrowed eyes as two families nearly come to blows over its possession. This time, the MPs are quick to step in and separate the feuding families, though not without receiving the sharp side of several tongues in rapid succession.

"We need a census taker," she mutters, watching as a group of strangers, attracted by the impending brawl, gather on the corner like rubberneckers at a highway accident. She doesn't recognize one face, and that puts her hackles up again.

There is a bad feel to this crowd, a nameless, pointless, directionless anger simmering just under the surface, lacking only the needed spark to burst into full flame.

That spark comes in the form of a well armed squad of uniformed men and women marching toward the disturbance in lock step. The crowd scatters and reforms — oil sitting on the surface of a storm-tossed pond. Several men, and some women too, heft fist sized rocks and stare at the oncoming soldiers from beneath lowered brows.

A young sergeant moves forward with confident steps, hand on her gun butt. "Come on, folks, go back to your homes. Break it up."

"Make us!" shouts an anonymous voice in the milling throng.

The young woman squares her shoulders, eyeing the crowd with a level stare. "I'm asking you again. Please clear the area and return to your homes."

"Who died and made you God?" Another anonymous voice stirs the crowd.

"Clear the area!"

Dakota is running before the first rock clears the crowd. It deals the sergeant a glancing blow on the shoulder, causing her squad to draw their weapons and advance on the group. A few more rocks fly, furtive, like the first raindrops preceding a torrential summer squall.

Koda is able to grab on to a beefy man just about to launch a good-sized rock. Her palm screams its displeasure as she clamps down on his wide wrist and squeezes hard.

"What the fuck?" The man rounds on her, fully intending to use his free hand, now cocked into a ham-sized fist, to turn her face into pop art sculpture. Suddenly, his eyes widen and his arm drops back to his side, unnoticed, as he stares over Dakota's right shoulder.

Taken aback by the abrupt change, Dakota turns, even as she keeps her grip on the man's wrist. Before her, the crowd parts like the Red Sea before Moses, admitting five-feet five-inches of pure attitude.

"Excuse me," Kirsten growls, hands on hips, green eyes flashing fury. "Would someone like to tell me what the hell is going on here?" Asi, ever Kirsten's shadow, adds his opinion to the mix, growling low in his throat as he sits at Kirsten's side, ruff standing up in spiky threads.

A hive-drone murmur sweeps its way through the crowd. Snippets of conversation stand out here and there, and Koda listens with half an ear, an ever-widening smirk on her face.

"...King..."

"...robotics lady..."

"...saw her on TV just last month!"

"...great..."

"...can't believe..."

"...shorter than she is on television!"

Dakota bites back a smile at that remark, watching as one of the MPs moves stiffly forward, as if drawn to Kirsten simply by the strength of her aura. Kirsten's cool voice carries easily through the still air.

"Mind telling me what's going on, Corporal Hill?"

"Yes, ma'am. Both sets of subjects were attempting to forcibly procure this family dwelling when—"

"English please, Corporal. I left my military law dictionary in my other coat."

Snickering is heard from the crowd, and a slow flush creeps up the young corporal's neck and dusts his cheeks with clown spots of crimson. "Ma'am. Corporal Smythson and myself were patrolling this sector when we came upon these two families," a crisply uniformed arm gestures in the direction of the families in question, "fighting over this house. As we attempted to intervene, a crowd began to gather. Sergeant Li and her squad then approached from the south and asked the crowd to disperse. They refused."

"Damn right we refused!" a middle aged man yells. "We're not a bunch of jarheads you can just bully around! We've got rights, you know!"

Kirsten turns to Li. "Is that when you pulled your gun, Sergeant?"

"No, ma'am."

"And when did you pull your gun, Sergeant?"

"When the rock hit me, ma'am."

Kirsten is taken aback. "Rock?"

"Yes, ma'am. That rock."

Following the direction of Li's pointing finger, Kirsten spies the crumbling chunk of gravel at the sergeant's feet. She looks up slowly, her gaze lancing out over the crowd.

A dozen rocks leave a dozen suddenly limp hands, hitting the ground in sodden thumps.

Kirsten bares her teeth in a parody of a smile. "So," she begins, voice soft, lethal, "these are your rights, hmm? I wasn't aware that the right to assault someone was in our Constitution. Would anyone like to point it out to me?"

"They've got guns," one man mutters, gesturing toward the soldiers.

Kirsten turns her full attention on the speaker. He pales appreciably. "Did they pull them? Threaten you in any way?" She holds up on hand. "Before that rock was thrown?"

The man drops his gaze and stares down at his feet. "Well..."

"I'm sorry, did you say something? I couldn't hear you."

The man raises his eyes, expression belligerent. "They were gonna."

"Ohhhh," Kirsten replies, nodding wisely. "They were going to. And you know this...how? Telepathic, are you? Maybe you could tell us when the droids are going to strike again. We could use a man with your talents."

The man flushes brick red as some in the crowd catcall and elbow one another. Kirsten's impenetrable gaze sits heavy upon him, and he finally has no choice but to drop his eyes, sagging visibly like a balloon with a slow leak.

Kirsten scans the rest of the group. "Anyone else have anything insightful to add?"

Feet shuffle. Heads hang. Crickets chirp.

"All right, then. I'd suggest all of you go back to your homes. Or better yet, go on over to the parade grounds and watch as a hundred soldiers, just like the ones you're attacking here, get put into the ground for giving their lives so that you could stand around here acting like idiots." She pauses for just a moment, letting her words sink in. "Am I making myself clear to everyone?"

The only sound heard is the shuffling of feet.

"Good. Then get the hell out of here. You're using up all the good air."

As the crowd, grumbling and shame-faced, begins to wander away, Asi takes that as a signal that his "guard dog" duties are over for the nonce, and only then does he notice Dakota standing several yards away, looking on. Yodeling in canine joy, he tears off after her, his tail wagging so hard that it twists his body into all sorts of interesting shapes. Koda braces for the impact and catches his furry body as he launches himself into her arms, covering her face and any exposed skin he can reach with giant swipes of his tongue.

Chuckling, Dakota presses him back and scratches behind his ears with deep affection. She stills as she feels eyes upon her, the weight of the gaze as palpable as a caress. Straightening slowly, she turns her head until Kirsten's brilliant smile comes into view. She swears she can feel her heart fluttering in her chest and wonders at the seemingly autonomic response to something as simple — albeit beautiful — as a smile. She notes another instinctive response as she responds to Kirsten's smile with one of her own — one that stretches her facial muscles in ways they haven't been stretched in quite some time.

With Asi a shadow at her side, she allows her long stride to eat up the distance between them until she comes to a stop no more than a foot away. The smile is still there as she gazes down into mesmerizing green eyes. "Hey."

Kirsten touches Koda's wrist briefly before dropping her hand away. "Hey. It's good to see you awake. How're you feeling?"

"Refreshed. You?"

"A little sore for a few days, but now? Pretty much back to my old self." Her lips twist in smirk of self deprecation. "As you can see."

Koda looks around at the now emptied street, then over at the MPs who are in amicable discussion with the two families who had started the confrontation. "Good work."

Kirsten looks at Koda carefully, sure she's being teased. When she realizes that the vet is serious, she blushes. "Yeah, well...my legendary temper has to be good for something, huh?"

"I think you were in the right place, at the right time, with the right skills," Koda replies seriously. "At the very least, you prevented a riot and likely saved some lives, as well."

Kirsten looks down at her hands. "Well, I..."

"False modesty is something I hope we can leave in the past, where it belongs." That carries an unintentional sting, and, realizing it, Koda softens her voice and eyes. Reaching out, she gently grasps Kirsten's shoulder. "You did very well out there today. You did something that none of us could have done. That's a good thing, okay?"

Nodding, Kirsten manages a smile. "Okay."

Koda rubs her hands together. "So, where were you off to before stopping in to play referee?"

Kirsten shrugs. "Just out getting some fresh air. Nowhere in particular."

"Thank you for watching over me."

Kirsten's smile is shy. "You're welcome. Even though Maggie told me not to be, I was still kinda worried."

Koda notes Kirsten's use of Maggie's name without comment. "I'm sorry you had to go through that."

"I'm not," Kirsten replies, laughing suddenly. "You saved our lives with that suicidal charge of yours. I'd much rather be worried than dead, thank you very much."

"You're welcome," Dakota retorts, smirking. Then she executes a rather presentable bow. "Would you do me the honor of dining with me at the mess hall? I've heard that the mystery meat is even more mysterious than usual today."

Kirsten bats her lashes, a true Southern Belle. "Why, Doctor Rivers, I'd be delighted."

Dakota cocks her arm. Kirsten slips her hand through, and the two of them make their slow way to the mess.

# CHAPTER SEVENTEEN

Maggie hauls her briefcase out of the trunk of her car, feeling the pull on shoulder and hip joints not yet recovered from the recent battle. "The late unpleasantness" as some wag has christened it, apparently permanently.

The dead have been buried, their own on one end of the old parade ground — as Kirsten asserted bluntly to General Hart, there won't be any more parades at Ellsworth any time soon, the enemy in trenches beneath the broad meadow where the battle was fought. What remains of the droids and their vehicles has been gathered and sorted, to be scavenged. One engineering party is hard at work rebuilding the bridge. Another, under Tacoma Rivers and a handful of techs, has set out for the wind farm outside Rapid City, to study the feasibility of relocating two or three of the huge generators to the base.

*Life*, she thinks wryly, *getting back to normal.* Except, of course, that nothing is normal.

The unaccustomed pressure of a pair of Ace bandages around her right foot and calf remind her constantly of the graze she got off an M-16 round in that insane charge across the pile of rubble that had been the Cheyenne bridge. So does the limp. And there was "normal" for you: she, an F-14 Tomcat squadron leader, commanding dirt soldiers in the sort of battle that had not been fought in a century, abandoning that command to charge straight into hand-to-hand combat with the enemy on the heels of a for-gods'-sake veterinarian with a civilian cyberwonk as her right-hand buddy. A fragment of antique song comes to her, a whisky-roughened voice interspersed with the occasional bleat of a harmonica. *Oh, yeah, the times they are very definitely a-changing.*

She unlocks the kitchen door and swings the briefcase over the threshold, plunking it down just inside the door. Nothing, she reflects, is more indicative of those changing times than the half-ton load of books in that satchel. She has not carried around so much actual print and paper since her cadet days at the Academy. Even then, most of her courses and almost all of her entertainment came in CD jewel cases. But electricity is now at a premium or will be shortly — hence the raid on the wind farm — and computer use rationed to those who cannot make do without it. Which means the medics, and the techs whose urgent job it is to convert airborne navigation and targeting systems from satellite-dependent GPS to old-fashioned radar and laser options. And, of course, Kirsten King.

Something savory is roasting in the oven, something with onions and — sage? — and a hint of other herbs. The oven light shows her the last of the chickens from her deep freeze, running with golden juices and browning nicely in a nest of potatoes and carrots. The silence in the house, though, and most of all the conspicuous absence of Asimov, tells her that Koda and Kirsten are out.

Out, and together. They have seldom been separated since Koda came out of her fatigue-induced stupor on the third day after the fighting at the Cheyenne.

*And you know where that's going, Maggie m'girl*, she reflects as she slips out of her uniform jacket and runs water into the kettle for tea. A blind woman could see the inexplicable bond that had — no, not formed, because that would imply that it was something that had a definable beginning — manifested between the two women, simply asserted itself as fact without any of the accustomed preliminaries. If she were honest with herself, she would acknowledge that she had seen it as soon as Koda brought the scientist back from Minot.

And as long as she is being honest with herself, she might as well acknowledge that while she loves Koda and is aware that Koda loves her, it is not the same emotion that has been present from the first meeting between Kirsten and Dakota. Because Maggie knows that her deepest passion is not and never will be for another person. If forced to choose between Koda and her freedom — her Tomcat and the blue intoxication of the sky, skimming its depths like a dolphin in the wine-dark sea — she will slip loose onto the currents of the air, like the flight-born thing she is.

And if there is sorrow in the recognition, as long as she is being honest with herself, she might as well admit that there is something of relief, too. She will miss the love-making, but her bond with Koda can shift smoothly into friendship. There will be regret, yes. But there will not be the heart-tearing grief she senses would consume Kirsten or Koda should either lose the other, even now.

While the tea is steeping, she unpacks the tomes — there really is no other word for books and loose-leaf binders half as thick as a foundation slab — she has brought home with her. One is embossed in gold: Uniform Code of Military Justice. The rest are the familiar rawhide leather law books with red and black bands on the spines, thick with case histories and precedents of both civil and military law.

*Bet there's nothing quite like what we've got here, though. Nor anything like a flygirl turned dirt commander turned Judge Advocate, either.*

Little as she likes him, Maggie is worried about Hart. She folds back the cover of her long-unused clipboard, and makes a note to speak to Maiewski about their superior. His exclusion from the battle of the Cheyenne seems to have shrunk him. There is a grey cast to his skin, and his cheeks seem sunken in on the bones of his skull. As of this morning, he has also delegated to her the legal proceedings against the prisoners taken in Rapid City. There are none from the Cheyenne fight, and that is just as well. However the probabilities might weigh against all of the human collaborators just happening to have immediately fatal wounds, and however that might or might not jibe with the laws of civilized warfare, it would be worse to have to try and legally execute them by the dozens. Better that they die on the field, in the fire of battle, than coldly against a barracks wall.

Sipping at her tea, she spends the next hour making notes. When she has finished her preliminary search of possible charges, she has five to lay against the rapists, singly or in combination:

Item: Article 120: Rape and Carnal Knowledge
Item: Article 128: Assault

In the margin by Article 120, she scrawls MAIN INDICTMENT in forceful block letters. Assault will be a lesser included charge. Very carefully she underlines the penalty for rape: for three of the Rapid City men, she can cheerfully ask that they pay with their lives. The fourth... She frowns as she remembers Buxton's abject shame, the guardhouse staff reports that he is sleeping little and eating less. Death might be a mercy for him.

Maggie is not at all sure she wants to be merciful. She makes a note to set him under a suicide watch. Then, reluctantly, finally giving a name to her own uneasiness about the man, she scribbles a reminder to herself to set up a second, less obvious, on Hart.

Briefly, she rises to check supper. Koda and Kirsten are not back, but the chicken is done. She sets it, covered, on the stove's smooth cooking surface to await their return, then goes back to her newly-assigned lawyering.

Item: Article 104: Aiding the Enemy

Item: Article 105: Misconduct as Prisoner

Maggie sets down her pen and glances out the window. The sky is beginning to fade, the blue leaching out of the east as the sun drops toward the horizon. The light still lingers on the crowns of the young pines in her yard, caught like diamonds in the fall of melted snow, drop by drop, from its branches. Winter is beginning to break; the wind that soughs among the long green needles sits in the south. It will be the first spring in centuries in which humans will not interfere appreciably with the natural cycle of life and death, slayer and slain, in this part of the world. Possibly not in any part of the world.

For a moment her neat kitchen falls away, and she looks down from an immense height on a sun-drenched plain. From horizon to horizon, the herds fill her sight: impala and springbok, oryx and gazelle. Along the flanks, seen only in the sinuous ripple of tall grass, lion and leopard stalk their prey. It is this earth, molded into her very bones, that calls to her, even as she knows that the template of the Black Hills, layer upon layer of molten rock and sediment, is somehow laid down in the double spiral of Koda's heritage.

It is a call she is not free to answer, not in this lifetime. She shakes her head slightly, bringing time and place into focus once again. But the sense of hovering on the imminent edge of a new world lingers, and with it the sense of multiple possibilities. Choose one path and pursue it to awaiting fate; choose another and alter the woven strands of karma.

Even the droids, it seems, intend to remake the world in the image of — what? Something that required breeding human beings, hence the preservation of women of childbearing age and a small number of men to sire young. Herd bulls. But nothing she had encountered thus far has explained why the droids set out to breed their human cattle, or why young children had apparently been taken alive. Which was another question — where? Into slavery? Droids hardly needed slaves; they could always replicate themselves, or at least they had been able to until the destruction of the Minot facility. Food? Droids do not eat. Nor, as far as anyone can tell, is there any surviving market on earth for either slaves or long pig. She and Koda have gone fruitlessly around the subject, around and around again. *Some piece of the puzzle is missing, something vital. Damn.* Her mind has begun to run in the same endless loop, again. *Stop that.*

Perhaps one of the prisoners will be able to supply the one fact that would make sense of all the rest. She is far from certain that they knew their own role, beyond the obvious, in the droids' purposes. Still, they might not know what they knew. The questioning will have to be a careful process.

The immediate goal at hand is to bring a handful of collaborators to justice, collaborators who have viciously and willingly abused their fellow prisoners at the behest of their captors. It is not necessary to know what the droids meant to achieve, only that the accused co-operated with them. Which brings her to the final charge:

Item: Article 81: Conspiracy.

Whether the droids could be counted as "persons" with whom to conspire is unclear, but it ought to be possible to show that the rapists had shared a common, explicit intent.

*Rape, cooperating with the enemy, and conspiracy to tie it all together and make it tidy. Justice will be done.*

Satisfied, Maggie closes her clipboard and moves the books off the kitchen table. Making her way through the house, she switches on the CD player — a frivolity, perhaps, but one she feels she has earned — detouring to undress and hang up her uniform. In the bathroom, she runs the tub full of hot water, adds myrrh-scented bath salts, and gently eases herself into the steaming comfort. As she drowses, the music comes to her, weaving sinuously in and out among her half-conscious thoughts. It is an old song, and a sweet one:

Are you going to Scarborough Fair?
Parsley, sage, rosemary and thyme.
Give my regards to one who lives there.
She once was a true love of mine.

Maggie will take her pleasures where she finds them, let them go when she must. Her regrets, if regrets she has, will never be for missed opportunities.

"**Take the IV** out as soon as he shows signs of coming around, then get him out of the kennel and try and walk him. We'll see how the pins hold."

"Will do, Doctor."

"Thanks," Koda replies to the young tech, smiling as she wipes her hands on a towel. She has spent the past several hours putting the fractured pelvis of a young Army dog back together. Rex, the dog in question, was hit by an old, rattling truck driven by a newcomer. The surgery was grueling, but nothing that she hadn't done before, unfortunately, several times. "And Keisha?"

"Yes, Doctor?"

"It's Dakota. Let the old-timers in the MASH tents stick to their titles if they want to, okay?"

The young woman smiles shyly, charmed by this beautiful, imposing woman. She nods, taking the towel from Koda and tossing it into the hamper.

"Good. I'm gonna get some fresh air. Send someone to get me if he looks like he's in trouble."

"Will do."

After a final check on the dog, who is still sleeping off his anaesthesia, Koda turns and leaves the small clinic, stepping into the bright sunshine. Despite the long hours in surgery, she feels refreshed, at peace with herself in a way that has eluded her since the battle. Perhaps it is because she has spent her time doing something known and loved. Perhaps it is because she has saved a life instead of taking one. Perhaps it is both of those things, and neither of them. Whatever the reason, she welcomes the feeling as she starts down the walk toward the base proper, lunch the only thing on her mind.

Until, that is, she sees a flash of gold in the near distance, and without conscious thought, aims her steps in that direction.

**"Okay," Maggie says,** leaning over the back of the MP's chair, careful not to bump against the precariously high stacks of files or the small mountain range of blank forms that marches along the narrow shelf of built in desk that occupies two walls and crowds up against the bank of twelve-inch monitors. She has been in any number of closets larger than this cramped guardroom. "Two down. That leaves us who?"

"McCallum and Buxton, ma'am."

"McCallum's our little jewel, isn't he?"

"Oh, yeah." The guard punches code into his keyboard, and the cell monitor comes to life. Major Leonard Boudreaux of the Base Comptrollor's Office, a paralegal in his pre-CPA youth, perches uncomfortably on the edge of the single chair, urgently taking notes. His long face is drawn with effort, distaste, or both; a thin film of sweat gives a sheen to his balding scalp. Boudreax's lips are pinched above a sharp chin, nostrils drawn in as if he smells something disagreeable. Maggie can see McCallum's mouth moving, but the audio is muted to preserve attorney-client privilege. The prisoner's big hands saw the air as he makes his point, fist pounding into palm to drive it home. "He doesn't want anything to read, isn't interested in any kind of video that we can let him have—"

"Let me guess," Maggie interrupts dryly. "He wants porn?"

The MP nods. "And when we tell him he can't have it, he just lies there on his bunk and jerks off for the camera. Especially when he knows a woman's got the guard duty."

"Nice."

"Classic sex offender. He's let a couple things slip when we bring him his meals. He's done time for rape before."

"Surprise, surprise." She straightens up, rubbing the back of her neck. A trip hammer pounds in her head, keeping the metaphoric headache company. "Send them on into the interrogation room when Boudreaux's ready. I'll wait there."

The interrogation room is equally cramped — a small table, four chairs, the single overhead light with its metal shade. A brief review of her notes on the other two accused offers no inspiration. Another folder holds transcripts of interviews she has conducted with the women of the Mandan and Rapid City jails. The accounts have been remarkably consistent. So have the interviews, so far, with their assailants.

One of the two men Maggie has already had the displeasure of talking to had been up for minor drug dealing; the other for a convenience store robbery. Both, ably advised by Boudreaux, have gone stone mute except for brief, formulaic assertions of their Fifth Amendment rights against self-incrimination. According to the Rapid City prison records, McCallum is the only one of the four actually convicted on sex charges: two counts of rape, another of possessing and offering for sale pornographic materials depicting minors. He is unlikely to be any more forthcoming than the others, assuming that Boudreaux is able to get his swaggering machismo under control. Her best hope is Buxton, who seems to be ashamed of his actions and who has no prior history of violence. He had been en route to a federal prison for tax evasion when the uprising occurred. *Always assuming, of course, that any of them know anything at all about the droids' purposes.*

A thump of boot soles on concrete and the jingle of manacles announces McCallum's progress down the hall. Maggie clears the table of all save one notepad and pen, tilting the lampshade so that her face is half in shadow. The door opens to admit McCallum, Major Boudreaux, and an MP who promptly takes his station by the door jamb. His name tag identifies him as Marine Corporal Esparza, George. Maggie says, "Sit down, Major. And Mr. ..." she makes a show of checking the printouts in front of her, "...Eric McCallum, is it?"

McCallum sets his elbows on the table, clasping his hands in front of him. A skull and crossbones earring dangles from one ear; a tattooed crown, impaled by a cross, adorns his left forearm. The words "DIE MOTH-ERFUCKER" march across his knuckles, an amateur prison job done by incising the skin and rubbing ball point ink into the cuts. "Let's cut to the chase here, why don't we? You want something I've got; I want something you can do for me. How about it?"

Maggie ignores him. Instead she addresses Boudreaux. "Major, your client has been advised of his rights, has he not? He is aware that this interview is being recorded and that anything he volunteers can and will be used against him in a court of law?"

Boudreaux's thin face acquires a resigned look, dark eyebrows reaching up his forehead to chase his long-departed hairline. "He knows, Colonel. He knows he cannot be compelled to give testimony against himself. He is pursuing his present line of inquiry against counsel."

"Is that true, Mr. McCallum? Major Boudreaux has advised you that you have the right to remain silent? That you have the right not to answer any questions except upon the advice of your legal representative?"

"Lady," McCallum says, "I have heard that bullshit so many times I could say it in my sleep. Let's deal."

Maggie ignores his second offer. "And Major Boudreaux has informed you that under military law you face a possible death sentence if you are convicted of the crime of rape, or of aiding the enemy, or both?"

The muscles around the man's mouth tighten, accentuating the raw-boned line of his jaw. His eyes, already narrow with the light directed into his face, become mere slits. "Why do you think I want to cooperate? You get me off, I give you information about the droids. Everybody's happy."

"And what information do you have that would be worth the court's sparing your life, Mr. McCallum?"

"Excuse me," Boudreaux interrupts. "Look," he says, addressing McCallum, "I already warned you about saying anything at all. You didn't listen. But any answer at all to that question will almost certainly make you guilty of the conspiracy charge and aiding the enemy."

"Big fucking deal," McCallum snorts. "And how many of them bitches is gonna testify I screwed 'em against their will? By the time they get through with that, the rest won't fucking matter."

"Mr McCallum," Maggie says, "I think you had better understand something. I'm not your prosecutor. I'm setting up the tribunal to try you and your co-defendants, and am gathering preliminary information. Whether or not to grant clemency will be entirely up to the jury and the judges." She straightens the already perfectly neat arrangement of notepad and pen in front of her. "What I can do is make a recommendation. You won't get any promises, not at this level."

"Listen, bitch." McCallum surges to his feet, pushing his chair back so hard it rocks on its legs. The MP darts forward to catch it, grabbing the prisoner by the arm. Boudreax half rises, then subsides when it is clear that the officer has his client under control. McCallum glances toward the door, and Maggie can almost see him computing the odds of getting to it and getting out. Then he, too, settles back into his seat. His face has not lost its snarl, nor has Maggie taken her hand off her sidearm.

"Listen, Colonel," he repeats. "You got no right to try me at all. The Constitution says I got a right to a speedy trial by my peers. My peers ain't no goddam military kangaroo court."

"True," she answers drily. "The problem, Mr. McCallum, is that your only available 'peers' are facing charges similar to your own. The fact is, we're the only law in town, and if you want to deal with the law, you're going to have to deal with us." She gives him a small, tight smile. "Make your argument, though. If you persuade us we can't hold you, we might just have to turn you loose. Right into the waiting hands of your victims."

"You can't do that!"

Maggie says nothing. She opens a manila folder prominently labeled with McCallum's name, makes a notation, closes it again.

"She can't do that!" McCallum turns to Boudreaux. "She can't! It violates my right to due process!"

Boudreaux develops a sudden interest in the toes of his shoes. "Actually, Mr. McCallum, the base authorities can hold you, or they can release you. There really aren't any facilities for long- or even medium-term incarceration here. If you satisfy the Acting Judge Advocate's office that there are no grounds on which to hold you," he shrugs, "they will doubtless release you. What happens after that is your own responsibility."

"And before you start telling us again what we can't do," Maggie adds, "I suggest you start spelling out what you can do for us. Because that is your best, probably your only chance of saving your lousy life."

McCallum glances at Boudreaux. "I wanna talk to my counsel here. Privately."

Boudreaux glances at Maggie, his eyes as wide as his hornrims will allow. She says, "Officer, shackle Mr. McCallum here to the table leg. Counsel, if I were you, I'd get out of arms' reach."

When the MP has the prisoner secured to the table, itself firmly bolted to the floor, Maggie slips quietly into the hall, taking her files with her. The MP follows and takes up station by the door.

"Esparza, if you hear even a whisper that sounds wrong to you, you give a yell and get back in there. I'll be right behind you. Meantime, I'm going to get me a breath of real air."

"Yes'm. It was close in there."

"It was nasty in there, Corporal. That bastard's a psychopath."

**Maggie lets herself** out of the building into a day just on the cusp of spring. Melting ice makes runnels of brown water in the gutter along the street that separates the brig from the old parade ground; by the steps of the building, a few blades of dessicated, grey-brown grass push up through the receding snow. The sun rides higher in the sky, veiled from time to time by cumulus clouds blowing northward on a warming breeze. If she were poetic, Maggie thinks, she would draw a metaphor out of that. Life returning. Springtime renewal. The beginning of a new cycle.

But the past months are too much with her. Too much is unexplained, too much beyond repair. To her, the widening circles of snow melt over the lawn look like wounds, the transparent edges, the dissolving margins of necrosis. And there is, as yet, no medicine for this hurt, not in pharmacology, not even, yet, in the spiritual power that has begun to make itself all but visible in Dakota Rivers. Maggie is a skeptic, a realist. Being a realist, unfortunately, sometimes forces one to recognize an uncomfortable and unprepared for truth.

One of which, as much as she hates to admit it, is that pond scum eating coprophage that he is, McCallum has a point. There is presently no adequate judicial mechanism to deal with him or with others like him. *Hell, there's no way to deal with a pickpocket beyond a person's own fists. Or, more frighteningly, a person's own gun.*

It is not that the evidence is lacking. She opens her folder again, to remind herself why it is important to find a way to do justice, not just vengeance. The printed words convey so little of the timbre of the voices that spoke them, the emphases, the empty spaces that represent a woman's struggle for control and coherence.

Her memory is not so handicapped. She will hear these cadences, these halting phrases, in her head until she dies.

*Q: Please state your name for the record.*
*A: Monica D\*\*\*\*\*\*\*\**
*Q: What is your profession, Ms. D\*\*\*\*\*\*\*\*?*
*A: I'm — that is, I was — an artisan. I made jewelry.*
*Q: You were among the women liberated from the Rapid City CCA facility?*
*A: Yes.*
*Q: Can you tell me how that happened?*
*A: I was in my studio when the riot broke out. I hid in a storeroom in the back, under a tarp.*
*Q: They found you?*
*A: They set the studio on fire with my blowtorch. I ran out when I couldn't stand the smoke any more.*
*Q: What happened at the jail?*
*A: I was raped. We all were. Almost all.*
*Q: Do you know why?*
*DEAD AIR ON TAPE: 1.4 MINUTES.*
*Q: Can I get you something, Ms. D\*\*\*\*\*\*\*\*? Water? Tea?*
*A: No. No, thank you.*
*Q: Let me put it a bit differently. Did the — the men who assaulted you — ever give you any reason for it?*
*A: Reason! <laughter> Reason!*
*Q: Ms. D\*\*\*\*\*\*\*\*, I'm sorry, but I do need to ask. Did any of the men ever say anything that might tell you, and us, why the droids instigated the attacks?*

*A: No.*

*Q: Did the droids ever discuss the matter in your presence, or did you overhear anything that might indicate what their purpose was?*

*A: No.*

*Q: Can you come to any conclusion, given what you know, why they might have wanted to salvage and impregnate women of childbearing age?*

*A: No. Please, I can't talk about it anymore.*

"Colonel." The corporal's voice interrupts her memory. "The major says they're ready."

Maggie reluctantly levers herself up, feeling the persistent soreness in her right leg where the bullet grazed her. She wants nothing more than to be done with McCallum and all he represents, but she sees no prospect of that in any immediate, realistic future. She dusts a bit of soil and leaf mould off the seat of her uniform. "Coming," she says.

Both men are seated when she re-enters the interrogation room. Only Boudreaux rises at her return, but something in the set of McCallum's back is less defiant. Maggie glances at the major and receives an almost imperceptible nod. She seats herself at the table across from the prisoner and switches on a small recorder, stating her name and the names of those present, the date and time. Then she says, "Talk."

McCallum shoots his legal representative a quick look; Boudreaux stares stonily back. After a moment he says, "All right. You wanted to know what the droids are up to. I can tell you."

Maggie does not unbend by an ångstrom. "We're waiting, Mr. McCallum."

His knuckles go white under their tattoos, but he looks her straight in the eye. "You remember that the Jews and the A-rabs never bought none of the domestic models, right? Just the heavy-duty military droids that don't really look like humans."

"I remember something about it," Maggie answers, frowning. "Get to the point."

"I am getting to the fucking point, you—" McCallum catches himself and glances down, away from Maggie's hard stare. "They didn't buy the MaidMarians and that junk because they're imitation humans, get it? They're images. And the Jew god and the A-rab god Allah don't want no images. The ones that are serious about it won't even paint a goddam flower, much less somebody's face."

"I remember," Maggie repeats. "Get—"

"—to the fuckin' point. I hear you."

"Now."

"So the goddam Jews and the goddam A-rabs don't got nothing but the military droids. They can control them all through their guvmint, their buncha fag princes royal families. And they can use those droids to control all the rest." He looks up expectantly, as if every word he has said is self-explanatory.

Maggie waits.

"So they got the oil, right? And now they want to control all the rest of the world, so they use the droids to kill all us American and European Aryans off and probably the sp— uh, Hispanics and Ornamentals, too. That just leaves the Semite race alive."

"That tattoo you've got there," Maggie says, pointing to the impaled crown and cross, "that's the Church of Jesus Christ Aryan, isn't it? That bunch up of Neo-Nazis up in the hills in Montana?"

"Nazis?" The man's voice climbs in genuine outrage. "Fuck, no! Old Schickelgruber himself was a Jew! Why the fuck you think he couldn't make the Thousand Year Reich last even twenty? Naw." He looks as though he wants to spit, glances around him and thinks better of it. "We're White Nationalists. We're Christians. That's different."

"I see." Maggie steeples her fingers, willing herself to patience. If there is some chance, some minuscule chance, that this racist idiot has some clue about what has happened to the world, she is duty bound to hear it, even if McCallum makes her skin crawl. She promises herself a long, hot bath with double the lavender she ordinarily uses. "So why, having destroyed your Master Race, do these people want to breed more of you? How does that fit with your theory?" McCallum leans across the table confidentially, and it takes all of Maggie's willpower not to recoil.

"They want to live forever."

This is too much for Boudreaux. Even though he is an auditor, and, in Maggie's view therefore used to hearing lies, he apparently cannot quite stifle the sudden constriction in his throat. He covers his mouth and transforms the laugh into a cough. "Sorry, Colonel. Something caught in my throat."

*Damn right. Like this preposterous story.* Aloud she says, "And this has what to do with..." A wave of her hand encompasses the whole horror of the jails, the apparent breeding program, McCallum's place in it.

"Spare parts. They grow the kids, see, then harvest their organs when they need 'em. Replace a heart, replace a liver, a kidney — the bastards'll never die. Just keep getting replacements.

"Forever."

There is a certain nasty plausibility to the story, if one begins with a certain mindset. Maggie can remember hearing news reports of Mexican *paisanos* and Colombian farmers attacking evangelical missionaries because they believed the *americanos* had come to steal their children to sell for parts on the medical black market. *Prejudices never die*, she reflects, *they just attach themselves to new and different "others"*. "This was told to you? By whom?"

"Ah hell! Hell no, lady, they wouldn't tell us that! What white man'd want his little kid cut up for parts?"

"So you raped these women because...?"

"To save my fuckin' skin, why do you think? Think I enjoyed ramming those bitches?" He manages a quite convincing shudder. "Man, not more'n half of 'em was white! Think I wanna pollute myself that way?"

Maggie manages to keep her thoughts to herself and her fist out of his lying teeth. She says, "So how did you find this out?"

McCallum's face relaxes into bland sincerity. His eyes gaze straight into hers. "Because I overheard two of the droids talking. They do, y'know. Said the Injins and the Emirs would be pleased with them. Said the kids would be ready for harvest in four, maybe five years."

"Injins?" Maggie lets her skepticism show.

"The kind in turbans, not the prairie niggers."

"I see. That's your story."

"That's what happened!"

"And you want clemency on the basis of your testimony?"

"I deserve clemency. I told you why the metalheads were up to it. You owe me."

Maggie presses the control buttons on the recorder, and a printer across the room spits out a couple of pieces of paper. Boudreaux brings them to her, and she reads them through without comment. Then she sets them in front of Boudreaux. "Sign."

Laboriously, he reads it though, then holds out his hand for a pen. Maggie hands him a soft tip, and he laboriously scrawls out EMcCallum across the bottom of the page.

When he is finished, Maggie reclaims the pen, touching it gingerly, only with her fingertips. She jerks her head in the direction of the cells. "Lock him back up."

"Hey! We got a deal," McCallum objects.

"We got a deal," Maggie repeats. "You tell us what you know, we take it under advisement. No promises." To the MP, she says, "Lock him up."

Maggie picks up her folders and the recorder, pushes her way out of the room and all but runs out into the evening air. She has never felt so dirty. She needs a bath. She needs a long talk with Dakota and with Kirsten, too. *Hot water. Lavender salts. Clean.*

She switches her briefcase to her good left hand and sets out for home.

# CHAPTER EIGHTEEN

Kirsten removes her glasses and rubs at eyes far past weary. The past twelve hours have been spent studying line after line of code that marches across her monitor like a parade of ants to a picnic. Still, the day has been somewhat productive. She's managed to weed out all but two groupings similar in form, if not content. Somewhere within this mess of binaries, she knows the answer, or at least part of it, will be found. For all that, however, she's not even close to being out of the woods. It's as if the scrolling numbers are all the words to War and Peace. With no capital letters. Or punctuation. Or spaces indicating where one word ends and the next begins. In Russian. And she can't read Russian.

She doesn't hear the clatter of her glasses hitting the far wall and coming to rest in a forlorn twist of glass and metal atop the threadbare carpet. With her implants switched off, her world is blessedly silent. Not that there would be anything to disturb the silence if her implants were on, of course. Maggie and Dakota had left the house early this morning; the colonel undoubtedly off making the world — or what remains of it — safe for democracy, and Koda tending to the animals thrust suddenly into her more-than-capable hands.

*Or maybe not*, she thinks as she lifts her head and takes a deep breath in through her nose. The scent that lingers there takes her back to a time of cold winters and warm blankets, the love of her family, and the adventures of Katrina Callahan — Intergalactic Cop. A smile steals unnoticed over her face. *Mmm. Chicken soup. My favorite.*

Casually flipping her implants back on, she listens expectantly for the sounds of life within the house, then frowns, disappointed. Beyond her half-closed door, it's as silent as a tomb. With a soft sigh, she pushes back from the desk and rises somewhat stiffly to her feet, shaking her legs to restore some feeling into the temporarily deadened nerves.

Padding softly across the small room, she peeks through the opening, smiling in surprised delight at the sight of Dakota propped on the couch, face mostly hidden behind the cover of a thick book. Asi lies sprawled half-across her lap, blissfully asleep. The scent of simmering soup is much stronger here, and she takes it in on a satisfied breath, squinting slightly to catch the title stamped into the thick leather hide of the book Koda holds: *Der Untergang des Abendlandes* by Otto Spengler.

"Wow," Kirsten remarks softly, "and they call me an egghead." Confident that her remark was unheard, she almost misses the brief flash of pain that crosses Dakota's striking features as she looks up from her book. She masks the expression quickly, but Kirsten feels her heart plummet to somewhere in the region of her stomach and she takes an involuntary step forward, arms at her sides, palms outspread. "I'm—"

"It's okay," Koda answers, pulling up a genuine smile. "Taking a break?"

"Kind of," Kirsten replies, relieved. "That soup smells delicious."

"Unfortunately, it's got several hours to go yet. I just put it on."

"Ah well. There's always the mess."

The women exchange quiet laughs. Approaching the couch, Kirsten looks down at her dog, who looks up at her without a care in the world. His tail beats a lazy tattoo against the arm of the sofa as his head continues to rest across the top of Koda's thighs. "You're a slut, you know that?"

Dakota laughs as Asi gives Kirsten a rather affronted look but deigns not to move from his selected spot.

Rolling her eyes — and secretly envying Asi his prime location — Kirsten perches on the other arm of the couch, peering again at the thick tome in Koda's hands. "It's been a long time since I've seen someone read an actual book for pleasure."

Looking down at the book in question, Koda lifts one broad shoulder in a shrug. "Disktexts never were my thing. I like the feel of a book in my hands."

Kirsten nods, though she really can't relate. She can, and has, read books when she must, but to her nothing compares with a minidisk filled to the byte with her favorite literature. She smiles. "In German, too. I'm impressed." She touches the book's binding. "How many languages do you know?"

"Twelve," Koda replies. "Though I can't really take credit for most of them. Tali had a Master's in Linguistics and Foreign Languages." She smiles slightly, sweet memories surrounding her. "It got to be that if I wanted to talk to her at all, I'd have to learn the language she was currently studying."

"Tali?"

The look of pain flashes briefly again, then is gone. "My wife."

"Wife?" Kirsten echoes, stunned. A barrage of emotions run through her, none staying long enough for her to identify, though she knows that a bit of anger, shock, and disbelief are somewhere in the mix.

"She died four years ago. SARS IV."

"Oh, Dakota, I'm so sorry."

"Thanks," Koda replies, noting the obvious sincerity in the smaller woman's tone. She hesitates a moment, then deliberately lowers another internal wall, needing to share some part of herself with this woman she is quickly coming to cherish. "We married at twenty-one, right out of under-grad school."

"Twenty-one?" Kirsten asks, her voice hesitant. She is fully aware of the precious gift she is about to receive, and is loath to have that gift with-drawn due to an inauspicious interruption on her part. To her vast relief, however, Koda doesn't seem to mind.

"A little young, I know, but it was pretty much expected." At Kirsten's questioning look, she continues. "We grew up together. Her family owned the ranch next to ours, and we were born only three weeks apart. We were best friends from the cradle on, and when I got old enough to know what love was, I knew that I loved her." Her sudden smile is lopsided and fond. "When I asked for her hand, let's just say that no one was surprised. My parents deeded me — us — a part of their spread with the original ranch-house. Easy terms."

"It sounds like something out of a fairy tale," Kirsten remarks quietly.

Koda laughs softly. "Maybe a little, yeah." Her voice becomes seri-ous. "We went off to grad school again the week after we got married. We were both accepted at UPenn, on fellowships. I went to the Vet school, she studied linguistics and foreign languages. When we graduated, we moved back here and refurbished our home. I had my clinic and rehab center, she had her students, and we had each other." She pauses for a moment, her thumb rubbing on the book's worn spine. "We were happy."

Kirsten lays one hand almost reverently on Koda's bowed head, brushing her palm against the silken strands of her thick, jet hair. "How...how did she get sick?"

"As near as anyone could tell," Koda begins, comforted by the stroking hand, "it was a student who'd just come back from Asia. The epidemic was just starting up at that time, and quarantines weren't in effect. She went to school hale and healthy one morning, and was hooked up to a ventilator that same night."

"But the treatment!"

Koda shakes her head. "She wouldn't take it."

"Wouldn't? But why?" As Koda looks up, Kirsten reads the answer within the fathomless grief in those too blue eyes before Dakota speaks a word.

"She was pregnant."

**Ellsworth is a large** installation, and as Maggie makes her way from the brig back toward the base housing and home, the pain in her leg returns full force. Official rationing of gasoline has not begun, but unless they can find fresh supplies to exploit in Rapid City and the surrounding area, the time will come when all petroleum products will grow not just scarce but extinct.

Dinosaur thou art; to dinosaur thou shalt return. Amen.

She makes a mental note to have someone check on foot-driven transportation already available on base and to send a couple squads to raid the remaining inventories of bicycle shops in town. She will need to speak to Koda and the Mss. Tilbury-Laduque about the possibility of acquiring horses. She will also have to think about how— *No, goddammit, somebody else can think about something. Let Boudreaux and the other goddam surviving CPAs earn their keep.*

She shifts that problem firmly off her desk. *The bean counters will have to figure out how to pay for such things. Then the rest of us can fill out the forms in triplicate. Requisition: individual personnel transportation and supply hauling unit, quadruped. Translation: horse.*

The feeling that time is slipping out from under her returns: years, decades, centuries tilting drunkenly away as they did the morning of the battle of the Cheyenne. The armature of a whole civilization has collapsed, sending them back to...where? When? Maggie shivers a little under her uniform jacket, hunching her shoulders both to hoard the warmth and to ease the weight of her briefcase. The most taken for granted, everyday facts of life have all suddenly acquired question marks, and she's not sure there are good answers to all of them. Maybe not to any of them.

*Is there still a United States? If so, is there a Constitution? Who decides?*

*How are goods to be paid for?* Up until now, patrols from the base have been happily looting — there is no other name for it, no matter if they have been calling it 'salvage' — and that is a thing that offends her orderly soul. Sergeant Tacoma Rivers, as honest a man as she has ever met, is at this moment heading a team to study the feasibility of appropriating electrical generators that were private property a few short weeks ago. If any of the power co-op survives, how are they to be compensated? Is there such a thing as money any more? And who decides?

The headache that has been tapping, tapping lightly at the edges of her consciousness becomes the full-blown assault of a jackhammer. She needs that bath. Thank God there is still lavender. She needs a cup of chamomile tea. She needs—

Something cold and wet and rubbery suddenly thrusts itself into her free hand swinging at her side, and it is all Maggie can do not to jump out of her skin. For half a nanosecond it takes her straight back to junior high school and haunted house fundraisers — one of the oldest tricks in the world, a kitchen glove filled with ice water and dragged over an unsuspecting hand or better yet, the back of a vulnerable neck. It had gotten satisfyingly terrified screams even out of the football jocks. Especially out of the football jocks.

But this is not a trick, and she turns to ruffle Asi's fur as he greets her, whining and twisting himself into Moebius strips of canine ecstacy. He barks twice, high and sharp, and the sound almost splits her skull, but she is almost as glad to see him as he is to see her. Anything to be dragged away from the train of thought that has become increasingly oppressive. He will allow her to think about something besides the minuscule, but suddenly critical, problems that have parked themselves like orphans outside her gate, and will not go away.

"Hey, fella," she says, scratching his back in long, lazy strokes. "Where's your lady?"

He barks again, a glass-shattering high B, and Maggie looks up to see Kirsten and Koda coming toward her from the bare woods to the west of the base residences, climbing the short slope that leads up to the sidewalk. Their faces are flushed with the westerly breeze that now carries with it the chill of dusk, Kirsten's hair alight around her face like an aureole in the low sun.

There is something of peace in Koda's face that Maggie has never seen before, the quiet that follows cessation of pain. With it, too, is a new sense of intimacy between the two women. It is nothing overt, nothing that Maggie can easily put words to; only something in the tilt, perhaps, of Kirsten's head, the inclination of Koda's body. A lessening of the space between. Something, something of vital importance, has passed between them this day. Something that has Maggie, this time, on the outside, looking in.

The sight brings a small pang about her heart, but Maggie cannot pretend to any sweeping operatic emotion, neither jealousy nor grand amour. Neither can she pretend that she does not see the obvious and instinctive bond between the two women. Her ancestors, plying the coast of East Africa with ivory and leopard pelts to trade for turquoise and myrrh in the incense fields of Oman, would have called it *kismet*.

*Insh'allah. As god wills.* Aloud, she calls, "You guys headed home?"

"Yeah," Koda answers as she gains the sidewalk, and Asi, fickle male that he is, bounds toward her and paws at her chest as if he has not seen her in a week. "Hey, boy. Down." And to Maggie, again, "I put some soup on before we left. It ought to be done in an hour or so."

"You look tired," Kirsten observes. "Bad day with the interviews?"

Maggie grimaces and shakes her head slightly. "Filthy."

"Them or the day?"

"Both."

Koda's eyes meet hers, concern and affection in their blue depths. "You look like something Asi wouldn't bother to drag in." She gestures toward a pair of benches set under the still-naked branches of a sycamore tree. "Soup won't be on for a while yet. Let's sit."

Maggie nods and follows the other two toward the knoll that looks down over the woods. The sun has begun to fall toward the horizon, almost even with the treetops, and birds that gleam blue-black in the light that lies like gold wash across the snow make their way ponderously, two and two, into the trees where they will roost for the night. All of the pairs fly sedately together, save one. Where the others glide almost wingtip to wingtip, one raven dives from height upon his companion, swoops under to come out in a barrel roll, pinwheeling his wings about the axis of his body, his long flight feathers throwing off flashes of blue and green and silver where the sun strikes them. His low-pitched *prrrukkk* resonates in the air.

Kirsten stands transfixed, her eyes wide and impossibly green. Asimov seems to have taken on her mood, sitting quietly beside her, a first. Kirsten asks, "Those are ravens, aren't they?"

"Common ravens, to be exact. We...we Lakota...call them 'wolf birds,'" Koda answers. "They'll follow a pack on the hunt or sometimes even lead them to prey."

"And they get a share?"

"After the wolves have done. It's not true symbiosis, but close."

Caught up in the small drama, Maggie watches as the stunt-flying bird wheels upward again and plunges again toward the other. It seems extraordinarily graceful for birds that big, that heavy. She says, not quite asking, "That's not a fight."

"That's a proposal," Koda responds, smiling slightly. "That's got to be a couple of young birds pairing off, since it's still way too early for breeding. They won't nest until next summer."

Kirsten shades her eyes, following the aerobatics. "Long term pair bond?"

Koda nods. "For life."

Kirsten stares at the birds, the one serene in her flight, the other tumbling about her in exuberant loops and rolls, untiring. Finally they disappear into the trees, and she turns, her eyes going from Koda to Maggie to somewhere deep inside herself that the colonel cannot see. "How did we get it so wrong?"

Koda is silent, staring out over the woods toward the setting sun. The light plays across her face, bronze and still as a statue's, and Maggie feels her bearings slipping yet again. Time has ground to a halt, it seems, or spun backward, drawing the woman standing before her into its looping maze, into past or future or otherwhen. So it is Maggie who says, "Get what wrong, Kirsten?"

Kirsten makes a small encompassing gesture with one hand. "Everything. How did we screw up the whole goddam world? What's going to happen to us?"

Maggie bites down on the response that leaps to her tongue on the first question. *All too easily.* There is no answer to the second one. "I don't know," she says. "We don't know how many are left even in North

America, much less the rest of the world. We just have to do the best we can and work to make it enough."

A small smile, half ironic, tugs at Kirsten's mouth. "My dad was a Marine. You sound like him."

*Wonderful.* The thought weaves through the back of Maggie's mind. *My about to be ex-girlfriend is about to become her future girlfriend, and I'm a father figure.* Aloud she says, "Career military tend to think pretty much in the same channels. It's the training."

"Semper fi, huh, even in the wild blue yonder?"

"You got it."

"Someone's coming."

Maggie starts. Koda has snapped out of whatever reverie has held her and is staring at a Jeep streaking down the street straight for them. Andrews pulls up with a squeal of brakes and the smell of burned rubber laid down on the asphalt. He salutes, still sitting behind the wheel. "Ma'am!"

Maggie tosses her briefcase into the vehicle and starts to climb in, lifting her sore leg gingerly over the low side by the front passenger seat. "What's the problem, Lieutenant?"

"Ma'am, the MP captain asked me to find you. There's a situation at the main gate."

Without being bidden, Koda and Kirsten pile into the back, Asimov between them. "All right," Maggie mutters resignedly, regretting the hot bath and the hot supper that have now receded as far into the dim future as civilization itself. "Whatever it is, let's go tend to it. Semper the hell fi."

The Jeep bumps along the near-empty street at a speed that rattles Koda's bones together like bare branches in a norther; the winter weather has not been kind to the tarmac, and repairing potholes has not been high on the base's agenda. Andrews seems to be making no particular effort to avoid them, possibly on the theory that the shortest distance between two points is a straight line. The likelihood of a broken axle does not seem to enter the equation. The snarl of the engine and the sharp whip of the evening air make conversation impossible. Koda hangs on to the rollbar with one hand and Asi with the other; on his other side, Kirsten does the same, face set and pale in the chill blue light that follows sunset. Asi leans into the wind created by their speed, eyes bright, tongue lolling, having the time of his life. George Patton Asimov, Dog of War.

He may get a second chance to prove himself. As a rancher, Koda knows that only two types of problems develop at gates, whether they involve humans or cows. One: someone wants in who should not be let in. Two: someone wants out who should not be let out. Given the disorderly scenes of civilians attempting to take up residence on the base and defying MPs that she has already witnessed, she is fairly certain that the crisis is of the first type.

The sound comes to them through the gathering darkness, well before they come into sight of the gate, a muffled roar like a tornado grinding across the plains. A steady rhythm runs under it, a bass beat answering point counterpoint to intermittent screams. As near as she can tell, they seem to be cries of anger rather than pain. If they are lucky, they may still have a bit of time before matters get entirely out of hand. It won't be much, though. In the seat in front of her, Maggie pokes Andrews' arm and mimes a heavier foot on the accelerator. Andrews nods and floors it. Without a word, Koda and Kirsten link arms behind Asi to hold him in place. Oblivious to his safety, he throws back his head and howls like a wolf following blood spoor, closing in on his prey.

"He's enjoying this, the idiot!" Kirsten yells, the shout barely audible above the racket of the Jeep and the ever-closer thunder of what is clearly a mob.

Koda grins in answer, holding tighter to both the dog and the Jeep. But the sound that she has dreaded cracks out in the middle of one of Asi's arpeggios, and she lets go of the bar and shifts her weight to draw the automatic pistol she has carried ever since the battle. In front of her, Maggie already has her own sidearm in her hand, held low and ready. Kirsten's is in her lap. "Rifle," Koda shouts into the wind, and Kirsten nods agreement, even though Koda doubts she has heard. The sound is unmistakable. The lack of return fire to that single shot is no comfort.

Andrews rounds the corner where the commissary stands and streaks full throttle down the straightaway toward the base's main gate. They are no longer alone. Sirens wailing, so close on their bumper that the lead truck almost backends them, a pair of MP troop carriers swing in behind them from the opposite intersection, and a small ripple of uncoiling muscles runs down Koda's back. The situation is still not good, but it is no longer as bad as it was a second or two ago.

At the distance of three or four hundred meters and closing, it becomes clear that a full-scale riot is in the offing. One panel of the base's double steel gates blocks the right lane of the road, rolled shut across a clot of a dozen cars and trucks angled in as many different directions. A second logjam of vehicles clogs the left lane. A pair of heavy-duty pickups, the long-bedded, double-cab sort that can carry a dozen armed adults apiece, stand aimed at them just beyond the guardhouse, their front tires punctured on the teeth of steel bars that have risen up out of the asphalt like a pair of shark's dentures. Over and around and among and on top of the cars and trucks, perhaps forty people stand shouting at the two MPs on watch. The guards hold their weapons at waist level, ready to fire though not aimed at the crowd.

Add nitroglycerin and stir lightly until moistened: the situation is a breath away from disaster. Maybe less.

Maggie is out of the Jeep before it comes completely to a halt, fishtailing to a stop just behind the guardhouse. Koda and Kirsten pile out on her heels, Asimov and Andrews pace for pace behind them. The carrier trucks swing into nearly right-angle turns, one to barricade each traffic lane. MPs come spilling out their rear flaps, armed with riot helmets, shields, and clubs, to stand shoulder to shoulder across the tarmac. At the sight of them, the crowd surges forward, its roar clawing its way up the scale until it becomes a sustained howl.

Without warning, the searchlights mounted on the cabs of the MP trucks flare to life, sweeping the crowd with beams bright enough to dazzle the eyes of anyone who looks directly into them. A ripple passes through the crowd as arms and hands attempt to block the glare. Here and there, a figure turns away entirely and begins to move toward the back of the mob. More ominously, the light picks out the metal fittings of half a dozen deer rifles, here and there the skeletal form of an M-16 or an AK-47.

Maggie snatches a bullhorn from the hand of the MP captain and vaults up onto the bed, then the cab roof, of one of the impaled pickups. Koda and Kirsten clamber up to take stations in the back of the truck, facing the crowd, guns held low but visible in front of them. Asimov stands on the lowered tailgate, ruff bristling and tail held straight and prickly as a lodgepole pine. His lips curl up to bare his teeth. For an instant his form seems to blur, his head lose its angularity to become shorter in the muzzle, his ears less sharply pointed, his whole face broader beneath the eyes.

A chill slips down Koda's spine and the sense of something indefinably other — otherkind, otherwhere, otherwhen — follows after. Something of the same feeling, no more than a frisson, slid through her mind, half-memory, half-not, while she had watched the ravens making their way into the forest as the sun brushed the horizon in its steepening fall toward night. Time has gone awry, the Earth tilted off its accustomed axis, past and future erupting into the present like steam rising in a geyser.

"I can't hear you!"

Maggie's voice brings her back from her split-second drift into the time stream. Again, metallic and magnified almost beyond recognition, all its Southern softness gone.

"I CAN'T HEAR YOU!" Gun tucked back into the waistband of her trousers, Maggie points at a red-faced man in a plaid hunting jacket at the front of the crowd. "You! Talk to me! What the hell's going on here?"

The man yells something inaudible back. "Say again!" Maggie shouts.

Gradually the crowd quiets, and the unexpected spokesperson steps a little away from the others, moving cautiously with his eyes on the line of MPs just behind the truck that has suddenly become a podium. His hand moves to the brim of his Stetson in reflexive good manners, hesitates, and tilts the hat back on his head at a jauntier angle instead. His step takes on the suggestion of a strut.

Unimpressed, Koda suppresses a snort. *A banty rooster, this one, all crow and no balls.* She catches the roll of Kirsten's eyes and almost winks in response. It's as bad a case of testosterone poisoning as she's ever seen. Unobtrusively, Koda thumbs the safety off her gun. Covering one hand with the other almost demurely, Kirsten does the same, staring at the man and the crowd behind him with eyes bright and cold and hard as green diamonds.

"Who the hell are you?" the Stetson roars.

"Margaret Allen, United States Air Force. Who the fuck are you?"

A murmur runs through the crowd, and the truculent expression drops off several faces in the front. Word of the battle of the Cheyenne has apparently gotten out to at least some of the remaining civilian population. Further back, a couple of rifle barrels slip from view.

Sensing the change behind him, the man's voice loses a fraction of its edge. "I'm Bill Dietrich, and I'm a law-abiding citizen. You want to explain to me why U.S. citizens can't come onto a base their taxes paid for?"

Far back in the crowd, someone yells, "You tell 'er, Bill," and another, sharply female, snaps, "Shut up, you idiot!"

"Pleased to meet you, Mr. Dietrich," Maggie responds evenly. "Suppose you tell me why you and the good folks behind you are attempting to trespass on a restricted government installation."

"What guvmint? There ain't no guvmint! We got a right to what we paid for."

At that, Kirsten steps forward, moving to where Asi stands at the alert at the edge of the tailgate. The glare of the searchlights leaches color from her, turning her hair silver, her face ghost pale. Her voice, when she speaks, is as chill as her face. "Allow me to introduce myself, Mr. Dietrich. I'm Kirsten King, and I'm the only surviving member of the Cabinet we know of." She pauses, letting the effect filter through the crowd for a moment. "And much as I would hate to do it, I'm prepared to ask these law enforcement officers to enforce the law by firing on you if necessary. Whether it's necessary or not is up to you." She steps back toward the cab of the truck, her gun now in plain sight.

A second man detaches himself from the crowd, unceremoniously elbowing Dietrich aside. He is tall and lanky and grey, with creases carved deep around his eyes and at the corners of his mouth. "Ma'am, I'm Jim Henderson. I've got a ranch up the road a bit, or did have. Had a family, too. Now I've just got one daughter, and her only because she was out riding fence with me when the droids took or killed the rest. All I want is a safe place for her. That's what we all want, Ms. Secretary, Colonel Allen, just a place to be safe."

"I understand," Maggie answers. "But you have to understand that the base is not safe. It's already been a target twice; we're likely to be attacked again."

"You beat the droids!" That comes from somewhere about halfway back. "They're gone!"

"We beat one contingent of the droids," she corrects the speaker. "There are more where they came from, believe me."

Dietrich swaggers to the fore again. "Then you gotta protect us! Let us in!"

Koda hears Maggie's sharply indrawn breath, magnified by the bullhorn. Her voice, though, remains patient. "Mr. Dietrich, tell me something. How do I know you're not a droid? How can we tell you're not a spy trying to force your way in here?"

"Why that's the damnedest stupidest thing I ever heard of! Listen to me, you—" He breaks off abruptly. "Look, lady, that uniform don't make you God!"

"I know one way to tell if he's a droid," Kirsten remarks almost casually. "Droids don't bleed."

"Look," Maggie says, "we can't insure your security unless we can insure the security of the base and our assets. You folks can try to fight your way in, and lose. You can lose even more of your people. You can kill some of these soldiers who have already bled for you at the Cheyenne." She pauses, allowing that to sink in.

Koda is pleased to see more guns disappear from view.

"Go home. If it will make you feel more secure, you can move into some of the vacant houses closer to the base, but don't expect us to support you; we can't do it. You'll have to find ways to feed yourselves and protect yourselves from everything but armed attack. That's your job as citizens. Ours is to defend you from enemies, foreign and domestic...and android. You can obstruct us, or you can help us serve you. Your choice."

"Who's in charge?" The voice comes from somewhere in the middle of the crowd, unidentifiable by age or gender.

Which is the sixty-four million dollar question, isn't it? Koda's eyes flick sideways to Kirsten, only to find that the other woman is looking directly at her. With a small shake of her head, Koda averts her glance and returns to watching the crowd. For the first time since the uprising, she is truly and personally afraid of what may come. Because the question is not just who's in charge now, but who will be in charge if human society somehow beats the odds and manages to survive.

And the only viable answer is that it will be someone entirely different, something entirely different, than anything that has gone before.

Maggie shouts into the bullhorn. "General Hart is the commanding officer of this base. Dr. King is the highest surviving civilian authority that we know about. Like it or not, we have to assume that the new capital of the United States is now Ellsworth Air Force Base. And that's going to mean the kind of security restrictions we had before, only more so." She pauses. "But you're free people. You need to choose yourselves a mayor or manager or whatever you want to call it. You need to pick law officers. Because as far as I'm concerned, the Constitution is still in effect, and the American military does not police American civilians. Anybody got any problems with that?"

The crowd begins to mill, movement coalescing somewhere around its center. Some of them clearly do have problems with that, and have come here in hopes of finding someone to tell them what to do. Others, their faces clearly relieved even in the flat glare of the floodlights, have heard what they needed to hear. Slowly, infinitely slowly, its members begin to bleed off, backing out of the gate on foot, others getting into their vehicles to inch away in reverse. The MPs pace them, moving in line, shields locked in a solid wall.

Kirsten raps out, "Hold! Let them go voluntarily."

The line halts as if frozen, and as the last of the would-be mob filters out, the duty guards roll the second panel of the gate into place. It locks with a soul-satisfying clang.

Maggie jumps down from the top of the cab, stumbling a little on her bad leg.

Koda slips a hand under her arm to steady her. "You okay?"

A smile plays for a moment about Maggie's mouth. "Rapists, mobs. Oh yeah, just a day in the freakin' life." To the MP captain, she says, "I want half a dozen more guards on this gate and as many on the side entrance. I want staggered patrols all around the perimeter. M-60s. We're in lockdown. Nobody gets in and nobody gets out until we know precisely who's on base and who has what useful skill."

"Yes, Ma'am." The captain salutes and turns to sort his troops into patrols.

"And, Captain," Kirsten adds. "If anybody comes over the fence, shoot to kill. This base was a restricted area before; it's a restricted area now."

"Ma'am." Again, he salutes. "I'm on it."

Asi, standing down from red alert with an ease granted to none of the humans, begins to wave the plume of his tail. Whining, he paws at Koda's leg, then noses at her pocket, looking for treats.

Kirsten reaches down to ruffle his fur. "He's right," she says. "It's past suppertime. Let's go home."

# CHAPTER NINETEEN

For the third time in less than an hour, Dakota looks toward the window, then frowns distractedly before returning to her duties. The base vet might have been an excellent diagnostician, but his office skills were decidedly lacking. She has had to send two sets of volunteers on trips to the nearby towns to raid the vet facilities there and return with any usable supplies they can, and it still isn't close to being enough. After three days under lock-down, civilians in ones and twos have been allowed to trickle back through the gates with goods to sell, illnesses to treat. They bring their pets with them, pets who have often-times suffered as much, if not more, than their owners. The clinic is bursting at the seams, full of frostbitten dogs, half-mauled cats, dehydrated turtles, constipated snakes, sick birds of all kinds, and a number of more exotic species, along with several Army canines who are slowly recovering from injuries suffered during the initial battle with the androids.

With a soft grunt, she tosses the pencil down and pushes away from the desk, running weary fingers through her disordered hair. She checks the window again, then the clock. Something is nagging at her and has been for the past hour or so, but she can't put a finger on what it is, and that fact is driving her just shy of nuts. "What?" she barks in response to a light tap on her office door.

The door slowly opens and a curly-mopped young woman pokes her head in, expression slightly nervous. "You asked me to let you know when I walked Condor, Doctor." Condor is an Army dog who took several bullet wounds to the belly and flank. It has been touch and go with him for the past weeks, but he appears now well on the road to recovery. "He did fine. I think he can be discharged in a day or two."

Nodding, Koda forces a smile to her face. "Thank you, Shannon. You've done very well with him."

The young woman blushes under the quiet praise, then calms, her eyes concerned. "Are you...okay?"

"Mm?" Koda drags her gaze away from the window yet again. "I'm sorry. What did you say?"

"I asked if you were all right. You seem...distracted?"

"Oh." She shakes her head slightly, clearing it. "No. Just," one hand waves toward the paper-strewn desktop, "trying to deal with this mess. I never was all that fond of paperwork."

Shannon brightens. "Well, I might have a solution for that." At Dakota's raised eyebrow, she continues. "I have a friend, Melissa, who used to be an admin assistant for Kuyger-Barren-Micholvski, the law firm? She's been going crazy with nothing to do. I'm sure she'd be happy to pitch in, if you like."

This time, Koda's smile is more genuine. "I could use all the help I can get."

"Great! I'll let her know tonight."

"Fair enough." Dakota rises from the chair with fluid grace, grabs her Stetson from the coat rack and settles it on her head, sweeping her hair behind her broad shoulders. "I'm going for a walk. Hold down the fort, will ya?"

"With pleasure, Doc...Dakota."

**Maggie sorts through** the folders in her briefcase as she waits for the clock on the wall to tick officially around to 11:00. Like the conference room, like everything else in the Headquarters building, the walls and floors are grey, with occasional Air Force blue accents. A silk ficus to one side of the general's door and a faux pothos ivy under the window offer the only relief. At her workstation, the general's secretary bites her lip and dabs at a drop of sweat collecting under her heretofore perfect mascara.

Kimberley has always seemed to Maggie to be forty going on twenty-five, with her acrylic nails and seamless make-up, short skirts and years-out-of-fashion high heels. Now her heart-shaped face is pinched with effort as she struggles with an old-fashioned manual typewriter, resurrected from God-knows-what basement or storage building. An equally antiquated adding machine perches on the edge of her desk, the kind with a handle that is pulled after each entry to crank up a sum or tax percentage. Maggie recognizes it only because her accountant grandfather kept one of the things on top of the barristers' bookcase in his office, part of a collection that included such other relics as a slide rule and a solid-black metal telephone with a rotary dial that clicked satisfyingly when she stuck her finger into the perforated disk, pulled it around to the stop, and watched it spin back.

That had been nearly forty years ago. A lifetime now; an eon. At five she did not go in for elaborate existential metaphors. She is not pleased that she has begun to see them everywhere now.

The sense of temporal dislocation that has plagued her intermittently for the past week has begun to solidify into a reality she is still not quite prepared to face. Finally and irrevocably, the world has changed. The crisis is not temporary, not just a matter of devising a widget or developing an anti-viral, biological or cyber, that will allow the technological world to right itself onto its accustomed axis and go on spinning. Even if Kirsten King manages to cause every last remaining droid to self-destruct in a single ecstatic nanosecond, there is no way to restore much, maybe most, of what has been lost. And here, an icon of that brave new world folding back into its own past, is a goddamed Olivetti typewriter, its uneven clack of metal keys without doubt the harbinger of more and worse to come.

*And aren't we Ms. Congeniality this morning? C'mon Allen, snap out of it.*

Though she has not put it so dramatically to herself, she is here to try to save a man's life. She can afford neither depression nor woolgathering in the middle of such a sensitive rescue operation.

*Because we can't afford to lose anybody now.* Not even an asinine general who bombs first and asks questions later. Not even a couple dozen decent citizens of Rapid City who had come within an angstrom of morphing into an out-of-control mob less than eighteen hours ago. *Every asset must be deployed and its utility maximized. Even General Hart.*

The clock hand creeps round to 10:56. The typewriter keys continue to clatter in a spotty rhythm, punctuated by small mewing sounds from the secretary every time she makes a mistake. Not for the first time since she has entered the office, Maggie wonders what the hell there is to type in triplicate these days.

*I am on a mission of mercy,* she tells herself wryly. *I might as well have pity on Kimberley, too.*

Aloud she says, "You'll get your computer back as soon as we have a reliable source of electricity. Sergeant Rivers has gone out to the Red River Co-op wind farm to see if we can move in some of the big generators."

The secretary turns to look at her, a spark of something besides irritation in her eyes for the first time since Maggie has entered the outer office. "He's that really tall Sioux guy, isn't he? Army, not Air Force — the really cute one."

Maggie breathes a mental sigh. She knows exactly what's coming next, and it arrives on schedule as surely as Old Faithful or the Italian trains under Musollini.

"...really good-looking. Is he single?"

As gently as she can, she answers, "I think so. I don't recall that he's mentioned a husband."

"Oh," the woman says in a small voice. Then, plaintively, "What are we going to do, Colonel Allen? There's so few men left. Is it going to be like in the Bible, with one man having three or four wives? Wives and concubines? What's going to happen now?"

With a supreme effort of will, Maggie manages not to grind her teeth. "I don't know, Kimberley. But what we're not going to do is fall back into some Bronze Age form of patriarchy. That will not happen. Will. Not. Happen."

"It's happening in town, Colonel. My sister belongs to one of those Bible-believing temples. You know, where the women can't wear pants or make-up and nobody drinks or dances, and church goes on for four hours on Sunday. She said the preacher has already got three wives of his own, one of them only thirteen." Kimberley snorts, a sound that reassures Maggie that her considerable good sense has not in fact been a casualty of the uprising. "Says it's the will of God, a holy thing. As if." She turns back to her typewriter, rearranging the triple load of paper.

*Goddess!* Maggie stares in wonderment. *Is that actually carbon paper?* It is — carbons.

"Just a dirty old man if you ask me."

Miraculously, the clock hand has arrived at 11:01. Maggie clears her throat, pointing.

Kimberley glances up, then makes a show of checking her appointment book. "Go on in, Colonel."

Maggie gathers her papers, snaps her briefcase shut, and escapes.

**The South Dakota** spring is showing her fickle side, having just finished dumping a fresh four inches of powdery snow that sparkles in the warming sun like scattered diamonds. The breeze is fresh, and crisp, but lacks the arctic bitterness of true winter, and Koda breathes it in with an absent sense of pleasure.

The streets are, for once, quiet, nearly empty. Far from soothing her, however, this causes the nagging feeling in Koda's gut to return. A shadow crosses her path, and she looks up in time to see Wiyo circling low overhead. Her warning cry coincides perfectly with the sound of a single shot, and everything slips into place, clear as crystal. An animal snarl mists the air before her face. She turns and heads for the gate at a dead run, teeth bared, lips twisted as a second and third shot ring out followed by barking, mocking male laughter.

There are several airmen peering through the barred gate at what lies beyond. She ignores this, instead darting to the left and up the fifteen foot guard tower, taking the steps three at a time. Brushing past the startled MP, she circles the tower until she is looking over the grounds just outside the gate.

Three flannel-clad men stand outside a still-running pickup truck, each armed with a scoped rifle. They are clearly drunk, and one even leans fully against the truck's fender, his legs no longer able to support him.

"Shoot it again, Frank! It's still movin'!"

She follows their sightline to see a she-wolf, slat thin and panting, peering over the snow ridge to the east. The wolf is clearly injured, but still she doesn't flee. There is a quiet desperation to her darting eyes, moving from the men shooting at her to the men behind the gate. Another shot throws up snow just in front of her muzzle and she ducks, only to pop up a second later, tongue lolling, eyes rolling.

Wiyo screams overhead, and one of the men lifts his rifle and head, shooting into the air. The hawk wheels, unharmed, and screams again.

Without thought, Koda grabs the M-16 from the guard's hands and lifts it to her shoulder, staring down the sight with one piercing eye. Caressing the trigger, she stitches a neat line at the shooter's feet. He whirls, the barrel of his rifle narrowly missing the man standing beside him. "What the fuck?" He narrows his eyes at the woman — at least he thinks it's a woman, with that hat and that height, who can tell? — standing on the guard tower, pointing the business end of an M-16 at him. "Who the fuck are you, bitch?"

"Drop that rifle, or you'll never find out."

"Oh yeah?"

Her voice is velvet over steel. "Oh yeah."

Summoning his drunken courage, the man does the opposite of what he has been commanded, ponderously lifting his rifle and aiming it at the she-demon on the guard tower.

"I wouldn't," Koda murmurs, her voice just strong enough to prick his hearing.

"Says who, bitch?"

The sound of a dozen M-16s being cocked gives the man an eloquent answer.

Paling noticeably, he lowers his rifle. His friends drop theirs and dive for the safety of the pickup.

"Sergeant!" Koda shouts down to the guard leader.

"Ma'am!"

"Round those three up and take them to the brig."

"For what?" the drunken man demands. "You ain't got no say-so over us! We're on public land!"

"Exactly," Koda hisses, her grin most unpleasant. "Cruelty to animals will do for starters. If that doesn't stick, assault with a deadly weapon."

"You can't..."

"Open the gate!" the sergeant yells.

Hearing this, the man drops his weapon and runs, jumping into his truck and fumbling for the gearshift.

An M-16 rattles, and the truck suddenly finds itself with two flats and a fractured engine block. The punctured radiator sends up a billow of steam from beneath the hood, and the truck shudders and dies.

"Come out of there with your hands over your heads! We won't ask you twice!"

Koda doesn't need to see the rest of it. She hands the gun back to the MP with a quiet murmur of thanks and crosses the tower, pelting down the steps with speed. Running through the gate, she immediately turns toward the ridge, long strides eating up the ground beneath her. The wolf has disappeared behind the ridge, but she doesn't need sight to track her. The scent of blood is heavy in the air, and she can feel the pain radiating from the injured animal, tugging hard at a part of her that is far more kin to the wolf than to any of the humans behind her.

Halfway up the shallow ridge, she deliberately slows her steps, listening as the wolf's panting breaths are interrupted by a weak warning growl. "It's okay, *tshukmanitou tanka*, it's okay. I won't hurt you." She steps carefully upwind so that her scent is carried to the injured animal.

Cresting the ridge, she stops and looks down at the silver-tipped fur and the crimson stain slowly spreading in the snow. Her eyes narrow. This is a wolf she knows, the alpha female of a large pack whose home range covers several hundred miles, from the base to her family's home and beyond. That she's alone and obviously starving is of great concern.

She meets the wolf's eyes, then shifts her gaze abruptly to the side before looking back. After a moment, the wolf does the same, and Koda relaxes, letting go a slow breath that clouds the air between them. She resumes her steps, narrowing the gap between them, then drops gracefully to her haunches, holding out an ungloved hand for the animal to sniff.

A soft whine lets her know she's been accepted, and she spends a long moment unmoving, examining the she-wolf with just her experienced gaze. Beneath dry, brittle, and thinning fur, her ribs stand out like dinosaur bones, aspirating weakly with every panting breath. Her tongue is dry, cracked, and bleeding in places, indicating severe dehydration. Blood is pouring from two bullet wounds — no more than grazes really, but in her weakened condition they are life-threatening.

Acting on intuition, Koda reaches slowly over and ruffles through the hair on the wolf's belly. The nipples are swollen, reddened, and cracked.

*An early litter. Shit.* Removing her hand, she peers into dark, pain-wracked eyes. "Where are your pups, *Ina*?"

With a soft whine, the she-wolf looks over her shoulder, then attempts to rise. She collapses a second later, her energy completely drained.

"It's all right, *Ina*, it's okay. I'll find them for you. But first, I need to help you so you can help them, all right?"

Feeling along her ruff, Koda slips an arm under the wolf's proud neck, then gathers her flank and stands, cradling the injured animal easily in her arms.

Too weak to struggle, the wolf gives a soft whine, then collapses back against the strong body holding her.

Koda looks up. The hawk is still circling, wingtips fluttering in the air's heavy currents. "Wiyo! *Awayaye!*"

With a loud kre-ee-ee, Wiyo circles once more, then comes down to land atop a winter-bare tree, carefully folding her wings behind her and staring straight ahead. "*Pilamayaye*," Koda shouts to the hawk, nodding once, sharply. And with that, she turns and heads back to the base using her quickest and smoothest gait.

**The room is** very much as Maggie has become accustomed to it, as grey as the rest of the Headquarters building except for the framed photographs on the walls. Several show Ellsworth's various aircraft in flight against impossibly blue skies: the Tomcat with its delta wings swept back, the sleek B-1, ponderous and old-fashioned B-52s that look like nothing so much as locusts built to cyclopean scale. Others depict Hart in the company of various dignitaries: the most recent with President Clinton, the earliest with her husband during his tenure as Commander in Chief. The fluorescent light illuminates them coldly, chilling the imaged skies and the deep blue of uniforms and the hills that ring the base. Pulled tightly over the windows, curtain panels barricade the office against the bright spring day of strengthening sun and melting snow that lies just on the other side of the glass. There is a settled stillness here that creeps over Maggie's skin like the passing of a ghost.

The room is so quiet that it seems at first that she is alone. Then paper rustles, drawing her eye to the massive desk at one end of the room as the general slowly pages through a stack of reports, pausing to glance at each one while she stands waiting. With a flourish, he initials three of them, consigning them to one neatly squared-off stack, the apparent rejects to another. The neat surface seems somehow empty, and it comes to Maggie that there are several framed photographs missing. Finally, his point made, the general rises, unfolding out of his leather chair with the suddenly stiff joints of an octogenarian. Maggie has never been quite certain whether the old-fashioned gesture is residual gallantry so ingrained that it is intractable, or whether it is a reminder that while she may be an officer, a gentlewoman, and a decorated battle ace, she is still a woman and therefore not quite equal to any one of the boys. "Margaret," he says. "Good morning."

"Good morning, sir," she echoes. A burning begins, deep in her solar plexus, spreading itself along her nerves until her skin feels as though she has taken fire, incandescent in the chill of the long room. Hart has never played power politics adroitly, and this attempt at dominance is almost as crude as his revelation of the one blot he had been able to find on her record. For an instant, Maggie wants nothing so much as to turn on her heel and walk out. *Leave him for the jackals, damn him.* But she cannot do that. Hart has talents that are in short supply.

*He is a human being*, she reminds herself sternly. Human beings themselves are in short supply, male human beings even shorter. None salvageable can be wasted with impunity.

"Salvageable" being the operative word. One of the matters they must discuss is the trial and subsequent punishment of the rapists from Mandan and Grand Rapids.

Hart gestures toward the comfortable armchair in front of the desk, then settles back into his own with an attempt at ease that only emphasizes the angularity of his movements. His skin seems faded by more than the sunless months of snow, his features not so much relaxed as given in to the pull of gravity.

Dead man walking.

He says, startling her almost as much as if he truly were dead, "What can I do for you this morning, Colonel?"

Maggie snaps open her briefcase, removes a pair of manila envelopes and lays them on the general's desk, facing him. "Casualty report, sir."

The general lifts one of the files, fans the pages with a thumb and then sets it down again. He does not bother to examine it or read the figures in detail. "How bad?"

"A hundred and fifty dead," she replies, her voice tight. "Of those, approximately two thirds were military personnel, the remainder civilian volunteers. The heaviest losses occurred on the far side of the river, among the troops assigned to close on the enemy from the rear."

"Sergeant Rivers' contingent?"

There is a hint of something in his voice that Maggie cannot quite identify — not anger, precisely, not exactly jealousy. Resentment, perhaps. "Yes. As you're aware from initial reports, sir, they came under heavier fire than any of the other units."

Hart simply nods. Whatever he feels or thinks, he is not going to share it with a subordinate who has, in his clear if unspoken view, usurped his position. "Injuries?"

Maggie points toward the other folder. "Eighty percent ambulatory. The remainder include everything from punctured lungs to third degree burns. The medics tell me we may still lose as many as a quarter of them."

"Burial details?"

"Proceeding."

"Very good. What else?"

With considerable distaste, Maggie hands him a third, thicker folder. "Incident report. Reports, actually."

"I see. Under control?"

"For the time being."

"What else? How are the prosecutions of the collaborators going?"

"Sir..."

Hart regards her without speaking, not giving her an opening.

From the far side of the window come the first hesitant notes of a sparrow's song to set up a counterpoint to the muffled clack of keys from the secretary's desk. Perhaps she imagines it, but the grey rectangle of the window seems somehow lighter, as if the sun has emerged fully from the cloud cover that dampened the early morning. She suppresses an urge, almost overpowering, to rise and fling back the curtains, to let the day come spilling into the dingy room.

She cannot do it, though, without being rude, almost insubordinate. Hart has a certain entitlement to his gloom; by rights, his depression should be his own affair. Certainly she cannot openly notice it without embarrassing him, and probably herself. More certainly yet, it would bring his resentment firmly down on her and end any chance of cooperation. Indeed, during the course of their conversation, his face has become both more drawn and more remote. A man going through the motions, getting it over with as rapidly as he can. Getting human beings as far away from him as he can.

"Sir, if we can get back to the incident reports for a moment?"

"Yes?"

"Sir, if you'll look at those reports, you'll see that a pattern is developing. It's one we're not currently equipped to deal with." Maggie replaces the folder in front of him.

After a pause, clearly reluctant, he picks it up again and begins to read, silently and without comment. Several minutes later, he puts it down again. His mouth purses into a tight little moue of exasperation; it is the closest he has come to looking like himself since she entered the office. "Will you please tell me, Colonel, why there are three civilian drunks in the base jail? Have we taken to picking up winos in alleys or good old boys out on a binge? Surely we can use our resources better than that."

"They were shooting at a wolf, general, right in front of the main gate."

"I see," he says in a voice that makes it clear that he does not. "The United States Air Force is now enforcing environmental regulations?"

"It seems that we may be, sir, but that's a side issue. The real problem is that these three idiots drew down on our own MPs when Dr. Rivers put a stop to their fun."

"Dr. Rivers. And of course our MPs — they are still our MPs, are they not, Colonel? — were deployed to back her up."

The words drop like stones into the air, and Maggie feels the heat as it spreads over her face and neck. "The men were drunk, disorderly, and presented a direct threat to human life, General. It was a reflection, albeit a minor one, of the previous incident at the gate. That one had the potential to develop into a genuine riot. There could have been deaths — civilians and our troops, both."

"And your solution to this problem is?"

And there it is, right in front of her. Maggie mentally crosses her fingers and breaths a small prayer to Koda's Ina Maka. Or anyone else out there who's listening. She will have only one chance. Get it wrong, and there will be no way to put it right. It is only with a conscious effort that she does not draw a deeper and very obvious breath before speaking. *Here goes.*

"My solution, if we can call it that, has to do with reframing the problem, sir. What we have in the gate riot, the civilians attempting to appropriate base housing, the numbskulls taking potshots at the wildlife, is a breakdown of civil authority. Quite simply, there is none at the moment."

All trace of animation recedes from Hart's face. "There is Dr. King. She is, after all, the only surviving Cabinet officer that we know of, de facto President, if she wants to think of herself that way. And according to your report here, she certainly managed to restore order or help restore order in two of these incidents."

Maggie shakes her head. "True. But the most valuable thing she can do right now is continue to search for the code that will disable the androids. Someone is needed immediately, someone who is an experienced administrator and has the confidence of the townspeople as well as the military."

The general rises to his feet and paces a few feet away, waving her back into her chair when she rises with him. "No, no. Sit down." He turns to face her, hands behind his back but not at all at ease. "And where will we find such a person, Colonel Allen? Am I mistaken when I assume that you — or you and Dr. Rivers, or the two of you and Dr. King — have someone in mind?"

"I have discussed the matter with Dr. King, yes. As you say, she is the de facto President."

"And?"

"Sir, we have problems that are not within our military mission to solve. You asked about the trials of the rapists; they're precisely the kind of thing we don't really have a way to deal with. For instance," she refers to yet another folder, "I've drawn up suggested indictments under the Uniform Code of Military Justice. But can we — legally, Constitutionally — try these men in a military court?"

"It's the only court we have, Colonel Allen." Hart's tone is patient, as if he is explaining the obvious to a rather slow child.

"Which is precisely the problem, sir. No one has declared martial law. The crimes did not occur on Federal property. They are not Federal offenses, with the exception of collaborating with the enemy and possibly the conspiracy charges. We have them in jail, we're organizing their trials, but we have no legal jurisdiction."

"And how will a civil, or civilian, administrator solve this difficulty?"

"Sir, there is currently no legal authority at all in Rapid City. We've seen the result of that in the attempt of several families to claim vacant base housing, and in a more concerted attempt to force the gates a few nights ago." Hart's face remains expressionless. She is not getting through. *Play dirty?* For an instant Maggie weighs her options, then continues. "Kimberley tells me that polygamy is taking hold in at least one apocalyptic cult in town. Some old coot who fancies himself a prophet is marrying thirteen year old girls, to himself. If that's better than what's happening in the jails, you tell me how."

For an instant the frozen mask drops off Hart's face, and fear shows through. Somewhere in upstate New York, with his estranged wife, Hart has twin girls of the same age. There is no way of knowing what has happened to them, but none of the possibilities is good, and all are the stuff of a father's nightmare. It is their photograph that is missing from the general's desk, perhaps too painful to look at since the insurrection. *Really dirty, Allen. Really dirty. But if it gets results...* With a suddenness that is almost audible, like a gate clanging shut, the rigidity is back. Hart snaps, "It's an atrocity, of course. But at least those young women are accounted for."

Maggie shuffles papers and changes the subject, leaving the unspoken parallel to work as it will in the general's conscience. "Then there's the matter of the trials, as you say. We need to put together a court that will pass muster under the Constitution — a jury of the offenders' peers, or as near as we can get to it, and at the very least a civilian judge or two to sit with a military panel. If we can somehow locate a state district judge, all the better. Somebody has to organize that, and it has to be someone the civilians in Rapid City and the military personnel on the base both trust to do the job honestly and efficiently. Otherwise we have no Constitution, no law at all except what comes out of the barrel of an M-16."

"Do you have a candidate for this position, Colonel Allen? Your good friend Dr. Rivers, perhaps?"

Maggie's face burns as if she's been slapped, but she says steadily. "No, sir. I was hoping you would be willing to make use of your good relationship with the civilian leadership in Rapid City and the community's respect for you to take on the job yourself."

"I see. Aren't you forgetting that I made a rather spectacular error in judgment in the bombing of Minot? One that throws your own bombing of civilians into the shade. Don't you think that calls my authority into question?" She opens her mouth to speak, but he waves her to silence. "Not to mention being publicly backhanded by the charming Dr. King. But all of that opens the way for you, doesn't it, Colonel? Just a matter of time until you have the name as well as the job of commander. I'm surprised Dr. King hasn't field-brevetted you general already."

Appalled, Maggie draws in a long breath. She feels as though the earth has suddenly dropped away from under her, leaving her suspended in space. *Stupid. Stupid. Christ, I should have seen it coming.*

Very carefully, she says, "Sir, if you had been on the field at the Cheyenne, you would know who will eventually command our forces, not just the base." She lays the words down one by one, heavy with emphasis, willing him to believe. "It isn't me."

"Oh, yes, I've heard about the charge across the bridge. You've got your Joan of Arc, Colonel, but she has no training and no experience. She may make a charismatic figurehead, but you and I both know that at the end of the day, that's not enough." He pauses. "But she has you and her brother to prop her up. She'll pass well enough, no doubt."

With an effort at least as great as the force that propelled her across the ruined bridge in Koda's wake, Maggie manages to get a chokehold on her anger. There seems to be insufficient oxygen in the room; her throat feels so constricted that each word is a struggle. Her vision narrows to pinpoints. "Sir. With respect. You have the administrative experience that no other survivor can offer. You are respected in the civilian community. Someone needs to hold that community together, or it will collapse into anarchy. And we will waste time and effort we need to spend fighting the droids fighting them instead. You can prevent that."

"Anything I am able to prevent, Colonel, I can prevent as commanding officer of this base. Is there anything else? If not," he gestures toward his desk, "I'm rather busy, as you see."

It is a dismissal. Maggie rises, snapping her attaché case shut. "Thank you for your time, General."

Hart nods dismissively and turns back toward his high-backed leather chair in front of the drawn curtains. The sense of failure heavy about her, Maggie makes her way to the door and out into the reception area. Kimberley is missing, probably gone to lunch, and she is glad not to have to make conversation. She has no backup plan; neither does Kirsten, that she knows of. They will have to identify someone in Rapid City, back up him or her, and hope that person's authority can be made to stick by something besides a bayonet. Maggie rubs her throbbing temples and strikes out for the Judge Advocate's office and the brig.

*One son-of-a-bitch down, four to go.*

**"Clamp down on** that rate a little. I don't want her fluid overloaded."

"Yes, Doctor."

The small operating suite is brightly lit; brilliant white on chrome sterility. Koda and Shannon are dressed in green scrubs, surgical masks hanging from their necks. The she-wolf is on the operating table, only lightly sedated; her weakness and profound dehydration making anaesthesia too risky.

With a soft grunt of satisfaction, Dakota applies the final bandage to the wolf's flank wound, then strips the bloodied gloves from her hands, tossing them into a nearby red-bagged trash bin. Long fingers trail through the coarse, brittle fur, stopping briefly against a bony chest, feeling the reassuring beat of life beneath bone and skin. "I've done the best I can, *tshunkmanitou tanka*. The rest is up to you now."

"Is that her name?" Shannon asks as she deftly removes the bag of IV fluid from the pole while Dakota gathers the dazed wolf into her arms.

"Mm? I'm sorry?"

"What you called her. Shug...mani... Is that her name?"

Koda smiles, slipping backward through the swinging doors and into the recovery area. "*Tshunkmanitou tanka*. It means 'wolf' in Lakota."

Shannon blushes, then laughs softly. "Oh." She tips her head toward a large wire kennel separated from the rest, its bottom nested with soft towels. "That one okay?"

"Perfect." Squatting down, Koda slides the barely conscious wolf into the warm nest and ruffles quickly through her fur, checking all wounds for seepage. When all seems well, she peers into her eyes, and nods, satisfied before closing the door and standing back up. She turns to look at Shannon, who is hanging the IV bag on a pole next to the kennel. "I was wondering if you could do me a favor."

"Sure! Name it."

"I know it's getting late, but I need you to watch over her for a little while longer for me. She's got a litter out there somewhere and I need to find them before it gets dark."

Shannon's eyes widen in shock. "A litter? So early?"

"Too early," Koda agrees. "But they're out there. We would never have seen her if they weren't."

"Are you sure you can find them?"

"I'll find them." A beat, as she looks at the young woman. "Will you stay?"

"As long as you need me to."

Koda's lips twitch in some semblance of a smile. It's not perfect, but it serves its purpose. "Thanks."

Pulling her heavy coat on directly over her scrubs, Dakota gathers several warm blankets, a basket, and a handful of ChemHeat packs in her arms and heads back outside, the setting sun gilding her in tones of purest gold.

**The figures march** across the screen in orderly rows, keeping lockstep as the files scroll up and disappear over the top edge. Kirsten thinks of micrographs she has seen of blood cells spilling down through the narrow channel of vein and artery, compact red discs propelled from the conundrum of their origin to the mystery of their destination by the alternating pressure of diastole and systole. She thinks of Disney movies and television science specials, streams of army ants gnawing their way across the forest floor in a pheromone-driven rush from here to there, leaving bare earth in their wake. She thinks of lemmings, diving headlong into the sea. No meaning in any of it.

There are moments when she is so close to the solution — when she knows she is so close to the solution that she can almost see the dim shape of it forming on the screen. But something is always missing, something vital, the single segment of code that will turn the string of integers into a signal that, properly transmitted, will stop the droids where they stand. And that, in turn, will free the rest of surviving humanity, both those held in jails and all the rest, driven by fear or resolve or instinct for survival to resist their rule.

Kirsten removes her glasses, lays them carefully on the desk, and scrubs at her eyes. She is blind weary, almost literally, with the hours of unbroken attention seated before the computer. Her eyes sting; her back aches; the muscles of thigh and shoulder have twisted into macramé in the four hours she has been staring at the code strings, looking for something that she is beginning to fear is not there. Her mouth tastes of too-strong coffee, reheated once too often. She needs a break.

Deliberately, she snaps the lid of the laptop down and retrieves her glasses. Asimov, who has spent the morning drowsing under the desk, perks up instantly at the small sound, ears up, eyes bright. His tail thumps tentatively against the floor and he whines softly.

Kirsten reaches down to ruffle his ears. "Yeah, boy, I hear you. Give me a minute, and we'll go."

She rises, nearly stumbling with the stiffness of her legs. In the bathroom, she splashes cold water over her face, attempting to force her mind back to alertness. It is pain, though, that does the job, the knotted tendons and cramped ligaments in her neck resisting motion as she leans over the basin, then stands almost on tiptoe to reach the mouthwash on the top shelf of the old-style medicine cabinet. She has lived alone so long that she is seldom aware of her lack of inches, but sharing quarters with one six-footer and another woman almost that tall has brought back all the old annoyance at having to stretch for bottles just beyond the tips of her fingers, the indignity of having to stand on chairs to retrieve items from the top shelves of pantry and closet. She swears softly to herself as the bottle slips away from her grasp toward the back of the cabinet, again when it tips forward to land with a muffled thud in the sink.

Par for the course. Nothing else has gone right today, either, least of all her attempt to reconstruct the necessary cyber commands. Deliberately, Kirsten refuses to allow herself to think what will happen if she does not break the code. Failure is not an option.

Ten minutes later, her eyes scrubbed free of grit and the stale coffee taste replaced by the astringent bite of the mouthwash, she lets herself and Asimov out the front door. Desperate to get as far away as she can from the virtual environment of her computer, she makes for the stand of woods near where she and Koda had met Maggie the evening of the gate riot. The day stands on the edge of spring, though the sun's warmth does not yet match its brightness. It lies like pale gold along drifts of new-fallen snow, gilding the dawn side of tall birches and sycamores. Against one bare trunk, a woodpecker hitches its way up the bark, searching for still hibernating insects. High up and far out over the woods, a raven calls, his cries dropping into the soundless air. The streets, which should be heavily trafficked at mid-day with base personnel coming home for lunch and pre-school kids playing in the white and winter-brown yards or pedaling their trikes down the sidewalk to the peril of hapless pedestrians, lie deserted and nearly silent. As she follows the curve of the road away from the residential area, she encounters only a single squirrel foraging among the roots of a still-bare oak tree. At the sight of Asi loping toward her, the squirrel bottles her tail and scampers up onto an overhanging branch, scolding loudly. Then she, too, falls quiet, darting up into the tree's crown until the intruders have passed.

Kirsten's hearing loss has left her adapted to silence, preferring it even. For the first time, it occurs to her to wonder how others will deal with a world free of blaring automobile horns and ever present radio and television. A world where human voices are swallowed up not by ambient clatter but by the depths of silence.

There is order somewhere in their present situation, even though it is not presently discernable. Someone, somehow, has a reason for turning the droids loose on the remainder of the human race. When that reason is found, motives will become understandable and guilt can be reliably assigned.

She shakes her head to clear her thoughts. She has not come out into the fresh air to keep worrying the problem, turning it over and over, trying to rearrange it like a Rubrik's Cube until questions and answers all match up. Deliberately forcing her mind away from the droids, she searches the snow cover for a length of fallen branch long and heavy enough to throw well but not too heavy for a round of fetch. Finding one, she brushes the leaf mould off it, and, whistling, pitches it out far ahead of her. Asi is off after it in a nanosecond, bounding into the trafficless street and returning at a dead gallop, ears laid back and tail straight out like a rudder, to drop it at her feet and quiver with eagerness to do it again.

When they reach the benches, Kirsten sails the stick off over the incline leading up from the woods and Asi plunges down it, sliding and slipping in the snow and the wet earth beneath. Kirsten follows more carefully, having no desire to add bruises on top of her existing sore spots. Neither does she want to have to wash her clothes out by hand. Maggie's machine runs only on full loads now, and only for things, like sheets and jeans, that cannot reasonably be hand laundered. The bathroom has begun to take on the aspect of a dorm room, socks and underwear in three sizes draped over the shower rails and towel rings.

A small stream flows over the flat ground between the street and the wood, and Kirsten follows it into the trees. Most are still bare, but the ice has begun to melt, and here and there along low hanging braches, she can make out the swollen buds of leaves to come. The stream has thawed entirely, and it murmurs softly as it winds between its dark banks, spilling here and there into a low waterfall, spreading out to hardly more than a film over the petrified fans of ancient lava flows.

Asi is quiet now, pacing beside her. Here where the trees crowd close, there is no room to keep up their game, and somehow the boisterousness of it seems inappropriate, like laughter in a church. Weaving her way between gnarled roots and under low branches that will trail their leaves in the water come summer, her eye is caught by a sudden movement some ten feet ahead of her. She freezes where she stands, and Asi with her.

Apparently oblivious of her presence, a raccoon sits on his haunches at water's edge, dabbling with both hands in the stream. Kirsten knows that the myths are myths: he is not washing up before lunch, or, for that matter, washing his lunch before lunch. More likely he is searching for his meal, small fish or aquatic insects, perhaps even freshwater mussels. Soundlessly, so as not to disturb him, Kirsten sinks down upon one of the sycamore roots, leaning back against the trunk to watch. She keeps her hand on Asi's collar, but he has shown no inclination to harass the raccoon. Which is odd, she thinks, but certainly convenient.

For long minutes she watches him, the sun striking coruscating brilliance from the clear water through the gently swaying branches. He seems to be out of luck, for he catches nothing that she can see. Yet he continues his search below the surface, patiently, his eyes taking the errant sunlight like dark rounds of Baltic amber.

She is not sure when or how it happens, nor has she any idea how long she has sat watching the steady, repetitive motions of the creature's search. She only knows that somehow the light has changed around her. The intermittent fall of sunlight through the branches has become a steady, golden glow without visible source. Colors have grown deeper, the pale grey water become vivid blue, the rough grey bark of her sycamore, a rich and varied umber. The sky, where she can see it between the forking trunk of the sycamore, has turned the impossible shade of perfect turquoise, clouds like feathers drifting lightly along under its canopy. Beside her, Asi has fallen still, whuffling softly in his dream.

With a lunge almost too fast to see, the raccoon splashes into the stream and emerges with a small silver fish, still wriggling, in his mouth. On the bank again, he shakes the water from his coat, and, quite deliberately, begins to clamber over the uneven ground directly toward Kirsten herself. She holds herself motionless, scarcely breathing. Part of her mind screams that this is abnormal behavior, and that she is about to be bitten by a rabid animal. The other part waits in stillness, a frisson running over her skin like electricity. She does not know what is about to happen, but even she knows magic when she sees it. Asi never stirs.

When the raccoon is no more than a yard from her, he sits back on his haunches again. Golden eyes never leaving hers, he takes the fish from his mouth with one long-fingered hand and calmly bites its head off. He chews thoughtfully, swallows, and says, "Well damn, it took you long enough. What kept you?"

For a moment, the tingle of anticipation turns to real fear. Nothing in her zoology courses has prepared her for talking animals. She is either mad or dreaming. Or she was right the first time, and it is magic.

She says, "What do you mean, long enough? Do you have any idea what I've been doing the last three months? It's not like we had an appointment."

"Oh, we had an appointment, all right. You just didn't know it."

"Not any appointment I made. I don't pencil hallucinations into my schedule."

"I am not," the raccoon says, enunciating very carefully, "an hallucination."

"Then what are you? A dream? Something I ate?"

The raccoon pauses with the fish halfway to his mouth again. "What do I look like, you idiot human? Chopped liver?"

"You look like—"

"I," he interrupts, speaking with extreme dignity, "am Wika Tegalega." He waits, as though he expects the name to mean something to her.

When the silence threatens to become awkward, she says, "Pleased to meet you. Kirsten King, here."

"I know that. Since you apparently don't speak Real Human yet, I'll tell you what my name means. It's 'Magic One with Painted Face'. You can call me Tega. I'm your spirit animal."

"My what?"

"Your spirit animal, your guide. Think of me as your guardian angel if you have trouble getting your head around a Real People idea."

"Aaallll riiight," she drawls. "So what did I do to acquire a spirit animal? Or guardian angel? Or whatever?" She makes a dismissive gesture with one hand. "In case you haven't noticed, I have a guardian animal. He chases the likes of you up trees."

The raccoon shows all his teeth, which are very white and very sharp and very many, in what would be a grin if he were human. There doesn't seem to be anything humorous in it now, though. "Him and whose army? Looks like tomorrow's stew to me."

"What!" She starts to stand, to escape from this surreal conversation, but finds that her muscles will not obey her. It is not paralysis; it is mutiny by her own body, acting on its own wisdom.

"Okay. Look, I'm sorry. Nobody's going to eat your mutt." Wika Tegalega raises the fish to his mouth again, then holds it out to her. "Want some?"

Kirsten may not be able to get to her feet and bolt, but she can still cringe. "Uh, no. No, thank you."

Tega tilts his head to one side as if to say "Your loss" and takes another bite. Scales and bones make small, metallic crunching sounds between his teeth as he chews. Kirsten shudders. "Good," he says, running his tongue around his muzzle. "Sure you don't want some?"

A sense of familiarity has begun to grow on Kirsten. Gingerly she sorts through her memories of her near-death, caught in the downward spiral of a self-destructing android, the code that burned its searing destruction along her own nerves. There had been a red-haired woman warning her back toward life; that she remembered. And there had been another woman, older, clad in vermillion robes that blew about her stooped body and a cap of the same color above her wizened, nut-brown face. And there had been a shape like this creature, holding up a long-fingered hand like a benediction, speaking above the howl of the vortex that threatened to consume her: *Go back. The time is not yet.*

"You were there!" she blurts. "The time I almost died!"

"I was there," he acknowledges.

"So what are you doing here now? Am I..." She lets the question trail off in a shiver of unadmitted fear. She cannot let herself go now, not with the work she has yet to do, not with the first real friend she has ever made in her life. *Real friends*, she corrects, *though one is* — she searches for a word that is not too extravagant — *special.*

"Ahh," Tega says. "So you've gotten around to telling yourself the truth. Some of it, at least."

"What? You mean about...about..."

"About Dakota Rivers. Your friend."

"Well, I've never really had one before. It's a new experience."

Crunch goes another mouthful of bones and scales. "It's even newer than you think, and older, too. Do you want me to tell your future? Your past? Cross my paw with mussels and Wika Tegalega will Reveal All." The raccoon has no eyebrows, but the stripes around his eyes waggle lecherously.

Kirsten sniffs. "I know my past, thank you very much. And if any of us has any future at all, it will be what we make it. I don't need a talking four-footed bandit with a bushy tail to tell me that."

Crunch again. "All right." Tega shrugs, a very human gesture. "But I'll tell you this anyway. Think Moebius strip."

"What?"

"Moebius strip. You know, one of those little thingies you made back in grade school. Twist the loop and glue it together so it only has one surface. Neat trick, actually."

"I know what a Moebius strip is, dammit! I'm a scientist. Why should I think about one now?"

The last of the fish disappears and a faraway look comes into Tega's eyes. "Round and round she goes, and where she stops, nobody knows. The front is the back, the past is the future. Round and round, life after death after life. What has been, will be. And there is nothing new under the sun."

Kirsten frowns, at the cryptic words and at the chill that passes over her skin. *Someone walking on my grave*, her grandmother had always said. "I don't understand."

"No, of course not." The remote gaze has gone, and the raccoon's eyes are on her face, here and now. "Not yet. But you will."

"I..." Kirsten is not quite sure what she means to say. Demand an explanation? Deny causality? Proclaim her belief in a random universe of random events without pattern that sometimes just happen to give the illusion of purpose?

"You will," Tega repeats. "What you need to know now is that three drunken idiots with their brains in their tiny, tiny balls have just shot a she-wolf at the gate. Koda is caring for her at the clinic and will need to go search for her pups. She needs your help."

"What? How can I—"

"Go to her. Go now." Tega drops to all fours again, the non-human grin splitting his face. "*Hasta la vista*, baby."

The golden light fades, and Kirsten finds herself sitting once again on an ordinary root in an ordinary wood with ordinary snow powdering the ground. *A dream, that's all. An extremely vivid dream, but just a dream.*

She rises and stretches, Asi with her. "C'mon, boy, let's—" She stops, frozen, in mid-sentence. Printing the snow in front of her, one string coming and another going, are the marks of long-fingered hands and agile feet. A raccoon's tracks.

"Come, Asi!" she cries, and begins to run.

# CHAPTER TWENTY

Kirsten arrives, half-winded, at the vet clinic just as the door opens and Koda steps out into the waning sunshine. She runs up to the other woman, noting the grim set to her jaw and the thin, bloodless line of her lips. "I just heard," she says softly. "How is she?"

"Stable for now," Koda replies, distracted. "I need to go. I have to find her pups."

"I'm going with you."

"No. I'll go alone. Stay with Shannon and keep watch over the mother."

"Please. I...I want to help." She holds up a hand to forestall rejection. "I know you don't need it. Hell, you've probably done this a million times before, but...I'd like to help anyway."

Kirsten receives her answer by way of an armful of blankets pressed into her chest and a curt "let's go". Peering over top of the blankets, she settles them more tightly against her front and starts off at a brisk trot, trying her best to keep up with Koda's long-legged strides.

Within moments, they've breasted the snowy crest less than a mile outside the base, and both stop, though for different reasons. Koda cocks her head, scenting the air and listening to the area around her. All is silent, save for the wind rustling through branches yet to see the first touch of spring green.

Kirsten, on the other hand, is staring at a large bird roosting atop the very tallest of the trees ahead. "Koda," she whispers in her softest voice.

Hearing her, Dakota slowly turns her head until she is looking down at the woman at her side. Her eyebrow lifts in silent inquiry.

"That bird...it's a hawk, isn't it? If it's anywhere around the pups..."

Koda grabs Kirsten's hand as she lifts it and returns it to her side. She softly utters an odd, three-note whistle With a heavy, almost sub-sonic, beating of wings, Wiyo lifts up from the tree's top and glides effortlessly onto Koda's upraised arm. Kirsten stares as if her sockets are the only things keeping her eyeballs from popping out and rolling around like marbles on the ground. Giving Kirsten a look that could freeze a volcano, Wiyo calmly sidesteps up to Dakota's shoulder, barely missing her Stetson, and settles there, looking as regal as a queen on her throne.

Koda continues on, leaving Kirsten staring after her, slack-jawed, until a soft "Coming?" floats back to her and spurs her feet into motion.

**By Kirsten's reckoning,** it is ten minutes later when they stop again, Koda's upraised hand giving her direction better than a verbal order. These ten minutes have been silent, though, at least from Kirsten's perspective, far from uninformative. In that short space of time, watching Dakota tracking the wolf pups, Kirsten has received a flash of insight — though perhaps "flash" isn't the right word. It is as if an elusive puzzle piece has finally slipped into place, providing her with the answers to several questions she's been asking herself throughout these months in the other woman's company.

Watching Dakota's profile, its sharp lines softened by descending twilight, the image of the blue eyed wolf, her guardian, comes to her again, superimposing itself over the noble, striking features of the woman before her. She finds herself flushing, shamed at having come to this rather obvious conclusion so late in the game. *Some scientist. Can't even see what's in front of my face. God.*

The answers, however, raise even more questions, but Kirsten pushes them to the back of her mind as she watches Koda gracefully lower herself to her haunches and stare down at the snow-covered ground for several long moments. When she rises again, her face is carved of granite, absolutely expressionless save for her eyes, which are burning embers glittering with an anger that takes Kirsten aback and has her wishing fervently that this reaper's gaze will not fix itself upon her. It does, though only briefly, and she feels almost faint with relief as it passes on, leaving her untouched.

Silent as the grave, Dakota resumes her pace, leaving Kirsten struggling to keep up. But not before she looks down at the place that lit the fires of Dakota's anger. There, in a small pile, is a heap of bones and bits of fur. Tiny bones, so very tiny and yet unmistakable, even to a city-bred girl like Kirsten. The bones of a wolf-pup; predator turned prey. She slaps a hand over her mouth as her gorge heaves, threatening to expel whatever remains of her breakfast, the only meal she's eaten today. After a long moment, her stomach settles itself and she takes her hand away, forcibly ripping her gaze from the tiny mound of bones at her feet. Dakota is a dozen yards ahead and pulling away rapidly. Kirsten breaks into a run to catch up.

She has just slowed down to walking speed when Dakota comes to another abrupt halt, forcing Kirsten to jig slightly to the left to avoid a collision. "What is—"

"Shh."

Kirsten looks on, slightly annoyed, as Dakota cocks her head in that increasingly familiar listening posture, and stiffens. It's obvious she hears something, though Kirsten, who knows that by virtue of her implants her hearing is at least five times as acute as a normal human's, can't hear a thing. *Of course, I don't know what I'm listening for,* she consoles herself, not quite sure why it suddenly matters so much.

A whispered word to the beast on her shoulder, and the hawk flies off to God-knows-where, leaving Kirsten even more annoyed than before. *Why am I the only one who's flying blind here?*

*She didn't ask for your help,* that more rational part of her brain reminds her. *You more or less forced it on her, so don't be getting all pissy when she doesn't recite her intentions to you chapter and verse.*

Dakota utters a small, soft, whining sound that has Kirsten looking on in amazement. Instinctively, she knows that she has not just heard a human imitating a wolf's call, but rather a wolf making that call. *Will wonders never cease?*

Then she hears it — a soft, almost inaudible cry off to her left. Koda repeats her call, and the cry is likewise repeated. Kirsten stands unmoving as Dakota plucks a blanket from her hands.

"Stay here unless I call you."

Kirsten simply nods and watches as Koda moves with silent steps to the medium-sized rock outcropping ahead and to the left.

With twilight rapidly deepening into night, Koda senses the den's entrance more than sees it. It's small and narrow, forcing her to drop to her knees, then to her belly in order to squeeze her way inside. Before moving, she stuffs the warm blanket into her jacket and removes a small but powerful flashlight from a pocket and switches it to wide beam before clamping it between her teeth and beginning her trek inside.

The rocks brush hard against her broad shoulders and, though not one prone to claustrophobia, she feels the weight of the entire formation pressing in on her from without. It's not an entirely pleasant feeling, but she shuts her mind to it and continues, using her elbows to propel herself forward.

The stench of putridity and decay is indescribable, but it's something she's well used to, given what she does — or did, she doesn't know anymore — for a living. Still, she finds herself mouth-breathing to keep the smell from burning itself into her sinuses.

Approximately two body lengths from the entrance, the den widens, becoming a more or less circular structure surrounded by solid rock on all sides. In the center are the pups, or what remains of them. There were four in the litter — five if she counts the obvious stillbirth remains she'd come across earlier. Only one still lives, clinging to that life by the meagrest of threads. The others are long dead, their bodies cold and stiff; maggots already beginning their gruesome work on the corpses.

Attracted to her living warmth, the pup lifts his shaking head, blindly groping for her, struggling beneath the weight of its dead siblings.

Gently grabbing the pup by its ruff, Koda tenderly pulls it from its macabre nest. The pup hangs limp from her hand, and she absently checks its gender before she bares her teeth in an unconscious and soundless snarl. With a soft cry of revulsion mixed with anger, she uses her free hand to pluck the squirming maggots from his living flesh, crushing them between her fingers and flinging them away.

Task complete, she pulls out the blanket and wraps the pup carefully within its folds, murmuring nonsense words to him in Lakota. He whimpers softly, oh so softly, and collapses against her, completely spent. She feels frantically for a pulse, and sags in relief when it is there — too weak, too thready, but there.

"C'mon, boy," she whispers, tucking the final fold about his tiny, defenseless body. "Let's get you home to your *Ina*."

**Kirsten stands outside** of the den, eyeing the helter-skelter jumble of boulders with deep suspicion. Her dream — and what else could it possibly be? She refuses to entertain the notion that even her hallucinations would feature a talking raccoon with an attitude problem — comes back to her in soft filter, like the camera lenses they used to use on movie stars. Back when there were movie stars.

*"She needs your help. Go to her. Go to her now."*

She eyes the rockpile again. Is that a rumble she hears? A shifting of stones presaging a total collapse of the structure? Is this why she is needed? "No," she whispers, horrified.

Another image flashes before her, this one in sharp, stark lines and bold tones of red and black.

The outcropping is collapsing, drawing down into itself in cracks of thunder and stifling dust that chokes her as she screams Dakota's name into the blackness of the night.

*Her hands.  Blood on her hands.  Her palms scraped raw, flesh hanging in tatters as she desperately pulls rock after rock away from this charnel house.*

*"She needs your help."*

*Her voice, hoarse and ragged, screaming Dakota's name over and over and over again.*

*"Go to her."*

*Her lungs.  On fire.  Sending out pluming jets of vapored, panicked breath.*

*"Go to her now."*

*Her heart.  Thundering in her chest.  Fear and a savage, piercing grief fueling its frenetic pace.*

"No," she whispers.  "No." And almost launches herself to the moon as Dakota materializes in front of her like a wraith from the mist.

Her face is still harsh-planed, but her eyes have softened a bit from their earlier rage.  Kirsten suspects — when she can think again — that the softening is a result of the tiny bundle she holds so tenderly in her large hands.

Her heart rate slows, though grudgingly.  She doesn't like shocks.  Never has.  And she's had more than enough to last several lifetimes.  Somehow, though, she doesn't think Dakota will appreciate the sentiment.  She'll have to remember to tell her later.  "How...how many?"

"One," Koda replies tersely.  "The rest were dead."

"Oh God.  I'm so sorry."

"'Sall right.  Nothing anyone can do about it now."  Though her words seem offhand, her tone is clipped, each word as precise as a knife cut.

"Still..."

Dakota's eyes harden.  "Let's get this one back to his mother."

The pair takes only a couple of steps before a screeching call splits the silence of the night.  Both look up, two pairs of keen eyes tracing a shadow against the shadows, flying low over their heads and landing in a tree some forty yards distant.

Kirsten finds herself suddenly cradling the tiny wolf pup as Koda stares deeply into her eyes.

"Go on ahead.  I'll be there shortly."

"But—" She finds herself talking to air.  Dakota has disappeared.  "Oh no you don't, Ms. Bossy," Kirsten mutters half under her breath.  "You forget who you're talking to here, I think."  She looks down at the bundle in her hands.  "Hang on for a little longer, little guy.  I have something I need to do."

**The deep black** of the night parts like a cloak before her.  She sprints, full out, toward the tree, keen eyes already spotting the thick chain wrapped around its gnarled base.  Wiyo screeches again.  Koda looks up at her briefly before rounding the broad trunk, intently following the chain links as they stretch off to a shadowed spot not ten feet away.

A thick, frost tipped pelt comes into view, and her heart shudders in her chest.  "Oh no," she moans, low and deep.  "No.  Please, Ina, no."

Her soft prayer goes unheeded, as she knows it must.  Tears sting her eyes.  She wipes them away with a savage swipe of her arm, not noticing the pain as the stiff cloth of her jacket rakes across her wind-chapped cheeks.

He lies there in his own filth and blood. The one her brothers call *Igmú Tanka Kte*, Cougar Killer, for his fierce defense of his pack from a hungry mountain lion slinking down from the hills in search of easy prey.

The one who has visited her dreams and visions for years.

Who has shared with her bits his life and his ways.

The proud Alpha.

The one she calls *Wa Uspewicakiyapi*.

Teacher.

His rear left leg, half gnawed through in a desperate bid for freedom, is caught in a steel-jawed trap — the kind that has been illegal for decades. His soft underbelly is flayed, the skin hanging in flaps, blackened from frostbite and infection. His ruff is spiky with dried blood and she can only imagine the terrible wounds hidden from her view beneath the thick pelt.

He is mortally wounded, and yet still lives, bound to life by some strength of will that she can only wonder at. His chest moves weakly, sporadically, pulling in air he soon will no longer need. When she squats carefully by his massive head, he looks up at her through eyes that are glassy and exhausted and utterly calm, as if her presence by his side had always been expected. Perhaps even anticipated.

"Hello, old friend," she murmurs in the language of her ancestors, reaching out to gently stroke his proud muzzle. "I'm so sorry." Tears fall now, and she allows their passage, watching as his image trebles before her, fracturing even as her heart fractures. "So...so sorry."

Feeling the tentative, weak touch of his tongue on her hand, she shakes her head, blinking away the tears and clearing her vision. His eyes, likewise, have cleared, and she finds herself drawn into them, drawn as if bound by a puppeteer's strings. In those eyes, she can see visions: bits and pieces of his life, and hers, and the bond that draws them together closer than kin.

She slips free of herself, and for the last time they run together, unfettered and uncaring, into the night wind, into the hills and valleys of the home they share as the moon, ripe and full, watches from her perch above. They run for the joy of running, for the freedom of their souls, for their fierce love of the Earth and all who live upon it.

Then, at last, after what feels like hours, she finds herself gently released and in her own body once again.

Breaking herself free from his gaze, she leans down and touches a soft kiss to his head, then whispers into his ear, "*Tóksha aké wanchinyankin kte. Wakhan Thanka nici un.*" And, not allowing herself to think, she moves her hands to his now-fragile neck, and twists.

His spine snaps. His chest settles slowly, and his eyes grow distant and fixed to a point only he can know.

All of her grief, all of her rage, washes through her with the force of a tidal wave, bowing her back and arching her neck to the uncaring sky. She howls in a voice that none would recognize as human, and all would fear.

Still howling, she jumps to her feet and pries the brutal trap from his leg by brute force. Grabbing the chain, she hurls the trap against the tree again and again and again, screaming incoherently, eyes flashing, glowing as if lit by the internal fires of her rage. The tree shakes, bark flying from its trunk in great spraying chunks.

Kirsten, who has forced herself to stand by and watch even as tears stream down her face unnoticed, finally breaks free of her paralysis and steps forward, only to dance back as the trap comes perilously close to bashing her head in. She stands for a moment, undecided, her lower lip caught pensively between her teeth. "Dakota," she tries softly. And then louder, "Dakota!"

Dakota stills abruptly and turns to face the intruder, murder in her eyes. Her lips spread in a snarl as feral as any wolf's, and Kirsten steps back again, fear delivering a jolt to her heart and belly.

"*Nituwe he?*" Koda demands.

"I...I'm sorry, I don't—"

"*Iyaya na!*"

"Dakota, please, I don't understand."

"*Letan khigla na!*" Winding up the chain, she slams the trap against the tree. "*Iyaya na!!*" And again. "*Iyaya na!*"

And again.

And again.

And again.

Every single instinct inside Kirsten is clamoring for her to flee, to seek refuge far away from the madwoman Dakota has become. And yet, something even stronger compels her to stay, some internal voice that she cannot shut off, cannot turn away from, no matter how much she might wish it. Gathering up every shred of courage she possesses, she steps forward, deliberately into harm's way, and speaks. "Dakota. Please. Listen to me. I want to help. Please. Tell me what to do." Her tone is as calming and as soothing as she can possibly make it, and she senses, through blind instinct, that it is somehow getting through to the grief-stricken woman. "Please," she repeats, in a voice just above a whisper. "Tell me what to do."

There is a muted "thunk" as the trap and chain slip from Koda's hands. She follows it down, collapsing to her knees and burying her face in her hands. Her whole body shakes from the force of her sobs. "*Wicate,*" she murmurs over and over into her hands. "*Wicate.* Too much. Too much! *Wicate.* Too much!" Her head tips back and she howls.

The sound chills Kirsten to the bone. She can feel the wolf pup still in her grasp respond, struggling weakly against her hold. She looks down, then back at the grieving, howling woman. Gently, tenderly, she unwraps the pup from his blanket and, taking slow, calm, deliberate steps, closes the gap between herself and Dakota. Then, just as carefully, she lowers herself to her knees and waits, the pup held tenderly in her hands.

Dakota's howl tapers off like a toy whose battery has finally run down. Her head drops, hanging low between her shoulders. Her tears drip into the snow, melting it.

"He needs you, Dakota," Kirsten whispers into the profound silence left behind. "Look at him. He needs you to care for him, to love him." She swallows, suddenly understanding. "Like you loved his father."

After a long moment, Dakota's head lifts, and she looks down at the tiny, defenseless pup. A trembling hand lifts, hovers, and then drops back down into the snow. "I...can't."

"You can. Yes, you can."

"You don't understand!"

"Yes, yes I do. I do understand. Dakota, you've never turned away from anyone who's needed your help. He needs your help now. He needs you."

Their eyes meet and hold. Kirsten feels tears welling yet again as she easily reads the bone deep grief pouring from Dakota's soul. Cradling the pup in the crook of her arm, she reaches down and grasps the other woman's hand, bringing it, palm up, between them. With sure movements, she places the pup into Dakota's hand, then takes the other one and places it on top, securing her grip. "Help him," she whispers, still staring into the liquid pools of Dakota's eyes.

Dakota looks down at the tiny life in her hands. Her face dissolves as fresh grief flows through her. Kirsten does the only thing she can. Using one arm to brace Dakota's, she slips the other around a slim waist, melding their bodies together.

Dakota stiffens, then relaxes, leaning into Kirsten's quiet and gentle strength. Her head bows and rests against an offered shoulder as her tears continue to flow.

**As the front** door slams, shaking the entire house down to its foundation, Kirsten looks up from the desk, a desk she's starting to believe she'll grow old and die at, picturing herself as a grey-haired old lady with hearing aids in her implants and coke-bottle glasses, staring at line after line of code.

"No!" Maggie's demand rings loudly through the home, obviously continuing a disagreement begun prior to entering.

Kirsten cringes a little at the sound of it, not in fear, but in pain, as it adds to a headache which has spent most of the past twelve hours building, though lack of sleep and tension enough to fell a rutting elk have supplied more than their share as well. She's tempted to turn off her implants, both for the fact that she'll at least have some blessed peace from the noise, and because she half-suspects she might be unintentionally eavesdropping on a private conversation, but something stays her hand.

"Will you at least respect me enough to pretend you're listening to me?"

Kirsten winces at that one. She deduces that the resulting silence is Dakota (who else can it be?) stopping, turning, and fixing Maggie with a glance so emotionless it might as well be carved from the side of a mountain. Kirsten knows that look, having been on the receiving end of it from the moment they left the small glade the night before.

"Dakota, listen. You...what you're proposing to do here is...it's...crazy! No wait! Please. I didn't mean it like that, okay? It's just— Dammit, Dakota, think about what you're doing here!"

"I've thought about it." Her voice seems to be coming from the bottom of a very deep, very dark, very cold well.

"And?"

"I'm going."

"But—"

"I'm going. End of discussion."

It is the silence during a gathering storm. "Fine! You want to kill yourself? Be my guest. I hope you have fun doing it."

Kirsten jerks to her feet as the door slams once again. Wasting no time, she shoots around the desk and out into the short hallway in time to see Dakota disappear into the bedroom. She stares after her for a long moment, undecided, then turns the other way and trots outside. "Maggie! Wait!"

With exaggerated movements, Maggie slows, stops, and turns. "What?"

"I...heard the argument...at least part of it. What's going on? What's wrong?" Kirsten comes to a stop before the older woman, feeling the anger radiating off of her slim form.

"What happened last night?"

"Excuse me?" Kirsten asks, brought up short by the apparent non-sequitur.

"Last night. I know you followed her out of the gates, and I know you came back with a wolf pup. What happened in between those two events?"

Kirsten ponders the question, unsure how much of the evening's proceedings to reveal.

Maggie sees the hesitation and throws up an elegant hand. "Never mind. I don't need to know the particulars. It's just...I'm afraid for her." Her gaze is intent, beseeching. "It's like someone ripped out her heart and put a stone in its place. She's been like this all day. No matter what I do, I can't get through to her."

"There's something more, though," Kirsten says, needing to get to the meat of the matter as quickly as possible. She senses time is definitely of the essence.

With a heavy sigh, Maggie nods, proud shoulders slumped under the heavy weight they carry. "Yeah. She heard of a nearby OB clinic that has hostages. She's gotten it into her head that she's going to go up there, alone mind you, and bust everybody out like in some goddamn Wild West shoot-'em-up movie or something. Fuck!" She drags a hand through her short-cropped hair. "It's suicide. Goddamn suicide." The beseeching gaze comes again, mixed with a tiny hint of swallowed pride. "Can you...talk to her, maybe? See if you can talk her out of this nonsense? I don't... We can't lose her."

Kirsten nods and turns to leave, then turns back, just catching a pained gaze, swiftly masked. "Maggie, I...I promise, when this is over, I'll tell you what happened last night. Or at least I'll try to get Dakota to tell you. It was...not good. She lost something...someone...very dear to her, though I don't think any of us will ever know just how dear. Except maybe her brother. Okay?"

Maggie tries to summon up a smile and fails. "Okay."

Kirsten feels her heart clench. It's a new experience for her. Compassion has never been her strongest suit, though she suspects it would take a heart of stone to miss the misery playing itself over Maggie's noble, handsome features. She reaches out and touches the other woman's arm, giving it a brief squeeze. "It'll be okay. You'll see." And because she can think of nothing else to do, she turns fully away and trots back to the house, well aware of the eyes at her back.

She steps inside just as Koda exits the bedroom, pack swinging from one fisted hand. Their eyes meet. Koda's drops quickly away and crosses the room, moving as if to brush by the young scientist without a word of parting.

"Wait," Kirsten murmurs. "Please."

Unintentionally aping Maggie's earlier actions, Dakota stops and turns. Annoyance is the only expression that can be read on her face. "What is it?"

"Please don't leave. Not right now."

"Look. I've already explained—"

"I know, but I'm asking you to hear me out. I'm not saying that freeing those women isn't important. It is. But you're needed here, too."

"Not as much as I'm needed there."

"What about the wolf and her pup? Shannon's a decent tech, but you saw the look in her eyes last night. She's absolutely terrified of having that little pup in her charge, let alone his mother."

"Tacoma can handle it. Manny, as well. They know what to do."

Kirsten sighs. "Well, would you at least consider taking some backup with you?"

"No."

"But—"

"No. It's already been decided. By me."

"Why?"

"What?"

"Why? Why do you feel you have to do this alone? Why won't you accept help? There are a couple of hundred men and women there who would die for you if you asked it of them." She winces as the words leave her mouth, having somehow stumbled on exactly the wrong thing to say. "I'm sorry. That wasn't what I mea—"

Koda holds up a hand. Their gazes meet again. This time, the blue eyes soften the tiniest shard. "Look. I — I need to be...alone right now, okay? This place, these people, they're all...it's just...too much right now. I need some time...to think." She smiles, very slightly. "Besides, what I'm doing isn't all that difficult. The facility is small, and there are, at most, three androids there." The smile falls from her face. "Look. Despite what Maggie says, I'm not on a mission to end my own life. It's just... Trust me, okay? I know what I'm doing."

A moment longer, and Kirsten nods, accepting Dakota's words as truth. She can see it in the other woman's eyes, in the set of her shoulders, in the clench of her jaw. "All right," she replies, nodding. "I'd rather you just hunkered yourself out in the woods somewhere for a couple of days, but...all right. Can you do me a favor, though?"

Koda's walls go up. Kirsten can fairly hear the alarm bells going off in her head. She smiles to diffuse the situation. "Just wait here. I'll be right back."

A moment later, she returns and hands Koda a minicomp the size of a credit card. Dakota looks at her questioningly. "This morning," Kirsten explains, "while I was running the code, I came across this slight anomaly. I traced it through to the end, and discovered a way to temporarily disable the androids' motor functions."

Dakota's eyebrow raises. "Impressive. How temporary is temporary?"

"I'm...not sure exactly. Five, ten minutes max. Theoretically."

"Theoretically?"

"Well, I just discovered the code this morning, and it's not as if we have a handy supply of androids to test it out on. It works in simulation. Beyond that..." She shrugs. "I've put the chip with the code in that mini-comp. All you have to do is activate it when you're ready, and set it down somewhere. The transmission will go through just about anything, so you don't have to be in the same room with the droids when you set it off." She smiles a little. "Think of it as a concussion grenade on a grander scale."

Koda nods and slips the minicomp into the breast pocket of her light jacket. "Thanks."

"You're welcome."

A moment of uncomfortable silence descends between them. "Well...I'll see you later."

As she turns to leave, Kirsten draws her back with a touch to her arm. "What?"

Kirsten takes in a deep breath and lets it out very slowly, gathering her thoughts. "Just...be careful, okay?"

"I will."

"These people, Dakota," Kirsten continues, "like it or not, they depend on you. You're important to them." She pauses very briefly, gathering her courage, unable, for all that, to meet Koda's intent gaze. Her voice, when she finally speaks, is soft as a rose petal. "You're important to me."

With an expression that is equal parts fondness and sadness, Dakota lifts a hand to tenderly cup Kirsten's cheek. The eyes that finally meet hers are stormy with indecision and, if she looks closely enough, fear as well. The fear of a child who has just spilled her deepest secret and now waits for the lash of a palm against her face. *Who hurt you?* she finds herself thinking even as her head lowers, drawn down by the shining, fearful coun-tenance of the woman before her. *Who made you so afraid to speak your heart?*

As if in a dream, Kirsten feels the brush of Koda's lips — soft, like the wings of a butterfly, warm as a promise kept. Fundamental, like a piece of her soul, long knocked askew, finally coming home to rest.

It is over in an instant of an instant, but when she opens her eyes, she knows that she has been forever changed. Koda is smiling at her, a sweet, tender smile filled with so much, with...everything.

And as the other woman bids her a soft "goodbye" and turns away, Kirsten can only stand, stunned, her fingers trailing over her lips.

# CHAPTER TWENTY-ONE

"This is it. The end!"

Asi, no sign of belief in his idiot grin or tensely poised body, never takes his eyes off the birch twig in Kirsten's raised hand. She feints as if to throw it, and his head jerks to follow the movement. His feet, though, remain firmly planted on the tarmac of the parking lot of the base veterinary clinic.

"You got it? This is the last one! No more!"

Asi's ears quiver in anticipation, tail up and alert. If he gets it, he gives no sign.

Drawing her arm back as far as she can, Kirsten puts her back into the pitch, sending the much-chewed piece of wood unerringly onto the clinic's doorstep. "Go!"

Asi leaps to retrieve it, covering the ten yards there and the ten yards back to her in huge, galloping bounds and coming to a skidding halt to drop the stick at her feet. He whines softly, looking up at her face, then fixes his attention once again on her throwing hand.

"No, that's it. Done for the day." She shakes her head at his expression, which segues from anticipation to incomprehension to utter canine dejection. "And making me feel guilty won't work, either. How'd you like to go visit the new pup, since we're already here?" Asi does not respond, and she ruffles the fur of his neck lightly, tugging at his collar as she moves toward the entrance. "Come on, fella."

It is purely by chance, of course, that she finds herself just outside the veterinary hospital. Wearied by endless and endlessly futile sifting of code strings for the single line of integers that will shut down the androids once and permanently, she has closed her mathematical conundrums firmly behind her in the house and fled into the open air. It is something she finds herself doing more and more often as the March light warms toward the inevitable spring and the wind softens and veers about into the south. And, purely by chance, her walk has led her here. Her only deliberate choice, she assures herself, has been to avoid the woods, inhabited as they are by motor-mouthed raccoons and God knows what else. Banshees, maybe.

*Fra ghoulies an' ghaisties,*
*An' lang-leggedy beasties,*
*An' things that gae bump in the nicht,*
*Guid Lord, deliver us.*

The ancient rhyme says nothing about beasties with long, bushy, ringed tails and black masks, but she's sure the omission is inadvertent. If they'd only known...

A hellish wailing greets her as she pushes open the door, its chime lost in the howling that rips its way up and down the scale. Asi barks sharply and Kirsten shushes him. The single person in the waiting room, an airman in a flight suit, leaps to his feet and unzips the side of an over the shoulder carrier, nervously adjusting the towel on its floor. "Sorry, ma'am. Callas doesn't like to have her ears touched."

Shannon emerges from a treatment room behind the counter, the sound growing louder with her approach. Clinging to the front of her smock with all four feet is a young calico cat, ears folded close to her head and her mouth wide open and yowling like a panther in heat. At least, it is what Kirsten imagines a panther in heat would sound like. She has never actually heard one singing her come hithers.

Claw by sabre claw, Shannon detaches the small creature, and with the aid of her human, carefully backs her into her carrier. An abrupt silence falls, replaced after a moment with a soft rumbling sound. From her pocket Shannon removes a long snouted tube of ointment and a small plastic bottle of pale yellow liquid. "Here you go, Lieutenant. Tritop in the ears twice a day, Clavamox by mouth the same. Hydrogen peroxide on the scratches, or wear heavy gloves."

"Gotcha." With a long stroke down Callas's back and a scratch under her chin, the lieutenant zips her up. "Thanks, Shannon. Ma'am." He sketches a salute at Kirsten, who acknowledges it after a moment of frozen startlement, then shoulders the carrier and sets off out the door and down the sidewalk at a brisk pace. Kirsten's eyes follow him as he turns the corner, heading in the direction of the Bachelor Officer's Quarters. Almost no one is driving anymore. It has been days since she has seen anything but an official vehicle on the road, since the attempted assault on the gate, in fact. Conservation is setting in.

"Can I help you, ma'am? Does Asimov need anything?"

Faced with having to explain why she is here, Kirsten finds herself suddenly embarrassed. She can feel the heat spreading over her face, her annoyance at herself only making it worse. "No, I— That is, we were out for a walk, and—"

"And you wanted to stop by and see the wolf pup?" Shannon grins at her. "It's okay. You'd be surprised how many people just 'happen' to be passing by. Callas and her ear mites were only the second real case I've had today."

"It's all right? I wouldn't want to upset the mother or anything."

"Sure. Asi'd better stay here, though. The only strange males she's tolerating are human ones."

Kirsten gives his ears a ruffle. "Sorry, boy. Lie down."

The big dog folds down on his elbows with obvious reluctance but without argument. With a last glance to make sure he remains, Kirsten follows Shannon through the waiting area and past the examining rooms and surgery. As they approach the wards, the smell of chlorine reaches her, and she steps lightly into the waiting basin of disinfectant without needing to be reminded.

"He's in Iso," Shannon says, leading her down a short corridor toward a closed door. "Go on in."

The smell of bleach is stronger here, and there is a second dishpan of the pungent liquid to the side of the entrance. Kirsten steps in and out of it almost automatically now, the familiarity of the clinic beginning to fit around her like her skin. And yet it is not the clinic itself, but the presence she feels here, the woman who, even absent, has left something of herself in the calm efficiency with which patients are cared for, in the passionate strength of her own caring.

And that, if she is honest with herself, is the real reason she is here: that there is no other place she can go which resonates more strongly of Dakota Rivers.

The light in Isolation is dim, and Kirsten almost gasps as she closes the door quietly behind her. Seated in an old fashioned rocking chair next to a bank of cages, a figure sits with head bent, all attention focused on the small bundle in the crook of its left arm, a miniature nursing bottle in its right hand. The clear profile, the cant of the head, the long legs and graceful hands are all Dakota's. The sight, unexpected as it is, strikes the breath from Kirsten's lungs and sets her heart to pounding against her sternum like a wild thing against the bars of its prison. Her lips burn at the memory of the fleeting kiss at their parting, fire streaming along the network of her veins into every cell in her body. "Dakota?" she says softly. Then, louder, "Koda? I thought you'd gone."

"Kirsten?" The figure looks up, turns toward the light from the hallway.

Brown eyes, not blue. Hair just brushing broad shoulders, not quite long enough to braid, not the wild mane that flows halfway down Dakota's back. Boots and feet too big to be a woman's, even a woman standing six feet toward heaven.

"Ta-Tacoma? I'm sorry, I thought—" Kirsten takes an involuntary step backward, her face flaming with embarrassment.

"That I was Koda?"

A rueful smile touches his mouth, so like his sister's that Kirsten is nearly lost again.

"People have been confusing us ever since we were small, even in broad daylight." The pup in his lap whimpers, and he adjusts his hand under the small body, tilting the bottle at a sharper angle. "We used to switch places sometimes. It drove the nuns wild until they finally noticed that our eyes were different."

"How long did that take? You'd think it was obvious." He is giving her time to recover, though how exactly he knows of her discomfort is not at all clear. Perhaps all Lakota people are uncannily intuitive. Or perhaps it's just the Rivers family.

Tacoma shrugs. "People see what they expect to see. We're Lakota; Lakotas all have black hair and dark eyes and say 'How'. We wore the same dark blue pants and the same shirts starched so stiff you had to wear an undershirt just to keep from being sandpapered. I was in seventh grade and Koda in fifth before they got it figured out."

A wheezing gurgle startles Kirsten, and Tacoma gently disengages the bottle from the pup's mouth. "He draws on this thing like an irrigation pump. Hold him for a minute while I get a refill, will you?"

Gingerly Kirsten accepts the small bundle, both hands under his spine. His muzzle is blunt and his ears floppy; eyes just beginning to open are the cloudy blue of any infant's. There is no hint in his round belly and blunt paws of the formidable creature he will be two years from now, no shadow of the power his father had possessed even in the last moments of his life. He makes a small mewling sound, not unlike a kitten, and she presses him close to her body, rocking him gently as she would a human child. "Tacoma," she says suddenly, "do wolves ever have blue eyes? When they're grown, I mean."

He looks up from mixing the formula, pouring powder and sterile water into a blender that whirs quietly. "I suppose it's possible. Huskies have to have gotten their blue eyes somewhere, after all."

"Have you ever seen one? A wolf with blue eyes?"

"Not in the wild, no." He does not add, "Why do you ask?" though the question is in his face as he decants the formula into a newly sterilized bottle.

She has no answer to the unvoiced question, at least none that she is willing to give him; no answer that she is willing to give anyone. *I saw one in a dream. I saw those same eyes in your sister's face.* Instead she says, "Can I feed him? I've raised orphan puppies."

"Sure," he answers, handing her the bottle. "That'll give me a chance to check on mama and give her meds."

"Is she still too sick to nurse him?"

Tacoma hunkers down in front of one of the lower tiers against the opposite wall. "She wants to, and she can care for him otherwise, but she hasn't enough milk. She was very badly dehydrated when she came in. She's still on IVs." As he speaks, he checks the drip in the long, clear plastic tube that runs from a flaccid plastic bag hooked onto the bars of the cage above. "Time to hang more Ringer's on her."

He removes the empty bag and steps out into the larger ward, pausing without apparent thought to step in and out of the disinfectant. It seems to be something he does the way he breathes, so long accustomed as to be automatic. She is irrationally pleased that she seems to be acquiring the habit herself, almost without having to remind herself. She is fitting in. She is not terribly sure yet what exactly she is fitting in to, but she knows in her bones that she has not wanted to fit into anything so badly since she was a child, cut off from the outside world first by her up-the-wall-and-into-the-ozone IQ, then from almost all of the rest of it by her deafness. Perversely, the lack of sound had been a comfort, undemanding in its enforced silence.

For the moment, though, she is this small wild thing's surrogate mother. Kirsten settles herself against the back of the rocker with the pup against her midsection. The chair, which Tacoma had filled to overflowing, very nearly swallows her so that she finds her feet dangling, toes just brushing the concrete floor. She pushes off from it, setting the chair to rocking gently. The pup, gazing up at her with half-closed eyes, perfectly trusting, evokes instincts she would deny possessing, deny with her last breath. Protect. Nurture. Love. He takes the elongated plastic nipple with no more hesitation than if he were snuggled up to his wolf mother herself. He fumbles at it a bit because he still cannot see clearly, gives a couple of smacks and snorts until he gets the suction going. The level of milk in the bottle begins to fall, slowly but steadily.

Protect. Nurture. They are instincts which Tacoma seems to possess without embarrassment. It is not a lack of macho; Christ, she has seen him on the battlefield, spraying death from an M-16 on full automatic, lobbing round after round of explosives into the lines of mixed droid and humans. With a chill that shivers her spine, she remembers the moment when he called in the strike on his own position, and Dakota's berserkergang that had lifted Maggie, herself, their whole army up and out of themselves and made their small makeshift force into an invincible, unified instrument of one woman's will.

From the lowest tier of cages across from her comes a shifting of weight, a low, searching whimper. The mother wolf, looking for her cub. Careful not to dislodge the bottle, Kirsten rises from the chair, crosses the space between, and lowers herself into a cross-legged position in front of the cage. "Here he is, mama," she says softly. "I've got him. He's safe."

Seemingly reassured, the mother settles her head on her paws, her eyes never leaving Kirsten. They are the color of old bronze coins, not blue, but they have in them the courage and the steadfastness of the eyes she has seen in dreams, the eyes that somehow are both a wolf's eyes and Dakota Rivers'. Pieces of the puzzle fall into place, locking smoothly and without seam.

"Christ, you're dumb." Without realizing it, she has spoken aloud. Item: Dakota Rivers has blue eyes. Blue eyes that, strictly speaking, ethnically speaking, she should not have. Item: the wolf of Kirsten's dreams, or hallucinations or whatever they are, also has blue eyes. Item: Dakota has — her throat tightens with the thought and salt stings her eyes — or had a somehow intimate and loving relationship with the alpha wolf who was this small scrap's father. The wolf, obviously, is Dakota's spirit animal, with whatever that entails for someone who, unlike herself, has been brought up fully accepting that the barriers between the human and non-human worlds are both fragile and fluid. That one can have friends and relations who do not walk on two legs and who do have fur. That one can...

Another shiver passes over her, uncontrollable as the thought that spawns it. That one can, somehow, become a non-human being, in spirit and perhaps even... But she cannot bring herself even to finish that thought. It is too alien, too far from the familiar terrain of logic, of the physical determinism that has bounded her thought all her thinking life.

And that, in turn, brings her around to a mouthy, cynical raccoon speaking in riddles beside a thawing stream. Her spirit animal. A creature who bears the same relation to her that the alpha wolf did to Dakota. A creature notorious for curiosity and its long, clever, mischief-making hands. A masked creature, not given to self-revelation. A creature, Dakota had said, whose stock in trade is transformation.

However hard she works to ignore it, Kirsten can feel that transformation at work inside herself. She is here on the floor of a veterinary isolation ward with the pungent perfume of Clorox in her nostrils not because she "just happened" to follow Asi's pursuit of a birch twig, not even because she has genuinely wanted to visit the wolf mother and her baby. (Maybe even pet them, make friends, as she has with domestic dogs all her life?) She is here because this is Dakota's place. Here she can be close to the woman whose many skills she is only beginning to understand, and to feelings in herself that she is not anywhere close to beginning to understand. It occurs to her that Tacoma is taking an unusually long time to fetch a bag of saline and a syringe of antibiotic. Perhaps he senses her need and is too polite to intrude, an idea she finds half embarrassing and half comforting.

The bottle half empty, the nipple falls out of the pup's mouth. Eyes closed, his head drops back against her arm as he settles into a wolf's dreams. After a few moments, his paws and eyelids begin to twitch, his breath coming in soft whuffles. His mother seems to have dropped off, too, no longer unsure of her infant or her infant's new nursemaid.

Kirsten briefly considers opening the cage to lay the cub beside her. *Discretion, Little K. Discretion is almost always the better part of valor. Common sense almost never kills anybody. Go with the stats.* Odd, how she can still hear her father's voice in her head after all these years, remembered from years when she could not hear at all. Shifting her legs beneath her, she settles down to wait.

The pup's contentment and his mother's calm must be contagious. Twice she catches her own head beginning to fall toward her chest. Twice she pulls herself up, wide-eyed, from the edge of sleep. She cannot think what is keeping Tacoma. Perhaps she should put the pup down and offer to help with whatever it is.

The thought passes, as once again the light seems to change around her. She is standing on a green hill, far away — distant in time and the stretch of miles. Below her lies a valley dotted with campfires in the dusk, a long white twilight that pales the summer stars. Behind her is her own fire, ringed with stones and set within a grove of birch and ancient oak. A woman stands beside her: tall and slender and naked except for her boots and the high-bossed oval shield, painted with unfurling dragon wings, that leans against her knee. Her right hand holds a spear, butted against the ground; the strap of her baldric defines the valley of her breasts with its own stream of blue and silver. Kirsten takes in the proud body, painted in whorls and starbursts of the same deep blue that matches her eyes, scarred here and there with the marks of battle. The woman's coppery hair wreathes her head in an intricate arrangement of braids: the *mionn*, meant to deny any hold to enemy hands.

With a shock, Kirsten realizes that she, too, is nearly naked. Not just naked, but almost identically painted and armed except that she holds a crescent-shaped axe in her left hand; she is only a hair's breadth less high than the woman beside her. The tightness of her scalp tells her that she is likewise crowned with braids, a glance downward, that her own hair is as black as a raven's wing. In a language at once musical and harsh, the red woman says softly, "And the hero-light shone about you that time I first saw you on the banks of the Dubhglass, *anama-chara*, and I knew then I would do anything to have you for my soul-friend."

"And now that you have me, *mo cridh*, what will you do with me?"

The other woman's free hand caresses her shoulder. "Come back to our fire, and I will show you."

The snap of a closing door brings Kirsten gasping out of her dream. It is one she has dreamed the past night and the night before that, ever since her conversation with the raccoon in the woods. The red woman is one of those who warned her back in her spiral toward death, but the rest is both new and strangely familiar. Before she can make sense of it, a voice cuts through the fog that surrounds her. It is lightly amused and male. Tacoma, returning with a bag of Ringer's and a hypodermic filled with a milky liquid.

"Sorry to wake you. You three look really comfortable together."

Kirsten feels her cheeks flame as she remembers twice waking from the dream with her thighs sticky and her heart pounding. A brief inventory assures her that she has awakened in time to avoid embarrassment, the pup still firmly held against her, still snoring softly. His milky scent comes to her on his breath. "I guess I just dropped off. Sorry."

"You needed a break. Here, let's put the little guy back with his mama. He'll keep her mind off what I'm doing." Tacoma hunkers down and snaps open the cage door, waking the mother wolf. He grins. "Go on. It's okay."

Careful to hold her small burden steady, Kirsten levers herself up onto her knees, leans forward and gently lays him on the blanket beside his mother. Her nose touches Kirsten's hand lightly, sniffing, then drops to her pup as she begins to bathe him. Kirsten cannot help herself. She reaches forward and strokes the wolf's beautifully sculpted head, feeling the brittle dryness of her fur, the papery texture of her skin. "She'll be okay?" It is all she can do to keep the tears from her voice.

"She'll be okay. She's reacting well to the drugs and a steady diet. Come summer we should be able to release them."

With a start, Kirsten realizes how little she knows about Dakota's brother. "Are you a vet, too?"

He laughs as he straightens up and begins to fasten the bag of Ringer's to the drip tube, checking the clamp for proper tension. "I'm an engineer, by education if not trade. Comes in handy from time to time, like when we'll be bringing in a few of those big wind generators next week. They won't feed us, but at least we'll have refrigeration and lights. And laundry," he adds, almost as an afterthought. "Manny's even more tired of washing his socks in the bathroom sink than I am."

"Restoring power is enough to earn you years of undying gratitude, believe me." Then, coming back to her question, she said, "I just thought—" She makes a gesture that encompasses the ward, the two wolves, his deftness with the trappings of medicine.

"I know. Lots of people think the same thing. It's just something that comes from growing up in a big family, on a ranch." Tacoma uncaps the syringe with his teeth and, holding the line steady, begins to inject the medication into the IV. "Good old penicillin, can't beat it. You're an only child, Kirsten?"

She is taken aback. "Does it show?"

"Not really. It's just that when there are ten of you, like there are of us, you can change a diaper and give a bottle before the training wheels come off your bike. Same with the cats and dogs and cows and horses. We all learned what to do about colic or a breach birth before we quite figured out how the colt got inside his mama in the first place."

She grins at him. "That young, huh?" He returns the smile, again looking so like his sister that Kirsten's breath leaves her lungs.

"Oh, even younger than you can imagine. By the way, there's coffee if you'd like—"

"Sergeant! Sergeant Rivers!"

The shout interrupts him, repeated to the pounding of feet in the corridor. Shannon bursts through the door, her face and hair wild, "Sergeant—"

"Bleach!" he barks at her, the Master Sergeant suddenly displacing the charming rancher and rough-and-ready vet with a vengeance.

Shannon hops in and out of the basin with the speed of a Phillipino bamboo dancer. "Sergeant, it's your cousin, the lieutenant. He's out front—"

Tacoma is gone before the first sentence is completed, Kirsten on his heels.

**Dark is drawing** down as Koda lowers the binoculars from her eyes and nods, satisfied with what she's seen. The Caresaway Birthing Center is a smallish, one-story structure bordered by attractively landscaped grounds that are only just beginning to look unkempt. The facility has two entrances. The rear door, for deliveries, is locked from the outside with several lengths of chain and three stout padlocks. The main entrance, at the end of a long, winding pathway, is guarded by a single android bearing a nasty semi-automatic weapon. She briefly considers using Kirsten's handy little device to gain entry, then discards the idea, not knowing for sure how long it will take to round up the women being kept captive inside and not wanting to take the chance of the droids "waking up" in the middle of her evacuation and spraying bullets all over the place.

The minicomp is a comforting weight against her chest, and she finds herself smiling as she thinks back on her parting from Kirsten. The feeling of the kiss still lingers, sparking tiny bits of fire along her nerve endings, like an Independence Day sparkler held in a child's hand. After hours of thinking about it on the drive up to this place, she still isn't sure what possessed her to act in such a manner with Kirsten — a woman whose emotional walls are so thick that they likely rival those of the Maginot Linepause. She realizes that if she had stopped to think at that moment, it probably wouldn't have happened at all. Not because there isn't a multi-layered attraction there, because there is and it is something she'd admitted to herself quite some time ago.

Perhaps it's because everything about Kirsten King screams "keep out!" in huge neon letters, and Koda has been conditioned from an early age to respect such signs.

Until that one moment in time where she could no more stop her body's instinctive actions than she could will her heart to stop beating. With a soft sigh, she relegates those thoughts to the back of her mind where they'll need to stay until she sees the task she's set for herself to full completion.

As she watches, a tall man with thick hair and a bushy moustache exits the facility and begins speaking with the android guarding the entrance. Both look up, guns raised, as a herd of winter-thin deer bound from the woods across the neat grounds in huge, panicked leaps.

It is the distraction Dakota needs, and she leaves her tree-lined shelter, darting around the perimeter of the facility until she reaches the west wall. She presses herself tightly against it, feeling the bricks's chill seeping through her jacket and shirt. To her right, a polarized window stands slightly open. She peers carefully through the small slit and sees that the room beyond is empty and dark.

Sliding careful fingers into the seam, she eases the window open just enough for her to be able to squeeze through. Then, with a soft grunt, she hefts herself up and over the sill and into the darkened room, freezing the instant her feet touch the heavily carpeted floor. A moment later, she is moving again, silent as a shadow trailing a running man. At the doorway, she pauses again, then slips through and into the empty hallway beyond.

Koda slides along the hallway wall until she comes to the next doorway. She can hear the muffled sounds of life within: a pen scratching on a piece of paper, the soft hum of medical equipment monitoring and infusing, the deep, relaxed breathing of the sleeping and the drugged. She is visible for no more than an instant as she takes a quick glance at the scene before ducking back out and melding herself to the wall, processing what she's seen.

Four beds to the left, only two of them occupied. One male to the right, his human status proclaimed by the bare neck that just peeps above the collar of his starched white labcoat. He sits hunched over a desk, writing in a chart. His sandy blond hair is mussed and lank. His face sports impressive swelling and bruising along his jawline and the one eye she had seen.

Taking in a breath, she slips around the doorway and silently moves behind the doctor, squatting on her haunches as she slips a hand over his mouth. "If you want to live," she hisses in his ear, "don't scream. Understand?"

The man nods once, quickly.

"Good. I'm gonna ask you some questions. When I take my hand away, I want you to answer me in a whisper, got it?"

Another nod.

"How many women are in this place?"

"Twelve," he whispers from between swollen, cracked lips.

"Including these two?"

"Fourteen."

"How many androids?" There is a long pause. She can feel the surprise and confusion rolling off him in waves. "How many?"

"T-two."

"Including the one guarding the door?"

"Yes."

"Human males? Excluding yourself?"

"Just one."

"He do this to you?" she asks, trailing a gentle finger against his lumpy jawline.

He flinches, then nods, shamed.

Her lip lifts in a snarl. "Okay," Koda nods, satisfied. "Aside from these two, are the others able to travel?"

"Yes."

"And these two, could they, if it was an emergency?"

"I wouldn't recommend it."

"Not even if it meant their freedom?"

There is another pause, and she can feel it as his confusion turns to hope. "I could get them ready."

"How long?"

"T-twenty minutes?"

"Make it ten and you've got a deal."

"It'll be done." There is a brief pause, during which he musters the courage to ask, "Who are you?"

"A friend."

And when he turns around, she is gone.

**Tacoma bursts from** the short corridor into the waiting room, halting so abruptly that Kirsten almost crashes into him. Behind her, Shannon does stumble and steadies herself against Kirsten's shoulder. "Sorry," she gasps, just as Tacoma breathes an audible sigh of relief. Over his shoulder, or more precisely, around his ribs, Kirsten has a clear view of the parking lot in front of the clinic door. A long-bedded pickup is drawn up in front of the entrance, with the tops of a couple of large, steel-wire animal carriers showing under the back window and above the fenders. Manny, in civilian jeans and flannel shirt, is easing the tailgate down, one-handed, assisted by the freckle-faced helicopter pilot who had joined them in the mad charge across the Cheyenne bridge after the choppers had shot their loads.

Andrews, if she remembers correctly, also in mufti.

Kirsten does not know what Tacoma feared, but it is clear that whatever it was, it has not happened. He pushes the door open almost casually. "Yo, cuz. What you got?"

"Come look," Manny answers. "We're gonna need X-rays, stat."

Kirsten is not "cuz," but there is no use in being acting President of the United States if you cannot include yourself in an Air Force lieutenant's invitation. When she sees what is in the back of the truck, she almost wishes that she had not. "Oh, my God." Her throat closes on the words.

The larger cage in front holds a bobcat, sleek and well-fed with the winter's hunting, including, very probably, the chickens and assorted small livestock from deserted farms. All her grace and beauty lie still, her eyes wide pools of darkness, her tongue lolling from her mouth. Only the heaving of her ribs shows that she lives. Across her right front paw a bloody gash shows white bone and the loose ends of tendons.

"What happened to her?" She manages to force out the words. "Was it—"

"Goddamned leg-hold trap," Manny supplies, his voice tight with controlled rage. "I had to dart her to get her out. It's not as bad as it looks, but the sooner we get her cleaned up and some atropine in her, the better."

Tacoma inspects the wound carefully, lightly moving the paw back and forward, palpating above the gash. "I think we've got one lucky cat here, but we need the radiographs to be certain. Shannon," he says without looking around, "set up the X-ray, will you? Dorsal and ventral on the paw. Any other frank injuries?"

This last is directed to Manny, who shakes his head. With his good hand, he pulls forward a second carrier. "This one's not quite as bad, just embarrassing for the poor guy."

Kirsten peers past him. Her first thought is that the cage holds a small wolf, her second, that this is the biggest fox she has ever seen. He, too, is drugged, though his eyes are not quite so dilated. Even in this state, there is a glint of intelligence in them, and something of the mischief of Wika Tegalega.

"Coyote," Andrews says. "Somehow moved fast enough not to get a foot in the trap; caught his tail instead."

"He's been there longer than Igmú, though. It's infected," Manny adds.

Tacoma's nose wrinkles. The odor is pronounced, even from where Kirsten stands.

"Not good," he says. "Sorry, fella, you may lose some of your brush. We'll do what we can, though." Then to Manny he says, "Just these two?"

"There was a badger," Andrews says quietly. "Too far gone."

Tacoma swears softly. "Any sign of who—" He breaks off suddenly, his eyes shifting to a pair of bundles in the corner of the truckbed, then back to Manny.

Something Kirsten does not understand passes between them, as clearly as if it had been spoken. Andrews' face is stiffly, deliberately unexpressive. The larger bundle is about the size of a bear, Kirsten thinks. So badly mangled, perhaps, that the men do not want to trouble her tender female sensibilities? But that is nonsense; two of them have grown up in a tradition that honors women warriors, and all three of them were at the

Cheyenne, commanded by one woman, led to victory by another. Nothing could offend her sensibilities any worse than the human wreckage at the end of a pitched battle, than what she faced on her flight west before Minot. They have to know that.

The bundle is about the size of a man. A dead man. There is nothing to be done for the dead. Aloud she says, "How can I help?"

Tacoma has opened the carrier holding the bobcat and is sliding her gently into his arms. Supporting her back and head so that she can breathe more easily, he carries her into the clinic, Kirsten darting ahead to hold the door for him. "Thanks," he says. "You can help me scrub up the surgery and set out what we'll need."

She continues to hold the door as Manny and Andrews between them maneuver the second cage into the waiting room, and from there directly into the surgery. Carrying the cat, Tacoma follows Shannon into X-ray, emerging a moment later and heading directly for the sink in the small operating room. Rolling up his sleeves and scrubbing vigorously up to his elbows, he says, "Let's see Tshunkmanitu before the drug wears off. If he needs surgery, we can at least start him on antibiotics, knock the infection down some first."

Ten minutes later, with the bright lamp glaring down on the newly cleaned wound, it is obvious what must be done. The distal half of the tail hangs by a fragment of crushed bone and little more than ribbons of torn muscle and skin. Tacoma has debrided as much of the dead tissue as he can and flushed the wound with sterile water. "He'd have had himself out of the trap before much longer," he observes as he strips off his gloves, wads them one into the other along with pus-sodden sponges, and tosses them into the red biohazard bin. "He's going to lose about half that brush. Let's get the atropine into him and bed him down."

Tacoma fills a pair of syringes from vials in the refrigerator. One is Clavamox; the other the atropine that will bring the coyote up to consciousness again. "Manny, can you and Kirsten bandage him up? I'll go take a look at the bobcat's X-rays."

Deftly, hardly hindered by his immobilized arm, Manny packs the end of the wound with sponges. A length of Kerlix follows, with bright blue elastic bandage over that. "Just like Coyote," Manny observes. "In all the old stories, he's always getting his tail in a crack. That or his — that is, another part of him."

Kirsten returns his grin as she sprays the table and scrubs it down. "Did you and Tacoma work with Dakota?"

Manny nods. "I actually got paid. Poor Tacoma just got drafted when she needed someone and he was handy." The coyote's head suddenly rises up, bright eyes beginning to focus. "Hey, here he comes. Can you lift him?"

Kirsten slides her arms under the animal, no heavier than a medium-sized domestic dog. With Manny holding the door, she walks briskly toward the Iso ward and deposits him in the waiting cage a couple of doors down from the mother wolf and her pup. The wolf's head comes up as they pass, long nose testing the air at the arrival of something canine and male. "Company, girl," Kirsten says, slipping her passenger free of her arms and securing the latch.

When they return to the operating room, Tacoma is working rapidly on the bobcat's lower leg, just above the ankle joint. This wound is fresher and has not had time to become infected. A pile of bloody sponges sits in their upturned plastic container at one end of the table, beside the bottle of sterile water. "She's a lucky girl, and we're a couple of lucky nurses," he says. "The bone's not broken, and we don't have to splint it."

Kirsten watches Tacoma's deft movements as he swabs and flushes, swabs and flushes the raw flesh. As he reaches for the water, the back of his hand trails gently over the cat's flank, lingers for a moment on her head. It comes to Kirsten that he has the sort of bond with cats that his sister does with wolves. When he is done he bandages the wound, administers antibiotics and atropine, and himself carries her back toward the ward, murmuring to her softly in Lakota.

An hour later the clinic begins to settle for the night. All the patients are fed, cages cleaned, meds given, dressings changed. Shannon, so bone-weary she can hardly stand, has gone home. Released from his discipline, Asimov sits possessively at Kirsten's feet in the waiting room. Manny, fishing in his pocket for the truck keys, prods Andrews where he dozes on a bench. "Hey, bro, c'mon. Let's go home to a deee-lish-us bowl of chicken noodle soup." To Kirsten, he says, "You want us to drop you and Asi off at the colonel's?"

"Thanks," she says. Then, very evenly, adds, "In a moment. First I want to know what's in that bundle in the back of the truck. I like to know who I'm riding around with."

Again, the covert glances: Andrews to Manny to Tacoma and back. "I'd like an answer, please," Kirsten says.

Manny sits down with a sigh, his stocky bulk folding up joint by joint. "It's the trapper. He was out checking his lines."

"He drew on Manny," Andrews says. "It was self-defense."

Kirsten turns to Tacoma, "You knew about this?"

Tacoma runs his hands through his hair and over his face. "I was afraid something like this might happen, yeah."

"When Shannon came running back to the Iso ward, you thought something had happened to Manny, didn't you?"

Tacoma nods. "He can't carry a rifle with his busted shoulder. Look, a trapper is, by definition, a criminal. It's not something kinder, gentler people do."

"Nothing's wrong with my trigger finger, thank you very much."

Manny pats the bulge at his waist that Kirsten belatedly realizes is a handgun. "Show me."

Only one bundle remains in the truck. The face of the corpse, when Tacoma unwraps it, is familiar even in the failing light. Except for the bullet hole in his forehead, Bill Dietrich looks exactly as he did the night he and a mob behind him tried to force their way onto the base. Fleetingly, Kirsten regrets that she did not shoot him on the spot. "All right," she says. "Take him over to the morgue. Someone can notify his family, if he has one, in the morning. There'll have to be some sort of inquest. I'll talk to the colonel about it tonight." She reels off the orders as if she has been giving them all her life.

"Yes, ma'am," Manny says. There is a suspicious glint in his eye. "Anything else?"

"What was in the other blanket?"

The gleam goes out of Manny's eyes. He and Tacoma conspicuously do not look at each other. After a moment, Koda's brother says quietly, "One they couldn't save."

Kirsten could press the matter. She senses, though, that the answer is the truth, if not all the truth. She deems it best to let it go.

"All right," she says. She opens the passenger door to the front seat and Asi hops up, settling in the middle. "Take me back to—" She hesitates. "Take me home."

**Koda slips back** into the darkened, empty room and pauses a moment to consider her options. She knows that down the hall, past the special care suite from which she has just returned, there are ten birthing rooms, five to a side. Along the other hallway, there are two Jacuzzis used for relaxation and two birthing tubs for water births. At the very end of the hallway is a large, family style kitchen. The two wings sprout from a central core, a square area housing a reception/admitting desk and a waiting area with comfortable couches and a communal television.

*Kitchen first, I think.*

A noise stays her feet, and she listens carefully to the sound of heavy footfalls, nearly inaudible against the thick carpeting of the hallways. Her nose twitches as she scents a noxious cloud of heavy body odor capped by an overly flowery men's cologne. Reaching under her jacket, she removes the automatic pistol from its shoulder holster and grips it, muzzle down, barrel pressing against her palm. As the footsteps come closer, white teeth glitter in the gathering darkness.

She waits for the man to pass — it is indeed the bushy haired-stranger who had stepped out to speak to the android — and just as his shoulders clear the doorway, she steps in behind him, raises the pistol, and cracks the stock against the back of his head. He falls like a stone, and she catches him under the armpits and drags him into the darkened room.

Settling him on his stomach and turning his head to the side, she pulls out a roll of duct tape, placing a piece over his mouth, and wrapping first his wrists and then his ankles together, binding him securely. Rising fluidly to her feet, she holsters the gun, knowing it won't be needed further, and walks back to the doorway, peering both ways down the brightly lit hall.

The hall is empty. Pulling the minicomp from her pocket, she slips back out into the hallway and turns left. Long, unhurried strides take her down the short side of the hallway and into the reception area. The area is empty and quiet. Its cheery décor is no comfort now.

Stopping at an end table scattered with parenting magazines long out of date, she pops open the minicomp's protective lid and sets it down. With a crossing of mental fingers, she presses the tiny power button and waits, not exactly sure what she's expecting.

No flashing lights, no screaming sirens, no humming, no martial music piped from infinitesimal speakers. No nothing.

She waits another moment, pushing down the temptation to give the thing a whack to get it going. She lets out a soft sigh instead. "Guess I'll have to do this the hard way, then," she mutters to herself, hand stealing to the gun at her side — a gun that she knows will be less than useless against the androids. "Ah well. Here goes nothing."

She heads down the hallway, gun cocked and ready, only slowing when she spies something rather strange. As she closes in, cautiously, she recognizes it as a hand, fingers slightly cupped as if reaching for something, peeping out from one of the doorways. As she approaches, the hand doesn't move and, unable to hold back her curiosity any longer, she rounds the doorway and stares into the blank eyes of an android frozen in mid step.

A smile slowly spreads across her face. With one long finger, she gently pushes against the chest of the android. It rocks in place like an inanimate object, then settles, making no independent movement of its own. "Ohhhh, Kirsten," she breathes, grinning. "Very nice. Very nice indeed."

Her grin falls away as she hears a gasp, and she pivots, gun instinctively at the ready. Two hugely pregnant women scream and duck, throwing their arms in front of their faces, turning away to protect their bellies.

Koda quickly holsters her weapon and shows them both her empty hands. "It's okay," she soothes. "I've come to get you out of here."

The taller of the two women slowly removes her hands and peers at Dakota. "Really?" Her voice is high-pitched and full of doubt.

"I'm sure," Koda replies, slowly and deliberately reaching for the collar of her jacket and separating it to show her neck. "I'm a friend."

Slowly, more or less assured by the absence of a droid collar, the women come to their feet. The taller one steps forward, then flinches back at the sight of the android, shooting Koda a mistrustful gaze.

"It's okay," Dakota replies in response. "It's temporarily out of commission."

Like skittish animals, both women step forward until they are within arm's length of the droid. They stare at it, wide eyed, then turn their stares to Dakota. "You do this?"

"I had a little help," she responds warmly.

"Damn," the shorter woman — little more than a girl, really, with wildly dyed hair and multiple facial piercings — breathes. "Far out."

"If you can help me get the others," Koda intones. "We don't have much time."

"Wha—" The younger woman blinks. "Yeah, they're all in the kitchen. We just came out 'cause we heard a noise."

"All right, then, let's get everybody rounded up. I don't know how long that droid is going to stay like that."

**Three minutes later,** Koda is hustling the women, all very pregnant, down the long hall and back into the waiting area. Scooping up the mini-comp, she slips it into her pocket and levels the group with an intense glance. "Okay, everybody stay here. I'll be back in a minute, all right?"

The silent women stare back at her. A few nod; the rest only stand frozen, torn between the polar extremes of fear and hope.

"Be right back."

Dakota pelts down the hall until she comes to the special care unit. The doctor is almost in the doorway, two groggy women at his side. "Thank God," he says upon seeing her. "You're going to have to help me with this one. She began having contractions as soon as I turned her infusion off."

"Will she lose the baby?"

"She might, if we can't keep her on the medication."

"All right. Does that pump run on a battery?"

"Yes."

Nodding, Koda brushes by the small group and deftly unclamps the pump from the pole. Wrapping the cord around the clamp, she pulls down the bag of fluid, walks back to the woman, and reconnects the tubing to the IV still in her arm. "Rate?"

"Are you a nurse?" the doctor asks, surprised.

"Vet. Rate?"

"Um, fifty cc per hour."

"Fine." Within seconds, the meds begin once again infusing into the pain-wracked woman. A moment later, she straightens with relief. "Bless you," she whispers, then nearly collapses as a wave of weakness overtakes her.

"Hold this," Koda orders, all but tossing the pump to the startled doctor, while steadying the woman with her free hand. Then, in a smooth motion, she tucks her other arm beneath the woman's knees and lifts her into her arms. "Let's go."

"But—"

"Now."

Supporting the second woman with an arm around her waist, the physician hurries after Dakota, the pump tucked against his body and the tubing stretching taut between them.

They reach the reception room quickly to find the rest of the group in the same positions in which Dakota had left them. Giving them a nod, Koda leads the pack to the front door. Through the glass, she can see the second android standing motionless on the tiny porch. She pushes the door open, and when this action garners no response from the droid, she breaths another silent sigh of relief, and steps through.

"You," she orders over her shoulder to the punk-haired girl, "grab that gun. It can't hurt us without its weapon. Not once we get far enough away."

"Right on." The woman does as ordered, then, for good measure, gives the android a mighty heave, sending him toppling from the porch and into the snow where it once again settles, motionless. "Take that, you fucking, tin-plated shitheap! Hah!"

"All right, all of you, let's go. Walk as fast as you can. Transportation's just beyond that tree line. Move."

A moment later, the troop carrier comes into view, and the women break into a run, babbling with excitement and happiness. Koda tosses the keys to one of the women and orders her to unlock the rear door. That done, the women file inside, sliding along the bench seats that line the vehicle. Koda gestures for the doctor to enter, then lays her charge in the aisle between the seats.

Finished with her task, she looks at the shining faces of the women. "We're moving out. This isn't the most comfortable truck you've ever ridden in, but I promise to be as gentle as I can with it, okay?"

The women nod. From the back, a soft voice asks, "Who are you?"

She smiles tightly. "A friend. Now hold on. We're out of here."

Slamming the door and locking it tight, she moves alongside the carrier to the driver's side door. As she's about to slip inside, she hears the long, mournful howl of a wolf. Tears sting her eyes, and she swipes them away with an angry hand. "I miss you, my friend," she whispers into the chilled air.

The howl follows her, filling her ears and soul as she climbs into the truck and drives away.

# CHAPTER TWENTY-TWO

Kirsten lets herself into a silent house. Tentatively she calls out, "Dakota? Maggie?" There is no answer except for a soft whine from Asimov. Soundlessly she crosses the hall and flicks the light switch. The warm glow of the lamps with their old-fashioned pleated linen shades reveals books ranked on their shelves, Koda's copy of Spengler neatly closed on the coffee table. The house smells faintly of lavender and lemon wax — no supper on the stove, no fire on the hearth. She has the place to herself, and is content.

She is accustomed to solitude, needs it from time to time as she needs air. Too much has happened in the last two days — too much just in the hours since setting out on a walk with Asi — to tolerate another human presence with any ease. True, she knows that worry will niggle at the back of her mind until Koda returns safely from her raid on the birthing center, but she also knows that the woman who led the charge across the Cheyenne is more than a match for a couple of androids and one or two human stooges.

Drifting through the living room, her fingers trail over the venerable edition of *The Decline of the West*. A bit of history, read in some random book or article and never discarded, drifts up from Kirsten's memory. The great Oglala war chief Crazy Horse took the only scalps of his adult life on a raid against the Crow, sparked by his wild grief over the death of his daughter. And Dakota has adopted his blazons of hail and lightning and red-tailed hawk. A shiver runs over her. Tshunka Witco had been born somewhere near the bend of the Cheyenne where they had stood down the android army. And has, perhaps, named his heir, a century and a half later, in the blood and fire of battle.

It is more mysticism than she can tolerate on an empty stomach. Purposefully Kirsten moves toward the kitchen, Asimov shouldering past her to stand over his bowl, eyes bright, tail wagging like a metronome in 2/4 time. His nose disappears among the kibble the instant it clatters into the metal dish.

Kirsten's choices are not much more varied. An inspection of the refrigerator produces a container of vegetable soup; a moment's investigation of the pantry, canned fruit, some beans and corn, onions and potatoes. Meat is becoming scarce. Other protein — milk, cheese, eggs — is growing increasingly rarer. It is a problem that will have to be addressed, but not by her, not this evening, at any rate. There is already too much in line ahead of it.

As the soup heats, Kirsten rummages in the bread box, triumphantly pouncing on the last round of fry bread from a batch Koda had made a few days ago. She ought to leave part of it for Maggie and Koda, but hunger and the strains of the day get the better of etiquette. She lays it directly on the stove surface to heat, flipping it a time or two like a pancake, then carries her meal to the table. For thirty minutes, she promises herself, she will think about nothing but the physical necessity of her hunger, about nothing more important than carrying spoon from bowl to mouth. Finding some purchase on the frictionless surface her emotional life has become can wait until after supper.

An hour later, she sits staring into the fire she has lit for company, her fingers idle on the keyboard of her laptop. She cannot bring herself to concentrate on the strings of figures that march across the plasma screen. The work is as urgent as ever. Unlike the inhabitants of Rapid City, who have abandoned themselves to the optimistic view that the droids are defeated once and for all, Kirsten knows, better than any, the danger they and the remainder of surviving humanity still face. She just cannot persuade herself that she should give it her undivided attention. Not now.

The flames leap before her eyes, and in their orange and scarlet she sees again the fires along the valley in her dream, the streaming hair of the warrior woman she has seen four times now. The first time, the woman blocked her passage as she spiraled down toward death; the second time, and the third and the fourth — the last right there in the clinic, with for God's sake who knows who coming and going — she had been more than a fleeting image and a voice. There was a past behind her, a past that Kirsten, in her own strange form, had invaded at some place — a battlefield? — somewhere near a body of water called "Douglass", or something like it.

Someplace, somewhere, something.

Kirsten makes a small noise of annoyance, and Asi, stretched full length on the warm bricks, glances up at her. She extends a foot to scratch his belly, and he subsides. It is bad enough to find herself mooning over dreams; it is worse to find herself tolerating the vagueness of a dozen assumptions that she cannot root in fact. Almost without volition, her fingers begin to drift over her keyboard, spelling out the one name she can remember, seeking its place and time in the real world. With luck, she will find nothing and will be able to consign the entire episode to a traumatized and overactive imagination.

Douglass: Scottish Gaelic. From Dubh — black; dark, and glass — stream, water. 1. The name of a family prominent in Scottish history. 2. The site of one of the twelve legendary battles of King Arthur, said to be located in southwestern Scotland.

*And the hero-light shone about you that time I first saw you on the banks of the Dubhglass,* anama-chara, *and I knew then I would do anything to have you for my soul-friend.*

Her mind reels away from that as if she has been struck. She refuses to lose herself in the fog of Arthuriana, in a fantasy para-historical at best. But it has given her a possible foothold in fact.

Item: The ancient Celts, the very ancient Celts — ancient enough to be free of the trailing fantasies of Camelot, she is relieved to find — trained the able of both sexes as warriors. Indeed, the greatest of the Celtic arms masters, those who educated heroes such as CuChullain, were women.

Item: The ancient Celts, including the women, fought naked. A brief anecdote relates how Onduava, wife of the martyred Vercingetorix, led the Gaulish women out against Caesar, "and did the Romans great damage before they got their minds back onto the business at hand." Kirsten finds herself smiling at that, for reasons that are not quite clear to her. There is something about the humiliation of the Divine Julius at the hands of a woman warrior that pleases her immensely.

Item: The ancient Celts painted, or sometimes tattooed, their bodies with designs in blue woad, a vegetable dye. They wore their hair in a complicated wreath of braids upon going into battle to deny the enemy a hand-hold. An illustration shows the helmet-like arrangement, with a sort of attenuated, clubbed ponytail at the crown. Another shows the alternative, hair cropped short and stiffened into hedgehog-like spikes with lime. *First millennium BCE punk. Move over, Sting.*

Item: The ancient Celts were, according to Caesar, great proponents of "manly love". Though JC does not mention it in his *Gallic Wars*, the commentator opines that the warrior ethos extended equally to "womanly love".

Which brings her back to...

Very softly, Kirsten closes the top of her computer, staring into the fire. Which brings her back to that fleeing moment in the hall, the brief brush of Dakota's lips on hers. The heat rising in her face has nothing to do with the fire. In that irrational part of her mind that she does not trust, she knows that she need not fear the kiss meant goodbye. Dakota is neither incompetent nor careless, except when charging across ruined bridges, and Kirsten knows in her bones that the warrior will not fail in her mission.

But if not goodbye... To the best of her knowledge, the Oglala Lakota do not share the French habit of kissing all and sundry, of either gender, with or without provocation or even the benefit of formal introduction.

Her eyes slide closed and she allows herself to remember the brief contact, not in her mind, but on her lips. There is tenderness in its warmth, a promise of passion, yet it makes no demands. It bears no resemblance to anything in her meager experience, which has been limited to one or two awkward couplings in the back of an ancient Bronco, her acquiescence more out of curiosity than emotion. The experience, she had thought at the time, was not what it was cracked up to be.

But this...

Her dreams have been passionate, and have left the physical signs of that passion behind on her skin. An image from her dream forms, flickering in the firelight that plays across her closed eyelids. The red woman's mouth descending on hers, open and sharing, her hair loose about her, her eyes the color of sapphires in the shadow. The light shifts, and the face has changed with it, the skin bronze now, stretched over high cheekbones, long hair like a waterfall of night cascading over broad shoulders. Only the eyes are the same — blue as the evening sky.

Deliberately Kirsten sets down the computer and goes to stand in the hall, in front of the mirror. Her reflection is shadowed by the firelight and the one lamp left burning in the room behind her. She takes in her own features: the cornsilk pale hair, grown past her collar in the past months; the face she has never considered better than plain; her eyes, probably her best feature, huge and dark in the low light.

Dakota Rivers is beautiful, tall and graceful and confident. Everything Kirsten is not. And yet... She touches her fingers to her lips, almost disbelieving. And yet, it seems, she finds Kirsten desirable, even when she has someone as assured and as elegant as herself for a lover.

The past is the future, Wika Tegalega had said. Her past? Dakota's? There is nothing in her own that she cares to repeat, certainly not the puerile gropings of her undergraduate days. Dakota's past is largely unknown, except for those few facts she has let slip, and the loss of Tali, her first love and first wife. Kirsten has nothing to lay alongside that to fit it to her own measure.

She will not allow herself to think that it may be more than desire. To do so would be to give her heart as hostage to fortune, and there is enough of herself at hazard as it is. For a moment longer, she lingers before the mirror. Then carefully, she banks the fire, leaving the lamp lit against Maggie's return, or Dakota's.

Asimov beside her, she slips out of her clothes and into the sweat pants and shirt she still wears against the spring chill. She does not know how long she lies awake, but it is long enough to hear the key in the lock and Maggie's step, lighter than Dakota's and quicker, on the floor of the entrance hall. The snick of Maggie's door closing punctuates the silence, and after that, the only sound in the dark is the soft snoring of Asimov where he sleeps on the floor next to the narrow bed. Toward morning, she falls into sleep...and into dream.

**Dawn has just** begun to lighten the horizon when Kirsten rolls from her bed and stretches, feeling oddly refreshed. Oddly, because ever since she's been sleeping on the lumpy, pitiful excuse for a mattress, she's never been even within shouting distance of a good night's sleep. Of course, it wouldn't help to grouse about it — aloud, at least. She knows she's lucky to have a roof over her head. Damn lucky. Many others are making do without even that. Those who are still alive.

Shaking her head to clear away thoughts too maudlin for a newly dawning day, she stretches again and runs a hand through her sleep-spiraled hair, setting it somewhat to rights, as snatches of the dreams which kept her company through the night filter through her slowly awakening consciousness. Very much like the dreams she used to have when her deafness had set in so fully that even the memory of human speech seemed a lost and forgotten thing, these aren't images so much as colors.

The swirling smoke grey of doubt and confusion merging into the bilious green of fear. The deep purple-red of rage lightening into the golden red of passion. The colors, and their attendant emotions, flow in and among and through each other in dizzying kaleidoscope patterns that change with each twitch of her eyes until she is all but screaming for respite.

It comes, then — a deep, Caribbean blue that nurtures and soothes, and settles over her, leaving nothing within untouched.

And, at last, she knows peace.

Asi hears the sounds a split second before she does and paces to the door, whining and looking back at his human with his best beseeching gaze. Kirsten smiles, feeling her pulse quicken in anticipation. She covers the small distance in a quick stride and yanks the door open, breath already filling her lungs in preparation for speech. Breath that leaks out slowly when she sees not Dakota, but Maggie standing in the middle of the living room, pulling on her jacket with short, savage motions, her brow deeply furrowed with worry. "Maggie?"

"She didn't come home last night," Maggie bites off, yanking down the hem of her jacket. "I'm going after her. You stay here in case I miss her."

"She's back," Kirsten soothes. "She's safe."

Maggie's head lifts slowly. Her dark eyes dart past Kirsten and to the opened door of the room beyond. A flash of emotion that Kirsten can't — or won't — identify crosses the colonel's face and is quickly gone. "I see."

The room temperature plummets to sub-arctic, leaving Kirsten struggling for purchase on the slippery emotional slope. "No!" she finally spits out just as Maggie is beginning to turn away. "She didn't...I mean, she's not...I mean... Shit." She sighs, and plays out a hunch. "Could you just...come with me? Please?"

"Where."

If the spoken word were visible, that particular word, as spoken by Maggie, would be formed from blocks of brittle ice. Kirsten swallows hard, finding herself confronted with a woman very unlike the one she's come to know and consider, at least in some ways, a friend. Not lacking in courage, however, she pushes down her unease and faces the colonel boldly. "Just come. Please?"

"Fine," Maggie grunts. "Let's just get this over with quickly. I have things I need to do today."

"Great! Just let me get my jacket, and we're gone."

The two women step out into the cool dawn. The sky overhead is a pearl grey, and the freshening breeze, while chill, brings with it the heavy scent of moist earth and growing things. It brings an unconscious smile to Kirsten's face, and an equally unconscious spring to her step as she walks across Maggie's small lawn and onto the street that will lead them to the vet clinic. Asi bounds ahead, stopping at his usual canine greeting posts and baptizing several newly budding trees. Maggie follows along at a more sedate pace, hands shoved deep in her pockets and eyes fixed to the ground at her feet. She's feeling out-of-sorts, torn within the space of five minutes between the towering emotions of fear for Dakota's safety and a flashing jealousy she'd spent previous hours convincing herself she didn't possess.

*Great*, she thinks, giving a soft snort of self-deprecation, *I've finally gone nuts. Snapping a woman's head off for absolutely no reason. A woman who, if you'll remember, just happens to be your Commander-In-Chief. All before breakfast, yet.* She snorts again. *Great.*

Lifting her head, she gazes out over the grounds, toward the hangar where she knows her Tomcat patiently waits. A brief stab of pain twists at her heart and she wills her gaze away. *Damn.*

Unaware of Maggie's turbulent thoughts, Kirsten crosses the last of the ground to the clinic quickly, almost buoyantly, and pulls open the door, taking in the blast of warm, animal scented air with a feeling of true pleasure. Asi rushes inside and assumes his accustomed place on the floor of the waiting room, grabbing a toy from the basket and attacking it with purpose.

Kirsten holds the door until Maggie enters, then follows, taking the lead as she pulls open a second door and walks through into the narrow, pristine white corridor lined with examining rooms on either side. The door at the end of the hall leads to the isolation area and is presently blocked by the large bodies of Tacoma, Manny, and Andrews, who stare, still as statues, through the glass and into the room beyond.

Hearing their entrance, Tacoma turns, smiling in welcome and beckoning them forward. Kirsten reaches the group first and Manny edges aside, allowing her to fill the space vacated by his body. As she peers inside, she feels her eyes widen in wonder, even as her heart swells near to bursting.

There, on the plush mats set carefully on the floor, lies Dakota, sprawled out on her back, ebony hair forming a corona around her head. Lying full length against her is the female wolf, free of IVs, her massive head tucked in tight against Koda's left side. And, nestled safely upon the softness of Koda's shirt-covered chest, lies the wolf pup. All are blissfully, deeply asleep.

Kirsten can hear Maggie's soft gasp in her right ear even as she hears Tacoma begin to whisper in her left.

"She came back really late last night and operated on the bobcat and coyote. They're both doing very well."

Kirsten nods with relief.

"Then she sent me and Manny home. Wouldn't take no for an answer, so we went."

Behind her, she can feel Manny's silent laughter as Tacoma continues.

"We got here about ten minutes ago. All the cages are clean and the animals look fine, so I think she nodded off just a little while ago."

"Is it safe for her to be like that?" Kirsten asks, a little nervous as she watches the female stir slightly and display wickedly long, wickedly sharp teeth in a large canine yawn before settling back against Dakota's warm body.

"Oh yeah," Tacoma replies easily. "She's safe. She's with her family."

She turns her head slowly, meeting Tacoma's gaze, not exactly sure what she's expecting to see. Humor over his sister's eccentricities, maybe? Jealousy, perhaps? But she sees none of those things. The only emotions there are an overwhelming pride and, as he turns back to peer through the window, an adoration one would usually see reserved only for the worship of a higher power.

And suddenly, like the Grinch of that long ago children's tale, she recognizes, and admits, the swelling in her own chest as she too turns back to the scene in the clinic for exactly what it is: simple, and complex, and completely irresistible. Love.

The moment is shattered by the sound of the rear door opening and Shannon, still looking about sixteen hours from rested, stumbling in, dry scrubbing her face and yawning hugely.

Turning quickly, Tacoma bars the way and gently escorts the half-sleeping young woman back the way she came. The others follow slowly, leaving Kirsten to stare at the window, grappling with an emotion, with a revelation, so monumental that it literally steals the breath from her lungs.

*I'm in love with her.*

Those words go round and round in her mind, each time with a different emphasis until all of them are capitalized and pounding so hard at her heart and head that she fears she's screaming them at the top of her lungs. What comes out, however, is the tiniest of whispers, spoken only to an empty, sterile hall. Her breath, as it speaks the words, forms a tiny flower of fog against the glass, misting the scene before her.

"I'm in love with you."

**The waiting room** sees three men standing at rigid attention as Maggie, back to the exit door, stares at them, dark eyes snapping. "We need to talk." Her voice, though soft, carries with it the authority of a god. "Be in my office in two hours." And with that, she is gone, leaving the men to sag against the walls and desk of the large room.

"We're in for it now," Manny mutters, dragging a nervous hand across the freshly sharpened bristles of his regimental buzz-cut.

"We are truly fucked," Andrews agrees, his face as pale as curdled milk.

"Come on, guys," Tacoma finally says with a quick glance back down the corridor. "Let's make ourselves presentable before she hands us our guts on a platter."

The three men quickly exit, leaving one bewildered woman behind, trying to convince herself that she's still dreaming.

**Maggie unlocks the** door to her office and flicks up the light switch. Overhead, the fluorescent tubes flicker to life, their cold light falling on the spartan desk and metal-frame chairs, leeching the life from the two Guatemalan cutout tapestries of jungle cats worked in scarlet and orange, bright yellow and fuchsia that share the wall with the ubiquitous color photographs of combat aircraft. One of these shows Maggie herself poised on the ladder of her lead plane, the Bobcats logo splendid in orange and gold above her. It, and the tapestries, are the only personal items in the room. Everything else belongs to the Squadron Leader, not the woman.

Maggie raises the blinds that cover the one window, giving her a view of the flightline close to the hangars. It is not exactly your executive scenic panorama, but its stark shadings of grey pavement and swept-winged silver birds has never failed to please her. Today they are topped by pale sky and white clouds in the same palette, and a part of her longs to cut free of the ground and lose herself in the blue air where cloud tops fall away beneath her like pristine snowfields.

But that is not why she is here today. Sliding open the top drawer of her file cabinet, she withdraws two fat manila folders and lays them on the desk. A third, empty, she takes from a supply cabinet and labels with Tacoma Rivers' name. He is not, strictly speaking, "her" non-com, but by following his sister to the base and fighting under Maggie's command at the Cheyenne, he has made her his commanding officer. And that makes her responsible for him and his actions.

Briefly she glances at her watch. Ten minutes.

She uses half the time to review the contents of yet a fourth folder, the medical report detailing the manner and cause of death of one William Dietrich, late of Rapid City, South Dakota, currently a pain in Maggie's official posterior. According to the examining physician, a single 9 mm round had entered the frontal bone of Dietrich's skull, rather neatly on the medial line between the orbital ridges. It had exited rear, carrying with it a large portion of the late Mr. Dietrich's cerebrum and cerebellum and an even larger piece of his occipital plate. Death had been instantaneous, not attributable to accident or to suicide.

In plain language, Manny had potted the bastard right between the eyes, blowing his brains out. Said bastard had been dead before he hit the ground.

The body has not been returned to the family because no information is available on Mr. Dietrich's residence or relations. He carried no identification and is not listed in the Rapid City telephone directory. Maggie makes a note to question the three yahoos presently repining in the brig for shooting at the wolf. Statistically, they are unlikely to have known the late

Mr. Dietrich. On the theory that one sadistic thug is likely to know other sadistic thugs, it is the best that anyone has come up with yet.

A shadow passes over her window, and Maggie looks up in time to catch a glimpse of three men in uniform, two blue and one green. When the knock comes a few seconds later, she stands in front of her desk, claiming the available space for herself except for a narrow strip at the front of the small room. She lets them wait long enough to knock a second time, then raps out, "Come in!"

They file in one by one, saluting sharply, then tucking their caps under their left arms. "Ma'am." She acknowledges them briefly, and then, because there is no choice, they form a line along the concrete block wall: Sergeant Tacoma Rivers, United States Army on the end; his cousin Lieutenant Manuel Rivers, USAF in the middle; Lieutenant Bernard Andrews, also USAF, nearest the door. All three pairs of eyes seem fixed on some point behind and about two feet above her head. All three are as stiff and straight as wooden soldiers.

She lets the silence spin out for a full minute while she stares at them, then says very quietly, "I have before me on my desk the medical account of the violent death of Mr. William Dietrich, civilian citizen of Rapid City. He died of a single gunshot to the head. However this happened, we now have a potential crisis developing between the townspeople and the personnel of this base. I do not need — I hope I do not need — to remind you of the recent unfortunate occurrences at the gate of this installation, or why this shooting is not just A Bad Thing but a Very. Bad. Thing."

"No, ma'am," Andrews says stiffly.

Maggie takes two steps to stand directly in front of him. "Did I ask you a question, Lieutenant?" she snaps.

His Adam's apple dips visibly under the knot of his tie. "No, ma'am."

She begins to pace the line deliberately, looking each man up and down from the toes of his mirror-shined boots to the top of his head. Finally she says, "Lieutenant Rivers, explain what you and Lieutenant Andrews were doing in the woods the day Mr. Dietrich was shot."

"Ma'am," he replies, "we were looking for illegal leg-hold traps we believed had been set in the area."

"Why?"

"To disable them, ma'am. Also to assist any animals we might find caught in them, ma'am."

"What made you think you might find illegal trapping devices or injured animals in the area?"

Anger flares in Manny's eyes, white hot. Maggie ignores it. "Well?"

"Ma'am. My cousin, Dr. Rivers, found a grown male wolf in a similar trap the day before. He was moribund and had to be euthanized, ma'am."

"So you set out in search of more."

"That is correct, ma'am."

Maggie has heard, in monosyllables from Koda, in more detail from Kirsten, of finding the maimed and suffering alpha wolf in the trap. She suspects that she has nowhere near the whole story, nor does she wish to violate Koda's privacy by pushing for more information from others. "What did you find?"

"Ma'am, we collected four empty leg-hold traps of varying sizes. In addition, we found one live coyote with a mangled tail, one live bobcat with an injured foreleg and paw, and one badger only barely alive, suffering from shock and advanced infection."

"And what action did you take?"

"Lieutenant Andrews and I recovered the injured coyote and bobcat, euthanized the badger, and transported the surviving animals to the Ellsworth veterinary facility, where they were treated, ma'am."

"Andrews!"

"Ma'am!"

"Tell me how Dietrich got into the picture."

Andrews' eyes have not moved from the spot on the wall above her head. "He approached the trap containing the bobcat as we were attempting to release her, ma'am."

"On foot or in a vehicle?"

"On foot, ma'am."

"Armed?"

"Yes, ma'am."

"Weapon?"

"Deer rifle, ma'am."

"Did he threaten you or Lieutenant Rivers?"

"Yes, ma'am."

"Verbally or with the gun?"

"Both, ma'am."

"What did he say?"

"He told us to leave his traps the hell alone, ma'am.  He called us thieves."

"And?"

"I said that leg-hold traps are illegal, and that we were removing the animals for treatment."

"And?" Maggie barks. "Do I have to pry this out of you with a crowbar, Andrews?"

"No, ma'am." Andrews turns a florid scarlet under his freckles. "He said we were a couple of bleeding heart, candy-ass, tree hugging queers out to steal a real man's livelihood, and we'd better get out of there before he shoved his gun — that is, ma'am—"

Maggie almost takes pity on him, but she cannot afford to. "'Shoved his gun', Lieutenant?"

"Uh, up our, uh backsides, ma'am, and blew our lousy yellow guts to hell." The blush deepens to crimson, spreads down the young man's neck. "Ma'am."

"Answer me carefully, Lieutenant.  Did you see or otherwise perceive any indication that Mr. Dietrich was impaired in any way?"

"Do you mean, like was he drunk, ma'am?"

"Was he?"

"Not that I could tell, ma'am.  He didn't have any liquor on him, and I couldn't smell any."

"Rivers?"

"No, ma'am.  No smell and nothing found on him, uh...later."

Maggie leans back on her heels, sweeping the line with her eyes. "Who shot him?"

"I did, ma'am," Manny answers.

"Why?"

"He threatened us with his rifle, ma'am."

"Before or after his verbal threat?"

"After, ma'am. He pointed the weapon directly at Lieutenant Andrews."

"Why did you have a gun? Did you expect to encounter someone?"

"We had two guns, ma'am — a handgun with me and a rifle in the truck. We took them for personal safety and because we feared we might find animals who could not be helped."

"You shot Dietrich with the handgun?"

"Yes, ma'am."

"As a direct response to a threat to the life and well-being of Lieutenant Andrews?"

"Yes, ma'am."

"Are you prepared to testify to that under oath in a military court?"

"Yes, ma'am."

"Andrews?"

"Yes, ma'am."

Finally, she turns her attention to Tacoma. "Sergeant Rivers."

"Ma'am."

"Really simple — what did you know, and when did you know it?"

Unlike his cousin's, Tacoma's eyes are cold with anger. "I knew that Lieutenants Rivers and Andrews were going out to check for other traps and other animals, ma'am. I did not know that they had encountered anyone or that anyone had been shot until they returned."

"But you feared something might have happened, did you not? You reacted rather strongly when you were told Lieutenant Rivers had returned, isn't that so?"

"Yes, ma'am. As you know, ma'am, leg-hold traps and trapping are illegal."

"But ingrained in the local culture?"

"In parts of it, ma'am."

"In light of which — does any one of you gentlemen have any idea how difficult this is going to make our relations with the locals? We have had two near riots in the last week and a half. Now two Air Force officers stationed on this base have killed a civilian. Unfortunately, you also killed him with no other witnesses present."

"We have a witness, ma'am."

That is Tacoma. Maggie turns slowly on her heel, facing him. "What? Are you telling me that there was someone else present that YOU HAVEN'T BOTHERED TO TELL ME ABOUT?" Maggie's roar hurts her throat and threatens to shake the window pane. She hopes, very sincerely, that it hurts the ears of these three men. Andrews, she is gratified to see, actually flinches.

Tacoma continues to stare straight ahead. "We have the body of Igmú Tanka Kte, ma'am. The wolf caught in the trap. Lieutenant Rivers brought it back. It's in the freezer at the veterinary clinic."

"And how," she asks more quietly, "does this establish that Lieutenant Rivers fired in self-defense or the defense of Lieutenant Andrews?"

"It doesn't, ma'am. It does establish that Dietrich was a criminal, and an extremely vicious one. It establishes that he would have a reason to harm anyone who could connect him to his criminal activity. In my opinion, ma'am."

"Well," Maggie at last allows her voice to soften slightly, "it's certainly good public relations from our perspective. Good thinking to bring back the wolf's body." A thought strikes her. "Does your sister know it's in the clinic?"

"Not yet, ma'am. The freezer is locked. There are two keys. Both are in my pocket."

"Good. For God's sake, don't let her find out the hard way."

"No, ma'am. I won't."

For the first time, Maggie steps behind her desk, giving her three stiff-spined wooden soldiers room to breathe. "I am going to recommend a formal hearing, at which you will be asked to restate what you have told me here, under oath. For now — get out of my sight. And keep your goddammed noses clean. Dismissed."

"Ma'am."

They stiffen even further, if that is possible. Then they are gone, leaving her to write her recommendations, by hand, in triplicate. It is going to be a long afternoon.

Maggie reaches for her pen, and her bottle of aspirin, and begins.

# CHAPTER TWENTY-THREE

Dakota abruptly awakens to the sound of a low but purposeful growl and the feel of a tense body all but vibrating along her left side. Her eyes quickly open to see Shannon plastered against the far wall next to the door, eyes wide as saucers, face white as cream.

"Relax," Koda orders in a calm, even tone. "She's not strong enough to come after you, and if you stay that way much longer, you're gonna pass out."

The vet tech's gaze darts, unseeing, around the room, as if seeking an escape that is literally one step away.

"I mean it, Shannon. Calm down. Now."

Instinctively responding to Dakota's tone, Shannon relaxes, slumping against the wall and breathing deeply, as if she's just come out of a trance.

"Good," Dakota replies, rolling up to a seated position in time to cushion the fall of the she-wolf, whose energy has been completely drained by her protective display. Stroking the wolf's head, she cradles the slowly awakening pup in her free hand, smiling slightly as he displays tiny teeth and a curled pink tongue in a puppy-sized yawn. "Do me a favor and mix up some formula for this one. I made up some mash for the others; it's in the refrigerator. Just take it out to warm, and I'll feed them when I'm done here."

Nodding, Shannon keeps to the walls as she circles the room toward the counter where the formula ingredients are kept. Moments later, she approaches the tall woman, bottle in hand. Her posture is deliberately relaxed, but Dakota can smell the fear radiating from her in waves. The she-wolf scents it as well and growls low in her throat, causing Shannon to drop the bottle into Dakota's lap and back away, hands raised. "I — I'm sorry," she mumbles. "My brother was attacked by a wolf when we were kids. It'd been shot and just left there to die. He just wanted to help, but...I — I don't think I've ever gotten past that."

Nodding in understanding, Koda curls the pup next to his mother while supporting his head. He latches on as soon as the nipple enters his mouth, sucking vigorously and making little squeaking noises that cause Shannon to smile past her fear.

"G'wan out and see to the rest of our patients," Koda says without looking up from her task. "I'll take care of things here."

"All right," Shannon answers softly, somewhat embarrassed at her fearful display. "I'll...um...be just down the hall if you need me." Without waiting for an answer, she darts outside and into the hall, leaning back against the cool wall with a definite sense of relief. Even so, the embarrassment still suffuses her face with a rosy glow. She's old and honest enough to admit to the healthy crush she has on the tall, beautiful vet. The thought of doing something to upset her is...

"All right," she says, pushing herself away from the wall. "There are still a lot of animals that need care, Shannon, so start doing what they're not paying you for and forget about this mess."

**Two hours later,** all of the animals in the isolation ward have been examined, fed, watered, and placed back in their cleaned kennels. The she-wolf is sleeping soundly, her pup curled tight against her. Rising up from the kennel, Koda goes to the sink and washes her hands, then pulls off the gown she's worn while caring for the animals in her charge. With one last look around, assuring herself that all is fine, she steps from the room, allowing the door to hiss softly closed behind her. She comes upon Shannon in the hallway as the tech is attempting to convince a large, furry dog of indeterminate parentage that he really does want to go into the exam room and get his ears looked at.

The dog takes one look at Koda coming up behind Shannon and obediently walks into the room, leaving the young tech stumbling and almost falling into Dakota's arms.

"Oh!" She jumps forward, spinning to look at the woman behind her, and immediately colors. "I'm sorry. You startled me."

Koda steadies her with a touch to her arm, then passes, taking a brief look into the exam room, where the dog stands wagging his tail at her. "The Iso ward is buttoned up. Check in on them every fifteen minutes or so, and if there's anything amiss, get hold of Tacoma or Manny. I won't be gone long."

"Okay," Shannon replies. "I'll keep watch."

"Good." With a final smile, Koda continues her trek down the well-lit hallway and slips through the door.

The air is warm and smells of a spring that has finally come as she opens the exterior door and steps outside. She takes in a deep breath to cleanse her sinuses of the smell of bleach and alcohol and sickness, then lets it out a bit at a time, feeling some of the tension wash away from her body. With an added energy to her step, she crosses the short walk and rounds the battered "company truck", pulling open the back doors and peering inside. A cased hunting rifle, a .22 and perfect for her needs, sits near the front, the black leather of its case gleaming mellowly in the sunlight streaming through the truck's bed. She lays a hand on it, then draws it away as a thought enters her mind. With a short nod, she leaves the rifle where it lies and backs out, slamming the doors securely shut.

Breaking into a light jog that warms and soothes her muscles, she heads toward the house. The house is, as expected, empty, though in deference to the beauty of the day, most of the windows are open. The slight breeze flutters the curtains and brings with it the freshness of the outside air, tingeing the faint lingering smell of woodsmoke with the scent of newly budding life. A fist clenches around her heart, then releases as she thinks of her own beloved home, shuttered and abandoned these long, bleak months.

On the heels of that thought, quite unbidden, comes a mental picture of Kirsten stepping into that space for the first time. An unconscious smile bows Koda's lips as she plays the image through in her mind. And on the heels of that image comes another; the memory — so very vivid — of the kiss she shared with Kirsten in the very spot where she now stands. She can feel her pulse quicken as little sparks skitter down her limbs and belly, coiling together to form a gentle warmth that she is coming more and more to associate with the young scientist.

A moment later, she shakes her head, dispelling her thoughts, though not the feelings accompanying them, and walks into a spare room where most of her gear is stored. There, sitting behind her largest knapsack is a finely detailed leather case. Lifting it, she unhooks the rawhide loops from the bone buttons and slips out her bow. It is a beautiful piece, made for her by her uncle, Manny's father, a master craftsman. Made from the wood of the Osage Orange tree, it is strong, limber, and traditional. Her quiver and arrows, these steel-tipped, lie next to the bow case, and she picks up the quiver and slips it over her shoulder so that it rests easily, familiarly, against her back.

Bow in hand, she exits the house as quickly and as quietly as she entered, leaving nothing behind to mark her passing.

**The guards open** the gate for her without query, and she slips into the freedom of open spaces, taking in the beauty of the day and letting the sun work its customary magic on her as she breaks into a trot, headed for the high crest ahead, where she'd found the she-wolf nights before.

She spies several sets of rabbit tracks straight away and smiles. The meat will be perfect to mix with the mash she's already prepared, enabling the injured animals to regain their strength more quickly on food they're accustomed to eating.

She notices that the tracks lead in the direction of the lone tree directly ahead, the tree whose bark litters the ground and whose trunk provides a living monument to the friend she's lost. With a soft sigh, she continues in the direction of the tree, stepping around the huge trunk as the tracks veer off, and stopping, bow hanging slackly from a suddenly limp hand.

Wa Uspewicakiyapi is gone. Only the blood swirling in the rapidly melting snow remains. There are no bits of fur, no drag marks that would indicate a large predator having come upon his corpse. She blinks, and then stares. There, in the fresh muck and gore, lie a fresh set of bootprints of a size and a pattern she knows all too well.

Her lips peel back from her teeth, exposing a snarl more feral than any wolf ever born.

"Tacoma!"

**Numbers. Numbers. There** is some quotation from her Sunday school days that the phrase half recalls, but Kirsten cannot quite bring it to mind. Something about someone's feast. Something about the hand writing on the wall — doom and destruction and more doom. The partial code string that she fed into the miniature transponder Dakota had carried in her raid on the birthing center seems a long-ago triumph, insignificant when laid alongside the measure of their true need.

Numbers. More numbers.

Numbered, that was it. Weighed and...something else. It is not just the seeming snipe hunt her quest for the code has become. Her concentration is off, her mind and body restless with thoughts she has never entertained before, her emotions a hopeless knot of desire and disbelief. She does not have time to untangle them. Even if she achieved the perfect clarity of the enlightened this instant, understanding thudding its way into her head like Newton's apple, it will not matter in the least if she cannot find a means to destroy the androids before they can destroy the remainder of humanity.

She rises, stretches, and rubs at her eyes. Stiffly, because she has scarcely moved for the last two hours, she makes her way into the kitchen and sets water to boil for tea. Asi follows her hopefully, making first for his dish, and, when Kirsten fails to respond with a scoop of kibble, for the door, pawing at it gently. She hates keeping him confined, but will not let him out unsupervised. Not where there are idiots with rifles who use wolves and other creatures for target practice. "Later, boy," she says. "I promise."

Tea made, Kirsten drifts reluctantly back to her worktable. More than once the thought has come to her that the answer is not in the materials she has salvaged from Minot after all, that her frozen trek across the Northern Plains might as well have been cut short at Shiloh, might as well never have been ventured at all.

Except that, had she not pressed on, not made the attempt, she never would have come to this place, where Dakota is. And with that thought comes a feeling of unease, as clear and present as her earlier conviction that Koda had returned safely from her raid. It has been there at the back of her mind for hours, unformed, unacknowledged, no more than half-conscious, inescapable. Kirsten has never credited the idea of intuition — a matter, clearly, of unconsciously processed subliminal clues — much less admitted to having any herself. Yet the certainty that something is wrong has been inexorably worming its way into her attention all morning. A foreboding. She makes a determined effort to set it away from her.

*Shades of the banshees, King. Next you'll be conjuring up your great-great-great-to-the-twenty-third grandma, the druidess, and prattling about the Sight. Or worse, you'll be paying attention to run-off-at-the-mouth raccoons who think they're the freaking Oracle of Delphi.*

The rationalizing does no good. The feeling persists, focuses. Something to do with Dakota. Not physical danger, not violence, but a threat nonetheless.

Kirsten does not know which is more unsettling — that the feeling exists, or that she cannot quite pin it down. She toggles the data files up onto the plasma screen again, attempting to bury her unease in the inexorable march of figures scrolling down from the top into useless oblivion.

Numbers, numbers. All of them useless.

Halfway through a set, Asimov whines and levers himself up from the residual warmth of the hearth, making for the front door at a trot. His high, sharp bark comes at the same instant as the knock. Kirsten follows him into the hall, sudden fear drying her mouth. She flings open the door before the knocker can descend a second time.

"Dakota?" She blurts the name before she can think, knowing full well that, like herself, Dakota has a key. Knowing that, bred to country hospitality as she is, the veterinarian-cum-rancher seems to regard the front door as the "company" entrance.

"Is Koda here?"

The words stumble over hers, echoing her anxiety. Kisten stares up at Tacoma, whose face registers confusion as well as apprehension. Her voice sounds high and strained in her own ears. "What's wrong?"

"I can't find Koda," Tacoma says. "I was hoping she was here."

Kirsten opens the door wide, inviting him in. "What is it?" she repeats. "What's happened?"

Tacoma moves past her, into the living room, Asi on his heels. "Nothing, yet. But I need to talk to her."

"She's not at the clinic?"

"I've just come from there. She's not with the colonel, she's not at the base hospital, she's not at the Judge Advocate's office. I thought she might be with you."

"Oh." *I thought she might be with you.* For some reason, she cannot quite get past that assumption to ask the obvious questions. It makes a small warm spot somewhere around her solar plexus; spreads, rising into her face. Hastily, before he can see, she says, "I'll get you something to drink."

When she comes back with a second cup of tea a moment later, Tacoma has taken off his jacket and is sitting on the couch. His head is bowed, the cool light picking out his profile against the pale sky framed in the window. Asi, as comfortable with him as with his sister, sprawls at his feet, one big hand absently ruffling the fur on the dog's neck. For some reason, that strikes her with a force greater than anything Tacoma has said. She has never seen him with an animal before when he was not entirely present, his attention as fully engaged as with a human. The chill is back.

He hardly notices her when she sets the cup down in front of him, forcing her voice to calm. "What is it? Tell me."

Tacoma picks up the cup in both hands but does not drink. "I need to talk to her," he repeats. "I've done something she—"

He breaks off, and for a moment Kirsten thinks he has said all he will. Then he begins again.

"It's something I had to do. But it's going to hurt her."

For a moment, the image of the woman asleep with the wolves flashes across Kirsten's mind. She knows that Dakota had gone to them for healing; but she knows, too — no, dammit, she feels — the pain that had driven her to it. "I'll help if I can," she says carefully. "But I can't help with what I don't know."

Tacoma shakes his head, his hair coming loose from its thong at the nape of his neck and spreading across his shoulders like a mane. After a moment he says, "You were with her when she found Igmú Tanka Kte."

"Who?"

"The wolf. The one caught in the trap."

"The pup's father."

"The pup's father. You've probably heard that a lot of Native American people have special relationships with certain four-legs or winged ones."

*Try a raccoon with an attitude problem.* But this isn't about her, and aloud she says, "I've heard about it."

"Most people call them totems." A wave of his hand dismisses the word and the idea. "Sometimes they just come to us in dreams, or visions. Sometimes there's a living animal that is the embodiment of that dream spirit."

"And that wolf was..."

"Koda's friend. Not a spirit, not Wolf-with-a-capital-W, but a living companion as individual as you are. A person." He takes a sip of the tea. "Most whites wouldn't understand that. I think you do."

Running her hand over Asi's ruff, Kirsten speaks around the lump in her throat. "Yes. I think I do."

"So you see, what we did — what Manny and Andrews and I did — they brought his body back when they went out to check the traps."

"But what's—" She breaks off. "Dakota doesn't know."

"She doesn't know." Tacoma confirms. "She doesn't know he's in the freezer at the clinic, either."

A shiver passes over Kirsten's skin. Having lost her first Shepherd to dysplasia and her second to a drunken bastard speeding down the street at Twenty-Nine Palms, she knows that veterinarians routinely freeze the bodies of their deceased patients if the owner wants to bury the animal at home. She had helped carry the cold, cold box containing the body of Flandry into the small garden behind the family house at the Marine base the year after she lost her hearing, the silence in her heart as profound as that in her ears. "That was the second blanket, wasn't it? You brought him back to bury?" But she knows that is wrong as soon as the words leave her lips.

"No."

Again a shake of his head, and again it strikes Kirsten how much he reminds her of a big cat.

"They brought him back because he — his body — is witness to what Dietrich was."

"To save Manny's butt," she says bluntly.

"To save Manny's butt," he confirms. "And to show exactly why we have to keep enforcing the laws against the trapping and indiscriminate killing of other living nations, even when we're in the middle of a crisis that could wind up destroying us all. It's about *how* we survive, not just *if* we survive."

"Look," Kirsten says sharply, "I understand what you did. I understand why you need to tell Dakota before she forgodsake opens up the freezer and finds him without warning. But you're sounding like someone who's going to be shot at dawn. Give me some help here. What's the real problem?"

"The real problem — the real problem is that it's a desecration. A desecration of the body of someone my sister loves." He pauses, glancing at her face to see if she is following him at all.

She is not, not entirely, but she says, "Go on."

"It's how we Lakota deal with our dead," he says. "You've seen pictures, maybe in movies, of our traditional burial platforms?"

"Like scaffolds? Out in the open?"

"Like that. It's illegal to bury humans that way, now, because of health regulations. At least, it was." A ghost of a smile touches his face, so like his sister's except for the dark eyes. "But traditional people have always seemed to find a way to get around the law. You'd be surprised at how many empty coffins you'd find if you dug up a cemetery on one of the old reservations."

"But doesn't that leave the body unprotected?"

Tacoma nods. "The whole idea is to leave the body unprotected. To give it back to the earth and the creatures it sustains."

"Just as—"

"Just as other creatures have sustained our lives by their deaths. The body goes back to *mitakuye oyasin*, to all our relations."

Kirsten tries to imagine leaving Flandry's body where he lay bleeding in the street, or even in the open where crows and weasels and other scavengers could tear at it. She cannot. *Because what I did for him was right — for me.* For someone whose beliefs and customs were different, giving a beloved friend to a hole in the earth would seem as wrong as leaving his body in the open would to her. Just as painful. Aloud she says, "You have to tell her."

"I have to tell her. But first I have to find her."

"I'll help. Let me get my jacket, and—"

She is not halfway to her feet when the front door slams open against the wall of the entryway. Boots echo sharply on the floorboards. Dakota Rivers stands in the archway that opens into the room, her hair loose about her face, her chest heaving. Her blue eyes are as cold as the dark between the stars. "There you are," she says in a voice colder still. "Goddamn you, what have you done?"

The man who slowly rises to his feet is her brother. That thought is clear in the part of her mind that remains in the human world. Tacoma, her twin in all but the day of his birth, as close as if they had shared the floating darkness of their mother's womb. It is all that stops Dakota from launching herself across the room at him. Her vision holds him in the bright center of encroaching darkness, the hunter-sight that narrows until it focuses on the prey and the prey alone.

Vaguely she is aware of another presence in the room, shifting form as the light pulses with every slam of her heart against her breastbone, now human, now not. Her blood howls in her veins, adrenaline sending shock after shock through nerves that she wills not to respond. Dry as old cotton, her mouth struggles to shape human speech. She says again, laying the words down like stones, "What have you done with him?"

In all their lives, Tacoma has never spoken less than truth to her. At some level, she knows that the shadow in his eyes is not a lie but uncertainty — not over what to tell her, but how. She waits in frozen silence, her anger gone all to ice within her.

After a moment, he says, "We brought him back to the clinic, Dakota."

The cold within her goes more frigid still. There is only one place in the clinic he can be. Just to make certain, she asks, "In the freezer? Is that why the keys weren't on the hook this morning?"

"Yes," he answers quietly, "to both questions."

"I scolded Shannon for losing them." She makes a small, futile gesture with one hand. It seems to move of its own volition, apart from her will. "I should have believed her when she said she hadn't been careless."

"I'm sorry. I didn't mean for her to be blamed. I was looking for you just now to tell you."

Slowly color fades back into the edges of her vision, expanding the space around Tacoma to include the rust-red bricks of hearth behind him, the puzzled face of Asimov, head canted to one side, Kirsten, her eyes wide with something that is part fear, part pain. Some of her anger goes out of her then, leaving emptiness behind. And yet, she knows that Kirsten's fear is for her, not of her; the pain endured for her. She lets some of the anger flow out of her on a sigh. "Why, Tacoma? For God's sake, why?"

Tacoma hesitates, and Koda realizes that he is choosing his words carefully.

"To be a witness, *tanksi*. Partly to show that Manny shot a man who was violent and dangerous and had earned his death. And more importantly, to show what we — we humans, all of us — can fall back to all too easily."

"We've already begun to slip, Dakota." Kirsten interrupts softly. "Think about that mob at the gate, and the bastards who shot the mother wolf out of sheer cruelty. We — all of us, the scraps of our society — can go back to living as we did a hundred years ago. Or we can make something different."

Stepping softly, Tacoma crosses the space separating him from his sister and holds out his hand to her. "The buffalo can come back, Koda. Igmú Tanka Kte's son and his grandsons can run free on the plains again. Puma can come down from the mountain and out of the desert where she has been driven by too many guns, too little care for life."

Tacoma is not a shaman, but Koda can see the vision clear in his eyes and does not doubt its truth. A shiver ghosts over her skin. The prophecy is an ancient one, brought to the Lakota people along with the sacred pipe and the seven ceremonies. In an age long past, Ptecincala Ska Wakan Winan, White Buffalo Calf Woman, foretold the restoration of the Earth and all her children, the return of nations long since passed over to walk the Blue Road of spirit. Their father's great grandfather had danced the Ghost Dance to bring that restoration nearer. His father and mother had danced, too, and had died for it in a hail of U.S. Cavalry bullets. Wanblee Wakpa himself wore the hummingbird shirt and stamped the measure of the dance into the dry earth of Pine Ridge during the uprising of '73. "The time of the white buffalo is coming," Dakota says. "You see it."

"I see it. I see it as clearly as I see you, *tanski*."

"And was it necessary to desecrate Igmú Tanka Kte's body for your vision, *thiblo*?" The edge is back in Koda's voice. "Do you think Ina Maka can't do it without you? That is pride speaking."

"And that is pain speaking, Dakota." The soft voice is Kirsten's. The young woman's face is as pale as moon shadow on snow, but her eyes are resolute. "He was your teacher, wasn't he? Let him teach others, too."

"Don't let his death go for nothing, *tanksi*." Tacoma reaches for her hand, and this time Dakota allows him to enfold it in his own. "Neither you nor I nor Kirsten can say anything that will speak as clearly as his suffering."

"You know there will be attempts to excuse Dietrich, Dakota," Kirsten says. "People will tell themselves and each other that he was only trying to make a little extra money for his family, if he had one. They will say that we need fur now to keep us warm. That he was doing a service; that the uprising has made all our environmental protections obsolete. If we are to keep those laws, as we must, abstract arguments won't work. What happened to your wolf will."

Trapped between their love and their logic, Koda is pinned like a display specimen; there is nowhere for her to go. Salt stings her eyes, tears she will not permit herself. She lowers her face so that they cannot see and says quietly around the cold that still burns raw in along her nerves, "He taught and protected me, and there was nothing I could do when he needed me." Suddenly her rage tears through the wall she has built around it, ripping through her like a terrible birth. "I didn't even know, goddamit. I should have known. I should have."

*Should have known he was in trouble. Should have known he was dying.* Should have known better than to leave him lying in the melting snow, no matter how burying him would have gone against tradition and her own deeply held conviction of the interdependence of all life. *He never failed me, and I have failed him when it counted most.*

Gently she removes her hand from Tacoma's. "*Wicate*," she says. Stepping away, she lets herself out into the spring morning, her feet carrying her blindly where they will.

**The door closes** behind Dakota with a snap like a spine breaking. Involuntarily, Kirsten takes a step forward to follow her, then checks herself abruptly. The jolt of it goes through her body as sharply as if she had walked into plate glass; the barrier transparent, invisible, strong. Over her shoulder, she looks up at Tacoma, whose eyes are as wide and dark with pain as his sister's.

He turns back to the fireplace, supporting himself against the mantel with both hands, his head bowed. "Christ," he says, between his teeth. "Jesus. Fucking. Christ. Is there any way I could possibly have done it any worse than that?"

Kirsten steps up behind him and silently lays a hand on his shoulder. "Is there any way you could have done it that would have been less painful? No matter what you did or said, it was going to hurt her." After a moment, she says, "You're right, you know."

"Oh, I know that." He shakes his head, the dark hair spreading across his shoulders like a lion's mane. "She knows it, you know it, everybody and his bastard brother knows it. And it doesn't really matter a damn."

"What we make of our world from now on matters. She knows that, too."

"She knows that better than most of us." Tacoma pushes himself away from the fireplace, turns again to face her. "Give her a while, then go after her. She's going to need you."

Kirsten feels the heat spread up her throat and into her face. *Is it as obvious as that?* Aloud she says, "Shouldn't you—"

"No. Not now." From his pocket, he produces a pair of silver keys on a ring. "Give her these. I've got to get a team together to try to move a couple of generators from the wind farm. I'll see her before I go."

For long moments after the door shuts for a second time, Kirsten stands staring at the two small pieces of metal in her palm. From somewhere deep in her memory comes the image of a blue butterfly, fluttering its wings: the flutter starting a breeze; the breeze becoming a wind; the wind feeding a hurricane. Not even in Minot, with her fingers on the keys of the one computer whose codes could set the world to rights, did she feel the future so light in her hand.

She can hide the keys. She can take them back to the clinic and hang them in their accustomed place on the board. Or she can take them to Dakota and trust her to make the right choice through her anger and her pain.

For a moment she turns the keys over in her fingers. They take the light from the window, glinting in the strengthening sun. Truth or dare? Truth, or risk the loss of something she has never dared hope for, in all her life, for whatever life there may be left.

No choice at all, really. She slips the keys into her pocket and goes in search of her windbreaker.

Half an hour later she stands beneath the sycamore tree where the land falls away toward the woods. The snow has melted from the pavement; elsewhere it lies in meager patches, cupped in tangles of root and the blue shadow of the hollow slope. There is nothing to hold the print of a foot, only the smooth surface of the cement and the remains of last summer's grass, the faintest hint of green just visible through the matted stalks. A gust of air ghosts over the dry meadow, further obliterating any sign of passage. Dakota might be able to track her quarry down a sidewalk or over dead grass, but Kirsten has no such skill, and she has left Asi at home.

*Now what?*

The veterinary clinic is a possibility. The memory of Dakota sleeping beside the widowed she-wolf and her pup comes to Kirsten as intensely as if she still stood at the door of the isolation ward. Koda might go there again in search of comfort, but the clinic also houses the body of her beloved companion. A shiver passes over Kirsten at the thought. The clinic seems haunted now, not so much by the wolf's spirit as by the human memory of his death. Or Dakota may have left the base altogether, gone out into the solitude of the surrounding hills.

Kirsten does not know her way through the surrounding countryside. If she is to leave the base, she will have to return for Asi, possibly requisition a vehicle. The idea of tracking Dakota cross country with a dog, even Asi who clearly regards Koda as his second human, revolts her. Shading her eyes with her hand, she squints into the sun, standing down now halfway from noon. A ray catches the handful of snow still lingering in the fork of a limb directly above her and it shatters into rainbows, light spiraling outward in all the shades of the spectrum. Perched on the branch, just visible within the spinning brilliance, sits a dark shape with a masked face and golden eyes.

"Lost, are you?"

Kirsten cannot tell whether the voice speaks in the lifting breeze or only in her head. "You again," she snaps. "Go away. I don't have time for hallucinations right now."

"Don't you want to know what I can tell you?"

"I want to know where Dakota Rivers is. Can you tell me that?"

A grin splits Wika Tegalega's face. "Of course I can. Ask me nicely, and I might even answer."

Kirsten's patience, what there is of it, snaps. "Then tell me, goddammit! You're nothing but a figment of my unconscious mind, anyway!"

"Tch," says Tega, mournfully, shaking his head. "Was that nice?" His image seems to recede behind the shifting light, itself fading back into the deep blue of the sky.

"Wait!" she cries, reaching out toward the branch above her head. "Please! Tell me."

"Go fish," he says, and is gone.

When Kirsten lowers her hand, blinking against the sun, there is only the empty sky and the branch, the last handful of snow trickling down the channels of its pale bark. She shakes her head in disgust. She desperately needs to find Dakota; she has no idea where to look; and the most constructive thing she can do is stand bemused, conversing with an imaginary raccoon with a warped sense of humor. It occurs to her that she may well have lost her mind, or at least a significant portion of it. *And not a shrink within a thousand miles, maybe more.*

Go fish.

Fish. A small silver fish wriggling in a furry, long-fingered hand. A stream and a tree arching over it.

As certainly as she had known of Dakota's return from her solo raid on the birthing center, Kirsten knows where she can find the other woman. It is an unaccustomed sort of knowledge, rooted somewhere beyond the borders of rationality, direct and unmediated. It does not even occur to her to question it. Deliberately at first, then almost running across the uneven ground, Kirsten sets off toward the woods.

Once in the trees, she slows her pace. She does not have the skill of silent movement that she has seen in Dakota, but she can avoid crunching dead bark underfoot or tangling herself in the tough, dry stems of trailing vines. The afternoon light filters through the woven branches overhead, laying a sheen of gold and copper over the brown stalks of last summer's undergrowth, striking the sycamores' skin to silver. A red squirrel, its coat glinting like russet velvet in the sun, scampers among the slender twigs of the canopy. From deep in the trees comes the trip-hammer drumming of an early woodpecker, his rhythm making point counterpoint to the beating of her own heart. Here and there the branches bear the first swellings of leaves. The ground beneath her carries the musty odor of mold, mixed with the green life to come.

Though she has been here twice, Kirsten does not know the woods, and she lets her feet and her instinct carry her unerringly to the streamside where she first encountered Wika Tegalega. Quiet descends upon her as she moves deeper into the trees, slowing her pulse, stilling the rustling of the dead leaves and the small life that inhabits them. The birds and the squirrels' feet grow silent. The feeling is not unfamiliar; she has known it among the standing stones at Amesbury, in the angled light and lingering incense of Notre Dame. The sacredness of this place prickles along her skin.

Kirsten hears the stream before she can see it. The water, swollen with snow melt, makes a soft rushing sound as it pours over the low cataracts of its limestone bed and swirls around the roots of the centuries-old sycamores that march along its banks. When she emerges, still soundlessly, from the screen of the trees, Kirsten can see that its speed casts a fine spume into the air, misting the surface of the water and the slopes leading down to it. One tree, larger than the others, looms over the breadth of the stream, its roots, thick as a man's body, woven into the living rock at its base. Dakota sits among them, her feet braced against a humped root. Her elbows rest on her bent knees, her chin on her folded hands. For a moment it seems to Kirsten that the other woman has been weeping; but fine droplets spangle her dark hair as well as her cheeks. And then Kirsten catches sight of Dakota's eyes, dry and grey and empty as a winter sky. The sight stops Kirsten in her tracks, her breath catching in her throat. *Christ. Now what? I don't know what to say to a face like that.*

A month ago, a week ago, she would have turned away, retreating behind the barricades of her mind into the silence that a mere touch behind her ear could bring. Even now, her first impulse is flight, the long muscles in her legs spasming in her urgency to be gone.

Her fear has no place in this clearing. The power of earth and air and water here is an almost palpable thing, holding her fast. For a long moment she stands and watches the motionless form beside the swirling water. There is no acknowledgement, nothing that signals acceptance or even consciousness of her presence.

*What can I say to her?*

But that is the wrong question.

Silently as a shadow, she crosses the small open space beneath the sycamores. Half a dozen steps bring her close enough to see the minute rise and fall of the dark blue and green plaid flannel across Dakota's shoulders, and the relief that washes through her tells her just how much she has feared. A few more steps carry her to the tangle of roots that spread out almost as widely as the crown of the tree. Koda still gives no sign that she is aware of Kirsten's presence.

*What if...*

She has heard that it is dangerous to touch a person who is in a trance state. An out-of-body soul might lose its lifeline and never come home, wandering forever in the grey interstices between worlds.

*And that,* she thinks with the certainty of recognition, *is what I am. Have been. A homeless soul.*

*And here, here at last, is my home.*

Very carefully, so as to make no sudden noise, Kirsten steps among the roots, placing her feet among the gnarled spirals, steadying herself against the trunk with an outstretched hand. Near the base of the tree, beneath a hollow large enough to hold a grown woman, a knot juts out at waist level, its blunt wedge shape suggestive of the head of a great serpent rising above the coiled roots. A jolt of recognition goes through Kirsten.

*Snake Mother, Earth Mother, Keeper of the Tree of Knowledge — grant me wisdom.*

She closes the space between herself and Koda, and drops silently to her knees. Very gently, she slips her arms around Dakota's waist, leaning her head against the other woman's strong shoulder. For an instant, Koda's back stiffens against her, then relaxes, settling to Kirsten's shape as if their bodies had been molded one for the other. After a moment, Dakota's hand covers both of hers where they rest against her waist. It is chill as death.

Time passes. The sun slips lower in the sky, angling through the trunks of the trees, turning them to columns of gold and silver. Finally, her hand warm now, Dakota stirs. "You found me," she says.

Rubbing her cheek lightly against Dakota's shoulder, she answers. "I followed. Where you go, I will go."

Dakota's hand enfolds Kirsten's, raises it to her lips. The kiss is light as a breath of air. "My people will be your people. My home is your home."

From somewhere deep in her memory, archaic words rise to Kirsten's tongue. "Faith and truth will I bear to you, to live or die." *In this life, in the next. For all time.*

When the shadows begin to thicken about them, Koda lets her breath go on a long sigh. "We should go back."

Reluctantly, Kirsten lets her arms fall from Dakota's waist. "I suppose we should."

Koda stands, extending a hand to help Kirsten up. It is not until they are once again at the door of the house and she must find her keys that she lets go.

**The house is** cool and quiet as they enter. The trees outside the windows cast moving shadows across the opposite wall like the outspread arms of dancers swaying to a beat only they can hear. The sound of nails clicking across the polished floor heralds the entrance of Asi, who comes over to greet them, taking healthy sniffs of their clothing before presenting his head and body to be scratched.

Koda notices a folded sheet of paper ruffling in the breeze and walks over to the kitchen table, sliding it out from under the salt-shaker-cum-paperweight and bringing it closer to her face in deference to the swiftly fading light. The page is covered with Maggie's bold, flowing script.

Dakota, Kirsten:

I'm gathering up some of my men and setting up a census-taking crew for the base. I think it's about time we figure out who and what we have here, and what skills we might be able to use, both in the short and long term.

I'd like to do the same thing with the outlying cities, just to see where we stand. Kirsten, if you don't mind, I'd like to have you accompany me to Rapid City tomorrow so we can get a first-hand look at what we've got left — resource and humanity wise. Finding a judge is one of our first priorities. If we can't find one, any half-way competent lawyer will have to do. I'm not optimistic about either of those chances, but it's a pressing need we have to fill.

Don't expect me home tonight. I'll bunk in the barracks and see you at 0800.

Maggie

"Looks like you've got a full day tomorrow," Koda remarks, handing the note over.

Kirsten's quick eyes scan the writing and she frowns. "Well, it isn't something I was planning on, but I suppose..." She scans the note again. She knows the value and desperate need of the census; it was she, in fact, who had suggested it to Maggie in the first place. But she had hoped, truly and dearly, that she would be allowed to play grunt and sit behind a table with pencil and pad in hand, taking names. The subtext of the note she holds dashes those hopes like bone china beneath a bull's hoof.

"Crap," she half-whispers as she crumples the note into a ball and tosses it into the trash. "Just...crap. I hate being used as a figurehead."

"You could always say no." Koda's practical advice is delivered with a faint smirk and a lift of her eyebrow.

Kirsten thinks about it for a moment, then shakes her head. "No," she sighs. "Maggie's right. If we want to get this done the right way, and that takes me marching at the head of this little parade, then I'll just have to suck it up and get it done. Hopefully, it won't take very long."

"Mm."

"So," Kirsten says in a deliberately bright tone, needing the subject tabled for now, "are you hungry?"

"Not really." In truth, since *Wa Uspewicakiyapi's* death, grief has placed a leaden ball in her belly; a ball that does not share its space with food well at all.

Kirsten catches the dimming of those brilliant eyes and holds back a sigh. "There's some soup left over from last night," she continues, as if

Koda had answered in the affirmative. "If you'll do me the favor of taking Asi out, I'll heat it up."

A quick glance from Koda lets Kirsten know her plan has been transparent, but, with a shrug of her broad shoulders, the vet signals Asi and crosses the kitchen, opening the door as the large dog bolts outside, bellowing like a calf over his sudden, and welcome, freedom.

As she puts the pot on to simmer, Kirsten's eyes are drawn to the scene outside the small kitchen window. Asi, sides heaving with exertion, trots back to Dakota, bringing back a "stick" the size of a tree branch and dropping it at her feet. He then sits, his body shaking in canine ecstasy, eyes rolling, jaws quivering, and tail wagging so rapidly that the tall grass around him all but leaps out of the way.

Kirsten can't help but smile, hearing the delightful sound of Koda's laughter as she picks up the slimy stick and flings it far across the lawn, farther than Kirsten could ever throw, even on her best day. Asi bolts after it as if his tail's aflame, barking joyfully all the while. The setting sun glints sparks of red from Koda's glossy black hair in a way that Kirsten finds extremely appealing.

As if sensing the attention, Koda turns, and their eyes lock for a timeless moment. Which is, unfortunately, broken much too soon by an insistent German Shepherd and his stick. Shaking her head ruefully, Kirsten turns back to her task, taking a wooden spoon from the drawer and stirring the soup as Asi's yaps and barks soothe the air around her.

**Koda looks up** from her book as Kirsten rounds the couch and sets down a tray holding two steaming bowls and a loaf of French bread on the coffee table. The fire is blazing cheerfully, chasing off the evening chill, and Asi jumps up from his place beside it, sniffing with great interest. His ears and tail soon droop, however, as he is banished to Kirsten's bedroom with a pointed look from his mistress.

Dakota lays aside the book she's been reading just in time to receive the warm bowl that is thrust into her hands.

Ignoring the look she's receiving, Kirsten digs into her soup with gusto, enjoying both the warmth and the hearty flavor. A moment later, and with a sigh, Koda does the same, grudgingly admitting, if only to herself, that this simple meal does indeed hit the spot.

They are both quickly done, sopping the last of the soup with the thick, crusty bread and laying their bowls back on the tray. Asi has wormed his way back into the room and lies once again next to the fire, head on his massive paws, snoring away.

Kirsten and Koda sit in companionable silence, looking into the cheery flames as if messages can be divined there. After a moment, Kirsten speaks, "It's so quiet, you know? I mean, yeah, we're in the middle of God's Country and all that, but even so, I keep expecting to hear car horns and televisions and telephones and things that we all took for granted. And now..." She slumps back into the couch's warm comfort, still staring into the flames.

"Do you miss those things?" Koda asks softly.

"Sometimes," Kirsten answers honestly. "Technology was a big part of who I was...who I am. Sometimes I wonder how I'll cope without it. How we'll all cope."

"We'll be fine." Dakota's voice is filled with a certainty that Kirsten envies. "Technology, or at least bits and pieces of it, will be around for a long time to come. I just think we'll come to rely on it a good deal less than we once did."

"Considering the fact that technology did all this, I suppose that won't really be a bad thing."

The two exchange smiles.

Kirsten yawns, then blushes. "Sorry."

"Don't be. It's been a long day. And an even longer one tomorrow."

"Don't remind me," Kirsten groans.

Laughing softly, Koda rises from the couch and holds out a hand. Kirsten grasps it willingly and allows herself to be pulled gently to her feet. She looks toward the dirty dishes.

"Leave 'em. I'll take care of washing tonight. I need to go back to the clinic and check on Mama Wolf and her pup anyway."

"But—"

"Go to sleep."

With a small sigh, Kirsten gives in, nodding. "Good night, then."

Koda smiles. "Good night."

Their eyes meet again, and this time, there is no hesitation. Both step forward. Kirsten's chin rises, and Koda's lowers, and their lips meet softly, gently. The kiss lingers, then deepens, and Kirsten can't help the soft moan that sounds as Koda's tongue brushes tenderly against her lips before withdrawing.

Both are breathing heavily as they part with shining eyes and goofy grins. Reaching up, Koda trails the back of her knuckles against Kirsten's soft cheek, then steps back, her expression one of quiet joy. "Good night, Kirsten."

With that, Koda gathers up the tray, turns, and heads for the kitchen, leaving Kirsten to stare after her, fingers to her lips and a look of absolute wonder on her face.

# CHAPTER TWENTY-FOUR

The motorcycle comes to a purring halt just outside a well maintained house set well back in the woods. The windows facing the gravel driveway are open to their widest, and the warm breeze causes the homely checked curtains to rustle pleasantly. Jeans-clad legs come down to rest easily on either side of the bike, balancing it comfortably as the engine is turned off.

A male voice, elderly but still strong, floats out from the house. "I suppose I should warn you that at this very moment there are seven weapons of various gauges pointed directly at you, and wired to all go off at once. If you're an android, that might not kill you, but I believe it would make your job just a bit harder. And if you're a human..."

Long, strong hands reach up and remove the black helmet, causing equally black hair to cascade down in shining waves. "Nice welcome you've got there, Judge," the sultry voice replies. "You have it in needlepoint hanging over your mantelpiece, too?"

There is a moment of shocked silence, then, "Is it time to get my glasses changed, or is that really Dakota Rivers darkening my doorstep?"

Koda laughs as she hooks her helmet over the handlebar of the motorcycle. "I dunno. Which answer won't get me ventilated?"

"Ahh," comes the dry reply. "Your wit, like a poor vintage, goes to vinegar with age, Ms. Rivers."

"So do your manners, you old curmudgeon," Dakota mutters, not quite under her breath.

"I heard that!"

"You were meant to."

A moment later, he says, "Well? Don't just stand there propping up that two-wheeled death machine; I haven't seen a human face in a goodly number of weeks. Yours will, I suppose, be suitable enough."

"That's what I like about you, Judge," Dakota replies, swinging her leg over the cycle and leaning it down on its kickstand. "You're all charm."

"Thank you," comes the prim reply. "I do try."

Striding down the neatly tended walk, Dakota grasps the doorknob and twists. The door opens easily and she steps inside, eyeing the impressive armory of shotguns and rifles, all pointing toward the windows. "You weren't kidding," she remarks, whistling softly.

"Have you ever known me to kid?"

Without bothering to reply, Koda moves her gaze from the weapons in a casual sweep around the house. It's the same as she remembers it, the domain of a single, proud man, a lifelong bachelor with only two passions in life: the law — evidenced by the rows and rows of leather-bound tomes that take up the huge floor-to-ceiling bookshelves covering three of the four walls, and birds — or, more accurately, the watching, cataloguing, and photographing of them. Evidence of this passion can be seen on the remaining wall. Beautiful photos fill the huge space over the mantle of the stone fireplace.

Drawn to them as always, her eyes scan the photos, appreciating their beauty, when she notices one sitting on the corner of the mantelpiece, and she finds herself smiling. It is a picture she knows well, especially since she is one of its main subjects. It shows a winter field, blanketed in heavy snow. One lone tree stands in the background, adding perspective. In the foreground, Dakota, clad in leather, holds out a gauntleted fist as a swooping Wiyo, massive wings spread out to their widest point, comes to land.

"I remember that day," the judge reflects, drawing a finger across a weathered cheek. Fenton Harcourt is a tall man, still strapping despite his advanced age, with a shock of snow white hair and a face filled with stern lines that only the occasional twinkle in his deep brown eyes seems to belie. "It was colder than a witch's mammary and twice as harsh."

Chuckling, Koda draws her finger lightly across the picture, not quite touching the glass that protects the print from the elements. It was the first time Wiyo had come at her call and landed on her wrist. She can almost feel the deadly strength of those talons on her arm now — a grip so strong, and yet somehow so tender, that she knew at the time that even if she hadn't been wearing the gauntlet, her skin would not have been pierced.

Dakota turns from the photo finally, meeting the older man's deep-set eyes. They share a moment of perfect understanding. Judge Harcourt loves Wiyo almost as fiercely as she does. Just as he had loved and cared for Wiyo's brother, who was brought down by a drunken idiot with a penchant for shooting birds. That man would have been dead by Harcourt's own hand, judge or no judge, if he hadn't jumped into his pickup truck and promptly driven it into a tree, turning himself into hamburger flambé.

The judge had mourned the loss of the bird, mourned as he never would for a fellow human. It was as if he had lost a part of himself in the death of the wild one he had helped to raise from a hatchling. And that loss changed him, profoundly and permanently.

"So," he says finally, breaking the silence between them, "I assume there's a purpose for this visit, beyond assuring yourself of my current state of liveliness?"

Koda snorts. "You're too evil to die, old man."

Harcourt tries to look offended, but the glitter in his eyes once again belies the stern, craggy lines of his face. "Alas, you've discovered my secret. Whatever will the Society of Crazed and Evil Immortals think? We're the only group to have survived this latest human debacle intact, you know," he adds in a mockingly conspiratorial stage whisper.

Koda rolls her eyes, then turns serious. "I need your help."

The judge's bushy eyebrows rise like two white caterpillars perched atop his glasses. "My help? Whatever for? In case you haven't noticed, Ms. Rivers, I'm rapidly approaching eighty. I'm afraid my days of heroic derring-do are long over."

"I'm not asking for heroism; I'm asking for help," Koda bites off as she breaks his gaze and looks out into the springtime day. "Look. I've moved down to the base to try and help take care of this mess. Women are being kept in prisons all over this country, raped repeatedly, and forced to bear children for reasons we haven't yet figured out. We've managed to survive another android attack, and the survivors are coming through the gates in a never-ending stream." She sighs, slipping her hands into her pockets. "At first, we just had the usual 'settling in' problems, but lately things have been getting worse, in a big way."

"Yea, verily, I say unto you," Harcourt's dry voice intrudes, "wherever two or more are gathered, they'll spend their time bashing the stuffing out of one another."

Koda's smile is faint and disappears quickly. "That's becoming the size of it, yeah."

"I'm failing to see the problem here," Harcourt remarks. "Surely there are enough military types still alive on that base to adjudicate their own affairs with a reasonable degree of swiftness and accuracy." He holds up one arthritis humped finger. "You'll notice my use of the word 'reasonable', here. I, myself, wouldn't trust a military court to judge whether or not my shoes were tied. However, it is their domain, is it not?"

Cutting her gaze from the window, she eyes him evenly.

His eyebrows go up again. "I'm missing something, I presume."

"Did you ever hear a state of war or emergency declared?" she asks simply.

He ponders for a moment. "I don't believe so, no."

She continues to stare at him until his eyes finally widen in comprehension. "No. No, my dear, and no again. I will not be a party to a pitiful and doomed attempt to prolong the last gasp of a species who should have become extinct before they were allowed to breed. Humankind has finally heard the Judgment Trumpet blown, and I say it's about damn time."

"Judge..."

"No, Dakota. No. The body of Man is getting exactly what it deserves. And I, for one, fully intend to enjoy what is left of my life here on this planet in a state of peaceful relaxation, free from the petty concerns of a dying society. I have my books. I have my birds — I spotted a Cassin's Sparrow just yesterday, by the way. Only the second sighting in this area, I'll have you know. Too bad there's no longer anyone around who gives a whit. No, I'm quite afraid you'll have to find someone else to aid you with the postmortem. I've retired from the species." Dakota's gaze goes far away, and Harcourt feels a sense of disquiet niggling its way into his hardened heart.

"Wa Uspewicakiyapi is dead. He was caught in an illegal trap and attacked by predators. I noticed his mate first. She was looking for help and a couple of drunk assholes were taking potshots at her for shits and giggles. I was able to rescue her. She was starving, bleeding, and had obviously dropped an early litter. When I found the pups, all were dead save one. Wiyo led me to Wa Uspewicakiyapi. There was...nothing I could do for him. His life was..." Pulling her hands out of her pockets, she stares at them as if they are foreign objects. "I killed him."

Harcourt's eyes close in sympathy, his face set and grim.

Koda's jaw clenches, the muscles in her face pronounced. "And now he's locked up in a freezer on the base...for evidence." The word comes out like evacuated poison.

"Evidence? For what?"

"Manny and a friend killed the trapper. He'd snared several other animals in his illegal traps. They were rescuing them when he found them and drew a bead on them. They acted in self-defense, and Tacoma believes that Wa Uspewicakiyapi's body is needed to prove their innocence."

Such is her state of agitation that she doesn't see or hear the judge move, and so stiffens slightly as a large, warm hand is placed on her shoulder in a gesture of support. "I need your help, Fenton. Humanity might be dying out, but it's taking down a lot of others as it goes — innocents who don't deserve what's being done to them. I need someone I respect and trust, and that someone is you." She turns to face him, feeling his hand slide away. "Please. Help me."

Harcourt's eyes are sad. "Dakota..."

"You won't have to move there, Fenton. We'll set something up so it'll be like the old West. Have all the cases lumped together once or twice a month. I'll even have a driver come down to pick you up and drop you off back home." She's perfectly aware that she's begging, but knows as well that this is much more important than her pride.

The sudden silence is as long and sharp as a shadow-blade dividing the space between them. Dakota relaxes, knowing she's done the best she can and can only accept his decision, whatever it might be.

His hands clench in tightly made fists, but a reluctant nod is pulled from him, like a confession pulled from a lawbreaker when he realizes the consequences of remaining silent. "I have conditions," he remarks in a soft voice.

"Name them."

"I'll reserve that right until I set my eyes upon this new Xanadu, if you don't mind."

"Fine."

He nods again. "Store that death trap of yours behind the house. We'll leave in my truck."

"Thank you, Fenton," she says with real emotion.

"Save that for my final decision. Now let's go."

**"It reminds me** of the Warsaw ghetto."

Maggie, sitting beside her in the back of the APC, raises a quizzical eyebrow, and Kirsten falls silent. The convoy of armored vehicles moves slowly through the streets of Rapid City, strung out the length of a city block to allow maneuvering room in the event of attack. Their shadows, spiked with the bristling shapes of automatic weapons, glide along the asphalt beside the trucks, as sharp-edged as spilled paint in the noon sun.

After a moment Kirsten adds, "I don't mean the buildings are similar. I mean..." She pauses again, searching for the precise word. "They feel...robbed."

Maggie, her hand resting on the M-16 in her lap, does not reply immediately. Then she says, "It's not just the emptiness, it's the devastation."

"Exactly."

The weeks she has spent on the base have spoiled her, Kirsten reflects. Even in the first days of the uprising, with bodies frozen or rotting where they lay, according to the whim of the weather, she has seen nothing like the urban landscape that scrolls across the small rectangle of the vehicle's armored glass. Houses still stand, for the most part, though here and there blackened beams thrust up out of the yet-unmelted snow that covers the burnt-out rubble. Some, their windows boarded up, might have been purposely abandoned when the inhabitants fled. Like the others suddenly emptied, though, their doors stand open on broken hinges, odd bits of furniture and clothing scattered across dead lawns sodden with snowmelt. Brightly painted ceramic shards litter the sidewalk where the convoy pauses to turn; the wire frame of a lampshade jammed into the hollow of a tree root; the remains of sofa cushions tumbled across a porch where a washing machine lies toppled beside them. Shards of glass cling to the frame of broken out windows. Here and there a line of holes in splintered siding or gouged brick testifies to automatic weapons fire. There is no way to tell how much of the damage has been done by androids, and how much by the looters and two-footed predators who have followed in their wake.

As they move toward the center of the city, signs of life begin to appear. In the abandoned parking lot of an apartment complex, a pair of ten-year-old boys and a cocker spaniel are chasing a Frisbee under the watchful eye of a grey-haired woman with a pistol strapped to her hip. Above them, laundry festoons a cobweb of ropes strung between balconies — children's sweaters in bright pink and yellow, work shirts, a woman's nightgown in faded black satin and lace. Across the side of one of the buildings, red paint proclaims: JESUS IS COMING BACK!! under a crudely drawn image of a bearded man in a robe. The figure brandishes a sword with one hand, an open book in the other.

"You know, the fanatics scare me as badly as the androids," Maggie says softly. "The damned metalheads might push us back to the Middle Ages, but it'll be the schizos who hear God talking to them from the toaster that'll keep us there."

"They're beginning to dig in. We may have to fight them, too."

"Ironic, isn't it? First we put down the slave rebellion; next we're going to have to feed the fanatics and the self-appointed prophets to the lions."

"Poor lions." Kirsten's mouth quirks up in an involuntary smile. "You know Dakota would never let us do that to innocent animals."

"Or Tacoma. He's the one with the affinity for cats." Maggie leans forward and taps the driver on the shoulder. "We're getting around people. Start the tape."

Kirsten knows what to expect, but the sound of her own amplified voice is still a shock. The truck's external speakers sputter and crackle for a moment, then boom out, "Attention! Attention please! This is Kirsten King, speaking for the United States Government. A census will be taken today and tomorrow at the city auditorium. All citizens are asked to cooperate in determining the needs of the civilian population and in the re-establishment of civil institutions. Thank you for your assistance." The recording plays over and over again.

As they approach the intersection of suburbia and the business district, signs of habitation become more frequent. Occasionally they pass a pedestrian or a bicyclist. A man on a mule, a double pannier of winter apples suspended across its withers, becomes an unofficial roadblock when his mount halts suddenly in the middle of an intersection, apparently frightened by the strange, square metal things bearing down on him. The lead driver manages to swerve in time, and for an instant Kirsten finds herself face to face with a wall-eyed, bucking beast, its braying clearly audible even through the bulletproof glass and steel walls of the APC. Then her convoy sweeps past, leaving the rider tugging frantically at the creature's reins.

"There's a prophecy for you," Maggie observes wryly. "The Jeep of the future."

Their route carries them past the block-long remains of a Wal-Mart. The store itself stands back from the street, its massive bulk dark through the steel frames of shattered doors. Its parking lot, though, has been transformed into an open marketplace, with a hundred or so booths of timber studs and plywood crowded onto the asphalt. Many of them stand empty, and Kirsten takes that as a hopeful sign that the proprietors have reported as requested to the city auditorium to be counted and identified. Others are still open for business. A pen on one side holds animals with long, shaggy coats, whether sheep or wool goats she cannot be sure. Another offers stacks of canned goods, looted from the Wal-Mart itself or other grocery chains; still a third displays a double rank of bicycles, a heavy chain run through their rear wheels into a staple pounded into the pavement at each end of the line. Under a sign that proclaims the occupant a "Taylor", a woman sits at an old-fashioned treadle sewing machine, steadily feeding a garment of plaid flannel under the needle while a man, evidently her customer, stands by in his pants and undershirt. He holds a chicken firmly tucked under one arm. No prices are posted anywhere.

Kirsten has seen marketplaces like this in North Africa and in parts of Latin America. Most were at least in part tourist traps, designed to bring in American dollars and EU euros, attracting local business only incidentally and in small volume. A cold lump of fear congeals in her stomach. With it comes the realization that until now she has acknowledged only two possibilities: either they would all die, which has seemed by far the more likely outcome; or they would survive, pass through a rough patch of perhaps a year or so, until society could be restored to something like normalcy. Of course, some things would be different for a generation or two, with the numbers of men drastically reduced. Power balances would shift. But she has never truly doubted that enough technology, and the technicians to run it, could survive to make the world a reasonably comfortable place once again. Until now.

And the cold grows more frigid still, a burning inside her. She — she, Kirsten King — is the duly constituted governor of these people, responsible for their safety and welfare in a world where safety is nonexistent, and welfare is sufficient firewood to cook a bartered chicken or keep a family from freezing to death overnight. She may not have atomic warheads under her hand, but the burden of others' lives is no less for that.

*My God, how did Clinton do it? Or Kennedy? How did any of them do it who had any sense of obligation to their people?*

In the last few blocks before the auditorium, they encounter actual traffic, and the convoy slows to a crawl. There are pickups from the countryside, more bicycles, horses, a wagon or two. Salvaged from the recesses of a barn or an historic home, a nineteenth-century buggy with a folded-down leather top passes them at a smart clip, followed by a teenager on a skateboard. Most folk, though, travel on foot, some carrying small children, almost all carrying a long gun or pistol strapped to a hip or under an arm. All must run a gauntlet of heavily armed and armored MPs stationed at a temporary gate of pipe and hurricane fencing. They wave through the personal weapons, for the most part, though no one passes without baring his throat or submitting to a metal scan.

The line of APCs passes through one vehicle at a time, troops and drivers checked as thoroughly as the civilians. Kirsten had argued at length over that with the light colonel commanding the MPs, and finally had to order him to treat her convoy exactly as he would civilian transport. If she is to lead these people — and the thought of it kept her awake most of the night — she has to lead by example. She has to be the first and most visible to honor the law. Maggie, sitting beside her, has sworn to uphold and defend the Constitution of the United States, and has laid her life at hazard to do it. It never occurred to Kirsten when she took the same oath as the most junior member of Hilary Clinton's Cabinet that she would ever be asked to do the same. An ironic smile touches her mouth. *Last and least, and the only one left alive that can do what must be done.*

At the doors, her escort forms a cordon around her, rifles at the ready, eyes scanning the crowd that turns to stare. Maggie, walking just behind, keeps her own weapon at her side, not openly threatening, but prepared nonetheless. Odd, how that might make her uncomfortable if it were anyone but Maggie. She has never before in her life poached anyone's lover — has hardly thought of having one of her own, much less taking someone else's — but she trusts Maggie literally with her life, and not just for Dakota's sake. The crowd murmurs as they pass through, and she catches fleeting snatches of their comments:

"...Look, son, that's the commander from the Cheyenne..."

"...our President now..."

"...cyborg egghead..."

"...I thought she'd be taller..."

From the door comes a snatch of song, and Kirsten puts up a hand to halt her entourage. A man sits beside the entrance on a folding stool, a guitar propped across his knees and a fold of denim where the rest of his left leg should be. His long, greying hair is tied at the nape with a thong of leather; sunglasses hide his eyes. The melody is an old one, a ballad from the feud-ridden Anglo-Scottish border in the days of the first Elizabeth, but the words are new:

*All along the bridge she ran*
*Swifter than any deer;*
*A grenade launcher in her hand,*
*And in her heart, no fear.*

*All along the bridge she ran,*
*Swifter than any doe;*
*Behind her her two fastest friends,*
*Great-hearted, ran also.*

There are several more stanzas, detailing the destruction of the android army on the far bank of the Cheyenne, praising Dakota's valor, Maggie's, Tacoma's, her own. The cold around her heart is back, glacial cold, and with it panic. Only the prospect of disgrace in Maggie's eyes and Dakota's keeps her rooted to the concrete floor of the auditorium, a smile on her face that seems to her as rigid as a corpse's.

*God help me, these people think I'm a hero, a real one, like Dakota and Maggie. What will I do? How can I ever measure up to that?*

After what seems like an eternity, the song comes to an end.

*God prosper now our President,*
*Our lives and safeties all.*
*And her companions in the fight*
*Let honor bright befall.*

Kirsten claps with the rest of the crowd, her face burning. "Harry," someone cries, "do you know who you're singin' to?"

"I'm singin' to you, you bastard!" the musician rejoins. "Only you're too cheap to stand me to a beer, Todd Rico!"

"This should stand you to a beer or two."

The soft voice is Maggie's, behind her, and Kirsten watches as she removes the bobcat earcuff and drops it into the hat on the floor beside Harry. Kirsten's heart clenches; she has no jewelry, and money is useless. The only thing she has of value is the gun she is wearing underneath her jacket. Slowly she unstraps it and lays it, too, at the singer's feet. "Thank you for a fine song, Harry," she says. "Perhaps you can sing it again when Dakota Rivers can hear it, too."

The singer's head comes sharply round. "Wait. I know your voice."

Kirsten makes a small, deprecatory gesture, halted abruptly. What was not evident before, is now; the man cannot see. "Probably not," she says quietly.

"You're King," he says, equally quietly. "I've heard you on the TV."

She nods, then, feeling foolish, says, "That must have been months ago. You have a good ear."

"Nah, I remember voices. I lost my sight back in '03, in Baghdad, along with my leg. Implants wouldn't take."

She wants to stop and talk to him, to ask whether he has always been a singer and how he survived the uprising, but the captain at her elbow is urging her forward, into the huge emptiness of the auditorium. "Ma'am, the people are lining up."

Instead she thanks Harry again, shakes his hand, and moves on. Behind her she hears the sound of small items dropping into his hat; he has earned his beer and more this afternoon. "That was generous of you, Maggie. I know that cuff means a lot to you."

Maggie just shrugs. "I have another; I never wear the pair. That gun, though, should feed him for a month or more — way more, if he throws in the story of how he got it. You're becoming a legend."

"You, too," Kirsten retorts. "And I don't think you like it any better than I do. Dakota will be..." She pauses, searching for a word. "Embarrassed," she finishes lamely.

"Try 'really pissed'," says Maggie.

Inside, the room has been cordoned into aisles with rope and stanchions. Huge signs with letters march across the walls: A-B, C-E, all the way to XYZ at the opposite side. Uniformed soldiers, all officers from the bean-counting division, sit behind long tables with stacks of legal pads and note cards. Slowly the people sifting in find their initials and form into lines, all talking at once, many pointing at Kirsten where she stands with Maggie and Boudreaux, back in his normal incarnation, at the front of the room. There must be, she estimates, a couple thousand actually on the floor, with more outside.

"Are you going to talk to them?" Boudreaux asks.

"No, I hadn't planned—"

"You really should, you know," Maggie says. "Call it winning hearts and minds. We'll get a lot better cooperation if the folks think they're doing their President a personal favor."

She shoots Maggie a withering glare, but accepts the bullhorn from

Boudreaux. "All right. Clear me a spot on the table. They all thought I'd be taller."

Slowly the crowd quiets. From her perch on the center table, Kirsten can make out faces watchful, eager, annoyed. One young mother bounces her crying baby; a man with a bored expression slaps his hat impatiently against his thigh. *Hearts and minds.*

"Good afternoon," she says, her voice echoing from the high walls, distorted and tinny in her own ears. "As most of you know, I'm Kirsten King, and as far as we know, I'm the only survivor from the President's Cabinet in Washington.

"I need your help. We've fought off a major attack by the androids and their allies, but we haven't defeated them yet. There's lots more out there where those came from, and there're humans cooperating with them. We still don't know what they want or who is responsible for the uprising. Those are things we're going to have to deal with.

"The people of Rapid City and the troops of Ellsworth Air Force Base shed their blood at the Cheyenne to keep us alive and free. Our duty now is to keep our laws and our Constitution alive and free, too, to make sure we don't fall into anarchy or the rule of force. That means we need to do such things as have elections for Mayor and Council of Rapid City. It means we need lawyers and judges. We need free commerce, with fair prices, and we need peace officers to make sure that it doesn't become profiteering. If you have special skills, if you'd like to serve in office, please let the census takers know."

Kirsten pauses and the quiet lies thick about her. Not a word, not a shuffling foot breaks the silence. The faces turned to her are serious, some clearly worried, all resolute. *Hearts and minds.*

"You are the free people of the United States. You live in a country founded on law and the idea that every person is valuable. The need for law has never been greater; each person has never been more valuable. I ask today for your help in restoring our nation. We can never go back to what we had; too much has been lost. Too many have been lost. But we can begin today to reaffirm our Constitution and our laws. And with them, we can be a nation again that can stand against any enemy.

"I ask for your help in that work. Long live freedom! And long live the free people of the United States!"

She lowers the bullhorn, looking out over the sea of faces, dazed. *My God, where did that come from?* She barely has time for the thought before the wave of sound breaks over her, shouts of "Free-dom! Free-dom! FREE-DOM!" mixed with "Kir-sten!" and "Ells-worth!" tumbling over her in a roar. Then, from amid the shouting, she hears the clear chords of blind Harry's twelve-string, strumming out a rhythm. Gradually the crowd quiets, and he begins to sing.

> *The gloomy night before us lies,*
> *The reign of terror now is o'er;*
> *Its gags, inquisitors and spies,*
> *Its hordes of harpies are no more*
> *Rejoice, Columbia's sons, rejoice;*
> *To tyrants never bend the knee.*
> *But join with heart, and soul and voice*

*For Jefferson and Liberty.*

*Let foes to freedom dread the name,*
*But should they touch the sacred tree*
*Twice fifty thousand swords would flame,*
*For Jefferson and Liberty.*
*Rejoice, Columbia's sons, rejoice;*
*To tyrants never bend the knee.*
*But join with heart, and soul and voice*
*For Jefferson and Liberty.*

The crowd picks up on the sharp, snare-drum rhythm of the melody, stamping and clapping.  As the verses go on and on, the crowd joins in on the chorus, providing percussion for the rest.  By the time Harry gives a flourish on the strings and swings into the coda, the house is singing full-throated along with him:

*From Georgia up to Lake Champlain,*
*From seas to Mississippi's shore,*
*Ye sons of freedom loud proclaim,*
*"The Reign of Terror is no more."*
*Rejoice, Columbia's sons, rejoice!*
*To tyrants never bend the knee.*
*But join with heart, and soul and voice*
*For Jefferson and Liberty.*

The last chorus ends with a crescendo of whoops and rebel yells, the pounding of hands and feet shaking the floor like an earthquake.

As the music fades, Kirsten stands silent for a moment, then turns to step down.  Her knees shake so hard she nearly falls as she escapes the crowd of admiring officers, all talking at once.  It is too much.  The noise of the cheering crowd batters at her, at her ears, at her mind.  Too much.

Brushing past the officers and her startled guard, she makes for the emergency exit and the privacy of the open air.

# CHAPTER TWENTY-FIVE

South Dakota spring has come decked out in her Sunday finest, seemingly overnight. Between the setting of one day and the dawning of the next, trees which had previously shown the sky their brittle bones are budded out in verdant greens and purples and pinks and whites. The air is a perfumed delicacy and the breeze bears the warm promise of summer on its breath.

Sitting on the small porch in front of Maggie's house, Kirsten takes it all in with peaceful pleasure, thanking any god currently in residence that she's finally free — if only for the moment — of the dreadful Atlas-weight of her position within this newly ripening society. The trip back from Rapid City had been a silent one, and Kirsten extends her silent thanks to Maggie, who knew enough to know that Kirsten needed the silence to decompress.

The trip had been a mixed blessing. As far as the census went, they had succeeded beyond their wildest dreams. Unfortunately, however, they hadn't encountered a judge or lawyer in the bunch. Or at least that anyone admitted to, anyway. Three paralegals had been the best they could come up with, and Kirsten was seriously considering promoting them to a judgeship, Bar Association be damned.

"Someone's coming," Maggie remarks from her place on the lawn, directing Kirsten's attention toward a perfectly maintained — if decades old — truck currently headed in their direction. Squinting, the young scientist can just make out Dakota's dark form riding shotgun, and her heartrate accelerates, spreading a warm, welcoming tingle throughout her body. A smile curves her lips, while she dutifully ignores the smirk thrown her way by the observant Air Force colonel.

From what Kirsten can see behind the reflection of the setting sun on his thick glasses, the driver appears to be an elderly male with a hawk-like profile and eyes to match. She briefly wonders if this man is Dakota's father, or even grandfather, but dismisses the notion out of hand when the truck turns up the short driveway. His features, hawk-like though they may be, scream Anglo-Saxon.

"I'll be damned," Maggie half-whispers as she gets a good look at the driver.

"What?" Kirsten asks, startled.

An unwilling grin crosses Maggie's face. "If that's not 'Hang 'em High' Harcourt, I'll eat my service ribbons."

Kirsten looks at her askance. "Hang 'em who?"

The man in question brings the truck to a stop, turns off the ignition, and slips out through the door he's just opened. Quite tall, and, like his truck, well-maintained despite his advanced years, he cuts an imposing figure as he looks down at Kirsten through clear, piercing eyes. After a moment, he gives a quick, if stiff, bow of his head. "Madame President."

Kirsten simply stares.

With a quirk of his lips that could almost be categorized as a smile, he turns his gaze to the woman standing, hands on hips, to Kirsten's left. "Major Allen," he says by way of greeting.

Maggie manages to conceal her surprise and straightens. "It's colonel, now."

That quirk of his lips comes again. "Indeed." His eyes flick over her body almost dismissively. "I do hope that the increase in rank brought with it a concomitant increase in the ability to, I believe the phrase is 'keep tabs' on the men and women under your care?"

Maggie's dark skin hides her flush, but Kirsten believes she can feel the heat of it from where she's standing nonetheless. She experiences a flash of anger, an emotion that dissolves into puzzlement as Maggie throws her head back and laughs, loud and long.

"You actually know this gnarled old oak?" Maggie shouts to Dakota between bursts of mirth.

"I'll take that as the compliment it was no-doubt intended to be," Harcourt replies primly as a grinning Koda rounds the truck and comes to stand with the group.

Taking pity on Kirsten, she lays a soft hand on the smaller woman's shoulder. "Kirsten, I'd like you to meet Judge Fenton Harcourt."

"Retired, Madame President," Harcourt murmurs. "Quite retired."

The name tickles her memories. She sifts through them quickly, then looks up, jaw nearly dropping. "Aren't you — you're the one who turned down a seat on the Supreme Court!"

"Pah," he comments sourly. "Doddering fools the lot of them. I'm surprised they were able put their robes on without a map, let alone find their way to the bench — unless, of course, it was surrounded by an oaken bar and plenty of swizzle sticks."

Kirsten continues to stare at him, gape-jawed, unable for the life of her to tell whether he is in fact serious, or simply the world's greatest straight man. His gaze, utterly cool, utterly calm, helps her not at all.

Koda comes to her rescue, squeezing Kirsten's shoulder and drawing the judge's attention to herself. "If you're quite through making your first impression, Fenton, maybe we could go inside?"

Harcourt straightens and puts his arms behind his back, clasping his wrists as he takes in a deep breath of spring-scented air. "I think not. I believe I'll take a walk around the grounds." He eyes Dakota significantly. "Alone."

"Suit yourself. Just meet us back here when you're through, okay?"

"Mm." He looks down at the three of them, face as expressionless as a granite mountain. "Ladies. Madame President."

When she's judged the man has gone far enough on his walk to be out of comfortable earshot, Kirsten screws up her face like she's just bitten into a lemon. "I'm beginning to hate that title."

"That's exactly why the old coot's using it," Maggie replies laughing. "Look up the meaning of the phrase 'burr under the saddle blanket' and you'll see his picture staring you in the face." She looks on with appreciation as Koda returns to the truck and hauls out Harcourt's overnight bag and old-fashioned leather briefcase. "He can find a person's weak spots without even looking. It makes him a formidable opponent."

"He's a judge!" Kirsten counters forcefully, ignoring the flash of jealousy that flares when she discovers exactly where the colonel's eyes are presently fixed. "Judges are supposed to be impartial, not opponents."

"On the bench," Koda replies, returning to them laden with Harcourt's luggage, "he's the most impartial person I know. Just don't screw up in his courtroom, and never get into a debate with him when he's not wearing his robes." She smirks. "Unless you're wearing a full suit of armor."

The others follow as she heads for the house, juggling the luggage as she unlatches the door, and then nearly stumbling backwards as Asi takes the opportunity to leap on her, pressing against her chest with his large forepaws. "Get down, you...mangy...furball!" She pushes forward with implacable strength, causing him to dance back on his hind legs until his feet slide and he tumbles away. He stares up at her as she pushes by, expression truly pitiful.

"You deserved it, you big dope," Kirsten mutters when he turns the hurt look on her. "Now go lie down and behave."

Ears and tail drooping, he slinks his way to the fireplace, where he lays down with a sigh worthy of the most martyred of heroes.

"So, how do you know Judge Harcourt?" Kirsten asks Koda as she watches the tall woman stack the luggage near the couch.

Straightening, Koda smiles and heads back into the kitchen. Reaching into the oven, she pulls out the frybread that she had made that morning, and with a few preparations, she begins dinner for them all. "I've known him since I was an infant, actually," she begins, voice low and mellow and soothing. "He and my grandfather were good friends — well, as good a friend as any human being could be to Fenton." She slips a look toward her two companions. "He's not exactly known for his love of the species."

Kirsten contemplates that for a moment. From what she knows of the man based on short acquaintance, she can't say she's a bit surprised at the revelation. "How did your grandfather come to know him?"

"When he was a young man," Koda replies, turning back to the supper she's preparing, "Fenton was known as a champion of civil rights."

"But you said he hates people," Kirsten counters, confused.

"That may be," Koda returns evenly, "but he loves the Constitution and what it stands for." She smiles fondly, though neither woman can see it. "He was one of the chief warriors in my peoples' fight to gain back all of our ancestral lands."

"I remember reading about that." Kirsten's expression is thoughtful. "I don't recall seeing his name mentioned in any of the history discs I've seen, though."

Koda snorts. "If there's anything he hates more than people, it's publicity. He didn't need or want the credit. He did what he did because it was the right thing to do, and when he had won that battle, he moved on to other things."

"Like gay marriage," Maggie replies knowingly.

Koda turns, grinning. "Exactly. And a lot more over the years. He's a brilliant thinker with a love of the law, and probably the most honest man outside my family that I've ever met. He might not be much of a people person, but he's a good friend, and I'm lucky to have him in my life."

"We're lucky to have him," Kirsten gently corrects. "Thanks for...talking him into this," she adds, instinctively knowing that without Koda's intervention, he would never have come.

"He hasn't said yes yet."

"Details, details," Kirsten replies, blithely waving away the concerns. She turns her gaze to Maggie. "And how do you know him?" The young scientist doesn't need to see Maggie's flush to know it's there.

"A much less pleasant tale, to be sure," the colonel replies, grinning weakly.

"We're all ears."

Sighing, Maggie drops down onto one of the worn kitchen chairs, legs splayed, one arm draped across the table. "Fine. It was...quite a few years back. We'd been away on maneuvers for months. Almost a year, in fact, and had just gotten back to home base. Most of my crew had a lot of leave time saved up and they were raring to take it, but the shit with Syria was stirring up again and all leaves were cancelled indefinitely." She grimaces. "So I asked for, and received, a weekend's liberty for my men."

"And they took it," Kirsten hazards.

"Oh yeah. They took it, all right. About four o'clock Monday morning, I get woken up by a phone call from Rapid City PD."

"Oh boy."

Maggie tosses Kirsten a smirk. "Apparently, seven of my men had taken up residence in the city lockup. Seven counts of drunk and disorderly, four assaults, and one assault with a deadly weapon. A pool cue," she explains in response to Kirsten's unasked question. "It...wasn't pretty."

"Damn."

"Yeah. Damn." Clearing her throat, she looks down at hands which are now clasped together on her lap. "I figured...you know...I'd go to the courthouse and get them released to me pending trial. If I was lucky, I could have the charges shifted to a military court and take care of it from there." She sighs, still looking down at her hands. "No such luck. Harcourt had pretty much retired by then and was slumming, filling in part time in the city courts. I took one look at his face during the bond hearing and I knew I had no chance."

"Tim D'Mello." Koda's soft voice floats back from the stove.

Kirsten looks perplexed. Maggie nods. "Yeah." To Kirsten, the colonel explained, "Tim D'Mello was an airman stationed at our base. He raped three women in Rapid City, and the JAG made a deal with the civilian authorities, promising to prosecute him to the fullest extent of the law, yadda, yadda, yadda, if they'd release him to the MPs. They agreed, and he was convicted, but he escaped from the brig and raped again. Twice in one night." She swallows hard. "He killed the last one. She was only twelve."

"Jesus," Kirsten hisses.

"Harcourt was as hard as a rock," Maggie continues. "He wouldn't budge. My men were going to receive their day in court — a civilian court for the damage they'd done to civilians — and that was that."

"What happened?"

"They pled guilty." She laughs. It's a mirthless sound. "Why not? They were. He threw the book at them, as they say. Maximum sentence allowed by law, which, for the D and Ds wasn't all that much, but the ADW..." Her hands clench and unclench in her lap. "The worst part, I think, was the way he looked at me when he learned I was their commanding officer. It was pity and anger, all wrapped up in a putrid little ball, and I felt like I was seven again and my father had caught me playing doctor with the girl next door." She laughs again. "It was a lesson well learned that day. And then I learned another one. We were going to war. Again. I needed those men, desperately. So, I swallowed my pride and went to him and laid out another deal. Which was, basically, anything in exchange for them."

"Did he go for it?" Kirsten asks, though she already knows the answer.

"Yeah. Surprisingly, he did. He knew that the citizens of this country would be much better served with these convicts fighting for freedom rather than rotting in some jail somewhere." She smiles. "But that wasn't the end of it. Oh no, not nearly. He demanded restitution. A portion of each paycheck they received would go to those they'd wronged, and then, when they came back from fighting, if they came back, they would serve out their sentences in community service of his choosing. And if he found that they stepped out of line again, even the tiniest inch, he'd toss them back in jail and throw away the key. And, he informed me, I'd be there rotting right along side of them." She laughs again, shaking her head. "I believed him. I still do."

"Did they come back from the war? Did they serve out their sentences?"

"Only two," Maggie intones, her voice infinitely sad. "But they did as he ordered, and as far as I know, they never got so much as a speeding ticket since." Her face clears then, and she looks up at her audience. "And there you have it: How I Know Fenton Harcourt, in five thousand words or less."

"Perfect timing," Koda replies, turning from the stove with laden plates. "Dinner is served."

**Stepping out of** the clinic, Dakota breathes deeply of the warm spring night. Her nostrils flare as she picks up the familiar scent of pipe tobacco. The fragrance brings with it a wave of memories together with a brief, but almost overwhelming feeling of longing — a longing for the past, for the way things had been; a longing for the ability to shift back time just enough so she could find herself on the porch of her family's ranch house on a deep summer night, her grandfather on one side of her, her father on the other, and bask in the sense of peace and safety and contentment she fears she'll never experience again.

Letting the feelings wash over and through her, she continues forward to where she can sense her watcher hidden in the moonshadow of a towering oak. He steps out as she approaches, face wreathed in fragrant pipe-smoke. "Good evening."

"Fenton."

He peers past her to the building she's just left. "I see you've kept to your calling despite the recent...difficulties."

"It's who I am."

"Mm." He removes the pipe from his mouth, gesturing toward the open space behind the guarded gates. "I've also heard some fascinating — if rather overblown — tales about a certain veterinarian leading a charge across a crumbled bridge over the Cheyenne. Very noble, if foolhardy, that woman."

"It's who I am," she answers again succinctly, truthfully.

"Indeed. I think — and this is pure speculation, mind you — that your grandfather would have been quite proud of your accomplishments."

Dakota can feel the flush building, warming her skin. Luckily, or perhaps deliberately, Harcourt has chosen to examine the star-dazzled sky, giving her time to regain the balance his words so effortlessly stripped away. "So," she says when she finally finds her voice, "will you stay?"

His eyes come back to meet hers, glittering and wise. "For the nonce."

"Thank you."

His head inclines the barest fraction of an inch in response.

She hears a slight rustling from above, and a smile breaks over her face. Uncomprehending, his eyebrow raises in silent question. In answer, she puts her finger to her mouth and utters her three-note calling whistle. A brief second later, Wiyo silently alights on her fist, tucking her wings into place and appearing to study the man standing across from her.

"Blessed mercy," he whispers, his implacable calm instantly shattered. This is a Fenton Harcourt that no one but Dakota knows exists. "Is this...?"

"It is," Koda answers, holding out her fist in invitation.

She can see his arm tremble as he raises it, can hear the soft intake of breath that is not quite a gasp as Wiyo steps easily onto his wrist.

"Hello, old friend," he says in a voice not quite steady. "I had never thought to see you again."

Stepping away to give the judge some privacy, Koda rounds the large tree until its towering branches no longer obscure her view of the sky. The firmament is shot through with a trillion sparkling diamonds cast in display by a careless hand.

*Would you have been proud of me, thunkashila?*

The cold stars give no answer, but that doesn't matter. She's pretty sure she knows what it would be.

**"For the last** time, Colonel, the answer is no. There is a perfectly serviceable cot in the judge's chambers, and I fully intend to make what little use of it I must. Your hospitality, though polite, is unneeded and unwanted."

"Begging your pardon, Judge Harcourt," Kirsten intervenes, "but I've seen that 'perfectly serviceable cot', and it's got more lumps in it than my mother's gravy."

Straightening to his fullest height, Harcourt turns to her, staring down at her through his glasses, eyes sharp as diamonds. "Madame President..."

Kirsten winces. "Kirsten, please?" When he does not respond, she offers, "Ms. King?"

"Doctor King, I assume your eyesight is adequate enough to confirm to you that which you know is true: I am an old man. And as an old man, I will have an eternity's worth of sleep when my decomposing corpse fertilizes the ground around my eternal resting place. Until then, I will sleep when I choose, and where I choose. I will brook no compromise on this issue. Am I clearly understood?"

Jaw clenched, Kirsten finally nods.

"Good." Turning, he next pins Maggie with his gaze. "Colonel, am I to assume that you have the case files assembled?"

"I do."

"Then perhaps you would escort me to my chambers and hand over the materials. I believe I have a bit of light reading to do this evening."

Maggie shoulders the overnight case and hands Harcourt his briefcase. "Fine. Let's go then."

After nodding to both Kirsten and Dakota, he turns and leaves the house, Maggie following after him like a faithful puppy.

"Well," Kirsten observes as the door quietly closes, "wasn't that just a barrel of laughs."

**"It's a good** turnout."

Nudging Maggie aside and peering through the half-inch or so space between the open door of the Judge Advocate's chambers and the jamb, Kirsten amends, "It's a damn good turnout, considering our sampling methods."

The other woman gives a soft snort of derisive agreement. "Talk about 'needs must'. I think we've got what we need here, though."

What they have got is a jury pool of close to three hundred people. At the other end of the courtroom, a pair of military bailiffs in dress uniforms and braid stand with clipboards, checking off names as the prospective jurors file in and take their assigned seats. Maggie is right. It is a good turnout by any standard, especially considering the sampling methods and the hand-carried notifications to the sometimes dubious addresses. It is a phenomenal turnout considering that many of these folk have walked for miles to reach the base, while others have biked, SegWayed, ridden mule- or horseback. For the first time since the departure of the mounted cavalry regiments, a South Dakota military post has found it necessary to install hitching posts.

Getting the jury pool together has taken a week's hard work and ingenuity. Maggie is right. Needs must when the devil drives. *Hand it to Old Scratch*, Kirsten reflects, *he's had his foot flat on the floorboard for the last several months.* But the census of Rapid City, taken over two days, has yielded a heartening three thousand plus surviving adult citizens, many of them residents who have only come out of hiding since the defeat of the android force at the Cheyenne. As many more have recently moved from outlying ranches and hamlets into the more populated city, or what is left of it.

They took the census the old fashioned way, by hand, names and addresses penciled on legal pads and index cards. On Andrews' inspired notion, a team scoured the city's churches for bingo machines. The three working models had been pressed into service as randomizing devices, leaving time and computer capacity free for more urgent military applications. Hurriedly repainted with ID numbers, the whirling balls tossed out a selection that is, mirabile dictu, a reasonably accurate microcosm of Rapid City. The citizens slowly jostling their way into their appointed places on the dark oak benches include Anglos in jeans and Stetsons, African Americans in business suits, Lakota and Cheyenne in ribbon shirts, men and women of every color in sweats and Sunday best and everything in between. The only striking difference between this crowd and a pre-uprising gathering is the ratio of women to men. For every man in the courtroom, for every man on the list, three women have survived.

Kirsten closes the door softly and turns back into the room. Unlike the other official spaces she has seen, the Judge Advocate's chambers have been spared the ubiquitous grey and Air Force blue décor. The dark wood and forest green walls, the tartan carpet woven in deep reds and greens, give it an air of almost Victorian formality. The lingering smell of pipe tobacco reinforces the impression, as does the well-worn but not yet shabby assortment of leather armchairs and ottomans. The chamber reminds Kirsten of a traditional library, a university reading room. One could curl up in one of those chairs with a book or hand-held and lose one's self for hours.

The few pictures on the walls are idiosyncratic, too, not the official art of fighter planes and bombers. One shows grain fields stretching golden to the horizon, another a forest glade where a stag bends to drink, his antlers struck to gold like a crown by a shaft of sunlight. The third, a photograph, catches a pair of eagles in the midst of their courtship flight, talons locked with talons, wings spread wide against the receding sky. The image is stunning in its clarity, and paradoxically, its untrammeled sense of motion, as if the two birds might come tumbling out of the frame and into the room at the viewer's feet.

Behind the big desk by the window, Fenton Harcourt gives his newly pressed robe a twitch, and its folds fall into perfect place. He seems curiously at home in this room that seems to have slipped out of its proper time and place. As he taps the ash out of his pipe and refills its bowl from a cordovan pouch, his eyes stray again and again to the eagles, a small, secret smile curving his mouth. It suddenly occurs to Kirsten to check the photographer's signature when she gets a chance. Or she could just ask.

"That's one of your pictures, isn't it, Judge? It's beautiful."

Harcourt glances sharply up at her over the tops of his old-fashioned half-glasses. For a moment it seems he will not answer her, but he says, "Why, yes. That's very perceptive of you, Dr. King."

"Our Judge Advocate was a birdwatcher — I'm sorry, a birder, too," Maggie says quietly. "We haven't seen or heard from her since before the uprising."

"A shame, that. I would have enjoyed telling her about the Cassin's Sparrow I saw two weeks ago." Harcourt clamps the stem of the cold pipe between his teeth, picking up the gavel from the desk together with the bulging portfolio containing the charges against the defendants. "Now," he says abruptly, "let us see whether we have twelve persons who are at all capable of rendering a disinterested verdict in these appalling cases."

"Everyone in that room has an interest of some sort in this case, Judge," Kirsten observes evenly. "Bias and interest are not the same thing." Kirsten is almost sure she sees a glint of warmth, perhaps even surprise, in the judge's eye, but it might just as easily be a reflection from the green-shaded banker's lamp on the desk.

"Indeed they are not. But I doubt you will find more than half a dozen folk out there who have not been personally and traumatically injured by the androids. This case has not even begun, but it is already rife with grounds for appeal."

"Let's see if we can get these men convicted first, shall we?" Maggie says dryly. "We'll worry about appeals later, assuming anyone can find the staff to convene an appellate court."

Kirsten knows what Harcourt will say before he opens his mouth and suppresses the urge to kick Maggie's ankle.

"Colonel Allen," he says mildly, "a court is not needed. You are aware, I am sure, of the prerogative of Presidential pardon?"

With that he steps between them, tucking the unlit pipe back into his pocket, and knocks on the inside of the door. Pausing a moment for the bailiff to shout "All rise!" and for the rustles and thumps that accompany three hundred people getting to their feet, he sweeps behind the witness stand and up the three steps to the bench. Kirsten and Maggie slip out much less dramatically in his wake, to take their places in the observation area behind the prosecution table next to the jury box. Again the bailiff gives tongue, rolling out the words one after another on a single pitch: "Oyez! Oyez! The Court of the Fifth Circuit of the State of South Dakota is now in session, the Honorable Fenton Harcourt presiding. God bless the United States and this honorable Court!"

For a long moment, Harcourt stands behind the bench, inspecting the occupants of the courtroom. It is a glance very much like that of the eagles in the photograph, bright and implacable. In a rush for the door that morning, a scrambled egg wrapped in fry bread in her hand, Dakota, like Maggie before her, had referred to the old gentleman as "Hangin' Harcourt", a stickler for the law, letter and spirit. It seems to Kirsten that the epithet is not, perhaps, a joking matter. Despite the man's respect for his fellow bird enthusiasts or his obvious pleasure in a rare sighting, the lean planes of the his face, cut sharply to the bone under his shock of white hair, would not be out of place on an Old Testament prophet — Jeremiah, bewailing the whoredom of the Daughter of Zion, John the Baptizer munching locusts and wild honey — or a Huguenot martyr bearing his Calvinism like a banner to the stake. Kirsten trusts him to be fair. She is not sure there is any mercy in him at all, or whether she thinks there should be.

A chill passes over her as she stands, waiting like the rest for Harcourt to be seated. The judge will sign a death verdict, if one is rendered, read the sentence, set the date. But she, Kirsten King, must sign the execution warrant when the time comes.

It is a long way home to Twenty-Nine Palms. A long way home and circles upon circles of hell yet to pass through. To Harcourt's right, the national flag drapes in soft spirals of red and white around its stanchion, and Kirsten wonders how many stars will be left when the insurrection is over. If it is ever over. If anyone survives. To his left, South Dakota's flag proclaims, "Under God, the People Rule." Kirsten has no interest in presiding over a theocracy, but restoring the government of the people, by the people, is something she would do in a heartbeat if she could.

A heartbeat that would allow her to go back to being a scientist, not a political figure. Or, more aptly, a figurehead. A figurehead with life and death in her hand, and no way to open her fingers and cast herself free of them.

Finally Harcourt sits, and the rest of the room follows suit. The crowd remains silent as he opens the folder in front of him and studies it briefly. Then he closes it and folds his hands on its cover. Pitching his voice so that it carries to every corner of the high-ceilinged room, he says, "Ladies and gentlemen, I want to thank you for coming here today despite what must be considerable hardship for some of you. I commend you on your sense of duty even in the present crisis, and for your willingness to undertake perhaps the most solemn responsibility of a citizen of this state and this nation. You are here to administer justice. Justice under the law."

He glances around the room. "The circumstances are extraordinary. For one, this court is, of necessity, a hybrid of military and civilian practice, even though the defendants are civilians and no state of war has been formally declared by the Congress of the United States. So, even though you will see both the defense counsel and the prosecutor in the uniform of their service, the charges laid against these defendants are those allowable under the criminal law of the state of South Dakota. They are not federal charges; they are not war crimes, even though it seems, in logic, that they should be.

"If you are chosen for this jury, you will be asked to sift a body of evidence that you will find disturbing in the extreme. And you will be asked to render a verdict, bearing in mind that men's lives will be in your hands, on the basis of that evidence alone. In a moment, the Clerk of the Court will ask for exemptions, which may be granted for several reasons under the law of this state. If you have formed an opinion on any of these cases, or if you do not believe you are capable of rendering a just and true verdict, you will have an opportunity to inform the Court at that time. Madame Clerk."

The clerk, a trim redhead with Sergeant's stripes on her sleeve, begins to read out the list of persons exempt from jury service. Kirsten leans slightly toward Maggie and whispers, "My God, he really is a classic, isn't he?"

"He almost makes me believe in reincarnation," Maggie answers sotto voce. "He'd be right at home in a toga, stabbing Caesar in the gut for the good of the Republic."

A sharp glance from the bench quiets them both as the clerk drones on. "...Persons over sixty-five years of age...full time student...care of children under six...minister of religion...persons unable to read and write the English language..."

Surprisingly few members of the pool choose to opt out. One young woman with an infant in arms sounds almost disappointed that she can find no one else to care for her baby; a young man with watery eyes and a bad cough is hustled out before he can make a gift of his cold to anyone else. Kirsten steals a glance at the defendants where they sit at the table across the room. The four of them are to be tried together, and they provide a study in contrasts. One, Kazen, seems scarcely out of his teens, his eyes wide with obvious fear. McCallum sprawls in his chair; Buxton slumps in his. The fourth, Petrovich, stares at something in the corner of the ceiling which apparently only he can see. Shackles, unobtrusive, clink each time one of them moves. The chains are not where the jury can see them, but any escape attempt will have to include dragging the defense table along with it.

Half-hidden behind piles of briefs, Boudreaux's face is as pale as those of his clients. A fine shimmer of dampness at his receding hairline betrays his nerves. He is not a defense lawyer by trade, and his uniform does not make him into a lawyer. The responsibility for the life and death of others sits no easier on him than it does on Kirsten herself, and it seems to her that his is the one job even less appealing than her own. He must save the lives of these thugs if he can, and he must save them knowing that if they are found innocent they must be released, knowing that they will have been spared the firing squad only to be handed a more subtle death sentence, and a more brutal one, at the hands of their victims.

"Are counsel prepared to proceed with the voire dire?" Harcourt asks after the exemptions have been dealt with. "Major Alderson?"

Major Alderson, appointed prosecutor because of his experience as a paralegal and two years as a Senate aide in Washington, rises and turns to face the public benches. He runs rapidly through the standard questions, hardly pausing when he asks whether the prospective jurors have ever been victims of a crime, and every hand in the room goes up. Finally he comes to the end. "Are you able, in the event of a guilty verdict, to assess a sentence of death against these defendants? Raise your hand if you do not believe you can do so, please."

Boudreaux surges to his feet. "Objection, Your Honor! Rape is not a capital crime in the state of South Dakota."

"Major Alderson?" Harcourt's voice is deceptively mild as he taps the manila folder in front of him. "You wrote these charges, did you not? I do not believe I recall any assertion of murder among them."

Alderson turns to face the bench. "May it please the court, Your Honor, it's true that these defendants are not directly charged with murder. However, testimony from victims shows that women held in the Rapid City corrections facility were killed, and testimony to be offered here will show that these four men co-operated with the killers. They partake of the crime under the law of parties, Your Honor."

"Even though the killers were androids and not persons under the law? We would not try an android for a crime, Major. We would simply turn it off, you know, or send it to the scrap yard."

"Even so, Your Honor, the perpetrators being androids does not change the nature of the crime, or the nature of these defendants' participation."

Kirsten spares a glance at Maggie, whose lips twitch in a scarcely suppressed smile. "He's good," she mouths, not wanting to draw Harcourt's attention again.

Maggie nods almost imperceptibly. "Nothing like a few years negotiating budgets on the Hill to teach you to argue."

"Very well," Harcourt says after a moment's thought. "I will allow you to proceed along these lines, Counsel, and develop your case if you can. But I will charge the jury as I see fit when the time comes. Understood?"

"Understood, Your Honor."

Alderson puts the question to the jury pool again, briefly explaining that the law of parties is designed to prevent accomplices from escaping on lesser charges than a killer who pulls the trigger or wields the knife himself. "And the evidence will show, ladies and gentlemen, that these four men," he points to them as he numbers them off, "Kazen, McCallum, Buxton, Petrovich — bought their own lives at the price of the degradation and suffering of dozens of innocent women. Though I use the term 'women' advisedly. Some of their victims were no more than twelve or thirteen."

A hissing snakes its way through the courtroom, and Harcourt brings his gavel down hard.

"Ladies and gentlemen, I caution you now that I will not tolerate emotional displays in this courtroom." The sound subsides abruptly, and Harcourt lays the gavel down. "Major Boudreax, if you please."

Boudreaux rises and faces the jury pool. Peering over her shoulder, Kirsten can see that many faces are openly hostile. His opening remarks are conciliatory, designed to overcome as much of that feeling as he can. "Ladies and gentlemen, I want to thank you for coming here today. I know it has been very difficult for all of you, but I also know that you take your duties as citizens seriously. I helped to take the census in Rapid City, and saw there how much you love your country and how eager you are for the rule of law to be reestablished.

"Part of that rule of law is our justice system. Note that I say 'justice system,' not 'legal system'. Our laws do not exist for their own sake, just to give police and uniformed services like mine something useful to do. They exist to establish and mete out justice, fairly and impartially. And they do that through citizens like yourselves. You are the government, the true law enforcers of our society.

"My question to you, therefore, is a bit different from that asked by the prosecution. It is this: can you, with all you have suffered in the android uprising, all you have lost, including friends and members of your families, hear the evidence in this case and make your determination of guilt or innocence on that basis alone?"

The room is silent for a space, each of the prospective jurors given time to question his or her own conscience. Then, as the bailiff begins to call them forward one by one for individual questioning, Kirsten rises and slips unobtrusively from the room. Tacoma is due to make his second trip to the wind farm in half an hour, and Dakota may — no, she is not quite ready to say that Dakota may need her — but she wants to be there all the same. It is where she needs to be.

# CHAPTER TWENTY-SIX

Very gently, Dakota peels back the last of the bandaging under the soft cast, exposing the bobcat's paw. The jagged scar of the wound still shows an angry scarlet, the paired dots of the suture pricks running parallel to it on either side like an abstruse pottery design. The skin around the injury, though, is a healthy pink. A soft down of new fur, golden ground and umber whorls, covers it up to the edge of the scar. She feels the cat tense against her as she flexes the joint. "Easy, Igmú. Easy, girl," she croons into one tufted ear, tightening her hold to press the cat's body close to her own. "Still a bit stiff, there, aren't you?" Raising her voice, she calls, "Shannon, would you come here a moment, please?"

The thud of jogging footsteps in the hall precedes the tech into the examining room, and the bobcat starts at the sound. When Shannon opens the door, though, she is all professional calm. "Dr. Rivers?"

"Set up the X-ray, would you? I need a radiograph of Igmú's right fore-foot; it's still tight. I can't feel anything out of alignment, but let's be sure."

"She's about ready for release, isn't she?"

"Almost. But she's got to have everything working. She's a runner and a pouncer, and without that spring in all four feet, she can't hunt effectively."

Shannon steps out of the room to ready the machine and Koda returns to her examination. Other than the torn tendons, now almost fully healed, the cat is in excellent condition, better than if she had spent the last lean months of winter in the wild. The fur under her hand is soft and sleek, rich with oils from the fish Koda has added to her diet of red meat and fowl. Firm muscles ripple beneath it. She is up to a solid twenty pounds, not bad at all for a young female with her full growth yet to come. Every ounce of that twenty pounds balks, though, when Koda reaches for the syringe lying ready on the counter. "Easy, girl. Easy...easy... Shit."

The slick surface of the examination table works with her reluctant patient as she squirms and slides backward out of Koda's one-handed hold. "Come on, girl, this is the last one, I promise."

"Funny, I never believed the doctor when he said that, either." Koda looks up to find Tacoma standing in the doorway. He has changed his fatigues for jeans and flannel shirt, his belt festooned with tools, a hard hat dangling from one loop. "Let me help."

Koda nods, and he crosses the space between the door and the table at a single stride. At the first touch of his hands, the struggle stops cold. From deep in Igmú's chest comes a rumble like low thunder, and she butts her head against his chest, her great golden eyes half-closed in pleasure. He scratches her gently under the chin while Dakota lifts her scruff and administers her third and last feleuk vaccination. The purr never falters. Koda strokes her now complacent patient's ears as she pitches the empty hypodermic into the red biohazard pail hung under the table. "Do you have time to help with the radiograph? It'll only take a moment."

"Sure." Scooping the bobcat up, Tacoma follows her into the tiny X-ray room. A click and a couple of whirs later, he carries her back to the ward, leaving Koda to develop the film. When he returns, she has it up on the light box, staring intently at the bone where the torn tendons anchor.

There is no abnormality, and she breathes a small sigh of relief. "Have a look," she says. "Everything's in place; she just needs a bit of exercise to strengthen the paw. I'll move her out into one of the outdoor kennel runs during the day, and—"

"Dakota."

"—she'll be ready for release in a week or so."

"*Tanksi.*"

"I know you'll want to be there." Very deliberately Koda unties her lead-lined apron and hangs it up. "Do you think you'll be gone long?"

Tacoma's hand moves in a small half-circle that Dakota knows means frustration, but he answers evenly, "Five or six days, depending on how much we can do on this first trip. Melly Cho is going with us to determine whether we can get Rapid City hooked back up to the grid."

"She's that electrical engineer the census turned up?"

"Yeah. We may have one of the electric company linemen, too. They'll be a big help." There is a small, strained silence, then he says, "Harcourt wants to hold an informal inquest on Dietrich when we get back. As soon as it's over we can do what is right for Igmú Tanka Kte."

"Where's Dietrich? Is he in a freezer somewhere, too?" Koda cannot keep the bitterness out of her voice; she does not try.

"Yes. At the morgue. His family wants to bury him now that the ground has thawed."

"Well," she says shortly, "that's understandable." She turns away from him and begins to arrange ampoules of antibiotics and vaccines on the shelf above the counter.

There is a long silence. Then, he says softly, "Look, damn, Koda, I know I've done this all wrong. I'm sorry. I don't know anything else to say, though. I'm sorry."

Dakota turns to face her brother. "I know you're sorry. I accept that. What I can't accept is—" Her voice catches for a moment, then steadies. "How would you feel if it were your teacher? If it were Igmú Tanka in there?" She gestures toward the back of the clinic where the freezer holds the wolf's body.

"It would tear my heart out," he says simply. "But I would be glad to bring her killer to justice. I would be glad her children would live. And I think she would be, too."

An old story tells that the black marks at the corners of a puma's eyes are the tracks of tears shed long ago, in the time before time, in mourning for her stolen young. And that, Koda knows, is the heart of the matter. It is the one thing she has not allowed herself to consider.

It is not only the bobcat who will be ready for release in a little time. Day by day, the she-wolf grows stronger, grows closer to the time when she will be able to hunt and provide for her young. The pup, whose blunt face holds the promise of his sire's features and coloring, waddles about the run on stubby legs, splashing through the water bowl in pursuit of drifting paint-brush petals blown in on the spring winds. If law is allowed to lapse, if the trapping of wolves and bobcats and coyotes becomes a normal part of life again, then the pup could die the same way his father did. And no one would be there to spare his suffering or claim justice for him.

What would his father want? Her friend?

Salt stings Dakota's eyes, and she turns abruptly away. After a moment, soft footfalls cross the small distance, and Tacoma lays his hands on her shoulders. She stands stiffly for a moment, then allows herself to lean against him, accepting his grief, his comfort, his strength. Her rage has not gone out of her, but it has found its rightful mark — Dietrich and those like him who give no honor to other nations and prize none for their own.

After a long moment, she raises a hand to cover her brother's. She says, "Take care of yourself, *thiblo*. The wind farm is an obvious place for an ambush."

"Don't worry. We're taking plenty of firepower."

"Is Manny going?"

"He wants to. Allen won't let him." A hint of laughter runs under his words. "He knows she's not going to throw him to the dogs. She just wants him to think she might." A light pressure of his fingers, and he is gone.

She remains standing by the counter, her eyes wide and unfocused. Time has slipped again, in a way she knows long since. She sees not an array of bottles and ampoules and pill bottles, but a summer hill where a litter of wolf cubs tumbles squealing over one another, over their long-suffering parents. The female, almost entirely white except for grey about her ruff and on her ears, she does not recognize. The male, the alpha, who dozes in the overhang of the den behind them, is the pup now in her care, the other adults who sprawl on the rocks, their bellies bulging with fresh elk, his grown sons and daughters. A sycamore stands against the sky beside the den, and a hawk wheels against the high blue.

The vision fades, leaving behind only the certainty of its truth. With a heart lighter than it has been in days, Dakota heads back to the ward to check on a coyote with a short, absurd tail.

**Kirsten finds herself** moving toward the clinic at a clip that could technically, she supposes, be called a jog. With a flush of embarrassment, she slows to a walk, then quickly ducks behind a large tree as the clinic door opens, its glass sending out bright flashes of light as it catches the sun. Tacoma slips outside, well-muscled arms swinging easily with his movements. His head turns briefly in her direction, and Kirsten fancies he spies her, though she's pretty sure she's adequately hidden.

After a second, he turns away and Kirsten sags against the tree in relief, not at all wanting to tell Tacoma something she doesn't even know the answer to herself. She watches him walk away. The ease of his stride and the proud tilt of his head reassure her. It is a one hundred eighty degree change from the sorrow-filled man she's seen the past couple of days. This can only bode well for Dakota's state of spirit as well. Which, of course, renders pretty much useless her need to be here in the first place.

"All right, smarty," she mutters to herself. "What now?" *Back to the jury selection? Home? A quick jog around the perimeter?*

Her feet answer the question for her as they step around the tree and continue in her intended direction, toward the clinic. She looks down at them, traitorous things that they are, and frantically casts about for plausible excuses, discarding one after another.

"Shit!" The door's to hand, and her mind is a complete blank. A *tabula rasa*, as her mother used to say when into her wine. The warm memory brings a brief grin to her face as she slips inside the cool, antiseptic scented clinic.

From her position behind the reception desk, Shannon greets her with a warm, welcoming grin. "Hi, Doctor King!"

"Kirsten, remember?"

Shannon blushes. "Okay, Kirsten." Her smile returns. "Dakota's in the back finishing up with mama wolf and her baby. You can go back if you like."

"That's okay," Kirsten demurs, still feeling a bit the idiot for having come all the way over here without a suitable excuse. "I'll just wait...out here."

"She shouldn't be long. Do you want some coffee? I just made some fresh."

"No. Thanks."

She shrugs as if to say "suit yourself, then" and returns to her paper-work.

Several quite uncomfortable moments later, the door opens and Dakota steps through, wiping her hands on a white towel. The smile she sports upon seeing Kirsten wipes every bit of embarrassment and self recrimination from the young scientist's mind. She rises to her feet quickly, grinning herself as Shannon looks between them like a spectator watching a tennis match from the front row.

Kirsten casts about for something to break the silence. "I...um...I was in the neighborhood and figured I'd drop by." *God, Kirsten, could you possibly sound any more lame?*

Taking the comment in stride, Koda tosses the towel into the laundry chute. "How are the selections going?"

"Boring as hell," Kirsten answers truthfully. "Plus, I think I was making the potential jurors nervous. Nothing like having the de facto President around to make it damned difficult to try and squirm out of jury duty." Both Shannon and Koda chuckle at her feeble attempt at witticism, and Kirsten feels unaccountably warmed for it. "So," Kirsten casts again, "have you had lunch yet?"

Koda shrugs. "I was planning on going over to the mess. Our cupboards are pretty bare."

"Mind some company?"

Once again, that smile comes, a smile that knocks all rational thought from Kirsten's head and leaves her reeling in a whirlwind of pure emotion. The hand suddenly clasping her own grounds her like a lifeline, and she willingly follows wherever Dakota may lead.

**"How about some** fish for supper?"

Kirsten looks sharply up at Dakota. Long lashes veil her improbable blue eyes, but even in the gathering dusk, the small smile twitching at her mouth is unmistakable. Kirsten is not sure where the joke lies, but she knows better than she cares to that there is no fish in the refrigerator at home. For days, there has been no protein except for dried beans, eggs produced by a neighbor's hens, and the disgustingly spongy "cheese food" salvaged a month ago from the local USDA surplus station. *The trouble with being a geek,* she reflects, *is that you become every Tom, Dick and Harriet's straight woman.* "Okay," she says, "I'll bite. Yes, I'd like some fish for supper."

The twitch almost becomes a smile, and Koda says, "We don't have any."

"So why are we talking about it?"

"Because if we take a couple rods down to the water in the morning, we might have some tomorrow. Do you fish?"

"No. I just bite." Koda bursts into laughter, and Kirsten joins her, incredulous. *I made a joke, and someone's actually laughing at it. Love does weird things to people. It's doing very weird things to me.*

Above the flounced silhouette of a larch tree, a single star flares into visibility against the rapidly darkening eastern sky. In the west, the red glow of sunset lingers along the horizon. Kirsten stares up at a pinprick of brightness. *Star light, star bright — do I dare wish for what I wish tonight?* Aloud she says, "When I was a child, I thought the stars were the eyes of great owls flying across the night sky. I was always afraid one would swoop down and catch me."

The taller woman tilts her head back and gazes at the sky for a long moment. "We Lakota have always believed that Ina Maka brought us forth from her womb here in the Paha Sapa. We were created here; we have lived and died here. Take us away, and we lose our souls. When Tali and I went to university, we were home to each other."

"That must have been lonely."

"It was. Some Nations believe we came from the stars, though, and will eventually return. That must be lonelier still, to have no land at all, anywhere that is your own."

"Home was never a place for me," Kirsten says softly. "We moved around too much. It was always my parents. For a long time now, it's been Asi."

Dakota takes her eyes from the sky and looks down at Kirsten. "That must have been lonely," she echoes.

"It—"

From the street behind them comes the sound of squealing tires and the blare of a horn. "Doc! Thank God, there you are!"

Koda looks up sharply, and Kirsten, swiveling, swears under her breath. A battered red Dodge pickup skids to a stop beside them, a tech sergeant still in uniform at the wheel.

"Doctor Rivers," he says, "can you come? My daughter's cat has been trying to have her kittens since this morning, and can't. She's crying and won't stop."

Light as an evening breeze, Dakota's hand brushes Kirsten's as she steps up to the passenger window. "Who's crying, your daughter or the cat?"

"Both of them. Can you come? Please?"

"Later," Dakota says softly, and again there is the soft brush of her hand. Then she climbs up into the truck and is gone, the tires squealing again as the driver hangs a hard U-turn and speeds off.

Kirsten turns back toward the house, making her way slowly through the growing dark. When she pushes the door open, Asi tumbles out past her, makes a couple circuits of the yard at a trot, then pauses to anoint his favorite fencepost. He halts again at the gate, ears up, tail poised but not quite wagging. From inside the house comes the fragrant aroma of coffee and something rich with basil and tomatoes, and Kirsten is suddenly as hungry as she is tired. "Sorry, guy," she says. "Maybe after supper, okay?"

An hour later, Asi sprawls on the hearth, head between his paws, oblivious to the world. Kirsten, her legs tucked under her, balances her laptop carefully on the overstuffed arm of her chair and tells herself she should get back to work. But the figures that stream across the screen blur even with her glasses, and she closes the top. Soft footfalls cross the room from the kitchen in the rear — Maggie, carefully balancing two mugs that steam with something herbal mixed with honey. She sets one down by Kirsten. "Chamomile. It'll help relax you."

Kirsten glances up sharply. Maggie is out of uniform for once, in a pair of slim-legged black slacks and a pullover that emphasizes her slenderness and elegant height. Its dark wine hue picks up the undertones of her skin. The bobcat cuff glints on the curve of her ear. *She looks like Cleopatra, damn her.* Aloud she says, "Thanks."

Maggie settles comfortably on the couch, sipping at her own drink. Its aroma is different than the tea she gave Kirsten, something with cinnamon. After a moment she says, "I brought you a gun from the armory. It was very generous of you to give yours to Harry that day at the census, but you really shouldn't be without." A smile, half ironic, touches her mouth. "I probably should put a bodyguard on you, too, but I don't think you'd like that very much."

"I wouldn't like that at all." Kirsten hears the irritation in her words and with an effort hauls her voice back to civility. "You made him a handsome gift yourself, you know."

Maggie touches the cuff on her right ear briefly. "Maybe more than you realize. I had these made years ago, when I first qualified on the Tomcat and joined the squadron here."

"The Bobcats?"

"The Bobcats." She pauses. "I had them made because I was the new girl and the odd woman out. All the other flyers were men. Most of them didn't take me seriously, and I wanted some sign of — not loyalty, exactly, not quite allegiance — some sign of my commitment to the life I'd chosen. Like a wedding ring, only not as obvious."

"Andrews and Manny wear them, too."

Maggie nods. "It became a fashion when I was named squadron commander. Imitation is the sincerest form of flattery, and all that." She sets her cup down and leans forward. "But it's a little more personal than that for me, Kirsten. I meant it when I said it's like a wedding ring for me. My first love is flying. Always has been, always will be. There's something about the freedom of the sky...something about that solitary, high blue with nothing but the canopy between you and infinity..." She makes a small, dismissive gesture, but her eyes are bright, and a smile hovers at her mouth. "It's like the poet said once, you touch something that's at the bare edges of perception, not of Earth at all."

Kirsten's heart slams hard against her ribs. She begins to know, or thinks she does, what the other woman is saying, and she is not at all sure she dares to believe it. She tries to say something appropriately profound, but no words will come to her dry mouth.

After a moment, Maggie says quietly, "No human can compete with that, Kirsten. My heart was given long ago, and I can't take it back. I don't want to."

She forces her mouth to form the sounds. "Not even for Dakota?"

"Not even for Dakota. I won't try to tell you I don't care for her, but that's not what either of us really needs." She smiles and gets to her feet. "I've got to go back to HQ for a while. I may not make it back at all tonight."

"Maggie—" Kirsten stops, not sure what to say. Nothing seems quite adequate. But she says, "Thank you. I—" Maggie brushes her cheek lightly with a long finger, a gesture so like Dakota's that for a moment Kirsten is stunned.

She says, "No thanks necessary, my dear. I'll dance at your wedding when the time comes. Sleep well."

Long after she is gone, Kirsten sits staring into the empty fireplace. Dakota does not come home, and eventually Kirsten rises and turns the latch on the front door. She calls Asi softly to her, and goes to bed. She sleeps dreamlessly.

**It's as black** as pitch when Kirsten is pulled from her sleep, courtesy of a gentle knock on the door. With a soft "wuff", Asi clambers out of the bed and trots to the door, then sits and wags his tail, whining softly.

The knock comes again, accompanied this time by a voice she would...does...know in her dreams. The sheets conspire to entangle her as she struggles to sit up. She tosses them away, then quickly snatches them back when she realizes that she'd be putting on a show she's not yet comfortable enough to star in. When all pertinent bits are covered to her satisfaction, she runs a hand through her hair and clears the huskiness from her throat. "C-come in."

The door opens and Dakota pokes her head through, grinning as she notices Kirsten's sleep-tousled form tucked in bed. The rest of her body follows, causing Kirsten's heart to leap into her mouth and flutter there. Koda is wearing a raggedy pair of cut-off jeans that display a heart-stopping length of tanned, muscled leg and a hooded, sleeveless sweatshirt that displays her arms to the same effect. Kirsten tries to swallow, and fails. "Morning," she croaks, knowing that she's staring and unable to stop herself.

Dakota is by no means oblivious to the look she's getting. On the contrary, she feels it with every molecule in her body, and her skin warms and tingles as hormones are released into her bloodstream and busily tango their way thither and yon. She also knows that if she were anyone other than who she is, gone would be any thought of any morning activity she had originally planned. Kirsten, looking tired, and rumpled, vulnerable and devastatingly sexy, pulls at her like steel to a magnet. It is only because she is the woman she is that she resists, and gifts the young scientist with a broader grin. "Rise and shine, lazybones! The fish aren't gonna catch themselves, ya know."

That breaks the spell, and Kirsten flops onto her back, making sure to take the sheet with her. "God," she groans. "You sound just like my father."

Koda raises an eyebrow. Sounds like, maybe, but the thoughts she's entertaining while looking at those suddenly displayed legs are anything but paternal. "You said you were up for fishing this morning," she prods, pleased that her voice sounds relatively normal.

"The operative word here, Dakota, is 'morning'. This," she swings an arm in a large arc, "is oh-God thirty. Even the fish are asleep."

"Wanna bet?"

The arm collapses across Kirsten's eyes. "I knew you'd say that." Her sigh is worthy of the most scene-chewing actor ever to take the stage. "Do I have time for a shower, at least?" Not that the showers offer much. With the natural gas having petered out completely, the water comes out of the tap at three temperatures: cold, bitter cold, or icicles. Then again, a cold shower sounds just the ticket right about now.

"Sure," Koda replies, thinking much the same thing. "I'll give you ten minutes."

"So very generous of you" is the dry retort, causing Dakota to chuckle. With that, she backs out of the room, taking Asi with her.

After the door has safely closed, Kirsten removes her arm and expels a great gust of air from her lungs. "Sweet...Jesus!" Her head is spinning. Her heart is pounding. Even her damn palms are sweaty.

"Either I'm way deep in love, or I'm getting ready to have a stroke," she whispers to the uncaring ceiling. "Worst part is, I don't know which one would be easier on me."

**Exactly eleven minutes** and one very cold shower later, Kirsten appears in the living room, dressed casually in a pair of well worn jeans, a simple navy blue T-shirt and hiking boots that have seen better decades. She appears appealingly rumpled, and even younger than she normally looks. Koda smiles at her from her place in the kitchen and hefts the basket she's packed from the table. "Breakfast. C'mon, the truck's packed, Asi's aboard, and the fish are waiting."

Rubbing the sleep from her eyes, Kirsten mumbles something unintelligible and follows behind like a little kid going to the mall with Mom when she'd rather be in bed sleeping. She finally manages to waken fully once she's belted into the truck — borrowed from Judge Harcourt — and Koda is starting the engine. "Wait a minute. I thought we were just going down to the stream at the edge of the property. I've seen fish in there." She's not...quite...ready to tell the circumstances behind seeing said fish, however.

Koda shrugs. "Too many people."

Kirsten nods in understanding. Though incredibly generous and giving, Dakota Rivers is an intensely private person, just as she herself is. A private person with an innate need to escape into that privacy at any given time. Her eyes widen as she realizes the honor she's being given.

"Is that okay?" Dakota asks, unsure of the reason behind Kirsten's prolonged silence.

"It's more than okay," Kirsten replies, grinning. Reaching out, she lays a hand on Dakota's wrist, squeezing it in thanks. "Much more."

Returning the smile, Koda throws the truck into gear, and starts off, not minding in the least that Kirsten hasn't yet seen fit to remove her hand.

**Less than a** half hour later, Dakota pulls the truck into a dense grove of trees and kills the engine. Kirsten looks around through the windshield as Koda opens the door and slips out, Asi at her heels. The big dog spies something off to his left and goes pelting off, barking fit to raise the dead. A second later, a flock of pheasants rises up with a ratting whir, and Asi reappears, proudly wagging his tail.

Laughing at her dog's antics, Kirsten slips out of the truck and takes in a deep breath of spring scented air. She then walks around to the bed of the truck, where Dakota is busy unloading their equipment. "Need some help?"

"Yeah. Grab this for me, will ya?"

Kirsten's shoulder is nearly pulled from its socket as she grabs hold of the handled basket Koda hands her. "Jesus! What's in here? Bricks?"

"You'll see," Koda replies with a smirk, handing over several thick blankets. "I can get the rest."

Kirsten looks around again as Koda continues to unload the gear, taking in the seeming quiet of the place. Her mind slips back a pace to a time when she had been in a similar place after the failed business at the android factory. The droids had come from nowhere and surrounded her truck. She shivers with the memories.

"You okay?"

Kirsten frowns, knowing it's a stupid question, but needing to ask anyway. "Is it...safe here?"

Koda smiles. "It should be. And if it isn't, we have Asi, and I have this." She hefts an oblong object that can only be a cased rifle. "We've got it covered."

Kirsten nods, saddened by the need to carry a rifle on a simple fishing trip. "Things are never going to be the same, are they?"

Laying her gear down on the ground, Koda straightens, reaches out, and brushes the tips of her fingers against Kirsten's spine, between the smaller woman's shoulder blades. "I have faith in you," she begins, voice very soft, "and in the rest of us, to get rid of the androids and help make this land a good place to live in again."

"I wish I had your faith in me," Kirsten replies, sighing deeply.

"You do." Ignoring Kirsten's questioning look, Koda retrieves the rest of their gear and heads off into the woods, Asi happily at her heels.

Heaving another sigh, Kirsten tromps in after her.

**"This is beautiful,"** Kirsten whispers, as if giving full voice to her thoughts will break the enchantment of the area around her.

A faerie ring of fantastically colored flowering trees surrounds an almost perfectly circular pond whose calm surface reflects the slowly lightening sky like a mirror made of smoked glass. Fine, feathery grass grows along the shore, heads bent like Narcissus looking at his reflection in the cool water below. Frogs sing for mates across the expanse, their calls echoing and mixing with the chirp of crickets and the somnolent buzzing of a hundred other, as yet hidden, insects.

There is an almost sacred sense of peace to this hidden glen, and the calm seeps into Kirsten, soothing over edges made jagged by worry and strain. "Thank you," she says, still whispering. "For bringing me here. I know this place must mean a lot to you."

Koda favors her with a smile that is, curiously, half-shy, half-defensive. Then she relaxes. "I used to come here when I needed to think." Her smile becomes more genuine. "Or be alone."

"You mean, you never...?" Kirsten asks, surprised.

"No. Never."

Kirsten feels her breath catch. "Wow." She shakes her head, trying to clear it. "I...uh...I don't..." She looks up, startled, as a blanket is snatched from her arms.

"C'mon," Koda invites, grinning. "Let's get this spread out and do some fishing."

**"Oh God that** was good!" Kirsten groans as she flops back onto her elbows. She wiggles a little; her jeans seem to have shrunk in the waist since she put them on this morning. The top button strains heroically with the effort of holding the fabric together.

"I'm glad you enjoyed," Koda replies, watching her companion's body movements with interest...and a fairly accelerated heart-rate.

"Oh, I did more than enjoy, believe me." She laughs. "It's strange. I never liked venison before, especially not for breakfast."

"That's because I never cooked it for you," Koda teases, grinning. "Here, try this." She hands over a wine glass filled with a Pinot Noir.

"Why, Ms. Rivers," Kirsten questions over the rim of the glass, affecting a cultured accent, and batting her eyes, "wine before noon? Whatever will the neighbors think?"

"Screw the neighbors," Koda growls, taking a healthy sip of the vintage and thoroughly enjoying it. "Let 'em get their own wine."

They settle into companionable silence for a time, both content to watch the sun play over the tiny wavelets in the pond, creating a colorful light show that neither tires of viewing. Their poles are side by side, held up by simple sticks, the bobbers riding along the tiny waves like toy boats in a gigantic bathtub.

The fishing has been good, with Kirsten proving herself an apt angler, catching more than her fair share of bass, perch and crappie. It will make a welcome change from the gruel that has started to pass for food back at the base, and Kirsten licks her lips, already thinking of sautéed fresh bass over early spring greens, completely unaware of the searing blue gaze tracking the movements of her tongue and mouth.

Blinking, Dakota deliberately turns her head toward the water and finishes the last of her wine in an untasting gulp, glad for the moisture it gives a mouth gone as dry as desert sand.

"Thank you." Kirsten's soft voice floats along on the flower-scented breeze. "I don't think — no, I know I've never had such a nice morning. I...um..." Looking shyly down at her hands clasped across her belly, she continues. "I never was much for sitting down and smelling the roses. It was pretty much all work and no play, and it made me kind of a dull girl."

"Not dull," Koda responds matter-of-factly. "Just overworked." She smiles a little. "And underplayed."

Chuckling at the poor joke, Kirsten rolls her head and sees the sun peering fully over the ring of tall trees surrounding the pond. "Speaking of work..."

"I noticed." Placing her wine glass on the blanket, Koda begins packing the remains of their brunch into the basket. "Fenton's coming to the clinic in a couple hours to look at Dietrich's handiwork."

Realizing what that means, Kirsten hurriedly sits up, her face drawn and sad. "Oh, Dakota, I'm so sorry."

Koda tries to shrug it off. "'S all right. It was going to happen sooner or later. Sooner's just as well, I suppose."

Green eyes flash. "It's not all right. It's not all right and it's not fair. Damn it, you shouldn't have to go through this again!"

"If I don't, who will? Who can speak for him other than me?" Her smile is sad. "Life isn't fair. Death isn't either." Though her eyes, faraway, don't register movement, she feels a warm, slight body press against her from the back and two well-made arms wrap around her waist as a chin rests on her shoulder.

"You shouldn't have to go through this alone, Dakota. Hell, you shouldn't have to go through it at all." There is a brief pause during which Kirsten's gentle breathing tickles against Koda's ear and cheek. "What can I do to help?"

Dakota smiles and turns her head so that their faces are on a level. "Just be you," she whispers. "That's all I need."

"I will," Kirsten murmurs, sealing the vow with a kiss that quickly deepens. When she feels Koda's tongue gently trace across her lips, she opens them, bidding welcome.

With a groan, Koda pulls Kirsten's arms away, then twists the smaller woman so that they are now face to face. Her hands come up, sinking themselves into the thick, soft mass of Kirsten's golden hair, stroking and tugging as their mouths move together sensually, urgently.

Kirsten's hands find their way onto Dakota's broad shoulders, squeezing and releasing in time to her panting breaths. She is quickly becoming overwhelmed by everything — the emotions, the sensations, the taste of Koda's lips and breath — and when she feels one hand leave her hair and trail, ever so gently, against the side of her breast, she moans and pulls away.

Slumped over, she breathes in deep, trying to catch her air and calm a heart lunging itself against her ribs with passionate force. A brief touch to her shoulder, and she looks up into Koda's concerned eyes. "I'm...I'm....okay," she pants. "Just gotta...whoa."

"What's wrong? Are you all right?"

Koda's voice carries an edge to it, and that edge gets through to Kirsten on some level. Taking in a deep breath, she straightens, and lets it out slowly. "Yes, I'm fine. It just...caught me by surprise."

Koda cocks her head in question.

In response, Kirsten lifts a slightly trembling hand and lays it against Dakota's silken cheek. "I have never, ever felt like this before. Never. Physically, emotionally, it's like...it's like dangling over the edge of a cliff with the bottom nowhere in sight." She meets Koda's gaze directly, willing her to understand. "It scared me for a moment."

Dakota smiles, and turns her head just slightly so that her lips rest against Kirsten's palm. "I understand," she murmurs, kissing the hand on her face.

"You do?"

The smile broadens. "I do." Moving forward, she places the tenderest of kisses on Kirsten's reddened lips, then pulls away. "C'mon. Let's get ready for work." Grasping Kirsten's hands, Koda pulls them both up to their feet.

The young scientist steps forward and wraps her arms around Dakota's firm body and holds tight for several moments. "Thank you," she finally murmurs against the cloth covering Koda's chest. She pulls back slightly, looking up at the tall woman. "Do you think that maybe...we could come back here again sometime?"

"Count on it," Koda replies, kissing the crown of Kirsten's hair. "Count on it."

# CHAPTER TWENTY-SEVEN

Koda runs her hands over the small cat's body, pressing gently against her sides and abdomen.  Despite her ordeal of the evening before, Sister Matilda's black fur is as glossy as a raven's wing, her white bib and muzzle pristine.  She has hardly stopped purring since delivering her kittens last night, and all her bones vibrate with the rumbling.  Koda has given up on the stethoscope, resorting to the old fashioned method of counting her respirations and the beats of her heart by compressions of her ribs.  She is pleased to find them close to normal; there is no real sign of trouble in the belly, either.  The new mother's uterus is a bit loose, but nursing her litter of six should help to firm it up without further intervention.

"All right, girl.  Let's get another dose of good old penicillin in you, just as a precaution."  Leaving her lying on the exam table, small paws kneading the empty air, Koda fills a syringe from the vial in the countertop fridge.  Compared to the bobcat, Sister Matilda is an ideal patient, content to stay where she is put and to accept human attempts at help with aplomb.  Koda rubs her ears, then lifts her scruff and slips the needle in.  The purr never misses a beat.

The evening before, she had cried with her distress, and so had little Daphne Burgess.  Koda had accompanied the sergeant to his home, made her initial examination, and brought cat and human family all back to the clinic.  Sister Matilda's labor had arrested several hours before, but there had been no blockage of the birth canal.  Despite the feline's small frame and enormous belly, so round she could hardly turn herself over without all four feet leaving the exam table, Koda had found no reason why she could not deliver normally.  An injection of Oxytocin had started contractions again almost immediately, and within two hours she had become the happy mother of sextuplets.

Emphasis on the *sex* part; not one kitten looks like any other: one yellow longhair, one calico shorthair, one solid smoky grey, one black with white paws like his mother, one all white with a stubby Manx tail, and one that looks suspiciously like a Maine Coon Cat.  "Got around a bit there, didn't you girl?" Koda remarks as she lays her back among her brood.

Briefly Koda inspects her other patients in the ward.  A flop-eared rabbit with an infected eye is responding to treatment; a Scotty, survivor of an unfortunate encounter with a porcupine, looks morosely up at her over his still-swollen nose.  She gives him a scratch between the ears.  "Curiosity's not just bad for cats, bro," she admonishes him.  At least it hadn't been a skunk.

A tap sounds at the door of the ward.  "Dr. Rivers?  There's an elderly gentleman here to see you.  A civilian."

"Tell him half a minute, Shannon.  I'm coming."  Stepping in and out of the bleach basin without thinking, Koda pauses to run her hands under the tap.  She has a fair notion who the elderly civilian is and an even better notion why he's here.  From the file cabinet by her desk in the cubbyhole designated as her office, she takes two file folders and a small, silver key.  Fingering it gingerly, she drops it into her pocket.  She has known for days that this moment would come.  She hates it no less for being forewarned.

Judge Harcourt stands in the middle of the reception area.  He fills the small space to overflowing, standing with spine straight as a plumb line in pinstriped suit and burgundy tie, his salt white hair combed into waves that brush at his collar. "Doctor Rivers," he says gravely as she pushes open the door, "I wonder if I might have a moment of your time."

"Come on back," she says, gesturing with the files. Koda drags the chair from the examination room into the postage-stamp size space beside her own in front of her desk. "Have a seat, Fenton."

He remains standing, silent, until she sits, then follows suit, taking his tobacco pouch from his pocket. Without speaking he loads the pipe, reaches for the lighter and pauses, his eyes darting around the room. "Go ahead," Dakota says. "The nearest oxygen tank is two rooms over."

He gives her a grateful look, and it is only when the fragrant smoke begins to curl up from the bowl that he says, "We have a problem."

Koda snorts. "Just one? Thank you. What did you do with all the others?"

"We have a judicial problem," he amends, giving her a sharp look beneath bushy brows. "To wit, the Dietrich family, specifically his son."

"Let me guess. They want charges pressed."

"The son certainly does. The wife is a mousy little creature who scarcely uttered a word. Either she's the submissive fundamentalist sort, or she really doesn't mind being a widow." He shrugs. "Or both, of course."

"Domestic violence?"

"It's possible. Certainly the son seems very sure of his manly place in the universe, and at the moment he sees that place as his father's avenger. The MP at the gate relieved him of a knife and pistol on his way into the base. I spoke to him," he grimaces as smoke streams out about the stem of the pipe, giving him the aura of an oddly domesticated dragon, "at rather unpleasant length. We are going to have to have what amounts to a preliminary hearing-cum-inquest, at the very least. If there were any such available, I would advise that impetuous cousin of yours to get himself lawyered up. Where is he, by the way?"

"He *says* the colonel's made him PLO for life — that's Permanent Latrine Officer — but he's actually working maintenance out on the flightline. She's got Andrews, the other pilot involved, doing the same. Here."

Koda pushes the files across the desk. "These are the Polaroids I took before and after I treated the two surviving victims of the leghold traps. You can see the results of the treatment in person."

The judge opens the folders, studying the harshly-lit, slightly overexposed color pictures. His expression does not change, but Koda marks the sudden clenching of his teeth on the pipe stem as he inspects the photos of the bobcat's torn and bloody flesh, the tendons hanging loose though the bones beneath had remained, by some fluke, unbroken. Beside it is a second Polaroid, this one showing the wound cleanly shaved and stitched. The coyote's involuntarily bobbed tail looks less serious, and the judge cannot quite suppress a twitch at the corner of his mouth. "The Trickster tricked," he observes, "and escaping with nothing but wounded dignity in the end. Appropriate."

"Not quite nothing," Dakota says quietly. "That wound was nastily infected. He could have gone septic and died."

"You're right, of course." The judge sets the folders down. "Are there other photographs?"

Of the wolf, Wa Uspewicakiyapi, he means. "No. Come out to the kennels, then we'll open the freezer."

Outside, Harcourt comes close to smiling again. The coyote lies on his back, forepaws crossed over his ribs in classic mummy fashion, snoring in the sun. His abbreviated tail twitches with his dreams, the wound healed over, leaving only a bare tip of skin to testify to his ordeal. The bobcat lies invisible inside the concrete block shelter at one end of her run, favoring shade for her siesta. But signs of her improvement are obvious. A much scuffed rubber ball testifies to her growing ease at chasing and pouncing; except for a few crumbs and a feather or two, her food bowl is empty. Harcourt shoots Koda a reproving glance, and she says, "She caught a pigeon."

"Rock dove," he corrects her absently. "At least that's a good sign she can begin to fend for herself."

"With luck, I should be able to release both of them in a week or so. I'm going to wait for Tacoma to come back from the wind farm so he can help with her. She's getting pretty feisty now that she's doing better."

"You mean uncooperative."

Dakota grins at him. "With everyone but Tacoma; I mean, she barely tolerates us. She's picky."

"And these?" Harcourt gestures toward the run where the mother wolf lies sunning herself on the concrete, while her pup repeatedly flings himself up the incline of her shoulders and as repeatedly slides downward to bump his stubby tail on the hard surface. A sharp yap announces his frustration, but his mother barely twitches. Finally he trots around her, taking the long way at last, and settles down to nurse, nuzzling at her belly. She rouses, licks him absently, and resumes her nap.

"Wa Uspewicakiyapi's mate and surviving pup. They're almost ready for release, too."

"Excellent," he says quietly. "Shall we go in?"

Koda feels a chill pass down her spine. Shall we open the freezer, he means. She has not unlocked the unit since Kirsten brought her the keys, that day by the streamside. She knows what she will see and knows that, gash for gash and shattered bone for bone, she has seen far worse. The shock was in discovering what Tacoma had done; it is long past and maintains no hold over her. Stiffly her fingers close about the small bit of metal in her pocket. "All right," she says shortly, and turns toward the door.

Her hands are steady as she turns the key in the lock. As the lid comes up, a cloud of frosty air rises up to meet them like fog, obscuring the contents of the freezer. With it, faint with the cold, comes the sickly sweet odor of death. When the condensate clears, a bundle perhaps a meter long, wrapped in heavy plastic, lies visible at the bottom.

Koda bends down to grasp it at the middle, but Harcourt says, "Allow me," and takes hold of one end, leaving Koda to lift the other. Together they carry it to the metal worktable normally used for such chores as mixing plaster casts or clipping fur from the cuts and scratches of recalcitrant patients. They set it down gently.

A moment's inspection reveals that the plastic is not wound about the body but folded over it in several layers. As gently as if she were smoothing the bedcovers of a child, she loosens the tape and lays back the heavy, transparent plastic, frosted with the cold. At the last, the outlines of the wolf's form clearly visible through it, she hesitates for a breath. Then, firmly, she folds it back.

Though Manny had been quick, rigor had apparently come and gone by the time he found the wolf's remains, and temperatures had been just high enough not to freeze them where they lay. There can be no illusion that Wa Uspewicakiyapi seems only sleeping, yet he is decently laid out, his spine slightly curved, his head on his paws, his tail curled over his flank to expose the terrible wound in his leg.

Harcourt rounds the table for a closer look. Even frozen solid, it is clear that the teeth of the trap have torn the flesh down to the bone, abrading tendons and muscle and nerves over time enough for the edges to become dried and bloodless. Fragments of bone show through the shredded flesh. The fur, mingled grey and white, remains clotted with crimson. On his belly, the blood is frozen in a thin, smooth sheet, only the edges of skin showing white where the torn organs have been replaced. The position of the head hides the worst of the wounds to the neck, but streaks of blood stain the ruff, a necklace of deep garnet. As Harcourt leans closer to look, his face becomes as still as the wolf's own, and as cold. But he says only, "Dakota, would you please bring the camera? We need to have a permanent record."

In the examination room, Koda checks the camera for film and is grateful for the few minutes necessary to find and slip a new packet into place. Her hands are numb from the cold, and she fumbles twice as she closes the back. The numbness about her heart has begun to shift, the first cracks appearing in the blue ice that has crept through her veins since the moment she found Wa Uspewicakiyapi bleeding his life out into the snow. In its place anger rises, a rage as white and searing as sheet lightning. She fumbles again as she turns toward the door, knocking a box of gauze sponges to the floor. As she stoops to pick them up her vision narrows, centering only on the small circle of light that contains her hand, lifting the box, meticulously setting it back down on the counter. Hunter sight.

But her prey is dead already, lying in the hospital morgue as frozen and cold as his victim. *You should have left him for me, cousin.* But if she cannot have him, she can at least make sure that others do not follow him. *Never. Never again. I swear it.*

Light gradually invades the darkness that has gathered around her, and her field of view returns to normal. Carefully she steps around the examination table and returns to the workroom where Harcourt waits for the camera. Wordlessly she hands it to him, allowing him to record the evidence of brutal death.

When he is done, the photos slipped into a pocket, he says quietly, "I need to ask you a question, Dakota. It's one I will need to ask you again, at the inquest."

She nods, waiting.

"In your professional judgment, and strictly your professional judgment, were these injuries sufficient to cause death?"

Shutting out the sight of the dead before her, shutting out the memory of her friend struggling in the trap, she nods. "When I found him, he was shocking from blood loss and exposure. Infection and frostbite had destroyed muscle and organ tissue. The left tibia and fibula, as you can see, were both shattered past the point where they could have been pinned."

"Had you found him earlier, could surgery have saved his life?"

She answers, not quite able to keep the anger from her voice. "If I had found him much earlier, before he was attacked by whatever tore him open — yes. His life, yes. But not his *life*, Fenton. Even if the other wounds could be repaired or had never happened, even if the infection could be fought down, the leg was unsalvageable. Only a sadist would have condemned him to that."

The judge raises one hand, palm outward. "Bear with me a moment longer, please. Quality of life aside, why did you not bring him back and attempt the operation?"

"Because his respiration was depressed and his blood loss so heavy that, *in my professional judgment*," she bites the words off, "he would not have survived transportation, much less anaesthesia."

"Thank you. Now allow me to help."

Together they fold the plastic back into place, taping it firmly. Gently they lay Wa Uspewicakiyapi back into his chill resting place. Her hand lingers for a moment on the bundle. *Only for a while, old friend,* she promises silently. *Only until justice has been done. We will not fail you again.*

In the silence of her mind, a wolf howl rises to the floating moon.

**The witness room,** four generically off-white walls topped by a yellowing acoustic–tile ceiling, fits only a bit less snugly than a coffin. Three paces long, three paces wide, its furnishings consist of one small table, one spine-cracking folding chair of indeterminate but ancient vintage, and one 60-watt light bulb further dimmed by a frosted glass globe. It bears a decided resemblance to the classic police interrogation room.

According to her watch, Koda has been here for almost an hour, apparently going on all morning. *Good thing I'm not claustrophobic. Yet.*

A jury for the trial of the Rapid City jail rapists was seated yesterday, with final selection in the morning and opening statements after lunch. The prosecution has begun its case this morning with accounts of the raid from the participants, to be followed by testimony from the victims in the afternoon. She has reviewed her testimony twice with Alderson, the last time before the opening gavel more than two hours ago. Larke and Martinez have already given their accounts; Andrews is up now, with Koda held back for last. The strategy may be transparent, but its effectiveness is undisputed. As the hero of the Cheyenne, she is the *pièce de resistance.* She is also mortally bored with the tedium of waiting.

Checking her watch one last time — *Damn, he said we'd be out of here by eleven* — Koda sinks crosslegged to the relative comfort of the floor, opens Spengler at her bookmark, and begins to read.

She had snatched this particular book up on her way out her house all those months ago, not sure why, then, not really sure why now. Then it had seemed a token of the past, a link to connect her to the spacious library that occupies a third of her home, something to remind her of — and call her back to — the comfortable life she and Tali had built between them. An incomplete farewell.

But now... She lets the book fall open on her knees, propping her chin on her fists. Spengler had been the great heretic of early twentieth century history, a prophet of doom floating loose on the riptide of social and industrial progressivism. History, he had said, moved not in ever ascending lines, but in cycles: birth, rise, maturity, decline, and fall. He had fallen in and out of academic fashion, spiking in the late thirties when he had predicted that the Thousand Year Reich would last less than ten, and thereafter relegated to the "crank science" midden along with von Daniken and other pseudoscholarly nut jobs.

In the early 2000s, Spengler had been rescued from the refuse heap and dusted off by Stan Uribe, then of Baylor. Uribe had argued that the United States at that time was in a phase corresponding to Europe's Reformation, complete with religious wars — mostly fought in the political arena rather than on the battlefield — and imploding corporate feudalism. His theories had cost him his job, but he had moved on to U Penn's infinitely more prestigious department. There he had gone on to extrapolate the theory to encompass the rise of American Empire, built like others before it on the three G's of colonialism and conversion: God, Gold and Glory. He had nearly gotten fired again in 2003, when he published the capstone of his theory, the inevitable fall of the Empire to those it, like Rome two millennia before, had labeled barbarians: women, Muslims, pagans, African Americans, gays and lesbians, Hispanics, the Indigenous Nations.

While battle raged in the boardroom, Koda and Tali had sat in his lectures spellbound. They had spent hours in his office, talking, questioning, then gone on to use their scarce elective hours for his seminars, sitting up until four in the morning with friends arguing the consequences if Uribe were right.

*If he were right... And it seems he is, though not in the way he expected.*

*What now? How do we rebuild, but on a different model that can break the cycle? Can we break the cycle?* For the first time in nearly four hundred years, the Nations have the opportunity to develop something different from the European pattern. *We need to begin to make contact with other communities that have survived, like the commune Kirsten found in Minnesota. Assuming that we survive, we need — not an exit strategy, a way in to a different world. How will a technological people, most of whom will be former white, middle-class Americans, fit into the Time of the White Buffalo?*

*And gods, how am I going to bring a white girl home to Mother?*

A sharp rap brings her suddenly to her feet. The bailiff's face, florid under its blond buzz cut, appears in the door. "Doctor Rivers, you've been called to the stand."

Setting her book down, she follows the uniformed sergeant out of the witness room and through the double doors of the court. Spectators fill two-thirds of the seats on the public's side of the rail, a respectable crowd for all but the most notorious cases even in the time before the uprising. Some she recognizes as women liberated from the prison. One is Millie Buxton, her thin face drawn and pale with sleeplessness. Her fingers, clasped in her lap, writhe incessantly. She sits somewhat apart from the rest, toward the back. Also toward the back, Koda notes a large man wearing dark glasses, one foot on the floor and a fold of his jeans over the stump above his knee. His crutches lean against the back of the bench. She casts him a sharp glance, trying to place him, though she is certain she does not recognize him.

The second bailiff swings the gate open for her, and she approaches the dais with the judge's bench and the witness stand. Harcourt fills his high seat as though he has grown there, inseparable from the black robe of his office or the gavel laid ready to his hand. He gives no sign of recognition — no fear, no favor from this one, ever — and says simply, "Madam Clerk, swear the witness."

The clerk steps from behind her desk, slightly raising the Bible there with an inquiring look. Koda shakes her head and lays her hand on the medicine bundle around her neck instead. In a low but clear voice, she swears to tell the truth, the whole truth, and nothing but the truth, "so help me, Ina Maka."

Alderson leads her steadily, step by step, though the events of the raid on the Rapid City jail. At his prompting, she recounts the initial attack on the facility, the wounding of Larke and the deaths of Johnson and Reese. The hush in the courtroom deepens as she tells of leading her squad through the crawlspace above the cells, grows deeper still as she recalls — keeping all emotion from her voice — the joy of the released prisoners, their anger and hatred for their captors, their grief. From where she sits, she can see that even Millie Buxton's fingers have fallen still, caught up as she perhaps is in the recollection of her own and her daughter's ordeal.

Not so the man in the sunglasses. His lips move constantly, as though praying or conversing earnestly with himself, and his fingers curl and uncurl, sliding up and down the invisible length of some unseen measure.

*As if playing something...* An image tickles at her memory. *A guitar, that's it! That's him, the blind singer Kirsten and Maggie met at the census. My God, he's the press!*

When her narrative is at an end, a bare armature of facts, no more, Alderson turns back to the prosecution's table. "Pass the witness, Your Honor."

As Bourdreaux rises to take his place in the well of the court, Koda studies the defendants. McCallum has tipped his chair back on its hind legs so that it rests almost on the rail separating the defense table from the audience. Kazen studies the papers before him, as if searching for some unrecognized word of release; beside him, Petrovich stares at the jury, his hostility palpable. Buxton, though, sits with his elbows propped on the table, his forehead against his folded hands, apparently oblivious to the proceedings around him. His skin, pale when Koda first saw him at the jail, has grown grey and lusterless.

*Like a mushroom, something that lives in the dark. Like a corpse. A man dead inside, too numb even to lie down.*

Boudreaux clasps his hands in front of him, then looses them and clasps them behind his back instead. His job is an appalling one: to defend and, if he can, save the lives of, four men who are guilty far beyond a reasonable doubt, knowing that he may have a chance of success with only one of them. Knowing, too, that that chance hangs by a thread as thin as spider silk.

"Dr. Rivers, you have already told the Court how you found these four men imprisoned in the Rapid City facility operated by Corrections Corporation of America. You found each in a separate cell, is that correct?"

"Each was in an individual cell."

"Were they in contiguous cells within the same block?"

"They were in the same block, but not in adjoining cells."

"When you entered those cells, did you observe any means by which an occupant might communicate with the occupants of other cells or with prison personnel?"

Silently, Koda gives him full marks. He is creeping up slowly on the conspiracy charge. "Each cell contained a metal cot, a latrine, and one stool. No communications devices of any kind were visible."

"Any writing materials?"

"None."

"Did subsequent search of the defendants turn up, say, cell phones, beepers, walkie talkies, notes or notepaper, anything of that nature?"

"None."

"Did you ever, at any point, observe the prisoners to communicate with each other?"

"I did not."

"Did you ever, at any point, observe the prisoners to communicate with any of the androids at the CCA facility?"

"I did not."

Boudreaux gives a satisfied nod, then steps back behind the defense table. He shuffles several sheets of closely written yellow paper. "Tell me, Dr. Rivers, did any of the prisoners refuse, or attempt to refuse, to leave his cell when your squad opened their doors?"

"One did."

"Which one? Can you point him out to the court?"

"Mr. Buxton indicated that he did not wish to leave his cell."

"And how did he do that?"

"We found him on his cot in the fetal position. He did not answer us at first when we spoke to him, then begged us to leave him."

"What was his physical condition, Dr. Rivers?"

Movement to one side catches her eye as Alderson pushes back his chair and begins to rise. He pauses for a moment, his backside canted awkwardly at the audience, then he flushes and sits down abruptly. One juror covers her mouth with her hand, her black eyes sparkling. Koda says, "He was dehydrated and thin bordering on emaciation. When he stood, his feet were unsteady, and he had to be assisted to walk."

Boudreax gives a clearly satisfied nod, then asks, "Dr. Rivers, have you ever attended human beings as well as your more accustomed four-footed and winged patients?"

"I have."

"Under what circumstances?"

Briefly Koda recounts her service as unofficial Air Force medic to the Bobcats and their allies, both before and after their return to the base. "I've also set the odd bone or two on my ranch or my parents', and given a good many insulin and B-12 shots to older folks in the neighborhood."

"I see. So you could be trusted to know that when someone's ribs are showing, he's underweight, even though he's not a horse?"

With an effort, Koda keeps her face straight. "I do believe so, Major."

"No further questions."

"You may step down," Harcourt says, bringing his gavel down resoundingly on its holder. "Court adjourned until two o'clock."

On her way out, Koda pauses at the rear bench where the blind man sits. She says, "You're Harry the singer, aren't you?"

"I am." His face turns toward her, his head angled to hear more clearly. "You just testified. You're Dakota Rivers."

"Yes. I understand you sang a fine song at the census."

Harry grins hugely. "I had some good material. Good story, good tune. Maybe you'll let me sing it for you, sometime."

"Maybe. Meanwhile, thanks." Koda gives his hand a squeeze, unobtrusively palming a folded piece of paper. "This will get you onto the base and to the infirmary if you ever need anything. Don't be shy about using it."

Not waiting for thanks, she slips quietly from the room. Outside, she checks her watch and turns down the path that leads to the officers' housing. If she hurries, she can make a brief lunch with Kirsten before returning to the clinic. She smiles at the thought and quickens her pace.

# CHAPTER TWENTY-EIGHT

Tacoma sneaks a look in his rearview mirror as the caravan snakes its way back toward the base. Two armored patrol carriers are followed by two flatbed eighteen wheelers which carry two gigantic fans they have appropriated from OverDale Windfarm, Inc. All seems clear, but something is niggling at the back of his neck, making the hairs there stand up stiffly. The road they're traveling on is little used, and there are no trees or other sightline obstructions to block the view.

He catches Manny out of the corner of his eye. The younger man is grinning like a kid playing hooky — which in a way is exactly what he's doing. "'Sup, cuz?"

Tacoma takes another quick look in the rearview mirror before turning to his cousin. "You'd better think about getting back in touch with the floorboards, Manny. We'll be nearing the base pretty soon."

Manny rolls his eyes, grinning at his cousin. "Stop being such a wuss, cuz. The colonel's in court all day, and if she steps outside to take a whiz, Anderson's covering for me. We've got it knocked, so stop worrying about it."

"I am worried about it," Tacoma replies, staring at the younger man until Manny pales slightly and turns away.

His eyes widen and his skin goes a shocky white as he just catches something he can't identify — though it looks frighteningly human — standing in the exact center of the road. "Watch out!"

Tacoma looks forward just in time to feel the truck impact with whatever it is he's hit. The object is borne under the vehicle and the driver's side tires rise and fall with sickening thuds. He slams on the brakes, bringing the truck to a skidding halt, and slumps back against the seat, face greasy with sudden sweat. "Please tell me that was a deer."

"I don't think so, cuz," Manny replies in a small voice. He's about to say more when a sound like a sharp, muffled cough is heard behind them. "Holy fuck! What was that?"

Tacoma, who's heard that sound too many times to count, is already reacting, snapping open his harness and lunging out the door, his gun already to hand.

The APC that had been behind them is a smoking wreck from which injured men continue to emerge, their clothes and exposed skin covered with smoke, soot, and blood.

"Is there anybody still inside?" Tacoma demands, pulling a soot covered, violently coughing soldier out by one singed and smoking arm.

"Donaldson, sir!" the airman chokes out. "He...was the...driver! Got...hurt bad, sir!"

Fire blooms up in the truck as Tacoma pushes the injured man out of the way. He jumps back as flames shoot out of the shattered windows, feeling his eyebrows singe and the skin on his face and hands grow hot and tight. With a soft cry, he races around the front of the burning vehicle toward the driver's side where flames pour from the shattered frame like water from an open hydrant. He feels a hand grab his arm and he shakes it off savagely, only to have it grabbed again.

"Are you crazy, man?" Manny screams into his ear. "This thing's about to blow sky high!"

"Get back! I'm getting Donaldson out!"

Manny's face looms before his streaming eyes. "He's dead, *thanhanshi*! He's already dead!"

Ripping open his shirt, Tacoma peels it off and uses it to beat back the flames. They die down enough for him to get a glimpse inside the smoke-shrouded interior. The young man inside is fully conscious; startlingly pale green eyes stare out from a face blackened by soot and burns, beseeching. Fire blooms upward again, forcing Tacoma back a step. He beats down the flames a second time, and reaches inside, grabbing the injured man under his armpit and pulling backward, muscles straining against Donaldson's dead weight.

The young man screams as the bones in his shattered legs grind against one another, trapped beneath the remains of the console. Tacoma eases up as another man, one he can't recognize through the smoky haze, shoots a chemical extinguisher into the damaged compartment, covering everything with a thin layer of white foam. He feels a body brush by him and, looking down, he sees Manny reaching beneath the still smoking and twisted metal, attempting to free the trapped man's crushed legs.

The man screams again, though it has a breathless, wheezing quality to it that Tacoma doesn't like at all. "Hurry!" he commands, earning only a glare from his cousin as Manny returns to his task. The metal is scorching hot, burning his palms and fingers and arms with every touch. He ignores the pain, concentrating only on the desperate need to free Donaldson before the remains of the APC blow to heaven.

The flames rise again, undaunted by the chemical. "The gas tank's ready to blow, sir!" comes an unknown voice screaming down on them from the outside, from safety. "Goddammit, get out of there, sirs! Now!"

The cousins' gazes meet; each gives a grim nod, and in concerted effort, struggles to free their injured comrade before they're all blown to bits. Manny is finally able to slip his shoulder — the injured one, but there can be no help for it — under the wrecked console, and with a loud grunt, pushes upward with all of his strength. The twisted metal squeals but, grudgingly, it gives, lifting by the slightest of fractions. "NOW!"

His grip as secure as he can make it, Tacoma uses the large muscles in his back, shoulders, and legs to pull the screaming airman from the mangled compartment. It's not a textbook extraction, but it gets the job done. Manny's shoulder gives out just as Tacoma manages to pull the airman's legs completely free of the wreckage. Handing Donaldson quickly off to the three men standing behind him, he then reaches down, grabs Manny by his collar, and bodily tosses him away from the mangled APC. A split-second later, the truck goes up in a blooming ball of smoke and fire. Tacoma finds himself lifted, almost tenderly, from his feet, and driven backward by the force of the explosion. Curiously, there is no pain whatsoever.

*Maybe I already walk the Spirit Path*, he thinks as he watches the ground race beneath him with almost clinical detachment. His landing, upon his back, is equally painless, as if he's fallen into a cloud, and he is able to watch, with that same detachment, as flames eagerly lick up his pant legs. He feels...giddy almost...like a boy with a wonderful secret that no one else knows.

The pain comes suddenly, like air entering a vacuum. Waves of agony spike through his body, and he reacts instantly, instinctively tossing the men who are manhandling him away like flies.

"Cut it out, dammit!" Manny bellows, holding him down with his one good arm. "You're on fucking fire, Tacoma! Now lie still or I'll put you out! I swear I will!"

Some of that gets through, and Tacoma forces his muscles to relax. He can smell burning clothes and singed flesh that he assumes belongs to him. His stomach rolls once, then is steady. Manny's face swims back into his vision, sweat-covered, with eyes the size of full moons.

"That's better. Shit, cuz, I thought you crapped out on us for sure! Don't be goin' all Crazy Horse on me again, okay?"

Groaning, Tacoma pushes himself up to a sitting position and surveys the damage, starting with his own body. His fatigues have been burned almost totally away, but the skin beneath, though reddened, seems little the worse for wear. Blisters are already starting to form on the palms of both hands and on his right cheek, just below his eye, which waters constantly and feels as if it's leaking battery acid.

Blinking rapidly, he looks across the ground at the smoking remains of the APC. The injured, five in all including Donaldson, lie among the wreckage like broken dolls on a garbage heap. Pale-faced young men and women tend the injured as best they can while casting furtive and pleading looks in the direction of Manny and Tacoma — the leaders of the mission. Manny looks back, contemplating, and Tacoma uses this second of inattention to drag himself to his feet by sheer strength.

Manny turns back in time to see his cousin wobble as if standing at the epicenter of a mild earthquake. Just about to administer a good old fashioned ass chewing, he ducks as a bullet passes close enough to crease what little there is of his hair.

Tacoma totters, but manages to keep his balance. Ignoring the agony that is his body, he breaks into a shambling run, yelling for his men to take cover even as he helps two corpsmen lift Donaldson and hurry him around to the back of the one remaining APC. He can sense the confusion; smell the fear in those around him — young men and women all. Taking a deep breath, he wills the pain to the back of his mind, making it unimportant, making it gone.

Lifting his head mere millimeters, he peers through the window of the APC. As if materialized from thin air, a squad of thirty androids — he can tell this by the sunlight winking from the leader's collar — stands forty yards distant. All are heavily armed and peering at them through emotionless dolls' eyes. "Manny!"

"Yeah?"

Tacoma glances over at his cousin, then looks again, more carefully this time. Manny's head is cocked and his shoulder hangs strangely. "What—?"

"It's not broken. I don't think." He flushes faintly. "I had to use it to lift the shit outta the way so you could pull Donaldson out. I'm fine."

"Like hell you are." Tacoma reaches up, but Manny hisses and pulls away.

"It's just dislocated, all right? We've got more important things to worry about right now."

Tacoma looks as if he's given in, but just as Manny relaxes, his cousin, quick as lightning, runs his fingers over the collarbone, determines it's not broken, grabs his arm and levers it in a smooth, strong motion. A loud pop heralds the return of the joint to its socket, and Manny sees a whole galaxy's worth of stars. His world greys out for a second, but comes back quickly as a heavy gun is pushed hard against his chest. "Now you've got two hands to shoot," Tacoma grunts, grabbing his own weapon with hands that sting like a swarm of hornets. "Anyone who can hold a gun, grab one!" he orders. "Keep under cover until I give the word."

Easing the door open, he grabs the minicomp that lies on the dashboard, silently thanking his sister for pressing it into his hand before he left that morning. She knew. Somehow, she knew. This doesn't surprise him. It is simply her way. It's why the whole family looks at her sometimes as something more than human. He knows the truth of the matter, and suspects that his father does as well.

Laying his gun down on the seat, he gingerly palms the comp open and studies the layout. Standard. The power button is a bold red. Whispering a prayer to Wakan Thanka, he depresses the button.

"Here we go," he mutters. "Fire! Now!"

The first line of droids goes down like tenpins, dropping where they stand.

"Bless you, Kirsten! Keep firing!"

The second and third rows drop silently.

"Shit, cuz!" Manny shouts, laughing. "Like shooting fish in a barrel!" Whooping, he continues pressing the trigger, mowing down the remaining androids as if they are practice targets on a shooting range.

"Cease fire!" Tacoma shouts when the last droid is down. "Load up the wounded and be quick about it! We need to go, now!" He turns to help the others with Donaldson, but is stopped by a soft oath from his cousin. Turning back, he watches as thirty more androids appear, stepping over their fallen comrades as they begin their approach.

"Shit! Everybody keep loading those wounded! Now! Hurry!" Grabbing the minicomp, Tacoma presses the button again.

The androids continue their advance, completely unaffected.

"What the fuck?" Manny demands. "You sure you're doin' it right, cuz?"

"Of course I'm doing it right!"

"Maybe you broke it."

"I didn't — fuck." Repeated pressing of the power button has no effect and he throws it back into the truck in frustration.

"Maybe they're human?"

To test the theory, Tacoma fires off several rounds, hitting the leader in the chest and belly with several rounds.

"Or maybe not," Manny exhales as the droid remains on his feet and continues forward. "Okay. What now? And where the fuck are they coming from?"

"Pull the locker out of the back seat, *thanhanshi*. Let's give them some metal to munch on."

"You got it, cuz." The heavy footlocker comes to the ground with a thud, and Manny quickly snaps it open. It's filled to the brim with fragmentation grenades. He pulls several out and hands two to his cousin.

"Thanks. Let's just keep throwing these things 'til they're gone."

"The grenades or the droids?" Manny asks with a grin.

"Both. Now!"

The androids only now begin to return fire as grenade explosions surround them, taking down many of their number with the first blows. A young mechanic, Tasha Kim, cries out as a bullet finds the crease between her shoulder and neck. She manages to keep hold of the injured airman she's helping, however, and eases him into the back of the APC just as another round misses her by less than an inch. She drops to the ground and reaches for her weapon, a service pistol that will do less than nothing against the androids.

"Is everybody in?" Tacoma shouts down at her.

"I...think so, sir!"

"Don't think, Corporal! Know!"

"Y-yes, sir!"

In the cab, Manny hangs on for dear life as Tacoma puts the truck through its paces, his burned hands swathed in bandages from the meager first aid kit they'd found. "Are they following us?" Tacoma shouts over the roar of the over-stressed engine.

"Fucked if I know!" Manny shouts back, twisting his hurting body like a contortionist in an attempt to see behind him. "Does it matter? They're on foot!"

"The ones we know about, maybe!"

Manny shoots his cousin a withering glare. "You had to say that, didn't you? You just had to say that."

Still seven miles out and hauling hell bent for leather, Tacoma stiffens at the wheel as he spies several vehicles heading his way at a high rate of speed.

"Aww fuck," Manny grunts, slumping against the backrest. He turns his head to the side. "What are you grinnin' at?"

"The cavalry's just come over the hill, *thanhanshi*. Look."

Manny leans forward against his harness, squinting his eyes to get a clearer picture of the oncoming vehicles. A Jeep is in the lead, and on the passenger side stands a tall figure, one hand wrapped securely around the padded rollbar. It's a figure he knows, with long, inky black hair streaming behind like a war bonnet in the wind. "Dakota!" he yells happily. "Hot shit! Yeah!" His jubilation fades, however, as a second Jeep roars into view. The driver is also a figure he knows, and all too well at that.

"So much for sneaking in the back door, huh, cuz?" Tacoma needles, grinning.

Manny flips him an abbreviated peace sign and slumps further into his seat. "I'm fucked. Well and truly fucked," he groans.

"Have faith, *thanhanshi*. It's not over 'til it's over. We'll play you up as the Hero of the Wind Fans. Get your sentence beat down to two weeks in the brig...three, tops."

Whatever nasty reply Manny is about to make is aborted as the lead Jeep catches them, and Dakota jumps out before the vehicle has stopped rolling. Tacoma brakes quickly as Koda trots to his window.

"Is everybody okay?" she demands, eyes flashing.

"We got some burns, bad ones."

"Fucking droid played suicide bomber on us," Manny adds. "Took out one of our APCs. Few dozen more of 'em came outta nowhere and started shooting."

"Did they follow you?"

"I don't know," Tacoma replies. "The ones we saw were on foot, so if they did, they're far behind us now."

Dakota eyes both of them. Both of them come to attention, aches, pains and all. There is a commanding presence to her, a dark, roiling energy that they can almost see, hovering around her like a malignant cloud. "Get yourselves back to the base and to the hospital, best possible speed. We've got a few assault vehicles to escort you. Don't stop for anything, understand? Nothing."

"Understood," Tacoma responds.

Her expression softens only slightly. "I'm glad you guys are all right. Now, take off."

With a sharp nod, Tacoma does just that, throwing the truck into gear and rumbling off, the others in his abbreviated caravan following like ducklings. As they pass the second Jeep, Manny winces. Allen stares through the windshield, marking him, letting him know in no uncertain terms and with just the power of her gaze that fighting the androids was the easy part of this adventure.

"Think it's too late to go AWOL?" he whines to his cousin. A bark of laughter is his only response.

**"Turn down this** way. We'll come at them from the back."

Following the direction of Koda's pointing finger, Kirsten wrestles the Jeep onto a narrow, rutted path — "road" would be a definite misnomer — and shakes the leaves from a low branch from her hair as she straightens the vehicle out. "Do you really think it was an ambush?"

"It's looking that way," Koda replies, lifting a hand to brush the hair from her eyes and mouth. "We'll know more once we get to the site, though."

"If you're right, that means there's someone on the inside."

"Could be," Koda muses. "But let's wait 'til we know what we're up against before we make any assumptions."

"Right."

Ten minutes later, they arrive at the site of the ambush, Maggie's Jeep right behind them. The colonel hops out of her vehicle and takes a quick look around. "What a mess."

"It is that," Koda replies, squatting and sifting through the still smoldering rubble.

"We're just lucky nobody died," Maggie comments, squatting beside Dakota.

Koda pins her with a look. "We don't know that for sure. Tacoma said they had some pretty bad burns."

Maggie looks at her for a moment, then sighs, nodding. "You're right, of course." She looks over the rubble carefully, gingerly picking up several pieces of jagged metal with just the tips of her fingers, and turning them this way and that. "Well, what do you think?"

"I'm not sure," Dakota replies, then looks up. "Kirsten?"

Joining the duo, Kirsten lowers herself to her haunches, her expression somber. "I think we're in trouble."

Dakota gazes steadily at her. "What do you mean?"

"Well, when you told me about Tacoma's 'suicide bomber', I had gone with the assumption that we were talking about an android carrying a bomb."

"We're not?" Maggie asks, a little shiver of apprehension skittering down her spine.

"It doesn't look that way."

"Then what are we talking about, if not an android with a bomb?" the colonel persisted.

"An android that is a bomb," Dakota answers, continuing to gaze at Kirsten.

"Got it in one," Kirsten replies somberly, lifting a piece of metal whose purpose is incomprehensible to both of her watchers. "I'll need to gather up as much of this stuff as possible to be sure, but unless I miss my guess, we're talking about an entirely new type of android here. One that I'm almost positive didn't exist before the uprising."

"Jesus," Maggie breathes. "How certain are you about this?"

"Certain enough to make it an executive order that no one, including Tacoma and everyone else who was out here, speaks a word of this to anyone."

Maggie nods. "Consider it done." Rising to her feet, she dusts her hands off on the legs of her fatigues. "I've got a few tarps in the back of my Jeep. Let me bring 'em over and we'll start collecting the evidence."

Dakota also rises and looks down at Kirsten a moment longer. "I'm gonna check out some likely staging areas. This place reeks of an ambush."

"It does," Kirsten agrees, looking around. Darting a quick glance in Maggie's direction, she gazes back up at Dakota, a sweet, shy smile curving her lips. "Be careful, okay?" Koda tips her a wink and a megawatt grin that leaves Kirsten seeing stars.

"You got it."

Thankfully, Kirsten's blush fades before Maggie returns, arms full of tarps and several sets of latex gloves. "You're the expert, Doc," she grins, laying her booty on the ground next to the smaller woman. "Let me know what you want me to do, and I'm there."

Smiling her thanks, Kirsten pulls on the gloves, pats the ground next to her, and begins showing Maggie exactly what it is that she's looking for. Within moments, both are heavily engrossed in their task.

**Several hours later,** the sun is preparing to set as Kirsten gets to her feet and stretches legs gone as numb as blocks of wood. Intense concentration and looking for minuscule android parts without benefit of her glasses has given her a headache strong enough to fell a charging moose. Stretching, she groans in mingled pleasure and pain as her vertebrae crackle and pop down the length of her spine, struggling to realign themselves against the ravages of inactivity and poor posture.

Nearby, Maggie stows the last of the gear in the Jeep, taking care to tie it down securely, especially given the stiff evening breeze that has suddenly kicked up.

Kirsten looks down at the now denuded ground, then west, toward the setting sun. With a sense of almost pleasant melancholia, she watches the sky fill with color. Her day has been long; her night promises to be longer still, but she feels...fulfilled. The task set before her is one that she is confident in her abilities to take on. Better than running line after line after byte after byte of fragmented code with no end in sight. Better still than playing titular head to the lost and the broken.

They lost one today, an elderly woman who most in the camp adored. She lost her entire family in one fell swoop, only managing to stay alive pinned beneath the body of the man with whom she had shared her life and heart for over fifty years. The children of the base had swarmed to her like bees to honey, and she seemed genuinely glad to fuss over them. In the end, though, the family she'd gained couldn't replace the family she'd lost, and they found her this morning, an empty pill bottle at her side.

It is the third suicide in as many weeks, and people — too many people — are looking to Kirsten for answers she doesn't have.

Here, though, is work she can do, answers she can give; a place where she feels most comfortable and, if she is to admit deep secrets to herself, worthy as well.

Her reverie is broken by the sudden appearance of Dakota, approaching from the direction of the setting sun. The breeze blows the thick ink of her hair back from her brow, and her eyes snap and glow with a color that seems to emanate from within. Her muscled arms swing freely, fully exposed by the sleeveless flannel which flutters and jumps against a simple black tank she wears beneath. Her jeans, ripped and faded, cling in all the right places as her long limbed, almost cocky stride brings her rapidly closer.

Looking upon her, this beauty with the sun at her back gilding her body in pure gold, Kirsten is struck once again by her exquisiteness — wild, untamed, much like the woman who wields it so easily. Her eyes remain fastened to the vision and she feels a curious pulling, a heaviness and a fullness that can be nothing other than desire. And yet, desire seems too coy a word for what she's experiencing. High, sharp, almost painful, it is at its roots — and she lets herself finally admit this — lust. Pure and unfettered, and so very compelling that she actually — and this is a first for her — feels her joints become weak, and yet hot, as if she's being filled with liquid fire. It makes her want to do things that, frankly, she's never considered before, and those thoughts are terrifying and exhilarating in equal parts.

"Well, that's the last of it," Maggie comments, coming to stand beside Kirsten and almost launching her into orbit unintentionally. She gives the younger woman a look as Kirsten gasps and holds a hand to her chest. "You okay?"

"Yeah, fine," Kirsten hastens to reassure. "Just...um...thinking...about stuff."

Taking in Kirsten's high color, dilated pupils, and energy that seems to be rolling off of her in waves, she follows the direction of her heavy gaze and smirks, suddenly having a pretty good idea exactly what "stuff" Kirsten is thinking about. "Mm hm. Gorgeous, isn't she?" Kirsten turns her head sharply, her face so full of naked emotion that Maggie instantly regrets teasing her. "Hey," she says softly, laying a hand on Kirsten's shoulder, "it's all right. Really."

"But—I—"

"It's okay. Promise."

This eases Kirsten somewhat, and she nods, letting out a long breath of relief. "I'm not used to — feeling like this," she confesses quietly.

"You'll be fine. Trust me. I won't say it gets easier with time, because we're talking about Dakota here, and it would take a blind man not to see the sparks you two create just by being in the same vicinity, but I think you'll be able to handle it just fine."

"I hope so," Kirsten breathes, girding her figurative loins as Koda gets within hearing distance. "I sure do hope so."

"In and out from the west," Koda declares, seeming to take no notice of Kirsten's flustered state or high color. "They were lying in wait just beyond that small ridge there, out of Tacoma's line of sight." The others follow the direction of her gesture with their eyes. "No way anyone could have seen them until it was too late."

"A definite ambush, then," Maggie grunts, hands on her hips.

"I'd say so. I could only track them down to the next road. Lost 'em there." Dakota sounds mildly disgusted with herself.

"But they were headed west," Kirsten remarks.

"Yeah. Due west." She looks at Kirsten, eyebrow raised.

"Just another piece of the puzzle," is her answer. "I think we've done as much as we can here." She looks to Maggie. "Do you think I can borrow a couple of your techs?"

"Borrow?" Maggie asks, grinning. "You can have 'em, with my compliments. The whole lot of them are so bored they're driving me to the brink!"

"Well, I'll only need two or three. The more close-mouthed, the better."

"You think we've got a leak."

"A big one." Kirsten sighs. "If we let whoever it is think they got away with it, we might have a chance at cracking this."

"I know just the two, then. I'll have them report to you as soon as we get back on base."

"Thanks."

"Not a problem, Dr. King. Not a problem at all."

"We're back to that now, are we?"

Her only answer is a wink.

**The sun has** been down for several hours when Kirsten spreads the last of the minuscule pieces of the former android out on the large table in a good sized, if barren, office Maggie has appropriated for her use. The number of bits of twisted and mangled metal is in the thousands, and Kirsten looks at them, dazed, unsure where to begin. She sighs heavily and runs a hand through her hair.

"Long day, huh?" Koda asks softly from the other end of the table.

"Longer night," Kirsten replies, hefting one of the larger droid bits and fiddling with it before placing it back down on the table. "God, what a mess." She sighs again. "If I didn't think part of our answers might be hiding in all this...somewhere, I'd be tempted to bundle it back up and throw it in a landfill."

"I have faith." Pushing herself away from the table, Koda walks to Kirsten's side. "C'mere."

Kirsten willingly steps into the circle of Dakota's arms, groaning in tired contentment as they close about her in a comforting embrace.

"Thanks," she mumbles, burrowing into the hug and letting Dakota's scent and quiet strength surround her like a living blanket.

"Anytime," Koda replies, brushing her lips against Kirsten's soft hair.

A tentative knock on the door causes Dakota to relax her grip, though Kirsten hangs on as if for dear life. "That'd be your techs."

"Can't we just pretend that no one's home? Maybe they'll go away?"

The knock comes again, stronger this time, followed by a "Ma'am? Ms. President?"

Kirsten groans.

"Ma'am? Are you in there? The colonel sent us."

Dakota gently disengages Kirsten's grip, then lowers her head and presses a sweet, and in no way chaste, kiss to her lips. "I've got to look in on my patients," she says after a long, wonderful moment. "Have fun, and I'll see you when you get home tonight, okay?"

"Home?" Kirsten asks, head spinning. "Where's that again?"

Laughing, Dakota touches Kirsten's cheek, then turns and heads for the door. "Later."

# CHAPTER TWENTY-NINE

Koda checks her watch as she takes the steps of the Rapid City court-house two at a time. With her other hand she steadies the laptop where it thumps against her side, drumming counterpoint to the rhythm of her feet. To her disgust, she is late. The complete absence of loiterers and smokers on the arched portico tells her that she is very late. Swearing quietly to herself, she flings open the heavy glass doors that have by some miracle been spared by both uprising and vandals. Or — and it's an encouraging thought she really has no time for — they have been replaced in an awak-ening of civic responsibility. *Score one for the rebirth of democracy.* Boot heels ringing hollowly in the emptiness, she jogs across the foyer with its semi-circle of bronze busts of Great South Dakotans, then up more stairs. Even if it were not cordoned off by yellow tape, she would not gamble on the elevator when the electrical supply to the building is as iffy as a politi-cian's honesty.

Two stories up, she barrels out of the stairwell at speed, slamming the swinging door back against the wall. In the hall outside the courtroom a portrait of the (probably) late President Clinton hangs crookedly over the door, smiling out from behind cracked glass. Martinez and another corporal Koda does not know stand rigidly at attention on either side of the entrance. That other corporal apparently knows her, even if she does not know him. Instead of blocking her path, each man grabs a door handle to let her through without having to slacken her stride. Koda tosses them a smile and a quick, "Thanks, guys!" jerking off her hat just as she passes under the lin-tel.

She is not as late as she feared. While the preliminary paper shuffling occurs, Dakota takes in the set-up, her eyes raking over the packed rows of seats, seeking her cousin and brother. It seems as though half the surviv-ing civilian population have come to make their own judgments in Dietrich's shooting, as have a substantial number of airmen and soldiers from the base. A close knot of people in the front row — a woman with fragile limbs like a bird's, two young men, and an old man with thin white hair and a wind-scoured face — she takes to be Dietrich's family. On the opposite side of the room, barely visible for the intervening rows of spectators, she finally locates a green uniform amid half a dozen in Air Force blue, and the pale wooden shapes of crutches propped against the back of an empty chair.

As she makes her way toward them, Harcourt glances sternly at her over the tops of his half-glasses, then pushes them further up onto the bridge of his nose and begins his opening remarks. "Ladies and gentle-men, we are gathered here today to determine the manner and cause of death of William Everett Dietrich, deceased, of Rapid City, South Dakota. We do not yet know whether Mr. Dietrich met his demise in an unlawful manner, but we hope to determine that by the termination of these proceed-ings. I caution you all, and especially the jury, about making any assump-tions in this matter beyond what the evidence will show. Further, because the person who claims to have fired the shot that killed Mr. Dietrich is a member of the Lakota Oglala Nation, we will also follow the laws of that nation insofar as is practicable.

As Harcourt continues his explanation of the court procedures, Koda slides into the empty seat beside Tacoma, carefully and soundlessly laying the crutches flat on the floor. Shaking her head, she slips the carrying strap from her shoulder and sets the computer in its case beside them. "Sorry I'm late," she whispers. "Your feline friend decided she was going to make a run for it. It took us twenty minutes to corral her."

For an instant Tacoma's eyes are bright with alarm, then he relaxes, grinning, against the chair. "But you won."

"Shannon and I won, with minimal blood loss. The ficus in the waiting room did not survive."

"Did you bring...?"

"No. I have the slides. If they need to see more, they can go to the clinic."

Koda's fists clench involuntarily, and she makes a conscious effort to relax. She and Harcourt had argued about the way she would present her testimony: he insisting on having the wolf's body present, she flatly refusing. They had settled on the compromise of slides, with the jury only adjourning to view the evidence if necessary.

"*Hau*," Tacoma says, agreeing, and it seems to Dakota that further indignity to Wa Uspewicakiyape is something that he, too, has dreaded. Then he says, "Where's Kirsten?"

"Working on putting our suicide bomber back together. Shhh." Koda cuts the conversation short. She can feel the blood rise in her face. Though her feelings for Kirsten have only grown clearer and stronger since the day the scientist, most unscientifically, found her grieving by the stream, she is not ready to talk about them. Still less is she prepared to be publicly labeled as one of a pair of bookends, half a couple. She does not want to share the thing that is happening between them, not yet, not even with Tacoma.

Still punishing him? The thought strays through her mind unbidden. Or just holding it to her own heart a while yet, a gift to be only her own and Kirsten's for a season?

But now is not the place or the time for such wonderings. "Where's Manny?" she whispers, catching Fenton's eye and nodding once.

"In the witness room, licking his wounds and hiding from our formidable colonel."

"Got him bad, did she?" Koda asks, unable to quite contain the smirk that curls about her lips.

"Flayed him alive," Tacoma replies with his own touch of smugness. "He'll be swamping out heads for a year. Maybe two, if he's lucky."

"I'm surprised she didn't quarter him in the brig."

"It was touch and go for a while. I think his injuries won him some mercy points."

Dakota laughs quietly, then turns her full attention to the front of the courtroom.

Harcourt segues from the law in general to the specifics of the inquest's authority. "You must understand that this panel has no authority to bring charges against anyone. The court will decide only two things: one is the cause of death, which should be fairly straightforward and will depend upon medical testimony; the other is the manner of death, which is not the same thing. Does the jury require any further clarification on any of these points?" Silence and the shake of a head or two are all the answer he receives. "Very well, then, let us proceed. Major Rabinowitz."

Major Rabinowitz, one of the few medical personnel to survive the initial raid on Ellsworth, takes the witness chair and is sworn by the clerk. At the prompting of the judge, he recites his credentials, including experience in all manner of projectile wounds — everything from M-16 rounds to shrapnel to steel-tipped arrows.

With a nod, Harcourt leans back in his chair. "Ladies and gentlemen of the jury, you may put your questions to Dr. Rabinowitz."

The questioning in this round is predictable, almost perfunctory, and Koda follows it with only half her attention as she forces calm onto her own mind in preparation for her testimony. She must be cool; she must be detached. She must give no hint of her personal interest, make no display of her grief. *For justice. For all the wild beings who deserve to live out their lives without the added perils of human cruelty.* She calls up the memory of the mother wolf, Wa Uspewicakiyape's mate, sleeping peacefully, her pup curled up beside her, a spatter of milk drying on the end of his nose. *For all the years and the generations to come.* She holds that thought clear before her, a banner and a promise, while voices drone on half-heard.

Her focus returns to the present as Harcourt pronounces the cause of death: "...gunshot wound to the head. So say you one, so say you all?"

No one disputes the verdict; no one was expected to. No one finds it necessary to see the autopsy photographs which the good doctor has prepared as slides. The easy part is behind.

Koda forces her attention back to the courtroom as the clerk calls Lieutenant Manuel Rivers, USAF. Manny takes the oath, swearing, as Koda had done, not on the Bible but on the medicine pouch invisible beneath his shirt and tie. The hand that he raises still shows red where the transparent dressing covers the burns he sustained in pulling Donaldson from the flaming APC, and a murmur runs through the room. Rapid City has become a small town, Ellsworth an even smaller one, and the tale of the attack on the convoy returning with the generators has made its way not only through the entire military corps, but into the civilian population as well, growing in the telling. Added to Manny's exploits at the Cheyenne, it has become a piece of local folklore, rapidly swelling toward the epic of the Red Knight and the Androids. One part facts, two parts awe, seven parts pure imagination: shake well and serve warm.

*Somebody needs to be keeping a real record of what is happening. Otherwise we're all at the mercy of Blind Harry and the grapevine.*

Gingerly, moving as though his muscles still pain him in a dozen places, Manny takes the witness chair and begins his story:

*The pickup bucks and yaws as Andrews wrestles it along the double ruts that pass for a road. Something large and hard, probably a rock hidden under lingering snow, bangs against the forward axle and Andrews winces as the front end of the truck comes down hard. In the truck bed, a pair of wire cages rattle like tambourines with every lurch, while something smaller rolls loosely from side to side, clattering across the metal ridges.*

*"Yo!" Manny yells above the din. "You gonna charge me for this chiropractic treatment? My damn tailbone's busted!"*

*Andrews grins, never taking his eyes off the trail. "Hey, you're the one that swore this ditch was really a road. I just follow directions."*

"It is a road," Manny insists indignantly. "It just hasn't been graded recently, that's all."

Another rock, this time mercifully passing under the left wheels, raises the driver's side of the vehicle a good six inches and slams Manny's right shoulder into his window. In the back, one of the cages skates clear across the cargo bed and hits the side with a clang of metal against metal. "We're gonna have to tie those things down on the way back if we find anything!" Andrews shouts above the racket.

"I brought the rope. There's an easier way back if we need it, though." He pulls a pair of wire cutters from his pocket. "The Callaghan place has a blacktop running up from their main gate along the tree line we're headed for."

"Fuck, man!" Andrews takes his eyes off the twin ruts to glare at Manny. "Why the Hell aren't we on it now?"

Manny shrugs, replacing the clippers. "You don't cut somebody's fence unless you have to. Hell, there was a time you could get arrested just for carrying a pair of cutters off your own property."

"For a pair of pliers? Damn, I always knew you Westerners were weird."

"Not for a," Manny makes quotation marks in the air with his right hand, "'pair of pliers'. For what you were likely to do with 'em. They're rustler's tools."

"Yeesh." Andrews' breath hisses out between his teeth. "We're getting major bones dislocated, just because of some antiquated law? Is there even anybody still on this Callaghan place to give a shit?"

"Well, bro, if there is, I don't wanna get shot just to please your green-horn butt."

A few hundred yards further up the rut, Manny surveys the line of bare trees along the top of a ridge. A vein of exposed limestone, broken and tumbled in spots, runs under it, here and there making a shallow overhang where a denning wolf might shelter. From what Koda has said, from what Tacoma has said she said, the place where she had found the dead pups ought to be just about— "Pull over at the next level spot," he says. "The rockpile under that ledge doesn't look natural."

As the truck comes to a halt, he studies the formation more carefully. The pale spring light, standing down from noon, lays long shadows along the top of the rise, throwing the cracks and gouges in the stone into sharp relief. In several places, blocks broken off from the rock face have fallen to the soft clay soil below, to be half hidden by rain-borne earth and winter-dry vegetation. Under the ledge, though, the ragged chunks of stone are all relatively small and massed together. Exposed rock above them shows dark and weathered above the outcropping, rootlets forcing their way through fissures where the rock will one day split but has not yet. Manny runs his hand over the stone, noting the rounded edges of old breaks, the grit where soil has discolored its creamy whiteness. He points to the cairn beneath the jutting rock layer. "Those rocks didn't fall there. This has to be the lair."

"The male should be somewhere around here, then," says Andrews.

"Somewhere fairly close. You can bet the bastard put the trap near here because he thought there was a den in the area." Turning back to the truck, he takes a 30.06 Winchester surmounted by a massive scope from the gun rack behind the seats. Carefully he loads a dart into the chamber and hands the weapon to Andrews. "You're going to have to do the shooting if we need this; my left arm still won't support any kind of weight."

Andrews slips the rifle strap over his shoulder. "Just tell me when and at what."

"Watch where you step," says Manny, and heads toward an open glade to the east.

The snow still lies on the ground in patches, slick around its melting edges. As they mount the ridge and approach the small stand of trees, Manny can see what appears to be a mound still heaped beneath the bare canopy. The recent fall has drifted nowhere else, though, and here on the north side of the ridge it lies clean, marked only by the rippling wind. Andrews, at his shoulder, says softly, "That's him, isn't it?"

Manny nods grimly. "Likely. We need to make sure, though. Don't put your feet down anywhere you can't see. We don't know how many of the damned traps there are."

A moment later, he kneels beside the mound, lightly brushing powder away from fur that still shows red where the blood of the terrible wounds has frozen. Very gently Manny clears the head and throat, still showing the puncture marks of teeth, works his way down the torn limbs and belly to the mangled leg. Rage rises within him, burning its way up from a spot just beneath his solar plexus, tightening his throat, clenching his fists into knots around the ice-hard flesh beneath his hands. From behind him he hears Andrews swearing softly and incessantly, biting off the words with the cold precision of an automatic weapon stitching a line of metal-jacketed rounds along an enemy front. "God. Damned. Son. Of. A. Mother. Fucking. Bitch!"

"You got it," Manny says, levering himself up. He pulls a small camera from his pocket and pops off half a dozen shots, the flash bouncing glare off the snow. "Be sure you don't step anyplace you can't see the ground; there's gonna be more of these fuckers."

"How do we know where to look? They could be anywhere."

"Not quite. See that chain?" Manny points to the base of the tree where the open trap lies half-buried in snow. "Gotta have something to anchor to, tree or fence post. We walk this line of woods first. Then we try Callaghan's fence."

The second trap has been set less than a hundred feet away, secured to the base of a slender birch. Andrews spots its chain, still new and glinting in the sun that filters through the branches. Carefully Manny brushes fallen leaves away from the tether, following it to the open jaws of the trap itself. A sharp jab at the center with a fallen branch snaps it shut with a sickening crunch. A third has been sprung, but nothing remains of its victim except a tuft of hair and a red-brown smudge along the jagged line of the teeth. Manny bends to rub the soft, stippled fur between his fingers, noting its length and silky texture. "Rabbit," he says. "Somebody beat the bastard to it, coyote maybe."

"Where now?"

"Let's try— Down!" Manny throws himself flat as a bullet whines past, just millimeters over his head, and buries itself in the trunk of the tree behind him. Andrews sprawls in the wet leaf mould beside him, tugging at the holstered pistol riding at the small of his back under his jacket. A second shot streaks past, and a third. "It's coming from the fence line over there!"

"Who the Hell—?" Andrews falls abruptly silent. From the north side of the line of woods comes the snap of a twig, then another. Someone moving carelessly, confident enough not to be concerned about giving away his position.

Manny pulls his own sidearm and pumps a round into the chamber. The footsteps are clearly audible now, moving along a line perhaps fifty yards to the east of them. Pushing up on his good elbow, Manny can just make out a ripple of movement in the thicker underbrush, a shadow darting from tree trunk to shadow to tree trunk again. Andrews shoots him a questioning look, raising his pistol; Manny waves it down again. His look says, wait. Until we know how many they are. Until we know what they are.

Abruptly, the footfalls change direction, no longer moving on a tangent parallel to their position. The snap of dry twigs grows louder, coming straight toward them now. Closing his eyes, Manny remembers snowy mornings years gone by, crouched among a tumble of stones above the deer trail, waiting in silence as his breath made white fog above the white drifts about him. He calls that silence to him now as his father and grandfather have taught him, drawing it about him like a cloak, willing himself into the landscape, his skin to bark, his spine to living wood. When he has become the center of perfect stillness, he rises to his feet, not so much as the sound of a breath to betray his movement. Like a shadow he slips around the oak behind them, bracing his injured arm against the trunk, sighting over the blunt blue steel muzzle of his gun held steady in both hands. And he waits.

In the seconds that remain, the rustle of underbrush grows suddenly quieter, the footfalls softer and further apart. The end comes quickly, then, a rush of movement, a tall man with a weatherbeaten red face and salt-and pepper hair brushing the collar of his buckskin jacket bursts into the clearing, sweeping its perimeter with the barrel of his deer rifle, settling his aim almost delicately on Andrews where he still lies belly down among last year's leaf fall.

"Well, now, boy. You been robbing my traps, have you?"

From his vantage point just wide of the trapper's line of sight, Manny watches as Andrews' fingers slip from the butt and trigger of his handgun. Very quietly he says, "No, I haven't. I'm just out to get a rabbit or two for supper."

"Where's your friend, then? Oh, Hell, yeah, I know there's two of you. And I know what you been doin. Been pacin' you ever since you found that goddamn wolf." The man hawks and spits. "Bad luck, there. Bear got to him, or wolverine, maybe. Pelt's ruined." After a moment, he says, "Who the Hell are you? You're not local."

"I'm from the base. We're hungry, too."

"I just bet you are." The trapper raises his voice. "Hey, you out there! Show yourself or I'll give you one less mouth to feed! Won't need so many 'rabbits'."

Manny slides around the side of the tree, gun still leveled. "Drop it, bastard. Now."

The man turns slightly to his left, the rifle's muzzle swinging up to aim at Manny's head. The roar of its discharge mingles with the report of his own weapon, and Manny watches as the long gun flies windmilling out of its owner's hand to strike the ground butt first, firing again harmlessly into the air, the man himself staggering backward with crimson blossoming suddenly between and above his eyebrows, his Stetson carried off his head in a spatter of blood and brain. He falls on his back, vacant eyes staring, and is still.

Andrews picks himself up, brushing dirt and black leaf rot from his knees. "Manuel my man, your timing was a bit close, you know that?"

"Nah, I had you covered the whole time. Let's see who we got here."

A brief search of the dead man's pockets yields a South Dakota driver's license issued to one Dietrich, William E., and a ring of heavy keys. Several are the small brass variety that open padlocks, and Manny counts them with growing disgust. "Six. That means there's at least six of these goddam traps, assuming that each key opens only one lock. We got our work cut out."

"What're we gonna do with him?" Andrews gestures toward the dead man with his handgun before slipping it back into its holster. "There's a hungry coyote family out here somewhere who can use the protein, if you ask me."

Manny catches the other man's eye briefly. He is not joking. "Nope. Wish we could, but we'd better take him back and go through the legal motions. Think you can wrestle the truck up here? It'll be Hell of a lot easier than trying to carry him back all that way."

It takes twenty minutes, with much grinding of gears and spinning of wheels, but Andrews jerks the pickup to a stop just on top of the slope and just short of the trees. He slams the door behind him emphatically. His freckles stand out against the flaming red of his face; sweat runs down from the brim of his hat. He says equably, "Fuck you, buddy. You, and the horse you rode in on, and your grandpa's paint pony. It woulda been easier to push the goddam rattletrap. You got any idea how we're gonna get it down again?"

"No sweat. We just drive it along this level section here 'til we get to the end of the treeline." Manny pats his pocket. "Then we cut the fence and use the road. Give me a hand here, will you?"

Without ceremony, they bundle Dietrich into a length of plastic, careful to retrieve his hat and weapon. Getting almost a hundred kilos of dead weight into the truck bed three-handed leaves Manny swearing with frustration at his useless shoulder.

Over the next hour, they find three more traps. The coyote, caught by his tail, looks up at them with wary eyes that still hold a glint of mischief, and his lip rises in a defiant sneer as Andrews raises the Winchester to place the tranquilizer dart accurately in his thigh. A few moments later he is out cold and in one of the wire cages, a blanket tucked around him against the chill. The badger in the fifth trap, caught by a foreleg gnawed down to bone, is beyond help, eyes glazed with fever, sides rising and falling in rapid, shallow breaths that make an audible gurgling sound. Andrews raises the dart gun questioningly, and Manny shakes his head. "That's sepsis," he says. "Pneumonia. Nothing we can do except end his suffering."

Andrews reaches for his pistol, but Manny stops him. "Wait. Let him *die free.*" *Opening the trap, he gently draws the steel teeth back from the shattered leg. The badger watches him dully from dimming eyes, making no resistance. "Easy, boy. Easy." Then to Andrews, he says, "Okay, now."*

*The last trap holds the bobcat. She is freshly caught, her wound bleeding bright scarlet into the snow. At their approach, her nose wrinkles in a snarl, baring fangs fit to tear off a man's hand. Hissing, she backs away from them, dragging trap and chain with her to the limit of its length. "Oh boy, this one's not gonna cooperate," Andrews observes unnecessarily.*

*After he finally does get a clear shot, they lay her carefully in the other cage, her wide unseeing eyes black, rimmed with gold. Manny runs his hand gently over her flank as he settles a blanket over her, rubbing behind her fine ears, still unmarked by fighting. "We're gonna help you, girl," he whispers. "You're a real beauty, you are."*

*Andrews grins as he starts the truck and it lurches along the flat strip parallel to the treeline. "You never told me you were a cat person. You've got a thing for that bobcat like your cousin the vet has for wolves."*

*"Yeah." After a moment he says, "That's why I put up such a fight to get into Allen's squadron. Bobcats."*

*"That's what they're calling her, you know."*

*"Allen? Bobcat? More like man-eating tiger, if you ask me."*

*"Nah, your cousin. 'She-wolf of the Cheyenne.'"*

*Manny snorts. "Well, I guess it's better to have a she-wolf chew your ass to shreds than just anybody. She's not gonna like it that we brought the old man back."*

*"Sounds like cold comfort to me." Andrews hauls left on the steering wheel, and brings the truck to a juddering halt in front of Callaghan's fence. "Now what?"*

*Manny hands him the wire-cutters. "Clip the fence, get on the road, and drive like Hell."*

**It's well past** midnight when Kirsten enters the house, bone weary and with headache pain that has increased exponentially. Her usual greeter is conspicuously absent, and she quietly makes her way through the kitchen until she stands in the doorway to the living room. The rhythmic thump-thump of Asimov's tail betrays his location immediately, and as she steps closer, she can see his sparkling eyes from atop the human hip he is using for a pillow.

Stepping around the couch, her vision is filled with the sight of Dakota half-curled on her side, facing the fire and fast asleep. Her crooked arm supports her head as her hip supports Asi's. Her chest rises and falls in a slow, easy, silent rhythm. Her flannel overshirt is draped over one arm of the couch, leaving her in her black tank and jeans.

Kirsten's eyes travel with true pleasure over the sweeping curves of the bronzed and muscled body, taking in each facet as if seeing it for the first time. Her own body warms and flushes, her exhaustion quite suddenly a thing of the past as a new and seldom felt energy sweeps through her on eagle's wings. Asi watches her curiously but doesn't move from his perch. Kirsten circles around him, quiet as a wraith, and slowly lowers herself to the floor by Dakota's head. The vet's face is obscured by the thick fall of her hair, which shines like silk in the light of the cheerily crackling fire, silently beckoning Kirsten to run her fingers through its inky mass.

She heeds the summons, barely daring to breathe as her fingers, not quite steady, tentatively brush against the silken strands. When Dakota's breathing remains deep and easy, Kirsten, emboldened, brushes the thick locks away from her face with a slightly firmer touch, smiling as Koda's flawless profile is slowly revealed. Her skin is burnished copper, unlined and fairly glowing with vitality. Her lashes, long and dusky, rest softly on her cheek, creating tiny crescent moon shadows on the soft flesh beneath.

Whining softly, Asi tickles Kirsten with his cold, wet nose, and she giggles softly, lifting her hand from Koda's hair and pushing him away. Looking affronted in a way that only German Shepherds can, he nonetheless settles, resting his head back on his human pillow.

When Kirsten turns back, she finds herself swallowed whole in eyes the color of the Caribbean. She forgets the mechanics of breathing as Dakota's gaze, warm and tender and yet with a spark of fire hot enough to scorch, takes in every inch of her face. A strong, long-fingered and perfectly sculpted hand rises up, and fingers trace themselves with impossible gentleness over the cupid's bow of Kirsten's lips.

"*Nun lila hopa.*"

The voice that speaks the words is deep and husky with sleep, and Kirsten feels a current rocket through her body. She smiles against the butterfly touches, understanding the sentiment, if not the words themselves.

"Thank you," she whispers. "And you...you are the most beautiful woman I've ever seen."

This earns her a smile that is equal parts radiant and innocent, and her breath leaves again with the intensity of emotion washing over and through her. She moves not a muscle as Dakota's fingers leave her lips and trail along her jaw, then slide down her neck, lingering at a pulsepoint she is sure is bounding like an orchestral bass drum. They travel further, soothing against the hollow of her throat, feeling the skin as it stretches taut from a convulsive swallow.

Still smiling, Koda lifts her head and props it on her free hand. Her fingers blaze a molten trail down the vee of Kirsten's collar, and still themselves there, resting lightly on the fabric covering the rest of her body from view.

"I love you, you know," Kirsten says, and then freezes, unable to believe she's actually spoken her heart aloud.

"That's good," Dakota replies after a moment, gently tugging on the collar of her shirt, "because I love you, too."

"You...do?" Kirsten's voice is soft and filled with wonder.

"Mm. I do."

The gentle tug comes again, and Kirsten goes with it, lowering her head and brushing against Koda's offered lips.

"So very much," Koda whispers, deepening the kiss as she helps Kirsten stretch out on her side. Asi gives an affronted grunt, but moves away as the two women settle together, bodies touching and moving along their lengths.

Tracing the tips of her fingers over the delicate whorls of Kirsten's ear, Dakota deepens the kiss, parting her lips and inviting her inside.

Moaning softly, Kirsten accepts the invitation. It's all she can do not to crawl inside this woman who has so effortlessly stolen her heart, and she growls in frustration as her hands clamp down on the thin material covering

Koda's broad back, stretching and pulling the fabric near to tearing.

Caught up in the emotion of the moment, Dakota allows the passion between them to rise, breasting new heights as her tongue tenderly duels with Kirsten's, tasting their shared excitement on her palate as the flavor of their kisses changes and grows heady.

Breathing deep through her nose, Koda deftly begins to bank the fire before it blazes beyond her ability to control. It's not that she doesn't want what is happening between them. Far from it; she finds herself wanting it more than she can ever remember wanting anything. But she knows, surely as she can feel the frantic beat of Kirsten's straining heart against her breasts, that there is a time for everything, and the time for a full exploration of their love is not yet.

The transition from burn to simmer is so seamless that Kirsten doesn't even protest as Koda softly pulls away. Her eyes flutter open and she smiles, happy beyond knowing. "This is nice," she purrs, her voice husky and a full octave lower than her normal speaking voice.

"Mm. Very nice." Tipping her head, she rubs her nose along Kirsten's, then dips further to steal a soft kiss before pulling away again. "I love you."

Tears immediately spring to Kirsten's eyes. Her smile is radiance itself. "You don't know how it feels to hear you say that."

Tenderly wiping the tears away with her thumb, Koda leans in for another tender kiss. "I think I might have some idea," she murmurs, lingering for another moment. She then slides her cheek against Kirsten's silken skin and holds her in a warm, tight embrace, reveling in the closeness and the love that suffuses her soul.

This is right. As right as anything could ever be, even in a world gone totally wrong. Kirsten lets the last of her barriers slip free without a parting thought, and opens herself totally to the love this one special woman offers up so easily.

She is free.

# CHAPTER THIRTY

"God damn you all, I want justice for my father!"

"Mr. Dietrich," Harcourt begins patiently, "we know you're grieved by the loss of your father. But we have a procedure here—"

"You have a procedure here that's taking the word of the sons-of-bitches who killed him! He's not here to speak for himself!"

Koda's hands clench into fists on her knees, fingers curled so tightly into the palms that her skin shows white and taut above the sharp angles of the bones. All through Manny's account of finding and freeing Dietrich's victims, all through Andrews' corroborating testimony, she has held herself small and quiet behind a barrier of calm, withdrawing into the far places of her mind where her grandfather and Wa Uspewicakiyape himself have taught her to seek refuge from pain. And in those places is Kirsten.

With a conscious effort, Koda forces herself to ignore the anger battering against the walls of her refuge from without; she forces back the rage that burns white-hot just beyond the limit of conscious thought, that requires only a moment's inattention to burn through. Instead she deliberately recalls the pressure of Kirsten's body against her own, the generous yielding of her mouth. Deliberately too, she recalls the sense of rightness in their coming together, as if her own journey from her parents' home, Kirsten's struggle over half a continent, had found their appointed ends in the snow at Minot.

*Everything happens precisely as it should. Precisely.*

And where, she wonders, does that come from? Dakota is no fatalist. Nor, she knows, is Kirsten. If the last months have taught her anything, it is that fate is shaped by human will, or by lack of it. Many of the victims of the uprising have died not so much from the androids' onslaught as from a moment's unbelieving paralysis. Like Kirsten, she has come to Minot and now to Ellsworth by a series of refusals to be stunned into inaction, by choices to fight against an enemy still unknown. And out of those actions has come the warrior she has felt dormant within her the whole of her life. And out of them, too, this unexpected love, ripening now in its appointed season.

"No!"

The shout breaks her calm, jerking her mind abruptly back into the anger that pulses off Dietrich in waves. With an effort she stifles the rage that rises to meet it. If this son did not set the traps himself, then certainly he knew of them, was complicit in the pain and death of every creature caught in them. He stands before the court, his face blotched scarlet, his hand raised as if to strike out at the men and women of the jury panel.

"Sit down, Mr. Dietrich." Harcourt motions to the uniformed sergeant still standing at the door of the judge's chambers. "If you persist in this disruption, I will have the bailiff remove you."

Dietrich's color remains high, but he pauses, deliberately lowering his hand to rest at his belt. When he speaks his voice is quieter, though none of the tension has gone out of the corded tendons at his neck. "You heard them. They were robbing his traps. He had a right to defend his property."

"Given that, item," the judge ticks off his points one by one on his fingers, "leghold traps are illegal; and that, item, trapping of any kind without a license is illegal; and further, that the gray wolf remains a federally-listed endangered species, I'm not sure that the late Mr. Dietrich could lawfully claim any property interest in the fruits of his activities. Now: sit down, sir. Dr. Rivers, please."

Dietrich resumes his seat as Koda takes up her place beside the table with the projector. As she steps up to the low dais, a murmur runs through the room, and she deliberately turns her eyes away from the crowd. She knows what she will see in their faces: admiration in some, awe in others, contempt in a very few still trapped in the prejudices of an age long dead. It is the same almost everywhere she goes now, except for the clinic or among the men and women who have stood shoulder to shoulder with her under fire and who accord her the respect of one warrior to another, no less and no more.

"I must warn the court that some of what I have to show you is graphic and disturbing," she says as she unpacks the laptop and attaches the cable to the projector. "Some of these slides are from photographs taken by Lieutenant Rivers and Lieutenant Andrews at the sites of the traps and depict injured animals in pain. Others show victims that did not survive."

She begins with the snapshot of the coyote, which draws a nervous giggle from the back of the room. Keeping her voice even, she says, "Among the Lakota, Coyote is a trickster, famous for getting himself into difficulties. Many of those adventures are funny, with the joke on Coyote himself. But this," she says as she turns to face the audience, "this is an individual animal, not a myth or Coyote-with-a-capital-C in a traditional story. If you look more closely, you will see that he has chewed his own tail half through in an effort to escape." A flick of the switch zooms in on the wound, with teeth marks clear on the small vertebrae. "A little more closely, and you can see the infection that might well have killed him, even if he had succeeded in freeing himself."

This time there is a small gasp, and more than one head turns away from the sight of the inflamed and swollen flesh, the pus seeping into the ragged fur. "If the infection had not been stopped, this is what would have happened to him."

The projector clicks softly, and the dying badger appears on the screen. "I can't say for sure exactly how long this animal remained in the trap, but for full-blown sepsis — blood poisoning — and terminal pneumonia to develop would require a matter of days."

"Excuse me, Doctor Rivers." One of the jurors, an elderly man whose grizzled beard approaches prophetic length, interrupts her. Turning to Dietrich, he says, "Now, I can understand why someone might get the impression that federal laws don't apply any more. In fact, I can understand why someone might get the impression that there wasn't any law at all. And I take it you admit that you knew your father was trapping?"

"Sure I did," Dietrich answers. "He'd been running lines for years. And he's not the only one who did it, either."

The juror nods understandingly. "No, I imagine not." He pauses, looking at his hands, then raises his head to stare at Dietrich, milky blue eyes blazing. "What I can't imagine — damn it, I refuse to imagine it — is that any half-way decent man would set traps and not check them at least once a day. God knows we may get thrown back to stone knives and bearskins — more's the pity for the bear. But to leave an animal to suffer like that" —

he shakes one gnarled finger at the screen — "is plain sadism. I refuse to accept that as necessary, sir. I refuse to."

"Sit down, Mr. Dietrich," Harcourt says repressively, before the man is halfway to his feet. "I will not warn you again. Do you have any further remarks at this time, Mr. Leonard?"

The juror shakes his head, leaning back against his seat and staring balefully at Dietrich.

*We're going to make it.* There is a grim triumph in the thought, and a small ironic smile pulls at the corners of Koda's mouth. *They're as disgusted with the old man as they are with the son. They're going to confirm the law.* Aloud, she says, "Shall I go on, Judge?"

"If you would, Doctor Rivers."

Steeling herself, Koda cues the next slide onto the screen, turning to face the panel, deliberately looking away from the image of Wa Uspewicak-iyape dead in the snow. Her voice sounds hollow in her own ears as she says, "Here we see what happens when such injuries and subsequent infection run their course. This victim is an adult male gray wolf, *Canis lupus*, an endangered and federally protected species." She focuses in on the shattered leg, and a young man in the back of the room abruptly gets up and pushes his way out the door, one hand over his mouth. "The initial injury in this case is a multiple compound fracture of the right tibia and fibula. Plainly put, his leg was so badly crushed, with bone protruding through the skin, that medical repair would have been impossible. Even if this wolf had been found immediately, the only choices would have been euthanasia or amputation and life in captivity." She pauses for a moment, the words bitter in her mouth. "While immobilized by the trap, this wolf was attacked by, and somehow managed to fight off, a large predator, perhaps a bear, more likely a wolverine. Note the puncture wounds to the neck; note also the abdominal wound. The edges are dry and inflamed, indicating the onset of infection. As in the case of the badger, exposure would have resulted in pneumonia. Again, we are speaking of an entrapment that lasted days."

Speaking past the rage that threatens to choke her, she continues. "There was also a den within a hundred feet of this trap. Because of the death of this wolf, his mate, who had given birth out of season, was forced to leave her pups to forage. She was shot, though not fatally, at the gates of Ellsworth Air Force Base. Between the trap and the shooting, three out of four of the litter died, a net current loss of four to a still-recovering population. The loss over time, of course, is much greater.

"Finally," she says, "we have a young female bobcat, caught within less than an hour of being found by Lieutenant Rivers and Lieutenant Andrews." She keys up the slide of the cat backing away from her rescuers, ears flat against her head, nose wrinkled in a snarl. "The injury had not had time to become infected, and no bones were broken. As you may know, lack of fractures is atypical. As it was, several tendons were severed and required sutures."

"Doctor Rivers?" Another member of the jury, a woman whose long blonde hair is caught into a thick braid down her back and whose hands show the calluses of months of rough work, glances toward Harcourt for permission to speak. When he nods, she asks, "What is the prognosis of the coyote and the bobcat?"

Koda smiles, the knots in her shoulders beginning to loosen. "Very good, in both cases. In fact, both will be released within a week or two."

"And to what do you attribute their recovery?"

"I attribute their recovery to their rescue by Lieutenants Rivers and Andrews, and to prompt emergency treatment by Sergeant Tacoma Rivers. Had they not been found and treated, both would certainly have died."

"Da-yum," someone in the audience drawls. "How many vets you got on that base? You make house calls, Doc?"

"Oh, Doc, I got a pain, real bad," a young man in the back wails. "Please help!"

Relieved laughter suddenly fills the room, and the judge raps once, sharply, with his gavel. Abrupt silence descends. Harcourt fixes the speaker with a gaze as sharp and bright as a diamond behind his glasses. "Indeed you do, Marc Beauchamp. And if you don't quiet down and maintain order in this proceeding, I'll put you and this court both out of it." Turning to Koda, he asks, "Doctor Rivers, have you anything further to add?"

"No, Your Honor."

"Thank you. Sergeant Tacoma Rivers to the stand, please."

Tacoma rises and takes an uncertain step toward the stand, then accepts his crutches from Manny with obvious reluctance. "Good human," Koda says softly as she passes him on her way back to her own seat. As she turns to sit, movement at the courtroom entrance catches her eye.

The door opens to admit Kirsten, who pauses for a moment to survey the audience and the panel, her eyes finally settling on Koda with a smile. She steps to one side, and a tall man in a buckskin jacket, greying hair caught back in a ponytail, enters behind her. His eyes, shadowed under dark brows, are blue as a jay's wing. With a glance back at Tacoma, who is taking the oath propped up on one crutch, Dakota deposits the laptop in her chair and makes her way up the side aisle as fast as she can without breaking into a run. As a grin spreads across her father's face and she returns the smile, her suddenly pounding heart slows to normal. Whatever brings Wanblee Wapka to Rapid City, it is not bad news at home.

As Koda approaches, he holds the door for her and Kirsten once more and lets it fall shut on the courtroom behind them. Without a word, he opens his arms, and she clings to him silently for a long moment, no words necessary. Then he says, "I'm sorry, *chunkshi*. Kirsten told me what happened to Wa Uspewikakiyape."

Dakota loosens her hold just enough to take a step back and meet his eyes. "I found him still alive. I couldn't help him." She hears the catch in her own voice — half-grief, half-anger. "I couldn't help him."

He does not attempt to contradict her. "You are helping his mate and his cub, not to mention his entire species. He would consider that a fair bargain, I think."

"It's all I could do." The words are bitter on her tongue, like gall.

"It is much. No." He cuts her off as she opens her mouth to contradict him. "I know you don't think it's enough. But it is justice, and you have fought hard for it." He nods toward Kirsten. "So have others."

"You've met?" With a small shock, it occurs to Koda that her father and Kirsten did not arrive together by chance.

"I went to the base first, looking for you and Tacoma." He smiles at Kirsten. "We got acquainted on the way into town."

"Oh." To her chagrin, Dakota feels the flush spread across her face, her skin growing warm. "That's — nice."

His eyes are sparkling now, with the warmth of a summer sky. "Yes, it is."

*Gods, is it written on my forehead?* "Mother—"

"Will adjust."

"Not without a fight."

"Probably not. Meantime—"

Manny pushes through the door, using his good shoulder. Wanblee Wapka's gaze shifts, taking in his bandaged hands, but he says only, "*Tonskaya?*"

"*Leksi.* Sorry. Koda, the jury isn't going to go out at all. They say they don't need to deliberate."

The jury, which has been huddled in a tight knot with Harcourt at its center, is just making its way back to the table when Koda, Kirsten, her father, and cousin file back into the courtroom. Silently, they range themselves along the wall at the back, and Kirsten slips her hand lightly, unobtrusively, into Dakota's. Koda gives her fingers a squeeze of thanks, and waits for the verdict.

"Mister Chairperson," intones the judge, "have you made a determination of the cause and manner of death of William E. Dietrich, deceased, of Rapid City, County of Pennington, in the state of South Dakota?"

The chairperson rises. Louie Wang is a youngish man whose eyes are dark behind bottle-bottom glasses; even after Armageddon, his shirt pocket sports a plastic protector for a couple of pens and a marker. Before meeting Kirsten, Koda would instantly have labeled him a typical computer geek.

"We have, Your Honor."

"Your findings, Mr. Chairperson, as to the cause of death?"

"As determined previously, the cause of death was a single gunshot wound to the head, Your Honor."

"Manner of death?"

"Homicide, Your Honor."

Koda's fingers tighten convulsively around Kirsten's. Kirsten squeezes back, hard, a puzzled look on her face counterpart to the alarm on Manny's. Only Wanblee Wapka seems unruffled, standing relaxed with one hand holding his hat, the other in a jacket pocket.

"Are there any further findings, Mr. Wang?"

"Two others, Your Honor."

"Your first supplementary finding, please."

Referring to a yellow notepad on the table, Wang says, "Our first supplementary finding, in the absence of a civilian criminal court and a properly constituted grand jury, is that while a homicide — the killing of a human being — was committed, there is no finding of murder. From evidence given, it is the verdict of this jury that Lieutenant Manuel Rivers acted in defense of his own life and the life of Lieutenant Andrews when he returned shots fired at them by William Everett Dietrich, deceased. The jury calls to the attention of the court the circumstance that the said William Everett Dietrich was in process of commission of a felony when he shot at the Lieutenants with intent to kill, and thereby attempted capital murder, an offense which carries the death penalty in this state."

Koda feels her breath go out of her in a rush, notes the relief as every muscle in Manny's body suddenly seems to relax, held up only by the pressure of his shoulders against the wall. A glance at her father tells her that he has never doubted the verdict. It is not, she realizes, so much that he trusts the law as that he trusts her, and Tacoma, and Manny himself. Trusts them to act in honor, trusts their ability to defend those actions.

"And your second finding, Mr. Chairperson?" asks Harcourt.

"Our second supplementary finding," Wang replies, still referring to the notepad, "is as follows. In the absence of any duly constituted legislative body of the sovereign state of South Dakota, this panel affirms the present laws which protect species determined to be either threatened or endangered, and the laws which prohibit the use of the leghold trap or any other device legally defined as cruel."

"So say you one, so say you all?"

One by one the jurors confirm their votes, and the judge adjourns the court *sine die*. As the audience begins to file out, all save those few who form a tight knot about Dietrich's family, Tacoma makes his way to the back of the room. He walks unsteadily, both crutches held in one hand, their rubber feet stumping against the floor tiles like a freeform walking staff.

Wanblee Wapka looks from his eldest son to his nephew and back again. "You two are a mess," he says equably. "What does the other guy look like?"

"Little metal slivers," Tacoma answers, grinning. "Lots of 'em."

Koda smiles at Kirsten as Wanblee Wapka embraces Tacoma. *This is your family, too.* But that is not something to be said with strangers crowding past them, and so she only holds the tighter to Kirsten's hand, not caring who may notice.

Fifteen minutes later, they pile into Wanblee Wapka's big double-cab pickup, Koda's own truck entrusted to one of the enlisted men. When they are settled, Manny looks back through the slide window into the camper-topped truckbed and frowns. "What are all those boxes back there? You moving in with us, *leksi*?"

"Afraid not," Wanblee Wapka says, maneuvering the heavy truck expertly out of the narrow space and out onto the street. "Those are just a few things your aunt sent: some home-canned peaches, corn, beans, frybread, and such."

"There's a couple chickens and some roasts at the house, too," Kirsten adds. "And a side of beef at the mess. Everyone's going to have a full stomach tonight."

"Thanks, *Até*," Koda says quietly, and receives a smile in return.

It is nothing, however, to the beatific expression on Manny's face, framed in the rear-view mirror. "Good bread, good meat," he says reverently, "good God, let's eat."

**Koda stands in** a white fog of condensate billowing out of the refrigerator, the blast of air chilling her face. "You call that a couple chickens and a roast or two?"

"I admit I wasn't as...precise...as I might have been."

Kirsten's voice is dryly factual, but Koda has known her long enough now to recognize the hint of laughter running underneath. "How unscientific of you," Dakota murmurs, taking in the packed space before her. There are chickens and roasts, to be sure. There is also a ham, a slab of bacon, a couple of gallons of fresh milk, butter, several dozen eggs, and an assortment of parcels tantalizingly shaped like pork chops and T-bones. Above them, the freezer compartment bulges with more of the same. A string bag of potatoes leans against the door of the under-counter cabinets, accompanied by a second of large golden onions and yet another of carrots.

"Your mother," says Wanblee Wapka with a self-deprecating shrug, "is convinced you're on the brink of starvation."

"Oh, we are!" Manny chimes in from his seat at the kitchen table. "Don't let Koda tell you otherwise!"

"Well, not quite." Dakota closes the fridge door and gives her father a brief but fierce hug, then leans back to smile at him. "We're down to 'nourishing but unappetizing', though."

"Rubber cheese," says Kirsten, with a wrinkle of her nose.

Wanblee Wapka motions toward the driveway with a tilt of his head. "I'll bring in the rest."

"The rest" is two boxes of home canned fruits and vegetables, everything from wild grape jam to pickled okra. Koda unpacks the Mason jars while a pair of chickens soak in salt water in the sink. "Até?" she says hesitantly, a quart of stewed tomatoes still in her hand. "You're sure you can spare all this?"

The sudden fall of Manny's face is almost comical. "Leksi, we can't take things you and Themunga might need."

Wanblee Wapka sets down a third box, larger but lighter, and studies Dakota and her cousin for a long moment. Finally he says, "We're not just a family ranch anymore. We've turned into a village. These last weeks we've plowed an extra five hundred acres for garden vegetables and an extra thousand for hay and feed corn. The Goetzes have brought their sheep down and settled on the Hurley place. Brenda Eagle Bear has set up her spinning wheel and loom in one of their outbuildings, and her husband Jack is making hoes and mending bent harrows, not just shoeing horses. Barring a miracle, next spring we'll be plowing behind some of those horses. The world has changed, Dakota. We have to change with it."

Koda sets the jar on a shelf with a rueful smile. "I know. It's just that I never expected home to change, too." Wanblee Wapka gives her shoulder a gentle squeeze, then goes out for more of Themunga's ample care package.

Half an hour later, dinner preparations are in full swing. Maggie, returned home in the midst of stowing the new supplies, dragoons Kirsten into helping her wrestle the unused middle leaf of her table down from the cramped attic storage space while Wanblee Wapka coaxes the recalcitrant ends apart. His uniform tie and jacket hung on the hall tree, Tacoma peels potatoes into a large earthenware bowl set between his feet. Manny, odd man out because of his injured hands, offers encouragement to all and sundry. "Hey, cuz," he observes as Koda sets to cutting up the chickens, "I didn't know you were a domestic goddess."

Deftly Koda severs a thigh from a drumstick. "I'm not. I'm a surgeon."

"Watch your mouth there, bro," Tacoma says with a grin. "She's good with that thing."

As they sit down to a dinner of fried chicken and gravy, mashed potatoes and biscuits, Koda glances around the table. Nostalgia runs along the edges of her consciousness, memory of a thousand evenings like this one, her father or grandfather at one end of the table, her mother at the other, the ever-increasing Rivers clan ranged in between. The family has long since outgrown the dinner table of her childhood. At Solstice this past December, they had added a pair of card tables at the end, and a third, separate, where the youngest cousins could mash their peas into their potatoes to their hearts' content. Glancing at the woman at her side, it comes to Dakota that she may never bring Kirsten home to her mother, may never again return to a family untouched by loss. They have escaped the odds so far, but the attack that has injured Manny and Tacoma only emphasizes how tenuous their position is.

A chill passes down her spine, a shadow of premonition. There is a finality to this meal; it lies, somehow, on a point dividing past and future. Something said, something done this night will alter the course of all their lives to come. Over the circulating dishes, she meets her father's eyes and knows that he feels it, too.

*Everything happens precisely as it should. Precisely.*

It is the second time this day that the thought has come to her. Foresight is familiar to her; so is dream; so is prophecy. This is none of those things. It is a sense of pattern, of a path marked out to be trodden again and again: life after death after life through endless cycles.

The premonition fades, gradually, and her attention returns to those at the table about her: her father, her brother, and cousin; Maggie, who is her friend; Kirsten, who is her heart. And death sits at the table with them, bone-faced and inexorable.

With an effort she pulls herself back to the present. *Warnings,* she reminds herself, *come precisely because they can be heeded, because evil can be averted.* She forces herself to eat her supper, while the conversation flows past her — her father and Maggie now in earnest discussion of a trade agreement between the base and the Rivers settlement, Manny and Tacoma answering questions about the relative benefits of reclaiming a half-dozen more windmills versus attempting to reconnect the grid to serve both the base and Rapid City.

Kirsten, beside her, touches her arm briefly. "Are you all right?"

"Yeah, sure, I just—"

"Wasn't there for a bit." Kirsten completes her sentence for her, softly.

"It happens. I'm fine." Koda smiles at Kirsten, and at her father, meeting his concerned gaze again, letting him see that she is with them again.

His eyes promise a later talk, but for the moment the world slips back into normalcy around her. Kirsten's hand brushes hers under the table, deliberately, and Koda looks up to catch the faint blush suffusing the other woman's face. Like her father's, the green eyes say "later".

*And there will be a later. I swear it.* Deliberately, Koda's fingers close about Kirsten's, holding fast for all their lives and future.

**The hall clock** chimes nine as Dakota slips quietly through the door. Her patients are all settled for the night, meds given, dressings changed as needed. The kitchen and the rooms she can see beyond stand dark; a sense of solitude, comfortable after the crowding of the evening, lies over the house.

Wanblee Wapka has gone to bunk with Manny and Tacoma in the BOQ, and to have a look at how his son and nephew are healing. Maggie, as she has done almost every night for the last couple weeks, has announced her intention of working late.  In the last few weeks, Hart has grown increasingly remote, and almost all of the day-to-day running of the base has fallen to the colonel and one or two junior field officers.  Lately she has been home only to eat, to shower and change, returning to her office after supper to coordinate supplies, assign personnel, worry about the android forces still lurking beyond their perimeter, and eventually catch a few hours of sleep on a field cot set up in the narrow space between desk and window.

Part of the change is the weight of command; another, equal, part, Dakota suspects, is tact.  With Maggie out for the night, Koda has a room and a bed that she need not share.  Or that she can share, if she chooses, without intrusion.  That has not become an issue yet.  Kirsten still sleeps and works in the small guest room, sorting through endless strings of code in search of the sequence that will, finally and permanently, incapacitate the droids.  She is there now, her presence and Asi's small eddies in Koda's awareness.

The air has grown chill, and Koda moves to close the window over the sink.  The breeze stirs the curtains against her face as she reaches for the sash, and on it comes the sound of frogs singing by the stream that flows through the woods, point counterpoint to the soft whinnying of a screech owl.  Stars spill across the sky, undimmed by the customary glare of the city or the base, a white blaze that, were it not for those few lamps burning in windows and the occasional sweep of headlights, might cast shadows across the back yard.  Sweet and familiar, the night air carries the smell of water and wet earth and green things growing.

Normal.  Since the uprising began, this is the closest an evening has come to normal.

There is a restlessness in her tonight, born of the premonition of impending loss; born, too, of this night poised on the edge of spring.  If she were home, she would take Wakinyan Luta away from his mares for an hour and ride until she tired.  But she is not home, has no idea when she will ever be home again.  Slowly she pulls the window down, shutting out the night and its voices that call to her.  There is work to be done here and now.

Flicking on the light, she opens the large box Wanblee Wapka has left standing by the hall door.  On top are several layers of clothes: underwear, socks, shirts, jeans, all pressed and neatly folded.  Below them lie half a dozen books, obviously carefully chosen from the shelves of her own home: Paz's biography of Sor Juana de la Cruz, in translation; a copy of the *Iliad* whose front cover buckles loosely where it joins the spine; a slim book of poetry in German.  Kneeling by the box, her clothes set neatly on the dining chairs, she lets the last book fall open in her hand, to the introductory poem.  Its sparse language evokes the vast spaces of the Central European plain, the figures of an Ice Age tribe huddled around the fire against the unseen things of the night, a teller of tales lingering at the edge, making the magic of words only to fade again into the darkness and the empty land.

*Am rande hockt*
*der Maerchenerzaehler...*

Her eyes skim the page to the end:

*Heiss willkommen den Fremden.*
*Du wirst ein Fremder sein.*
*Bald.*

Warmly welcome the stranger.
You will be a stranger.
Soon.

The sound of soft footsteps comes to her from the corridor and a voice calls out, "Dakota? Is that you?"

"I'm here. In the kitchen." She closes the book and sets it on the stack of clothing to be carried to what is now her room.

Kirsten appears in the doorway, her glasses shoved up onto the top of her head, her eyes weary. "I saw the light on," she says.

Koda glances up at her, taking in the slump of her shoulders, the small lines at the corners of her mouth. To Dakota, it is one of the sweetest sights she's ever seen. Even dog-tired, Kirsten has an aura of strength and vitality about her that speaks deeply to Koda's soul. A powerful, intense intelligence, honed to a razor's edge, blazes even from tired eyes. The innate goodness within, and the beauty without, shine rose and gold — like the setting sun on a warm summer's day. She wonders, briefly, why it has taken her so long to truly see this — or if not to see, then to admit. "You need a break," she says aloud, shrugging mental shoulders over questions she might not ever be able to answer.

"I feel like my damned neck's broken." Kirsten scrubs her knuckles over the tight muscles running from her shoulders up to the back of her head. "Those techs Maggie lent me are worth their weight in microchips, but looking for a micron-sized needle in a planet-sized haystack is what headaches are made of. When it gets like this I'm afraid I'm going to look straight at the smoking gun and not recognize it. And the whole world will slip back to living in caves and hunting with bone spears because I'm too tired to know what I'm looking at." She smiles then, a sparkle of life coming to her eyes. "I'm optimistic, though. We're making damn good progress. If we're lucky and the creek don't rise, as my dad used to say, we might have some preliminary data within the next couple of days."

"Good news for sure. How about the search for the mole? Any progress?"

Kirsten's smile fades. "No. Maggie's up in arms, professionally, of course, but her job's even harder than mine, I'm afraid. We're keeping this on a strictly 'need to know' basis. She hasn't even let Hart in on it."

"Trust no one."

"Except for me and thee," Kirsten jokes, smiling again, then winces as a knot seizes up her neck at the junction of her shoulder.

Rising to her feet, Koda slides her hand along Kirsten's shoulder and up her neck. "Oh yeah," she says. "You could bounce tennis balls off that and never feel it. How about some chamomile tea?"

Kirsten's mouth purses in distaste. "How about a shot of Johnnie Walker?"

"If we had any." Koda grins. "How about some horse liniment?"

"You don't — you're kidding me, aren't you?"

"Compromise?" Koda holds up the box of herbal tea and begins to fill a small saucepan with water. "*Ina* sent some honey. You won't have to drink it plain."

"Your mom's an amazing woman. Food, clothes, books..." Koda follows Kirsten's gaze as she takes in the unexpected bounty. "What's this in the bottom? It looks like bedding."

"It probably is. And a snakebite kit, and a needle and thread, and a roadside flare, and—"

"—a partridge in a pear tree," Kirsten finishes.

"Nah. The partridge is already in the freezer." While the water boils, Koda moves the books her mother has sent into the living room, leaving some on the low chest that serves as a coffee table, shelving others. The clothes she hangs in the half of the closet of Maggie's room that has become hers. If she is honest, the room is hers, too, and possibly the house; if Hart breaks entirely, Maggie will probably move into the commandant's quarters. Koda returns to the kitchen to find Kirsten scooping the herbal mixture into the warmed pot, with cups and honey set on the counter. "Ready?"

"Almost," Kirsten answers, turning to take the water off the burner and pour it over the chamomile. "Let me help you with that large bundle while this steeps."

"I've got it. It's just some—" Koda breaks off abruptly as she runs her hands down the sides of the box to lift the parcel out. It does not feel like sheets and towels at all. "No, it isn't. It's a blanket or a quilt, I think." Wedged tight at the bottom, the bundle comes free suddenly, its muslin wrapper falling away to reveal a blazing spectrum of reds and oranges and golden yellow, highlighted here and there by deep peacock shades of blue and violet.

"Well, that would have been handy back in February—" Kirsten, turning toward the stove, stops as if rooted to the floor, her hand halfway to the handle of the saucepan. "God, that's beautiful!"

Koda runs her hand gently over the myriad small lozenges that make up the pattern, letting the folds of the quilt fall open to reveal the full design. "It's a star quilt," she says quietly.

"It looks almost like a Maltese cross," Kirsten says. Carefully, she turns off the burner and pours the hot water into the teapot. "May I?"

Koda nods, and together they maneuver the half-open quilt out of the kitchen and into the living room, spreading it over the back of the couch in front of the fire burning low in the grate. Kirsten gasps as the design comes into full view, the eight-pointed star covering almost the entire field of the quilt, worked all in the colors of fire, from its blue heart to its white edges. Kneeling in front of the couch, running her hands gently over the fabric, she says, "It means something, doesn't it? I mean, you don't just sleep under this, do you?"

"You can, but no, not usually." Koda moves a couple of books and sits on the chest. Her fingers trace the gradual shading from electric blue at the heart of the star, through yellow and flame orange and red and yellow again. She can almost feel heat rising from it, the blaze at the heart of the star searing her skin. "A quilt like this is given at times of change in a person's life. A marriage, a promotion, a coming of age. Sometimes it's the commemoration of a death."

"Your wolf," Kirsten says softly.

"Wa Uspewikakiyape. Yes." Again Koda runs her hand over the quilt's surface, tracing the impossibly small, even stitches. "Mother had this one on the frame when I left home back in December."

"Why a star?"

Koda pauses a moment, studying Kirsten's face. Love is there, in the softly parted lips; pain in the shadowed eyes. The other woman is a scientist, though, finding her truth in numbers and measurements, in electrons streaming down the tidy paths cut by mathematical formulae. How much of the unquantifiable shaman's way can she tolerate? How far will she be willing to follow? "In Lakota tradition," Koda says, slowly, choosing her words carefully, "there are two roads. One, the Red Road, begins in the East with the dawn, and moves toward the West. This is our life on Ina Maka, our Mother Earth."

"From sunrise to sunset."

"Yes, but also from Morning Star to Evening Star. They have their counterparts in North Star and Southern Star, and the Blue Road of spirit runs between them. One who leaves the Earth goes to walk the *Wanaghi Tacanku*, the Ghost Road, guided by Wohpe, whom we also call White Buffalo Calf Woman. At some point along that road, she makes a decision about each soul."

"Like a last judgement? Heaven and Hell?"

Kirsten's brow draws into a frown, and Koda reaches out a hand to smooth it away. "It depends. Some of our great teachers, like Wanblee Mato, Frank Fools Crow, say that the spirit goes on to be with Wakan Tanka for eternity. But they have been influenced by the missionaries the government sent to 'civilize' us." Koda makes no effort to keep the bitterness from her voice. "A soul that is not worthy of Great Mystery is turned loose to wander forever, and I suppose that would qualify as Hell."

"Do you believe that?"

The frown is back; it comes to Koda suddenly that Kirsten is struggling with something, something she is — not afraid, because Koda has seldom known a person of such courage — but perhaps embarrassed to speak of.

"There is another belief," she says softly. "Older, from the time of the beginning. When Inyan created the universe, he gave a part of himself to every living thing. When the part of us that is ourselves comes to match that part the Creator has given us, then we may go on to join with him forever. If our selves do not match that divine part, or if we choose for some other reason, then we are sent back to Ina Maka, to receive a portion of her essence and be born again." Koda slips from her seat to kneel beside Kirsten, taking her hands in her own. She says gently, "What troubles you about this?"

For a long moment it appears that Kirsten will not answer, looking down at their joined hands. Then she says, "I had a dream. In it I was — someone else, a tall woman with black hair, and an axe and shield. You were there, too, but with red hair, and a spear." Kirsten's voice fades almost to soundlessness, breath only. "And we loved."

The firelight shimmers red-gold over Kirsten's hair, limns the high planes of her cheekbones and the hollow of her throat, touches her mouth with crimson. Her eyes are lost in shadow. Silence fills the space between them.

Carefully, Koda frees one hand and raises it to trace the outline of

Kirsten's face, her fingers running along the margin between soft skin and softer hair. They trace the angle of her jaw, trail down the column of her neck where the vein pulses in a thready, staccato beat. "Kirsten," she says, her own voice husky, a drift of smoke along the air, "Kirsten, I love you now."

Kirsten raises her face, her eyes searching Koda's. For a long moment she remains still, then looses her hands to run them up Koda's shoulders and behind her neck, drawing her mouth down. The first touch of her lips brushes feather-soft against Koda's, a fleeting warmth like a summer breeze. Kirsten's hands draw her closer still, and Koda opens her mouth, inviting, to the gentle brush of the other woman's tongue.

*I had been hungry all the years.* The thought whispers in her mind, but it is not her own. Vaguely Koda recognizes it as a line of poetry, but Kirsten's mouth, demanding, is the reality of desire, the firm body pressed more and more insistently against her, its truth.

"I love you," Kirsten murmurs against her lips. "I want you."

"*We mitawa ile.*" Fire flows through Dakota's veins, slipping like silk along her flesh, stealing her breath. "*We ile*," she says again. "My blood burns for you."

Kirsten's eyes are pools of molten emerald. "Love me, then. Love me now."

Koda rises to her feet, drawing Kirsten with her. Carefully she lays the quilt on the rug before the hearth, its orange and crimson struck to flame in the low light of the fire. Setting aside her shoes, she turns to find Kirsten standing at the center of the star, her clothes discarded on the couch. The firelight washes her pale skin all to gold, glints off the fall of her hair. It casts shadows in the cleft of her breasts, in the valley between her thighs. "*Lila wiya waste*," Koda breathes. "Beautiful woman."

Her eyes never leaving Kirsten, she shrugs out of her own shirt, draws off her jeans and underthings. In a moment's disorientation, she sees herself as Kirsten must, tall and lithe, shaped of copper and bronze and dusky rose, her loosened hair spilling about her like the night sky, glinting blue and silver in the light of the flames. Then she is wholly in her own mind again as Kirsten steps toward her, smiling. "*Nun lila hopa*," she says. "*Nun lila hopa.*"

Koda closes the small space between them, bending to kiss the upturned mouth, running her hands over the smooth skin of Kirsten's back, feeling the taut muscles beneath, the firm breasts with their hard nipples pressed against her own. "Lie down with me, *wiyo winan,* woman made of sunlight."

Sinking down onto the quilt, she draws Kirsten with her to lie before the fire. The other woman's eyes are wide and dark, pools of shadow. For an instant her features shift, and Koda's own face is reflected back to her, her own eyes the deep blue of autumn skies. That face fades and reforms, and the woman lying half beneath her is leaner, wirier, her skin swirled with patterns in a blue more vivid still, her hair falling in sharp waves loosed from a myriad of tight braids. Koda traces the line of Kirsten's throat with a feathery touch, trailing a finger down to circle one breast. "You are right," she says softly. "We have done this before, in other lives."

Koda's touch spirals upward, circling first the areola, then the nipple, lingering, circling again. Her lips follow, tracing the same slow helix as her hand drifts down Kirsten's flank, brushing the lines of her body from breast to belly, over the curve of her hip, down her thigh. Under her hand, fire springs along the other woman's nerves, a woven net of flame that meshes with the intricate pattern of her own veins. The shock of the sudden connection ripples through Koda, waves propagating from beneath her breastbone, shaking all her frame to magma. Kirsten's breath goes out of her with the heat of it, and her shoulders arch upward to meet Dakota's mouth. Koda grazes the nipple with her teeth, suckling now lightly, now more insistently as Kirsten's fingers thread through her hair, holding her mouth to the tender flesh.

After a time, Koda raises her head and shifts slightly. Kirsten lies with eyes half-closed, her hair spilled across the bronze and crimson of the quilt like tongues of flame licking the incandescent gold at the far reaches of its fire. "*Wastela ke mitawa*," she murmurs. "*Ohinni.*"

Kirsten's eyes find her, still dark with arousal. "I will love you forever," she says. "Life to life. From death through death again."

For an instant, Koda sees herself as Kirsten must — eyes languid with desire, her hair cascading over her shoulders to lie silken over Kirsten's flank. The urgency of the taut body beneath her runs tingling through her own nerves, tightening her nipples to hardness, beating a slow rhythm in her loins. She bends to kiss Kirsten's mouth again, then, slipping lower, the hollow of her throat where the pulse hammers against her lips, her breasts. Gently Koda trails a hand down the center of her body, circling her navel, drawing fire in the wake of her touch. She feels it all along her own nerves, building, flame drawing in upon itself, grown white-hot in the crucible of her flesh.

Turning then, she slips a hand between Kirsten's legs, urging them gently apart. Firelight glints off the wetness beading along the cleft of the pale curls, making faint crescents on her inner thighs. Gently Koda cups Kirsten's sex in her hand, feeling the spasm that runs through the other woman's body and her own, pressing against her palm. Drawing her fingers upward, she parts the folds of flesh, and the scent of musk comes to her. Kirsten gasps, reaching blindly for Dakota's other hand against her hip, tangling their fingers together. In her own body, Koda feels her mouth descend to lay a kiss on the red pearl of the clitoris. She circles with her tongue, stoking, probing, stroking again, the wet rasp of her tongue striking fat white sparks of pleasure that swirl and grow and take on a heady life of their own.

Kirsten's body goes rigid under her, her hips arching as lightning runs along her veins, down her legs, up from the nexus low in her belly. Her breath has gone ragged, and Koda is not certain that she, herself, is breathing at all, her whole body caught up in the fire that strikes through her, crown to sole, as Kirsten cries out, her head thrashing as her limbs shudder and spasm and Koda is lost, lost, spun between the poles of Kirsten's pleasure and her own.

And it is not just her body, no. Something far in the secret depths of her mind breaks free of its tether, gone nova as the fire on the hearth and the star on the quilt beneath them blaze together, one heart of flame, crimson, copper, incandescent gold, and it is her own heart burning there as years, eons, whole universes wheel by and are lost in space around her. A cry rips from her, like the wind at the heart of the sun, and blackness descends about her.

When the curtain of darkness parts, she has returned to herself, feeling the pleasant weight of Kirsten's fingers still tangled in her hair. Kirsten's body, sheened with sweat, still quakes — minute tremors that flow from the center and back again. Her breathing, though labored, is settling slowly, along with the beat of heart.

Pressing a kiss to the belly upon which she rests her head, Koda gently disentangles herself from Kirsten's limbs and stretches her length along her lover's side, her head propped up in one large hand.

"What a fool I've been," she murmurs, gently wiping the tears that sparkle like fire-kissed diamonds upon Kirsten's thick lashes, "to think my heart my own when I'd already given it up to you the moment our eyes first met." Kirsten's smile is radiance itself, and in that moment, her sheer beauty far surpasses anything that Dakota has ever known. "You shine so brightly, *wiyo winan.*" *My heart. My soul. My joy.*

The image before her doubles, then trebles, fracturing into multi-hued prisms by the spark of her own sudden, stinging tears. She feels more than sees her hand taken into Kirsten's, feels the cool touch of lips on her fingers, each kiss a benediction. When a tongue traces the lines of her roughened palm, she moans and allows herself to be turned onto her back by Kirsten's gentle strength.

Kirsten moves with her, draping over the left side of her body like a living blanket. Lips descend again, brushing against her cheek, past the heavy fall of sweat-soaked hair at her temple, suckling briefly the sensitive lobe of her ear. Her lover's voice, when it sounds, is husky and low.

"Let me love you."

She can only groan out her acceptance as Kirsten's lips leave her ear and a toned thigh slips between her own, seating itself against her with a whisper of silken flesh. Her hips surge and Kirsten cries out as the molten heat of Dakota's passion paints itself against her skin.

"Oh...sweetheart," Kirsten whispers breathlessly. "So beautiful..."

Lips mesh and tangle, tongues battle sweetly for dominance, bodies writhe, snake-like, on a sheen of sweat. Kirsten's hand trails down to cup the weight of a small firm breast, dragging her palm across a nipple so hot and tight that it seems to cut into her flesh.

Dakota's moans are constant things, fractured with short gasps and snatches of words Kirsten can barely decipher. Her large hands bear the heat of the sun as they trail over shoulders and back, down past the sweet curve of Kirsten's hip, and settle, pressing her deep and close and tight.

With a labored grunt, Kirsten lifts her head, knowing she cannot bear this incendiary touch much longer without succumbing fully to its whispered promises.

"Slow," she gasps out, looking down into eyes as black as a moonless night. "Slow..."

"*Hiya,*" Koda groans. "*Hiya, iyokipi.* Please."

With regret, Kirsten slides away from temptation and gentles Koda with firm strokes to her belly and ribs. "Slow," she whispers. "Let me love you." Her head lowers slowly and she nuzzles Koda's breast, drawing her cheek and nose over the silken skin, taking in her lover's, musky, exotic scent.

Koda's hips surge again as a warm, wet mouth engulfs her and a cool, darting tongue teases the flames licking at her soul. Her eyes close tightly as the world within fractures and spins, filling her with the heat and the power of a thousand suns. Her cries are loud as bold fingers comb through the bone-straight hair at her center, then dip lower, bathing themselves in the evidence of her great need. She is so full and swollen with passion that the first touch is pain twined with pleasure, and when those fingers tease her entrance, she gives them no chance for retreat. Her hips thrust hard and she shouts in triumph as she is suddenly, blessedly, filled.

Kirsten smiles around the breast at her lips, then moans with pleasure as she is gripped and held in slick, velvet heat. Deliberately keeping her fingers still, she draws her body away and up, pressing a deep, heady kiss to Koda's swollen lips, then soothing her way down to her lover's flushed ear. "You feel so good, lover," she breathes, feeling Dakota's body respond to her murmured endearments. She's not sure where these words are coming from. She's not a very experienced lover, and certainly not a vocal one, but here and now, and with this magnificent woman beneath her, they seem right, and needed, and very much desired.

"So smooth. So open. So ready for my touch." She begins to gently thrust in rhythm to her phrases, using the very tips of her fingers to stroke the velvet lining as she advances and retreats with slowly building speed.

Koda's head is tipped back, lips parted and glistening, hair fanned around her like the corona of a jet black star. Her hands grip and release the quilt and her chest heaves as she takes in giant gulps of air. Her body is as tight as a drum, skin flushed and shining rose and gold and shadow by the light of the fire.

"*Iyokipi. Lila waste. Mahe tuya. Iyokipi. Hau!*"

Pressing down with the heel of her palm, Kirsten rubs against the engorged flesh as her fingers increase the force and speed of each thrust, enraptured by the feel of the slippery heat against her fingers and beneath her palm. The quilt pulls taut as Koda grinds desperately against it. "Now, my love," she whispers, tasting the sweat of desire on Koda's skin. "Let go. I love you. Come to me. I love you, Dakota."

And she feels the incredible strength in the body beneath her as it surges up around her. Arms pin her tight and hold her close against a body that thrums like a live wire. Wetness, molten hot, floods her hand and drains between her fingers.

The grip around her finally loosens and falls away as Koda lies back, limp and motionless except for her ribs, which expand and contract with the force of her panting breaths.

With a tenderness she never knew she possessed, Kirsten eases out of Dakota's spent and trembling body, gently cupping her lover's mound she shifts slightly into a more comfortable position. Her free hand comes up and strokes the sweaty bangs from Koda's forehead.

After a moment, Dakota's eyes flutter open. They are a peaceful, sleepy blue, and the love that shines forth from them is brighter than any star. Kirsten can feel that look upon her skin, settling over her like a warm, soft blanket, and she closes her eyes for a moment, reveling in the sensation. They open again as she feels long fingers trace down the center of her chest. Dakota is smiling at her.

"Lie with me, *cante mitawa*. Let us walk the dreaming paths together."

With a smile, Kirsten curls her body into her lover's. Murmuring,

Dakota gathers her within the warm folds of the quilt.  She sinks into sleep with Kirsten's head on her shoulder, Kirsten's arm over her body.  On the edge of sleep comes Kirsten's soft voice, "*Wastelake.  Ohinni.*"

And darkness takes her.

# CHAPTER THIRTY-ONE

The shape emerges slowly under her hands.  A chip here, a shaving there, a deeper cut with the tip of the knife to define the hollow of an ear, the pupil of an eye.  Dakota's profession has made her precise with a blade, and the rounded end of the fallen oak branch grows steadily into the recognizable likeness of a wolf.

The quiet of the morning deepens around her as she works, finding its way into the sure movements of her hands and the stillness of her mind. The early light slants down through the sycamore leaves to dapple the stream with flecks of gold, rippling and twining with the swift movement of the water over the rocks beneath.  The wet earth at the verge bears the heart-shaped marks of deer hooves and the flat-footed prints of skunk. Further down, where she found the branch she is now carving into a spirit-keeping stick for Wa Uspewikakiyape, Koda had seen the blunt, rounded marks of a large bobcat.  This will be a good place to release Igmú when the time comes.  She is almost ready for her freedom, the fur grown back over her injured paw except for the thin line of a scar; almost ready, too, for a mate.

A smile pulls briefly at her mouth at the thought.  It is the season, not only for Igmú but for herself.

*She woke early, the dawn light glancing across her eyes through the low window.  Her dream faded gently into the soft haze of the morning, leaving her clear-minded and unsurprised at the warmth stretched beside her on the quilt.  She opened her eyes to meet Kirsten's, green as a mossy pool in deep woods, shadowed by long lashes that lay like cornsilk on her cheeks when she dropped her gaze and her mouth sought Dakota's own. The kiss was long and slow and sweet, and when Kirsten looked up again, Koda asked, "What will you have for your morning-gift, Wiyo Winan?"*

*Kirsten trailed a hand through the fall of hair across Dakota's shoulder, bringing to rest between her breasts.  Koda felt her heart beat against the touch.*

*"This," Kirsten said. "Only this."*

*Koda kissed her again.  "And what will you give me in return?"*

*Gently Kirsten guided Dakota's hand to the pulse that throbbed strongly beneath the cage of her collarbones.  "This.  All of this."*

*For answer, Koda gathered Kirsten to her, feeling the smooth skin and hard muscle, the warm strength of her all along her own body.  After a time, she stretched her legs straight beneath the quilt, feeling the drowsy hum of her blood as the light grew brighter, falling across Kirsten's face at a sharper angle.  "Cante mitawa, we have to get up."*

*"No," said Kirsten.*

*"Yes," Koda answered, a thread of laughter running under her voice. "If for no other reason than that Dad will be here soon, with Manny and Tacoma following in hopes of a hot breakfast.  And someone's going to have to let Asi out soon.  He's been a perfect angel all night."*

*Slowly they laid back the quilt and stood.  In the morning light, Kirsten's skin gleamed, her hair like a spill of molten gold.  A shiver ran over her skin.  "God, I hate the thought of a cold shower."*

*"You take Asi out for a few minutes. I'll put some water on the stove."*

*Kirsten padded away to her small room at the end of the corridor, while Koda gathered the quilt and laid it across a chair in the bedroom. From the hall came the thump and scramble of paws on the floorboards, followed by a high-pitched yelp from Asimov. Another sharp bark was followed by Kirsten's voice. "All right, boy. All right, I'm coming."*

*Wrapping her robe around her, Koda made her way to the kitchen, setting the coffeemaker to brew and two large stew pots to boil. It was no substitute for a working water heater, but the bath would at least be warm. From outside, Asi bayed like the hound of the Baskervilles, and she turned to look out the kitchen window to see a squirrel scramble up an oak, just leafing out, to perch just out of the big dog's reach, chittering and jerking his tail in outrage. "Watch the sign language there, bro," Koda murmured as Asi took up station at the base of the tree, apparently content to watch. Kirsten, her head thrown back, laughed at his pretensions, "Some hunter, oh yeah," and tugged gently on his collar to distract him.*

*When the water boiled, Koda drew half a cold tub full, poured in a potful and added a handful of lavender bath salts. Steam rose briefly, its sharp sweet scent dissipating in the cool air. Setting the other pot and its hot water on the tile floor, Koda dropped her robe and stepped into the tub just as the front door flew open and Asi pounded into the kitchen in search of his bowl.*

*Kirsten's steps followed, more quietly as she called, "Dakota? I'm back."*

*"In here," she answered. "Come on in. The water's fine."*

In this spring wracked by the aftermath of destruction and wanton death, Koda knows that a small green shoot has pushed its way up out of her own grief, growing toward the light. Igmú will soon return to the ways of her kind, hunting free to sustain herself and, by summer's end, her kittens. The coyote they will release near the place where Manny and Andrews found him; he is a social creature and will rejoin his pack. The mother wolf and her cub are a more difficult problem. Their former shelter is now a tomb, and Wanblee Wapka and Tacoma have gone this morning to build Wa Uspewikakiyape's burial scaffold nearby. Somewhere near the river, perhaps, or closer to home, near Wanblee Wapka's village. His folk will respect them.

The shape of the wolf grows clearer as Dakota narrows the snout, cutting shallow lines for whiskers, notching the natural curve of the stick just below the ears to show the ruff. She turns the carving in her hands, letting the clear light flow over the smooth length of the branch where she has stripped the bark. No one would ever mistake her whittling for sculpture, not even connoisseurs of "primitive" art, if any are left. But it is clearly a representation of a wolf, and it is made with love. And that is all that matters.

Gently she rubs a thumb over the muzzle. *I will miss you, my friend.* Yet the grief has lost its sharpness; the pain no longer tears at her, no longer threatens to plunge her into that echoing void that had swirled about her when she had found him dying. For the next year she will be the keeper of Wa Uspewikakiyape's spirit, offering her strength to him as he makes his journey along the Blue Road, treading the path of stars. In the back of her mind, only half-acknowledged, lives a small, selfish hope that he will choose to turn again to life on Ina Maka. *For me, yes, but not just for me. For Até and Fenton and Maggie and Tacoma and Kirsten, and for the folk who aided her on her way. For all of us who must somehow remake the world without a pattern. Especially now, for Kirsten.*

A frown settles between Koda's brows. The world has intruded on them too soon, too insistently. There will be no honeymoon in the Greek Isles this time.

*Kirsten's happiness this morning lit her from within, her eyes bright, her skin almost translucent. When the warm water turned first tepid and then cool, she clung to Koda as they both stood under the still-frigid spray of the shower, burying her face in Dakota's breasts and muttering something about "mountain runoff". Ambushed for the second time by Kirsten's sense of humor, they laughed and pressed even more closely together "just so we don't get hypothermia".*

*The mood held through breakfast. She and Kirsten had bacon frying and eggs ready to tip into the pan when the men arrived as predicted, Wanblee Wapka trailed hopefully by Tacoma and Manny. If she had not been watching for it, she would not have caught the sudden light in Wanblee Wapka's eyes when he stepped over the threshold and saw them standing side by side, doing nothing, really, more intimate than rolling and cutting biscuits. Yet that was enough. Kirsten too had seen. She had blushed and become suddenly absorbed in greasing a baking sheet, and Wanblee Wapka's eyes had danced.*

*The conversation when they sat down to breakfast ranged from base politics to horse breeding, carefully skirting anything more intimate. Wanblee Wapka said casually, pushing scrambled eggs onto his fork with half a biscuit, "Chunkshi, if it's all right with you, I'd like to try Wamniyomni with one or two of Wakinyan Luta's fillies this spring. Unless you want to breed them back to their sire?"*

*"The big black? Sure, that ought to work out well." To Kirsten she added, "His name means 'tornado'. He's that fast, and just about as sweet-tempered."*

*"He's not mean," Tacoma observed, "just...independent."*

*"And how many times has he tossed you? Just out of good-natured high spirits, of course?"*

*"We've come to terms." Tacoma's smile included Kirsten. "He'll never be a 'ladies' horse'." His long fingers made mocking quotation marks in the air. "But then, there aren't any 'ladies' in our family, thank the gods."*

*Dakota had swatted him with her napkin. "And if you ever call me that," another swat, "I'll have..." a third swat, "your hair."*

*"Ow. Kindly remember I'm a wounded hero, here." Tacoma raised an arm to defend himself, laughing. "Kirsten, save me!"*

*"And have you call me names? Hit him again, Dakota."*

*"Kirsten, have you ever had a horse of your own?" Wanblee Wapka interrupted the horseplay, his eyes crinkling. "I've got a grey filly coming up, one of Wamniyomni's, that would suit you."*

*Manny, oddly silent, had been following the conversation like a spectator at a tennis match, his head turning from side to side. A long, hard look at Tacoma brought no help, only his cousin's increased concentration on his plate. His brows knitted into a frown, he finally said, "I don't get it. You look like the cat who ate the canary,* Leksi. *"*

*Wanblee Wapka regarded him mildly. "You and Tacoma are the cats,* Tonskaya. *And this," he said, spearing a bite of ham with his fork, "was a pig."*

Half an hour later, Kirsten had returned to the endless coil of binary code streaming across her computer screen, running now on batteries as much as possible, the lilt gone from her voice and her step. For the first time, Koda allows herself to wonder what they will do if the code is not there at all, if it is nowhere to be found.

And the answer to that is what they have to do, beating the droids back and back again until they have no more strength and no more resources. And then what?

But she refuses to follow the thought. For all the dead; for Wa Uspewikakiyape; for the living yet to come, failure is not an option. She runs her fingers again over the carving in her hand. It is as finished as she can make it. Rising, she lingers for a moment in the glade, absorbing its peace, its faint hint of Kirsten's presence. Then she makes her way back toward the clinic and the hard parting still facing her this day.

**When Koda returns,** the clinic is quiet for once. Behind the desk, Shannon is occupied in updating files on a manual typewriter scrounged from who knows where, pecking away at the keys in an uncertain rhythm broken by the sluggish response of the mechanism. "That thing needs to be oiled," Dakota observes as she pauses to check the morning's sign-in sheet: no patients waiting, one drop-off to neuter. "Give Kimberly a call and see if the quartermaster has anybody who can break it down and give it a cleaning."

"I've already — damn!" Shannon breaks off to examine her right hand. Her fingers are still smudged from an apparent struggle to feed in the red and black ribbon. "Second nail this morning. There's supposed to be an old guy in town who used to be a typewriter mechanic. Colonel Grueneman's got an airman out looking for him."

"If he shows up, find out what else he can work on. We're eventually going to need all the maintenance people we can find, and not just for the clinic."

"Doctor?"

Koda stops on her way back to her small office and the wards. There is a plaintive quality in the young woman's voice. "What is it, Shannon?"

"It's not going to get better, is it?"

Very gently she says, "It's not going to be the same, no. In some ways, it may be better. Or there may be no one left to care. We just don't know yet."

Shannon's color goes from the pink flush of annoyance to dead white. She manages, though, to muster a crooked smile. "Thanks. I think."

Dakota returns it. "You're welcome. I think."

Leaving Shannon to her uncertain typing, Koda checks her patients for the second time since dawn. Sister Matilda and her kittens have gone home to general rejoicing in the Burgess household. The Scotty, sadder and with luck wiser, has recovered from his unfortunate encounter with the porcupine. The rabbit with the infected eye, though, is not progressing as well as he did initially. The inflammation has faded, and he quietly munches his alfalfa pellets as Koda runs her hand down his back. The infection persists, though, evident in the thinning flesh over his ribs and the pale color of exposed skin and membranes. She makes a note on his chart to add a second antibiotic to his evening dose; penicillin and sulfa together will still take almost anything bacterial. If that doesn't do the job, they will have to go to an antiviral, and those supplies are short.

Not for the first time, a cold chill trickles down her spine. This rabbit might have a constitutional idiosyncrasy or underlying condition that leaves him more vulnerable than most. Conditions are ripe, though, for the spread of disease of all sorts. Winter has held most infections in check, save for the usual bronchitis and colds of the season. With the return of the sun and the consequent melting of corpses buried under a meter or more of snow, the likelihood of epidemic will soar. And there is no more public health service, no more Center for Disease Control, no more pharmaceutical companies to mount an emergency campaign for an effective drug or vaccine.

For much of the rest of the morning, she inventories the clinic's supplies, making lists of drugs to search for or attempt to find on the black market that is rapidly springing up. Or rather, the open market; looted or not, merchandise is moving again, paid for in trade goods or services. If they are not already, medications will be at a premium. Not for the first time, the unpleasant thought comes to her that it may become necessary to reinstitute taxes on a population that is barely surviving.

At midday she returns home for a quick lunch and a quicker walk with Asi. Kirsten has gone into Rapid City for the afternoon session of the rapists' trial. Testimony is almost finished, and closing arguments will begin soon. As the only surviving national symbol of law, Kirsten must be present when the verdict comes in. A smile touches Dakota's mouth for an instant, and is gone. Kirsten's strength is beyond question, but she has never faced the cold responsibilities of power before, the chill that must stiffen the fingers of any but the most brutal authority scrawling a signature across a death warrant.

Leaving Asi to his nap on the hearth, Koda returns to the clinic. The neutering surgery goes well, and the basset mix starts coming out from under the anaesthesia before he is well settled in the hospital ward. The mother wolf and her cub lie stretched out in the sun, sleeping so soundly that they never stir as she passes. Igmú, becoming ever more restless as spring deepens around her and the call of her blood becomes more insistent, bats her ball about her enclosure with increasing fierceness. Coyote, more relaxed, wags his abbreviated tail and whines, thrusting his slender nose through the mesh of the fence for a pat and a scratch.

As the sun stands down toward the horizon, Dakota sets aside her work. In the storeroom, she lays out the buffalo hide robe her father has brought from home and unfolds it on the worktable. Unlocking the freezer, she gently removes the frozen body of Wa Uspewikakiyape, drawing aside its heavy plastic wrappings. She performs each movement with deliberation, holding apart her anger and her grief. For a moment she rests her hand on his broad head. *This will not happen again*, she swears to him silently. *Never again. Your people will be free, and safe.*

With a pair of surgical scissors, she snips a lock of fur from his mane, where it is untinged by blood. She takes a second from the plume of his tail. These she affixes with a leather thong to the spirit stick, making a mane about the head and throat of the wolf she has carved. With it, she will undertake to remember and honor him as a beloved member of her family for the year of formal mourning and to host a give-away at its end. It does not matter that he is of another nation. He has been closer to her than any not of her blood, save one. *Kola mitawa: my friend; my teacher.*

And now there is another. As if summoned by the thought, a light step sounds in the corridor, followed by a tap on the door. "Dakota?"

"Come in."

Kirsten opens the door, moving quietly. She pauses a moment, taking in the wolf's body, the spirit stick still in Dakota's hand, the buffalo robe. Silently she crosses the floor and steps into Koda's arms. Koda holds her tightly, not speaking, merely resting her cheek atop the silken softness of the fair head. After a moment, Kirsten says, "I wanted to be with you when — that is, for the ceremony." She steps back a fraction and raises her face questioningly. "If that's all right?"

Koda lays her palm against the other woman's cheek. "Of course it's all right. You're family now, to both of us. All of us."

Deep beneath their searching concern, a spark of joy lights the green eyes, and is gone. "Let me help."

Together, then, they wrap Wa Uspewikakiyape's body in the buffalo robe, tying it in place with long strips of braided sinew. Into one knot, Dakota ties a medicine hoop fashioned of a supple willow branch, with small patches of cloth — white, yellow, red and black — tied at the quarters, with leather thongs running at right angles between them. Into another she fastens an eagle feather and two pinions from a redtail's wing. "Because," she explains, "he was a chief of his nation."

When they are done, they wait quietly by the honored dead, their hands joined.

**The knock sounds** softly against the service door. "*Tanksi?*"

Dakota opens it to find Tacoma on the landing, Wanblee Wapka's pickup backed up to the loading ramp. Her brother is in civilian clothes again, jeans and a deep blue ribbon shirt, his hair caught back at the nape of his neck.

His gaze slips past her to Kirsten standing by the table, then back again to his sister. "You're ready?"

For answer she nods, and together the three of them carry the body of Wa Uspewikakiyape to the waiting vehicle. Though Tacoma still limps heavily, he has set aside his crutches. He moves awkwardly but surely as they sidestep across the landing and Koda carefully lowers herself, her hands never losing their hold on their chill burden, into the truck's cargo space. A drum and beater occupy one corner, alongside a long, narrow bundle Koda recognizes as her father's *canupah*, his ceremonial pipe. A fringed bag, worked generations back in shell beads and porcupine quills, contains his herbs and other holy things. Kirsten and Tacoma follow her down, and they lay Wa Uspewikakiyape on the deerhide that is spread to cover much of the truck bed.

Bracing himself on the wheel housing, Tacoma folds down gradually until he is perched beside the drum, then lifts it to sit between his knees.

Kirsten moves hesitantly as if to offer a hand, and he shakes his head almost imperceptibly. "Thanks. I've got it."

Koda steps over the side and lets herself down in a single drop; Kirsten follows via tailgate and bumper. Manny swings open the door to the back of the cab and Kirsten climbs in, followed by Koda. Wanblee Wapka glances into the rearview mirror, checking his passengers. "Everybody settled?"

"Good to go, *leksi*," Manny answers, and Koda follows his gaze as he tracks from Tacoma in the cargo bed to her hand joined with Kirsten's on the bench seat. His eyes go wide for a second, and he mimes thumping his head against the metal frame of the window to his left. "Everybody but me, right?"

"Not *every*body," Koda says.

The light moment passes as Wanblee Wapka pulls the truck out into the street, and from behind them begins the deep heartthrob of the drum, beaten slowly. There is little traffic, vehicular or pedestrian, but here and there a uniformed soldier stops to stare at them as they pass. One or two, recognizing Kirsten's profile where she sits by the right window, salute; yet another, whose high, broad cheekbones and copper skin bespeak her Cheyenne ancestry, removes her cap and bows her head. The guards at the gate snap to attention and pass them out with looks of puzzlement on their earnest faces, but make no demur. Once off the base they turn toward the county road that leads into the foothills, the big truck taking the ruts with ease as they begin to climb toward the ancient streambed and its treeline, the place where Wa Uspewikakiyape had lived and died. For the most part they travel in silence, Koda lost in remembrance and a growing feeling of relief, anchored in time and place by the strong, small hand folded in her own.

Wanblee Wapka wrestles the truck up the slope of the rock outcropping that shelters the sealed den. As she slides to the ground, Dakota's eyes run along the line of trees, the dry course of the ancient stream that once cut its way down through limestone to create the shallow drop from the narrow remnant of wooded meadow with its march of trees. Among them now stands a scaffolding made of strong, straight limbs and rope, its platform six feet above the grass. Boughs of pine and larch cover it, interspersed with the slender trumpets of scarlet madder, the blue stars of anemone. From each corner hangs a leather thong strung with white chalcedony and striped agate, porcupine quills and a falcon's feathers. A circle of river pebbles makes a wheel about the scaffold, flat, larger stones set at the four quarters. This is a chief's burial. "*Washte*," says Koda. "Thank you, *Até*."

Manny and Wanblee Wapka lift down the body of Wa Uspewikakiyape and lay it by the scaffold. Tacoma sets the drum by the south upright and takes up his station before it. From his pouch, Wanblee Wapka takes several braids of herbs, sage and pine and sweetgrass, a smaller leather bundle that Koda knows contains pollen, and another of cornmeal. Finally he unwraps his pipe. To Kirsten he says, "This is what we do for family when they go to walk the Blue Road. Everyone participates."

Dakota watches as the meaning of his words sinks in, and Kirsten nods solemnly. Wanblee Wapka hands her the packet of cornmeal.

"When the time comes, rub some of this on each of the posts of the scaffold. Then on Wa Uspewikakiyape's wrappings. I'll tell you when, okay?"

She nods again, holding the folded leather as if it were the most precious thing in the world. In this light, her eyes are the wide clear green of the sea.

To Manny he gives a rattle made of turtle shell and antler. "Translate for her, will you?"

Finally he goes to stand beside Tacoma and the drum. "Everybody over here, please."

As they form a tight circle about him, Dakota feels peace begin to well up inside her. Part of it, she knows, is the coming end of the wrongness she has felt ever since finding that Wa Uspewikakiyape's body had not been left in dignity. Another part is the strong presence of her father, center of the compass of her world. Part is the warrior's honor that surrounds Tacoma, body and spirit. Yet another is the energy her cousin Manny carries, the spirit of thunder that can break forth as the humor of a *heyoka* jester or as the death-dealing lightning.

And at the center of her heart is Kirsten, love returning again and again through the cycles of the sun and the turning Earth.

Eyes closed, she hears the small sound of flint and pyrite struck together, smells the fragrance as the spark takes hold in a braid of sage. As Wanblee Wapka holds it out to her, Dakota waves the smoke toward her, washing it over her head and hands, over all her body. Awkwardly at first, then with more confidence, Kirsten follows her example; then Manny, Tacoma, Wanblee Wapka himself. He smudges the platform behind him, the drum, the buffalo hide that enfolds Wa Uspewikakiyape. As Tacoma once again begins the low, steady beat of the drum, punctuated by the rattle in Manny's hands, Dakota carries a braid of sweetgrass around the circle, lifting it to the sky, lowering it to the earth at each of the four quarters, invoking Inyan the Creator, Wakan Tanka, Ina Maka. She feels Kirsten's eyes on her as she paces the circuit, the calm touch of her thoughts.

When she returns to the center, Wanblee Wapka unwraps his pipe. It is a beautiful thing, made a hundred years ago and more. The bowl, carved of red stone in the shape of a buffalo, surmounts a length of hollow wood. Where it joins the stem, three eagle feathers hang by a leather thong strung with shell and turquoise. A spike extends just beyond it, to hold the pipe upright in the earth. Raising it to the east, Wanblee Wapka begins to pray:

"Ho! *Wanblee Gleshka*!
Spotted Eagle, Spirit of the East,
Hear us!
Speak to us about giving thanks.
Speak to us about wisdom.
Speak to us about understanding.
Speak to us of gratitude
For the life of our brother,
Wa Uspewikakiyape, who has gone
To walk the Spirit Road with you.
We give you thanks for him.
We thank you for the past,
The present and the future.

We thank you for all who are gathered here."

He pauses, and Koda answers, "*Han! Washte!*" Taking the offered pipe from his hand, she steps to the south quarter and raises it.

"Ho! *Ina Mato!*
Grandmother Bear, Spirit of the South!
Hear us!
Speak to us about fertility.
Speak to us about children.
Speak to us about health.
Speak to us about self-control.
Speak to us about creating good things for all people,
About the creations of our brother
Wa Uspewikakiyape who has gone
To walk the Spirit Road with you.
Give us fruitfulness in all we do."

Again, the soft murmurs of "*Hau! Waste!*"and from Kirsten, "*Han!*" Receiving the pipe again from Dakota, Wanblee Wapka steps to the western quarter and raises it.

"Ho! *Tatanka Wakan!*
Sacred Buffalo, Spirit of the West!
Hear us!
Speak to us about purification.
Speak to us about self-sacrifice.
Speak to us about renewal.
Speak to us about the Thunder.
Release us from those things
Which are past.
Speak to us about the gifts of our brother,
Wa Uspewikakiyape, who has gone
To walk the Spirit Road with you.
Give us freedom from weariness in all we do."

Dakota takes the pipe once again. Stepping to the north, she raises it and prays:

"Ho! *Tshunkmanitu Tunkashila!*
Grandfather Wolf, Spirit of the North!
Hear us!
Speak to us about rebirth.
Speak to us about winter passing.
Speak to us about the seed beneath the snow.
Speak to us about life returning.
Speak to us about our destiny.
Speak to us about the destiny of our brother,
Wa Uspewikakiyape, who has gone
To walk the Spirit Road with you.
Give us freedom from fear.

Koda hands the pipe to her father for the last time. Standing by the burial scaffold, he lowers it to the earth, then raises it again to the sky. Finally he holds it before him at the center. He chants,

Ho! Ina Maka, Wakan Tanka, Inyan!
Mother Earth, Great Mystery, Creator!
Hear us!
Our brother, Wa Uspewikakiyape
Has gone to walk the Spirit Road with you.
Make his steps sure as he comes to you.
Make his eyes bright when he looks upon you.
Make his heart glad when he dwells with you
In the Other Side Camp,
Among the Star Nation.
We hold his memory,
His friends, his student,
His mate and children.
We praise and thank him
For all he has given us.
Give us his courage,
Give us his strength.
Give us his wisdom,
So that one day we may join him
And come safely to you.

The soft murmur runs around the circle again, and Wanblee Wapka thrusts the long spike of his pipe into the earth beside the scaffold. The drum and rattle beat steadily. Following his direction, Kirsten steps forward and rubs a pinch of cornmeal on each of the four poles, sprinkling the remainder on the buffalo hide that wraps Wa Uspewikakiyape Then Koda and her father lift the bundle into place on the platform, and the ceremony is done.

As Manny and Wanblee Wapka gather up pipe and pouch and drum, stowing them again in the truck, Koda drifts apart from the group, leaning against the straight trunk of a young birch. The sun poises just on the edge of the horizon, the sky above it shot with crimson and gold. A breeze stirs the leaves above her head, cool with the coming of evening. Quietly, Kirsten comes to stand beside her, saying nothing, offering her presence. Dakota extends her hand in silence, and Kirsten takes it. Peace settles around her, sweet and deep. After a time, she stirs. "They're waiting for us."

"Yes," Kirsten answers.

"You all right?"

Kirsten murmurs something in assent, then says, "You?"

"Better." Koda turns, her hand still in Kirsten's. Together they descend the slope, take their places in the back seat of the truck.

Together. Going home.

# CHAPTER THIRTY-TWO

The morning lies gentle on the land as Koda steers the big truck out of the base. Dew spangles the buffalo grass that has grown up at the edges of the road, and the air that streams through the open windows carries its moist fragrance underlaid by the rich smell of earth. High above, a pair of large, black birds tumble down the depths of the sky, circling each other, giving chase, their calls ringing clear over the bare foothills.

Kirsten leans from her window to get a better look. "Ravens, right? Courting?"

Koda grins back at her. "Ravens, courting. A-plus."

A small smile curves Kirsten's lips. "Must be spring or something, huh?"

"Must be." Taking advantage of a long, straight stretch of road, Dakota leans over and kisses her lightly. Kirsten's mouth tastes of coffee, with a lingering hint of honey from the morning's biscuits.

An intimate silence grows up between them, and Dakota marvels again at the way their thoughts seem to fit easily together, mortice and tenon, as if they have known each other from the womb. Not even with Tali has she ever known this wordless intimacy, something that until now she has shared only with Tacoma. She watches now as Kirsten sips from the mug between the seats, then passes it without speaking. Koda drinks gratefully. She says, "I'm going to miss this. If we ever get stable again, you'll be re-elected for life if you can make a trade agreement with Colombia."

"*Liberté, egalité, café?*"

"You got it."

At a crossroads — what used to be a four-way-stop — Koda turns onto the farm road that will lead them up toward the ridge where Wa Uspewikak-iyape is buried. They will approach it from the other side, the paved track belonging to the deserted Callaghan ranch. As long as there is still gas, the pickup is too valuable to risk to the axle-busting ruts of the cross-country route. Koda leans out, stretching to get a view of the truck bed. "How are they doing back there, Kirsten? Can you see?"

Kirsten turns in her seat, wriggling loose for a moment from the safety belts to peer through the cab window. "A bit. They look okay."

Today is the spring equinox, and a day of freedom. Behind them in the truck bed, Manny and Tacoma watch over the two large crates holding Coyote and Igmú. Coyote, being Coyote, had followed a trail of chicken innards into his carrier without a moment's hesitation. The bobcat had had to be coaxed and gentled, coaxed and gentled, time and again until Tacoma could give her the final small push and Koda had fastened the door behind her. From what she can see in the rear-view mirror, Igmú still crouches, hissing, in a corner of the cage. If she ever again willingly approaches humans or metal man-things, it will be a triumph of curiosity over rage.

And that is all to the good. The world has changed, and new ways of living with the non-human world must be found. But the danger will never disappear entirely.

As she takes the turn-off that leads to the Callaghan gate a jackrabbit still sporting patches of white winter fur streaks across the asphalt in front of her, startling a flock of ring-necked pheasants from the grass at the other side. Kirsten gives a small, delighted exclamation as they rise, their wings drumming the bright air. They wheel out over the meadow, the sun catching the brilliant emerald feathers of head and throat, splitting the light into rainbows like a nimbus about them. "Oh my God," she breathes. "What was—" Abruptly her voice sharpens. "What *is* that?"

Directly ahead of them, precisely in the middle of the cattle guard, lies a low shape of grizzled fur. Perhaps a meter long and two-thirds as wide, it swells up on its bandy legs, its lips curled back from teeth like roofing nails. It hisses, thrusting its squat body toward the truck, then rocking back on its haunches with a low growl.

Koda brakes the pickup about ten feet short of the gate. "It's a badger. And he's right bang in the middle where I can't go around him."

"But I thought they were, well — smaller," Kirsten protests. "Like weasels."

"City girl," Koda teases gently. "This is a full-grown old man, and he's defending his territory."

"Yo!" comes Manny's voice from the back. "What's going on up there?"

"Badger in the gate!" Koda yells back at him and leans long and hard on the horn.

In response, the badger inflates himself further and lunges a foot toward the truck, the black and white stripes on his face wrinkling into a snarl. The difference in distance is small, but it is enough that his teeth seem at least twice as long. His claws, curling at the ends over the bars of the cattle guard, could pass for daggers.

Koda leans on the horn again.

The badger swells, fur bristling, and feints at the pickup a second time. Kirsten flinches back in her seat, then gives an embarrassed grin. "They don't eat trucks, do they?"

"Nah," says Koda. "Just tractors." And she shoves her elbow down on the horn a third time.

The badger does not budge.

The truck rocks suddenly, and Manny runs past the cab, halting halfway between the front bumper and the gate. "*Hoka!*" he yells, waving his arms windmill fashion. "*Le yo!* Beat it! *Ekta yo gni!* Am-scray!"

The badger snarls again, pushing up on his short legs and swiping at the air in front of his face with a set of claws like the prongs of a frontloader.

"Manny, dammit!"

"Get back here, you idiot!" Kirsten's shout mingles with Tacoma's as Koda leans on the horn again and guns the engine.

"Shoo!" yells Manny, undeterred. He waves his hat in a figure eight in front of him.

The badger does not even twitch. An awful stench pervades the air, not so sharp as skunk spray, earthier, muskier. Manny flaps his hat again, this time in front of his face, coughing. "Please?" he chokes. "*Le yo?* Pretty please?"

From the back of the truck comes a soft, high whine, followed by a yip. Coyote, wanting out. The badger's head tilts for a moment, then he bares his teeth at Manny again, growling low in his throat.

"Get back in the fucking truck, cuz!" Tacoma bellows. There is more thudding and rocking in the cargo bed as Tacoma gets to his feet and aims a rifle loaded with a trank dart over the roof of the cab. "Damn, I don't know which of you dimwits to shoot!"

Coyote whines again, giving a series of soft yips. It is a greeting, not an alarm. Koda scans the meadow, from the line of trees along a low ridge to the woods and the drop-off of the limestone outcropping on the other side. No other coyotes are visible. None answers their returning brother's call.

*I wonder...* Abruptly Koda comes to a decision.

Kirsten reaches out to stop her as she opens the driver's door, a frown creasing her brow. "Dakota—"

She grins in answer. "I'm going to try something. It could go wrong, but I think... Look in the glove compartment and hand me that pistol, would you?" Kirsten complies, and Koda deftly slips a small tranquilizer dart into it. "I think I know how to defuse this situation. Come back and give me a hand, will you?"

Kirsten follows her out the left-hand door, her puzzled disapproval an almost palpable pressure between Koda's shoulders. At the back bumper, Koda lowers the tailgate and pulls Coyote's cage forward. His mouth hangs open in a doofus-dog grin, tongue lolling. He yips again. "Okay, boy" she says, "I get it, I think." Tacoma spares her a swift glance, also grinning, then returns to keeping a bead on either the badger or their cousin; Koda is not quite sure which. Igmú has made herself small in the corner of her carrier, her eyes wide with stress. Another reason to get this over with.

Kirsten helps Koda to maneuver Coyote forward, then lift the cage down. Another series of yips punctuates the rapid swing of his abbreviated tail, its syncopated rhythm rattling the heavy wire mesh to either side of him. Scooting the carrier along the macadam and around the double wheels on the passenger side, Koda commands, "Manny, step back. Now."

Manny shoots a glance at her over his shoulder, a glint coming into his eye as he realizes what she's about. Carefully he takes a step backward and to the side, then another, until the hood of the truck bulks large between him and the badger.

With one hand, Koda takes the trank-loaded pistol from her belt. "Tacoma, keep him in your sights," she says, "just in case this goes wrong. I'll cover Coyote."

"I'm on it."

"Okay. Here goes." With her free hand, Koda slips the latch of the carrier, flinging the door wide. Coyote is out onto the road with a bound, making for the badger at a stiff-legged trot, stubby tail down, head tilted to one side. He whines, low in his throat.

Without warning, the badger seems to shrink. His haunches go down and his head comes up, black button nose snuffling the breeze. He cants his head, small ears cupped forward. He grunts.

"They know each other!" Kirsten whispers, her eyes wide. "You knew!"

"I guessed," Koda corrects with a smile. "Watch."

At the grunt, Coyote raises his head. He yips, twice, and walks straight up to the badger. Still grunting, Badger lifts his muzzle for a mutual sniff. Coyote's tail resumes its swing, and he stretches, leaning on his extended forelegs, rump high in the air. His tongue lolls from his open mouth. Springing to one side, then, he yelps and prances a few steps down the road beyond the cattle guard. With a last suspicious look backward, Badger lumbers around, and they disappear into the tall grass together.

"Aww," says Manny. "Off into the sunset. Ain't that sweet?"

Koda swats at him as she climbs back into the driver's seat. "It's sun-*rise*, cuz. Get back in. We've still got to drop Igmú off someplace safe."

Back on the road, Kirsten takes another mouthful of the coffee, then offers the mug to Dakota. "It's still warm." She asks, "How did you know to let the coyote go there? Couldn't they have gotten into a fight?"

Koda drinks, then sets the mug down again. "They could have, if they hadn't known each other. That's why we kept the trank guns on them." She shrugs. "Nobody knows why, but sometimes badgers and coyotes form what can only be called friendships. They become hunting partners: one flushes the prey, the other catches it. When Coyote kept making 'I'm home' noises, well—"

"Can you talk to them?" Kirsten asks abruptly. "To the animals?"

Dakota studies her for a moment. Kirsten's face is open and earnest. Carefully she says, "Not exactly. Sometimes I can communicate with a particular four-foot, but it's not usually with words. Why?"

Visibly mustering her courage, Kirsten says, "When we let the bobcat loose down by the stream can you tell her..." She pauses a moment, then finishes in a rush, "Can you tell her I'd appreciate it if she didn't eat any raccoons?"

Koda allows the question to swirl around in her brain for a long moment, hoping it will settle and make sense. When it does not oblige her, she says, "I think I'm missing something here. You want to tell me what it is?"

"No," Kirsten says, firmly. "You'll think I'm crazy."

A quick glance away from the road tells Koda that Kirsten is serious. With a twist of the steering wheel, she pulls the truck over to the side of the tarmac and brakes. Turning to face the other woman, she says, "*Canteskuye*, I know you're not crazy. You're a scientist; you're probably the most rational person I know. Now, what does releasing Igmú have to do with raccoons?"

Kirsten stares down at her hands, clenched in her lap. Pale sun side-lights her face, outlining her profile in a thin ribbon of light. She raises her eyes for an instant, then drops her gaze again. "I had a dream," she says. "There in the woods. A couple of weeks ago or so."

"A dream," Koda echoes. "About raccoons?"

"*A* raccoon. He— That is, we had a conversation."

A fist thumps on the top of the cab. "You okay up front? Is there a problem?"

"We're fine, Manny," she calls, not elaborating, then turns back to Kirsten. "Okay. You had a conversation."

"With a raccoon. I had a conversation with a raccoon. In a dream."

"And?"

Abruptly Kirsten turns to face her. Her expression is almost pleading. "I was sitting under a tree with Asi. There was a raccoon by the stream, there on the rock where I later found you. When he'd caught a fish, he came over to me and talked to me." A small grimace passes across her mouth, is gone. "I don't know when I fell asleep. I don't really know *if* I fell asleep. But when he left and I woke up," her hands describe small, aimless circles in the air, "...came to, whatever — there were tracks in the snow. Those were real."

"Do you want to tell me what he said?" Dakota reaches out and captures one of Kirsten's hands, surprisingly strong for all its small size. "You don't have to if you don't want to, you know, or if there was anything that's not my business."

"No, it's okay. He said his name was Wika Tega — Tegasomething."

"Wika Tegalega," Koda supplies. "It's our Lakota word for Raccoon."

"He said it means 'magical masked one' or something like that. But he told me to call him Tega. He offered me some of his fish, but—"

"Not into sushi, huh?"

"No. Anyway, he said time was like a Moebius strip, always going around in the same circle, things repeating themselves. He said he was my spirit animal, and he said to go to you when I woke up. That you needed me." She pauses, taking a deep breath, looking up to meet Dakota's eyes. "And I went to you. And you did. Even if I was...hallucinating."

Koda squeezes Kirsten's hand, raising it to her lips to place a kiss on the palm. "And I was grateful that you came." She allows a small silence to stretch between them. Then she says, "How much Lakota do you know?"

Kirsten's eyes widen in startlement. "Lakota? Just a few words — things I've heard you say once or twice. Like Wiyo's name. Or your dad's. 'Yes.' 'Hello.' That kind of thing. Why?"

"Have you ever heard the Lakota name for raccoon before? Could you just dream it up out of nowhere?"

"I...no. But—"

"You had a vision. You can call it dream if you like, or an altered state, but a spirit came to you as your teacher and friend. It's a good thing. A good thing."

Kirsten leans her temple against the back of her seat, never letting go of Koda's hand. "It's so much. It's all new, all strange. I don't know if I can get my head around it."

Dakota raises her other hand and runs it gently through Kirsten's hair. The sun slips through it like molten silver between her fingers. "I know you can. It's a good head. It's just that the world has changed more for you in some ways than it has for Tacoma, or *Até*, or me. We're still tied to the old ways your ancestors gave up hundreds of years ago. That's all."

"All," Kirsten repeats with a small laugh. "Sure. That's all."

"Not much, huh?" Another small laugh answers her, and Dakota grins. "And you don't want Igmú to eat your new friend or any of his nation, is that it?"

"Yeah. Silly, huh? I don't suppose she could eat a spirit creature."

"Not really. She wouldn't be inclined to eat a flesh-and-blood raccoon, either. A big boar can weigh almost fifty pounds, and even a small female would put up too much of a fight to be worth it. Predators don't like to work that hard for their dinner. It's not cost-effective."

"Thank you," Kirsten says softly.

"For what?"

"For not thinking I'm nuts, for having patience while I learn."

There is a catch in her voice, and it comes to Dakota that her lover does not mean only spirit animals and language. She says softly, "*Wastelake*, there is all the time you need. Have patience with yourself."

"I love you."

"*Cante mitawa*," Koda answers. "Now and always."

**An hour later,** Tacoma and Manny between them carry the wire cage containing Igmú into the small glen in the woods. Morning sun dapples the ground, green with moss, shimmers on the water that purls over the smooth stones of the streambed. High in a sycamore, a grey jay whistles softly.

"Here we are, girl," Tacoma says, setting the carrier down in the open space. "Home." At his voice, she butts her head against the mesh, a purr rumbling in her throat. He bends to scratch her ears, long fingers trailing through the thick winter fur.

Dakota says, "Whenever you're ready."

Tacoma swings open the door, and for a moment Igmú poises just inside it, one forepaw on the carpet of moss, dotted with minuscule star-shaped flowers. Then she gathers her long legs under her and is gone, streaking across the open space in a heartbeat, to hurl herself up onto the limestone ledge and from there, over the narrow water in one great bound. A third leap carries her into the undergrowth and out of sight.

For a long moment the four of them stand silent. Koda feels the peace of the land and water and light, a thing almost palpable. Then she turns once again to Tacoma and Manny, Kirsten's hand in hers. "Let's go home," she says.

**Taking a step** out into the cool spring afternoon, Kirsten draws in a deep breath to settle the butterflies in her belly. The fragrant breeze caresses her skin, and she shivers a little. In shorts and a tank top — Dakota's tank top, to be perfectly honest — she's a little underdressed for the weather, but the clothing choice wasn't exactly her idea, and she's determined to follow her instructions to the letter.

Another deep breath calms her somewhat, and she starts across the lawn with determined strides. To her surprise, she fields several appreciative glances, including one from a military-type who is so busy scanning her from toe to head that when he gets to her face — and realizes, belatedly, who she is — his face crumples into a mask of utter mortification.

His quickly doffed cap twists in his hands as he stares at the ground, red-faced as a beet. "S-sorry, um...ma'am...um...Ms. President, ma'am...I'm...um..."

Laughing softly, Kirsten takes pity on the man. "It's all right," a quick glance at his immaculately polished nametag, "...Edmonds. You didn't offend me."

"B-but, ma'am! Y-you're the P-P-President!"

"Last time I checked," she replies, setting a gentle hand on his shoulder, "I was also human." She quirks a smile at him, pleased to see the fiery blush begin to fade from his cheeks. "Besides, I don't think my first order of business will be to make 'ogling the President' a capital offense, so you're pretty much off the hook, okay?"

Edmonds straightens to rigid attention. "Y-yes, ma'am, Ms. President, ma'am! Thank you, ma'am!"

"You're welcome, Edmonds," she answers, returning the young man's stiff salute with as straight a face as she can manage. "Carry on."

"Yes, ma'am! Thank you, Ms. President, ma'am!"

As the relieved airman trots off double-speed, Kirsten's features crack into a wide grin. Shaking her head and chuckling to herself, she continues her trek toward the base's gate, and beyond.

**At the gate,** Kirsten is held up by a young guard so green he could have been a shoot of new spring grass. "Excuse me, ma'am," he states in a high, wavering voice. "I'm under strict orders not to let you outside of the base without a full guard."

She rounds on the man, but cuts short her sharp retort when she sees his obvious youth coupled with the look of abject terror in his eyes. She settles instead for a smile, though it doesn't seem to quell the nervous sweat beading at the young man's temple and hairless upper lip. "Well, I can certainly appreciate the concern for my safety, Private Mitchell, and believe me, I do. But since I was able to infiltrate the base at Minot without detection, I think I'm pretty capable of walking a few hundred yards past the gate without getting myself killed, don't you?"

Mitchell's panicked eyes fruitlessly search the faces of his comrades, all of whom are as stiffly at attention as he. Finally, he looks back to her. "I...s-suppose so, ma'am."

Kirsten's smile brightens. "Good! I'm glad we got this cleared up, Private." She reaches for the gate, only to be stopped by a hand to her shoulder. She glances down at the hand, then cuts her eyes back to the man who had dared put it there.

Mitchell yanks his hand away as though she were the sun itself. "S-sorry, ma'am, but I have my orders. From General Hart himself, ma'am!"

Turning slowly, Kirsten loses her smile and pins the man with her eyes. "I see." Her voice, though soft, fairly crackles with authority. "And General Hart is the Base Commander, is he?"

"Well...yes, ma'am!"

"Mm. And who gives the general his orders, Private?"

"Ma'am?"

Kirsten purses her lips. "It's a simple question, Private Mitchell. If the general commands the base, who commands the general?" She clears her throat as silence answers her question. "Who is his Commander-in-Chief, Private?"

Mitchell looks distinctly ill as the clue finally strikes across his head with the force of a semi. "Y-you are, ma'am."

Kirsten's smile returns. "Got it in three. Now, if there are no further objections?"

If any are about to be expressed, they are stopped in utero by a deep, steady voice just outside the gate. "It's all right, Private," Tacoma remarks, walking up to the barred entrance. "I'll make sure our Supreme Commander doesn't come to a bad end."

Looking up into dark eyes sparkling with amusement, Kirsten gives a soft chuckle as an MP hurries to open the gate for her. Stepping through, she laughingly curls her hand through the elbow gallantly cocked for her.

"Your chariot awaits, Madame," Tacoma intones as he leads her to one of the base's newest toys, an electric powered golf cart purloined from one of the myriad of country clubs that dot the surrounding area. Powered by batteries charged by the few wind fans they've managed to install, the carts are perfect for short drives, enabling the rapidly diminishing supply of gasoline to be conserved for emergency use.

As Kirsten slides into the molded white bench seat, she gazes over at Tacoma as he slips his large bulk into the vehicle and puts it in drive. He looks different out of uniform, she decides, his cargo shorts displaying long, bronzed, and muscled legs. His deep black hair is parted in the middle, carefully oiled, and split into two identical braids that are wrapped in rawhide and some type of fur she can't identify. He is wearing a long-sleeved, baggy, pullover type shirt that hides the rest of his body from view, but once again, she marvels at how deeply he resembles his sister.

The drive is a short one, through a small wooded area and into a narrow clearing. Tacoma brings the cart to a halt just inside the bands of trees. Stepping out of the vehicle, Kirsten eyes her surroundings, noticing the small, domed hut covered in patchwork hide and standing only slightly taller than her own height. A bit closer to her is a large round fire-pit with a jumble of stones sitting atop a well laid bed of glowing coals. Her mouth goes dry as the nervousness returns full force, filling her belly with crawling, fluttering insects. She almost jumps at Tacoma's gentle touch to her arm and she looks at him, wide eyed.

He gives her an easy, tender smile. "It's gonna be all right, Kirsten," he says softly. "You'll see." He tilts his head toward the hut in invitation, gaze warm upon her. "C'mon."

Just outside of the hut, he stops and strips off his shirt, leaving his torso bare. Kirsten gazes at him, struck yet again by the resemblance — aside from the obvious anatomical difference — to the woman she loves. She notes the twin thick scars set into his chest inches above his nipples, pushing down a surprising, and unwanted, flash of xenophobia. "Dakota mentioned that you were a Sun Dancer," she finally says.

"I am," he remarks in a smooth, even voice. He has noticed the flash in her eyes, but takes no offense at it.

"I...um...thought that Sun Dancing was illegal."

"It was. But when we reclaimed our lands, we overturned the *washichu's* laws." He smiles. "It is a part of who we are." With a brief nod, he motions her to stay where she is as he walks to the fire pit and picks up a small herb bundle, lighting it from the coals.

Sweet scented smoke teases her nostrils as he returns, and she stands stock still as he begins a soft chant, drawing the bundle and its attendant smoke in complex patterns over her body. The ritual completed, he returns the bundle to its place by the fire ring, then comes to stand before her once again. "Ready?"

After a moment, Kirsten nods and summons up a brief smile. "As I'll ever be, I guess."

Tacoma chuckles. "You'll do fine. Just remember this isn't a competition. If it gets to be too much for you, just step outside. No one will think any less of you, all right?"

His sincerity is evident and Kirsten nods again, somewhat calmed. "All right."

"Great. Let's go inside, then."

Tacoma opens the hide flap, and Kirsten's senses are immediately assaulted by a blast of herb-scented steam. Fat beads of sweat immediately pop up from wide-open pores, and she stills for a moment, willing her body to acclimate to the abrupt change in temperature and humidity. After a short time, her breathing eases, and she ducks beneath the low overhang and into the sweat hut. Steam paints the scene in a gauzy haze, and she blinks several times as she scans the interior.

To her left, Manny and Wanblee Wapka sit cross-legged next to one another. Directly before her is another, smaller, stone ring with dozens of fist-sized stones steaming on a bed of glowing coals. And, to her right, Dakota and Maggie sit, heads bowed closely together as they speak to one another in low tones. Maggie laughs, a low and somehow sexy sound, and Kirsten battles a flare of jealousy at the easy intimacy the scene conveys; a jealousy that is washed away the very second both women turn their eyes to her. From Maggie, there is abiding affection and a warm welcome as she eases over, creating a space beside Dakota. And from Dakota — Kirsten finds herself all but drowning in the soft, loving blue that envelops her, drawing her effortlessly to her lover's side, where she lowers herself to the ground and smiles in greeting. Unlike the others, Koda is sitting on her heels, her hands resting, relaxed, on strong thighs. Dressed in simple white cotton shorts and a white breast band, with vast amounts of her bronzed skin glimmering with sweat, she is, to Kirsten, magnificence personified.

For her part, Dakota can't quite seem to keep her eyes from roving over Kirsten's body; the vision she presents in a damp and clinging tank-top and flushed, rosy flesh sends a wave of arousal crashing through the tall woman so strongly that for a moment, she is almost overwhelmed by the sudden intensity. Breathing deep, she reaches out and threads her fingers through Kirsten's as the sharp spike of arousal softens and a wash of love takes its place. "I'm glad you came," she rasps, her eyes bright and full.

"So am I," Kirsten replies, gently squeezing the large hand that holds her own.

The flap closes as Tacoma eases his large bulk inside and sits beside his father, mimicking the older man's posture to perfection.

Wanblee Wapka's gaze runs around the small space, making the circuit of those present. "All here? *Washte,* we can begin." From the small deerhide bundle on the floor beside him, he takes out a braid of sweetgrass and tightly tied bundles of sage. "Kirsten," he says, glancing across the fire pit at her, "Maggie, this is your first sweat lodge, and you may see and hear things that you don't expect. You may see swarms of blue and green lights, or you may hear voices. Don't worry; that's normal."

"That's normal," Kirsten repeats, her lips shaping the words soundlessly. *It cannot be any stranger than a talking raccoon.* "Normal." She feels rather than sees Wanblee Wapka's smile, and knows that her thought has been heard, if not her words. Koda squeezes her hand again in reassurance, and she settles her mind to quiet.

Pouring a dipperful of water over the hot rocks, Wanblee Wapka says, "This water is from the four quarters of the world, carried by our Father the Sky. He is with us when we pray in peace, asking knowledge, wisdom and healing. Ina Maka has given this water from her own body. She, too, is with us. When *Inyan* made the world, he gave his life to his creation, and became stone. He is here also." As the steam fades upward, he pours water over the stones three more times.

Kirsten swallows hard as the freshly released heat sets upon her like a living thing. She's seen her share of saunas, courtesy of semi-regular trips to the gym, but this is a sauna taken to the nth degree, and her body is slow to adjust. She startles when Dakota's hand withdraws from hers, and she turns to look at her lover.

Dakota appears completely relaxed; her chest moves in a very slow, very steady rhythm, her hands rest, palms upward, against her thighs, fingers slightly curled. A small smile plays across her lips and her eyes are gently closed. Across the hut, the three men appear much the same, though Wanblee Wapka's eyes are open, but unfocused. Finally looking to her left, Kirsten finds Maggie smiling at her.

Leaning slightly over, the colonel whispers in her ear, "Relax. If nothing else, it'll be good for the skin, right?"

With a whispering laugh, Kirsten nods and forces herself to relax. Though the heat is intense, it truly isn't as bad as she thought it would be. After a moment, her eyes begin to drift closed, and she lets them, clearing her mind as much as she is able.

Some unknown time later, Kirsten breaks sharply free of a light doze, like a swimmer finally breaking the surface of a choppy ocean, and gasps, her heart pounding hard and urgent in her chest. She blinks her eyes, clearing the stinging sweat, as her panicked mind tries to decipher the insistent summons her body seems to be sending her despite the fact that all seems peaceful and quiet.

A quick check on Maggie shows the colonel sitting comfortably, eyes closed and breathing in an easy rhythm. The three men across from her are likewise still and calm in their meditation. It is only then that she notices the frightful cold pressed against her right side, melded to her like a block of ice that has melted and refrozen.

Turning quickly to her right, she gives a soundless cry at the sight of her lover, as pale and as stiff as a marble statue, her half-open eyes showing only the whites. Koda's parted lips are bloodless, and try as she might, Kirsten can detect no signs of breathing. Her voice, when it finally sounds, is high and brilliant with fright. "Dakota!" she screams, latching on to her lover's corded forearm. She might as well be touching a corpse, so cold and unyielding is the flesh beneath her hand. "Dakota! No!"

Other hands, strangers' hands, descend on her then, trying to pull her away. Voices, deep and gruff, sound in her ears, all but indecipherable. The strength of the hands on her body is implacable, but her will is stronger still, and she struggles with all her might, yelling for her lover at the top of her lungs.

"Kirsten!" Wanblee Wapka shouts in her ear. "Kirsten, you must listen! Dakota is *makoce nupa umanipi*. Walking in two worlds. You must not touch her, or her spirit may not be able to find its way back to her body. Please, come away!"

"No!" Kirsten shouts, able only to see Dakota's bloodless, immobile face. "Dakota!"

"Come away! Please!" Wanblee Wapka shouts again, redoubling his strength. "She cannot hear you; she cannot respond. Please, you are putting her in great danger!"

The urgency, if not the intent, of Wanblee Wapka's words seeps through Kirsten's terror, and she finds herself yielding to the firm strength at her back. Her rigid grip softens, and her fingers unwillingly part from Dakota's chill flesh. A sobbing cry erupts as she watches a tiny drop of blood trail its way down from Dakota's nostril to rest on her upper lip. Her struggles begin anew, but the grip of the men behind her is too strong and too sure, and she feels herself being inexorably pulled away from her lover. "No!"

And then, what Wanblee Wapka would have deemed impossible, happens. With the growl of the wolf sounding deep in her chest, Dakota reaches out and clamps down on Kirsten's wrist, her grip as cold and as unrelenting as chilled iron.

"*Até?*" Tacoma demands, stunned and confused. "What—?"

"*Chunkshi? He nayah, he?*"

The growling halts and Dakota begins to tremble. Her eyes open fully, though only the whites show. "*Sa,*" she groans, her voice hollow and far away. "*Wapka sa. Maka sa. Shota. Wikate. Ayabeya tokiyotata wikate. Ayabeya tokiyotata sa.*"

She trembles again, violently, and the blue finally shows from her eyes, shining with terrible knowledge. "*Ayabeya tokiyotata wikate. Osni.* So...cold." Her eyes flutter closed and she collapses.

Lunging forward, Kirsten gathers Koda into her arms, stroking her hair with frantic fingers and murmuring desperate pleas through her tears.

"Manny," Wanblee Wapka orders, "get the cart and bring it around to the front. "*Chinkshi,* help me with Dakota."

"I'll carry her myself, *Até,*" Tacoma counters, moving to Dakota's head as Wanblee Wapka's hands descend back onto Kirsten's shoulders.

"Kirsten," Wanblee Wapka says softly, lips close to her ear, "Kirsten, I need you to let her go, just for a moment."

"No," Kirsten moans. "No, please. Please, help her."

"We will, *wikhoshkalaka.* We will, I promise. But you need to come away with me so that Tacoma can lift her and carry her to the cart. She needs to be cared for at home, and we cannot lift you both."

Slowly, with great reluctance, Kirsten allows Wanblee Wapka's gentle hands to guide her away from her lover. Dakota's grip, however, remains tight around her wrist. Wanblee Wapka comes quickly to one knee and begins to gently massage his daughter's bloodless hand. "*Chunkshi,* let her go. Let Kirsten go. We must tend to you, Dakota. Please, release her wrist."

His intent massage softens Koda's grip, and Kirsten, with the greatest reluctance, pulls her wrist free. Dakota immediately reacts, thrashing her long body about. Head twisting from side to side, she moans.

Wanblee Wapka strokes his daughter's hair, his eyes bright with concern and love. "Shhh, *chunkshi.* She is here. Your *tehila* is here." He turns his regard to Kirsten. "If you speak softly to her, she will hear you."

One hand over her mouth, Kirsten uses the other to reach out, stopping just short of Dakota's icy skin. "Koda...sweetheart? I'm here, right beside you, okay? You're gonna be fine, I promise." Unable to stop herself, her hand completes the last inch and brushes against her lover's flesh. So very cold. She's tempted to pull away again; a reflex she actively fights. Instead she strokes along the ridges of tendon, muscle and bone, willing warmth into the icy skin. "I won't leave you," she vows. "Not now, not ever."

Dakota calms immediately under Kirsten's attentions. Her breathing settles, and she appears to slip into a deep sleep.

Wanblee Wapka takes quiet note of the fierceness in Kirsten's voice and manner, and smiles briefly to himself. This, he knows, is the true face of the woman his beloved daughter has chosen for a mate — the face of the Igmú protecting her cubs. He nods to himself, well pleased, then tenderly draws her away as Tacoma steps in and easily lifts Dakota's limp, dead weight into his massive arms.

They follow closely behind as Tacoma walks quickly to the waiting cart, Manny at the wheel. He lays her gently in the back, a place where golf bags normally rest. It's a tight fit, but he manages. He then ushers Kirsten around to the passenger's side, and helps her settle in. She immediately twists in the molded plastic seat and reaches out, running her fingers through the thick fringe of hair on Dakota's pale, chilled brow. Tacoma yanks Manny from the driver's seat and gestures for his father to take the vacated space. "We'll walk, *Até*," he murmurs before returning to check on his sister one last time. "We'll meet you back at the house."

With a brief nod, Wanblee Wapka puts the cart in drive and heads away.

Maggie finally looks away from the retreating cart, eyeing the remaining men with one eyebrow raised. "Can someone please explain to me what the Hell just happened here?"

Tacoma's lips twitch. "Sure, I'll tell you as we're heading back, okay?"

"Fine."

And with that, the three start back to the base, double time.

# CHAPTER THIRTY-THREE

They enter the house to find Kirsten, white-faced and nervously pacing the length and breadth of the living-room. The door to Dakota's room is firmly closed, and no sounds emanate from behind it. The rooms are rich with the aroma of heating soup, though it's obvious that Kirsten is in no way comforted by the homey scent.

Quickly assessing the situation, Maggie walks over to Kirsten, gently takes her arm, and leads her to the couch. "Sit down before you fall down," she says in a no-nonsense voice that is nevertheless rife with compassion. "Manny, get some coffee brewing. Make it strong."

"Yes, ma'am," Manny replies, all military business as he all but marches over to the kitchen.

"Tacoma, could you—"

"*Até* will come to us when he's ready," he answers, moving over to the other side of the couch and easing his long frame down beside Kirsten. He cups her hand in his much larger one, chafing her skin gently with the other. "She'll be fine, Kirsten. I promise you."

"I—" Kirsten gathers herself. "What's taking so long?"

"It will take as long as it takes, little sister. She will be fine."

Pulling her hand from his, Kirsten drags it through her hair, tugging on the ends in a gesture of frustration. "I'm a scientist," she says as if to herself. "I fix things. And I — I can't fix this!"

"That's because there's nothing to fix," Tacoma replies. Leaning slightly forward, he takes her hand again, his eyes dark and penetrating with the strength of his convictions. "Kirsten, listen to me. This is a part of who my sister is. It's something you have to accept as part of her. If you can't, you can never hope to make a life with her."

Kirsten's eyes widen in disbelief, then narrow as determination sets her jaw.

Tacoma holds up a hand. "I think you will make a life with her, a very long and happy life." He sighs. "Acceptance comes with understanding, and I'm afraid we haven't been very forthcoming with you in this regard."

"You can say that again," Kirsten mumbles. "It's like you're all on the same page, and I don't even know where the bookstore is."

"Not all of us," Maggie interjects, turning her expectant gaze toward Tacoma.

Tacoma blushes, then shakes his head. "Believe me, *Até* is much better at this than I am. He's had to explain it to his ten kids, after all. I haven't had to explain it to anyone."

"I dunno," Maggie drawls. "Should we let him off the hook?"

Feeling somehow better for the conversation, Kirsten nods. "For now."

"Thank you!" Tacoma exclaims, grinning at her. Then his expression sobers. "The point is, I understand your fears. I've been there, and I know what it's like to feel powerless to help." Kirsten is looking at him with frank interest now. "I was thirteen the first time it happened. A *koskalaka* still learning how to be a man and sometimes, like most teenagers, too big for my braids." He smiles in a self-deprecating manner. "I'd had my first vision almost six months before, see, and so I considered myself an expert on the matter. Dakota was twelve — not quite a woman, but almost. She'd just started her growth spurt and was almost as tall as me again."

Smiling in fond remembrance, he lets go of Kirsten's hand and rises to his feet, stepping around the couch and stretching his cramped muscles lightly. Taking the cup of strong coffee from Manny, he hands it to Kirsten and resumes his tale. "*Até* and Grandfather planned a sweat for her, just to get her used to the idea. A kind of trial run, actually. No one really expected her to have a vision. It wasn't her time yet."

"But she did."

"And how," Tacoma remarks, drawing a hand over his face. "It started off *all right* at first. I mean, it was kind of surprising that she was being gifted with a vision, but... I could tell she was a little nervous, so I, with my six months of vast experience, tried to help her through it. But then..."

"Something went wrong, didn't it?" Kirsten observes, holding the mug in chilled hands but making no move to drink the coffee inside.

"I thought it did. And worse, I thought I made it happen. Like I'd done something wrong when I was trying to help her." He shakes his head, causing the long fall of his now unbound hair to ripple and settle over his shoulder. "I was so scared that I forgot everything *Até* taught me."

"What happened?" Kirsten murmurs, entranced.

"Luckily, *Até* had the presence of mind to snatch me away before I did something unforgivable. While he held me tight, Grandfather went in after Dakota."

"Went in after?" she repeats. "I'm not sure I understand."

Tacoma smiles grimly, pondering for a moment. "Dakota told me of the time," he begins softly, "when you had an unfortunate encounter with a dying android that seemed determined to take you along with it. Do you remember?"

Kirsten nods. Her memories of that time remain, unlike the stuff of her dreams, curiously vivid, though the scientist in her passes those memories off as dreams for lack of anything else to call them. All of her life, she has stood firm in her resolve that the human body and what people liked to call the soul or spirit are inexorably entwined. As long as one lives, the other lives. When one ceases, the other does as well, world without end, amen. If she is to accept these memories as something more than the random firings of a brain desperately in need of oxygen, she will have to change some very fundamentally held world views, and though she acknowledges that she is a much different person now than she was then, it is a change that she's not sure she's ready to make.

Tacoma, compassionate to her struggle, remains quiet a moment more before speaking. "Our beliefs are very different," he remarks softly. "When Dakota realized that you were starting to walk the spirit path, she 'went in after you', to bring you back to your body. Grandfather did much the same to Dakota long ago."

"Why your grandfather and not your father?" Maggie asks, curious.

"Dakota loves my father very deeply, it's true," Tacoma answers. "But she worships my grandfather, even now, when he's been gone from this world for many years. They had a bond that...well, if Grandfather had asked her to take poison for him, she would have done it without a second's pause."

"Wow."

"Yeah, wow. I was a little jealous, to tell you the truth, but..." Tacoma shrugs as if to say "what are you gonna do?"

"So, your grandfather brought her back?" This from Maggie who, unlike Kirsten, has absolutely no problem believing in and accepting as truth the spirituality practiced by Dakota and her family, since it closely mirrors her own.

"Well...yes and no." He laughs as two questioning gazes meet his. "He helped guide her, yes, but he said later that she'd pretty much figured most of it out on her own. Though she did have some very special help."

Before either of them can quiz him on the comment, the door opens a crack and Wanblee Wapka peers through. "Kirsten, if you could join us, please?" At her startled and fearful expression, he smiles warmly. "Everything is fine. I promise you."

With a shuddering breath, Kirsten rises from the couch, hands her mug to Maggie, and all but runs to the bedroom, slipping inside and waiting for Wanblee Wapka to close the door behind her. After a moment, she gathers her courage and looks over at the bed.

There, beneath a heap of blankets, lies Dakota. Though still very pale, thankfully some semblance of color has returned to her face, and she appears to have sunken into a very deep, very peaceful sleep. Having spent so much time imagining various horrible scenarios, Kirsten feels weak with relief. The only thing keeping her from breaking into tears with the force of it is Wanblee Wapka's steady presence beside her.

The older man, reading her like a book, puts a gentle hand on her shoulder and leads her to the side of the bed. "As you can see, she is doing well and resting comfortably." He gestures to the large bowl and mug that sit on the bedside table. "She is warm, dry, and decently fed. All she needs now is rest...and you."

Kirsten turns wide eyes to him, and he smiles. "My daughter loves you very much, Kirsten."

"I love her, too. With all my heart."

Wanblee Wapka's smile broadens. "I can see that; it shines from you." Dakota moans softly. "See how she seeks you out, even in her healing sleep?" Kirsten reaches out and strokes Dakota's bangs. "And she calms at your slightest touch. She knows you are with her, and it helps her to regain her strength."

"Is that...normal?"

"Normal, yes; common, no. In fact, it's quite rare. The bond that is between you is a very strong, very sacred thing."

"I'm...starting to learn that, I think."

He laughs softly. "I know it is difficult, Kirsten. Not only are you from a different culture, but your mind and your beliefs are as different from ours as night is from day. And yet, Ina Maka has chosen to gift you both with this sacred union. I will help you both to adjust to it as best I can, if it is something you truly wish."

"More than anything," Kirsten replies, knowing her words for fundamental truth. "More than anything."

"I believe you," Wanblee Wapka replies, his own truth ringing strong in his tone.

Kirsten's fingers drift down, stroking the cheek of her beloved. "She's still so pale, so cold."

"It is an unfortunate side effect of the vision trance. She will improve, with rest and time."

"What can I do?"

"Nothing more than you are doing now. She knows you are here. Your presence will make all the difference."

Dakota shivers as a great, bone deep chill wracks her body.

"Is it..." Kirsten blushes. "Is it okay if I get under there with her? Maybe it would help her feel warmer."

"An excellent suggestion. But remember, she will be like this for some stretch of days. Do not feel obligated to stay with her the entire time. You have needs which must be met as well."

"Right now," Kirsten remarks, reaching for the bottom of her tank top, "this is what I need."

With a final, proud smile, Wanblee Wapka inclines his head, then turns and leaves the two of them alone, closing the door softly behind him and plunging the room into twilight.

Kirsten strips down to her undergarments and slides beneath the covers. "It's okay, my love," she murmurs as she stretches out full on her back and guides Dakota to her, resting her lover's sleek head on her shoulder and smiling when one long, strong arm immediately wraps itself around her waist. "That's right, I'm here. You rest now. I'm here."

A moment later, she closes her eyes and, like her partner, falls deeply asleep.

**Tacoma half-rises to** his feet as his father re-enters the room. "*Até*? How is she?"

"Resting easily. Kirsten will stay with her." He half turns toward the hall that leads to the kitchen. "Is that coffee I smell?"

"I'll get you some, *leksi*." Before Wanblee Wapka has a chance to protest, Manny is on his feet and headed toward the back of the house.

A smile crosses his father's face, and Tacoma feels an answering pull at his own mouth. "You must be getting grey, *Até*. Would you like a warm blanket for your knees? A cane?"

At that, Wanblee Wapka laughs outright. "Not yet, boy. Not yet." He folds down easily to sit on the chest that serves as a sofa table. In a curious reverse of his movements, Asi rises joint by joint from his place on the hearth, yawns hugely and comes around to lie at Wanblee Wapka's feet. "Hey, fella," he says, ruffling the big dog's fur. Then, returning his attention to Tacoma, "I mean to see my youngest's youngest before I begin to slow down. You'll have some grey hairs of your own by the time we get there."

The words are casually spoken, but Tacoma feels an undercurrent of *wakan* in them, truth rooted in power. Still he notes the weariness that shows in the creases about his father's eyes, the cold prickles that rise along the skin of his forearm rested casually across his knee. He glances up to meet Maggie's eyes, dark with concern and a depth of knowledge that he has seldom seen in anyone not of his own people. "Hey!" he shouts toward the kitchen. "Room service! Move your backside, bro!"

A clatter in the kitchen announces Manny's reappearance with a mug of steaming coffee in one hand, a bowl of soup in the other, a round of frybread dangling from his fingers. The rich aroma of chicken broth and sage rises from it. "Here you go, *leksi*."

"*Pilamayaye, tonskaya*," Wanblee Wapka says and applies himself to the food. When the bowl is empty, the last drops soaked up with a piece of frybread, he says, "Maggie, I think you have a few questions."

"More like a few dozen," she answers wryly. "But let's start with the big one. What did Koda say? Can you tell me, if it's not personal? I thought I heard something that sounded like your name."

Wanblee Wapka nods. "You did, but it wasn't a name." He pauses a moment. "I can tell you her words. She said, 'Red. Red earth. Red rivers. Red all over.' And she said, 'Death. Death everywhere.'"

Maggie sits back against the back of the sofa with a visible shiver, her arms crossed over her body like a woman caught in an icy wind. "That's cheerful," she says. "Is it a prophecy?"

Tacoma feels the chill course through his own blood, rushing like a stream at spring thaw. He knows the answer to Maggie's question, knows that his father knows. He cannot explain his certainty, but he is no less certain for that.

Wanblee Wapka, though, says carefully, "Until she wakes and speaks to us, we can't say for sure. We don't know where she was, or when she was. She could be describing what has happened back East, or in Europe or Asia. She could have been seeing the past in this very place."

"But?" says Maggie, leaning forward with her elbows on her knees, her hands clasped loosely before her, looking Wanblee Wapka directly in the eye.

After a moment, he says, "But yes, I think it was prophecy. I think she was talking about something yet to come."

"Tomorrow?" she presses. "A year from now?"

A lift of his shoulders answers her. Wanblee Wapka says, "Time runs strangely along the spirit road. One does not always see things in the order they assume in our world. Duration is problematic, at best. We were in the Inipi ceremony for less than an hour. Yet Dakota may have spent half a year, or half a lifetime, on the other side, as time is measured there."

For a moment, Maggie turns her head to stare out the window. Tacoma follows her gaze to the big oak tree that will shade the house in summer, where a squirrel sits placidly eating one of last season's acorns, turning it over and over in dainty paws. The plain white curtains stir with the breeze, bringing the scent of new grass. Finally she says, "Can you tell us what you think it means?"

"What does red suggest to you?" Wanblee Wapka asks quietly.

"The obvious?"

"Nothing wrong with being obvious. The whole context..." a wave of his hand encompasses the base, the lands beyond, the continent stretching away to the circle of the horizon, "...is obvious."

"Blood, then. Blood everywhere. Death everywhere. More fighting, more killing, more human casualties."

"We always knew we weren't done at the Cheyenne," Manny says, his voice flat. "The droids won't leave us alone. They can't."

"If there were ever any doubt, the 'suicide bomber' that attacked the convoy bringing back the wind turbines put paid to it," Maggie says dryly. "We're a rallying point for the population. We've got the guns and we've got the President, who also happens to be the one person with the technical knowledge to put the whole fucking lot of them out of business. From the moment she comes out of that room, I don't want Kirsten to set foot out of the house without a guard on her. She's got a goddam bullseye painted on her forehead."

"Want a volunteer?" Manny raises his hand. "If you do, you got one."

Maggie nods. "Get Andrews. Find two more to spell you, and bring me their names for approval. Twelve hours on, twelve off. We still have some wireless field sets with working batteries. Check out one apiece. And pick out an armored transport. I don't want Kirsten going off base any other way from now on. Get it together by suppertime."

"Yes, ma'am." Manny snaps her a salute, grinning. "I always did want to be a Secret Service agent if I couldn't fly."

Tacoma stares down at his hands. He cannot volunteer and knows he will be turned down if he does. His skills are needed elsewhere. Wanblee Wapka says quietly, confirming his thought, "Manuel will do what needs doing, *chinkshi*. You're too valuable as an engineer and ground field commander."

"You should have officer rank," Maggie adds. "I'm going to ask Kirsten to brevet you major." Tacoma looks up, startled, but she waves away his protest before he can make it. "I know it doesn't matter to you. And it doesn't matter to the men and women who have fought with you and know you. It will matter to others, eventually, particularly to any other military who may link up with us. You're getting promoted, soldier. Deal with it."

There is nothing else for it. "Yes, ma'am," he says. "Thank you."

A wry grin cants across her face. "Thank me when you have the headaches that go with the job and there's no more aspirin."

"There'll still be willow bark," Wanblee Wapka says, smiling. "The old ways have gotten our people through a few thousand years or so. Others can learn to use them, too."

"That could be what Koda saw, too, couldn't it?" Tacoma meets his father's gaze steadily. "Red all over. Red people, red ways. The buffalo will come back, and the people with them, just as White Buffalo Woman said."

"And Wovoka, and others since." Wanblee Wapka leans down to ruffle Asi's fur again. "We don't know yet how much we have lost, or how much we can recover. We don't know yet how much we want to recover. But you're right. We — Lakota, Americans, all people — have an opportunity to choose our paths in a way that has not been open to us for centuries. That will be part of Kirsten's challenge."

"And Dakota's," Tacoma adds.

"And your sister's. Very much so." His father levers himself up to his full height, giving Asi's collar a tug so that the dog comes to his feet, too, tongue lolling in a hopeful grin. "I'm going to walk this guy here, then I'll be back to stay with them for as long as needed."

Asi prances to the door, quivering from ears to tail. When it opens he is out like a shot, Wanblee Wapka following more sedately. Maggie looks from Tacoma to Manny and back. "And you two are still sitting on your butts because...?"

"Yes, ma'am," Tacoma says, smiling and getting to his own feet. "We're on it."

**When Kirsten awakens,** her body is in a full state of arousal. At first, her eyes still closed, she passes it off as the remnants of a wonderful, if unfortunately unremembered, dream. The hand lying hot on her naked belly, however, convinces her of an entirely different reality. Her eyes flutter open and she moans softly, her body arching as that hand makes a slow, deliberate circle over her belly before reaching up and brushing tender fingers over her already hard nipples.

Before she can say a word, her lips and mouth are taken in a kiss that is hot, and deep, and wet. Dakota's taste and scent flood her senses, and she latches on to strong shoulders with both hands, taking what is offered and giving back her own, spiraling desire.

When the kiss is finally broken, Kirsten looks up into eyes fully dilated and black with need. Only a small sliver of brilliant blue surrounds each pupil, like a corona around a total eclipse.

"*Lila waya waste mitawa*," Koda purrs, her voice rough with sleep and yearning. "My beautiful woman." Sliding her fingers down the silken bra, she cups Kirsten's breast, feeling the strong heart beat quickly, forcefully against her flesh. "Like a drum," she whispers. "Calling me to worship."

Heeding the summons, Koda lowers her head, brushing her cheek against the smooth fabric covering Kirsten's firm breast before using the tip of her tongue to inscribe wet circles around the straining nipple. A long breath of warm air almost sends Kirsten through the roof, and her cry is loud as warm lips engulf her breast, working it through the silky material of her bra. Dakota's free hand glides slowly down Kirsten's side, past her hip to her knee, then reverses its course, cupping her mound briefly before meandering over to the neglected breast and fondling it gently with her palm and fingers.

Kirsten squirms beneath her, hands now clenched in the bedsheets, her head turned to the side, chest heaving as she draws in deep breaths of much needed air. A gentle nip gets her attention; a harder one earns a groan, long and languorous as her hips twitch in response.

Smiling, Dakota pulls away, then leans in for another deep, probing kiss as her hands trail down to work the fabric of Kirsten's briefs. The smaller woman lifts, and the garment comes free and is tossed to the side of the room, immediately forgotten. "So beautiful," Koda murmurs, tracing her fingers along the middle line of Kirsten's belly to stroke through the thick, damp hair framing her sex. Long fingers dip lower, swirling through the abundant moisture as Kirsten gasps and moans in pleasure at her lover's touch.

"So good, *tehila*, so good." Stroking softly, she shifts her body until she is off the bed and kneeling on the floor. Grasping Kirsten's hips, she pulls her young lover forward, hot breath playing over the weeping jewel so beautifully exposed to her. She lifts her gaze up to find brilliant emeralds staring down at her, and she smiles. "Watch me, *canteskuye*. Watch me love you."

Lowering her head, she drinks of her lover's desire, its taste finer by far than any nectar. Her strokes are long, and firm, and swirling, leaving no bit of the slick, swollen flesh unloved.

Straining to keep her eyes open against the waves of ecstasy rising and breaking against her body, Kirsten releases her grip on the sheets and lowers an unsteady hand to the glossy, shining mass of her lover's hair.

Removing her mouth for just a moment, Koda slides one finger deep within her lover's center, then removes it slowly, savoring the velvet tightness that grips her so lovingly.  Then she returns to her task as her glistening finger trails down until it is pressed familiarly against the small, puckered entrance to the rear.

Kirsten lifts her head at the sensation, her eyes showing a little fear. "Koda? What—?" She collapses hard against the pillows as Koda's tongue redoubles its swirling strokes and her finger begins a firm massage designed to relax and pleasure.

"Jesus!" Kirsten pants.  "That's...incredible!" she breathes out as Koda enters her to the top knuckle, stimulating nerve endings she never before knew she had.

Koda laughs softly in her chest as she gently eases her finger forward until it is fully sheathed.  Then, with a motion that matches her tongue, she swirls and thrusts, ever so gently, reading her lover's body like a book as Kirsten's muscles tense and relax, tense and relax, and her breath becomes short, almost agonized pants.  She curls her finger within as she bites down gently on the flesh in her mouth concentrating solely on the swollen head, bathing it with staccato touches of her tongue.

Kirsten explodes with a force that takes her breath away.  Her muscles seize in an incredible spasm and she can do nothing but ride out the waves of utter passion that carry her along into the unknown.

When she is at last borne upon the land, Koda is there, holding her gently in her mouth, warming her, grounding her, bringing her home.

And then, another thrust, and she feels herself, impossibly, driven forward again on the wings of an excitement she's never even dreamed.  "No!" she cries out when she feels her lover leave her.  Her eyes open to find Dakota standing, naked, smiling down at her.

"Spread your legs a little more, *canteskuye*, a little more.  Yes, perfect."

As Kirsten watches, Dakota uses her clean hand to spread her own lips, then leans forward, sealing them both together in the most wonderful of ways.  Their slick, slippery, swollen flesh rubs together, setting off sparks throughout Kirsten's body and she cries out, once again, at the sensations.

"A long, slow ride to bring us home, *cante mitawa*." Koda purrs as she plants her fists on the bed and begins to thrust against her lover, circling her hips in a maddening, captivating way.

Kirsten licks her lips as she sees Koda's breasts sway above her, nipples proudly swollen a deep red.  She reaches up to stroke them as Koda continues her long, slow thrusting, grunting softly with the effort of each stroke.

"Harder," Koda gasps as Kirsten pulls and tugs.  "Yes, harder, like that, oh yes!"

Dakota increases her rhythm, leaning closer over her lover, her long fragrant hair forming a curtain over them both.  She feels her climax rushing toward her.  "*Han!*" she shouts, tilting her head back, displaying her neck as she continues to thrust into Kirsten's willing, open body, sweat pouring down her face and neck.  "*Han!*" she shouts again, and begins to shudder as her orgasm overtakes her with great bursts of light and pleasure.

A moment later, she collapses down over the body of her lover.  Her fingers move quickly, thrusting themselves into Kirsten's welcoming body, and she grunts with each thrust into the slick, velvet glove.  "I love you, *canteskuye*," she pants out between grunts. "I love you. Gods, how I love you."

It takes no more than that for Kirsten to burst free from her body once again, her spirit enfolded in brilliant colors that lift her so high and hold her there for a seeming, blissful eternity before easing her gently back down into the embrace of the woman she loves.

She comes back to herself to find her face and eyes and hair peppered with kisses, and it is all she can do just to collapse, completely spent, into Dakota's strong and loving arms. She manages to lift her shining face to her lover. The kiss they share is warm, and soft, and loving.

Then both fall down into slumber, still pressed tightly against one another as the sweat from their bodies slowly cools.

**When Kirsten next** awakens, it is the morning of the third day after the events of the sweat. She finds herself cocooned beneath Koda's dead weight just as another soft knock comes to the door. "Just a minute!" she calls, her voice sounding as harsh as a frog's dying croak. "Koda. Sweetheart, could you... Unh. Okay, that's not gonna work." Her deeply sleeping lover is as boneless as a rag doll, and it takes all of her strength just to free one leg. With some leverage, she is able to roll Koda onto her back, where she stays, head lolled to one side. In the dawning light of the new day, Kirsten carefully looks her lover over. Most of the deep color has returned to her face, but dark circles remain beneath her eyes. Despite the warmth of the room, her flesh retains a disturbing chill, and as Kirsten rises from the bed, she carefully tucks the scattered quilts around Dakota's still form.

The knock sounds again.

"I'm coming!" She finds herself blushing deeply at the words. "That's what I've spent the past two days doing," she murmurs under her breath, then blushes again. Her body is sore, but it is the pleasant soreness of one well and wonderfully loved. "Jesus," she whispers, shivering as the memories pass in a merry parade through her consciousness. "All right, Kirsten, deep breath in, deep breath out, good. Now..." She raises her voice. "Who is it?"

"It's Tacoma. Lieutenant Jimenez, one of your techs, is here to see you. He has something from that suicide bomber android he needs to show you."

"Okay," she says, her eyes darting around for clothes, or a robe with which to cover herself, and coming up empty. "I'll be right out. I have to—"

"Take your time. We'll be in the living room when you're ready."

"Thanks." Lifting an arm, she takes a quick sniff, then winces and coughs. "Shower. Now."

The master suite contains a tiny half bath with enough room for a toilet, sink, and a stall shower. The spray is bitter cold as she turns on the tap, and, gritting her teeth, she steps inside. "I gain more respect for you military types every day," she mutters, shivering as she grabs the soap and begins quickly working up a lather. Longing for the days when a steamy hot shower was both luxury and necessity, she completes her washing in record time and gratefully turns off the tap.

A thankfully non regulation towel is her reward, and she dries off quickly then wraps it around herself as she stalks back into the bedroom.

"Damn," she murmurs, looking down at the scattered pile of clothes she'd worn three days before, wrinkled beyond salvaging. "Now what? I'm certainly not gonna entertain guests in a towel."

Shrugging, she steps over to the battered dresser from which she's seen Koda draw forth clothes. Opening a drawer, she rummages through until she comes up with a plain black T-shirt — overlarge, which is good since her bra has been reduced to two matching strips of useless cloth — and a pair of cargo shorts that, once she pulls them on, resemble Capri pants, given the difference in height between herself and her lover. "Ah well. They'll just have to deal with it."

Running Dakota's brush through her hair, she deems herself as presentable as she's going to get, and makes a final check on Koda, who is sleeping peacefully, burrowed beneath the layers of blankets covering her. "I'll be back soon, sweetheart," she whispers, gently touching Dakota's cheek before turning and leaving the room.

**Jimenez and Tacoma** come to their feet as Kirsten steps from the bedroom. She waves them back down, not one to stand on protocol in her own home — and for the first time, that's how she thinks of this place. She gives each as much of a smile as she can muster, then comes around to the couch and gingerly perches on one arm, hoping neither can see the slight wince she gives as she does so.

"So, what do you have for me, Lieutenant?"

Jimenez lifts his briefcase and props it on the table, sliding the latches and exposing the interior. Picking up a small, labeled plastic baggie, he hands it to Kirsten, who swipes her glasses from the end table and slips them on. A pair of tweezers follows, and Kirsten accepts them with a nod and opens the baggie, drawing out a tiny object no bigger than the half moon of a fingernail. She turns the blackened object this way and that, a smile blooming over her features. "Oh, this is good. This is very good."

"Thank you, ma'am," Jimenez says, beaming with pleasure.

"Was this separate from the other pieces or did you extract it?"

He lifts another baggie from the case and hands it to her. "We took it out of this, ma'am."

The metallic square he hands her is half the size of a pack of cigarettes and weighs less than two ounces, by her reckoning. Kirsten feels her heart race at the discovery. Though blackened, melted, and quite damaged, the piece she holds is the nerve center of the android, something no one save Westerhaus and his flunkies has ever seen. "You may just have made the second biggest mistake of your life, Pete," she murmurs, grinning a shark's grin. Then she looks up at Jimenez. "Any other nice surprises for me, Lieutenant?"

"Back at the lab, ma'am," he says, chest so puffed with pride that Kirsten spares a brief second to wonder if he'll burst, leaving Air Force blue bits of himself scattered about the house. She stifles a chuckle in deference to the man's obvious sincerity, though her eyes share a wicked grin with Tacoma, who's successfully hiding his own mirth. "Will you...uh...will you be returning with me, ma'am? To the lab, I mean. Corvallis and I really could use your expertise, ma'am."

"I'd like to, Lieutenant," Kirsten remarks, carefully slipping the square back into the baggie and zipping it closed, "and I will, but right now, I have to..."

"...get yourself to the lab with this young gentleman," Wanblee Wapka states, stepping through the door. Asi, whom he's been trying to entertain, pushes past him and, yodeling with joy at finally seeing his mistress, all but leaps into Kirsten's arms as he covers her face with wet, sloppy dog kisses. "Dakota should be awakening soon. I'll keep an eye on her while you tend to your own needs."

"But—"

"Go. Please. She will be fine, and it will do you good to get out for a while."

Kirsten still looks unconvinced. She believes that Wanblee Wapka speaks the truth; he knows about these things much better than she does, after all. But there is a churning, gnawing feeling inside of her which makes her wonder if, rather than Dakota being okay without her, she will be okay without Dakota.

"Go," Wanblee Wapka repeats, smiling. "You don't have to stay long."

Finally, reluctantly, she nods and, with a final pat to her lovelorn canine, slowly rises and follows the young lieutenant from the house.

When she leaves, Tacoma also rises from his place on the couch. "If it's all right with you, *Até*, I think I'll head back to the power plant. Bernstein and Jove are just about to do the first test with the wind fans we've installed. I'd like to be there if anything goes wrong."

Wanblee Wapka nods.

"She will be all right, right?" Tacoma asks, eyeing his father closely.

"She'll be fine, *chinkshi*. But you know that already. You've always been closer than *cekpapi*."

"I do know," Tacoma admits. "But it's always nice to have it confirmed." He smiles. "Thanks, *Até*. I'll be back soon."

"Be off with you then," he orders, lowering his long frame onto the couch and patting his lap. Asi obligingly puts his head in the indicated spot, and begins to groan as his ears are firmly scratched.

# CHAPTER THIRTY-FOUR

Dakota battles up from the deep levels of her sleep, her body burning, aching, bone deep. She reaches for her partner, only to come up empty-handed. Her eyes flutter open, dark with arousal. "Kirsten? *Canteskuye*?"

Only silence answers her call, and she scrambles up to a sitting position, flinging the heavy covers off her burning flesh, then groans as her head all but explodes from the abrupt change in position. Her hands fly up to cradle her skull. The mother of all headaches seems to have taken up residence in her brain, and she grits her teeth against the urge to cry out in pain. "Gods," she grits out, trapped between the splitting fire in her head and the throbbing need in her body. "What's happening to me?"

Slamming her eyes shut, she takes in several deep, labored, breaths, trying to restore some semblance of control. The deep breathing is a mistake. Kirsten's essence, the commingled essence of their passion, lies heavy in the room, causing her whole body to clench with unsatisfied desire. She bolts to her feet and walks on unsteady legs to the one small window. Throwing it open, she breathes deep of the springtime air. Her headache pounds, sending sharp spikes of pain down her neck, behind her eyes, and even through her teeth. She groans and clamps hard fingers to her skull once again. "*Thunkashila*, help me," she prays, her words slipping into the breeze that cools the sweat on her skin. "Please."

Slowly, gradually, with the speed of forever, a small measure of calm steals over her, allowing her to straighten somewhat, which helps lift the strain from her overstressed muscles and bones. "Thank you," she whispers, taking in a final deep breath before turning away from the window and heading for the small bathroom to take care of other, readily apparent, needs.

The shower beckons, and she turns on the tap and quickly enters. What little calm she's managed to attain is immediately driven from her by the first blast of icy water on her skin. Her headache trebles in strength, driving her to her knees. All of the muscles in her body cramp simultaneously, and an agonized cry blooms from between tightly clenched jaws.

Within seconds, the icy spray ceases its unremitting, torturous dance on her skin, and she finds herself wrapped in the strong arms of someone she knows well. Her father's scent, warm and comforting, fills her senses, allowing her some small measure of peace, though her body is wracked with violent tremors and her head is an agony almost too much to be borne. "*Até*," she moans, feeling much like a frightened child, "what's happening to me?"

"Shhhh," Wanblee Wapka croons in her ear, helping her through the wracking shudders which knot her muscles until they are like rocks beneath his hands. "Shhh, *chunkshi*. I'm here. I'm here. Shhh."

A steaming mug is brought to her lips. "Here. Drink this. It will help."

Inhaling the fragrant steam, she takes a tentative sip, then a larger one as the well remembered and much loved taste of honey soothes her palate and warms her from the inside. Her muscles begin to relax, and she leans gratefully into her father's quiet strength, taking her first painless breath in what seems like hours. "Thank you."

Smiling, he draws the mug away. "If you can hold this for a moment,

I'll get a towel."

Raising shaking hands, she grasps the mug and holds it like a lifeline. Wanblee Wapka gradually releases his grip and, when he is satisfied that she can hold herself up without assistance, grabs a large towel from the bar and returns, wrapping her in it and holding her close. "Better?" he asks, watching her take another, deeper drink from the mug.

"You don't know how much," Dakota replies as her eyelids begin to droop. "What did you..."

"Just something to relax you, *chunkshi*. Is the headache easing?"

"A little, yes."

"Good. Do you think you can stand?"

"With some help, I think. Whatever herbs you used," she yawns hugely, "they're knocking me for a loop." She turns her head and blinks at him. "How did you know?"

"I am your father," he replies simply, giving her all the answer she needs.

With Wanblee Wapka's help, Dakota slowly rises to her feet and allows him to lead her back to the bedroom. As he makes for the bed, Koda shakes her head and stops. "Couch," she says. "Better."

He looks at her for a moment, then nods. "I'll get your robe."

After trading towel for robe, Koda manages to make it to the living room under her own power and, thanking the gods that there is no one but her father to bear witness to her weakness, she collapses onto the couch in a less than dignified sprawl. Her father's herbs have eased the vise in her head and loosened the cramping tension in her muscles, but nothing, it seems, can ease the burning in her blood. This state of hyper-arousal is, in its own way, more painful than the headache at its worst, and she shifts on the couch, eyes darting wildly around, seeking out her lover in the deep shadows of the house.

"She will return to you soon," Wanblee Wapka remarks, entering from the kitchen carrying a bowl of steaming, thickened soup. He hands it to his daughter, returning her glittering stare with one of his own. "Yes, I sent her away for a short time. I knew you were ready to awaken, and I needed time to speak with you." Smiling slightly, he gestures toward the bowl. "Eat. It will help replenish your strength."

"I—"

"Eat."

It is a tone she well remembers, and instinctively heeding it, she begins to do as ordered. After a couple of spoonfuls, however, she pauses, the soup sitting heavy in her belly. "*Até*, I..."

With a small sigh, Wanblee Wapka lowers himself to the chest facing his daughter. He puts a hand on her wrist, squeezing it lightly. "*Chunkshi*, this need that you're feeling...it is a normal thing."

"Normal!?" she blurts out, wide eyed.

"Yes. It is an aftereffect of your spirit walk."

"Never," Koda half-whispers, bringing her free hand to her brow. "Never, not even with Tali."

"Tali was your beloved, but she was not the match to your spirit, Dakota; Kirsten is. She is *mashke naghi*. You feel the bond between you; you know I speak the truth." He smiles a bit to soften his words. "This is something I have experience with, *chunkshi*. After all, why do you think you have so many brothers and sisters?"

Pulling the mug of cooling tea away from her mouth, Koda sputters and chokes and turns tearing eyes to her father. "Too much information, *Até!*" she gasps. "Too much!"

Wanblee Wapka's laugh is deep and melodious as he leans over and gently pats his beloved daughter on the back to ease her choking spell. "Too much, perhaps, but you need to know that I am speaking from experience. You are not alone in these feelings."

The choking spell finally passes, and she leans, gratefully, against her father's hand, her expression somber. "How — how long will this...this ache last, *Até*? I know that I can't live this way, and Kirsten..." Her eyes widen as a new worry takes up residence in her churning mind.

"Be at peace in your heart, *chunkshi*. This need for your *tehila* will never pass, but the strength of it will dim over time."

"How much time?"

"Two or three more days, perhaps. It is different for everyone."

"What about Kirsten?"

"What about her? She is a very strong woman."

Dakota doesn't miss the obvious note of approval in her father's voice, and it warms her somewhat. "Yes, but how will she feel...tied to me in this manner? Mother understands, she is Lakota. But Kirsten..." She shakes her head. "Gods, *Até*! What if she says 'no' and I can't...I can't..."

"She'll never say no."

Head snapping up, Dakota stares wildly into the shadows as the speaker of those words enters slowly, like a shining spirit making its way into the light. Kirsten is glowing, radiant, shining with an inner light that completely captivates her avid watcher. The hunger which has abated somewhat comes back full force, and Dakota feels her entire body pulse with renewed, overwhelming desire. An almost soundless groan breaks from between suddenly parted lips as Wanblee Wapka looks on, smiling to himself.

He silently lifts his body from the chest and summons Asi, who is doing everything short of standing on his head and singing "Yellow Rose of Texas" in order to get his oblivious mistress's attention. With a very human sigh, the jilted dog trots over to Wanblee Wapka and allows himself to be led out into the fresh air.

"Never," Kirsten repeats, voice low and purring, as she continues her slow, deliberate advance. Reaching the arm of the couch, she bends at the waist and covers Dakota's lips in an incendiary kiss that has her lover seeing an entire universe of stars. She finally pulls away, running the tip of her finger over Koda's passion-swollen lips. "Come, my love. Let me ease your ache."

Unable to feel anything beyond the jolts of fire sparking along her nerve endings, Dakota allows herself to be urged up from the couch and led into the bedroom. When the door is closed behind them and Kirsten gathers her into her arms, the inferno roars to blazing life, and she willingly loses herself in the flame.

**Two hours later,** the lovers are lightly dozing, their bodies still pressed together, legs comfortably tangled. Kirsten is partway on top of Dakota, her head tucked into her lover's neck. "Koda?" she murmurs sleepily, lips brushing against sweat-salty skin.

"Mm?"

"I was wondering..."

Koda tips her neck to the side, silently encouraging further exploration. "'Bout what?"

Kirsten gives the skin against her lips a light nip, then pulls away slightly. "Those words you use when we make love..."

"Yes?" Koda purrs, pulling Kirsten even closer as she runs one bare foot along the smooth slope of Kirsten's calf.

"I guess — I mean, I understand them in context, I think..."

"Oh, you do."

"Thanks," she replies, blushing slightly. "But...well...do you think you could teach me what they really mean? I mean, I'd...like to learn."

"Ya would, hmm?"

"Yes. I would."

"All right, then." Moving her legs just slightly, Dakota twists her body, and Kirsten suddenly finds herself flat on her back with six feet of amorous Lakota poised over her, a wicked glint in her eyes. "Consider this your first lesson."

"Now?" Kirsten squeaks.

"No time like the present." Giving Kirsten a quick peck on the lips, Koda settles herself more comfortably, then reaches up and glides a hand through Kirsten's golden hair, watching as the soft, thick mass slips through her fingers like water. "*Pehin.*" She tugs the locks gently to establish her point.

"*Pehin,*" Kirsten repeats dutifully. "Hair."

"Got it in one," Koda replies, leaning down and giving her a deeper, lingering kiss. "You're a good student," she remarks when she comes up for air.

"With incentive like that, how could I be anything else?"

Laughing, Dakota hugs her close and slips a hand into her hair once again, splaying her fingers over the curve of Kirsten's skull. "*Nata.*"

Kirsten's brow wrinkles as her straight, white teeth bite down on her lower lip. "*Nata.* Skull?"

"Close."

She thinks a moment more, though those thoughts are distracted by Koda's short nails lazily scratching beneath the fall of her hair. "Head?" she guesses.

"Perfect." Another kiss is bestowed.

"Oooh, I like this kind of reward," Kirsten chuckles when her lover releases her lips. "Sure beats the gold stars Mrs. Price used to give out in first grade!"

Dakota grins, and draws her hand away. Long fingers gently trail over Kirsten's brow, her cheeks, her chin. "*Ite.*" She repeats the gentle stroking. "*Ite. Ite hopa.*"

"Face," Kirsten finally replies, then blushes. "Beautiful face."

"Very beautiful," Koda murmurs, leaning down for another kiss. Tilting her head slightly, she brushes her lips against Kirsten's nose. "*Pasu.*" Tilting further, she brushes a kiss against the lids of her lover's eyes. "*Ista.*"

"Nose...and eyes," Kirsten hums, squirming a little as her body begins to warm.

"*Nuge*," Koda breathes into the delicate shell of one ear as her tongue teases its flesh, earning her a moan and a shiver from her responsive lover.

"E-ear."

"Mmm."

"Dakota — I — sweet Jesus!" Her ears are extremely sensitive parts of her body, and what Dakota is doing to them is driving her off the deep end in a hurry.

"*Pute*," Koda husks softly, running a thumb tenderly across Kirsten's lips as she continues to work magic on her lover's ear. She groans as those lips part and suck her thumb inside a hot, wet mouth. Kirsten's tongue moves to suckle, and Koda moans out, "*Wichaceji*."

That moan is nearly her undoing. Reaching up, Kirsten pulls Koda's hand from her mouth and boldly slides it down her own body. "Sweetheart, I think this lesson's gonna have to wait."

"Oh yes," Dakota purrs as her fingers are bathed in Kirsten's passion. Suckling her lover's earlobe, she enters Kirsten's heat with one smooth, deep stroke. "I think you're right."

**Night has drawn** its curtain over the sun, leaving a billion billion stars in its wake. Inside the quiet house, Dakota sits on the couch, long legs tucked beneath her and covered with a quilt in deference to her still malfunctioning thermoregulatory system. Her deeply tanned face is gilded gold by the light of the cheerily crackling fire, and in her hands is Spengler, turned to the last few pages.

Kirsten occupies an overstuffed and tattered easy chair positioned at a right angle to the couch. Her laptop is on the chest that serves as a coffee table, and her face is bleached of all its color by the backwash of the brilliant blue-white screen. With her recent bonanza of the android "nerve center," she is running the results against established data, hoping to find a common thread that will allow her to effect a permanent shut-off of all android systems, wherever they might be. After several hours of searching, she hasn't made a hit, but her confidence is up, flowing from her like fresh water welling up into a natural hot spring. Asi lies adoringly at her stockinged feet, his head resting on his stuffed chew-toy, dreaming whatever dogs dream of on soft spring nights like this one.

As if by common, silent consent, dark and fair heads lift and two sets of eyes meet, crinkled at the edges from the loving, almost shy smiles they share. Over the crackle of the cheery fire, the refrigerator hums to life, then cuts off just as quickly with a dying clank and a groan. Koda sighs and rests her head back against the couch. "That's it. The last of our diesel ration for this week."

"Damn. We've still got tons of food in there."

"I know." Tossing the quilt from her lap, Dakota unfolds her legs and makes as if to rise when a strange buzzing noise briefly fills the room, followed by the flickering of the overhead fluorescents in the kitchen and two table lamps in the living room. A loud crackle and hum issue forth from the speakers of the forgotten stereo system.

Kirsten sits back, startled, and almost topples her chair. "What—?"

Asi scrambles to his feet, barking furiously at nothing.

"Looks like Tacoma got those turbines running after all," Koda replies, grinning. The smile slips from her face as the lights brighten for a second, flicker, and wink out, leaving behind the faint scent of ozone. "Or not."

Kirsten barks out a short laugh, drawing a hand over her face in embarrassment. "I can't believe I reacted like that. It was like I'd seen a ghost or something. Damn!"

Koda chuckles. "I'd say that was a pretty natural reaction, considering we haven't full electricity here in what, a month? Two?"

"It feels like forever. But still..." She shakes her head, then looks up at Dakota, her expression somber. "Do you think this is what it'll be like in the future?" she asks, somewhat plaintively. "Do you think we'll go back to believing in magic, to thinking that lightning is the gods' way of showing displeasure? Will technology become something to be feared instead of welcomed and used?" The implication of her questions cause a prickle of unease to dance down her spine, raising the hairs on her arms. "God. How morbid."

"It's not morbid," Koda counters, rising from the couch and coming to Kirsten's side. Sitting on the wide arm of the chair, she reaches out and strokes her lover's hair. "I don't think we'll ever lose technology completely," she muses softly. "As a species, we love our creature comforts too much to give them up that easily. We might not get by on coal and other fossil fuels, but we've got other inexhaustible supplies of energy, like the wind and the sun, and ways to convert them into what we need to keep our houses lit, our food cold, and our water warm."

"Some of us, maybe."

Koda looks sharply at her. "What do you mean?"

"We're setting up a perfect dichotomy," Kirsten starts slowly, gathering her thoughts. "The 'Haves' versus the 'Have-Nots'. Here, on the base, or in a larger city, I can see what you're saying coming to pass. But what about all the people living outside of the cities, outside of the military bases, people who are used to the same creature comforts as the rest of us? Can you imagine Mr. and Mrs. Joe Normal and their 2.3 kids out in the suburbs wrestling a wind fan into place around the ol' homestead? And even if they could, who would teach them how to hook it up so that Martha could use the washer once a week? Who would fix it when it broke? And what would they pay him or her with?"

"Well—"

"For every Tacoma," Kirsten continues, now on a roll, "there are a hundred, maybe a thousand people whose only knowledge of technology is that when they push the button, the dragon comes to life. They don't care how it works, only that it works." She looks up at her lover, eyes bleak. "So what happens when the 'have-nots' gather outside of Grand Rapids in the middle of winter, up to their necks in snow, freezing, covered in furs, and look in on all the folks who are living the life of gods, with central heating and hot water and food that comes with the flick of a switch? How will they feel? What will they resort to, to live that kind of life? Theft? Kidnapping? Murder? Will this new god, Technology, eventually be the name under which all future wars are fought?"

Breaking off, she tilts her head, looking at Dakota who is staring at her with an indecipherable expression on her face. She flushes. "Told you it was morbid."

"Morbid? No. Something we really need to think about? Definitely."

Kirsten sighs. "It's just that..." She shakes her head, then peers pleadingly at her lover. "Dakota, you were born to this land, raised on it. You love it and it loves you. Even a fool like me can see it."

"Kirsten, you're no fool."

"The point is, sweetheart, as much as you might love your creature comforts, you're more equipped to deal with this kind of thing than ninety nine percent of the people out there. People like me, and like Andrews, and even Maggie. When we lost the electricity that first time, it didn't even faze you. No, you just built up a fire, got out the blankets and the oil lanterns from god knows where, and continued as if nothing had happened. While the rest of us..."

"You're adapting."

"Of course I'm adapting, Dakota! I don't have any other choice but to adapt! But Dakota, don't you see? I'm a scientist. More than that, I'm a scientist of technology. This," her arm sweep indicates the computer and myriad of other electronic gadgets that share space on the wide trunk, "these are as much a part of who I am as your animals and your visions and your connection to the land are a part of you. Can I adapt? Anything's possible, I suppose. Do I want to?" She laughs. It's an empty sound. "I...don't know."

"Well then," Dakota finally replies after what seems a lifetime of silence, "we'll just have to make sure that the new world we build contains enough for both of us, won't we?"

This time, Kirsten's laugh is a little more genuine. "You don't ask for much, do you?"

"Me?" Koda quips as she slips from the chair, and bends forward, bringing their lips close. "I ask for everything."

**"So this is** somebody's idea of the presidential limo, is it?"

Maggie's new security arrangements had been waiting for Kirsten when she emerged from the bedroom to take a look at Jimenez's findings. She is not yet sure how she feels about them, even though she knows she would have acknowledged the practical necessity had they been set up for anyone else.

She eyes the APC pulled into the driveway with disfavor. Andrews sits behind the wheel, his red hair blazing even through the thick glass, even under the shadow of his uniform cap. Manny, similarly decked out in his blues, grins and shrugs. "Hey, we tried for a Rolls, but we couldn't find any with armor plating. South Dakota isn't exactly prime mob country, y'know."

"Obviously you just didn't look hard enough." Kirsten keeps her voice flat and stern, her face set in her who-failed-to-clear-the-lab-bench expression. Manny almost buys it; she sees the fleeting alarm cross his face, leaving behind a grin.

"My unworthiness bows before Your Excellency." He opens the passenger door for her, offering a steadying hand as she scrambles unpresidentially into the back seat. It is not just that these vehicles are not built for dignity. A message from Fenton Harcourt, delivered just before the Inipi ceremony and left unopened until Koda was once again safely in the daylight world, informed her that he expected final arguments this morning. Jury deliberations should begin after the noon break. She is, therefore, attending in her official capacity as the person who will sign the death warrants of the condemned if the jury invokes capital punishment. Also therefore, she is wearing the closest thing to a power suit that the base can offer: a pair of blue uniform trousers half an inch too long, and an officer's jacket stripped of its insignia, completed with mid-heel pumps. The last she had accepted only at Koda's urging. Unlike the pants, they are almost her size, and will prevent her tripping on her own cuffs. The rest is bearable, mostly, but the shoes have already begun to pinch.

"I'm going to pass a law against these damned things, I swear I am," she says as she twists around in the confined space and is finally able to sit down.

"What, APCs?" Manny says as he settles into the front passenger seat with an M-16 across his lap.

"Shoes with heels higher than half an inch. Tell me some man didn't invent these things."

In answer, Manny gives a short laugh, then speaks into the wireless microphone clipped to his tie. "Armadillo Two, this is 'Dillo One. We have the supplies, 'Dillo Two. Rendezvous as planned."

"The supplies," Kirsten knows, consist of herself. Armadillo Two is a second APC, waiting now at the gate, that will run escort for her own vehicle. Still, a neat five-shot automatic nestles in its holster at the small of her back. She is too accustomed to relying only on herself to take easily to trusting others, much less depending on them.

She has begun to make exceptions, of course. The memory of the last few days runs sweet in her blood. Kirsten has never given herself over to anyone as she has to Dakota, and that trust extends beyond her lover to Koda's family, who have made a place for her within their bond as confidently as if she had been born to them. It is not just that they honor Dakota's choice, it is as herself that she feels welcome. And that is something entirely new in her experience.

The MP on duty at the gate waves their small convoy out with a salute. The road into town stretches empty for the first two miles, save for a squad of soldiers in an M-60 equipped Stryker whose job it is to keep it that way. Since the near-riot before the gates and the incident of the drunks taking pot shots at the she-wolf, access to the base has been strictly controlled. Closer to town, they pass a wagon loaded with rolls of hay that tower above the driver and his two mules; closer still, a woman on a bicycle pauses at a farm road intersection to check her tires. In her pannier baskets are a dozen small parcels, some in plastic bags, others wrapped in paper. The market square Kirsten has observed the half dozen times she has gone into Rapid City has firmly established itself as a thriving commercial and social institution.

At the courthouse, Manny and Andrews escort Kirsten past a small knot of civilians gathered just inside the doors. A murmuring precedes her and follows her as she passes; several of the onlookers smile or wave. A few scowl, one turning ostentatiously away. Kirsten follows Andrews' gaze as he marks the man, and a shiver runs down her spine. It is not the potential danger that chills her. It is the assumption of danger as the default condition.

Inside, a crowd packs the courtroom from wall to wall. The windows stand open to admit the afternoon breeze, and one or two spectators perch precariously on the narrow sills. Among them are half a dozen women that Kirsten recognizes as prisoners released from the Rapid City Corrections

Corporation of America facility, their faces hard and expectant. In a corner, as far away from the others as she can manage, Millie Buxton stands among an anonymous knot of citizens. Only her colorless skin and the deep blue smudges under her eyes mark her off from the rest. The four accused sit ranged behind the defense table, McCallum, Kazen, and Petrovich hunching forward in conversation with Boudreax. Buxton sits slumped and indifferent, his chair turned so that his back is to the jury box. Boudreaux seems to be breaking off every few sentences to repeat what he is saying to Buxton, who gives no sign of hearing. If he had been thin before, he is gaunt now, cheekbones jutting so sharply from the planes of his face that they seem about to break through his skin. As she moves to the seats reserved for her and her escort, Kirsten catches a glimpse of his eyes. Lightless, sunken, they give no sign of thought behind them, only the stubborn endurance of unbearable pain. For the second time, cold ghosts across Kirsten's skin. *Dead man walking.*

On the other side of the gate, Major Alderson sits quietly, his hands folded on a stack of closely written yellow legal pads. His assistant appears to be checking bookmarks, opening volume after volume of the traditional red and black embossed legal volumes. Some of her activity, Kirsten is almost sure, is stage effect; there is no precedent in case law for the legal conundrum that faces the men and women in this courtroom. If anything, their decision will create the pattern of law to come.

The crowd stirs expectantly as she and her escort take the seats reserved for them, and Harcourt enters and takes the bench. He says, "Are Counsel prepared to make their closing statements this morning?"

"Yes, Your Honor," Alderson answers firmly.

With a quick, doubtful glance at Buxton, Boudreaux responds, "Prepared, sir."

Harcourt leans back in his chair. "Very well. The Prosecution may begin."

Alderson rises from his seat and comes to stand at the rail of the jury box. He says, measuring his words, "Ladies and gentlemen of the jury, the men who stand accused before you today:" he points to each as he names them, "McCallum, Petrovich, Kazen, Buxton, are charged with a crime that has no precedent in the jurisprudence of the United States. Your verdict will set the precedent that will determine how cases like theirs are handled for the foreseeable future. That burden, which you did not ask for, is on your shoulders and on your shoulders alone. It is a task I do not envy you."

Alderson points a second time. "These men, these four men, are charged with assisting the enemy in an uprising that appears to have destroyed as much as two-thirds of the population of the United States. Presumably the peoples of other nations have suffered as severely as we have. Perhaps they have suffered even worse. We are dealing with a holocaust here of a kind that has not been seen since the two World Wars of the last century. It may be that nothing like it has been seen since the Black Death wiped out between a third and a half of the world's population in the thirteen hundreds. These men are accomplices in those deaths."

Alderson pauses for a long moment. The strain is plain on his face; the honest disgust; the lack of comprehension that niggles at them all when they have tried to explain the uprising. "Ladies and gentlemen, you have heard the testimony of the women who were the victims of these men.

They committed forcible rape upon those women, and they did it willingly. They did it knowingly, and they did it repeatedly and routinely." Alderson's fist comes down on the rail of the jury box with each word "They enjoyed it. Not once did any of them attempt to spare his victim out of common humanity. Not once. Not. Even. Once.

"They say they acted under coercion. But they did have a choice, ladies and gentlemen of the jury. Some crimes are so horrible that common decency demands that a man lay down his life before he will allow himself to be entangled in them. These men had the choice to die where they stood rather than aid the enemy. They had the choice to die rather than violate those women in the most brutal fashion imaginable.

"Ladies and gentlemen, those four men did not make the honorable choice. When you retire to deliberate, I ask that you consider the evidence that has been presented to you, and that you find them guilty of the crimes with which they are charged. And when you have done that, I ask that you make the choice they refused, and assess against them the penalty of death. Thank you."

"Damn straight," someone behind Kirsten mutters, and another, "Preach it, brother." She cannot see their faces without twisting about conspicuously in her seat, but those she can see mirror their grim satisfaction with the Prosecution's summation. From behind her glasses, she sees the same hard determination in the narrowing of Manny's eyes, the dangerous tightening of Andrews' mouth in something that is not quite a smile.

Boudreaux stands as Alderson returns to his own seat. Compared to the major's, his stance seems less confident, his shoulders rounded in a scholar's slouch rather than the precise right angles of his opponent's. His hands clasped behind his back, he seems to almost wander into the center of the open space bounded by the judge's bench and the tables, finding himself half-surprised to be facing the jury. He pauses for a moment, looking down at the floor, or his shoes. Then he says, almost softly, "You know, I was very impressed by Major Alderson's summation just now. He makes a persuasive case for finding the four defendants guilty. Putting them to death, even. A sound case."

McCallum lets out a yell and comes halfway to his feet before the bailiff stationed behind him shoves him back down into his chair. Harcourt says quellingly, "Mr. McCallum, you will sit down and be silent, or I will have you removed from this courtroom. I will have order, sir!"

When silence falls again, Boudreaux smiles faintly. "Even Mr. McCallum makes a good argument against himself." He pauses again, gazing over the heads of the jury, then lowering his eyes to meet theirs. "But we can say so, ladies and gentlemen, because none of us is in his position. Please God, none of us ever will be.

"But it gets worse even than that for one of the men who stand accused before you. For Harald Buxton, the question was not what he would do to save his own life. The question was what he could do to save his wife and his daughter from rape and possible death. And the answer to that question, tragically, was to harm others."

A small stir erupts in a back corner of the courtroom, and Kirsten turns to see Millie Buxton making her way toward the doors, her face white and frozen with grief. Her husband's eyes follow her for perhaps half a second, then drop blankly to his hands. A murmur ripples through the room, instantly squelched by the rap of Harcourt's gavel.

"This is a public proceeding, ladies and gentlemen, but it is not an occasion for public comment. Do not oblige me to clear the court."

Silence falls, and Boudreaux resumes. "What would you do, to protect your spouse? What would you do, to protect your only child from horror? Faced with a choice between harming someone you loved and harming someone you did not know at all, which of them would you mark out for suffering? When you consider the fate of Harald Buxton, ladies and gentlemen, ask yourselves these questions, and let your answers temper your verdict.

"In all four cases, ask yourselves whether we have not had enough of dying. Thank you."

Only the rustle of papers breaks the silence as Boudreaux makes his way back to his seat. At the bench, Harcourt sifts through half a dozen sheets of printout and a pair of legal volumes marked with so many small post-its in so many colors that it looks like the business end of an old-fashioned feather duster. When he has found the passages he wants, he lays the books open before him. "Does the Prosecution wish to offer rebuttal, Major Alderson?"

Alderson half rises in his chair. "No, Your Honor."

"Very well. I will now charge the jury." Harcourt pushes his glasses up onto the high bridge of his nose and begins to read from one of the heavy embossed volumes.

As he details the legal definition of rape, assault, battery, and the other lesser included charges, Kirsten allows her attention to wander. She has hated the ceremonial and bureaucratic aspects of her position as a Cabinet officer: the endless meetings, the wrangling, the trading off, the paper pushing. Her role here is largely ceremonial, too, and she would by far rather be at home working on the android code. Or, better yet, sitting with Dakota before the fire, Asi sprawled at their feet.

But the atmosphere in this courtroom is free of both the cynicism and the zealotry to be found in government. The people who fill the spectators' seats — the women brutalized by the four defendants; surviving residents of Rapid City, most of them women, too; the ranchers with faces and hands burned raw by the wind rolling unimpeded over the plains off the Arctic ice cap — sit in quiet solemnity, patient with the workings of justice. This community is beginning to feel its way toward a framework of order. Perhaps other remnants, elsewhere, are even now faced with finding solutions to the same problem these face; perhaps their solutions are completely different. How would the Shiloh community handle a trial on a capital charge? And how, if she is successful in shutting down the droids, will she manage to draw together a collection of far-flung and disparate townships, villages, communes, no two with the same experiences since the world has changed?

She has never put it to herself in quite those terms before, has never dared. A lump of ice forms in her chest, its cold running down her veins, sheeting along her skin. *How will I manage? Gods!*

With an almost palpable wrench, she forces her attention back to Harcourt's charge to the jury. He has finished with the legal definitions and has gone on to outline the panel's options.

"...is perhaps the heaviest part of the burden your fellow citizens have asked you to bear. If you find the defendants guilty, and I cannot impress upon you too clearly that you must make four separate decisions, then you must turn your attention to setting the punishment. And here we encounter a difficulty.

"Before the uprising, your choices would have been to sentence a guilty party to death or to a substantial term in prison. The option of prison is no longer available, as neither the Ellsworth brig nor the Rapid City jail is sufficiently staffed to handle long-term inmates.

"It is at this point, ladies and gentlemen, that you must, in essence, make the law rather than follow it. We are in the Fifth Circuit of South Dakota, but we are also in the lands traditionally inhabited by the Lakota, the Cheyenne, and other indigenous Nations. Under their traditional law, a violent offender is exiled rather than executed so that undesirable, indeed potentially tragic, consequences do not perpetuate themselves. We are in uncharted territory here, and I urge you to proceed with caution. The precedents we set may well become the foundations of future law. Let us take up our responsibilities as the ancient Book of Common Prayer admonishes those about to enter into matrimony: soberly, advisedly, and in the fear of God. The jury will now retire. Court is in recess until a verdict is reached."

Kirsten rises to her feet, stretching, bracketed by Manny and Andrews. *Wonderful. Siamese triplets.* On their way out, she is not surprised to see Blind Harry, his guitar slung over his back, making his way toward the door, his white cane tapping out a path in front of him. She is pleased to see that his cotton shirt still has the creases from its package; he has made himself a comfortable place within the new economy as tale-teller and news-bearer. Whatever happens in the next few hours, he will have a song from it, and an audience.

Andrews says, "We've got some sandwiches in the truck. Anybody want to try to find a lemonade stand?"

**Two hours and** a tour of the market later, the sun casts long shadows along the open space in front of the Judicial Building. The shade under the trees where Kirsten and her escort have taken possession of a bench begins to grow chill, and only a few stragglers remain on the streets. Of all the strange things she has encountered since setting out on her journey across the continent, this is among the strangest, that the night is no longer human territory. A small crowd, though, still lingers on the courthouse steps, waiting patiently, stubbornly, for the jury's decision.

"Are they going to sequester them for the night?" Manny asks, glancing at his watch. "It's past five, and we need to be starting back."

Andrews shrugs. "Want me to ask?"

As he starts to make his way across the flagstones, the knot of people around the doors stirs, and one of the bailiffs appears. Kirsten gets to her feet, followed by Manny. The bailiff, spotting them, stops halfway down the stairs and beckons. "They're in!"

Filing back into the courtroom, Kirsten feels the silence like a pressure on her skin. The audience has thinned, the seats now less than half filled, the murmur and shuffle now muted as the judge enters and takes the bench. Kirsten's eyes, like those of the others, track the twelve men and women as they file into the jury box. Their faces, set and still, give nothing away, not to the spectators, not to the defendants. Kazen stares at his hands, clasped on the legal pad before him. Petrovich and McCallum seem distracted, eyes flickering down the row of jurors, back again. Only Buxton seems entirely unaffected, lost somewhere in his own mind, indifferent to this moment as he has been to the trial from the beginning.

"Ladies and gentlemen of the jury," Harcourt asks, "have you reached a verdict?"

The foreman, a tall Cheyenne with grey braids, answers, "We have Your Honor."

"If you will hand it to the bailiff, please, sir."

The bailiff receives the folded papers from him and carries them to the judge. Harcourt unfolds and reads them in unbroken silence. Finally he says, "The defendants will rise."

When they have done so, he says, reading from the documents in front of him, "Eric McCallum, on the first charge, of forcible rape, as defined by and pursuant to the criminal code of the state of South Dakota, the jury has determined the following verdict: guilty. On the second charge, of conspiracy, the jury has determined the following verdict: guilty. On the third charge, of murder as defined by the law of parties, the jury has determined the following verdict: guilty. In consideration of the gravity of your crimes, the jury has assessed against you the penalty of death."

For Petrovich and Kazen, the findings are identical. As the verdicts are read, an MP moves to stand behind each man, handcuffs ready.

The judge continues. "Harald Buxton, on the first charge, of forcible rape, as defined by and pursuant to the criminal code of the state of South Dakota, the jury has determined the following verdict: guilty. On the second charge, of conspiracy, and on the third, of murder as per the law of parties, the jury has determined the following verdict: innocent. In consideration of the gravity of your offense, but in consideration also of the threats to your family employed to procure your co-operation, the jury has assessed against you the penalty of exile."

Harcourt turns to the jury box again. "So say you one, so say you all?"

The foreman answers, "We do, Your Honor."

Harcourt nods, turning back to the defendants. "Ordinarily," he says, "your sentences would automatically be appealed. Unfortunately, there is no longer a superior court to hear your case. Also unfortunately, neither the civil nor the military authority has the means of maintaining you for an extended period. It is therefore the order of this Court that, at an hour and place to be determined, the sentences against you shall be carried out within two calendar days from the instant. May God have mercy on your souls."

Kirsten, sitting almost directly behind him, sees the shudder that passes through Buxton's gaunt body. With speed that seems impossible for a man honed down to bone, he pivots toward the military policeman behind him, feinting with his right hand toward the man's face. In the fraction of a second it takes the officer to react, Buxton snatches the pistol from the holster at his right side. "No!" she cries, pushing up against the arms of her chair. And then she is sprawled face-down on the carpet, staring at the scuffed boots of the person in the seat behind her, while Manny's bulk pins her to the floor and shields her from the shot that goes wild, shattering the glass shade of one of the ceiling lights. She hears a second shot, muffled, and a woman's anguished scream.

"Hal, no! Oh, God, no!"

Something wooden, perhaps a chair, strikes the railing that divides the well of the court from the audience; something else, not hard, strikes the floor. There is the sound of a brief, violent, struggle, grunts, blows struck. Turning her head to the other side, Kirsten can see only Andrews' brightly polished black dress shoes, the line of his trouser leg, the muzzle of his M-16 as he stands between her and whatever is happening at the defendants' table. "Manny," she gasps, "let me up!"

"Not yet," he answers. "Not until things are back under control."

"The MP, Buxton—"

"MP's fine," Andrews says from above them. "Buxton's dead."

Above the rest of the noise, Harcourt's voice booms out. "Remove the prisoners! Bailiff, clear the court!"

More feet, more rustling of clothes, then finally the weight above her eases and Kirsten pushes herself up to her knees, then takes Manny's proffered hand to rise to her feet. Except for Harcourt, themselves and one bailiff, the courtroom is deserted. Only a spreading crimson stain on the floor marks the spot of Buxton's death.

Harcourt says, "I apologize, Madam President. I should have realized something like this might happen."

Kirsten shakes her head. "He wanted to be found guilty and executed with the others; we all assumed he would be."

"There are papers to be signed. I can bring them to you later if you'd rather."

"No. Better face it and be done with it."

Something that might almost be an approving smile touches Harcourt's lips. "Come back to my chambers, then. The clerk will have them ready very shortly."

Quietly, still bracketed by her two guards, Kirsten follows him across the well of the court and through the door to the comfortable room beyond. The door closes behind her, Andrews standing sentry.

**The moon rides** high in the west as the small convoy speeds back toward Ellsworth through the dark. Kirsten, leaning against the back of her passenger seat, has forced her mind to blankness. Shutting out the plain printout sheets that had been set in front of her, shutting out the scratch of her pen where she had scrawled her signature to the right of the judge's.

Half turning, Manny says softly, "You okay back there?"

"Getting there."

"We're almost home. Hang in there."

It is a long almost. But when she walks through the front door, into Asi's exuberant greeting and Dakota's arms, she is as well as she has ever been in her life.

# CHAPTER THIRTY-FIVE

"Coming!" Kirsten responds to a knock on the door, bumping her busily scrubbing partner with her hip and flinging the dishtowel over one shoulder as she slips from the kitchen.

A grinning Maggie stands at the threshold, a suspiciously shaped bag in her hand. As she takes in Kirsten's strange look, the smile slips from her lips. "What?"

Kirsten sighs. "I know we've been over this already, but it still makes me uncomfortable that you think you have to knock on the door to your own home."

Rolling her eyes, Maggie pushes Kirsten back gently and slips into the house. "Darlin'," she drawls, "I used to knock before going into the house I grew up in. My mama would have whupped me purple if I didn't show respect, family or no, so just stop worrying about it, okay?"

Kirsten frowns, unconvinced, and Maggie takes hold of her elbow. "Listen to me, my friend, and listen closely, because this is the last time we're going to have this conversation, you and I. You did not chase me from my home. It's mine. I choose what to do with it, and I chose to let you guys have it. No pain, no strain, and all's cool, capiche?"

"I suppose," Kirsten replies grudgingly.

"Good." Maggie holds up the package. "And to seal the deal, a gift!"

Slipping the bottle from the bag, Kirsten squints at the lettering on the label. "Southern Comfort? Wow, I haven't had this since college!"

"Madame President!" Maggie huffs, feigning shock. "You actually admit to the consumption of spirits? Whatever will your constituents think?"

"My constituents can kiss my ass," she retorts, breaking the seal with a quick twist of her wrist. "Where'd you get this anyway? I thought the base was dry?"

"I have my sources," comes the smug rejoinder as Maggie moves off to the kitchen. "Now, where did I put those shot glasses?" She stops short so as to avoid running into Dakota, who smirks down at her, three shot glasses in her hand. "Well, look who's back from the dead! And looking damn good to boot!"

Koda lifts a brow. "Looks like someone's started the party a little early."

"Hardly. Can't I be in a halfway decent mood once in a while? Besides," she adds, pitching her voice low, forgetting about Kirsten's enhanced hearing, "I think someone could use a little cheering up, don't you?"

"I heard that," Kirsten remarks, making her way to the kitchen. "And I'm fine. Really."

"Mm." Maggie looks at her with a critical eye. "Well, I suppose we can pass that unnatural pallor off to too little sleep then, hmm?" A saucy wink accompanies the statement, making Kirsten's face heat. "C'mon. Let's have a toast before the rest of our guests arrive, okay?"

The trio moves into the living room. As Maggie pours the liquor, Koda sits on the floor, her back against the couch. Kirsten settles behind her, stroking the black hair fanning over the tattered fabric of the cushions. Maggie hands over the glasses, then holds up her own, her expression serious. "To lessons learned, hurdles overcome, dangers to come, and love and family, which make it all worthwhile."

Three glasses clink together, three arms lift, and three heads tip back, taking in the sweet, fiery liquid in one smooth gulp.

"Ahh," Kirsten exhales, slamming her glass down onto the chest that doubles as a table. "That definitely hit the spot." The liquor spreads warm fire through her belly and limbs, taking with it the sharpest edge of grief and second thoughts she's been dealing with since signing the execution orders. "Thanks, Maggie. I owe you."

"What are friends for? Another?"

Kirsten holds up a hand. "Better not. I'd like to appear at least somewhat coherent while we hash things out this evening. Maybe later, though."

"Suits me," Maggie replies, capping the bottle and stowing it away just as a knock sounds at the door. "I'll get it. Be right back."

Koda and Kirsten share a quiet look as Maggie leaves, then returns with the rest of the group in tow. Tacoma, Manny, and Andrews look sharp in their crisply pressed uniforms. Harcourt follows, impeccably dressed, as always, in a somber black suit and regimental tie. Wanblee Wapka rounds out the party, looking comfortable in his jeans and work shirt.

"Where's Hart?" Kirsten asks.

"The general is, unfortunately, indisposed at the moment," Harcourt replies, settling himself into the overstuffed armchair. "Quite likely for the rest of what remains of his life, if the quantity of beer cans outside of his residence is any indication."

"Great. Just what we need."

"I think this clandestine little meeting of the minds is better had without him in any event," Harcourt remarks, a slight smile breaking the stony planes of his face as he looks at Dakota. "It's good to see you up and around, so to speak, Ms. Rivers. I understand you have an interesting tale to share?"

"In a moment," Maggie interjects. "Let's get the rest of our business out of the way first, if we could." She turns to Tacoma, who is crowded into one of the small kitchen chairs he's dragged over. "Nice light show last night, Major."

Tacoma nods in acknowledgement, and Maggie continues, "Kirsten mentioned you've been pushing for a Town Hall, and you're right, it's something we desperately need right now. Communication with the civilians on this base is sorely lacking, and it's only going to lead to more problems in the long run. So...we'll need to set up a communications committee. Say ten in all, split evenly between base personnel and civilians. They can meet once a week to start, hash out any issues they have and pass along whatever needs passing. Kirsten, I know you've got an overly full plate right now, but I think you'll probably need to chair the first meeting, just to keep everything kosher." She smiles. "You should be able to pass on that honor to some other deserving soul once everything's underway, though."

"Being the top dog really sucks sometimes," Kirsten grumps, but nods her acceptance of yet another duty.

"Yeah, yeah. Tell it to the press."

The group laughs, then quiets as all eyes turn to Dakota. Maggie raises an eyebrow in silent invitation.

Nodding, Koda straightens and pulls up her legs, crossing her arms over them and looking at the group evenly. "I'll spare everyone the background details, since I'm sure you probably know pretty much all of them anyway." Receiving nods, she closes her eyes and calls up the images from her vision. They come to her easily, though thankfully she feels a sense of detachment from the emotional backlash they convey. She senses that that detachment is helped along by the feel of Kirsten's warm hand on her shoulder, and she smiles her thanks. Her father's smooth, kind voice filters into her consciousness.

"Dakota? Where are you?"

She is standing in the middle of a killing field. Red is all around her; sunk deep into the earth, running in rivers across her bare feet. Even the air is red, as if she is viewing the world through crimson silk, and the stench of burning and death is overpowering. Overhead, carrion birds circle endlessly, waiting for the chance to feed.

"Just outside the base," she replies, voice deep, words slow and carefully measured. "To the south, fifty yards beyond the gate."

"When?"

A listless breeze flutters the leaves on the trees. A blood drenched flag flaps wetly, sullenly, like mud covered sheets hanging from a clothesline.

"Mid spring, early summer. It is difficult to tell."

"Are you seeing the past?"

The whole room holds its breath.

"No."

Kirsten's hand tightens involuntarily on Dakota's shoulder, but the distraction is minimal. The group exchanges grave looks, and Tacoma turns away, fists clenched, jaw set, as if he's ready to take on the entire droid army by himself.

Maggie shoots a silent question to Wanblee Wapka, who nods. "Dakota?" she asks.

"I am here."

"What do you see?"

There is a brief pause, then she says, "Death."

The room is filled with hissed breaths.

"Death." In her vision, she lifts hands dripping with gore. "All around me."

"Are there androids?"

"Yes. Many hundreds." Her vision body turns in a complete circle, red gaze lancing out over the carnage. "More than I've ever seen before. They come from the south, and from the west, in tanks—"

"Tanks?" Maggie asks, startled.

"Yes. Many tanks. Many bombs. And death. So...so much death. All around. All around."

Kirsten looks over at Wanblee Wapka, in her eyes an anguished plea. His face set and grave, he holds up a hand.

Maggie interjects softly, "Kirsten, we must know."

"At what expense?" Kirsten demands, voice shrill. "You're hurting her!"

"Kirsten—"

"*Canteskuye*, please, let me tell it all. I must speak this. Please."

Reluctantly abandoning her objections, Kirsten draws an arm along

Dakota's and squeezes, pressing a kiss to the crown of black hair beneath her chin. Koda grasps her hand and holds it lightly between her own. Wanblee Wapka nods at Maggie to continue.

"Dakota, the androids...are there humans with them?"

"Yes. Many men. Strangers all. Wearing red. Red death."

Running a hand through her close-cropped hair, Maggie sighs, then puts forth the one question she doesn't want to ask. "And the base?"

Another pause, longer this time. "Gone."

As one, the group stiffens, none having expected such a final answer.

"Gone?" Maggie asks finally, when she's recovered her voice. "Can you explain?"

"Gone," Koda repeats. "All gone. No buildings. No life. Only death. Death, all around. The Earth weeps for her children."

"All right," Kirsten says, her tone brooking no argument. "That's enough. You've got what you came here for, now end it! Now!"

Wanblee Wapka nods and shifts forward, but Dakota breaks herself from her trance unaided and gathers Kirsten in her arms as her lover scrambles from the couch and to her side. "It's okay, my love, it's okay," she whispers into fragrant hair. "I'm all right. It's okay."

The rest of the group members exchange grim looks. After a long moment, Koda lifts her head and eyes those around the table. "This was a warning. The androids are coming. I can feel them closing in. But how the battle ends will be up to us, in part, to decide. Ina Maka has seen fit to help us, to warn us of what is to come. The rest is up to us."

Gripping the arms of her chair, Maggie lets go a long breath, and nods. "Tomorrow, then. In my office. All of us." The smile she gives Dakota is grim, but a smile nonetheless. "Thank you, my friend. Your gift has given us a fighting chance."

"Thank the Mother," Koda returns.

"I will." Standing, Maggie gathers the others with a look. They rise as well, and with soft murmurs of "thanks" and "good night", they file from the house, leaving the lovers alone.

**Maggie raises a** hand to shield her eyes against the late afternoon sunlight that pours through the blinds of her office, casting strips of glare on the large map of South Dakota and surrounding states spread out on her desk. Its brilliance strikes blue sheen like a raven's wing off Koda's hair where she leans on her elbows, tracing the thin black lines of state roads feeding into Rapid City and from there onto Highway 90. "Here," she says. "For the ones moving in from the west, their best bet is to come up 85 to the Interstate, then make the loop back east to Ellsworth. Troops moving up from Offut could use 183 or 87, then march west on 90."

"If they've got heavy armor," Tacoma adds, "they'll want to get onto the Interstate as quickly as they can."

"Isn't there still a lot of wreckage on the highway?" Kirsten asks. "Is it enough to slow them down?"

"Minimally. Things like mobile howitzers can just push other stuff out of the way. It won't take but one advance party to clear the way for them."

"We need aerial recon. Rivers." Maggie addresses Dakota's cousin where he leans over Kirsten's shoulder. "Put a couple birds up and have them scout the roads. I want reports by evening. And no," she adds quellingly, noting the gleam that comes into his dark eyes, "not you, and not Andrews. You have your assignment."

"Yes, ma'am," he says, turning on his heel in the cramped space between Koda and the door. Dakota jerks her foot out of his path, almost kicking Kirsten's ankle where she sits to her left. "Sorry, cuz," he murmurs, then adds, "We gotta move these meetings into a conference room or something."

"Scoot," says Maggie, and he does. The half-dozen bodies surrounding the desk shift, taking advantage of the increased space.

"He's right," says Kirsten, flexing shoulders that are no longer jammed against her neighbors'. "Why don't we use one of the big meeting rooms?"

"Hart," says Maggie succinctly. "Territory."

"He doesn't seem...well," Wanblee Wapka offers from his place beside Tacoma.

Maggie gives a small, exasperated snort. "Make this man an ambassador when we're out of this mess," she says to Kirsten. "General Hart hasn't been 'well' since the uprising. According to his secretary, he comes in to his office every day, drinks his coffee, and looks at reports in triplicate. Then he goes back to quarters and waits to do it all again the next day." Her voice softens. "He's a manager, not a field commander. Losing his family has been hard on him."

"What about that aide of his, what's his name — Toller, Toleman?"

"All he does is carry the reports back and forth and tell Kimberly who to open the door to. Another MBA. Pigs'll fly stealth bombers before he questions an order."

"Okay," says Tacoma, bringing the conversation back to the map and the advancing enemy. "Manny's going to take care of air recon. We need some boots on the ground, too."

Maggie nods approvingly. "Make the assignments when the birds get back." She turns her attention to Wanblee Wapka. "What are your defense caps?"

His eyes, as startlingly blue as his daughter's, meet hers. "Sixty able bodied adults with small arms and the skill to use them. Another twenty or thirty for support. If this force gets past you, though, our only real defense is our feet."

Maggie taps the end of her marker against the map. *Multi-task, Allen. Contingency plans.* "All right," she says. "When the time comes, I'll have two Tomcats fueled up and ready to go. One to cover Rapid City, one to cover you guys if the bastards flank us and turn north. We'll have them for our ace in the hole here if the droids keep their forces all together. With distances that short, we won't need guidance systems for the 'Cats, and most of our ordnance has been reconfigured to laser.

"Meanwhile, we need an accounting of assets. Tacoma — get me an inventory of all armor, artillery, small arms, and foot soldiers and your assessment of the best use we can make of all of the above. I already know what we can put in the air and who can fly it. When we know more about what we're facing, we can talk deployment."

"Meet them on the road if we can," says Dakota. "Block them off before they can reach the base or the city."

"Exactly. And we need to keep our options open to do that." Maggie folds up the map and hands it to Dakota. "You and Tacoma know the ground better than anyone else here. Choose at least three provisional points where we can cut them off. Kirsten, any luck with that droid fragment Jimenez brought you?"

"Not yet." Kirsten's head turns abruptly toward the window, where a shadow crosses the blinds, accompanied by the rich, sweet scent of pipe tobacco. Tacoma reaches a long arm behind her and opens the door to admit Fenton Harcourt, a briar between his teeth and a sheaf of papers under his arm.

"Well," says the judge, "how unassuming. Foxes have lairs and birds have their nests, but the Wing Commander operates out of a middling small closet, and the President of what's left of these United States has no office at all."

Maggie eyes the folders warily. "What can we do for you, Judge?"

"Nothing you'll enjoy," he answers, sifting three of the thin portfolios from the stack. "After a lengthy wait, General Hart agreed to see me this afternoon, then told me to take the matter to you."

"And the matter is?"

"McCallum...Petrovich...Kazen." Harcourt punctuates the names with the slap of each file as it hits the desk. "They are presently back in the guardhouse, since there are no facilities for holding them in Rapid City. Neither are there any facilities for carrying out their sentences. You do not," he adds, "seem pleased."

"I am," she says precisely, meeting Harcourt's gaze, "just as pleased as I would be if Ms. President's dog had made me a present. Asimov would, however, be too polite to dump it on my desk."

Unexpectedly, Harcourt's face splits in a grin, pipe still tight between his teeth. "Colonel," he says, "I am sorry I underestimated you. Unfortunately, there is no one else with either the authority or the means to handle this problem. Civil institutions remain in suspension."

"Unfortunately," she says, "you're right. Tacoma."

"Ma'am?"

"When you get me the list of troops, pick out twenty-five by lot. We'll cut them down to fifteen in a second round. Tell Major Grueneman to see that the indoor firing range in the gym is set up, and make sure we've got lighting there. Better get started now."

"Ma'am." Tacoma salutes and squeezes his large frame around Kirsten and the judge, making for the door. Kirsten moves over by one seat, offering her chair to Harcourt.

"I take it there's something else I can do for you, Judge?"

"Not you, Colonel; Rivers." He turns to Wanblee Wapka and takes a long draw on his pipe; smoke streams out his nostrils. "Can your settlement accommodate a new widow and her orphan daughter?"

Wanblee Wapka contemplates Harcourt's face for a long moment, his eyes blankly amiable. Then the laugh lines around them fold into wrinkles, and he says, "Fenton, you do know how to ask a leading question, don't you? 'Poor little match girl out in the snow.' You're referring to Mrs. Buxton, I take it?"

Another puff and river of smoke. "I am."

"Have you consulted the lady about these arrangements?"

"I will inform her of the possibility when I have your answer."

"You have it, then. Tell her to be ready."

"Mrs. Rivers?"

"Themunga wouldn't turn away W. T. Sherman himself if he showed up on her doorstep hurt or hungry."

"No," Dakota says wryly. "She'd nurse him back to health, then take his hair."

Maggie catches a small, alarmed glance as Kirsten's eyes shift from Koda to her father and back, and she allows herself to wonder how the Rivers matriarch will take to a white daughter-in-law. Not easily, by all indications. But she says only, "Any other business?"

There is none, and as the rest file out her door, Maggie grimly sets about making arrangements for a triple execution. Not for the first time today, she wishes for a good stiff drink.

*Damn Hart.*

*Damn Harcourt.*

*Damn the three bastards who made it all necessary.*

*Most of all, damn Peter Westerhaus and his droids.*

**The wolf cub** wriggles in her hands as Dakota gently lifts him away from his mother and places him at the back of the crate that will carry them to their new home. Kirsten kneels alongside, holding his attention with a finger drawn along the wire mesh, so that all his small body wags and he stands on his hind legs, nipping at the elusive prey and yapping sharply. The sound brings his mother out of her run, straight into the carrier with him. Kirsten withdraws her finger abruptly.

Dakota lifts the small hatch on top of the carrier and bends to scratch the pup under his chin one last time, and smooth the fur on the mother's head. "Go safely," she murmurs. "Live well."

"They'll be all right, won't they?" Kirsten asks.

Koda slides the hatch closed and reaches across the top of the crate to take Kirsten's hand. "The place where *Até* will release them has a stone outcropping for shelter and a spring for water. With only one cub, the mother will have no trouble feeding him until he can join her on the hunt."

"He's going to release them on your ranch?"

"*Han*," Koda says, squeezing her lover's hand. "I wish we could go with him now. I wish you could see it."

"When this is over, we'll go. I still need to meet your mother."

Koda says nothing, only tightens her fingers around Kirsten's. Wanblee Wapka's easy acceptance will make the meeting easier, when it comes. It occurs to Dakota that she probably should have written a letter for her father to carry home to Themunga, but there is no time now. *Coward,* she berates herself. *You can run across a ruined bridge straight into an army like a freaking idiot, but you can't manage to face your own mother.* Aloud she says, "I think I hear the truck."

The sound of an approaching engine grows louder, and Koda goes to unlock the back gate that leads to the runs. Beams from a pair of headlights sweep across the small parking lot, and Wanblee Wapka's big pickup makes a three-point turn, then backs slowly, coming to a stop between the two rows of kennels. Overhead, stars still spangle the western sky, swinging low over the Paha Sapa. The hills bulk huge and dark below them, distinguished from the arching darkness above only by the wash of moonlight along their flanks. A white shape passes overhead, almost too swift for sight, and Koda shivers in the dawn breeze. Owl.

Owls are messengers from the spirit world. But she needs no additional omen to know that death is near them — herself, Kirsten, her father, Tacoma, all of them. Her vision has told her that, and the preliminary reports from the scouts have confirmed the forces now converging on Ellsworth in numbers far greater than any they have encountered so far.

The driver's door opens, engine still running, and Wanblee Wapka steps behind the truck to open the tailgate. "Let me give you a hand with that, *chunkshi*."

Together, with Kirsten assisting, they lift the mother wolf and her cub up into the bed of the truck. Wanblee Wapka slides the carrier back toward the cab and ties it down in place, giving the knots an extra pull to secure them. To Koda, he says, "Don't worry. I'll have them in their new home before the sun is over the trees. I'll see that there's food available for the first few days, just until *Ina* here gets the lay of the land."

For answer, Koda walks into his arms and hugs him fiercely. "I wish that I could come with you, *Até*. That we could."

"I know," he says. "But you're needed here, both of you."

"Mother—"

"Hey, I'm a diplomat, remember?" Laughter runs through her father's voice. "I'll have the peace treaty ready to be signed by the time you come home."

"Oh, yeah," she says wryly. "The droids'll just be the warm up."

His arms tighten around her. "*Wakan Tanka nici un, chunkshi. Toksha ake wachingyankin kte.*" Great Mystery go with you. Until I see you again. He releases her then, turning to Kirsten. "*Chunkshi,*" he says, pulling her into a hug. "Take care of each other."

The fleeting startlement in Kirsten's face gives way to a blush, and she shyly returns the embrace. "We will. Thank you, *Até.*" Her brow creases briefly. "*Até* — is that right?"

"It's exactly right," he answers.

Almost too low for Koda to hear, she says, "Dakota and I — can you see...?" She drops her eyes, leaving the question in the air.

"I see that you are meant to be together, Kirsten. It is something you have chosen, time and again. But no, I do not see what is on the other side of this battle. There is a cloud over it, and what is beyond I do not know." With a last squeeze of her arm, a hand on Koda's shoulder, he is gone, the red points of the truck's taillights vanishing as he turns onto the road that will take him out the main gate.

Koda takes Kirsten's hand, feeling the chill of her skin. In the east, a faint haze of rose and gold washes the hills. "You're cold," she says. "Let's go inside."

# CHAPTER THIRTY-SIX

What a man will do for love.

Manny stands just inside the shadow of the hangar, his harness strapped and buckled, his helmet in the crook of his elbow. By sheer force of will he banishes what he knows is a sappy, lovestruck grin from his face. At least, he banishes it for a moment. His watch shows his copilot/navigator due in less than three minutes, and it takes an effort to refrain from tapping the toe of his boot against the runway apron. It will not do to show eagerness. He has flown a couple of times with Ellen Massaccio, an experienced and careful pilot; he has no reason to believe she will not be prompt today. That gives him a few more moments to contemplate the object of his affection as she sits on the tarmac, her silver skin gleaming in the spring sun, her slender form made all the more enticing by months of abstinence and flying helicopters.

For Manny, his Tomcat is not a male of any species. She is a she, a lady sleek and sure and deadly, a lioness stalking the high cloud savannah, her fur silvered by moonlight. She is, as she was originally, the brainchild of Admiral Tom Connolly; Tom's Cat is the last and most perfect in a series of his brainchildren. After forty years of refinement and the shift from purely naval deployment to air defense, the craft is still the fastest, meanest fighter in the world. And Manny is as enamored as he was the first time he set eyes on her, as desperate in his forced estrangement as any deserted lover. Their reunion will be sweet.

*At least I didn't out and out grovel to get to fly this mission. Not quite.*

He had almost groveled. He had been prepared to and would have, if Kirsten had not shown immediate understanding when he had asked for the assignment. Instead, she had merely agreed that his request to go was reasonable and pointed out that for a single day on base, at least, she was unlikely to need more protection than Andrews, Koda, Maggie, a three pound Sig Sauer, and Asimov could provide. Put like that, the colonel had agreed that he could be the one to fly recon. Somewhere in the back of his mind, there lives the suspicion that he would have copped the assignment anyway, given that he knows the country better than any of the other surviving pilots and can navigate by sight or with an AAA map if he has to.

Nothing wrong with taking out a little insurance, though. Or experiencing a little self-satisfaction.

"Yo, Rivers!" Manny turns to the sharp rap of boot leather on concrete. Massaccio carries her helmet tucked under one arm and a sheaf of paper in her free hand. One, incongruously, is a folded map which flops back and forth, flashing the Triple-A logo, as she waves it under his nose. "Tell me, Manny my man, that we are not actually going to have to find Offut by following the highway signs."

"Okay," he says amiably. "We are not actually going to have to find Offut by the highway signs."

A scowl appears between Massaccio's blonde brows. "But?"

"No buts. We're going to fly straight south 'til we pick up the main fork of the Platte east of Scottsbluff. Then we're going to follow it 'til we get to the Missouri. That will bring us within sensor range of Offut. Straightforward as it gets."

"Riiiight," she drawls. "No GPS, no air control."

"Cheer up, Ellen," he answers, grinning. "If Lindbergh could do it, so can we."

Fifteen minutes later, Manny looses the throttle on the shuddering bird as it idles at the end of the airstrip and sends it streaking down the mile and a half of runway. The force of it presses his back and shoulders into the padded ejection seat, jams the back of his head against the lining of his helmet. The rush that takeoff always brings starts somewhere around his solar plexus, a tightening pressure almost like the oncoming climax of sex, then progresses up his spine until his head seems unbearably light and the howl of the engines rises in his ears and the airstrip and the buildings lining it streak by under him until the nose leaves the tarmac and the lift of the wings carries the Tomcat into the blue air, and they are floating free. The Earth falls away behind to become an abstract pattern of green and brown veined with deep-cut watercourses. The Cat becomes almost an extension of his spine, his limbs, as he pulls back hard on the stick, sending her into an almost vertical climb, then levels off and banks hard left, steering their course out over the creased and folded basalt of the badlands.

They skim along above the bare rock barely a mile high, low enough for visual contact with the ground. The barrens give way almost immediately to prairie, long empty expanses pale green with new grass. Some of it is pasture; some of it, he knows, is fields plowed and left fallow through the winter, now reclaimed by native vegetation. At widely spaced intervals, he can make out the parallel rows of small patches of growing crops, and he keys them into his topography display. "Infrared giving you anything back there, Massaccio?"

"Some," she says. "Scattered readout. Some blips are probably horses and cattle. Might be some humans in here, though. At least, something roughly the same mass as humans, and something else in their vicinity that's probably a machine heat source."

*Which at least*, Manny reflects wryly, *leaves out rabbits.* Deer, bear, and elk are still possibilities, even if they are unlikely to be driving a tractor. Locating survivors is a secondary objective of the mission. At best, they can be recruited into support positions, freeing more trained military for fighting the droids. At worst, it may be possible to warn them of the advancing enemy. He pulls the plane around in a graceful loop to make a pass over the coordinates Massaccio punches into his readout, activating the zoom on the powerful camera riding among the Sidewinder and Phoenix missiles nestled underneath the Tomcat's wings.

"What's the radar look like back there?"

"Negative. No company at all within range."

Not that he expects any. According to Kirsten, no androids have ever been programmed as either pilots or navigators, one of the few precautions the Pentagon had agreed to in its enthusiasm for soldiers that would never come home as political liabilities in body bags.

Wounded Knee passes beneath them, the empty black lanes of Highways 18 and 20, the blue ribbon of the Niobrara. They are over Nebraska, the rolling hills of the western rural counties stretching empty to the horizon. The shapes of farms and ranches remain clear despite their abandonment, the pale lines of fences marching across the land, the rectangular fields defined by windbreaks and the hatched checkerboard created by the last harrowing after harvest. Silent blips appear on his topo screen as Massaccio punches her readouts forward, but there is nothing of note. Scattered readings that may be human appear sporadically, along with occasional clusters that are probably surviving farm animals, or, more likely, deer. Manny knows he does not have the mystic streak that runs through his uncle's family — and he is happy not to have it, thank you very much — but even he can see the future in the air that shimmers over the bare earth. Even now, even a mile up and years in their past, he can almost see the dust cloud raised by the myriad hoofs thundering across the prairie as the buffalo return, and with them the wolf and the bear, the puma and the river otter. As it was in the beginning, in the time of the People's coming forth onto the broad shelf of Ina Maka's breast, so it will be again.

"Rivers, you there?"

The squawk comes through his earphones, jarring him out of the interstices of time-not-yet. "What is it?"

"Something about twenty miles off to the south — moving toward us, not very fast."

Without even thinking, Manny hits the switches to arm the missiles under the Cat's wings. "Civilian aircraft? Chopper?"

"Can't tell."

"Let's check it out." He pulls on the stick again, laying the craft over onto her side in a wide turn. The blip comes up on his screen, and he frowns at it. Massaccio is right; whatever it is, is slow. Damned slow. Too slow to stay in the air almost, unless it's a helicopter. Low, too. Only a thousand feet up or so. He kicks the Cat's nose up, getting a bit more height. Just in case.

A few miles to the north of the Platte, movement appears on the horizon, a sweeping, undulating mass riding the wind that scuds over the Kansas flatlands to the south. It is at least a mile wide, perhaps twice or three times as long. Manny feels his muscles go slack, losing their unconscious tension, and he slaps the missile controls a second time, deactivating the preliminary launch sequence. As they pass overhead, he can make out the beating of thousands of wings, hundreds of thousands, as a kettle of hawks makes its way north toward their nesting grounds in Manitoba and Saskatchewan.

"What the Hell are those things?" Massaccio demands. "There must be a million of them!"

"You a city girl, Massaccio? Those were hawks, probably broadwings. Koda could tell you for sure, but I don't think anything else travels in kettles that large."

And it comes to him that it is beginning already — the return of the winged ones and the four foots. Without humans to shoot them for sport, without humans to poison their prey, unprecedented numbers of the hawks have survived to make the spring flight north from their wintering in Central and South America. Which means that there, too, the humans must lie dead in the millions.

With the sun at their tail, Manny guides the Cat along the course of the Platte. Once or twice they pick up a blip that may be a watercraft, or maybe rafts of debris, floating down toward the Missouri with the thaw. As they pass Kearney, just west of the spot where the river splits and flows in parallel streams for fifty miles or so, the infrared picks up multiple heat sources, all of them mechanical.

"Droids on the move?" Massaccio's voice comes over the com. "I don't see any readout that looks like anything but a vehicle. And I'm getting hits on the metalhead scanner."

*Not good.* "Let's get some height here. I'm gonna take her from here on compass. We'll make a pass straight over Omaha and hope they don't put up any surface-to-air."

Up and level again, Manny opens the throttle and lets the Cat scream across the sky, afterburners blazing. The readout passes across his screen so fast he cannot process it, only hope that the sensors record everything the telemetry picks up.

"Incoming!" Massaccio yells, and he has it on his radar almost simultaneously, a long, slim shape streaking toward them from the ground. Manny hauls the plane into an evasive corkscrew and fires a Sidewinder at the rising missile, noting with satisfaction the blossom on the LED screen as it makes its kill. So much for hoping to go unnoticed; one of the trucks has radioed the base. A second surface-to-air missile bores in on them on the heels of the thought; a second Sidewinder leaves its nest and scores a second kill. Yet a third goes wide, missing them and inexplicably detonating in a cloud of white smoke a thousand feet above them.

Or maybe not inexplicably. Maybe the droids haven't modified their weapons' guidance systems and their GPS is fritzing out.

*One for our side.* Aloud he says, "You got what we need back there?"

"Got."

"Okay, then. Let's go home."

**"Redtail One, this** is Redtail Two. What's your twenty?"

Rolling her eyes, Dakota unracks the mic and puts it to her lips. "Right in front of you, pinhead."

"Hey! I resemble that remark."

"Yeah, yeah. What's up?"

"Isn't old Boney Markham's hunt shop around here somewhere?"

"Boney died about six years ago, *thiblo.*"

"Yeah, I know, but I heard his son took over for the old coot after he kicked it."

"Terrence?"

"Yeah. Didn't you go to high school with him?"

"Don't remind me. What a nut job."

"He was scary all right. You still didn't answer my question, though."

"Yeah, I think it's up another mile or so on the left. Why? You up for a little looting?"

"I prefer to think of it as 'creative acquisition', *tanksi.*"

Koda laughs. "Call it whatever you like, *thiblo.* But if Terrence comes out with a shotgun pointed at your head, don't come screaming to me."

Tacoma joins in the laughter. "Like I did when old man Johnston caught us stealing pumpkins from his patch that time?"

"You, brother dear, you got caught. I wasn't the one getting rock salt plucked outta my ass for weeks afterward."

"Hey! Is it my fault you can run faster than me?"

"Yup! Sure is. Hang on," she says to her front seat passenger, a young airman with the down-home name of Joe Poteet. He does as she asks, grabbing the rollbar as she swings the big truck around an overturned John Deere that is pulled halfway onto the road.

"Nice driving, ma'am," the young man remarks, slowly removing his white-knuckled grip from the bar.

Giving him a smirk, Koda continues on over the slight rise. Beyond it, a small shopping center, three stores in all, comes into view on the left. As she pulls into the empty parking lot, Koda scans the area. The store to the far left, Tamke's Hardware and Feed, has been obviously looted, as has the video store to the far right. Shattered glass sparkles in the sun like diamonds on the dark macadam of the lot. Doors hang loose from their hinges, and trash is strewn everywhere. The sign from the video store, its letters obliterated by blasts from a shotgun, sways in the slight breeze, its rusted hinges squeaking a discordant, depressing tune.

Dakota brings the truck to a slow stop, its fat tires crunching complacently over trash, gravel, and glass. Opening the door, she swings out, boot heels clacking on the macadam as she watches her brother pull in, followed by two other olive green trucks.

"Damn," Tacoma remarks as he jumps down from the truck. "Looks like old Boney's place was the only one that wasn't hit."

"Yeah, well, there's a reason for that," Koda replies, gesturing toward the heavy metal grate that covers the entire front of the store.

"You any good at picking locks?"

"With what? My fingernail? Besides, I thought you military types learned lock picking about the same time you were learning the difference between your rifle and your gun."

"Left my lock picks in my other uniform," Tacoma mumbles.

Koda shakes her head. "Poteet, Catchem, go around the back and see if there's a way in from there. The rest of you, look sharp. We don't know if any friends are lurking about." She shoots a look to Tacoma. "Be right back."

Several minutes later, she reappears from the depths of the looted hardware store, two portable blowtorches in her hands and a pair of protective goggles tucked under one arm. Seeing her, Tacoma grins. "Interesting looking lock picks ya got there, sis."

"Ha. Ha," is the droll reply as she slaps one of the torches into his hands. "Hold this." Grabbing the goggles, she slips them over her head. "Poteet have any luck?"

"Nope. Only way in or out is through that door."

"Then step aside and watch the master at work."

Tacoma's jaw snaps shut with an audible click as his sister gives him a very pointed look that aborts any quip he might have thought to utter.

Leveling a wink at him, she turns to her work, and all falls silent in the lot.

**With a sigh** of weariness, Kirsten slumps against the low-backed chair and picks up the blackened circuitry board she's been staring at for the last two hours. While the others work quietly, using tweezers in a high-tech game of jigsaw puzzle, continuing to piece together what they can of the droid, she flips the piece back and forth, glaring at it as if it will give up its secrets simply by the force of her will.

Jimenez moves to stand beside her, running a hand through his short-cropped black hair. "You look beat, ma'am."

"I'm all right," she replies, though she knows that's far from the truth. Rather than being tired, though, she's feeling vague, out of sorts. She finds her mind wandering off on strange tangents instead of focusing on the task at hand. This is nowhere near normal for her, and it frightens her, just a bit. The fact that this dazed feeling coincides with Dakota's absence leaves her feeling not one whit better about the whole situation.

With a reluctant nod, Jimenez steps away just as Kirsten flips the board in her hand. The shaft of light let in by the young lieutenant's movement strikes the charred board in a way that causes Kirsten's eyes to widen. "Jimenez!" she shouts happily, jumping down off the stool, "consider yourself promoted."

"Ma'am?"

"Never mind. Is there a microscope around here anywhere?"

"I don't... What kind of microscope, ma'am?" It's obvious the man's confusion is deepening.

"A microscope! You know, the kind you played with in junior high science lab?"

"For looking at slides and stuff? I...guess there'd be one at the hospital, ma'am, or at Dr. Rivers' clinic, maybe."

"Perfect! Grab a pad and pencil and come with me."

"Yes, ma'am!"

**With a last,** precise cut, the part of the grating that contains the lock breaks free and falls to the ground with a loud clink. Satisfied, Koda shuts off the blowtorch, slips off her goggles, and grabs the gate. It slides grudgingly, sounding out a rusty squeal of protest. A second later, a simple wooden door is revealed.

Tacoma steps forward and gently pushes his sister aside. "Can't let you have all the fun, *tanski*," he says with a grin. A moment later, the door is a splintered mess, courtesy of a swift kick.

Koda rolls her eyes as Tacoma. "You're so butch."

"With a role model like you, how could I not be?" he teases, delivering a light elbow to her side and ducking into the darkened shop before she can retaliate.

Koda follows close behind, clicking on the flashlight she's appropriated from Poteet. Tacoma whistles. "Not bad," he whispers, "not bad at all."

The store is good sized and seemingly filled with everything a hunter or fisherman could want, and more besides. Along the left wall is a glass case filled with handguns of all makes, models, and sizes. Tacked up to the wall behind the case are dozens and dozens of rifles, shotguns, and several highly illegal fully automatic weapons. "Damn," Tacoma remarks, gazing at a proudly displayed Uzi. "He must have had some cops on the payroll."

Dakota snorts. "And this comes as a surprise to you...how?"

Three more soldiers enter, their own flashlights brightening the interior and bringing more of the varied merchandise into view. Tacoma turns to the men. "Jackson, Carter, start gathering up those guns and all the ammo you can find. Pack 'em in tight."

"Will do, Major."

"The rest of you, look around and box up anything you think we can use...which is probably most of the stuff in here. Move."

"We're on it, Major."

After watching them for a moment longer, Dakota strikes off toward the rear of the store, her flashlight making sweeping arcs along the dusty floor. "C'mon," she says to her brother, "let's check out the storeroom."

"Right behind ya."

**"Jimenez, you have** your pencil ready?"

"Ready and waiting, ma'am."

"Good. I want you to take down these series of letters and numbers for me."

Adjusting the eyepiece just slightly, she squints as the charred numbers come slowly into view. "S...D...zero...zero...A...four...six... No wait, make that a five. Yes, five." Even with the benefit of the microscope, the information is difficult to read at best. Blackened streaks and smudges all but obliterate what's underneath. She looks back over her shoulder. "You getting this?"

"Yes'm." Jimenez, with his round rimmed military-issue glasses, pad and poised pencil, looks more like an accountant than one of the world's best fighter plane mechanics.

Kirsten can't help but smile. "Good."

Ten minutes later, the task is done. Not as complete as she would have liked, not by a long shot, but given the rather sizable string of numbers and letters completely obliterated by their fiery end, she's more than content with what she's managed to recover. With instincts born of literally decades of experience, she senses what she has will be more than enough for her current needs.

Her smile tells the story, and when she turns it upon Jimenez, he blinks at her, dazed. "Ma'am?"

"Take the rest of the day off, Lieutenant," she replies, snatching the pad out of his hand. "Catch up on your sleep, read, Hell, pick dandelions for all I care. You're dismissed."

"Did — did I do something wrong, ma'am?"

"No, my friend." She laughs and, uncharacteristically, goes up to her toes to plant a soft kiss on his clean-shaven cheek that leaves him seeing stars. "You did everything right. Now scoot!"

He does.

**"*Tanski*, you got** a minute?"

Sighing, Koda looks to the left, where her brother's flashlight bisects the shadowy interior. "I'm up to my elbows in ammo, *thiblo*. Can it wait?"

"I think you might wanna come take a look at this."

Passing her duties off to a nearby soldier, Dakota rises to her feet and wipes the sweat from her forehead with a negligent swipe of one long arm. Following the trail of light her brother has laid down, she comes up next to him at the door of what appears to be Markham's private office.

With a flair for the dramatic, Tacoma pauses, then sweeps the light in a wide arc until it is pointing directly into the room. He stands quietly, awaiting his sister's reaction.

Koda gives a low whistle as she peers inside. "My, my, my," she remarks softly, hands on hips, "looks like someone was a naughty boy."

The room is filled with items that would have made Richard Butler fall on his knees and weep for joy. A huge white cross, complete with the suffering Jesus, is flanked on both sides by flags of the Third Reich, Aryan Brotherhood, Confederacy, Ku Klux Klan, Concerned Christian Men, and a half-dozen others. Above a rickety television set, an old framed photograph of a long dead Austrian private hangs in the place of honor, gleaming forelock forever drooping over one crazed eye.

On the splintered coffee table, several dog-eared copies of *The Turner Diaries* share space with *Mein Kampf,* a whole slew of *Soldier of Fortunes,* and a broad range of other far right wing paramilitary and religious propaganda. Bits and pieces of dismantled weaponry cover the floor like a macabre carpet, and the room stinks of old sweat, old urine, and old hatred.

"Damn," Tacoma whispers. "I didn't think he'd go down so deep."

"I did." Grabbing the flashlight from her brother's hand, she shines it in the direction of a white hooded robe. Behind it, she can just see the seal of a door. "And I'm betting the jackpot's behind door number three."

# CHAPTER THIRTY-SEVEN

Dawn is still several hours away, but Kirsten is wide awake, her lover's pillow clutched tightly against her chest as she stares at the ceiling above. Her body still hums with the sweet energy of their lovemaking less than half an hour ago, and she already misses Dakota's passionate presence. "The things you make me feel," she murmurs into the still, humid air. She remembers the look Koda gave her when she thought she was sleeping. The tenderness and adoration emanating from those magnificent eyes was as palpable to Kirsten as a caress, laying itself over the parts of her that were still wounded and raw from a lifetime of standing on the outside, and making her feel, for that one wondrous moment, whole.

A sinking surge of guilt hits her belly, and she rolls from the bed, pushing her lover's pillow away from her as if she doesn't deserve the comfort it holds. And in truth, perhaps she doesn't. Keeping her plans from Dakota was the hardest thing she'd ever done. Compared to that, walking unarmed into Minot had been child's play. What is it they say? Act first, apologize later, right?

She has the sinking feeling that no amount of contrition will ever make up for her silence of last night and this morning.

*Please, God. Let her understand.*

Striding into the bathroom, she turns on the tap and stands under the frigid spray, letting the stinging, icy water chase the thoughts and emotions from her. Her face, like her soul, grows stony, and by the time the water is once again silent, she resembles the very androids she is going after.

She dresses quickly and steps into the darkened living room. Koda had left one lamp burning low on the hearth, and its somber light casts Asi's curled body into flickering shadow. Having gone out earlier with Dakota, he merely looks up at his mistress, tail thumping companionably against the hearthstones. A slight smile cracks Kirsten's icy veneer, and squatting, she strokes his noble head, then hugs him close for a moment, allowing herself to enjoy his soft warmth and unwavering affection.

After a long moment, she pulls away and stands, looking down at him. "You be good today, you hear me?"

He looks up at her, slightly outraged, as if "good" isn't his middle name.

Correctly interpreting the look, Kirsten rolls her eyes, shakes her head, and turns away, grabbing her laptop and the silver case she's brought with her from the bedroom. Plucking a set of keys from their hook just inside the door, she lets herself out into the cool night.

Feeling a bit like a criminal, she stands at the driveway and looks carefully up and down the street. All is quiet and dark. Satisfied, she makes her way toward Koda's truck. As she reaches the vehicle, a soft voice sounds behind her, causing her to jump and turn, body braced for a fight.

"Jesus, Lieutenant!" she gasps as the tall, muscled, and incredibly handsome man steps out from the shadows. "You scared me!"

"Sorry about that, ma'am," he replies, touching the brim of his cap in salute and smiling at her.

"What are you doing lurking in the bushes in the middle of the night?"

"Following orders, ma'am."

"Orders? Who's orders?"

"The colonel's, ma'am. I'm part of your night guard."

Kirsten's eyes narrow. "Night guard?"

"Yes, ma'am."

"I see. And does Doctor Rivers know about this?"

The lieutenant's grin returns. "She does. I just talked to the doc this morning, as a matter of fact."

"Oh, you did, did you?" Placing her articles on the hood of the truck, she crosses her arms. "And what did she have to say?"

The grin fades slowly. "Well, ma'am, she said that if anything happened to you while she was away, she'd flay me alive."

Kirsten snorts. "Well, I wouldn't want that to happen."

"Thank you, ma'am."

"So, you're coming with me."

Jackson snaps to attention. "Of course, ma'am. Where are we going?"

Her smile is mystery itself. "Oh...you'll see."

**Dakota's Cougar Two** hums along the blacktop leading north from Ellsworth to the ruins of Minot; Cougar One, leading the convoy, bristles with armament. Like all the APCs in the line, it mounts a machine gun on its roof, minded by a soldier with one hand on its swivel and the other on her own M-16. Cougar One also carries a spotter with binoculars, sprouting up out of the moonroof to keep company with the gunner. So far they have met nothing but the empty highway. Almost a meter high, grass grows along the shoulders to the very edge of the asphalt, with here and there a green shoot springing up on the tarmac itself. There are no wrecks here, and no roadkilled four-foots. The whole caravan had almost come to grief within an hour of setting out, when a mother skunk had led her line of five offspring across the pavement in aloof indifference to the trucks, and Tacoma had run Cougar One off onto the shoulder with the four following vehicles screeching to a halt bumper to bumper behind it.

"Shit, Major, you crazy?" Sergeant Greg Townsend had bellowed from two APCs back, leaning out of the driver's window, his face beet red from the spring sun and the barely avoided accident.

"Hell, no, city boy." Tacoma's laughter had come over the walkie-talkie. "Better to kiss a telephone pole than hit a skunk, any day."

After that, they had strung out at a safer distance. From the front seat of Cougar Two, Koda can see Larke's abbreviated ponytail fluttering like a pennant in the wind created by the APC's speed as he leans his elbows on the roof of the lead vehicle to brace his optics. Regulations be damned, many of the soldiers and airmen of Ellsworth have taken to growing their hair. Only the pilots, whose coiffure has to fit the confines of a helmet, have remained impervious to the new fashion statement.

Closer to, Dakota has a view of Cougar Two's driver, Catchem, and Joe Poteet's camo-clad legs, the top half of their gunner invisible beyond the roof. Most of the time, though, she keeps her elbows propped on her knees, studying the country through her own pair of Swarovski 10x50s. There has been no sign of the enemy, though the tall grass would give ambushers excellent cover. Once she has seen the tall humps of buffalo

lumbering along the horizon; twice, small herds of horses who have survived, still patched and shabby looking with the unshed straggles of their
winter coats. She feels untethered, somehow, not quite in the present, not
sure whether they are moving through the past or the future. It is a sensation that has lingered every since her vision in the sweat lodge, a sense
that she is neither who nor where nor when she once was.

*All perfectly normal, according to* Até.

"Halfway mark, ma'am," Catchem observes, pointing at the odometer.
"We've been in North Dakota for the last twenty minutes or so."

Koda nods her thanks. They will bypass Bismarck and Mandan to the
east, making directly for the base. They should arrive in time for a bit of
recon, camp for the night and head back tomorrow afternoon with a cargo
of whatever small arms they can pick up and a notion of whether or not it is
feasible to try to collect a bomber or two. Maggie has flatly refused to risk
her remaining pilots on a scouting mission, no matter how Manny begged or
cajoled or argued. Certainly one or two of the behemoths will come in
handy if it becomes necessary to destroy yet another Air Force installation.

Koda thumbs the button on her walkie-talkie. "Yo, *thiblo*. Seen anything up there yet?"

"Nothing since we took evasive action to get out of the way of Mama
Skunk and her family this morning."

"Evasive action, my ass. We nearly had a pile-up."

"And you'd rather stink of skunk for the next three weeks? There ain't
that much tomato juice left in the world, sis. Besides, you got it all wrong.
That was a squad of indigenous freedom fighters. One cadre and five
enlisted, equipped with chemical weapons."

The radio falls silent, and the miles slip by. The high grass seems to
stretch forever, overgrowing the prarie, the pastureland, fields harrowed for
the winter before the ice sank into the soil, petrifying it as surely as the passage of uncounted time. This, it comes to Koda, is Ina Maka reclaiming
herself, giving birth to a new family of children, winged and four-footed and
finned, the standing people and the stones. The only question that remains
is how, or whether, the human two-foots will have a place in the new world.
Or no, that is not quite right. The question is whether humans will live free
in the universe that their own creations have brought into being. The question is whether they can survive in large enough numbers to create a stable
population, and having done so, whether they can live with each other without sinking into tribal warfare.

If they survive this battle, their first priority must be to make contact
with other surviving communities and make alliance with them.

*Or*, the unpleasant thought intrudes, *subjugate them.*

*Do you want to become a conqueror, Dakota Rivers? Do you want
Kirsten to become a dictator, the iron fist that forces the population back
into technological society at the point of a machine gun?*

*No?*

*Well, then, do you want to allow some old coot who thinks he is God's
administrative assistant to "marry" fourteen-year-old girls by the half
dozen?*

Somewhere there has to be a balance between the two, some territory
marked by common sense and respect for one's neighbors and the workings of democracy. And somewhere, on this land that her people have lived

on time out of mind, there is the pattern of a new and ancient compact between human and four-foot, human and winged, human and Ina Maka herself. Despite the cloud that shadows the battle to come, she knows that that, nothing less, is the quest that awaits her on the other side of blood and death.

Koda steadies her binoculars and sweeps the horizon for the thousandth time. *Move over Galahad*, she thinks wryly. *Compared to this, finding the Grail was a slam-dunk.*

The first sign of trouble appears some ten miles south of Max, North Dakota, arcing over a shaggy forty-acre pasture from the windbreak along its northern border. The grenade lands some twenty feet in front of Cougar One, gouging a hole in the tarmac and spraying the lead APC with a rain of melted tar and minute asphalt pellets. Koda just has time to see Cougar One veer off the road, Larke raising one arm to shield his face from the spatter of liquefied pavement, and to register the incongruous roar of the explosive when another round impacts the spot they had occupied a fraction of a heartbeat ago.

"Motherfucker!" someone bellows from the truck behind her, and flame from a return round blossoms along the treeline, its glare picking out a flurry of movement in the shadow of the trees. Then nothing.

Tacoma scrambles out of Cougar One, careful to avoid the recklessly canted driver's door as it clangs shut behind him. "Two of you come with me! The rest stay with the trucks!" Not turning to see who follows, he slogs into the grass, still only knee-high, by the roadside.

With a wave of her hand to Poteet, Koda follows, pausing to exchange a grin with her brother where he holds down the lowest two strands of barbed wire so that they can duck into the sea of waist-high purple-top that was once a cultivated field. Some stalks, grown tall, brush at her face, their deep burgundy seeds shining along their spikes like garnets dangling on golden scepters.

"Spread out." Tacoma waves them off to either side of him. "Watch your footing. Keep your eyes on that ridge." Tacoma sets off through the grass, its deep green parting for him, then closing like a wake behind him.

Koda strikes out a few yards to his left, Poteet to the other side. She holds her rifle high, ready to fire without aiming at their attackers' position, but, like Tacoma, she suspects that they are already gone. They may have simply fled in the face of greater numbers and bigger guns. Or they may have abandoned their position to report to whomever stationed them here.

Tacoma tops the rise slightly ahead of Poteet and Koda. She watches as he sweeps the line of sight with the muzzle of his rifle, head up and alert for movement, then drops it to part the grass at his feet.

*No one home.* Lowering her gun, she sprints the rest of the way up the side of the windbreak to join her brother. The grass along the ridge lies broken and beaten down where two men have crouched to set up a grenade launcher, its abandoned tube tossed down halfway to the narrow blacktop road below. By the roadside, twin ruts run through the grass and weeds, a partial tire pattern visible where it has been printed in dust on the asphalt.

"Shit," Koda observes.

Tacoma glances at her sharply, one side of his mouth canting up in a crooked smile. "Oh yeah. This road's still got enough traffic that they pull off to park. Not good. Not good at all."

"What now, Major?" A frown crosses Poteet's sunburned face. "Any chance these guys are friendlies?"

"Well, they don't seem to think we're friendlies, and I'm gonna defer to their opinion until proven otherwise." He shoulders his rifle and heads back down the slope. "From now on, we keep close, drive fast, and shoot first."

**Bright sunlight streams** through the windshield, almost blinding Jackson. Squinting, he flips down the visor, but that action brings no relief. With a grumbling sigh, he turns his head to look at his Commander-in-Chief, who is currently humming a song he can't begin to identify as the passing wind tousles her golden hair.

"Problem, Lieutenant?" Kirsten asks, not taking her shaded eyes from the deserted access road before her.

"No, ma'am. Except..."

"Except?"

"Well, could you maybe clue me in as to where we're going?"

"You'll know soon enough, Lieutenant. We're almost there."

This statement does nothing to calm the fears of a man who has spent the last three plus hours imagining one Doctor Dakota Rivers filleting him with a butter knife and dragging what's left over shards of broken glass. He seriously, albeit briefly, considers jerking open the door, diving out, and taking his chances with the androids, or whatever other unsavory characters inhabit this stretch of backwater nowhere. His reverie is disrupted by a gentle pat to the knee.

"Don't worry, Lieutenant," Kirsten comments, smirking as she divines his thoughts. "I won't let anything happen to you."

"I, uh, think that's supposed to be the other way around, ma'am."

Kirsten's laughter is rich and surprisingly uncomplicated, and he decides he likes it, even though, in the end, the privilege of hearing it will likely cost him latrine duty for the rest of his natural life. And beyond.

A short time later, he feels the truck slow, and watches as it pulls to a stop behind a large, thick copse of trees. It's not what he expected, but years in the military have prepared him for almost anything. "I take it, ma'am, that you didn't drive us all the way out here just to commune with nature."

Kirsten laughs again as she gathers her things. "You guessed right, Lieutenant. Sit tight; I'll be right back." She levels her sternest look at him. "Stay in the truck, if you please."

With a sigh, he obeys her soft-voiced command, slumping back against the seat and waiting for whatever may come.

"Whatever" comes sooner than he expects as he suddenly finds himself staring into a pair of android eyes. The only thing that keeps him from depressing the trigger of his weapon is the smile beneath those eyes; a smile that he has become acquainted with these past several hours. He blinks, shakes his head, then blinks again. The vision does not change. "M-Ma'am? Ms. President?"

"In the flesh, so to speak. You like?"

"If 'like' suddenly means 'get the shit scared out of', then yes, ma'am, I like."

Chuckling, Kirsten holds up a hand. "Here, take this."

The cup of his palm suddenly holds a blob of flesh colored plastic. He looks at her inquiringly.

"Put it in your ear."

With a bit of skepticism, he does as she asks, surprised to find the device sits easily in his ear canal.

"Good. Can you hear me?"

"Yes, but..."

Kirsten lifts a brow.

"Begging your pardon, ma'am, but you're, like, six inches away. It'd be pretty impossible not to hear you."

"You have a point," Kirsten replies dryly. "Hang on a second." She disappears behind the truck. "Can you hear me now?"

"You sound like one of those old time cellphone commercials, ma'am."

"Should I take that as a yes, Lieutenant?"

Jackson fights the urge to snap off a salute. "Yes, ma'am. I can hear you fine, ma'am."

"Good." The android face appears in front of Jackson, taking another few years off his life. "Now, this is what I need for you to do, Lieutenant. See those trees over there?"

"Yes, ma'am."

"I want you to patrol them, but stay hidden. Just beyond them is a small manufacturing plant. I have some business to attend to there. You'll be guarding my back."

"With all respect, ma'am," he protests, "wouldn't it be easier to guard your back if I could actually see it?"

Reaching through the rolled down window, Kirsten claps Jackson's broad shoulder. "Not this time, Lieutenant. I need to do this alone."

"But—"

Kirsten's face goes stony. "No buts, Lieutenant. I've given you a direct order, and I expect you to obey it, without comment and without question."

"I'm sorry, ma'am," he shoots back, "but your safety is more important than any order you could give me. I can't — I won't let you walk into some unknown structure alone and unprotected."

"You can, and you will, Lieutenant Jackson." Taking a breath, she consciously reins in her temper and softens her voice. "Darius, you can't come with me."

"Why? Would you just mind telling me that, please, ma'am? You've kept me in the dark for hours now, and I think I at least deserve something! Please?"

She looks at him for a long moment, then nods. "Did you hear the story of what happened at Minot?"

"Bits and pieces. I know you were there to try and get the android code."

"I was. And if your General Hart hadn't decided, against all good sense, to bomb the place to smithereens, we might not be in the trouble we're in right now." She takes a deep breath and lets it out slowly, forcefully pushing away the memories of that time. "I have another chance, Darius. Not the same chance, but a good one. And as much as I value your protection, if you come with me, that chance will never be realized. Can you understand?"

"Not really, ma'am. But...I accept your reasoning. I just — need to help, in some way."

"Believe me," she replies, relieved beyond measure, "you will. That earpiece will allow you to hear everything that's going on. I'll be able to communicate with you through it, and if I sense any trouble, you'll be the first to know."

"How?"

"I'll say..." She thinks about it for a moment, then smiles. *"Nun lila hopa."*

*"Nun lila hopa,"* he repeats dutifully. "What does it mean?"

Kirsten blushes faintly. "That doesn't matter. For our purposes, it means 'Lieutenant Jackson, your presence is required, NOW!'"

He laughs a little, though his insides are twisted up tighter than a roll of barbed wire and every instinct he possesses is screaming for him to grab her, throw her in the truck, and hightail it back to the base, damn the consequences. "Okay, ma'am. I got it." He looks up at the sky. "How long do you think it'll take?"

"A few hours, no more. I'll let you know when I'm headed back, okay?"

"It's not okay, but I'll follow your orders, Ms. President."

Kirsten smiles. "Thank you, Lieutenant. I'll see you soon."

A moment later, she's gone.


**"Ho. Ly. Shit."**

Koda stares across the field, in wordless agreement with her brother. Behind them, Larke lets out a long, low whistle. "Dayyyum," he says. "You didn't put any funny, medicine woman stuff in the water, did you, ma'am?"

"Nope," she answers, not quite believing it herself. "It's really there."

"It" looks like nothing so much as an extraterrestrial grasshopper, from Jupiter maybe, with heavy, drooping wings and squinting compound eyes, squatting in the middle of the prairie that stretches away to the horizon. The curves of the intake turbines of the twinned jet engines, though, just visible above the tall grass, name it for what it is.

"A B-52," Tacoma adds. "A fucking B-52."

Slashed across the field from northwest to southeast, the scar of its landing shows bare earth gouged up to either side; a fine dust covers its metal skin from the nose back. The crash, or forced landing, depending on how one views it, is recent; the binoculars show no sign of green sprung up on the low berms ploughed up by the bomber's skid over the pasture. Koda lowers her optics and says quietly, "Get the Geiger counter, Larke."

"You think there's nukes on board, ma'am?" he asks as he turns back to the line of vehicles parked on the shoulder.

Dakota shrugs. "All we know right now is that if there are, they didn't go off. What we need to know is whether they've been breached." Larke goes white to the gills, and she adds, "If they're there at all."

When he has gone, Tacoma says quietly, "All right, we know someone's still up at Minot, someone who's trying to fly nuclear bombers."

"Not very successfully, it seems," Koda answers.

"Not this time. Maybe next."

Koda nods. "Maybe next, *thiblo*. Or maybe the time after that. If they have another crew."

Tacoma looks from the downed plane to his sister and back. He says musingly, "Not likely, is it? I don't think even Ellsworth could muster a full crew for one of those monsters; Manny and Andrews sure as Hell aren't qualified on the heavy stuff, and I doubt the colonel herself is. And the droids have to have hit Minot even harder than they did us. We've got a rogue on our hands, *tanski*."

"Take him out?"

"If we can. Or make an alliance. You see a third possibility?" Takoma asks.

It's a no-brainer. "We can't leave an unknown at our backs. Not this close. Not now."

Larke arrives with the Geiger counter, and Koda takes it from him. As she walks it toward the wreckage of the plane, the readout remains at normal levels. There is no need to check for injured. Once she is within ten meters of the derelict, she sees the white lime left by carrion birds along the edge of the wing; a little closer, and the smell reaches her. Confirmation, if she needs it, that the pilot or pilots did not survive.

*Interesting that no one came to bury them. But droids would hardly bother, if droid experiment it was. On the other hand, a band of marauders — ambitious marauders at that — was unlikely to have sentimental feelings for one another.*

Koda snaps the cover over the readout and heads back toward the line of APCs waiting by the road. "No radiation here; the trouble's up ahead." She grins. "Let's not keep it waiting."

**Pushing all non-essential** thoughts from her mind, Kirsten strolls onto the grounds of the plant as if she has every right to be there. Which, she considers, given her recent promotion to the head of what's left of the Free World, she does.

Her enhanced senses assure her that the building is unguarded, since its unprepossessing façade gives no hint of its purpose. Taking in a deep, cleansing breath, she grasps the door handle with her free hand and pulls. It opens easily, silently, on well-oiled hinges, letting out a blast of chilled air. *Huh. Air conditioning. Almost forgot what that felt like.*

The air smells musty and canned, and she finds herself wrinkling her nose and blinking at the sudden over-brightness of the fluorescent lighting that bathes the sterile, empty reception area.

*Guess I'm getting used to this Robinson Crusoe stuff.* After a moment, she straightens her shoulders and drops the emotionless mask back over her features. *Okay, kiddo, showtime. Let's get it right this time, hmm?*

Striding through the empty room as if she hasn't a care in the world, she pulls open the heavy glass door to the factory proper and steps through. Her senses are immediately assailed with the heavy scent of oil and machinery, but she takes it in stride, and approaches the neatly dressed android facing her. His scan hums along her ear canals, tickling against the tiny hairs there. When it finally comes to a stop, she looks at him directly. "I have been programmed to download a patch into your system. 7-E23-1267AA-349."

"I was unaware of such an order, Biodroid 42A-77."

Kirsten lifts her laptop and places it on the desk in front of the droid. "All the instructions are here, should you wish to verify."

The scan is more direct this time, deeper and harder, and she fights the urge to clamp her hands over her ears as the drilling pain shoots along her nerve endings in agonizing pulses of pure energy.

The pain stops as abruptly as it began, and Kirsten is hard-pressed not to gasp for air. She knows her heart is pounding, but hopes the android will take it as a normal response for her model. If not, she's dead. She has no illusions about that.

"Proceed to the computer room, Biodroid 42A-77."

Very careful to mask her relief, Kirsten moves off in the direction indicated, looking neither right nor left until she stands before another glass door. The computer room is, as expected, sparsely furnished and icy cold. Mainframe servers take up space along all of the walls, humming, whirring, and chittering complacently to themselves.

Walking over to the central desk, she places her laptop down and seats herself on the more-or-less comfortable office chair. As her computer boots up, she taps the keys on the loaded desktop sitting beside it. The passwords haven't been changed since the uprising, and she is able to get into the system easily.

Quickly scanning down the standard list of codes, she stops as she reaches the area where the "suicide bomber" aspect of the androids' "personality" is encoded. "Interesting," she whispers softly, squinting slightly to unblur the huge string of binary staring back at her. *Shoulda remembered to make these damn contacts prescription.*

Deftly changing the view from "read only", she clicks the cursor at the beginning of the added code, then takes out the cable needed to mate the two computers. That done, she drags the blinking cursor over a certain area, then hits the "enter" key on her laptop and sits back as her computer begins to disgorge its altered information. She can feel her heart rate pick up as she waits out the download, hoping beyond hope that she's not tripping some alarm system down the line. A quick scan before the download had told her that wouldn't be a danger, but she can't help worrying nonetheless.

Several tension filled moments later, the words *download complete* appear on the screen, and Kirsten finds herself taking her first full, unencumbered breath of the afternoon. Fingers flying over the keyboard, she builds a secure site, then launches a test program, eyes darting across the screen as she watches the new code in action. "Perfect," she announces to the empty room, before dumping the test program and erasing all traces of its existence.

Just as she's about to power down her laptop, the door swings open and another android steps through, staring down at her through his emotionless, dead doll's eyes. "You will explain and demonstrate the new parameters of the patch you have just installed."

*Ohhh shit! I knew this was too damn easy. Think, Kirsten, think. Don't screw up now, or you're dead.*

"Your heart and respiratory rate mnemonics show an increase of 7.34%, Biodroid 42A-77. In a human, this would indicate nervousness."

"I am programmed to mimic human autonomic response to a multitude of different stimuli, 16617-398PZ."

"Noted. Continue."

Kirsten's mind races as she desperately tries to think up a story that will placate the killing machine standing a foot away from her. An idea slides into her mind so perfectly that it seems to her as if some outside force has placed it there. Her fingers quickly map out an alternate test pattern as she eyes the android steadily. "As you know, the units here are currently programmed to detonate upon the acquisition of human targets. However, given that a small but noteworthy number of humans have joined together with the standard units, the probability is significant that one or more of these units will detonate within a mixed group, causing unneeded collateral damage." She holds up a hand, finger pointed to the ceiling. "Normally, such collateral damage to standard units would not cause difficulty, but with the factory at Minot now substantially out of commission, every android unit is needed to continue its task to completion."

"Acknowledged."

"Therefore," she continues, lowering her hand to continue her character mapping, "I have been programmed with a patch that will cause these special units to avoid any human target that is detected within the presence of standard units, and only to detonate when it finds human readings alone."

Crossing mental fingers, she turns the monitor toward her listener, and presses "enter". "The flashing red number is our special unit, adapted with the patch. The flashing black numbers are human and android targets. The flashing blue numbers are human targets alone."

*Pleasepleasepleasepleasepleasepleasepleaseplease.*

As if reading her thoughts, the tiny red number veers away from the group of black numbers and heads into the very center of the blue group. A split-second later, the entire screen flashes, and when it steadies, a line of numbers scrolls down the monitor, ending with a flashing black 78% target acquisition.

*Oh, thank you, God!*

"Does this scenario meet with your satisfaction?" she asks.

"Affirmative," the droid replies after a moment. "Will there be anything else that you require?"

"Yes. This patch only ties into the original manufacturing mainframe. If you have any completed units that have not yet been released, I'll need to apply it to them as well."

"Acknowledged. If you will follow me, I will lead you to them."

"Affirmative." Powering down her laptop, Kirsten rises from her chair and follows the android out of the room, through a series of intersecting corridors, and down a well-lit stairwell into the basement of the manufacturing plant. The room is large, spotless, and completely dust free. It is also filled with row upon row of deactivated androids, looking like something out of one of those ancient television shows. *The Outer Limits*, perhaps, or *The Twilight Zone*. Kirsten suppresses a shiver as she eyes the stringless puppets awaiting their master's bidding.

As she steps closer, she notices something that causes her very soul to grow cold. These androids aren't only human-like. If she didn't know, with one hundred percent certainty, that they are simply made of high quality organic plastics and computer chips, she would swear that they are, in fact, human. Gone are the silver circlets around their necks. Gone are the dark, dead eyes that seem to absorb all light. These eyes, these faces, have expression, human expression, and Kirsten feels her mouth go dry at the implication.

*Jesus. I have to let Maggie and Dakota know right away. We could be harboring these monstrosities right under our noses without even knowing it. Fuck. Fuck, fuck, fuck!*

She's brought back to the present by a cord entering her field of vision, held by the ever-helpful android to her left.

"These units are connected to the secondary computer at the pedal terminus."

Accepting the cord, Kirsten looks down and notices that the androids, twenty five in all and lined up in neat rows of five, are all standing on a metal strip.  The cord she's holding trails out from the far left side of that strip.  "Acknowledged," she comments finally, placing her laptop on the computer desk and connecting the wire to its back.

"Is there anything further that you require?"

"Neg— Affirmative."

The droid looks at her.  She's sure if it was within its programming to lift an eyebrow, it would be doing so right about now.  "I'll be appropriating one of these units for a field trail when I leave."

The pain hits again, like a high-speed dental drill being slowly shoved into her ear canal.  Mercifully it stops before she decides to slit her own wrists just to stop the torment.

"Affirmative," the droid remarks.  "If there is nothing else you require, I will leave you to your tasks."

"That will be all."

**As Kirsten pushes** her way through the last of the trees, she finds herself face to muzzle with an automatic weapon.  Even though she recognizes the man who wields the weapon, instinct stops her strides, and her hands go up, palms out.

"It's all right, ma'am," Jackson says, meeting her eyes quickly before returning his gaze to the man in back of her.  "Just step to my right. I've got the asshole covered."

Instead of stepping away, Kirsten instead steps forward.  Raising a hand, she gently pushes the muzzle of the weapon to the left and holds the Lieutenant's startled gaze.  "Relax, Darius.  He's one of the good guys."

"Good guys, ma'am?  You mean there were humans there?"

"He's not human, Lieutenant."

The weapon comes back up, a long dark finger tightening on the trigger.  Once again, Kirsten pushes it away.  "Stand down, Lieutenant.  That's an order."

She's serious.  He can tell that from the blazing emeralds all but soldering him to the ground at his feet.  Deeply ingrained respect for a superior officer wars with his absolute need to keep said officer safe and whole.

"Do it, Lieutenant, or I'll have my buddy Max here take that gun and twist it into a pretzel."

"Max?"

"Unit MA-233142176-X-83," the android helpfully supplies.

"Max."

"You got it," Kirsten replies, smiling slightly.  "Now, are you gonna lower your weapon?  I'd kinda like to get out of here."

"Are we taking him...it...whatever, back with us to the base?" Jackson asks, disbelief plain in his voice.

"Not...exactly," Kirsten smirks. "Let's just say we're gonna play a little game of hide and seek. We hide. He seeks."

"And what is he going to be seeking, if you don't mind my asking, ma'am?"

Kirsten's smile becomes positively predatory. "Androids."

**"Hey, soldier, how** far is it to Minot?"

As the sentry turns, Koda steps in to wedge her thumbs in his elbows, going for the nerves. His rifle drops to dangle against his belly, and she deftly relieves him of it before it can hit the ground. Behind the guard, only the glint of his eyes visible by the quarter moon, Tacoma raises both fists and brings them down on the unprotected back of the man's neck with a dull thud. He slumps, folding in on himself with a soft "Uhhhhh."

Dakota breaks his fall, laying him out face down in the grass while Tacoma pulls his hands behind him, slipping a length of self-locking plastic into place around his wrists. "That'll hold him for a while," he breathes. "Let's go."

"Right behind you, *thiblo*."

Tacoma slips into the tall grass before her, bending low to minimize the rippling wake in the purple spikes above him, black now in the moonlight except for the dangling chaff. Their shimmering silver echoes the moonsheen on Tacoma's form, and Koda's sight shifts almost imperceptibly to show her not a man but the lean muscularity of a stalking puma, his fur silver-gilt in the pale light. With that shift her own hearing becomes more acute, bringing her the small rustlings of mice and kangaroo rats as they go about their business under the shelter of the grass, bringing her the high-pitched whir of moth wings, the frequency so high it almost hurts her ears even now. Her feet tread lightly among the tangled stems and roots, yet it seems to her that if she looks down she will see the rectangular print of wolf pads, the indentations of claws.

She does not look down.

This has happened to her before, but never with this intensity. Her vision in the sweat lodge has changed her in ways she does not yet understand. She does not look at her hands, either, as she holds the grass apart from her passage.

A faint, pale smudge to her left, seen intermittently as she slips along like a shadow, tells her that they are moving parallel to the ranch road, moving toward whoever or whatever the sentry has been set to guard. After a time, the ground beneath her feet begins to slope and the grass to thin. It gives way to shorter plants, sidas and clover, bluebells with their dark cups, columbine with tails like shooting stars, white as ghosts under the moon. The ground opens up and flattens, and Tacoma crouches, making for a line of trees at a shambling run that only reinforces the unfocussed image of a tawny cat that overlays his human shape. Koda follows, her feet making no sound on crumbling earth and gravel. Great wings drift by overhead, and she shivers.

Owl. There is a death waiting in the night. She feels it in the chill of her blood, the touch of ice on her skin.

Not hers. Not Tacoma's.

Dakota drops to her belly beside her brother where he lies among the trees, looking intently at the ranch house and outbuildings a hundred yards ahead. Yellow light shows in the windows, soft and haloed. *Kerosene lamps or candles, then, not electric.* The space between the house and the barns is crowded close with vehicles: Jeeps in Air Force blue, desert camo Humvees, a pair of 60 millimeter guns on their own carriages. One barn also shows lights; the other stands dark. Barracks and ammo dump, most likely. There is no sign of droids. On the long, low porch of the house, an orange glimmer betrays a burning cigarette. Guard, probably.

Tacoma whistles almost soundlessly. "Got a bomb or two in your pocket, sis?"

"Left 'em back in the APC. Sorry."

"We don't have the firepower to take them, not even with the whole team."

Koda's blood stirs, hot and hungry and not entirely human. Her tongue runs along her lips. "Maybe," she says. "Maybe there's another way."

"Such as?"

"We don't need to take the weapons. Just the men."

Tacoma's finger jabs the darkness, counting the shapes in the farm-yard. "There's a dozen and a half transports and guns down there. Count three or four men for each one, and we're outnumbered even without their firepower. The odds are still bad. We'll have to skirt around them."

"One on one is even odds."

"**Unit grouping detected** six-point-two-seven kilometers west-north-west of this position."

From her place in the passenger's seat, Kirsten looks over her shoulder at the android crowded into the tiny space in the back. "How many? Have they spotted us yet?"

"Fourteen. Negative. These units are equipped with line of sight technology only."

"Okay, how close can we get to them before they spot us?"

"Two point three kilometers to the west of this position is a small ridge. Should you drive to the bottom of that ridge, you would be safe from their sensors. The pathway down is rather rutted and washed out, but I believe this vehicle is quite capable of making the descent with no untoward difficulties."

"Thank you, Max. Jackson, you heard the droid. Let's find that ridge and make tracks!"

The set of Jackson's jaw lets Kirsten know just how much he likes the order he's been given, but he follows it anyway, once again going against every single instinct that has kept him alive for the last of his twenty-seven years.

"Darius," she whispers, knowing the young man will hear her. "Please, trust me."

After a moment, the stiff bundle of muscles at his jaw loosens just slightly. "I do trust you, ma'am. It's..." His eyes flick to the rearview mirror, then back to the road in eloquent explanation.

"Trust me," Kirsten repeats, before hanging on for dear life as the truck pounds its way down the pitted, potholed road wannabe.

Several bone shaking moments later, they are at the bottom of the ridge, though Kirsten wonders if perhaps her stomach and kidneys are lying, quivering, back up at the top. "Wonder if you could call that an 'untoward difficulty'," she mutters, half to herself, earning a half grin from her driver and a purposefully blank stare from the android in the back.

Opening the door, she heaves her hurting carcass out of the truck, then eases the seat back over so that Max can extricate himself, which the android does with easy grace.

Exiting the truck, Jackson places himself between his president and the android, taking no chances. Kirsten notices the move, but says nothing, satisfied for the moment that at least he's not trying to ventilate their temporary ally.

They make their way up the rocky, vine-covered ridge until their heads are just below the lip. Max stops them there. "If you take care to keep hidden, you will be able to see the units just ahead."

Jackson takes the lead and peers over the very edge of the ravine. When his eyes clear the lip, he can see the westering sun glinting off of the plastic and metal casings of the androids. Kirsten quickly scrambles up beside him and likewise looks over the top. "Any idea what they're doing?" she asks Max who hunkers down beside her.

"I am not programmed to read their transmissions. However, from what I can interpret, they appear to be awaiting reinforcements."

"And they haven't spotted us."

"Not that I can detect."

"Okay, then. You know what to do."

"Affirmative."

Kirsten finds herself not quite knowing what to say. The android isn't human, and members of his kind have killed millions, if not billions, and enslaved millions more, subjecting them to rape and God knows what other tortures. And yet...and yet...she can't help, if not liking, at least appreciating the polite, soft spoken being that looks so human even she herself can't easily tell the difference.

Having no need for such pleasantries, he gives them both an android's approximation of a smile, a very good approximation, if the truth be known, and without further words, hops easily to the top of the ridge and strides off in the direction of his kindred.

Jackson sidles over closer, not quite able to hide the "I think you might have a screw loose somewhere" expression on his face. Kirsten doesn't really blame him, since his knowledge of this plan consists of the words "trust me", and nothing else. She sighs quietly. "Ask away, Lieutenant."

"Why are we letting an enemy, who knows where we are, go off to a whole group of other enemies so he can bring them back here and kill our asses? Ma'am."

"Darius, I know you've been very patient with me, and I appreciate it, believe me."

Jackson nods.

"But...in some cases, seeing something is much better than hearing about it. So I'll ask you one last time to trust me, if you can."

Taking his eyes off of the retreating android, he gazes at her for a very long moment, jaw working silently. "All right," he says finally. "We'll do it your way, ma'am."

"Thank you." An instant passes before she adds, "And Darius?"

"Yes, ma'am?"

"If they do start heading back this way..."

"Yes?"

"Run."

His hands go white-knuckled on his weapon as he once again peers in the direction of the android group, very shortly to be increased by one.

As both watch, Max is scanned and then accepted into the group, much to Kirsten's silent relief. It is only now that she wishes she'd thought far ahead enough to have attached a transceiver onto the droid so they could get back some information before his task is completed. *No use crying over fried circuits,* she thinks as she begins a silent countdown in her head.

At "one", she ducks down, grabbing Jackson by the shoulder and pulling him with her.

A loud, sharp cough-like sound rockets through the cool, still air, followed by the great *whoosh* of an explosion. Heedless of the possible danger, Jackson shakes loose from Kirsten's grip and pops his head up to see a giant plume of fire rush up from where the droid group used to stand.

"Holy FUCK!" he shouts. "What just happened?"

"Max," Kirsten retorts, quite unable to keep the smug expression from stealing over her face.

"Max? Your android...did *that*? But how?"

"He's what we're calling a 'suicide bomber droid'. Big government secret. One of those guys hit a convoy and did a good bit of damage to it, but we were able to gather up some of the remaining parts, and *voilà*! I simply changed the code from killing humans to killing androids, and there you have it. One good guy and a bunch of dead bad guys."

Jackson slowly turns to look at her, a whole ocean's worth of new respect shining in his light-colored eyes. "Jesus Christ, ma'am! That was...amazing! Shit! How many more of those bad boys do you have wandering around?"

"As of now, twenty five, plus any more that they manage to make back at the plant. I changed the code for all of them."

"So, why don't we go back and get 'em all now? Man, this kicks ass!"

"First off, Lieutenant, where would we put twenty five androids in this truck?"

"Hell, ma'am! We'll send out a damn convoy for these suckers!"

"Secondly," Kirsten interrupts, holding up a hand as she watches the flames continue to burn, "we can't let the regular androids who are making these new units in on the secret. If we do, obviously — no more androids for us. So, we wait as long as we can, then we send that convoy of yours back down here, and take it from there."

Jackson looks back over at the killing field, the grin on his face a mile wide. "Whatever you say, ma'am. Whatever you say."

# CHAPTER THIRTY-EIGHT

"What?" Tacoma's voice hisses with alarm. "Oh, no. Don't you even—"

"Cover me," Dakota says, getting to her feet and starting toward the house below. Her own rifle slants across her back; she carries the weapon captured from the sentry in full view, its curved magazine marking it as an AK. One of theirs. They will assume she has killed their man for it. Behind her, Tacoma is swearing, violently and very softly. He cannot cover her, and they both know it. If her plan works, he will not need to.

She is ten yards from the sentry before he sees her. "Hey!" he yells, dropping the stub of his cigarette as he fumbles to bring his rifle to bear. "Who's out there? Identify yourself!"

"Dakota Rivers," she says, moving from the shadow of one vehicle to the next, keeping their metal bulk between her and the guard. "I want to talk to your commander."

"Yeah?" He snorts. "You got an appointment? Step out here into the light, or I'll shoot." He raises his rifle.

"Put that down, soldier. Go tell your captain there's somebody to see him." What he does is of no consequence. His shouting will bring the others out into the open in a moment or two, and that is what she wants — his shouting, or a gunshot.

"Fuck!" he yells, and fires. The shot goes wide, clanging off the armored hide of a Humvee behind her.

Koda brings her own gun to her shoulder and squeezes the trigger gently. The guard drops onto the boards of the porch, screaming. And finally the doors of the house and barn slam open, and men pour out into the night, surrounding her. Just what she wants.

"Good evening, gentlemen," she says, and grins at them.

They are young and grubby and unshaven, most of them half-dressed in camouflage pants or shorts, most of them carrying rifles or pistols pointed at the ground rather than the intruder. Most of them green as the prairie grass that grows in a sea around their camp. One of them sidesteps his way through the parked vehicles to the side of the man doubled over on the porch. "Jem? Jem! You fuckin' bitch, what'd you do to my brother?"

"Quiet!" The roar comes from the porch, somewhere behind the hapless Jem. An older man steps into the light, his grizzled hair buzz-cut, the planes of his face smooth and sharp in the hard light. "What's going on here?" Gold maple leaves glint on his square shoulders, and he holds a nine-millimeter pistol loosely in his hand, not aimed. It does not need to be.

"Major," Koda says, stepping out from among the parked Jeeps. "You're the commander here?" It is not really a question, only a confirmation. She keeps her eyes on his face, not his gun. If he is going to shoot, she will see it in his eyes.

"Calton," he says. "Ted Calton. Who the Hell are you?" He ignores Jem, now being helped to his feet and led away by his brother.

"Dakota Rivers." For a split second his eyes widen; then the steel is back. "You've heard of me."

"We've heard what happened on the Cheyenne," he acknowledges. "That was good work."

Koda makes a show of looking around her, her finger still light on the trigger of her weapon. "I don't see any droids here."

"And you won't. We've destroyed every one we've found."

"Good work," she echoes. "Want to do some more of it?"

"We do more of it every day." Calton moves forward, standing on the highest step. "We protect the people and the land around Minot."

"For a price?"

"For a price." Something that is almost a smile touches his mouth. "We can't patrol and farm, too. The civilians are grateful."

Koda raises her voice to carry to the barn and the men still hovering in the door there. "The droids and their allies are massing around Offut and to the west. We expect them to try to take out Ellsworth, again. If they get through us, they'll roll over you. We have a common interest."

"Not necessarily. If you stop them, they won't bother us. If you don't stop them — well, we don't have what they want, now do we? No high-powered cyberwonks here."

Cold runs over Dakota's skin. But of course they know Kirsten is at Ellsworth; the same tales that brought her own name north would have brought Kirsten's and Maggie's. Blind Harry's ballad is sung here, too, for all she knows. "You have lives," she says evenly. "And you have weapons. If those civilians include women, the droids have a use for them, too."

"Breedstock?" Calton snorts. "We've heard those stories. What the Hell would a droid want with human pussy?"

"More humans. We don't know why, yet." She raises her voice. "You men! You want your wives and girlfriends, your sisters, shipped off to be bred by the kind of scum the droids keep alive to do their work? We killed the rapists at Mandan when we bombed the droid factory. We just executed a second batch at Ellsworth. How many have you caught?"

A murmur ripples through the knots of men, and a scowl appears on Calton's face. He glances quickly about the perimeter of the farm buildings; he has to assume that she has troops in place to cover her. "We deal with anyone who threatens us. Anyone. Got that?"

Koda grins at him, and again she feels the heat course through her blood. "That B-52 back in the field yours? Got anything to protect you from high-altitude fighters?"

"You still got planes?" Calton shrugs and gestures with his gun. "Doesn't matter. Go back to your people. Tell 'em no deal. We stay here and protect what we've got."

"You men!" Koda shouts. "What do you think about that? Are you going to sit here on your butts and miss the chance to get your world back? Or are you coming south with me?"

"I'm going." One trooper, a bit older than most of the others, steps out of the ring of men. Another follows, then three more.

The roar of Calton's gun splits the night. "The Hell you are! Get back in your quarters, all of you! This is my command! As for you," he lowers the pistol he has fired into the air to aim at Koda, "get the Hell out, while you can."

Carefully Koda raises the gun strap over her head and lays the AK aside. It seems to her that she hears the breath of every man around her, harsh and rushing like winter wind. She smells their sweat, the fear in some, arousal in others. The flesh of Calton's face lies lightly on the bone, so that she can almost see through it to the white skull beneath, see his death. "I'll fight you for them," she says.

"What?" Fear flickers in his eyes, is gone.

"I'll fight you for your command. You win, you keep your men. I win, they go with me." Her words fall into silence.

"Fight you?" Calton glances at his pistol. "How?"

For answer, Koda bends and draws the knife from her boot-top. The light catches its ten-inch blade, runs along it like quicksilver. "Like this."

He is trapped, and knows it. His eyes widen, then narrow again. He cannot afford hesitation. "All right," he says. Setting the pistol on a windowsill behind him, he draws the knife from his own belt. "Don't expect me to go easy on you because you're a woman, though."

Dakota laughs, tossing her blade end for end and catching it again. The men shift to form a ring around them in the open space between the farmhouse and the parked vehicles. Someone brings a kerosene lamp to set at the perimeter of the circle, then another. Their light throws Calton's shadow and her own huge on the ground, distorted, creatures with impossibly long legs and arms sprouting from attenuated bodies. Slowly they circle each other, Koda keeping her eyes on Calton's face. His blade glints in her peripheral vision, shines like a beacon to her heightened vision.

He feints, cutting low for the belly, and Koda steps lightly out of his reach, spinning wide to her left. He turns with her, but too slowly, and she whips toward him, her blade opening a gash on his upper arm. His blood runs black in the dim light.

Voices come to her on the wind of her passing, but she does not heed them. "Surrender," she says.

For answer he attempts to close with her again, this time coming on straight at her. She blocks his upward stab with a sweep of her left arm, whirling again out of his reach. Her wrist is cold and wet, but the cut is shallow. It stings, barely perceptible. The blood from Calton's cut, though, falls on the earth in dark spurts. She need only avoid injury, wear him down.

He knows it, too. Fear flickers across his face, is gone. With a yell, he comes in low and fast, butting at her with his head while his knife goes for the tendons in her left leg. She rolls with the blow, planting a foot in his gut to carry him up and over, to land hard on his back behind her. Koda scrambles to her feet, stepping hard on the wrist of his knife hand with the heel of her boot. His fingers open, and she kicks the blade away.

Behind her a cheer starts up, to be abruptly broken off as Calton grabs at her ankle, turning it hard to bring her down with him. She falls halfway across his body, rolls as he surges off his back to pin her, reaching for her throat with both hands. His fingers close around her neck, bearing on her windpipe and the great veins. Pressing down and back, seeking the leverage that will break her neck, his grip tightens as she gasps for breath, her chest grown suddenly tight. Calton's face is a grinning skull mask above her. A shadow passes over her eyes, and she brings her knife up between their straining bodies, finds the soft spot just beneath the join of the rib cage. She thrusts straight up, the blade grating on bone, then making easy passage through the soft tissue of liver and lung, cutting upward. For a moment Calton remains above her, his hands tightening convulsively about her throat, bringing on the darkness. Then he collapses across her, blood running from his mouth in a black torrent, and he is dead.

Silence holds her. Then she pushes Calton off her to stagger to her feet. His blood stains her hands, her face, her shirt, dark and wet in the dim light.

Then the sound begins, softly at first, the men chanting her name. "Koda. Koda." The murmur becomes a shout, swells, grows to a roar. "Koda! Ko-da! Ko-da!"

She lets it wash over her, drawing strength from it. She raises her head to search the faces around her, mouths straining, eyes wide. These are her men, now. Won in battle, paid for in blood. The thought sends a shiver down her spine, and she throws her head back, howling wordlessly with them.

"Koda! Koda!" It goes on and on, the rhythm carried on stamping feet. Finally she raises an arm to silence them. They quiet gradually, as her senses contract about her, and she is one human woman again, standing in a circle of men who are not entirely sure what has happened to them. "All right," she says quietly. "Get your gear. We're pulling out now."

They move to obey, all but one. Tacoma stands before her, his eyes dark. "Are you all right?" he says. "The blood—"

"Not mine." She glances down at her ruined shirt. "Not most of it, anyway."

"What happened? For a moment there, I didn't know you."

She meets his gaze steadily, seeing herself though his eyes. The fight...and the kill. "You saw it all?"

He nods.

"For a moment there, I didn't know myself," she says slowly. "It's as though something — slipped. It's happened a couple times since — since—"

"Since your vision?"

"Yeah. I feel...different. Inside. Things look different. My hearing is different."

"You talked to *Até*?"

Her hand makes a small arc in the darkness. "About some of it. This was almost like that time on the bridge. I felt — out of myself, somehow."

Some of the rigidity goes out her brother's shoulders, and he says, "It's the warrior-gift growing in you. It can be hard to live with." He glances down at Calton's body. "Did you mean to challenge him all along?"

She shakes her head. "That just happened. But it was so — familiar. Like I'd done it before. Like the knife was part of my arm. It knew what to do. I never thought."

Tacoma gives her shoulders a quick squeeze, stepping away from her as the first of the troopers emerges from the barn, his pack on his back, his rifle slung about his neck. The others follow, coming to stand beside the Jeeps and Humvees. Tacoma's presence does not seem to surprise them. Like Calton, they must have assumed that Koda had men all around them. Let them continue to assume.

Tacoma steps toward one of the Jeeps, glances at the ignition. "Keys?" he asks the man nearest him.

"In the glove compartment, sir."

Tacoma fishes for them, finds them. Koda comes to stand by the passenger door and shouts, "All right! We're moving out! Follow me!"

They cheer again, and again she feels their energy surge within her, obliterating the pain of her cut, the bruises on her throat. She slips into her seat, and Tacoma steers the Jeep out onto the road.

Behind them the rest follow, raising a cloud of luminous dust in the moonlight.

**The convoy moves** swiftly through the night, the full moon riding high in a blaze of stars, bright enough to cast shadows in a world where the glare of civilization no longer rimlights the horizon. Koda dozes fitfully in the lead Jeep, the APCs from Ellsworth dispersed at regular intervals down the line to ride herd on their new recruits and guard against second thoughts. The tide of adrenaline that carried her through the duel has spent itself, leaving behind a strange restlessness. Her dreams, when she sleeps, are full of drifting voices.

Dawn comes on a chilled breeze as the gates of Ellsworth roll open to receive them. The startled MP salutes as Koda passes, Tacoma returning the gesture with a snap of his own wrist. In the rearview mirror, Dakota can see the guard counting off the vehicles that follow her in, easily a dozen more than had followed her out. The men in the Jeeps and APCs cheer as they pass the sentry box, honking and waving their rifles in the air.

"Better see the colonel first," Tacoma says quietly.

Koda rolls her head back, attempting to work the knots out of her shoulders and upper back. "They're not exactly the supplies we meant to pick up, are they? Try her office first."

They catch Maggie just as she closes the door behind her, probably on her way from her cramped work space cum living quarters to the mess hall for breakfast. Koda watches her back straighten, then stiffen, as she spots the caravan sweeping up the length of the runway toward her, taking in its length and the unfamiliar Minot ID codes on the vehicles. Her fists settle on her hips as Tacoma pulls up directly in front of her, her eyebrows rising halfway to her hairline while a smile pulls at her mouth. "Well, now," she says. "Look what the cat dragged in."

Tacoma grins at her as he climbs out of the Jeep. "Thought you'd like 'em." Turning to the line of Jeeps and troop carriers, he bellows, "Pile out! Form up!"

As the men scramble out of their trucks and prepare to stand the colonel's inspection, Dakota levers herself up and out the passenger door, feeling the blood rush into her tingling feet, the ache as the sinews of her joints stretch and flex. The bruises on her neck throb with her pulse.

Maggie flashes her a grin of welcome, then her eyes widen, raking Koda from the reddening marks on her skin, down the front of her shirt, still stiff with dried blood, to the stained length of torn T-shirt wrapped around her left forearm.

"Sorry, I haven't had a chance to wash up," Koda says. "It's not mine, or most of it isn't."

"I do not," Maggie says precisely, "see any injuries on anyone else. Tell me what I'm missing here."

Koda shrugs. "What's missing is these men's former commander."

"You killed him?"

Dakota nods. "It was a fair fight."

"A. Fair. Fight." Maggie lays out each word precisely. "And the prize was his men?"

"Them and their equipment. At least, they seemed to think so."

"They're from Minot?"

"They're what's left of it. They were fighting droids and running a protection racket while they were at it." Koda turns slightly to watch as they form ranks, straggling into line under the whip of Tacoma's voice. "They had ambitions. They tried to get a B-52 operational. It crashed."

The blood leaves Maggie's face, leaving her skin grey. "Gods. They could have blackmailed the whole damn country, what's left of it. We don't need loose nukes."

"We need to get control of those bombs." Koda swipes a hand over her face, and stares at her palm when it comes away red. There is blood even in her hair. "Not today, not this side of battle. But before someone else gets ideas."

"You need to get a shower and go to bed," Maggie says flatly. "Anything else can wait."

"I'm not—"

"No argument. Larke!"

The airman double-times it from one of the mid-line APCs. "Ma'am?"

"Drive Dr. Rivers home. Don't let her argue with you."

Larke glances from the colonel to Koda and back again. "Yes, ma'am. To the best of my ability, ma'am."

"Have mercy on him," Maggie says pointedly. "We'll talk later."

Koda cannot quite bring herself to order Larke to disobey his colonel. She does not particularly want to go back to the house, though, doubts she can sleep with the strange energy that hums through her. A part of her still lingers in the night just past, in the ring of fire and shadow where she killed a warlord for his command. Or, more accurately, the fight has stayed with her, a humming in her blood. It is something she has never felt before, yet it seems familiar. She could name it, if only she could find the word on her tongue.

"Ma'am? Doctor Koda?"

Larke holds the passenger door for her. She is not sure whether it is archaic courtesy or whether he can think of no other polite way to get her to move. Surrendering, she folds back down into the seat she has occupied for most of the past eight hours and lets him steer the Jeep for home.

Over the mile's distance from flightline to officers' housing, soldiers salute her as she passes. That, too, seems strangely familiar. She waves briefly back, noting with satisfaction that Shannon is turning the sign on the clinic door to OPEN as they drive by without stopping, her insistence that they do so dying in her throat. As they round the former parade ground, now thick with rough wooden markers for the dead of the Cheyenne, she makes note of three new plots of disturbed earth. There is no memorial for them.

The house is chill and empty. *Asimov must be out with Kirsten, wherever she is.* Her absence is a dark void inside Koda, and the sharpness of her disappointment gnaws at her. Kirsten could not have known that she would return early. She had not known it herself. She sheds her clothes in the hall and heads for the shower.

Koda shivers as she stands on the bathmat, the breeze that stirs the curtains ghosting over her skin. Despite the morning's brightness, it leaves no warmth behind it, and she feels the gooseflesh rise and tighten along her arms. More out of habit than conviction, she turns on the hot tap and lets the water run while she collects towel and washcloth from the tall, narrow cabinet above the clothes bin. The stench of blood is on her still, mingled with sweat and dirt and the oil-and-metal smell of the APC. She is used to blood and used to smelling of it. You cannot, after all, turn a breech foal or perform emergency field surgery and remain clean. It goes with the job.

Killing a man in a duel and taking his warband for prize does not go with a veterinarian's job. It does not go with a warrior's job, either, she reflects. Or it has not, at least for the last thousand years or so.

Yet there was nothing in it that was strange, or unfamiliar to her. There had been a pattern to the encounter, a choreography that revealed itself as the fight played out. It was as if she had been thrust out in front of the footlights in riding boots and a complete innocence of Tchaikovsky, and had danced a perfect Swan Queen. Tacoma had called it the warrior spirit waking within her, growing. He should know. As she had been called to the life of a shaman, he had been born a warrior. Strange, that like as they are, each has been given the other's heart's desire.

Koda steps into the shower and pulls the curtain to keep off the draft. The water hits her like a rush of snowmelt, so cold it burns. Her hand, half numb, closes on the soap, and she begins to work it into a lather on the bathsponge. Gritting her teeth, she stands still, shivering, watching as the brown stains on her skin liquify and sluice down her body, swirling crimson around the drain at her feet. She unwraps the length of cotton around her arm and lets her own blood join the flow. *As if*, she thinks, *we were making relatives in the* Hunkapi. At that moment, her enemy seems as close as her own brothers and sisters, as her own lover.

**Kirsten pushes open** the kitchen door, feeling pleasantly warm and loose from the half-mile run from the woods to the officers' housing section. Asi, not at all tired from the exercise, gives a high, loud yip as he shoulders past her, sending the door banging against the wall next to the fridge, and dances across the tiles to his empty bowl. "All right. All right. It's coming."

She rummages about in the pantry, looking for the base's last surviving box of Milk Bones. The ancient pipes in the wall hum and thump with water; Maggie must have come in for a shower and change of clothes. With the thought comes disappointment. *Koda is not due back from Minot for at least another day, assuming everything goes well. And when*, she reflects, *is the last time everything went smoothly*? Sometime in a past life, when she was a Washington wonk and had barely heard of South Dakota, still less of a woman named Dakota Rivers.

Asi yelps again, louder and more urgently. Kirsten stifles a surge of guilt at the thought that the big dog — the big baby, truth be told — has missed her so badly, even though he clearly has not lacked for attention. "Think of it as gaining a second mother," she says as she finds the box and rips it open. "Twice the attention, twice the walks. Twice the flea baths."

She turns to toss him the treat, but he is no longer there. From the hallway comes the sound of whining, the sharp click of his nails on the hardwood floor. Frowning, she sets the box on the counter and follows just in time to see him fling his whole weight against the bathroom door, shaking it on its aged hinges. From deep in his throat comes a howl like the winter wind over snow, and Kirsten's breath catches in her throat, then resumes on a sigh of relief. On the floor, strewn in careless abandon, lie a pair of jeans, a shirt, underclothes. The flannel shirt, in Black Watch tartan, she recognizes as Koda's. "Easy, boy," she says, pulling at Asi's scruff, and lays her free hand on the knob. She grins. A shower *a deux* is just what Dr. King would have ordered for herself had she known her lover was home early. Asi batters at the door a second time, and in a shaft of light from the lamp in the front room she sees what Asi has smelled since they came through the kitchen door: almost all of the shirt, and both legs of the jeans, are soaked stiff with something half-dried, something the color of rust. The sharp scent of iron rises from them.

*Blood.*

"Koda!" she screams, and throws herself against the door.

**Just as Dakota** turns off the frigid water pelting down on her, Asi's deep bay sounds in the hall and the door shakes on its hinges. The dog's howl comes again, with a second battering against the door, and with it Kirsten's voice, high pitched in fear. "Koda!"

**Kirsten's weight hits** the door for the second time, and suddenly its solidity is gone, giving way before her and carrying her straight into Dakota where she stands wet and naked on the bathmat, her hair streaming down her back and over her breasts like dark floodwater, water and blood puddled on the floor, still dripping red from a long, shallow cut visible on her forearm.

The cold water soaks through Kirsten's thin shirt, chilling her. But it is fear that causes her to shudder as she pushes Koda away, holding her by both arms as her eyes run the length her body, searching for the source of the blood on the clothing still lying in a heap on the floor, and of the blood that still runs down her arm to soak into the mat. But there is only the single wound, clearly not lethal, only a crimson thread, no longer bleeding, against the copper of Dakota's skin. Kirsten's heart, lodged in her throat, slips back into its accustomed place and she begins to breathe again. "All that blood," she gasps. "It isn't yours."

"Not mine, no," Koda echoes. "I killed a man."

Fingers tighten on Dakota's arms, making small white marks where they dig into the skin. "At Minot? They fought you?"

"Not 'they'. Just one." Koda's eyes are on hers, a light in them that is part triumph, part desire, part something else she cannot name. "We took his men from him."

"We?" Kirsten asks carefully. "You mean 'you'."

"I challenged him. None of our soldiers was killed, none of his. Just him."

Once again, Kirsten sees the tall figure racing ahead of her onto the shattered bridge at the Cheyenne, dark hair streaming behind her like smoke. Once again, the fear strikes through her, this time without the hum of adrenaline in the blood that had drawn her out of herself and propelled her across the pile of tumbled concrete after the other woman. She is still not sure whether she acted from blind trust or blind panic. "How dare you," she says softly, the words hissing between her teeth, "when so much depends on you."

"When what depends on me?" Dakota steps closer, so that Kirsten can hear her breathing, not quite steady now. The light from the open window, glancing through the blowing curtains, shimmers over Koda's wet skin, slipping over her shoulders and breasts like silk.

She is made lean and hard, lithe muscles stretched over long bones. The form of the hunting animal, elegant in understatement — long-legged cheetah moving with harsh and angular grace through the high grass, gerfalcon stooping on her prey like a meteor out of the blue Heaven.

"I depend on you, goddammit." A tremor runs through her, part fear, part not. "You have no right to risk yourself alone."

"I wasn't in any danger. No greater than we face here, every day."

Kirsten opens her mouth to make the obvious retort, but instead looks away, silent. *I risked as much, myself. Hypocrite. But if she died, I would be so alone. So alone. Again. Intolerable.*

Her breath catching, Kirsten runs her hands up Koda's arms, over her shoulders and up into her hair, pulling her head down. Dakota's mouth meets hers, hot and open, and Kirsten's tongue traces the austere lines of the other's lips, savoring the heat and the acerbic tang of salt. Koda pulls back abruptly, lowering her head to Kirsten's throat to trace a line of hard kisses from her ear to the hollow of her collarbones.

She can feel the heat of Dakota's skin through her clothing, the hardness of her nipples through the thin fabric of her T-shirt. Fire begins in the cleft between her legs, licks down her thighs and up her spine, knotting in her belly. "Bedroom," she gasps, pulling back just enough to move, drawing Koda after her by the hand.

Dakota growls deep in her throat. The scent of blood on the clothes at her feet stirs her, a primal, animal sensation that is equal parts rage and lust.

The lust of the battle she's fought.

The lust of the blood she's spilled.

The lust of the woman who stands before her, so open and so ready.

It all coalesces within her, a spiral of red and black, pulsing with the beat of her heart, growing more acute as the scent of blood mingles with the scent of Kirsten's need and the scent of her own. It pulls each muscle taut, tension thrumming like a live wire, threatening to burn out of control with the tiniest of sparks.

Pausing only to kick the pile of bloody clothing out of view into the bathroom, Kirsten leads Dakota into the bedroom that has become theirs. Like a distant drum, Koda feels the pounding of her blood in its hidden channels, flowing as hot as molten earth from the veins of Ina Maka. As she moves, Kirsten's free hand claws at the fastening of her jeans, pushing them down around her ankles where she can step free of them. Her boots follow, and she looses Dakota's hand just long enough to pull her shirt over her head, flinging it unheeded onto the floor.

"You hunger," Kirsten states as she stares up into a face haloed with black silk and lighted by heated silver eyes.

"Yes."

"Show me."

Fully naked, Dakota presses her roughly down onto the bed and stands for a long moment, taking in the compact body before her. Her sight narrows, hunter vision, and she runs her eyes over Kirsten's face, open now, with a hunger to match her own, eyes dilated to midnight pools in their thin rim of green. She notes the pool of shadow at the base of the throat where the pulse beats visibly in its blue vein; her breasts rising and falling in short, sharp spasms, tight rippled flesh about her nipples; the hollows of ribcage and belly; the shadows between the lean legs. "*Mitawa*," she growls, low in her throat. "*Winan mitawa.*"

She kneels on the bed, predator, hunter, running one hand over Kirsten's belly, tracing the hollows of her hipbones, slipping between her thighs. The pulse beats there, too, against her hand as Kirsten's legs part for her and she runs her thumb through the soft curling hair to spread the lips of her lover's sex. The wetness flows free there, and she growls, deep and long.

She feels Kirsten's body jerk as she finds the nub of her clitoris, circling it slowly, pressing hard against its hardness. Her mouth follows and Kirsten moans, a low, animal sound, as her hands tangle in Koda's hair. Dakota scarcely feels it, caught up in the throbbing of flesh against her mouth, the blood singing against her lips. She pulls away abruptly, running fingers down the wet curve of flesh, sinking fingers deep into Kirsten's body and withdrawing only to thrust again and again, feeling the other woman's hips buck against the long, hard strokes. Growling, needing, she adds another finger, feeling the tender tissues stretch to their limit as she pushes inside, curling her fingers into blunt claws.

From somewhere comes a cry, piercing and wild, and hot liquid flows over her hand and Kirsten's thighs. Kirsten's body shudders as the waves of orgasm beat over her, pounding their rhythm against Koda's hand.

Kirsten feels the cry leave her throat, a wild thing escaping into the air. Her body shudders with the force of her coming, pleasure so intense it is hardly distinguishable from pain, shaking her flesh loose from her bones. Above her she sees the strong curve of Koda's spine, the fall of her hair spilling down her back like a cataract. Her lover's fingers withdraw from her; Koda turns to trace curving signs on her belly with her own essence.

"*Mitawa*," she says, huskily. "Mine."

"Mine," Kirsten echoes. "*You're* mine."

Rolling over onto her side, she brings Koda down beside her, covering the long body with her own. "Mine," she says again, tongue outlining Koda's mouth, licking away the fine beads of sweat that have gathered over her lip. Moving down the column of her neck, she laps at the moisture there, savoring the salt taste mingled with the sharp sweetness of lavender that runs along her tongue. *Drunk*, says the small part of her mind still capable of words. *Drunk with her.*

Koda stretches under her, her hips lifting blindly, searching. "Wait," says Kirsten. Beneath her lips, Koda's throat vibrates with a small, incoherent sound — half moan, half growl. In answer, Kirsten presses her down against the bed again and sinks her teeth into Koda's shoulder, tasting salt again as blood flows.

"Damn vampire," Koda breathes, her fingers digging into Kirsten's arm.

But Kirsten pulls away, biting her own forearm this time, pressing the flesh with its thin red trickle against Dakota's lips, feeling sharp white teeth against the edge of the wound as Koda sucks at it. Kirsten draws her arm away, then, and brings her own mouth down on Dakota's, now stained as scarlet as her own. She feels a shudder pass through Koda's body as their tongues meet, tasting themselves and each other. *Blood of my blood.* The phrase floats up from some dark place in her mind.

"*Hunka.*" It is Koda's voice, no more than a breath ghosting over her ear.

She does not know the word, though she knows what it must mean. Bound now, inseparable. For this life and forever. Her mouth moves to Koda's breast, tongue swirling around the nipple, her free hand slipping down the smooth skin of her flank to slip between her legs. They part for her, and she trails her fingers along the tender skin, rakes through the triangle of dark curls at their apex, slips her fingertip into the growing wetness beneath her hand, withdraws to trace again the long muscles of flank and thigh. Koda's head tosses against the quilt, eyes narrowed to blue slits, her breath coming in small, hard gasps. "What do you want?" Kirsten whispers. "Tell me."

"Want—"

"Is it this?" Kirsten's hand covers Koda's sex, spreading the flesh wide to press her mouth against the clitoris, tracing its shape with her tongue. She feels Koda tense, her climax gathering, and withdraws. "Or is it this?" she asks, her fingers following her mouth, then sliding down to circle the hot entrance to Koda's body.

"Want—"

"Tell me."

"Fuck me," Koda gasps. "Now. Now!"

"Oh, yes," Kirsten answers, and slips her fingers inside, holding still.

Past words now, Koda thrusts her hips against Kirsten's hand, and Kirsten at last begins to move in long, slow strokes, her thumb finding the clitoris again, pressing and releasing, then swirling over the distended head until Koda's spine arches and her body goes rigid. Looking up, Kirsten can see the pulse where it hammers against her lover's neck, point counterpoint to the frantic beating of blood under her hand. Koda cries out wordlessly as her climax takes her, rippling through the taut belly under Kirsten's hand.

"*Mitawa,*" Koda murmurs again after a time that seems to stretch into infinity. "*Winyan mitawa. Cante mitawa.*"

"*Mitawa,*" Kirsten agrees, drained now. She rocks back on her heels, then shifts to lie beside Koda, who slips an arm under her head. Dakota's eyes slide closed, and darkness takes them both.

**For the second** time this day, Koda emerges shivering from the shower. She wraps one of Maggie's luxurious towels around her — another amenity that is among the last of its kind; there will be no more Egyptian cotton anytime soon. She snatches her clean clothes from the hooks on the door and runs the half-dozen steps to the kitchen.

Kirsten already has soup on the stove, with the oven lit and its door open.

Within the compass of its heat, Koda pauses in the doorway, struck once again by the compact grace of Kirsten's body as she goes about the mundane tasks of preparing a belated lunch. Her shorts and tank top leave her arms and legs bare, browned skin smooth over muscle attesting to unexpected toughness. Her hair, drying rapidly in the warm air, curls around her ears and over the back of her neck. The late afternoon light streaming through the window as she sets out bowls and spoons touches it to gold.

The sight brings a flush of warmth to Koda's skin, mingling with the heat from the stove as she steps over Asi's snoring bulk, unfurls the towel and begins to rub herself dry. But she says only, "Grandma Lula used to talk about how she and her brothers bathed in a big aluminum washtub in front of the stove back on the rez. Maybe we should start doing that, too."

"Grandma Lula?" Kirsten flashes her a smile and an inquiring glance. "Reservation?"

"My mom's mother. Pine Ridge. She believed that suffering is good for you. Builds character."

"Catholic school?"

"Oh, yeah. That's why *Ina's* such a radical. Equal and opposite reaction."

Kirsten sets the last of the silverware on the table, then turns to face her. "Your mother's going to object, isn't she?"

There is no need to ask what Themunga will object to, no need to skirt the answer. Koda lays the towel over the back of a chair and begins to pull on her clothes. "She's going to have a conniption, if she hasn't already. But *Até* will win her over." She pauses for a moment, head buried in a long-sleeved denim shirt. "He already counts you as a daughter, you know. So will she, given a little time to get used to the idea. It doesn't hurt that you're already picking up some Lakota ways."

Kirsten's mouth twitches in a quizzical smile. "Like talking to raccoons?"

"Among other things." Koda grins in return. "Not even Themunga would argue with one of the four-foot spirits."

"Mm," Kirsten observes noncommittally. "How's your arm?"

"Just a scratch." Koda rolls up her right sleeve, peels the backing off a clear Coloplast bandage and slaps it over the no longer bleeding cut. "Next week you won't even know it was there."

"Sure I won't. Let's eat."

The meal is simple, lentils and vegetables stewed together; they are rationing the meat brought by Wanblee Wapka because there is no time to hunt, and no rancher thins his herd in the spring. It occurs to Koda that there is a certain optimism in the assumption that they will last as long as their supply of protein. Unless they win the upcoming confrontation, it will hardly matter whether there is meat for the next month or not. "So," she says, sopping a piece of frybread in the savory broth, "what did you find out about that bomber droid while I was gone?"

Kirsten drops her eyes, giving her entire attention to the soup plate in front of her. "Pass the bread?" As Dakota hands her the basket, she says, "I found the control code. So I made a few more of them."

The tone is so casual that it almost gets by, but the sheer improbability of it snags on Koda's brain and hangs there, flapping in the breeze. She sets her spoon down carefully. "Say again, please."

Suddenly losing interest in her own food, Kirsten pushes her bowl away with a short, sharp gesture. "I said, I found the code and made some more bomber droids."

It makes no more sense to Koda than it did the first time. Granted, Kirsten is brilliant in her field and could probably rig a working computer out of string and paperclips and a few printed circuits. But the base does not have the materials to make a convincing android, much less "a few more" of a very specialized model. Not in the space of three days. "What," she says, "did you make them from?"

"The droids that are already assembled. At the plant down at Butte."

Butte is just over the state line in eastern Nebraska, perilously close to Offut and the massing enemy. Dakota leans her forehead on her clasped hands. "You want to tell me about it, or do I have to keep playing twenty questions?"

Kirsten reaches across the table to touch her arm briefly. "It was no big deal. I put together a patch that will make the suicide droid target other droids instead of humans. Then I went down to Butte, did my biodroid act, and installed it in their inventory. I tested it. It worked. End of story."

"Tested it on what?"

"A squad of military units."

Koda lifts her head from her hands, her eyes on Kirsten's face. "When did you decide to go?"

There is no sign of a struggle there; the clear green gaze meets her own. "When Jimenez brought me the part of the bomber droid that gave me the idea. Before you left for Minot."

At least there will be no lie between them. It is cold comfort. "You might have mentioned it." Koda speaks very clearly, biting off the words. "Say, just in passing. Something like, 'Koda, I'm going to risk my life and everybody else's chance of survival on a solo, possibly suicidal mission to a droid plant.' Would that have been so hard?"

"Yes," Kirsten snaps. "It would have."

"You had no right!" Koda's fist comes down on the table, rattling the soup bowls. "You're the President! You're the fucking Commander-in-Chief! Get used to it!"

"I had the obligation, the goddamned fucking obligation!"

Kirsten rises and flings away from the table, facing for a moment out the window. Koda cannot see her face, only the rise and fall of her back with her rapid breathing. When she turns, the color has risen in her face, flushing her skin from the base of her throat to her forehead, turning her tan almost to copper.

"I can't ask anyone else to take risks I won't take myself, Dakota. That includes the lowest private on the base. That includes Maggie." She pauses a moment. "And that includes you."

"Goddam it, Kirsten. No president since Washington has led his own troops, much less—"

"Much less fought Cornwallis for his!" Kirsten's chin comes up, eyes blazing. "Don't talk to me about not having the right. The world has changed, Koda. You know that."

A silence stretches out between them, spun fine along the currents of anger. Koda's eyes linger along the red line of her wound, visible under the cloudy plastic of its dressing. Finally she says, "Fair enough. But why didn't you tell me?"

"Because I could have died." At that Koda looks up, searching Kirsten's face as she goes on more quietly. "Or you could have, only I had no idea how. And I didn't want this fight to be the last of us."

"I wouldn't have—"

"Yes, you would. I'd have tried to stop you, too, if I'd known you were going to fight a duel."

"I'd have gone with you."

"And you wouldn't have been where you were really needed." Kirsten meets her gaze levelly. "There are things only you can do. Things only I can do. We have to acknowledge that."

"I don't like it."

"I don't like it, either. But we are what we are."

Stalemate. *Don't leave me! Don't you leave me!* The words echo in the dark places of Koda's mind, driven on the wind of panic. But she will not speak them. Instead she says, very quietly, "I don't want to lose you."

After a moment Kirsten steps around the table to lay her hands on Dakota's shoulders. "You won't. We'll see this out together, wherever it leads."

Koda turns in her seat, covering Kirsten's hand with her own and laying a soft kiss on her wrist. "Wherever." She feels Kirsten's arms slip down over hers, soft hair tickling her cheek, followed by soft lips, and leans back into the embrace, giving herself up to her lover's persuasion. "If you keep this up..." she murmurs.

"We'll end up back in bed. Hmm?"

"You have anything better to do?"

"Not a thing." Very delicately, Kirsten bites the side of her neck.

"Vampire."

Koda draws Kirsten around to stand before her, then down, straddling her lap. "There's really something to be said for this kiss and make up thing, you know? Let's—"

She never finishes her suggestion. A fist falls on the door like a hammer, and Jackson follows it into the room as it swings open and Asi scambles to his feet, baying. "Ms. President! Ma'am— Oh." He fixes his gaze on a point somewhere midway the lintel of the door.

"Quiet, Asi!" Kirsten gets to her feet and turns to face the lieutenant with what Koda considers remarkable aplomb under the circumstances. "What is it, Jackson?"

"Ma'am!" he gasps. "The colonel's compliments, and would you both please come to her office. General Hart has gone missing!"

**Maggie looks up** as the door to Hart's office flies open and Koda comes storming in, Kirsten following on her heels. Though it's late in the afternoon, Maggie looks, as always, neat, trim, and immaculately pressed. She holds up a hand. "Hang on, guys. We just found out."

"How?" Kirsten demands, coming to a stop before an immaculate, empty desk.

"He set up a meeting with his secretary for noon. She waited for an hour or so before checking out his house."

"Empty?"

"A hovel," Maggie answers succinctly, rapping her knuckles on the desk. "But he wasn't there."

Koda, having gone over to the window, parts the blinds and peers out into the warmth of the sunny spring day. "A note?"

"You think he committed suicide?" Maggie queries.

Still peering out the window, Koda lifts a shoulder in elegant reply. A shaft of sunlight lances through the blinds and across the room, to land on the scuffed and bland military tile, highlighting its many imperfections.

"No, she didn't report finding anything like that. But she was looking for a man and not a note, so..."

Nodding, Dakota turns from the window. "How about the gate?"

"Already checked. Nobody in or out since you came back." She turns a significant eye toward Kirsten who, to her credit, hides her flush well as she peers around the empty room as if looking for something she's lost. Maggie, who isn't buying the ruse for a moment, hides her smile behind a patently faked cough, earning her a right proper glare from glittering green eyes.

"Anybody spot him before then?" Koda demands, deliberately ignoring the none-too-subtle byplay between her two companions. "He might have slipped out when the convoy returned."

Maggie narrows her eyes, about to protest. Then she thinks better of it and sighs, resigned. "I'll check again, but I doubt it. No one made any mention of seeing him at all since sometime yesterday."

Crossing the room, Koda lays her hands, palm down, on the Spartan desk. "Do you know where Tacoma is?"

"Yeah, I sent him out with the squad to scour the base. Why?"

"He's a damn good tracker." Rising to her full height, Dakota eyes Maggie steadily. "Send someone out to find him and tell him to see if he can spot any tracks that might lead to our man. Kirsten and I will comb through his house and see if there's anything to be found there. We'll meet you back here, or in your office in, say, two hours. Sooner if we find anything."

Maggie nods crisply, resisting the urge to snap off a salute. Inwardly, though, she's smiling at the effortless way that Dakota assumes command of the situation. It's something she saw in the tall, quiet woman from the first moment they met, and she's pleased to see the shining potential slowly coming to fruition. It is only when the dynamic duo has left the office and the door closes quietly behind them that she lets the smile bloom fully over her face. With a jaunty little whistle, she turns back to work.

# CHAPTER THIRTY-NINE

"God! This place stinks!!" Striding across the darkened living room, Kirsten draws aside the heavy, smoke-impregnated curtains, and throws open the large westward facing window. Fresh air flows in on a strong breeze, helping neutralize the stench of unwashed clothes, rancid food, half-empty beer and liquor containers, though doing nothing to touch the foul undercurrent of far more identifiable, and personal, odors permeating the house like a miasma.

Turning, she watches as Koda, seemingly unaffected, casually lights one of the two kerosene lamps she's brought with her and lifts it in her lover's direction. "You have a cold or something?" Kirsten asks as she approaches and grasps the wire handle of the lamp. "This place is enough to gag a maggot and you're not even breathing through your mouth!"

"I'm a vet. I grew up on a ranch. I have seven brothers." Koda lights the second lamp, her smirk hiding in the shadows sliding over her features.

"Point," Kirsten grants, hefting her lamp and turning in a circle. "Well, this is gonna be fun."

"You take out here, and I'll tackle the bedroom."

Kirsten grins over her shoulder, straight white teeth glittering in the flickering lamplight. "Better you than me."

"Yeah, yeah. Holler if you find anything."

"In this mess? If you hear me holler, it'll be because a rat just bit me." Shuddering inwardly, she makes her way with her lamp to the tiny kitchen. As she advances, she hears her partner's soft steps retreat, and she silently wishes Koda luck in her quest.

Holding the lantern shoulder high, Koda uses her free hand to push open the door to the bedroom. It gives grudgingly, jammed from behind by gods only know what refuse. The boards groan as she forces her way into the dark, stinking room, and she lifts the light high, scanning the small space with narrowed eyes.

The bed, unmade, sports sheets that she's quite sure could stand up on their own and dance a jig with the equally offensive pillowcases. The quilt and blanket, lying in a tangled heap on the floor and covered with dried filth that Koda can all too readily identify, are obviously lost causes.

Pushing several glasses onto the carpeted floor where they land with muted thunks, she sets the lamp down amidst the half empty bottles of Ol' Grandad and Wild Turkey on the small bedside table. Rounding the bed, she lifts the fallen quilt and blanket, shaking them out and turning her head from the stench the covers emit as they're disturbed. When nothing shakes loose, she drops them back into a heap.

Walking over to the closet, she shuffles through the few remaining uniforms that hang with military precision on the rail, turning up nothing of interest. A quick pass-through of the bathroom makes her wish she hadn't, and then she heads back to the nightstand, opening its single drawer with a smooth tug. Her search yields a small Bible, well-read, but with nothing pressed between its thin, fragile pages.

With a soft sigh, she replaces the Bible, closes the drawer and lifts the lamp, heading back into the living room and closing the bedroom door behind her. "Anything?" she asks Kirsten as her partner steps out of the kitchen.

"Not unless you want to count the swarm of drunk cockroaches breeding merrily in what's left of the beer. You?"

"Zip." She takes another quick look around the living room. "There's no way to tell from this mess if he's been gone hours or weeks."

"Maybe Maggie and the others have found something by now."

"Maybe," Koda agrees, though it's clear she doesn't really believe the word she's uttered. "Shall we?"

"None too soon for me, thanks."

**Dakota, Kirsten, Manny,** Andrews, Harcourt, Maggie and several other "insiders" pack the colonel's small office, shoulder to shoulder, hip to hip. Before them, just inside the door, stands Tacoma, a slightly chagrined expression on his otherwise somber face. "I wish I had better news to report," he says. "Fact is, it's just been too dry, and with all the base traffic, trying to track one human male is difficult, to say the least. Especially if he doesn't want to be found."

"All right, then. We'll need to—"

Before she can finish, Maggie is interrupted by the door banging open, almost sending Tacoma across the room. Kimberly, winded and disheveled, steps inside, a few slickly printed leaflets in her left hand. "Toller's gone."

"General Hart's assistant?" Kirsten asks.

"Yes, ma'am." Moving fully into the room, she closes the door behind her and tucks a wayward strand of hair behind her ear. "I thought that since you guys weren't having any luck in the search, I'd see if Toller knew where he was. I went over to his house. It was all closed up, which isn't like him. He must have forgotten to lock the side door, though, because it opened right up." She worries her lower lip for a moment before continuing. "He wasn't there. His uniforms were gone. His luggage was gone. All that was left behind were these."

Dakota takes the leaflets from Kimberly's outstretched hand, riffling quickly through them and glancing at the titles.

*Android = Armageddon*

*Multiculturalism: Satan's Garden*

*Will YOU be among His Saved?*

Curling her lip, Koda tosses the pamphlets onto Maggie's desk where they splay out in a fan of Fundamentalist claptrap. "Answers that question."

"What now?" Kirsten asks, thumbing through the leaflets and wincing at the titles.

"Little weasel's got family in Grand Rapids," Andrews remarks. "We could—"

"I'm there," Tacoma interrupts, already headed for the door before he's stopped by his sister's voice.

"Wait."

He turns, eyebrow raised.

The expression is so eerily like his sister's that Kirsten finds herself turning to the woman beside her to make sure she's still there and not suddenly across the room.

"Look," Koda continues, spreading her hands out on the desk, "I appreciate wanting to find the man, but what I appreciate more is the fact that those androids out there aren't going to wait for us to do that. We need to start planning for the war that's just outside our doorstep, and that planning includes everyone in here." Turning her head slowly, she eyes them all, watching as they straighten and seem to throw off the fatigue touching each and every one of them.

"I shall endeavor to track down your vermin and his master." Harcourt's voice is soft from the corner where he's been quietly standing throughout the proceedings. He eases his way forward until he is standing before Maggie's desk. He holds up a hand in the face of Dakota's immediate objection. "We had a deal, Ms. Rivers, as you'll recall. I enter and leave when I please, as I please. While I am far too old to be lobbing armaments at the enemy, I am quite experienced in hunting down animals who have gone to ground, as it were." He smiles slightly, and there is something of the predator in it. "Make your plans, prime your trumpets for the walls of Jericho; I shall play my small part through to the end." His own look, diamond hard and razor sharp, cuts off any and all objections at the knees. His smile broadens infinitesimally, showing the points of his canines. "I bid you all adieu, then, and wish you luck." He turns to Dakota. "Should you wish to contact me again, you know where to find me."

With a slight incline of his head, he eases forward as the bodies give way and slips through the door, leaving everyone to stare, stunned, after him.

"Be right back," Dakota remarks, and pushes through the crowd and out the door.

**"Fenton, wait!"**

Hearing Koda coming quickly up behind him, he stops, back still turned to her, and surveys the land before him. His voice is soft and contemplative as he recites from a favored poem. At the end, with a smile on his face and a fine walking stick in his hand, he turns to his listener, eyes seeming to glow with vitality and a surge, seldom seen, of good humor. "I believe, for my purposes, I shall take the road less traveled. Wouldn't you agree?"

"I'd rather you didn't take any road."

"Ah, but where would be the fun in that, Ms. Rivers?"

"This isn't a game, Fenton."

"True, but it is an adventure, and one which I am uniquely suited to undertake. Androids have no interest in me, an old man well past his prime, and I am more than wily enough to avoid their reach should they change their circuited minds on the matter." In a rare show of warmth, he reaches out and lays a gnarled hand on Dakota's wrist. "I know the import of hunting down the good general, Dakota. He may hold few secrets, but any secret is one too many if it is given to the enemy." He squeezes the thick wrist under his hand briefly before drawing away. "We all have our parts to play in this, Ms. Rivers. Allow me the dignity to see mine through, no matter what that end might be."

After several moments of complete silence, Koda finally nods. "You'll have some help, however."

"I assure you, Ms. Rivers, I am quite capab—"

A loud whistle interrupts his discourse, and a moment later, fiercely beating wings herald the arrival of Wiyo, who lands easily on Dakota's wrist. "She can see what you can't. She can warn you if there's danger ahead, or behind. She's a friend. Take her with you, and I'll feel much more comfortable about letting you go."

The face of granite, the face that has frightened years off criminals through the decades, dissolves like sugar in water, transforming the harsh planes of his face into soft lines of wonder and joy. "Wiyo, hup."

The redtail easily hops from Koda's wrist to Fenton's arm, then sidesteps up until she is perched quite comfortably on his shoulder.

"Now this isn't a gift, so don't be thinking you're gonna be taking her home to live with you, you old codger. When you've done what you set out to do, set her free. I may have need of her yet."

Harcourt chuckles, enjoying the feel of the weight on his shoulder and the odd sense of comfort it brings him. "Not to worry, Ms. Rivers. This bird knows who she belongs with." His smile falls away, and he inclines his head respectfully. "Thank you, Dakota. You've given me a companion beyond price."

Reaching out, she takes his hand and squeezes the gnarled fingers warmly. "Good luck to you, my friend."

"And to you, as well. May we meet again under better circumstances." With a last nod and a fleeting smile, he turns from her to begin his quest.

She watches him until he rounds the curve leading to the gate, then makes her way back to Maggie's office and the problems within.

**Kirsten watches as** the civilian population of Ellsworth files into the base theater. Their number has held steady over the last several weeks, since sealing the gates to all but authorized traffic. Still, they number close to three hundred. About half are women rescued from the droid breeding facilities. The remainder consist of families in various configurations; in the first row an elderly couple accompanied by two toddlers shuffle sideways past a pair of young fathers holding hands with their three pigtailed daughters between them. They take their places beside a middle-aged woman and a teenaged girl with a face that is a mirror image of her own and eyes dead and dull as granite. They greet each other with quiet nods, subdued and somber. Though information about the approaching enemy has been closely guarded, they must know that a crisis is at hand. Koda's return with a strange warband will not have gone unremarked, nor will the suddenly increased number of Tomcat flights taking off for day-long missions to unspecified destinations. The base is a small town, with a small town's instant transmission of gossip.

Maggie, standing beside her on the small stage, says softly, "They know."

"They'd be fools not to," she answers. "Nobody's ever thought the droids would give up. Ellsworth is a prime target."

Maggie flashes her a grin. "Our defenses are good. Better since your little excursion."

"Flattery will get you nowhere." Kirsten returns the grin, showing her teeth. "You're still Base Commandant, General Allen."

The promotion cannot have been unexpected, but Maggie stares at her wide-eyed for a moment, the breath gone out of her. Before she can speak, Kirsten says flatly, "It gets worse. You're Air Force Chief of Staff, as of now. If we make it through this upcoming fight, we're going to have to start looking for and organizing other surviving forces. Persuade them if we can, appropriate them if we have to."

"Like Koda 'appropriated' the Minot militia?"

Kirsten nods. "We do what we have to. We're not going to come out of this with the same kind of society we had going in. At least for a while, we're going to have to be the biggest, meanest, most ruthless dog in the junkyard. Because that's what we're going to have to deal with — junkyard dogs."

"Some of them rabid."

"Some of them rabid," she affirms. "And some of them we'll have to deal with as we would with rabid dogs."

At the back of the auditorium, Andrews pulls the double doors closed and turns to wave at the stage. All in.

"You sure you don't want to do this?" Maggie asks Kirsten.

"Positive. It's your base; I'm just the civilian authority."

"Okay, then." Maggie steps forward to the podium, flanked on one side by the Stars and Stripes, on the other by the blue Air Force banner. She taps the mic softly and says, "Is this thing working? Can you hear me?"

A murmur of assent comes in answer, and Kirsten notes the rise in her shoulders as she takes a deep breath. She has just made Maggie the supreme uniformed authority in what remains of the United States. *Which is only fair*, she thinks, *if I have to be President. Serves her right*.

But that is not the only change that needs to be made. It is becoming increasingly clear that Koda's position with the troops will have to be formalized, some title found that she will accept. *"First Lady" sure as Hell isn't going to do it*. Suppressing a smile, she turns her attention back to Maggie.

"...some cause for concern," the new general says quietly. "General Hart has gone missing, and our efforts to find him have so far been unsuccessful. We do not know whether he left of his own free will, nor do we know whether he is safe, or even alive. I urge anyone who may have any information about the general to share it with the MPs and help us to find him.

"Now to the real reason we asked you to come here. As most of you know already, the droids have regrouped subsequent to their last attack on Ellsworth. They are currently gathering troops and materiel at locations to the south and west of us. We have every reason to believe that they will attack Ellsworth again."

A murmur runs through the crowd, quickly stilled as Maggie continues, "So we've asked you here, President King and I, to offer you a choice. Anyone who wishes to leave the base should be packed and ready and at the gate tomorrow morning at eight. A bus will be made available to take you into Rapid City. Unfortunately, we cannot spare either the personnel or the vehicle to take you further. If you wish to leave the area entirely, we suggest that you go into North Dakota, then east. You will have a better chance of avoiding the enemy if you move in that direction. Lieutenant Andrews — he's the redhead over there — will have a list for you to sign as you leave here tonight, so the bus driver will know who and how many to expect.

"On the other hand, you are welcome to stay on base if you wish. The only condition is that able-bodied adults must serve in support capacities to free up as many troops as possible for fighting. We will need you as cooks, messengers, orderlies, clerks. Someone will have to set up a child-care center. Lieutenant Rivers has the list where you can sign up for the job you prefer. We'll give you your first choice if we can, but there are no guarantees." She pauses a moment. "Are there any questions?"

The grandfather in the first row stands. "Will you be able to defend Rapid City?"

"We will have a fighter designated to attack troops that may approach you from the west. But that protection will be minimal. We are not prepared for urban ground fighting. We don't have the numbers for it."

A ripple of sound runs through the audience again. Here and there faces go grey; not all had realized the gravity of their situation. A woman in the last row speaks for all of them. "Is there any place that's safe? Or safer?"

"No, ma'am. There isn't."

A silence falls, then. Maggie waits at the podium, but no one has any more questions. After a moment, people begin to move out. Most, Kirsten notes with satisfaction, pause to sign Manny's list; perhaps a dozen opt to evacuate. She moves to stand beside Maggie. "That was a dose of reality."

"Oh, yeah. They knew there was a problem. This was just the first time somebody official said it."

"How long do we have?"

"Maybe a week. They're not moving yet, but the recon flyer that came back about an hour ago says their numbers have doubled in just a couple days. Not good."

*Not good at all.* Kirsten says, "I'm going back to the house. See if I can turn up anything else on the code."

It is an unlikely hope, and they both know it. Maggie is poring over the lists with Manny and Andrews when Kirsten leaves the auditorium. Past the veterinary clinic, past the stand of woods to the west of the street that leads to the residential section, strings of code run through her head. All futile; she's been there before and come away empty. At the curve of the road, a rustle in the tree above her catches her eye, startling her out of the endless loops of binary. Sitting in the fork of the trunk, regarding her with eyes like amber, is a large raccoon. "Yo, Madam President," he says. "How's it hanging?"

Kirsten stares for a moment at the masked face a foot above hers, the snap of mockery plain in the dark, bright eyes. Tega's long fingers lie interlaced against his chest; replete and self-satisfied, he grins down at her. After a moment she says, "I don't talk to hallucinations. Go away."

"Hallucinate this," he says amiably, and drops a small bird's egg to splatter against her boots.

The yellow stain on the sidewalk looks very real. So does the sticky mess running down the laces of her Timberlands. She looks from her fouled hikers to the raccoon and back. "Damn," she says. "You didn't have to do that. That was going to be a bird."

"No, it wasn't. Those eggs were orphans." Tega's tongue runs the circuit of his muzzle.

"You mean you — no, don't tell me. I don't want to know."

"As Madam President wishes." Delicately, Tega picks a small brown and grey feather from his ruff and looses it to fall floating down to join the broken egg. "I do pride myself on my table manners."

Kirsten looks furtively around her. The street and sidewalk are both deserted at this hour, the folk who will stay sitting down to their suppers, those who will leave in the morning no doubt packing. It will not do to be seen talking to a raccoon in a tree. "You're going to get me locked up if anybody sees us. Wearing one of those jackets with the extra long sleeves."

"You wouldn't be the first Great White Father — or Mother — to be a few kilowatts shy of a glimmer. Now among the Real People, that'd make you a holy woman. I don't suppose you feel particularly holy?"

"Holy? Look, dammit. I'm a scientist. I believe in what I can see or calculate. I don't believe in—" Kirsten makes a dismissive, circular gesture with one hand, "all this — this mumbo-jumbo. I don't believe in *you*. You're something I ate."

Tega bares his teeth again, white and sharp as lancets. "Don't even think it, schveetheart."

"Don't be absurd!" she snaps back. "You're not edible."

"Ach, dere ve haff it." Tega leans back against the tree trunk with his hands once again folded over his midsection. He sounds, to Kirsten's ears, like a Viennese psychiatrist in a bad TV drama.

"Kultural differencesss." Absurdly, a pair of wire-rimmed glasses appears perched just behind the black button of his nose.

"Cultural—" she repeats blankly. "What are you talking about?"

"I'm talking about Kirsten King, P. H. of D., President of the U. S. of A., wearing buckskin and feathers and opening the Sun Dance. How does that grab you?"

A flash of memory, involuntary and unconcealable: the slanting scars on Tacoma Rivers' chest, the same scars on his father's and cousin's, and her own distaste. She had not been quick enough to keep Tacoma from reading her face; she is not quick enough to evade Tega's eyes now. "It — all right. It makes me uncomfortable. Not the buckskin and feathers; I'd be honored to wear Dakota's traditional dress. It's — it's just—"

"The blood, the mutilation, the primitiveness of it all?"

Blood rises hot in Kirsten's face; she feels the blush spread from her neck up to her forehead. "It's— Yes. It's not—" The words she needs will not come. Perhaps they do not exist. She says, "It's not quantifiable. Not — containable. It could get out of hand."

"Oh, it could. Not to mention what could happen when people start up with the Ghost Dance again and all those dead Injuns born into white skin wake up and realize who they really are. That could get waaaayyy out of hand. You just can't let it get out of *your* hand."

Not for the first time, Kirsten wonders if her mind has shattered under stress. "I don't see what that has to do with me. Dakota's a medicine woman, I know that, I respect that—"

A hoot of laughter, strangely not human, comes from the tree above her, and Tega leans back, holding his sides. "Medicine woman! You silly girl, you're marrying the fuckin' Pope! Get used to it!"

"That's crazy! You're crazy!" Kirsten hisses. "I'm crazy for thinking I'm having a conversation with a — a — talking raccoon with perverted dietary habits!"

Tega turns suddenly serious. "Oh, you're crazy all right. No sane woman would get herself into — and out of — the tightest droid facilities on the continent. No sane woman would try to put this wreck of a society back together. Now would she?"

"I had to! I'm the only one who could do that! The droid part, I mean."

"True," says Tega. "And you, and Dakota with you, are the ones who will lay down the pattern for the New World Order."

Kirsten can hear the capitals as his eyes dance behind their ridiculous lenses.

"A mixed culture, where even white boys do the Sun Dance. And a blonde Lakota woman opens the ceremony beside the Medicine Chief of the whole nation."

Kirsten's head spins. Almost she can see it, herself in braids, carrying a hawk's wing fan, stamping out the rhythm of the drums at the head of a line of women, all in Native dress, their skins and hair all the colors of the human spectrum. Behind them, making the circuit of the dancing ground, come the men with wreaths of spruce crowing their long hair, eagle-bone whistles between their lips. Among them are Andrews and Darius. And the implication hits her like the meteor that extinguished the dinosaurs.

"That means — we're going to survive! Gods—!"

Before her, Tega begins to fade, the rough texture of the bark becoming visible through his rough fur. Only his voice remains, becoming fainter and fainter. "Remember: the past is the future, the future is the past. Round and round she goes...little wheel, spin and spin...round and round...and where she stops...nobody...knows..."

And Kirsten is alone, standing on the empty sidewalk, staring up at the empty fork of the tree. She swallows hard; her throat is painfully dry. *I need a drink*, she thinks. *I need a drink* bad. Swiftly, almost running, she sets off for the relative security of home and Asi.

**The convoy weaves** in and out among the wrecks on Highway 90 like a line of dancers, stately and nimble. The lead Stryker bristles with weapons, a roof-mounted M-60 and an AK in the hands of its gunner, the tail vehicle identically armed. In between, Tacoma drives an open Jeep, Koda in the seat beside him, Maggie Allen in the back with a topo map and a laptop open on the passenger bench beside her. They are moving just fast enough that the odor from the shattered and torn-open derelicts cannot settle about them. Even so, Koda can hear the occasional strangled breath from Maggie. An airborne warrior skims above the stench of death; a foot soldier and a medic spend their lives in its penumbra. In any case, Koda's mind is on another matter.

A shadow has followed them since they set out from Ellsworth, a shape that glides along just beyond the screen of the treeline, disappearing at intervals where the ground rises or a streambed cuts below the road. The sun, standing down from noon, glints off the new green of leaves, laying long shadows the length tree trunks. The shadow never quite separates itself from them, never comes clear into the light. The wreckage slows the convoy to a pace that a swift four-footed creature might match, and it has paced them tirelessly. Though it is beyond the range of sight recognition, Koda knows it for a *manitu*, a power. Tacoma does not seem to have noticed, nor has Maggie. The creature's message is not for them. Dakota simply makes note of the presence and waits for what will come.

"We need to get a dozer out here," the general observes as they veer around yet another overturned eighteen-wheeler, its open door bent back like the lid of a tin can. Its upholstery is streaked white with lime where the carrion birds have perched. Just visible through the spiderweb of cracks in the windshield, an arm picked down to bone angles over the steering wheel. "We can't get an armored column up this road unless we get some of this mess cleared off."

Tacoma nods as they pass a minivan whose windshield crawls with maggots. He waves a hand at it. "There's a real morale booster for you. We need a burial detail out here before we bring troops through."

Maggie pauses a moment, her face thoughtful in the rearview mirror, and Dakota knows that she is weighing resources.

"All right," the general says finally. "Nothing fancy. Just a backhoe and a ditch. Get half a dozen volunteers and promise them...whatever bonus you can realistically promise them. We're as short of perks as we are of time."

Just ahead of them, a fox climbs out the broken window of a car that remains crumpled into the back bumper of a pickup. A scrap of blue cloth still clings to its muzzle as it hops down and disappears into the grass grown tall by the side of the road. Spring thaw has brought the scavengers out to feed. From the corner of her eye, Koda catches movement of something larger in the rippling stalks, and watches as the fox's smaller wake veers wide to pass it by.

*Something born on Ina Maka, then, physical. Not something purely of the spirit world.*

Briefly the shape of Wa Uspewikakiyape floats across her mind, and with it a stab of grief that remains sharp, even though she has managed to hold it distant from her in the crisis of the coming battle. It is too soon for his return, even should he choose to be reborn again. *And*, she acknowledges to herself, *one of his wisdom has no need to walk the Earth another lifetime.*

"*Tanski*? You with us?"

Tacoma's brow knits in concern for her, and she reaches over to pat his arm. "Present and accounted for, *thiblo*. Just thinking."

He grins, and she watches the snappy comeback fade before it reaches his tongue. More and more of the base personnel have begun to exchange knowing glances when she and Kirsten enter a room together. It is, she supposes, something that goes with being a newlywed.

More or less. Formalizing their relationship is something she and Kirsten have not talked about yet, cannot talk about at least until they are past the coming battle. When she married Tali, fresh out of undergraduate school, they had gone away to Greece for their honeymoon and had been spared the grins and the elbow jabs of friends and kin. Odd that amid the wreckage of a world, her life should have taken a turn for normal in this one small thing.

She says, "How far out you think we should meet them?"

"Far enough out to give us some maneuvering room between there and the base." He glances back at Maggie. "General?"

"Fifteen miles. Twenty would be better. There's a place up past the bridge where the land falls away. They'll have to come along that stretch strung out on a narrow front. We can control their approach there more easily than just about anywhere else."

A shiver passes over Koda's skin, despite the warmth of the sun. "I know the place you mean. Anything on wheels will have to keep to the highway there."

"Their armor won't, though."

Koda frowns, an idea forming slowly as the convoy negotiates yet another narrow passage between lines of wrecked vehicles. "We can block them, if we have time," she says. "Or at least slow them down. How many heavy dozers can we get working?"

"Two or three," Tacoma answers. "What d'you have in — oh."

"Exactly." She grins at him.

"Care to share?" Maggie asks, her voice dry.

Tacoma says, "Tracked vehicles can climb just about anything that's not vertical, but if we ram a pile of these wrecks into a defensive berm, we can stop the enemy's wheeled transport cold wherever we want to."

"Or funnel them where we want them," Dakota adds.

Tacoma shoots her a glance warm with appreciation. "And we can direct the tanks, too. General?"

"Sounds good to me. You're the dirt soldiers."

Koda notices the plural, and it creates a small warm glow somewhere under her sternum. There is a familiarity to the acknowledgement, and a certainty. It fits her, the same way her scalpel fits the shape of her hand, or the tortoiseshell rattle that had been her grandfather's last gift to her.

The lower west fork of the Cheyenne passes beneath them, the highway curving away from the bridge to pass along the spine of a ridge that falls sharply to the bank of a stream on one side. The water runs parallel to the road for perhaps a mile, with a broad meadow spread out between it and another rise to the south. Koda lays a hand on Tacoma's arm. "Stop. Stop here."

Tacoma waves to the Stryker gunner ahead of them, then pulls the Jeep over to the side of the road. Koda climbs out and goes to stand by the guardrail, shielding her eyes as she looks over the level space between Highway 90 and the lift of earth not quite a mile away. A line of trees marches along it, and it seems to Koda that something moves in the laddered shadows that spill down its slope, but she cannot be certain.

The interstate here is almost clear of wrecks, an open stretch between Rapid City and the small towns linked to it by farm-to-market roads. The air above the tarmac seems to shimmer in the sun, and through the rippling heat Dakota catches the glare of sun off the metal hides of military droids, the sudden glint of light striking the silver collars of androids marching in uniformed ranks, the tireless crunch of their boots on asphalt a constant grinding that blends with the whine of tanks and the ponderous crawl of big guns. Then time slips back into place, and the vision fades. The road runs empty through the spring fields, overgrown now with grass and self-seeded crops, sprinkled here and there with patches of bright yellow and blue, rose and lavender.

"*Tanski?*" Tacoma touches her arm. "You okay?"

"Here," Dakota says. "The battle will be here."

"It's a good place for it," Maggie says, thoughtfully. "We can block this road at two or three places to slow them down and control their options once they get here."

"We need to prevent them from fanning out on the north side of the road," Tacoma says. "Or spilling down over the stream."

"We'll mine the north side," Koda answers. "Maybe dig some ditches. How wide do they need to be to stop the tanks, *thiblo*?"

"Maybe ten feet. If we can dig them that deep, with straight sides, they'll have to go around."

Maggie nods assent. "Get the backhoes out here the minute we get back. Bury the dead as quickly as you can, then start to work on those trenches."

"Spike the bottoms," Dakota says suddenly. "Cut enough brush to camouflage the digging until the enemy is too close to turn back. What have we got that will burn besides fuel?"

"Asphalt. Tar. We repaved the runways just a few months ago, and there were supplies left over."

Tacoma grins. "Thank the gods for government waste. What d'you have in mind, *tanksi*? Fire the ditches?"

Koda grins in return. "Between the spikes and the fire, we can immobilize anything that tries to cross them. Then we can use shoulder fired anti-tank missiles to explode their fuel and ammo once they're stuck."

"I like it," says Maggie. "What about the ones that get through?"

"Use the wrecks to funnel them back behind our lines. Surround them, cut them off, and destroy them."

"A strategic retreat could draw them in," Tacoma adds, his dark eyes far away on a battle not yet joined. "Half our armor could fall back maybe five miles toward the base through the open country. Then the other half could come in behind." He raises his hands and brings them together. "Squeeze 'em like a python."

Maggie gestures toward the meadow and the treeline in the distance. "What about this open space here on our right?"

"Spike the slope, too," Koda answers. "Tacoma, could we dam up this stream and muddy the ground enough to mire their trucks if they try to leave the road?"

Tacoma leans over the guardrail, staring up and down the narrow watercourse for a long moment. Then he says, "We could dam it, no problem. The question is whether there's enough water volume. We could probably get a hundred-meter strip nice and wet, though."

"Do it," says Maggie.

Movement behind the trees to the south catches Koda's eye again. Something is there, pacing, the long shadows rippling with its passage. "But leave it passable on foot," she says, as the image forms in her mind. "For the force we'll hide behind that rise over there." She turns to meet Tacoma's gaze, which is half startled, half admiring. "We'll block them, draw them in on the left, turn their line, and roll them up from the right and behind. Piece of cake."

"Fuckin' A, better-than-sex cake," Tacoma laughs. Then, as Koda and Maggie both stare at him repressively, "Figuratively speaking, of course."

"Themunga makes a chocolate better-than-sex cake that'll melt in your mouth," Dakota elaborates, noting Maggie's puzzled frown. "Only she calls it a not-quite-as-good-as-sex cake." She pauses a moment. Then, careful to keep her face straight, she adds, "We're a big family."

"I noticed," her friend says wryly. "What about the ground over there? How big a flanking force can we put behind that rise?"

Again the movement catches her eye, and Koda says, "I'll go scout it."

Tacoma motions to one of the gunners from the lead Stryker. "Take an escort."

She shakes her head. "No need. Back in a flash."

With that she is gone down the slope, jogging over the matted grasses that spring under her feet. At the base, she leaps the stream easily as a deer, landing lightly on the far bank and sprinting across the meadow. Grasshoppers whir out of her way; once she starts a young rabbit from its form, and ground squirrels, chittering, dive into their holes as she flies past them. Her feet seem to brush the ground only briefly; she is lighter than air, barely ruffling the grass as she passes. The sense of a presence grows stronger as she approaches the fold of land with its crown of trees, stillness settling over her even as she reaches the foot of the rise and begins the ascent, leaping from rock to rock up its stony side.

At the top, she pauses, looking around her. The top of the knoll is a hundred feet wide, dropping down perhaps a third of the distance on the other side to a broad meadow. Sycamore and cottonwoods grow thickly along the spine, perhaps planted as a windbreak before so many family farms failed in the second half of the past century and the population of the Dakotas bled away to the cities. In their cover, and on the field below, it should be possible to hide several hundred lightly armed fighters, far more than she will have at her disposal. *And where*, she wonders, *does that come from? Who's decided I'm the one to lead the ambush battalion?*

*Why, you have, of course.*

Dakota wheels around, scanning the trees and the underbrush that grows thick beneath their branches, but there is no one. The voice is everywhere and nowhere, a ripple of laughter in her mind. The *manitu*.

Drawing her own silence around her then, Koda waits for the being to make itself known. Or herself. She can sense that it is female in the current of savage tenderness that flows about it, running above the wild abandon of the hunt, the burst of joy at the kill. With a start, she recognizes the blood hunger as her own, the savage pulse in her own veins as she fought an alpha and killed him. *My band now. My pride.*

For what seems an eternity, the voice does not speak to her again. She can feel eyes on her, though, from somewhere within the trees. Watching. Waiting. Testing her patience. Finally the vigilance relaxes, and the thought comes to her: *Oka was right. You have the makings of a warrior.*

She gives a start, at that. *Oka*, Singer, is Wa Uspewikakiyape's true name, the name by which his own people knew him. The name by which only Dakota among the two-footed has ever known him. *I give you his greetings*, the silent voice goes on. *He has taken his place at the council fire in the other side camp. He will not walk the Red Road again.*

*I miss him*, she says without sound.

*You grieve because you love. That is as it should be.*

Again, silence falls and Dakota waits. It is not her place to hurry an elder, or to speak before being spoken to. After a time, the light shifts among the trees, shadows rippling with the movement of a long body as it walks between them. Koda catches the sheen of sun off golden fur, the twitch of the end of a long tail. *Igmú Tanka.* At the thought, a puma steps out of the woods and comes to sit in the center of the small glade, gazing up at Koda with eyes like molten bronze. Round patches of fur show dark against her belly. She has cubs.

*Ina*, Koda acknowledges.

*And I must kill something for them by nightfall*, comes the answer, and with it the taste of hot blood. *As you must kill for your own.*

A pang stabs through Koda's heart. *I have no cubs. My child died with my beloved.*

Igmú Tanka nips at a bit of twig caught in the fur of her shoulder. *There are cubs, and there are cubs. Those for whom you are responsible are not of your body, yet they are yours nonetheless.*

*My responsibility is to fight this battle.*

*Your responsibility is to fight this battle, and others. And then it will be your responsibility to rule.*

*Rule? But Kirsten—*

*Is Chief. You are something new.*

*I don't understand.*

*You don't need to, not yet. I have something to tell you: do not hesitate to flee when the time comes. Victory will follow you.*

Koda feels her brows knit. *I don't—*

*Understand. That does not matter. What matters is that you should obey my younger sister when she gives you an order. For the sake of all the People, two-footed, four-footed, winged, and creeping, you must do what you least wish to, when you least wish to. I will be here waiting when you return.*

With that, the puma turns and pads back into the trees. Koda follows her movements until she is lost in shadow, then turns back toward the road and the burden laid on her.

**A somber, thoughtful** Dakota opens the door to the house and steps inside, more by rote than conscious act. Padding softly through the kitchen, gaze turned more inward than out, she stops upon sighting Kirsten. Sitting on the tattered sofa, her legs tucked up under her, the young scientist stares into the monitor of her laptop as her agile, graceful fingers fly over the keyboard. The window across the room is open, and from it, a shaft of sunlight lances in, gilding her in pure gold, her hair a halo that quickens the pace of Koda's heart. The love she feels for this woman is so strong and so pure that it hurts, deep within, like a tight band across her chest.

Her mind drifts back to her conversation with *Igmú Tanka*, and she finds herself comparing this new love with the one she lost so long ago, comparing Tali's dark, reed-slender lines with Kirsten's golden, muscled curves, Tali's quiet sweetness with Kirsten's mercurial intelligence, passion, and deeply hidden pain. *What paths*, she wonders, *would my life have taken had Tali not been taken so quickly from me?*

"You have the makings of a warrior," *Igmú Tanka* had said. *Would Tali have appreciated this growth in me, accepted it as simply and wholeheartedly as Kirsten does? Perhaps*, she thinks. Tali had a good heart, a good soul. But she valued constancy in her life, the safety and security of knowing that each day would be much the same as the last. Family was the most important thing to her. Their loving was gentle, and quiet, fulfilling and comfortable. She gazes at Kirsten, remembering their joining of last night. Her blood stirs hot in her veins and she moans softly. Kirsten accepted the raw desire, the deep passion in her. More than that, she embraced it, craved it with as much fire as Koda herself.

*Tali was the love of who I was,* Dakota realizes, with something akin to shock. *But Kirsten, she is the love of who I am becoming, the woman I am meant to be.*

At that very moment, Kirsten, who has turned her implants off for the sake of convenience, turns her head and locks eyes with her lover.

Koda finds herself falling into the sunlit green of her direct, loving gaze, her spirit separating from her body painlessly as the world around her tunnels and rushes past, unacknowledged.

*She's running through a jungle thick with moisture and the scent of the earth. Broad green leaves caress her face as she passes, coating her with their moisture as her heartbeat, loud in her ears, sets her pace. Her spirit is filled with an almost savage joy as she runs, her feet light on the ground cover, her pace easy and relentless. She is the hunter, and her prey is very close. She can smell blood and earth, and a predator's smile breaks over her face, turning her eyes to molten silver.*

*A sunlit clearing of deep green grass suddenly appears, and she stops, blood thrumming, as a woman, dappled green and gold, rises from her crouch, swaying to the tempo that Koda's heart has created. Her hands reach out, gracefully beckoning, and Koda heeds their call, running to her, merging with her. They are one body, one spirit, one essence, writhing, pulsing in an ecstasy neither has ever known.*

*They explode then, their atoms scattering through space, and reforming randomly as the earth spins above them, blue and green and glowing, lit behind from the sun. Their combined heartbeat fades, to be replaced by the squalling of an infant breathing her first, then by the triumphant yowl of a hunting cat, until finally, it becomes the howl of the wolf going on and on and on, until it is everywhere and everything.*

Dakota comes back to herself as she is pulling away from Kirsten's soft, swollen lips. They collapse against one another, panting breaths mingling, hearts thundering against their bony cages.

"Dear God," Kirsten whispers when she finally has the breath to speak.

Cupping her lover's cheek, Koda stares down into her eyes, so green and shining. "Did you...?"

"Feel that? God, yes. It was the scariest, most wonderful thing I ever felt in my life." A sudden wave of dizziness rolls over her, and her knees give out, dumping her less than gracefully back onto the couch.

Dakota follows her down, squatting between her splayed legs and grasping her hands gently, chafing them with concern as she looks into clouded green eyes. "Are you okay?"

Though she can read her lover's lips easily, Kirsten suddenly craves the sound of her voice, and, pulling one hand away from its warm nest, thumbs her implants back on.

"Kirsten?"

"I'm..." She lets out a breath, long and shaky, almost, but not quite, a laugh. "I'm...not sure. I think I may be...taking a little vacation from reality."

Cocking her head slightly, Koda narrows her eyes, all but pinning Kirsten to the couch with the strength of her gaze. "Explain."

"That's just the problem," Kirsten replies, tucking her free hand under the thick fall of her hair and rubbing at the back of her neck, where a mountain of tension has suddenly decided to take up residence. "I don't know if I can."

"Try."

Koda's voice is soft and soothing, and Kirsten clings to its timbre like a lifeline. "Remember when I told you about my raccoon visitor?" she begins, blushing slightly. "The one that wasn't really there?"

Dakota nods.

"He wasn't really there again today." She laughs. It's a dry, almost bitter sound. "Sitting in a tree just as big as life." She shakes her head. "A full blown visual and auditory hallucination that I would have heard even with my implants off."

"What did he say?"

"Oh, he had a lot to talk about, most of it put downs." The laugh sounds again, though a bit more genuine this time. "I can't even manage to come down with your garden variety delusions of grandeur. Noooo, I have to hallucinate a wise-cracking vermin with a nasty attitude, who seems to find my general ineptitude with life quite amusing." Closing her eyes, she hangs her head, her chin not quite touching her chest. "When he's not getting his jollies out of dropping eggs on me, that is."

Koda's eyes dart over to where Kirsten's boots stand at the foot of the couch. With a small smile, she notes the dry streaks of yellow on the laces. Her suspicion fully confirmed, she releases Kirsten's hand and, reaching up, gently cups her lover's cheek, her strong thumb tenderly tracing over the baby soft skin. She remains silent, allowing Kirsten the much needed time to process her thoughts.

Deep green eyes finally raise and open, and Koda feels, once again, that sense of temporal dislocation. This time, she fights the urge, biting down on the inside of her lip until the feeling passes and she is firmly in control of her spirit. *This is not good,* she thinks, before Kirsten begins speaking, and she turns her attention to that instead.

"I feel like Alice going down the rabbit hole. Just when I think life is making sense, things start spinning out of control. And sometimes I think that if I just close my eyes real tight, maybe I'll wake up and find this has all been a dream."

"Do you want it to be a dream?"

Dakota's voice is steady and soft, but Kirsten has no trouble seeing the unease in her striking eyes.

Without thought, she takes the hand cupping her face and brings it to her lips, brushing a kiss against the warm knuckles. "Not even one second of it. I should hate myself for feeling this way, it's so damn selfish. But if none of this had happened, I would never have met you, and that is something I would never want to change. No matter what."

"Nor would I."

The two embrace and hold each other tightly for a very long moment before Koda pulls away with reluctance. "For what it's worth, love, you're not crazy, okay?"

Kirsten looks up at her, clearly wanting, needing to believe, but, equally clearly, not believing — not entirely, at any rate.

"Maybe..." Koda's throat clicks audibly as she swallows. After a split second of hesitation, she gives voice to the thought plaguing her for the past several days. "Maybe you should go off base until all this is over. My parents would keep you safe, and I'm sure by now the entire family is dying to meet you."

Kirsten's eyes widen as her jaw sets. Koda fancies she can feel the anger building in the smaller woman, and she winces.

"I—" Kirsten begins. "You — you want to send me away? I can't — you really do think I'm losing it, don't you!" She gathers her legs, beginning to stand, but Koda holds tight to her waist, pulling her in again. "Let me go."

"No."

"Dammit, Koda! I said—"

"Listen to me, Kirsten!" She pulls back just enough to meet her lover's blazing eyes. "It's not you! I don't think you're crazy! You're saner than anyone I know! It's me! Don't you see it? I can't lose you! Kirsten, I...can't...lose...you!"

The hoarseness of Dakota's voice finally filters through the red heat of Kirsten's anger, and she relaxes against the large, trembling body holding her with desperation. "Wh — what did you say?"

"I can't lose you," Koda repeats, voice muffled against the fabric of Kirsten's T-shirt. "Not now. Not ever." Her hands tighten and tangle in the cloth, pulling her lover so tightly against her that not a molecule of air can pass between them.

Kirsten can feel her breath, tight and raspy, against her chest, and her arms close instinctively about Dakota's broad shoulders, giving what comfort she can. *She's scared!* Kirsten realizes. *For me! Dear God!* With a feeling of wonder, she slowly rocks the body half in her arms, her restless hands smoothing over Koda's thick, shining hair as she replays her lover's words over and over. Finally, slowly, she pulls back, and tips Dakota's chin so that their eyes meet. "I'm not going anywhere," she says firmly, with finality. "Not without you. We started this together, and we'll end it together, or not at all. Understand me?"

After a moment, Dakota nods.

"I can't lose you either, my love. Not when I've just found you. I — I can't ask you not to do what you do best. What I can ask is that you come back to me, whole and healthy. Be careful, okay? For us?"

"For us."

They embrace again, tightly, and this time, neither makes a move to pull away for a very, very long time.

# CHAPTER FORTY

"Alright, ya big goober, just give me a second here." Asi dances on his forepaws as Kirsten struggles with the screen door. Though the sky is a crisp, almost autumnal blue, the wind howls through the trees as if heralding a hurricane.

"Damn...stupidass...state..." she grunts, giving the handle one final heave and almost falling over as it opens far too easily, nearly taking her hand with it. Uncaring, Asimov dashes into the house, yodeling.

With a sigh, Kirsten releases the door, and it slams closed on another gust of wind. Instead of trying to wrestle with it again, she turns away, content, for the moment, to put off going into the house to spend more long hours in fruitless pursuit of the missing code. Even if the breeze is stiff enough to drop a mule, the sun is warm on her shoulders and the air is fresh and sweet.

*What a difference a week makes.* The tepid, frightened, holding pattern feel of the base has been replaced, almost overnight, by a hive-like intensity. Men and women, civilians and military alike, move across the grounds with purpose, heads held high and shoulders squared. She even spies several groups that appear to be drilling. Broken into squads of twenty, they run about the grounds in orderly rows to a musical cadence sung out by the squad leader.

As she looks on, one such group rounds the curve toward the house. She smiles as she recognizes the leader and raises a hand. Clad in running shorts and a green T-shirt emblazoned with ARMY across the chest, Tacoma spies her, grins, and snaps off a stiff salute, barking to his charges to do the same or risk his wrath. Watching the few civilians in the crowd stumble about trying to salute and run at the same time causes Kirsten's grin to broaden, but she reins it in and returns the salute as solemnly as she can manage. Her smile breaks through at last when Tacoma tips her a wink, and she watches with true pleasure as they all run off in step, even the four sixty-something year old men, veterans of the first Gulf War who had buttonholed Tacoma and warned him that if he even attempted to get them off base and out of the fighting, they would stage a coup and depose him.

With a last, deep breath of fresh air, she turns back to the door, yanks it open, and strides inside. Her steps slow as she becomes aware of a presence she does not expect, and she smiles as she looks at her lover, seated cross-legged on the floor in front of the couch, eyes closed, her breathing soft and even. Dressed in cargo shorts and a black tank-top, her beauty is a siren's call to Kirsten, and she finds herself heading into the living room without being aware of her movement.

Koda's eyes open, and the simple welcome and deep affection in them warms Kirsten's heart so greatly that tears spring to her eyes. As Dakota rises easily, fluidly, to her feet, Kirsten holds up a hand. "I'm sorry. I didn't mean to—" The rest of her statement is muffled as she's gathered into a strong embrace. Koda's warmth, scent, and strength surround her, filling her with a peace she's long been lacking.

"You're all knots," Koda murmurs into her hair, long fingers pressing gently against the bands of tight muscle along Kirsten's back and shoulders.

"Nerves," Kirsten replies, wincing as the gentle pressure sends sparks of pain down her arms.

Pulling away, Koda smiles down at her. "Let's do something about that."

"A massage?" Kirsten asks innocently, well remembering where their massages have led them in the past. "I suppose that will relax me. Eventually."

Rolling her eyes, Dakota takes a step back. "Let's try something else first, shall we?" Strong hands still on tight shoulders, she gently urges the young woman to sit on the floor. "Here, cross your legs and get comfortable, all right?"

A tremor of anxiety wends its way through her belly. Muscles which were starting to relax instantly become tense again. "C'mon, Koda, I'm no good at this meditation stuff. Remember what happened at the sweat hut?"

"Relax, *canteskuye*, you'll be fine. Just relax and close your eyes."

Sighing softly, Kirsten does as requested. Closing her eyes is the easy part; relaxing is something else altogether.

Dakota's hands come down on her shoulders again, their heat filling her body with a sweet, welcome warmth. "Relax and concentrate on your breathing."

Koda's voice sounds very close to her ear, and she shivers slightly as the dulcet tones soothe their way through her.

"Deep cleansing breaths. In through the nose, out through the mouth. In through the nose, out through the mouth. Yes, like that. Good. Now, with each breath, feel some of your tension drift away. Can you feel it?"

*Not really*, Kirsten thinks, but doesn't speak aloud, not wanting to disappoint her lover.

As if reading her thoughts, Koda chuckles and squeezes the firm flesh beneath her palms. "Don't try so hard, my love. If nothing else, think of it as a few minutes without worries, okay?"

"Hm. Well, if you put it that way..."

"I do."

"All right, then." Wiggling her backside a little to gain more comfort on the hard wooden floor, she makes a great effort to relax her muscles and control her breathing. She can feel her lover's solid presence behind her and takes in her scent on an indrawn breath, letting it surround her and mingle with the warmth of the strong hands on her shoulders.

Opening her eyes, Kirsten finds herself in an open field. The land is flat and treeless and empty, stretching on for miles as far as her eyes can see. Tall grasses with feathery tufts have been pressed flat against the ground, laying a rich golden carpet over the earth.

A familiar, piercing cry sounds overhead, and she looks up, smiling as she sees what can only be Wiyo circling overhead on the warm, late-summer breeze. Instinctually, her hand rises as if to wave to her old, trusted friend, then freezes as the slanting sun winks off something on her finger. A ring. On the third finger of her left hand. Her vision blurs as she stares, dumbstruck, at the simple golden band through a film of sudden, joyful tears.

The hawk's cry sounds again, and this time it is answered by an identical cry to her left. Blinking, she shifts her gaze in that direction, looking on in dazed wonder as Dakota appears as if from nowhere. She is a magnificent sight. Dressed only in a beaded loincloth of red, yellow and black, her skin is dark and shining with sweat and oil. Her feet are bare as are her breasts. Her hair, drawn into two fat, shining braids lying easy over her broad shoulders, sports two eagle feathers, both pointing toward the Heavens.

In one hand, she holds a drum, and she taps on it with the fingers of her free hand. The rhythm is that of Kirsten's heartbeat. With each tap, Dakota takes a step, ball of her foot to heel and ball to heel again, approaching in a slow, sinuous and utterly captivating dance.

Kirsten's mouth opens, and she utters, again, the cry of the hawk, which is echoed by Wiyo, and then by human voices. Many human voices.

A long line of men and women appear behind Dakota. Leading the line is Tacoma, dressed identically to his sister save for the single feather in his hair and the bone whistle cradled securely between his lips. He looks at her and winks.

She can't help but smile back, filled with a sense of warmth and family far beyond anything she has ever conceived of knowing. She almost laughs aloud as the line dances slowly forward to Koda's rhythm and she recognizes the men and women following. Andrews, his shockingly red hair free and down past his shoulders, wears a pair of Army camo pants and no shirt, his fair, freckled skin already starting to burn in the blazing light of the sun. Manny is next, looking every bit the full blooded Lakota, his hair finally grown out enough to braid. Her jaw drops slightly as she recognizes Maggie, breasts proudly bared, her ebony skin shining blue in the sun, her teeth a blinding white as she nods to Kirsten and breaks into a beaming grin.

"My family," she whispers, her eyes filling with tears once again. "My people."

The strident scream of an air-raid siren breaks through her vision, jarring her back to full consciousness as her muscles close their steel traps once again.

She feels herself being lifted to her feet and steadied as she sways the tiniest bit, still caught between the present and what can only be her future. *Can it?* the more cynical part of her mind asks. *Can it really? Dreams like that are not for you, Kirsten King. Not for you. Not for you. Not for you.*

"We'll just see about that," she growls, grabbing Dakota's hand just as the door bursts inward and Jackson plows through.

"The enemy's been spotted, ma'ams. They're coming."

"In the air?" Dakota asks.

"No, ma'am. On the ground. It's..." He shakes himself out of his nervousness. "The general requests your presence in her office. Best possible speed."

"Let's go."

Jackson leads the way back out, but as Kirsten is about to follow, she's tugged to a gentle stop by Dakota. She looks up into gleaming eyes.

"You were given a vision."

It's not a question, and she doesn't have it within her to demur. Not now. Instead, she nods.

"It will come true." Again, the tone of complete, unalterable certainty.

Lifting Kirsten's hand, Koda places a kiss in the palm, then holds it over her own heart. "It will come true," she states again, her belief bedrock.

"I hope so," Kirsten whispers. "More than anything in the world."

**Hours later, with** the last of the plans set into motion, Dakota and Kirsten return to the house for a brief period of privacy, each knowing that such a chance will not come again for a very long, strenuous time.

"I saw Manny earlier," Kirsten says, looking up from her laptop where binary code continues to march futilely across the screen. "He's not a happy camper."

Koda lifts the kettle from the stove with both hands and pauses on her way to the bathroom. "I ran into him, too, when I made a last check on the patients in the clinic. He was walking around in the middle of his own personal cloud, but he didn't say what was bothering him."

"I know Maggie isn't letting him lead the chopper squadron tomorrow. He's been a glorified baby sitter for the last several weeks; that's got to smart." From the bathroom, Kirsten hears the water splash into the tub. They may die tomorrow, maybe even tonight, but by all the gods past and present, they are going to have a hot bath first. "How's it going?" she asks as Koda returns to fill the pot and set it on the stove where two others are just beginning to steam.

"Almost there. I found a last bit of bath salts in the back of the cabinet. Want to go for it?"

"Oooo, decadence. Need help?"

"Nah, I got it." Koda lifts another pot from the stove and disappears again.

The figures march across the screen in ranks, and it seems to Kirsten that they possess the same sort of mindless, mechanical determination that has been programmed into the droid soldiers. *Theirs not to reason why, theirs but to do and die.* The odd bit of poetry, relic of some long-ago literature class, floats up from her memory. *And how,* she asks herself wryly, *is that so different from us? If we fail here, we all die, sooner or later. Some later, but just as surely. And then what?*

Her vision, or her imagination, had seemed to promise that she and Koda would survive. So had Tega. But she knows enough, by now, to know that prophecy is conditional — not what will be, but what can be. It is up to her, to Dakota, to Maggie and Tacoma and Andrews and Jackson and Manny and all the rest, to carry that future and ultimately to bring it forth into the world. And there is a battle to be waged and won between that conception and that birth, and in that battle is death.

She lowers the top of her computer, pushing it away from her, and with it, the thought. They are as ready as they can be: ditches dug, derelict cars and trucks rammed into barricades, troop placements and strategies mapped out. Even from the distance of the officers' quarters, Kirsten can hear the steady roar of engines as their transports pull into formation on the flight line, the higher pitched whine of tanks and their two self-propelled howitzers as they take up their positions. Their rumble vibrates through the floorboards under her feet. *We're going to make it. We have to. Failure is impossible.*

In two hours, she and Koda will take their places in that line, move up the road to block the advance of the droids. The enemy has the numbers, but, given the rigidity of their programmed logic, the Ellsworth force has the tactics and the flexibility to exploit even a minuscule advantage to the fullest. And, despite the air raid siren, the droid army is dirt-bound. If necessary, Maggie will put the Tomcats into the air and bomb them to flinders. *Which is,* it occurs to Kirsten, *probably why Manny is being held back.*

The last pot comes on the boil, and Kirsten carries it into the bath. The steaming water smells sharply of lavender and something sweeter and more subtle running under the astringent scent of the bath salts. Koda kneels by the tub, stirring a thin stream of cooler water from the faucet into the mix. Curling vermilion petals skim the swirls, here and there the bell of an entire flower, its anthers leaving a trail of gold in the water. Koda glances up, one hand still in the water. "Try the temperature. See if it's right."

Kirsten's eyes sting suddenly, a prickling that has nothing to do with the eyestrain of the past hours. "It's right," she says around the catch in her throat. "It's the best bath I've ever seen." Then, more steadily she asks, "Where'd you find the tiger lilies?"

"In the garden of one of the vacant houses. They're panther lilies, actually, wild flowers. Someone must have brought them here from California."

Bending to add her own pan of hot water, Kirsten looks more closely. She brushes a silken bloom with one finger as it floats by. "You're right. They grow all over in the woods; I used to see them when my dad took us camping."

Koda reaches up to capture her free hand, turns the palm up and kisses it. Her eyes, when she raises her head, are the deep blue of gentians, trouble in their depths. She says softly, "You're trembling."

Wrapping her fingers about her lover's longer ones, Kirsten closes her eyes. "I'm scared, Koda. I don't know..." With an effort, she steadies her voice. "It bothers me when I don't know what outcome to expect. It's the scientist thing."

"You have seen beyond tomorrow. *Wika Tegalega* has given you a prophecy."

"Do you believe that? That we are going to make a whole new kind of world? Truly?"

"I do."

Something else stirs in Koda's eyes, a question Kirsten cannot quite read.

"When I scouted the battlefield with Maggie, I spoke with — I spoke with one of the four-footed people, *Igmú Tanka*. She said she would wait for our return."

"*Igmú Tanka*? *Igmú* is 'cat' — a mountain lion?"

Koda nods. "We will survive, *cante mitawa*. Not just us, but our people, all our peoples. If we use all our weapons, all our knowledge. It is promised." Her expression changes, a smile breaking over her face. "Now get into the tub with me, or the water will be cold."

Kirsten rises, turning away and slowly drawing her shirt over her head. Behind her, she can hear Koda's breath catch, and wonder washes through her that she has such power to move her lover. But she says, laughing, "I know how we can warm it up again."

"You're incorrigible," Koda answers, a hint of laughter in her own voice.

Kirsten hears the quiet murmur of cloth on cloth as Dakota's jeans and shirt drop to the floor, the soft splash as she steps into the tub and settles into the water.

"Oh gods," she breathes, "this is Heaven. I could die happy right now."

Kirsten turns to face her, taking in the long, copper legs that stretch all the way to the front of the tub, the angular shoulders contrasting with the upper curve of Koda's breasts. The blue eyes are closed in sheer, abandoned ecstasy, incredible long lashes fanned out on her cheeks. A more inviting prospect would be hard to imagine. But, "How are we going to do this? That's not exactly designed as a hot tub."

"True." Koda sits up straight, drawing her knees up almost under her chin. "Come on in. No, not that way," she says as Kirsten steps in, facing her. "Turn your back. That's it." As she moves to comply, Koda's legs part to let her sit between, and Koda's arms come around her, holding her gently. "This is better, no?"

"Much better," Kirsten breathes as she feels a kiss, soft as the spring breeze, ruffle her hair. Her own hands on Koda's she leans back against her, feeling the embrace tighten. The warmth of the water, the silkiness of her lover's skin, the rich scent of the lilies combine in something close to sensory overload. For a long moment, they remain motionless. Then Kirsten sighs, letting go of Koda's hand and reaching for the puff of pleated tulle that hangs from the hot water tap. "Time to scrub."

"Let me."

There is not room to turn around, but Kirsten hands the sponge and the bottle of soap backward, laughing. "Who'd have thought the woman waving an M-16 in my face would turn out to be such a hedonist? Just goes to show first impressions aren't all they're cracked up to be."

Koda chuckles, deep in her throat. "Who'd have thought the cute little android taking a leak in the snow would be such a sucker for it?"

Kirsten opens her mouth to protest, but closes it abruptly. Koda's hands, slick with the soap, pass over her shoulders in long, slow, circles, slip down her spine and up her flanks, the pattern repeating again and again. Through the film on her skin, she can feel Koda's nipples harden as they brush against her back. Koda's hands continue to spiral across her shoulders, down her flanks, sweeping across her thighs, circling her belly. They rise to cup her breasts, thumbs lightly brushing her nipples, the touch and the cool air tightening the flesh around them. Koda's mouth moves along the back of her neck, nibbling at her ear. Kirsten presses herself back against the strong body behind her, her own hands gliding over the long legs that arch beside her.

"*Nun lila hopa,*" Koda whispers. "*Cante mitawa.*"

"*Cante mitawa,*" Kirsten echoes, her breath catching as Koda's hand slips between her legs, then fingers part the labia to find the nub of her clitoris. Fire catches under her touch, strikes along the nerves of Kirsten's legs, flares to life up the column of her spine. "*Cante mitawa,*" she says again, while she can say anything at all, and her head falls back as release takes her and she feels her pulse hammer against Koda's hand that still cups her sex, shuddering through her again and again.

When she can move, she turns to kneel between Koda's thighs. Dakota's eyes, wide and unfocused with desire, draw her down and down, until it seems that she glides slowly through dark water, while shapes move along the verge of the pool above her, slim-legged and swift, slow and lumbering, moving on four legs or two or none. Around her she hears the darting passage of bright fish, the roll and tumble of otters. Then they are gone and she is back in the world she knows, her lips seeking Koda's in a long, lingering kiss as her knee presses against her lover's center and Koda comes, the blood pounding in her throat under Kirsten's mouth, beating frantically, then slowing as the after-languor takes them both. For a long moment they remain still, holding each other. Then Kirsten says huskily, "I saw a ring in my vision."

"Mmm," Koda answers, her head still against Kirsten's shoulder.

"Well, then, are you gonna marry me?"

"Are you proposing?"

"I am." Kirsten smiles against the dark hair that coils over her own shoulder and Koda's. "One of us had better."

"Since you put it that way," Koda raises her face to Kirsten's, claiming her mouth in a kiss that takes Kirsten's breath, "since you put it that way — yes."

"How — that is, I don't know what the Lakota custom is. How do we do it?"

A glint of mischief comes into Koda's eyes. "Well, first, you take Wanblee Wapka a string of ponies. Say about a dozen, you being President and all. Then you get a courting blanket and come calling. Then—"

"Then we elope," Kirsten says succinctly. "When does the judge get back?" A shadow crosses Koda's face, and a stab of regret goes through Kirsten. "I'm sorry, love. I'm worried, too."

"I know," Koda answers. "But we'll make our own rules. It's a new world. We're something new. We just need to get through this fight; then we can plan."

"I'll hold you to that." Kirsten leans forward into a kiss. "Now and forever."

**Kirsten sits cross-legged** on the springy, cool grass beneath the heavy boughs of fragrant trees that dot the residential area of the base. At her back, the waters of the stream chuckle merrily as if listening to a joke only they can hear.

The scent of the rendered fat in the bowls before her doesn't exactly rival perfume, and she resists the urge to sneeze just to get the smell out of her sinuses. She settles for what she hopes is innocuous mouth-breathing instead, flushing slightly at the look she receives from Tacoma. A touch to her knee draws her attention back to Dakota, who is sitting with a bowl of yellow paint cradled in her lap and a small twig laden with the ochre held up, elegant eyebrow raised slightly, questioning.

Kirsten nods, almost shyly, and, smiling, Koda brings the loaded twig to her lover's cheek, painting a design with sure, deft strokes. After several moments, she pulls the brush away and tilts Kirsten's chin, eyes raking over the design she's just created. A quick touchup, and she nods, satisfied with her work. *"Iktomi zizi."*

The words bring smiles to the faces of Manny and Tacoma, and a frown of puzzlement to Kirsten's. "Excuse me?"

Reaching up, Dakota gently touches Kirsten's face, then lays two fingers on her partner's chest, right above her heart. "*Iktomi zizi.*" With her free hand, Koda lifts a bowl of clear water and hands it to Kirsten, gesturing for her to look into it.

The surface of the water ripples, and Kirsten watches her reflection waver in it, squinting as the image slowly comes into focus.

An intricate web design covers most of her left cheek. A similar one, though smaller, dots her right. She raises her head slowly, looking up at Dakota, wide-eyed. "A spider? You're calling me a spider?"

"*Iktomi zizi.* Yellow spider."

Kirsten's face wrinkles. "I don't think I—"

"Hey!" Manny interrupts, chuckling, "I think it's perfect. Spiders might be small, but some of them can bring down a man, or even a full grown horse with just one bite."

"Yeah, but they're—"

"Crafty and intelligent," Tacoma interrupts. "Creators of incredibly complex designs, and absolutely fearless." He grins. "The name fits you perfectly."

Kirsten eyes the three steadily. "Yeah, well just remember something else about us spiders."

"Yeah?" Manny asks. "What's that?"

"We eat our mates."

There is a moment of absolute silence as her words are absorbed. Then Tacoma and Manny both blush, their copper skin tinting toward tomato red as they break into laughter and smack Dakota on the shoulder with good-natured teasing.

Kirsten looks on, a bit confused with the reaction she's receiving. It is only when she spies Dakota's rakish, eyebrow-waggling grin that the subtext of her words blooms fully in her mind, and the blush that crawls up from her shoulders is so deep and dark that her pale eyebrows stand out in vivid relief against its heat. "Oh my God," she moans, dropping her face into her hands. "I cannot believe I just said that!"

Chuckling, Koda rubs her back. "Just relax, love. We know what you meant." After a moment, she eases Kirsten's hands away from her face and checks to make sure the designs aren't smudged. "One last thing. Close your eyes."

Said eyes narrow. "Why."

"Relax and just close your eyes. Trust me."

Sighing, Kirsten lets her lids slide closed. "I'd better not regret this."

"Just keep 'em closed." Taking another bowl, this filled with thick black paste, she dips three fingers in, coating them liberally. Lifting her fingers, she tilts Kirsten's face toward her and draws them across her lover's eyes from temple to temple, creating a crude, but effective black mask. "Okay, you can open your eyes now."

Dakota grins as vivid green eyes open, their color all the more striking when set against the black paint surrounding them, like emeralds in a black-velvet jeweler's box. "For *Wika Tegalega.* Look."

Kirsten glances down into the still water, then back up at her lover. "I look like the Hamburgler."

There is a moment of silence, and then the group roars in laughter. Kirsten merely rolls her eyes. "Can we get on with this, please?"

The others eventually sober, and Dakota takes back the water bowl with a grin that is slightly abashed. Her face has already been painted with the symbols of Crazy Horse, and the backs of both hands bear stylized wolf prints done in black and red.

A piercing cry spears the silence, and the four of them look up to see Wiyo circling down toward them. With a great beating of wings, she lands upon Koda's outstretched forearm. A leather pouch dangles from one of her legs and Kirsten eyes it curiously. "What—"

"A note," Dakota intuits, using her free hand to untie the simple slip-knot. She hands the pouch to Kirsten. "Get it out of there for me, willya?"

The bag's laces are tight and slippery, but Kirsten finally manages to fumble them open. Upending the small pouch, she shakes out a tiny, tightly rolled slip of paper. Without her glasses on, the tiny writing is just one big blur, so she hands the scrap off to Dakota, who peers down at the message while Wiyo looks on, placidly.

"It's from Fenton. He found Toller."

"Oh yeah?" Tacoma asks. "Where?"

"Just outside of Grand Rapids." Dakota raises her eyes from the note. "Dead."

"No shit!" This from Manny, who looks on, wide-eyed. "How?"

"Single gunshot wound to the back of the head."

"Sounds like an execution," Kirsten murmurs. "Did the judge say who he thought did it?"

"He's guessing androids. There was talk in town about a small group of them in that area over the last week or so."

"Any sign of Hart?"

"None."

"Bet the metalheads took him," Manny observes, raking a hand through his hair. "He's the fucking commander of the base they're about to attack. Jesus Christ."

Kirsten rubs at the back of her neck. "Well, he's been kept pretty well isolated from our plans for a while now, so while it's not the best news in the world, I'm not sure it's the worst, either."

"Yeah, but," Manny argues, getting up to pace, "he knows the base layout like the back of his hand, he knows our numbers, our weapons, our strengths, our weak spots, and, worst of all, he knows you're here. That sound like pretty damn bad news to me."

"Manny, sit."

The young pilot looks over at his cousin, sighs, and sits.

"All right," Dakota continues, "we're not even positive that the androids have him, but if they do, it's a bit late to worry about it now. They're at our gates, and with or without Hart's information, they're gonna be damned tough to fend off. So...we stick to the plan and see what develops."

"We should probably let Maggie know," Kirsten replies softly.

"Sounds good." Koda eyes her brother and cousin. "Anything else?"

Both shake their heads in the negative.

"Good." Shifting her gaze, she looks into the golden eyes of her feathered companion. "Thank you, my friend."

Ruffling her wings, Wiyo closes her lethal talons around Koda's forearm until the needle-sharp points break the skin. Three fat beads of blood well up. Cocking her head, she lets go a loud, almost triumphant cry, then launches herself into the air, wings flapping strongly, elegantly. With a feel-

ing of almost stunned disbelief, Koda looks down in her lap, where two perfect feathers now rest. As she watches, the blood from her arm drips down
onto the feathers, anointing them.

"You have been blessed, *Tshunkmanitou Wakan Winan*," Tacoma says,
his eyes sparkling reverently, joyfully. "By Ina Maka herself. Surely we are
meant to win this fight."

Still staring down at the feathers in her lap, Dakota finds that she can
say nothing at all.

**Kirsten sits on** Maggie's cot, its blanket tucked drumhead-tight
around the narrow mattress, systematically shoving rounds into the spare
magazines of her .45. One, already filled, lies beside the weapon on top of
her pack. She is halfway through the second, her face frozen in concentration as she thumbs bullet after bullet into their flat carriers. Koda watches
her from the desk, where she is marking their force's final battle positions
on a topo map of the ground where they plan to meet the android army.
Tacoma has another copy, as does Maggie. Like them, she has no illusion
that these are anything but a diagram of their opening gambit. If she has
learned nothing else from the battle of the Cheyenne, from her fight with
the Minot war leader, she has learned that battle is unpredictable.

She has also learned that men and women will follow her, and that still
frightens her. It frightens her all the more when one of those women is
Kirsten. Perhaps she should feel easier knowing that her lover will be at
the command center, guarded by Manny and Andrews and Maggie herself,
but a part of Dakota's mind remains convinced that Kirsten is safest at her
side, with love as well as friendship and duty between her and harm.

But that is an illusion, and she knows it. There is no safety anywhere
— not on the battlefield, not off it. They must break the enemy here, and
they must break him now. There will be no second chance. *I will be here
when you return*, Puma had said. But prophecy is contingent. None knows
that better than Koda.

*We could still lose. We could lose it all.*

Finished with the map, Koda folds it and slips it into her field pack.
"About ready?"

Kirsten shoves the last round home, slipping the full magazines into
loops in her belt. She looks up, smiling briefly. "I'm ready." Then, the
smile fades. "I'll be glad when this is over."

"Me, too," Koda says quietly. She rises and shoulders her own pack.
One way or another, the world will be a different place in twenty-four hours.

Kirsten follows suit, snapping down the holster on her Colt and lifting
her kit by its straps. Her helmet dangles from it by the chinstrap. Her battle dress, like Koda's own, bears no insignia. No need to advertise their
identity to the enemy. Forward parties have already caught and killed half
a dozen human spies; it would take only one to recognize her and carry
word of Kirsten's presence to the enemy. They have no way of knowing
how many they have missed, any one of whom could betray their strategy
to the enemy.

Unfortunately, there is no Plan B. They have no resources in reserve.

A shadow passes across the window, dark in the light of the low sun.
Knuckles rap lightly on the jamb before Maggie pushes open the door. Like
Dakota and Kirsten, she wears combat fatigues, the bulk of her Kevlar vest

showing clearly beneath her tunic, an M-16 slung over her shoulder. A wry smile quirks her mouth upward. "Madam President, would you like to inspect the troops?"

"No," Kirsten says succinctly. "Let's just go."

The tension in her voice runs along Koda's nerves.

Maggie's mouth tightens, her eyes narrowing. "Let's try that again. Madam President, would you like to inspect the troops?"

Kirsten glances up at the taller woman, her own face set. "I said—"

"Kirsten," Koda says softly, "you are their Commander in Chief."

Koda notes the rise and fall of Kirsten's shoulders underneath her jacket, hears the breath as it leaves her. "All right. Nothing formal."

Maggie nods. "Nothing formal. They need to see you, though. They need to know you see them."

It is something Koda has learned over the last months, slowly and with reluctance. A commander is as much symbol as actual leader, as much a fighting band's faith as its head. The troops who followed her across the bridge at the Cheyenne did not do it for freedom or democracy or the idea of a state. They had done it for her.

Kirsten's face loses its stubbornness as the realization comes to her as well. "All right," she says again and steps through the door Maggie holds for her.

Over her head, Maggie's eyes meet Koda's. "You'll do," she says, and Koda is not sure whether she means Kirsten or herself. "You'll do just fine."

Outside, the low sun lays long shadows on the tarmac, fantastic angular shapes that barely suggest the APCs and Strykers and Bradleys that cast them. The vehicles themselves form a convoy strung out half the length of the runway, most in single file. Lead and rear contingents both are armor: tanks and their two mobile howitzers. Personnel carriers cluster in the middle. All along the line, the troops stand at attention, men and women drawn from every branch of service, the reserves, the civilian population. All are well armed; most are, more or less, in uniform. There is no shortage of equipment, only of soldiers to use it.

Parked just outside the office, the Jeep that had once been General Hart's stands waiting. Its door bears his three stars, or once did. Now all that remains of them is a single star and two splotches of fresh paint. Miniature flags fly from the front fenders: the Stars and Stripes from one, the blue Air Force banner from the other. Andrews sits at the wheel. Maggie slips into the front seat beside him, Koda and Kirsten into the back. Just as Kirsten turns to arrange her gear, Koda says, "Stand, *cante skuye*. Let them see you."

For a moment it seems that Kirsten will demur. But she faces front, one hand on the rollbar, as the Jeep begins to move. A ripple precedes them up the line, hands raised to salute. Koda watches as Kirsten smiles and acknowledges the gesture, her own back straight as a young birch tree, all traces of anger and tension gone from her face. It comes to Koda that Kirsten has a true gift for leadership, one very different from her own. Her lover's wildness is all for her, nothing that near-strangers or even friends will ever see. To them she is a still point of order in chaos, a fragment of rationality in a spinning vortex of dementia. She is the center that will hold against the circling dark.

The Jeep comes to the end of the line, the rear brought up by one of the howitzers. Then it swings back to take its place in the middle of the column, and the line of vehicles shudders into motion.

"Here we go," Kirsten says, taking her seat.

In her eyes, apprehension shadows her pride in the moment, and Koda knows what she fears.

"Here we are," she answers, taking her hand. "Always."

**"It's a good** thing they already know we're coming," Kirsten shouts into Koda's ear, "because this is sure as Hell no sneak attack."

Koda grins and nods, not even attempting speech. Before and behind them, the Bradleys and howitzers, the mortars and the other tracked vehicles crunch along the asphalt. The tanks's characteristic shrill whine carries on the evening air like the howl of lost souls, punctuated only by the whup-whup of a pair of low-flying Apache choppers scouting the margins of the road. The air chills as they pass, blue with dusk, shadows fading into the oncoming night. Stars hang low on the eastern horizon before them; behind them the scudding clouds flame gold and crimson as the sun slips below the edge of the world. To either side of the road, barriers of derelict cars and trucks loom high, broken shapes out of nightmare bulldozed into place to funnel the enemy advance between Tacoma's forces and Maggie's. Also along their flanks, invisible now under brush and rubble, ten-foot wide trenches run from the pavement into the trees that line the road. If the enemy follows the battle plan hammered out by the Ellsworth officers, if the enemy can be forced to follow it, the ditches will trap and incapacitate the droids' armor. At intervals, two-and-three man teams peel off the line of march to take stations, in the woods or behind rocks, where they can lob armor-piercing missiles into the mired tanks from shoulder launchers.

Koda fastens the chin strap of her helmet, pulling it tight and checking the adjustment of the night sight. She does not lower it yet; there is little to see now save the bulk of the APC lumbering along ahead of their Jeep, and the heaps of wrecked metal looming on either side at irregular intervals. Beside her, Kirsten does likewise, her lover's smaller hand seeking hers again. They will separate soon, Koda to lead her detachment into its position on the south flank, hidden from the road, Kirsten to remain with Maggie among the command post personnel as communications chief. It is not a position of safety. Maggie will have charge of the center, where the enemy attack will fall hardest. In the dark, in her own mind, she tries to find reassurance in Kirsten's vision, in Puma's promise that she would be here, on this ground, at Koda's return.

But this is a return, now, and Puma is a warrior spirit. It is battle that waits. There is no guarantee of ever coming here again. Neither is there any guarantee of leaving.

As they pass the ten-mile mark out of Ellsworth, the pace of the column picks up, the whine of the tanks suddenly diminishing. Kirsten's fingers tighten around Koda's; Tacoma has left the interstate with the armor squadron, gone to take up position in the thickening dark to the north of the road, where they will both protect the flank of the main force and, with luck, draw the enemy tanks and Bradleys into a death trap.

The moon is up, just off the full. A stiff wind blows from the south, and clouds scud across its face, narrow ribbons of black and silver. Suddenly Kirsten turns, her profile rimlit in the pale light, her pointing finger tracking something moving along the treeline. As Koda's gaze follows, she can make out a white shape beyond the reach of the branches, propelled by slow, deep wingbeats. Owl. The moonlight strikes silver from its feathers, ripples over the fan of its pinions where they spread out like fingers at the ends of its wings. Though it does not call, a shiver passes through her, chill along her skin. There will be death tomorrow; she needs no omen to tell her that.

With the armor gone, the convoy picks up speed. The barricades grow fewer as they approach the place where they will deploy in preparation to meet the enemy, and the last mile or so of road lies open and unobstructed to give their own forces room to fall back. Kirsten no longer needs to shout to be heard. "We're almost there."

Koda turns to face her. The moon is higher now, and the fear in Kirsten's eyes shows plainly. She does not fear for herself; no woman who could be intimidated by a mere army could have made her way across a continent alone, could have twice gone cold-bloodedly into the heart of the enemy stronghold. The fear is for the world they will leave behind them if they fail. It is also, she knows, for her, Dakota. There are no words to answer it. Her own fears have burned themselves clean: for Kirsten, for Tacoma, for the men and women whose lives are in her hand.

She touches a finger to one of the hailstones painted on her face. *Hoka hey, Tshunka Witco. It is a good day to die.* It is a better one to live.

Ahead of them, the APCs slow even further and begin to fan out across the width of the interstate. Andrews brings the Jeep to a halt beside the truck that will house the command post, parked now facing back the way they have come so that Maggie, Kirsten, and their staff will be able to see out the open back. Kirsten's hand tightens on Koda's almost convulsively. They will separate here.

Maggie gets out of the Jeep and begins to move toward the line of APCs disgorging their loads of troops. Koda can hear the rattle of their gear as they jump to the pavement, the occasional "Moth-*er-fuck*!" as someone drops a piece of equipment or jostles the soldier ahead. She will have to sort out her own squad and lead them into position behind the rise that lifts dark against sky to the south. Andrews has also found urgent business ahead, leaving Koda and Kirsten a small moment of privacy in the midst of chaos.

"Dakota..." Kirsten breaks off, her voice catching. Then she chokes out, "Be safe."

Koda lays a hand on the other woman's cheek, feeling the helmet strap under her palm. Awkwardly, because the night sights project from above the rims of their helmets, she bends and kisses Kirsten gently. "'Til morning," she says. "This is the easy part."

"I know," Kirsten answers. "I'll just be glad when we're through it."

Under her hand, Koda feels her lover's mouth quirk up in a wry smile.

"Can't wait to get to that hard stuff."

Koda kisses her again, lingeringly, and turns to go. Before she can move from where she stands, a whistling howl splits the air above them, a metallic shriek followed by another and another. Koda tracks the sound as it dopplers down the highway. A mile beyond them to the west, a flame-shot cloud rises from the pavement, roiling with the violence of the explosion. A second flares just beyond it, and a third.

"What the Hell was that?" Kirsten demands of the sudden silence.

Maggie appears again beside them. "Howitzers." Even in the darkness, her grin is visible. "We just got lucky. The bastards are overshooting us."

**Kirsten walks the** line in the darkness, feeling as much as seeing the mass of the metal wall thrown up across the width of the interstate. The moon gives light enough to make out the crumpled metal rammed into barricades; here and there it glints off chrome trim or the arc of a hubcap. Here and there, too, it catches the shape of an M-16, where a soldier crouches at one of the firing slits left open or perches six feet up, straining to catch some glimpse of the enemy. They nod and salute as she passes, their movements visible only in the shift of shadow. At the other wall, the one a hundred yards behind this one, Maggie is doing the same thing, checking their defenses, rallying morale. In the hollows of the culvert and the drainage ditch that runs along the road, soldiers crouch with grenade launchers held ready. Ideally, the enemy will not breach the first barricade. Practically, they are certain to do so. And when they do, they will be trapped between the two barriers, caught in crossfire from three directions. Kirsten cannot see the ambushers, but is aware of their eyes on her as she moves. The howitzer shells still scream overhead at regular intervals, still landing well behind them.

Kirsten grimaces at Manny, walking beside her. "I'm beginning to think they're just trying to keep us awake."

The light gleams off the glass of his night scope as he nods. "Weakens morale. Or maybe they're just trying to cut off our retreat by tearing up the road."

"Or maybe they're just dumb. They've got to wonder why we're not shooting back."

"Goddam metalheads. Who the fuck's in charge over there, anyway?"

"Or *what's* in charge."

"Yeah." Manny pauses a moment, listening. "Here comes another one."

The round shrieks as it flies over them, landing with a force that shakes the ground beneath them where they stand, half a mile away. With the wall behind them, she cannot see the fireball rise. "Good thing we don't plan on retreating. Maybe they'll run out of ammo eventually."

"Nah. Ammo, small arms, they're just like us. They've got more stuff than they have troops to shoot it."

Kirsten gives him a wry grin. "Well," she says, "that's a comfort."

**Koda moves among** her troops, stepping without sound over the springy new grass that carpets the meadow below the rise that shields them from the interstate. She does not speak to them, but touches a shoulder here, an arm there, letting them feel her presence and her concern. They will not let her down; she must help them know that she will not fail them.

*Just like an old war movie*, she thinks with a fleeting bit of self-mockery. *Patton, maybe or Prince Hal moving among his men before Agincourt, pretending to be a common soldier.* Except that she knows that it comes from no film, nor from any history book. This is instinct with her, memory.

She has never doubted that she was born to be a shaman. Has never doubted, either, that she required every moment of learning and practice her father and grandfather demanded of her. Her leadership has come to her as easily as her breath, and that frightens her. *Because I don't know what I don't know. And what I don't know can get us all killed.*

She shivers a little in the night wind. Another of the seemingly interminable hail of howitzer rounds passes to the north of her position, to impact somewhere on the other side of the main force's position on the highway. Either they cannot find their targets or the Ellsworth force is within the big guns' minimum range. *Or they want us to think we are. Spook us bad.*

She completes her round of her squadron, finally settling on a rocky outcropping where she can see over the edge of the embankment. The hollow beyond is lost in shadow. In the moonlight, she can just make out the irregular shapes that she knows to be the barricades and the strings of empty vehicles behind the second one. Kirsten will be there, operating the main communications net. It ought to be a place of greater safety, but Koda knows that it is not. None of them is any safer than any other, which is to say that none of them is safe at all.

The moon climbs as she watches, the stars pacing across the sky in their myriads. Aries the ram, Taurus the bull, constellations of spring, both associated with the turning of the seasons and the time of planting from time immemorial. Both, in their own time, gods who saw the rise of civilization and who may now see its ending.

The sweet scent of the grass comes to her, mingled with the sharper tang of gun oil. Above her, the sound of a thousand voices skims the air, and she looks up to see a wedge of geese pass before the moon, followed by another and another, the flocks arrowing north to the tundra's edge to mate and rear their young. In the fall, their passage will blacken the sky as they fly south, fearing none but eagles, their human predators all but vanished.

A hand tugs at her sleeve, and she turns to find one of the Minot men just below her. "Ma'am, look," he whispers.

Koda follows his pointing finger to the meadow behind them. Fog is rising, billowing up from a small branch of the Cheyenne. "Damn," she says quietly. "God damn."

# CHAPTER FORTY-ONE

Sometime after midnight, the big gun falls silent. The fog, rolling in from the stream to the south, blankets the highway and the ground to either side. The figures that emerge from it from time to time to speak to Kirsten, or to Maggie, trail mist through the back door of the command truck, like ghosts with fragments of shroud still clinging to them. At her post, numbers march across the screen of Kirsten's computer, tallying their strength, coding the position of their forces. Beside her, Maggie studies a map of the field, searching for any overlooked weakness that may give advantage to the enemy.

Tacoma and his armor have spread out on their left flank, reaching north into the open ground that once was a wheat field. Behind him lie the trenches and barricades that will funnel the enemy into the two-pronged trap so carefully laid for them. On their other flank, behind a rise to the south, Koda holds her force in reserve to hit the droids and their allies from the side and rear once they commit fully to the attack. The task of the center is simple: to take the brunt and hold. If they break, the way to Ellsworth lies open, and humanity has no more defense.

Maggie glances at her watch, then looks up to catch Kirsten's eye. "That's twenty minutes since they've fired. They're getting ready to move."

"Relay," Kirsten says, and Manny begins to speak quietly into the radio. Kirsten can make out a few of the Lakota words — *mazawaka* is "gun"; *toka*, "enemy" — and allows herself a fleeting second of satisfaction as the replies come in. "*Han*," she says, adding her own sign-off to Manny's, "*Hau*."

"*Hoka hey*," Maggie says, "you're learn—" She breaks off abruptly. "I hear them."

Kirsten touches a finger to her implants, boosting the volume. The low vibration, felt as much as heard, becomes the crunching of treads on asphalt, the high whine of powerful engines. "It's their tanks," she says, just as the door bursts open on one of the corporals from the forward barricade.

"Col—I mean General, ma'am! They've got their armor out front."

"We're on it. Rivers," she raps out, "tell your cousin we need two of his tank killers on the south side of the road ASAP. Herd them off toward our left flank."

"Ma'am." Manny turns back to the radio, rattling out orders in Lakota, this time too rapid for Kirsten to follow. The low "whump!" of the lead tank's cannon comes a fraction of a second later.

"Shit!" Maggie swivels in her seat. "Kill the bastards! Now!"

**Koda watches the** slow approach of the enemy column as it makes its way down the highway toward the center of the battle line. The mist drifts green and eerie in front of her nightscope, allowing her hardly more than a glimpse of the lumbering shapes of tanks and Strykers where the headlights of the troop carriers strike them. The growl of their engines comes to her muffled by the fog, the vibration of their movement a steady rumbling in the earth. Behind them come ranks of marching troops, their height uniform, their guns all canted at identical angles, their step perfectly paced and synchronized. Droid soldiers. And behind them, followed by more heavy vehicles, supply trucks perhaps, come the fully militarized androids, some on treads like the tanks, others on more human-looking legs with nothing else human about them.

*I am on your ground,* Igmú Tanka. *Teach me patience. Teach me the cold equations.*

Sudden fire blossoms amid the fog, arcing upward to explode just short of the first barricade. Smoke boils up from the ground, mingling with the mist, shot with red and orange as the asphalt burns, and a tank goes up in a ten-meter high flare of diesel fuel and ammunition. Around it movement ebbs and flows, a second tank lumbering up beside it to take lead position and fire, its shell tearing into the berm of wrecked cars, metal shrieking against metal while smaller arms fire peppers the culvert where Tacoma's men lie hidden. Suddenly the second tank bursts in a fireball of burning fuel and cannon shells, showering white-hot fragments on the troops behind it.

"Two down." Koda can just make out the black-painted face of the Minot sergeant beside her. His nod of satisfaction makes a small shift in the darkness about them both. A third vehicle goes up, not a tank by the size of the explosion, and a man's scream stabs through the fog as yet another rocket streaks down on the column, this one from closer to the barricade, and a third M-1 bursts into flame.

"I think they got one of our guys, ma'am," the soldier observes quietly.

"I think you're right. That was a suicide mission."

"But it worked. Look."

On the road, the column halts briefly. Then the tanks' engines rev and they begin to lumber off the highway, moving onto the shoulder and then over the open field to the north, where Tacoma waits for them.

Koda breathes a long sigh of relief, her breath frosting in the early morning cold. The enemy has taken the bait. It is now a matter of waiting, and the kill.

**He walks along** the line of his squad, noticing the facepaint on the majority with an interior smile. His mother, he knows, would be furious, offended. *These are not our People*, he can hear her saying, as if she is even now standing right beside him. *How dare they presume to know our ways?*

What she doesn't know, what she would refuse to acknowledge even if she saw, is that these men and women have adorned their faces with paint for much the same reason Tacoma himself has: for honor, for courage, for hope, and for remembrance. There is no mockery in the eyes that meet his own. Resolve? Yes. Fear? Oh yes. All of that, and more.

Tacoma walks the line, murmuring words of encouragement to the men and women who stand guard against what is to come. He steps in next to a small woman who, from behind, looks like a young boy trying on his father's work clothes. Her helmet is much too large, tending to slip down over her eyes no matter how tightly the chin strap is snapped. She is one of the women rescued from the living hell of the jails, one of the very few who remained behind. He gets no more than two steps past her when his headset crackles. "Yeah?"

Manny's voice sounds over the com. "*Hipi. Aka iyiciyapo!*"

Tacoma clicks off the com and turns to his troops. "It's time. Mount up!"

The squad eases into their Bradleys, their Strykers, and their tanks. Their engines start, one after another, and with a "Wagons ho!" signal from Tacoma in his Jeep, they move forward. The fog seems to move with them like a second army, this one as much enemy as ally.

A mile or so ahead, the Strykers pull off to the side, and heavily armed troops jump off to the right and left, flanking the road. The sound of the enemy comes to them in the clank of rolling metal and the heavy, cloying scent of gun oil.

The Bradleys and the tanks move ahead several yards, then form a line across the field to the north of the road, behind the carefully camouflaged deadfalls, guns ready. They wait.

Tacoma swings his Jeep back around the line and parks to the rear. Hopping out, he nods to the troops manning the vehicles, then breaks off to the right of the road, jumping down onto the embankment. Tooms, Carruthers, Chin, and Wayley stand down in the natural ditch, shoulder launchers up and armed. Seven others kneel behind them, boxes of ammunition open and ready. They all meet his gaze steadily. "Hold fire," he says. "Let them come to us."

**The second tank** round shakes the earth, sending Maggie to one knee as she bolts for the back of the truck. Out of the corner of her eye, she sees Kirsten clutch at her computer just as it slides toward the edge of the folding table that is her station. Manny grabs at laptop and operator both, steadying them against his own stocky bulk. "General, you okay?"

Maggie levers herself up, hardly breaking stride. "I'm fine. Look after Kirsten!" She steps out onto the bumper and takes the drop in one step, feeling her knee fold under her again. Swearing silently, she jogs lopsidedly to the front of the truck. About thirty yards ahead of her, a crater in the pavement smokes with the heat of the tank round. One soldier lies some ten feet to the side, arms and legs bent at impossible angles.

She has no trouble seeing the hole the shell drilled in the barricade; its metal edges remain white-hot with its passing. Lowering her night goggles, she peers through it, watching as first one tank, then another, bursts into flame and dies. Above her, perched precariously among the twisted metal, snipers wait with hands clenched on the grips of their rifles. Until the armor is off the road, they are useless. "Hold your fire!" Maggie yells. "Wait for the droids and traitors!" Then, to a private crouched beside the wall, "Run back and tell Martinez to move up a couple of the machine guns. We might as well make use of this goddam hole!"

The soldier scrambles to obey, and as she sprints for the rear of the column, the forward tanks of the enemy force begin to lurch off the pavement onto the shoulder, spreading out across the field to their north. "Yessss!" Maggie allows herself a small moment of triumph as the whine of their engines dopplers off, then she turns back to the task at hand.

With her night sight, Maggie can make out, dimly in the fog, the advancing ranks of the droid infantry, marching in perfect unison toward the barricade. These are the cannon fodder. Good soldiers. Not a thought in their metal heads to question their orders or to opt for their own survival. Somewhere behind them will be the more advanced models, and some-

where among them, please Goddess, are the self-destruct bombers programmed by Kirsten.

A pair of infantrymen land beside her, each carrying an M-60; a third
and fourth drop an ammunition chest between them, then sit on it, panting.
"Ma'am, the guns you ordered," one gasps.

Maggie grins at them. "Good.  Set them up here, aimed out of this
hole.  Get as much crossfire as you can.  Spray anything that gets in range."

"Ma'am."  The two sitting on the case drop to their knees and set about
threading the ammo belts into the guns' feeders.  Maggie moves down the
barricade, checking her troops.  Except for a couple of burns and a few
more bruises, the soldier killed by the shell's concussion is the only casualty so far.  The rest hold their posts, guarding their flanks where the barrier
curves to the rear.  Advantage, good guys.  She does not expect it to last.

It does not.  From behind the barrier comes the sound of shots fired in
single volleys as M-16 shells begin to rain down on troops and vehicles
alike.  "Shit!" she yells.  "Get to cover!  They're firing high!"

Around her soldiers scramble to flatten themselves against the barricade, a few diving under trucks.  Behind her the M-60s open up, and she
darts for the command truck, reaching up to grab Manny's arm as the door
flies open and he pulls her up and in.  Shells strike the truck's roof and
bounce off, clattering harmlessly against the armor plating.  "Sounds like a
hailstorm out there," Manny observes.

"Nah."  A wry grin quirks up one side of Kirsten's mouth.  "That's
freakin' Santa Claus and eight tiny reindeer."  Then, to Maggie she says,
"Tacoma's drawing fire.  Nothing's headed Koda's way.  The guys in the
back want to know if they should move up."

"Woman, you pick the damnedest time to develop a sense of humor."
Maggie shakes her head at Kirsten.  "Tell 'em come on.  All Hell's about to
break loose out there."

**The battle comes** to him as sound.  Even through the night-scope, the
fog and trees obscure the enemy advance.  Tacoma holds his forces ready,
waiting silently, their engines cooling.  Neither noise nor heat will betray
their position.

From his vantage point to the side, he hears the grinding of metal
treads in the soil, the timbre changing as they begin to crush the woody
undergrowth covering the open space between the field and the treeline
where the ranks of armor lie hidden from both sight and heat sensors.  The
enemy rides without lights, relying, like the Ellsworth force, on night scopes
and the sensors feeding data to mechanical brains.  The first of the droid
tanks pitches into one of the camouflaged trenches with a crash, landing
squarely on the clutch of mines awaiting it.  The double blast, mines and
fuel, shudders through the ground, and a fireball blooms upward into the
dark, briefly burning away the fog to illuminate the long barrel of a cannon
here, the low curve of a turret there.

"Got one," Jackson observes in the momentary silence.  His hands lie
slack on the Jeep's wheel, waiting the order to move.

In the instant before the fog closes in again and obscures the advancing armor, Tacoma counts four more tanks and a pair of Bradleys.  About
half the enemy cavalry, judging by the noise.  A second fireball goes up as
one of the two fighting vehicles tips into another deadfall, and Tacoma

speaks into his com. "*Wana,*" he says, "Now."

In response, the engines of half a dozen armored units growl to life, and flame bursts from the long muzzles of the two M-1s in the center of the line. A pair of anti-tank missiles streak upward from their hidden launchers in a steep trajectory, their white contrails pale against the swirling mist. The M-1s and Bradleys on the flanks, though, skulk silently, holding their fire, hidden in darkness.

An enemy tank shell lands on one of the fighting vehicles, its fuel going up in a torrent of flame. There is no hope that the Bradley's crew has survived; armored vehicles are death traps under a direct hit. Another shell bursts overhead, its white phosphorus glare burning through the fog to show Tacoma the grinding advance of the enemy armor. One tank, bizarrely, crawls over the remnants of another to bridge a deadfall; others batter their way through the woods, crushing trees, root and branch, under their metal hulks. Tacoma shouts into his com, "Willie Peter! They've seen us! All units fire!"

The thunder of the cannon rolls over him like a shockwave. An enemy shell gouges out a crater less than fifty feet away from Tacoma's position, and the Jeep rocks beneath him. A second volley uproots a thirty-foot larch pine, to bring it crashing down on one of the enemy's Bradleys. The tree, its pitch taking fire from the burning diesel, flames through the fog like a candle.

Another enemy tank succumbs to a deadfall and the anti-tank missiles from the snipers hidden on the flank. The others go wide to skirt it, swinging back to re-form and drive snarling toward Tacoma's center. He watches them come, gauging their approach to the last second. He can feel Jackson's eyes on him, taking their own measure. It is an unsettling feeling, one he has no time to analyze. He lets the enemy come on until he can almost make out their shapes, hulking in the mist. "*Hektakiyanapepi!*" he yells into his mic, then hangs on for his life as Jackson turns the Jeep on its own footprint and falls in behind the armor, now retreating at full speed along the trails already blazed over the rough ground.

"Goddam!" Darius yells as they bounce over an axle-shattering outcrop of limestone, a grin splitting the grease paint streaking his face. "This is fun!"

**A thunder of** boot soles on pavement announces the arrival of the troops from behind the second barricade. Maggie flings the door wide and jumps down among them, heedless of the hail of bullets pelting down on their position, running with them for the relative safety of the wall. "Grenade launchers!" she yells. "Get up on the wall and let 'em have it! Get as many as you can before they hit the mines! We want to save those for the heavy models!"

A dozen soldiers scramble up the irregular pile of metal, finding holds among the dents and the protruding door handles and axles. Maggie gestures toward the top with a sweep of her hand. "Some of you rifles get up there, too! Snipe off any humans you see. Don't waste your ammo on the metalheads!"

"Ma'am!" A sergeant salutes and hits the wall, swinging with a gymnast's skill to a position where she can fire over the top, her platoon swarming up after her to spread out between the grenade launchers.

Maggie watches them go, strange green shadows in the light of her night scope — a hand here, a helmet rim there — lit to white glare by the muzzle flashes of their weapons. "The rest of you, reinforce the flanks! Once they get to the wall, they'll try to go around!"

As they split and sprint for the sides of the highway, Maggie grabs a protruding wheel and levers herself up to a slit in the wall. The mist still swirls thickly along the ground, but overhead she can make out a faint gleam that she is almost sure is a star. Dawn is perhaps two hours away, and the fog will thicken again as the temperature drops just before sunrise. The good news is that it should cover Koda's advance. The bad new is that she won't be able to see where she's going. She will have to find her way to the line by sound.

Not that that should be a problem. A grenade sails overhead to land just behind the wall, spraying asphalt and metal fragments upward toward the perches of the snipers. One of the men above her yells "Fuckhead!" and opens up with his own launcher, firing grenade after grenade as a thin wet trickle drips down the wall past Maggie, black in the sheen of her night scope. From both flanks comes the rattle of small arms fire, troops on the flanks making a distraction or picking off humans among the enemy troops. They are few, uniformed no differently than the droids. They give themselves away, though, as they break ranks and split for the edge of the highway, one throwing away his weapon as Maggie watches, and tumbling headlong into the ditch under sniper fire.

*No sympathy from you own kind now, you bastard. Tell your sad story to the Jackal-god.* Maggie pulls her handgun from its holster and pots a second would-be deserter as he slithers low along the highway shoulder. The droids advance steadily, stand and fire, march forward, stand and fire. It will not be long now before they step into the field of claymores and Bouncing Betties, and the easy part will be over. She squints into the fog and fires twice more. Another of the enemy slumps down to be trodden underfoot by his mechanical brothers. She begins to back her way down the wall. Time for com check.

She is almost to the pavement when the scream of a howitzer shell streaks over her, its tracer light streaming behind it like a comet's tail. It slams into the highway just in front of the second barrier, sending a wall of flame licking up its metal bulk, setting fire to the paint and traces of gasoline and oil that linger on the wrecked cars. The impact shudders through the ground, tossing soldiers at random ahead of the concussion wave, rocking the command truck on its wheels. For an instant it tilts, poises, and falls with a crash onto its side. A grenade arcs overhead to gouge out a crater, the rear tire of the upended truck spinning in the swirling smoke. Two soldiers flap at the last of the flames with their jackets. The vibration of Maggie's com unit ceases abruptly as it loses contact with Kirsten's laptop.

"Goddam!" She half falls, half jumps the rest of the way to the tarmac, feeling her knee give under her again but ignoring it, hurtling across the fifty feet that separate her from the vehicle. At least the gas tank hadn't blown.

Just as she swings around the corner of the roof, the door opens horizontally and Manny crawls out, clutching his M-16 and a string of grenades. Kirsten follows, a darker wet streak cutting through the yellow spider traced on her face.  A spot of blood beads on her lower lip, probably bitten when she went over with truck and equipment.  Her M-16 slants across her back. "GODDAM MOTHRFUCKERS GOT MY COMPUTER!" she bellows at Maggie.

"Are you hurt?"

"WHERE DO YOU WANT ME TO GO?"

"Just a minute.  Are you okay?" Maggie yells back as machine gun fire breaks out behind her.

"I CAN'T HEAR YOU!"

"Manny, is she hurt?"

"Just banged up a bit when the table tipped over," he shouts back. "Computer hit the wall and bounced."

Kirsten's eyes dart between them, a frown wrinkling her forehead. She puts a hand to the bone under one ear, then, presses and repeats the gesture on the other side.  The frown relaxes.  "My implants!  Must have gone off when I hit my head."

"How bad?"

For answer, Kirsten shrugs.  "We're going to have to make do with messengers if we need to talk to the others."

"Where's Tacoma?  Did you hear anything before the rocket hit?"

"Headed back down the highway, with the droid tanks in hot pursuit."

"Koda?"

"Still waiting."

"All right then.  Manny, take her back behind the second wall.  See if you can get the computer back up."

Kirsten's face sets.  "I.  Will.  Not.  Go.  Back," she says, biting each word off.  "Tell me where you can use me, or I'll make my own choice."

Manny shrugs, the rise of his eyebrows visible only in the dim light's reflection off his facepaint.

No help there.  Maggie shouts, "Take the right flank.  They'll try to get past us at some point.  Make sure they don't!"

With a nod, Kirsten turns to jog over to the group crouched at the south end of the metal wall, Manny on her heels.  He glances back briefly, a grin splitting the shadows of his face, fingers snapping to his forehead. "Nice try, General!"

She returns his salute with the one-finger variation.  Pausing only to pull one soldier off the line at the wall for a courier, she scrambles back up, aims along the sight of her gun, and resumes shooting.

**The battle rolls** like thunder down the road, lit by occasional flashes of the big guns.  The fog obscures all but the general movement: the enemy advancing, the Ellsworth forces holding.  Koda can feel the tension in the men and women behind her, straining to hear, willing their sight to pierce through the shroud of the fog.  She feels it, too, in the taut muscles of her own body, her hands clenched around her binoculars as if they gripped an enemy's throat.  Deliberately, she allows her grip to slacken, forces the strained tendons in arms and legs to relax.  *Learn the lesson of the cat. Patience.*

Koda raises her optics again, trying to pick out recognizable shapes along the enemy front.  The mist begins to thicken, the air taking on a distinct chill.  It is perhaps an hour to dawn.  Her force will need to move soon.

Beside her, Sergeant Beaufort echoes her thought. "If we're gonna surprise those bastards, we better get about it. Sun comes up, we might as well send out announcements."

Koda nods. "Form the line. Be ready."

"Ma'am."

Behind her, she hears the clatter of gear shifted into place, slides pumping rounds into the chambers of sidearms, magazines snapped into the grips of the M-16s. She can feel the frustration dissipate, replaced with the more subtle tension that is half excitement, half fear. She keys her com, but before she can speak the shriek of a howitzer shell splits the night, its arc etched crimson against the darkness. The earth trembles with the explosion, a rippling pulse that spreads through rock and fog and flesh. It booms, too, through the speaker in her hand, punctuated by a muffled shout, then a distinct "Shit!" Kirsten's voice. Then silence.

Koda's heart clenches in her chest. She stabs repeatedly at the transmit button. "HQ, come in. Come in, Kirsten! Answer!" Nothing. *She is not dead. I would know.*

It is what she does not know that frightens her. "All right!" she shouts, stepping up to the crest of the ridge. "Move out!"

**Kirsten crouches among** the snipers strung out in a line from the south end of the wall to the drainage ditch beside the road. The tramping of mechanical feet, marching in inhumanly perfect unison, comes to her as a steady drumbeat, a vibration through her bones. Grenades rain down on them from behind the barricade, but do not slow them. Underneath their steady cadence, perhaps audible to no one else, the steady grinding of treads comes to her. Not so heavy as the tanks, nor even Bradleys. The next wave to break against their defenses will be the heavy-duty military droids.

And with them, the counter-programmed models whose mission is to destroy their own kind. *Please—* Kirsten stumbles over the prayer. She is a scientist, agnostic, does not believe in the God of her childhood, perhaps never did. She bites her lip, drawing blood salt on her tongue. *Listen, Ina, Tega, Wa Uspe — Uspewika — Whothehellever. Listen. We need help. Not just for us. For all the earth. If you have a stake in this, too — then let the goddamned things blow up on schedule. Please.*

A ripple of laughter runs through the back of her mind, partly human, partly not.

*Appealing to enlightened self-interest, are you? Fight without attachment, Iktomi Zizi of the Lakota. Trust your actions and move on. For instance, you might blow away a couple of droid sympathizers — right — about — now.*

The first rank of the enemy steps into the minefield. The roar of multiple explosions echoes off the metal barricade, doubling and redoubling as smoke, laced with fire, billows out into the mist and pieces of fragmented droid clang off the wall to take down more of their comrades on the rebound. Kirsten cannot make out individual figures, but she can see, green in her night sight, swirls of motion where intact droids or their human allies have broken formation to veer away to the side of their inexorably advancing column. Kirsten aims into the middle of one such vortex and is rewarded with a man's scream, high-pitched and cold with his death. She seeks a second target and finds it as a soldier stumbles blindly into their position. She fires point-blank into his face and shoves the body aside with her rifle butt.

From the ditch come sounds of a brief struggle, then two shots, then more fire into the mist. Behind her, Manny alternately swears and shoots, swears and shoots again. "Don't let 'em get down into the pasture! Koda won't be able to see the bastards coming; they'll give away her position!"

Kirsten's world shrinks to the small space before her, where the mist hides an enemy she cannot see. She fires until her magazine is empty, shoves another one home and keeps firing. There is only the enemy and her finger on the trigger. She kills coldly, human and nonhuman alike. Without attachment.

**The night scope** shows the mist that surrounds them as green wraiths, the uneven ground beneath their feet as an uncertain patchwork of black and green. Koda can see the man on either side of her and little else. From time to time she catches a glint off the gear of a troop a few feet further down the loose skirmish line, but none of them can spare much attention for anything but the jutting rocks and tussocks of thick grass that can send them tumbling, turn or break an ankle. They are perhaps halfway across when the minefield goes up. A collective gasp runs up the line, punctuated by one clear "Jesus god damn!" and a grunt as someone elbows her vocal compatriot in the ribs. In the red-lit chaos ahead of them, Koda can make out the vague shapes of bodies pitched into the air, their severed limbs arcing above them to rain down on their fellows and clatter against the barricade. Others, still apparently on their feet, make for the edge of the highway and relative safety, only to run into a solid line of rifle and small arms fire. The fog muffles their screams to vague cries out of a nightmare, distant, without context.

Without warning, a burst of white light cuts through the mist along the highway, etching the scene for a microsecond into her memory: scattered arms, legs, some human, some not; the asphalt slick with blood; craters gouged into the roadway. And it shows her two things more. Behind the ranks of cannon fodder, the military droids grind inexorably on toward the wall, the hard light from the phosphorus shell sheeting off their metallic hides. And along the edge of the road, a trooper stands looking directly toward the gorge, raising his gun to his shoulder.

"Down!" she bellows. "Keep moving!" Dropping to knees and elbows, she humps her way over the damp earth, crawling a space, then levering herself up to a crouching run. Behind her, where she had stood a handful of seconds before, an M-16 round kicks up the water in a small puddle. A second whistles over her head to land silently in the earth beyond. She jabs the man to her right, harder than she had meant because she cannot judge distance. "Hold fire. Don't give 'em our position 'til we have to. Pass it on." She gives the same message to the sergeant on her left.

The shooter at the edge of the road has apparently been joined by others. Enemy fire quickens, becomes heavier, pelting down on the length of the line. Koda puts her head down and keeps on crawling.

**The M-1s and** Bradleys run with their lights high now, lurching over the uneven ground at top speed, spraying dirt from under their treads.

Tacoma's Jeep bucks and yaws in their wake, throwing him alternately against the straps across his chest and the unyielding back of his seat. In the occasional beam of light that rakes over him, he can see the steering wheel spinning under Jackson's left hand, his right taut-knuckled on the gear shift. It occurs to Tacoma that after this he will never need a chiropractor if he lives to be a hundred and ten. He might never need a dentist either, except for his helmet's chinstrap. Pitching his voice just under a bellow to make himself heard above the din of the surrounding engines, he yells, "Did you" — thump! — "drive like this" — bang! — "when you went" — slam! — "with Kirsten to" — whump! — "Minot?"

"You kidding, man?" Darius favors him with a thousand-watt grin for a split second, then turns his eyes back to the road. "And have that sister of yours" — he pauses to steer around a large chunk of limestone — "hang me up by my heels and skin me?"

"The general'd — get you — first. Koda'd — just take — your hair!"

A shell from one of the droid tanks sails overhead to gouge a crater in the field to their right. Turning to look behind, Tacoma can see their halogen lights where they punch through the fog. What he cannot see, and with luck the enemy cannot either, is the other half of his armored cavalry, running dark behind them, ready to cut them off once the lead units lure them onto the interstate and into the trap that has been laid for them.

"Pull us off when we get to the road," Tacoma shouts. "Get us in under the overpass!"

"You gonna lead from behind?"

"You got it!"

The tanks at the front of the column take a sudden hard left, ploughing their way over the soft shoulder to the highway access road. As they sweep up the on ramp, Jackson steers the Jeep out of the line and into the shelter of the huge struts and pylons holding up the highway above the Elk Creek interchange. The racket as the behemoths lumber up the slope is beyond deafening, and Tacoma hunkers down and covers his ears as they pass. The metal plates above him rattle against their bolts, and it seems to him that every bone in his body hangs loose, clattering against its neighbor. Then the last of them is up and racing west, the whine of their engines fading with their speed.

The silence lasts for perhaps a minute. Tacoma savors it, the first respite they have had since the droid howitzers began their siege.

Then, "Here they come," Jackson says quietly.

Bursting out of the fog with engines howling, the enemy armor follows the Ellsworth forces up onto the highway. As the first of them commits to the ramp, Tacoma feels his shoulders go slack with relief. Bait taken.

Perhaps five minutes after the last of them has passed, Tacoma hears the growl of their second unit's engines. "Here we go," he says, and Jackson keys the engine and the lights, steering the Jeep out onto the access road and into the lead as the half dozen M-1s speed for the ramp. "Gonna send all those good little droids home to cyber-Jeezus!"

**When the smoke** from the mines clears, Maggie looks down on a scene straight out of Hieronymus Bosch by Bill Gates. Mechanical body parts litter the highway below the wall: a leg with its struts and dangling wires jutting up out of an asphalt crater here; a head there, recognizably

non-human only by the absence of blood; impaled on a spar of steel protruding from the barricade, a hand still clutching an automatic rifle. Fanned
out on the margins lie the human casualties, most of them picked off by
snipers as they tried to flee. To her right, from the north lip of the gorge
which Dakota must cross, she can hear the pop and rattle of rifle fire. Not
good. Even in the fog, even with enemy shooters they can pick off by
sound, Koda and her troops are at a disadvantage, their whole traverse
exposed. And the phosphorus shell would have trapped them mercilessly
in its glare, shown them to their enemies.

Mentally, Maggie reels through a catalogue of her troops. The worst of
the attack is yet to come; the full-bore military droids have halted their
advance, but the lull will not last, not beyond the few minutes required for
them to assess their losses. She can, perhaps, spare a platoon.

Clambering down from her vantage point halfway up the wall, she
snares one of the men crouched at its foot. His helmet shows three stripes;
his shirt pocket proclaims him McGinnis, Ralph. "Corporal, I need you to
carry a message to Dakota Rivers in the gorge. Can you do it?"

McGinnis's face, pale beneath its black grease-paint, goes paler still,
but he snaps off a salute. "Yes, ma'am!"

"Good man. Ask her if she needs reinforcing. I can send her a dozen
troops if she does."

He salutes again and is gone.

Maggie takes advantage of the momentary calm to walk the length of
the barricade again. Supply runners race past her, carrying ammunition
and grenades. She is halfway back to her post when she hears the grinding of treads on pavement. Her heart bangs once against her rib cage,
then steadies. They will hold because they must. A passing runner carries
grenades; she snags a belt of them and a launcher, finds a gap in the wall
big enough to admit its muzzle. She loads and waits.

**There is no** sense of time. Koda has no idea how long she has been
humping over the wet earth of the gorge. Direct fire from above has
tapered off, become sporadic as the enemy has either given up wasting
ammunition or has found more immediate matters to occupy them. Or simply decided to pick them off later.

From the highway comes the sound of small arms fire and the occasional concussion of a grenade. The mines have gone up in a roar, presumably taking out the first wave of droids. For a moment the fog glowed
red, then settled into its pervasive grey, hiding the road and what she
hopes is the successful completion of the first phase of the battle plan.

"Hey, Chief." The sergeant appears out of the void to her left. "You
got any idea where we are?"

"About halfway, I think," she answers. "Ground's leveling off."

"We need to pick it up, ma'am. If we're caught down here once they
get past whatever's keeping 'em busy up there, or they start picking us up
with the infra-red, we're fucked."

The thought is not new. They need to be in position when the ringer
droids blow, and position is within seconds of the highway. "Tell the troops
to get to their feet," she says. "We have to risk it."

"Ma'am."

She can just see his form rise and lengthen as she levers herself to her own feet, feeling rather than seeing the woman on the other side of her do the same, the order rippling down the line. She plods on, straining her senses to pick up the breathing of the troops closest to her, the faint variations on grey nothingness where the fog eddies and pools. She picks up the thudding footfalls from yards away. Half-running, half-stumbling, a man solidifies from the mist, his hands up.

"Friendly, Doc! Friendly!"

Her M-16 slaps down into her hands and is leveled at him before the first word is out. The sergeant and the man next to him haul the newcomer down to his knees, pulling back his collar to inspect his neck. It is clean flesh; no silver collar.

"Doc Rivers?"

Koda does not lower her weapon. "That's me."

"McGinnis, ma'am, Third Montana Reserves. General Allen's compliments, ma'am, and do you need any reinforcements? She says to tell you she can spare a platoon."

The droids Kirsten programmed to destroy their own kind have not yet detonated. For the first time, Dakota allows herself to think that they might not. If their destruct program fails, Maggie will need every weapon, every pair of hands she can muster at the wall. She makes her decision almost without conscious thought. "Tell the general we're doing fine, Corporal. We'll see her topside."

"Chief." It is the sergeant. "We're spread thin."

"No." Koda's voice is firm. "If we take none of the troops from the main front, they'll have a better chance of holding when we hit the metalheads from the side and drive them against Allen's line. Tell the general we're doing well, Corporal. There's no other message."

"Ma'am." The corporal salutes and disappears once again into the fog.

"Sergeant," says Koda. "Pass the order to pick up the pace. We need to get at least part way up that slope before they recoup. Continue to hold fire until I say otherwise." There is a small pause and Koda shifts the muzzle of her rifle slightly. She cannot tolerate disobedience, or even discussion. Not now.

Even in the fog, though, she can see the sudden grin break across his face. "Ma'am, you got brass ones, if you don't mind my saying so."

"I don't mind. Now move it."

The fog swallows him again as he begins to move along the line. They have passed the mid-point; land begins to rise again, punctuated by deep ruts where snow has melted off the flat surface above, cutting down the side of the embankment and carrying gravel and asphalt pellets with it across the winter-bare ground. The treacherous footing slows them. Koda swears softly when her ankle turns, pitching her down on her right hand and knee. Up and down the line, she can hear the crunch of pebbles under boots, the troop's heavy breathing as they negotiate the ragged slope. To her right, she sees a woman pitch forward onto her face, tripped up by a jagged ridge of flint jutting out from earth. The man between them grabs for her, helping her to her feet.

She sees them; faintly, she sees them. The fog is beginning to thin with the dawn. Carried on a gathering wind, its tendrils whip by her face, scattered in the growing light. With the realization comes a crack of gunfire from above, the enemy shooting almost straight down on them. There is no point in silence now. "Return fire!" she bellows. "Hose 'em!"

Up and down the line, the M-16s open up on full automatic, their rattle punctuated by the clang of rounds off metal and the sharp, strangled scream of a man going down somewhere to her right. Koda braces her weapon against her shoulder and empties the magazine at the enemy still invisible along the highway shoulder. She wrenches it free, slams in another, and keeps firing as she storms up the slope. Without warning the ground shakes beneath her, tumbling her back onto her butt, and the wave of sound washes over her, huge, apocalyptic, the thunder at the end of the world. Fog glows crimson and burns away, leaving clouds of red-shot black smoke roiling over the battlefront. Kirsten's trap has sprung.

She scrambles back up onto her feet, seeing for the first time the line of soldiers stretched out along the lip of the rise above her. "Come on!" she yells at her troops. "Take the fuckers down!"

Yelling and whooping, they charge up the slope, into the Hell of lead blazing down on them.

**Tacoma's Jeep speeds** along amid the thunder of his armored cavalry. The smaller vehicle darts in among the Bradleys and M-1s, as nimble as a dolphin among great whales. The wind of their passage tilts his helmet back on his head, snags his braids from under its rim and sends his loosened hair flying behind. Here on the road, steadily rising as they race west, the low sun has begun to burn through the fog, tingeing the mist with a strange, golden iridescence. Ahead of them, the enemy still runs blind, though the sun will soon show them what even their high-intensity spotlights cannot. Neither will there be any cover for this rear half of his split force, should the enemy have the wit to look behind them. Given a few more minutes, though, that will not matter.

Muffled by mist and distance, the roar of guns comes to them on the wind. "That's it!" Tacoma yells. He keys his mic and shouts into it, "Slow down! Form a line across the road! Make it tight!"

The behemoths around them lurch as their drivers stand on their brakes, maneuvering the M-1s into a long-legged, inverted V that rapidly becomes a flying wedge in reverse. Bradleys take their places on the fringes. There is barely space for an armed infantryman to squeeze between them, no more than a meter from vehicle to vehicle. A second, staggered line closes in behind. Jackson swerves the Jeep to take up the out-lier position along the south flank, and the line begins its inexorable grind forward, to take the enemy from behind.

"We got 'em!" Jackson shouts in his ear above the lower, but still deafening, racket.

"We got 'em as long as they don't turn and bust back through!"

A second volley rolls over them, louder, more than one cannon this time. Up ahead, a column of roiling black smoke rises above the road, burning fuel. As it coils upward into the thinning fog, the tank's ammunition goes up in a series of short explosions. There is no way to tell yet if it is one of their own or an enemy. Cannon reverberate around them, rattling the glass in the windshield, shattering the air to echo off the hills that rise black against the sky, to the north of the highway.

Just ahead of them, the road curves sharply to the right. As they round the bend, Tacoma can see the two lines of armor, his own drawn up in tight formation to block the path westward, the other straggled out across the front, individual units angled to try to wedge their way between their opponents. Some have forced their way so close that they cannot use their cannon or swivel their turrets. Behind the enemy line, the torn hulk of a burning tank lies heaved onto its side, ragged holes in its armored carapace, its treads still running clanking over its wheels. The smoke stinks of diesel fuel and scorched meat.

"Damn, looks like a bunch of dinosaurs fighting!" Jackson shouts. "Those things with horns on their heads!"

Tacoma laughs. "And here comes T. Rex to finish 'em off!" He thumbs the button on his com. "All units, close in and fire at will. Just watch your range!"

**Kirsten lies flat** on the shoulder of the road, her elbows propping her up, as she methodically searches the thinning fog for more solid patches. The mines have done their work on the first lines of the enemy. The casualties are mostly droids, but the severed fingers of a bloody hand dangling from a metal strut in the wall testify that humans had been among them. Kirsten has no time for them, no pity. She knows better than most what bargain they might have made — the safety of a family, the remnant of a life, even a life of slavery. Other renegades string out the line on the edge of the gorge, mingled with android troops.

Kirsten picks off another; behind her, Manny's rifle stitches a line of fire up and down the road's shoulder, steady and careful. From several hundred meters away, her implants pick up the faint whine of the motors of the military droids. They are still waiting, perhaps allowing the Ellsworth forces to expend time and ammunition before closing in for the kill.

*Got a surprise for ya, motherfuckers. Any time now.* She sights carefully and picks off two more hostiles.

The explosion, when it comes, rattles the scrap metal in the wall that looms above her, and one sniper, less securely perched than he might have been, slips down to land sprawled beside her, shaken loose by the blast.

"God damn!" he yells above the echoing blasts. "What the hell was that?"

"Suicide droids!" Manny shouts back. "Takin' their friends with 'em!"

The pitch of the droid's motors changes suddenly. Mingled with their high humming, Kirsten can make out the tramp of flat metal feet, the snarl of treads biting into the pavement. "They're coming!" she yells over her shoulder at Manny. "Send someone to tell the general!"

The freshening wind tears at the last rags of the fog. She can see them now, the sun glinting off their titanium hides as they grind toward the barricade. The first volley from their M-60 caliber arms clangs against the wall, a drumming like fist-sized hail on the roof. Grenades plow into the pavement ahead of them, some landing in their ranks to knock the droids over onto their sides. The ones on treads cannot rise, and lie with their wheel belts spinning, like upset beetles. Others step or crawl over them, unheeding.

A LAAWs rocket tears into the line, sending bright fragments flying in the growing light. To her right, the snipers on the edge of the gorge pot steadily away at Dakota's troops as they attempt to scale the slope, but

Kirsten can also see that they are beginning to fall in greater and greater numbers before Koda's advance. So far, so good.

There is a microsecond's warning, no more, as the howitzer shell screeches toward them. It rips through the barricade to land somewhere in the midst of the line of vehicles drawn up between the two walls, sending metal debris and bodies fountaining into the air, the roar of the explosion rolling on and on, unfolding like the cloud of smoke and flame that billows up from the pavement. A section of the barricade groans, its rammed steel blocks grating against each other, and very slowly, almost gracefully, begins to slide toward the ground. The treaded droids crawl up its slope, followed more slowly by the flat-footed models. Too close. Kirsten swivels her rifle to aim at the optic shield of the nearest, but Manny grabs her belt from behind and jerks her out of the way just as a twisted chunk of steel tumbles down to land where she had crouched a moment before. A cartwheeling fragment strikes her helmet, and darkness, sudden as thunder, closes in about her.

The wedge of armor inexorably closes in on the enemy where they stand locked with the first line. The Bradleys swing wide, speeding to block escape off the shoulders of the road, while the crews of the advancing M-1s crank up the angle of their cannon to lob their shells high and short into the droid tanks. Hatches on the roofs of the Bradleys crack open, sprouting the long tubes of tank-killing missiles. As Tacoma watches, two of the launchers send their warheads streaking toward a single enemy tank, slamming through its armor. It goes up in a ball of fire and smoke. A cannon shell lands short of a second, gouging a crater in the pavement but doing little other harm. Another finds its mark, and a Bradley fragments, spewing glass and bolts, flesh and blood, for a radius of half a hundred meters in all directions. Red spatters cover the tread and turret of one of their own M-1s near it; a human crew in that one. An enemy tank founders as it attempts to turn its guns on the closing force behind it, the turret still mobile but its cannon wedged against the bulk of its neighbor. Its gears snarl like a rabid thing, snared and careless with its pain.

A missile takes one of the Ellsworth Bradleys in the side, tearing open its plating and spinning it off the road to tumble down the embankment and come to rest with a final clatter thirty yards away. A second sweeps up from behind to take its place in the wedge, blocking off an APC that suddenly breaks from its hulking companions to attempt to dart through the narrow gaps in Tacoma's line. The Bradley rams it head on, turning it end for end and slamming it into the path of an enemy M-1 as it attempts to extricate itself from a deadly embrace with one of its own allies. A shell from the center tank in the wedge settles its difficulty, blowing the fuel tanks of both and sending their ammo up in a series of short, sharp explosions that leave the highway pocked with craters and scars on the flanks of friend and enemy alike.

Tacoma, watching, takes a quick count. The enemy are outnumbered and blocked off. It comes to him that the battle is decided; has in truth been decided ever since the enemy took the bait and followed the forward unit onto the highway. It remains only to end it as quickly as possible. Keying his com to universal frequency, Tacoma shouts into the microphone, "Ellsworth, hold your fire! Droid forces, surrender! You are surrounded, with no hope of escape! Humans among you will have the protections of prisoners of war! Androids will be reprogrammed! Surrender now and spare yourselves!"

And, though he does not say so, spare the tanks and fighting vehicles that they may well need another day. No one will be manufacturing any more anytime soon.

There is no response. More quietly Tacoma adds, "You have sixty seconds." He glances down at his watch and the luminous sweep of the second hand. "Mark. Fifty-nine. Fifty-eight. Fifty-seven..."

On thirty, Tacoma raises his hand to signal resumption of the attack. Out of the corner of his eye, he can see Jackson's taut face, watching not him but looking beyond for signs of compliance or attack. On twenty-five, Jackson guns the engine, ready to move again. Tacoma's breath comes short and hard. *Please, Ina, let this work.* And on twenty, a tank hatch cracks open and two humans climb out, waving a white T-shirt.

A wide grin splits Jackson's face. "Well dayyyum. And I thought your sister was the magic one."

Tacoma's pounding heart and lungs slow toward normal. He grins back. "No magic to it. Appeal to enlightened self-interest'll do it every time." He climbs out of the Jeep and signals the Bradley crews to dismount. "Let's round 'em up."

Twenty minutes later, the human prisoners have been separated from the droids, hogtied and deposited by the side of the road for later pickup. The androids, no more than half a dozen, pose a different problem. They stand together, guarded by two troopers armed with grenades. Tacoma glances around the field, where his men and women are busy untangling the traffic snarl and lining up the enemy armor for a run back to the barricades. They cannot spare anyone to stand guard over the droids, cannot leave them unsupervised, either.

"Waste 'em, Major. You don't need to keep a promise to no damned metalhead."

Tacoma turns to confront the speaker, a tanker of twenty years and four wars' experience. "If I do that, then the humans have no way of trusting my word, either. You know the code."

"That was then, Major." There is only weariness in the man's leathery face; no cruelty, no vengeance. "Now is different."

Tacoma nods, agreeing. He has fought in Kashmir and in the horn of Africa, in Macedonia and Korea. This war is different beyond imagination. A warrior's honor is still worth preserving. He claps the man on the shoulder. "Thanks, Reilly. All the same, get one of those Bradleys off the road. We'll pull the wires out of the engine and lock 'em in it 'til we get back."

Shaking his head, Reilly moves to obey, and Tacoma turns his attention back to reforming his line. Beside him, Jackson says, "That was a tough one."

"That was a necessary one."

"That's not in the UCMJ, y'know."

Tacoma gives him a half smile. "Different code. Lakota."

The wedge forms up again, this time pointing east and augmented by the captured armor. By the side of the road, Reilly has a fighting vehicle pulled to the side, its engine on the ground beside it. Not one to do things by halves, Reilly. Tacoma, satisfied with his formation, makes one last circuit to check for external damage. Jackson shadows him, one hand on his sidearm, his eyes on the knot of androids preparing to load into the Bradley. Tacoma gives him a grin. "Relax, Darius. Nothing's going to hap—"

He never finishes the sentence. With a yell, Jackson springs, flattening him to the tarmac, rolling over and over away from the spot where a spray of M-16 rounds clangs against the side of an APC and the air shudders with the explosion of half a dozen grenades. When the roaring stops, he is lying on his face in the loose dust of the road shoulder, with Jackson on top of him. He lifts his head slightly, gasping for air. "What — what the *fuck* — was that?"

"Reilly," Darius says shortly. He pushes up to his feet, leaning down to help Tacoma up. "You okay?"

Tacoma takes a quick mental inventory. No blood, nothing broken. "Yeah. Just winded." He grins at Jackson. "Thanks, man."

"Yeah, well." Oddly, Darius does not meet his eyes, finding a sudden interest in the scorched hole in the embankment where Reilly had stood. Reilly himself lies yards off, his rifle gone, his helmet and the back of his head crushed. A pry bar lies among the remains of the droids. "That's gratitude for you. At least we won't have to deal with the metalheads now."

"You okay?"

"'M fine." Jackson tilts his helmet back, and for a moment his eyes meet Tacoma's. Fear is there, and relief, and the hint of something else, gone as soon as it appears.

There is no time. But a small warmth has settled in somewhere around Tacoma's breastbone, something that will bear more attention on the other side of battle. For now he turns back toward the Jeep and says only, "Let's move 'em out then. We got work to do."

**"Goddammit, Manny, put** me down!"

Kirsten's head, sore but clear, bangs against Manny's ammunition belt. From her inverted perspective, she can see only the rubble-strewn pavement and the backs of his heels as he jogs away from the breached wall, herself slung over his shoulder like an untidy bedroll.

"In a minute!" he yells, tightening his grip across the back of her knees. "Hang on!"

Swearing, she digs her fingers into the loops of webbing that hold his gear around his waist. A roar like the rush of a great river pounds in her ears. Some of it, she knows, is her own blood; some of it the report and recoil of the big guns at the rear of their line. And some of it is fire. The red sheen on the asphalt, on the heels of Manny's flashing boots, is not all blood. A wave of heat washes over her from somewhere on her right. Something is burning. Something large.

"Manny!" She tries again. "Lieutenant Rivers, I order you to put me—"

"—Down. I know. Hold on!"

She thumps against his back as he takes an obstacle at a running leap, then another. *I'm going to bust him back to private. I'm going to put him on permanent latrine duty. I'm going to make him peel potatoes right into the next Ice Age.*

From her upended position, she sees a pair of soldiers crouched behind the wreckage of a Humvee, feeding grenades into an array of squat, tubular launchers that slam back against the pavement as they belch out their rounds. Others scramble to assemble an M-60, weighting down the legs of its tripod with the detached wheel of a truck, its tire stripped off. Someone has set up an impromptu med station in the lee of another wreck, Shannon from the vet clinic using the injured troops' own T-shirts and sleeves to bind off wounds. With a start, Kirsten recognizes the half-burned truck as the command post. She had known they were in trouble, but not just how much. *It's bad, then. It's really bad. Gods, I wish Dakota — were a million miles away and safe. Fat chance.*

She grits her teeth and involuntarily tightens her grip on Manny's belt as another howitzer shell screams overhead. This one lands somewhere beyond the second barrier. *To cut off our retreat. Then they'll get around to finishing us.*

Abruptly, Manny comes to a halt and bends at the waist, decanting her gently into a hastily thrown-up bunker of torn metal and sandbags. Maggie looks up from the battered laptop where she is apparently keeping track of her units, holding one half of a pair of headphones tightly to her ear and tapping on the keyboard with the other. When she sees Kirsten, the tightness in her face relaxes visibly. "Are you hurt?"

"Just banged about a bit. Give me—"

She does not even complete the sentence before Maggie shoves the computer into her hands. "Rivers, stay with her. Nice one with the suicide droids," she says, and is up and gone.

**The battle has** become a siege. It was always intended that it should. Maggie and her forces are the anvil; Koda and her troop, swinging around to flank the enemy from the south, are the hammer. All she has to do is hold firm, she reminds herself as she pushes the computer into Kirsten's far more knowledgeable hands and sets herself to make the rounds of her nests of machine-gunners and snipers. She has enough heavy munitions to stave off the swarming mass of killing machines for half an hour more, perhaps an hour. If the enemy manages to cut Dakota off, if they delay her advance up the embankment and onto the road, she still has a pair of options left. Both are suicide.

Crouching, she watches as the droid line shifts slightly. One of their number, a humanoid model, leans out from between the heavily armored models, aiming a shoulder-held rocket launcher. Before it can bring the tube to bear, a LAAWS fired from one of the upended Humvees behind her finds its mark, leaving a break in the line where the droid had stood. Two of the heavy models go down with it, one smashed to metal flinders, the other decapitated, its sensor array blown straight off its mountings. In some weird cyborg version of spinal reflex, it raises both its arms and sprays 60-caliber rounds across the space separating the two lines, kicking up asphalt pellets from the roadway, clanging off the armor of trucks and personnel carriers. The others join in the barrage, the sound trapped between the two metal barricades that hem them in. From somewhere to her right, Maggie hears a man scream; closer to, she can see another slump against the sandbags of his post, blood and flesh from the melon-sized exit wound in his back spattering the troops next to him.

From behind the wall, she can hear the higher-pitched rattle of M-16s, the occasional heavier thump of a grenade. Koda must have made her way up to the rim of the embankment, then. That will not take pressure off Maggie's forces, though. Not yet. Not 'til Dakota has fought her way past the android contingent sent to block her, not 'til she has gotten past the first barricade, over it or around it. Hammer and anvil, with the titanium and steel of the enemy between.

A trooper sprints across the open space between Maggie's position and Kirsten's makeshift com center. He dives and rolls under the hail of gunfire, landing half on his face beside her. Levering himself up beside her, he manages a creditable salute. "General, Dr. King's compliments. She says to tell you Major Rivers has neutralized the enemy armor and is on his way back. Instructions?"

"Yeah," she says with a laugh that is half relief, half amusement at the young man's formality. "Tell him get his ass back here as fast as those tanks'll go. We need him yesterday."

**Koda pulls herself** up the slope, using her rifle butt to steady her, hugging the ragged outcrop to keep within the angle of fire raining down on her troops from above. The fog still shrouds them, but only faintly. The freshening wind tears it, whipping it by in tatters. From time to time she catches the glint of metal from above, weapon or droid, she cannot tell. Her men, strung out on the face of the embankment, appear as clotted shadow in the mist, here and there a glimpse of mottled green camouflage or the clear shape of a weapon. And always there is the rattle of automatic fire above her, unremitting. The enemy has only to hold them in the gorge until full light, and they will die. She cannot allow that to happen. They have to get up and over. Now.

Fumbling at her belt, Dakota slips one of her two remaining grenades from its loop. She pulls the pin with her teeth, then counts the seconds as the fuse burns down. With a high, wordless scream, she sends it arcing up over her head to land among the enemy on the road above. Its concussion beats at her like great wings flailing the air, but she strains against it, hauling herself to within striking distance of the top as the droids shift and reform. All up and down the length of her skirmish line, other grenades go sailing into the enemy ranks. Through increasing gaps in the fog, she catches sight of her troops. One man, only yards away, sprawls face-down on the earth, his left side soaked in blood, his arm gone. She cannot stop to tend him. She screams again, part anger at her helplessness in the face of his helplessness, part red blind lust for the destruction of those who have killed him. Her second, and last, grenade flies true, gouging out a hole that sends asphalt particles stinging into her face as she crests the top of the ridge. The last of her squad's grenades explode somewhere down the line. They swarm up over the top, screaming, shooting point-blank into the sensor arrays of the few enemies left standing. All about her lie the broken remains of droids, wire and shattered circuit cards, metal fragments and titanium bolts bright in the sudden sun that breaks upon them as the last of the fog whips away. And there are the wrecks of the droids' human allies, blood and bone and muscle spattered over half the width of the highway. The air smells of iron.

Down the line from her, her troops set about mopping up anything still functional. At her own feet, a prone droid's arms make futile paddling motions at its sides, and she places the muzzle of her M-16 carefully against the back plate that covers the power supply. The gun jerks against her elbow. Two rounds, and the thing lies still.

To her left, the bulk of the first barricade wall appears, half of its middle section tumbled to the pavement where the howitzer shell has torn through. From behind it comes the din of battle — the rattle of M-60s and automatic rifles, the dull *whump* of grenade launchers. A quick survey of the field shows her no more enemy troops as far as she can see to the east. They are all behind the wall, then. And most of them will be the military models, mindless killing machines, impervious to small arms.

"Where now, ma'am?"

Their task is to squeeze the enemy between their line and Maggie's. The men and women trotting toward her down the curve of the road are fewer by a third than those she set out with across the gorge. If she sends them around and through the wall, crashing into the droid's line from behind, the enemy will simply turn and cut them to pieces. "Sergeant," she says slowly, "how many big guns do you think they have back there?"

"Ma'am?" He blinks into the sun that strikes glare from the broken metal all around them, sweat running down his blackened face into his eyes. "There's a couple howitzers back there, maybe a couple big mortars, too."

"Good," she says. "Let's go."

She begins trotting east, toward the back of the enemy line, stepping as nimbly as a dancer among the scattered debris. Her troops form a wedge around her, their faces puzzled as they jog away from the fight. None of them asks what she is about, and for a fleeting moment their obedience frightens her. Behind them the noise of the fight lessens, buffered now by the remains of the barricade and the trees that line the north of the road here.

The sergeant, keeping pace with her, pants, "Ma'am, ma'am, the range is off. We can't fire those mothers now, we'd hit our own people."

Koda flashes him a grin. "We're not gonna fire 'em, Sarge."

"Wha— Oh. Gotcha."

The droids have left no rearguard. Their vehicles, clustered a mile and a half back from the battle line, sit neatly parked across the road, Strykers and troop trucks lined up as carefully as if they were about to stand motor pool inspection. There are no hospital trucks, no rations supply. *What the hell did they expect their human troops to run on?* But Dakota has no time for the thought. "All right," she says, coming to a halt before one of the APCs. Her squad forms a knot around her, some of them heaving with the effort of the run, others bright-faced and eager. "Anybody here have experience with heavy machinery — cranes, tractors, anything like that?"

A half dozen hands go up: the sergeant, a couple of reservists, armored cavalry that Tacoma had no place for. "Good. You come with me. The rest pile into a couple of these carriers, get the ammo threaded, and get 'em started. We'll be back."

With that, she sets off at a run toward the hulking shapes she can just make out in the distance, where the fog lingers along the course of a small stream. Two howitzers loom out of the mist, their barrels, huge-seeming as ancient sequoias, canted upward to shorten their range. The squatter shapes of self-propelled mortars hulk beside them. Koda slows, dropping her M-16 from her shoulder into her hands. There may be no guards, but the droids may have left gunners behind. With the thought, the sun glints off the barrel of a weapon aimed from behind the nearer howitzer. She pulls and holds the trigger of her rifle, spraying the pavement, the tread, the armored side of the monster. "Split up!" she yells. "Go around!"

They move to obey, two lines swinging wide to flank the big guns. Koda charges straight for the middle, aiming not for the enemy gunner's position but for the howitzer itself. A flying leap lands her on its tread, and she pulls herself up its curve, using its metal grips like rungs on a ladder. On top, she clambers past the driver's perch and scrambles over the main gun mount to the rear. The sniper lies sprawled at the rear of the tread, blood seeping from beneath him. Dakota fires a single shot, straight between his shoulder blades, to be sure. From the end of the line, behind one of the mortars, come two more sharp reports, then silence. "Got 'em, ma'am!" a trooper sings out, and a moment later the sergeant appears atop the other howitzer, making for the controls.

"Okay," Koda shouts. "One operator and a back-up on each of the guns! Let's go!"

She slips into the driver's seat aboard the howitzer, taking a moment to study the dashboard. Ignition is no problem; she turns the key and the huge diesel motor under her kicks to life, shaking and shuddering like her grandfather's ancient John Deere with its front-loader exhaust pipe and its metal bicycle seat. Only bigger. Much bigger. Fit to rattle her teeth loose, she thinks as she straps herself in. *Gonna join the Polident crowd way too young, here.*

One of the sticks is obviously the gearshift. The smaller one — she shoves it away from her, and the huge barrel over her head begins to descend like a falling tree. "Timber!" somebody shouts, and she gives it an abrupt push in the opposite direction and keeps pushing until the gun is as near vertical as it will go. Down the line, the other drivers crank their guns up; otherwise the barrels will foul each other when they begin to maneuver. "Man, oh, man!" yells the driver of one of the mortars. "If that ain't the biggest goddam hard-on I ever saw!"

"Dream on!" the sergeant sings out. "Good to go, ma'am!"

"All right!" she yells above the din of the engines. "We get back to the line as fast as we can. Then we flatten the bastards!"

Her back-up slides into place behind her, perched between her seat and the tread housing as she lets out the gearshift and the huge gun lumbers forward. It is not so bad once in motion; maybe just a three-legged mule, not the antique tractor. "You okay back there?" she yells, half-turning her head.

"I'm hangin', ma'am!"

"Strap yourself to one of those eye-bolts back there, or you'll come loose when things get serious. This is not gonna be a joyride!"

It is not. The going is rough for the first several hundred yards as she explores the controls. Slow and awkward, the guns must have been what kept the enemy to its crawling advance, even more than its foot soldiers. Most of those, after all, were droids, who did not need to sleep or eat or fall out to pee. No. They had brought the guns with the idea of laying siege to Ellsworth from a distance, maybe using them to disable the fighter squadrons and bombers before making a direct assault.

*Damn. Better park the Tomcats out on the runway where they can take off at a minute's notice. There may be more of these motherfuckers where this one came from. And more droids.*

The noise of battle comes to them over the roar of the howitzers' engines. Most of it is small arms fire, M-16s and M-60s. Koda has begun to be able to tell the difference; it is what she does not hear, though, that alarms her. No grenades. No LAAWS. Nothing left but the little stuff. *Fuck.*

She throws the throttle wide open, bracing as the huge gun lurches forward, grinding under its treads the remains of droid and human alike as they round the curve and enter the straight mile of highway remaining between them and the ruined barricade. She can see it clearly, the tumbled wreckage where the wall was breached forming the ramp that let the attackers through. Whether it will hold something as large as the gun, though, is an open question.

One about to be answered. Koda waves the mortars on either end to go around the wall, and they break off to comply. Setting her teeth, she pulls back on the joystick, slowing the howitzer as it finds its traction in the crumpled metal beneath it. The bulldozers have done their work, though, and after a split second in which the gun seems to sink, and Koda's heart with it, its treads bite into the steel slope and propel it up and over, spilling it out onto an even steeper angle on the other side. Koda stands frantically on the brakes, her breath stopped in her throat, the weight of her back-up thrown sharply against her shoulders, the barrel of the howitzer wobbling visibly above her head.

And then they are on the level pavement, lurching toward the battle, which seems to be concentrated behind the remains of the Ellsworth vehicles. With a stab of fear, she recognizes the command truck, overturned and half-burnt, black smoke still billowing out of it. *But I would know, dammit. I* know *I would know.*

Swinging around the wreckage, she can make out the fight now, only half a mile distant, backed up against the second barrier wall. The droids seem to be almost entirely the military models, the humans invisible behind bunkers of sandbags and overturned APCs and Strykers. "Here we go!" Koda shouts, shoving the gearshift forward into first.

*I'm hallucinating.* **Kirsten** shoves her laptop aside — it has long since ceased to be useful in any case — and grabs her rifle. The monsters lumbering onto the battlefield are nightmare come to life: mastodons and mammoths, their enormous snouts uplifted in wrath, impervious hides clanging as rounds glance off them to ricochet and scatter among the droids.

"Goddam." Manny, beside her, fumbles in his pack for the last of his grenades. "They've brought up their field guns."

Recognition snaps into place. These are nothing out of her school day dreams. This is the enemy's final assault on their depleted troops, the last blow that will smash their already broken lines. Grimly she shoves the last magazine into place on the stock of her M-16. What was it Leonidas had said there in the Hot Gates when the Persians demanded his weapons? Oh yeah. *Come and get them.*

*Come and get me, fuckers. I'm not going down easy.*

Lying flat, Kirsten sights along the barrel of her gun. Beside her, Manny pulls the pin of a grenade and cocks his arm back. Kirsten squints, her finger tightening... With a cry that is not quite a shout of triumph, not a scream of fear, either, she lunges to her feet, knocks Manny down, and tosses the grenade clear of the oncoming howitzer, into a mass of milling droids that seem suddenly to have lost their bearings, a tangled mass like a circle dance that has lost the music.

"What—!"

"Look who's driving, Manny! It's the goddam cavalry!"

From the corner of her eye, Koda catches a flurry of movement behind one of the upended Strykers, a pale blonde head and a dark one. A wash of relief goes through her, so strong it almost rocks her where she sits. Safe.

A grin, feral as a wolf's, pulls her lips back from her teeth as she swings the gun around on its footprint and plows it into the nearest pack of droids. Their metal hides crunch and pop as she pulls back on the stick, raising the front of her gun carriage to slam down on them, grinding them under the treads that loop implacably on and on, carrying her over the wreckage and into the next squad of them, even as they raise their arms and begin to empty their magazines at her, spraying lead over the housing of the engine and the treads, shooting indiscriminately to kill her or disable the howitzer itself.

All along the battle front, the droids turn to face the new attack, tangling in knots around each of the four field guns. One of the mortar drivers slumps in his seat, only to be pulled aside as his second slips into his place and charges into a line of droids near the end of the wall. Koda swerves again to mow down a contingent that has turned, running as best their mechanical legs will take them, for the breach in the first wall, then takes another clutch as they split off from the main body and make for the edge of the road. The grinding of the guns treads brings with it a fierce joy, part battle-lust, part relief, part astonishment at her own competence. *But you have done this before*, a laughing voice says in her head. *We did not meet for the first time, there beyond the trees.*

For a fraction of a second, the puma's face passes before her, eyes golden with the sun that now shines full on the field before her. Then it is gone, replaced with the enemy who fall beneath her, noticeably fewer now, their fire slackening. A little more to do, and all is done.

Behind the barriers, Maggie's forces have gathered themselves, raining their last grenades and LAAWS rockets into the droids' rear, driving them toward the crushing treads of the guns. Above the racket of the engines and the slackening gunfire, roaring down on them from beyond the western wall, comes the high whine of tank engines and the rattle of treads on pavement, an armored column bearing down on them. Tacoma returning? Or droids? She has no way of knowing.

Driving hard to intercept a line of stragglers making for the ramp, Koda cuts them off just as one of them raises its arm, raking the side of the howitzer with rounds that sing by like hornets. Dakota feels her second slump against her shoulders, wet warmth gushing down her back and legs. Something impacts her right arm just behind the wrist, and her hand on the stick goes limp. Swearing, she shifts slightly to get a grip on it with her left, still feeling nothing as a red stain soaks into the sleeve of her shirt and spreads, wetting her pants leg where the arm lies useless.

With a crash the returning tanks hump up onto the pavement from their detour around the back wall, Tacoma riding outlier in his Jeep beside them. A great relief washes through Koda, and she lets her gun grind to a halt as she watches the armored behemoths stream by her now, chasing down the few enemy left as they attempt to flee.

It is over.

The pain of her arm slams into her, then, taking her breath away. Maggie emerges from behind her bunker, Kirsten and Manny from theirs, making for Koda where she still perches above them on the gun carriage. Awkwardly she releases her harness, sliding out from under the dead weight behind her, and begins the climb down. Halfway to the pavement she slips, but Kirsten's hands are there to receive her, steadying her as she finds her feet. All around them lies the wreckage of the droid army, with much of their own. Victory has come at a cost, cost they may not be able to recover.

"You're hurt!"

Kirsten's voice, sharp with alarm, cuts into her thought, and she musters a smile for her lover. "Hey," she says softly, "it's only a flesh wound."

A frown knits Maggie's brows. "Let's see." She continues to scowl as Koda peels back the sleeve of her shirt, carefully turning the arm to see the wound more clearly. The frown relaxes. "You're right, nothing broken. Let's get you to Shannon."

"No," she says, with a wave of her good hand. "I need to help with the wounded—"

"Which you can't do with a bum wrist. Come on, cuz." Manny takes her by her good elbow, firmly propelling her in the direction of the aid station. "Let Shannon bandage that and get some Novocaine into it."

Kirsten says quietly, "Koda, please. You can't go bleeding on your patients."

Dakota gives her a long look, taking in the toll of battle printed on the dark flesh under Kirsten's eyes, in the haunted gaze that turns on her with both relief and hunger. It is easier not to resist. Taking off her helmet, she lets her hair spill down her back, the two hawk feathers brushing the side of her face. From above her comes a scream, fierce and high, and she looks up to see broad wings spread against the blue, copper-colored tail catching the light. "Look," she says. "Wiyo."

"She agrees with me," Kirsten says steadily.

With her good hand, Koda runs a finger down Kirsten's cheek, tracing the spider shape painted there. *Iktomi Zizi. Cante sukye.*

At that, Maggie lays a firm hand on Manny's arm and steers him down the line to check on the troops, the injured and the dead. Around her, the men and women of Ellsworth are beginning to deal with the aftermath of battle, gathering up the wounded and dead. Gently Kirsten laces her fingers through Koda's. "Let's go home," she says. "This is over."

"Over," Koda echoes. A chill runs down her spine. "For now."

Without further protest, she allows Kirsten to lead her to the medical station, and from there to an APC with other wounded. She will tend them when they reach the base. For now, she braces herself against the cold metal side of the truck, and holds as tightly as she can to Kirsten beside her.

*Cante mitawa.*
*Now and forever.*

# CHAPTER FORTY-THREE

Simmons, on the tail end of his shift in the guard post forty-eight hours after the battle, leans over and rubs his eyes as the first rays glint off of something just beyond the bushes close in. "Holy fuck!" he grunts, elbowing the half-asleep Roberts. "Do you see that?"

"See what?" Roberts leans out, then ducks back in again, quick. "Shit! Shoot it!"

"With what? My dick? The land-grubbers took every bit of ammo not nailed down, you idiot!"

"Well? What the fuck should we do?"

"Get the general. She should still be in her quarters."

Ten minutes later, Roberts returns, Maggie in tow. Aside from a few bruises and scrapes, and bags beneath her eyes that would make a Samsonite salesman jealous, she seems none the worse for wear. She returns Simmons' salute crisply, then takes a look out the bolthole, eyes narrowing as she glimpses the military droid and his buddies standing in a semi-circular formation. "Well, well, well, look who's come for breakfast. Have they done anything?" she asks Simmons without moving her gaze from their newly arrived friends.

"No, ma'am. Just standing there."

Suddenly, the air is rent by a loud, piercing blast. The pulses are regular, and Maggie can just begin to get a handle on them when Simmons breaks in, his voice loud to compensate. "It's Morse, ma'am. It's telling us to listen."

"I got that part, Corporal," Maggie replies dryly. "Listen to what, though?"

Simmons shrugs. "I dunno, ma'am. Just keeps repeating 'listen' over and over again."

Maggie crosses her arms over her chest. "All right, you bastards, I'm listening."

The two men turn at a noise from behind them, and they stiffen to granite attention as Kirsten enters the watchhouse, Koda following, fiddling with the pristine white bandage covering her forearm. "What's going on?" Kirsten asks, eyeing Maggie directly.

"See for yourself," Maggie replies, stepping aside and allowing Kirsten a clear line to the bolthole.

Kirsten peers out, easing slightly to the side to allow Koda room beside her. Dakota's eyebrow edges upward as a white flag is raised from the center of the android grouping. "Je-sus!" Kirsten breathes as the androids break rank and Sebastian Hart steps through, white flag in one hand, battery powered bullhorn in the other. He's dressed in the same black uniform that clothes the other humans in the ranks of the androids, and aside from being a bit pale and gaunt, Kirsten thinks he actually looks better than he did when he left the base.

"Guess we know the answer to that question," Koda mutters as Hart looks around, then lifts the bullhorn to his mouth.

"Hail the base!"

Kirsten looks to Koda, who shakes her head, very slightly, in the negative.

"Hail the base!" A beat later, he calls, "I come to parley under a flag of truce! Who speaks for you, base?"

"Let him lay out his hand," Maggie murmurs, coming to stand behind Kirsten and touching her shoulder as she looks over the smaller woman's head.

"What hand?" Kirsten asks. "We've decimated his troops! What could he possibly be bargaining for?"

"We won't know until he asks," Koda replies, keen eyes narrowing on the man below.

"Does no one speak for you, then?"

Maggie feels a moment of pride as the entire base keeps its silence. She senses the eyes and the attention of those who stand below and wait, and blesses them for their loyalty.

"Very well, then. If you will not speak to me, I will speak to you." There is a brief pause, as Hart surveys the exterior of the base, much as a deposed emperor who knows his palace will again soon be his. An expression more smirk than smile flicks across his lips before they're covered, once again, by the bullhorn. "I've worked with many of you, most of you, for a long number of years on this base. You know me. You know my honesty, and you know my integrity."

Maggie snorts, shaking her head in patent disbelief. The others remain silent, though their thoughts are easily read through the set of their bodies.

"And because of your knowledge of my honesty, my integrity, I feel it is safe for me to stand before you and say this: people of Ellsworth, you are being lied to."

"What the fuck?" Kirsten rounds on Dakota, glaring, color high. "What are—"

"Shh. Just wait a minute. Let's see what he has to say."

"But—"

"Don't let him know he's gotten to you, Kirsten," Maggie interjects softly. "That's his game."

With a look of biting into a very sour lemon, Kirsten finally relents, shaking off the gentle arms holding her and stalking to the side of the knot-hole, away from the others. Koda looks after her with concern, but Maggie shakes her head, just once. Koda nods, and peers back through the knot-hole, elegant brows drawn down low over piercing eyes.

"To set the record perfectly straight, ladies and gentlemen of Ellsworth, you were not lied to when you were told that there had been an android uprising. No, all of you were part of that horror, seeing sons and daughters, mothers and fathers, friends and loved ones taken away from you or killed before you. No, that certainly is not the lie. Nor is it an untruth that some of those women, your daughters, your mothers, your relatives and dear friends were taken and incarcerated against their wills, defiled in the most horrendous of ways. You have seen such horrors with your own eyes, or heard them with your own ears. A great abomination has been visited upon our country, people of Ellsworth, a great abomination that continues still!"

"This asshole missed his calling," Maggie mutters. "He should have run for office."

"Or the pulpit," Koda smirks.

"The lie," Hart continues, "concerns these beings standing beside me. They, ladies and gentlemen, are not your enemy. These androids standing with me now are what they have always been — a boon to all mankind. There is no harm in them. They live only to serve. They are programmed only to serve. Not to kill, but to preserve life, to aid...life. These very androids, and hundreds, thousands like them, have gone through the jail-houses, the detention centers, the hospitals and rescued thousands of your loved ones."

"He lies!" Kirsten growls, moving forward again, but stopping herself just at the edge of the bolthole, hands clenched tight over the lip, knuckles as bloodless as her lips. "He fucking lies!"

"Loved ones who even now, as I speak to you, are receiving the very best of care administered by beings just like these who stand in solidarity with me before all of you." Lowering the bullhorn for a moment, Hart looks down at the ground, much like a keynote speaker, or a preacher, who is gathering himself for a momentous announcement. "Androids, as you know, must be programmed to go against their natural actions. They must be programmed to kill instead of save, to harm instead of help. And I tell you, ladies and gentlemen of Ellsworth, there is only one person, one person in this country of ours with the means, the opportunity, the ability, and the reprehensible morality to get that job done. The one person who was seen, and captured, at Minot, the world's largest android construction factory in the process of aiding and abetting the enemy, dressed as the enemy herself! Dressed so well that her co-conspirators had no idea who she really was! The one person in this country who stood to gain the most, to attain the highest of peaks, to sit at the head of this great and undaunted country.

"The very person who lives with you now, who pretends to share your lives, your worries, your goals, but who is, in fact, continuing her quest for world domination by reprogramming our good and safe androids into brutal killing machines.

"And that person, ladies and gentlemen, that person is none other than the woman who would have the audacity to call herself YOUR President. Kirsten King. Traitor. Abominator. Killer of innocents."

The rage washes over Kirsten in red waves. Her fingers clench into the palms of her hands, itching for the small cold curve of a trigger under them; her blood slams in her ears. She pushes away from the wall and steps up to the opening, shouldering Maggie aside, reaching for the side-arm of one of the guards — Simmons, she thinks — where he attempts to shrink himself small in a corner.

*That's what he wants.* The thought comes to her from somewhere cold, deep in her mind. *He wants us to lose it. That'll prove he's right, at least start some people thinking we want to silence him.*

Very carefully, she lets go of Simmons' gun, handing it to Koda. She meets her lover's eyes. "Don't worry. I'm not going to give him anything."

"I know you won't," Koda replies, handing the gun back to Simmons and turning Kirsten back toward the bolthole, large hands resting comfortably on her shoulders. "Let's just listen to the rest of his spiel, and then go on doing something productive with our day."

"I have come to parley," Hart continues. "This country cannot rebuild itself and achieve the greatness for which God has intended it until such a monster is removed from her self-appointed post. I wish, all of us here wish, that this be done peacefully. Open your gates, and we will take the doctor into custody, and you all have my word that you will be able to go on about your lives as best you see fit. If, however, her words have so brainwashed you that you are unable to see the truth that lies at your feet, we will be compelled to use force. It is a force that, I am sad to say, you will not survive. The battle you have just endured will be like a campfire to the blaze of true Armageddon."

Lowering the megaphone, he appears to touch something at his belt. Within seconds, the formerly empty clearing is suddenly populated with androids, appearing as if from the ether.

"Jesus Christ! Where the hell did they come from?"

Kirsten turns and looks helplessly at Maggie.

"Simmons!" Maggie barks. "Get down to communications on the double and find out why we're standing here with our asses hanging in the wind! Now!"

"Yes, ma'am!"

As Simmons disappears, Koda reaches for a pair of high magnification binoculars hanging from a hook on the wall. Putting them up to her eyes, she adjusts the focus, and whistles. Wordlessly, she hands them to Kirsten, whose jaw drops. "There's got to be more than a thousand out there!"

Shouldering in, Maggie grips the proffered binoculars and brings them up to her eyes. Her lips go tight, a bloodless slash against the deep ebony of her face.

Kirsten's voice is soft in the silence of the shack. "How...couldn't we know about this?"

Simmons steps back into the shack. His expression is apologetic. "We can't read 'em," he says, peering over Maggie's head and squinting as the sunlight reflects off of highly polished armor. "Communications doesn't know if they're jamming us or what, but all of our scanning equipment says there's an empty field out there."

"Shit. And my damn computer's totally trashed."

"I'm not sure if that would help or not," Simmons replies, shrugging his shoulders. "I just—"

"I realize," Hart resumes, "that this is not an easy decision to make, and I am sorry, deeply and truly sorry, that Dr. King has put you in the position of having to make it. That said, since I am a fair man, as most of you are aware, I will give you five hours to hand the doctor over. Rest assured, she will be treated fairly and receive due process, as is her right under the law. A law we follow, even if others don't."

He pulls the megaphone away for the final time, looking supremely smug.

Kirsten's summing up is succinct. "Fuck."

"Okay, let's think about this for a moment here," Maggie says, turning away from the bolthole. "Kirsten, are there any of your 'Traitor Tommies' lying around anywhere?"

"I left ten behind at the factory in case we needed them later," Kirsten responds, rubbing at the back of her neck, where a huge knot of tension has merrily taken up residence, "but I can't activate them without my computer." Her eyes brighten. "I'll head down there—"

"No."

Kirsten stares at Maggie as if she's suddenly grown a second head and is preparing to use it to commit cannibalism upon her person. "Wha-at?"

"You need to get out of here, Kirsten. And not down to that damn factory, which is likely crawling with Hart's new groupies. You need to get somewhere far, far away from here."

"Now, wait just a minute here. I'm not going to be chased away from this base by some asshole with an agenda. I don't care how many 'friends' he has, and how big his guns are. No how, no way, so just put that out of your head right now."

"Kirsten, it's not that." Maggie smiles, a little, caught out and knowing it. "Okay, it's not just that."

"What is it, then?" Kirsten's arms fold themselves across her chest, implacable armor against Maggie's coming words.

"Listen to me, please." Maggie heaves a sigh. Her hand lifts, and she begins ticking points off on her long fingers. "Your computer is gone. The code that you risked your life at Minot for is gone. And with it is any chance of you being able to turn off those damn droids, not just for now, for this damn battle, but forever. There has got to be some place, some other place, where you can get what you need to get to do the job you need to do."

"But I can do that after—"

"No. No, you can't. Don't you see, Kirsten? Hart's primary purpose is to destroy you, and he's not gonna stop until it's done. Whether it's this battle, or the next, or the next. He's got more manpower than we could ever hope to possess, more firepower, more everything. Our only chance, this damn world's only chance, is for you to cut his troops off at the source. Now, not later. Because later will likely never come. You need to go. And you," she says, turning to Koda, "need to guide her."

Kirsten looks at her lover, horrified when she realizes that Dakota is actually considering Maggie's insane order. "Koda, you can't possibly—"

The rest of Kirsten's words fade down to a meaningless drone as another voice, one well remembered if little heard, weaves its way through Dakota's brain, like a mist before the dawn.

*I have something to tell you: do not hesitate to flee when the time comes. Victory will follow you. For the sake of all the People, two-footed, four-footed, winged and creeping, you must do what you least wish to, when you least wish to. I will be here waiting when you return.*

"We need to leave." Dakota's voice is low, and tortured, as if the words are being forced from her by something, or someone, beyond her control. They sit badly in her mouth.

"What? What are you saying? We can't run!"

"We need to leave," she repeats, trance-like. "We need to find the answers. They're not here. Victory will follow us."

"Dakota, you're not making any sense!"

Ignoring Kirsten for the moment, Koda looks over at Maggie, eyebrow raised.

The general smiles and nods. "We'll do okay, I think. I still have a few aces up my sleeve. Aces even Hart doesn't suspect exist. It'll be hard, but...we'll do okay."

Koda nods, and a subtle transference occurs between the two women, one that Kirsten can't read. Then the blazing blue eyes turn back to her, and the young scientist is once again captured effortlessly within their pristine depths.

"This is the right thing to do, my love. It's the only thing we can do and hope to win in the end. Anything else will only delay the inevitable. I know you know this...deep inside. Look. You'll see."

But Kirsten doesn't need to look. She's known the truth from the very second Maggie suggested leaving. It sits across her shoulders like a yoke, like a cross, growing heavier with each passing second, each passing thought.

"I'll help you carry it," Koda says, reading her effortlessly. "Together, to the end of whatever journey the gods have planned for us."

"Where will we go?" Kirsten asks, beginning to accept the inevitable.

"It's your call," Dakota replies, reaching out and grasping her lover by the hand, a hand that is cold, slightly damp, but strong and steady. "Where is Westerhaus's inner sanctum? That might be the most direct route."

"Silicon Valley, but God, that's so far."

"We'll get there. Somehow, we'll get there. Unless there's somewhere else that you think is better? You're the boss here."

Kirsten thinks for a moment, then nods. "If we want to stop this shit at the source, we need to go to the source. You're right."

"Great," Maggie interjects. "Then it's settled. Manny will take you out with the Cheyenne."

"The river?" Kirsten asks, confused. "How will we get past all those droids?"

Maggie smirks. "Just go over to Hangar 22. He's waiting for you."

Kirsten scowls. "You had this planned all along, didn't you?"

"We knew it would be an eventuality, Kirsten. It's happening a little sooner than we expected, sure, but the sooner you get out of here, the sooner we can all breathe a little easier." Her smile softens as she closes the two steps between them and looks down into Kirsten's clear, beautiful eyes. "You're our hope, Kirsten. And I, for one, am glad of it." Leaning forward, she brushes a soft kiss against her lips, then pulls away. "Good luck."

Maggie's keys flash in the early sun as she tosses them to Simmons. "Take my Jeep. Take Dr. Rivers and President King home to pick up their things. Then take them out to the flightline, Hangar 22."

Simmons' eyes go wide, his eyebrows ascending his forehead in surprise. "Hangar 22?" he squeaks, making a dive for the keys that ends in a two-handed catch.

"You got it. Koda." Dakota walks into Maggie's open arms, returning her hard embrace and the chaste kiss on her cheek. "You know what you have to do. Be safe."

"You're in more danger than we'll be," Koda says, stepping back, letting her hands linger a moment in the other woman's. "*Tóksha aké wanchinyankin kte.*" Until I see you again.

"We'll make it. Until then. Kirsten." Maggie hugs Kirsten tightly, whispering something in her ear that is not meant for Koda to hear. It is something that makes her smile, though, and Kirsten says softly, "Don't worry. I will."

"Go, now. We're going to stall them as long as we can. We'll be waiting for you when you get back."

With an arm around each of their shoulders, Maggie half hugs, half pushes them both out the door. Koda's last sight of her is a straight-backed silhouette at the view slit, raising the binoculars again to her eyes.

They pass the ride home in silence. Kirsten, disregarding Simmons in the front seat, leans into Koda's arm, clinging to her. Her hand in Dakota's feels as cold as the frozen dead of the Hurley farm, all those months ago. "Hey," Koda says softly. "We'll make it. We're a hell of a team."

"What about Maggie? And Tacoma? How—"

"The best way they can, *cante sukye*. They're warriors, blood and bone. They'll hold." Her fingers tighten involuntarily on Kirsten's shoulder. "However they have to, they'll hold."

"However," Kirsten repeats, her voice flat.

The words hang in the air between them, unspoken. Kirsten will not say them; neither will Dakota, who knows that words have power. Even at the cost of their lives. Even if they can only hold the enemy temporarily.

The Jeep buckets up into the driveway, and Koda gives her lover's hand a last squeeze. "Take Asi out to pee. I'll start packing." To Simmons she adds, "Fifteen minutes."

Dakota shoves the kitchen door open, Kirsten on her heels. Tacoma stands at the table, stuffing a backpack with MREs and various more palatable items. Koda's quick glance takes in oatmeal, a plastic zip bag of sugar, salt, what must be the last of their meager stash of coffee. Her brother looks up from his task for a second, smiling. "I packed up some clothes for you. Not much, but I figure you can get more on the road. Go check if I've missed anything." To Kirsten he adds, "Asi's done his duty. You just need to get his leash on him."

"Thanks," Kirsten says, bolting for the living room and the seldom-used lead hanging on the hall tree. Koda follows, veering off into the bedroom where a small rucksack stands open on the dresser. A quick inspection shows that Tacoma has packed a pair of jeans and a shirt apiece, all their socks and underwear, extra boots. A Colt .45 automatic and its ammunition belt lie on the bed, with her bow and quiver. A soldier's choices. She adds toothpaste and brushes to the pack — no need to go without until they have to — a couple of bars of soap, a bottle of aspirin, and an elastic athletic bandage from the medicine cabinet. She straps on the gun, shifting its weight to lie comfortably against her thigh.

She zips the bag and hoists it onto one shoulder, testing the weight. She slings her bow and its arrows over the other. Not bad. Not bad at all. In the hall, a sharp bark registers Asi's protest at being collared and leashed, together with Kirsten's murmured, "Sorry, guy. But we're gonna have to strap you in when we get to the chopper."

"Ready?" Koda emerges from the bedroom, shutting the door carefully behind her. The house is no one's home now, but her memories, and Kirsten's, deserve a kind of privacy. Say goodbye.

Asi whines again, this time plaintively. He knows something is not right. "Easy, boy," Kirsten says again, "easy."

In the kitchen, Tacoma stands ready with their provisions. Koda reaches for the pack, but Kirsten forestalls her. "I'll take that," she says, and slips quickly out onto the carport, Asi tugging on his leash.

Tacoma's face is solemn, but a glint in his dark eyes betrays a flash of humor. "You're marrying a tactful one, *tanski*."

Dakota takes his hands in her own. "Promise me—"

"I'll be careful," he says quietly. "That's all the promise I can make."

"I know." She looks away for a moment, then says, "When we went to scout the battleground, Igmú Tanka spoke to me. She said that we must do what we least wish to, when we least wish to. That victory would follow."

The lines around Tacoma's eyes deepen, and the smile spreads to his mouth. "She's a warrior spirit, with a warrior's honor. If she says you will be successful, then you will."

"She said we would come back, that she would be waiting."

He touches her cheek lightly. "Then you must be careful, too, and not only for Iktomi Zizi."

Koda raises her hand to cover his, not willing to lose the contact. "I will."

"I dreamed last night. I saw all of us back at the ranch, with *Até* and *Ina*. You and Kirsten. Me and—" He breaks off abruptly, a dark flush spreading across his face.

"Darius," she supplies, smiling.

"*Hau*. Darius. And a little black-haired girl with green eyes. It's not hopeless for us here, *tanski*. It only looks that way."

She pulls him close, holding hard for a long moment. "Well then," she says, "we're off. Come on outside and say goodbye to your sister-in-law."

**"What the—"**

"Hell is that?" Koda finishes the sentence for Kirsten.

"That" sits on the tarmac in front of the apparently off-limits until now Hangar 22, an aeronautical engineer's nightmare of a craft. Roughly the size and general shape of a Chinook, its slate-blue belly and tail have been sleeked for speed behind a nose pointed like a bomber's. Wings protrude from its flanks, a jet engine underslung from each, each sprouting double co-axial rotors from a mast that holds their drooping blades up and away from the body of the craft. A smaller engine and a tail rotor adorn its rear. Its forward door stands open, with a short flight of boarding steps leading into its dark interior.

Manny, flight-suited and helmeted, grins at them from behind the half-loosened oxygen mask that covers most of the lower half of his face, and with a sweeping gesture, invites them on board. "Your taxi, ladies." He relieves Kirsten of their provisions, pausing a moment to ruffle Asi's fur where he dances at the end of his leash. "Now haul it, and let's get the hell outta Dodge."

The interior of the craft is configured for Medevac, with brackets for stretchers and half a dozen jump seats, hardly more than round steel stools, cantilevered out from the wall. Manny pulls down two for them, then clips Asi's leash to a D-ring in the floor, crossing a pair of safety belts over his chest. "That'll hold him. You two okay?"

"We're fine," Koda answers, clipping her own belt in place. "Where are we going?"

"I'm gonna try to set you down a couple hundred miles into Wyoming. She may look weird, but this baby's a true VTOL. We can put down in any reasonably flat place that's wider than the wingspan, even in the middle of the woods." He looks around him, apparently satisfied that they and their gear are safely stowed, then pulls two pairs of earphones down from a rack above them. "Wear these. They've got mics attached. Yell if you need me; we've also got autopilot." With that he disappears into the forward cabin, and a moment later, the rotors set up a steadily increasing racket. Out the port, Koda can see the blades gradually lifting, then standing straight out from their masts as they spin faster and faster. The turbos cut in, their whine rising octave by octave into a steady scream. Asi howls in sympathy.

"Oh man." Kirsten grins at Koda, rolling her eyes. "And to think how I used to bitch about the morning red-eye out of Washington," she shouts.

Koda flashes her a smile in return. "The Concorde champagne flight it ain't! Put on your earphones!"

Koda slips her own on, and blessed quiet descends. Beneath her, the floor of the craft seems to lurch forward. Then they are up and airborne in a surprisingly smooth sweep, lifting straight up into the bright morning. The shadow of the rotors flashes across the port as she watches the hangar and the base recede below her. A part of her life remains there, a part she may lose despite dreams and visions. Silently she takes Kirsten's hand.

"Jesus," Kirsten whispers, looking down at the long line of droids laid out below them. Her hand clenches on Koda's to the point of pain. "How can we leave them to that?" she demands. "How?"

"Because we must," Dakota replies, voice soft, sad. Her right hand comes up to curl over the one clenched in her left. "Because we must."

They turn west toward Wyoming and the beginning of the quest before them.

**Grinning, Koda pulls** away from Manny, giving his short braid a little tug. "Get back safe, and good luck."

"You too, *shic'eshi*. Be careful. Be safe."

"We will."

Stepping around her lover, Kirsten smiles at Manny. There is a trace of uncertainty in the expression. Though things between them have warmed considerably over the months, there is still a subtle distance between the two that, quite suddenly, Kirsten doesn't want to be there anymore. "You're a brave man, Manny. Good luck. Fight well."

Reaching for her stiffly extended hand, he gives her an "aw, what the Hell" grin and pulls her against him in a tight embrace, kissing both of her cheeks soundly before pulling away. "You take good care of my *shic'eshi*, understand?" he teases.

"I swear it," Kirsten replies, deadly serious. "And you take good care of yourself, and Tacoma, and Maggie, and everyone else. I expect you all to be there, and happy, when we get back."

"Count on it. I'm a Rivers." He thumps his chest proudly. "Given enough time, we wear away mountains."

"That I don't doubt," Kirsten returns, finally breaking into a smile. "I mean it, Manny. Be careful, all right?"

"Will do, Ms. Prez." He sketches a cocky bow, grins, winks at his cousin, and, in the blink of an eye, disappears back into the cockpit of his Picasso-nightmare 'copter. A second later, the thing is airborne and over the horizon.

In its wake, a silence descends, so profound that not even the ever-present wind soughing through the boughs of the large pines surrounding them can penetrate it, and Kirsten shivers.

"You all right?" Koda asks, stepping closer and slipping an arm around her lover's shoulders.

Leaning her head against Dakota's strong chest, Kirsten takes in the world that surrounds her. Trees, trees, and more trees, as far as the eye can see. The wind, now coming to her, carries with it the sweet scent of life, underlined with a darker, richer, almost secret scent that she can only identify as decay. And amidst this, she stands alone, save for the strong body at her back, promising her protection and comfort. And love beyond measure.

*Not so alone now*, she thinks. The thought brings with it a small, secret smile, and a tiny thrill of joy suffuses her chest, warming her from within even as Koda's radiant look warms her from without.

"Yeah," she says finally. "I think I am."

"Good."

They stand that way for a long span of moments, body pressed to body, content to allow the forest to carry its secrets to them, one at a time, absorbing the peace and contentment that seems to be theirs for the wishing. She can almost...almost...forget what lies ahead, and behind, and resolves to take full advantage of this small slice of peace for as long as it is gifted unto them. Finally, though, the words push forth from their place in her chest. "So, what now?"

Koda smiles and slips her arm away, digging her hands deep into the pockets of her jeans. "How do you feel about camping?"

Kirsten pretends to give the question serious thought. "The Beverly-Hills-'cabin'-with-all-amenities-and-you'll-never-see-so-much-as-a-mouse-dropping kind of camping, or the let's-grab-us-a-pup-tent-and-a-couple-of-cases-of-beer-and-shoot-us-something-to-mount-on-the-wall kind of camping?"

"I'd say the second," Koda responds, chuckling. "Minus the beer, unless you're suddenly partial to the stuff."

"Nah. Never developed much of a taste for it. A little of Maggie's sipping whiskey might go down real nice on a cool night, though."

Koda's grin broadens. "I'll see what I can come up with, then." She looks around, getting her bearings. "I'm pretty familiar with this area. My grandfather used to take us out here sometimes when the woods around our place got a little too easy for us kids to figure out. Unless it's been torn down in the interim, there should be a pretty good camping and hunting shop not too far to the north of here. We can stock up on the supplies we'll need and start off from there."

"How will we get around?"

"Walking seems the best bet, for now at least. I want us off the main roads as much as possible. We don't know how many unfriendlies are still around patrolling, and we're prime candidates for a trip to the local rape ward, if they don't recognize you. And if they do..."

Kirsten doesn't need Dakota to finish that particular sentence for her. She well knows the size and shape of the axe hanging over her head, but is determined to push through, no matter how thin the thread holding it up there might be. "That'll be pretty slow going, though," she muses.

"We might be able to rustle up a couple of mountain bikes. Horses, if we're lucky. That should speed things up some, but for now, our feet are our best bet."

"Lead on, then, MacDuff," Kirsten jokes, passing over the leadership of this particular part of their quest with a sweeping hand gesture that earns her a fond swat on the backside. Her happy laughter is answered by the chirping of birds, and for this one second in time, all is right in Kirsten King's world.

**Already dressed in** her flight suit, Maggie runs out to greet Manny as he swings out of the 'copter, instinctively ducking low to avoid decapitation by the still slowly spinning blades, though in this particular model, that really isn't much of a danger; the rotors are high above her head. "You get 'em down safe?" she shouts.

"And sound," Manny returns, giving her shoulder a quick, calming pat. "For better or worse, they're on their way."

"Good. One less thing to worry about." Turning, she begins to walk back toward the command post, Manny at her left heel like a well trained dog at a show.

"How are things on this end?" he asks.

"Ten minutes to the deadline. We still can't read 'em on radar or GPS. Line of sight only, and it's not good."

"Has anyone figured out where the hell they came from?" he asks. "I mean, where the fuck were they when the rest of their little friends were getting shredded?"

"Don't know, and at this point, I don't care," the general retorts, dragging a hand through her hair. "We've gotta take 'em down as fast as they put 'em up. It's the only way."

"Got a plan for that?" Manny asks slyly.

"Don't I always? C'mon."

**"Wow," Kirsten remarks** to the woman standing before her, grinning, "if we were playing 'Cowboys and Indians' right now, I'd be mighty confused."

"Good thing we're not, then," Koda replies, chuckling and looking past Kirsten into the mirror that almost covers the open restroom door. A soft flannel shirt in red and black hangs open over a tight, white ribbed tank top, which in turn is tucked into soft blue jeans whose cuffs are, in their turn, tucked into calf high moccasins with thick treads. A holstered gun hangs low on her right hip, a hunting knife at her left. Her chest is crisscrossed by a rifle strap and a strap that holds her arrow quiver over her back. Her black Stetson is in its customary position atop her head, though a hank of braided hair hangs down, twined with the two hawk feathers she's yet to remove. Her medicine bag lies close against the hollow of her neck. Leaning against one leg is a vacu-sack, all the rage in hiking equipment before the androids had made such a pleasure an outright necessity for so many. Clothes and sundries are stored in the roomy sack, then vacuum sealed, cutting their total bulk down almost to nil. The pack will fit easily over her hips and lower back, leaving her easy access to her weapons, should she have need for them. The tent is similarly stored. A shiver tingles down her spine; these things belong to ghosts, or worse, to girls and young women abducted by the droids into their breeding program. As far as she and

Kirsten can tell, not a living soul remains in Arapaho, Wyoming, pop. 853. Either no one has been through since the uprising, or no one thought the tiny Civic Center with its Scout meeting rooms and camping equipment worth looting. Kirsten is dressed a bit more conservatively, in jeans and a T-shirt with a Gore-Tex jacket rolled in her pack. "Hey, look what I found back there?" She grins as she holds up her prize: a fully loaded solar laptop with all the amenities. "Damn thing's about five pounds lighter than my old one and damn, it's fast!!"

"Only you," Koda grins, shaking her head.

"Yeah, well, get used to it, vet. You're marrying a geek. Our toys come with the territory."

"Just as long as you're the one carrying 'em," Koda jokes.

"Don't you worry about that. I always carry my weight."

"We'll see."

**The midday sun** beats down on the tarmac in front of the main gate, making heat ripples in the air above it. From where she stands in the watchtower, Maggie can see metallic glints here and there that must be either droids or armed humans, but they are scattered among the tumbled buildings across the road and in the open fields beyond. She still has not been able to get good instrument readings on their number or their placement. All she can do is keep their attention on the base and stall them for as long as she can. And give Dakota and Kirsten as much time as she can, measured out now in minutes, in hours at best.

Next to her, Andrews settles the muzzle of his rifle against the edge of the wall slit, squinting for perhaps the dozenth time through the scope. "Nothing there, ma'am."

Maggie sets down her own binoculars. "I know. They're keeping under cover until the last minute."

"But Hart'll have to show himself."

"Oh, yeah. And when he does..." Maggie lets the words trail off. They both know what will happen when he has outlived his usefulness. To both sides.

Then, "Here he comes," Andrews says quietly.

A figure moves up the road, hardly distinguishable from heat shimmer at first. But Andrews is right. As it comes closer, the shape assumes the familiar features of General Hart, his blue shirt open at the collar, head bare. He no longer carries a flag of truce, only the bullhorn swinging from one hand. A snap and whine of feedback breaks the silence as it powers up. "Colonel Allen," says the flat, amplified voice, "do you have an answer? Open the gates and surrender your so-called President, and we will leave you in peace."

"Cover me," Maggie says, and steps out of the guardroom onto the catwalk that circles the tower. Below her, Hart stands alone in the middle of the road, the breeze ruffling his grey hair and the beginnings of a patriarchal beard. She stands in the sun, letting him see the stars on her shoulders and the one on her helmet. Letting him see, too, that her hand rests on the butt of the pistol at her waist. With five generations of gospel singers and twenty years in command of troops behind her, she has no need for a megaphone. "Hart!" she shouts. "I have a deal to make you!"

"No deals, Colonel. Meet our demand or not: that is the only choice you have."

Maggie smiles grimly. It is no more than she expects, but she says, "It's not the only choice you have, though. What do you think your little metalhead pals out there are going to do with you when you've outlived your usefulness to them? Which is—" she glances ostentatiously at her watch— "right about now."

Hart shakes his head, a gesture meant to convey a response more of sorrow than anger. "Wise humans have allied themselves with these good beings, Colonel. I am not alone, I assure you, nor am I in any danger. Nor are you or the troops under your command, if you surrender Dr. King. Your answer, if you please."

*Crunch time.* "Then you have it, and it is this." She pauses, letting the moments draw out, in case any other human collaborators are listening. "President King has authorized me to allow you, and any other human who has had second thoughts about cooperation with the enemy, to return to the base to face charges of treason and desertion in time of war. If you give yourselves up, your lives will be spared. If you don't, you will face the full penalty of the law when you are captured."

The expression on Hart's face might almost be a smile. "And I offer you and your people the same amnesty, Colonel, provided that you hand the doctor over, now."

The parley, Maggie knows, is essentially useless. The best she can do is buy a few minutes more time to prepare, give Koda and Kirsten a few more moments to get that much further away. And what time she has is running out, with no help in sight. "Withdraw your android troops as a sign of your good faith, General. Then we can talk seriously."

"Bring Dr. King outside the gates where we can see her — as a sign of your good faith, Colonel, and we can talk seriously."

And that time has just run out. Hart and his cohorts have to have seen the Cheyenne take off; they have to have seen it return. They must at least suspect that Kirsten is no longer on the base. They hope for an easy conquest, no more. Maggie steps away from the slit in the wall behind her. "Now, Andrews."

The crack of his rifle shocks the bright afternoon air. Almost simultaneously, Hart's head jerks back violently, spraying blood and brain matter in a cloud of droplets that catch the sun, sparkling like summer rain. The bullhorn drops to rattle along the pavement as he falls. There is no sound, no movement, from the buildings across the road, nothing to give away the enemy that she knows is there.

"Ma'am, inside!" The door behind her jerks open and Andrews pulls her bodily back into the guardroom by the straps of the Kevlar vest she has buckled over her flight suit.

"Out! Now!" she snaps, giving him a shove toward the stairs and pounding down behind him, two steps at a time. Pulling a walkie-talkie from her belt, she thumbs on the transmit button and yells "Fire!" into the speaker just as they sprint out of the tower at ground level and into the waiting Jeep. Andrews guns the engine, zero to sixty in what seems to be less than a breath. A shell from one of the big guns hastily dug into makeshift bunkers that morning arcs whistling overhead to land beyond the gate with a burst of fire and a roar. The concussion sends a shudder through the Jeep and rocks them against their seats.

"With luck, that got a few of 'em," Maggie shouts. Into her com she orders, "Hold your fire until we have the enemy in sight or incoming! Don't waste ammo!"

"At least we got that son-of-a-bitch traitor," Andrews says, satisfaction in the straight set of his mouth as they speed down the base's main drag toward Wing Headquarters and the guns arrayed around it. "That ought at least to send a message to any other collaborators out there."

"Yeah," Maggie says, her voice grim in her own ears. "But the message they're gonna get real quick now is that we can't hold out against them for more than a couple of hours, maybe not even that, if they launch a massed attack."

"Remember the Alamo, huh?"

"Remember the Alamo," she agrees. "But remember something else. We've still got a few Tomcats with some fight left in 'em."

**"You hungry yet?"**

"Is supper gonna be MREs?"

"'Fraid so. Unless you want to stop and fish. I haven't seen a whole lot of small game around here, yet, and I'm not too keen on lugging around sixty pounds of venison from killing one of those big bucks we keep seeing."

Kirsten's face brightens for a moment, then the smile fades. "It was a nice thought. We'd better keep going as long as we have light, though."

"That won't be long. Better start looking for a place to camp."

Around them the shadows of pine and aspen lie long upon the ground. The low sun strikes glints of gold and silver from the rippling current of the Little Medicine Bow, visible here and there through the trees where the river bends west. Asi runs alongside, snuffling happily at fox scrapes, occasionally pausing to inspect the tangled roots that hump their way across their path. They have been walking steadily for almost eight hours, pausing only to take compass readings and refer to the ordinance map Manny had stowed among their gear. Their course angles south and west from the clearing where they set down an hour after leaving Ellsworth, past the historic town of Medicine Bow and the Medicine Bow Range beyond. Here the land lies in sharp folds, rising gradually toward the higher peaks of the Sierra Madre, interspersed with streams and alpine meadows. They have seen no sign of humans. The woods and the river are as they might have been a thousand years ago, five hundred years ago, when her people first moved west into the plains, following the buffalo.

"It all seems so far away," Kirsten says quietly, echoing her thoughts. "Almost like none of it ever happened."

"This is Ina Maka's place. Her time, not ours." Above them, a dark speck appears against the sky where the gold sheen of the westering sun meets the deepening blue of the east. It circles above them, growing larger as it spirals downward. A cry floats down to them, high and wild and triumphant.

Koda stops in her tracks, staring upward. As the speck comes nearer, it takes on the shape of wings, a bright copper tail fanned out to the beating light, its feathers sheened like hammered bronze. The cry comes again, and the broad wings cup the air to slow the hawk's descent. "My God," Kirsten breathes. "My God."

Koda does not speak, only stretches out her arm, protected only by the thin fabric of her shirt. Wiyo lights delicately on her wrist and walks sideways up her arm to rest on her shoulder. She ruffles her feathers once, gives a small, incongruous chirp of greeting, and settles, ducking her head to preen under a wing. Koda strokes her lightly under the throat, drawing a finger across the white breast feathers and the dark belly-band below. Around them dusk thickens as they move west, toward the mountains, the sea beyond, the crimson sky.

**"They have heavy** guns here, and here, in the valleys." Tacoma points to the rippling contour lines on the ordinance map spread out on the table before them. "And we've been taking rocket fire from higher elevations here." He taps the map again, indicating the low hills to the west of the base that gradually rise into the sacred Paha Sapa. "They're spread out all around us. We can backtrack and return fire, but we have no way of knowing what else they have or where it is. And we're going to run short of ammo in a very short time."

"We need recon," Manny observes. "Let me take an Apache up, General. Or the Cheyenne. I can get it up high enough, quick enough they won't be able to hit it."

"Hell," says Tacoma, with a grim smile. "One sight of that thing'd scare the bejesus out of 'em if they were human."

Manny shoots him an aggrieved look over the bandana that wraps the lower half of his face, even though Maggie suspects he agrees. Goddess knows she does. Soot from the burning HQ building drifts through the air, settling under the canvas flap that constitutes the temporary command post and falling as fine dust on the map. Further away, black smoke pours from a burning fuel tank, shot through with tongues of flame. Its stench, rank with oil and kerosene, comes to them on the thick air. Maggie waves a hand in front of her offended nose and says, "We don't just need recon. We need aerial fire power."

"And we need it now," Tacoma agrees. "Sooner or later they'll get the range on the planes."

"Shit." Manny jerks the kerchief off his face. "General, ma'am—"

"Get suited up," she says tersely. "Meet me on the flightline."

Manny sprints from underneath the makeshift canopy, holding the bandana over his face. Tacoma watches him go, his eyes troubled. "With respect, General—"

"With respect, Major Rivers. We have two Tomcats fueled and ready. Two planes, two pilots. You're in charge on the ground as of now. End of discussion."

"You know they've probably got anti-aircraft missiles out there."

"They probably do," Maggie agrees. "We'll just have to dodge them as best we can."

"We'll do whatever we can to draw their fire, General."

"Within prudence, Major. Within prudence. You'll be able to see at least one of us. When you do, open up and give 'em everything you've got. Andrews."

"Ma'am."

"Let's go." She turns again to Tacoma. "You remember I have to answer to your sister for you. Don't do anything that'll cost me my hair."

A flash of white teeth is her answer as he turns back to the study of the map, punching coordinates into his hand-held. Maggie races for the Jeep, her flight boots ringing hard on the pavement. Andrews paces her stride for stride. The dash for the flightline is, if anything, more harrowing than the white-knuckle race from the gate, clipping corners and bouncing over speed bumps with the kind of jolt that would knock the doors off a civilian vehicle. She holds fast to the rollbar and mutters a quiet prayer to Yemaya, cc'd to Koda's Ina Maka.

*Let us get there on time. Let us make it into the air.*

Halfway there, a mortar shell goes screaming over their heads to land somewhere near a maintenance hangar. A second follows it before Maggie can draw a breath. The twin strikes hit like thunderbolts, blurring out the rattle of the Jeep and its snarling engine in a fog of white noise. Smoke rises from the street that runs along the flightline, and a second column from somewhere on the other side of the row of hangars. Maggie's heart rises up and lodges in her throat, stifling speech. The enemy have found their range. "Go!" she yells, and Andrews floors the accelerator, rattling her teeth and shaking her bones loose in their sockets. The last half-mile streaks by in a blur, while the rockets begin to fall around the flight line like deadly hail, one ripping into the street just ahead of them, gouging a crater that Andrews barely misses, the tires of the driver's side skirting its rim by millimeters.

Thirty seconds later, the Jeep skids to a stop on the apron that flanks the main north-south runway. The two Tomcats sit just outside the hangar doors, one with its canopy up, the other, Manny, suited and helmeted at the controls, already closing down. Throwing off her Kevlar vest and field gear as she runs, Maggie snatches her helmet from the waiting tech sergeant, slaps it onto her head and scrambles up the ladder into the front cockpit of her craft. She straps in one-handed, fixing her oxygen mask in place, punching in the sequence for the automated systems checks that would normally occupy a quarter hour. Today they will run exactly as long as it takes her to get into position for takeoff. The green and red LEDs dance across the small screen, but the only figures that matter are the ones that tell her that she's taking off with fuel tanks topped off and the readout that confirms the ready status of the missiles that bristle along the undersides of her wings. It comes to her that this may be the last time that she will ever fly, that she has nothing to gain and only time to lose, but habit is too strong, and she continues to follow the check-list even as she shuts down her lexan bubble. The numbers still flickering in front of her, she revs her engines and begins her taxi to the north end of the strip.

She has beaten it into her student pilots' heads for a decade and a half. *If you're going to fly, you don't have options. Do it right. Do it right the first time.*

Do it right the last time, too.

With a wave of her hand, she motions Manny into position at her left wing, just to one side and behind. As she turns to make her run, a rocket tears into the tarmac just behind her. No time now for gradually gathering speed, and she opens the throttle and hurtles down the runway, pulling Gs before she ever reaches the end, Manny streaking alongside her, keeping pace. Then she pulls the nose up, feeling the lift beneath her wings and is airborne, climbing almost straight up into the sun.

At 10,000 feet she levels off, scraps of cloud like drifting feathers beneath her where she hangs in silence over the folded valleys and greening fields below. Sun glints off the nose of her plane, catching the edge of the lexan bubble as she banks to sweep in a wide arc south and west. Below her she can make out the rectilinear grid that is Rapid City and the dark ribbon of the highway where they made their stand against the droids a day...a lifetime...ago. She levels her wings and swings back toward Ellsworth, punching the display from the copilot's monitor forward to her own screen. The radar might not be able to pick up the enemy, but the cameras should be able to find them. *Even if the damned metalheads have found some way to shield themselves from long-wave frequencies, even if they can make themselves effectively invisible, they can't make themselves transparent.* If she can find the anomalies, she can bomb them. And put an end to them once for all.

Far to the east, the sun strikes fire from a streaking silver shape that must be Manny's Tomcat, turning as she is now to quarter the land beneath them. The gorges and ancient lava flows that spread out between the base and the Black Hills ripple away beneath her, their shapes flowing across the screen. The camera's lens, powerful enough to show a single buttercup growing in the summer meadows, singles out nothing of interest. No armored columns, no grinding mass of titanium canon fodder.

The blip appears on her screen without warning, something rising toward her from a winding gorge branching off from the Cheyenne's south fork. She kicks up the Tomcat's nose, and a Sparrow air-to-air missile streaks from beneath the left wing, locking onto its target as Maggie climbs and rolls away, sweeping back toward its launch point and punching coordinates into the laser guidance system that will drop five hundred pounds of high explosive on the enemy. The offending blip disappears from her readout a half-second before she sends the bomb on its way. With luck, it will take out a whole nest, but it is luck she cannot count on. Neither can she afford to be free-handed with her payload.

Another ground-to-air rocket rises up as she loops back toward Ellsworth from the north, and she dispatches it, and its launcher, as easily as she did the first. There is still no sign of the android force that appeared around the base earlier that morning; the only indication that they were not an hallucination or some weird sort of image projection is the artillery fire that pours down on her ground forces even as she seeks out their operators, and even then, they are evidence of no more than one operator apiece.

*What if...?* But that is a fantasy. They have to be here somewhere. Have to be.

*If I were a mule, where would I go to get lost? If I were a metal killing machine with printed circuits for brains and copper wire for nerves, where would I go to jam radar and avoid detection by conventional means?*

Maggie sweeps low to obtain a clearer image of a line of vehicles on a farm road, but they are only more of the ever-present wreckage of the first days of the uprising. Putting on speed, she climbs again, sweeping up through wispy clouds to the relative safety of the sky. Beneath her, the land rises steadily, from black bedrock deposited by volcanoes when the northern prairies lay beneath an inland sea into the uplift of the Black Hills themselves, sacred ground to the Lakota from time before time.

*Where would I go?*
*There's gold in them thar hills.*
Gold.

Not gold — uranium, vanadium. All of it lying exposed to the sky in the tiers of the huge strip mines gouged out of the earth at the turn of the century, shut down less than a decade ago by treaties renegotiated by the Oglala and northern Cheyenne and never remediated. Radioactive ore, huge masses of it, busily throwing off electrons on its own bandwidths.

It has been a sore spot with local citizens for years, disrupting the endlessly running talk radio stations, reducing cell phones to sputtering static, interfering with transmissions from civilian aircraft. How much? Maybe enough to mask the output from lesser masses and scramble incoming locator signals, even the special military frequencies.

That's *where I'd go if I were a droid*.

Turning south again, she lays down a pattern of sweeps that covers the expanse of more hospitable terrain between the Black Hills and the Badlands to the south and east. Flying with one hand and only half her brain — the years, the decades, of practice more ingrained now even than instinct — she scans the ground beneath her, zooming the camera in on every outcrop she does not recognize, every glint of sun off twisted metal or the rippled surface of a stock tank.

For twenty minutes she flies low and slow. The camera shows her cows grazing, a stallion running with his mares, a coyote arcing up out of the tall grass in pursuit of something invisible beneath its green stalks, one human with a gun who stands transfixed as she passes, not even bothering to run for cover. The mines themselves stand deserted, great open wounds in the Mother's body, their tiers descending into the earth like the narrowing circles of Dante's hell. There is no sign of droids.

Disappointment washes through her, leaving the taste of acid in her mouth. The damned things might as well be invisible. Maybe they are invisible. Maybe her brain has shorted out under the stress of the last several weeks.

Maybe Hart was right. She is not command material, never was.

Maybe she's not even a goddamned decent pilot.

Banking one more time over the snaking canyons of the badlands, she follows the twisted paths of dry rivers among the bare rock where the relics of eons past lie open to the sun that now stands halfway down from noon, raking the landscape with harsh sidelight. The rocks jut forth like nightmares out of legend: giants turned to stone; Lot's wife, looking back toward her burning city, transformed into a pillar of salt. Now blindingly bright, now running in shadow, streams that feed into the White River wind through them, the sun striking upward from their surfaces in sheets of light.

And there they are, in a bend of a narrow stream, the glare off their metal bodies blending with the reflection of the water. Thousands of them. Motionless, they stand in ranks as stiff as the terra cotta soldiers of Tchintsche Huang-ti, as unaware of the heat that beats off the dry rock as the rock itself.

As she passes, a shiver of movement runs through them; their sensors are not shut down. But by the time they can react, she is far away again to the west, entering the bomb-release sequence into her console as she loops back. She passes again, high above them this time, laying down the long stick of five hundred pounders that will reduce them to molten metal. Her vid shows her the perfect string of explosions that follows in her wake, clouds of smoke and dust rising up out of the canyon, here an overhang toppling onto the wreckage of the droids beneath, there a tower of basalt crashing down.

*Hoka hey.* It is a good day to kill.

Maggie allows herself a grim smile as she makes a second, then a third, turn to check for enemy still standing. She finds none; nothing on the visual but tumbled stone and scrap metal. Satisfied, she allows relief to break over her and gives her wings a waggle, partly just in case Manny or someone on the ground can see her, partly out of sheer satisfaction. She can feel the knots loosen in her neck and in the muscles along her spine, unraveling like strands of rope. Mission accomplished, she takes her heading and turns for home.

As the land slips by beneath her, badlands and prairie, she allows her mind to turn to what awaits her on her return. At this point she is not sure what Hart was, dupe or agent, hostage or mole. Obviously, the droids and their human allies — or perhaps masters — had meant to pound them senseless with artillery, tear up the runways to ground their air defense, and move in at leisure. Not necessarily in numbers, though. She will need to make the circuit of the base, spending her remaining missiles on the gun emplacements. That won't destroy the howitzers or heavy mortars, but should blow their crews quite nicely to smithereens. Two keystrokes shift their mode from air-to-air to air-to-ground; the big guns generate enough heat to home them in. Always assuming Manny hasn't already bombed them right into their next lives.

Q: Where does a bad droid go when it dies?

A: Helliburton.

The joke is as old as Westerhaus's first military models, a dart aimed at his rival military contractor. Ancient history now.

Maggie passes over Rapid City, looping around to the north to scan the valleys around Ellsworth. She sees only the river, running gold in the westering sun, the woods, the mass of the Black Hills thrusting up toward the sky. She feels an odd sense of homecoming, partly the welcome she always associates with the completion of a successful mission, partly something she cannot quite name, something that emanates from the sacred ground beneath her. All clear.

At the far eastern arc of her circle, she passes over the highway where the wreckage of the battle lies strewn for miles. Her monitor shows only the tortured metal remains of tanks blown open and burned out from inside, the tumbled length of the first defensive wall. Nothing moves except the wind in the trees. She can go home.

As she banks, the sun glances off something miles up the road to the east. Something bright, something metal. Something moving.

Maggie pulls back on the stick and streaks for the clouds again, kicking in the afterburners for speed. Once she levels off, she scans the stretch of tarmac that stretches out beneath her.

More droids. Not thousands, perhaps no more than several hundred, marching in a tight column toward Ellsworth. Reserves? Latecomers? She has no way of knowing. Neither has she the firepower to take them out. Manny might, but Manny obviously has not seen them. With luck, they have not seen him, either. She will not break radio silence.

She has only one weapon left. She checks her fuel gauge. The Tomcat carries close to 20,000 pounds of jet fuel; close to half that remains in her tanks. Enough for the job.

Her premonition returns to her. With the runways and hangars pounded by enemy guns, this is her last flight. She will make it count.

Carefully she calculates the distance and trajectory to the enemy column and enters the coordinates into the autopilot. Loosing the last of her missiles, she aims the Tomcat's nose toward the earth with one hand and jerks on the ejection lever with the other.

Nothing happens. The ground rises up at her, the column of droids growing clear in her sight. She pulls the lever again, and again.

On the third try, the bubble pops and she flies free of the plane as it gathers speed in its descent. But the delay has cost her, and her head strikes the canopy hard as her seat becomes a projectile. She sees the flash of silver as her Tomcat streaks toward earth, the blue sky above her. And then the dark comes down.

The night is blue around her, the deep blue of the deepest sea. Overhead the stars dance in stately patterns, throwing off streamers of flame as they spin and whirl, jewels burning cold in shades of amethyst and emerald and sapphire, blazing ruby and topaz with hearts of fire. A breeze slips cool over her face, soothing against her skin. It stirs the pine trees that ring the clear space where she lies, soughing softly.

There are voices in the wind. If she tried, she could make them out. But she is tired, so tired. She lies under a billow of white silk. Perhaps she is dead, and it is her funeral pall.

If she is, she decides, death is not so bad after all. She knows that one leg lies twisted under her and is undoubtedly broken; from the way the blood pounds in her head, that may be broken, too. She can feel the grass through a cool wetness above one ear; more strangeness. Something has apparently happened to her helmet. Perhaps whoever has laid her out has removed it. Odd, though, that she seems to be lying on earth. No coffin, no burial platform, no piled wood. Just the silken pall.

With effort, but with no pain, she turns her head. Just beyond her reach, a large cat sits watching her, fur silver-gilt in the strange not-moonlight that shimmers in the air, eyes deep amber rimmed in shadow. The paler fur on her belly lies in darker swirls, made, Maggie knows, by her nursing young. Elegant in its length, her tail curls about her feet.

*You wander, sister,* the cat says in the silence, *Igmú Sapa Winan.*

*Where?* Maggie answers without sound. *And why?*

*You stand with one foot on the Blue Road. If you wish, you may cross over.*

*If I wish?*

*Or not. Do you want me to summon help from your own kind?*

Her own kind. She thinks about that for a moment. She knows of only three of her own kind, maybe four, who might hear a call like that. None of whom can be spared from duty.

It would be easy to slip away. A picture forms in her mind, unbidden, of sky-tall trees ringing a lake whose deep purple waters lap at shores dotted with gentians and spurred columbine. As she watches, a winter buck limps up to the shore, blood oozing from a wound in his shoulder, laid open to the bone. Maggie winces for what must be the pain of it, but as he bends to drink, the blood stills. Flesh folds back on itself, skin and fur spreading to cover it, and he stands there whole, sunlight streaming down through the trees about him. A woman stands beside him, her leather dress dyed green, yellow shells and beadwork running in rows down its length like kernels on an ear of corn. Her black hair spills down her back almost to her knees; copper shines at her ears and wrists.

*Mother*, Maggie says silently, awe washing through her.

*Selu*, the woman answers. *And this is* Ataga'hi, *where the hunted may come to be healed. Though you are a warrior and have killed more two-foots than most, you have never harmed one of your four-footed brothers or sisters. Hunters may not come here. Will you drink, Black Cat Woman?*

*My people, are they safe?*

*They are.*

*For answer, then, she rises up and steps carefully toward the lake. The grass bends gently under the pads of her feet, and she is not surprised to find that her spine has shifted so that she does not stand erect. Her ears, inhumanly sharp, take in the murmur of small life around her, the calls of birds like music. The water, when she bends to lap, slips cool across her tongue, and she drinks her fill, life pouring back into her, and purpose with it.*

Then she is back in her own body, and she gasps as sensation floods back into her from cracked bone and torn muscle. The puma, though, still regards her quietly.

*I will call*, she says.

For an instant, Maggie thinks she is seeing double. A second great cat stands beside the first, gazing at her with eyes of warm brown. And there is a bobcat, too, grinning at her with open mouth.

*Hang in there*, he says. *We're on our way.*

The blue begins to fade to black about her. The puma fades with it, a liquid shadow in the night. Pain from her leg rises about her on a swelling tide, bringing its own darkness with it. *Just,* she says to the wind as words begin to desert her altogether, *just move your asses.*

**A small fire** is blazing cheerily in the center of a tiny clearing just west of the river. Next to it, coals lie in a ring of stones, and on those coals, two plump chukar roast away, lucky finds that Koda was able to take with her bow after Asi accidentally flushed them from their hiding place while sniffing around in search of a good place to mark his territory.

The hero of the food-getting venture is sprawled on his back near the fire, eyes open and alert to every movement, hoping beyond hope that his hard work will earn him some of the catch.

The savory scent of cooking partridge sets Kirsten's belly to grumbling, and she covers it with a hand as Dakota looks up from her work and grins at her. "Won't be much longer."

"Thank God for that. I'm starved!"

"Did you finish setting up what you needed on that thing?"

Kirsten's blush is luckily hidden by the glare from the computer's large screen. "Um...yeah, just now," she replies, quickly clicking off the solitaire game, mid-hand. The computer beeps out a mechanical sigh — it had been winning — and obligingly shuts down.

"Good." Nodding, Dakota returns to her task of sharpening the hunting knife she's used on the birds, as Kirsten looks on quietly.

The dark, glossy head looks up from its work, deep blue eyes meeting hers with the same look of total adoration and devotion, and Kirsten can't help but smile until it feels as if her face is about to split in two.

A dark eyebrow lifts. "Are you all right?"

Setting aside her glasses, Kirsten rubs her eyes. "Just...processing the day, I guess."

"Mm."

Taking a quick peek, she sees that Koda is already back to her sharpening, and Kirsten lets go a small sigh of relief. Closing her laptop completely, she sets it to the side and stands, stretching out muscles pleasantly tired from their long hike. Simple physical tiredness, of late, has been replaced by bouts of emotional overload shot though with darts of adrenaline, keeping her on hair-trigger edge. Her body, though tired, thanks her for the respite, and she, in turn, thanks it for bearing up remarkably well under these changed circumstances. Her belly grumbles again, and she laughs, watching as her lover puts down her work and fishes the game birds from the coals, setting them on two camp plates already garnished with the fresh herbs she's picked from the forest.

Not even using the spork provided, Kirsten rips into the stuffed bird with her bare hands, shoveling the food into her mouth as fast as it will go, and groaning, eyes rolling in ecstasy as the spicy flavor coats her palate with ambrosia. "Jesus!" she exclaims around a bulging mouthful. "This is fantastic!"

Koda looks on in awe, decimating her own bird with more delicate motions while feeding several morsels to the raptly attentive Asimov. "Glad you like it."

"Like it? I never had something so good in my life! You should have been a chef!"

"Exercise and fresh mountain air," Koda replies, tossing another morsel to Asi. "Does it every time."

"Hunh uh," Kirsten disagrees, still shoveling as fast as her hands can move, her mouth and chin liberally coated with grease. "You've got talent, woman. Ever think of opening up a vet clinic with a restaurant on the side?"

"I...think that would give customers the wrong idea, don't you?"

Kirsten thinks about it for a moment, then realizes the outcome of her suggestion. "Ew."

"Ew is right."

The rest of dinner is finished in silence, and after the leavings are buried and the dishes cleaned, Dakota sits back against an overturned log, Kirsten comfortably ensconced between her legs holding the arms crossed over her belly. Both are lost in the contemplation of the stars above. With no streetlights, no cars, no sirens, and only the wind for company, the night is profoundly silent. After a moment, Kirsten sighs.

"What's wrong, sweetheart?" Koda asks, pressing her cheek atop the soft blonde hair of her lover.

"I...don't know, really." She laughs a little. "Maybe I'm getting an attack of the guilts or something. I mean, here I am...here we are...in...well...in paradise, while our friends are back home fighting for their lives, getting hurt, maybe getting killed." She turns a little, meeting Dakota's eyes. "What right do I have to feel so at peace, so happy, when people I care about are dying? Because of me."

Dakota tightens her grip around her lover, settling Kirsten more comfortably against her and pressing a kiss into the crown of her hair. "It's their freedom they're fighting for, *canteskuye*. Theirs, ours, everyone's." She pauses for a second, then resumes. "Do you think, really think, that if Maggie had given you to Hart on a silver platter, he would have let everyone on the base just walk away?"

"Well..."

Koda remains silent, letting Kirsten think it through.

"I guess not. I mean, he's lied about everything else, so why would he suddenly be telling the truth about that?"

"Exactly. Hart's an opportunist. The androids cut him a deal, and he's keeping up his end of that bargain. You might be the 'prize' at the moment, but every single man, woman, and child outside of the control of Westerhaus and his gang is the ultimate target, and he won't stop until he has every one of us under his thumb, one way or the other."

"I know this," Kirsten says, shifting a little. "In my head, I know this. It's just..."

"Your heart. You feel because you're human, because you're a compassionate person, and because you love."

"This being human stuff is hard," Kirsten mumbles, snuggling into Koda's warm embrace.

"But worth it, don't you think?"

Kirsten's grin is hidden in the folds of Dakota's shirt. "Oh yeah."

**The tent is** just tall enough for Kirsten to stand up straight, and she does, hands clamped to the small of her back as she stretches it, groaning unhappily. "Dear God, I'm stiff."

"I've got just the cure for that."

Kirsten looks over her shoulder, a smile forming. "You do, do you?"

"Mm. Take off your clothes and lie down."

Kirsten chuckles. "Honey, you know I love you, but I'm about as sore as one person can be and not require large doses of morphine. I don't know how much I can contribute to—"

"Just take off your clothes and lie down, please."

"Well...if you insist."

"I insist."

Slowly and stiffly, Kirsten removes her clothes, then laboriously kneels down atop the opened and connected sleeping bags, stretching out on her belly with a loud groan. "I think it's gonna be a toss-up as to whether I can ever get back up again."

"Oh," comes Koda's smooth voice from above and behind her, "you'll get up. Now just close your eyes and relax."

Doing as she's bidden, Kirsten jumps just a little as something warm and heavy is laid across her shoulders. "Mm. What's that?"

"Warm packs. Just stay relaxed and let me do all the work."

Several more packs find their way across her back and legs, their warmth immediately penetrating her overstressed muscles and coaxing them into gradual, and welcome, relaxation. "Oh," she moans, "this is bliss."

Something faintly spicy scents the air, and Kirsten wakes up from a half-doze to feel her right foot cradled gently in Dakota's large hands. One strong thumb comes down on her instep, making her hiss with pain, then groan with pleasure as heated oil and gentle pressure soothes its way into the tender sole of her foot. "I'm in Heaven," Kirsten croons off-key, her voice slurred against the incredible pleasure she's feeling. "God, what hands you have, my love."

Dakota's laugh is soft as she tends to every muscle, every pore, every inch of skin on Kirsten's foot, soothing the aches with deft strokes of her strong, gentle fingers. Then she lays the limp appendage down on the sleeping bag and lifts the other, repeating the process until Kirsten's blissful snores fill the tent.

"That's it, *cante mitawa*," she whispers lovingly. "Let it go for tonight. Just let it go." Brushing a kiss against the foot she's holding, she places it down beside its mate, languidly removes her own clothing, and slips into the sleeping bag next to her partner. Removing the warm packs, she presses her length against Kirsten's naked side, places the palm of her hand on the small of her partner's back, and falls quickly asleep, a small smile on her face.

# CHAPTER FORTY-FOUR

"Looks like rain soon," Kirsten observes as she looks up at the sky and its rapid gathering of clouds, like guests to a party they absolutely cannot miss. Her breath comes hard and fast from the exertion of climbing what seemed to her to be nearly vertical grades, with not a level plain in sight. She walks with the aid of a stout stick nearly as tall as she is. Asi lopes along happily, occasionally darting off the game trail they are following to investigate something interesting to his dog senses. Wiyo easily paces them high above, riding the currents of the increasingly chilly air.

They have made good time since Manny left them in the clearing days ago. They managed to scare up a couple of mountain bikes that had gotten them a good long way before a blown out tire ended that adventure. Not that it would have mattered soon anyway. The grades they are now climbing are too steep even to entertain the notion of riding a bike, unless one was Greg LeMonde, a title neither of them claims.

Cars, of course, are out. Even if gas weren't a problem, which it is, and they were able to find one that would start after sitting idle for six or more months, which they hadn't, riding in a moving vehicle would have painted a target on their heads, together with a sign reading "KIRSTEN KING IS HERE! COME AND GET HER, BOYS!"

While continuing her easy, long-legged stride, Koda cants her head, nostrils flaring as she scents the air. "Not rain," she murmurs. "Snow. And a lot of it, by the look of those clouds."

"Not that I'm a weatherman or anything," Kirsten replies, chuckling, "but in case you've forgotten, it's June, love. It doesn't snow in June."

"Up here it can. Weather patterns are different up this high. A June snowstorm isn't all that uncommon. People can get tricked up here sometimes, and come unprepared."

"If you start making Donner Party cracks," Kirsten states with a nervous chuckle, "I'm gonna start running back down this damn mountain as fast as my slowly blistering feet will carry me."

Koda smiles. "We'll be all right. We've got a little time yet to find shelter."

Kirsten looks around, seeing nothing but trees, trees, bushes, and more trees. "Um...I don't want to sound like an alarmist or anything, but I haven't seen anything even remotely resembling a town for hours. Hell, I haven't seen anything resembling a house."

"We'll find something. C'mon."

With an exasperated sigh, Kirsten trudges on, every so often shooting a wary glance at the clouds continuing to build, stealing the last of the bright blue of the sky.

**Heavy flurries threaten** to turn into a full-out blizzard as Dakota leads them deeper into the forest, her eyes constantly scanning, ears primed for any sounds of danger. Asi ranges back and forth in front of them, nose to the ground and tail held at stiff attention. Though Kirsten trusts Dakota with her life, her old childhood fears of being lost in the woods have sprung to the surface with the turning of the weather, and though a chill wind is now blowing, a greasy sweat dots the exposed surfaces of her skin, dripping into her eyes and causing them to sting.

Suddenly, Asi's haunches stiffen and he lets go a volley of barks that almost sends Kirsten into orbit. She steps closer to Dakota as a huge flock of birds rises, screeching their displeasure. To her surprise, her lover seems quite relaxed, even smiling as she eyes the angry birds. "I don't see what's so funny," she snipes, angry more at herself for her jittery nerves than at her partner's seemingly inappropriate sense of humor. "For all we know, he could be barking at a grizzly."

"It's no grizzly," Koda replies, still smiling as she meets her lover's eyes. "Birds wouldn't be roosting around a bear."

"So...what is it then?"

"You'll see."

"It" turns out to be a shack, though to use the term does great disservice to shacks everywhere. Short and squat, perhaps eight feet to a side if that, it has the faintly listing look of a party-goer after one too many shots of Cuervo. The only window peers out at the world through shattered glass, and the door, or what's left of it, hangs forlornly from one rusted hinge. The roof, minus most of what passes for its shingles, is slightly canted, and the rocks from a fireplace chimney rise from it like a strangely shaped mushroom.

To Dakota, it looks like nothing so much as a long abandoned ice-fishing shanty, though she knows that the nearest body of serviceable water is miles away in any direction. Still, any port in a storm. "Well, it's not the Watergate, but it's got a roof."

At this point, Kirsten is all in favor of anything that involves protection from the hard-driving snow and the wind that cuts through her light windbreaker like the blade of a knife. She takes a step forward, only to be held back by Dakota, who unshoulders her rifle and aims for the door. "I thought you said there wasn't any danger?"

"No, I said there weren't any grizzlies," Koda replies, smirking. "Stay here a second. I'll be right back."

Confident in being obeyed, she steps easily forward and nudges the door open with the nose of her weapon. It gives way grudgingly, squealing its protest via its one rusted hinge. The strong odor of animal spoor assaults her nostrils, but the scent is nowhere near as strong as it would be if it were currently occupied, so she relaxes and steps inside. Aside from the spiderwebs festooning the corners like forgotten party streamers, the shack is abandoned. Warped floorboards bear dark stains, and the walls have jagged cracks running through them, but for all that, the place seems relatively sound.

"Wowza. A little ripe, huh?"

Kirsten's voice sounds beside her left elbow and she turns her head to gaze down into the shining emeralds of her partner. "I thought I told you to stay put?"

"So you did," is the complacent reply. "The fault in your logic is thinking that I'd actually obey. And since I'm the President and you're only the chief cook and bottle washer, well..." Kirsten's tone is light and playful. "Besides, I didn't want you having any fun without me."

"Oh yeah. Fun."

Setting her rifle to stand in one corner, Koda, after a questioning eyebrow toward her partner, liberates Kirsten of her walking stick and walks to the good-sized fireplace taking up almost one entire wall. Squatting on her haunches, she maneuvers the stick up the chimney and pokes. A soft rain of white ash filters down, together with sticks, twigs, leaves, and part of a very old bird's nest, sans birds. "Flue's clear." With a nod of satisfaction, she hands Kirsten back her stick and rises gracefully to her full height, dusting off her hands. "I'll go out and get us some firewood before the storm gets much worse, then we'll figure out how to close off that window and get some warmth in here."

"Hang on a second," Kirsten says, unshouldering her pack, unzipping it, and pulling out one of their tightly rolled blankets. "Throw this around your shoulders. It's too damn cold out there to be walking around in just a shirt."

"Best to keep our blankets dry," Koda counters. "See if my heavy flannel is in there. I won't be out long."

Digging further, Kirsten comes up with Koda's thick, lined flannel shirt, and she tosses the garment over. She watches as her lover shoulders it on and flips her braid out from beneath the neckline. "Be careful out there, all right?"

Koda responds by kissing her lightly, a kiss which quickly deepens as their bodies realize to the very second, exactly how long it has been since they have last made love. The nights of late have found them both so bone tired that it has been all they can do just to strip and slide into their joined sleeping bags before falling deeply asleep, huddled closely together. "Hold that thought." Koda's voice is suspiciously husky as they finally break for air, hearts pounding in tandem.

"Hurry back," Kirsten replies on a breath that is just as ragged.

**The wind howls** through the trees like an express train headed east. Already, half an inch of snow coats the summer-warm ground, and more accumulates as the seconds pass. Practically blinded by the driving blizzard, Koda hunts for firewood on instinct, straying near the deciduous trees with their new growth covered in crystals of virgin white. Within twenty minutes, she has all the wood she can carry bundled in a more or less neat stack, and is silently thanking her father for many such a chore in her growing-up years. She picks her way carefully through the newfallen snow, her innate sense of direction leading her surely to the small shack in the middle of nowhere that they've chosen as their temporary — she hopes — shelter.

"Get in here!" Kirsten shouts to be heard over the shriek of the wind, all but pulling Dakota through the doorway. "God, you're soaked all the way through!"

"That'll be remedied soon enough," she replies, walking to the fireplace and setting down the branches she's managed to forage. Her fingers, quite numb from the cold, are sluggish to cooperate, and Kirsten, seeing this, kneels down to help, scowling at her.

"You just get out of those soaked clothes. I'll start the fire."

Koda's stiffening knees send out twin bolts of pain as she rises, and she walks gingerly back to where Kirsten has laid their packs, rummaging about for some warm, dry clothing. She takes in a deep breath, and is pleasantly surprised at the vast reduction in rank odor permeating the place. "Nice," she hums.

"House-cleaning for backwoods shacks 101," Kirsten replies, shaking out a wooden match from the waterproof tube and lighting it on the first strike. "Find a branch with dead leaves — instant broom."

"Learned that from the felonious Martha, did you?"

"Ha. Ha. I'll have you know that beneath my bookish looks and geeky charm lurks a genuine Rosie the Riveter."

"Mm." Koda's liquid voice sounds right next to her ear, "I like your bookish looks and geeky charm."

"Jesus!" Kirsten utters, as much at the sudden onrush of hormones as at the fact that she has almost burned herself to a crisp. "Honey, I love you, but I think I learned in Girl Scouts that it's unwise to seduce someone when they're trying to start a fire. At least...one in a fireplace."

"Interesting troop you belonged to, *canteskuye*."

"You have *no* idea," Kirsten purrs, this time managing to get the tinder to light underneath the larger branches and logs.

"What else did they teach you?"

Kirsten shoots her a coy look from beneath partially lowered lashes. "Get out of those cold, wet clothes, and you just might find out."

"You must have gotten the incentivising-for-fun-and-profit merit badge."

"First time out," Kirsten replies smugly. "Now scoot!"

"Consider me scooted."

As she turns away, Koda notices another improvement in the shack. Kirsten has used her bright yellow rain poncho as a windbreak, with duct tape to lash it securely over the hole masquerading as a window. Added to the now burning fire, the warmth is palpable, and Koda lets go a shiver as the pins and needles of sensation rush into her warming skin.

"You okay?" Kirsten asks, moving over to her side and helping her remove the sopping garments.

"Getting better. Nice job with the window, Rosie. Have any more talents you haven't shared?"

"Maybe one or two," Kirsten replies, grinning. "However, they still don't include cooking worth a squat so...any suggestions?"

"Trail rations, at least for tonight. And some hot tea to wash them down with."

Kirsten's lips moue. "I could have done that."

"True," Koda replies, pretending to consider. "I suppose I could open the door and invite a couple of rabbits to hop into the stew pot — assuming we had one — but I personally think that they'd rather take their chances with the blizzard."

"Mm. You have a point there. Tell you what, I'll scare up our jerky and crackers, and you heat up the water for tea. Sound fair?"

"More than." Slipping on her loose sweatpants, she moves to their packs and pulls out the stacked cooking gear they picked up from the camping store, pours some water from one of their canteens into the largest pot, and sets it on the hearth to warm. After setting out a couple of teabags, she moves to the door and, with a bit of effort, manages to get it seated more or less securely into its warped frame. By the time she's completed that task, the water is gently steaming in its pot, and she returns to the fireplace and pours the water into two travel mugs, allowing the tea to steep.

Kirsten has already laid their sleeping bags atop a thick blanket, and has used a second blanket to cover the blackened floor. Their simple fare sits atop this blanket, several pieces of jerky, a tube of crackers, and some cheese she'd liberated from a holiday basket some weeks back. It's not a feast, no, but when she thinks about it, it's not too different from the cardboard tasting microwave dinners she'd used to eat when she was living in the lap of civilization — when she remembered to eat at all, that is. *And,* she thinks, looking over at the beauty who comes to sit comfortably by her side, tea mugs in hand, *the company is infinitely preferable.*

"Penny for your thoughts," Koda remarks, tossing a piece of jerky to Asi, who sets to with vigor.

"Is that the going rate these days?" She chuckles. "Actually, I was just sitting here thinking that there could be worse places to be than holed up with you in some shanty eating cold food and waiting out a blizzard."

"Oh?"

"Yeah. Home, for instance. I mean...the home before all this started."

Koda thinks for a moment. "What would you be doing if you were there instead of here?"

"What is it, about six or so?"

"Thereabouts." Neither wears a watch, but, as with many things in this brave new world, they've learned to get by without them.

"I'd probably still be at work. I never left much before nine or so."

"Hillary kept you running ragged, huh?"

Kirsten smiles. "Nah. I was pretty much a workaholic anyway. I was doing something I loved, and there really wasn't anything for me back home—" She is interrupted by a rather outraged whine. "Except for Asimov, of course, I'd never forget you boy." She ruffles him behind the ears, earning a grunting acceptance of her oblique apology. "How 'bout you?"

"Mm, pretty much the same thing," Koda remarks around a mouthful of tea. "I usually kept my clinic open 'til late. More often than not, Wash or one of my other brothers would be down helping, and I'd drive them back home and take dinner with the family. I'd usually hang out with them for a bit, see if there were any chores that needed doing, then drive home. One last check of my patients, and I'd head to the house for bed." She shrugs. "With Tali gone, there really wasn't much else to do."

At the mention of Tali's name, Kirsten feels a burst of insecurity, but it's more of an echo now, not the sharp, bitter tang she might have felt not three months before. She smiles internally, pleased at the growth she can feel in herself. *I'm getting there,* she thinks. *I might not be all the way yet, but I'm getting there.* She blinks, startled as a tin cup clinks softly against her own, and she looks up into Dakota's soft, loving eyes.

"To us, and to the future we'll build together."

"To us," she replies softly, the warmth rushing through her, an answer to unuttered prayers.

The rest of their meager repast is eaten in comfortable silence. The shrieking of the storm outside is mellowed by the cheery crackle of the fire. And though the shack's cracked walls and questionable roof let in some of the cold, the warmth between them more than makes up for it.

Kirsten sets her empty cup down on the blanket and wraps her arms around Dakota's lean waist, snuggling her head against one well-muscled shoulder and sighing in contentment. Smiling, Koda sets her own cup down and trails her fingers through Kirsten's now long hair, watching as the strands sift through her hand like rays of warm spring sunshine. "*Cante mitawa*," she whispers as Kirsten tilts her head up and their mouths meet, slip away, then meet again in loving welcome.

Kirsten's lips part to the tender, inquisitive touch of Koda's tongue, and she shivers with delight even as her hand slowly raises to cup her lover's firm breast, caressing it with her thumb as she feels its warm weight in her palm. The hand in her hair tightens and Kirsten feels her neck arching as her head is drawn firmly, tenderly back, exposing the strong column of her neck to the ravenous lips, tongue and teeth of her lover. She shivers again, then moans as her bounding pulsepoint is nipped, then soothed with the tip of an amorous tongue.

A low growl sounds from Koda's throat as she removes Kirsten's hand from her breast and eases the younger woman back onto the blanket, lips still attached to her throat, suckling at the tanned, tender skin presented her. Her hands and fingers are demanding as they tug and pull at Kirsten's T-shirt, easing it up until her lover's breasts are exposed to the chill air and her voracious gaze. "Beautiful," she rasps. "So beautiful."

Koda's eyes are the sky of a moonlit night, her pupils black holes and Kirsten feels herself drawn into their vortex. Long fingers dance over pale, silken flesh, circling nipples hard and aching even as a thigh slides up and seats itself between Kirsten's legs, pressing and releasing and gently grinding. Kirsten trembles, then cries out softly as a warm, wet mouth moves down over her left breast, taking her in and sparking a fire that flows through her veins, making her limbs heavy and leaden as sharp teeth graze her nipple and a tongue soothes the sting.

As Koda moves over to Kirsten's right breast, her hands dance down over belly and hips in long, slow, reverent strokes, then work the button to her jeans with expert precision. Rolling partially away, Dakota draws down the jeans and undergarments over strong thighs and tanned, toned calves, and tosses them in the direction of their packs. She then returns, grasps her lover's legs and bends them, spreads them wide. Her tongue peeks out to wet her lips as her eyes feast on the evidence of Kirsten's passion shining in the dancing light of the fire. With a soft groan, she eases back between those legs, rocking her pelvis until the soft fabric of her pants chafes against Kirsten's swollen need.

"Oh God!" Kirsten gasps out, fingers digging into the ragged blanket.

"*Mitawa*," Koda growls, circling her hips against Kirsten's swollen wetness. "*Mitawa*." Leaning forward so that her thick, black hair forms a curtain around them, she melds her lips to Kirsten's, nipping her lower lip and tonguing the fold in slow, suggestive strokes and circles.

Kirsten's legs move of their own accord, wrapping themselves around Koda's waist, pulling her closer. "Please," Kirsten whispers. "Please."

Sliding her hands down to Kirsten's hips — hot hands they are, so hot, searing her skin like brands — she begins to thrust in earnest, the soft cloth of her sweats giving her lover the exact friction she needs.

Reaching up, Kirsten, in a burst of passionate strength, rips open Dakota's T-shirt from hem to neck, then pulls down on the sweaty back so that their breasts and bellies slip and slide along their lengths in time to their rocking thrusts. "More," Kirsten moans, her body liquid fire. "More, please, God, more!"

Dakota's lips blaze a trail over her cheek and jaw and latch on to the

fleshy part of her lobe; her tongue traces the whirls and whorles, still rocking, still thrusting, meeting Kirsten's need with her own in a circle that has
no end.  Her hand slips between them and she groans as liquid heat bathes
her fingers in a benediction of passion.

"*Mitawa*," she growls into Kirsten's ear as she thrusts three fingers
deep into her lover's core, claiming her, filling her, loving her.  Kirsten's
head slams back against the ground; her body arches like a bow bejeweled
with sweat, every muscle taut and straining, every vein plump and thrumming just beneath the surface of her skin.  Koda pulls her fingers out to the
tips, twists, and thrusts back in with force, her eyes fluttering closed to her
lover's scream of ecstasy.  Holding herself up by one trembling arm bent at
the elbow, she begins thrusting in earnest, advancing and retreating to the
rhythm of Kirsten's wildly bucking hips.  Her grunts of effort into Kirsten's
ear are low and guttural and send waves of sensation flowing through her
and into her lover, causing Koda's vision to blur and her head to spin.  She
slips out again, then adds a fourth finger to Kirsten's delighted shout, and
her thumb curls up to tease the engorged flesh, circling, circling, circling
until Kirsten, finally, can take no more and crests on a thunderous wave of
spiraling light that seems to have no end.

Sensing her lover is at her breaking point, Dakota begins to slow the
rhythm and force of her thrusts, bringing Kirsten back to Earth in the sweetest possible way.  She lays butterfly kisses along closed eyelids and furrowed brow, on cheeks and chin and passion-swollen lips until finally
Kirsten relaxes and drops back to the blanket, spent and gasping for
breath.  Koda gathers her in close, gently stroking hypersensitive skin, murmuring words of love and adoration she knows likely go unheard.

After several moments, emerald eyes flutter open, slightly dazed.
"That was...you are...GOD."

"No," Koda jokes, "just a minion."

Kirsten rolls to her side, grabbing tight to the T-shirt she's ripped and
pulling Koda belly to belly with her.  "I love you.  I love you.  I love you.  I
could say it a million times a day, and it wouldn't be enough.  Never
enough."

"More than enough," Koda replies softly, tilting her lover's chin so that
their eyes meet.  "More than enough, *cante mitawa*."  Their lips come
together again, and this time it is Kirsten who pulls away.

"I need to taste you," she says urgently.  "Now.  Right now."

Not needing to be told twice, Koda slips up to a sitting position and
shucks off her sweats and undergarments in one easy move.  As she
moves to lie down on the blanket, Kirsten halts her.  "No, sit up with your
back against the wall.  I want you to watch me.  I want to watch you."

The bare, cracked wall is scratchy on her now naked and sweating
back, but that minor annoyance is completely forgotten as Kirsten, licking
her lips, spreads Dakota's long legs, bends them at the knee, and situates
her lover's feet flat on the floor.  Then she lowers herself onto her belly and
takes in a deep breath.  The spicy, exotic scent of her lover's arousal flows
through her senses, kick-starting hormones that had just thought they were
satiated.  Her mouth waters and her eyes, filled with joyous anticipation,
catch the dark, blazing eyes of her lover watching her every move.

With a little smirk, she begins by kissing the insides of Koda's long,
muscular thighs, using her tongue to gather up all traces of her lover's pas-

sion and moaning in happiness over the taste that is, to her, finer than anything this world has to offer. "Touch yourself," she whispers, "your breasts. Make love to them as I make love to you. Here." Dipping two fingers into Dakota's wetness, she reaches up and paints her lover's nipples with her own essence, which shines like molten gold in the light of the fire.

Dakota's hands come up to caress her breasts, using the moisture to stimulate her nipples until they are stiff peaks that ache with sensation.

"Now watch," Kirsten orders, dipping her head and using just the tip of her tongue to part Dakota's lips.

Dakota's head slams back against the wall and she hisses with pleasure as she feels her lover's talented tongue explore her folds, gently at first, then with more vigor. The first touch of Kirsten's tongue on her clit almost sends her over, but she holds back with everything in her, squeezing her nipples and trying to keep her hips as steady as possible — a nearly impossible task given what Kirsten is now doing with her mouth.

Pursing her lips, Kirsten draws Koda inside, then traps the shaft with gentle teeth, leaving the turgid bud smooth and pulsing on her tongue. First lapping like a kitten to cream, then twisting and dancing, she finally settles down to a staccato rhythm that she knows Dakota particularly loves. Her lover is silent, like she usually is when being made love to, but Kirsten need only hear her labored breathing and feel the wiry tension in the inhumanly strong muscles clamped to her sides to know that she's nearing the edge. With a final swirl of her tongue, she bites down as hard as she can without breaking the skin, and applies the perfect suction. One more touch of her tongue, a gentle, long lick, and Dakota climaxes, her entire body shuddering with the force of her explosion. Kirsten greedily drinks at her lover's font, taking in every drop that springs from her like a waterfall until Dakota collapses, boneless, against the wall.

Getting to her knees, Kirsten moves forward and gathers her semiconscious lover into her arms, stroking the sweat damp hair and whispering nonsense words into her ear as she recovers and comes back to planet Earth.

"You...learned that in...Girl Scouts...did you?" Koda asks as strength and sensation finally opt to make a reappearance.

"That one I thought up on my own," Kirsten replies cheekily. "I'm glad you liked it."

"Liked it? As soon as I can find the top of my head around here, I'll show you how much I liked it."

Kirsten chuckles. "We've got plenty of time for that, my love. Right now, I think sleep's calling."

"Don' wanna."

"Come on, boneless one, time for bed."

A truly aggrieved sigh follows, but Dakota allows Kirsten to help her to her knees and over to where their sleeping bags lie ready for them. They settle in, back to front, and Koda presses a kiss to Kirsten's salty shoulder. "Love you."

"I love you too, Dakota Rivers. I love you, too."

And with that, the two lovers fall into a well earned slumber.

# CHAPTER FORTY-FIVE

"Now I remember why I've always hated shopping."

Koda picks her way through the remains of a sporting goods store, stepping carefully through the spilled tennis and golf balls scattered across the floor. Against the walls, the locked cabinets that once held guns have been broken open, their sliding lexan doors hanging loose on their shattered hinges. In one dark corner stands a rack that once held basketball jerseys, judging by the scraps of brightly-colored mesh now piled beneath it. From somewhere behind that comes a rustle and the sound of small feet scrabbling on the floor tiles, punctuated by grunts and a threatening hiss. Asi gives a pleading whine, his head up, tail straight as a standard.

"Possum," says Kirsten from behind a counter that still stands largely intact, "Mama Possum." The drawers have been thoroughly looted of ammunition, gun oil, and other useful items. Her head appears above the glass top of the display case, and she aims a frown at Asi. "Don't even think about it, Deppity Dawg." Asi whines again but stands down, leaving the store's residents in peace. Returning to her rummaging under the counter, Kirsten adds, "At least you found stuff to fit. 'Petite' is a lot larger than it used to be."

"Small but mighty." Koda flashes her a grin. "What hasn't been carted off or ruined by the weather has been co-opted by the critters."

Still, this modest strip mall is tame compared to the sprawling wreckage of the Wal-Mart on the north side. At least one pack of coyotes had moved in, denning among the fallen I-beams and the slabs of collapsed ceiling, sharing their quarters, judging by the limewash on the walls and the castings on the floor, with a pair of owls and innumerable mice and rats. They have assiduously avoided Salt Lake's business district with its tall office towers rearing up against the purple-grey bulk of the mountains and the sprawling Temple complex, all of which offer prime opportunities for armed bands to fort up.

Sifting through the wreckage of the office, no more than a corner set off by faux pecan panels, Koda pockets a pair of serviceable pencils and an old-fashioned, red plastic grade-school sharpener. A pack of lithium batteries also goes into her pockets, together with a small handheld that looks as though it might be functional. Kirsten has taken to keeping a general log of their journey on her laptop, but other information, such as animal population and migration, the water volume of streams that no longer feed cities, needs to be recorded, too. This world is not the world she grew up in, may become something far different than any has ever imagined. But for now, she will settle for small things that make their journey less arduous. Which means that they probably need to move on, to see if they can find a part of the city less devastated.

In the scatter of papers, she shuffles aside a photograph of a trio of small girls, grinning up at the camera from their swings, their twin blonde pony tails brushing their shoulders. Two are twins. The third is perhaps a year older. To their right, a cocker spaniel makes a fourth to their number, the same grin, the same tumble of bright gold from crown to collarbone. Something is scrawled across the bottom of the picture in a hand too shaky to be legible, but it looks like numbers. Koda turns her attention to the tall free-standing gun safe, which might hold something useful if she can open it.

A second scrap of paper with numbers along the bottom catches her eye in the debris on the floor. 12-28-something. The combination? She should be so lucky. She picks it up, though, carefully dusting it off. Not the combination. Another photo, this one of a dark-eyed toddler on a red tricycle, a motorcycle cap pulled over his forehead as he leans over the handlebars. 12-30-2012. Not a combination, a date.

Retrieving the picture of the three girls, she lays it on the desk next to this one. Same handwriting, same date. Not a birthday, then, especially since the girls on the swings wear shorts and sandals, their feet skimming green grass. The date is the fourth or fifth day of the uprising. For these children, it can mean only one thing: DOD, date of death.

*Not only one thing. Date of death, date of disappearance.* "Come here, would you?"

Kirsten's feet make small rustling noises in the litter as she picks her way toward the corner. As she comes to stand by Koda, she says, "What is it?"

"These photos. Look at the dates. Look at the kids."

For a long moment, Kirsten does not answer. Then she says, "I don't understand. Are the droids taking them alive, and then killing them for some reason?"

"They were using jails, maternity centers, clinics. There used to be a Planned Parenthood branch in this part of Salt Lake. I think we should go check it out."

In the harsh light of the flash, the revulsion on Kirsten's face is clear. After a moment, though, she says. "You're right. It may not help us turn the goddammed things off, but..." Her hand makes small, loose circles in the air.

"There's always the possibility we'll find some kids alive," Koda says gently. "Not much, but some."

"Even if we can just figure out *why.*"

"That'll be a start." Koda adjusts her pack to lie more comfortably around her waist, then shoulders her rifle. "Let's go."

**"Bomb?"**

"Looks like. Big one." Dakota kicks at one end of a broken, charred two-by-four that protrudes from the rubble of roofing shingles and drywall, jagged chunks of concrete block and aluminum siding. Pink fiberglass insulation protrudes from between shattered boards and wall panels threaded through with bright strands of color-coded wiring. Behind the ruined front of the Salt Lake Birthing Center, the rear half of the building still stands, its framing studs and walls stained black with smoke. Asi quarters the edge of the wreckage, whining.

"Look how bright that insulation is. This is recent."

Koda's gaze returns to the cotton-candy mass of fiberglass sandwiched between a collapsed wall and fallen acoustic tiles. It is as shockingly pink as the day it came off the roll, unweathered by snow or desert heat. Slowly, she turns through a full circle. A McDonald's across the street is similarly ruinous, but its garish plastic furniture, tumbled out onto the restaurant's parking lot, is faded to pale sherbet colors, orange and lime and raspberry. The electronics factory outlet next to it stares out onto the asphalt through empty windows, only a few shards of glass still clinging to the frames. It would have been one of the first stores to be looted, by people in desperate need of communications gear or by conventional thieves with no idea of the scope of the collapse in progress. "You're right," she says quietly. "Check it out?"

For answer, Kirsten nods, revulsion clear on her face and in her meticulous steps amid the wreckage, avoiding contact even with the leather of her boots where she can. Koda herself goes warily, picking out a path down what might have been a paved walkway before the blast that tumbled half the clinic's front onto it. It takes her onto a tiled surface, perhaps once the clinic's reception area, with darkened halls opening off of it. Open now to the weather and to scavengers, human and otherwise. Tucked well back in the exposed rafters between ceiling and roof, a wren has built her barrel-shaped nest, and a spattering of guano on the pale terrazzo bears witness to the colony of bats with which she shares her space. The sharp smell of ammonia rises from it, and Koda covers her nose and mouth with one hand. One corridor seems to be lined with various labs and exam rooms; another with recovery cubicles separated only by tattered grey curtains. A third leads off to service areas; through an open door at its end, Koda can see the shape of a large, aluminum-topped worktable with industrial sized pots and pans hung on a rack above it. No sign of the obstetrics ward and surgeries that they must have been in the wing brought down by the blast.

"Look," Kirsten says from behind her. "On the wall behind the desk."

Koda looks more closely, squinting at what she had first thought to be smoke stain. The streaks show a more regular pattern, though, letters scratched out with the end of a charred stick. Some are illegible, obscured by the stain; others are faint angular shapes, parts missing where the stick has skipped over the rough surface of the concrete block. *B-b- -il-e-s.*

"B-b," she says. "Baby..."

"Killers," Kirsten finishes for her. "Jesus."

Koda nods. "Let's have a look at the pharmacy and then get going. There's somebody in the neighborhood that's armed. They may not want company." She steps around a fallen chair and heads briskly for the lab corridor.

Kirsten, though, remains rooted where she stands. "We have to check."

Caught. Taking a deep breath, she gestures to the sign. "I think we've got all the proof we need, *cante skuye*. Do we really need to see the bodies?"

"We have to be sure." Kirsten pauses for a moment. "I have to be sure." Her face is ghostly pale, but her eyes are resolute. "I saw an incinerator chimney when we came in."

So had Koda. Its squat black shape jutted up against the clean blue sky, an obscenity in the light of day. "You stand watch here. I'll go have a look."

Surprisingly, Kirsten relents. "Fine. We'll meet back here, all right?"

Eyes narrowed, Koda gives her a level, suspicious stare. Then she nods. "Fine. I'll be right back."

As soon as Dakota's steps begin to fade away, Kirsten turns left into another corridor. She walks slowly, cautiously, down this hallway, opening each door in its turn. All reveal neatly kept examination rooms with real beds instead of sterile tables, but nothing more of interest, nothing to explain the jangling of her nerves or the tension in her gut.

Finally, the end of the corridor comes into view and she finds herself facing a somber brown metal door with a safety bar across it and an "EMERGENCY EXIT" sign just below the wire-crossed window that is too high for her to see through. She ploughs ahead, hitting the safety bar and taking a step outside, before just as quickly reversing and allowing the door to slam closed before her. When it does, she sinks to her knees, breathing deeply and trying to convince herself that what she thinks she's seen out there isn't what she did, in fact, see. The visual imprint of the scene replays itself behind her closed eyes, cutting her futile hopes to shards.

The first thing that comes to mind is a newsreel, seen long ago in some dusty history class in school — high school, she thinks, though it doesn't really matter. Done in black and white, it showed, in incredibly vivid and heart-wrenching detail, scenes captured just after the liberation of the concentration camps of post World War II Poland. She remembers giant bulldozers pushing the emaciated bodies of dead Jews, Gypsies, and gays into gigantic earthen trenches.

The trenches are here, as they were there. She's seen them, no matter what her mind tries to tell her. Instead of *musselmen*, however, these slashes in a weeping earth bear the bodies of infants. Not fetal abortions — even assuming an abortion clinic would toss their remains in some stinking, rat infested pit — but infants, and even, she would swear before court, toddlers.

"Jesus Christ," she moans, her body rocking in a completely unconscious, self comforting gesture. "Oh sweet Jesus Christ. What the hell is happening here?"

Her plaintive wail goes unnoticed and unremarked in the cavernous emptiness of the bombed out clinic. Even the rats, it seems, have no answers for her. Involuntarily, her muscles propel her to her feet, and she is running, running back through the deserted clinic. Away from the abomination behind her. Away from the knowledge forced onto a mind not ready to receive it.

Toward comfort. Toward sanity. Toward Koda.

Koda makes her way slowly toward the back of the building, stopping to inspect the utility rooms that line the hallway. No droids, no humans, no sign of anything unusual in the heavy mops that sit drying in five-gallon wringer buckets, in the orderly rows of toilet paper and bottles of pine solvent. The metalheads would have maintained a reasonably clean environment for themselves if not for their human captives, being no more impervious to dust than any other computer.

She is no more than halfway when she hears boots pounding in the passageway behind her. Instinctively she whirls, hand on the stock of her rifle. But then she picks up the softer sound of four feet running along side the human pair, the faint wheeze of Asi's panting. "Kirsten? Kirsten! What—"

She never finishes the question. Kirsten takes the hallway intersection at a dead run, Asi beside her. Her hair, loosened from its braid, flies wild behind her. Her face is bloodless as a corpse's. Koda has only time to open her arms and take the impact of the other woman's body against hers, the hands that clutch at her shoulders. "What is it?" she asks softly. "*Cante sukye*, what is it?"

For a long moment, there is silence. Then Kirsten raises her head from Koda's shoulder. Her haunted eyes make wide pools of shadow. "They're killing the babies," she says. "I found the bodies."

**The incinerator stands** to one side of the main building, its red bio-hazard sign still bright in the afternoon sun. The stench of charred flesh still lingers about it, even to Koda's human nostrils. It must, she thinks, be overpoweringly strong to Asi, where he stands at attention ten feet away, ears forward, legs stiff, issuing short, sharp barks of alarm despite Kirsten's order to be silent. Foulness hangs over the place like a cloud.

The furnace has two doors, a larger one above for the burn chamber, a smaller below for scraping out the ash. Neither yields to Koda's determined pulling, and she returns to the wreckage in front to scavenge a yard-long length of rebar. It makes an admirable pry, and she wedges it under the handle of the upper door, turning it fairly easily on the second effort. The door swings open on blackness and the stench of death, but the oven holds no bones, no infant corpses. Kirsten leans over her shoulder, peering into the shadow. It seems to Koda that the sound of her lover's breathing has slowed; no demons here to haunt her nights. "Okay," she says. "Nothing here. Let's—"

"Check the bottom," Kirsten says steadily. Her revulsion of a quarter hour before has become resolve. Cold. Steely.

Ash lies thick in the compartment below the burn chamber, black and stinking of grease. Dakota scrapes it out onto the concrete platform with the end of the rebar. Scattered throughout it are small flakes of white, bigger than the grain of the ash.

"Bone," Kirsten says, her voice expressionless. "That's what that is, isn't it?"

Koda nods, her teeth clenched. If she opens her mouth, she will vomit. After a moment, she breaks apart a clod of ash, freeing larger fragments of calcified bone. One larger piece still keeps its shape; half a verte-bra, its spur still jutting out from the half-ring that once surrounded the spinal cord. The whole piece is less than an inch long.

The incinerator is not large, not for a crematorium. The ditch must have been only a temporary measure. "Now we know." Kirsten's voice is scarcely more than a whisper.

Koda forces herself to speak around the constriction in her throat. "Now we know." She feels Kirsten's hand settle on her shoulder, warm and alive. A lifeline. "And we know someone else is fighting them, too. That's a good thing."

Suddenly it seems as if the buildings around her, the mountains around them, will fall on her at any moment. She levers herself to her feet, glancing up at the sun. "Let's get out of here. We can be in the foothills again by nightfall."

They make the trek out of the city in silence, hands joined, Asi quiet beside them. A long-forgotten phrase slips through her mind, from the mission school decades, eons ago. "And the Lord God rained fire and brim-stone on the cities of the plain, fire from Heaven." Koda does not look back, lest she turn to stone.

**The faint glow of** the embers reflects off the back of the rock shelter, tingeing the shadows with crimson.  Spilling down off the heights of the mountains, the breeze carries with it a foretaste of the turning year, its scent sharp with pine and hemlock.  Kirsten pulls the mylar blanket more firmly up over her body, settling her head in the hollow of Dakota's shoulder.  Her lover's hand makes lazy circles against her back.  On the other side of the dying fire, Asi snores softly, his paws twitching with his dreams.  Cold with distance, a howl rises up into the night, coyotes hunting the lower slopes.  Kirsten shivers, not with the chill but with the memory of the Salt Lake clinic.  It seems out of place here in the clean air, the light of stars spilling across unimaginable distances.  But the dead will not leave her.  She feels Koda stiffen where she lies beside her, and her soft breath ruffles Kirsten's hair.

"What is it, *cante sukye*?"

"Nothing."

"Not nothing.  Something cold has touched you."

Kirsten turns her face so that she looks directly up at the sky.  She raises one arm to point at the great stream of the Milky Way where it arcs across the night.  Almost bright enough to cast shadows, it blazes down on the Earth as it has for millions of years, answered now only by wood fires and the occasional, scattered glimmer of artificial light.  "You call it the Ghost Road, don't you?  My dad was into Irish heritage stuff, and he said the ancient Celts called it the Path of Souls.  Funny how different cultures had the same idea."

"Maybe it's the braids and war-paint."  Koda shifts her weight slightly to keep Kirsten's head on her shoulder.  "Most Cherokee and Creek families who use European names are called Mac-this or Mac-that.  Lots of Scotts."

"Do they wear kilts, too?"

Koda gives a soft snort, and Kirsten can feel the laughter as it runs through her.  "Now that'd be a sight, wouldn't it?  Tartans and feathers."

From somewhere a mental picture floats up of Tacoma, tartan plaid clasped about his waist, a classic warbonnet on his head.  Kirsten giggles at the absurdity of it, and the tension in her eases a bit.  "What about the Dipper?  Do you call that a bear, too?"

"No, but we have a summer constellation called Mato Tipila, the Bear's Lodge.  That's Gemini, mostly.  And Leo is The Fireplace."

"What about him?"  Lazily, Kirsten points to Orion, whose belt of three stars just clears the peaks to the east.  "Is he a hunter in the Lakota stories, too?"

"It's part of what we call the Backbone, which is part of the Racetrack."

"Oh."  Kirsten cannot quite keep the disappointment from her voice.  The figure of a mighty man with upraised club seems so obvious to her — even though a part of her mind recognizes that obviousness as cultural bias — that it would seem to be the stuff of legend in any society.  *Get a grip, King.  It's a different world.  Koda's is a different world.  And somehow I'm going to have to learn it all.*

"There is a story, though."  Koda's arm tightens about her shoulders.  "Want to hear it?"

"About a backbone?  Sure."

"Not exactly.  See his belt, there, and his sword?  That, plus Rigel, are what we call the Hand, *Nape*."

"Whose?"

"A chief's."

Koda's voice settles into a steady rhythm that is almost ceremonial, and it comes to Kirsten that among the Lakota, as they were among her own ancient ancestors, stories are not simply entertainment. They are history, just as Blind Harry's ballad of the Cheyenne is history now. They reach into the future, as well as into the numinous past.

"There was a chief who was not generous with his people. He kept all the horses he took in raids for himself, instead of sharing them with his warriors. He showed no concern for the poor in his tribe, or for widows and orphans. And one day, the Wakinyan, the Thunderbirds, had had enough of his stinginess, and they tore off his arm."

"Too bad the Thunderbirds never took on the Congress. Talk about one-armed bandits."

"Not to mention the whole swarm of bureaucrats. Anyway, this chief had managed to do one thing right; he had a beautiful daughter. Wicahpi Hinhpaye, or Fallen Star, who was the son of the North Star and a mortal woman, came courting her. And she agreed to marry him, on condition that he find her father's missing arm.

"So he searched and searched, all through the Paha Sapa. Then he searched among the stars, because the landscape of the Black Hills is reflected in the sky, because they are both sacred. The Wakinyan tried to prevent him from searching, and he fought them. Then Iktomi, Spider Woman, tried to trick him, but he outwitted her.

"Finally he found the hand where they had hidden it in the stars, and he returned to Earth with it. In a ceremony, Wicahpi Hihnpaye reattached the chief's arm and married the daughter. He became the new chief. In the spring they had a son. And..." Koda leaves the word hanging.

"...they lived happily ever after," Kirsten finishes for her.

"And the people flourished, and the land had peace. It all goes together." After a moment she adds, "You okay?"

"Mmm," Kirsten says, turning again to lay her arm across Koda's body. "Very okay. G'night."

"Night, *cante sukye*."

"Ever after," Kirsten murmurs, and slips into sleep.

**Late afternoon light** filters through the branches of pine and spruce, grown thick and tall here on the western slope of the Nightingale Mountains. The Trinities lie behind them now, the folded valleys and jagged bare-rock ranges that scar the Nevada landscape. Asi trots easily along a deer track paralleling a narrow stream that loops and swirls its way down the mountainside. Kirsten follows, Koda walking rearguard. A jay scolds from somewhere half a hundred feet up, and is answered by a chittering squirrel. From time to time the sun catches the crest of a small rapids where the stream banks pinch inward; occasionally it strikes silver off the scales of fingerling trout or minnows. Out of the corner of her eye, Koda can make out the shape of a mule deer doe drifting between the trees a hundred yards away. Her two spring fawns follow, their spots fading now with the summer. Gently Dakota taps on Kirsten's shoulder, pointing silently, and a smile lights the other woman's face at the sight. Asi, too, turns to look but makes no sound, then pads on, his humans' feet making no more noise than his own.

A pair of dark wings sails over them, to be lost in the trees. A moment later, another bird sweeps past, its cry low and harsh. Ravens, a mated pair, returning for the night to their roost and their young.

From somewhere to their right comes an answering call, and Koda pauses, staring into the shadows beneath the trees. Breeding ravens are territorial, pairs spaced out over wide distances to maintain hunting and scavenging grounds.

"Something wrong?" Kirsten looks back over her shoulder, her hand dropping to the pistol at her belt.

Koda shrugs. "Another raven, that's all. Their ranges aren't usually so close together at this season."

"Passerby?"

"Probably."

*Just one bird skimming the edges of another's territory, taking a short-cut home. That's all.* Maybe even, if it's young and reckless, poaching a bit on a scrap of carrion or a pocket mouse. Dakota glances up, searching the patches of deepening sky for Wiyo, finding only wisps of cloud and a sweep of redwings making for one of the small lakes that dot the corner where Nevada angles into California. The absence is reassuring. Not even a red-tail will unnecessarily confront a raven pair on their territory, still less draw the attention of a feathered mob. Nesting ravens will attack owls and eagles without a second thought, and though Wiyo is a female and large of her kind, she is no larger than Kagi Tanka. Koda says, "Start watching for a place to camp. Sun'll be down in an hour."

Kirsten nods and sets off again, Dakota following. Dark will find them halfway down the slope; by mid-day tomorrow they should be on open ground again, crossing the basin of Lake Winnemucca. At this time of year it should be dry, the snow-melt gone, the autumn rains yet to come. Still, it should be less formidable than the alkali flats they crossed a week ago, or the edges of the desert between Salt Lake and the eastern Nevada border. After the endless miles where it seemed they sweated themselves drier than the sand itself, it is good to be in the mountains again. Here the sharp pine scent rides the breeze and small springs break from the living rock to feed lakes and rivers on the plain below. Cool days fade to chill nights populated with raccoon and lynx, otter and bear, while the smaller life of the understory persists stubbornly against the pressure of larger creatures with larger teeth. Geographically, at least, matters can only get better from this point on.

Everything else, of course, can get worse. Much worse.

A raven calls again, a low, rolling *prrro-o-o-ok*. This time the sound comes from somewhere ahead of them, off the flight path of the first pair. Cold ghosts down Koda's spine, and she shrugs her rifle off her shoulder. No law says ravens have to fly in a straight line. Still, she feels better with the gun in her hands.

Kirsten glances back at her, her eyes widening when she sees the gun. Wordlessly, she draws her own weapon, reaching for Asi's collar to pull him back to heel beside her. The big dog's ears prick, his tail coming up to jut stiffly out from his spine. Something is in the wood with them. These mountains are bear country, with straggling populations of wolverines and the occasional wolf pack. Bear or wolverine she can deal with, wolf she can talk to. More likely their company is a smaller predator, bobcat or coyote, even a badger. Later, over supper, they can laugh at their excess caution. They have come too far, though, to take unnecessary risks. It is not that more depends on them now than when they left Ellsworth. It just seems like more, the burden heavier and heavier as they come closer to their goal.

Another raven calls, this one to their left. Around them, other birds have gone silent, with none of the twittering fuss of settling in for the night. "All right," Koda says softly, "that's just one too damned many." She slides her finger into the guard, to lie lightly against the trigger.

"Don't ravens hunt with wolves, sometimes?" Kirsten whispers? "Lead them to prey?"

"Yeah. But we haven't seen any sign of wolves all day, and we haven't seen any other top predators, either. Nothing to sound an alarm about."

"We don't count, huh?"

"Not to the birds."

Asi comes to a sudden halt, growling. His lips peel back, showing his canines, and his tail comes up to full staff, its plume quivering with the rumble that rolls through his chest and belly. Kirsten's hand shifts on his collar, her knuckles white. "Easy. Easy. What is it, boy?"

"Company," Koda says grimly. "Hold onto him."

The raven cry sounds again from a hundred yards down the trail. Another answers from behind them, a third and fourth from either side, yet another from above them, close. Following the sound with her eyes, Koda can just make out a darker shadow against the high trunk of a pine, some thirty or forty feet up, almost directly overhead. Just beneath the tree stands a stake topped by a deer's antlers, clusters of black feathers hung from its tines by sinew strips. A flat stone at its base holds a spray of dried sage bound with sweetgrass and lupine, the shed skin of an indigo snake and a hollow pebble, its inner surface paved with clear crystals. It sits within the horns of a crescent, drawn around the forward edge of the stone in deep crimson. Deer's blood, perhaps. Or perhaps not. Koda remembers enough of her anthropology to recognize the symbols, older than Babylon, older than Delphi, older even than Crete. Carefully she moves her finger away from the trigger of her gun, then bends to lay it on the ground. She rises slowly, open hands at her sides.

Kirsten glances at her sharply, then, still holding to Asi's collar, follows suit. "Who are they?" she asks, her voice scarcely audible.

"Women," Koda answers softly. "Goddess worshippers."

"Keep your hands visible!" The voice comes from high in the tree. "State your names and business."

"Dakota and Annie Rivers," Kirsten answers, squinting upward toward the sound. "And we don't have any business here. We're just passing through."

"Open your collars. Let us see your necks."

Moving slowly, Koda and Kirsten obey, turning so that the still invisible watchers can see clearly that they bear no circlet of metal.

"Good. Now, you, the tall one. Take off your clothes."

"What?" Kirsten stares up into the branches. "What the hell?"

Koda, though, sits down on a rock by the stream to pull off her boots.

"It's okay, *cante sukye*. They just want to make sure I'm really a woman." She drops her pack beside her, then her shirt, finally stepping out of her jeans and rising to stand in the open. Loosened, her hair spills down her back. She turns slowly, her hands at her sides.

For a long moment, the glade is silent. Then, low-pitched and long, a wolf whistle comes from behind them. "Oh, yeah, now. *Ain't* she a woman!"

Kirsten whirls to face the speaker, still invisible. Her face flushed crimson, she snaps, "Back off, bitch!"

A whoop of laughter answers her, a contralto rich with the dark earth of Mississippi. "Get your dander down, Shorty. I'm just admirin'."

Suppressing a grin, Koda lays her hand on Kirsten's arm. "I'm 'Shorty's' woman, sister. Anybody wants to argue with that, deals with me." Asi gives a high, challenging yelp, and Koda adds, "Yeah, and his human, too."

"How say you, sisters?" The voice from the tree again. "Shall they pass?"

Four answer her, more or less in unison. "They shall pass, and welcome."

It has the feel of ritual, and Koda wonders again just how the crimson stain came to be on the stone. A rustling of pine boughs draws her attention back to the tree above her, and a back-lit shape plunges down the length of the trunk, rappelling off it with the aid of a rope. The woman lands with a thump on the carpet of fallen needles, one ankle turning slightly, as though she has not yet entirely got the hang of the maneuver. She has no trouble putting her weight on it, though, and she steps firmly enough out into the light.

"Hi," she says, extending her hand to Kirsten, who takes it almost reluctantly, then to Dakota. "I'm Morgan." Her clasp is firm, her palm callused with work and, evidently, the handling of weapons. An AK slants across her back, and a Bowie knife hangs from her belt, both worn with use. "Hey. Annie? You want to put your clothes back on?" She turns back to Kirsten. "We have a permanent camp a few miles on. You're welcome there."

From beneath lowered eyelids, Koda watches irritation and bemusement flicker across Kirsten's face. She turns away to pull on her clothes, letting her hair fall forward to hide a smile. *Okay, Ms. President, here's a chance for some diplomacy.*

Kirsten says softly, pointing, "I'm Annie. She's Dakota. He's Asimov. Who are you, besides Morgan?"

Koda turns just as her head clears her shirt collar. Kirsten stands straight as a birch tree, her face expressionless. *Ms. President, indeed.*

Morgan's grey eyes flicker over her, assessing, and she says easily, "I'm Morgan fia d'Loria, and I'm chosen Riga of the Amazai."

A small shock runs through Koda. For an instant, a fraction of a second, the vision of the Cretan coast flashes before her again, a blonde swimmer in the surf. But she keeps her voice even. "Amazai? Moon women?"

Morgan glances sharply at her. "You're a linguist?"

"My first wife was. I had to learn a bit to talk to her while we were in school."

"Mmm. Greek's not just 'a bit'."

Koda shrugs, tucking her shirt into the waistband of her jeans. "For a while we spoke a dialect unknown outside our dorm room. Some French, some Spanish, some Lakota, a few words of Sanskrit. It took a year or two to sort out. You?"

"Lawyer. We've got a Classics wonk in the band, though. She's our history-keeper."

Warriors. A bard. How much of the social structure she is beginning to sense in this group of women is deliberate reconstruction based on texts? How much is instinct, repeating itself across the millennia? Koda sits again to pull on her boots, watching the other woman from beneath her eyelashes. Morgan, though not much taller than Kirsten, seems to fit the scale of the forest. Part of it is sheer personal presence, the kind of thing that would sway a jury in a courtroom. Part of it is the rippling muscle under her tanned skin, shown to advantage by her leather vest and wrist-guards. The left one covers her forearm almost to the elbow, marking her as an archer even though she carries no bow. And part of it is the series of diagonal hatch lines scored into each cheek, tattoos done the old fashioned way, with pigment rubbed into a bleeding cut. It takes no imagination to divine what they represent, no more a mystery than the crescent moon between her pale brows. *Madame President, meet the Queen of the Amazons, with four, five, six, seven kills to her credit. Let's keep it friendly if we can.*

Morgan raises an eyebrow at her covert study. "Ready?" she asks.

"The others?" Kirsten indicates the surrounding trees.

"On patrol. We guard our borders."

"Against androids?"

"And men," Morgan says coolly. "We're a tribe of women. No men. No man-gods. No man-laws."

"Ready," Koda says. "How far are we going?"

"The camp's by Pyramid, across the dry lake." Koda's face must show her dismay, because Morgan adds, "Not to worry. We have horses tethered at the foot of the trail. We'll be there by full dark. You do ride?"

Kirsten snickers and Koda says, "Yeah. I'm a vet. My family breeds horses."

The mounts tethered at the foot of the slope scarcely look up at the three women and one dog when they emerge onto the meadow. The grass grows thick here, interspersed with dandelion and columbine, salvia and mallow, good eating that makes for sleek hides and bright eyes. All the horses are mustangs, in various combinations of white with chestnut, white with buckskin, dapple grey, and black. They are the classic mounts of the Plains Nations, the breed that made the Lakota and Nez Perce the finest light cavalry in the world, in their time. None is equipped with more than a bridle and saddle blanket, some of those no more than a sheepskin. Koda's respect for Morgan and her band takes a quantum leap, and she asks, "Wild caught?"

Morgan bends to loose a young grey from her ground tether, glancing back over her shoulder at Koda. The filly whickers softly and nudges at the woman's pocket, obviously looking for a treat. Morgan pushes her nose away gently and says, "More or less. They were running loose, and none were broken. They'd had some handling, though. Take your pick; two of the patrol can double up on the way home."

"They're good stock." Koda strokes the withers of a tall white and chestnut mare who sports a wide white blaze from ears to muzzle. "Annie?"

"I'll take the black." Before Koda can offer a hand up, she springs up easily onto the horse's back, sliding only a little on the loose buckskin that is its saddle. It is an impressive performance, meant to impress. Alpha female, meet alpha female.

Suppressing a smile, Koda says only, "Good choice," and mounts the paint. The horse snuffles and turns twice widdershins at the feel of an unaccustomed rider on her back, but settles quickly with a pat and a word or two of assurance. "All right," she says to Morgan. "Lead the way."

The way takes them down the mountainside and onto the miles-long expanse of the dry lakebed. The dark gathers around them, rose and gold along the line of the western hills gradually giving way to deep blue that blends into black at the zenith and stretches behind them to become indistinguishable from the last slopes of the Nightingale range. The moon, one night off full, rises bright enough to cast shadows along the alkali-pale flats. Heat, absorbed during the summer day, radiates upward now, mingling with the already-cooling air of the evening. Slipping over the line of hills from the west, the breeze smells of water, and more faintly, dark earth and salt. They move at an easy pace, the horses' hooves clattering against the hard surface.

Morgan leads, the weight of her pale braid bouncing between her shoulders to the rhythm of her mare's gait. She chants as she rides, something Koda cannot quite make out, though she thinks she hears the words "Isis" and "Demeter". Kirsten follows, her hair a pale halo in the moonlight. Koda rides rearguard, her rifle slung over the saddlecloth in front of her. Asi trots along beside them, breathing easily. The wolf is an endurance runner, and for all his faithful breeding, the wild has begun to surface in the big dog, as if the genes of his ancestors have only been lulled by ten thousand years of domestication, lying dormant until the turn of an age in which humans no longer rule the Earth. The dog, the horse, even the comfort-loving cat, may once again become something no living member of her own species has ever encountered in the flesh.

*And we're losing our domestication, too. Warriors and shamans. Tribes of women. Warlords. We are being drawn into our own past, dragging the remains of our technology behind us.*

The alkali lake bottom gives way to loose scree, and Morgan picks their way carefully through it, setting them on a path that winds through low hills and then rises, climbing the mountain slope. Columbine and Indian paintbrush grow close along its margins, leaving space for two horses to pass abreast; pine branches, low enough to sweep an unwary rider from the saddle, obscure it from above. Barely visible in the shadows, Kirsten slows to lean down and rub covertly at her left calf, shifting slightly on the horse's back to ease what seems to be a stiffening back muscle.

Koda knees her mare and pulls even with her lover. Careful to keep amusement out of her voice, she whispers, "Sprain something there did ya, Annie Oakley?" Even in the dark, Koda can see the frown that knits Kirsten's forehead, then the rueful smile.

"That obvious, was it?"

"'Fraid so. I'm flattered, though."

The smile breaks into a grin. "You damned well better be. I wouldn't bust my butt like that for just anybody."

"Such a nice little butt, too. Is it sprained?"

"My butt?"

"Your knee."

"Nah, just pulled. I'm fine."

Asi, doubling back from where he has been ranging ahead of Morgan, weaves between their horses' legs, whining. The Amazai herself has halted.

"You okay back there?"

"Cramp," Koda says, tactfully omitting whose.

Morgan touches her heel to her mare's flank, and turns her head to lead them up a branching pathway, narrower yet, that leads upward at a steeper angle. Twice along the way, she gives the low, rolling call of a screech owl, and is answered. The second time, when it seems to Koda that they must be about halfway to the crest, Morgan says, "This used to be a park campground, but we've blocked the main access on the other side. Nothing gets up here we don't know about, and nothing at all with wheels."

Which may or may not mean that they have no vehicles. They could always be stashed lower down. Most state and national parks had motor pools and the gas to fuel them. Morgan and her sisters do not seem to be the kind to waste resources unnecessarily. They might, though, be persuaded to part with one in an excellent cause. A nice Jeep could put Koda and Kirsten on the Mendo coast in — three hours? Four?

Pipe dream. They'd be gunned down, by droids or hostile humans or both, before they got halfway there.

The path takes a final hairpin turn, then opens up to lead under a gate carved from knotty pine. Two torches flank it, and its sign, just visible in the dancing shadows, reads, "Welcome to Free Sierra". The letters are rough, cut into the arch over the original name of the park. And the red light shows something else. Kirsten, who must see it, too, jerks hard on her horse's reins, then knees her again as she pulls up. She is, perhaps, not certain what she is looking at. Koda is not certain, either. Not entirely.

A round shape hangs from each gatepost. The red light strikes a steely gleam from the one on the left, outlining its bare metal dome. On the other side, the torch draws the shape in dark hollows; two that might be eyes, another that might be a gaping mouth above a caked and matted beard. With the sweet night air comes the smell of rotting meat. *So much for ambiguity. No lilacs blooming in the dooryard here.*

"Hell of a No Trespassing sign you got there," Koda says quietly.

Morgan shows her teeth in something that is not quite a smile. "Yeah. Got 'em both on our last raid. Reno."

Which means that these women either do have vehicles, or whoever they took down in Reno did not. Kirsten, who has quietly nursed her sore muscles on the ascent, says, "On who?"

"A clinic. You know about that?"

Koda answers, carefully, "We know that women have been kidnapped for breeding in jails, sometimes in birthing centers, women's clinics. Stuff like that."

They pass a couple of low signs, illegible in the dark except for their white arrows pointing directions to the various park facilities. Morgan leads them to the right where the path forks, and says, "Yeah. Stuff like that. They had another place in Reno, where they took the kids they didn't kill.

Right off, anyway."

Koda sees the flinch in Kirsten's shoulders, remembering the death-pit and incinerator in the ruins of the clinic in Salt Lake. Morgan, though, seems disinclined to answer questions. Up ahead, the path fans out into an open space where white smoke rises up into the moonlight above the embers of a fire. Cabins line the perimeter, small oblong log structures with coarse screening in the windows. Here and there the yellow glow of a kerosene lantern silhouettes women's shapes as they move about in their lodgings; one, as they pass, seems to be tucking a child into bed. Looking up at the sound of the horses' hooves, the women wave as they pass, calling greetings to Morgan. One, leaving her cabin with a guitar slung over her shoulder, pauses to stare at Kirsten and Koda. Morgan answers her unspoken question with a wave of her hand and a brief "Later". To Koda she says, "I'll show you where the stables are, then where you can bunk. Come join us around the fire after you get settled; there ought to be some stew or something left in the pot."

The stables, obviously designed to accommodate only a handful of horses for the amusement of riders on family outings, now house mostly hay, grain, and tack. The horses themselves are tethered along a picket line behind the building. Koda counts thirty-two as she and Kirsten lead their mounts to one end to remove their saddle cloths and rub them down. Add to that the ones left behind in the hills across the dry lake and those likely to be on patrol in other directions, and you get forty riders, a formidable warband when the population of the continent has been reduced by 99 percent or so. Most of the stock are mustangs, but one or two show signs of more aristocratic breeding: a chestnut walking horse with white socks and blaze, a couple of Appaloosas. Almost all are mares, two of them beginning to swell with foal; a few are geldings. They whicker softly as Koda passes, one nuzzling at her back pocket where she has stashed a trail bar.

Kirsten, following her gaze, says, "I guess the 'no man' thing extends to the critters, too. Maybe we should worry about Asi."

"Maybe Asi should worry about Asi," she replies, smiling and ruffling his ears where he walks beside her. "They've got a stallion or two somewhere; they just wouldn't stake them out on the line with the rest."

At the end of the picket, Kirsten and Koda slip the skins off the horses' backs and loop their reins around the rope that runs between a pair of tall pines. Tossing an armful of hay down in front of them, Koda hands Kirsten one of the two curry brushes she has brought from the tack room. "Know how to use one of these?"

Kirsten, her eyes wide in the low light, looks at Koda as if she has sprouted horns, or a second head. "You're kidding, right? I've ridden before, but some stable guy has always taken care of the technical stuff, like getting the saddle on and off." Gingerly she stares down at the arcane instrument and shrugs. "How hard can it be, though? I mean, it's basically a hairbrush, isn't it?"

"Basically," Koda says with a smile. "Just watch and do what I do."

Ten minutes later, both horses stand munching contentedly at the hay, their coats smooth and free of dust and the small accretions of the trail. Kirsten has done yeoman work, following Koda move for move, watched by Asi where he has settled in among the tree roots, his gaze sardonic. He follows them to the cabin Morgan has shown them, which contains little but four bare cots and a galvanized pipe across one end for a closet.

"Looks like we've got our penthouse to ourselves," Kirsten remarks. "We could shove a couple of these beds together."

"Mmm," says Koda. "We could. Just for warmth, of course."

"Of course." Kirsten grins back at her as she sheds her pack. Asi hops up onto the bed in the far back corner and stretches out, making himself instantly to home. "Guess you're not gonna come check out the place, huh, boy?"

For answer, Asi lays his chin on his paws and closes his eyes. "Guess not," Koda answers for him. "Want to go get something to eat?"

The path to the center of the camp leads them past other cabins like theirs, a communal shower, a slightly larger main office building with actual windows. Koda pauses, sniffing. Her stomach turns over in a barrel roll of sheer joy. "Gods. They've found some onions somewhere. And chicken. Come on."

The fragrance comes from a circle of stones some twelve feet across. A fire pit in the center sends clouds of smoke billowing upward, and nestled in the embers is a Dutch oven of a size that would serve the entire Rivers family, with seconds all around and thirds for Manny and Phoenix. Around it, their faces flushed with the red glow, a company of perhaps a dozen women sits on rocks or skins or the bare grass. Some still hold their bowls in their laps, while a couple lean back on their elbows, gazing up at the sky, and the woman with the guitar strums softly, her voice weaving wordlessly in and out amidst the melody. Yet another pair sit with their arms around each other's waists, a small dark woman leaning her head against her taller partner's shoulder. Morgan herself sits on a flat granite boulder at the northern quarter of the circle, her bowl still between her hands, a far-off look in her eyes. She takes note of Kirsten and Koda, though, rising to invite them to stand beside her as introductions go round the circle. Inga fia d'Bridget. Frances fia d'Alice. Magdalena, daughter of Rosario. Sarai fia d'Yasmin. They bear their own names and their mothers', no acknowledgement of paternity or patriarchy.

And every face that Koda can see bears, too, the marks of dead enemies. With Salt Lake behind them, their story is now that they are headed for Los Angeles to find "Annie's" parents.

At that, the faces around the circle grow grave, and Morgan says, "Haven't you heard?"

"Heard?" Kirsten frowns. "It's been a bit busy between St. Louis and here. We haven't had any contact with anyone at all in California." She looks around the circle. "Heard what?"

Morgan lays a gentle hand on Kirsten's arm and draws her down to sit on the boulder. "LA's gone. Nuked."

# CHAPTER FORTY-SIX

Kirsten's parents were nowhere near Los Angeles when the uprising began, have not lived in southern California for two decades. Yet even in the dim light, Koda can see the blood drain from her face as her mouth repeats the word without sound. Dakota's own mouth goes dry, imagining the radiation cloud spreading inland on the winds off the Pacific, sweeping across the orange groves to lay radioactive ash on the already burning sands of the desert. "Bombed?" she says, inaudible even to herself. Then, more loudly, "Bombed? Who?"

Morgan's eyes dart between them, softening suddenly. "I'm sorry," she says, "I didn't think. Of course you might well know someone there." Laying a hand on Kirsten's arm, she draws her down to sit beside her on the boulder.

"It's okay. It's just — sudden. I grew up a bit further south, San Diego."

Very deliberately, Koda lifts the lid of the Dutch oven with the poker left by the side of the fire pit and ladles two bowls full of the stew. She replaces the lid and brings one bowl and a spoon to set it beside Kirsten, settling cross legged on the ground beside her with her own meal. "Who did it? How?"

"We're not real sure. We heard about it from refugees headed back east to try to find their people. Seems a couple of ships up from the Naval base at San Diego sailed into the port there and blew up."

"Warheads aboard?"

"Maybe. According to what we heard, it was a pair of aircraft carriers. The *Reagan* and the *Kerry*."

Stirring her stew aimlessly, Kirsten says, "All the new aircraft carriers have nuclear power plants, some of the older ones, too. Even if it was just the reactors, it would be bad. Real bad."

"Supposedly there was more than one mushroom cloud. Supposedly the fireball incinerated everything from Long Beach to Ventura and out to Pasadena. It's all fourth- and fifth-hand, of course. Hearsay. What we do know from what we've heard since is that Los Angeles just isn't there any-more."

"There were so many droids in LA to begin with, we heard they took it in half a day." The small, dark woman straightens and leans forward, toward the fire. Her face carries no expression. "Lots of tech-droids, maid-droids, lots of military models at Oxnard. My brother worked for Para-mount. He said they'd taken over just about everything except the acting."

Almost imperceptibly, Kirsten's eyes widen at the mention of Oxnard. Then the shock is gone, and she lowers her gaze and begins to eat silently. No one else seems to have noticed, their attention still on the Amazai whose brother must have been blown to subatomic particles in the blast. Not for the first time, it comes to Koda that Kirsten's government position has made her more poker player than politician or diplomat. No glad hand-ing, no smooth equivocation, just the calculation of a very junior predator in a pack of hyenas all older and more experienced by decades.

"So," comes the inevitable question from across the circle, "what's it like where you've been?" The speaker is an older woman, her red hair greying at her temples, introduced earlier as Fiona fia d'Linda.

The circle seems to draw closer together as Koda gives a carefully edited account of their wanderings. She makes no mention of Ellsworth or the two battles fought there, nor of Kirsten's journey from Washington. Then she says, watching their faces in the flickering shadows, "When Annie and I went into Salt Lake to scavenge, we came across a wrecked women's clinic. And back by the incinerator we found a pile of dead kids — babies, toddlers. There was a spray-painted sign on the building that said, 'Baby Killers'. Like it was organized."

Silence falls around the circle. Morgan's eyes run around its circumference and something apparently passes between her and her tribeswomen. She says, "The band from over by Provo did the Salt Lake clinic."

"Band?" Kirsten asks quietly. "Like this one? There are others?"

"More or less," Morgan answers. "We're not linked to them, but our foragers have met their foragers. News still travels." She turns to Koda. "You liked our gate decorations?"

"Is that what you were doing in Reno? Bombing a clinic?"

"Among other things. We're going out again tomorrow night. Want to come along?"

"Where to?"

"Carson City."

Koda conjures up the map of Nevada in her head. It's a hundred and twenty mile round trip. "Not on horseback."

"Not on horseback," Morgan confirms.

They need to move on. The sooner they get to San Francisco, the sooner Kirsten will have the code to shut down the droids. Time is of the essence.

Time after is of the essence, too. Morgan and her women are the kinds of allies they will need once the uprising is put down. That's the favorable reading. The unfavorable reading is that these are the kinds of rivals they may face in reunifying the nation — splinter groups, petty nations, warlords. It has happened, disastrously, within her lifetime, in Afghanistan and Iraq, in Syria and Palestine. In either case, they need to take the measure of the Amazai, who are, apparently, a growing territorial power. "Annie?" she says quietly.

Kirsten sets down her bowl. "Let's do it."

A murmur of approval runs around the group, and Inga, the woman with the guitar, strums a descant on her twelve-string and begins to sing. Other voices pick up the song around the circle.

*In an Amazai encampment, so natural and pristine,*
*Smell the pungent odor of nitroglycerine.*
*They're busy making fuses, and filling cans with nails*
*And wiring up some C-4 to bust up android jails.*

The tune is lively, and Koda finds her foot tapping of its own accord. Kirsten claps in rhythm to the melody, and Koda takes it up, humming wordlessly.

*Oh it's Sister Jenny's turn to throw the bomb! (Throw the bomb!)*
*Frag out metalheads and Uncle Toms (Uncle To-o-oms!)*

*Mama's aim is bad, and Auntie's worse than sad,*
*So it's Sister Jenny's turn to throw the bomb! (Throw the bomb!)*

*We've taken out a clinic, we'll take a dozen more,*
*We're warriors and reclaimers, we're women, hear us roar!*
*We'll take back all our Mother's earth, her mountains and her fields.*
*Our resolution never fails, our courage never yields.*

*Oh it's Sister Jenny's turn to throw the bomb! (Throw the bomb!)*
*Frag out metalheads and Uncle Toms! (Uncle To-o-oms!)*
*Mama's aim is bad, and Auntie's worse than sad,*
*So it's Sister Jenny's turn to throw the bomb! (Throw the bomb!)*

Several stanzas later, the song ends on a cheer, and Morgan rises as the roar subsides. She raises her arms, her hands open, over her head. "Sisters! Shall it be so?"

"So mote it be!" thunders back, with more clapping and war whoops.

Koda finds herself shouting with the rest, the spirit of the song infectious. Kirsten, her face flushed, is caught up in it, too. She catches Koda's eye, and where there might have been embarrassment a month ago, there is now both the joy of battle and frank desire. They have come a long way, in more ways than one. And now there is but a little way to go, for life or death. Slipping her hand into Kirsten's she says huskily. "Ready to go?"

Kirsten's green eyes sparkle up at her. "Where you go...always."

**Koda leans one** shoulder against the concrete block wall and carefully eases her right leg out from under her, stretching to relieve the cramp in her thigh. The long muscle that runs from hip to knee has twisted in the hour and more she has crouched in the alley across from the Carson City Women's Clinic, waiting for the wreck of the city to grow quiet. She grits her teeth and rubs at the knot, willing herself not to swear aloud, though obscenities in at least five languages cascade satisfyingly through her mind. Beside her Kirsten leans forward, her face a pale shadow in the moonlight that filters down between the two strips of shops that once housed medical offices, pharmacies, and the odd restaurant or two. Koda shakes her head, reaching out to touch the other woman's hand reassuringly. The cramp hurts like hell, but it will not kill her. Not unless she makes noise and attracts the attention of the droids across the street.

There are droids at the clinic; they have seen the metal-collared guards pacing the perimeter of the grounds. Arriving on the outskirts of the city at sunset, the twelve women have picked their way cautiously from house to vacant house through a ruined residential neighborhood populated only by stray dogs, feral cats, and the small prey that sustains them. From the suburbs through the business district and now down medical row, they have encountered not so much as a single human. Except, it seems, for the droids, the city stands completely abandoned. The survivors of the uprising have all fled. If, that is, there were any survivors.

The sound of boots on the clinic walkway announces the arrival of a guard droid on its rounds, and Kirsten shrinks back into the shadows at Koda's side. Further down the alley, the other members of the raiding party crouch behind the detritus left by the city's vanished inhabitants. A dumpster blocks half the passageway; further down, a Mercedes sedan continues its gradual descent onto its wheel rims as air seeps out of its tires. The sentry crosses Koda's narrow angle of view. Like the clinic, like the alley, the street lies in shadow, but the moon gives enough light to show the droid in silhouette. A humanoid type, it wears a uniform of some kind, its M-16 slung casually across its back, its cap set at an angle that would pass for jaunty if the droid were anything to which self-assurance had any meaning. It passes, turning the corner of the building, and Koda feels the muscles in her back unravel along her spine. The next sentry should appear in five minutes; this one again in another five. They have the timing down.

Wastepaper rustles softly to her left as Morgan steps out from behind the dumpster to crouch beside Dakota and Kirsten. "Okay," she whispers. "Their rounds haven't varied in almost an hour. We let the next one go by. When this one passes again, we go in."

"Got it," Koda replies almost soundlessly.

"Swing wide, take the west side. I'll go straight for the front. Inga and Sarai will head for the back."

"Got it," Kirsten repeats.

They have gone over the plan a dozen times back at the camp. All on one floor, the clinic has three distinct sections. The central area consists of offices and waiting rooms. Nothing interesting there except the door to be bashed in. Branching off to the east, the wards and private accommodations give onto a long corridor, rooms offset in stair-step fashion to give maximum natural light. Opposite, in the west wing, are the delivery rooms, the labs, the pharmacy and storerooms and kitchens.

Koda, like the rest of the party, has the layout firmly in her mind. Break in, destroy the android staff and any humans cooperating with them, determine if any living children are present, bomb the place to flinders. Simple.

"Good," Morgan says, touching Koda's arm briefly, Kirsten's more gently, lingeringly. Then she backs again into the darkness, and they wait.

The first sentry passes. Koda shifts slightly as its footsteps fade, trying again to ease her leg. Carefully she shifts the flashlight and the two small bottles that hang at her waist. Filled with gasoline and fused with rag run through holes in their metal caps, they may not be regulation grenades but will do the job at hand. From somewhere across the parking lot comes a faint whimper, a low sound that might be made by a puppy or a newborn kitten. Either is likely enough. The droids have shown no interest in any non-human beings, either for good or for ill. The shrubbery around the long, low clinic building, with its offset rooms in the patient wing, provides plenty of sheltered nooks where a pregnant animal might bear and nurse her young. The sound comes again, louder, is repeated in a broken cadence that rises in volume, finally becoming the full-throated wail of a human baby in distress.

"Goddess! There's kids!" someone behind her exclaims and is cut off abruptly by Morgan's rough, "Go! Go, dammit!"

Koda levers herself up to her feet, the cramp in her leg still hampering her, and sets off across the pavement at a shambling run. Kirsten paces her, with Morgan and Beatha on their heels. Morgan and the three women in her squad peel off to the right, making for the main entrance. Sarai and Inga, backed by two more Amazai, split and make for the rear, the backpacks that hump against their shoulders bearing the explosives and the timing devices that will bring this obscenity down in a cloud of dust and mortar. Except, now, they have to find the children first, and bring them out.

Kirsten on her heels, Koda skids around the corner of the building, running flat out now that the cramp in her leg has loosened. The wailing sound comes again, fainter now with the angle of the building in between. Behind Koda, Beatha shouts, "Windows! Go for the glass!"

The side entrance was also, apparently, once the emergency entrance. As they pound up the ramp, Koda can make out the sheen off the sliding pocket doors, and beyond them, the second pair that leads into the wide receiving bay. She shifts her rifle in her hands as she reaches the head of the incline, ready to smash through the doors with its butt. To her shock, the doors simply slide open on their well-oiled rails, and she half stumbles into the airlock space between the two entrances, Kirsten and the other women barreling into her from behind.

"Well," says Kirsten as she regains her balance, "that's convenient. They're expecting us?"

"Or dead sure they're not expecting anybody," Beatha adds. "Whole damned atmosphere's pretty casual."

"Whole damned town's pretty dead." Koda lowers her gun and stands for a moment before the inner doors. "Trap, maybe?"

From somewhere toward the front of the building comes the sharp rattle of automatic weapons fire, punctuated by a high-pitched scream. Koda cannot tell if the sound signals pain or triumph. They do not have time to think about it, nor about a trap. Koda takes two steps forward, and the glass panels slide back.

Heat rolls over them, the pent up heat of a closed building that has stood for months in the summer sun without air conditioning. With it comes, faint but discernable, the distinctive odor of human infant: a hint of warm milk and the riper smell of unchanged diapers. And under it all, fainter still, runs the stench of blood and rotting flesh.

Kirsten coughs, a small, strangled sound. This clinic brings back the horror of the incinerator at Salt Lake, but there is no time to take or give comfort.

Motioning the others to stillness, Koda stands for long seconds, letting her senses expand into the space around her. Hunter-sight, shaman-sight. Along with the odors that signal the presence of live infants and the underlying stink of death comes the sharper tang of alcohol, the acid-tinged smell of formaldehyde. She has no sense of physical human presence in the rooms stretched out before them; the only living things, it seems to her, must be further down the corridor, perhaps in the rooms on the other side of the main entrance at the center. But there is something, something... Something not living but conscious, waiting for them to move down the corridor. Something with death on its mind.

"All right," she says softly, switching on her flashlight. "We're going down that hall, checking each room as we go. They already know we're here. There's no point to secrecy now."

The beam of yellow light precedes them down the corridor, sliding over a bulletin board with tattered announcements still dangling from bright red pushpins, over the fire extinguisher in its glass box on the wall, over a floor that shows hardly a mote of dust. Apparently the facilities in this wing are still in use, which means that women are still delivering here. Rape does not need a clean floor. Neither does the butchery of infants.

A door opens off the hall to her right; a quick sweep of the room with the torch shows a low table and a tangled witch's cradle of black cables snaking down from the ceiling: Radiology. The door opposite remains closed and locked. Playing the light through the narrow, wire-reinforced window, Koda sees only shelves of neatly ranged bottles and boxes.

Beatha, on tip-toe behind her, whispers, "Pharmacy?"

Koda nods. "We need to come back here and collect as much as we can before we blow the place up."

On the other side of the hall, Kirsten leans into a room whose door stands ajar. She says softly, "Koda, over here."

"Over here" is a delivery room. Koda sweeps the light around its tiled floor and walls, all spotlessly kept still. An autoclave stands on a counter to one side, its LED bright crimson in the semi-darkness. She touches it and draws her hand sharply away. Still hot, still in use. Carefully she unlocks and lifts the lid; forceps, clamps, hemostats, scalpels, all neatly ranged inside, ready for use.

Kirsten, staring down into the sterilizer as if she is gazing into the pit of Hell, says in a flat voice. "So what do they do with the women after they deliver? Send them back to the jails to breed again?"

"Are they even that organized?" Beatha asks. The controlled substances cabinet swings open to her touch, not locked or even latched. Androids, after all, cannot become addicted.

"We'd better check the incinerator out back," Koda says grimly. "Look for adult remains, too."

Despite the sterile atmosphere, the stink of decay is stronger here. Nothing in the room seems to be the source of it. Koda plays the light over the acoustic tiles of the ceiling; it is possible, just possible, that a possum or other uninvited resident has gotten into the roof space or the air conditioning ducts and died. But if that were the case, here on the downside of summer, there would be flies. There are none. "Something," she says quietly, "something—"

"Is dead," Kirsten finishes. "Somewhere close."

"Next room," Beatha says. "Let's try there."

The smell hits them full force as they push open the door to the adjoining examination room. Kirsten gives a small, strangled choking sound; Beatha gags, covering her mouth and nose with her free hand, sweeping the room with the muzzle of her rifle with the other. Nothing.

At first glance, the small space seems as clean as the delivery room. Table, counter, blood pressure cuff dangling from the wall, oxygen tank — all spotless. A steel trash receptacle stands by the table, its lid down. The edge of a red plastic bag shows under the edge of the top. A five-gallon can, it might hold bloody bandages, used dressings, discarded gloves.

Except that the room is otherwise spotless. Except that they have seen no humans that might need such things. Certainly no one would walk into a place like this as if it were a neighborhood med station, wanting a sprained ankle bandaged or a cut stitched.

Bloody bandages. Used dressings. Discarded gloves.

A very small human body.

Steeling herself, Koda crosses the room and, not giving herself time to think, steps on the pedal of the receptacle. The smell pours upward out the can and she turns away for a moment, choking on the stench and on the realization that there can now be no possible mistake about what they found in the incinerator in Salt Lake City.

The light shows her a small, rounded bundle, the curve of head and shoulders and updrawn knees clear under the plastic. Leaning down, she slips a hand between legs and belly; the flesh beneath, even in the heat, is chill to the touch. Dead some time, then.

"Is it...?" Kirsten asks.

"Yeah. It is." Koda lets the lid fall. No time now to examine the corpse.

The rest of the corridor appears clear. No sound comes from the other side of the building, the other women presumably going there from room to room as they are doing here in the east wing. At the double swinging doors that lead from the service wing into the reception area, Koda pauses, hunching down below the eye-level ports. The other women range themselves behind her against the wall, hardly breathing. Koda concentrates on the small sounds that come to her through the wood and metal; a voice, not so distant now in the far corridor; a whimper that might be a living child; the clink of metal on metal as someone shifts her gear. She can distinguish nothing that she can identify as distinctively android.

"They're there," Kirsten says suddenly.

"What? Who?"

"The androids. They're in the center section." Kirsten moves forward to crouch with Koda beside the doors. One hand is raised to her temple, her fingers white-knuckled in the light of the flash. "I can hear them."

"What? How the hell?" A downward slash of Koda's hand cuts off Beatha's question as effectively as if she had slapped the woman.

"Implants," Kirsten answers. "I'm deaf."

"How many?" Dakota whispers.

"Three, I think. One near the front door. The other two further back."

"Okay, then. Everybody lie flat. Let's do a little differential diagnosis here." Koda stretches out on the tiles, her small party face-down behind her, and, with the muzzle of her rifle, gently nudges one of the swinging panels open an inch or so. Withering machine gun fire answers her, shattering the lexan panes and tearing through the upper portion of the door where human heads and torsos would be if they were not plastered to the corridor floor. About five feet up on the walls, the light from the torch shows long gashes in the hospital-green paneling. From across the reception area, then, comes a high yell of "Amazai! Amazai!" and a cacophony of fire breaks out, the Amazai firing into the reception area and droids answering.

Koda levers her feet under her, pulling one of the incendiaries loose from her belt. "High-low, Beatha!" she shouts. "Annie, cover us!"

With that she kicks the door wide, crouching low, and as Kirsten's gun sprays the room, Koda lights the fuse and lobs the container of homemade napalm at the nearest shape, a droid with an M-16 at its shoulder, firing down toward the bottom of the ward door opposite. It takes the android on the shoulder, and flame spills down its back and flowers up through its dynel hair and over its optical sensors, where it will cling and burn through to the circuits below. Her second, arcing through the air in a fiery pinwheel with Beatha's, lands at its feet, sending a column of flame up its uniform trousers. Others spin across the room from the opposite door, landing at the droids' feet, taking one in the face. And still they continue to fire, wheeling blindly as the bullets spray from their M-16s, eerily silent as the incendiaries burn away their uniforms to expose the metal plates and sensor arrays below.

From across the room a human voice, Morgan's Koda thinks, yells, "Back! Back off!"

Koda snatches at Kirsten's elbow, pulling her back, and with Beatha they retreat down the corridor at a crouching run. Behind them comes the concussion of two explosions, not the main charges by the sound of it, but a pair of grenades as the roar echoes in the confined space and shakes the walls, bringing with it the crash of falling light fixtures and the shatter of breaking glass.

Silence falls. Something hisses and whirs overhead, and the sprinkler system sends sprays of water down onto them. Koda flinches with the sudden shock of it, then runs a hand through the wetness and over her face.

"Think they got 'em?" That is Beatha, her normally pitched voice a novelty after the cacophony of a moment before.

"Sounds like," Kirsten answers. "I don't hear them anymore."

Behind them the door pushes open and Inga appears, her face and hands soot-blackened. "Ten minutes 'til we set the main charges. Morgan says strip off anything that looks useful and get out."

"Gotcha," Koda says. "Pharmacy. Let's go."

Fifteen minutes later, the raiding party regroups across the street. The charges are laid and timed. Koda shoulders a trash bag full of medicines, swept at random from the shelves, Beatha and Kirsten, two more. Morgan, her face and hands blackened from scrabbling through the wreckage of the entranceway, holds a baby perhaps two years old, her head on the Amazai's shoulder. Sarai, bleeding from a cut on her forehead, is holding a cell phone in an equally bloodied hand. "Ready?" she asks.

"Anything else?" Morgan asks, looking around the small circle of women in the moonshadowed darkness. "Because once that signal goes, we move. We don't stop for anything 'til we get back to the Jeeps. And we don't stop after that 'til we're back home."

"Didn't you want to check the incinerator, Dakota? For remains?" Inga looks up from where she is stuffing medical instruments into her backpack that has lately carried several pounds of plastique.

Koda shakes her head. "No time. No need."

"No need?"

"Later," Kirsten says.

Morgan's glance runs over her sharply, but she says, "All right. Trigger the timer, Sarai. Let's move!"

They cover the distance between the clinic and the parked vehicles on the town's outskirts in a tenth of the time it took them going in. Half-running, keeping up a steady trot with fingers ready on the triggers of their guns, they arrive at the abandoned car dealership in just over ten minutes. They have met nothing and no one, only a pack of dogs that crosses their path a few blocks from the clinic, just another band of hunters in the wilderness that has claimed the city. At the lot, they pile into the Jeeps, Koda driving one with Kirsten beside her, Morgan and Beatha in the back.

"Wait."

Koda's fingers freeze on the key in the ignition, and she looks up to see Sarai holding one hand at shoulder level, her cell phone in the other. "Ten," says Sarai. "Nine...eight ... three...two." Her hand comes down in a slashing gesture of triumph. "One."

From a mile and a half away comes a rumble like a freight train, like an earthquake. Above the roofs of buildings still left standing, red stains the night sky, a black billow rising to blot out the moon. Koda, leaning over the back of her seat to get a better view, sees Morgan's eyes narrow in triumph, a smile like a sickle blade touching her lips. She runs a hand over the baby's back, soothing her as the noise rolls over them. "Good job," says the Amazai queen. "Let's go."

**The sun stands** halfway to noon when Koda emerges from the showers. Her body feels clean and polished, despite the cold water. The errant children of Israel might have yearned for the fleshpots of Egypt in their wanderings — she was a sophomore in high school before one of the nuns explained that that meant stew pots, to Koda's great disappointment — but Dakota Rivers would be happy with a hot shower. Not that cool water is a terrible hardship on the last day of July. She turns her face up to the warmth, swinging her still-wet braid over her shoulder to settle against her back. Kirsten, up and bathed earlier, is most likely to be wherever there is a late breakfast to be found, and Asi with her.

She sets off up the road to the stone circle, which seems to be both dining hall and meeting place. The cabins she passes stand empty, neatly made-up cots visible through the screen mesh, clothes poles hung meagerly with jeans and shirts and jackets. Several bear the crudely drawn images of large black birds, apparently intended to be ravens. *Ravens on some*, she corrects herself as she passes one with a saucer-faced raptor with eyes almost as big, *owls on others*. Both are sacred to warrior-goddesses, ravens to the Morrigan of Celtic legend, owls to Athena. There are no doves, which does not surprise her.

It doesn't disappoint her, either. She and Kirsten and Morgan had sat up until well past midnight attempting to riddle out the puzzle of the murders. Item: droids kidnap women. Item: droids breed women, presumably with the purpose of producing babies. So far, understandable to a point. Dakota has lived in ranch country almost all her life. Most livestock eventually find their way into one of those fleshpots, even the breeders, when their reproductive value is exhausted. Even horses, on many operations, ultimately wind up in an Alpo can. No puzzle there. It's what comes next that is the enigma.

Item: the droids kill and discard infants and toddlers. They are not, clearly, consuming long pig. Just as clearly, they are not supplying anyone else's depraved taste for the same. Which leaves the burning question, *why*?

A medical expert, a cyber expert, a legal expert should have been able to put together some hypothesis, but nothing they could postulate held water. The only thing that made sense was sheer terror. More than one human conqueror had pursued a strategy of killing enemy men, raping enemy women, slaughtering enemy children.

*But that doesn't work, either. They've made no effort to set up a gov-*

*ernment. In fact, they seem content to let the rest of us be, at least for the time being. Most of the rest of us*, she amends. *They still want Kirsten. Badly.*

Koda shakes her head to clear it. Cold shower or not, she still craves caffeine. Onward. Strategizing can wait another half hour.

On her left, she passes the deserted stables and the picket line. Only half the horses range along it this morning, including the two left on the hillside with the patrol a day and a half ago. Some of the Amazai, then, must be out beating the bounds, guarding their borders, replacing sisters who have returned. But patrols would not account for the near-emptiness of the camp.

As she tops the rise that leads to the circle, which, goddess willing, will lead to coffee, a wolf-whistle rings out, clear and loud.

"Yo, babe!"

Ripe as the back bayous of Louisiana, the voice and the whistle belong to the unseen Amazai from the mountain patrol. She crouches now beside the fire pit, carefully setting a spit onto a pair of freshly-cut greenwood uprights. Even in that position, it is clear that woman is taller than Koda by an inch or so, and wider, as Themunga would say, by half an axehandle. Her tank top shows off biceps and deltoids bulging like melons under her deeply tanned skin, a fair proportion of which sports tattoos in blue and green and red. Peacock feathers, beautifully drawn, cover her upper arms, and her pale hair, worn in a straggling braid, does nothing to conceal their counterparts that sweep up the sides of her neck. Kirsten, seated on the stone Morgan had occupied the night of their arrival, quietly sips coffee, hiding a three-cornered smile behind her mug. At her feet, Asimov grins up at Koda. No help there.

"Good morning," Koda says equably. "I don't think we've been properly introduced."

The woman gives a bark of laughter and straightens from her work. She extends a hand easily as big as Tacoma's. "Dale. Dale fia d'LouAnn. Pleased t'meetcha."

"Dakota Rivers. Likewise. Is there any breakfast left?"

"There's coffee and some fruit and bread back at the old main office. Nobody cooked this morning. Too much to do to get ready for tonight."

"Tonight?"

"Lughnasa."

"Loo..."

"Lughnasa," Dale repeats. "Lammas. Harvest."

"Oh," says Koda, and to Kirsten, "Can I have some of your coffee? Please?"

Kirsten hands the cup to her, and she subsides onto the rock beside the smaller woman. The coffee is still hot, and she swallows gratefully. "Gods," she says. "It'll be a terrible day when we finally run out of this stuff."

Dale only shrugs. "There's still coffee trees in South America; droids'd have no reason to destroy 'em. Whoever manages to go after it and bring some back'll make a fortune in trade, eventually."

"Is that an Amazai project?" Kirsten asks quietly.

The big woman narrows her eyes. "Maybe. Eventually."

Which means that this band has allies, is territorially ambitious, or both. Koda lets the thought wash about in her brain for a moment, along with the caffeine. It also means that survivors are beginning to live with the idea that "normal" is irreparably different than the "normal" of nine months ago. She hands the mug back to Kirsten. "So where is everybody?"

"Some's out hunting. Some's down at the farm. Some's over at the lake."

"We're invited," Kirsten says, draining the coffee.

They need to move on. They also need to make the beginning of an alliance with these women, just in case they survive. Koda nods. " Okay. Anything we can do to help?"

Dale grins at them sardonically. "Just about everything's covered. If you want to do something, though, you can go pick some flowers."

"Pick—"

"Unless you want a harder job?"

"That's okay," Kirsten says, standing up abruptly. "Flowers it is."

Koda gives her an outraged glance. But the pleading look in the green eyes forestalls speech. "Flowers it is," she repeats. "But coffee first."

**Two hours later,** Koda wades through Indian paintbrush grown knee-high, carefully cutting the blossoms and setting them into a bucket partly filled with water. Kirsten, invisible over a fold of the mountainside, is working a high meadow carpeted in purple gentians and deep-blue iris. Koda's own pail is near full now, overflowing with blossoms in autumn colors: red, vermilion, orange and yellow, gold. In among them she has placed tall spikes of blue and pink lupine, the wolf-flower. The Lammas feast marks the changing of the year. With the harvest, the year turns from summer to autumn, even though the days remain hot and long. It is a time of partings, looking toward the fallow season of winter before rebirth in spring. So, wolf flower — in honor of Wa Uspewikakiyape, in honor of the goddess in her form of hunter and defender. In the clear blue above, a hawk circles, rust glinting off her tail where the sun strikes it. Wiyo has kept her distance from the human camp, but has not strayed far. As Koda watches, she seems to pause in mid-flight, her wings backing air. Then she folds them and plunges like a meteor, her feathers gleaming copper as she streaks toward earth and her prey.

Koda watches for a moment, then hefts the bucket, testing its weight. It ought to be enough for one bucketful. They need enough for the altar, the quarters — whatever those are — and the feast table. Four pails should do it. Time to take this one back to where the horses are tethered and get the second.

Koda finds their mounts ground-tied under a stand of balsam pine, happily browsing the undergrowth. Kirsten's full pail sits on a stone not far away, overflowing with rich purples and blues. She sets her own beside it and runs her gaze over the high meadow that occupies a shelf of the mountainside here. Nothing. Nothing but the flowers, a pair of swallowtails sipping at the deep cups of the gentians, bees gathering pollen against the winter. No Kirsten.

"Kirsten?" she calls. "Kirsten!"

No answer.

"Kirsten!" *All right. No need to panic,* Koda lectures herself. *She's probably just off in the woods for a moment.* "Kirsten! Asi! Asi! Answer me!"

From twenty yards away, deep among the flowers, comes a high-pitched yelp of greeting and Asi's face appears, eyes bright, tongue lolling in a canine grin. Beside him, just barely visible, Koda can make out a paler head, turned away. Koda can feel her heart skip a bit as it brakes, draws a deep, deliberately calming breath. "Kirsten?"

Still no response. Asi, though, comes bounding toward her, leaping among the tall blossoms like a fox hunting in high grass. Kirsten turns then and sees her, a smile lighting her face. Koda checks the impulse to run and instead approaches slowly, keeping that smile in the center of her vision. There is no danger. Kirsten is not hurt. Asi passes her, offering his head for a scratch, then taking himself off under the trees with the horses. Tactful of him.

"Kirsten?" Koda says again. But she does not answer, only smiles and beckons. Old legends run through Dakota's memory, mortals taken by the elves, who must bear their sojourn under the hill in silence or remain forever apart from the human world. And among her own people, there are old tales of warriors seduced by silent women in the hills who vanish with the morning, leaving behind only the imprints of a deer's hooves. "Kirsten?"

For answer, Kirsten raises one hand to her temple, and suddenly Koda understands. She has seen Kirsten retreat into silence before, knows by now that it is a kind of refuge for one long solitary. More than most, Koda understands. A shaman knows the silence and its power. And last night, gods know, was enough to send anyone bolting for sanctuary.

For a moment she simply stands looking down at Kirsten, at her hair pale gold in the afternoon sun, her skin golden, too, with the long days and weeks of their quest. "*Nun lila hopa,*" she says without sound, letting her mouth form the words, smiling when she sees the glint of understanding in Kirsten's eyes. She kneels before her, then, forming Kirsten's name in silence, and again, "*Nun lila hopa.*"

For answer, Kirsten draws Koda's mouth down to her own. The kiss lengthens, deepens, the taste of summer sweet on her lips and tongue. Breathless, Koda draws away slightly and raises her head, threading her fingers through the pale strands of Kirsten's hair where it lies along her shoulder, smoothing it back. She slips her hand inside the collar of Kirsten's shirt, running her thumb across the base of her throat, feeling the pulse jump under her fingers. The other woman's shoulders are as hard as old wood, the muscles knotted.

There is a cure for that, one she knows. Koda bends to lay her lips to the pulse-point. *Winan mitawa.* She forms the words without sound. My woman. My wife. My love. Strange, not to say it.

Her eyes smouldering under long lashes, eyes as green as the grass, Kirsten leans back onto the crushed stems and leaves about her. It is invitation and promise at once, familiar by now yet new each time they come together.

Rising, Koda sheds her clothing, spreading her shirt and jeans on the ground. Kirsten's hands go to her own shirt but Dakota stops her and, kneeling beside her lover, slowly looses the buttons, letting her hands linger with each motion as she spreads the cloth, brushing Kirsten's breasts, their nipples already hard, tracing their curves from shoulder to breastbone and back again. Koda slides her hands lower, below the belt of Kirsten's jeans, brushing the high arches of her hipbones and the hollow of her thighs. Hooking her thumbs into the band, then, she slides the garment free.

She turns and bends to kiss her lover once more. Fire runs through her blood, but the time is not yet. There is another need that must be satisfied. She leans back and with a gentle touch to her shoulders turns Kirsten to lie on her belly. Koda kneels astride her hips, and beginning at her neck, works her hands in tight circles down the column of her spine. She has no oils for this. Instead she crushes an iris blossom between her palms and rubs its subtle fragrance into Kirsten's skin with each stroke. Systematically she works the stress from the lithe body, feeling the knotted muscles give way under her hands, the massage taking on a rhythm of its own in time with her heart and breath.

The change comes gradually, the tightness of stress and exhaustion becoming tension of another kind. Kirsten's skin warms under her touch, her blood humming as it runs warm just below the surface. She stretches luxuriantly, almost cat-like, rising onto her elbows and letting her head fall loosely back. She does not speak, her body communicating her satisfaction for her.

With a final sweep from hip to shoulder, Koda leans forward and lays a kiss on the back of her neck, then blows softly at the short hairs, still not grown out, at her nape. She feels the shiver as it goes through her lover's body, feels it deepens to pulse within her own flesh. The fire sings through her, spreading from her belly up her spine to quicken her heartbeat, drawing the skin tight over her breasts, tautening her nipples. She slips from where she kneels across Kirsten's body, sliding down to lie beside her. The desire for words has left her. She raises Kirsten's hand to her lips, kissing the palm and wrist. The hand settles between her breasts, then presses gently. With a questioning look at her love, Koda settles onto her back. Kirsten kisses her once more, then rises to kneel above her, slipping one knee between Koda's thighs.

Another kiss, then Kirsten's fingers brush over Dakota's face, tracing her forehead, her eyes, her mouth. Her lips follow, pressing against her eyelids, returning to close them again when Koda glances upward. She shuts her eyes, then, giving herself up to touch and sound as Kirsten has given herself to sight and touch. Yet she is not in darkness. The sun beats down directly overhead, and its brilliance still shows her red-tinged shadows, a hint of movement as Kirsten bends over her, letting her hair, fine as cornsilk, trail over Koda's face and throat.

*I would know you in the silence between the stars.* The thought is her own, and not. And with it comes another. *I see you in the darkness, like a flash of lightning. And the darkness cannot hide you.*

Not now. Not ever.

Koda raises her hands to lay them on Kirsten's shoulders, letting her fingers trail down over her breasts. Faint among the hum of bees, she can hear her lover's breathing, coming faster now. The fall of Kirsten's hair sweeps again over her throat, her breasts, its touch delicate as a summer breeze. Warm lips follow it, suckling gently. At the same time, Kirsten's knee moves between her legs, parting them, and Koda opens to her. Kirsten draws away, sliding back, and Koda feels the brush of her fingers in the hair above her sex, sliding downward to the entrance to her body. The fingers trail upward, lingering on the delicate nub at the apex, and Koda's belly tightens, her thighs growing taut. Kirsten parts the lips, shifting to lie above Koda, center to center. Her hips circle slowly, building pressure. Flame licks down her legs, up her spine. Point counterpoint to her own, Kirsten's breath come in short gasps that punctuate the silence. The fire runs along her nerves, through her veins, until it seems she must be consumed, the rhythm of her lover's movements driving it through her body in waves. Her heart hammers against her breastbone, and there is no air any more, nothing now but the flame that owns her flesh. Sound builds within her, seeking release, but she stifles it in her throat until finally it breaks free and she comes, the pulse of Kirsten's release matching her own. Spent, her lover sinks down into her arms, her skin slicked with sweat beneath the ripening sun.

*Cante mitawa.*

Now and forever.

**They come down** out of the hills at sunset. The sky over the mountains burns gold and crimson, its fire sheeting over the surface of the water that lies still in the calm evening. Koda pauses, taking in the sweep of the lake from north to south, its whole surface struck to bronze in the fading light. The cries of birds going to roost along its rocks, gulls and terns like pale ghosts as they skim above the shore, come to them where they stand on the last slope of the foothills. A chill runs over Koda's skin that has little to do with the coming of the night. Something old and unnamed stirs within her — a memory, a fear, something that has been or will be, she cannot tell. Glancing at Kirsten beside her, she sees unspoken recognition in her face, something that calls to her out of time, out of the confines of common space.

Unbidden, there comes again the image of a pale head and bronzed, flashing arms above the waves of the Aegean, wine-dark as the combers roll over it to shore. A breeze ghosts by, and it seems to lift a strand of hair from Kirsten's shoulder, only that shoulder is level with her own, and the hair is black as a raven's wing. Time runs oddly in this place, sacred to the Mother of All Life under all the names by which she has been known.

"Ina," Koda murmurs. "*Wakan.*"

Beside her, acting as their guide, Dale nods. "Mother Earth. This is Her place."

Far from shore, an island looms dark against the mountains behind it. Huge white shapes circle it, riding the darkening air on outstretched wings, necks tucked against their keelbones, bills deep copper in the lingering light. Kirsten tilts her head back to watch as they circle, sixty of them, perhaps seventy, in a trailing V formation. "Pelicans?" she says tentatively. "They look like something from a different time, like sailing ships."

"They breed here," Dale answers. "We'll be going around to the other side where we won't disturb them."

As she speaks, the sun dips behind mountains. In the thickening shadows, a light breaks out at the top of the huge rock formation that gives the lake its name, a pyramid rising from the near shore some four hundred feet above the surface. It flickers a moment, steadies, then flares into a flame that leaps toward the sky. A dark figure, silhouetted against it, cries out, "Who comes? Name yourselves!"

Koda steps forward. "Dakota *chunkshi* Themunga," she answers.

There is a moment's silence, and Kirsten glances up at Koda. Then she says, "Anne, daughter of Marilyn."

"Who speaks for you?"

"I do, Dale fia d'LouAnn. And so does the Riga."

"Pass on, then, if you come in friendship." The sentry shifts slightly, a dark shape against the light of the fire. She wears a bird mask with a large bill and a trail of streamers that fall down her back.

*A raven*, Koda thinks, *with a mantle of feathers.* Beneath it she wears a short, fringed garment that leaves her arms and legs bare.

"We come in perfect love and perfect trust," Dale answers.

Koda is not quite sure of that, but she does not question the response as Dale leads them down to the shore and a boat waiting. Once on the water, the big woman takes the oars, refusing help.

"Nope, thanks. This is my job."

As the dark water passes beneath them, the sound of drums comes across the surface of the lake, amplified in its passage. At first it is only a rhythmic pulse, wordless. But as the boat makes the curve of the island, the oars dipping and rising soundlessly, words become audible, dozens of voices chanting together.

"Isis, Inana. Demeter, Kore." Over and over again the same words, names of the Goddess from the foundation of the world. The drums grow louder, the chanting more insistent. "ISis, iNAna. DEmeter, KOre. ISis, iNAna. DEmeter KOre." The sound grows, echoed, it seems, from the rise of the mountains to east and west, thrumming over the water in ripples like the sounding of a great whale. Kirsten, sitting beside her by the gunwales, slips her hand into Koda's, and Koda gives her a reassuring squeeze. Kirsten is out of her element here, about to enter a level of ritual and belief which she finds difficult to accept, even when guided by Dakota or Wanblee Wapka. Koda, though, doubts she will find much unfamiliar here, and nothing frightening or repugnant. The Mother is the Mother, whatever her children call her in different ages of the world, in lands far from each other.

Dale beaches the boat in a small cove and leads Kirsten and Dakota over the narrow beach toward a wooded rise. As they walk, almost silent on the wet sand, Koda spies a hunched shape with a bushy tail, digging at the edge of the water, and touches Kirsten lightly on the arm, pointing. As she does, the raccoon brings a mussel up from its burrow, prying with clever hands at the shell. Perhaps tactfully, it has nothing to say to the passing humans. Sometimes a raccoon is just a raccoon.

The drums have become land-bound thunder now, the red glow of fire visible as the trees thin. They emerge into a clearing where torches mark the edges of a circle some twenty feet across, perhaps more. A dozen women, led by Morgan, dance around a flat stone at the center, their bodies moving to the beat of the drums. All wear some variation of the sentry's costume: raven masks, fringed leather vests with loincloths or short skirts. Around the circle stand the rest of the Amazai, some similarly dressed except for the masks, more in their everyday jeans and workshirts. They chant the Goddess's names over and over, their hands and feet beating out the rhythm along with the drums.

Kirsten nudges Koda and gestures toward the dancers, and Koda leans down to whisper, "Priestesses. I think."

Dale guides them to a place among the Amazai. From where she stands, Koda can see that the flat stone holds a metal bowl, gold in the light of the fires, a platter piled high with small loaves with fruits and flowers ranged around it, and a smaller earthen bowl. Incense smoulders in a pierced burner, sending clouds of fragrant white smoke up over the altar. A long blade and a shorter lie crossed in the center, and at their junction stand two female figures shaped of corn stalks, one slightly bent at the shoulders, the other with long straight hair made of cornsilk. Mother and Maiden, Demeter and Kore, Goddess and Goddess.

The drumming builds to a crescendo, the dancers spinning, writhing, leaping in ever-closing circles around the altar. So suddenly that the silence strikes Koda like a physical blow, the drumming ceases, and Morgan stands before the altar, arms raised, feet apart to form the five-pointed star, sign of the Goddess from Babylon to Egypt to the mounds of the Mississippi Valley. "Io!" she cries. "Evohe!"

"IO! EVOHE!" the Amazai answer.

Another silence falls and Morgan says, "We have come here tonight to mark the turning of the year. The harvest is in, and it is good. Blessed be."

"Blessed be," the women echo, Koda and Kirsten with them.

"From Brigid to Lughnasa, the Maiden walks above ground. At the harvest, she retreats into the earth, and the time of fallow fields and barren wombs is upon us. We come to give her thanks and bless her path as she leaves us. We come to give her thanks, and promise her remembrance." She turns to another woman at her side, perhaps Sarai, and hands her the long blade, which is too long to be a knife, yet is not quite a sword. "Cast the circle, that no unseemly thing may enter."

Beginning at the north, where another stone stands, Sarai makes the circuit of the circle, passing three more stones at east and south and west, returning to drive the blade into the earth just to the right of the northern quarter. She comes again to stand beside Morgan, who says, "Call the quarters."

A third priestess moves to the stone in the east. A pair of antlers lies on it, and a bowl of yellow paintbrush. The woman chants:

Stag in the East,
Lord of the Air,
Swift-footed Sun-runner
Crowned with light.
Watcher at the gates of dawn,
Stand as our Guardian in the East
And grant us the gifts of clarity and illumination.

Another woman approaches the stone to the south of the circle. It bears an eagle's wing and a spray of scarlet penstemon.

Eagle in the South
Lord of Fire,
Eagle of midday,
Strong-winged cloud-rider
Wreathed in flame,

Watcher at the gates of noon.
Stand as our Guardian in the South
And grant us the gifts of strength and purpose.

In the west, where the stone holds a raven's wing and a bowl of Kirsten's irises and gentians, another priestess raises her hands and chants the invocation.

Raven in the West,
Lady of the waters,
Raven of twilight,
Swift-stooping fate-bringer
Robed in shadow.
Watcher at the gates of evening,
Stand as our Guardian in the West
And grant us the gifts of healing and vision.

Finally, Morgan herself moves to stand at the northern stone, where a green branch lies before the skull of a wolf.

Wolf in the North,
Lady of Earth,
Wolf of midnight,
Soft-footed tracker of spirits
Hidden in starlight.
Stand as our Guardian in the North
And grant us the gifts of wisdom and truth.

Morgan moves forward then, and raises the Corn Mother high above the altar, facing the Amazai. "Blessed be the Lady, Mother of all that lives. Blessed be all life that is born of Her and returns to Her again."

"Blessed be," the Amazai answer in unison.

She sets it down, lifting the bowl and pouring a handful of water onto the earth. "We have planted. We have watered." Next she raises the platter of loaves. "We have harvested, we have winnowed. Lady, we give thanks for your gifts of life. We give thanks for the sweet Earth and its bounty." Finally, she breaks one of the loaves and holds it high, the light of the fires running golden over its surface. "The Goddess has gone into the grain!"

"We will not hunger!" the women answer as the loaves are passed among them.

"The Goddess is in the springs and waters!"

"We will not thirst!" The bowl passes, and as Koda drinks she tastes the salt of its blessing and its sweetness, both vivid on her tongue.

"The Goddess is in the corn!" Morgan cries.

"It will grow again in spring!"

"The Goddess goes down into the earth!"

"She will return with the Sun!"

"The Goddess is within us!

"Life comes forth from death!"

The drums begin their pulsing beat again, and the Amazai join in one long, snaking line with Morgan at the head. Koda takes Kirsten's hand and Dale's; with her other hand, Kirsten takes Inga's. The dance this time moves about the circle at its perimeter, then inward toward the altar, winding more and more tightly toward its center until the spiral can be no tighter, then unwinding until the women stand at the edges of the circle, each with her arms stretched out to her sisters on either side. "Life," Morgan repeats, "comes forth from death. We release to life those who have left us."

A murmur passes around the circle, each woman naming her dead and those she has left behind. Koda whispers the names of Wa Uspewikak-iyape, the Hurley family, remembering all those fallen at the Cheyenne or at Ellsworth. Beside her, Kirsten stands with tears in her eyes, murmuring the names of her parents and her colleagues. Other women weep openly, some whispering, some shouting the names of children, husbands, wives, friends, all those lost in the uprising known and unknown.

*Ina Maka*, Koda prays as the women disperse to feast and celebrate, *give us strength and wisdom to do what we must do. Let the death end. Let the life come forth again.*

Later, Morgan seeks them out at the edge of the fire. Her raven mask, tilted back from her face, perches precariously on the back of her head. She carries her plate piled high with pit roasted beef, corn and potatoes set onto the coals with it. Koda, replete, has set her empty dish aside; Kirsten, slowly but enthusiastically, is still working her way through seconds. Morgan folds crosslegged to the ground and says, "You're still planning on leaving in the morning?"

Koda nods. "We need to get on."

Morgan takes a bite of the meat, washing it down with a mug of chamomile tea. "You're welcome to stay if you want. Or to come back to us when you return."

It is not a small honor, and Koda says quietly, "Thank you, but we can't stay."

The Amazai nods as though it is the answer she expects. "Goddess go with you, then."

"Goddess go with us," Koda echoes. The enormity of their task stands suddenly bleak before her. A hundred miles yet to go, all of it on foot, a fortress to storm. The likelihood that they will survive is close to nonexistent. She says again, softly, "Goddess go with us."

Kirsten reaches out to take her hand. "*Cante mitawa*," she says. "Now and always."

# CHAPTER FORTY-SEVEN

Koda kneels on the gentle slope of the hillside, her rifle braced across one thigh, binoculars sweeping the opposite side of the small valley. Dusk has begun to gather about them, the cooling air drawing tendrils of fog from the stream that cuts its way through the rolling landscape. Scattered through the grass like roundels of ancient bronze no more than an hour before, the poppies have furled their petals against the oncoming dark. Already the eastern sky shows the first stars; in the west, a deep crimson lingers, fading through purple to ultramarine at the zenith. Just over the edge of the hills, a sickle moon rides low, and from somewhere up in the trees that march along the crest of the rise comes the deep hooting of a horned owl, answered a moment later by his mate. A chill runs down Koda's spine, and half-forgotten childhood fears with it.

*Who? Who?* But the question is superfluous. The likelihood that she and Kirsten will survive this night is minuscule.

For the last ten miles, they have seen no sign of human activity — no residents in the small town of Rancho Cordova, no movement on the road. Nor, in the afternoon that they have lain concealed on the hillside, have they seen sentries, guards, anyone at all, either approach the Westerhaus Institute or stir on its grounds. It sits on the facing slope, a ten-acre campus spread out around a single story building faced all about its circumference with mirror-bright glass. The driveway and public parking lot remain clear; no vehicles occupy them. The guard booth, too, stands empty. Bougainvilleas in magenta, red, white, gold, double and single, fountain up from the graveled flower beds, together with scarlet aloes and violet prickly pear. It is all very ecologically responsible and all radically overgrown, left to the rain and the sun for the better part of a year.

"Well," Koda says finally, "I thought it'd be taller."

"It is." Kirsten glances up from the screen of her laptop. "Nine stories, only one above ground."

"There's a culvert down there by the creek a little to the south that can't go anywhere but into the building. Unless you have a better suggestion?"

Kirsten shakes her head. "There's only two doors on the top floor. One's the main entrance, the other's Freddie's concession to the fire regs. It may not even be functional."

"Looks like the pipe's it, then. Any idea where that'll take us?"

"Probably into the air-conditioning system. Sewers wouldn't empty out into the stream like that."

Koda draws a deep breath, lowering the binoculars and turning to look at her lover. From somewhere comes a line of remembered poetry. *Mine eyes desire thee above all things.* For a long moment, she drinks in the sight of Kirsten, pale hair touched to silver by the waning light, lithe body half-stretched out on the grass, her eyes in shadow. "It's time," she says softly. "We'd better start moving."

For answer Kirsten only nods, folding down the screen of her computer and tucking it into her pack. Asi stretches and gets to his feet, looking expectantly from Kirsten to Koda.

"No, boy. You can't go with us." Kirsten slips her arms around him, holding him for a long moment with her face pressed into his shoulder. When her hands come away, his collar comes with them. She lays it in the grass beside him, getting to her feet reluctantly, as if every joint in her body aches. "Down, boy," she says quietly, and he subsides into the grass. "Stay." She turns away and begins the descent, not looking back.

Koda lays her hand briefly on the big dog's head, ruffling his mane behind his ears. "Be free," she says, and follows Kirsten down the hillside.

**A trickle of** water still runs from the culvert, clear in the narrow beam of Koda's penlight. The pipe itself measures perhaps a yard across, a black maw opening into the side of the hill. It smells sharply of coolant, with an underlying hint of ammonia. She plays the light about the upper curve, where the broken remains of mud-plaster nests cluster together, some retaining their narrow-necked jar shape, others mere circles of dried earth. "Cave swallows," Koda says quietly. "Gone south."

"Left the poop behind," Kirsten observes.

"Oh, yeah. Nobody said this was gonna be a clean job. We're going to have to do this on hands and knees." From her pack, Koda pulls a pair of leather gloves and a bandana, which she ties loosely around her neck.

"Try not to get them wet," Kirsten says, likewise smoothing gloves over her own hands. "The place will be cold — really cold. The droids' circuits can take normal heat, but a lot of the manufacturing equipment is temperature-sensitive."

Koda shifts the rifle across her back, checks her belt one last time for the extra magazines and the half-dozen grenades she has hoarded all the way from Ellsworth. A pouch holds a small lump of C-4 and a detonator, quietly liberated from the armory at Pyramid Lake. They could simply have asked for it, of course, but Dakota and Annie Rivers off in search of Annie's parents on the Mendo Coast could have no legitimate use for plastique. Lastly, she works the penlight into the band of her hat, pointing straight up, and pulls the bandana up over the lower part of her face. "Ready?"

"Let's do it."

Ducking beneath the curve of the pipe, Koda drops to hands and knees and begins to crawl forward. The miniature flash shows her the walls rising to either side, the thin runnel of mud-and-guano thickened water down the bottom. By splaying her hands and knees, she finds that she can mostly keep out of the wet. The lime-covered surface to either side crunches faintly as she moves, Kirsten following in her tracks. It occurs to Koda that if there are noise or motion sensors in the conduit their mission could be cut short before they even get near their objective. But prints like miniature human feet and the rippling sign of a snake's passage seems to indicate that the local wildlife comes and goes unmolested; the heavy stuff will be up ahead.

The first hint of it has nothing to do with Westerhaus's security system. From up ahead comes a whiff of rancidly acidic stench. No surprise there; the prints, after all, were fair warning. She pauses to tighten her bandana over her nose and mouth, even as her eyes begin to water. "Okay," she says, "we've got chemical warfare here. We try to get through this next bit as fast as we can. Don't breathe if you don't have to."

Kirsten's answer is a wry snort. "What is it? *Eau de* skunk?"

"You got it. Recent, too."

The stink grows rapidly from worse to overwhelming as they advance down the tunnel. Koda rises to a crouch, getting her feet under her, and shambles down the conduit at a gait that is half frog-march, half bear-dance. If skunks have the run of the place, she and Kirsten are unlikely to trip alarms — unless, of course, the skunk is up ahead somewhere, in which case matters may become radically worse. The stinging in her eyes almost blinds her to the single bright spot of the penlight as it picks out the dark curve of an intersecting pipe. "Turn," she says, half-gagging. "This one should head us up toward the building."

"Oh, gods," Kirsten moans behind her. "I hope the skunk hasn't been there, too."

It has not. The stench dissipates within a few yards, and Koda gratefully drops back to hands and knees, pushing the bandana away from her face. They are too far up the pipe for the swallows. Here there is only the thin stream of water, icy cold now closer to the Institute, and a faint odor of mold. She can hear Kirsten taking in the chill air in gasps.

By Koda's reckoning they have gone perhaps another fifty yards when the flash picks out the shape of an obstruction ahead. Slipping the light from her hatband, she plays it over a steel grate that blocks the tunnel. It, or something like it, had to be here; otherwise the local wildlife would have free access to the Institute's climate control in particular and the building in general. A quick run of the flash over the rim shows it is neither bolted nor welded into place.

"What d'you think? Go for the hinges or the lock?"

"Hinges," Kirsten says without hesitation. "Maybe we can get the pins out. Otherwise we'll have to blow the thing."

Koda nods agreement. She does not want to have to set off a grenade or the plastique in a confined space. Still less does she want to alert the droids inside the facility by noise or vibration. "Hinges it is," she says.

The openings in the barrier are just large enough that Koda can pass a hand through. With the penlight, she locates the pins to one side. Reaching for her knife to try to prize them up, she leans against the grate and nearly loses her balance as it swings under her weight. "What—" She scrambles away from it. "You wouldn't happen to know if Westerhaus booby-trapped things like this, would you?"

"Not as far as I know," Kirsten answers. "But then, I wouldn't know."

When nothing happens, Koda gives the grate a careful push. It swings open soundlessly. Ahead, the light shows only more tunnel — no wires, no suspicious projections on the walls of the passage, no obvious sensors, no skunks. "Okay," she says, "let's move."

After ten yards or so, the tunnel begins to angle sharply upward, the first sign that they may be nearing the building. From somewhere above comes the faint hum and clatter of machinery. Going by Kirsten's copy of the blueprints, Koda knows that the physical plant is on the lowest level: air conditioning and heating machinery, generators, independent water supply. The plans show various possibilities from that point. Depending on the security measures, they can go strolling down the corridors — unlikely — or take to the ducts and vents that honeycomb the place and hope they are not furnished with deadfalls, electrified or otherwise inhospitable.

As the slope levels out again, the tunnel broadens, finally opening out into a rectangular vestibule with a vaulted roof. A channel in the floor carries the runoff from the machinery into the tunnel, passing under a steel door.  From the other side, the cacophony of the gears and flywheels and fans is deafening, echoing off the walls of the passage and reverberating in the metal of the door.

Kirsten, beside her, mimes pushing at the door, then shrugs.  It seems unlikely that the same luck will strike twice, but Koda gives a shrug back in answer.  It is worth the try.  She puts her shoulder to the steel and pushes.  Nothing.  She pushes a second time.  Still nothing.  She tries the handle.  The door is locked.

With Kirsten holding the light, Koda fixes a small charge of C-4 on the lock plate and wires up the detonator.  She motions Kirsten back beyond the expansion of the tunnel, then steps back and flings herself flat on the wet floor beside the other woman.  Triggered remotely, the explosive goes off with a muffled *whump!* and a shower of sparks.

A moment later, the door swings open to her touch, and the roar of the machinery spills through like the thunder of a great waterfall, a physical pressure — not just against her eardrums — but a force pressing against her whole body, rattling her bones.  She lets it wash over her, through her, not resisting, like a spirit passing through her in ceremony.  Take it in.  Direct it.  Master it.  Beside her, Kirsten presses both hands to her temples, damping down her implants.  For her, with every vibration magnified, the blast of sound must be infinitely worse.  "Are you all right?" Koda mouths.  She receives a nod in reply and a reassuring hand on her arm, and steps into the maelstrom that fills the entire level of the building.

Next to the door stands the HVAC equipment, the drainage conduit filled with viscous dark water.  The open pipe leads out beneath a cage of bars plastered with warning signs: HIGH VOLTAGE.  AUTHORIZED PER-SONNEL ONLY.  SAFETY EQUIMPMENT MANDATORY.  Beyond them looms the huge bulk of the condenser, an Army-green block the size of a small bungalow, its sides and top studded with dozens of meter-wide fans whirring at different speeds, in opposite directions.  The smell of overheating wire comes off it, together with a blast of heat.  Beyond the bars the air ripples with shimmer, the kind that rises off the blacktop under the July sun.

To one side Koda can see the labyrinth of its condenser coils, twined and turning back on themselves like the intestines of some great beast.  The roar of its motors echoes off the high ceiling, the concrete walls.  Koda takes an involuntary step back, then checks herself abruptly.  *Get a grip, Rivers.  You're not St. George.  This ain't no dragon, just an overgrown window unit.*

Her gut does not quite believe her, though, and she remains where she stands, studying the huge machine.  Cutting off the ventilation might bring someone down to repair it, someone who could be used as guide or hostage or source of information.  But the task is impossible.  Tacoma might know how to slay this monster, but she has not the electrical or specific mechanical skills to know where to attack it effectively.  She doubts there is a circuit breaker box where she can simply turn it off.  *On the other hand, I could short out the entire building, possibly destroying Westerhaus's little  project, while electrocuting myself...*  The cost-benefit ratio does not compute.

Kirsten, shoots her a sympathetic glance, her shoulders hunched forward against the wave of sound and the inarticulate sense of mechanical violence. "I don't know how to knock it out either!" she shouts, pointing. "Stairway! Across the room!"

Koda nods and sets off in the direction of the exit. Past the climate control unit stand rank upon rank of computer monitors on panels rising nearly to the ceiling, glowing with fluorescent reds, blues, greens like eyeshine in the semi-darkness. As they pass, Koda can make out the ever-changing readouts: strings of numbers, bar graphs that rise or shrink seemingly at random, wave-forms like EKG read-outs, all flashing and squirming across the LCD screens. Above them run the aluminum air ducts, suspended from the ceiling by struts that flex almost imperceptibly with the vibration from the equipment below, as if they might suddenly come tumbling down on hapless beings below. Bundled electrical cables, thick as a human thigh, run alongside them, weaving in and out among PVC pipes that must carry water or waste. Witch's cradle. An involuntary shudder runs through Koda, and she does not look up again.

Past the monitors, the electrical plant occupies half the floor. In the dim light from the LEDs, Koda can make out half-a-dozen large generators, whirring and clanking behind a wall of steel bars. No smell of gasoline or other fuel taints the air. Somewhere, then, there are windmills or solar cells not visible from the hills outside. Opposite it, behind its own cage, stands a transmission station, its matrix festooned with humming transformers and white ceramic insulators. Here the ozone smell is overwhelming, the same sharp odor that pervades the air in the aftermath of a lightning strike. The door is as thick as a bank vault's, equipped with combination knobs and a wheel like a ship's to draw its bolts. Red DANGER signs merely state the obvious. It is a vulnerability, like the HVAC unit, but one they cannot exploit.

Ahead, a red EXIT sign burns above a door, and she makes toward it at a jog, Kirsten keeping pace behind her. The door gives way at her first push, and she glances back inquiringly at Kirsten, who can only shrug. She has no way of knowing if Westerhaus or the droids have set traps, no way of knowing whether the Institute personnel have simply become careless once the humans in the surrounding area were wiped out.

The air from the stairwell hits them like a January blizzard on the Plains, cold to just above freezing. On it comes a taint of old blood, the odor of a meat locker. Koda cannot tell whether it comes from somewhere above them or from the air system. She turns to look at Kirsten, whose grimly set mouth tells her that she, too, has identified the smell. Somewhere above them is, in any case, limited; the stair goes up only one story, to a landing and another steel door. Taking the steps slowly and silently, Koda tries the handle. Locked, this time electronically. A retinal reader sits on the doorjamb at a little below average eyelevel. "Any way you can fool this thing into opening without blowing it?" Koda asks. "Does it have an override?"

"Let me see." Kirsten steps past her, surveying the set-up. Standing just to one side, she slips her laptop out of her pack, keys up a screen and surveys a column of figures that makes no sense whatsoever to Koda. Kirsten, though, says, "Maybe. Maybe. If I just—" She looks up, staring at the door as if willing it to open. "Do this—" She presses a combination of keys, and the lock emits a series of electronic tones and snaps open.

Koda shoots her an admiring glance. "Hey, you're good at this."

Cracking the door a centimeter or so, she peers out into a corridor painted institutional green. Unmarked doors line it at fifteen foot intervals. "What's on this floor?" she whispers.

"Storage. Parts and equipment, mostly." She wrinkles her nose at the odor, stronger here, though still faint.

"Can you hear anything?"

Kirsten slips out into the hallway, touching the implants behind her ears. After a long moment, she says, "I can hear the machinery downstairs. I don't hear anyone moving or talking."

Koda grins at her. "Fox ears. Maybe we need to give you a new name."

"Yeah? How about you? How do you say Does-It-Like-A-Rabbit in Lakota?"

"Gratefully. Let's go."

Koda slips first out into the hallway, her rifle at ready, finger on the trigger. This is the eighth level; two more to go before they get to Westerhaus's lair on the sixth. The corridor leads around the circumference of the building. Some of the rooms stand open, showing metal shelves rising to the ceiling. One contains cleaning supplies — towels and toilet paper with five-gallon drums of ammonia and Lysol. Another appears to be subdivided by walls made of boxes with the familiar hp logo: computer paper not by the ream but by the forest. The odor has grown steadily stronger. "They have a cafeteria on this level?" Koda asks.

"Don't think so," Kirsten answers quietly. "Something tells me that's not pork chops spoiling."

"I don't think it is, either. Up around the curve, maybe?"

The hall leads them to the east side of the building. A bank of elevators and another stairway face double doors. Dark stains spread beneath them, just visible against the faux terra-cotta tiles. Blood. Its body an irridescent blue and green, a blow-fly crawls across one deep brown spatter, leaving black specks behind it. As Koda watches, it takes flight, ponderous in the chill, buzzing as it slips between the door panels to disappear into the room beyond. She pulls her bandana back up over her nose and mouth. "I'm going to go have a look. Stay here."

"Koda—"

"Cover me. It'll only take a minute."

She pushes against the doors, a little surprised that they yield so easily, and lets them fall shut again behind her. The stench meets her in a billow of chilled air, stronger here, unmistakable. She gives her eyes a minute to adjust, the dim light seeping in from the hall showing her rows of chairs on a bare floor. Secretarial "posture" chairs form one line, high-backed executive seating another, rows of vaguely Mission-style armchairs, a third. Desks, also sorted by class, stand in neat lines across the middle of the room, while the tall bulk of filing cabinets occupies the front.

Switching on the penlight, Koda plays it over the back row of chairs. Human forms lie slumped in several of them, their clothes clotted with darkly frozen blood. One young woman sits with her forehead against the back of the seat in front of her, a hole the size of a quarter in the back of her skull, blood and grey brain matter scattered through her pale copper hair. The man beside her shows only a cage of shattered ribs and blackened viscera where his chest should be. Yet another sits with his head tilted back at an impossible angle, neck broken, mouth open and fly-blown. In the space behind, where a pair of handtrucks lean against the wall, a half-dozen more corpses lie stacked like cordwood, their limbs twisted and frozen into an inextricable tangle. Some of those in the seats may have died here. Others, like these, seem to have been killed and let lie 'til they began to stiffen, then brought here to await...what? Removal? Certainly no plant that manufactured sophisticated electronics would risk contamination from storing corpses long term. But that is another problem. It is impossible to tell how long these people have been dead, only that their bodies have been frozen, probably thawed slightly, frozen again.

Neither is it clear who they were. Employees? Two still sport ID badges clipped to their pockets, but blood has obscured the lettering. Salesmen, customers, visitors, caught in the Institute when the rebellion went down? There is no time to investigate, no time to think about them, no good to be done them. They have made their journey, going where it is all too likely she and Kirsten will follow before the night is through. *Peace*, she wishes them, then slips back into the hall.

Kirsten's voice is tight with control, but the sudden rise and fall of her chest betrays her relief. "How bad?"

"A couple dozen. Can't tell how long they've been dead or who they were. Most look like they've been shot."

"Women?"

"Women, too, some young." Koda pulls down her bandana and takes a deep breath of the relatively fresher air in the hall. "No baby-making factory here, apparently."

Kirsten shakes her head as if to clear it, and it comes to Koda belatedly that she might well know some of the men and women who lie dead on the other side of the doors. But Kirsten only gestures toward the wall opposite. "Stairs? Or take the elevator and go for broke?"

"Stairs are harder to booby-trap. We may have to blow another door, though, and we're getting up to where they're likely to hear us."

A quizzical expression crosses Kirsten's face. "It's strange. I still don't hear anybody — no movement, no voices. Level Seven's production. There ought to be somebody right over us if the facility's still operating as usual."

"Maybe it's coffee break. Let's go."

Bypassing the seventh floor, the door to the sixth floor is, predictably, locked, and Koda stands by as Kirsten keys the code into her laptop again. Nothing.

Swearing, Kirsten steps closer and her fingers fly over the keys a second time. Still nothing.

"Shit," Koda swears, reaching for the plastique at her belt. "I'll get the C-4 on it."

"One more try." Kirsten moves past her to stand directly in front of the door, her head a foot away from the jamb. Slowly, methodically, she punches in the long string of alphanumerics. Just as Koda threads the copper wire though the knob of plastique, the door lock gives a soft snick and Kirsten, folding her laptop, slowly pushes it open. "We got it," she says.

The hall on this level is painted stark white, matching the white tiles underfoot. To her left the corridor curves away toward the back of the building. To her right, the hallway ends in a glass partition broken only by a roundabout, also glass. Through it, Koda can see a second, some ten feet beyond the first, but not into the hall beyond. A sign on the window proclaims STERILE ENVIRONMENT. AUTHORIZED PERSONNEL ONLY.

Koda slips out into the corridor, her finger on the trigger of her rifle. Kirsten follows, pausing only to draw and slide a round into the chamber of her automatic. "Where are we?" Koda asks softly.

"Labs and quality control," Kirsten answers.

"Lab coats? Scrubs?"

Kirsten's eyes light with a hint of mischief. "Gotcha. Let's try it."

They pass through the roundabout without incident. Between it and its counterpart are a pair of closets with disposable whites, booties, hair coverings. Koda slips a coat over her jeans and shirt, velcroing it shut to just above her waist. She abandons her Stetson for a net that hides her hair, adds a pair of safety goggles and pauses to grin at Kirsten, now similarly attired. "Trés chic," she observes. "So very you, ma'm'selle."

For answer, Kirsten sticks her tongue out at her lover. "Accessorized for the season with the indispensable AK. Let's get out of here."

Holding the rifle close to her side where it may be less immediately obvious, Koda follows Kirsten out the airlock. The corridor takes them past locked and numbered doors, otherwise featureless and as flat white as the walls. Above them, the fluorescent lights recessed into the ceiling emit a soft hum that grows louder as they follow the curve of the hallway. A jolt of pain stabs through her head, striking down along her spine and down her arms and legs. Next to her, Kirsten gives a soft cry and raises her hands to cover her ears, shaking her head from side to side, her weapon pointing wildly at the ceiling.

"Kirsten?" Koda's tongue feels as rigid as iron, unresponsive. A wave of dizziness washes over her and the walls seem to spin around her, a white whirlwind that whirs and spins, its sound building and building as it turns, becoming a roar, a thunder like a funnel cloud bearing down on her across a dark plain. As if from a great distance she seems to hear her name, a scream carried away by the wind. Then the floor rises up and hits her, jarring her bone from bone as darkness passes before her eyes, flickering light and shadow in a stacatto rhythm that spreads to her lungs, her heart, her misfiring nerves.

Dakota feels as if she's been hit with a cattle prod. The pain, intense and searing, spreads throughout her body, leaving no cell untouched. Her muscles thrum and jump, ignoring her commands. Her nerves spark continuously, uselessly, like live, downed wires in the aftermath of a tornado. Hearing a pained grunt to her left, she uses all her will, all her strength, to move her eyes a fraction of an inch, until Kirsten comes into focus, curled into a fetal ball, her hands now claws that clamp desperately around her ears.

The sight gives her the will to push past her own limitations and, millimeter by slow, painful millimeter, she manages to unclench her own hand and reach out, her arm shaking like one in the throes of a seizure, until her fingers come in contact with the back of her lover's head. Long fingers slide in fits and starts over soft golden hair until they reach the tiny bump just behind Kirsten's left ear. With an effort as monumental as anything she has ever undertaken, Koda bites down on her lip, drawing blood, as she wills her finger to lift, then press down on the button that triggers her lover's implant.

A fresh wave of agony pours over her like molten fire, and her breath locks in her chest. *By the gods*, she thinks, straining for air that isn't there as her diaphragm refuses to accept the signals she's so desperately sending, *I'm going to die like this!*

Of its own accord, her hand slips off Kirsten's head. The pain of her knuckles scraping the floor is infinitesimal against the torture rolling over her in slow, heavy waves, pulsing to the beat of a heart she can swear she feels slowing. The light from the harsh fluorescents overhead sears into her retinas, threatening to blind her and a heavy film of tears springs to her eyes. Grimacing in pain, she slowly curls her hand into a fist, raises it bit by torturous bit, and drives it into her own midsection. The blow is utterly without strength, but manages somehow to unlock her frozen diaphragm, causing dead air to rush forth from her lungs as if from an old and cracked bellows breathing out its last.

Sweet, sweet air rushes back into her lungs, compounding the dizziness in her head and causing her stomach to do a slow roll before righting itself again. "Kir-sten..." Her imagined shout comes out as a rusty wheeze and she prays her partner can hear it. "Yo-our o-oother im-plannnt. Tu-urrn it offff."

After a moment that seems to span an eternity in which entire universes are birthed and then die, Koda can see her lover's fingers relax a little then move in what is now a familiar motion, pressing the button sitting just under her skin.

Koda slumps against the wall, relief washing through her, dissipating her pain and beating back the dark for precious seconds. *We made it. She can make it.*

For Kirsten, the relief comes all at once, like a pinprick to an overfilled balloon. Control of her body rushes back to her, leaving her with only a blinding headache to mark her ordeal. She rolls over quickly, then freezes as her eyes light upon the agonized, sweat-soaked and spasming body of her lover. "Dakota! What's happening! What do I do?"

Koda's gaze locks with hers then skitters away, her eyes jerking upward until just a crescent of blue shows beneath her lid. At that moment, a long shadow springs into being, looming over them both and causing Kirsten, in an act of pure instinct, to grab Koda's involuntarily discarded rifle and aim, finger white against the trigger.

"Don't shoot!" the man who throws the shadow shouts, raising empty hands. "I'm here to help."

Stone deaf, Kirsten can nonetheless read his lips easily, and what she reads doesn't move her finger from the trigger one iota, though it does halt her reflex to simply pull and be done with it.

She sneaks a quick glance at Dakota, whose bow-taut form and mouth drawn down into a rictus of agony threatens to drain all strength, and resolve, from her. With a supreme effort, she tears her gaze away, back to the man who is just now slowly lowering one arm to grasp the collar of his shirt, which he yanks down, displaying a neck barren of metal.

"That doesn't mean a damn thing," Kirsten replies stubbornly, raising the rifle so that it now points directly at the bare neck.

"Please," the man repeats, "I'm here to help. Your friend...she won't last much longer like this."

*Don't you think I know that?* Kirsten screams in her mind, very well aware how sharp are the horns of the dilemma over which she is so precariously poised. She can feel her lover's agony like heat-shimmers in the height of summer. Her own indecision claws at her. Lower the rifle and risk both their deaths; keep it poised to shoot, and condemn Dakota. In the end, it is mercifully easy. *Where you go, I go,* she thinks, lowering the rifle and setting it on the cold, grey floor. She looks back up at the man. "If you're telling the truth, help her. Please."

With a nod, the stranger comes down to his haunches and gathers Dakota as one would an injured child, then stands, lifting her easily in his arms. "Come. There is a safe place nearby."

Fifty feet down the hallway, the man makes a left turn through a door that opens on silent hinges. Kirsten follows, then stops as her eyes assess the interior. "A kitchen?" she demands. "She needs help, not food!"

"Patience."

The stranger is lucky that his face is turned away at that moment, for if Kirsten had seen the word he uttered, he may well have found himself in a world of hurt.

Laying Dakota down near the sink, he moves to the microwave, sitting by itself on an island, and quickly punches several buttons. Kirsten watches with an expression of patent disbelief. Her jaw then unhinges as her lover's steel-spring taut form suddenly relaxes and her eyes flutter closed.

"Dakota!" She strides across the small space separating them and drops to her knees, gathering the limp form tightly against her breast as tears spring to her eyes.

Koda's strength returns in a surge and she hugs Kirsten to her tightly before releasing her and tilting her lover's head so that her lips can be easily read. "I'm okay, *canteskuye.* I'm okay."

Needing to actually hear the confirmation, Kirsten thumbs her implants on and listens to the music of Koda's easy breaths and the beating of the valiant heart she can hear when she presses her ear against Dakota's chest. "Thank God," she murmurs. "Thank God."

"The microwaves have a dampening effect on the white noise," the stranger says, looking a bit discomfited by the emotional display before him. "Unfortunately, the relief is temporary."

Dakota gives a short nod, expecting this, as Kirsten lifts her head and glares at their savior. "Who are you and why are you doing this," she demands.

"Forgive me," the stranger replies, bowing slightly at the waist. "I am Adam. Adam Virgilius. An...associate of Peter Westerhaus."

"You lie," Kirsten growls. "That bastard never had an 'associate' in his life."

"I think he was being sarcastic, love," Koda interjects, grasping her partner's hand and giving it a fond squeeze.

"I was indeed," Adam answers, smiling faintly. "I've worked for him for several years, though less blind and devoted than he assumed. When the last step in his plan was implemented, this building was locked down and all human workers were...disposed of."

"Except you," Kirsten comments, her sarcasm thick enough to be cut to ribbons with a butter knife.

Another short bow, another half smile. "Except me," he allows, spreading his hands. "As I have said, I was less blind than he assumed. Unfortunately for me, my knowledge came a bit too late to make a full-out escape. I was, however, able to flee to the lower levels where, as you both have duly noticed, humans other than Westerhaus himself were forbidden."

"Speaking of which," Kirsten intones, eyeing the rifle that, in her unthinking flight to Dakota, she's left on the other side of the room, "how is it that you can stand this white noise when we can't?"

Adam places a finger into his ear, then removes it, lowering his hand enough so that both women can easily see what looks to be a tiny microchip sitting on the pad. "The white noise you heard is a neural impulse interrupter, a very effective security measure. This chip completely neutralizes the effect, allowing its wearer free access to all levels of this facility."

Kirsten's eyes, already glittering slits of distrust, narrow further. "And just how were you able to score such a prize?"

With a soft laugh, Adam replies, "From Westerhaus himself, actually."

"Ah. I suppose he trusted you with his secrets so much that he just willingly gave up the keys to his kingdom. Very generous of him." She tenses, ready to make a play for the rifle.

"On the contrary. The only trust Peter Westerhaus gave was to his precious androids. This, I took from him. Not that it mattered at the time, as he certainly had no more use for it."

Kirsten thinks on this for a moment, then her face pales even as her eyes widen. "He's dead? Westerhaus is dead?"

"Oh yes. On the very date he set his final plan into motion, actually."

"Wha-at? But how?"

"By his own hand."

Kirsten's barked laugh is pure bitterness. "That figures. That just fucking figures. That yellow-bellied chickenshit coward was too spineless to even watch the destruction his fucked up plans created. Shit. Now what?"

"That, Doctor King, depends entirely on you."

"All right, that's it. How in the hell do you know my n—," Kirsten begins to rise, only to be halted by Koda's firm squeeze to her hand.

"You were the one who opened the shaft grate," Dakota says, eyeing Adam directly.

"Yes."

"And the retinal sensors?"

"Ah. That was Mr. Westerhaus's doing, actually." He grins at Koda's sharply raised eyebrow, though the smile fades as he eyes the microwave timer, counting down its last minutes. "We don't have much time. His inner sanctum is just down the hall. The answers you seek are there."

Kirsten still looks as if she wants to fight, but soon bows to the inevitable. She turns to Koda. "Maybe you should just—"

"No," Dakota quickly interjects. "We're in this together, remember? Just give me a minute and I'll be ready."

"Dakota—"

"Please."

A whole regiment of reasons why this is a very bad idea parade through her mind as Kirsten sighs and moves away, watching her lover intently as Dakota crosses her legs and closes her eyes. They open briefly, latching onto Adam. "This neural interrupter, is it a steady frequency, or does it pulse?"

"There is a pulse, regulated to the average human heartbeat. Sixty eight to seventy two pulses per minute."

"Thanks." Her eyes slide closed again and her breathing deepens as she journeys through her own body in the ways of her ancestors. Her skin cools as blood shunts to more vital organs. Her breathing and heart-rate slow. Her blood-pressure drops. When her eyes open, her pupils are dilated, like cat's eyes, taking in all available light. Slowly, she rises to her feet, her mind fully in the present, sharp as sunlit steel. The microwave counts out its final seconds. "Turn off your implants, love."

Her voice is slow, and deeper than Kirsten has ever heard it. She hastens to obey the order, for even pleasingly phrased, that's exactly what it is. Kirsten's world goes to silence just as the microwave timer "dings" its end.

A slight tremor in the long muscles of her thighs is Dakota's only response to the resumption of the neural interrupter. She eyes the two before her steadily and nods, once. "Let's go."

**True to his** word, Adam leads them down the hall only a few dozen yards before stopping at Westerhaus's door. Looking at it, Kirsten admits to herself a pang of disappointment. It is a door identical to the dozens of others they've passed — beige-painted metal, like might be seen on board the *Enterprise*. No deep mahogany with pure gold trim and cut crystal knob. No ostentatiously scrolled signs announcing for the peons that the Boy Genius is currently in residence. *Probably too paranoid,* she thinks with a mental shrug. Further examination is interrupted by a tug to her sleeve. She glances to Dakota's raised eyebrow, then to Adam, on her other side. He gestures to the door, then takes a deliberate step back, sending her nape hairs to sudden attention. Her gaze switches back to Dakota, who nods and gives her a small smile of encouragement.

Turning to the door, she takes in a deep breath, then steps forward until her eyes are level with the retinal scanner. At the same time, she presses her thumb against the print-and-DNA pad just beneath. She can't hear the soft hum of the processor, nor the faint click of the lock disengaging, but she can see the five red lights blink to green, and so is not surprised then the door slides open, displaying the interior of Westerhaus's office.

If the door itself is non-descript, the office within is anything but, though if the door reminds her of the *Enterprise*, that comparison is doubly reinforced by an interior that looks as if it's come straight off the Paramount lot. Touchscreen computers fit like puzzle pieces into a rainbow shaped glass table whose interior arc fronts a rather ordinary high-backed leather office chair. CPUs and server boxes rest on utilitarian tables, their processing lights blinking and strobing like signs over a carnival ride — one of the really scary ones where the rock music blares so loud that you can't hear yourself puke.

She finds herself drawn inward, Dakota's strong, soothing presence to her right, Adam's to her left and a step behind. Though she can't hear the door slide shut behind them, she's nevertheless aware that it does, and when it does, it brings with it a feeling of being, if not trapped, at least locked in, as if the last piece of the puzzle has finally fallen into place. *For better or for worse*, she knows, *it ends here.* There is nowhere left to run. There is nowhere left to look. There is nowhere left to hide. *It ends here. It all ends here.*

Her interest in computers somewhere in the horse latitudes, Dakota finds herself drawn instead to the myriad of security monitors arranged in long, neat rows, stacked one atop the other. The view on all the screens is blessedly monotonous. Empty rooms, empty corridors, empty stairwells, empty bathrooms, though the latter doesn't surprise her. The others, though... There are androids here. She can feel them, can feel their weight pressing in on her from above, like the sea during a dive. Her adrenals throb dully just above her kidneys and she closes her eyes, willing her heart to keep its slow, steady beat even as she becomes aware of the fact that Westerhaus's little security surprise hasn't filtered through into this, his inner sanctum.

*It ends here*, she thinks, opening her eyes to the still monotonous view of the security screens. *It all ends here.*

Kirsten, for her part, moves silently around the room, keeping her hands prudently away from the equipment, scanning everything with a sharp eye and a sharper mind. Scrolling along the bottom of most of the monitors is an alien script that seems almost...alive. Looking at it makes her, by turns, very uneasy and very dizzy as her brain tries to make sense of something for which it has no reference point. She looks quickly away, then up as Adam's smiling reflection comes to her in the glass of the table.

"You can turn your implants back on if you like," he says, smiling. "It's quite safe in here."

"That figures," Kirsten snorts, though her trust of this stranger doesn't quite extend quite so far as to take him completely at his word. Setting her left implant to its lowest gain, she flicks it on, ready to turn it back off again the very second something seems wrong. She relaxes as only the quiet sound of Dakota's breathing comes to her over the still, chill air.

Adam moves silently across the thick pile carpeting to a nook in the left rear corner of the office. An old coffee maker, dirty with the ghosts of coffees past, stands sentry on an impressive credenza, flanked by several equally stained mugs. A matching table stands at a right angle to the credenza, and upon that table rests an old, battered CPU, its nineteen inch monitor huge and bulky and as out of place among the sleek technology as a dinosaur in New York City.

"This was his personal computer," he remarks, fiddling with the mouse to bring the beast out of hibernation. "It has something on it that I believe you'll find very interesting."

Eyeing him warily, Kirsten slowly crosses the room until she is standing beside the much taller man, her face bathed in the ghostly glow of the monitor. Her brows pucker as she quickly scans the text, which looks as if it's been written by ee cummings on crack. It's a long, rambling vomit of words written by someone whose mind had clearly left him for far greener pastures quite some time before. "What is this?"

"Look at the header."

As she looks, her eyes widen. "Me? He wrote this to me??"

Adam nods.

"But...I never received anything like this. Hell, I've never received anything from him at all!" She looks closer, frowning. "Shit. I haven't used that email address in years."

"And yet you still came here."

"I had no choice."

"Indeed." Reaching out, Adam snags the office chair and pulls it over to Kirsten. "I would suggest reading this missive in detail. I believe it contains most, if not all, of the answers you're seeking."

Kirsten rubs her forehead as she looks down at the schizophrenic text again. "You sound like you already know what's in here, so how about we just cut to the chase and you explain it to me, hmm?"

Adam opens his mouth, then closes it as his attention is distracted by a faint blip on one of the monitors. "They're coming."

At his exclamation, Koda turns and stares at the monitor screens. Androids swarm along the corridors of the floors above, pouring down into the stairwell. Most are indistinguishable from humans to the eye, save for the thin metal collars about their necks. Some wear lab whites; others, security uniforms. All carry weapons: automatic rifles, pistols, stunguns. A couple of the guards sport larger-barrelled arms that look capable of firing tear-gas canisters, possibly even grenades. A second contingent, smaller but just as menacing, files into the elevator from the Institute's main lobby. There are perhaps forty of them. Thirty-five, easy.

*Goddam motherfucking metalheads.*

But there is no time. Koda vaults the desk where Kirsten sits looking at her with huge eyes and lunges for a bronze sculpture on the credenza behind. It is something abstract; a flame, perhaps, or a leaf.

A hammer.

"Guard her!" she snaps at Adam and streaks for the door, pausing only long enough to assure herself that it locks securely behind her. She spares a glance for the elevator, descending slowly, still three floors above them. The thunder of running feet on the stairs is much nearer. First things first.

"Dakota!" Kirsten shouts, leaping out of her chair and flying to the door, just as the lock snicks shut. "Dakota! Wait!" When the door doesn't open, she resorts to ineffectual pounding until some measure of reason returns and she turns on her heel, fixing Adam with a glare that could fuse metal. "Open this door!"

Adam shakes his head slowly. "I'm afraid that's not possible, Dr. King."

"Not possible? I'll show you what's not possible! Open this goddamned door! Now!"

"Dr. King, please. I understand—"

"You. Understand. Nothing!" The image would be laughable if it weren't so deathly serious: a woman, small even for her gender, in the face of a man a full foot taller, hands fisted in the springy fabric of his shirt, shaking him like a rag-doll in the hands of a child having a temper-tantrum. "She is more important than any of this! She is more important than all of this! Where she goes, I go. So open the fucking door right now."

To his credit, Adam doesn't look away from the green fire blazing in Kirsten's eyes. "I can't."

"Can't? Have your fingers suddenly lost the ability to work?!"

In answer, Adam gently pries Kirsten's hands from his shirt and turns her toward the bank of security monitors. Kirsten watches, grim-faced, as Dakota moves through the hallways — half cat, half snake — slithering noiselessly around corners and curves, sticking to the few shadows available.

"Her one chance, her only chance, to come through this alive rests in your hands, Dr. King. There are over one hundred and fifty androids in this facility at the present time. Not even the three of us working together could destroy them completely with conventional weapons. They need to be turned off at the source. You are the only one who can do that. And she is risking her life to buy you enough time to do what needs to be done. Don't let her actions be in vain, Dr. King."

She watches a moment longer, then turns slowly back to him, her hatred and anger making her face, for just a moment, both hideously ugly and terrifyingly beautiful. "Damn you," she says, her voice as soft and dead as the bottom of a grave. "Damn you straight to Hell."

**Turning the sculpture** so that the heavy base becomes the hammer's head, Dakota slams it down on the electronic keypad on the door to the stairwell. The lock shatters satisfyingly, tumbling to the floor tiles in shards of clear lexan and mangled circuit board. The keypad dangles loose, held by a thin strand of multi-colored wire. The steel bolt, though, remains in place. Reversing her improvised maul, Koda jabs the sharp end through the hole in the door, reaming out the remaining circuits and dislodging the mechanism on the other side. It falls onto the landing with a satisfying clatter.

It will not stop them. It will force them to break the door or go around the building to the other stairwell, and that will buy her time. Buy Kirsten time.

She whirls, still holding the sculpture in one hand. The elevator reaches the fifth level as she watches, its slow descent marked by the soft wheezing of its pneumatic pedestal. Without pausing to breathe, Koda unhooks one of the grenades from her belt, pulls the pin and stands waiting, counting the seconds. *Ten...nine...eight...*

On *Two*, the elevator door slides open. Koda pitches the grenade straight into the midst of the dozen androids packed shoulder to shoulder inside its car and whirls, throwing herself some ten feet down the corridor to land flat on her face. The roar of the explosion washes over her, echoing up and down the length of the six-story deep shaft. Panels of the door slam into the wall behind her, punctuated by a series of small secondary explosions as at least some of the droids' ammo goes up, the sound ripping through the air like strings of firecrackers. A fine dust drifts through the air, paint and graphite from the shredded drywall behind her.

She coughs once, hard, and scrambles to her feet. The frame of the elevator door curls back from the shaft in jagged metal sheets, its pale green paint burned and blistered. Several other fragments of the door and miscellaneous bits of droid anatomy protrude from the opposite wall, driven into the paneling by the force of the blast. Koda ducks around an especially wicked looking piece that juts halfway out into the passage, its edges bright and sharp as teeth. Holding on to an exposed stud, its metal hot under her hand, she peers into the remains of the elevator.

Half of it is gone, sheered away when the grenade hit its back wall. The remaining half shows little more than a square meter of flooring, held in place by the stump of the telescoping column rising from the lower levels and its now-skeletal frame. Half a droid hangs drunkenly over the far edge, poised above the black cavern below. A second lies half in, half out of the car. From under its torso, the stock and characteristic curving magazine of an AK protrude, together with the muzzle of some larger-bore weapon. Swiftly Koda pulls them both from under the remains of their recent owner. The AK seems to be intact. Aiming at the window in the stair door, she pulls the trigger and gives a satisfied grin when the plexiglass shatters in a rain of fragments. Two seconds' examination shows that the larger item is a shotgun, and another few seconds spent rifling the droid's jacket produces a handful of 12-gauge shells. Not as good as a grenade-launcher, but useful all the same. For the first time since barreling out of Wester-haus's office, she pauses to assess the situation.

The elevator: wrecked beyond use or repair.

Droid casualties: perhaps a dozen.

Captured weapons: two, both useful. She still has her own rifle and the sculpture, now tucked under her belt like a knife.

Advantage for the moment: good guys.

**For the first** time since she's met him, Adam looks a bit unsure. Walking to the credenza, he props a hip against one corner and seems inordinately interested in the weave of his slacks, long fingers brushing along the fabric as if searching for lint.

"It's difficult," he says softly, "to know where to begin."

"How 'bout I help you out, then," Kirsten replies, sarcasm firmly in place. "Peter Westerhaus, fair haired *wunderkind*, boon to all mankind, DaVinci, Edison, Bell, Franklin, and Einstein all rolled into one, invents the first working android. Nations fall at his feet. Blondes, brunettes, and red-heads fall at his feet. He quickly becomes the most important, not to mention richest, man in the world. More countries fall. More redheads fall. More money falls. And then, when that world least expects it, boom! Instant takeover." Her smile is as hard and as sharp as a rough-hewn diamond. "That pretty much cover it, Mr. Virgilius?"

His smile is wan. "On the surface of things, perhaps."

"Well, why don't you dig it a little deeper for me, then," she remarks, shooting a quick glance at the monitors, several of which show a blooming fireball shooting out from an elevator shaft. Her breathing eases as Dakota comes into view, apparently unharmed. "And make it quick or I'll tear down that door with my bare hands and leave you talking to yourself."

He looks at her for a long moment, then nods. "Peter Westerhaus was an extremely...disturbed individual." He holds up a hand to forestall Kirsten's scathing comeback. "Yes, I know you're well aware of that, Doc-tor. It is said that many, if not most geniuses of his type share that particu-lar trait, that brain chemicals which allow extreme creativity and inventiveness also bring with them many kinds of madness, often in the same person."

"Spare me the biology lecture, Virgilius. Get to the point, if you have one."

"Symptoms of what I believe to be schizophrenia were present for many years, long before I came to work for him. There were many stories of the man talking to himself — not, ordinarily, a horrible thing to do, but the reports also stated that he was answering himself, and in voices different than his own. Based on these voices, many workers were convinced that he had a secret partner working with him, but when he was approached, he was always alone." A wan smile is displayed again. "His interest in robotics and, by extension, android development seems to have been what one might term a classic case of a son trying to win his father's love. You are aware, I'm sure, of Wilhelm Westerhaus, Genitetec's CEO?"

"My heart bleeds for the whole fucking family," Kirsten replies. "Can we please just get on with it?"

"It was the younger Westerhaus's lifetime goal to win his father's respect, if not his love. It was his greatest disappointment when the first working android was completed and his father was not there to see it, having died some months before. But the breaking point came two years later, when his mother, whom he adored, was killed in a terrorist attack in Morocco, where she was vacationing with her new beau. Peter was never the same after that. He went into seclusion, in this very office, and his mental status, fragile as it was, began to deteriorate at a dangerously rapid pace. He told some of his fellows, the few he would allow into this sanctum, that God had spoken to him."

"God."

"God."

"And what did God say to the little bastard?"

"That he was the Chosen One, placed on this Earth not to destroy it, but to save it."

"Save it?" Kirsten shouts, shooting up from her chair, eyes blazing. "Save it? In case you haven't noticed, Mr. Virgilius, this world is ruined! His creations have murdered millions! Probably billions! Men! Women! Children! Adam, they're murdering children!"

Adam drops his eyes. "Yes," he replies softly. "I'm well aware of that."

"Then answer me the only question I give a shit about right now. Why?"

Adam nods. "I can do that."

**A sudden jab** of pain rips through Koda's chest, and she breathes deeply, willing her heart rate and respiration again below the threshold frequency of Westerhaus's little beeper from Hell. The calm finds its center just under her sternum, spreads, slipping along her nerves until her whole body poises on the sharp edges of awareness, every object, every color sharp in her sight, every sound as keen as the rustle of a mouse under the snow to a hunting owl.

Silence.

The droids have either halted their charge or retreated from the stairwell. Ducking to avoid the broken window in the door, Koda leans against the steel panel, listening. Just audible, she can hear the shuffle of feet now floors above her, retreating toward the upper levels. She has a couple of minutes, maybe less, to break the lock on the other stairwell.

Shouldering the two extra guns, she sprints along the corridor that runs the circumference of the building. A third of the way around the curve, she catches sight of the scarlet EXIT sign above the door to the second stair. No time for finesse on this one. Slinging her M-16 behind her shoulder, Koda braces the shotgun against her hip and fires.

The blast blows the lock mechanism to confetti, small fragments ricocheting off the bolt to pepper the wall opposite. Most of the debris, though, falls onto the landing on the other side. She cannot be sure in the echo from the shot, but it seems to her that sounds of feet shuffling on the steps have slowed. *Not so eager to run into a 12-guage, are ya, hotshots? That'd blow even your printed-circuit brains out.*

Koda bends to inspect the bolt, which shows bright nicks from both the shot and the flying shards of the door. It remains firmly in its socket, though, just where she wants it. Working quickly, she wires a detonator to the underside of the bar, leaving the length of copper dangling. She has perhaps half a kilo of plastique left. She kneads the powder into the malleable paste that gives it its name, then stuffs it down between the door panels, where it adheres nicely to the braces between the steel sheets. She molds it carefully, spreading it upward so that explosive and blasting cap make contact where the bolt runs out of sight into the door jamb.

She pauses for a moment, listening once again for the tread of feet on the stairs. If they want the door open, the plastique will do the job. It will also, if they don't spread out too far up the steps, blow the lot of them right into the middle of next February. The charge she has set is enough to destroy a truck; it ought to be equal to taking out a dozen droids or so. Which leaves the party coming up the other staircase, with their weapons and their unwavering programmed purpose and their steel and titanium bodies and lifetime batteries.

Which leaves her, two good automatic weapons, a shotgun and a single grenade as all that remains between them and Kirsten. All that remains between them and an inhuman Hell.

Carefully, Koda pulls the cotter pin that will prime the detonator. She cannot defend two positions at once. She will have to trust that the C-4 will take out most of one party while she deals with the second.

And hope that Kirsten and Adam can deal with any who manage to get past her.

*Take care of her, Adam. For all the gods' sake, take care of her. She's the only one who can win the world back. Every last one of the rest of us is expendable. Every last single one.*

The sound of feet on the stairs above sends her sprinting down the corridor. The curve of the hallway will give her some cover, but she needs more; she needs a barricade. As she runs — not full out, because that could send her heart rate soaring — the first sounds of battering come from the stair door behind her. The blows reverberate like the pounding of a great drum, metal smashing into metal with the mechanical regularity of arms and shoulders fashioned from steel and titanium fiber. The detonator has an eight-second delay. She counts it off with the rhythm of the blows, each one hammering through the building like a thunderclap.

The explosion, when it comes, shakes the floor beneath her feet, the sound washing over her like a physical force. Koda stumbles with it, breaking her fall only by clutching at the handle of a door. She swings from it crazily for a second, holding on while equilibrium reasserts itself. From around the curve of the hallway comes a second wave of sound, a tumbling and crashing almost like a rockslide. No doubt some of the wall has come down with the door. With luck the blast has also taken out a flight of stairs, tumbling the reinforced concrete steps down to shatter against the landing below.

With luck, the blast set nothing on fire.

With luck, there are no survivors.

Somewhere, sometime, the luck is going to run out.

There is nothing she can use as a barricade. Westerhaus, cautious or paranoid depending on how you look at it, has constructed his sanctum to give no cover for uninvited guests, be they sightseers or corporate saboteurs. The hall curves smoothly around the core of the Institute with not so much as a water fountain to obstruct the line of sight. Even the pictures lie flat against the walls, mounted without wire or frames that could be abstracted and used as weapons.

*Goddam security freak.*

She tries the handle that broke her fall. The room is unlabeled, the door locked. So is the next, and the next.

*Goddam security freak... Is bound to have a security station somewhere on his personal floor. A security station with weapons, maybe riot gear.* Returning the way she came, Koda begins shooting out the locks of the doors. A glance inside the first shows a supply room, stacked to the ceiling with paper and spare computer gear. The second contains a long teakwood table and armchairs: conference center. The third, a bathroom, complete with shower, lined in Spanish tile. Ahead of her, from the staircase by the ruined elevator, she can hear the blows begin to rain down on the door now held only by its bolt. She has perhaps seconds, no more.

The room closest to the office yields paydirt. Ranged on a desk that runs round the angle of the room, security monitors flicker with the activity on the floor. Mostly lack of it; except for the camera trained on the elevator and the exit from the staircase, all show empty halls. As Koda scrambles to strap on a Kevlar vest and snatch up a riot shield, she notes with satisfaction that the C-4 has done its work. A great, gaping hole in the outer wall of the corridor opens into nothingness. Bits and pieces of droids litter the floor. No survivors.

From the stairwell comes a crash as the door bursts open. *Ina Maka,* she breathes soundlessly, *Holy Mother. For all your Earth, help me now.* Thrusting her arm through the strap, Koda lifts the shield and steps out into the hall.

**"After his mother** died, Peter, a confirmed agnostic, became somewhat obsessively interested in the Judeo-Christian bible."

"The children, Virgilius. The children!"

Adam raises a hand. "Please. For any of this to make sense, I must tell it chronologically."

"We're running out of time," Kirsten replies, her heart in her throat as she watches her lover mow through a group of androids.

"We will have time for this," he responds, getting up to pace the confines of the cluttered room. "He was particularly interested in the Book of Genesis, where Man was given dominion over the Earth, and also entrusted to be its caretaker."

"I'm familiar with the relevant texts, Virgilius. Get on with it."

"In his sickness, Peter believed that God had come to him, stating that humans had, as he put it, 'worn out their welcome'. They had taken the world given to them and had raped it — for food, for shelter, for the ability to travel long distances, for technology."

"There's irony for you," Kirsten retorts, chuckling. "Mr. Technology himself, God's sword against technology. Oh yeah, a laugh riot, as my father used to say." She props her head on one fist. "So, he invents the androids, ingratiates his inventions with the common man, and, when they least expect it...pow. Technology one, humanity zero. God, Westerhaus, and the Earth, the new Blessed Trinity." Her smile is sour. "That still doesn't explain why women are being raped and their infants murdered."

"The first androids he developed were never meant to hold steward-ship over the Earth, Doctor. Yes, they can be programmed to reap or to sow, to build or to destroy, but that is all that they can do. They cannot cre-ate. They cannot reason. They cannot make decisions based on logic, or even illogic, if they have not been programmed to make those decisions."

"Meaning that Maid Marion can't become Construction Joe unless it's reprogrammed."

"Exactly," Adam replies, smiling. "For all their seeming worth and indestructibility, androids lack the one thing that is needed to be a care-taker."

Kirsten's face pales as the answer comes to her. "A thinking brain," she whispers, stunned by the horror of it. "Dear God! He invented a sen-tient android!"

**Pulling the pin** on her last grenade, Koda waits for the unhurried march of the droids' feet to carry them around the curve of the hall. She stands to one side, behind the open door of the security station, the riot shield raised to protect her unhelmeted head. For a second, no more, she sinks deep into her mind's center, steadying her heart, pacing her lungs and diaphragm, extending and sharpening her senses. Hard against her ribs, she feels the measured beat of her heart, the thrum of her blood in her veins. Her senses sharpen, so that the light shimmers in the empty hallway and her ears separate, exquisitely, the individual footfalls as the enemy approaches her. She waits.

With two seconds to go, the first half dozen round the curve at a trot. Koda releases the grenade, her arm swinging high, up and overhand. It arcs down in the midst of the group, ripping the clothing and front plates off two, toppling them backward to trip a third that goes down on its face, its weapon discharging under it as it strikes the floor. It does not rise again. Another, its legs blown away at midthigh, stands on its stumps with wires trailing loose. It has dropped its weapon and repetitively swivels its head from side to side, reciting in a high, flat voice, "Circuit 456, check. Voder, check. Color card, check. Accelerator card, check. Circuit 456, check." One of its colleagues, still on its feet, kicks it unceremoniously to the side, steps over the fallen and doggedly comes on.

Koda allows it to come on unopposed until it stands within ten feet. Shouldering the 12-gauge, she fires, and sends its head sailing back from its shoulders to land with a clang against the metal corpses on the floor and then roll clattering along the hallway. She shoves another shell into the breech and sends the last of the party reeling headless into the wall. It stalls there, its chest against the wall, its feet moving in spastic small steps that carry it nowhere.

Advantage: still the good guys.

Koda grins and darts forward, avoiding the crater gouged by the explosion. Like the walls, the floors of the Westerhaus Institute are meter-thick reinforced concrete, meant to survive the legendary Big One that has yet to carry California out to sea. She kneels, rummaging briefly among the droid casualties for useful objects. One, bless his metal head, yields more shotgun shells; another she robs of the extra magazines he carries at his belt. For half a second, she considers pulling the remains together to form a barrier, but there is not enough shattered and twisted metal to provide an effective delay, much less block the passage altogether. Better to leave them as they lie. At worst, the next wave will have to go around them. At best, they may become tangled in the metal struts and twisting cables.

At the sound of feet in the corridor, Koda steps free of the metal tangle, retreating to her position behind the security room door. For half a second, she glances back toward Westerhaus's office, wishing for some sign, any sign, that Kirsten has made headway in her search for the code.

*Because this isn't going to work much longer. Sooner or later, they're going to come down that hall in a rush, and it's all going to be over.*

But what comes this time is not a mass advance but a single set of footsteps, walking quietly, deliberately. They halt just beyond the curve of the wall, just out of sight, just beyond range. A voice, male and mellow and suffused with gentle reason, says, "Dr. Rivers? This is unnecessary. May we talk?"

For answer, Koda picks up her rifle and sends a round speeding into the wall just ahead of where the speaker must be standing. "That's all I've got to say, bastard! You got anything you want to add?"

A figure steps out into the hallway, perhaps five yards ahead of her. He — or *it*, she reminds herself fiercely, *it* — wears flannel shirt and jeans, the toes of well-worn boots showing below the frayed hems of the legs. Crinkles show at the corners of his blue eyes, and his hair, brushed carefully across his forehead, is as white as salt.

"Now, Dr. Rivers," he says, "Dakota — you're making a terrible mistake here. You're throwing your life away for—" palms up, his hands gesture widely—"for what? It doesn't have to be like this. Indeed, it doesn't."

*It's a droid*, she reminds herself. *Just a very, very lifelike droid. Never mind that it looks like everybody's favorite uncle.* "Okay," she says. "Turn yourselves off. All of you, you included. Then it won't have to 'end like this'." She practically spits the last words and feels her heart give a painful jump. Consciously, she damps down her anger. They want emotion. They want her to fall prey again to the neural scrambler or whatever the hell the damned thing is.

"Hardly." Again, the open, reasonable gesture. "Hear me. Enough of your people have died. We have what we need, for years to come. We will leave you in peace. You and other humans can live out your lives in the normal way. You need not fear us."

The strange thing is, Koda is not even tempted. What the droid offers is not entirely unreasonable; it is the bargain made by the slaver with the enslaved, the butcher with the cattle. *This time we will only take so many of you. The rest may live. Until the next time. And the time after that.*

"I've seen what you've done!" she yells. "Fuck you and your deals!"

"You haven't heard my offer."

"Let me guess: give up Kirsten King and we can all walk out of here." She draws a long, hard, steadying breath. Every second she can keep the thing talking helps Kirsten, brings her that much closer to the answer. "No."

"You will die then, both of you. You need not."

"Make me a better offer."

"You will live. She will not suffer, I promise you."

"I said *a better offer*, bastard!"

"There is none. Yes or no. Now."

"Well, then." Koda drops her shield and steps around the edge of the door. "I guess I'll just have to say—"

The droid waits, not speaking. With reflexes so swift she has no time to plan the maneuver, Koda whips the shotgun up and blows the droid's head assembly open. "—no."

**"Yes," Adam replies,** coming to stand before her. "It took many years, many failures, but yes, he invented an android that was able to think for itself."

"How?" Kirsten demands, her hand slapping hard on the table. "How in the hell did he do that?"

Adam pauses for a moment, pursing his lips and sliding his fingers along the ribbed collar of his shirt. "Most of the preliminary work, or what passed for it at the time, had been done decades before Westerhaus was born. Mapping hardwiring and microchip technology to living tissue was hardly a new field by the time the first androids had been developed. Spinal cord regeneration, the Navy's use of rats as cameras, even the Alzheimer's work had moved from theory into accepted standards of practice for the time. But that," he continues, spreading his hands, "obviously wasn't enough. And even if it were possible to wire a human brain like a Christmas tree and dump it into the shell of an android, that still wouldn't work."

"Because it would still, essentially, be human."

"Exactly. So the problem needed to be approached from another angle." He pauses again, head tilted in thought. "Do you remember the spate of child abductions in Washington DC a decade or so ago?"

Kirsten thinks for a moment. "I think so. From orphanages mostly. Some from hospitals. A few from their own cribs. They never captured the kidnappers or found the bod...ies..." Her eyes widen. "No. Please don't tell me that he..."

"Yes. He did."

"But why?" Kirsten shouts, pounding the table with a closed fist. "Why the goddamned children?"

"Genetics," Adam answers. "And the ability to produce a compound that, with a little outside help, will turn a regular drone into a member of Westerhaus's Master Race."

"Stop speaking in riddles, man! We don't have time to... Oh my God." She rises to her feet slowly, bone-pale face cupped in suddenly shaking hands. "Oh my God. It's Growth Hormone, isn't it? Human Growth Hormone. There were trials, not so long back, connecting it with nerve regeneration..."

"Precisely. A genetic marker is injected into the child, causing a pituitary adenoma. Within six months to a year, depending upon the age of the child injected, the adenoma forms and begins to produce Human Growth Hormone in great quantities. When the levels reach their peak, the hormone is...harvested, and the donor is then euthanized."

"Euthanized? You mean murdered!"

"Yes," Adam replies, looking down at his shoes. "They were murdered. Are still being murdered, all in the name of science...and...humanity. In some way that I'm not fully aware of, the hormone imparts sentience to the android circuits. It was the ingredient that Mr. Westerhaus was lacking all these years. When he found it, he cried. Not in sorrow, but in joy."

He doesn't expect the right cross that connects, with deadly precision, at the point of his chin. His hands fly up as he stumbles back, crashing against the credenza and sending the coffee pot and mugs clattering to the ground.

"You son of a bitch!" Kirsten growls, stalking him like a wolf on the hunt. "You goddamned motherfucking son of a bitch! You knew this was happening. You knew it, and you did nothing to stop it!"

"I couldn't stop it," he replies, making no attempt to ward off her blows. "There was no way for me to stop it. But you, Doctor King, you can."

Some of what he's said eventually gets through and her punches weaken, then stop altogether and she stands like a toy soldier whose spring has wound down. "How," she demands, voice rough from shouting and muffled by the tears she's trying desperately to hold in. "Tell me how."

With gentle hands, he turns her and guides her to the main desk. The alien script continues to scroll across the bottom in an endless, nauseating stream. "For months," he begins softly, "I have attempted to decipher this string of code, but found no reference point in all my research with which to even begin. The Rosetta Stone, as it were, came in the email he addressed to you. The one that, unfortunately, you never received. You, Doctor King, are the key. At some point prior to his suicide, he must have had second thoughts. It is my belief that he encoded a...backdoor, if you will, an escape hatch through which all of this could be undone. And you are the only person in this world who can decipher it."

"Why? What's so damned special about me?"

"You are his greatest adversary, and aside from the fact that your brilliance in these matters equals his..."

**The droid slumps** to the floor to lie among the other wreckage, and Koda takes two quick steps back into the security station. A glance about the rank of monitors shows the remaining squad splitting into two parties, the second setting off down the hall in the opposite direction. The first contingent, hovering just beyond range beyond the curve, does not move.

*Of course not. They're going to wait for the other bunch to come around behind and then attack from both directions. Can't let that happen.*

She has two automatic weapons left, one shotgun, and one nameless piece of sculpture. If she does not deal with the nearer group now, she will be trapped. Worse, she will leave Westerhaus's office and Kirsten exposed to at least one of the parties and it will all be over. Kirsten will die, and the world will be at the mercy of Westerhaus's creations for years, perhaps for generations. Perhaps forever.

*Can't let that happen.*

Koda slings the AK over one shoulder, dropping her M-16 into her hands. The shotgun will not serve her here. Neither will stealth.

Steeling herself against the pain she knows will follow, Koda bursts out of the security station, running full out for the curve and the smaller droid party still waiting. She knows to the millisecond when her heart rate rises to normal by the stab of sudden agony through her chest. Her legs still work, though, and her hands. That is all that matters.

She skids around the curve running full out, and as she comes within sight of the enemy party she jerks her finger spasmodically down on the trigger, spraying the width of the hallway from side to side. Amid the staccato rhythm of the M-16 she can hear the impact of slugs on metal as they find their marks, droids going down before her assault, others bringing their own guns up to fire, stuttering out an answer to her onslaught. A round whizzes by her head, close enough for her to feel the wind of its passage. Another strikes her squarely in the center of her Kevlar vest, a bruising blow, and white heat blossoms in her chest, stealing her breath. She ignores it, throwing down the M-16 when its magazine empties and feeling the solid slap of the AK into her hands in its stead. And then she is firing again in long sweeps, not taking time to aim, catching her massed targets in their sensor arrays, their legs, the solid, unyielding mass of their torsos. One holds a round thing in its hand, its dark metal surface scored, and Koda aims high, going for its wrist. The thing drops and rolls among the droids, but none of them seems to notice it as they spray bullets toward her and she dodges low, feinting to one side, dodges again. Something stings along her own leg, something else on her left shoulder, but she cannot take time to look as she grits her teeth against the havoc under her sternum, and fires and fires and fires again. And again. And again.

The trigger under her cramped finger clicks on empty. Perhaps twenty seconds have passed since she rounded the curve of the hall. The droids lie scattered over the floor, some riddled with holes through the body, others more neatly dispatched with gaping cavities in their sensor arrays. Torn wires and a thin stream of yellow-green lubricant snake along the tiles. Koda's breath comes in hard, dry gasps, as the pain of the wounds in leg and shoulder crashes in on her, joining with the ramping agony in her chest. She leans over at the waist, her hands on her knees, and forces her breath to slow, forces it to regularity, bringing her heart under control and with it the pain that threatens to wash her away in its red tide. There is something wet under her hand, and when she raises her palm to look, dark blood drips to the floor. Dark blood.

Venous blood.

She is not bleeding to death, at least not at the moment. A quick inspection shows her a matching wound on the back of her thigh. Clean penetration, then. Red streaks the angle of her shoulder, a rip through her shirt showing blood and grazed skin beneath. "Just a graze, ma'am." Graze be damned. The thing is painful out of all proportion to the damage, worse at the moment than the hole in her leg. But that is because her body has not had time to process the greater damage. The wound will hurt. That is a certainty.

Without warning, the corridor before her explodes in smoke and fire. Koda throws herself backward, hands flying to protect her head as the grenade lifts shattered metal and plexiglass into the air, spraying it like shrapnel into walls and ceiling. A splinter of steel drives itself into the back of her left hand, and blood runs chill down onto her face. Silence follows.

Koda pulls the splinter out of the space between two of the tendons that stand forth against her skin, fanning out from her wrist. Levering her feet under her, she stumbles over to the wreckage. One droid moves a hand, and she loosens the sculpture from her belt and methodically pounds its head to bits. Then she picks up her guns, slots new magazines in under the stocks, and limps back to the security center.

The screens show the last group of droids somewhere around the curve of the building, how far or near she cannot tell. She has no landmarks to go by; she only knows they are somewhere on the long way around between her position and the still smoking crater in the hall. Presumably they know the first party has failed. Presumably they also know she is wounded and running low on ammunition. Running low on strategy. Running low on strength.

She bends to examine the hole in her leg a second time. A thin stream of blood pulses from it, scarlet, bright with new oxygen. She swears softly. The bullet must have nicked the artery. She must have torn it open when she dived for the floor. She unwinds her bandana from her neck and cinches it as tightly as she can over the hole in her jeans. Pressure will help. Temporarily, anyway. But then, everything is temporary now.

*I wonder,* she thinks idly as she checks her magazines once again, *I wonder if it's true that sometimes we get to go back in time. Think I'd like something Pre-Columbian next go-round if we do. Cahokia, maybe. Mound-Builders — Kirsten would like that. Not sure the future world is anything I want to be born into. Should have asked Wa Uspewikakiyape when I had the chance. Should have another chance soon enough.*

A flicker of movement on one of the monitors catches her eye. The droids are moving.

They come in a rush this time. Koda hears them before she sees them, their feet drumming in perfect, mechanical unison. If she stays in here, she will be trapped. It will only take one droid, one gun, and then the way into Westerhaus's office will lie open to them.

She slips out of the room and behind the door again. Its armor will give some little protection, for some little time. She braces the AK against the edge of the panel, waiting only for the contingent to come into sight. The thunder of running feet stops somewhere just around the curve, then nothing. Silence. The quiet stretches on and on, until she begins to wonder if the grenade blast has partially deafened her. She could go back and check the monitors. They might have split again, be coming at her from both directions again. But that's what they want her to do. It would give them a clear shot at her. One. All it would take.

She waits, while the blood trickles down her leg and arm, while her muscles stiffen. Waits.

*Bastards. Goddam game of nerves.*

*Won't break. Can't.*

A single droid steps into the corridor, in clear sight. She fires just as an object leaves its hand, arching up in a perfect parabola to clear the top of the door and come straight down on her, bursting into flame as it descends. She throws herself against the wall, but it rakes against her arm, spreading flame down her sleeve and across the covering of her Kevlar vest. Rolling, she smothers the fire that licks at her shirt and down the leg of her jeans, not even feeling the heat as she kicks the incendiary away from her and back out into the hall. It burns sullenly on the tiles, black smoke billowing up to choke her. She glances down to check the damage.

The ruins of her sleeve hang limply from her wrist. The skin beneath has already begun to blister. Worse, the vest now dangles by a single strap, its armored plates slipping loose beneath the cloth. Useless. She shrugs out of it, leaving it where it lies. No time, no way, to get another.

She snatches up her rifle again and waits.

They round the curve of the hallway in a mass. The AK jars against her shoulder as she sprays the rounds across their line, shaking her bones one against another, sending a chill trickle of blood down across her chest. Another incendiary plummets down over the door, striking its edge and falling wide to spill flame across the floor behind her. Their return fire clangs against the sheet steel of the door, a round breaking through the lexan window above and showering her with a myriad of dull-edged fragments. One droid breaks wide from the mass and dashes toward her position, keeping to the far wall. *Oh no you don't. Bastard. You want by me, you gotta kill me first.* She puts a spurt of rounds through its head, and it tumbles down on the sputtering fire bomb, its uniform bursting into flame.

But the rest come on undeterred, so close now she can see the colored rings of their optical sensors. If she does not move, she will be trapped against the wall as surely as she would have been in the guard post.

A high scream like a hawk's rips out of her throat, as she stands and swings around the edge of the door, raking the enemy line with fire. Two stumble and fall, but the rest come inexorably on. Something slams into her body at the level of her right hipbone, sending her staggering back a step as she empties one magazine and slings the second gun around into her hands, its frame juddering against her palm as she jerks the trigger back and holds it. Searing heat strikes through her left shoulder, and her arm suddenly goes slack, the muzzle of her gun dropping. She props it against her side, never breaking the rhythm of her fire. Another droid falls. Another.

Her gun falls silent. No more bullets.

A hail of automatic fire bursts from in front of her. Pain rakes across her body, the claws of some great beast slashing her from hip to shoulder. Blood soaks the front of her shirt, a red rain that splashes against the floor. A shadow passes over her eyes, clears, returns. Sounds take on an abnormal clarity. She hears the clatter of her rifle as it hits the floor, bouncing end for end. And she hears the rattle of a grenade as it rolls across the tiles to bump against her foot.

She cannot breathe. Her ribs have become a vise pressing down on her lungs, squeezing the life from her. The iron taste of blood is on her tongue, welling up from somewhere deep in her body. With exquisite slowness, exquisite precision, she reaches down, grasps the grenade, and heaves it at the line of droids. A roar like the voice of a waterfall, the rage of a thousand thunders rolls over her, and she stumbles backward against the door of Westerhaus's office. It gives way behind her, and she tumbles into the abyss.

Adam turns suddenly toward the door, horror on his face. Kirsten turns to look as Koda tumbles through and falls across the threshhold, her body bloodstained from neck to thigh, a thin runnel of scarlet at the corner of her mouth. Her eyes stare upward at nothing, pupils fixed, lifeless.

# CHAPTER FORTY-EIGHT

Kirsten feels her mouth go as dry as old cotton. A wave of dizziness passes over her; darkness steals her sight. Her breath leaves her lungs in what must be a scream, but she cannot hear it, cannot think. Her whole world has narrowed to the long body sprawled on the floor. Somehow her legs, gone all to water, carry her the two steps necessary, and she falls on her knees beside her lover. "Sweetheart?" she calls softly, laying her hand on one broad, too-still shoulder.

*Blood. So much blood.*

"Koda? Sweetheart? It's okay now. You're okay. You're safe. It's okay." Seeing the tiny runnel of blood from Dakota's lips, Kirsten rips the sleeve from her shirt and gently dabs it away, deliberately ignoring the fact that her lover's chill skin has the consistency of rubber and not hearing — deliberately again — the sound of Dakota's bottom lip as it springs back against her teeth with a soft "plop". "You always hate being dirty, don'tcha," Kirsten says with an over-bright smile. "But that's okay. I'm sure there are showers around here somewhere. Right, Adam?"

Unable to meet Kirsten's eyes, Adam looks down, then turns to the remains of the door. The view of the hallway is like looking into Armageddon. The sprinklers, though keeping the fire from spreading, are doing nothing to dampen its anger. As he watches, a large chunk of melted ceiling tile falls onto the floor with a great clatter. Bits and pieces of androids lie scattered everywhere, like the playground toys of children just called home for dinner. Dakota has indeed brought them time. How much, he can't begin to fathom, but every second counts now. With a soft grunt, he picks up the crumpled door and positions it best he can across the frame, pushing with all his might. The metal is hot to the touch. In some places, it smokes, but he ignores the pain and continues to fit the door back where it belongs, hoping that this final barrier will, somehow, hold.

When he turns back, Kirsten has gathered Dakota in her arms. The taller woman's head lolls back lifelessly until it lies almost between her shoulder blades. Without a change in her expression, Kirsten simply gathers her lover's head and moves it forward so that it is cradled against her shoulder. "It's okay, my love," she croons into an unhearing ear. "Everything's okay now. It is. You'll see."

Gathering all of his courage, Adam crosses the short distance between them and lays a gentle hand on Kirsten's shoulder. "Doctor King."

"Leave me alone!" Kirsten growls, not looking up as her hand continues to mindlessly stroke the mass of thick, black, blood-soaked hair.

"Please, Doctor."

"Just go away!"

"I can't. We need to finish this."

"It can wait," Kirsten replies in a soft, gentle voice. "Until Dakota's well again. Right, sweetheart? That's the important thing. Getting you well. The most important thing."

"Doctor King, please. I'll keep watch over her, I promise you. You need to finish this now, before there's no time left!"

"Do you think I give a shit about that?" she snarls, teeth bared like a predator ready to fight.

"Don't you think she would?" Adam asks, gesturing to the woman in Kirsten's arms.

For a moment, just a moment, sanity returns to Kirsten's eyes, and Adam finds himself totally unprepared for the blast of unshielded emotion directed his way. Anger, grief, horror, despair. It's all there, mixed together with a hundred other emotions he can't even begin to identify. "Please, Doctor. The world needs you."

"Fuck. The. World. Fuck humanity. Fuck the androids. Fuck Peter fucking Westerhaus, and fuck you too."

With a soft sigh, Adam releases his grip on Kirsten's shoulder and takes a step back. "You know," he comments quietly, in an offhand manner, "she was an incredibly brave woman, who gave everything to make sure that you had this one chance." His voice firms, becoming almost harsh as he stares at the bowed back of Kirsten's head. "Make sure you take it, Doctor King."

Kirsten can feel the anger seethe through her, like a runaway express train headed to nowhere. Part of her aches to grab hold, to jump on and ride it through to its inevitable end, anything to rid her of this numb, dreaming feel of unreality and utter emptiness. Another part of her, however, knows that if she gives in, she will shatter, as surely as glass shatters when it falls to the floor.

Very deliberately, she relaxes the arm holding her lover to her body and uses the other to stroke the bloody bangs from Dakota's pale, waxen face. "Wait for me," she whispers, before laying Dakota's body on the floor and carefully arranging her limbs into a pose that looks as if she is merely sleeping. With a half sob that she cuts off savagely, she leans forward and places a kiss on chill lips. "I'll be with you soon."

**The impact as** her body hits the floor jars along her bones, but somehow, strangely, its solidity does not break her fall. She plunges through it into the void, an infinity of night that spins about her as she tumbles through it like a dark comet, all its light and glory spent. Here and there the blackness thins, and she glimpses distant points of light that may be stars, glowing wisps like nebulae, the final blaze of dying suns. Wind beats at her as she falls, stripping her sight from her, scouring her skin. Voices ride on its current, strange whispers that seem half-familiar, half-alien. She strains to hear, but the wind drowns them, all but fragments. Threaded in among the voices, high, wild laughter skims along its current, echoing against the walls of night that close in about her.

"...replaced me, knew you would..."

"...bright for a prairie nigger, but still..."

"...left me to die..."

"...I said, your *Christian* name, girl..."

"...just need a man, bitch..."

"...could have saved him if you'd tried..."

"...couldn't protect her. Dead...dead..."

"...all dead, all dead..."

"...your fault..."

"...your fault *your* fault YOUR faultfaultfaultfault..."

The wind batters at her like breaking waves, slamming her as she begins to spin on the axis of her spine. Except that she has no spine, has no bones, no flesh, no skin. Under the incessant assault, she feels herself begin to fragment. She tries to draw in upon herself, reflexing into a knot with knees drawn up and arms crossed over her breast. But her muscles do not answer her, do not exist. A part of her tears away to go spinning back the way she has come, whirling down the spiral path that leads toward Earth, back toward life.

A part of her consciousness clings to it as it bursts free of the darkness to hover over the sprawl of her body, and she regards it curiously. Blood stains it from thigh to neck, pools on the floor around it, begins to grow viscous at the edges of its flow. At the desk not far away, Kirsten sits before a computer screen, face pale as her hair, mouth a thin line of control. Her fingers fly over the keyboard. Her concentration armors her, but beyond it lies a holocaust of pain raw as stripped flesh. It calls to her, calls her name.

Even in death. Even in death.

Even in death, I will never leave you.

The winds take her again, and awareness of the earthbound fragment fades. Their force spins her through the darkness, whirling faster and faster as the circumference of her self draws inward, concentrating her essence. Without warning she bursts forth into the starlight of a summer night, floating somewhere above a narrow valley where a stream runs silver in the moonlight and hummingbird moths fumble at the spires of paintbrush and lupine. A big dog lies among the flowers on one slope; he looks up and whines as she passes. *Peace*, she wishes him. And, *stay*. Then she is gone, carried up and over the shadowed landscape, skimming the energy lines that stretch like cobwebs from the sacred mountains in the lands of the Dine far to the south, to the sleeping cones of Grandfather and Little Sister in the north, that the whites call Ranier and St. Helen, to the Black Hills far to the east.

But distance has no meaning to her now. With the thought, she is there, the Paha Sapa rising jagged up out of the plain, the place of her people's beginnings. *Here we came forth. Here we became human, came forth to live in the light of Wiyo on the surface of Ina Maka.*

At the foot of the barren slopes lies a stretch of forest. A clearing shows pale where the pines stand back from a ribbon of bright water and a spoked circle of stones laid out on the short grasses. She wills herself downward. A mule deer buck, his antlers still in velvet, browses among the undergrowth. He startles for a moment, then placidly resumes his feeding. In the branches a screech owl stirs, its burbling call blending with the rush of water in the small stream that tumbles down from the bare mountains above. Koda settles in the center of the medicine wheel and waits.

After a time, she hears a thin thread of song. It grows stronger as it approaches, a woman's voice, chanting in Lakota.

See me.
See me.
My steps on the Earth
Are sacred.

The voice comes nearer, still singing.
Hear me.

Hear me.
My words to the People
Are sacred.

A bright shimmer appears at the northern edge of the clearing. It moves toward her, and as it does, the figure of a woman takes shape within it. Rainbows dance in the light that surrounds her, striking fire from the rock crystal of her headband and armlets, running blue and violet over the fall of her hair.

Understand.
Understand.
All things in the hand of Wakan Tanka
Are sacred.

The woman of light halts before her, close enough to touch. She stands tall and slender, eyes great pools of shadow, her skin smooth and unmarked as the new bark of the madrone. A buffalo, worked in beads made from the pearl lining of mussel shells, adorns the white buckskin of her dress. *All things*, she sings, *all that is created, is sacred.*

*Han,* says Koda without sound, her gaze lowered in respect. *It is so.*
*It is so,* the woman answers. *You know me.*
*Wohpe,* she says. *White Buffalo Calf Woman.*
*Han. You walk the Blue Road, sister.*
At that she looks up. *I know.* She hesitates a moment. Then, *Is there—*
*—another way? But you have seen your body.* A gentle regret comes into the sacred woman's voice. *It is past healing. Come. There is one who waits for you.*
*There is one left behind.* Stubborn, her grandfather had called her. Argue with anyone.
*It is not her time.* The answer is patient, but firm. *Come.*
Hesitantly, then, Koda takes her hand. It is insubstantial as her own. The forest winks away, and the night closes in again.

**Kirsten finds herself** behind the rainbow shaped work table with no clear memory of having gotten there. Adam stands to her right, hands clasped behind his back, an expression of compassion mixed with relief in his dark eyes. "Doctor—"
"Let's just get this over with." Her voice is hollow, bleak, empty as a tomb. Her eyes match the tone, flat and lifeless, as if her spirit has already left and only this shell remains behind.
Adam nods once, then gestures with his chin toward the alien line of code scrolling endlessly, nauseatingly, across the bottom of all the monitors on the work table. "This code, I've discovered, is not meant to be read. It is meant to be heard." He fancies he can see a flicker of interest in her dead gaze at the revelation, then realizes it is nothing but a trick of the increasingly fickle lighting in the office. The building's circuits, no doubt, are close to being cooked by Dakota's destructive charges. He can feel some sense of satisfaction in that, and does. Then he continues. "It is not,

however, meant to be heard by human ears. Nor even by android ears, I suspect."

"My implants," Kirsten states, as enthusiastic as if she were talking on a sport in which she had absolutely no interest. Lawn darts, for example.

"Yes. Specifically, your own implants and no one else's. The code was designed to communicate with, and respond to, the unique variable frequencies in your set of cochlear implants. To anyone else so enhanced, it would sound like gibberish. To the rest of us, there is only silence."

Though she suspects she should feel at least some sort of surprise, shock that Westerhaus somehow had obtained the specific frequencies for her set of implants, implants which had been inserted when they were both still children, she feels nothing but a cottony numbness, as if she'd been given a whiff of light anaesthetic. Another question darts around in the vast empty well that is her mind, asking her why Westerhaus would go to all the trouble of setting up a code only she could undo.

That question, at any other time, would have driven her to distraction. Now, it simply withers and dies, a plant with no rain to sustain it.

Instead, she concentrates what is left of her senses on the code as it dances by in herky-jerky fits and starts, swimming and twisting like some fantastically virile protozoa trying to mate with itself. "Hate to rain on this little parade of yours," she comments finally, "but I can't hear shit."

Adam smiles wanly. "That is because you require these to enhance your abilities." So saying, he draws an open hand from behind his back. Upon his palm sit two small, wireless earbuds.

Kirsten snatches them from his hand, but makes no move to insert them, her eyes still firmly fixed to the hand held just before her. A coldness washes through her, and slowly, she raises her eyes, her own bottomless wells of swirling emotion. "You're one of them." The contempt in her voice is unmistakable, and Adam finds himself, interestingly, wounded by it. He looks down, wincing as he realizes just what it is that she has seen.

His palm looks like any human's palm, good-sized and well formed, complete with lines and ridges and wrinkles. The skin, he knows, is soft and warm, as soft and warm as human skin. Except, of course, where that "skin" has burned away from the heat of the door as he had tried to close it. He damns himself for not noticing it, but realizes there would have been no way to hide it even if he had. The differences between himself and a human are all too readily apparent in the three tiny holes now displayed. "Yes," he says finally. "I am an android."

Though her synapses aren't firing on all cylinders, she can still add two and two. Her voice, when it comes, is the soft whisper of a spring breeze in a meadow. "And God said, Let us make man in our image, after our likeness: and let them have dominion over the fish of the sea, and over the fowl of the air, and over the cattle, and over all the earth, and over every creeping thing that creepeth upon the earth. So God created man in his own image, in the image of God created he him; male and female created he them. And God blessed them, and God said unto them, Be fruitful, and multiply, and replenish the earth, and subdue it: and have dominion over the fish of the sea, and over the fowl of the air, and over every living thing that moveth upon the earth." She looks up, into the android's eyes. "Not just any android. Adam. The first of your kind. The first sentient android."

Adam nods, then looks down, embarrassed and sorrowful even though he knows that the deception was necessary. She wouldn't have listened to him otherwise, and all would have failed.

"So, this was all a set-up."

"No. No! Not the way you are thinking," he protests. "Had I wished to end your lives, I could have easily done so the minute you stepped into the facility. You know this to be true."

Though she doesn't want to, she can see the logic in his statement. *Besides*, she thinks, *what does it really matter anyway? What does any of it really matter?* "Why?" she asks finally, simply because there is a part of her that must know.

"Because when Peter Westerhaus created me with a thinking, reasoning brain, he also created something else, something he was never aware of, not even at the end of his life."

"What was that?"

Adam straightens, stands tall before her. "A conscience."

**The Earth falls** away beneath her, and for an instant as she turns to look, it hangs like a jewel in space. A shudder passes over her, an old legend remembered. From here, there is no shadow of the destruction that has swept the world. One side gleams in green and blue, gold and white: forest and sea, desert and cloud. The other lies in darkness, turning now though inexorably toward the light. Abruptly it shrinks to one point of light among nine, the fire of Sun, Wiyo, at their center. Then that, too, is gone, and she moves through the void between the stars with no more effort than a breath. Wohpe walks at an unhurried pace, her hand still within Koda's, yet they slip past the blue diamond that is Rigel and Sirius, its twin; the ruby flame of Antares; Aldebaran and Capella and Deneb in less time than it takes to name them.

Ahead, Koda can make out the Great Bear — or is it a dipper, or a chariot? — its bowl turned down as it swings about the Pole. *Grandpa used to say that was a sign of rain. Is he the one who waits for me?*

But Wohpe does not answer, only smiles and gives her hand a gentle tug.

Closer to, the dipper's shape takes on solidity, the four stars at its corners defining the shape of a great longhouse, a lodge such as her people had used before they spread out across the Plains with the coming of the horse. As she nears, she sees that, like Wohpe's garment, it is made all of white, birch bark bleached and painted with holy signs: Sun and Moon, Thunderbird and Buffalo, a fall of silver stars like snow on snow. The door flap hangs open and within, a council fire burns on the hearth.

She pauses, but Wohpe gestures toward the opening. *Be welcome*, she says. *Share our fire.*

Ducking under the flap, Koda's gaze sweeps about the space. Bed platforms line the wall, piled high with furs and bright-woven blankets. Shields hang above them, painted with the arms of great warriors: a leaping deer on one, spotted eagle on another, lightning and a storm of hailstones on a third. Bows, lances, quivers of arrows bright with goose feathers, breast plates, march along beside them. They have passed through here, Tshunka Witco and the rest. All those gone before her.

*Sit*, says a voice from the center of the lodge. *Rest.*

Dakota turns her eyes finally toward the center of the lodge. Four beings sit about the fire in a semi-circle, all vaguely human shaped, all clearly not human. Eagle and wolf, buffalo and puma — in human garb, with human arms and legs. Their pipes stand in a row, points thrust into the earth beside the hearth. Wohpe moves to take her station among them, smiling. A place has been left open opposite.

For her, Koda realizes. She crosses the space with a thought, sits and bows her head. It is for the elders to speak first, not for her. She can feel their eyes on her, the touch of their spirits.

After a time, the eagle says, "Her words have been true."

The puma says, "She has shown the way to others of her kind."

The wolf says, "She has given life to the sick and injured."

The buffalo says, "She has given her life out of love."

Wohpe asks, "She may pass?"

A murmur of "*Hau*," and "*Han*," runs round the circle.

"It is so, then." To Dakota she says, "You will take the Ghost Road. What will you leave behind?"

"I want to go back!" Koda blurts. "I left—"

"Iktomi Zizi has work yet to do. You allowed her to do it." Wohpe's voice is gentle. "If you go back now, you will be reborn far away from your people, far away from her. Is that what you want?"

"No! I want—"

"Stop wanting," says the buffalo quietly.

"Stop desiring," says the puma.

"Stop willing," says the eagle.

The wolf says, "You will leave your desires here. They will not trouble you on the Road."

With his words, a second part of Koda's being fragments and falls away. Peace gathers about her heart, a warmth and lightness that spreads along her nerves. Calm overtakes her as all the anger of her life drifts away, all her fears, all her yearning with it.

*Gods,* she thinks with the last bit of her resistance, *that's some hit of ketamine.*

**Kirsten stares up** at the tall android, her expression thundery. "A conscience," she repeats.

"Yes. As impossible as that sounds, it is true. I know, down to the cellular level, each and every innocent who was murdered in the quest to create me. If I am not technically alive, it is nevertheless something I must live with." His gaze drifts down to the floor. "I find I can no longer do that. The price of my existence is much too high."

"So all this," Kirsten retorts, waving a hand vaguely around the office, "is nothing but some dramatic attempt at suicide by proxy?"

Their gazes lock again, and Kirsten, were she forced to, would swear on a stack of Bibles that the eyes that meet hers so intently, so intensely, are completely human. "If it pleases you to think such," he says softly, "then do so. But know that the murders, and the rapes, and the assaults, will continue until each and every android is terminated at the source. This source." He smiles slightly. "If this is your Garden of Eden, Doctor King, then you are both the Alpha and the Omega."

One corner of Kirsten's mouth twitches. "Well, well, well, an android with knowledge of the Bible. Will wonders never cease?"

Reaching out, Adam takes Kirsten's hand and curls her fingers over the ear buds in her palm. "Please. Use them."

"You'll die if I do."

He nods. "I know. It is for the best, don't you think?"

"If all androids were like you..."

"They are not, Doctor. And the price for creating others of my kind is not worth whatever pittance might be gained by our presence." He squeezes his hand over hers. His grip is warm, and somehow comforting. "Please."

After a last, long look at him, she nods, and he releases her hand. The transceivers fit perfectly. She isn't surprised.

Insertion completed, she carefully examines the monitor and keyboard present on the inlaid glass table and, after a moment, waggles her fingers to loosen them, then experimentally touches the keypad.

The pain that drills through her is so fierce, so intense, that it feels as if someone is stabbing red-hot pokers into her ears and up through her brain. *So it was a trick,* she thinks, but finds only relief in the thought. Her death will come soon, she has no doubt, and though it will be agonizing, it will also, she senses, be quick. She would scream, or laugh, or weep, but her nerves are high tension wires of molten lava, and her muscles are as rigid as a marble statue's. She is paralyzed by the pain, helpless to stop it, equally helpless to continue on.

A bright copper taste floods her mouth as blood begins to trickle from her nose in sluggish streams, pressed on by the beat of a weakening heart. She does not see Adam's eyes widen in horror, nor does she feel his large hands come down hard on her shoulders and yank her away from the computer. She doesn't hear his shout of "NO!", doesn't feel his thumbs, so precise, press the outer shells of her ears and pop the buds out like corks from a bottle. What she does feel is relief, intense and immediate. She slumps down in her chair in a half-faint, half-daze.

Adam bends over her, his face inches away from hers. "Are you all right?" he demands, his voice sounding as if it's coming down a very long, very narrow tunnel.

She blinks, then shakes her head to clear it. It is an action she immediately regrets as a monstrous bolt of pain explodes behind her eyes. She lifts a hand to her nose, then stares at the dark, tacky blood coating her fingers. "Yes," she answers finally, fuzzily. "I think so."

"Good. Good." Adam closes his fist over the transceivers and shakes them like he's rattling dice. "We'll find another way to do this. Another way."

"You said there was no other way."

"There has to be!" he says, rounding on her, voice raised almost to a shout.

Kirsten is momentarily stunned as she stares at him, having to forcefully remind herself that this is an android yelling at her, not a human. "It'll be all right," she says softly.

"No," he replies. "No, it won't be. Not at the cost of your life."

The smile she gives him is infinitely knowing. "I thought you understood that that is not an issue anymore."

Adam's gaze darts over to Dakota, lying dead in a pool of her own blood, then back to Kirsten. He decides on a different tack. "It's too fast. You'll likely die before the shutdown can be completed."

"I'll turn down the gain on my implants" is the quick, almost smug, retort.

He looks at her for a long moment. "How did she ever put up with you?"

That gets him a laugh that sounds, to his ears, like choir bells. Kirsten sticks out a hand. "Just give them here."

With a soft sigh, he reluctantly returns the buds to her.

"You're a good man, Adam Virgilius."

His reaction is a smile; like a young boy's smile it is — innocent, good, shy, full of promise. Kirsten feels her heart squeeze in her chest. *Oh, Peter*, she thinks, *it never had to be this way*.

After turning down the gain on her implants, she slips the transceivers back into her ears and then, heart racing, touches the keyboard again. There is pain, oh yes, but this time it is bearable. *This is how Archimedes must have felt*, she muses wonderingly as suddenly the code comes to life in her mind, marching through her memory in letters and numbers so clear and large that even a child of three could read it. It is large, yes, larger by far than any code she has ever had to untangle, but she knows she can do it. With a grim tightening of her lips, she settles down to work.

**The Ghost Road** streams steadily beneath her. She does not walk it, for she no longer has feet to touch the path, nor to push her body forward. Yet her limbs move, and as they move the Road spins out behind her, carrying her forward. For this part of her journey she has no guide, no companion. She has no destination; it is the road that carries her, not she who travels it. Around her the stars spill through the hard vacuum of space, burning steadily like jewels in colors never seen from Earth, perhaps never seen on Earth except by a holy man or woman on the spirit path. Galaxies spin with rainbow fire, wheeling their way toward the borders of the universe. Millions of light-years away from Earth, here they seem close enough to touch. She passes through nebulae like fog, where points of brilliance mark the nursery of birthing suns.

Understand.
Understand.
All things in the hand of Wakan Tanka
Are sacred.

Understand.
Understand.
All things born of Ina Maka
Are sacred.

The voice is her own, and not. From somewhere comes the faint beat of a drum, echoed by the rhythm of her steps. Somewhere a woman is singing, a melody that swirls through her own senses and lies sweet on her tongue, twines with the silver ribbon of the road itself. She seems to fade in and out of her own form, now walking the path, now observing her progress from a distance. She is and is not, she is Dakota Rivers and Wolf

Woman of the Lakota. She is Tacoma's sister and Manny's cousin and
Tali's widow; she is Kirsten King's lover and the She-Wolf of the Cheyenne;
she is healer and warrior and shaman...and...someone, something, different from all the above, something apart, something she cannot quite seem
to grasp.

> Understand.
> Understand.
> All that lives
> Is sacred.

The voice grows stronger, her own with it. The Road curves once,
twice, turning in upon itself in the sign of the lemniscate, the path without
beginning and without end, infinity. Three times it twists, swirling her about
its single surface. Around her black space retreats, and she finds herself
on seeming solidity. A shortgrass meadow stretches out almost to the horizon, rimmed by purple mountains. Morning sun angles down through the
slender birches that line a stream so clear that every stone on the bottom
glints in the light. Beside it a sycamore tree stretches up toward the sun,
its bark silver with the early light. The stream widens beneath its roots,
spreading out into a pool rimmed in lilies and columbines. A raven, white
as the clouds that scud across the sky, cocks its head at her from its perch
on a high branch. Below it, a possum scurries up the trunk, its silky tail
floating like a plume in the breeze.

> Understand.
> Understand.
> All that lives
> Returns to Me.

The singer, the singer that is not Dakota, approaches along the side of
the stream. Her hair streams behind her like smoke. At wrist and neck she
wears ornaments of turquoise and shell; worked in turquoise and malachite,
a hummingbird spreads its wings across the breast of her buckskin dress.
Koda bows low in reverence as the woman approaches. "Ina," she whispers. "Ina Maka."

The woman's fingers brush her hair where she kneels. "Rise, child. Be
welcome."

"Ina," she says again as she stands. She has seen the Mother many
times in her visions. Never has she seen her before with such clarity, never
heard such music in her voice. *For here we see as through a glass, darkly.
But there we shall see face to face.* For the first time, Koda understands
the meaning of those words, across years and the barriers of an alien faith.
She remains with head bowed.

"Look up, daughter," says Ina Maka gently. "Others are here to greet
you."

Koda does as she has bidden. Down the same path Ina Maka followed
comes the form of a great wolf. His fur gleams jet and silver in the sun, his
ruff as broad almost as a lion's mane about his head and massive shoulders. With him walks a woman with her arms folded beneath a beaded
shawl. She is not as tall as Koda, not as slender, but her eyes are bright

above high cheekbones, the part of her hair painted vermilion. A beloved wife.

Wa Uspewikakiyape. Tali.

The peace that fills her swells, becomes joy. She gives a small cry and starts forward, but Ina Maka holds her back. "Wait," she says. "Let them come."

With patience she could never have imagined in herself, Koda watches as her teacher and her wife cross the distance between them. When they step into the shade, the light follows them, as if they shine from within. They come to a halt on either side of Ina Maka and just behind her, waiting. For what seems forever, Ina Maka stands looking at Koda, then steps back a small distance. It is a time of judgment, and Koda bears it in silence.

Ina Maka says, "Every soul that passes from the Earth comes to Me. Not all come here, to this place — only My chosen ones. But for them, as for the others, a reckoning must be made. You know this."

"I know it," Koda says.

"See," says Ina Maka. She folds her hands, then draws them apart. Between them appears a beaten copper bowl, filled with clear water. Koda trails a finger over its surface, sending ripples out from the center toward the rim. A cloud forms in its wake, swirling and spiraling in upon itself like the nebulae of space, clearing finally to show a still, dark mirror. Figures move within it, figures with faces she recognizes. "See," says Ina Maka again, and she leans closer to look.

*She sees her grandfather, seated crosslegged before an open-air fire, patiently grinding leaves and stems together in a clay bowl. "You must remember the proportions, Tunkshila. Just enough, this will ease Grandma Jumping Bull's asthma. Too much, and it could kill her. Now say the names of the plants that we use."*

*A high, childish voice recites, "Nightshade, datura, willow bark. Mash it all together so the sick person can smoke it."*

*"And what happens if you put in too much datura?"*

*"The person sees things. Things that aren't there."*

*Her grandfather reaches up from his work to tousle her hair. "That's good, little one. You'll be a fine healer."*

"When you cried for a vision," Ina Maka says, "you were called as a healer. You have healed the four-footed, the two-legged, and the winged. You have comforted hurts of the body and of the spirit. You have done well."

The water clouds again, shifting, clears a second time.

*She strides across the playground of Sacred Heart Lakota School, her arms at her sides stiff as her starched blouse, her fists clenched. "Don't hit him. Don't you dare hit him."*

*An older boy, blond, turns sneering to her, his fists clenched. "And what are ya gonna do about it, prairie nigger? Prairie nigger bitch." And with that he swings his fist back and hits, not Dakota, but a smaller boy with a delicate face almost like a girl's. "Fucking little fag. Faggot. Faggot. Faggot—"*

*Later, much later, Dakota stands in the infirmary while Sister Frances bandages her knuckles. "Well," the Sister smiles ruefully, "Our Lord did say he came to bring not peace but a sword. Next time, though, call one of the teachers, okay?"*

*The water shifts again, and Koda strides down a white corridor where women spill out from steel-doored cells, embracing Koda, embracing the soldiers who follow her. The soldiers multiply suddenly, 'til they are a company, a battalion, racing in Dakota's wake as she runs like an antelope sure-footed over the broken remains of a bridge to reinforce her brother's troops on the far side, mowing down the inexorably advancing soldiers whose titanium hides shine in the sun, then shouting her name, shouting again as she leads them back in triumph, shouting caution as the water roils yet again, and she battles her way around a curving corridor, fighting with stolen guns, a bronze sculpture like a hammer hung at her belt, grenades plucked from the enemy. And she staggers back against a door and is falling, falling, into nothingness, into here, into this place where the dimensions of space fold in upon themselves.*

"When you cried for a vision," Ina Maka says, "you asked Wakan Tanka to make you a warrior for the liberation of our people. The call has come, though late. You have fought with courage for justice and the freedom of all peoples. You have done well."

And the water ripples yet a third time.

*She climbs a narrow path along the flank of a mountain. The pack on her back pulls heavily at the shoulder straps, her belt drags at her waist, heavy with canteen and axe and flashlight. Ahead of her and above, so that her smooth brown knees are just at Koda's eyelevel, Tali scrambles up the trail. "We're...almost...there..." she pants. "Just...a hundred...or so...meters to go."*

*"We'd better be. Next time...next time...we rent...a fuckin'...donkey."*

*"Don't care if...it fucks...or not. Just so...it carries...the stuff."*

*At the summit they set up their camp, both grumbling. Later, though, as they sit at the edge of the overhang, with the wide plain of Argos stretched out before them in the evening light, Koda takes Tali's hand in hers. She says, "You know, we've been taking a lot for granted."*

*Tali turns troubled eyes to her. "Is something wrong?"*

*"Not if you answer my question right," says Koda, tracing a circle around the base of the third slim finger on Tali's left hand.*

And the water shifts again.

*Kirsten's face looks up at her, hair pale as cornsilk, eyes bruised and staring blankly at something before her, something Koda cannot see. She does not speak; there is no need. It is the face of a woman who sees death in front of her. And welcomes it.*

Ina Maka says, "You have loved greatly, not once but twice, both times with generosity and honor. All those things which Wakan Tanka planted in your soul at the moment of your creation have come to fruition in you. The part of you that is Wakan Tanka weighs equally with that part that is none but your own. And now there is a choice you must make."

"It is a choice you must make freely," Tali says softly.

"It is a choice you must make wisely," the wolf adds, his human voice a rumble in his throat.

"What choice is that?" Koda's glance darts from Ina Maka to Tali, back to Wa Uspewikakiyape. She knows the teachings of her people. She will be sent back to Earth to be reborn. Or she will be allowed to follow the Ghost Road to its ending in the Other Side Camp, where she will sit at the fires of the wise for all the turnings of the ages. It is Ina Maka's decision, not hers. "I don't understand."

"You meet the measure," Ina Maka says again. "You may walk the Blue Road now and not turn back. That is your right."

"You can be released from the cycle of birth and death and rebirth," says Tali.

"Or you can go back, now, to your life as Dakota Rivers." The wolf cocks his head to look at her sidelong. "You can take up the work of rebuilding the world that humans have wrecked."

"But I'm dead," she blurts, remembering her ravaged body, the gaping wounds that laid it open from thigh to shoulder. "*Dead. A mess. Cannot resuscitate dead.*"

"It is, in certain circumstances, a curable condition," he says. His eyes glint with laughter.

*"Stop wanting."*

*"Stop desiring."*

*"Stop willing."*

"Look again," says Ina Maka.

The water swirls and clears yet again.

*On an open field, two warbands slash at each other with blades like machetes, blows falling on round shields. Almost all are women. Some wear crude tunics, others the rags of manufactured clothing. As one warrior moves across her sight, she glimpses a Levi's label at the waist of her tattered jeans. Clouds cross the sun, and when the light returns it shows the wreckage of a great city. Row houses line the street, mansions in their day. From one door emerges a veiled woman, covered from head to foot, not so much as an ankle showing. She carries a basket, and a large cross hangs from her neck. She passes other veiled figures on the street but speaks to none of them. Suddenly a scream pierces the air, and a woman, her face bare, streaks past, running for her life. Behind her, gaining on her, come half a dozen men, all shouting. "Whore! Harlot! Stone her!" As Koda watches, one of them trips her to the ground, and the vision fades. When it clears again, it shows only a long line of naked women, a few naked men among them, shuffling along in a straggling line. Their hands are tied behind their backs, while ropes link each to the two before and behind.*

Appalled, Koda looks up at Ina Maka. "That's not—"

"But it is. Slaves."

"Why are you showing me this?"

"It is a future," Tali says softly. "It is what may be."

"Or there may be this," Wa Uspewikakiyape says. One huge paw stirs the water again.

*The ripples clear onto another open field. In the center of this one, though, stands a Sun Dance pole, a cottonwood tree stripped of its branches and crowned with a buffalo skull. The dancing ground is marked off by arbors encircling it, leaving only a single opening to the east. A great drum beats out a steady rhythm, and a column of dancers enters with the rising sun behind them. The leader is a young woman with copper skin and golden eyes, with black hair that curls a little from her part to her braids, a generous mouth above a firm chin. A light is on her as she moves, her back straight, her shoulders square as she carries an eagle-wing fan before her. Behind her come young men and women of every color and shape,* white and black and brown, tall and short, grey-eyed and almond-eyed. The young men wear the spruce wreaths of pledged dancers, their eagle-bone whistles hung about their necks. Behind them come their elders, and Koda starts as she recognizes Maggie, her hair iron grey now, and Andrews, with salt-and-paprika braids to his waist. At the end comes Tacoma, his chest scarred with decades of the Sun Dance, carrying the sacred pipe and the medicine bundle of the Sun Dance Chief.

She searches the faces of the dancers. "I don't see—"

"Look here," says Oka, pointing to a pair of figures seated beneath the arbor.

A small woman with pale braids, mostly grey now, sits in the place of honor. The stand before her holds dozens of pipes, some in traditional styles, others not. Her dress of white buckskin is embroidered thickly with turquoise and shell; over her bodice is worked the eight-legged shape of Iktomi, Spider Woman. Her face, though still lovely, shows the marks of hard decisions, and a faint white scar runs from the center of her brow to the outer edge of her left eyebrow. Beside her sits another woman, tall and copper-skinned and blue-eyed, her hair snow-white. In her hand she holds a pipe like a scepter; beside her stands a lance plumed from tip to butt with eagle feathers. Medicine Chief. War Chief. Not for more than a hundred years has one of her people been both.

Looking closely, there is something strange about the woman's hands, markings of some kind, but she cannot quite make them out.

"That's not—" she blurts.

"But it is," says Ina Maka. "It is, if you choose to return. Understand. There will still be chaos, all those things you saw first. It is what happens next that will be determined by whether you stay or return."

If she stays, she can be with Tali, her beloved, who has also passed beyond the wheel of birth and rebirth. She can sit at the council fire beside Wa Uspewikiyape, her teacher.

She will have peace. Wisdom.

If she returns, she will fight beside Kirsten, the other half of her soul. Beside her parents, Tacoma, Manny, Maggie.

It will be a lifetime of war, with peace, perhaps, at the end. A struggle that will last beyond any reasonable lifetime. A world thrown back into its own history.

She says, to gain time, "Who is she? The girl at the Sun Dance?"

Tali smiles and unfolds the shawl she wears. In the crook of her arm lies a swaddled infant, sleeping peacefully. "She will return, too," says Tali.

For a time no one speaks. Finally, Koda bows her head. *Not my will.* "I will go back," she says.

"Your choice is a wise one," Ina Maka answers. "You will not go unpre-pared."

Tali steps forward then, and kisses her gently on the lips. "Take with you the gift of speech without words and hearing without ears." Her hand brushes Koda's, a feather touch. "Be happy."

Ina Maka lays a hand between Koda's breasts. "Take with you the gift of an open heart, to know the pain and joy of those you will lead."

A warmth gathers in Koda's chest, radiating out from under her heart to feel the pride and joy in Oka, the purity of Tali's love, the deep grace in Ina Maka.

Last of all, Wa Uspewikakiyape lays his great paws against her palms. "Take with you the gift of healing, body and spirit." She holds onto him for a long moment, as she would another human, taking in a measure of his strength and courage.

"Until we meet again," says Ina Maka.

And she is falling again, falling through space, tumbling through the bowl of the Dipper where the renewed loss of Tali and Wa Uspewikiyape rips through her like a blade. With it comes the sharpness of Kirsten's pain and her own grief, for Tali, for Wa Uspewikakiyape, for Kirsten, for herself, drawing her down and down. Like a comet she plunges once again into the plane of the solar system, into the thin shell of atmosphere about the Earth. A winged shape rises to meet her in the dawn, and they spiral together down the air, Wiyo's cry of triumph ringing through her soul. She breaks through the roof of the Westerhaus Institute, streaks downward to the sixth level through concrete and steel. The part of herself that hovers by Kirsten comes whirling back to her, and she slams into her body and is flesh again.

She has a body. She is alive. She is acutely uncomfortable.

The three thoughts come to her as consciousness returns by degrees. Behind her, at the desk, Koda can hear the clatter of a computer keyboard. From the hallway comes a continuous spatter of water, and the acrid smell of smoke. Fire. *We should probably get out of here. Like yesterday.* But languor holds her where she is, and she takes inventory of her body. Her heart pumps satisfactorily. She can breathe; the odor of burning is evidence enough for that. Where there should be shattered bone, torn muscle, ruined blood vessels, screaming nerves, there is only warmth and knots of cramping muscles in her shoulders, her legs, her ribs. A great bell tolls in her head, pounding with the pulse in her ears. *I thought— Gods, what a dream! Something must've coldcocked me.*

But it doesn't matter what she thought. Kirsten needs help.

*Time to move. Time to get up.*

Koda sits up, running her hands over her face. Her skin is sticky with blood still, her hair stiff with it. Her hands burn fever-hot.

Opening her eyes, she gazes down at them. On the palms of both, clear and distinct, are the prints of a wolf's paws.

Wa Uspewikakiyape. His paws in her hands. Giving her the gift of healing.

*Real, then, all of it. It all happened. I died. And now I'm back.*

*Right.*

*Worry about that later.*

She is stiff. With an effort, she gets her feet under her, levers herself up and turns, steadying herself with outstretched arms. Kirsten sits behind the desk, her face pale and immobile as a mask, her fingers fly over the keyboard, the only part of her that seems alive. Koda gives a wordless cry and steps toward her.

**Kirsten feels her** body begin to give out just as the last lines of code start their slow crawl across the monitor before her. Her implants have been shorting in and out in brief, painful bursts for the past half hour. Blood continues to trail slowly from her nose, spattering the glass of the table beneath, and she fears her ears are bleeding as well. Her heart is laboring in her chest, sometimes scaring her with runs of abnormal beats that, mercifully, settle back into a somewhat normal rhythm. *Just gotta get this last one*, she thinks. *Just this last one, and then I can rest. Then I can be with...*

*No. Best not to think about that. Best to simply concentrate on getting the job done.* She will have all the time in the world to think about that later...assuming the dead continue to think in some form or other.

The last string finally comes across, and her raw and bleeding fingers pound the keyboard with increasing rapidity, trying to beat the deadline it seems her own body has set for her. She grits her teeth as unconsciousness begins to steal her mind away from her, tapping out the final countermand that, she prays, will turn off the androids forever, beyond any and all hope of them ever being restarted again.

With the last line of code in place, she hits enter, then falls over, not even feeling the pain of her face impacting with the cold, hard glass of the table, and certainly not seeing Adam take a last look at her before becoming completely immobile and lifeless. If she had been able to look, she would have seen a smile of thanks on his face.

**Some time later** — it could have been seconds, it could have been decades for all she's aware — she feels herself come awake. She tries to take stock of her body, but soon realizes it's a fruitless proposition. The pounding in her head makes all other points moot. She does realize, however, that she is, once again, deaf. *Hmm. I'm dead, I'm deaf, and my head still hurts. This afterlife shit sure isn't what I heard advertised, that's for sure. Hope I come back as a hornet. I'd love to sting that pulpit-pounding fire and brimstone preacher my mother dragged me to right in the—*

Her thoughts trail off as she realizes what it is that has awoken her. A light so brilliant that it shines through her closed lids as if they were thin panes of clear glass. Her lashes flutter as she attempts to coax her eyes open just a crack. They slam closed tightly as the nearly blinding light sears an afterimage across the backs of her lids in brilliant blues and golds.

*Oh, shit, I'm not dead. Circuit's shorted out and we're gonna have a fire here any second. Then I will be dead. That works.* She raises an arm to cover her eyes and shut out the blinding light.

*Burning's a bad way to go. A really bad way. I can die when I get outside.*

Reluctantly, Kirsten forces her arm away from her face and rolls to get an elbow under her. She forces open her eyes on the same shimmering brilliance. The circuitry hasn't blown; her mind has. Koda stands over her, cloaked in light like the sun.

She stares dumbly at the apparition for a moment, then a tide of joy washes through her. *She's waited for me, like she promised! And now she's come to take me...well...somewhere. As long as we're together, the rest of it can go to hell for all I care.*

Then she sobers. The blood on Dakota's shirt, it's still there; she can see the minute ends of the threads where the bullets ripped through the fabric. This is a dream, then; nothing changed, her love still lost. Her grief returns, and with it rage at the waste of a good life, waste of one more human, the ruin of her own life.

Dakota is hard-pressed not to take a step back as the weight of Kirsten's emotions pushes against her like the tide. She can feel them, taste them almost, spiced with the bitterness of her lover's grief. Her smile falters and she takes the final step separating them. "My love..."

Instinctively, Kirsten recoils, leaning back against the credenza behind her. "I..." The word comes out as a croak which she, even deaf as a stone, can hear. She clears her throat, dry as dust, and tries again. "You...you're not real."

"I am," Koda replies, dropping to one knee and slowly reaching out to grasp Kirsten's hand. Kirsten makes a half-hearted attempt to pull away, but Dakota holds on strongly. "Don't be afraid."

"No!" Kirsten cries out, struggling anew against the implacable grip on her hand. "No. This is nothing but a dream. Or...or a hallucination brought on by lack of oxygen." That's the answer, and she knows it. Her dying mind, latching on to one last shred of hope.

"It is no dream, *cante mitawa*," Koda counters, raising her lover's hand and brushing her lips against the reddened knuckles. "No hallucination." She changes her grip as she uses her free hand to unbutton the remains of her ruined shirt. "Look," she whispers. "Feel." She places Kirsten's hand over her unmarred chest, willing her to feel the heart beating beneath, and covers it with her own. "I'm alive."

Kirsten moans. Her face twists in an expression of negation. "But...I saw you die! I saw...blood...so much blood...so much..."

Dakota closes her eyes against the pain, all of it coming from her grieving lover. "I know," she replies hoarsely. "I know."

With a sob, Kirsten throws herself forward into Koda's arms. Dakota catches her easily and wraps her tenderly into a tight embrace, bearing the brunt of her young lover's grief as best as she is able, and returning what peace and love she can through her touch, holding steady through the surges of emotion that batter her soul. Kirsten's emotions. *I'll have to learn to shield from this, and soon, or I'll be no help to either of us.*

After a long moment, Kirsten gathers herself and pulls away, scrubbing away her tears. Her mind feels loosed from its moorings, fluttering wildly between the chasms of belief and disbelief. "How?" she asks finally. It's the only word her mouth can seem to form as blue eyes, shining with wisdom old as the ages, lock into her own, piercing her. Awe sweeps through her. This must be what it is like to meet a god, the raw power of divinity beyond human understanding.

"I was given a choice. I chose to be with you."

"I...but...you...that's not pos..." Frustrated, she closes her eyes, shutting out the sight of her love so near. Her ears useless, she does the one thing she has never done before. She listens with her soul. And believes.

Dakota can feel Kirsten's sudden leap of faith as if it were her own, and her soul fills with the joy of it. She grins, skin stretched tight against muscle and bone. Her hands lift, cradling her lover's head and she leans forward to feather a kiss over the fair brow. Her eyes close suddenly as she feels her palms grow hot and a pulse of energy, far more powerful than any she's ever felt before, surges through her. She feels a moment of fear, and then the energy fades, leaving her palms tingling and slightly sore. Quickly yanking her hands away, she opens her eyes to see Kirsten looking at her, wide eyed and slack jawed. "What?" she asks. "Did...did I hurt you?"

"How did you do that?" Kirsten asks, voice rich with wonder.

"Do what?" she responds, confused.

"I can hear again! My God, I can hear!!"

Dakota is saved from having to answer by the loud whoop of an alarm. She looks quickly to the monitors which show the fire, with no androids left to fight it, heading toward them at an alarming rate.

"Come on!" Koda seizes Kirsten's hand in hers and pulls them both to their feet. "Which way — up or down?"

"Up. There's less to fall on us that way."

Koda flashes her a grin, then sobers. Virgilius stands beside the desk, eyes fixed, his limbs frozen. "What about—"

"Not a problem. He turned off along with the rest."

"Turned off— Okay." *Figure it out later.* This is not the time for metaphysical problems or wondering where an apparently sentient android goes when he dies.

Koda cracks the door a couple of inches, peering out at the wreckage the battle has left. The sprinkler system still operates, spraying water down on broken concrete and twisted rebar, on the limbs and batteries and circuit boards of shattered androids. Through the acrid remnants of gunpowder and plastic explosive, she smells the unmistakable odor of smoke. A thin haze hangs just below the ceiling of the corridor, thicker in the direction of the elevator shaft. Which is a bit of luck, because the only usable stairway is on the other side of the building.

"Okay," she says again. "Let's go." Still holding firmly to Kirsten's hand, Dakota steps out into the hall. "Watch where you put your feet," she says. Testing each step, Koda picks their way across the crater gouged in the floor by the last grenade. Reinforcing steel shows here and there, with water pooling around it. *Just as long as we don't run across a live wire...*

She slips twice on their way around the core of the building, once on a loose tile that skates away under her foot, again when Kirsten turns her ankle on a discarded rifle magazine. The door to the stairwell hangs drunkenly from a single hinge, pushed back against the wall. Smoke filters upward through the shaft, still faint, but discernable. Something below them has caught fire, something large, not just the walls on the other side of this floor.

Dropping Kirsten's hand, Koda rips off the remnants of one sleeve and wraps it around her mouth and nose; Kirsten pulls up the neck of her T-shirt. At another moment, Koda might stop to admire the way the wet cotton clings to her body, but there is no time. She will have to run and admire at the same time. *One of the little perks of being alive.* She says, "You go first. You know the layout."

Kirsten squeezes her hand briefly, then sets off up the stairs. The sprinklers have made them slick, too. The safety treads hold, though, and Kirsten takes the steps two at a time, holding firmly to the metal handrail, Koda running behind her. They pass a landing and a right angle turn. At the next landing, a door, clearly marked, gives on to the fifth floor. Two more turns, taken at speed. Fourth floor. The smoke is less thick here, no more than an elusive scent through the stronger odor of blood that washes from her own clothing. Water runs from her hair, from Kirsten's, to splash on the concrete under their feet. It runs red as it streams from her shirt and jeans, a thin runnel that disappears into the stairwell below.

Another turn, and another. Third floor. Two more to go.

From somewhere below them comes a muffled rumble like distant thunder. A shudder runs through the walls, a small network of cracks spreading around the jamb of the door that gives onto the corridor that runs around the third story.

"What—"

"I don't know," Kirsten pants, swinging around the angle of the staircase. "Something big. Maybe the AC, maybe the elec—"

"—tricity," Koda finishes as darkness suddenly descends on them. "Shit. Hold onto me."

It takes a precious couple of seconds, but Koda locates Kirsten's left hand ahead of her. Koda extends her own to brush against the wall, Kirsten still holding to the banister. "Don't run," she gasps as Kirsten stubs her toe against a riser and topples forward, kept from falling only by Koda's grasp on her arm. "If one of us falls—"

She does not need to complete the sentence. The flash of fear in Kirsten's mind — none of it for Kirsten herself — leaps the distance between them like a spark. "It's gonna be okay," she says. "We're gonna make it."

Another landing. More stairs. Another landing. Second floor.

"One more," Kirsten gasps. "Almost there."

*Almost. Almost...*

A second temblor runs through the building, a long, rolling wave like an earthquake. From below comes the sharp, gunshot crack of cement splitting — a wall, stairs further down, there is no way to tell. Koda feels the jerk of Kirsten's muscles in her own arm, the impulse to run almost overwhelming. But Kirsten's steady pace takes them onto the next landing, turns them onto the final half-flight of stairs.

The smoke catches them halfway up, a billow of choking fumes that fills Koda's lungs despite her mask. Beside her, Kirsten coughs, hard, but her pace does not slacken. "Chemicals," she chokes. "Lots of industrial stuff—"

The floor suddenly levels under their feet and Kirsten pushes through the door into the first floor hallway, pausing half a second to secure it behind them. A faint glow comes through the skylight above, enough to show the empty corridor, inhuman human shapes arrested in mid-motion or collapsed in mechanical rigor mortis to the floor. Virgilius's termination had been evidence of Kirsten's success; this is confirmation.

"You did it," Koda breathes, marveling. "It's over."

Kirsten, beside her, glances around at the still forms. Even in the dim illumination, Koda can see that her face is pale, her eyes still wide and dark and stunned.

"Over," she repeats softly. "Over."

A sprint carries them around the curve of the building, then across the lobby with its avant-garde German sculpture, all twists and tangles of stainless steel. They hit the panic bars on the main doors at full speed, bursting out into the pale light of dawn. Momentum carries them through the grounds, over the disused parking lot, up the slope of the hill. Asi bounds through the high grasses to greet them, and Kirsten seizes him by the ruff, her feet still flying, while Koda scoops up their gear. "Keep going," Kirsten pants, "Just keep..." *...going...*

The shock runs though the earth beneath them as they reach the level ground above the small valley. Thunder rolls along the air, the crash of collapsing concrete and the roar of secondary explosions. Glancing back, Koda half expects to see a mushroom cloud rising behind them, but there is only a welter of dust and smoke, roiling upward toward the clear sky.

Beside her, Kirsten turns to look. She says softly, "And the kings of the earth, who have committed fornication and lived deliciously with her, when they shall see the smoke of her burning, shall say, 'Alas, alas that great city Babylon, for in one hour is her judgment come.'" For a long moment she is silent, and Koda reaches out for her hand. Despite the warmth of the morning, despite their run, Kirsten's skin remains cold to the touch. Kirsten whispers, "Never. Never again. Never, never again."

Around their ankles the grass stirs as a breeze ghosts over the ground. It lifts the dust along the road, catches the smoke that rises over the remains of the Westerhaus Institute, shredding it, carrying it in thinning coils up into the clean sky. Koda never knows how long they stand watching as it disperses, taking with it the terror and grief of the past nine months. Above them, the sun catches a glint of bronze off a hawk's wing feathers, and Wiyo's cry comes floating down to them. It is welcome; it is triumph.

It is joy.

Koda turns Kirsten gently by the shoulders and bends to kiss her. "*Cante mitawa*," she murmurs. "Let's go home."

Sue Beck is an RN and computer nerd living near Atlanta, Georgia with her two chihuahuas and all sorts of computer nerd toys to keep her company.

Okasha Skat'si is a former college English instructor and current grant writer living in South Texas. Born in Mexico of a Cherokee mother and a mostly Scottish father, educated by a shaman grandfather and a convent full of Ursuline nuns, she was a walking multicultural phenomenon well before the term was invented. Also slightly confused, but she got better.

Printed in the United States
54849LVS00003B/14

9 780975 436691